THE SAINT MARY'S DUET BOX SET

SJ SYLVIS

AUTHOR'S NOTE

Good Girls Never Rise is the first book in the St. Mary's Duet. The St. Mary's Duet is a **DARK** boarding school romance intended for **MATURE** (18+) readers. This duet is labeled as dark due to the dark themes (strong language, sexual scenes, and situations) throughout. Be aware that it contains **TRIGGERS** that some readers may find bothersome. **Reader Discretion is advised.**

WELCOME TO

WHERE

GOOD GIRLS NEVER RISE

S.J. SYLVIS

PROLOGUE

Two Months Ago

GEMMA

Branches slashed and whipped against my skin as if razor blades were being chucked at me from a short distance, but the pain the tiny sticks and leaves inflicted over my flesh was nothing more than a brief thought as fear wrapped itself around every last limb, pushing my feet farther and farther away from the place I'd called home my entire life.

The last few hours had completely spun my world upside down, and then again and again until my sketchbook was being shoved in my backpack and my shoelaces were being tied over my feet.

It was nearing dusk, the sun slowly dipping behind the thick clouds. Soon, he wouldn't be able to find me. Soon, I'd be gone, far and away from him and everything he'd ever done or said. His beliefs and corrupted plans for me would be nothing more than panic-inducing thoughts that the breeze of the ocean would whisk away.

The second the guidance counselor pulled me into the principal's office, I knew what a grave mistake I'd made. My sketchbook laid right there in the center of Principal Malcoy's desk, opened to the last sketch I'd done while waiting for the final bell to ring. I hadn't even known it was missing. How careless was I?

It was obvious that they'd flipped through the rest of the drawings, if their faces had anything to say. Slack-jawed, glassy-eyed, suspicious glances to my body, particularly my wrists.

Another branch seemed to come out of nowhere as another piece from earlier filtered into my head: *"Gemma, is there any truth to these drawings? Is someone hurting you at home?"*

My fingers slipped underneath the straps of my backpack as I continued dashing through the trees. My heart flew through my chest as Tobias' face came to the forefront of my brain, and I tried pushing that away too.

"Gemma, these are disturbing. And if this is something that is occurring, you need to let us know. We are here to help you."

Now, looking back to a couple of hours ago, I shouldn't have trusted them. I shouldn't have trusted them at all. The only person I should have listened to was Tobias. He may have been more like a ghost these days, but the venomous truth had never been more clear to me than at that moment: *Trust no one, and just survive, Gemma.*

My foot caught on a tree root as I thudded down to my knees. My jeans had holes in the front, and I knew I was bleeding by the sharp sting against my skin. I hopped back to my feet, regardless.

"I hate that it came to this, but my niece is mentally ill. It's why I've kept her home for most of her life. My mother, Anne, home-schooled her along with the girls at the group home. Once my mother had her stroke and the group home was shut down, I was forced to send Gemma to public school for the remainder of the year. The state,

no matter my stance in the judicial system, wouldn't allow for her to continue homeschooling without a parent or guardian's help, and given the fact that the state does not require homeschooled children to have educational records other than an affidavit, a social worker thought sending her to public school would be a good starting point. I've had full custody of Gemma since she was a young child, right after her mother committed suicide." My uncle's lies had shot through the closed door of the office, and fear squeezed against every inch of my body, and before I knew what I was doing, I was running.

And I was still running.

I would run for the rest of my life if it kept me away from him.

My *uncle*, Judge Stallard—one of the most sought-out judges in the entire country with more sway in this town than Jesus himself—was a bad, bad man who did things to me that I once thought to be normal but learned, very recently, were not.

Running was never my intention—not until Auntie had her stroke and the group home was shut down. Not until the social worker discovered that the judge of our quaint town had a niece no one had ever heard of. Not until I started getting curious and began snooping in his office when he was gone all day, working cases with criminals that were no worse than he was. Not until I'd found the old photos and videos that he'd taken of my mother when Tobias and I were in the same exact room as young babies. And now...now things were even worse.

Running was my only option, Tobias missing or not. I had to hope, with every last ragged breath I took in the forest beyond our manor of a home, that Tobias was somewhere safe and knew better than to come back for me.

He always promised he would.

But that was then, and this was now.

Now, my only option was to survive, just like he'd told me to.

My foot snagged on yet another firm root in the ground, but I was able to right myself and keep on running. My hands were still clenched around the straps of my backpack as the sun continued to disappear to make way for night. Brown strands of hair stuck to my sticky skin, and just as I reached up to push them away from my eyes, I tripped again, but this time, there was no root in the ground that caused me to fall.

Instead, there was a towering figure at my back, and without even looking behind me, I knew whose shadow it was.

"What did I tell you about good girls breaking rules, Gemma?" His hand clasped my ankle, and I was whooshed backward, the breath in my already tight chest seizing and clawing to be let out. "Now, you'll have to be punished."

Even through the sound of rapid heartbeats drumming in my ears, I could hear the sinister, sick pleasure in his tone.

Right then, I knew what a terrible, hasty mistake I'd made by trying to run away without a plan.

And now, I'd have to pay.

CHAPTER ONE

GEMMA

RAIN TRICKLED down the side of the window in an ingenuous manner, unknowing of all the evil in the world. It was innocent and free in ways that I would never be but so desperately wished I could. I was the good girl—naive, soft, quiet, submissive—but I was the furthest thing from pure. I wasn't shielded from the bad in the world. Instead, I was thrust head first into purgatory. Every single day was an uphill battle of wading through everything I'd ever been taught.

The moisture of the sky fell over my shoulders as Tobias' words echoed throughout my head, *"I'll come back for you. Just do as you're told, Gemma. Survive."*

In some ways, the rain pounding my skin and soaking my long chestnut hair felt like a rebirth, like I was cutting through the choppy waves and coming out stronger on the other side. St. Mary's boarding school, the strictest boarding school in the Western Hemisphere, probably terrified most. But it was like a beacon in the dark to someone like me. Even through the slanted rain, the building appeared like a haunted mansion with its cracked stone pillars and castle-like steeples. The archway was ominous, and the dark and looming clouds surrounding my new home should have scared me off.

But I wasn't afraid of the dark.

I'd looked pure evil in the eye before, and this place wasn't evil.

Creeping up the steps, my luggage bumped along the cobblestone beneath my shoes. I opened the door and stepped inside, inhaling the scent of aged, ancient books and stagnant dust. The entryway was gloomy, and a single chandelier hung above my head, casting the room in a dim light. The floor was wet below my feet as rain continued to fall off my gray jacket, and the ends of my hair looked black instead of the warm brown color they really were as they hung like ropes over my shoulders.

My head swung to the right as a tall, oak and wrought-iron door opened, and a man popped his head out. "Gemma?"

I swallowed before speaking. My voice was hesitant and hardly audible, and I hated that because, although I felt stronger here than I ever had before, I still fell back into that vulnerable, insecure version of myself that I'd been forced into since a young child. "Yes."

The man's expression changed for a slight moment. His green eyes dipped, a tight wrinkle etching itself onto his forehead. He squinted deeper before he shook his head, as if clearing his mind of something, and gave me a warm smile. "Please, come in. You can leave your bag right there. Do you have any more? I can send someone to grab them."

Shifting in my squeaky shoes, I quickly shook my head. "This is all I have."

His eyes dipped again as he glanced at my small suitcase then back to my face. "Okay, well, please come in."

The long, checkered hallway was unmoving and quiet as my shoes squeaked along the waxed floor. I wrapped my arms around my slender torso, feeling self-conscious as I brought attention to myself. The second I was through the heavy door, the man gestured over to a seat in front of his desk.

I eyed the shiny name plate on the mahogany surface: *Headmaster Tate Ellison*. Scanning the man again, and his large office, I'll admit, I was skeptical. He didn't look like a man in power. He was warm and inviting. The green in his eyes was charming, and the dark hair on his head was messy and looked in need of a haircut. In simpler terms, he was *boyish*. There was no way he was over the age of forty.

His crescent-like smile met his eyes as he sat down behind his desk. His chair screamed out a squeak when he leaned back, placing his hands behind his head. He was at least wearing a dress shirt and tie, but it was wrinkled. Richard said St. Mary's was strict, but the headmaster looked anything but. Then again, I couldn't really trust myself to judge.

"Gemma. Welcome to St. Mary's. I'm sure your..." The headmaster looked leery, eyeing me skeptically before clearing his throat and placing his elbows on his desk. "I'm sure your Uncle Richard has told you a bit about our school and our rules, yes?"

I swallowed again, unmoving in my seat. "Yes, sir."

"Do you have any questions?"

Did I have any questions? *Oh, did I ever.*

"No, sir."

He shifted uncomfortably in his seat, glancing away. "Your uncle wanted me to call him as soon as you arrived. Let's do that, yes?"

Was he asking my permission?

I flushed, likely more uncomfortable than he was. I knew why I was uncomfortable...but why was he?

The headmaster reached over and grabbed his phone, his office so quiet I could hear the dial tone on the other end. I glanced around the room, eyeing the worn books lining the shelves and the globe that sat on the very edge of his desk. There was a framed map behind him, and I zeroed in on the United States. I had no idea where I wanted to go when given the chance, but it would be somewhere sunny and near a beach. Somewhere where I could just *be*.

"Judge Stallard," Headmaster Ellison said, his voice stern —much different from the warm tone he had used when he welcomed me into his office. *And there it was—that power.* "Gemma has arrived."

Chills broke out along my arms as I heard my uncle's voice. I cringed internally at the word *uncle*, feeling a hot burn zip through my chest. Judge Richard Stallard wasn't technically my uncle, even if I—and everyone else—referred to him as that. Richard and I weren't blood related, and I took comfort in knowing that. Although, maybe if we were blood related, he wouldn't treat me the way that he did.

His voice was muffled, so I leaned forward, pretending to mess with my soggy shoe. *"Thank you for calling, Tate. I don't feel the need to remind you of the stipulations of my niece, but please remember to keep a careful eye on her. She has run away before, and I wouldn't put it past her again. I know you will follow through with your word to keep tabs on her."*

I slowly sat up in my seat and found the headmaster eyeing me stoically. His gaze never left mine as he said, "I can assure you that our school is well protected, and we watch our students very carefully." It might have been my imagination, but I swore the headmaster's lips twitched as the words left his mouth effortlessly.

Richard's voice boomed, and my stomach coiled. *"Don't forget...your family owes me this favor, so make sure you watch my niece. Call me if anything unsettling arises. She has a wild imagination."*

The headmaster continued staring at me as he assured Richard, again, that he would keep a careful eye on me. I began to sweat and quickly glanced away when he thrust the phone in my direction. "Your uncle would like to speak with you, Gemma."

I swallowed, and it felt like swallowing a bunch of bees. My hand shook as I grabbed onto the phone and placed it to my ear. "Hello, Uncle," I croaked.

"Gemma," he reprimanded. "You've made it safely. Good." *Was it, though?* "I hope this teaches you a little lesson. You have given me no other choice. I can no longer trust you." My nostrils flared with my rising anger, and for once, I didn't hold that back. I was too far away from him to feel that unyielding amount of fear. "The headmaster will be keeping an eye on you, and if I hear that you are doing things you shouldn't be doing and bringing unwanted attention to yourself or this family, well...you know what happens when you break the rules."

My throat squeezed as if his hands were back around it. "Yes, sir. I understand," I said, pushing down that anger that made me burn from the inside out. *Survive, Gemma.*

"Good girl. Now hang up and go get acclimated with your surroundings. At least now I know you're safe and tucked away somewhere, and you won't do anything foolish. And don't forget, sweetheart...I have ties with everyone."

How could I ever forget? Did he truly think the thought had escaped me after last time? Judge Richard Stallard was a very powerful man. I thought he was bluffing before, likely due to my perfectly sheltered life that he'd created for me. But I wouldn't be caught off guard again. I wouldn't make the same mistake twice—because my life truly depended on it.

Tobias told me to survive, and that was exactly what I was doing.

Surviving.

The line disconnected, and I gave the phone back to the headmaster. I eyed him a little differently now, much more hesitantly than before. Richard said that the headmaster, or at least his family, had owed him a favor, and it was never a good thing if you owed Judge Richard Stallard something.

As soon as the headmaster dropped the phone back to the receiver, he opened his mouth to say something to me, but it rang just as quickly as his lips parted. We both eyed it suspiciously, me assuming it was Richard calling back to give me another open-ended warning, because he could never just say it once, or even twice, but over and over again. My hand still ached from the last time he'd made me write my *mistake* down over and over again.

The headmaster abruptly answered the phone. "Headmaster Ellison." His expression faltered for a moment as the other person spoke, but he quickly recovered. "Send him to me immediately." His voice was gravelly, a hint of anger beneath the surface. I glanced away, almost too afraid to look any longer. If the headmaster knew Richard...well, who knew what type of man he was. "And as for her," he started, his voice a little softer, "I'll be down to discuss the situation with her as soon as I talk with my nephew. Thank you, Mr. Clark."

As soon as I heard the receiver click down, I peeked up at the headmaster. His tired eyes were shut tightly as he pinched the bridge of his nose. The room felt tense, and I almost shot out of my seat to leave, but he slowly dropped his hand and gave me yet another reassuring smile.

"I'm sorry about that, Gemma. I have a situation with my..." He cleared his throat. "With another student. Do you mind sitting out in the lobby for a moment while I talk with him? Afterwards, I will take you to your room and get you settled."

"Oh, of course," I answered, climbing to my feet. I glanced down at the arms of the leather chair I was sitting in, noticing the crescent-like shapes that my nails had put there. My fists clenched. I hoped he didn't notice.

The headmaster quickly followed behind me, opening the door before ushering me to a bench that was right beside the door. "This won't take long, Gemma."

"It's no prob—"

Both of our heads turned to the sound of slow, shuffling feet down the hall and the lingering echo of a whistle. The headmaster groaned at the sight of a student slowly walking across the black-and-white checkered floor, the same checkered floor that I had stood on just minutes before in all my soaking glory. But now, there was a shift in the air. The white-and-black checkered floor seemed to be put down, tile by tile, just for this person to stride over. A flush started over my cheeks, my body suddenly feeling very hot.

The boy was very tall with broad shoulders, and he was sporting black pants that hung on his slender hips and a white dress shirt that was untucked at the bottom. Almost all of the buttons were undone, allowing a thin sliver of chest to show. A striped maroon-and-gold tie hung loosely around his neck, and then, over his shoulder, he was holding a matching maroon blazer with what seemed to be one single finger.

The closer he got, the hotter I burned. My tongue was stuck to the roof of my mouth as he continued down the hall with incredibly too much swagger, and I hoped that neither he nor the headmaster spoke to me, because I wasn't sure I could form a sentence.

I'd noticed boys like him before, at my old school, before my *uncle* had ripped me away. They were amongst the popular bunch, the ones that made my skin a little prickly. But this boy? He was downright dangerous because he was so captivating. I couldn't look away, even though I wanted to. Even though I needed to.

His chin tipped to the headmaster when he was only a few yards away. I noticed the red flush over his cheeks and neck and the mark of a purple blotch just below his ear. *Did someone hurt him? Or was that...*

"What's up, Uncle Tate?" He smirked, his chiseled cheeks lifting in that delicious bad-boy way.

I swallowed, the gulp working its way from my throat down to the very bottom of my belly. Suddenly, the boy's eyes flicked over to me, half hiding behind the headmaster. His head tilted in a predatory way, and I almost squeaked. *Almost.* The blue in his eyes matched the sky perfectly, except they glittered with something I'd only ever dreamed about.

"Get in my office right now, Isaiah." I shifted my attention between the two, and the headmaster's eyes were no bigger than slits across his face. Isaiah hissed a laugh under his breath as he swiveled swiftly on his shoe and walked into the office.

I let out a held breath when the headmaster turned toward me. "Please excuse me for a moment. This won't take long."

My lips stayed sealed as I nodded because I was honestly unable to speak. As I sat down on the bench beside the door, I waited until he shut it behind him, and then I scooted all the way up to its hinges. I could hear their voices on the other side, despite the large oak door acting as a barricade.

Isaiah's laugh lingered through the air, and something in my stomach fluttered.

I pushed my back against the hard wall behind me as I continued to eavesdrop.

Listening and observing in the shadows and behind locked doors was my only source of power. After all, it was how I began to learn the truth.

CHAPTER TWO

ISAIAH

MY UNCLE WAS ABSOLUTELY livid with me. My lips rolled together as I fought to keep the smile off my face. He slammed his hands onto his messy desk and leveled me with a stony glare.

"Isaiah. What the fuck."

A laugh was lurking in the back of my throat. "Did you just curse, Uncle Tate?"

The sound of his hand slapping against the desk again did nothing but heighten my amusement. "I'm not your uncle right now. I'm the headmaster. As much as I'd like to believe that what Mr. Clark said was a blatant lie, I know better. So go on. Start from the beginning."

Oh, this was going to be interesting. I leaned back in the leather chair and placed my forearms down on the arms, gripping them with my hands. I ran my fingers along the small divots embedded into the leather, glancing down to the tiny moon-shaped cuts into it. "Who's the girl out in the hall? We get a new student?"

My uncle's face—excuse me, *the headmaster*'s face turned a deep shade of red. "Isaiah, so help me God. The SMC is already threatening to expel you! You understand that, don't you?"

Of course I fucking understood that. SMC stood for St. Mary's Committee. In other words, they were the glue that held the school together. All school decisions were run through them, as were disciplinary actions.

"Do you *want* me to tell your father of all the havoc you've been setting forth since stepping foot into St. Mary's? If I'd told him about the fake IDs, or the fights, or the sneaking into girls' rooms," he growled, "or any of it...you'd be twenty feet underground, surrounded by nothing but stone walls and men twice your age breaking every bone in your body for the fucking fun of it. The committee is ready to throw you out on your ass, and your father will be livid."

I glanced away, my chest rumbling with animosity. "Why haven't you told him, then?" I asked, looking my uncle dead in the face. "You keep threatening it, but you have done no such thing. So why? And the SMC has been threatening to expel me for over a year."

My uncle and father were nothing alike. My father was all business, and my Uncle Tate, despite being in charge of St. Mary's, was lax. He didn't typically get angry, but if he did, he got over it quickly. He had a soft spot for troublemakers.

My uncle's eyes narrowed as he dropped his head. His hands came up, and he ran his fingers through his hair all the way to the base of his skull before giving me a look that had me wavering for a second. "Maybe I will, Isaiah. I thought..." He cleared his throat before clasping his hands together. "I thought I could help you. I've been you, Isaiah. I *was* you." His voice grew louder, and he glanced at the door behind me before lowering it again. "I know what it's like to be the black sheep. I'm trying to help you, Isaiah. That's why I sent you to

Ms. Glenburg for counseling, plus the SMC wanted something done with you. They wanted to see the potential in you
that I see." He chuckled sarcastically, and I took a deep
breath, watching him with a careful eye. "So tell me why."

"Why what?" I asked, sounding bored.

He leaned back in his seat, glaring at me. "Why did you
seduce her? That's the only reasonable explanation. Some
may blame the adult in this situation, but"—my uncle crept
forward, almost in a menacing way, before leaning his arms on
his desk—"I blame *you*."

I sighed, a small smile playing on my lips.

"Start talking. Or you can kiss any amount of freedom you
have away this very second."

I peered up at him and saw that he was actually serious
for once. *Fuck.*

"Fine," I started.

And then I spilled the dirty truth.

*"ISAIAH." Ms. Glenburg grabbed onto my hands. Her skin was soft
against mine, and she flushed the second I raised an eyebrow at her.*

*We'd been having these weekly sessions for about a month now,
and each one, she got a little closer to me. Today, she even went as far
as touching me. Naughty, naughty.*

"Yes, Ms. Glenburg?" I asked slyly.

*Her hands moved from mine, and she took a shaky breath. My
gaze went to her chest as she inhaled, her breasts spilling out of her
low-cut, dressy top. I couldn't help but wonder if she had worn it for
me. If only she knew I was playing her. If I was a decent guy, I may
have felt a little bad. She thought she was in control, but she was
wrong.*

*"Are you going to be truthful today? Are you going to tell me why
you have been so defiant? Why you've been acting out against your
father? How you've ended up at St. Mary's?"*

I shrugged, loosening the tie around my neck. We were alone in an empty classroom. Her classroom. Ms. Glenburg was the school counselor, but she also taught a few elective courses like psychology and sociology. It was poetic that a woman like Ms. Glenburg could be fooled by me when she actually studied the human psyche for a living.

I leaned forward into her space. She didn't move, and her dark-red lips parted as a breath escaped her. "Why don't you tell me, Ms. Glenburg? You've been studying me for weeks now. Why do you think I act out?"

God. It was so easy to toy with her. I knew it was wrong, but that was what I was known for. Why not live up to the standard, right? My uncle was foolish if he thought someone like Ms. Glenburg could change me.

"I think you act out because it's the only form of control you have."

I shifted my eyes from her tits to her eyes. "Go on."

She moved in her seat, recrossing her legs. "You have no control over your life. You were sent to a strict boarding school without your consent. From what you've told me, your college is already decided. Your major. Your job afterward to work with your father. You have no control over anything, so the only thing you can do is grab a hold of your behavior."

Fuck. *My stomach tightened with her words. I didn't like that she was indicating that I didn't have any control over my life. I also didn't like that what she said made sense.*

Something evil stirred inside of me at the very thought of my father treating me like I was a fucking puppet in his game. In a way, Ms. Glenburg was right. My choices have been made for me since I was born. I didn't have control in most aspects of my life, and that made me irate.

"You don't think I have control, Ms. Glenburg?" I asked, shifting closer to her. My hand fell onto her knee, and she gasped.

"I—" she stuttered, staring at my hand on her bare skin, sitting nice and still below the hem of her skirt.

"That's not true, Ms. Glenburg." I smirked, glancing at her lips. "I'm in control right now."

"Are you?" she whispered.

My hand stayed on her knee as I glanced over my shoulder. "You said my father has control over my life, but I don't see him anywhere in this room." I gave her a sheepish look. "In fact, I don't see anyone in this room..." My finger trailed over to the inside of her leg. "Except you."

She swallowed, her cheeks rising with color.

"Do you want to see me in control, Ms. Glenburg?" I would show her that she was wrong. *My father didn't have control over me.*

Or did he?

"I'm not sure," she answered breathlessly.

I smiled at her as my hand moved higher up her leg, disappearing underneath the dark fabric. I took my other hand and gently took her glasses off the bridge of her nose and placed them onto the desk beside us.

Ms. Glenburg was twice my age—somewhere in her thirties—but she was still hot in this authoritative sort of way. Either way, I still would have been in this situation, but it was to my benefit that she actually did get my dick hard.

"I thought we were telling the truth here," I said as my hand stopped moving up toward her center. "You asked me to be truthful, but are you being truthful, Ms. Glenburg?"

She gulped before licking her lips. Her hazel eyes held that hungry look in them, like she wanted me to fuck her.

"Do you want to see me in control?"

Her words were as rushed as her breaths. "I could get fired for this, Isaiah." Try 'you could go to jail,' since I'm technically a minor, but that was just semantics.

"Then we better not get caught."

Her hand was wrapped around my tie within a flash, and she pulled us both to the desk as her legs parted around my waist. Her *fuck-me eyes were droopy and hooded as she peered up at me from lying back on the hard wood. I placed both hands beside her head, her blonde hair spilling out all around her.*

A jolt of blinding excitement went through me at the thought of getting caught. It was a rush. A rush I'd welcome over and over again until I no longer had the chance.

"You're wrong, Ms. Glenburg. I am in control." I dipped my head down and captured her lips with mine. My dick pushed up to meet her warm pussy as her skirt hiked its way to her hips. Her hands went to my biceps as her tongue swept in my mouth, taking every bit of my lust that I gave her.

A whimper sounded from her as I backed away and found her wet panties. A wicked smile formed its way on my mouth as I pushed the silk aside and ran my finger over her slick slit. She arched her back, one leg wrapping around my back, as her hand dove underneath the dip in her blouse to grab herself. "Already so wet," I teased, my finger rubbing over her swollen clit. "Tell me," I whispered, ready to finger-fuck her. "Have you been wanting this from the beginning?"

Ms. Glenburg was panting as I stared down at her, her eyes barely open. "I've wanted this since the second you stepped in this school, Isaiah. You're not like the others. You aren't a boy. You're jaded."

That was when I let my finger sink into her warm walls. They constricted almost immediately as she moaned loudly. So greedy. I have to admit, this was my first time fucking around with an older woman, but I was definitely enjoying it. She knew what she wanted, and she wasn't afraid to go after it.

Her hips curled as she palmed her tit. I reached my hand up and unbuttoned the rest of her top as I pumped her faster.

"I want to fuck you," I said, wondering if she'd actually agree to it. This was too easy. If my uncle saw this, he'd have a fucking aneurysm.

"You're the one in control," she moaned.

"That I am," I said as I pulled my finger out and unbuttoned my pants. She pushed herself back onto her desk, papers floating to the

ground wistfully, and spread her legs. I reached up roughly and pulled
her panties down past her legs and dropped them to the floor.

Just as I had the condom on and placed myself at her entrance, the
door swung open, and in came a cart full of janitorial products along
with Mr. Clark who looked like he'd seen a ghost.

"Oops," I muttered as Ms. Glenburg peered back.

If only I could have been in Mr. Clark's position and see what he
saw: me, a student, hovering over a teacher with my dick in my hand
as Ms. Glenburg lay spread open on top of her desk with her chest on
full display.

She quickly sat up and covered herself, trying to talk her way out
of it. She was flustered, rushing her words out so quickly it sounded
like she was speaking a foreign language.

"Okay!" My uncle slapped the desk again and brought me
back to reality. "That's enough!"

I smirked as I began buttoning the rest of my shirt, the
buttons sliding into their slots effortlessly. I shrugged. "You
said you wanted to know."

"Isaiah." He leveled me with a stare. "Did you truly fuck
her—"

"I didn't fuck her," I interrupted him after crossing my
arms over my chest. *But I would have if I hadn't been*
interrupted.

He glared at me, and I rolled my lips again, trying to
hold it together. I knew I was pushing his buttons, probably
a little too far, but I couldn't help it. I was a little
worked up.

My uncle sat back in his seat and rubbed his chin as if he
were the one studying me now instead of her. I kept a hold of
his stare for a few seconds as he squinted at me, analyzing me,
scrutinizing me. Then, I began glancing around his stuffy,
crammed office with entirely too many weird artifacts, like

the fucking ancient globe at the end of his desk. Did it even have the correct continents on it?

"You felt threatened."

I shifted my attention back to him without changing my posture. "Excuse me?"

"She made sense. She saw right through you. It made you angry, so you did the only thing you could think of, and you turned on your charm to prove a point."

I clenched my jaw. "And what point would that be?"

His eyebrow lifted. "You wanted to show her, and me, and maybe even yourself that she was wrong. That you *do* have control." He chuckled, throwing his hands up with astonishment. "She was right. That's exactly why you act out."

"No, it fucking isn't." My temper was rising. My fists were clenching around the arms of the chair as I dug my nails into the same crescent-shaped marks that were already there.

My uncle took a deep steady breath, running his hands through his unkempt hair once again. "Isaiah." His green eyes wrinkled at the edges. *Fuck. This was it. He was kicking me out.* I wanted to pull my own hair out. I felt very unstable at the moment, completely unsteady in my seat, even though my feet were planted firmly on the ground.

"Spit it out, Uncle."

"This is your last chance. Do you hear me?" My hands unclenched slightly. "I want to help you. I do. Stop fucking up on purpose, because I can't keep turning my head at the big things. I'll lose this school, and that's the last thing I or anyone here needs."

I said nothing, and we stared at each other for far too long. We were having an unspoken conversation about all the things our family was mixed up in—neither one of us wanted to speak of it. He got out, but it wasn't that easy for me.

"Isaiah," he repeated

I held my hand up. "I hear you."

His stern gaze that resembled my father's all too well fell. "You do have a choice. You know that, right?"

I scoffed, pushing myself back into the chair forcefully. "You don't truly believe that, do you?"

My uncle looked away, thinking for a moment before shaking his head and standing up hastily. He walked around his desk, as I sat lazily in the chair in front of him, and propped himself on the edge. Leveling my chin, I locked onto his gaze.

"This is your last chance, and as much as I don't want to say those words to you...I have to. If the SMC finds out about this or anything else you impulsively do, they will likely expel you, and then your father will get involved." He pushed off the desk and began walking past me toward the door.

Silence filled his office as I stood up, keeping my back to him. I peered up at the large, framed map that was plastered to the wall behind his empty chair. How easy would it be for me to just walk away? To flip my father the bird and leave the family name behind like my uncle?

But it wasn't that easy for me. There were casualties to that.

Like Jack.

I wouldn't do to him what Jacobi did to me.

I wouldn't leave him in the dark to fend for himself. I didn't feel much these days, other than anger, but I knew, deep down, Jack meant the most to me.

My uncle's voice hit me from behind. "You could make the same choice I did."

I spun around quickly and glared at him. My rebellious, rule-breaking, gave-zero-fucks persona had vanished like quicksand between my fingers. "I won't do that to Jack."

His hand was on the doorknob, but before he twisted it, he sighed. "Then get it together, because the SMC will eventually get tired of my excuses for you, and they will go straight to your father to let him know you've been expelled. There will be no more chances."

I scoffed again, ready to walk out the door and push this conversation away. "So what are you saying exactly? That I should stop fucking teachers?" I laughed under my breath, trying to get back to my calmer state.

His jaw was tight. "Yeah, Isaiah. That's exactly what I'm saying. The SMC is already breathing down my neck." The green in his eyes hardened to stone. "If you are expelled, there will be nothing I can do to help you. And that's if they let me keep my job after saving your ass over and over again. You do know where your father will send you, right? He'll send you right to the Covens. Tell me you understand. If you think St. Mary's is bad, you'll be in for a rude awakening there."

I didn't think St. Mary's was all that bad, but I didn't say that. Instead, I grumbled, "I get it. I know what the Covens is."

"Good." He swung the door open and grinned. "Now, as your punishment, you're going to take our new student, Gemma, to her room—322—and give her a tour of the school while I go do damage control."

I rolled my eyes. That was it? *That* was my punishment?

Before I walked past him and into the hall, he pulled me back by my shirt and whispered, "She's a good girl. Take her to her room, show her around, and then leave her alone."

I snickered when he let go of me. "Don't worry. Good girls aren't my type, Uncle."

CHAPTER THREE

GEMMA

"GEMMA!" The headmaster walked out of his office with his nephew following closely behind him.

I quickly averted my eyes away from Isaiah, although I couldn't ignore the dip in my stomach when our gazes collided. "Isaiah will be giving you a tour of the school, and then he will take you to your room to make sure you are settled." He glared at him once before giving me another warm smile. "I'll be sure to check on you later before lights out."

My lips gently tugged upward as he turned and began storming down the desolate hallway, leaving me alone with a guy my age for the first time in...ever.

Isaiah and I stood beside each other for a few painfully awkward seconds before he broke the silence with his cool voice.

"Did you enjoy the conversation?" he asked, his head tilting to the side as he scrutinized me. His blue eyes twinkled with something that should have warned me off, but surprisingly, I kept a hold of his stare.

"What?" I asked, feigning confusion.

He smirked, but it didn't quite reach his eyes. I followed the flicking of his chin to the wooden bench I was sitting on seconds ago. "When I went into my uncle's office, you were sitting wayyy over there." His gaze met the spot I was in when I had first sat down. "But when we came out, you were pushed all the way up to the door. So, I'll ask again." His eyebrows rose for a split second as he casually placed his hands in his pockets. "Did you enjoy hearing that I fucked a teacher?"

Did he really just ask me that?

My tongue was heavy in my mouth. Like if I were to speak, my words would tumble out in the wrong order.

The fluttering of my eyelashes tickled my cheek as I continued staring at him. The longer we looked at each other, the harder my heart beat. The pounding was deafening. It was so thunderous I wondered if he could hear it too.

After a few more seconds, Isaiah laughed under his breath before rolling his eyes. "My uncle was right. You are a good girl."

My fists instantly clenched with his words.

"Don't call me that," I snapped, feeling the skin of my palm split open from my nails. I gasped at my outburst and looked behind me, as if Richard was going to pop out of a hidden corner and drag me to the basement to repent for my sin of not only talking to Isaiah with such a harsh tone but for just talking to him in general.

When I turned back around and met Isaiah's face, he was grinning wildly. His white teeth glimmered behind his perfect blush-colored lips.

"Hmm," was all he muttered before reaching down and grabbing my bag. He spun around and began walking down the hall. I followed after him because I wasn't sure what else I was supposed to be doing. But I was still agitated that he had provoked me, and even more so that I had acted on it.

The hallway grew darker the farther we walked, as if we were stalking toward the pits of hell. The strangely bare walls stole my attention before I found myself standing below a large staircase that had dark, wooden, decorative handrails that seemed to go on for forever.

Isaiah glanced back at me, still sporting a smirk between his chiseled cheeks, before he began hopping up the stairs like an Olympic athlete, holding my one suitcase in tow. His long strides pulled him quickly, and I struggled to keep up, but before long, we were standing on the landing with two more sets of stairs on each side.

"To the right is the girls' wing, and to the left is the boys'." I nodded, and he continued on. "We aren't allowed to go to the other wing except for special circumstances. But some of us break the rules." My brow crinkled, and he had a hard time keeping his face straight. "As in, boys sneak into the girls' rooms, and sometimes the other way around...depending on the type of girl." He started inching toward the right set of stairs, walking backward as he smiled at me. "We won't have to worry about you doing that, though. Right, Good Girl?"

I ground my teeth and inhaled all the oxygen that I could.

He laughed, and I wasn't sure I liked the way my heart squeezed at the sound. I was naive, and I had a hard time reading people, but I knew he was making fun of me. And I didn't like that. Not one bit. It made me feel small, and I was really freaking tired of feeling small.

"Stop calling me that," I bit out, crossing my arms over my chest.

He chuckled and hastily turned around and skipped up the rest of the steps. I waited a few seconds, calming down the heat stirring in my belly before stomping up the rest of the stairs. He was all the way at the end of the hallway by the time I reached the top, but I could hardly see him through the thick darkness.

The hallway was long and deep, laid with dark-red carpet underneath my feet. It was bathed with an eerie light from the few sconces on the wall in between each set of doors, and if I believed in ghosts, I would certainly be feeling a little bit uneasy at the moment.

"Are you coming?" Isaiah shouted. "Or are you afraid of the dark?"

I didn't answer as I crept along the soft floor, running my finger along the grooved, walnut-colored wood. So far, St. Mary's seemed like an old medieval castle that was turned into a boarding school. And for all I knew, it was. Each door I'd passed was thick, dark wood with intricate carvings in the mass of them. They each had iron-clad doorknobs with chains attached at the bottom, and for the first time since setting foot in this place, a chill raced down my spine.

I was a few steps away from Isaiah, the warm glow of a lantern light shining on the side of his face, making him that much more beautiful. I gritted my teeth at the thought that came through, but it was suddenly gone as the sound of one of the chains ricocheting off another came from behind me. Panic set deep into my bones, and I ran straight into Isaiah's hard chest, bouncing off him like I'd hit a brick wall.

"Whoa," he blurted as his strong hands wrapped around my upper arms, steadying me.

I gasped at the touch. Sparks flew. Heat sourced from his palms, and when he let go, I instantly took a step back.

"Isaiah?" a girl whisper-yelled. I quickly spun around and saw a pretty girl with long lean legs step out of a door. "Sneaking into the gi—" She stopped talking when her eyes dropped over to me. "Oh. Who's this?"

Isaiah groaned, his words clipped. "New student. Go back to your room, Callie."

She huffed as she crossed her arms over her chest in a bratty manner. "Who are you? Father Isaiah? Telling me to go back to my room..." She huffed out the last part of her sentence, and Isaiah snickered.

"I remember you calling me daddy a few nights ago, so yeah, I guess you could call me that." My mouth dropped open slightly, and then she yelled, "Fuck you, Isaiah," and then swiftly turned around and slammed her door.

Wow.

"Let's go, Good Girl," Isaiah whispered in my ear, and I jumped before following after him again.

He waited until we were stopped in front of what I assumed to be my new room to say, "If you're afraid of the dark, I suggest getting a flashlight."

I gingerly peered up, still feeling a bit vulnerable that I was so spooked from the sound of chains that it had me running into him. And if I was being honest, I was a little embarrassed to admit that his and Callie's little spar distracted me enough to make me forget about the chains all together. That was very unusual. "I'm not afraid of the dark."

Isaiah studied me with an interested look before raising his hand to knock. "Then what *are* you afraid of?"

The chains were clamping around my wrists. The gag was being stuffed in my mouth. "Nothing," I answered as he rapped his knuckles on the door. "Nothing at all."

He kept his icy-blue gaze on me as the door opened up. Before I brushed past him, his hand clamped down on my elbow, and he whispered his hot breath into my ear, "And here I thought good girls didn't lie, *Gemma*."

Heat spread over my skin like I was standing in the middle of a burning room. I inched my head to the side, my neck more exposed than before. "Well, maybe I'm not a good girl, *Isaiah.*" Then, I ripped my elbow out of his grasp and entered my new home.

It took him a few moments to follow after me, and I was certain it was because he was as surprised as I was at my behavior. I wasn't sure what had come over me. I had never, in my entire life, talked to someone as confidently as I had just spoken to Isaiah. I felt in control but totally out of control at the same exact time, which made absolutely no sense at all.

What I did know was that, without Richard breathing down my neck and watching me with his dirty, beady eyes, I felt at ease, and that wasn't good even in the slightest. Letting my guard down around anyone, especially Isaiah, would only bite me in the ass down the road.

I wouldn't make the same mistake twice.

My lungs burned as snippets from the last few weeks filled my head, but they quickly disappeared as I let my gaze scour around my new room. My mouth fell as I took in the beautiful, glowing fairy lights that hung from every corner, making the small area seem like some sort of fairytale instead of the dungeon that I'd expected.

"I know," a girl announced, snagging my attention. I glanced to the center of the room and saw a petite girl with shoulder-length black hair. Her smile was as bright as the pink on her lips. "It's weird coming from a creepy hallway to a room that's..."

"Beautiful," I finished for her, looking up to the ceiling that had some type of 3D paper butterflies taped to it. The room was all things light and fluffy, which were two things I wasn't really familiar with. I would be lying if I said it didn't make me feel lighter, though.

"Gemma, this is Sloane. Sloane, this is Gemma, your new roommate."

She smiled again as she walked over to me and held her hand out. "Welcome to St. Mary's."

I took it cautiously and glanced at Isaiah who was staring at me intently with an unreadable expression on his face. "Alright, I'm out," he finally said, still keeping me pinned to my spot.

"I thought I was supposed to get a tour of the school?"

"I'll give you a tour," Sloane said, dismissing Isaiah.

My shoulders immediately dropped in relief. Being around Isaiah was exhausting, even if it had been only for a few minutes. I was acting way out of character with him for some reason. It was better this way. I'd be able to keep myself in line by getting a rundown of St. Mary's from my new roommate rather than *him*.

He made me feel...something. Something I wouldn't allow myself to feel because I already knew it would be a distraction.

"Great." Isaiah slapped his hands together. "I'll see you around, Good Girl." He winked at me, and my face flamed.

As soon as he left the room, Sloane laughed. "That's Isaiah for you. He's a lot, huh?"

I thought very carefully before I spoke. "He makes me nervous," I said, and although it was true, it wasn't the first word to come to mind when answering her. Isaiah made me feel excited and maybe a bit scared. And hot. Really hot. Like, sweat-was-coating-my-back hot.

She nodded, her straight, shiny, ebony strands swaying. "He makes all the girls nervous. He's a bad boy, though. Through and through." She sighed. "You should probably stay away from him, or you'll end up in the closet."

The closet? I absolutely hated that I was so out of the loop on just about everything teenage-girl related. It only took a few days at Wellington Prep to realize that high school was not what I had expected—or what I was taught. I had learned a lot from watching others my age navigate their *normal* high school lives, and the things I'd overheard at the lunch table made me blush just being near someone who had done them. I was curious, too. Really curious.

I nodded in Sloane's direction, pretending I knew what she was referring to with the closet thing, but I really had no idea. I could only guess that it was something my dear Uncle Richard wouldn't approve of, though.

"Well, anyway," she started, shaking away the conversation. "Let's get you settled. I'm glad to have a roommate again. My last one had to..."—Sloane averted her eyes—"leave pretty abruptly."

"Why?" I asked curiously. "Did she break a rule or something?"

Sloane threw her head back and laughed as she pulled up my suitcase for me and placed it on the bed opposite of hers. "Oh, Gemma. We all break the rules here."

My stomach fell. *Then why would Richard send me here? Was it a test?*

"Is this all you have?" Sloane asked, tucking her hair behind her ear. She glanced around my body and jutted her lip out.

"Um. Yes." Seeing the confusion on her face, I quickly added, "I just wasn't sure what to bring, so I only brought the essentials. I mean, we get uniforms here, right?"

She eyed me curiously, her hazel eyes showing a lot of depth behind them. "Yeah. We do. But we don't have to wear them after classes end. You're welcome to borrow my things if you want. I have tons of clothes. My parents feel bad for sending me here, so they always send me new things."

"They feel bad?" I asked, taking a step closer to my bed.

Sloane popped back onto hers with a whoosh, her legs dangling below. She was a tiny person. She hardly reached my 5'5" frame.

"Yeah." She grabbed a small pink, sequined pillow and wrapped her arms around it. "They're both in the military, and they both deploy a lot. My grandma used to take care of me, but she got Alzheimer's, so she's in a nursing home now. There was no one else I could stay with, so they sent me to the best boarding school in the nation." She shrugged. "At least I'll get into a good college, right?"

College. Such a wistful thought.

I began to turn around to empty out my suitcase that had nothing significant in it, except for one discolored Polaroid photo of me, my mom, and my brother, when Sloane asked, "What about you? Why are you here?"

Awkwardness hung in the air like the stench of spoiled meat as I tried to come up with something that wouldn't raise too many questions and, again, something that wouldn't make me seem...different. I had a serious battle of what was considered normal and what wasn't.

"Are you one of the good ones? Or bad ones?"

My second pair of jeans were like dead weight in my hands as I pulled them out of my suitcase. "What do you mean?" I asked, looking for a place to put my clothes.

Sloane nodded to the chest of drawers pushed up against the wall next to a desk that had nothing on it but a pamphlet of some sort.

I get my own desk?

As I walked over to it, Sloane sat up a little taller. "Yeah. Are you an uber-smart student, and your parents sent you here for a better chance at a college? Or are you an orphan with a bad past?" Her last assumption was said jokingly, but it really wasn't that far off from my real life.

Clearly seeing my confusion, Sloane chuckled while giving me an incredulous look. "You don't know much about St. Mary's, do you?"

Not a single thing. That actually wasn't necessarily true.

Richard had told me all about St. Mary's, but I trusted him about as far as I could throw him, and spoiler alert: he was three times my size.

I shifted on my feet nervously. "Not really." I glanced down. "My uncle sent me here. That's who I lived with... before now."

Pity was clear on her soft expression, but it was totally unneeded. Being sent here was an upgrade. "Oh. I'm...sorry?"

My heart had a slight dent as I pushed away any sad lingering thought that involved my mom and Tobias before I put my hand up. "It's okay. But to answer your question..." I had to force the lie out. "I'm here for academics mostly. Plus, my aunt isn't well, and my uncle works a lot, so it was better for all of us for me to come here."

The lies were bitter on my tongue. Like I'd taken a mouthful of battery acid. That wasn't true at all. Richard was forced to put me in Wellington Prep a few months ago because some of the girls at the group home, who had to relocate because of Auntie's sudden debilitating stroke, talked to their social worker about *the teen who lived in the house with Judge Stallard,* thus raising too many questions. Then, I seemed to blow my chances for a normal life at a normal high school because I'd shared things with the wrong people.

I really could trust no one that Richard knew. In fact, I couldn't trust anyone but the one social worker who was relentless in figuring out who I was and why I was living with Richard in the first place. And I didn't even really trust her, either.

I quickly darted my eyes away as Sloane's began to look suspicious. I rummaged through the rest of my things, shoving them all into the empty drawers as a distraction, when she finally spoke again.

"The headmaster will love you."

"Why do you say that?" I asked, slowly turning around.

She laughed lightly, tucking her shiny hair behind her ear again. Her other hand played with the glittery sequins on the pillow.

"Because the more fucked up you are, the more he likes you. He has a soft spot for the really messed-up ones."

My mouth fell open as a knock sounded on the door.

Sloane slid her feet to the ground and patted my arm. "Don't worry, Gemma. We're all a little fucked up at St. Mary's. You'll fit right in."

Then, she bounced to the door and opened it, leaving me feeling like I had rocks in the bottom of my stomach.

CHAPTER FOUR

GEMMA

PULLING down the maroon blazer I was wearing, I shivered. Nerves were making my skin tingle and itch like I was standing on the edge of a cliff with someone behind me, ready to push me below into an abyss of icy-cold water with an uncertainty of everything I was about to crash into.

Yesterday evening, after Sloane deemed me as *fucked up*— which was more or less a good thing because she insinuated that it was pretty normal around here—the headmaster walked into our room, holding a pile of new uniforms in one hand and a cardboard box in the other.

Sloane excitedly went through the box as the headmaster gave me my schedule and handed me a school map in case I got lost after my tour with Isaiah, which never ended up happening. I didn't tell him that, though, because I was more relieved than anything.

As soon as the headmaster left our room, Sloane laughed and said in a sing-song voice, "See?" She ushered toward the cardboard box. "He likes you."

When she pulled me over to the box, the heavy rocks in my stomach turned to dust. Inside were school supplies, a laptop, and some twinkle lights that Sloane draped over my bed posts. It was the only thing on my side of the room that said, *"I'm loved,"* as I literally had nothing else to my name, not even a nice blanket, but that was okay. I slept better last night than I had in months, which wasn't really saying much.

Picking up my new journal on my way out the door this morning, Sloane draped her arm through mine and led me down the dark, windowless hallway with tons of other girls bustling around. I even saw a few running over the blood-red carpet with towels perched on top of their heads, yelling that they were going to be late for breakfast.

Sloane and I were right on time.

"Here," she said as she handed me a tray and nodded over to the lunch line. The cafeteria was just as medieval as the rest of the school. Large, wooden tables sat parallel to one another with seats fit for a king on both ends. On the sides were long benches, which seemed to be where mostly everyone sat.

"Wow," I whispered, pulling steaming oatmeal—which seemed to appear out of nowhere—onto my tray. The smell of cinnamon filled my senses, and I sighed wistfully.

Sloane nodded back at me. "I know. The food is pretty good here."

I said nothing as she pulled me by the elbow toward a table closest to the two French doors. We sat at the end, near no one in particular, but before long, the entire table was filled up, and everyone was whispering and staring in my direction. I pulled at my white collar underneath my scratchy maroon blazer and rubbed at the hives along my neck.

I was used to going unnoticed, pushed away into the shadows, keeping my mouth shut, and following the rules. I was submissive and quiet by nature because I knew my place, and

I knew what would happen if I stepped a toe out of line. So this? This was awful.

"Everyone..." Sloane slowly stood up, gaining everyone's attention. My face was on fire as I dipped my head down low, my dark locks swaying over my face. Part of me wanted to straighten my spine and prove to myself that I wasn't that quiet, passive girl I was bred to be, but old habits died hard. "This is Gemma. My new roommate."

The entire dining hall went quiet except for the clanking of silverware and opening of milk cartons. Sloane cleared her throat, and I peeked up to what felt like five million pairs of eyes on me. I scanned over their faces quickly, like the fast forwarding on a VCR, and felt a tiny bout of disappointment. At first, I wasn't sure why. I didn't expect—or want—to make many friends. It was too hard for me to keep up my *normalcy*, not to mention keep my story straight. And also, I had big plans that didn't involve a single person here. But when the French doors clamored open again and everyone's attention swung toward them, I realized right then why I'd felt the slight twinge of disappointment.

Isaiah. I'd been scanning the long dining table for him. I'd been searching for those icy eyes that had sparked something to life in me yesterday.

My face flamed even brighter with the thought. I was wading in unknown waters, unknowingly chasing after something so completely foreign to me that I didn't even know what to call it.

Sloane plopped back down beside me, picking up her spoon and pushing it into her gooey oatmeal. "And just like that, the attention is off of you."

I blinked several times, unable to look away from Isaiah and what looked to be his pack of friends as they slowly prowled into the dining hall with so much commanding, hot authority I actually started to sweat.

"Wh—what?" I stuttered, trailing over each of them before landing back on Isaiah. They were all flawless. Each and every last one of them. Tall...some leaner than others, but they all appeared to be in good physical strength—like Tobias. I could still see him through the darkness of my room as he did a million and one push-ups in the middle of the night when he knew I couldn't sleep. He always stayed until I fell asleep, even when I begged him to go back to his room so he didn't get in trouble.

I sighed softly, pushing away the memory. Isaiah and his friends' school blazers fit their broad shoulders tightly, and somehow they each had a type of *air* surrounding them, like they were totally unbothered by a single thing in the world. Lazily hot, with so much confidence that everyone was forced to stare. Authoritative, in a way, which was something that *wasn't* completely unknown to me.

I quickly turned my head from the pack of guys as yet another hush fell over the dining hall. Sloane dipped her head closer to mine. "I knew the Rebels were about to walk through the doors. That's why I made a quick intro of you, knowing the attention wouldn't last long when they walked in. Figured it was better to get it over with than drag it out, right?" She went back into her own personal bubble, giving me room to breathe before shrugging. "You're introverted. You're a lot like my last roommate, and she would have *hated* having attention on her."

My lip twitched at the corner. It was a nice thing that she did, whereas before, I kind of wanted to knock her chair over for putting me on the spot. "Thank you, Sloane."

Her pearly whites beamed behind her pink lips before she stuffed more oatmeal in her mouth. She was pretty when she smiled, and it was a friendly one, at that. I kind of wanted to be her friend, even though I knew the friendship wouldn't last long. But it felt like we were on that path, and I wasn't sure I had it in me to pretend that I didn't desperately want someone in my corner.

I began eating my breakfast even though my stomach was in knots. The silver spoon in my hand continued to slip through my sweaty fingers as I brought another spoonful of the cinnamon oats up to my mouth. The dining room had picked up some more chatter, and I noted a bunch of people pulling out their cell phones. I had a cell phone, but it was mostly for show, given to me by Richard before I started to attend Wellington Prep. I'd never really used it because he told me he could see everything that I did on it, so I hardly touched it. Even the mere thought of giving him even more insight to who I was caused a slight chill to blanket my skin.

Sloane laughed softly beside me as she put her phone down on the table. She shook her head and mumbled, "Jesus."

"What?" I asked, placing my spoon beside my bowl. I couldn't stomach another bite of my breakfast, even if it was delicious.

Sloane caught my eye briefly. "There's a new post on Mary's Murmurs." Seeing my confusion, she shook her head. "Sorry, I forgot you have no clue what I'm talking about. Mary's Murmurs is the gossip blog for St. Mary's." She rolled her eyes. "It's usually all about who the Rebels are fucking or their latest bad-boy drama."

The muscles along my face stayed nice and steady as she continued on, but I felt the heat rise to my cheeks.

"Today, it's about Isaiah." She laughed under her breath, and my heart slipped in my chest at the sound of his name. *Why? Why did it do that?*

My voice cracked at first before I cleared my throat. "Who writes on the blog? How do they know all the gossip?"

Sloane shrugged. "No one knows. The Rebels love the

attention, though, so they just go with it. They're so full of themselves."

She said the last part in half awe and half disgust. It was like she was annoyed but also fascinated. I had to admit, I kind of was too. Not annoyed but maybe a little intrigued. I wanted to ask more about them. Why they were called the Rebels and why everyone was so drawn to them besides the obvious reason: *because they were really, really attractive.*

Slowly, *very* slowly, and discreetly, my gaze traveled over Sloane's tray lined with an assortment of breakfast foods, to the dark wood of the dining table underneath it, to my oatmeal, and then down the long dining table, past all my new classmates. I locked onto the chair at the very end—the one fit for a king.

I gasped, my breath hitching in the back of my throat.

Sloane's voice hissed in my ear, but I hardly registered it. "Why the hell is he staring at you like that? Or should I say glaring?"

My eyes bounced between Isaiah's, the ice-blue color summoning me to submit. Submit to what? I wasn't sure. But I felt my legs shaking underneath the table. My heart skipped a beat, my stomach somersaulting to the point that it was convulsing inside my body.

A harsh ring sounded out around my ears, and it quickly took me out of the stupor. I jerked back, my head snapping back down to my oatmeal. Sloane's hand fell onto mine, "Come on. It's time for class."

My movements were jerky. I was shaky when I stood up from long bench, the sturdy wooden legs scraping slightly along the intricate tiled floor. My fingers clutched around my notebook as my paper schedule crumpled between my fingers.

"Are you okay? That was weird, right?" Sloane asked, weaving her arm back through mine like before. Relief settled in my bones as she pulled me along because I wasn't sure I could walk straight, and also, I was so glad to be out of Isaiah's grasp.

"Yeah, I'm fine," I answered after peering behind my shoulder. I braced myself for the pair of piercing blue eyes again, but Isaiah was gone.

CHAPTER FIVE

ISAIAH

MY JAW ACHED from clenching it every few seconds. I narrowed my eyes on the petite, chestnut-haired girl running her deft fingers over the drawing pencils with a laser-like fascination. The muscles along my forearms bounced as my fists squeezed tighter, hot blood soaring through my veins.

"Fuck. She is hot as hell. Who cares if she spilled the tea? We usually welcome the talk." Brantley's voice was low, a grumble almost, as he stared at Good Girl—who apparently wasn't as good as I had pegged her to be.

The little snitch.

Let's go back to two hours ago, when my uncle called me into his office at the crack of fucking dawn.

My hair was still damp from my shower as I wrapped the maroon tie around my neck, not bothering to tighten it around the collar of my white dress shirt. I knew my uncle would look at me disapprovingly, but I truly didn't care—and not just because it was well before the sun had even peeked through the gloomy clouds. In general, I just didn't give a fuck.

The hallway was silent as I swiftly made my way to his office, the door slightly open with a faint glow coming from the heirloom lamp on his desk.

His head popped up as I stepped through the threshold. I hoped he could sense the irritation coming off me in thunderous waves, but like me, he most likely didn't care about my feelings toward him.

"Isaiah."

"Uncle," I said in the same tone he used as I threw myself down into the seat I'd occupied no less than twenty-four hours ago when he'd caught me with Ms. Glenburg, who—I'd noted—had already left the premises. "Is this my real punishment for *almost* fucking a teacher? I told you I'd get my shit together. No need to drag me out of bed at six in the morning."

My uncle sighed, clearly annoyed. He leaned back in his leather chair and steepled his fingers together. "The SMC has called for a meeting."

"Okay, so?" I said, flicking my eyes down to my uncle's coffee cup that was steaming above the brim.

What would he do if I just grabbed it and downed it? Nothing?

"So," my uncle seethed. "They already fucking know you were caught with your hand up a teacher's skirt! Who did you tell about Ms. Glenburg, Isaiah?"

My mouth opened slightly in shock. There was a dip in my cool facade that I wore like a second skin. My uncle interrupted my thoughts, slapping his hands down onto his desk in his usual frustrated manner. "Did you tell the rest of your alpha pack?" His face scrunched as if he was fed up with the entire situation. *That made two of us.* "The Rebel Boys?"

"It's just the Rebels," I clarified.

The group was born long ago—before I or my uncle

attended here. It was a century-old society set within the thick, damp walls of this dark boarding school, originating from the Latin word, *Rebellis*. The history behind the group was that there needed to be order within the students. The students that came here in the far past were from two separate upbringings. Split right in half. Some were orphans—sent from an orphanage a few blocks over with no one to answer to and with no one to teach them right from wrong. The others were descendants from parents who did illegal shit but who were also prestigious in the outside world. It was still like that—with the students, I mean. I fell into the latter of the group. My last name was well-known. My family was wealthy, and we were considered high society. But that didn't mean we were good. My father was a piece of shit. He dabbled in crime behind the scenes of his business investments and charitable dues. His bad side was elusive to many.

The walls of St. Mary's were secure, though, like a completely different civilization breathed here rather than in the real world where there was true crime and death. The Rebels, at least a century ago, were the ones who ruled the school, set forth rules, and kept others in line, all while causing havoc in their own way. It wasn't like that anymore. It was more or less a myth. The group had been dormant until Brantley, Cade and I came here. Our other friend, Shiner, knew all about the Rebels and their...traditions...and that was when the elite group had started up again.

And as the story stated in the old journal that we'd found, the Rebels changed and evolved over the years with the different generations. One group was like a family evolving, branching the students together like a giant tree. But others were more like a hierarchy. I'd like to think the current group of Rebels, the one I was a part of—which consisted of me, Brantley, Cade, and Shiner—was a mix of the two. Again, we were more of a myth, a fraternity of sorts, but for some reason, students still came to us if there was a problem. And we definitely ate up the fame because with fame came perks, and the perks were always *hot*.

My uncle's voice rang out, "That's right. The Rebels. Tell me, does Nash know what you, Cade, and Brantley know?"

My jaw flexed. "You know Shiner doesn't go by Nash anymore." *He hated his first name.* "And no, he doesn't." My jaw ticked again. "And to answer your question, I didn't tell the boys."

Yet.

It wasn't that I planned to keep Ms. Glenburg a secret. I meant to tell the Rebels at some point, but if the SMC was as close to expelling me as my uncle said, then they'd likely cut me for good if they knew what had happened with me and Ms. Glenburg. I wanted to be on full lock-down when I spilled the dirty details, so there wasn't a chance of loose ears lingering around.

Uncle Tate pinched the bridge of his nose. "Well, the SMC knows, and I'm almost certain they will be going above me to call your father." He sighed. "They are far beyond believing my excuses for you. I can't be your alibi any longer."

I swallowed roughly, a roll of anger flying down each and every vertebra in my spine.

My eyes locked with his, and we stayed like that until I broke the dense silence. "So, what are you saying? They're expelling me? And then Dad will come up here to personally throw me into the Covens to control me even more? He won't let that happen. He needs me here."

There was once a time where I would have done anything to make my father proud. Now, though, it was the complete opposite.

My uncle's face dropped for a moment, guilt covering each and every woven line on his forehead. "I—I don't know. Just"—he took a moment before he glanced up at me—"get your shit together. I'll call your father in a few and figure out what's going on and see if he knows anything. I'll deal with the committee and do everything I can to keep you here. You need to make better choices, though." The lines of his face sharpened. "I'm being completely serious, Isaiah. You're going to need to get your grades up. Stop fucking around. For the love of God, get an alibi—someone who can collaborate your excuses—and stop getting caught doing shit. I want you to have your freedom here, because God knows you've never had it before, but there's only so much I can do for you."

A heavy feeling weighed on my chest because I could sense the urgency in his voice. I could feel the trickle of fear in the back of my head when I thought of my father and how he'd react if I was expelled. If I didn't stop rebelling, if I told him that I wouldn't be following in his footsteps, that I'd be taking the high road like Jacobi did...*fuck*. I wasn't afraid for myself. I was afraid for Jack.

"Okay," I finally said, and my uncle's head snapped up, shocked.

I was shocked too, but when it came to Jack, things hit a little differently. There was a miniscule part of me that felt something when it came to him. A slight opening in my numbness.

"I have it under control," I said, climbing to my feet.

His head tilted, and the shadows from the dim light on the edge of his desk clearly showed his skepticism.

"I don't even want to know. Just..." He glanced away. "Figure out what path you're going down, and stick to it. Yeah?"

I nodded, going toward the door, feeling all sorts of fucked up. Not only from the conversation with Uncle Tate but also from wondering how the hell the SMC could have known about me seducing—definitely using that word lightly here—Ms. Glenburg.

The only two people who knew, other than me and Ms. Glenburg herself, were the janitor and my uncle. And I knew that Mr. Clark hadn't told anyone. He and my uncle went way back. Mr. Clark knew more about my family than anyone else at this school. In fact, he had turned his head many times at my questionable behavior. Hell, he'd even helped me sneak back into the school after I'd left to be my father's errand boy in the middle of the night.

Then, it clicked.

There was one other person who could have known.

It didn't hit me until I walked into the dining hall for breakfast, after Brantley and Cade continued to prod me about the gossip on the stupid fucking blog that couldn't seem to talk about anything else other than me and the rest of the Rebels. Honestly, whoever filled their time with writing for the thing was desperate for my dick. Let's just put it that way. But that was when I saw her.

She was a little ray of sunshine sitting there at the table with Sloane. She stood out contrastingly compared to everyone else. Fucking gorgeous, *pure*, all things good—but there was something dark about her too. I wasn't sure if it was her features, where her skin was smooth and porcelain-like, completely flawless and angelic, but her eyes were sharp and vivid. They struck you when they latched on. Then, there was yesterday when she bit out a response to me but also blushed and clammed up afterwards. She was split down the middle. Soft but hard, light but dark. Looking at Gemma was like breathing in fresh air...but with black, murky lungs.

It was her, though.

The good girl. Gemma.

She was the only other person who could have known.

Mrs. Fitzpatrick's voice, in all its shrill glory, snapped me back to reality. Brantley and Cade were both staring at

Gemma with a devious look in their eye as she sat, completely unaware of anything going on around her.

"Okay, class. I want you to pick one object in the room—I don't care what it is—and start drawing." Mrs. Fitzpatrick's hands clapped, the sound reverberating around the room. "I just want to see where your potential is! There is no right or wrong way to do art, friends! Let's get creative!"

My lip curled as I took my eyes off Gemma and brought them back to my boys. "I need to talk to her alone." I flicked my head to her as she swiped a lock of brown hair out of her face. She began drawing on the paper in front of her, appearing even more angelic than before. She was completely focused, heedless of anything else—even me—as I stared at her, plotting something in the back of my head.

"We're on it," Cade said.

I grabbed my pencil and grinned, watching my boys divide and conquer.

Alright, Gemma. It's payback time.

CHAPTER SIX

GEMMA

I LEARNED LONG AGO that you had to find good in the littlest of things. The minute of silence in a house full of people you hated. The smell of coffee in the morning, even if you knew you weren't going to get a cup. The sun on your face, even for a fleeting moment, before a tsunami-like storm hit the grass below your feet.

This right here. This moment was good.

The pencil felt light in my hand, the metallic shine of the lead on the thick paper in front of me was like a little sliver of hope on this awful day. I couldn't shake the unease that had laid deep in my belly after breakfast this morning. My skin prickled underneath my brand-new uniform during my first two periods. I wasn't necessarily anxious about being at St. Mary's, because it really was better than home, but I did feel apprehensive when it came to people staring at me—and trust me when I say *everyone* was staring at me.

So, this moment here? Art class? Are you kidding me? This forty-five-minute class made up for the lingering gazes that kept following me around the expansive hallway this morning.

Art was my happy place. Art was the one thing he couldn't take from me. I always found a way back to it, even when I felt like my creative streak had vanished along with all rational thinking. Somehow, drawing was what grounded me. I got lost in it.

It felt like home, and that was a comforting thing to feel when you were a hostage inside the place you'd lived all your life. Not to mention, art had saved my mental state so many times I'd lost count.

My hand continued to flick over the thick, high-quality paper as my pencil moved languidly, sketching the small clay figurines on the top of a nearby shelf. I chose to sketch the first thing my eyes landed on, because as soon as Mrs. Fitz-patrick said, "Sketch", I jumped at the opportunity.

"Hey, that's really good."

The deep voice was close, and my head popped up quickly, a rushed breath leaving my mouth as my fingers wrapped around the pencil in my hand. I landed on a set of deep, honey-colored, almond-shaped eyes that sent a rush of warmth through me.

"Oh," I croaked. "Thank you." I smiled shyly and then put my attention back to my paper.

My heart started to skip in my chest when his presence grew heavier. He was still standing beside me, a little too close for comfort. But maybe he was just admiring my art work.

"I'm Cade," he offered as he plopped himself down in the next chair.

The art room wasn't set up like a traditional classroom, although I couldn't really be certain what a traditional class-room was since I'd only ever gone to one high school, and it was for a brief time, but it didn't look like my first two periods' rooms at all. Instead of desks sitting in an organized manner, there were several rectangular tables set up in different directions all over the room. There didn't seem to be any rhyme or reason to why they were placed where they were placed, but I kind of liked it like this. It wasn't so direct. It was a little messy and completely out of order.

It was strange that things out of order felt right to me when I'd been taught all my life that there was no middle ground. It was black or white, straight or crooked, right or wrong. There couldn't be an in between. Ever.

"I'm Gemma," I said, going back to my paper while trying to ignore the heat I felt from his skin radiating onto mine. A sense of urgency whipped through me, telling me to move away from him, but I didn't. I didn't move because I knew in the back of my head I wasn't feeling that urgent need to flinch because of him as a person. It was because of something else entirely.

Tobias' voice tickled the back of my brain: *Survive, but don't believe a single thing he says. He has plans for you, just like he did for Mom.*

Not everyone was bad, and I had to start trusting my gut more than trusting what I'd been told over the years. I knew that now.

Cade and I worked in silence for the next several minutes, and soon, I felt myself getting lost in my sketch again. My eyes moved back and forth from the little figurines and their ornate details every few seconds, making sure I got every last thing correct when he muttered, "Shit."

Glancing over briefly, I saw that he was staring at me.

"Can you do me a favor, Gemma?" His voice was sweet, genuine. Maybe even a little desperate.

I paused, my heart slowing. Placing my pencil down on the desk, I gulped a big lungful of air before looking over at him. Strangely enough, another wave of warmth went through my body. It was like I had taken a steaming cup of tea and gulped it down quickly, feeling the hot liquid coat my throat all the way to my stomach.

"Um, sure." I hated how my voice came out like a whisper. I'd always been a quiet person. Richard used to ask if I was afraid of my own voice, and honestly, around him, I was.

Cade tilted his head across the room, his jawline sharp as he angled it away from me. "Can you go over to that door right there." I followed his line of sight. "Yeah, that one," he confirmed. "Can you go and move that curtain out of the way? The end of it blew onto the statue that I'm drawing. Probably from the air vent."

"Oh, yeah. Sure."

"Thanks. I just don't want to lose my line of sight by walking over there. Drawing doesn't come easy to me." His eyes shot down to my sketch. "Unlike you." His smile was soft, and two dimples formed on his cheeks. He seemed nice, but when I glanced back at his eyes, they said something different. I couldn't pinpoint it exactly, but where his smile said he was innocent, his eyes did not. Either way, I chose to ignore it because there was no sense in being outlandish. I was nice, and it was okay to help someone, even if I was always taught to keep to myself. I hopped off my stool and began walking over to the statue he was drawing, feeling proud that I wasn't letting old habits decide my every move at St. Mary's, despite how out of my element I was.

The art room was the one place in this entire school, at least so far, that wasn't dimly lit. There were recessed lights above my head and a million other standing lamps placed all over the room. It was bright in here, so bright it took my eyes a moment to adjust when I'd first crossed the threshold.

Just as I was passing by a dark, half-opened wooden door on my left, likely a supply closet, a hand wrapped around my upper arm, yanking me into a dark area that smelled of acrylic paint and old, musty art supplies.

I yelped, immediately looking down to the hand on my arm, which was pointless because the room I was pulled into was dark. The only light source was the door outlined from the other side.

A gritty voice simmered in the darkness. "Who did you tell?"

My heart slammed against my ribcage as the hand on my arm tightened. My stomach bottomed out as I was dragged even farther into the closet only to be pushed forcefully up against a shelf with my next breath.

My eyes immediately began scanning the area, straining against the bleak darkness for a way out. *Always look for an escape first.* There was only one door, the one I was pulled into, and the person in front of me was blocking it, so that was out. *Look for a way to protect yourself second.*

Wait. I shook my head, clearing my thoughts and bringing myself back to the present. *You're not in that place, Gemma. You're at school.*

A short burst of air left my mouth. "Get your hand off my arm," I very calmly demanded, keeping my voice steady and my feet firmly on the floor. The rising anxiety was there in the back of my head, scratching the walls of my brain with panic, but I pushed it away, knowing I had been in much more compromising situations in the past. Being shoved into an art closet in the middle of art class was like child's play.

The firm grasp on my arm dropped, the scent of something enticing gone, and then I heard a shuffling noise before the click of a light which then shined down on my head. I glanced up to the single light bulb swaying above me before coming down and almost choking on air.

Isaiah's head tilted as our eyes collided. His gaze was like an icy stake being thrust into my chest, cooling me and burning me at the exact same time. The feeling was new and perplexing, and I felt my head tilting too. What was it with him? Why did it feel like he shocked me to life when he was near?

"Who did you tell?" Isaiah snapped again, this time while running a hand through his dark hair. His jaw clenched on the sides as his plump lips turned into a disapproving scowl. My body grew hot. The sip of tea I metaphorically had earlier when Cade looked at me, warming me on the inside, was *nothing* compared to latching onto Isaiah. It was similar to walking under a steaming shower after rolling around in the snow, the hot water washing over every inch of my flesh, burning the coolness instantly.

"Wh—what?" I stuttered, unable to catch my breath.

Isaiah's eyebrow hitched as he crossed his arms over his school uniform. "I knew you were eavesdropping yesterday when I talked to my uncle—in the privacy of his office, might I add—but I didn't peg you to be like the rest of the girls here. I didn't think you'd run your gossiping little mouth, especially after only being here for what? Twelve hours?"

My cheeks caught fire.

I *was* eavesdropping. I'll admit that. But I didn't tell anyone a single thing. Who would I have told?

My lips parted, and his eyes instantly flew down to my mouth. I felt a tugging on my stomach that was beyond unfamiliar, so I brushed it away before saying, "I don't know what you're talking about."

A rough chuckle rolled out of his mouth as he threw his head back, the muscles along his neck growing more prominent with each echoing laugh. "Here's the deal," Isaiah whispered, taking a step closer to me after abruptly ending his laughter. My eyes widened as his chest brushed against mine. My back was firmly pressed into the shelf behind me, causing a lone paintbrush to fall down to the ground with a slight thud. My breathing had quickened, and my pulse was speeding, but it wasn't out of fear. Isaiah was strong and commanding. He was definitely confident, and after seeing him this morning in the dining hall, and how everyone else seemed to gravitate around him, I understood why. But he didn't scare me—not in the way I was used to, at least.

Isaiah's chest was still pressed against mine as he gingerly reached up and brushed a stray hair out of my face. My cheek tingled where his fingers touched. "Oh, *Good Girl*." He laughed under his breath in a condescending tone. "You kind of owe me now."

That stupid nickname he had obviously given me after meeting yesterday stirred up a bunch of shit that I'd pushed away from the moment I got into that town car to attend St. Mary's. It sent me straight to the red, and although I had a really good hold on my emotions, anger especially—a survival tactic, no doubt—I found it hard to keep myself in line when he said that. My hand reached up, of its own accord, and I smacked his away from my face. I peered up into his smug expression and seethed, "*Do not* call me that."

Whoa. Did I really just do that?

His lip twitched at my tone, and I could feel the weak girl inside of me, the one that was shattered long ago, pulling me back. But I stood my ground, tilting my chin upward as my brown locks fell behind my shoulders. "And I don't owe you anything, *Rebel*." He wanted to give me a nickname? I'd give him one right back.

Surprise flashed across his face—and probably mine too. *Why was I acting like this?* I knew right then that Isaiah was dangerous to be around. He did something to me. Breathing his air gave me confidence and a feeling of power that I had never felt before. I found myself relishing in the feelings he was planting inside of me.

I went to push my way around him, eager to get out of the

tiny, dark room that apparently had me morphing into someone I wasn't, when his hands clasped onto my wrists.

I paused, my heart thudding to a complete stop. "Did you or did you not tell someone about me and Ms. Glenburg? Because I have to say, you just stirred up a bunch of shit for me." His voice lowered as he brought his head down to my ear. My entire body went haywire as his warm breath graced the sensitive skin. "I know you heard the conversation, Gemma."

I gulped, tilting my head over so he had better access to my neck. *What the hell was I doing?* I couldn't stop. I didn't want him to leave my personal space. I wanted him to keep breathing down on my neck like he was, because…I *liked* it. I liked it a lot. "I was eavesdropping." My voice was low and breathy. "But I didn't tell anyone."

There it was again, his hot, minty breath mingling over my skin, causing goosebumps to rise. "Are you sure about that? Because if you did tell someone, I will find out."

This time, I pulled my wrists out of his grasp, and I basically ran to the door. I peeked over my shoulder, my chest rising and falling like I was in PE instead of art. Isaiah was staring at me intently, looking completely unbothered in his school uniform. He was effortlessly attractive, and he knew it. "I'm sure, so again, I don't owe you anything."

And with that, I threw the door open and stepped back into the art room, breathing in the fresh air that wasn't nearly as intoxicating as Isaiah's.

But as soon as I took a deep breath and felt my shoulders relax, they shot up to my ears again because every single set of eyes, the teacher's included, were staring directly at me. And when Isaiah stepped out of the closet, I could see the wheels already spinning inside my classmates' heads.

A deep, throaty chuckle sounded as he walked past me. I stared after him, feeling my body go numb at the rumors that were likely about to be floating around this desolate boarding school.

Isaiah turned around on the heel of his shoes and began walking backwards, smiling from ear to ear at me like the devious bad boy that he *obviously* was. Once he slid back onto his stool, the classroom as still as if it were empty, he slyly said, "I guess I know who will be featured on the gossip blog tomorrow...with a new story." My eyes drove into his with a burning intensity. He winked. "Consider us *almost* even, *Good Girl.*"

I was on fire from embarrassment as he spun around in his stool, putting his back to me. Cade and another guy stood beside him, snickering as they, too, winked at me.

Isaiah had no idea what he just started.

CHAPTER SEVEN

GEMMA

MY STOMACH GROWLED LOUDLY as I sat on my bed with my knees pulled up to my chin. The junky phone that Richard gave me months ago laid untouched beside me on the fluffy cobalt-blue comforter that had somehow appeared on my bed along with a few girly pillows thrown on top for good measure.

When Sloane had walked in earlier, after all of our classes were finished, she paused while taking off her maroon blazer that fit her like a glove and laughed.

"See?" She grinned, nodding to my bed. "He loves you."

"Who loves me?"

A deep voice from the past tried to weasel into my head with insults about no one loving me, but I pushed it away as I focused on my roommate.

She gave me a pointed look, kicking the shoes off her feet, which went flying across the room. "Headmaster Ellison. He obviously got those"—she nodded to my blanket and pillows —"for you—unless someone sent them from home?"

I couldn't stop the sarcastic laugh from tumbling out of my mouth. "Definitely not."

Sloane smiled, but it didn't quite reach her eyes.

We'd both fallen into easy silence while doing our homework after she'd asked about my day and complained for a solid ten minutes about the fact that we didn't have any classes together. I peeked up at her a few times from my desk, watching her type something on her computer, unbeknownst to her that I was literally sweating while trying to focus on my own homework, which took me no more than an hour to complete. Auntie was very thorough with my studies over the years, and a lot of the time, the only thing I had to occupy myself with was reading the textbooks she and Richard supplied me with. As sad and boring as it was, learning was the only thing I had to look forward to in my childhood.

But as each second passed with Sloane buried in her computer, my stress levels rose. Sloane didn't say a single thing about Isaiah and the whole art-supply-closet ordeal, so I assumed the news hadn't reached her yet. I had a big feeling that Sloane was definitely the type of friend who wouldn't let something like that slide under the rug. But what did I know about having a friend?

After another hour, she asked if I was ready to go to dinner, but I told her I wasn't hungry. Her lips pursed, but she didn't push me on it. She only nodded after asking me one last time before slipping out of the door, and I hadn't seen her since.

That was when I turned my cell phone on and laid it beside me. I knew Richard would hear about the rumor of Isaiah and me—whatever the "rumor" was. For all I knew, it would get back to Headmaster Ellison, and he would call Richard, letting him know what his *niece* was up to. I didn't know much, but I knew enough to know that if a girl was shoved inside a closet with a boy, especially one as popular as Isaiah, the rumors would be juicy.

I remembered every last thing down to the smallest of details from when I'd attended Wellington Prep for those few short months before coming here. *Sex. Parties. Drugs. Drinking.* I drank it all up in huge gulps as I stayed behind in the shadows, hoping no one would pay attention to the judge's *strange* niece as I eavesdropped on classmates and their gossip. Rebecca, the only other person in the senior class that talked to me, usually filled in the gaps for me. She didn't know it, but she taught me a lot. She brought me up to speed. And one thing I knew with absolute certainty, from attending Wellington Prep and Rebecca's short, one-sided friendship, was that high schoolers were vicious with their gossip, and scandal was the one thing that fed it.

I was lucky to have made it out of Wellington Prep without ever being the center of anyone's gossip. I knew how to blend in, and not many people paid me any attention, except when Ms. Weltings started *really* looking into my drawings, which was what landed me in St. Mary's in the first place. Although, now that I was here, I was wondering if Richard knew all there was to know about this school. He certainly acted like he did, but I also knew that one of his personality traits was acting arrogantly confident in every situation he was ever in. Even if he flew blindly, he still acted as if he knew every last detail. He made it seem like St. Mary's was a prison. A punishment. A way to keep me under lock and key while also getting the social worker off his back. It was his subtle way of reminding me that I was his and that I needed to follow the rules. As soon as I turned eighteen, the social worker would no longer look into Judge Stallard's hidden niece. There would be no need to pretend that he followed the laws that he so righteously protected. I was his, and his to do with whatever he pleased. Or so he thought.

Several shaky breaths shuddered from my chest as I glanced back down to my phone, seeing nothing but a blank, black screen. And then the door flew open. Sloane quickly darted inside our room, wearing tight jeans and an off-the-shoulder shirt that was knotted in the front, showing off her flat belly. The chains on the other side of the door jingled, and my stomach twisted at the sound before she slammed it shut and placed her hands on her hips.

"Holy hell, Gemma!" Her mouth gaped, and my face flamed almost instantly. *Here we go.* "You're here for less than twenty-four hours, and you score a closet date with Isaiah Underwood?"

The realization hit me head on, like the final snip of a thread. *A closet date.*

I flew up from my bed. "No! That is not what happened!" I let out a tiny growl and started pacing the room in my short sleep shorts and plain t-shirt. "He set me up. He thinks I'm the one who told that blog thing about him and the teacher!" I flung toward her, probably looking no less than a frantic mess. "But I didn't, and I told him that!" Anxiety from Richard finding out that I was caught in the closet with Isaiah was causing me to act erratically, and I would be lucky if Sloane still wanted to be my friend after I just rushed toward her like a rabid animal.

Her features were pulled together tightly, a little wrinkle in the center of her eyebrows from the confusion. "How did you end up in a closet with him?" She shook her head, her raven hair swaying as she walked toward me and pulled me back to my bed to sit me down by pushing on my shoulders. "Take a deep breath, and start from the beginning."

So, I did. I told her everything that Isaiah said to me in the closet. My mouth was like a speed boat, zipping through choppy waves, plowing down every single red light that my brain was throwing out.

When I was finished spilling everything, Sloane let out a loud, breathy sigh and popped up from my bed. She began pacing the floor back and forth, nibbling on her thumb, just as I was seconds before. "Okay, listen." She glanced at me, and I scooted up to the top of my bed, eyeing my phone that was still beside me. "It's not a huge deal. I mean, you totally have a crush on Isaiah—that much is obvious from the red on your cheeks when you talk about him—and it's odd that you can't see that yourself, but whatever. Everyone has had a crush on Isaiah, and by crush, I mean every girl would strip themselves bare and spread their legs wide for him. But this will all blow over soon. The blog will post about Isaiah's latest closet date, and then something juicier will happen, and it'll be over."

My heart sunk even deeper in my chest. Sloane had it all wrong. I didn't care what anyone thought about me at this school. That wasn't my issue. The issue was this rumor making its way back home. If Richard learned that I was in a closet with a boy, he would be here faster than I could even pack my getaway bag.

There would be no escaping him.

There would be no grand plan to elude him and his sick future for me.

And there would be no finding Tobias.

"Hey, hey." Sloane's hand landed on mine, and I flinched before recovering and glancing up to her soft features. "It's not a big deal. I swear. Everyone has been featured on that stupid blog, Gemma. Don't sweat it."

A weak smile graced my lips as I snuggled down onto my bed, dropping my head onto the comfiest pillows I'd ever felt. Sloane left the room for a few minutes, doing something in the bathroom before coming back into our room and sitting back on my bed. I scooted over to the very edge, pressing myself against the wall as she lay down and pulled her computer to her lap.

"What are you doing?" I asked, rolling to my side, clutching the cell phone in my hand with an empty feeling carving out my stomach. I was dreading the moment it would ring.

Nerves began eating away at my hot skin when a heavy bout of anxiety fell on my shoulders. *What if he just comes here and drags me back home? Like, gives no warning and just shows up?* I silently shuddered.

"High school is hard. Especially this one since we can't even escape all the bullshit." She laughed under her breath. "So, I'm being a good friend and lying here with you as we watch some cheesy movie on Netflix."

A little bit of warmth seeped in when she said the word friend, but I didn't let myself show anything on the outside. Instead, I asked, "What's Netflix?"

Sloane's head whipped toward me, the side of her face illuminated by her laptop screen. "Girl, where have you been?"

Hell. Hell is where I've been.

CHAPTER EIGHT

ISAIAH

I COULD ALWAYS FEEL when someone was watching me. The skin along my neck would prickle, the beating of my heart would thud a little harder against my ribcage, my eyes would snap to each and every last corner of the room I was in, waiting to see that overbearing shadow of what my future held. The SMC had nothing to do with my father's line of business, but their watchful eyes were just a mere glimpse of what it would be like when I took over his position. If I hated the SMC watching me, waiting for me to slip up so they had grounds for expulsion, how would I feel with the law circling every so often, ready to catch me in the middle of a massive gun exchange? Not to mention the enemies. Their presence was heavy and, at times, imperceptible. Some of them could be lethal and blend in better than a fucking chameleon. I knew better than anyone just how lethal human beings could be.

My phone vibrated for the fifth time since yesterday, with my father's name flashing along the screen. If I didn't answer soon, I knew he'd throw a goddamn hissy fit, so I finally snatched it from my pocket while swiping the apple out of Cade's hand.

"*Fucker,*" he mumbled under his breath.

"Hello, Father," I answered into the phone, taking a bite of the red flesh. The sweet juice hit my tongue, but it wasn't nearly enough to take the bitterness out of my tone when it came to talking to Carlisle Underwood.

He growled on the other end, hardly noticeable, but I could detect his piss-poor mood even being locked away at St. Mary's. "I hear you've been wreaking havoc on your uncle's boarding school. Is that true?"

I took another bite of my apple, shifting my eyes down that long wooden table lined with numerous plates of food until I landed on Gemma. "What are you talking about?" I asked, wiping my mouth off with the back of my hand.

Damn. Cade was right. Gemma *was* hot. Really fucking hot. Hot in the way that she didn't know she was hot. It was a pity that she was like the rest of the girls here: hungry for gossip and as shallow as the fucking kiddie pool.

My father's voice got louder on the other end. "Did you fuck a teacher?"

There was no hesitation on my part when I answered, "No."

Cade nudged my elbow, and I shot him a look. He mouthed, "Party?" Then he swirled his index finger around in the air. I knew what he was asking, so I gave him a curt nod and watched as the hushed whispers broke out along the table.

"Did you only call to ask about my sex life, or did you call for a less exciting reason?"

Now there was no hesitation on his end. "Both. I've heard rumors of Callum's son dabbling in the business. Is it true? Have you found out anything useful?"

Oh, right. The whole reason I was at St. Mary's.

I huffed out a sarcastic laugh, annoyed at how my blood pressure was spiking. My hand squeezed around the apple so hard juice began to seep out of the sides. "Can't just let me be until I graduate, eh?"

"I can't have you acting like a fucking immature fool, especially with Bain there."

My gaze shifted from Gemma, who was smiling shyly at something Sloane had said with her head barely even visible from the shelter of her hair, over to Bain.

Bain was the bane of my existence—no pun intended. Our fathers were rivals in the gun-trafficking business. They were both competitive, always trying to beat each other out of sales. They were shady as fuck. Both domineering. Both living up to the legacy that their fathers, and their fathers before them, and so on, left to carry out—thus Bain and I being forced to fall into line to carry the legacy out once the time came.

But the difference between Bain and me was that I wanted no fucking part in what my father did for a living, and Bain was the exact opposite. He was already a miniature clone of Callum.

And Callum was a shitty human being. I had my eye on Bain—and not only because that was what my father not so subtly demanded when he thrust me into this godforsaken boarding school.

"You have a choice to make, Isaiah." *He couldn't be serious.* I'd never had a fucking choice. "You can join the business as a snake. Or you can join as a lion." My jaw clenched tightly as I suddenly became very focused on the conversation with my father. "Stay unknown to Bain, fly under the radar, and knock him on his ass when you two meet again in the future. *Or* I can rip you out of that school and throw you into the Covens where you'll come out more lethal than I am."

A deep chuckle left my chest as I rose from the table and began striding through the dining hall with my phone pressed to my ear. Once I was away from wandering eyes, I gritted through my teeth. "You won't rip me out of this school because you want me here to spy on Bain." I was too valuable.

My father laughed in the most narcissistic of ways. "You might not give me a choice. Your uncle says the committee is ready to throw you on your ass." He paused, and a hot sensation of dread crept over my shoulder. I glanced behind me, only to see the long, dark hallway with shiny white and black tiles along the floor and nothing else. "I want you to listen very closely to me," he snarled. I swallowed, clenching my fist tightly with my ears perked. "Get your head out of your fucking ass, boy. This is real life. This is a real business. You're right. The last thing I want to do is send you to the Covens. Not because I necessarily care where you are until it's time for you take over—because, frankly, you probably need the discipline that comes with the Covens—but more so because you need to do your fucking job."

I was shaking with anger. My limbs vibrated as I held tightly onto the phone, wanting to smash it into tiny little pieces.

My father's voice sunk into my bones as the words came through the line, "Clean your act up and figure out how to dazzle the committee so they don't expel you. Fuck, just do your goddamn job. If not, you won't be the only one going to the Covens."

I stilled. "What does that mean?"

"Jack could use some discipline too, I guess. Think of this as a bargaining chip. Fuck up, and you both will be shipped off until the time comes that I need you. Do you understand that?"

Fucking piece of shit. My throat clogged, and I clenched my eyes. "Yes."

"Yes what?" I noted the uptick in his voice.

I swallowed my pride because I was quickly brought back down to reality when he brought up my little brother. "Yes, *sir.*"

Then, the line went dead, and I quickly shoved my phone into the side pocket of my blazer. My fist reared back quickly, and I pounded into the wall, feeling pain rip up from my fingers all the way to my neck.

Fucking Jacobi. It wasn't fair to blame my older brother for wanting out and leaving me behind, but I did. I fucking did.

———

MY SWOLLEN KNUCKLES still ached a little as I tore off my white button down and flung it back into my bag. Lockers were being shut all around me, and for a moment, it felt like I was back in my old high school, surrounded by precious trust-fund babies with their biggest worry being what kind of car their mommy and daddy were going to give them for their birthday, only to wreck it hours later.

A low growl came from me as I scanned the locker room. It was the only modern part of St. Mary's. Everything else was dark and dreary. Old and primeval. Even the weather was uncanny as rain seemed to constantly fall from the clouds.

"What did you do to your hand?" Shiner stood beside me as he whipped on his lacrosse shirt, nodding to my hand.

"Nothing," I snapped as he shot me a wary look, but with his usual easygoing personality, he brushed me off quickly.

Shiner's real name was Nash, but he refused to be called that, so he went by Shiner. Actually, mostly everyone called him One-Liner-Shiner. He gained that nickname his freshman year when it only took him one line to get the entire female senior class in his bed. The legacy had stuck, too. Shiner was a bit of a manwhore, but most of us were. After all, what were we supposed to do while attending a boarding school that didn't even allow us to have cell phones during class hours?

As soon as we were all geared up for lacrosse practice, Cade rushed out in between our warm-up laps. "Where're we getting the booze for tomorrow?" he asked, bending down to touch his toes in a stretch. I held my lacrosse stick tightly in my hand, glancing at the dark clouds above our heads, wondering when it was going to start raining—because it *always* did. "Some of the girls have some shit stashed." I cracked my neck, looking out along the field and over the grassy hills that laid behind the bleachers. St. Mary's stood in the distance, appearing like a castle—a broken castle for broken princes and princesses was more like it.

"Nice," Cade muttered before sticking a foot out and tripping Shiner as he ran another lap.

Cade cackled as Shiner fell to the ground, his brown hair flopping on his head. "What the fuck, Cade."

"Payback's a bitch, Shiner."

"Payback for what?" I asked, staring at my two friends. Cade was towering over Shiner, who had made himself comfortable on the grassy land beneath his back. He even went as far as bringing his hands up behind his head and crossing his ankles. "Fucker claimed the new girl for the party before I could."

My head snapped down to Shiner who was grinning deviously like the smug fuck he thought he was. "Not happening."

"You already had her!" Shiner's mouth fell. "It was the headline on the stupid blog."

Cade snickered, glancing at Coach who was about to

round us up. "You're on that damn thing more than anyone, Shiner. You love it. So, are you calling yourself stupid, too?"

I rolled my eyes at their banter. "For one, I don't share. You know this. And two"—I walked over and stood directly above him, peering down into his face—"I'm not finished with her."

I felt Cade's stare driving into my temple. "You're not?"

Pointing my lacrosse stick at Cade, I answered with, "Nope," and then stalked off to the huddle that was beginning to form.

I wasn't finished with Gemma.

She just didn't know that yet.

CHAPTER NINE

GEMMA

THE NEXT FEW days at St. Mary's were better than I'd imagined, but that wasn't necessarily saying much because I had expected it to be pretty shitty. I kept waiting around for the blog post to show, the same one that Isaiah taunted me with, and by day three, I was feeling relieved that I hadn't heard or seen anything about me being in the closet with him.

Sloane and I got into a good routine, and I met a few other girls too. My stress levels began to fall with each passing day of no calls from Richard, but when Friday rolled around, there it was. Just like Isaiah had said.

I snatched Sloane's phone out of her hand during breakfast, and the blood drained from my face. There was a picture of me, walking through the hallway with my head tugged low, my worn and tattered books clutched to my chest. My chestnut hair was draped around my cheeks like a veil, shielding me from everyone.

The headline was all that I thought about during class. I

didn't even look back at Isaiah and his friends during art. I didn't look at anyone.

"People have already moved on," Sloane said, tugging me by the fabric of my blazer toward an arched doorway that looked as if it belonged in a Catholic church. A thin stream of light fluttered through the colorful stained glass, making the green a little more vibrant than before.

Once she pushed the door open, I felt the warm heat from the sun land right on my face. I breathed out a sigh, feeling lighter than before when we were stuck inside the school with people no doubt murmuring about me behind my back, despite Sloane lying to make me feel better.

"They have not," I said, trying to find it in me to laugh. I came up short, and after a few minutes of walking in silence with Sloane by my side, she came to a sudden halt.

We were both standing up on a grassy hill overlooking St. Mary's on one side and some sort of sports field on the other. I could see a huddled circle of guys in the middle, all holding large sticks.

"What are we doing?" I asked, bending down and pulling up my socks a little higher. It wasn't cold out, but there was a tiny bite to the air which likely meant rain was soon approaching.

Sloane eyed me skeptically as I stood straight again, ignoring my question. "Why are you so worried about this? About being on the blog? Why does it bother you so much?"

I darted my attention away from hers, looking back down to my shoes. I'd only known Sloane for a few days, and I already wanted to tell her everything. That was how it was with Sloane, though. There was something special about her. Something welcoming. I wanted to be her friend in a way that I probably never could.

I shrugged, lying through my teeth. "I just don't want people thinking I'm like that right off the bat."

Sloane shuffled on her feet, the grass crunching underneath her weight. "Gemma." Her voice was low as a few girls walked past us, smiling. Sloane smiled back sweetly, whereas I glanced away. As soon as the girls were out of earshot, she shot me a look that had me wavering. "I like you..."—she glanced down to the field—"but I can tell you're lying to me."

"I'm not," I blurted, feeling the anxiety of losing the first friend I'd ever had.

God. How totally pathetic did that sound?

I sighed, bringing my arms up to cross over my chest. My lip teetered in between my teeth as a whistle sounded from the sports field. "I have..." *Shit. Should I be saying this?* I peeked up at Sloane, and she was waiting patiently, her delicate features loose and unbearing. "My uncle is really strict." The words rushed out like water breaking through a dam. There they were. Out there in the open. The first of many secrets I'd buried underneath this nice and tidy boarding school uniform.

Sloane's dark, delicately arched eyebrows crowded together. Her thick lashes fanned over her cheeks as she thought for a moment. "What does this have to do with your uncle?"

My legs were shaky as my chest constricted. "He'll find out, and I'm not really allowed to have..." *Anyone.*

Sloane's bright-pink lips formed an *O* as recognition dawned on her. "A boyfriend? Don't worry about that, Gem." Her smile reached her eyes as she grasped my arm, intertwining ours together. "There's no way your uncle will find out."

My stomach seemed to swallow itself. "He knows the headmaster."

Sloane threw her head back and laughed freely as we continued walking down the grassy hill toward a set of bleachers that were pretty empty except for a few lingering girls huddled together, watching whatever sport the guys were playing down below.

"Gemma, the headmaster isn't going to tell your uncle anything. Trust me."

I wanted to trust her; I really did. But I didn't trust anyone.

Shaking my head, I sighed and took my arm out of hers as she turned and leaned over a chain fence separating the field from the metal bleachers. "Trust *me*, Sloane. My uncle will find out." My gaze shifted from her to the field, and just like that, a buzz went through me. A jolt of something hot started from the very bottom of my stomach, zipping all the way to my burning ears. I gulped when my eyes collided with Isaiah. He was several yards away, glancing up to where Sloane and I were standing as he took the bottom of his shirt and brought it up to his forehead, wiping away the sweat. My eyes instantly dropped to his torso, and my lips fell open.

Sloane giggled. "Oh my God, your face is blood red, Gemma."

I sucked in a breath and quickly whipped around, putting my back to the field. "What? No, it isn't!"

Sloane laughed even harder. "Don't worry, it happens to us all. Those Rebels are *hot*. I'll be the first to admit it."

"Damn straight they are!" a few girls who were sitting on the bleachers called out from behind us, fake fanning themselves. "Tell us!" One girl grinned down at me. It was Callie. The same girl that I saw the first night I was here. She was still sporting her school uniform—we all were since school had just ended a little while ago—but her white blouse was untucked and tied in a knot right under her bra that was peeking from below. Her long, blonde hair was braided but not in a childish way. It was cute and preppy, and I was a little envious.

"What?" I asked, suddenly feeling *extremely* self-conscious.

Callie's group of friends laughed as she deadpanned, "How was he in the sack? Hopefully still as good as when I had him a week ago!"

In the sack?

Sloane must have sensed my confusion, because she stepped forward, placing her hand on my arm. "Oh, shut up, Callie! We all know Isaiah turned you down at the last party."

My lips parted as I tried to make sense of what they were talking about. It took me a while to catch on to what they were referring to, and it made me hate Richard even more. I was good at blending in and acting like I wasn't the strangest, most naive seventeen-year-old on the planet, but I was. I was so out of my element it wasn't even funny, and I couldn't just ask Sloane to fill me in because that would raise too many questions, just like it did with Rebecca at my last school. The thing was, I wasn't a normal teenager. I hadn't experienced the things most kids my age had. I knew that. It was just really hard to accept.

As I further listened to Sloane and Callie argue back and forth about the Rebels, I eventually caught on and interrupted Sloane when she growled—yes, actually growled.

"I didn't do anything with Isaiah."

"That's not what he said," another girl piped up, giving me a once-over. I ignored the urge to hide myself.

"Well, he was lying." Blood rushed to my skin, and I wanted to turn around, stalk down the grassy field, and yell at Isaiah for making everyone think something of me that wasn't true—which, to be honest, was completely out of character for me. But still, I could feel a smothered scream trying to climb out of my chest. I was angry. Really angry.

Another girl leaned forward. "Why are you denying it? It'll only make you more desirable if you admit being with him. He's the most popular Rebel there is. I bet all the other boys will want a taste of you now. Shit, maybe even I want a taste of you."

Callie rolled her eyes as her friend giggled. I knew right then what type of girls these were. I noticed girls like them at Wellington Prep. I'd overheard their conversations many times during class and even in the bathroom. I didn't quite understand their power play, but I envied them all the same. They didn't bow down to anyone. It seemed as if nothing scared them. They were fearless, and they definitely knew their way around a boy's heart...and body.

Sloane huffed as she pulled me around, putting our backs to the group of girls once again. "Ignore them. They're just bored."

My mouth spoke before my brain could tell me to stop. "I don't really understand. Do they not like me now? Or do they like me even more? Did she seriously say she wanted a taste of me?" That was weird. Right?

Sloane gave me a side-eye, and *shit, I messed up.* "Gemma?"

My teeth scraped along one another as I gulped. "Yeah?"

"Just how strict is your uncle?"

Strict was an understatement.

"Uh, why?" I gulped again. My fingers began playing with the cotton hem of my skirt nervously.

"You just seem..." *Weird.* "Different. Like you're...sheltered in a way?"

Silence passed between us as I debated my next words. There was a sudden halt to the conversation. A fork in the road. *Surely telling her I was homeschooled most of my life wasn't a huge deal, right?* It was the stuff I was taught and punished for that would raise suspicions. It wasn't even that I wanted to protect Richard. I wasn't *not* telling her certain things for his benefit, but it was purely for mine. I had to act smart, form my plan, and crush him like a Mac truck when the time came. If he knew I was spouting off things that he wanted to stay private because he *knew* they were wrong, he'd rip me away despite the suspicions from the social worker. He'd find a way to keep me stowed until the time came where he could use me for his own sick desires. It would be difficult, but he would find a way if he truly had to.

My head fell back down to the field until I landed on Isaiah again as I debated what to say to Sloane. This time, he wasn't looking at me. "I guess I am kind of sheltered. I was homeschooled for a really long time."

I felt the breeze from her head snapping in my direction. "Is St. Mary's your first school? Like...ever?"

"No." I followed Isaiah's tall, lean frame as he jogged down the field, holding a stick. I wasn't sure what sport they were all playing, but it actually looked kind of fun, even if this small, angry part of me wished that he would trip.

Turning to look at Sloane again, I found her watching me intently with her hazel eyes, obviously hungry for more information. "What sport is that?" My head tilted toward the field.

Her face blanched. "Um. It's lacrosse."

I nodded, tucking my hair behind my ear to watch them again. One guy flung his stick hard toward another one who was standing in front of a net. A ball went flying through the air. The girls behind me cheered loudly before erupting in gleeful laughter. I jumped at their shrill outburst, and then my shoulders slowly dropped. A feeling of despair snuck up behind me, like a ghost coming up and brushing its translucent fingers over my flesh. My heart sank as I let myself feel the envy burning my blood.

I'd missed out on so much, and in the past, I'd never really let myself dwell on that because when you're in an internal battle with yourself, filtering through what was the truth and what was a lie, resentment over not going to a real high school and having normal experiences seemed so trivial in the grand scheme of things.

But standing here, without Richard looking over my shoulder and no threats being whispered into my ear, I felt it. I felt that unbending amount of loss and anger, all wrapped up in one atomic bomb, ready to unleash at the first taste of freedom.

"Gemma?" Sloane saying my name kicked me out of my troubled thoughts. My eyes refocused as I landed on her soft expression. "One, I have so much to teach you." My cheek twitched as the bitterness slowly disappeared. "And two"— her eyes sparkled as she glanced back down to the field —"Isaiah is totally walking up here right now."

I gasped, a breath getting stuck in my chest. My head whipped to the right, and there he was, shirtless, striding up the field with a wicked grin sitting right between his high-arched cheeks.

"And he has his eyes on you."

CHAPTER TEN

ISAIAH

M<small>Y</small> <small>ATTENTION</small> never once left hers. From the moment I saw her standing up above the lacrosse field, my plan seemed to get brighter and brighter in my head. Like a neon sign, blazing its iridescent colors in my direction.

She was beautiful, even more so as I got closer to her, and I didn't use that word often. I stopped walking for a second. I didn't think that I'd *ever* used that word to describe a girl.

But fuck, Gemma's face was beautiful. Even the air around her was beautiful. It was as if the sun was shining directly on Gemma and no one else.

I noticed Sloane standing beside her, turning her attention to me and then back to Gemma a few more times before nodding. A leaf crumbled beneath my shoe, and just like that, Sloane was glaring at me.

Wonder what I did to piss her off?

I quickly thought back to the last party, but *nope,* definitely didn't get caught up in her at any point that night.

"Sloane." I dipped my head as I brought my hands up

around my neck, pulling my bundled-up shirt tighter as it draped around my shoulders. I was shirtless and sweaty, but neither Sloane nor Gemma seemed to be affected by that. *Weird.*

Flicking my eyes to Gemma, I noticed that she wasn't looking at me. It was as if I didn't exist at all to her. If only she knew that that made her much more alluring to me.

"Don't you *Sloane* me!" Sloane snapped, placing her hands on her hips.

I heard a snicker behind my back, telling me that Cade and Shiner had finally caught up to me.

I clicked my tongue against the roof of my mouth and leaned my forearms on the metal fence, falling in between the two girls. "Why the cold shoulder, Sloane?"

She huffed as I looked toward Gemma again. The sun caught a few strands of her hair, making the chestnut color even richer. "Because!" she snapped, clearly irritated. "Poor Gemma over here is *stressing* because of your little show earlier this week! The whole school thinks she's a slut."

Cade wandered up beside me, running his hand through his sweaty hair. "Oh, now, come on. Isn't that every little girl's dream? I heard that being a slut in high school nowadays is like being prom queen. It means you're popular."

"Not every girl wants to be popular." Gemma finally turned herself toward us and leveled me with a stare that touched every single cell in my body. My stomach dipped, and my tongue darted out of my mouth as I licked my lips. *Oh, I like her.*

"Hmm," Cade murmured beside me, leaning back on the fence as he looked out toward the field. The girls were on one side, us on the other, but I suddenly had the urge to jump over the metal rod so I could be on the same side as Gemma.

"Make it go away." Her voice was soft and hesitant, but I could sense the fierceness lurking behind with urgency.

Silence fell over the group of us. We were all staring directly at Gemma who had dropped both of her arms down to her sides. She was on the taller side, at least taller than Sloane, with lean, long legs. The skirt she wore fell to about mid-thigh, much like all the rest of the girls at St. Mary's, but Gemma seemed to wear it best. Her skin was creamy and smooth, her cheeks flushing with the tiniest bit of pink.

I slowly swung my attention to Sloane, who had her lips pursed together in my direction, waiting for my answer. Her eyebrow suddenly cocked upward, and I appreciated how she didn't bat her eyelashes at me. Sloane had been attending St. Mary's since the time I had, so I knew her pretty well, but we'd never been alone in a closet together. She had never thrown herself at me like the rest of the female population, and I'd never pursued her because I didn't need to pursue anyone, really.

I kept my gaze trained on Sloane even though I wanted to look at Gemma in the most agonizing way. "Sloane, did Gemma tell you about Ms. Glenburg?"

Everything around me ceased to exist as I kept staring down into Sloane's hazel eyes. This was something that my father had instilled in me long, long ago: how to read people. Their mannerisms, their breathing, their eyes. I'd watch and then decipher the next words that came out of their mouth very closely. It was a quality that my father needed in his line of business, I supposed—and fuck him, but he taught me well. I could see through someone as if they were water in a glass cup.

The skin around Sloane's eyes wrinkled as she threw her hands up. "What? What about Ms. Glenburg?"

She looked to Gemma, who had kept her face expressionless, and then back to me. "Stop trying to change the subject, Isaiah. You may be considered the top dog at this school, but you need to fix this for Gemma until—"

"Until what?" I inquired, suddenly even more interested.

"Nothing," Gemma snapped at me. Her soft and hesitant expression morphed to anger as she locked onto me, and I felt a flame blaze within. "Let's just go, Sloane."

I didn't want her to go, but just like that, Gemma had turned her back on all of us and began walking down the grassy hill toward St. Mary's. My eyes trailed after her, following the smoke from the fire brewing inside of her.

Sloane narrowed her gaze on me. "Seriously, Isaiah. Not everyone likes attention. I know that's hard for you Rebels to understand, but figure out a way to get her out of the spotlight before she gets in trouble." Then, she growled at me like a rabid dog before ruffling her black hair in her hands with frustration. "Oh. And Gemma didn't tell anyone about you and that teacher, whoever it was. She had only talked to me that night, and she didn't say a word."

I assumed as much, since there wasn't even a flicker of recognition on Sloane's face when I mentioned Ms. Glenburg a few seconds ago. Thankfully, the blog didn't release any names, likely because they didn't even know who it was. Teachers came and went at our school often—probably because of students like me who liked to cause trouble. *Oops.*

Before Sloane followed Gemma, who was already down to the side door of St. Mary's, I asked, "Why would she get in trouble?"

"Just never mind. Get it taken care of. I'm done with letting my friends get walked all over by Rebels." Sloane shifted her attention to Cade briefly before whipping around and running after Gemma.

I turned to see Cade's face fall.

"Did she know...?" I asked, not wanting to dive too much further into choppy waters with his situation.

He pushed off the fence, sighing. "Probably. She and Journey were close. They were roommates." Then, he shook his sweaty blond hair out. "But Sloane is right. Not everyone likes attention, even if we thought she deserved some payback."

I heard Shiner in the distance as he walked beside Cade. "I like the attention."

Cade grunted, "Shut up."

Finally pushing myself off the fence and taking my eyes away from the door that Gemma had disappeared into, I realized the validity in Sloane's statement. Not everyone liked attention, and even glancing at Gemma brought attention.

CHAPTER ELEVEN

GEMMA

"THERE'S A PARTY TONIGHT, and we're going."

Well, with a statement like that... I warily looked over at Sloane who was shoving an Italian sub into her mouth. The dining hall was open pretty much all day on the weekends and didn't close until curfew, which was 9:00 on Friday and Saturday. On Sunday, it went back to normal hours: curfew at 7:00 and no later.

Still gripping my cell phone in my hand, waiting for Richard to grace me with his nightmare of a voice, I began picking at the fruit salad on my plate and glanced down to a few other girls that Sloane had introduced me to last night before lights out.

"I can't," I whispered, feeling uncomfortable.

"Why?" one of the girls asked. Peeking up through a few strands of my hair, I saw that it was Mercedes, one of the girls I met last night. She lived just across the hall.

I shifted in my seat, unsure of how to answer the question. I'd never been in this situation before, sitting with other girls my age, having small talk about a party that was going on later in the evening. It was nice, don't get me wrong. I'd thought of this exact moment and played it out in my head every night when I'd get home from Wellington Prep. I'd watch the girls during lunch, listen to their easy conversations, and wonder if I'd ever get that. And now that I was kind of living that dream and enjoying it, I knew it wouldn't last forever. None of this would. *But I still wanted it.*

"Um..." I started.

Sloane placed her sub back down on her tray before wiping her fingers on a napkin. She swiped at a few stray crumbs stuck to her black shirt before taking her hands and placing them on my forearms, squeezing lightly. "Listen, I know you said your uncle is strict, but there is no way he will find out that you went to a party. I mean, we're locked away in a boarding school, Gem."

I lowered my head, not wanting anyone else to hear me. "But my uncle knows Headmaster Ellison. What if he catches us and then tells him?"

Mercedes giggled. "Trust us when we say the headmaster won't tell your uncle. He knows so much stuff about me"— she glanced around the dining hall as if she were looking for someone in particular—"and he has yet to tell my parents, who, by the way, are on the committee."

"The committee?" I questioned, even more leery than before. *What freaking committee?*

I looked between the two girls and watched as Sloane grabbed her fork. She started shoving a bite of salad into her mouth seconds later. Not only did she have a greasy Italian sub on one end of her tray, she had a colorful, healthy salad on the other. She said something about *balance* when Mercedes commented on her two choices of food but quickly moved on and muttered through her chews. "Yeah. So the way it works is that Headmaster Ellison basically has the final decision on everything, but there is a committee—the SMC—that votes on grants, educational shit...discipline...and"—she shrugged —"whatever else it is they have meetings about. I don't know and don't really care. I just know that the headmaster has covered for us both on numerous occasions."

My face must have shown my confusion when Sloane added, "The only people the committee has beef with are the Rebels, and that's because they think they rule the school and are always doing stupid shit to get a rise out of them."

Mercedes laughed. "Especially Isaiah. They hate him."

That garnered my full attention. I was still totally infuriated with Isaiah over the closet thing, and not only was I appalled at how one look from him could make my chest tight but also elicit angry little fires throughout my bloodstream at the same time, I was also confused. And intrigued. I wanted to know more about him, and I didn't understand why. "Why do they hate him?"

Sloane rolled her eyes. "Because he's the baddest one of the bunch. He's always sneaking out and doing shit he shouldn't...like having sex with a teacher."

He didn't actually have sex with her. I knew that from listening in on his conversation, but I kept that to myself.

I looked back and forth from Sloane to Mercedes as they took the conversation in their hands, talking in between bites. "What teacher was it anyway? The blog, as usual, was vague as shit."

Sloane looked perplexed. "I'm not sure. I haven't seen Ms. Hayes around, but also...I haven't seen Mrs. Lanning either... or Ms. Glenburg."

Mercedes' mouth dropped. "Mrs. Lanning is married. It can't be her."

Sloane dipped her eyes down, casting her a look. "Isaiah is hot as sin and looks way older than he actually is. Not to mention he can basically convince anyone to do anything. I'm certain that even married women have fantasized about having his head between their legs." She paused as a grin graced her face. "And I mean *both* heads, if you catch my drift."

Mercedes and a few other girls laughed as they all began talking about Isaiah and the rumors that followed his legacy.

My cheek tinged with pain as I bit the side of it while listening to their conversation. My heart flopped as I silently agreed that Isaiah was very attractive. Quite possibly the hottest guy I'd ever seen in real life. Granted, all I had to compare him to were the guys at Wellington Prep and the imaginary ones in my head that I'd conjure up from the books I'd sneak from the girls at the group home, but he had all the perfect attributes. The ones that were used to describe the perfect specimen of a male.

Dark hair that somehow made the sharp lines of his face stand out even more. Icy eyes surrounded by a mass of thick, dark lashes. Tall and strong. And there was just a little something extra to him that made your heart zing with one look. But despite thinking all those things, it didn't take away the fact that I was still angry with him. In fact, it felt like a betrayal to myself that I felt something when his eyes were on me. It was far beyond what my little innocent brain could decipher, but my body felt alive when he was near. *I* felt alive. Maybe that was why I had no issue snapping at him the last few times we had spoken. It was like my subconscious was aggravated that he had some affect over me.

"No," Mercedes' voice brought me back into the conversation. She shook her wild, curly hair out. "I think he's hot because of his behavior. Did you see him kissing Breanna last weekend? The way he gripped her?" Mercedes fanned herself. "It was so...possessive, and for some reason, he made it hot."

Sloane snickered into her sub, eventually throwing her head back and laughing loudly.

I kept my mouth shut as envy filled up the gaps inside my chest that had been opening since I was young enough to know what jealousy was.

I didn't feel it often, but once I got to Wellington Prep, and I was able to breathe life for the first time in *ever*, I didn't realize how much more there was beyond the walls of my bedroom. Even the girls at the group home that Richard's mother ran wouldn't throw me a bone to let me know that my life was completely and utterly fucked up. I even thought that the books I'd sneaked from them were purely fiction. I had no idea there was any truth to them.

It was good that I was feeling that envy, though. That meant that I'd broken through yet another wall Richard had built in front of my eyes, demolishing it swiftly with the sudden curiosity of what else was out there.

"He's picky about his girls, though. Have you noticed that?" Mercedes took a sip of her drink. "That's why I've never tried to get his attention. I'm not sure my ego could take the hit if he turned me down."

"Isaiah would be an idiot to turn you down," I said before I could stop myself. "You're pretty perfect, if you ask me."

Mercedes' cheeks flushed as she smiled at me, but then her smile quickly fell, and I wanted to suck the words back in. *Should I have kept that to myself?* But it was true. She was the most welcoming of the girls I'd met so far, except for Sloane.

"I'd be an idiot, huh?"

My eyes widened at the voice coming from behind me. *Oh my God.* I understood now why her smile had vanished. Was she trying to warn me?

Isaiah's scent, something clean but enticing, wafted around me as he took a seat to my left. I kept my eyes on Mercedes, who was blushing even more than before. *Shit, now what?* Taking a quick pause to think, I then pushed my tray out in front of me. I tilted my body toward him, glancing at his hot, somewhat arrogant smirk. *Show no fear.*

"Yeah. You would be," I calmly stated, backing my opinion with confidence. "Mercedes is great."

Our eyes caught, and I swore everything else around me melted away. Just like that. I was certain the sounds from the dining room were still there: the silverware scraping against the bowls and plates, the low chatter of other students, even the distant whirring of the air conditioner, but I couldn't hear a single thing except the thumping of my heart in my ears. I was brought to life in those few seconds staring at him. Air whooshed into my lungs. My blood rushed through my veins. Everything sparked as our gazes caught.

What was it with him? Why couldn't I seem to function correctly when he looked at me?

Isaiah's head tilted just slightly, a small twitch of his perfect lips. His inky hair was laying untouched on his head, longer on the top than on the sides. "Gemma," he whispered, snapping our moment in half like a twig breaking in the middle of the forest.

My brows crinkled, my eyes slanting. One tip of his chin and the flicking of his eyes to someone standing beside me caused me to finally shake myself free.

"Gemma?" the headmaster's voice sounded from behind me. I glanced up at him quickly in horror, seeing him staring at Isaiah disapprovingly, like the other day when I'd first arrived at St. Mary's. I slowly glanced around the dining table, wondering how much time had passed. Sloane's lips were smashed together as she stared at me. Her short black hair was tucked behind both diamond-studded ears. Mercedes' eyebrows were shot straight up, her fork frozen in mid-air with a piece of lettuce dangling off the side.

There was a hush that came over the table as the headmaster bent down to my level. "I need to see you in my office, please."

A blinding white light flashed before my eyes. The floor underneath my feet felt like slippery mud. My limbs were trembling as I shot straight up from the table, banging my knees off the bottom ledge.

I couldn't even bring myself to look at Sloane, and definitely not Isaiah, as my shoulders caved in on themselves. My feet shuffled along the shiny floor as I felt every ounce of freedom I'd managed to grasp slip through my fingers.

This was it.

It was over.

My one chance was gone.

CHAPTER TWELVE

GEMMA

I COUNTED each and every square on the checkered floor as I followed the headmaster. Nothing but our breathing—his leveled and mine erratic—sounded in the long hallway, and before I knew it, we were walking into his office.

Ping-ponging my attention back and forth from one end of his office to the next, noting almost instantly that we were alone, I found myself relaxing a fraction.

Richard wasn't here. Yet.

"Gemma." The headmaster bowed his head to the chair at the foot of his heavy desk.

Shuffling farther into his office, I lowered myself down onto the leather seat, grasping onto the arms for dear life. Fear like no other crept over my shoulder, whispering dreadful things in my ear. Every time I shut my eyes, I could see nothing but a dark, wet concrete floor and chains swaying from the ceiling.

"He's coming to get me, isn't he?" I whispered, feeling

myself tighten. *Shit. Shit. Shit. I knew he'd find out about the rumor.*

The headmaster didn't sit behind his desk. Instead, he perched himself at the end, his shoes peeking into my line of sight.

"No."

"No?" I repeated, thinking over the little word carefully. The word no typically stood for something negative, at least in my life, but right now? It was full of sunshine and rainbows.

A light chuckle came from him, and I finally glanced upward, leery of what I'd find. "I just wanted to see how you were doing. I saw you made friends with Sloane, and..." The headmaster looked up at the ceiling as if contemplating something before bringing his green eyes back down and smiling. "Mercedes?"

Pushing my back onto the hard chair, I swallowed nervously. "Oh, um. Yes, sir. They're nice."

His heavy brow line deepened. "You don't need to call me sir, Gemma."

I let out a breath, bringing my hands to my lap. "My uncle told me—"

"I'm pretty positive your uncle told you a lot of things. Please do not call me sir. I want you to be comfortable here, and I can tell you're pretty uncomfortable right now."

Not necessarily uncomfortable, just extremely cautious.

"And..." He sprung up off the edge of his desk and walked around to sit in his chair. I eyed him the entire way. He was even more relaxed today than when I had met him at the beginning of the week. He wasn't wearing a tie but instead was wearing dark jeans and a button-down shirt, his hair a little messy on top. I had to admit, he was perplexing. "Gemma, did you hear me?"

Shit. No. I was too busy trying to figure him out. "Oh. I'm sorry. What did you say?"

"I said I can tell you don't trust me."

"I don't trust anyone except my brother." I was quick to answer him, and almost instantly, I wanted to slap myself. There was a definite dent in my heart as I spoke aloud about Tobias for the first time in a very long time. *Why did I say that?!*

I saw the shock on his face before he had a chance to recover. "You have a brother?"

My chest was wound so tightly that I could hardly breathe. "Yes. A twin." *Should I have been telling him this?*

The headmaster reached out and grabbed a green folder, opening it and placing it in front of him. Every muscle inside my body begged me to move forward just a bit, to see what was inside, but I didn't want him to think I was digging, so I stayed still in my seat. A few pages were flipped, the head-master licking his finger once or twice, before he set it back down and brought his gaze back to mine. "So, where is your brother, then?"

If only I knew.

A few seconds passed as I had an internal war with what I was supposed to be sharing with the headmaster. I didn't trust him, but there was a very strong part of me that wanted to. I didn't know why. For some bizarre and unexplainable reason, he felt familiar to me, and not in the way that I'd seen him passing by on the street. It was something more. Some-thing that made me feel safe, which, in the same breath, made me feel unsafe.

A knot made itself known in my throat. My chest grew even tighter, and the girl inside of me that longed for her brother, and longed for a way out, banged her fists against the contents of my brain, but at the exact same time, there was a door being slammed and a lock being clicked. *Don't trust.*

"You know what?" I switched my eyes back to him as he smiled. "Never mind that, okay? I called you in here for a few reasons, actually, and none of those were discussing your trust with me."

The headmaster, again, stood up from his desk and came around and plopped himself on the edge in front of me. One of his legs was touching the ground, the other was hiked up over his knee. "Your uncle wants you to check in every Monday with him, and he wants you to use the phone directly from the school instead of your cell phone. I told him you could come down here each Monday evening before curfew."

Can't wait. "Okay, thank you."

He nodded and glanced away for a moment. "I need you to know something, though."

I wavered before reluctantly saying, "Okay?" which came out more like a question than anything.

"As headmaster of this school, I take my students very seriously. I like to give them freedom and a chance to make their own decisions." Heavy silence filled the office before he continued. "You don't trust me, and that's okay because you don't know me. But you can come to me with any problems you may have..." His sentence trailed at the end as we had some weird, muted conversation with one another. I couldn't be sure, but I felt like he was skirting around what he truly wanted to say, and before I could nod my head in understanding, he leaned forward and lowered his voice. "And I mean *any* problem. It doesn't have to pertain to school... Do you understand what I'm trying to say?"

Don't trust. Don't trust. Don't trust.

My pulse quickened at his words, and the fear and loneliness I'd felt almost all my life—even more when Tobias left—came crashing down at the exact same time thunder rolled above the school. I jumped in my seat, taking that as a sign to keep my mouth shut. *If he only knew just how badly I wanted to trust him*. But I wouldn't. The only person I could truly trust was myself, and sometimes, I even questioned that.

"Also," the headmaster moved right along after I didn't answer him, and I was thankful. I was thankful because I wasn't sure what to say. "Mrs. Fitzpatrick was impressed with your artistic ability." He laughed, moving around to his desk again, acting as if we didn't just have a heavily deep conversation about trusting one another. "Actually, that's putting it mildly. She said you were brilliant. That you had the skill of Picasso himself."

That brought an instant smile to my face. A real, down-to-my-soul smile. "Really?" I asked with true surprise. I surely thought Mrs. Fitzpatrick would think poorly of me after seeing me pop out of a closet with Isaiah on my heels. *Jerk. A hot jerk, but still a jerk.*

"Yes, really." He grinned before pulling the green file open again. After flipping through a few papers, he read aloud, "Gemma has the potential for a full-ride scholarship to almost any prestigious art school in the nation, with a portfolio. Each and every piece she created for me in her few months of attending Wellington Prep blew me away, and I have been an art teacher for almost twenty years. Please give her a safe place to let her creative streak shine, because if you give her a chance, she will flourish."

My lips parted, and my cheeks were on fire as I sat there dumbfounded.

"I took it upon myself to contact your old school for transcripts since your uncle has yet to get them to me."

There was a reason for that, I was sure.

"Oh," I whispered, wondering what else he got from Wellington Prep. Did they tell him about my journal? About what was inside? About what Richard, my not-so-real uncle, had told them? The tips of my fingers prickled with the need to snatch that green folder from his hands.

"So, after talking with Mrs. Fitzpatrick, we've decided to let you use the art room at any hour of the day, except for after curfew or, of course, during your other classes."

Hope blossomed in my chest, warming me up from the inside out. "Are you serious?"

He nodded, this time grinning so big I could see his white teeth. A flash of something whipped through my head at the familiarity of his smile, but after a fleeting second, it fell, just as the feeling of warmth had vanished. "Just..."—he glanced away—"your uncle has made it very clear that you are to focus on your studies and *not* art."

That wasn't surprising in the least, especially considering what had happened at Wellington Prep.

"But...you're allowing me to use the art room? Why?" I couldn't help the words tumbling out. I was beyond confused. There were too many mixed emotions floating around my head, jumbling up my thoughts. From the second I stepped my wet shoe into St. Mary's expansive entryway on Monday, I'd been in complete disarray. Isaiah, the headmaster, Sloane... all together, mixed with the thick walls of this place, tucked away in the middle of the forest on the very brim of Washington...made me feel something that was almost taunting in a way: *safe.* I felt safe.

But I wasn't. I wasn't safe until I was far, far away from Richard. He had ties with this school in some way, and even if Headmaster Ellison had been all but forthcoming about his rocky skepticism regarding Judge Stallard himself, I wasn't totally sold on the idea that I was untouchable here.

If Richard knew of even one tiny misstep from me, I'd never ever get a way out. For all I knew, he was putting together a plan right this second to fend off the social worker and any unanswered questions and take me back. But still, I wanted to know why the headmaster was allowing me to do something *my uncle* forbade. I needed to make sense of it all.

"Because," the headmaster whispered, finally answering me, "you remind me of someone."

CHAPTER THIRTEEN

ISAIAH

"BECAUSE YOU REMIND ME OF SOMEONE."

Hearing my uncle and Gemma get to their feet and walk over to the door of his office, I scooted back slightly from the hinges and rested my back along the stone wall behind me.

Gemma was the first to walk out, stopping dead in her tracks at the sight of me sitting in the same spot she had sat a few days ago, when *she'd* eavesdropped on *my* conversation. There was a slight dip in her brows, her pale lips pursing. She recovered quickly, darting further away when I shot her a wicked grin. I cocked an eyebrow as if I were saying, "*See? I can eavesdrop too.*"

"Isaiah?" My uncle cleared his throat, breaking Gemma and me away from our silent spar. She quickly shot me a withering stare before turning around and walking down the hall in her tight skinny jeans, which I may have preferred over her uniform. The uniform showed smooth legs, but her jeans fit her like a glove, showcasing her tight ass and curved hips.

My uncle cleared his throat again, and I finally tore my longing stare away from Gemma. "What do you need?"

I really only came down here to ask why my uncle needed to talk with Gemma, but after I'd heard their voices filtering through from the other side of his office door, I couldn't help but listen.

I needed—*okay, fine...*I wanted to know more about Gemma because there was absolutely more to her than met the eye. At first, she looked innocent, and there was no doubt in my mind that she was. She was shy, blushed a fuck-ton, which was actually kind of cute in a way, and fell into herself anytime there was attention on her. But she had a fire inside of her too. Gemma was fueled by something. Something dark and unforgiving. I was beginning to learn that she was hard to read, but all in all, she appeared good and respectful. For fuck's sake, she called my uncle *sir,* and each and every teacher adored her. I'd heard them discussing her in the teacher's lounge the other day when I bluntly walked in to use the vending machine that was off limits to students. Gemma was a good girl, even if she hated when I used that little pet name, and I wanted to know more.

After striding into my uncle's office and plopping myself down onto the leather seat at his desk, noting it was still warm from Gemma, I hiked a foot onto his desk. "What did the SMC say?" I had been acting nonchalant since we'd talked last, but after speaking with my father, I was on edge. I hardly slept. Instead, I stayed up until three, playing video games with Cade, and I *never* did that. Video games were like a suspension from reality, and although my reality sucked, I still liked to be in control of it.

He grunted. "You're on probation."

I paused. "What the fuck does that mean?"

My uncle ran a hand through his hair, looking more tired than usual. He put his back to me and angled his head up to the ancient map framed on the wall behind his desk. I followed his line of sight, roaming my gaze over each and every valley of earth, reminding me that there was so much more out there than this dreary place I called home.

"It means you have one more chance. You and Ms. Glenburg put them over the edge."

My nostrils flared as my boots thudded to the floor. "I talked to Dad."

He cocked his head over his shoulder. "I did too."

Silence fell upon us as it often did when my father was brought up. I ground my teeth, gripping onto the arms of the chair tightly. "He threatened Jack."

That had my uncle turning around with a disapproving scowl etched on his features. His hands graced his hips angrily. "Of course he did." Shaking his head, he sat down into his seat.

"So, I basically can't get kicked out of St. Mary's and also have to keep tabs on Bain, who loves trouble as much as any of us."

The scratching of my uncle's hand against his pebbled five o'clock shadow caused my eyes to drop down. He huffed out a sarcastic laugh, but I stayed silent. Thinking. Pondering.

"Why exactly can't *you* give my father updates about Bain?"

I'd never really thought of it before because when my father forced his little scheming plan of sending me to boarding school to keep watch on his enemy's son, Bain, I didn't really care. I was happy to be away from him and his bullshit, albeit a little worried about Jack, but with our nanny and Mom's nurses as a buffer, I was sure Jack was *mostly* fine. But now I was wondering. And I mean, did I have a choice? No. But why did I have to be his little spy when my uncle was the headmaster, for fuck's sake?

His answer came swiftly. "That's easy, Isaiah. Your father doesn't trust me."

I squinted. "That makes no sense. You're his brother."

My uncle darted his eyes away from me. "And you're Jacobi's brother. Do you trust him?"

I grunted. *Touché.* It wasn't that I didn't trust my older brother—he'd never blatantly lied to me—but I had been betrayed by him, and that was similar enough.

"The real question is"—his hands came and rested along the desk—"how are we going to keep you out of trouble but allow you to keep an eye on Bain? I know that when you sneak out, it's because of him, and the SMC will not allow me to make excuses any longer. I cannot be your cover. The SMC no longer believes my lies."

His admission didn't phase me. I knew he was aware that I snuck out, because he was always the one that had the final say in punishments, even if he wasn't the one who had caught me sneaking back in. It infuriated me beyond belief that Bain always snuck back in undetected, though. He was a sneaky little fuck.

My fingers came up and drummed against my chin for a second. "So, I need to quit getting caught or at least have a better cover for when I do get caught…"

"And you need to get your grades up. You're smart, Isaiah. So why on earth are you flunking?"

I chuckled under my breath before shrugging.

"You're so defiant. You're failing your classes on purpose, aren't you? Another one of your attempts to gain control like Ms. Glenburg had pointed out."

Whatever. I wanted to stew in silence, annoyed that they'd somehow made sense of my behavior that even I hadn't realized, but I didn't have time for all of that. They could take their Freud bullshit and do with it as they pleased.

I sighed, rubbing the back of my neck to ease the tension.

"I think I have just the plan that can knock out each of those things."

He raised an eyebrow, wafting his hand out for me to continue.

"What do you know about the new girl?" I asked as my cheek lifted.

His face faltered. "No." The word was like a bullet being fired.

"You haven't even heard my plan."

He snickered. "I'm certain that whatever it is, the answer is still no."

I propped my leg back onto his desk, ignoring the way it made him scowl. "Hear me out. Good Girl can be my tutor. You said I was on probation, right?" I didn't give him a chance to confirm. "I'm assuming they're going to be paying close attention to my grades along with my behavior. I'll get my grades up with my '*tutor*,'"—I used air quotes around the simple term—"and she can also be a damn good cover. An alibi." My leg fell to the ground as I sat up taller, feeling the smallest amount of desperation kick in. "You can write a note that she and I have permission to use the library after lacrosse practice, which gives me a pretty good excuse to be out of my room and roaming the halls after curfew, and on the nights that the SMC is suspicious of or doesn't believe my bullshit, Gemma can lie and tell them that I was with her, studying. They would *never* suspect a girl like her to cover for a guy like me. She's too...*good*."

He gave me an incredulous look, but he didn't say no. "And you just expect her to lie for you? You are right. She is a good kid. She's timid, and sweet, and I'm assuming she's honest as well. What if she doesn't lie for you, Isaiah? What if she tells them straight up that you were not with her?"

My desperation, along with the anger that my father had instilled after our conversation, was beginning to rise to high levels. "Then I'll fucking convince her! Do you have a better idea, Uncle Tate?" I took a deep breath before cursing under my breath. "I didn't care much about what Dad had to say when he sent me here. Fuck him. But he threatened to send Jack to the Covens. Jack!" My voice grew louder. "He's fucking nine years old."

Another round of silence fell upon us, hushing my loud outburst. My chest was heaving, and for the first time in a while, I lost my control in front of another person. I felt a little unhinged.

My uncle didn't say anything. Instead, he brought his finger and thumb up to his nose and punched the bridge of it. Then, he moved to his temples and began massaging them. I needed to do the same because my head began to pound the moment I brought up my little brother.

After a few more seconds of silence, I leaned my elbows down on my black jeans. "Do you have a better idea?" My chest ached, the muscles along my neck tensing. "I know it's my fault the committee isn't happy with me—that's on me. But you're right. Half the time, the reason I get caught doing shit I shouldn't is because of Bain. He somehow twists shit, and he never gets caught sneaking back in after going in fucking circles. He always manages to sneak away without getting into any trouble at all."

"That's because Bain has been taught all his life to evade authority. His father has been grooming him from a young age."

I often forgot that my uncle was once in the same position I was in. That he was once a part of the family business, and he likely knew more than me.

"So was I," I answered, flicking my eyes to him.

He gave me a grin. "You're right, but there's a difference between you and Bain, Isaiah. You don't want to please your father like he does. And also, you're not the bad kid that everyone thinks you are."

I joked. "The committee says otherwise."

Another stretch of silence passed as he thought for a moment. His eyes wandered all over his office as he had an internal battle with himself. Then, he shook his head. "I suppose you can carry on with your plan...but don't break that poor girl's heart. She's...fragile. She can be your tutor." He glanced away as he mumbled under his breath, "It would probably do her good to make some more friends around here." After a moment, he locked back onto me. "She can lie for you on occasion, if she's up for that, but do not force her into anything she doesn't want. Every girl at this school seems to be wrapped around your finger. Don't mess with Gemma."

My lips ached to give him a cocky grin, but instead, I stood up from the chair and began walking toward his office door. "Don't worry, Uncle Tate. I won't corrupt the good girl."

I was certain he mumbled, *"Yeah fucking right,"* under his breath, but I couldn't be sure.

CHAPTER FOURTEEN

GEMMA

"AND THIS IS where we usually hang out on the weekends before curfew..." Sloane's voice trailed as she plopped herself down onto a couch with a ridiculous number of frilly pillows scattered on top. Her small frame was nearly invisible as the cushions swallowed her up.

Glancing around the dimly lit room, I found a few standing lamps and some candles resting along a high book-shelf, their flame flickering back and forth. The room was dark but comforting. I could totally see myself getting lost while sketching in here.

"Come sit with us," Mercedes said as she pulled a book from the shelf across the room. "What did the headmaster want?"

Slowly sitting down on the floor over a multicolored woven rug, I crossed my legs and rested my back against the couch Sloane was lying lazily on. There were a few other groups of students in the...lounge?...but they all went back into their own conversations after scanning me from head to toe.

"Oh, um." I teetered my lip back and forth. "He wanted to talk about my past transcripts and let me know that I could use the art room whenever I wanted."

"The art room?" Mercedes sat at the end of the couch, wiggling underneath Sloane's legs.

"Yeah." I smiled shyly, pulling my long sleeves farther onto my hands to hide my wrists.

"Oh, yes, didn't you know?" I quickly straightened at the sound of Cade's voice. He strode into the room, looking just as dreamy as he did in art, except I knew those honey-brown eyes could be deceiving. Sliding down beside me, resting his shoulder against mine, he peered over at me. "Gemma is quite the artist. You should have seen her sketch in art the other day."

I hastily moved my arm away from his, annoyed that he was touching me. "It would have been nice if I could have finished my sketch. But someone took advantage of my generosity." *Shit, why did I just say that?* What was it with these guys that fired me up?

A girl from a few seats down snorted under her breath. Mercedes smashed her lips together as Sloane mused, "Okay, I officially love my new roomie."

I wasn't sure why she said that, but I assumed it was because I had talked back to Cade. It wasn't on purpose, but I was still a little bitter that he had tricked me and worked alongside his friend to corner me in the closet. I was amazed at the confidence I had when allowed to speak my mind for once.

"Uh-oh. Someone's bitter." My eyes moved swiftly over to a pair of black combat boots that were so close to touching my own shoes I could have moved a centimeter and they'd have been joined together. I refused to travel the length of his legs to meet his face.

"Of course she's bitter," Sloane mumbled. The couch cushions moved behind my back, so I knew she'd sat up. "The school thinks she had an infamous closet date with you after one day of being here."

Brantley, one of the other Rebels that Sloane had pointed out during breakfast, made an appearance. "Did you hear that? Your closet dates are infamous, Isaiah."

Cade made a high-pitched whistling sound. "I don't know about you, but I think I hear some jealousy in Sloane's tone."

"Absolutely not," she was quick to rebuttal. "I don't screw around with Rebels."

Brantley stepped closer to us. "Who do you screw around with then?"

I finally turned around and glanced up at Sloane. She and I hadn't talked much about *her* since I'd arrived here. We'd talked about the school, a little about my life, but not so much hers. That probably meant I was a bad friend. I needed to ask more questions, get to know her a little better.

Sloane's face stayed even, but I saw the smallest amount of pink spread over her cheeks. Before she could answer, Isaiah cleared his throat, and the tip of his boot hit the edge of mine.

Finally, I brought my attention to him, craning my neck back to peer up at his tall stance. I tried to brace myself for the impact, but my stomach flopped anyway.

The angle of his jaw was even sharper from where I was sitting, the edges of it looking like a sharp blade. His blue eyes were icier than ever, too, but somehow soft as he peered down at me. "Can we talk?"

My mouth opened, but nothing came out. Butterflies were definitely swarming my stomach. I gulped when I pressed my lips together again, suddenly feeling dizzy. *Say no.*

I needed to say no. He made the entire school think I had done something with him in the art supply closet. He was the whole reason my cell phone was burning a freaking hole in the back of my jeans, just waiting for Richard's cold voice on the other end telling me he'd seen the blog post on Mary's Murmurs. I wasn't sure how to access the site, but Richard was a smart man. He'd figure it out.

"I think you've rendered her speechless, bro."

Another voice came from beside Cade. I think it was Brantley. "I think you've rendered everyone speechless."

Isaiah and I both took a quick scan of the room, realizing everyone was staring at our little moment. Not a single person was speaking. Their attention was solely on us.

It didn't take long for my body to grow hot. Gasoline was poured over my head, and their scorching eyes were the match. If there was a mirror in front of me, I wouldn't even have to look to know my entire body was flushed.

Once I peeked back at Isaiah, his head moved slightly. My breathing had quickened, the couch cushions behind my back shifting again, telling me that Sloane was about to swoop in and save me.

"Fine," I whispered, slowly climbing to my feet. Isaiah dipped his head down to my legs and then back up again. The single movement of him scanning me from head to toe made the room spin. I was in a time warp. Time had passed, I was sure of it—maybe only a few seconds—but to me, I felt it had paused all together. I was rooted to the floor, my feet becoming heavy in my shoes, but eventually, the moment was gone, and I trudged after him.

See? I could do this. I could get past the way he made me feel when he looked at me. *It was fine*. Isaiah Underwood would not become a distraction. And plus, I was pretty sure the only reason I was feeling so erratic around him was because I'd been so starved of human interaction my whole life. It had nothing to do with the way his blue eyes seemed to burn a little brighter when he locked onto me.

The very second Isaiah and I stepped out of the lounge, we were met with the quietness of the long, empty hall. A trickle of a faucet dripped in the distance as I tiptoed after him, my shoes barely making a noise on the floor. The water dribbling and the pounding of my pulse were like an orchestra playing in my head, but it quickly came to an end when Isaiah halted in front of me. I made sure to keep a good distance behind him so I didn't fall into the hard planes of his body again like the first night we'd met. I slowly looked at his attire from behind, seeing that he was wearing black jeans and a red-and-black flannel shirt that was rolled to the middle of his forearms, and I hated that my stomach dipped.

"Come on." Isaiah's hand wrapped around my wrist, and my eyes shot down to where he was touching. I was suddenly thankful I had pulled my sleeves over my hands before taking a stroll with him. *Why was he touching me?*

The art room was dark, uninhabited by Mrs. Fitzpatrick, but Isaiah didn't bother turning on any of the standing lamps as the outside light shined through the far windows, basking the room in a faint outdoorsy glow.

The shuffling of his cool, casual stride gained my attention as he strolled over and flicked my earlier sketch that hung from a piece of string over Mrs. Fitz's desk.

"You're talented, Gemma."

I said nothing as I shifted on my feet. Isaiah's cheek lifted in a coy grin, and although every submissive, rule-following bone in my body broke with my intense stare on him, I didn't dare look away. That was the girl Richard molded me into from the time I could walk, and I didn't want to be her anymore. I would look at Isaiah all I wanted, and I'd talk to him like I wanted, too. Maybe I'd even take it a step further just to spite my dearest Uncle Richard all together.

"What do you want?" I asked, surprised at how leveled my words came out.

Being alone with Isaiah somehow gave me even more confidence than earlier when I'd talked back to Cade. And that was extremely enticing. Nerves still littered my belly, but a small part of me craved to feel that electric current of anticipation he gave me. Standing here, staring at him all alone in a dark room had the realization coming into view. The very second Isaiah came into my line of sight that first day at St. Mary's, he opened up something that was buried deep within my soul, and I'd been chasing the high ever since. I hadn't even realized it until this single moment. *Did I like the way my stomach dipped when he looked at me? Did I enjoy talking back to him?* I think I did. I think I liked seeing his reaction.

Isaiah laughed under his breath, the sound making my lips ache to do the same. Then, he hopped up on the edge of the teacher's desk, his long, black-jean-clad legs dangling an inch above the floor. "Alright, Good Girl. I have a proposition for you."

I snorted, and surprise flashed on both of our faces. "A proposition?" I rolled my eyes before backtracking as anxiety whipped through my body from the shadows of my past. I cleared my throat as I moved to take a seat on the stool in front of my usual desk. *Did I just roll my eyes at him?* The last time I'd rolled my eyes, I'd been punished. Badly.

"Hmm," he mused, hiding a smile. "I really like that you don't put up with my shit. You are quite possibly the only girl I've ever met who isn't affected by my charm."

Cocky, much? I thought his statement over for a moment, placing my arms on the art table in front of me. I pulled my sleeves down even farther onto my hands, clasping my fingers over on the cotton to stay glued to my palm. It wasn't that I wasn't affected by his charm, because I was, it was just that I didn't know what to do with it. I didn't know how to flirt.

Wait. I shouldn't be flirting with him. I was *not* affected by his charm.

"Who said you were charming?"

Isaiah's face split in two, the smallest dimple appeared on his cheek, and I locked onto it. Okay, fine. Maybe he was charming—at least the dimple was. "You are"—he scanned my face once more, the dimple still there—"very interesting, Gemma."

I ignored his statement because I didn't even know how to respond. "Did you take care of the blog? Did you get it taken down like I asked?"

Isaiah's legs stopped swinging for a moment as his smile fell. "You're afraid of your uncle finding out?"

My head whipped up, a piece of my hair getting stuck to my lip. I hurriedly swiped it away, watching as Isaiah focused on my mouth before he said, "Oh, yes. I can eavesdrop too, Good Girl."

I recoiled instantly. "Stop calling me that."

His large hands shot up in mock innocence, another smirk gracing his chiseled face. Even from across the room, I could see the mischievous glint in his eye. "Okay, okay. I'll stop calling you that"—he paused—"if..."

I made a throaty noise, dropping my head. "I should have known there'd be an if." *There always was.*

His voice cut through the air. "I'll stop calling you Good Girl if you do me a favor."

I treaded slowly. "What favor?"

He shrugged. "For starters, I need you to...uh, tutor me."

My face scrunched. "Tutor you?"

He nodded before glancing away. "And on occasion...I might need you to cover for me. A white lie here or there. No biggie."

I jerked back, my fingers clenching down over my sleeves. "You want me to lie for you? What kind of favor is that?"

I was confused, and for a split second, I thought he was teasing me again. Maybe he wanted to see if I'd fall for his good looks and arrogance like every other girl did. Maybe he wanted to see if I'd be willing to do whatever he wanted. But one look from the near ground-breaking level of hope in his eyes told me he was being serious.

He wanted me to lie for him?

Why?

CHAPTER FIFTEEN

ISAIAH

"You're serious?" she asked, completely and utterly dumb-founded. Gemma glanced around the room, her hair swaying from one side to the other, before landing back on me. "Why would I lie for you? And to whom?"

She rolled her pretty green eyes, the same eyes that somehow sparkled even without any lights on. It was like they were the light themselves. "This is a joke. Isn't it? You're trying to see if you have any sway over me because you're hot and *charming*." The word dripped from her mouth with pure distaste, then she flew to her feet and shot me a dirty look. She mumbled something under her breath about this being a test then said, "Leave me alone, Isaiah. I do not have time for this."

I hopped down too, my boots thudding to the floor as I ran after her. Gemma was small, so her feet didn't carry her nearly as fast as mine did me. "Wait," I called out, wrapping my hand around her waist from behind. She gasped as I pushed the heavy door shut with my other hand. "I'm being completely serious with you," I whispered into her ear, leaning so close to her I could feel her warm heat cover me like a blanket.

She ripped herself out of my grasp and darted underneath my arm, panic set deep into her features. My eyes narrowed. It was damn hard to read her. One second, she was acting timid and innocent, the next she was rolling her eyes and spouting off insults.

"I can't figure you out." My sentence came out as a whisper, and to be honest, I didn't even mean to say it out loud.

Gemma put enough distance between us that the entire line of lacrosse players could stand comfortably.

She wrapped her arms around her slender waist. "Why would I lie for you? And to whom?" Her left eyebrow was raised, and her lips were pursed. "And tutor you in what class?"

I stayed put, giving her the space she desperately sought after I had leaned into her warmth. "All of them. After lacrosse each night, I'll need you to tutor me in the library after curfew." She opened her mouth to protest, but I held up my hand. "The headmaster already said he would write us a note, excusing us if anyone asked what we were doing out past 7:00."

Gemma seemed to think that over carefully as her fingers clenched even tighter over the sleeves of her shirt. "We don't even have any classes together."

My head slanted as I took a step toward her. "We have art together."

She huffed. "How could I forget that? You shoved me into a closet the first day here."

There she was. That fiery girl who excited me more than I'd like to admit came back just as quickly as she'd left. I took another step toward her as she sighed loudly. "I can't tutor you, and I definitely can't lie for you." She took a step back.

Hope crashed and burned around me. "Why not?"

She shifted, her feet shuffling on the floor. "Because I'm... supposed to be focusing on my own studies." She hesitated for a quick second. "And my uncle doesn't allow me to be alone with boys."

With *boys*, she said. As if I were a boy. The things I'd seen and done made me lose my boyish vibe years ago. But I already knew this would be an issue with her, given the conversation I'd overheard earlier. I didn't hear the entire conversation between her and my uncle, but I heard enough. Her uncle was strict. I got it.

"Your uncle doesn't have to know. He won't find out."

Skepticism washed off of her in waves as she shook her head and glanced to her feet.

I took a step closer to her. "I can promise you that he won't." Was it an empty promise? Maybe. But who was going to run to Gemma's uncle and tell him that she was tutoring someone? Who even cared? It seemed so trivial.

Gemma began biting her pale lip, and there was a strong urge that begged me to swipe at it. It began at my neck and traveled down to my fingertips, causing them to twitch. Her lips looked soft, and her mouth was kissable as fuck—especially when she insulted me.

Gemma began shaking her head again as she took another step back. I could feel my grasp on her loosening. The war she had brewing on whether to consider my proposition was slowly becoming nothing but useless words floating around an empty room. My tone was eager and almost pleading. "He hasn't found out about the blog, right?"

She paused, looking right past me, as if looking me in the eye was going to do something. "No thanks to you."

I fought a smile. "That's because no one knows about it but the students. It's for school gossip. Most of the parents and guardians that send their children here want rid of them.

What makes you think they're checking some random blog on the Internet? Everyone outside of these walls is under an illusion that St. Mary's is a strict boarding school without the normal shit that comes with teenagers, like drama and gossip." *Among other things.*

"The two things teenagers thrive on."

My eyes slanted as I tried to read her again. There was a hitch of melancholy in the way she'd said that. "But not you?"

Gemma finally brought her emerald eyes back to mine, the shine in them a little dimmer now. "No. Not me. I prefer to stay away from the spotlight."

I clenched my teeth because, unfortunately, even just tutoring a guy like me would bring nothing *but* the spotlight. Rumors would spread like wildfire. They already were just from me asking her to "talk" in the lounge moments ago.

"I really need this," I whispered, showing her a side of myself that I'd never in my entire life showed anyone before. *Desperation.* But shit. I was. I was desperate. Jack wouldn't survive at the Covens. He was a good kid. And if I got expelled, that was exactly where he'd go. My father did not bluff. I was in a shit position.

Gemma paused, her tightened features dropping for a fraction as she scanned over my face. Her lips softened into a sad smile, though the moment was fleeting because, after a second, she seemed to clam up as she shook out her long brown hair and breezed past me. Her clean and girly scent clogged up my senses for a second, making me forget my purpose.

But when I heard the door open, I quickly spun around. "I'll give you whatever you want," I said with her back to me. She peered over her shoulder, giving me a glimpse of her smooth cheek. "It doesn't have to be a favor. Let's make a deal. You give me what I need, and I'll give you something in return. What do you need? Money? I have plenty." Shit. Now

I truly was sounding desperate. Money? Did I just offer her money? *What the fuck was I doing?* I was quick to change my pace. "You name whatever you want, Gemma. I'll give it to you."

A loud swallow came from her throat, and I felt the hope lingering in the air right in front of me. But then *poof,* it was gone within a flash. Gemma clenched her eyes, and instead of saying anything, she stepped out the door, leaving the echoing slam the only thing I could hear.

Fuck. That did not go as planned.

CHAPTER SIXTEEN

GEMMA

GLANCING DOWN TO MY OUTFIT, I cringed. "I..." My voice was as wobbly as my feet in the heels Sloane had lent me. "I feel weird."

Sloane popped her head out of the bathroom with one eye full of dark makeup and the other bare. "Don't! You look fucking hot, Gem." *Gem.* A slice of the past rushed toward me. The only person to ever call me Gem was Tobias. *Cue the ache in my chest.*

"It's true. You do!" Mercedes was flinging clothes out of Sloane's dresser. The scattered articles of clothing covered our floor like a new rug.

Looking back into the mirror, I trailed my eyes down to my smooth bare legs and back up to the tight leather skirt that hit my upper thighs. The mesh, black, long-sleeve shirt hugged my body tightly, showing off my slender waist and medium-sized chest. The only compromise that Sloane and I had was letting me wear a long sleeve shirt. She had questioned my request but didn't push me on the matter, thank God.

"Here." Mercedes came up from behind me, wearing nothing but her pink bra and matching underwear with a full face of makeup, handing me tall boots. "I can tell you're uncomfortable, so this will help. It'll cover up some skin." She smiled at me through the mirror. "You look killer, though. You have this good-girl vibe to you, but"—her eyes trailed all over my face—"your features are…so striking. Intense. But like, in a good way."

There was that phrase again: *good girl*. The small muscles along my belly clenched as I bent down and pulled off the strappy heels, placing them nicely at the bottom of Sloane's bed. Mercedes threw me a pair of socks, and after sliding the boots on, I did feel a little better.

Turning around and glancing at the knee-high leather boots, I felt less revealed and more myself. I was used to covering up, so showing this much skin was a rarity, except for those dark nights I pushed clear into the back of my head. *Nope. Not now.* I would not think of those things on the night of my first party with my two new friends.

"Are you going to tell us what Isaiah wanted today? Or are you still going with your story that he wanted to apologize for shoving you into a closet under false pretenses?" Sloane walked out of the bathroom, looking like a totally different person from the girl I'd met a few days ago with the fairy lights hanging around her bed. Red lipstick covered her lips so eloquently that she reminded me of a doll. Her hazel eyes were shadowed with dark-gray, shimmery eye shadow, and for a moment, I wished I was like that. I wished I'd had the opportunity as a young girl to play around with the makeup that lined the shelves I'd seen at the store with Richard's mother on our monthly outing. She'd scold me each and every time she saw me looking and would tell me that makeup was a sinner's poison. That if I touched it, I'd turn unworthy and end up like my mother.

The smallest amount of fear had seeped in at the memory, my heart thumping hard. Now that I was older and away from the looming threats and uncertainty that surrounded my mother when she'd *disappeared,* I knew Auntie's words were empty at best, but it still sent me into shock.

"Want some?"

Want what? I looked down to the red lipstick Sloane was holding and quickly shook my head. Clothes were still being thrown behind her head as Mercedes huffed and stomped around.

"Not tonight. Maybe next time, though."

Sloane smiled, the softness of the gesture not matching the intensity of her makeup. She looked dark and mysterious, and I felt a little envious of how confident she was.

I'd watched in silent awe as Sloane went over and grabbed a few pieces of clothing and flung them out to Mercedes. She snatched them quickly and started to shimmy her way into them.

"I love you," Mercedes sighed, running her hands down the front of her short purple dress. "I wish I was roommates with you two instead of Shayna." She rolled her eyes. "She kicked me out for four hours today while she messed around with one of the Rebels."

Sloane laughed as she sat on her bed to put those same strappy heels on her feet that I'd removed from mine. "If I were into the Rebels, I'd probably do the same."

Mercedes paused, silence encasing us all. Then, she began to giggle. "You're right. Me too."

My face was hot as they began talking about some of the other guys they'd like to spend four hours with. As they talked and I listened, my inexperience seemed to drive me away from their conversation, and my mind began drifting to

Isaiah and then to the rest of the Rebels. They were the only guys I'd really come into contact with since arriving here on Monday, and I couldn't deny their popularity with not just the girls, but with everyone. They were just *it*. Prestigious. Protective. Strong. Superior. Their ability to command a room was irresistible. I'd learned that much just from watching them in the dining hall and earlier, in the lounge, after I'd left Isaiah high and dry in the art room. I didn't last long when returning to Sloane and Mercedes after our talk, because my mind was reeling, and the nerves never left, especially with what seemed like a million pairs of eyes on me. *Everyone* was staring at me, wondering what Isaiah wanted to talk about. So, as soon he had walked back in, his intense gaze landing right on me, I excused myself and came back to my room, opened up my brand-new journal from the headmaster, and mindlessly sketched until Sloane got back with Mercedes in tow. That was hours ago, and I was still feeling antsy.

"Seriously," Sloane chided. "Tell us. There is no way Isaiah called you away from everyone to apologize. That boy doesn't say sorry."

A nervous tremor went through my body, zipping and whirling, telling me that Isaiah's little chat was not far off in my brain, even though I kept pushing it away. I, unfortunately, didn't have my pencil in hand at the moment, so I couldn't just...turn off my thoughts.

The thing was, I didn't *not* want to tell them about our conversation, but I still needed to process it, and I would be lying if I said I was totally put off by the idea. It wasn't until he declared, *"I'll give you anything you want,"* that made me pause. I'd been secretly weighing my options, and every time I'd tossed up the two choices, my body would fizzle out. *Life or death. Servitude or freedom. Stay or flee.*

And not only was I conflicted with him *asking* me for a favor instead of demanding it, but he could actually give me something in return that could propel my plan to get out of the trap that my life was in. So far, I didn't have this grand plan like I'd hoped to form the second I was away from home, but with Isaiah's tempting words in the back of my mind, things began to spin. It was a plan that could likely kill me later if I were caught. It was something that could probably kill him too, if it came down to it.

Sweat began to break out along my forehead at the thoughts and my ears began to ring. I was suddenly very angry that I was even put in the position where I had to think of these things in the first place. I was angry at my life, and my *uncle,* and sometimes—even though it made me feel irrevocably guilty afterward—I was angry at my mother. Angry that she somehow landed in Judge Stallard's lap and chose to stay even after she could have left. I knew that she wouldn't have stayed as long as she did if she knew everything that I knew now, but didn't she sense he wasn't a good person? Didn't she feel the same dark and unforgiving feeling in his touch that I felt? I knew Tobias did.

I cleared my throat, springing up suddenly from my bed and walking over to the mirror to glance at the fragile, clear-faced girl in front of me that desperately wanted to be strong and courageous. "I think I do want some makeup, Sloane." I peered over my shoulder, and I could see the confusion on her face but also the excited sparkle glimmering in her dark-framed eyes.

She bit her lip, her white teeth straining brightly against the red stain. "What changed your mind?"

I shrugged, running my eyes down my outfit. "Let's just call it...spite."

She looked at Mercedes, and they both got the evilest yet amused smile on their faces. Then, they rushed at me and got to work.

———

THE HALLWAY WAS EERILY quiet as Sloane and Mercedes pulled me along. I was stuck in the middle of them, my hands clasped in each of theirs. Mercedes gave me a tight squeeze, her palm colliding with mine.

"We should probably tell her about the types of parties the Rebels throw."

My heart caught at the mere mention of their name. Sloane whispered back to Mercedes, her warm breath hitting the side of my face. "She's never been to a party. She won't know the difference."

Mercedes' hand clenched on mine. "You've never been to a party?"

"Don't make her feel bad, Mer." Sloane didn't give Mercedes a chance to apologize—not that she needed to. I knew I was the odd one out in this trio. "But just a heads up—"

"What if we get caught?" I interrupted her, my heart slowly sliding down my body like a sticky sludge as the resentment from an hour ago turned into blinding anxiety.

We had to wait until the clock hit a certain time for us to sneak out and travel down the windy stairs to the main level of St. Mary's, and that was when I really began thinking about what I was doing. If we got caught and Richard got word that I was sneaking around at night after curfew, he'd likely come to St. Mary's himself to punish me, if not just take me all together.

Chills ran down my spine as we continued walking down the long hall. The only guidance we had were the flickering sconces on the walls, which seemed to get dimmer with each step we took, until we landed in front of a door at the very end of the long corridor. The tall, arched wood creaked as it opened, and once it shut, we were enveloped in pure black. I couldn't see a single thing in front of me, and without knowing it, I gripped onto both Mercedes' and Sloane's hands again.

They didn't let go, though, or laugh. They intertwined our fingers together, and my breathing calmed. After a few seconds of standing in the dark, a deep voice startled me. "Names?"

Sloane answered for us, and we heard, "I trust you to inform the new girl on our rules?"

She answered, "She'll be fine. She'll sit this one out." Then, she began pulling me forward. *Sit what out?*

My boot splashed in something wet, and for a split second, I was taken back to a different place at a different time. A coldness set in my bones, and I shivered, which definitely didn't go well with the already high anxiety swarming my body. "Are you okay?" Sloane asked, stopping her stride for a second.

My voice croaked, and I hated that. I hated it so much. "Yeah. I just don't like dark, damp places." My eyes still hadn't really adjusted. "Where are we? And you didn't answer about getting caught. What if we get caught?"

My nerves were getting increasingly worse, and I was certain it had everything to do with being in this place surrounded by familiar smells and sounds.

"We're underground," Mercedes answered.

I whipped my head over to her even though I couldn't see her. "Underground? Like a basement?" The fear in my voice was like getting hit by a bus. I hoped they didn't detect it too much.

Water sloshed as Sloane stepped forward, pulling us again. "Yeah. It's basically soundproof. And we won't get caught. The headmaster is usually asleep by now, and even if we did get caught, he'd tell us to go back to our rooms, and that'd be it. He's cool, Gemma. He lets us be *us*."

I breathed heavily through my nose, trying not to let the musty smell of the basement get into my head. *This is St. Mary's. Not home.*

"Okay," I answered, feeling irritated all over again at the mere glimpse of the past. I shook out my shoulders and nodded. "I guess it's time I learn what a real high school party is like, right?" *Screw you, Richard.*

Sloane and Mercedes both laughed, the sound echoing throughout the emptiness of the hall. "Oh, Gemma. This is *nothing* like a real high school party."

"No?" I asked as we continued walking forward. The closer we got, the more I could hear a slight thumping of music.

"No." I could hear the smile in Sloane's tone before she grew serious. We stopped in front of something. The air grew dense, the gap of emptiness closing. "And no judging. Okay? This is where we get to pretend we're not trapped in a creepy boarding school away from our families, acting like we're normal teens, because we aren't."

I swallowed back the fear and felt confidence slide back in. "I know all about not being normal, Sloane." *Trust me.*

She breathed out a light laugh and then opened the door.

CHAPTER SEVENTEEN

GEMMA

IT WAS JARRING. The lights, the music, the smells, everything. It took a few moments for my eyes to adjust, the mascara on my lashes feeling heavy as I blinked several times, trying to figure out what was in front of me.

Sloane and Mercedes didn't let go of my hands as they pulled me farther into the room. Multicolored lights danced along their features, making their hair look blue. The music vibrated off my bare skin, and it felt intoxicating. I stifled a gasp as I drank in the scene as if I hadn't had water in years.

"What—" I muttered, still being dragged by Sloane and Mercedes.

Sloane pulled me from the front, tipping her head back to see my reaction. "Hope you're ready to dance." Her voice was hardly audible from the loud music coming from the speakers, and I couldn't believe that I'd hardly heard it at all from outside the entrance.

The warm breath from Mercedes graced my ear as she

shouted, "The only good part of St. Mary's, besides the hot boys, are the parties. It almost makes it worth it."

"Almost?" I shouted back, glancing over several of my new peers that I had barely even imprinted into my brain since getting to St. Mary's. They looked like they were having fun. *Was this what I had been missing out on during all those years in the basement?*

She huffed a laugh over my shoulder but didn't say anything else to me.

It was obvious that Sloane and Mercedes—and probably almost everyone else that attended St. Mary's—felt that it was kind of like a prison. There were curfews set in place, no one was allowed to have a vehicle, and we couldn't leave the school grounds. But to me, it was freedom in the form of castle-like walls with chains hanging from iron-clad doors. St. Mary's was better than home. Home was *my* rendition of prison.

This boarding school was so much better than feeling like your very flesh was being eaten away as someone stared at you from across the dinner table, taking their longing eyes and dragging them down your arms and back up to your face again. Every bone in my body would break, and my stomach would recoil when the word *Daddy* flew effortlessly from my lips, as if it didn't fucking kill me to call him that.

Survive, Gemma. Just survive.

I tasted the bile in the back of my throat but clamped my teeth together and calmed my pulse as I was brought back to the present, still gripping both Sloane's and Mercedes' hands. I'd realized my palms were squeezing theirs when they both glanced over to me with suspicion.

My fingers flew open, releasing theirs. "Sorry," I mumbled, hiding my embarrassment.

Mercedes tucked a wavy piece of hair back. "It's okay. It's a lot to take in." She paused, glancing out to the open area in front of us that was packed with everyone moving and shaking their hips.

I'd never been to a school dance, or party, for that matter. The only social gatherings I'd ever been to were the ones that Richard would take me to with his closest and most trusted colleagues to save face. *Here is my niece that I took in when her mother went off the deep end. She's a good girl. She's polite and smart. Isn't that right, my dear Gemma?*

The *only* indication that this entire scene was normal for people my age was from some conversations I'd eavesdropped on at Wellington Prep or during the rare occasion that Auntie would let me into the group home for an hour or so, where I gulped up as much information as I possibly could without seeming too interested.

I was *technically* supposed to be a member of the group home that Richard's mother ran after my mother had left, but Tobias and I stayed in the main house with him because the group home was for girls only, and Tobias and I threw a fit when they had tried to separate us as young children. Who could blame us? Our mother had been ripped away at such a young age—so young that I could hardly remember what her laugh sounded like. If it weren't for the old photograph of her, I don't even think I'd be able to visualize her face. Or maybe I didn't want to. The only thing I could remember for certain was that I'd never felt safe again after she left. Ever. Not even when Tobias and I would sneak into each other's beds late at night because we were both sad and scared. Seeking comfort with each other didn't last long, though. Richard grew more furious each and every time he found us together.

He hated Tobias. He hated him so much.

Richard's mother didn't mind Tobias much. In fact, I think she may have favored him over me, along with most of the girls she took care of, but after her stroke a few months ago, leaving her basically brain dead, the group home diminished in its entirety.

That was when things began to get interesting.

Judge Stallard suddenly had to explain why there was a random girl living in his house that wasn't on record and had no ties to the group home—none that anyone was aware of anyway. From what I'd gathered over the years, it seemed that my mother had been one of the girls at the group home. Maybe even one of the first. I'm not sure how or why my mother ended up living in Richard's house, but that didn't really seem to matter in the grand scheme of things.

What did matter were the rumors of me and Tobias that started from the girls who attended the group home before Auntie had her stroke. Social workers flooded the home, having to place each and every girl into a foster home or a different group home. I'd even heard talk of sending some of the girls to jail, which never made sense to me, but that was where they learned that there was a teenaged girl—*me*—living in the main house.

Judge Stallard was favored in the court, obviously, and had many—*too many*—ties with police, lawyers, and even social workers, but you couldn't buy everyone. (His words, not mine.) There was one social worker in particular that continued to poke around, thus landing me in Wellington Prep and now St. Mary's.

It seemed things just got messier after he sent me to school to save face. Richard could no longer trust me, and I could no longer trust him.

"Have you taken it all in yet?" Sloane asked thoughtfully.

Swinging my eyes away from hers and back around to the ocean of bodies swaying, I really let myself look. Mercedes was right; we were definitely in the basement of St. Mary's. There wasn't a single window that I could spot, which made me a bit itchy to think about, the floor beneath my boots was hard and dirty, and there was a smidge of dampness lingering in the air. Huge pillars were standing upright around us with glowing lights winding around the durable stone almost as if the stone pillars were holding up the entire school above our heads. There was a long table beside the curved door that we'd walked through that had various sizes of glass bottles on the top that I recognized as alcohol from Richard's bourbon addiction.

But my attention was strictly on the bodies jiving and thrusting along one another as an upbeat song came through the speakers. They were sweaty. Girls' hair stuck to their foreheads, their dresses and skirts pushed up high, showing off their legs. Most of the guys were off to the side, watching the floor with likely the same amount of awe that I currently had in my expression.

A door opening across from the dancing bodies snagged my attention away for a split second before I went back to watching what was happening in front of me. It was like a drug, watching people dance and just *be*. My stomach hollowed out, jealousy surging through my limbs, causing them to twitch. I stepped a foot forward, wanting to let loose just like they were. Everyone looked so free and happy, and I craved that. I could almost taste it on my lips.

I wanted that. I wanted to feel that euphoria that I'd only ever felt when I was sketching, too lost in my own world to realize that I was actually living in my own version of hell.

"Now the real party can start," Sloane said, a sultry tick in her tone.

"What?" I muttered, still unable to look away. One of the guys came up behind a girl. It was Callie, the girl that had taunted me on the lacrosse field the other day.

"The Rebels are here."

My attention was whipped away when the words left her mouth, and almost instantly, I locked eyes with Isaiah. He was taller than mostly everyone in the room, easily able to look over the dancing bodies and pin me to my spot.

A rush of heat swept through me, causing my breathing to quicken. I watched with bated breath as his thumb came up and swept over his bottom lip, never once looking away from me. His friends had moved away, but he didn't step a toe in either direction.

He was staring at me, and I was staring at him.

Blue lights illuminated his cut cheekbones, his jawline sharper than usual from the dancing shadows, and then he flicked an eyebrow up, questioning me.

It was almost as if he knew I was considering his deal.

I gulped back the unyielding amount of anxiety and fear trying to claw its way up my throat at the thought of Richard sniffing out what I was up to. But if I wanted to avoid my future and disappear into thin air so he could never *ever* have me, I needed a plan.

I ran from him once out of fear, and it was a stupid, hasty decision on my part.

I wouldn't be that stupid again. I needed a plan, and Isaiah was going to help me with it. He just wouldn't technically know it.

CHAPTER EIGHTEEN

ISAIAH

WHAT'LL IT BE, Good Girl?

The party was in full swing tonight, everyone already buzzing on the hard liquor we'd snagged from some of the girls—not a hard task when you fucked their brains out for a few hours, making them come more times than they even thought possible—at least according to Shiner. And knowing him, he likely wasn't bluffing on that front.

Cade, Brantley, Shiner, and I were late, but that was only because I had to devise a plan with them regarding Bain. I knew he and his fuck boys, who were nowhere near as trustworthy as the Rebels, would be here, and I had a feeling he'd be a pain in my ass tonight. He was a sneaky shit. He often liked to slip out during these parties, and I usually had to tail him so I could keep an eye on his movements for Dear ol' Daddy and stupid fucking vengeance, but I knew I needed extra eyes tonight. I had a pretty big feeling someone would steal my attention, and I was right. I'd been here for three seconds, and I'd already found her.

"You comin'?" Brantley shouted over to me as the door clamored shut behind us. My heavy boots were stuck as if they were cemented into the floor as I kept a hold of Gemma's watchful expression. She was all the way across the party, a lengthy amount of distance between us, but still, every nerve ending in my body was aware of her being. We'd locked eyes almost the second I stepped foot into the room.

She looked different tonight, wearing clothes that weren't hers and makeup that didn't quite belong on her soft face. She looked hot, don't get me wrong, but she didn't look as angelic as she did in her schoolgirl uniform. More like an angel that was scorched by a sinner's touch.

A little sexy, a little dirty, but still shining as bright as the goddamn stars.

"Yeah," I muttered, my eyes still fastened tightly to hers. There was a definite unspoken conversation happening between Gemma and me at the moment, even with pounding music and moving bodies in between us. The only problem was that I couldn't read her like I could most people.

With that frustrating thought, I moved my attention away, feeling the dip deep in my core as I followed the rest of the Rebels toward the makeshift bar. I snagged one of the neon-colored plastic shot glasses and tipped it back, letting the burn of Fireball coat my throat. Wiping my mouth with the back of my hand, I quickly searched the room, waiting to find Bain. After all, he was the main reason I'd come tonight.

No.

That wasn't true.

I came to see Gemma. I was prepared to corner her and break down that very shaky wall she'd hastily thrown up earlier when I'd brought up my little plan. She'd hesitated when I offered her money. She'd glanced over her shoulder, just briefly, seconds before opening the art room door and running away, but I could see the minor crack in her strong-girl facade. Gemma needed something, and I hoped I could be the one to give it to her, at least for Jack's sake.

The Covens. My chest grew tight at the mere thought of my father sending him there.

Part of me wanted to call up Jacobi and flip my shit on him—*again*—for leaving us in the dust, but I refused to grace him with a phone call. He didn't deserve to hear my voice or know how Jack was doing. Because fuck him.

The sound of my knuckles cracking caused Cade to grimace. "What's eating at you, bro?" His lips flattened as he leaned in. "You're usually much more chipper on Saturday evenings."

Shiner elbowed me and waggled his brows. "Yeah, I mean...it's Claiming Night, bro. What the fuck is the sour mood for?"

Claiming Night was a century-old tradition founded by the original Rebels themselves—at least according to the history Shiner had found. It'd evolved over the years with each group of Rebels, but the same rules applied. If you wanted to get fucked, prepare to get claimed, and the girls at St. Mary's? They *loved* the idea of being claimed, especially by one of us. They all had daddy issues—no judgment here, I get it—and they craved the thrill that came with these parties. They desperately wanted our hands gripping their willing bodies tucked away in a dark corner.

"It's the new girl, yeah?" Brantley sighed from behind me, tipping another shot back and gasping at the end. "Fuck, that burns." He chuckled, running his hand over his short hair as he threw the hot-pink cup behind him. "But it burns so *damn* good."

"The new girl doesn't want our boy," Shiner sang loudly over the music. "That's what's wrong with him."

I grunted, crossing my arms over my chest as I watched Sloane and Mercedes drag Gemma in her fuck-me leather boots across the floor. The lights of the party played peek-aboo over her slight curves, and the bare skin on her upper thigh made blood rush right to my dick. "That's not what's wrong with me," I snapped, suddenly irritated as fuck that every other guy was watching her cross the party with her two new friends.

Being jealous wasn't my usual M.O., and I wasn't even sure why I was jealous. Was it because I needed something from her and she wasn't willing to give it to me? Maybe. Or maybe not.

I didn't really have time to decipher it all.

What I needed was for Gemma to let me claim her for the night so I could get her alone long enough to rehash my earlier advance. *Fuck, that sounded dirty.* I cracked my neck, evening my breath. I just needed to get her alone so I could work out some type of deal with her. There was something she needed, and I'd give it to her in exchange for what I needed. All she and I had to do was convince the SMC that my grades were improving due to her excellent tutoring skills, and she had to tell a tiny lie for me on occasion. It wasn't that hard. I just needed the SMC off my back and to take me off probation so I didn't have to worry about being expelled.

Easy day.

"Are you sure about that?" Brantley raised his eyebrows at me. "Looks like they're headed over this way." A wicked grin spread along his face, and my fist begged to wipe it off. "Shall we see which Rebel Gemma likes better?"

I scowled and drove my eyes into his. "Don't, Brantley." Something potent hit my blood, and I hoped he caught my slight warning. Brantley, along with Cade, knew all about the real reason I was at St. Mary's, because their fathers were in the *family* business. My father was their fathers' boss, for lack of a better word. We'd all seen shit that we wished we hadn't. Our lives weren't normal, and our upbringings would probably make grown men recoil, but that wasn't saying much for the students that attended St. Mary's. We were all a little fucked up in one way or another. It just depended on the cards each was dealt that determined whose life was worse.

"Has anyone spotted Bain yet?" This question came from Cade as Brantley and I continued staring at one another.

"I have," Shiner commented from the other side of me.

Shiner wasn't aware of what my father did for a living or that Brantley, Cade and I knew of each other before we all began attending St. Mary's. I knew my father had told their fathers to send their sons here at the same time I'd shown up, as a sort of intro to what our futures held, but Shiner somehow made his way into our friendship, and I liked him. He had our backs even if he was unaware of some things. He also knew the ins and outs of this school since he'd been attending here longer than any of us, and that came in handy.

Shiner's face remained relaxed as he stared out into the party. "Bain has eyes on your girl, Isaiah."

My blood ran cold as I sharpened my gaze on the room and landed on his beefy stance. Bain was surrounded by a group of guys, who'd all wanted to be a Rebel but didn't quite make the cut, in the far corner of the basement. Each and every last one of them stood back with their arms crossed over their chests like they were gangsters, gazing out onto the floor with their tongues half hanging out of their mouths as they watched Gemma, Sloane, and Mercedes on the dance floor. Bain's mouth twitched as he kept watching Gemma, my attention bouncing back and forth between him and her.

Nope.

Before I could even stop myself, knowing damn well that when he saw me with her, he'd want her *that* much more, I made my way onto the floor, leaving the rest of the Rebels behind. Gemma was in between Sloane and Mercedes, her dark hair tumbling down her back and framing her heart-shaped face as she stood with her back ramrod straight, watching everyone around her dance like their lives depended on it.

Sloane ruffled Gemma's hair as laughter rushed out of her. "Come on, Gemma. Dance like nobody's watching!" she shouted.

Gemma nibbled on her lip, slowly looking up at everyone around the room who was undoubtedly staring at her, until she saw me. Her eyes widened, the dark makeup surrounding the vivid green color showing me just how out of her element she was.

"What is it?" Mercedes asked, pausing her moving hips for a brief moment.

"It's me," I answered, coming around and lazily putting my arm around Gemma's tense shoulders. She sucked in another breath as our bodies touched, and Sloane gave me a warning look. Her hands graced her hips, but just before she could spit out whatever came to mind, the lights went out, and a voice sounded out from the speakers. *"It's claiming time."*

CHAPTER NINETEEN

GEMMA

I GASPED, my body frozen with pure, blinding anxiety. "Claiming time?" I asked, wincing at the unease evident in my tone.

"Isaiah," Sloane's voice warned from somewhere close by. "She is not ready to be claimed. Pull her off to the side —*now*."

Isaiah's arm that was draped over my shoulders didn't even move a fraction. "Relax, Sloane," he whispered. "Don't you trust me?"

She scoffed quietly. "No. Not even a little bit. Quit fucking around."

My heartbeat sped up to an inhuman speed. Short puffs of air escaped my chest as I willed my eyes to adjust to the darkness. The room was quiet...so quiet I could hear everyone's breathing. Confusion filled my senses, making them stall out altogether. I was frantically trying to get my mouth to open to ask what the hell was going on, but my tongue was twisted in a perfect knot with confusion.

Music suddenly cut on again, playing so loudly that I flinched. I snapped my head over to the nearest speaker, wishing I could see into the bleak darkness. "Breathe, Good Gi—" Before Isaiah could say anything else in my ear, a cold hand firmly grabbed my elbow opposite of him, and I was whooshed away, just like that.

Panic coursed through me, and I jerked my arm back so hard I stumbled over my own feet. I knew it wasn't Isaiah as his arm fell from my shoulders quickly, and his voice and body heat were long forgotten. A cold fear washed over me in thunderous waves, and I had to silently scream at myself to remember that I was far, far away from home at the moment.

"Let me go," I seethed, pulling my elbow back again. Whoever it was that had me let out a dark, rich chuckle. The music was still blaring, but he was so close to me I felt the rumble of his chest along my arm.

"Now, now, new girl." His alcohol-ridden breath tickled my ear, and my nose turned upward just before I tripped over something. The grip he had on my elbow grew tighter as he kept me upright. "I just wanted to claim you for the night. You want claimed, don't you?"

"What does that even mean?" I asked, my voice muffled by the upbeat song. My head was spinning with the mix of darkness and loud music. Everything was in overdrive from the second Sloane and Mercedes had pulled me down the dark hallway after curfew. I should have just stayed in my room and scoured through endless articles revolving around Judge Richard Stallard himself to see if I could uncover anything about what he may have done with my brother.

But *no,* I just had to come to this party with Sloane and Mercedes, for some godawful reason.

I knew the reason, but at the moment, I wasn't going to admit it. Not now.

A finger trailed over the side of my face as the guy's voice penetrated my ear again. I wasn't sure where we were in regard to where I was standing a few seconds ago, because whoever it was that had me in his grip dragged me several feet away, and I didn't even know in what direction. "They didn't tell you the rules of tonight? They didn't explain what Claiming Night was?" He huffed, his hand on my elbow tightening again as he pushed his body into my backside. Swallowing back the bile and the familiar feeling of disgust, I pushed my fear away and tried to level my breathing. *Survive, Gemma. Just survive.*

I shook my head, no longer resisting. My eyes shut as my shoulders loosened. I'd been in this position too many times before to let myself get all riled up. I knew how to calm myself down and just *deal.* Richard wasn't behind me, demanding that I call him *daddy.* I wasn't in a pit of emptiness where no one would hear me scream. I was at St. Mary's, and I was fine.

But was I?

"Let me go," I demanded through my silent protests of wanting anger to outweigh fear. Something thick and hard graced my back from the guy who ripped me away, and I bit down on my lip as I recognized what it was. My eyes closed. An empty black abyss was all I could see, yet somehow, it grew even darker. *No. You're fine, Gemma.*

Flashbacks began assaulting me, hidden memories creeping out of their vaults and taunting me in the back of my brain. I felt the tremor in my limbs, my body quaking with my rising stress levels.

His voice was muffled, morphing into something from the darkest parts of my soul. "They say you're a good girl, Gemma. But are you?"

And just like that, I was snapped back to a place I never wanted to be again.

. . .

THE FLOOR WAS hard and cold. Blood seeped from my bare, wet knees. Misery seemed to be the only thing to keep me afloat. It was the only thing I could feel. I was numb, except for that tiny amount of sadness that was allowing the tears to fall ever so gracefully over my dirty cheeks for the last...however long it had been. Time seemed to pause but move quickly at the same time down here.

A faint glow of light swept underneath the covered window, and that was how I'd been keeping track of the days, but when I was in and out of consciousness, it was hard to know if an hour had passed or an entire day. The only indication that I knew actual days had passed was because Richard's tie was a different color from the last time he'd come down here.

My eyes drooped again, my wrists aching from the metal digging into them. They were sore and weak as I hung below. Sometimes they'd be lowered, and I could rest my face on the cold dirty ground, but other times, I'd been extended. See? Time kept passing.

I snapped to attention, the metal chains ricocheting off one another, as the door opened and shut again. My brain told me to flinch from fear, but my body must have been too weak, because it didn't seem to move again after the initial startle from drowsy to alert.

My head hung as my arms were extended high, and the ends of my hair were a dark-gray color from the wet dirt coating them. The strands were thick bands of mud, hardly moving at all. His shoes were the first thing I could focus on, the shiny black of them gleaming and making my eyes hurt.

He shuffled past me, going behind to hopefully unchain me. This had to have been the longest he'd ever left me down here. With Auntie basically dead, no one came to check on me. Not that she did much, but it was comforting to know I wasn't truly alone when he'd get in these foul moods.

My arms fell with a thud, the chain screeching as it finally let up. My elbows cut as they hit the gritty concrete I'd been resting my knees on, and I cried out as much as I could with the dryness of my throat.

"Was that punishment enough, Gemma? Are you ready to be a

good girl?" he asked, a chummy tone in his voice like he was doing me a favor.

I wanted to spit at him, but that would require me to have strength to raise my head, and it would also require me to have actual saliva in my mouth, and I had neither of those things at the moment. Not to mention, he'd broken me. He broke that blazing, fiery spirit I'd had when I'd decided to stand up to him like Tobias had. It was a mistake. I knew that now. But I was hopeful. I was hopeful he'd send me to the same place he sent Tobias—wherever that was—but how wrong was I?

My head was jerked backward as his hand wrapped around my hair. "I asked you a question. Don't make me repeat it." He cursed under his breath as a dry yelp escaped me. "I will be damned if you act like your mother. I wasn't able to break her from that defiant streak she had, but I'll be sure to break you. You will be what I want and nothing more."

A strangled cry left my lips as my chest caved. "Y-yes." The word croaked out of me like a dying frog, and it damn near killed me.

"Yes, what, baby girl?" he whispered into my ear, pressing his core into my back. Something girthy rammed into my spine, and I silently belittled myself for learning what it was—which, ironically, was the start of what had landed me in this stupid predicament in the first place. Nothing got past Judge Stallard. With my Auntie gone, I thought I could be sly and figure out everything Tobias whispered to me in the mere minutes before he disappeared, but I was wrong. Richard checked on what I'd been up to. He knew every last Internet search I'd ever made.

Swallowing back nausea, I whispered through labored breaths, "Yes, Daddy."

A lone finger traced my bare spine, a shiver of chills coating my skin. He hummed in agreement as his fist tightened around my hair again. My head hurt when he'd pulled on my strands a little tighter. "If you're curious, just ask me." His warm sigh brushed over my shoulders. "You're almost eighteen. The perfect age. I can teach you all there is to know about the human body. Just wait, little one." And just like that, he dropped me back to the ground, my knees all but shattering with the impact.

"WHAT THE FUCK."

I gasped, my eyes springing open quickly as lights blinded me from above. My palms immediately went to cover them as I moaned, and that was when I realized my cheeks were wet. *Why are my cheeks wet?*

"Isaiah, back off," a voice said, sounding seriously concerned. "Calm down."

A growl sounded. "Calm down?" Then a loud gruff. "What the fuck did you do to her, Bain?"

Who is Bain?

"Gemma?" Sloane whispered. "Are you okay?" Soft hands wrapped around my wrists, and I let out a shaky sigh, and then I quickly snatched my arms away at the thought of my sleeves being pulled up too high. *Shit.* I flung my eyes back open, clenching my fists so tightly my nails dug into my skin. Despite Sloane's dark and edgy eyeshadow, I could see that she was truly worried about me.

"I'm..." I began to sit up. "I'm—fine." *Oh my God.* Did I say anything while I was out? Did I do something?

She took her plump red lip into her mouth, and she eyed me cautiously. Her hand gingerly went up to my forehead, and she raised her eyebrows, as if asking my permission. I gave her a slight nod, and she rested the back of her hand on my sticky skin. "You're in a cold sweat. Did you pass out?"

"Or did you knock her out?"

I turned my head to see Isaiah—in all his righteous glory, might I add—glaring directly at a guy I'd never seen before.

Isaiah's scowl was deep and furrowed; angry lines sliced over every angle of his face. He looked...intense. Two of his friends—one of them being Cade—stood in front of him, almost like they were a barrier between him and the other guy, who was looking pretty damn smug.

"I didn't knock her out, Rebel. Calm the fuck down." His laugh was a haughty one. It reminded me of Richard's. "She passed out or something. One second, she was standing in front of me, and the next, she was down. She slumped in my arms." He shrugged like it was nothing.

"And so you fucking dropped her?" Mercedes was standing off to the side of a room that I didn't recognize with her hands on her hips. *How did I even get in here?* Sloane was still checking me out, feeling my forehead again and frowning. Then, her hand went behind my head, and she gasped.

"You're bleeding."

Isaiah flung his attention to me so fast I jumped, causing my knees to buckle together as I sat on the floor. The glacial color of his eyes grew even colder as he zeroed in on me and then to Sloane's bloody fingers.

"Think first, act second," Cade said to Isaiah under his breath, not loud enough for everyone to hear, but I definitely picked it up, thanks to my well-honed listening skills. The other friend of Isaiah—who I now recognized as Brantley—had stepped toward Bain. Bain looked completely bored with the entire situation and not at all intimidated by Isaiah's murderous glare.

I knew right then that I didn't trust Bain. Just looking at him from down below made my stomach twist in knots, and that wasn't just because he'd been the one to send me into a full-on panic blackout. I just didn't get a good feeling from him. His dark eyes were hungry for something as he flicked his attention down to me, and after being around evil my entire life, I could tell, without a doubt, that he was corrupted in some way or another.

A light touch on my chin startled me as I continued

staring at Bain. My head pounded violently as I flinched, but then my attention was gently snagged away with the turn of my face. Isaiah was crouched down to me, his brows lowered, his icy eyes filled with worry. "Did he do something to you, Gemma?"

Gemma.

He called me Gemma instead of Good Girl.

Why did that bother me?

"Not intentionally." *But was he planning to?* I was suddenly aware that I was the center of attention in a very small room with way too many eyes. I cast my gaze downward, but Isaiah was quick to raise my chin again, his thumb brushing ever so lightly over my skin. "I blacked out," I admitted, blinking rapidly as he ping-ponged his attention between my eyes. I knew there were other people in the room. Too many people. But something about breathing the same air as Isaiah made me feel safe yet vulnerable at the same exact time. It was like I *wanted* to tell him all my secrets—even the scary ones that I preferred to hide from. "It's not the first time. I'm fine."

My lips parted as his hand came up and cupped the side of my face, weaving his fingers into my hair. My body was instantly awake, my head no longer pounding with pain but swimming with something else. It felt like I was floating. My body flushed; my skin prickled. His lips fell open slightly, and I glanced down to his mouth at the sound.

"For fuck's sake. You think I'm bad? You're about to make the new girl orgasm on the spot with that lustful look you're giving her, and she's fucking bleeding. You're a kinky fuck, Underwood. All I did was whisper in her ear, and yet I'm the one to blame?"

Isaiah's jaw hardened at the same time his nostrils flared. His hand dropped from my face, taking away the small escape of the situation with him. Then, he popped back up to a standing position.

He barked an order out to Sloane. "Take Gemma back to her room, and make sure to clean up her gash. Keep an eye out for a concussion."

"And you'll deal with Bain?" she asked with disgust as her hand wrapped around my arm. Mercedes came over and helped me up, too. The room spun a little, but I wasn't sure if that was from falling or from the up-close-and-personal encounter I'd just had with Isaiah.

Isaiah said nothing as I glanced back at Bain. He was staring at me intently, his eyes narrowing and his head slanting ever so slightly. Something flashed across his face, but before I could focus on it too much, I was pulled out of the room and enveloped in the dark hallway yet again.

CHAPTER TWENTY

GEMMA

SLOANE AND MERCEDES were both sound asleep on Sloane's bed, both of them snuggled underneath the lush lavender comforter. I nibbled on my lip as I reached back behind my head, my fingers diving underneath my thick hair, to make sure it was still okay. After we'd made it back up to our room from the party, Sloane went to work on cleaning the cut, inspecting it thoroughly with the flashlight on her phone, all while cursing out Bain—the guy who had tried to *claim* me— under her breath.

I stayed silent as she and Mercedes listed all of Bain's bad qualities, the two of them rambling on for what felt like hours. Apparently, he was the black sheep of St. Mary's, and he wasn't someone you wanted to be claimed by. Sloane could attest to that firsthand, although she didn't go into details.

After finally gaining the courage to speak again and agreeing that I would stay away from Bain, I very reluctantly asked what "claiming" was. Mercedes shot Sloane a worrisome look, as if they didn't want to tell me. I think they thought I was going to judge them, but I was the last person who ever would.

"Being at a boarding school doesn't give us a lot of free time to date or anything. We have curfews and can't really leave the premises, except for special occasions, and even then, it has to get approved by the SMC. But the rumor states that the Rebels, long ago, started something called Claiming Night. It's where the boys claim a girl for the night, and they fuck or do whatever, and come morning, everyone goes back to their normal boarding-school life filled with nothing but academics and shitty memories of their families who shipped them away in the first place."

I stayed silent as she and Mercedes gauged my response. A dreadful feeling of disgust and embarrassment slithered through me over the fact that this Bain guy thought I wanted him to claim me, and even hours later, it was still sitting nice and heavy in the pit of my belly like a bucket full of stones.

If I hadn't passed out in my fit of panic, what would have happened? And what about Isaiah? Didn't he say he was claiming me before Bain snatched me away?

A rush of heat swept over me. I clenched my legs tighter, ignoring how I kind of liked the idea of Isaiah wanting to claim me, and stared down at the laptop the headmaster had gifted me a few days ago.

I was already high on anxiety, with a pounding headache from the night's events, so opening up the laptop was just putting a cherry on top, but sleep was out of the question. And so was sketching. Taking pencil to paper was usually therapeutic for me, but sometimes, when I got too into it, I would have the same blackout spell that I'd had earlier, where I'd travel back to the not-so-distant past, and that was the last thing I needed at the moment. *No, thank you.* One traumatic visit from the past was enough for me.

Dropping my knees to sit cross-legged, I pulled the laptop closer, glancing at Sloane and Mercedes to make sure they weren't about to catch me searching stuff on the web that I *"shouldn't under any circumstances"* be searching, per Richard's threats. But if I wanted to get on with my plan, I needed to learn all there was to know about Judge Stallard and his many, many connections. I hoped it would lead me right to Tobias.

The keys of the laptop were cool under my touch, my fingers shaking slightly as they rested along flexible rubber. The ache in my head wasn't nearly as bad as before, but the brightness of the screen in the dark room caused my eyes to burn.

I'd just opened the search engine, my heart pounding wildly, the echo of it almost deafening in the near silent room, and that was when I heard a slight *ping*. A soft gasp escaped, as if it had sprung right out of my nervous stomach. My gaze widened at the little box in the far-left corner that said I had a new message. I had no idea what it was. I had hardly used my laptop since getting here, but the more it blinked, the more I panicked. Sweat started to form on my hairline, my head thumping in sync with my rapid heart rate. *Breathe, Gemma. Just breathe.* I shut my eyes, removing my hands from the laptop, and counted to ten before I went into a full-on spiral like earlier.

When I opened my eyes again, I glanced at the girls asleep on Sloane's bed. Mercedes had shifted a little, likely from hearing my little outburst, but her chest was moving softly like before.

After bringing my attention back to the glow of my screen, I took a steady breath and clicked the flashing icon. I hadn't even realized I was holding my breath until I began to see stars dance in front of my vision. A heavy burst of air left me, staring at the words in the message.

GOOD GIRL, *meet me in the hall in five.*

·   ·   ·

As each second passed, my heart thumped harder. Blood rushed to my ears as my skin grew slicker with sweat. I reread the message a few more times before another one came in.

Stop second-guessing yourself. *I won't bite.*

My fingers hovered over the keyboard as I tried to convince myself that it wasn't a trap. There was no way Richard knew I was sitting upright in bed in the middle of the night on a laptop he didn't even know I had, messaging me as if he were Isaiah. That was...irrational.

Isaiah? I typed, still needing the confirmation.

He messaged back within a second.

Who else calls* you Good Girl? *Of course it's Isaiah.

A sarcastic laugh threatened to escape my lips. If he only knew that he wasn't the only one who called me Good Girl.
    Feeling brave, I typed out another response.

How did you know I was on the computer and that I'd get your message?

·   ·   ·

ANOTHER PING SOUNDED as I bit my thumbnail.

I DIDN'T.

I SWALLOWED as I ran my hands down my face. Then I typed, **How do I know it's really you?**

I WAS STILL RIDDLED with anxiety as I chewed on my nail, rereading the messages, when it showed he had sent another. A spark started in the center of my chest as the next message had a picture attached. It was of him grinning at me. His inky hair was messy on the top, his chin tipped upward showing off the harsh angles. His icy eyes, surrounded by a thick band of black eyelashes, looked playful and not at all like the dangerous, smug boy I'd met just a few days ago outside of his uncle's office.

Another message came through as another rush of heat swept through me.

I'LL BE outside your door in two minutes. We need to talk.

I SAT on my bed for another thirty seconds, staring at the empty search engine box as I contemplated ignoring Isaiah. I could slip underneath my blankets and push my laptop away, pretending like everything was fine and that this entire night never even existed, but he was right. We did need to talk.

Butterflies fluttered in my belly as I pictured him outside my room, waiting for me. A small smile tugged on my lips, which I quickly wiped away as I swung my legs over the bed, placing my feet on the soft rug.

Tiptoeing over to the door, I glanced back at my two new friends, making sure they were still asleep, as I gently placed my hand on the iron knob and slowly turned it.

Oxygen filled my lungs with my deep breath as I silently reminded myself there was no other option for me. Isaiah said he'd give me anything if I tutored him, and I knew, deep down, I wouldn't get another chance like this. I was going to think of this as a transaction. A deal. I would do what I needed to do in order to get what I needed in return.

So what if I found him slightly attractive? So what if my body sizzled like I was on fire when he was near? So what if he made me feel alive for the first time in my entire life? He was also arrogant, smug, and had a niche for breaking rules. *Obviously*. Isaiah needed me to tutor him and lie to...someone, for whatever reason, and there was no question about it—I'd do it because I had to. I was surviving, just like Tobias told me to. I desperately needed money and probably even a fake ID, and those were two things I knew for certain Isaiah could get for me after hearing his conversation with his uncle.

He and I would strike a deal, and then, when the time was right, I'd be soon forgotten by everyone.

Even him.

CHAPTER TWENTY-ONE

ISAIAH

THE WALL WAS solid against my back, and my feet were steady on the firm ground, but my heart rate was anything but. I stood in the girls' hallway with nothing but small flashes of light from the lanterns flickering with the obvious rising tension.

Even though it had been hours since I found Bain hovering over Gemma's lifeless body in one of the rooms in the basement, I still felt keyed up. Not only did Bain get me completely riled by just simply being himself, but when he pulled his fucked-up shit with Gemma, I pictured myself strangling him. From the moment she was pulled out from under my arm during claiming time, I felt unnervingly frantic.

The most frustrating thing about it all was that Cade was right: I couldn't do anything to Bain. My father would go ballistic if I outed myself or our family, and not to mention, I was under probation with the board. I couldn't do shit—not when Jack dangled in the crossfire. My father knew exactly what he was doing when he had threatened him, and I hated him for it.

It seemed Bain knew that I couldn't do anything, too. His smug, shit-eating grin nearly caused me to slice my hands open with my nails as my fists clenched together. When he walked past me, after having words about the *rules* of claiming, I saw the coy glint in his eye, that all-superior, pompous attitude that had him holding his head up high like he was untouchable.

He wasn't untouchable. Maybe at present, but not in the future. If only he fucking *knew* who I was.

The door slowly swung open, and all thoughts of Bain vanished right in front of me.

One long, bare leg stepped out into the hallway first, and the orangey glow of a candle flickered at the perfect time to show Gemma's quiet figure slipping into the hallway. The heavy door shut quietly behind her as she continued gripping onto the iron chain before it bucked against the wood.

Her soft footsteps were silent as she padded over to me. My lips twitched as she got closer. The oversized shirt she was wearing reminded me just how fragile she actually was.

"Hey," I breathed out, still leaning back onto the wall. I remained casual, but there was definitely something urgent tugging on the inside.

"Hi," she squeaked, glancing up at me with her doe-like eyes. Her attention shifted down both ends of the hall, and that was when I pushed off and clasped my hand in hers.

Her breath hitched, staring directly at our connected palms. A hot flare of desire punched me right in the chest with the sound of her lips opening, and that was when I began pulling her down the long corridor. Her bare feet shuffled over the dark-red carpet, and I quickly darted my eyes away from the dark polish on the ends of her toes. *Even her fucking feet were attractive.*

We stopped abruptly, and Gemma damn near ran into my back. "Sorry," she whispered, a bundle of nerves backing the word as it flew out into the silent hall.

"Shh," I hushed, gripping her hand a little harder, making our palms connect yet again. There was really no need to grab her hand, but there was a strong part of me that needed to touch her. It was very unsettling.

I opened the door to the closet lined with extra linens and pulled her through, shutting it as quietly as possible behind her.

"Where are we?" Gemma's hand tightened on mine when the bleak darkness surrounded us.

I pulled her a little farther into the deep closet, all the way until we got to the back. "We're in the linen closet. It's almost time for the duty teacher to walk the girls' hall, but we should be safe here."

"*Should* be safe?" She put a clearly implied emphasis on the word "should", and I couldn't help but chuckle.

Her voice grew stern, and I was instantly pissed that I couldn't see her angry expression. "Why are you laughing? I think I've used almost all my luck in the not-getting-in-trouble department lately. I'm bound to get caught for something soon. I am not a lucky person, Isaiah. And I don't break rules."

Her dark silhouette shifted in front of me, and I was pretty certain she had her hands propped on her hips. "Then why'd you come?" I asked.

She huffed, her warm breath hitting me directly in the chest. She didn't answer, though, and a heavy silence filled the small space.

I took a step toward her, finally able to make out her body as my eyes began to adjust in the room, and I wrapped my hand around the back of her head gently. I didn't know what I was doing or why I couldn't seem to take my hand away, but when the soft waves of her hair fell gracefully over my skin, I whispered down into her space. "Is your head okay?" My fingers continued to move around tenderly, feeling for a bump that I was certain was there.

The entire Bain situation didn't make sense to me, and when we'd questioned him further, he seemed to talk himself into circles, laughing casually every so often. Shiner came in during the tail end of the conversation, after shutting down the party as I demanded when Gemma was ripped out of my arms, and he was ready to throw down with Bain.

Shiner couldn't really understand why we wouldn't just throw fists for him fucking up Claiming Night by breaking the rules, but in order for him to understand, I'd have to tell him who my father really was, why I was at St. Mary's in the first place, and yeah, that really wasn't on my to-do list. Brantley had calmed him down in the end, and eventually, Shiner let it go. But he wasn't wrong. Bain absolutely needed to be knocked down a few notches. Body-snatching the new girl out of someone else's arms definitely crossed over quite a few claiming rules, and he fucking knew it. The question was, why did he do it?

"My head is fine," Gemma's voice cracked. My fingers were still woven in her hair as I rubbed the back of her head, relishing being so close to her.

Shit, what the fuck was I doing?

Not only was my body humming with something new and exciting with her so close, but my dick was beginning to twitch. There was just something about a good girl being shoved into a dark closet with me that turned me on.

Just as Gemma let out a wistful sigh, something echoed out in the hall, and she screamed. I flung my hand over her mouth and pulled her into my chest, shushing her. "Fuck," I muttered under my breath.

My uncle's words echoed throughout my head: *Stop getting*

caught. There are no more second chances. And this was exactly why I needed her to get on board with the tutoring thing. If that were already established, being out of our rooms after curfew wouldn't be that big of a deal right now, and I wouldn't have had to shove her into a fucking closet to talk.

If this were a week prior and I was in a closet with someone, mere seconds from getting caught, I'd probably make my chosen girl moan loudly just for the fun of it, but that was before my father had threatened Jack and I was put on probation with the SMC. Now, I was on thin fucking ice, and I wasn't stupid enough to jump on it.

Her head shook back and forth along my chest as my hand fell from her mouth. She whispered quietly, "Sorry. This is why I don't like breaking the rules. I'm not a thrill seeker. I can't get into trouble."

I stayed silent for the next few minutes, listening for movement. Gemma was still a warm cocoon of all things *her* pressed against me until my arms began to relax. Then, she slowly took a step away, taking her warmth with her, and I watched as she reached up and ran her hands down her face. *I wished I could see her expression.* Not that I'd be able to read her. She was guarded better than the fucking El Chapo.

I cleared my throat lightly. "So, what is it that you need from me so that you'll agree to tutoring?" I asked, cutting straight to the point. I wasn't sure how much longer I could stand in a dark, stuffy closet with her standing so fucking close to me.

"And lie..." she half-whispered. "Isn't that what you said the favor was? To tutor you and lie for you?"

I chuckled. "Yes, and I'm not at all surprised that you didn't forget that little piece."

She shifted, just barely, but I noticed. It was surreal how hyper-aware I was of her slightest movements. "Who will I be lying to?" she asked, as if she were still contemplating her decision.

"The SMC."

She was quick to reply. "The committee?"

"You know about the SMC?"

"Yes. Sloane and Mercedes were talking about how the SMC hates you. They said that they hate you the most out of everyone..."

Her voice trailed at the end as if she felt bad for what she was saying. I snickered, unable to help myself. "Yes, and I'm just absolutely wounded that they hate me." My lips split as I held back a laugh. "I'm trying to get in their good graces. That's why I need a tutor. I gotta get my grades up."

She paused for a few seconds. "I don't think you're telling me the truth. You're the type of guy who couldn't care less if someone didn't like him or the choices he made."

"Not true," I hummed, thoroughly enjoying the conversation with her. "I care if you don't like me."

She paused. The closet grew quiet. My lips were pressed together as I tried reminding myself that Gemma and I were about to strike a deal and that I needed to take it seriously. But instead, I was toying with her.

"I'm just messing with you," I said in a low voice, trying to remember the whole point of this conversation. "I mean, it would be nice if we could be friends." *Why did that word sound so fucking bothersome?* "But we don't have to be anything more than tutor and student, if you want to get technical. You tutor me, and the nights when I have to dip out early, you lie and say I was with you the whole time. That's all."

Time had passed. I wasn't sure how much, but it had to have been a while because I was becoming very observant of the smallest movements from her. I could hear her soft breathing. I could feel her body heat, smell the scent of her shampoo.

"Why?" she finally asked, her voice no louder than her quiet breaths. "Why do I need to lie? Why do I need to cover for you? Where will you be going?"

"Sometimes I need to leave the school at night, and since I'm on probation, I'm kind of out of second chances for redemption." That was all she was going to get from me. I couldn't dive any further into why I leave on occasion. I just couldn't.

She shifted on her feet and crossed her arms over her chest. I wished it wasn't so dark in the closet so I could see how her legs looked in that oversized shirt again. Did she even have any shorts underneath? Or just her panties? *Fuck. Pay attention.*

"You're on probation because..." She hesitated, and my head tilted, waiting for her to finish. "Because of you and... and...the teacher having..."

"Sex?" I hardly concealed my amusement. "You can say the word, Good Girl. It's not dirty unless you make it that way." I paused. "And we didn't have sex."

The air whooshed as she quickly stepped forward, placing her hands on her hips. "I know I can say the word!" she whisper-snapped.

I smashed my lips together to hide my laughter, but her arms dropped, and her hair fell forward like a shield. "I'm sorry," she started. "I don't know why you make me so...angry. There's just something about you that—"

"Gets you all fired up?" I smiled. "I noticed...and I like it."

Her head moved a fraction. "You like when I'm rude to you?"

My lips curved. "I kind of like that I have an effect on you."

"No one said you had an effect on me."

I laughed, knowing very well that I *did* have an effect on her.

Gemma took a step away from me, as if she could hear my thoughts. Then, she straightened her shoulders again. "So...you need me to tutor you to help you get your grades up and lie for you on the nights that you have to leave the school to do..."

Fuck. I held my breath, hoping to God she didn't ask what I did when I left the school. I wouldn't tell her. I'd have to lie, and for some reason, lying to a girl like her just felt wrong.

She sighed. "Whatever. That doesn't matter. So, I need to tutor you and lie sometimes...if anyone asks?"

It sounded like she was beginning to accept my proposition, and I felt instant relief at her words. "Yep." I pushed myself back a little farther and propped my leg up behind me onto the linen-lined shelves. "So, you're in, then?"

Her whisper cut through the air like a knife. "No one said I was in."

I suppressed a frustrated growl. *Goddamn. Was she toying with me now?* "But you're considering it. I saw the way you paused earlier when I said I'd give you anything you wanted."

Another heavy bout of silence filled the sultry closet that was no longer smelling like linens but more so Gemma. Something soft and girly. I liked it so much I wished I could taste it. I bet she tasted sweet.

"My uncle cannot find out." Her words were laced with venom but dripping in fear. "He wouldn't be happy if he knew I was tutoring you."

"You mean Judge Stallard?"

I *felt* the uptick in her stress level. The change in the tiny room was nearly suffocating with her tension. "You...you know my uncle? By name?" She stumbled over her words, and part of me wanted to reach out to steady her.

"I don't personally know him," I answered swiftly. "But

after going through the trouble of removing the blog post from Mary's Murmurs, I wanted to know just who your uncle was and why you were afraid of him."

"I'm not afraid of him." Gemma shot forward, as if her getting closer to me was going to convince me of the bald-faced lie coming out of her mouth. She was afraid. No amount of shoulder straightening, chin lifting, or confident stance was going to fool me. Her small frame nearly quaked with fear at the sound of his name coming from my lips.

Giving in, I sighed. "Whatever you say." And then I took a step toward her. "Then let's talk about payment because the sooner we do this, the better."

A slight nod in the dark was all I got.

CHAPTER TWENTY-TWO

GEMMA

"You want what?" he asked as he stood over me in the dark closet.

A slight dip in my stomach filled with disappointment at the leeriness in his voice. If he wasn't able to pull through, I'd be devastated. *I needed this.* "I want fifty thousand dollars and a fake ID."

I watched as his arms came up behind his neck for a slight moment. "The money I can do, no problem. But a fake ID is going to take some time." Then, he paused as hope consumed me. "Why do you need a fake ID, Good Girl?"

"And that's another thing..." I prefaced my next request with as much confidence as I could muster up. Being shoved in a tiny closet with him—*again*—was making me feel all sorts of bold. "No questions."

I could hear the grinding of his teeth before he reluctantly agreed. "Fine. Same goes for you, then. No questions."

My brows furrowed. It was a fair trade-off, but I already

had questions nibbling away at my tongue, which annoyed me to no end. Why did I care?

"Who said I cared enough to ask questions?" *I totally did.* "You can do whatever you want as long as you can get me what I need."

He let out a light chuckle, and for some reason, I liked the sound of it. "I can get you the money and a fake ID, but you need to stay quiet about me leaving early or not showing up at all. No one can know I'm sneaking out of St. Mary's. Not even your friends."

"You mean Mercedes and Sloane?" I thought for a moment. *Were they actually my friends?* Yes. I guessed they were.

"Yes. Mercedes' parents are on the SMC."

I nodded, even though he couldn't see me. After thinking for a moment, I snuck a glance at his dark figure. "Okay, so..." My voice was shaky, and I was so frustrated by it. He probably thought I was a nervous wreck twenty-four-seven. "You need me to tutor you and cover for you, and I need money and a fake ID."

"Do we have a deal?" he asked in a voice so low I felt my stomach dip.

"Yes," I rushed out, feeling as if I'd just taken a leap off a cliff. Isaiah took a step toward me as I was finishing my thoughts. "But no one can know what I've asked of you. No one." If Richard knew I was asking for money and a fake ID, he'd know I was planning on running again. I mean, he already knew I wanted to run—I'd already tried—but I also knew he thought that my last punishment broke me. It nearly did. But even with broken pieces, I'd still run. And this time, I was going to be smarter. I would succeed no matter how good I was at playing the dutiful good girl he thought he had a future with. I wasn't his little doll to do with what he wanted, no matter how I portrayed myself to him. That was all part of the game.

Survive, Gemma. Just survive.

Isaiah's hand gently grasped onto my wrist, pulling me out of my thoughts. I flinched the second he touched the bumpy skin before remembering that we were in the dark, and he couldn't see the marks. "Shh." The word floated out of his mouth and tickled my skin like a feather. He pulled me closer to him and slowly turned me around, putting my back to his front, before pointing at the light seeping underneath the door.

Panic wrecked me in waves, havoc causing several stress-inducing scenarios to play out in my head. It was like I was watching a series of movie trailers, but I was the guest star being thrown back into a pit of hell.

"Someone is out there, so be very, *very* quiet, Good Girl." Isaiah's whisper did nothing to alleviate my stress. In fact, it might have made it worse.

I nodded with the pounding of my heart drumming in my ears. Isaiah gently pulled me back farther into the closet and behind a standing shelf of what I saw to be more linens. Laundry detergent and his body wash filled my senses, calming me for a fraction, before the door swung open, and a golden stream of light filtered through the tiny area.

Isaiah's hand instantly covered my mouth, and his other arm snaked around my waist, pinning me to his front side. His chest was sturdy along my back, his breathing calm and not at all frantic with fear like mine. I was damn-near hyperventilating, and my vision was growing fuzzy. *Shit. Shit. Shit.*

Isaiah shifted behind me silently, and his arm around my waist loosened. I was so full of fear and stress that we were going to be caught I almost grabbed onto his forearm, but then something switched.

My chest was still heaving, but instead of being consumed

by dreadful nerves, I was focusing on something else happening. Isaiah's hand was wrapped over my mouth with his breath tickling the side of my neck, but his other hand, the one previously wrapped around my torso, slipped up past my long t-shirt and landed on my bare stomach.

I sucked in a quick breath, wondering what he was doing, when my skin broke out in millions of tiny goosebumps. He traced small, soft circles lazily over my flat belly, and I leaned back into his embrace. Something tugged in my core, and a needy spark jolted between my legs at the constant feel of his skin along mine. *Okay...whoa.*

My eyes jolted open when his lips touched the side of my neck. For a few moments, I just stood there, frozen, mesmerized by his warm mouth on my body, but as soon as he let up, he whispered ever so quietly in my ear, "Calm your pulse, Good Girl. They're just restocking the linens."

And as soon as he said those words, the door slammed shut, and the light was out.

Another moment passed, and when the coast was clear, Isaiah took a hefty step away from me, taking a little slice of my dignity with him. What was that? How...how did he manage to keep me from spiraling? When fear came in huge waves like that, it usually took me under. That was the thing with fear, though. Right? If you let it simmer for too long, you could get lost in it. Fear wasn't a bad thing. In fact, it made you aware and kept you sharp, but if you let too much of it in, well...that was when it took you down. *Did he touch me on purpose? Did he just...distract me? And did I like it?*

A harsh swallow came from beside me before he mumbled under his breath, "Things are going to get awfully interesting between us."

My brows furrowed, but then he said, "We better get back soon before housekeeping comes back with more linens. Mrs. Dunes should be done with her watch by now, anyway."

My voice was breathy. "Okay, yeah. Good idea."

I shuddered at my awkwardness, but I was so flustered by what had just happened that I couldn't delve in that too much.

We were silent as we walked side by side down the hall. I put enough distance between the two of us that there was no way he hadn't noticed, but the space didn't allow the tension in the air to dissipate even in the slightest. We were both a little on edge. I wasn't really sure why he was, but as soon as we popped back out into the quiet hallway, I noticed the tense way he held himself. Wide shoulders tight, fists clenched, corded jaw muscles moving back and forth.

My hand hit the iron knob of my door, but before I could turn it, he cleared his throat quietly. "We start Monday. I'll let my uncle know you've agreed to tutor me."

I nodded briefly, unable to look at him. "Will I be lying to him too? If he asks me about our tutoring sessions?"

"No."

So, his uncle knows. Interesting.

Isaiah took a step toward me, wafting his clean-scented body wash into my personal space again. "The SMC might not even question you. You're more of a cover for me. They usually catch me in the act of sneaking out or back into the school. If they see me in the hallway, I'll just say I was tutoring with you. I highly doubt they will even ask you anything."

I kept my eyes trained to the red carpet on the floor beneath our feet. "And if they catch you in a lie? Or me? Then what?"

"You won't get into trouble. Trust me."

My head finally snapped up as I locked onto his eyes. It was too dark in the hall to see the light-blue color surrounded by dark lashes, but I didn't need to see them to know they were full of conviction. "I don't trust anyone, Isaiah."

His tongue darted out to lick his lips, and that familiar pull from earlier made itself known in my lower belly. "Well, you're gonna need to trust me." A slight tug on one of my long pieces of hair was as good as him saying goodnight as he turned around swiftly and strode down to the opposite end of the hall and made a turn into the darkness.

CHAPTER TWENTY-THREE

ISAIAH

"YOU'RE FAILING 90% of your classes." I brought my eyes up to the laptop screen, seeing that the face on the other side was Mercedes' father.

The SMC consisted of ten members. Five teachers, my uncle—the headmaster—three parents, and one of the school's biggest benefactors. We all sat at a long, rectangular table in the library before the sun even made daybreak. They were all on one side, sitting across from me, each holding an angry, disapproving glint within their expression that was clear even on the parents' faces through the computer screen.

Even my uncle appeared disappointed.

He was still pissed about the Bain ordeal on Saturday night. He'd somehow figured out what had happened with Gemma. He knew we threw parties occasionally, but he'd never caught us in the act or even knew where we held them. For all he knew, we crammed into one dorm room. But regardless, I think he trusted me and the Rebels to handle things if they ever got out of hand—which was precisely why Saturday was cut short. I may have been a rebellious menace most of the time, but I wasn't okay with what Bain had done.

My uncle leaned forward onto the shiny table and angled the laptop that had the three parents on videos, "Isaiah is aware of his grades. We have come up with a solution."

"You have?" That came from Mercedes' father again. He didn't like me. He'd never met me, but I'd seen enough of his face over the last year for disciplinary reasons. "Please do tell, Tate. I would love to know how you are covering for your nephew again."

A strike of annoyance cut through me. Maybe even a little guilt, too.

"He isn't covering for me. It was my idea. My uncle threatened to kick me out of St. Mary's himself, actually." I leaned back onto my hard-backed chair, briefly smelling the dust that lined the bookshelves behind me, and raised my chin. "I found a tutor, and she has agreed to help me with my school work in the evenings after lacrosse until I get my grades up."

Mrs. Dunes' head slanted, her plump rosy cheeks lifting in amusement. "You found a tutor? Who, may I ask?"

I knew what they were thinking. I could read it all over their faces. They weren't taking me seriously and likely thought I'd seduced someone into tutoring me. Again, it drove a stake of annoyance through me, but also, I couldn't really blame them. "Gemma Richardson."

Silence raced through the group of teachers. They shared quick looks with one another, which were hardly noticeable to the naked eye.

"Who is Gemma Richardson?" one of the parents asked through their muffled microphone. I was pretty certain it was

Abby Clinton's mother by the similarity in features, but I couldn't be certain.

"She's our new student. Very smart and driven." My uncle's voice held a hint of authority, one that he didn't often use.

Another parent snickered. "What is this? A joke? I'm sure the school's bad boy has already had her under the bleachers."

I laughed. "As if I've ever taken a girl under the bleachers." There were far better places to fuck someone than under the bleachers. I may have been an arrogant asshole, but I did have some dignity. I wasn't a goddamn animal.

My uncle shot me a death stare, his green eyes widening and his mouth set in a deep scowl.

I rolled my eyes and wiped off my smile. "Honestly..." I leaned forward, eyeing the parent who had said such a comment. "The new girl isn't really my type. Plus, she's one of the only girls at this school who isn't trying to get me to fu—" I stopped myself before the word came out. "...date them," I was quick to add. "Your daughters don't count. They stay clear away from me, and I stay clear away from them."

That wasn't true, but I was trying to get into their good graces, after all, so I felt the need to add that in.

"Faculty?" Mercedes' father asked, drawing all of our attention to him. "Can you back up what Isaiah is saying? Mercedes has told me a little about their new student. It is on par with what the headmaster has said. She also said that Gemma was very quiet and, overall, a nice girl. I would like to hear your comments, though."

I glanced down to the benefactor, to see what his opinion on the matter was, but he was out cold. Mouth open and everything. I suppressed a laugh.

Each of the teachers shared looks again and nodded amongst one another. Mrs. Fitz was the first to speak.

"Gemma is a wonderful addition to our school. She is

sweet and smart, from what I gather, and an amazing artist. I don't see her becoming swayed by Mr. Underwood at all. She is too focused on her studies—on art, to be exact."

Mrs. Dunes spoke next. "She is very mature. Well beyond her years. Attentive in class."

Mercedes' father garnered our attention again, his brows lowered. "Okay, so she has agreed to tutor you. But why?"

I sighed. "It's simple, really. She's just...nice." I was totally fucking lying out of my ass. I mean, I was certain Gemma was nice. She seemed to have a caring, nurturing side about her, but that wasn't at all how the conversation went down when I'd asked her to tutor me in the first place. Granted, I had asked her to lie for me and to cover my ass too, but that was beside the point.

"You mean to tell me...you asked her to take time away from her own studies and free time, and she just...agreed. Just like that?"

"Yes," I deadpanned. "They'll tell you." I nodded my head to the teachers. "Gemma is nice. There's no other way to say it. I told her I needed help getting my grades up and asked for her help, and she said okay. As simple as that."

Mr. Cunningham nodded. "She is a sweet girl. She helped me pick up the books I'd dropped the other day when every other student laughed—your children included. And then, she called me sir afterwards, as if I had done her the favor."

The other teachers were all commenting on how nice and sweet Gemma was when the benefactor let out a loud snore. I laughed under my breath, and then it seemed the conversation began to shift.

"Okay, fine. That's settled, then. We will give you a month to get your grades up."

Thank fuck.

"Hold on now," Mercedes' father interrupted Abby's mother who was very much ready to get out of the meeting.

"What about your behavior? That is more of a concern of mine than your grades. Mercedes tells me all that goes on in the school, and you are always the star of the story."

I highly doubted Mercedes told him much of anything. Or maybe she told him about the things that didn't involve her. Mercedes wasn't necessarily a rule-breaker, but she wasn't a saint either.

Sighing internally, I put on a fake face and acted apologetic for the first time in my entire life. "Listen, I know I've been nothing but a nuisance to you and the rest of the SMC since attending St. Mary's, and I understand I have burned most of my bridges with you all." I glanced down to the table and then back up to the faces staring at me. "But—"

"But he understands that this is his last chance at redemption. Most of his time will be accounted for. School during the day, lacrosse afterwards, tutoring in the evenings. Isaiah and I had a long talk, and he is aware that this is the last straw, and he didn't like the alternative."

My uncle was right. I didn't like the alternative, but neither one of us could come out and say what that alternative was to the SMC. None of them knew what the Covens was or who my father truly was—at least I hoped not.

There was a long pause on the computer as the SMC took in what my uncle was saying. Most of their eyes swung toward me, and for once, I didn't wear a mask. I didn't try to hide my desperation or cover it up with a smug grin. I showed them that I was serious, because truthfully, I was.

Ms. Glenburg said I didn't have a choice in anything except my behavior, but she was wrong. I didn't even have that choice. My father's threat was as clear as the water in the Maldives. I either did my job or Jack would suffer the repercussions. That wasn't much of a choice, was it?

"One month for an improvement in grades," my uncle stated, pulling the computer to face him. "And no more excuses for behavior. No more fighting. No more sneaking out of the school or into the girls' hallway. No more ditching class."

Someone from the computer said, "And no more seducing teachers."

The benefactor had woken up at some point, and the old, gray-haired man snorted in amusement, which truly didn't help matters.

"Yes, and no more seducing teachers." My uncle caught my eye over the computer and gave me a look.

I threw my hands up with mock innocence. "No more seducing teachers. Got it." My eyes briefly caught Mrs. Dunes, and her round cheeks were a bit redder than before. I bit the inside of my cheek to hold in a laugh so I didn't blow my last chance with the SMC.

"We will have another meeting in one month, Isaiah. Prove to us that we didn't just make a mistake by not expelling you due to your uncle's convincing—*again*."

"Yes, sir," I replied coolly, standing up and pushing my chair out from the table. "If we are done here"—I began adjusting my tie—"I need to get to breakfast if I want to be on time for class—something Mrs. Dunes will probably appreciate."

"Yes, yes." My uncle waved his hand out. "Go."

And with that, I turned around and walked out of the library, feeling the smallest amount of relief settle in.

———

LEANING BACK onto my stool during art class, I continued to gaze at Gemma. We'd missed each other this morning during breakfast, so I wasn't able to let her know that everything was a go for tutoring this evening. She, Sloane, and Mercedes had skipped out for some reason, and I couldn't help but think that reason was me. After all, Gemma would barely even look at me from across the room now.

That really didn't sit well with me. How the hell was she going to spend the evenings *tutoring* me if she couldn't even look at me from across the room? She needed to loosen up some. She was always so...serious. Cautious, too.

"Better fix that hard-on before the bell rings," Brantley laughed from beside me.

I snapped my attention down to my pants before rolling my eyes, knowing damn well I just fucking fell for his stupid joke. His chest shook as he busted up with laughter, and Cade joined in with him.

"Fuck off and quit thinking about my dick," I snapped, bringing my attention back to Gemma. She was sitting on her stool, looking like a poised schoolgirl with her spine straight and shoulders pulled back. Her hair was in one long braid that I imagined wrapping around my fist as I fucked her. *Fuck. Wait. That took an abrupt turn.*

I shifted on the stool again, taking my eyes off the soft skin of her legs peeking out from below her plaid skirt. I was already imagining myself kissing her breathless, which I absolutely could not do. It would be a huge mistake. I'd end up fucking her one way or another, because there was no way you could kiss a girl like that without wanting more, and then things would get messy between us. She was definitely the type of girl to let her feelings get involved, and that just couldn't happen—not with someone like me, at least. Plus, I couldn't have my cover-slash-tutor hating me and backing out on our deal now, could I? I was much smarter than that. Mixing business with pleasure was never a good idea. *But damn, I hadn't screwed around with anyone since Ms. Glenburg, and I didn't even get to finish.*

Cade began pulling on his backpack, even though the bell hadn't rung yet, while Brantley slipped his backwards baseball hat onto the top of his head, knowing very well Mrs. Fitz would scold him to take it off until he was out of her class. "Have we seen Bain anywhere today? How's he lookin'?"

My gaze snapped to Cade as my blood pulsed. "What do you mean, 'how's he looking?'"

Cade's eyes widened as he shot a panicked look to Brantley. "Apparently, you haven't seen the latest blog post."

That stupid fucking blog.

Clenching my jaw, I placed my feet from the stool back onto the ground, glancing to Gemma once before looking sternly into Cade's *oh-shit* expression. "Explain."

Cade looked about as uncomfortable as Mrs. Dunes today when the SMC had brought up me seducing Ms. Glenburg. Brantley rubbed his forehead roughly with his free hand. The bell rang, and I slapped my hand down onto the table. "Get on with it!"

"Shiner didn't listen to you. You know how pissed he was that the party got shut down..." *That could only mean one thing.*

"And you're just now telling me this?" My voice shook with unshed anger, and it killed me to keep it low. Gemma was seconds from rushing out the door, still keeping her attention away from me, which I found to be irritating, but thankfully, at the last second, Mrs. Fitz placed a hand on her arm and began talking to her with a glitter of awe in her eye.

I shot up out of my seat and gripped my backpack forcefully. I glared at Cade and Brantley before turning back to get my eyes on Gemma. "Tell Shiner he is on my fucking shitlist. I specifically told him to drop it." I was silently cursing myself for not taking a closer look at Bain this morning, too.

Cade mumbled under his breath as I began walking past. "Maybe it's time we clued him in, bro. He wouldn't have done it if he knew..."

I cut him another glare, and he threw his hands up innocently. "It was just a suggestion." Then, he nodded to the door where Gemma was standing. "Just FYI, the article said a Rebel—unnamed, of course—attacked Bain, fighting on Gemma's behalf because of what he'd pulled with her on Saturday. Probably why she's avoiding you."

Great. "I want that shit taken down *now*."

"We'll get it taken care of," Brantley urged. "We thought you already knew and had talked with Shiner."

I grimaced. "Well, I didn't, and now things are about to get messy."

CHAPTER TWENTY-FOUR

GEMMA

WATCHFUL EYES FOLLOWED my every move. They trailed me as I walked down the hallway, as I washed my hands in the girls' restroom, even as I sat in the back of World History, listening to a lecture on the Seven Seas. Everyone was mumbling under their breath and whispering about the blog post that I was featured on—*again*—so by the time I rounded the corner to art, I was ready to crumble.

My stomach was already filled with nerves, and the thought of being in class with Isaiah, who I hadn't seen since our linen-closet meeting Saturday evening, truly made me want to vomit all over the place. *Did he attack Bain? Was it all a rumor?* I wasn't sure, and neither was Sloane or Mercedes. The three of us huddled over Sloane's phone this morning while eating granola bars for breakfast as we read the blog post, mortification swallowing me up whole, not even bothering to spit out my bones afterwards.

On shaky legs, I gripped my sketchbook tightly to my

chest, relying on the fact that I was about to be in my favorite class of all to get me through the rest of the day. I purposely left my crappy cell phone in my room, already too keyed up over everything to be bothered with the fact that I still had Richard's threats echoing in the back of my mind.

I shuddered at the thought of *Uncle Richard* flashing across the screen with an incoming call but then froze when a hand reached out from a hidden corner at the end of the hall. I was pulled through as a light shriek clamored out of my mouth. My first thought was that it was Isaiah, because it'd been twice now that he'd shoved me into a small space to *talk,* but when my eyes adjusted to the dark crook blanketed in cobwebs, I froze.

Bain. It was the first time I'd been up close and personal with him—well...besides Saturday night.

"What are you doing?" I asked, keeping my voice steady, even though my heart currently had wings and was flying right out of my chest. "Coming to claim me against my will again?" I mentally smacked myself for not keeping my mouth shut. *What was going on with me?*

Bain's left eye was pretty swollen, and if the lighting were better, I was certain I would be able to make out the ashy-colored bruises. His dark eyes were stern, and for a second, I swore I saw his pupils dilate. "I have a little message for you, Good Girl."

I snarled, my lip rising with disgust. Then, I paused for a millisecond, realizing that the last few times Isaiah had called me Good Girl, I didn't recoil like normal. *Weird.*

My tongue stayed tied as I pulled my arm free from his touch. I eyed the light from the hallway from behind his wide stance. If I just slipped past him quickly and kept my back to the other side of the wall, I'd make it out and into the open area. But running wasn't a specialty of mine, and without having a solid plan of escape, I needed to stay put. I knew that from experience.

"A message for whom?" My voice didn't shake with my question, and pride filled me.

But just because I didn't seem afraid on the outside, didn't mean I wasn't on the inside. Bain gave me the creeps. He had given me the creeps on Saturday, especially when we were in a pitch-black room, and he gave me the creeps now. There was something cold in his touch. Something that felt too familiar to me. "Your little boyfriend, that's who," he snarled, squinting his other, uninjured eye at me. "Tell him that I know who he is..." He huffed out a laugh, and I pulled back even farther from his space, annoyed that his breath was touching me. He pushed his unbuttoned white cuffs up to his elbows before grinning at me wickedly, pausing for dramatic effect. His square jaw dropped as he reached a finger out and stroked the side of my face, despite me pulling away. "And it won't be long before I know who you are too. I recognize you. I just don't know where from yet."

I felt the blood drain from my face as he trailed his nail over my cheek, like he was summoning the blood to leave my body by the request of his finger. Then, he spun around and left me standing in the dark, spider-infested corner alone as the late bell rang throughout the hall.

I hurriedly rushed into art, and I'd been a frazzled mess since.

Mrs. Fitzpatrick was still talking with me about the painting I'd done early yesterday morning before breakfast as all my peers were still asleep in their beds when I felt the looming danger from behind. I knew Isaiah was staring at me; I could feel his eyes the entire class. The skin on the back of my neck was prickly, and Bain's words played on repeat as each second passed.

I recognize you. Did that mean Bain knew Richard? Did he know me? Better yet, did he know what went on behind closed doors? Richard was very private when it came to me, except for when he'd drag me to his elite dinner parties that consisted of other shady businessmen and politicians. I didn't realize it at the time, but the way they'd talk to me and run their hot gazes over my body told me all I needed to know now: Richard's closest allies were not good people. Not at all.

I wouldn't have been surprised if they knew the details of *my uncle's* plans for when I turned eighteen. He didn't think I knew, but I did.

"Gemma." Isaiah's hand wrapped around my small bicep just as I began walking out of the art room like I had a fire trailing me. "Wait up."

Blinking through thick moisture, which infuriated me to no freaking end that my thoughts had caused such a thing, I glanced up to his face.

The blue color of his eyes caught my attention first, and for a single, fleeting moment, I felt at peace. Calm. But then everything came tumbling back into view, and my lips turned downward.

"We need to talk," I rushed out, feeling the words waiting to explode out of my mouth.

"Come on," he said in a low voice as some students passed by but not without looking at us with their greedily receptive eyes. Drama: it was what made high schoolers thrive.

I shifted my attention to Cade and Brantley as they tipped their heads to us and walked away with furrowed brows and phones in their tight grasps. They definitely looked like they were up to something.

"They're taking the blog post down. I didn't know about it until right now. I know you feel uncertain that it won't get back to your uncle, which it won't, but I'll get it taken care of." Isaiah pulled me into the classroom beside the art room that must not have been used in quite some time, because it smelled of dust and had white sheets draped over every last piece of furniture. He shut the door behind me quickly, pulled me away from the dirty glass window, and let go of my hand.

He stood back and watched me with a careful eye, and I did the same to him. A small, barely noticeable flutter of butterflies swarmed my stomach, and it seemed all my thoughts disappeared. He wore his maroon school blazer today, which fit his wide shoulders perfectly. His tie was still a little loose around his neck, his tanned skin peeking out from the top of his unbuttoned white shirt. His coal-colored hair fell over to the side in a deliciously messy way, and before I knew it, my mouth was gaping, and heat was blasting to my cheeks.

Words died on my tongue as I went to say something, because not only was I checking Isaiah out, but I think he was doing the same to me. His eyes were locked and loaded on my bare thighs as I squeezed them together, and I swore there was a strong magnetic pull that was almost forcing me over to him. *Wait...why did we need to talk again?*

"Um," I finally managed to breathe out. The short word seemed to bring us both back to reality as his head snapped up, and his icy eyes left my legs.

"Fuck. Right." Isaiah shook his head and leaned back onto the sheet-covered desk.

I stayed exactly where I was to begin with, too afraid to get any closer. "Did you attack Bain? Did you do that to his face?"

His jaw was tense. "No." Then, he shrugged. "That's not to say I didn't want to, though. But I'm on probation with the SMC, remember? I can't afford to get in trouble."

I sighed in relief but shifted nervously in my new shoes that had magically appeared on my bed yesterday morning when Sloane and I got back from breakfast. She laughed and rolled her eyes playfully, mumbling something under her breath about the headmaster. "Bain talked to me before class," I said, pulling my blazer sleeves down over my wrists.

Isaiah's eyes hardened before he shrugged off his jacket and crossed his arms. "He talked? Or did he do something else?" The hardness in his gaze made me gulp.

Just how dangerous was Bain? And how dangerous was Isaiah? My inner voice whispered the answer to that question before I answered him. "He said to tell you he knows who you are."

Isaiah's chest heaved, and I watched as veins popped out over his hands. "Was that it?"

My gaze shot down to my new shoes. They shined with the little bit of light coming through the window as rain slashed at the glass. "No."

"Good Girl..." Isaiah was closer now, and I quickly brought my head up to see where he was. His strides were slow and casual as he approached me, stirring up the dust in his wake. "I know you don't trust me, but if it has to do with Bain, I need you to tell me."

My tongue swiped over my lips as my heart thumped against the walls of my chest. A really big part of me wanted to trust him, but I had a really hard time trusting myself to do so. My judgment was skewed. After all, I'd trusted Richard for seventeen years before I'd learned that all he was, was a devious man hiding behind the gavel in his hand.

But in the end, my heart won against my mind. "He said he recognized me...and that he'd soon know where from."

The only reaction I got from Isaiah was a slight twitch in his eye.

I wrapped my hands around my torso as a sort of

strength-inducing embrace. "If he knows me, then he likely knows my uncle, and—"

"He's just fucking with you to get to me," he interrupted me.

"I don't know." My mind was spiraling as I thought over Bain's words. It was the way he looked at me that had me thinking otherwise. *What if he did know me?* Could he have seen me at one of the gatherings Richard made me attend in the past? I didn't look many people in the eye at those frivolous, high-society parties because I knew I'd be punished later. "I don't trust him."

Isaiah's lips moved, showing off a grin. "I thought you didn't trust anyone." His slight smile grew wider, and I stared at his perfect white teeth. "We haven't even established a friendship yet, and you already trust me?"

I pulled back. "No one said that I trusted you." I paused, crossing my arms over my chest. "And no one said we would become friends."

He shrugged. "But you wanna trust me."

My brow furrowed as my arms flexed across my body. "I do not." And it didn't matter if I was lying. I wouldn't trust him. I wouldn't.

His smile caught my eye, and I swore the breath left my body like a soul ascending to heaven. "And you want to be friends with me." He reached over with his long arm and flicked my braid off my shoulder. "And that's a start, Good Girl."

A flicker of warmth basically caught me on fire at the mere sight of his dimpled cheek. *I couldn't be friends with him.*

Isaiah erased the open space between us until we were a foot away from one another. I tipped my head back to look at him and saw that his light expression had morphed into something darker. "Are you rethinking things now? With Bain making threats?"

I clenched my teeth together to suppress anything that wanted to run out of my mouth. It was hard to keep my thoughts straight with Isaiah this close. Something danced over my skin as if he was touching me. But he wasn't. It was scary how exhilarated I got with him near. Almost scarier than Bain knowing who I was.

"No. But if he found out what I was really up to, what you were getting for me, and he told my uncle..." I trailed off, my brain almost screaming at me to shut the hell up. "Just never mind. I don't want him running back to my uncle and giving reports on me. That's all."

Isaiah pushed his hands into his pockets, and as I peered up at him, all I could see was the side-eye he was giving me. "Your uncle must be a force to reckon with if Bain can inflict that much fear into you at the mere thought of him making the connection." He glanced away, watching raindrops trail down the window. His sharp jaw was the only thing I could focus on. "If you want out, you need to tell me now so I can come up with a better plan to get my ass off probation."

"Out of what? Tutoring?"

His icy eyes found mine again. "Yes."

Panic pushed me toward him, my shaky hands grasping into his forearm. "No!" The word was a jolt of desperation flinging through the empty room. "I need what you promised me." I needed it so badly I could almost taste the freedom on my lips.

His arm flexed under my touch, and I immediately dropped my gaze to his mouth.

"Good. Because the SMC already agreed to allow you to tutor me. We start tonight." Our eyes locked, and something passed between us. A bond? An understanding? I wasn't sure what it was, but something seemed to click into place for me.

"I'll meet you in the library at seven, then." The panicked

tone of my voice had vanished with relief, and Isaiah's grim frown had morphed to his normal, sly grin.

"Make it eight. I have a lacrosse game tonight."

I nodded. "Okay. I'll see you at eight." I began to turn away before his hand reached out and snagged me back.

"You should come to the game."

My brow furrowed as his hand stayed on my arm. "Your lacrosse game? Why?"

His eyes darted away, and his sly grin was nowhere to be found. His dark brows were slanted over his eyes as he stared at the window again. There was an unfathomable pull in my chest that made me want to reach out and place my hand on his, letting him know that whatever he was conflicted about was fine—which confused me altogether. Why did I even care if he was conflicted about something? Where was this coming from? Boiling anger began to surface at my irrational notion to make someone like him feel better. Isaiah and I weren't friends, and last I checked, he had thrown me into a closet on the first day of school as *payback*. I didn't know a single thing about Isaiah, and my need to put his feelings over mine was going to need to make a swift turn right out of this room.

But then... My mouth opened, and the words that came out surprised us both. "I'll come to your game." *What?!*

He snapped his attention back to me, and he sighed out a breath. "Good." And just like that, he walked over to the door and held it open for me. I began walking out with my lips sealed because I was so appalled by my behavior.

Right before I stepped back into the hall, Isaiah leaned down and brushed his lips over my ear. Goosebumps broke out along every inch of my skin, and unlike before, when Bain and I were in close contact and I'd had fear slithering through my veins, Isaiah caused nothing but an exciting thrill of butterflies to flutter across my belly. That was, until he said, "Do me a favor. Stay away from Bain."

His hand left my arm, and his breath no longer tickled my ear. I swallowed roughly and nodded curtly before he left to walk down the hallway with his unknowingly pretentious stride.

CHAPTER TWENTY-FIVE

ISAIAH

I STALKED into the locker room, whipped the maroon tie off my neck, and threw it to the floor. Cade flicked his eyes over to me as he was pulling on his white lacrosse jersey. Just as soon as it was over his head, I barked out a demand. "I need everyone on the field but you, Shiner, and Brantley."

"Bro," Cade started. "The game's in thirty…" His sentence trailed off because the look I shot him caused him to close his mouth quickly. "Everyone out. Now!" he shouted, waving his hand in the air. The rest of our team paused, some with their jerseys on, some shirtless and mid-laugh. It didn't take them long to see that something was going on with us, and they knew better than to ask. Locker doors were slammed, lacrosse gear was snagged, and soon enough, they were all filing out of the locker room, and it was the four of us surrounded by metal lockers, empty showers, and the echo of my racing heart.

As soon as the last person piled out—Mason, that slow fuck—I shot a venomous look at Shiner before giving no indication that I was about to take my fist and plummet it into his pretty-boy face. I watched for a split second as his expression went from confused to *oh fuck* before my closed hand landed on his cheekbone with a loud thud.

"What the fuck, Isaiah!" Brantley stepped in between us the second I pulled back, and his brows clearly showed his anger. "What are you doing?"

My hands immediately went to my hips, creeping underneath my jersey. I ignored the pain in my hand from punching one of my best friends, but that was what happened when you deliberately disobeyed an order that I gave.

Granted, Cade was right earlier. Shiner was in the dark, and it was biting me in the ass, but I wanted to set this conversation off on the right foot, friend or not. I needed him to understand that there were bigger things at play here. Because what he didn't know was that innocent lives quite literally dangled in the crossfire when it came to me and Bain and this school. A little punch to Bain's face from Shiner was all in fun childish games to him, but to me? It wasn't. It wasn't a game at all.

"I looked you right in the face, and I told you to drop the Bain thing." My voice was calm as I leveled Shiner with a glare. His hard cheekbone was red and swelling, but it didn't deter from his narrowed eyes and clenched jaw.

"And I didn't listen," he bit out. "I don't think that fucking deserves a punch to my face, does it? This isn't the fucking mafia, Isaiah."

My voice echoed against the metal of our lockers. "If it were the mafia, I would have chopped your fucking hand off." Something my father would have no issue doing.

Brantley was still standing in between us as a buffer, but he didn't need to any longer. I wasn't going to do anything else. My intention was to get Shiner's attention, and I needed him to shut his bantering mouth for more than three fucking seconds so I could get out what needed to be said. "There are things you don't know, Shiner," I started, dropping the firmness in my voice for a split second. "Things you are better off not knowing."

He huffed, shaking his head with what seemed to be disbelief. "Yeah, no shit, Isaiah." His chin tipped to Brantley and Cade. "You three have something going on, a secret bromance or some shit. I'm not fucking blind. I've seen the way you three have silent conversations."

Cade scoffed. "It is not a bromance, you fuck."

I ignored Cade and crossed my arms over my jersey. "Well, congratu-fucking-lations, Shiner. Welcome to our fucked-up lives." I flashed a look to the clock hanging over the door, seeing we had fifteen minutes to get on the field before Coach came in here and chewed our asses for skipping out on warm-up. "Sit the fuck down and listen, because I'm only going to tell you this once."

Shiner glanced at Cade and Brantley as they slowly came over and stood behind me, backing me with my decision to tell Shiner that we weren't just a bunch of bad-boy shitheads trying to get through their senior year at a stuffy boarding school by pulling pranks and skipping classes. In fact, we were trying to drag this year out as long as possible because what awaited us afterwards was nothing but stripped-away freedom with danger on the horizon at all times.

"My father didn't send me to St. Mary's just to get rid of me, like most students here," I started before shooting Cade and Brantley a quick look over my shoulder. "I'm here on behalf of my father. We all are." It almost killed me to say his name out loud. Not the name he used to front his many contributions to orphanages and group homes. Not the name that was signed off on checks for donations and charitable goods. No, I meant the name that others had been known to shiver at the sound of. The name that I'd someday take as my own, even though it cut me in half to think about.

"Your father?" Shiner asked, cocking a brow.

"Yeah. My father...*The Huntsman*."

———

After Shiner finally picked his jaw up off the locker room floor and wrapped his head around what I'd told him, the four of us rushed out onto the field with our crosses in hand.

The air was dense with fog, the sun completely forgotten by the coverage of thick clouds. Our cleats stuck in the wet ground as we kicked back clumps of mud to the opposing team every so often. We were already in the second quarter, and just when I was getting in the zone and giving myself that break from the everyday nagging of my father's voice in the back of my head and his threats laced with sin over sending Jack to the Covens, Shiner came up behind me with his crosse in hand, eyes set on a defender on the other side of the field. "I can't fucking believe that your father is *The Huntsman.* Like..." He gasped for a breath of air, ready to jog past me. "*The* fucking Huntsman. Shit, Isaiah." I caught the look of anguish on the tight creases of his eyes, and I shook my head.

"It's whatever," I muttered. "Get your head in the fucking game. We're down by two." I brushed off the pity he was unintentionally giving me and acted like my father being the Huntsman wasn't a big deal, but it was. God, it fucking was. My father was feared by most. When people said his name out loud, they shuddered. Death followed everywhere he went. He'd killed people. He'd killed people right in front of me. I'd felt someone else's blood splatter across my face as he held the cold gun in his hand. The same cold gun that he'd later sell in his multi-million-dollar illicit trade business.

People knew of the name, even if they were in no way affiliated. The elusive Huntsman was the center of the news most
of the time, while my father kicked back and laughed. I was
certain the authorities had given up trying to put a face to the
name.

I blinked away the thoughts as Shiner nodded sharply
before sprinting past and slyly cross-checking someone twice
his size, causing their body to thud to the ground. Mud splattered over the side of Shiner's white jersey, and I grinned.
That's what I'm talking about. Fuck the future. Seeing Shiner
cross-checking a prestigious pretty boy from Washington
High was what I needed to bring me back to the present.
Washington High's biggest concern was fucking up a game of
lacrosse in front of their girl. Mine? Mine was keeping my
brother out of hell and keeping myself in check long enough
to find a way out for both of us. But right now, I'd focus on
this. The game.

After Shiner cross-checked the opposing player, causing
the ball to fly through the air, Brantley snagged it and began
working his way down the other side of the field, where I
trailed him, body-checking a few guys of my own who stood
too close. My gaze wandered momentarily, locking onto
Gemma for the fifth time in the last half hour. She sat in the
same spot on the metal bleachers, with Sloane on her right
and Mercedes on her left. She stuck out like a sore thumb
because she was in a completely enthralling trance of the
game. Every other girl around her was chatting away or
laughing with their heads thrown back, but not Gemma.

Her eyes followed me. Even with the disadvantage of
distance, I could feel her lingering gaze. My lungs burned
with the thought, which was something new for me, but it
was a flame I'd gladly keep lighting.

Because for once, I felt something more than dreadful
numbness and the smallest amount of trepidation. Gemma,

the Good Girl, gave me a spark of hope that I could keep Jack safe, and that wasn't something I'd felt in a long fucking time. I think the last time I'd let myself feel anything other than blinding anger was before Jacobi up and left me high and dry with our fucked-up father.

A smack to my back brought reality down on my shoulders again. The sounds were back, the wetness of the light rain pelting the skin of my arms. "You're talking about me getting my head in the game?" Shiner tapped me against the back with his crosse, and if we weren't in the middle of a game, I'd take mine and slice it behind his knees to make him fall. "You get *your* head in the game. Don't worry. Gemma isn't going anywhere, and Bain is tucked away nicely on the top bleacher with his eyes on Callie. He isn't even paying attention to Gemma."

I sighed, wishing I believed what Shiner said, but I knew, deep down, that Bain had his eyes not only on Gemma, but on me too.

Fucker.

CHAPTER TWENTY-SIX

GEMMA

LACROSSE WAS PROBABLY the most entertaining thing I had ever watched. The way each player chased after a ball with unyielding determination on their faces, kicking up mud and grass with their heavy strides down from one end of the field to the other. The strength in their arms as they used their stick for protection and what seemed to be a sort of weapon, beckoning the ball to a certain side of the field.

It was fascinating. The whole experience. From sitting on the bleachers in my favorite black jeans and borrowed St. Mary's lacrosse shirt from Sloane, with two of my new friends on each side of me, to the sounds of other people clapping and cheering in the background and whistles being blown that the game was coming to an end. It was all so...*normal*. The smallest seed of happiness planted itself inside of me, and it was hard to fight its sprout as Sloane and Mercedes dragged me toward the chain-link fence separating the field from the bleachers.

"What are we doing?" I asked as their expressions were

set on the field toward the left side. I followed their gazes and watched as a bunch of guys whipped off their helmets and wiped away the sweat dotting their foreheads.

Mercedes sighed wistfully as she rested her chin under her hand. She leaned against the wet fence without looking at me. "Checking out Washington High players."

"Oh," I answered, looking at each and every one.

Sloane snorted out a laugh. "Pretty sure Gemma isn't interested in Washington's players, Mer."

I sucked in my bottom lip, shrugging. "They're okay, I guess." Then my gaze wandered over to St. Mary's side of the field, and I immediately started comparing the two teams.

Aside from both teams wearing jerseys, albeit different colors, and being damp from sweat and the short spurt of rain we'd gotten halfway through the game, they were nothing alike. It seemed our guys were taller, stronger, and broader. Wide shoulders, chins held high. Each and every last one of them—even the few that I didn't recognize—looked determined and resolute. Determined to do what? I wasn't sure, as they'd already won the game.

My heart flipped when I saw Isaiah standing toward the end of their bench, talking with Cade, Brantley, and Shiner. He ran a hand through the sweaty ends of his dark hair, shaking it out slowly. Then, I ceased to exist altogether when he snaked a hand up underneath his jersey, showing off a stomach lined with hard muscles. His head tipped backward as if he were massaging a shoulder muscle or something, and then he slowly twisted his neck, making his well-defined Adam's apple bob up and down.

My throat closed. My legs prickled with heat. He was… He was really, *really* attractive. I felt a slight crack in my chest as I continued to stare. Isaiah was so beautiful that it was scary to look at him. In the few months at Wellington Prep, I'd hardly noticed any of the guys because I was too busy taking in everything else that was so new to me. I was in overdrive. But here? Away from my home and that town? I noticed *everything,* and the tingling in my core did not go undetected.

"Gemma!" Sloane's tone was loud but playful as I snapped my attention to her. I shoved a thick piece of brown hair behind my ear, feeling the heat sear my skin. A gust of cool, moist air wafted around us, but it didn't cool me down in the slightest.

"What?" I asked.

She and Mercedes both laughed but quickly stopped as wet footprints began to approach. We all turned our attention to a group of guys who began to walk up the muddy field, still in their hunter-green uniforms with smirks gracing their faces.

"Hey." One of them nodded to us as he seemed to lead the pack. "Did you babes enjoy the game?"

"We sure did," someone said from behind us. "You boys played a good game."

The leader of the pack, with his damp blond hair, looked over our heads, and his eyes lit up.

"Thank you, *beautiful.*" The interest in his voice was totally obvious, even to me. Sloane, Mercedes, and I all turned around to see who he was talking to.

"*Figures,*" Sloane mumbled, turning her back to Callie. "She's already fucked everyone at this school, so she has to start scouting newcomers."

I whispered back to Sloane, even though she had no issues verbally insulting Callie. "What's the point if they just up and leave after the game, though?"

Mercedes answered for her. "She's just looking for a quickie, probably. Callie has no self-worth. She uses guys and sex to make herself feel better." She paused before pulling herself out of my space. "I'm not judging...that's just what it seems like, anyway."

And before we knew it, the fair-skinned, blue-eyed Washington High player was jumping over the fence, and he and Callie were sneaking off behind the bleachers. The unwanted feeling of curiosity tickled the back of my brain as I turned back around. I wondered for a fleeting moment what it would be like to be her. To be a girl who wasn't afraid of what it felt like to be with a guy like that. I wasn't even sure what it felt like to kiss someone...well, not really. Not a guy I wanted to kiss, at least. Not a guy who made my skin tingle with something enticing...like Isaiah.

Sloane and Mercedes moved down to the group of guys that were still standing near the fence, and I followed reluctantly, curious to see them in action. My mouth was glued shut as Sloane took a piece of her hair and wrapped it around her finger, laughing at something one of the players whispered in her ear, and Mercedes blushed as a shy smile found her lips. I felt the jealous snake curl around my neck. I wanted to do what they were doing: garnering the attention of guys, flirting, all of it. I wanted that. I wanted to be comfortable enough with myself to do what they were doing. Would I? *Could I?*

My heart raced as I watched as one of the boys who had dark-brown hair and a scruffy jaw began to approach me. I started to panic, looking at Sloane and Mercedes for assistance, but then someone cleared their throat. *Isaiah.* I bristled at the excitement that came with seeing him so close. *When did he walk up here?*

"What are you doing, Graves?" He cocked an eyebrow as the sentence effortlessly flew from his mouth but dropped it when he moved his attention over to me. "Hey, Gemma. Did you enjoy the game?"

Mercedes and Sloane stopped talking mid-flirt and stared

a hole in the side of my head. Cade looked at Isaiah suspiciously, and I was suddenly aware of everyone's eyes on me. Again.

Isaiah's eyes were soft and inviting, but I saw the same look in them as I had earlier when he'd asked me to come to the game. It was as if he was conflicted about something. The blue color was warm, like an ocean in the middle of summer, but cold too. Glacial. The words were unspoken, but they were lingering in the air with our silent exchange. *Trust me.* My feet shuffled along the sidewalk, and I inched closer to the fence separating us. He was still sporting his jersey, although the white fabric was dotted with specks of grass stains and mud. His lip tipped upward, his eyes exuding the smallest flicker of approval before he glanced at the Washington High player. Then, he quickly whipped his attention to the bleachers behind my shoulder and narrowed his eyes.

Confusion filled me as something passed over Isaiah's face. Cade moved closer, and his gaze followed Isaiah's, eyes hardening at the last second. Just as I began to turn around to see what they were glaring at, Isaiah rested his elbows on the metal rod between us. His mouth twitched as he leaned his head beside mine, pushing my thick hair, which was now wavy from the moisture in the air, off my shoulder. I squeaked out a surprised sound as my heart thudded to the ground when Isaiah's hand crept into the back pocket of my black skinnies. My entire body hummed as a jolt ran down my leg and back up to my heart. *I liked it when he touched me.*

Isaiah smelled like the outdoors, and for some reason, that was comforting to me. "I know you're confused, but just trust me." He paused, and I swore I could feel his lips brush my skin. "Please."

Uncertainty swept me off my feet, and just as my thoughts unmuddled, Isaiah whispered along my ear again. "I'm going to kiss your cheek." My breath caught, and before I could react, he quickly moved his mouth from my ear, and he placed his soft lips on my high cheekbone in front of everyone.

My teeth clamped down over my plump bottom lip before I could allow myself to smile. It wasn't a fake smile either. It was a real, ripped-from-the-deepest-parts-of-my-soul smile, which was exactly why irritation soon followed.

I wanted to ask what the hell he was doing and why he thought it was okay to touch me like I was his, but God, there was a secret part of me that liked it. I liked it too much, and liking it took away the fear of Richard somehow finding out that someone had touched me, *kissed* me—even if it was just my cheek.

But before I had the chance to clear my head and say anything, Isaiah quickly pulled back, whipping his hand out of my pocket and putting a safe distance between us. "Meet me outside of the locker room in twenty. We can walk to the library together for tutoring. Sound good?"

I blinked a few times, trying to steady the earth below my feet. "Ye—yeah," I said, finally letting my lip plop from my teeth. *What the hell was happening?* I knew I was naive and completely uncertain in this situation, but everything about this encounter was confusing to me, and I was pretty sure it had nothing to do with my lack of social skills.

Isaiah shot me a nod just as someone began to walk behind me. Glancing over my shoulder, I saw that it was Mrs. Dunes. A tender smile graced her face as we locked onto one another, and I saw that she was wearing the same St. Mary's lacrosse shirt that I had on but with dangling silver earrings that looked to be lacrosse sticks hanging from her ears. Her gaze briefly moved to Isaiah, and she gave him the strangest look before sighing and walking down to the side door of the school.

Then, someone shouted in the distance, taking all of our

attention. The guys from the opposing school seemed to recognize the catcall, and they began saying their goodbyes to Sloane and Mercedes and a few other girls from Callie's tight-knit group of friends—not before giving up their numbers—and they turned to leave. The one that had spoken to me before Isaiah swooped in and sliced the moment in half raised his angled chin to Isaiah and chuckled. A moment passed between them, and then they all turned around and stalked down the wet grass to their teams.

My brows crowded with even more confusion as Sloane tipped her head over the fence to look down at me. "Did Isaiah just say you were tutoring him?"

I opened my mouth but was interrupted by MaryAnn, one of Callie's closest friends, as she popped in between us. "Um. Did Isaiah Underwood just kiss your cheek? In front of everyone? Does that mean it's true what the blog said? Are you two...a thing?"

"What? No! I'm...I'm just tutoring him. That's all." That didn't explain the whole kissing-my-cheek thing, but I'd figure that out later when we were alone and I could ask what he was thinking.

Blonde ringlets bounced off MaryAnn's shoulders as they fell with relief when she flipped around to lean her back on the fence. "That makes sense. You're definitely not his type."

A sting of annoyance pelted me just as Sloane scoffed. "What makes you think that Gemma isn't good enough to be his type, MaryAnn?"

She shook her head. "No, no. That's not wha—"

Mercedes leaned forward into my line of sight. "Yeah. Gemma is gorgeous, and she's—"

"Late." Headmaster Ellison appeared out of thin air, and I jumped in my spot, whipping around so hard I hit my back on the chainlink fence. The second our gazes collided, I was smacked face first with reality.

It was Monday.

It was Monday at 7 o'clock.

I was supposed to call home every Monday at the same exact time, and Richard did not like to be kept waiting. Shit. How could I have forgotten?

Dread slithered into my veins, making all the happiness I'd felt in the last few minutes turn to stone.

"Let's go." The headmaster's voice wasn't disciplinary or even angry, but it did hold a certain amount of caution to it, which told me that he'd likely already been graced with a phone call, demanding to know why I was late.

Richard was probably waiting by his phone, and the second it hit 7:01, he dialed up the headmaster and threatened something.

Probably his life.

CHAPTER TWENTY-SEVEN

ISAIAH

STEAM from the locker room surrounded me so thickly that I hoped I could duck away from the guys and snag my clothes before meeting up with Gemma outside in order to evade more questions. After dropping the "my father is the psycho they call the Huntsman" bomb on Shiner earlier, there wasn't time left for me to fill them all in about the deal I'd made with Gemma. So, when I treated her like she was something more than what any girl here had ever been before, Cade nearly combusted with questions. It was the sight of Grayson from Washington High that threw me off course. There was a flame of jealousy that flickered through me when I saw the way he was looking at her, but a wave of protectiveness quickly dimmed that light, and I took control of the situation. Grayson had no business talking to anyone at this school, and he knew it. His father was just as much a rival as Bain's was to my family, which meant that he and I were a conflict of interest. What was mine was mine, and he was not coming near anyone or anything at St. Mary's. I already had

Bain to deal with. I didn't need Grayson fucking poking around too.

I fended Cade off long enough to shower the sweat and mud off my body before he was able to corner me again, and I reluctantly filled him in. Curfew was soon, and I didn't have time to be chatting like little old bats at the hair salon on a brisk Saturday morning regarding my little show with Gemma.

Just as I slipped my black Vans on and stood up to leave the locker room, thankful that there were no more questions being thrown at me, Brantley's palm came down on my shoulder, and he squeezed my sore trap muscle. I yelled out in agony and slapped my hand over his, peeling his firm fingers off my muscle. I bent it backward until he screamed out and flung forward, cradling his hand that I nearly snapped in half. "Don't fucking touch me, Brantley. I'm sore as fuck."

He stood up, red-faced, but then quickly recovered. "You gonna fill us in on you and Gemma? What was that about?"

I shot a look at Cade, and he threw his hands up in protest. "I didn't say anything." How the fuck did word get around so quickly in this school? Brantley hadn't even been nearby when I'd bent down and kissed her cheek. *That soft, rosy fucking cheek.*

Shiner chimed in after Cade. "And *now* you're staking a claim on the new girl in front of everyone? First your father, and now this?" He scoffed out a sarcastic laugh, whipping off his towel with no regard to anyone else in the locker room.

I cringed, looking away. "Shiner, no one wants to see your dick."

He made a sarcastic noise. "Psh, they don't call me One-Liner-Shiner for nothin', Isaiah. Everyone wants to see my dick."

We all paused, and then Brantley shook his head. "I thought about it, and nope, still don't want to see your dick."

Cade laughed under his breath as he pulled a shirt over his head. We all ignored Shiner as he got dressed.

"Seriously, though. What's going on? Why did you make a scene like that? Are you trying to get Bain to fuck with her again? Because we all know the only reason he pulled that shit on Saturday was because he had watched you with her earlier that day."

A few of our other players walked into the room, also drying off from the shower. I eyed them briefly before shooting the rest of the Rebels a look.

"She's tutoring me because I'm on probation with the SMC." I shrugged. "As for the other stuff..." I trailed off, nodding to our midfielders briefly. I told them, "Good game," in a gruff voice and then began leaving the locker room. "I'll explain later."

I wasn't going to lie; I'd had the sudden urge to jump the fence and wrap my arm around Gemma's waist over the fact that Bain and Grayson were looking at her like they wanted a piece, but the main reason I'd put on the show was because they needed to know their place. At least, that was what I was telling myself.

Things with Grayson would slowly die off. He wasn't near Gemma enough to be much of a threat. But Bain? There were only two choices: I could try to keep my distance and hope he'd move past his little game of using her to get to me, or I could get even closer to her and make sure he stayed the fuck away.

I knew Bain. I knew his games. I knew most of his moves before he did. I saw the way he was looking at her and then at me. There was the smallest glint of excitement in his eye. Leverage. He wanted to hold something over me. It was becoming clearer and clearer that Bain didn't dislike me because of who I was in this school but more so because of who I was outside of it.

He'd told Gemma that he knew who I was, and I was beginning to believe it. It was possible that he wasn't bluffing.

I couldn't seriously consider Gemma and myself to be more than what we were now, even if my blood ran hot with her near. She couldn't be my girlfriend or anything even remotely close to that. I wasn't staking a claim on her like Shiner had said.

I didn't stake claims on anyone, not only because no one held my attention for long, but because I'd never in a million years give myself the chance to feel something like that for someone.

Having a girlfriend, or even just a relationship with someone that went further than the surface, wasn't in the cards for me. It was a no-go. It would be nothing more than a trap. Could people fall in love? Sure. Would I? No. I wouldn't allow myself the luxury because if I did that, then that would mean there was one more person that could get caught in the web of some very dangerous and illegal shit.

My own mother was a casualty in my father's little game, and even at age nine, when I was still so goddamn naive and impressionable, I knew I wouldn't do that to another woman. I wouldn't fall in love and bring an innocent being into a world full of lies and pain—almost always emotional but sometimes physical too. A rough swallow worked itself down my throat as broken and fragmented memories came rushing in at the sound of my mother's bones snapping. That same cry for help I'd shouted years ago almost worked its way to my lips, but I clenched my fists until my knuckles went white, and I exhaled a deep breath.

I'd make damn sure that Gemma and I went our separate ways after I was taken off probation with the SMC, so that way, there wasn't even an inkling of suspicion that she truly meant something to me after it was all said and done.

Because she didn't. She was just a means to an end. A

glimmer of hope that Jack would be fine—for now. *But then, why was I trying to protect her so fiercely?*

After letting the locker room door shut, rather aggressively, behind me, I scanned the hallway for Gemma but came up empty-handed. This addition to the school was built only a few years ago when my uncle had taken over the position of headmaster. Sports weren't always a necessity at St. Mary's, but my uncle fought with the SMC, arguing that sports were a great way to get aggression out that most of the students here were burdened with. That was why our lacrosse season was all year long. We had practice games during the off season with the schools that were close by to *'give the students something to look forward to.'*

After stalking down the hall, I pushed open the swinging door and was met with fat, thunderous clouds and a light mist of rain. I jogged along the sidewalk, past the bleachers, and made my way to the back entrance of the school, pulling open the brass-handled door, and slipping inside with even wetter hair. I flung the damp ends back and forth and let my eyes adjust to the dark entrance until I spotted Sloane and Mercedes a few yards away.

But no Gemma?

Mercedes was pulling her wild, spiral curls up into a bun when I approached them, and her cheeks instantly ripened with color. "Where's Gemma?" I asked, ignoring the way she blushed.

Sloane looked suspicious, her eyes crinkling on the sides. "She had to go with the headmaster." She darted her attention away as if she were hiding her concern. "She looked..."

"Scared," Mercedes answered quickly, actually looking me in the eye for once.

A weird notch of concern hollowed out in my chest, and I casually pushed it aside. A cool breeze wafted around our ankles as the door opened, allowing Cade and Brantley to walk through. I had no idea where Shiner was, but I could only guess it had to do with a set of warm lips.

My attention went directly to Sloane as she lightly growled under her breath at the sight of Cade. Then, she turned toward me. "I'm going to go look for Gemma."

"No."

She raised her dark eyebrows, her short hair swaying over her shoulders with the jerky movement of her head. "Excuse me?"

Tipping my head to the rusty clock above the archway, I said, "It's almost 7:30, which is curfew on game nights. By the time you grab something from the dining hall, it'll be time for you to go back to your rooms. I'll go find her. We have tutoring soon."

Sloane flicked an arched eyebrow up. "Right...*tutoring.*"

Mercedes' voice was small when she spoke up beside Sloane. "But won't you two get in trouble if you're out past curfew, like the rest of us?"

"The SMC has allowed for Gemma and me to tutor after lacrosse in the evenings—after curfew."

Sloane rolled her eyes. "Has Isaiah ever cared if he got in trouble, Mer?"

Cade spoke up as soon as I turned my back and began striding down the hall. "Want me to grab you girls something from the dining hall? He's right. It's almost curfew."

Sloane didn't miss a beat. "No one wants anything from you Cade. We all know how you don't show up when needed anyway."

I wanted to laugh at the insult because neither I nor the rest of the Rebels usually got turned down for anything. Cade being insulted by someone would have been fucking hilarious had there not been a reason why Sloane hated Cade so much. I knew, without even looking back, that Cade's face was an

ashen gray. He knew why Sloane hated him too, and it fucked
with his head.

Rounding the corner of the long entryway, I found myself
alone. Everyone would soon be tucked away in their rightful
halls: boys on the left, girls on the right. I hadn't heard from
my father since Friday, but I yearned to hear from Jack. Just
for confirmation that he was doing okay, more than anything.

I didn't trust my father, and my mother was too far gone
to take her word on much of anything these days.

Pulling my cell phone out of my pocket, I quickly typed a
text to Jack and then slid my phone back into my jeans. My
uncle's office door was shut, so I leaned my head against the
thick wood to have a listen.

A loud, stern voice played on the other side, the end of a
sentence filling the office. *"Were you studying? Or were you doing
something you know I wouldn't approve of?"*

My brow furrowed as I tried to decipher the reasoning for
that question. Then, my frown deepened when Gemma's
tender voice came next instead of my uncle's. "Yes, sir. I was
studying."

The man's voice, who I assumed to be Judge Stallard,
didn't let up. "Are you alone? Where is the headmaster?"

A pause on Gemma's end. "He's in here with me."

"And how often do you go into his office alone, young
lady?" There was an icy-cold bitterness to his tone that had
my shoulders squaring and teeth clenching. It was obvious
that Gemma was fearful of her uncle, no matter how many
times she defied such a notion, and I could see why. He didn't
scare me, but I understood why he scared her, if his tone was
anything to go by. My breath hitched with anger at the
thought of someone scaring her, and I had a primal urge to
barge into the office and rip the phone off my uncle's desk.

Gemma didn't hesitate when she answered her uncle.
"Only to call you."

"I don't know if I believe you," he sneered, and just as I was about to turn the knob to make it known that Gemma was *not* alone with the headmaster like her uncle was insinuating, the door flew open, and my uncle stepped out, red-faced and aggravated beyond belief.

He quickly shut the door, eyeing me briefly, as if he knew I had been standing there, and rested his ear against it just like I was. *Well, shit, I now knew where I got it from.*

My uncle rolled his eyes at me, loosening his tie from around his neck as we both listened to Gemma and her uncle, who was still on speakerphone.

"The headmaster just left the room. I'm alone now. There is nothing going on. I'm following the rules. I'm in my room by curfew each night, and I'm doing everything you've asked of me."

Gemma said her uncle was strict, and she wasn't lying. He sounded like a real son-of-a-bitch, to be honest. I didn't like him.

"Good." His voice was gruff, and there was a clunking on the end of the phone, like ice sliding against a glass cup— likely surrounded by amber liquid. I knew that sound by heart. "And your art? You've stopped sketching, yes? If I hear that you've been sketching up those—"

"I'm not. You asked me to stop, so I did."

Something loud banged on his end of the phone, and my brow furrowed again, trying to piece together what was going on. "Did you just interrupt me?"

"I—I..." Gemma's voice grew leery, and I found myself praying to God that she would dish out that same fiery spirit to him that she did to me. *Who did he think he was, talking to her like that?* I almost laughed at the thought. I knew men like him. I knew men like him so well it made me see red. He sounded just like my father—high on power and hungry for violence.

"I'm sorry," she finally managed to say, and that notch in my chest seemed to hollow out.

"I'm sorry?" he asked. "I'm sorry..." The way the words floated out of the speaker made it seem like he was insinuating something only he and Gemma were aware of. I cleared my head, shaking it slightly against the wood, trying to get a better read on him, when Gemma's fear-laced voice turned cold and empty.

"I'm sorry...*Daddy.*"

My eyes flung to my uncle's, and I jerked back slightly. *Did she just call him...Daddy?*

A very loud and muffled sound of breathing made its way past the wood door, and it sounded an awful lot like a moan. My head was spinning in different directions, all of which resulted in barging inside my uncle's office and snapping the fucking phone in my hand, but I fought to keep myself present and grounded. Calculated behavior was better than impulsive behavior. I'd take this little moment and stash it away for a later date and use it to my benefit if it ever came to that.

"That's right. I am your Daddy," her uncle finally said after more heavy breathing. "And soon enough, you'll be home, back where you belong."

My heart began thumping a little harder at his words, and I didn't know why. What I did know was that I didn't particularly enjoy the thought of her leaving and not coming back.

"I will talk with you next Monday. And this time? Don't be fucking late." There was a strange sense of awareness as the words trailed from his mouth. Like there was a threat to be delivered. Maybe a silent one.

"I won't be late," Gemma answered. "Would you like to speak with Headmaster Ellison before I head up to my room? It's almost past curfew."

"No," her uncle answered sharply. "Go back to your room.

You know I don't like when you break rules. Remember what we say?"

"Good girls don't break rules." Then the line went dead.

Just as my uncle and I pulled back from the door, both of us looking equally as perturbed, the loud bang of the phone slamming into the receiver told us all we needed to know.

Gemma's uncle thought he had her wrapped around his finger, but he didn't. Because Gemma was angry.

CHAPTER TWENTY-EIGHT

GEMMA

MY ENTIRE BODY twitched as I stood above the headmaster's mahogany desk with my hand still on the phone. I slammed it so hard onto its receiver that my arm went numb. His voice was like a million little spiders crawling into my ear and filling my head with unjust lies and bigoted thoughts that only stemmed from years of looming threats and punishments. I hated him. I hated him so much I felt a scream threatening to tear through the empty room. But instead of screaming or taking the globe off the end of the headmaster's desk and throwing it against the wall, I peeled my fingers away and counted backward from ten until my breathing grew less erratic.

My stomach churned as I continued to replay his words: *you'll be home soon, back where you belong.* I couldn't. I couldn't go back there. I wouldn't survive. If this thing with Isaiah didn't work out, I wasn't sure what I would do.

The money I could probably do without. I would make ends meet one way or another. There would be no other choice, but it was the new identity that was my true ticket. I needed a fake ID with a new name. A way to blend in without raising flags to the officials—the officials that Richard had spent years forming relationships with so they could stay nestled in his deep pocket.

Being a judge came with many perks, and having everyone on your side—police chiefs, fire officials, attorneys, judges, you name it—meant that if I were spotted, I'd be tucked away nicely in a police car and taken right back to Richard himself.

I should know. It happened before.

This was no speculation. It was a very real possibility.

I pushed the heels of my palms into my eyes to force away the frustrated tears before the headmaster walked back into his office. It was already awkward enough that he had heard my *uncle* insinuating that something was going on with the two of us while on speakerphone. Crying in front of him would only make things worse.

The look on the headmaster's face flashed across my mind, and he was no less than mortified. But knowing Richard, that was his plan in the first place: embarrass the headmaster and conjure up some power play to show that *he* was in charge here, not the other way around.

A long, drawn-out breath left my chest just as the door swung open again and in walked Headmaster Ellison. My hands lifted from my eyes immediately, and I tried to force out a smile, which only turned to shock when I watched Isaiah walk in after his uncle.

"Isaiah," I blurted, startled that he was now standing in the office too.

His lips curved at the sight of me. "Already ditchin' me for tutoring?"

Shit. I was supposed to meet him outside of the locker room. I darted my eyes around the room, searching for a clock to see what time it was. I was never sure how much time had passed when Richard was involved. Anger and fear seemed to contort my senses, and everything was skewed.

"It's almost curfew," Isaiah said, coming a little closer to me. My heart skipped inside my chest at his nearness, and it surprised me. It surprised me that I could feel something other than that lingering fear and resentment that I was always left with after playing the dutiful niece. "Good thing we have the okay to tutor after curfew, yeah?"

The headmaster was standing behind his desk, opposite of Isaiah and me. He eyed us both cautiously before clearing his throat. The red tie around his neck was looser now than it had been when he grabbed me from outside a little while ago. "If anyone gives you trouble for being in the library after curfew, send them to me." His dark brow rose at Isaiah, like he was silently threatening him, but when he turned toward me, his expression softened. "Same time next week, yes?"

I stared at the headmaster from across his desk for a few moments, eyeing him subtly as the same familiarity that I'd felt on that first day tinged my senses. *Maybe I could trust him.*

I stilled. *No. Don't trust.*

"Yes, sir." I nodded and quickly turned to look at Isaiah because I was ready to get out of his office with Richard's voice lingering in the open air. Everything felt tarnished after he spoke. Once I locked onto Isaiah and got over that dip in my stomach that kept happening when he was near, I hesitated.

Trailing past the sharp curve of his cheek and straight jaw, I moved down his tight black tee and found his hands in fists. His posture told me that something was wrong. It was as if he was angry, which was confusing to me—much like earlier when he had leaned in and kissed my cheek before disappearing back down to the field. The more I was with Isaiah, the more I learned just how complex he was. Or maybe it was just that he threw off my senses. I felt so jumbled near him.

After glancing back at Isaiah's face to decipher what was going on, I saw his laser-like stare locked onto something on the headmaster's desk. But no sooner than I snapped my head down to the messy contents on top, Isaiah grabbed a hold of my hand, stealing my attention away and completely blinding me.

"Let's go, Teach." Isaiah pulled me behind him, his calloused hands—likely from holding that stick in his tight grip during lacrosse—brushed over my soft palm. I let him lead me like a blind fool because his hand in mine muted something that screamed *urgent* in the back of my head.

I glanced back once at the headmaster and watched in a daze as he picked up a file and shoved it in the top drawer of his desk before slumping down in his chair.

He was definitely upset about something, and I had a very strong feeling that it had to do with me. *Great.*

———

As SOON AS Isaiah and I were out of his uncle's office, I felt like I could breathe again. The hallway was a little brighter, and the long, narrowed corridor leading to the dining hall was bathed in a warm glow from the overhead chandeliers. The air was fresher, and soon, my senses were filled with the scent of delicious warm food that made my stomach roll from hunger. *My weekly phone call was done. I survived.*

Isaiah's hand was still in mine, but I didn't pull away or comment on it. I was silent as we walked, too captivated by everything else around me that seemed to mute the dark voice lingering in the background. "Is that why you don't like when I call you Good Girl?"

I paused, my feet stuck to the black-and-white floor

beneath my shoes like cement. My eyelashes fluttered with shock as I tore my hand from his. My head flung up, and all I saw were two icy eyes peering down at me. "Wh—what?" My heart drummed against my chest.

Panic set in when his lips set into a firm line. "Just answer the question."

"Were you listening to my phone call?" Embarrassment flooded my cheeks, and a small amount of horror seeped in. How dare he listen.

There was a small twitch of Isaiah's mouth that I zeroed in on, which sent a new batch of fire to my blood. "Just like you listened to me and my uncle the first day we met?"

My eyes shifted to the floor, suddenly feeling stupid, because he was right. I had eavesdropped on him first, so I guessed I kind of deserved that. But I was still annoyed, and just as I was trying to rationalize why it was okay for me to eavesdrop and not him, he interrupted me.

"I was listening in, yes, but regardless, your uncle wasn't exactly quiet on the other end of the phone. And surprisingly enough, you can hear very well through that thick door." I stayed silent, mulling over what I should say next. I was upset with myself that I didn't even think about the fact that the headmaster could hear the conversation on the other side of the door after he'd very abruptly stepped out. And I had no idea that Isaiah was even out there. I grasped at the conversation that I was trying my hardest to push away, replaying it in my head to figure out what I had said.

"Answer me," Isaiah pleaded. His voice had a sternness to it, and there was a tiny divot in between his brows.

"I thought we said *no questions asked*." I shifted in my shoes, crossing my arms over my chest. A few students staggered out of the dining hall, holding cans of soda, passing us by as slowly as possible. They looked at Isaiah and then to me, and I wasn't sure what we looked like to everyone else, but I assumed it looked as if we were sparring. Isaiah was staring down at me sternly, and I was peering up at him with one eyebrow raised, waiting for his response.

I heard a loud sigh escape him and maybe even the light sound of a growl as he spun around on his heel and stormed through the dining hall doors. Another group of students had quickly shot out of his way as he stalked into the large room with as much authority as Richard had in the courtroom, and then their attention went to me, likely wondering what I'd done to make the top Rebel of the school so angry.

I was wondering the same thing. Shouldn't I have been the angry one in this situation?

And why was there a small part of me that was feeling out of sorts, knowing that Isaiah was angry at the moment? Was he angry at me? Why was I even concerned that he was angry in the first place?

Stepping farther into the nearly empty dining hall, I watched as Isaiah moved like some sort of predator as he casually swiped food from the line, even as the workers were putting it away. He didn't even bother paying as he turned back around with his eyes dead set on me standing in the same position that he left me—arms crossed, one eyebrow raised.

His dark hair fell onto his forehead as he came closer, then he thrust a bag of chips into my hand and stormed past me, knowing I'd follow. Even if I didn't follow him, I'd see him in a few minutes anyway as we both headed to the library for tutoring, and not to mention, I was through being intimidated by people or letting their behavior affect mine. That wasn't the new Gemma. That was the old one that Richard had formed between his slimy fingers.

The halls were empty and dark as we walked down them, side by side, eating our separate bags of chips. The only sounds were the bags crinkling and our very subtle chewing.

My tongue was burning to yell at him or spew something angry, mainly because he had stormed off, acting as if I was the one who had just eavesdropped on his conversation and not the other way around, but as soon as we were in the desolate library and the door slammed shut behind us, something else entirely came out of my mouth, stunning me right there in the entryway.

"Yes." *Wait. What are you doing, Gemma?!*

Isaiah was a few steps ahead of me, his tall stance nothing but a dark shadow in the enormous room with tattered books lining the shelves. His back went still.

I belittled myself silently, irritated that I had answered his question that we both should have forgotten about, but it was like an invisible power had coaxed me into it. There was something heavy weighing on me from the very second he brought it up. Like he pushed away one of my many masks and saw beneath my stony glare that I was certain didn't intimidate him at all.

My voice broke in all the wrong spots before I cleared my throat and tried again. "Yes, that's why I didn't like it when you called me Good Girl. That's why it made me angry."

I saw a tremor rip up Isaiah's spine, and I swore he grew another three inches as I stared at his back. It only took him seconds to recover, but I knew that what I'd said had jolted him. He turned around quickly, the bag of chips still in his hand. "Then I won't call you that anymore."

"No!" I blurted, pushing myself farther into the library with desperation hot on my heels.

It wasn't hard to see his muscles tighten with the moonlight filtering through the far windows. "No?"

I swallowed, keeping a hold on him. Why couldn't I just stop talking? Why was I spilling the dirty truth all over the library floor as if I hadn't spent years hiding from it? "Don't stop calling me that."

The faintest of smiles touched his lips as the bag crinkled in his hand. "Okay..." He dragged the word out before rubbing his thumb over his bottom lip and then licking the salt off. "But why? It's apparent you don't like your uncle."

Understatement of the year. "I don't." I wrapped my hand tighter around my bag of chips, feeling incredibly vulnerable for saying that out loud. If Richard heard that confirmation come out of my mouth, I'd be chained up for weeks until I proved to him that it wasn't true. "But..." I looked away, almost suffocated with the words that wanted to come out.

A throat cleared from behind me, and I jumped so far I bumped into Isaiah. His free hand wrapped around my waist to steady me as I searched the dark library for whoever had made themselves known.

"What are you two doing in here?" The librarian, who I recognized from the other day, pushed her glasses up so she could see us better. "It's after curfew. The library is closed, hence the lights being off."

The older woman skittered her gaze past me and locked onto Isaiah. "Out after curfew again, Mr. Underwood. I wish I could say I was surprised." The cool disappointment was clear in her tone, and for some reason, that set a fine line of protection through me.

Stepping forward out of Isaiah's grasp, I plastered a soft smile onto my face. "Actually, I'm here to tutor Isaiah. Didn't the headmaster tell you?"

She eyed me cautiously. The whites of her eyes moved quickly as she scanned my face. "He did no such thing."

I peered back at Isaiah. I could tell she didn't believe me; there was a certain hitch to her voice along with a knowing glint in her eye. Knowing what? I wasn't exactly sure. She probably assumed I was one of the willing girls that Isaiah shoved into closets to mess around with. My face heated at the thought—more so because curiosity tickled the back of my brain again.

I slowly turned back around. "Well, the headmaster said that if anyone gave us trouble, to direct them to him. Isaiah is failing his classes, and I was asked by the SMC to tutor him in here after lacrosse to bring his grades up." I smiled sweetly, and it felt like I was falling into my past self whenever I was questioned by Richard when he thought I was lying about something. I could play this part well—so well that it felt like slipping into my own skin. "We can walk down to his office together, if you'd like. I don't mind at all. It'll give Isaiah a chance to gather his study materials anyway."

The woman looked at Isaiah and then back to me. The library keys dangled in her hands as she jostled the books in her arms. I could see the leeriness fade as she bounced her attention back and forth between us again. "That's okay, dear. I can check with him on my way out. Just make sure you two lock up when you're done."

I smiled once more. "Of course."

Before she turned around, she leveled Isaiah with another withering stare that only older ladies seemed to possess. I silently laughed, remembering Auntie giving that look a time or two. "Don't get crumbs in my library, Mr. Underwood. Or else you'll be doing Mr. Clark's job. Got it?"

Without even looking back, I could hear the cunningness in his voice. "Yes, ma'am. I'll lick them up if I need to."

The older woman's face flickered with shock before she let out an exasperated sigh and spun around. Her long dress swayed as she hurried to the door, and then she slammed it shut.

My free hand found my hip as I spun around. "Really?"

Isaiah's cheek lifted as he casually shrugged. "What?"

"You'll *lick them up* if you need to? Who even says that?"

Isaiah's smile grew wider, and my eyes went right to the

THE SAINT MARY'S DUET BOX SET

dimple in his cheek. I felt my own lips tingle with the need to smile but gritted my teeth together so I wouldn't. If there was one thing I'd already learned from Isaiah, it was that he didn't need any more encouragement.

"Her reaction was entertaining. Could you imagine what she'd do if I actually bent down and licked the floor?" He paused, looking thoughtful. "Do you think she'd be mad?"

I sighed. "I think I can see why the SMC is tired of you. And it has nothing to do with your grades."

His hand fell to his chest as if he were gripping his heart. "Ouch. Bring back the nice Gemma who just batted her eyelashes at the meanest old bat in this school and somehow got a smile in return." He chuckled. "I didn't even know Mrs. Groves could smile."

I rolled my eyes as I breezed past him, heading straight to one of the long tables. "It's called having respect." I knew everything there was about that tiny word. Richard made me memorize it, and I was pretty sure I could recite the Merriam-Webster definition in my sleep.

Isaiah's bag crinkled again, and I peered over my shoulder, watching as he tipped his head back and put it up to his mouth to eat the leftover chip crumbs. A wistful thought flew through me as I recalled seeing Tobias do that on the rare occasion that we were given an unhealthy snack as a child. A small bag of chips to us was a once-a-year treat.

Pushing the thought away, I shouted over my shoulder to Isaiah. "Better not get those on the floor."

The now-empty bag had vanished from his face as a devilish smirk appeared. The silvery moonlight hit the side of his chiseled jaw as he flashed me his white teeth. Then, he lifted his finger and popped it into his mouth, sucking it to remove the salt from the tip. My small, teasing smile instantly vanished as something forbiddingly hot fell to the bottom of my stomach. I jerked my head away and pulled out my chair, slinking into it as sweat coated my hairline.

I heard his shuffling feet before he appeared at the other side of the table. The chair creaked as he sat down, his empty bag of chips lying beside my half-full one. "You think I don't have respect for authority?" he asked as he leaned back onto the chair, tipping it back far enough that I just *had* to look at his face. "I told her I would clean up after myself."

A breath left my lips. "You made her uncomfortable."

He smirked. "I can't control others' reactions."

My brow creased as Isaiah pushed my bag of chips to me, nodding to them. I gingerly stuck my hand in the bag and pulled a chip out, not bothering to put it up to my lips. "But you can control your actions," I reiterated, pushing the chip back into the bag. "Actually, now that we're on the subject of *actions*...care to tell me what was up with earlier? Why did you kiss my cheek in front of everyone?"

And why did I like it?

Isaiah stilled, his chair balancing on only two legs. I glanced up at the small lamp that sat on the table between us, and my fingers itched to turn it on so I could see his face better. "I'll answer yours, if you answer mine."

I knew very well what he was referring to, and the last thing I wanted to do was talk about the phone call he'd overheard, so I deflected the topic as if it were my main reason on this earth. "I think we better get to studying. What do you need help with first?"

Isaiah's arms came down and rested on the glossy wood that separated us. I kept my eyes trained to the dancing shadows along his forearms that seemed to move every other second as his fingers drummed over the hard surface. "I thought you trusted me, Good Girl."

My eyes moved to his, and it drove me mad that I couldn't see the blue color. I suddenly found myself reaching over to the light in between us and clicking it on. "I already told you I don't trust anyone."

His head tilted, his thick black eyelashes falling once, then twice. "You trusted me earlier when I leaned in and kissed your cheek. Didn't you?"

I did. The muscles along my mouth tightened, and I was left speechless.

"So, tell me, Gemma. Why do you still want me to call you Good Girl? Now, after knowing that your uncle calls you that—which I am one hundred fucking percent certain isn't in an endearing way—I'm going to need an explanation."

The beating of my heart grew in speed as I stared up into his cool eyes mixed with uncertainty and something else I couldn't quite decipher. Every single part of me was screaming to abort this conversation and put him and his pleading face in his place, but there was a teeny-tiny stab in my chest that had me pausing. I didn't owe him an explanation. I knew that. So why was I considering it?

Could I trust him? Would it be so bad to trust someone here? The hollow part of me grew deeper as my heart continued to climb in speed. The thumping was hard—I could feel the beat in every corner of my body—until I just let go. I blurted out my answer, and it was like thunder cracking in the background. "Because every time you call me that, it cancels out each time he has called me that." I licked my dry lips as I shrugged. "Maybe if you say it enough, it'll erase them all."

Silence filled the library, and it was just as heavy as my vulnerability. There was no change in Isaiah's facial expression, no hitch of breath, nothing. Isaiah only stared at me. He stared at me so long that I began to grow uneasy, and I wanted to slash at the air to make the words disappear. But that was the thing with words. Once they were out, they were out. There were no take-backs.

Anger began to seep in at Isaiah's lack of response. I wasn't even sure what I wanted him to say, but I needed him to say *something*. Anything. Another few seconds passed, and I finally straightened my spine. "Was that enough trust for you?" I snapped, leveling my chin and glancing away. Shame settled in my bones, weighing me down to the chair as if I were permanently one with it now.

"I kissed your cheek earlier to protect you." His words cut through my anger for a second.

"What?" I asked, completely confused.

Isaiah repeated himself. "I kissed your cheek earlier to protect you."

"I heard what you said. I just don't...understand." My brows puckered for a second before I recovered. "Protect me from who?"

Isaiah pushed my chips toward me again. "Eat, Gemma. The dining hall is closed, and I've heard your stomach growl three times now."

I brushed the chips away, too eager to know his answer. "I answered you. Now you have to answer me."

The biggest, megawatt smile appeared on Isaiah's face, and the warm glow of lamplight shone on that stupid dimple again. "Oh, is that how this is gonna go, Good Girl? An answer for an answer?" His brow hitched. "That can lead to some very dangerous places."

I ignored his grin, sitting up taller in my seat, feeling slightly exasperated. "How is placing a kiss on my cheek going to protect me?"

"Why are you so afraid of your uncle?"

I placed my hands down on the table. "Why are you so dead set on not getting expelled?"

He leaned forward, our eyes leveling. "Why are you always scribbling in your journal?"

Anger brewed. "Why did you tell me to stay away from Bain?"

"Have you ever been kissed?"

A soft breath left my mouth as my eyes jolted down to Isaiah's lips. The traitorous pair that they were betrayed me right there on the spot. I thought for a hopeful moment that Isaiah didn't notice, but by the twitch of his upper lip, I knew that I'd been caught. *Isaiah: 1, Gemma: 0.*

"You haven't, have you?" His smile fell, and when I met his eyes, my cheeks flooded with heat. *And shame.* There was a whole lotta shame that came after the initial feeling of embarrassment. His jaw tightened at the edges as his chest filled with air. Once he let his breath out, I did the same. I hadn't even realized I was holding mine until I watched his chest expand. "Bain will try to use you to get to me. I kissed your cheek to show people that you were mine. I was making a point."

Why did his words sting so much? What? Did I want Isaiah to kiss my cheek for any other reason? No. That couldn't even be a possibility. I had enough to worry about. Isaiah was already close enough to becoming a casualty in Richard's games if he caught on to our agreement. If Isaiah and I somehow became more than what we were now, it would only seal his fate. No one was allowed to touch me, and I knew it killed Richard to know that there were people here who could see me—and possibly touch me. Even if they weren't looking at me in the way that he did.

You are mine. I held back a shudder as his voice filtered in, but it was quickly replaced with resentment and anger. I wasn't his. And I wasn't Isaiah's either.

My face felt tight. "I'm not yours." The words were like a slap in the face with how much anger stewed behind my lips. "And you think something as simple as kissing my cheek will keep people away?" I laughed bitterly. "People take what they want, Isaiah."

Isaiah cracked his knuckles before placing them back down onto the table. "It'll take much more than a simple brush of my lips to keep Bain away from you. But at least it's a start." Isaiah leaned back, clearly unphased by my temper-tantrum, and pulled his phone out of his pocket. "People will start talking, Gemma. And soon, there will be a lot of specu-lation about us. More eyes on you means Bain will have even less of a chance to mess with you."

I shifted my gaze away, slightly embarrassed that I had just lost my cool and a little annoyed that he wasn't even looking at me. My eyes squinted as I glanced at the library doors, swearing that I'd seen a shadow pass by, but that was likely my head messing with me because I suddenly felt exposed. "So…" I started as silence encased us. "You kissed my cheek so people would talk? And watch me?" My hands fell to my lap. "I'm not really a big fan of having eyes on me." *This was already off to a bad start.*

"I know." Isaiah finally glanced up at me from his phone. His expression was soft, but his voice held an undeniable amount of sternness to it. "But there are things you don't know, Gemma. There is a lot more riding on me staying at this school than I'd ever care to admit."

Silence pressed on us, as if we were stuck in that tiny linen closet again. "And there's a lot more riding on me getting my hands on a new ID than I'd ever care to admit."

Our eyes clashed together again, and I swore time had stopped. Everything had stopped existing except for the two of us. There was something heated about our conversation, like hot coals seconds from bursting back into flames. I felt the walls caving in, the room growing smaller.

But then, Isaiah's phone buzzed, and the moment was gone. The air conditioner kicked back on, and the papers on

Mrs. Groves' desk fluttered to life. I watched as Isaiah ran his hand through his dark hair, pushing it off his forehead to reveal two slashes of brows.

My chin jerked when he raised his phone in his hand. "Duty calls."

"What?" My voice was all breathy, and I quickly shook my head. "Wait. We're done for tonight? We didn't even study."

His lips curved. "I don't need a tutor, Gem."

Gem. "I thought you were failing your classes?"

Isaiah stood up, hovering over me. "I am. But it's not because I'm incapable of learning. I just don't do the assignments."

My mouth opened as I peered up at his tall stance. "Oh." I began to stand up, feeling somewhat bothered by the fact that Isaiah was pretty much just using me as a cover and that he didn't actually need my help studying. But then again, I was using him too, so I had no right.

Isaiah grabbed the chips off the table, and I stood back and watched as he swiped the crumbs back into the bags. His gaze shot to mine at the last second, and his brow hitched. "Should I lick it to be sure, or..."

My lips begged to curve upward, but I didn't allow myself to smile. I only sighed and shook my head, acting as if I were just as exasperated as Mrs. Groves was earlier, but I wasn't.

As soon as Isaiah flipped the lamp off, he came up behind me and opened the door, allowing me to step into the hallway. His arm brushed mine as he reached over and turned the lock, and even though I was wearing long sleeves, tingles still flew to my skin. My blood was humming as he walked in stride with me. The hallways were empty, the lights dimmed to a minimum. I peeked up once, only to see him staring straight ahead with his face completely free of anything going on inside his head.

Leveling my gaze with the hallway, I took even breaths,

willing my body to behave in the way that it always had before, but the truth was, I'd never been alone with a boy as much as I'd been alone with Isaiah since coming to St. Mary's. It seemed the more we were pushed together, the more silent exchanges we shared, and that only led to my body reacting in ways that scared me. It scared me because I had the strongest urge to step in front of him and beg him to *see* me. To put his eyes on me and learn of everything that lurked inside.

That was the total opposite of who I was. I didn't want anyone to look at me. I didn't want anyone to see what was on the inside, because it was dark there. It was really, really dark. But still, Isaiah Underwood and his hot and sultry looks and random dimpled grins were becoming more and more alluring to me. It was the way that he could somehow coax me into speaking my mind, instead of hiding behind shy smiles and hidden thoughts, that was enticing. In a way, Isaiah *was* seeing me, and that was because I wasn't holding much back when it came to him, and I had no idea why.

Once we'd rounded the girls' hallway, he stopped, stepping in front of me. His dark hair swayed down on his forehead again, and I wanted to push it away just so I could see him better. "I need your phone number."

I stumbled over my words even though I'd just spent the last several seconds practicing leveled breathing. "Wh —what?"

His lips moved slowly. "I want your phone number, Gemma."

"Why?" I asked, still very aware that he was only a few inches in front of me. If I breathed too deeply, I bet our chests would brush.

His brow furrowed, another stray piece of dark hair tumbling down. "Because I'm not done with you, but I have to go do something." He slowly raised his hand and brushed his hair back, showing off his clear skin.

I rocked back on the heels of my shoes, feeling the pressure intensify in my chest. "I can't give you my number."

His head slanted. "What do you mean you can't?"

I blew out a breath, placing my hands into the back pockets of my black jeans. "My uncle will likely pull my phone records. He gave me the phone before I got here, and I haven't touched it." I felt stupid for asking my next question, but I did it anyway. "Can you see who people call? Or text? He can look that up, right?"

Isaiah looked to the tall ceiling above our heads and sighed. "Yes." I heard the grinding of his teeth before he shook his head. "Okay, don't worry. I'll figure something out." His phone vibrated again. He didn't even bother looking at it. "Don't come back out of your room tonight. Okay?"

My brow furrowed as I glanced around the dark hall. "Okay..." I wasn't sure why he said that, but either way, I wouldn't be leaving my room.

Isaiah's brows crinkled for a fleeting second before he recovered. "And if anyone asks, we were tutoring together until ten, okay?"

"Until ten?"

He nodded sternly, his jaw hardened to stone. "I have to go. Go back to your room."

On top of Isaiah's pushy words, I detected a very small amount of pleading, like there was caution lingering there. I was curious, but not curious enough to ask. Instead, I nodded and then began walking past him before his arm caught me around the waist, and he pulled me backward. His breath moved over my ear, and my entire body heated with excitement. "If I'm ever not around and something happens, you can trust Cade, Brantley, and Shiner. Okay? Find them if you need something."

I swallowed past the hot knot in my throat. "Isaiah, I already told you I don't trust anyone."

His chuckle hit me in all the right spots. "You trust me, Good Girl. Even if you want to pretend that you don't." His arm slowly dropped from my waist, and I almost pulled it back over before I realized that would have been completely insane. "I'll see you tomorrow."

He began walking in the opposite direction, leaving me standing there with my skin warm and my heart moving in triple speed.

My blood didn't stop rushing until I got to my room and slammed the door shut behind me, not even remembering that Sloane would be on the other side. But that was what Isaiah did to me. Being around him made me see nothing *but* him. He had some crazy, uncontrollable power over me that shunned everything away except his icy eyes, which sent me into overdrive. It was terrifying.

Sloane gasped as I stepped inside our room, pausing right in the middle of it with her black hair in a messy topknot and huge pink, fuzzy slippers that looked like bunnies below her legs.

"What on earth are on your feet?" I asked, halting as I locked onto the two fuzzy creatures.

"Where have you been?!" She rushed over to me, the bunnies' heads bobbing back and forth. "Isaiah said he was going to look for you, and I know you had tutoring, but I've been worried. The headmaster ripped you away, and I'm not going to lie, you looked spooked." Sloane placed her hands on my shoulders. She looked over my body quickly, her eyes running over my face and clothes. "I do not trust those Rebels for even a second. I don't know what Isaiah is playing at, but are you really tutoring him? He isn't stupid. I've seen his SAT scores. Is there something else going on, because I have never in my life seen him kiss a girl's cheek like that. It was innocent and tender, and those are two adjectives that I would never use to describe Isaiah Underwood. When he has his eyes on someone for claiming, he ravishes their face greedily before the lights even go out." She glanced away, like she was reminiscing about something. "Not that anyone complains. It's just...he doesn't do the whole *sweet* thing."

"Um," I started, glancing at her big, round eyes. "Yeah, we are just tutoring." I knew I couldn't tell Sloane about our secret conversations in the bleakness of night, tucked away in dark closets or dusty classrooms. Especially because those conversations seemed to circle my past and hidden secrets.

Sloane dragged me over to my bed and pushed me to sit. "Then why did he kiss your cheek?" She then ran the four feet to her bed and hopped up on top, scooting all the way to the wall. "This is so unlike him. Usually, he's a *wham-bam-thank-you-ma'am* type of guy. Not the type that would randomly kiss someone's cheek and bat those eyes, tutor or not." She thought for a moment, looking distrusting. "What is he playing at?"

Unlacing my shoes, I asked, "What does that mean? Wham-bam-thank-you-ma'am?"

Sloane placed her hand to her lips, muffling her next sentence. "You are more innocent than I thought." Her hand dropped. "I have so much to teach you."

Just as Sloane was about to continue on with her rambling, there was a faint knock on the door. Both of our heads swung in that direction. Sloane mused, "Expecting someone?"

I shook my head, the teeniest amount of anxiety creeping over my shoulder. Would I ever not be afraid that he was coming for me? "Who would I be expecting?"

Sloane slowly climbed off her bed and walked over to the door. A weird sense of urgency flew through me and seemed to push me off my bed. What if it wasn't Richard, but it was Bain? Isaiah's words echoed through my head, remembering that he was silently begging for me to stay in my room for the rest of my night. He'd said that duty called, which ended our "tutoring session" much quicker than I had anticipated. Did Bain know Isaiah had gone somewhere and he was coming to mess with me?

"Wait," I called out as I followed Sloane. "Let me get it."

Sloane's face dropped, her pink lip jutting out, but she didn't protest. Instead, she stepped out of the way, the fuzzy bunnies flopping on her feet. My heart thudded against my ribcage as I slowly opened the door and peeked down the hall. It was hard to see with the flicking sconces, but a familiar, broad-shouldered lean body was walking down the hallway slowly, as if he didn't have a care in the world.

Isaiah?

Sloane bent down and grabbed something before pulling me back and quietly shutting the door, hardly making the chain on the front rattle at all. A note was crumpled in her hand along with a familiar bag of chips. "I think this is for you." She smiled as she handed the note to me.

With a less-than-stable hand, I opened the piece of paper that had my name written on the top in huge lettering.

Don't think I forgot about you not eating, Good Girl. Eat your chips. I need my tutor well-fed.

A surge of something warm rolled through me, like the sun finally gracing the skies again after weeks of thunderous storms. I fought to keep my heart relaxed and smile at bay, but I failed miserably at both—something Sloane most definitely managed to point out.

CHAPTER TWENTY-NINE

ISAIAH

I EYED Cade's sleeping form on his bed through the darkness of our room, stepped over the PlayStation controller that had fallen from his hand sometime in the night, and headed for the door. I snagged my tie off the back of my chair, whipped it on over my damp hair, and exited my room as quietly as possible.

I'd never cared in the past if I had woken Cade up—or the rest of the hall, for that matter—but it was way before the moon disappeared and gave way to the sun, and also, I didn't want anyone to know what I was up to.

My Vans shuffled along the red-carpeted floor as I pulled out my phone and reread the texts between me and my little brother. He was fine but had mentioned spending a lot of his time with Mary, our lifelong nanny who could take someone down with a frying pan if need be. She was a stocky woman with olive-colored skin and eyes like the sea. Her crazy, curly hair had begun to gray the last time I saw her, and wrinkles now lined her round cheeks, but she was still the same woman who had stepped in after Mom's *accident,* and she'd been there for me and Jack ever since.

I trusted Jack with our nanny, but I didn't trust him with our parents. *Such a healthy, happy family we had.*

Once I stepped onto the landing, I eyed the girls' hallway briefly before Gemma's face had flashed behind my eyes. Not that it was the first time I'd thought of her this morning. I thought of her from the moment my alarm sounded, drifting me out of my sleepy fog. I'd wondered briefly if I had dreamt of her too, because her vivid jade eyes and pouty mouth were the first two things in my head this morning.

Or it could have had something to do with the fact that I was about to go snooping in my uncle's office for that file titled "Gemma Richardson" that he not so subtly shoved into the top drawer of his desk yesterday.

If my uncle were smart, he'd guard that file with his life. Because one way or another, I was getting back into his office, and I was reading all there was to know about Gemma and her secretive life, along with her extremely suspicious uncle. *She called him Daddy.* What the fuck was up with that?

A growl sat deep in my throat as a strangely possessive feeling came over me, causing my shoulders to tense and my jaw to clench. I wasn't sure why I felt so agitated over Gemma and her life that she obviously wanted to keep private. I hardly knew her, although it didn't feel that way when we were alone. I was eager to touch her and be close to her, but I had no right to feel protective. Maybe it was because her uncle reminded me so much of my father. I wanted to destroy all the Carlisle Underwoods in the world— not just my own flesh and blood. That was another reason why I despised Bain so much and the way he looked at her. She was a toy to him. A toy he wanted to break just because I'd touched it first.

Stepping down off the last step, my phone vibrated in my

pocket. I reached in my black pants and read the latest blog post from Mary's Murmurs. After Gemma seemed so put off by the whole blog post and being featured on it, I'd set up alerts for new posts. Her uncle would likely never learn of Mary's Murmurs, but after last week's scandal, I'd made a decision to become informed of all things in this school— even the insignificant gossip that filled the halls.

The top headline was bolded, like always, and my name was the first to be seen.

BAD-BOY REBEL, ISAIAH UNDERWOOD, TO BE SNAGGED BY OUR NEWEST STUDENT, GEMMA RICHARDSON.

RUMOR HAS it that Gemma is tutoring Isaiah in the late evenings, but is that all that's going on? Is Gemma Richardson the beauty to our beast? Beautiful, quiet, shy, and seemingly naive to all the bad in the world. Is she Isaiah's ticket to a clean slate? Can she help him with his grades...and more? Or is he her ticket to life on the wild side? Only time will tell.

I CHUCKLED UNDER MY BREATH, putting my phone back in my pocket. They had one thing right: Gemma was beautiful. Everything about her was beautiful. Her eyes, her skin, the curve of her cheek, the soft flesh of her waist as my arm snagged around her last night. Gemma was the full package, guarded or not. Was she my type? No. But that didn't seem to deter me from thinking about her twenty-four-seven, now did it?

When I reached my uncle's office, I placed my ear to the

door and listened. Oftentimes, my uncle would fall asleep at his desk and wake the next day, looking disheveled and confused until he was able to get his hands on some of the coffee in the dining hall, so I needed to be certain he wasn't trapped behind his desk from the night before.

Silence filled the other side, but the uncertainty was still there as I turned the knob slowly, noting that it was unlocked. I pulled the door open, glancing inside with hesitation.

My uncle *was* in his office. But he wasn't asleep. Instead, he was staring directly at me.

"What are you doing?" he asked, raising a wary eyebrow in my direction. He was standing beside his desk, holding a paper in his hand with a cup of coffee in the other. *Fuck, he's already up and has had his coffee.*

I only paused for a second. "Oh, hello, Uncle." There was a light and airy notch to my tone, completely bypassing the fact that I had just walked into the room, looking suspect as fuck.

His eyebrow didn't lower as he continued to stare at me.

I walked in a little farther, my tie still loose around my neck. A fire was burning in his wood-burning fireplace on the other side of the room, the flames licking with intensity as I shut the door behind me.

"Trying to break into my office?" My uncle's eyebrow finally fell, but the wary expression only worsened.

I shrugged. "No. Just wanted to catch up. How ya been?"

"Isaiah, what do you want?" He took a sip of his coffee before sighing.

I sat down in the seat at the foot of his desk, the one that I was sure Gemma had sat in the night before. "I came to check out that file you stashed away last night."

My uncle's eyes flicked up over the brim of his coffee mug.

The cup hid his mouth, but I heard the words plain as day. "I knew you'd be back."

I leaned back in the leather chair, propping my feet up onto his desk. "You did, did you?"

Placing the mug down, he walked over to the fireplace and put his back to me. His hands were clasped behind him, and a dense silence filled the room. The popping of embers was the only sound to break the quiet every few seconds.

I was the first to speak as I lowered my feet to the ground and walked to stand beside him. "What do you know about her?"

His chest inhaled and stayed like that for so long I turned my head and focused on the fire. Whatever it was that he knew, he was struggling with it. That part was clear. What was also clear was that I was eager to know everything. If it were anyone else, I wouldn't care. I wouldn't have come back here early this morning to see what the file had said. It would have left my head the second my uncle had shoved the file into his desk.

Gemma was quite literally digging herself underneath my skin, and she didn't even know it. I had no reason to want to know more about her, but I did. I desperately did, and I couldn't blame that on wanting to protect her from Bain. This had nothing to do with him at the moment.

Finally, my uncle exhaled, the fire fanning underneath his heavy breath. "I do not trust her uncle. The things he has told me don't match up to her file. She'd apparently been homeschooled until two months ago, then sent to a nearby prep school, and then he abruptly ripped her away from it and called me to send her here."

"And what did he say when he called you?" I waited a beat. "*Why* did he call you?"

I slowly turned and fixed my attention on the side of my uncle's profile. He stared into the fire as if it were challenging him to look away, which he wouldn't because, deep down, he was an Underwood, even if he didn't claim the name, and Underwoods never backed down from a fight. "He's, uh... I owed him a favor. He asked me to take in his niece because she was a troublemaker."

I laughed without hesitation. "A troublemaker?"

He scoffed. "Yeah. And it's obvious that it's not true."

We stood in silence for a few more minutes before he turned his head to mine, and I did the same to him. We locked eyes, held each other there for too long before he said, "He's hiding something."

I nodded once. "So is she."

"She's fragile and scared."

"Scared? Yes. Fragile? Debatable." I thought back to her snarky little attitude the first couple of times we'd talked. She may have been shy at times, and she blushed so much it was actually cute, and she was definitely afraid of her uncle, but she had a fighting streak in her. She wasn't as breakable as my uncle thought.

My uncle sighed again before walking back over to his desk and slumping down behind it. "She reminds me of someone I used to know." He looked back at the fire instead of at me, and it was like he wasn't fully there. Like he was revisiting the past as the orange and red flames coursed with life. "She was a fighter by nature, but she was sweet, too. Kind."

More silence passed between us, and I finally went back and sat in the seat I was in before. I was sure the sun was beginning to rise, and I was eager to get to the dining hall to not only see Gemma, but to catch sight of Bain too. He'd disappeared last night when he'd snuck out during my tutoring session with Gemma. That was why things had been cut short, and it infuriated me that I'd lost track of him. I never did that. The only good thing was that I'd made it back to my room without being caught by the duty teacher.

"Have you talked to your father?"

I shifted uncomfortably at the change in the conversation. "No. I did talk to Jack, though. Mom must be feeling down lately. He said he's been spending a lot of time with Mary."

"That's probably a good thing."

My mouth stayed closed, but it was the truth. Mary was a sense of normal, and normal was what Jack needed.

"Gemma needs a phone."

My uncle's head fell to the side as his mouth slanted. "I can't give her a phone. How would I explain that if anyone found out?"

I shrugged. "How do you explain giving her a laptop, blankets, and those extra uniforms?"

His eyes narrowed. "How did you know I did that?"

"Uncle Tate"—I crossed my arms over my chest—"you know I have my ways."

He rolled his eyes and rubbed his hand over the scruff on his chin. Then, he pulled his bottom drawer out and scooped up something before dropping it on his desk. Several phones clinked together from his arms. "Take your pick. It'll only work on the Wi-Fi, so pick one that is adaptable to your phone for messaging."

"Thanks," I muttered, picking up a phone that was identical to mine. I assumed they were confiscated in the past when phones were banned, or maybe students had accidentally left them behind and didn't want to come back here for even a second to grab it. I didn't really care. All I cared about was Gemma having a phone. Not only so I could talk to her when I felt like it, instead of waiting for her to get on her computer to chat, but also because Bain was a troublesome thought in the back of my head when it came to her.

Gemma needed a way to call me quickly if he decided to corner her again, which I knew he would. Bain was a lot of things, but stupid wasn't one of them. He would wait until I wasn't near to do so.

"Keep her close, Isaiah." I shook myself from the thoughts and regained focus on my uncle as determination covered his features like a steel mask. "I have an inkling that something much bigger than what we think is going on with Judge Stallard."

"What do you mean?" I asked, eyeing the clock. Breakfast started in five minutes.

He shook out his unkempt hair. "He doesn't have any siblings."

"Who doesn't?"

"Her uncle, Judge Stallard. He said Gemma is his niece, but he doesn't have a sister or brother. Nor does he have a wife—or anyone in the family with the Richardson surname." He looked around his office at nothing in particular. "I've looked into it. I don't think Gemma is related to him—which makes me wonder where she came from."

I let out a breath as I stood and placed Gemma's new phone in my pocket. "Well, that's... interesting...and, quite frankly, not comforting in the fucking least."

The things going through my head were dark and twisted, which I knew were a direct result of how I grew up. I wasn't a stranger to gruesome upbringings and traumatic pasts, but it didn't sit well with me to think those things about Gemma.

"I suspect abuse."

My heart stopped, and my back went rigid.

"So, keep her close, Isaiah. We do not want a repeat of Journey." My uncle was remembering exactly what I was. I looked down at my hands hanging down by my sides, the veins pumping some seriously hot blood throughout. I still felt Journey's limp body in my arms as I handed her off to Cade.

"I've got it under control," I said before stalking out of his office and shutting the door behind me. My eyes clenched tightly as I ran a hand through my hair, tugging on the ends slightly to get myself to clear my head. A few heavy breaths left my tight chest, and just like that, I was fine.

For once, I was thankful for all the fucked-up shit I'd seen as a child. At least now I had the capability and threshold to deal with traumatic shit and push it away until it disappeared altogether.

Did that make me fucked up?

Probably.

But hey, we were all a little fucked up at St. Mary's.

CHAPTER THIRTY

GEMMA

My fingers ached the next morning, and up until just a few moments ago, charcoal had covered every inch of my hands. Now they were red and raw from scrubbing them in the sink so no one would suspect that I was in here instead of in my room, tucked away underneath the comfy blankets that were given to me by the headmaster.

After Isaiah and I had parted ways last night, and Sloane had finally drifted to sleep after drilling me about Isaiah and our tutoring session, I couldn't sleep. Not a single freaking wink. Which wasn't at all unusual, but since arriving at St. Mary's over two weeks ago, I had slept better than I had in months. Ever since Tobias was sent away, my dreams had been more potent than normal, and they occurred more and more as I aged. They felt more real than reality, at times. It was terrifying, and every time I closed my eyes last night, all I could hear was Richard's voice lingering in the back of my head. His familiar sickening breath of pleasure that floated through the phone after I'd given in and called him his favorite little pet name caused my stomach to twist with unease, and I knew the only way to untwist it was to get it out.

I needed to spill everything onto the canvas—my outlet.

So, at around five in the morning, I climbed out of bed, tiptoed over to the bathroom, and hurriedly got ready for the day. A quick shower, moisturizer, a little bit of lip gloss (just to spite Auntie), my uniform, and I was out the door and creeping along the dark hallway with only the flickering sconces as my audience. Nerves pushed at my belly with each corner that I turned, wondering if it was okay to be out of bed that early in the morning, especially given Isaiah's warning. But the sun was going to peek over the tall, lush trees any minute, so I kept going. And I had to admit, breaking the rules—even by a few minutes—felt good. Dangerously good.

The very second I stepped in the empty art room, I breathed in a sigh of relief. It only took me minutes to gather my supplies and get ready. I pulled my damp hair into one long braid, freeing any stray pieces from my face, and slipped my blazer off my shoulders. I draped it over a stool, my lips twitching when I saw that I'd placed it on Isaiah's stool that he sat on during class. Next, I took my white blouse off in case I got charcoal on it, because I knew I would. I was only in my knee-high socks, maroon plaid skirt, and a tight, white tank top, which sent a chill over my skin.

But then, I got to work.

Time flew by, and before I knew it, the hallway lights were turned on, and the clock showed that I had been working for nearly two hours. Breakfast was soon, and I didn't want to make Sloane worry, so I rushed over and washed the charcoal off my skin before standing in front of the canvas with my raw hands. I scanned the creation that I had no recollection of even creating. Sketching had always been a release for me. A way to work through my secrets without revealing a single thing. My head was in a different space. *I* was in a different space.

I was there, reliving whatever horrendous memory that wanted to resurface, and in a way, it was therapeutic. It was a way for me to take control of the situation and then toss it right the hell out of my head.

But it never really left.

A shaky breath fell from my lips as I looked at the smudged charcoal. It was mostly the color of ash, but some parts were darker than others. It was a messy, rushed sketch, but that was exactly why I liked it. In the middle of the canvas, it was me—half of my face, at least. I trailed down the sharp black curve of my button-like nose and the shadows around my right eye. The arch of my high cheekbone was encased with long stray hairs, and my lips were split, like I was gasping for air. Then, on the other side of the canvas, where the rest of my face should have been, were the words *Good girls don't break rules,* over and over again, getting messier and even more smudged as they trailed down the entire length of the paper. The words blended with my face, and something in my chest cracked. Animosity and the slow burn of anguish tore through my soul as I quickly spun, taking my eyes off the shattered girl that I'd drawn.

The sudden urge to whip back around and tear it into pieces consumed me as a scream clawed at my throat. I was fighting like hell to make the torturous memory disappear. I even glanced down at my hand to see if the blisters were still there from the last time he made me write the phrase over and over again until my hand had bled, but no. The only thing I saw were the scars that circled the diameter of both wrists. The shiny skin that was lighter than the rest of my golden flesh.

Counting backward from ten, I stared at the ceiling, calming myself. Movement outside the classroom door was beginning to catch my eye, and I knew I needed to get a move on. Forcing the sickly feeling of the past from my mind, I hurriedly ran over to Isaiah's stool and grabbed my blouse and blazer. I pulled my shirt up and over my head, not once looking at the mirrored, charcoaled version of me. I knew I couldn't leave the canvas sitting out in the open like that, and Mrs. Fitz and I had never discussed what I should do with my projects if I were to use the art room like she and the head-master had suggested, so I did what any sane person would do. I unclipped it from the easel and ran over to the supply closet—the one that Isaiah had pulled me into on that first day—and hung my work in the very back, near the broom that looked as if it hadn't been used in years. The ends of it were frayed, and cobwebs hung off the wooden stick as dust danced around me. *Perfect.*

It was vital for me to keep these sketches a secret, and I was too proud of the actual work to throw them away. I made the mistake of letting someone else see them once, and that bit me in the ass.

Just as I shut the supply closet door, a deep voice floated around me, causing me to freeze.

"I was wondering if I'd find you here." Isaiah's tone was light and airy, and it was a welcomed sound from the angry and panicked beating of my own heart.

"Isaiah," I started, then I felt stupid because I seemed to always address him by his name when he popped up out of nowhere. It was like my brain and mouth were no longer connected when he was within sight. Clearing my throat and hoping that my cheeks didn't give away my embarrassment, I asked, "What are you doing here?"

He leaned back onto the table that he usually sat at, his feet somehow still touching the floor as his butt rested along

the edge. He was utterly beautiful sitting there, and my
fingers twitched to sketch him instead of the nasty memories
that kept resurfacing. There was a shadow under his jawline,
and the maroon blazer he wore was snug around his biceps
and cut off just below his waist, showing his slim hips and
black pants that led to his shoes.

Yes, Isaiah was definitely the definition of dark and
dangerous.

Until he smiled.

Which he was currently doing at the moment.

Wait. Did I miss something?

"Did you say something?" I asked, quickly darting my
attention away.

He hummed out a laugh and stood up from the desk. His
strides were slow and easy as he walked toward me, causing
my heart to jump up to my throat. *What was he doing?* Just as
the panicked thoughts began to consume me, his finger
graced the bottom of my chin, and he tipped my head backward. My braid swung behind my shoulder, and I watched in
awe as he brought his other hand to his mouth. A flush
started to creep up my neck as his tongue darted out from
behind his soft lips to lick his thumb. I felt the slick pad of
his finger swipe over my cheekbone, just below my left eye,
and I almost fainted.

I was hot. Burning up. I was completely captivated by
whatever was forcing me to stay in his tight grasp. Something
throbbed within, and desire annihilated any reminder of the
inexperience I had. The entire room was festering with
flames. I wanted to kiss him. *Did I really want that?* I did. I
knew I did. I wanted to know what it felt like to be kissed by
him.

"You had something black on your face," he said, still
keeping his hand on my chin.

"Charcoal." The single word had cracked around the edges like a firework.

He nodded once, our breath mingling together as we stared at one another. His eyes held something wild and tempting, and I really, really wanted to chase after it.

"What are you doing to me?" His question was nothing more than a raspy whisper as his hand left my chin, and he finally stepped away, allowing me to breathe again. His fingers ran through his dark hair, ruffling it a bit, and I just stood there, completely and utterly dumbfounded. Did he mean to say that out loud?

My lips were still parted as Isaiah crossed his arms over his chest and lowered his gaze. "I thought I told you to stay in your room."

Blinking myself back to reality, I pulled down my blazer sleeves and leveled my chin, forcing out a lie. "I waited until curfew was over."

His angry slash of an eyebrow hitched. "You've been in here for hours, which means you left your room before the sun even came up."

I pulled back. "How—"

Isaiah shot up from the desk he was leaning against and crept toward me. "Your hair is messy," he said, reaching out and pushing a piece of brown hair away from my face. "You had charcoal on your cheek." His lip twitched, and I couldn't seem to tear my eyes away as he crowded me again. "And I went to your room to grab you this morning, and Sloane couldn't seem to find you." He sighed before flinging his blue eyes to mine. "Leave a note next time."

My heart hiccupped at what sounded like panic in his voice. "Why did you come to my room?"

There was a beat of silence that lasted a second longer than I wanted. Isaiah's thick lashes lowered as he glanced away. "You shouldn't be in the halls before curfew is up, Gemma. Not alone, anyway."

"But why?" Isaiah's jaw was bracketed with tension. "Does it have something to do with whatever you had to do last night? Does it have something to do with me covering for you?" I couldn't seem to stop the questions from spilling out.

His growl was low, but I heard it. "How long have you been in here? Please tell me it hasn't been all night."

A sarcastic noise left my mouth as I threw his words back at him from the night before. "I'll answer yours, if you answer mine."

My lips curved at the sight of his narrowed eyes and dimpled cheek. "My uncle does not give you enough credit." Then, my slight smile fell. I swore he was talking in riddles. What did that even mean? "Tell me, Good Girl. Are you this snarky with everyone? Or just me?"

The tiniest laugh left my lips. "Just you."

He grunted with a half-smile before grabbing onto my hand and pulling me toward the classroom door. Butterflies coated my belly that I hastily pushed aside, pretending they weren't there. The second we were in the hallway, he pulled his hand away but glanced down at me. "For some reason, I feel privileged."

"Privileged?" I asked, glancing back up at him.

He nodded, looking straight ahead as we walked side by side. "I kind of love that you dish it back out to me and no one else."

I fought a laugh. "Why would you love that?"

His dimple reappeared just before I saw Cade, Brantley, and Shiner walking toward us from the dining hall. The bell rang over our heads, and I cursed myself for getting so caught up in my sketch—and let's be honest here, I was caught up in Isaiah licking that freaking charcoal off my face too—that I had missed breakfast altogether. Sloane was probably busting at the seams to ask me where I had gone so early this morning.

Just before the rest of the Rebels appeared in front of us, Isaiah bent down and whispered into my ear. "I love it because it means you trust me enough to be yourself, and even though I'm probably unworthy of a girl like you trusting someone like me, I'll take it anyway."

He winked as he pulled back and then began walking in stride with the Rebels, who'd all dipped their chin at me like they were approving something, and I felt the pride swell. I liked the fact that Isaiah said he felt unworthy of me, and I liked that his friends seemed to approve of me, too. I was beginning to like a lot of things that I shouldn't, and as the hallway began flooding with students from breakfast, all trying to get to their first class, I was left standing there, feeling my inability to trust someone disappear right into thin air.

Deep down, I knew I needed to control the butterflies that had been dormant in my belly for so long. I knew that Isaiah's intentions were good, and he probably didn't even realize that the simplest of touches made me burn on the inside. He wasn't really flirting with me or insinuating that he wanted anything from me other than what I was already giving him. He said it yesterday: he had kissed my cheek in front of everyone to prove a point. But still. My thoughts were muddled when we were brought together. I wasn't living in fear, or hiding from the past, or even contemplating my next move. Instead, I was secretly watching out for his dimple to reappear or waiting for that scorching heat to wash over me when he'd glance down to my mouth, even as fleeting as the look was.

Somehow, the bad boy of St. Mary's, who I'd found to be egotistical right off the bat, put a pause on my dark and troubled thoughts, and I didn't realize it until now, but that was exactly what I was starved for. I was ravenous for Isaiah Underwood and for the way he silenced all the shit in my head, and I found myself looking forward to seeing him again later, even if I knew there would eventually come a time where I wouldn't see him ever again.

CHAPTER THIRTY-ONE

GEMMA

WALKING INTO THE LIBRARY EARLIER, I had felt a little pep in my step. I'd been like this all day. My cheeks were twitching to smile for no reason at all other than the fact that I was beginning to feel ease settle over me with the hint of freedom chasing after my heels.

I wasn't sure if it was because I'd sketched this morning, or maybe it was because I was able to sit down in the dining hall with people my age who really weren't all that different from me—even given my upbringing—and eat lunch with them. Or maybe I was feeling elated because I'd gotten the highest grade on my English 4 test—thank you, Auntie, for making me read *Jane Eyre* in one single sitting last year. Or maybe it was because I was truly feeling at ease without two dark and beady eyes staring at me from across the dinner table each night just hoping I'd mess up so he could fulfill his sick pleasures and punish me.

"What's all this?"

My body hummed at the smooth voice coming from

behind me. Spinning around with my uniformed skirt still on, I raised my brow at Isaiah, all fresh and clean from his shower after lacrosse. *He smelled so good.*

"This," I answered, flipping back around to hopefully hide my heated cheeks, "is called tutoring, Isaiah. How will you explain the pair of us just sitting here if someone walks in? We need study materials. We have to actually act like we're tutoring, right? Even if you say you don't need it."

I didn't give him a chance to answer as I sat down in the same seat I used last night, moving a piece of paper off my laptop.

Isaiah mumbled something under his breath as he pulled his seat out and slumped down, looking all relaxed. His long legs were sprawled out in front of him, his feet hitting the tips of my shoes, making my toes tingle.

"What was that?" I asked, opening my laptop to distract the tingling in my legs. The light of the screen was so bright in the dimly lit library that I had to close my eyes. The librarian had shut most of the lights off before leaving me alone in the expansive room with as much life and history that one person could hold lining the deep shelves.

"I said I guess I should do my homework since my grades really are shitty."

I smiled. "Killing two birds with one stone. Who knew you were smart under all that no-cares-given attitude?"

Isaiah chuckled, pulling something out of his pocket. "I may act like I don't have a care in the world, but that's not true."

I glanced up to his face, and we caught each other. Deep down, I knew there was much more to people than met the eye. More than anyone, I knew such a thing. Whatever was on the outside was most definitely more potent on the inside. It was obvious that Isaiah was troubled, as was I. Although, I tried to hide it as best as I could.

Isaiah's black lashes swooped down to whatever was in his hand, and I followed his line of sight. "If I didn't care about anything, then I wouldn't have gone through the trouble of getting you this." He pushed something black and rectangular in shape across the table, and my brows furrowed. I moved my laptop to the side with the search engine still open and tucked loose pieces of hair behind my ear.

"What's this?"

"A phone."

My eyes rolled of their own accord. "I know I'm a little backward, Isaiah, but I'm aware that this is a phone. I'm just wondering why you're handing it to me."

His hand fell to mine as he wrapped his fingers around my wrist. My eyes jolted to the skin-on-skin contact, and everything in my body seized. It wasn't because he was touching me, although that made me feel warm, but it was more so because of what part of me he was gripping onto. If he saw my wrists...

"Because you need a way to get a hold of me."

I swallowed back a tightness in my throat as I looked up at him once again. His hand was still wrapped around my wrist, and the longer it stayed there, the more my heart thudded. "And maybe I want a way to talk to you other than the lame student chat."

I said nothing as I stared at his face. I didn't know what to say. My body was frazzled for many reasons.

Isaiah's palm finally left my wrist, and I jerked it back, putting it in my lap. He didn't seem to notice the dip in my mood.

"The phone only works on Wi-Fi, but you can still text me and use the Internet. I put my number in there, along with the rest of the Rebels', and added a few apps I thought you might like."

My lashes fluttered against my cheek a few times before I

regained the ability to speak. "How did you even get this?" I turned the device in my hands a few times, inspecting it. This was nothing like the phone Richard had given me. It did look a lot like Sloane's and Mercedes', though.

He shrugged, leaning his arm on the chair beside him, looking nothing less than smug. "I have my ways. I just needed peace of mind that you had a way to call me if..."

"If what?"

"If Bain said something...or cornered you again." He glanced away. "He won't do it if I'm close by."

My pulse began to drum. "He's been pretty silent since the other day." With every breath I took, it seemed my heart pounded twice as fast. I hadn't forgotten about Bain or what he'd said to me. But he hadn't said anything since. In fact, I'd hardly seen him at all. It seemed our schedules didn't align, and I was thankful for that, but he was still a quiet thought lingering in the back of my head. He was nestled up right beside my dearest Uncle Richard.

Isaiah's gaze heated, his eyes appearing like shards of glass. "Never trust a snake that's silent, Gemma. Bain may be quiet, but I can assure you he is still just as deadly." The muscles along Isaiah's temple flickered. "Bain and I have history, even if he doesn't exactly know how deep that history runs yet. He has it out for me and would like nothing more than to have power over me. He sees you as a bargaining chip or a way to get back at me, because I've given you attention, and not to mention, you're one of the sole reasons I'm not being expelled—something Bain would fucking love."

There were too many questions floating around my head, and even though I'd always been told to keep my wandering tongue silent, I still wanted to ask him more. I wanted him to elaborate. What history did they have? Why did Bain want Isaiah to get expelled from St. Mary's? But I didn't say a word because just as soon as my mouth opened, the library doors flew open, and Cade's glare traveled over each and every table until he landed on us.

"Ever think about checking your phone?" Cade looked agitated as he walked over with his set jaw and slight scowl.

Isaiah slowly looked back to see Cade, who had his hands pressed to his hips. His chest was heaving. *Did he run here?*

I watched as Isaiah pulled his phone out of his pocket. His eyes scanned whatever it was that he was reading, and then a feral growl left his mouth. "You don't know where he went?"

"No. And the car hasn't moved."

"Who? Bain?" I asked before I could stop myself. I *almost* shrunk back into the chair from past experiences of speaking out when I shouldn't have, but that wasn't me anymore. I didn't have to stay quiet to stay safe. I wasn't going to get punished for asking an innocent question.

Cade's mouth flung open as he snapped his gaze back to Isaiah.

Isaiah shot him a look that I couldn't put my finger on, and then his features softened a little as he looked over to me. "Tutoring is coming to a sudden halt." Isaiah pushed himself from the table, his tall stance looming over me like some type of enticing nightmare. His inky hair fell onto his forehead, and the blue of his eyes that were warm seconds ago turned glacial. "If anyone asks..."

"I know. I know. We were here, tutoring together."

His lips twitched so subtly that I doubted he even knew he did it.

Before Isaiah left, I asked, "Should I go back to my room? What if someone comes in here and doesn't see us sitting here? Like someone on the committee?"

"I don't think anyone is actually going to come in here. All the teachers who are a part of the SMC dip out right after school unless they have hall duty."

A leery feeling of unease settled over me. "Are you sure?"

Isaiah sighed as he ran his hand down his face feebly. I could be his alibi like he wanted, but if someone actually came here and asked where he was, what would I say? It was one thing if they asked me the next day. It was another if they were standing here looking at an empty chair.

Cade mumbled under his breath as he looked away, too, clearly thinking of a new plan. Silence fell over our group as I sat in the chair with the new phone in my hand and my laptop pushed to the side as Isaiah and Cade both stood above me with a tenseness in their shoulders that even I could feel.

My fingers grasped the phone tightly. "I'll just text you if someone comes in here. I'll say you ran back to your room for a book or something." I paused. "Unless you are leaving school grounds?"

Cade spoke this time, looking at Isaiah. "The car hasn't moved. He didn't leave the school—yet."

Isaiah's brows knitted together as he gripped the back of the chair he was standing above so tightly his knuckles began to change color. His gaze pierced mine once more as he said, "Text me if anyone comes in here. And I don't just mean a teacher. If any other student pops in here, don't trust them."

A chill flung to my limbs as Cade let out a grunt. "Still think your plan of showing Bain that Gemma was yours the other day was a good idea? Because now he's really unpredictable."

"Did I have a choice?" If looks could kill, Isaiah would be a cold-blooded murderer right about now. But so could Cade. He had those dreamy, all-American-boy features, whereas Isaiah had dark and dangerous ones, but when he narrowed his eyes and clenched his jaw? Thunder rolled. Watching them stare at one another was like watching a hurricane brew over an ocean. "I saw the way he looked at her after our initial conversation when I'd asked her to tutor me in the first place, and then at the claiming?" He shook his head with rising anger. "Bain isn't stupid, Cade. You know that. It's either I keep my distance from her and act like she's nothing more than a piece of fucking dirt on the bottom of my shoe"— *Ouch.*—"which I fucking can't because she's my..."

"Tutor," I answered, inserting myself to the conversation so they'd both remember that I was sitting right here even though they were acting like I wasn't. *A piece of dirt on the bottom of his shoe?*

"Exactly." Isaiah's voice was tight around every single word, and my stomach flopped. "She and I are being thrown together no matter what, so it's either I keep a close eye on her, or..."

Cade sighed, crossing his arms over his chest.

"Or nothing. You're right. We know how Bain gets when he becomes...centered on something." I slowly raised my chin and looked at Cade. His sentence threw me off course because the anger that was just radiating off him was no longer there, but instead, there was anguish. His big brown eyes deepened as they found the ground. His shoulders dropped. His breath was unsettled.

"I've seen him looking at her too," Cade said. "But is it because of you? Or because..."

Isaiah huffed. "Probably both."

Silence encased us all again as they stared at each other, obviously sharing a silent conversation that made me feel pretty damn insignificant.

Pride washed over me as I opened my mouth. "Is anyone going to fill me in? Because it sounds like you two are talking in code, and I don't like to be left in the dark." A simmer of anger began to brew right after pride. I'd been in the dark my entire life. I'd been lied to, forced to keep my mouth shut, and physically thrown into a dark basement so I was *"protected"* from certain things. Being unaware of your surroundings or things that were going on around you was nothing less than dangerous. I deserved to know what was going on. I'd always deserved to know what was going on around me. It had just taken a while to realize that.

"There isn't time right now." Isaiah shook his head and began typing something on his phone. "Cade is going to walk you back to your room when I give the go-ahead." He glanced up at Cade briefly before beginning to walk away. "She shouldn't be alone if we can't find him. I don't trust him. If anyone comes in here asking why you're here, just say it's a group tutoring session or something."

The tiniest growl left my lips when Isaiah dismissed me. Both boys snapped their attention to me as my hands flung to my waist. "I've been lied to my entire fucking life." I paused for a split second at my choice of words before continuing. "I've only been told certain things because..." I trailed off, pushing away the past, gripping onto my rising anger. "It doesn't matter why. What matters is that something is going on that pertains to me, and I deserve to be brought up to speed. I am so tired of being dismissed because I'm a *good girl.*"

One second passed as my heart whacked against my chest. Blood rushed to my fingertips, and I wasn't sure what it was, but I was *mad*. Was I finally just at my threshold for all the bullshit in my life and taking it out on Cade and Isaiah? Maybe.

My fists tightened even more as Isaiah's mouth split wide, and he let out a laugh that only fed my rising temper. "How often do you curse, Gemma?" Cade chuckled under his breath, and I pursed my lips. "You're seriously adorable when you're angry. I might just start pissing you off to see your reaction." Then, he grinned at me and turned around, leaving me standing there with fumes coming out my ears.

I stomped my foot like a five-year-old would, but to be honest, I don't think I'd even done that as a child, let alone at seventeen. "Isaiah!" I barked. "You will tell me what's going on, or else I won't be your alibi if the SMC comes knocking." An evil grin slid onto my face, and I *loved* the fact that I had power. I loved it too much. "How easy would it be for me to tell them that you leave during our tutoring sessions to sneak out and go do God knows what."

Isaiah threw his head back and laughed without even looking at me over his shoulders. "You'll continue covering for me, Good Girl." I crossed my arms over my chest, feeling that surge of power dissipate. He continued walking to the door as he talked. "Or did you forget about our deal? Didn't you need something in return? A fake ID or something?"

The door shut seconds later, and my arms slowly fell in defeat. Isaiah was right. How could I forget that he was my ticket out of here? That he was the one carving my path to freedom? That he was paving a way for me to hopefully find my brother? It was scary that Isaiah could take my worries and turn them to dust within seconds, making me forget all that had weighed me down in the first place.

When I turned toward Cade, he was standing there with his arms still crossed and his gaze pointed to the ceiling like he was trying his hardest not to look at me.

"Will you tell me what's going on?" I asked.

He laughed sarcastically, bringing his gaze back down. "Not a chance in hell. Isaiah brought you into this; he can be the one to deal with the repercussions."

"Rude," I whispered under my breath, plopping myself back down into the chair. I pulled the laptop over and began typing furiously into the search engine, pretending that Cade wasn't standing just a few feet away and that Isaiah didn't just leave me in the library, totally empty-handed and restless. He wanted me to cover for him, but he wouldn't tell me why?

Whatever. Fine. It wasn't like I was willing to tell him my secrets either. But it seemed that both of our secrets affected the other in ways we didn't want to admit. He said he was protecting me, but how was I protecting him when it came to Richard and my secrets? After it was all said and done, if Richard somehow learned that Isaiah was the one who gave me the necessities to get away from him, would he go after him?

I sighed, easing the stress from my shoulders as I tried to be proactive with my time. I typed the words *Judge Stallard* rather aggressively into the search engine and hit enter, waiting to dig into every last thing that Richard was related to. Knowledge was power, and maybe something would pop up that would lead me to Tobias. Maybe the smallest of clues would appear, and I'd know where to start once I got out of this school with my wad of cash and new ID. Nothing like distracting myself with a little search that Richard would nearly kill me for. It was all part of his control: him knowing everything about me, and me knowing nothing about him.

"Judge Stallard?" Cade startled me, and I had no idea that he'd even moved from the other side of the table.

I slammed the laptop shut. "Stop snooping," I snapped.

Cade's brown eyes widened. "What? You can trust me. Maybe I can help with your little search there."

"I *do not* trust you," I said, even though there was a really small voice inside of me that told me I could.

Cade's lips twitched. "I'm bothered that you don't think I look trustworthy."

I raised my chin. "You *do* look trustworthy, and that's exactly why I don't trust you." I began pushing the laptop open again with my fingers. "Plus, you were the one who tricked me the first day in art when Isaiah pulled me into the closet."

Cade's shoulders slumped for a second, his light hair

falling into his eyes. "Well, shit. I did, didn't I?" He batted his thick eyelashes at me. "I'm sorry. Do you forgive me?"

A smile tickled my lips as I fought to keep them even. "Does batting your eyelashes like that really work on girls?" I knew for fact that it did. I'd seen him in action a couple of times this week. His target always seemed to fall into his lap like he was some type of female magnet.

A huge grin covered Cade's face. "Of course it does." He pulled out the chair beside me and rested his hands behind his head. "But for the record..." He glanced away. "I won't betray your trust. I promise. I won't look at your computer anymore."

I wanted to believe that. I really did. A warmth settled into my bones, and it seemed to spread over my skin. I pushed my laptop the rest of the way open, only peeking at Cade a few times before I typed enter on the search engine again and began reading all there was to know about Richard. For some reason, the bitter taste I'd always had didn't surface like usual when his round face appeared in front of my eyes. Instead of feeling that rising panic, I felt powerful. Like digging up all this information was giving me a sense of strength against him. The last time I'd started to dig, he caught me red-handed, and it did not end well. Even when I groveled at his feet and acted like the devoted and loyal girl that he wanted me to be, he still punished me.

Out of the corner of my eye, I saw Cade shift with his phone in his hand, but he didn't look at my computer screen again. I wasn't sure if he was making a point not to look because he said I could trust him, or maybe he just didn't really care. Either way, I was relieved. My chest untightened as each second passed with his head down, and my breaths eventually resumed to their lazy rhythm as I scrolled over articles and newspaper headlines.

That was, until I felt a vaguely familiar feeling creeping up behind me, causing my fingers to pause over the keyboard. I glanced at the little time icon in the corner and saw that it was well past curfew—something the rest of the Rebels didn't seem to care about.

I peered over my shoulder slowly, prepared to see something or someone standing there, but all I saw were sky-high bookshelves and an empty, dark aisle that led to the back of the library.

"What's wrong?" Cade asked, putting all four of his chair legs back onto the floor.

"I...don't know." I bristled at my rising anxiety. I was probably feeling uneasy because of all the searching I'd done. My subconscious was poking at me to tread lightly. "It's probably nothing. I just feel like we're not—" My sentence came up short when something thudded in the back of the library. There was a flash of movement, and within seconds, Cade was up out of his seat, and he was pulling me up and pushing me behind him. I stumbled onto the edge of the table with the phone Isaiah gave me clutched in my hand and my face pressed to Cade's back.

"Text Isaiah and tell him we're going back to your room right now." His grip on my arm tightened, and within seconds, we were heading for the door.

"Wait!" I shouted. "I need my sketchbook." I had no idea what was going on, but there was a feeling of urgency in my blood that was instinctual. If someone found my sketches, things would get bad—fast.

"What?" Cade's face was a mix of pressing caution.

"Please," I begged, trying to whip my arm out of his grasp.

The shadows over his face deepened, but he dragged me with him to the table, keeping his eyes trained to the back of the library. I hurriedly swiped the worn sketchbook off the table, and then we were out the door.

"Stay quiet since I'm technically not allowed to be out after curfew." His hand loosened a little. "So let's not get caught."

"I wasn't aware that you cared much about that."

Cade's chuckle was short and sweet, but he stayed silent the rest of the way to the girls' hall. We didn't run into anyone else. The hall was just as unmoving as it usually was during curfew hours. I pulled the phone up during our walk and began texting Isaiah, which Cade had to help me with because I had no idea which button to press. Just as we reached the girls' hall, Cade's phone began vibrating, and he answered it quietly.

"Check the library," he whispered, glancing behind us once. "There was a loud thud in the back, and instead of investigating, I decided to take Gemma back to her room." Then, the line went dead, and Cade pushed his phone back into his jeans.

"Was that Isaiah?" I asked, watching the darkened corners of the girls' hall. We were almost to my room now, and thankfully, the duty teacher hadn't made her rounds yet, but I still felt unease moving through my blood like sludge. I was on edge—likely with good reasoning.

"Yeah." He glanced down at me. "He said to tell you to stay in your room all night."

I rolled my eyes, but before I could say anything, Cade sighed. "And he said to put an emphasis on the words *all night*."

My lips twitched as I pulled the phone out and texted him again.

ME: Yes, your highness. I will stay in my room.

. . .

HIS RESPONSE WAS INSTANTANEOUS.

ISAIAH: **All night.**

"JUST LISTEN TO HIM."

I pulled the phone to my chest and glared up at Cade. "Again! With the snooping!" I whisper-yelled. He was worse than Tobias when I used to hide my sketches from him.

Cade's lips curved, but he said nothing as I quietly opened my door and slipped inside.

Sloane popped up off her bed, her hair falling back behind her shoulders. She sighed before plopping back down onto her pillow. "Finally! I've been waiting for you to watch our show. Tutoring with Isaiah should take, like, one hour, max."

A light laugh floated out of me as I tucked the new phone into my pocket, pushing away Isaiah's text from my mind, along with everything else. I was safe, and that was all that mattered at the moment. "Let me get changed for bed, and we can watch it. You didn't have to wait for me, though. You could have skipped ahead and filled me in later."

She sucked in breath. "Absolutely not." She peeked up at me just before I went into the bathroom. "And you better never watch without me. Our friendship depends on it."

I couldn't even hide my smile as I shut the door behind me.

CHAPTER THIRTY-TWO

ISAIAH

I'D WAITED until mostly everyone was in the common room to slip out early Saturday afternoon. Cade and Brantley were currently creating a diversion and getting everyone stirred up over our lacrosse game that ended with thrown punches to the other team.

The Wildcats didn't accept that we'd beat them in the last few seconds of the game, and a few of the guys had words, and before I knew it, Shiner was flying over our goaltender's back to defend him after a sucker punch to the jaw.

Coach brushed it under the rug, although I was sure my uncle had heard all about it.

I, for one, did not partake in such felonious acts. In fact, I was the one who had pulled Shiner off and held the peace. There was definitely a time for throwing punches, and being on probation with the SMC wasn't one of them.

Before leaving the common area, I found Shiner attempting to one-line one of the girls that Bain often frequented, which stole Bain's attention away instantly. Which meant my plan had worked like a charm.

Gemma was nowhere to be found in the common area, but that was because she was in the art room, and I was fine with that, knowing we had eyes on Bain at the moment. The last few nights of tutoring had been tense. Aside from a few bantering comments about how I needed to do my homework so the SMC felt that she was doing her job as my tutor, along with quick, heated glances from me that I was certain she didn't even notice, we'd mainly kept to ourselves. I had a feeling she was still angry about the fact that I hadn't given her any more information on Bain, but it was better that way.

Cade, Brantley, and Shiner had been on their A-game with keeping up with Bain after Tuesday's slip up, and he'd yet to leave the school grounds like he had in the past. Bain had fucked with us the other night, as if he knew there were eyes on him. I'd had a suspicion for a while now that he was getting antsy, and Tuesday confirmed as much. There was no one in the library after Cade had taken Gemma back to her room, and once we were done searching the darkened library aisles, finding not even a single page of a book out of place, Bain suddenly reappeared and slipped back into his room after we'd gotten back. It was a damn miracle that neither of us had gotten caught by the duty teachers scouring the halls that night.

Shaking the feeling of pressing anxiety from my shoulders, I crept up the stairs and walked down the hall slowly. It didn't take long to find myself in front of Bain's room, and I was inside the dorm even quicker since I had the master key—well, a copy of it, at least. Something I wasn't sure my uncle knew, considering I'd stolen his and made a replica the first week I'd arrived here.

I knew it would come in handy eventually. *Always think ahead, Isaiah. Cover your bases.* A swallow worked itself down my throat as one of my father's lessons came to mind. He'd always taught me to think ahead, and even though I hated him more than anything in the entire fucking world, I'd stayed true to that piece of advice. I had a backup plan for every aspect of my life—except for being the heir to my father's business. There was no backup plan for becoming the Huntsman, because that meant harming Jack, and I wouldn't do that. Jack was my limit.

As soon as the door clicked behind me, my gaze grew sharper and my ears more alert. I wasn't sure what my father wanted me to find. He'd been too cryptic over the phone yesterday, and I wasn't in a spot where I could question him further. I could only assume it was related to drop-offs and sales, though. I knew Bain's phone would likely hold the most information, but that would be much tougher to snag, so his room was my first stop.

I stepped over his bundled clothes on the floor and lifted up his mattress, searching for any makeshift holes inside for hiding spots. The pillows in my hands were just the same as any other pillow, soft and fluffy, lacking any weight that would indicate something shoved inside. His dresser was full of boxers and extra uniforms, along with a few pieces of street clothing for after classes and weekends.

Just as I stepped back from his desk, something caught my eye. *A Polaroid camera?* My brows pinched as I picked it up and inspected it. Then, I placed it back down quietly and searched the rest of his room for what I was absolutely certain would be here.

I stood in the middle of his floor, searching every corner of the room until I paused, staring at a book. It wasn't unusual to have a book on your desk at a boarding school, right? But what was unusual was that it was neatly pushed up against the back end of his desk. Each book was ramrod straight, almost looking like a decoration that would be on a

shelf in a house versus an actual textbook that the school had
given us.

My finger ran down the spine slowly, and instead of skin-
like leather touching the pad of my pointer, it was plastic.
Hard, unbending plastic. As I tipped one book back, the
entire thing moved in one fluid motion, revealing the smallest
cutout in the wall.

What a fucking idiot. I changed my opinion from earlier.
Bain was stupid.

The hole wasn't any bigger than a few inches wide than it
was tall. There were frayed pieces of drywall all around the
edges, and as I reached inside, I easily grabbed the photos.

I flipped through them quickly, knowing that, at any given
moment, Bain could head upstairs. The guys were instructed
to text me the second he stepped out of the common area,
but still, that wouldn't give me much time to exit his room
without running into him. It was doable, though. Otherwise,
I wouldn't be here.

The first few pictures were of Journey, which was no
surprise to me. Everyone knew of his obsession with her, and
although her accident was ruled just that—an accident—I
still suspected he had something to do with it. I didn't buy his
alibi when we'd cornered him, and without anyone suspecting
that someone was at fault other than Journey herself, no one
else had questioned him. I wasn't convinced, though—not
with the things I knew. Which was another reason why I
didn't want Gemma alone—not with a direct threat from
Bain himself.

After pushing aside the few stalker-like photos of Journey,
who had obviously been unaware that her photo was being
taken, there was one of Ms. Glenburg that had me snarling.
Not out of protection, because from the looks of the photo,
it was quite obvious that she wasn't just lusting over me but
over Bain as well. Her tits were on full display in a lacy bra

with what I assumed to be Bain's thumb in her mouth. Her red lips were wrapped around his finger with hollowed out cheeks as she sucked. I didn't give a flying fuck that Bain seemed to be having some sort of an explicit relationship with her. I wasn't jealous in the slightest. But what I did care about was that the next photo was of me as I hovered over her with my hand up her skirt.

That fucker.

Bain was the one who told the SMC. It shouldn't have been much of a surprise that he'd been following me—my suspicions have been there for a while, especially with what he'd said to Gemma. But now that I was certain he was the one trying to get me kicked out of St. Mary's, that likely meant he knew I was following him and reporting back to my father on his whereabouts. Did he know my father was the Huntsman? Or did he just know my father was in the same line of business as his? Most of the time, you could put a face to someone's name, but what name did he know my father by? Carlisle Underwood? Or the Huntsman?

My teeth gritted together so hard my jaw throbbed. Finding this meant that Bain knew too much. I knew calling my father was inevitable. He needed to know that Bain was onto me, but what did that mean for me? For Jack?

I shoved the photo of Ms. Glenburg behind the next, careful not to crinkle the edges, but when I settled on the image in front of me, my fingers clamped down.

Golden brown hair fell down her back in those luscious waves that I found myself wanting to touch out of the simple notion that they looked soft. Her bottom lip was sucked into her mouth as she stared at the computer screen in front of her. Even through the bad quality of the photo, I could see the intense look in her gaze as the screen illuminated the perfect planes of her cheeks and—*was that Cade beside her?*

It was. My firm grip grew tighter, the edges of the photo

bending in my fingers. This photo was taken Tuesday, after I'd left Gemma in the library with Cade as I searched for Bain's sneaky ass.

Goddamnit. My heart began climbing in speed, the thumping so hard my chest rumbled. I cracked my neck as I shoved the photos back inside the hollowed part of the wall.

My phone vibrated, and I angrily pushed the fake book back in its place and read the text.

CADE: on the move.

I WAS out of Bain's room before I even put my phone in my pocket. My strides were slow and easy down the hall, and I knew I appeared as I usually did on the outside, but I was burning with a million little fires on the inside, all of which formed a blazing circle around Gemma.

A feeling of protection like no other had surfaced, and I wanted to find Bain, shove him up against a wall with my hand wrapped around his throat, and demand he never look in her direction again.

There were two reasons Bain would be taking photos of Gemma, and none of them settled well with me. He was either interested in her because of me, or he was interested in her because she reminded him of Journey. Both options added on another layer of anger that all stemmed from my fucking father.

Which only made me hate him more.

CHAPTER THIRTY-THREE

GEMMA

AFTER SPENDING MOST of my day in the art room, I was feeling better than before. The week had been interesting. I was finally getting in the groove of my classes and finding myself more relaxed than ever with Sloane and Mercedes, whereas before, I was a little nervous to be hanging out with them in fear that I'd act too suspicious or say the wrong thing, but things were becoming easier for me. Everything seemed to be looking up, except for my tutoring sessions with Isaiah, which were nothing more than a nerve-wracking ending to my day.

I wasn't afraid to be around him, but I found myself glancing up at him every few minutes as we'd work silently in a room that seemed to have an even eerier feel since Tuesday night. I was also a little perturbed with myself, because even though I was half-angry with him that he still hadn't given me any information on Bain and the vague threats or even answer my question about who was in the library that night with Cade, I still found my breath faltering when we'd lock eyes for the briefest of seconds. It lit me on fire each and every time, and then after I cooled down, I would berate myself for even looking up in the first place.

It was maddening.

He was maddening, and I didn't even think he meant to be. It was just my body's reaction to him. I kept blaming it on curiosity that came with never being alone with a boy, or feeling hands on me that belonged versus hands on me that were forced, but whatever it was, I couldn't seem to get it to stop. The thoughts that were put into my head like tiny little seeds were fed and watered by Isaiah's icy eyes and perfect, arrogant mouth. I couldn't avoid him—or the wicked thoughts that made my skin itch.

And tonight, there was another claiming party that Sloane and Mercedes were dragging me to—something that Isaiah was well aware of. It was made known at the breakfast table yesterday morning when Sloane had very loudly demanded that I go. Even despite the whole incident that happened last time, she wouldn't hear of me staying in our room. Once it was decided that I'd go, which I really only agreed to because she was making such a scene, Isaiah's gaze slid right to mine and then ripped right past me, as if he were looking at someone from afar.

"I can't believe Isaiah gave you a phone." Sloane was doing her makeup in the bathroom, but she'd kept the door open so Mercedes and I could still chat with her.

"That is really odd." Mercedes glanced up before looking back at her nails that she was painting red polish onto. "Why did he even get you a phone? Don't you have one already?"

Unease settled in. I really liked Mercedes and Sloane, and I truly did hate that I was keeping them in the dark, because what a contradiction that was. But in order to keep things in line, I had to evade the truth some. "Yeah, well..." I glanced away, unable to look either of them in the eye. "He wanted to be able to get a hold of me about our tutoring sessions. Sometimes he runs late because of lacrosse and…" The hole in my chest was getting bigger as I forced a little bit of the truth out. "My uncle is pretty strict, and he checks my phone records. He wouldn't be happy about me texting someone that he had never met—especially if it were someone like Isaiah." That was definitely putting it mildly.

Mercedes let out a loud laugh. "My dad would lose his shit if he knew I was even talking *about* Isaiah. My father doesn't even want me to look in his direction."

"Isn't your dad on the SMC?" I asked as she glanced back at her nails.

She blew out a breath, her blush-covered cheeks puffing. "Yep, so he *really* doesn't like Isaiah since he knows of everything that he's done." A light laugh left her. "Well…the things he's been caught for."

There was a question at the tip of my tongue that caused it to burn. "Why are you at St. Mary's, Mercedes?"

Sloane was sent here because her parents were in the military and deployed often, but I wasn't sure why Mercedes was. She was nice. Really nice. And if her parents were on the SMC, that meant that she actually had parents, and well… something didn't quite add up. Sloane said everyone at St. Mary's was a little messed up, but I didn't get that from Mercedes. I didn't really get that from Sloane, either. But then again, did people get that from me?

"Because Mercedes' parents want her to get into Harvard or some ritzy school like that."

I shifted on the bed. "And you can get into one of those schools by going here?"

Mercedes shrugged. "St. Mary's has an excellent reputation for getting students into the Ivy Leagues—or at least a well-credited college. It was the closest high-end school to my hometown, so they decided to send me here instead of allowing me to attend regular high school with fewer chances at getting a good education. Or so they say."

I began picking at the threads on my blanket. "So, St. Mary's is considered to be a high-end school?" I thought back to Wellington Prep. It was absolutely the type of school that could get you into an Ivy League college—or at least that was what mostly everyone had talked about when I attended for those brief two months. The curriculum there was on-par with what it was here, but of course, nothing like what Auntie used to make me do.

Sloane laughed. "I'd say so. It's expensive to go here if you're not on a scholarship. My parents had the same thought that Mercedes' did. It is one of the only boarding schools in the nation that produces Ivy-League-destined graduates, even despite some of our shitty upbringings. It's like the SMC thought we had nothing else to do but study, so they made the coursework hard as shit." She rolled her eyes at the last part of her sentence but quickly changed her tune as she gave me a pointed look.

"I have a question for you, Gemma."

My attention bounced to Mercedes and then back to Sloane, my fingers now basically tearing the blanket apart. "Okay?"

"Where do you keep sneaking off to in the middle of the night?"

My heart halted as my fingers stilled.

Mercedes' voice squeaked. "She's sneaking off? What? To where?"

"Is it to see Isaiah?"

I sucked in a breath, sitting up taller. "What? No!"

"Is that why he's always looking at her?" I snapped my attention back over to Mercedes. *Wait, what? When does he do that?*

Sloane pointed her straightener at Mercedes. "Exactly

why I'm asking! He kissed her cheek the other day, and ever since then, he has been watching her like a hawk." Her lips pursed as she glanced back at me. "What exactly are you two doing while tutoring? Is it him you're going to see in the middle of the night?" She sucked in another breath, her chin dropping. "Oh my God. Are you guys having sex?" She placed a hand to her heart. "I swear to God, if he takes your virginity and then breaks your heart, I will burn him alive with my flat-iron! You are too sweet. God, he will ruin you! I knew this tutoring thing was such bullshit! It makes no sense!" At some point during her rant, she'd begun waving her straightener around the small bathroom like a maniac.

Mercedes hopped off the bed. "For the love of God, put the straightener down before you burn St. Mary's to the ground, Sloane!"

I couldn't help it. A loud laugh escaped from my mouth, and once it was out, I couldn't seem to stop. I couldn't remember a time in my life where I'd ever laughed so much, and I didn't even know why. Was it because I was elated that she didn't know I was sneaking off to the art room to draw the most horrific yet beautiful depictions of my most buried memories? Or was it because she threatened to burn Isaiah alive on my behalf? Whatever it was, I liked it. I was laughing hard. It only took a few seconds for Mercedes to start giggling and then for Sloane too.

We were all mid-laugh, trying to catch our breath, when a knock sounded on the door. I jumped to my feet quickly, but Mercedes brushed me off. "It's probably Callie. I told her to bring me my necklace when she was done getting ready."

Relief settled in, and I relaxed again. I wasn't even sure who I thought would be on the other side of the door, but with how things were going lately, I was skeptical that they would stay normal for me. "Isaiah and I are not having sex," I said to Sloane, finally addressing what she'd assumed I was doing when I left my room. Maybe I'd laughed so hard because the idea that I was sneaking off at four in the morning to go do the one act that was absolutely forbidden to me above all else was so absurd it was hilarious.

"Yet." Sloane pointed her straightener at me, and I laughed again.

"Put that down before you really burn St. Mary's to the ground." I pushed off the bathroom door frame. "And what do you mean by *yet?*"

"I mean... I see the way he looks at you, Gemma." She began straightening the last few strands of her black hair. "I know you say that you're just tutoring him, but he...I don't know. It's like he can't stop looking at you. Even when he's at lacrosse practice. His eyes find you every time he takes a break."

Just as Mercedes began opening the door, she rolled her eyes at Sloane. "It's true."

I let out a tight laugh, trying to figure out a way I could brush off her speculations of Isaiah. Even if he was looking at me as much as she said he was, I was certain it was because of the Bain thing. They didn't know that Bain had made that vague threat against me. They didn't know that Isaiah was concerned that Bain was going to try to use me as some type of pawn to get back at Isaiah for whatever it was that they were feuding over.

"Oh!" Mercedes' tone was like the squeak of a mouse. "Headmaster Ellison."

My thoughts faltered as I glanced at the door and caught the eye of the headmaster. He was staring directly at me, and my stomach somersaulted. *Oh no.*

"Umm..." Mercedes looked between us. "So sorry, Head-master. I'll go back to my room."

His expression changed swiftly with the slight shake of his head. "Oh, there's no need for that, Mercedes."

She stepped back farther into the room, closer to me now. Her nail polish lid was still off, and the strong scent flew under my nose. "But...it's after curfew. I should be in my room."

"Oh?" The headmaster smiled deviously, and it shocked me because, for some reason, the way his lips tipped upward was so...familiar. A warmth settled over me. "I suppose that may be true." His statement was more of a surmised one at that. He winked innocently at Mercedes and then caught my eye again. "I just came to see if Gemma was adjusting well with everything. Especially with the new tutoring gig. We didn't really get a chance to talk much on Monday after you left my office. But it seems like you're doing just fine."

He was definitely surprised by this but also looked... happy? I had to admit that Headmaster Ellison was very confusing to me. I really wanted to trust him, and there was something about him that I connected to almost instantly, but there was also the smallest voice in the back of my head, reminding me not to trust a single person—least of all someone who owed Richard a favor. Their initial conversation was not far from my memory.

I nodded. "I'm doing okay." My lips smashed together as Sloane and Mercedes came to stand beside me. "We were just"—I glanced at both of them—"having a...girls' night. Is that okay?"

The headmaster was bewildered by my comment. Something flashed along his features before he smiled. "Of course." He looked at each of us. "Have a great night. Don't tell the other girls I let you three have a sleepover." He chuckled. "Although, I assume this is a common thing around here? I don't make a habit of coming to the girls' wing often." Then, he nodded once and muttered a goodnight awkwardly before shutting the door.

The three of us stood in the middle of the room for a solid minute before Sloane said, "That was weird as fuck."

Then, we all started laughing again.

––––––

THE SPLASHING of water beneath my feet sent a thrill of exhilaration up my spine. My stomach dipped with excitement, which was a vast improvement from the last time I'd walked in the tunnel underneath St. Mary's. After the headmaster had left the room, Sloane, Mercedes, and I commenced our *"slumber party,"* which just involved getting ready for the party. Sloane had taken the straightener to my hair, even if I was a little hesitant at first because of how she had been aggressively waving it around all night. But in the end, my darkened mess of brown waves had fallen over my shoulders like a shiny sleek curtain.

It was amazing the transformation I'd had in the few short weeks I'd been at St. Mary's. I had been away from home for less than a month, and with each passing day, I felt Richard's slip on me lessen more and more. It was a troubling thought as I walked arm in arm with Sloane and Mercedes to attend a party that revolved heavily around something that had always been presented as *bad* to me. I was taught that breaking rules was bad and so was anything beyond that. In the past, the thought of breaking rules would have sent me into a spiral of panic, but now? After being away from Richard and that house? And everything that reminded me of what I'd missed out on and what I had lost? Like Tobias... I was welcoming the feeling of rebellion. It wouldn't last forever. I knew that. But the contrast between home and here was transformative in a way. Like the iron shackles were off my wrists. Metaphorically and literally. I was almost thirsty for what was to come of tonight—whatever that may be.

Suddenly, Isaiah's face flashed within my thoughts, and something achy came over my body. Then, I began sweating as Sloane's and Mercedes' arms, intertwined with mine, pulled me along the abyss.

We were getting closer to the door of the party, and I could feel the thumping of bass underneath my feet. I pulled down the sleeves of my shirt to cover my wrists when Sloane stopped walking.

I looked over at her, even though it was pitch black. "Sloane?" I asked as trepidation came rushing to the surface. "What's wrong?"

"Gemma." Her voice echoed against the empty walls surrounding us. "I need to ask you something else."

The excitement I had been feeling moments ago fell so hard I listened for the splash below my feet. "Okay..."

"What's going on, Sloane?" Mercedes whispered. "We're almost to the door."

"I know," Sloane whispered back. "But I don't want to ask this around anyone but you."

Now dread was really starting to set in. Sloane's arm unwrapped from mine, and the scratchy material of the long-sleeve sweater she lent me rubbed against my arm. Then, she grabbed a hold of my hands and gave them a quick squeeze before rushing up and pushing my sleeves past my wrists.

I jerked back from instinct, trying to unwind myself from both her and Mercedes.

"What are you doing, Sloane?" Mercedes' voice was still low enough that if anyone were to come up behind us, they wouldn't hear, but to Sloane and me, it was like a rubber band snapping in the wind.

I began shoving my sleeves back down, knowing that it

didn't really matter because it was so dark that no one would be able to see.

"Why do you do that?" Sloane asked, ignoring Mercedes. "Why do you hide your wrists?"

Mercedes gasped, and my brows furrowed with confusion.

"Gemma." Her voice was sweeter this time, and her hands found their way back to mine. "Are you...suicidal?"

I paused before Mercedes broke the heavy silence. "You can talk about it, okay? It's important to talk about it. We're here for you."

My mouth opened, then shut, and then it opened again. "I'm not suicidal."

That wasn't to say it hadn't crossed my mind once or twice in the past, but only in the darkest pits of my head did I ever have those thoughts, and as soon as I'd said them, the voice of Tobias would cut through with his steel armor and sword, slashing them away no sooner than they came in. *Survive, Gemma. Just survive.*

And I would. I'd spend every one of my breaths trying to survive, just so I could find him.

Neither Sloane nor Mercedes said anything, and it was probably because they didn't believe me. I couldn't blame them, though. I was quiet and kept to myself a lot. I disappeared for hours at a time, and I couldn't imagine what they'd think if they ever saw my sketchbook.

"Then why do you shove your sleeves down? Why do you never wear a t-shirt or undress in front of me?"

"It's not because I'm hurting myself," I answered with full honesty, and I wished I could tell them the actual reason I shoved my sleeves down. The words were on the very tip of my tongue, and for the briefest of seconds, I almost said them.

"Then why?" Sloane asked, completely dumbfounded. If I could see her face, I bet she'd look skeptical.

I sighed. "Because I broke the rules." I sucked in a sharp breath, intertwining my fingers with both Sloane's and Mercedes' through the sea of darkness. I began pulling them farther, and once we reached the door to the party, I squared my shoulders and raised my chin. "And good girls don't break rules."

CHAPTER THIRTY-FOUR

GEMMA

A GUST of air whipped my straight hair around as I pulled Sloane and Mercedes into the room. The party was in full swing. Everyone's faces were familiar to me now, and it seemed as if we were the last to arrive.

Sloane's hand clamped on mine as the door shut behind us. "What does that even mean?"

"What?" I shouted over the loud music, eyes catching on the dancing lights that fluttered around.

"What does breaking the rules have to do with your obsession with pulling your sleeves down?"

My mouth clamped shut, and after a few seconds, Sloane swung herself around and cut through my view of carefree classmates.

Her black-winged eyes dropped slightly, her pink lips frowning. "Are you sure you're not..." She looked to the left as someone walked by. As soon as they were out of sight, I took my hand from Mercedes, who was still holding on tight, and I placed my palms on Sloane's hardly covered shoulders.

"I *promise* you I'm not hurting myself. That's what you think, right? That I'm..." My voice trailed off as I tried to remember what I'd learned in psychology class during those brief months at Wellington Prep. "Cutting?" I said this as a sort of question because I couldn't remember if that was the correct terminology.

But I must have been right, because Sloane briefly nodded.

"I'm not." I smiled gently, seeing that there was the smallest flicker of sadness in her eyes. I wondered what that was all about. She looked sad for a moment...or affected. "There is a reason I cover my wrists, but that's not why."

Mercedes' hand touched my arm. "You don't have to tell us all your secrets, Gemma. But please come to us if something like that happens. Okay? If you...feel alone."

My brows crowded in, and even with the chaotic happenings around us, I felt a sort of bond form between our trio. "I promise," I answered, suddenly feeling very lucky to have them by my side even if I knew I wouldn't be able to reach back out to them after I left St. Mary's for good.

They shared a worrisome look but both ended up shooting me a little nod before my hands fell from Sloane's shoulders. We clasped hands again, catching the eye of a few other groups of students who all stared at me like I'd shown up naked instead of in what I actually wore.

My eyes glided over my outfit, and my stomach tumbled. There was a lot more leg showing tonight than at the last party. And even though I wore a skirt during the day for class, I'd always worn knee-high socks so there was only a thin sliver of thigh peeking most days. But tonight, Sloane had talked me into wearing her ankle boots—Doc Martens was what she'd called them, completely baffled that I didn't know the name. She'd lent me a black mini-skirt that hit mid-thigh but had a gold zipper down the back that seemed overly accessible to anyone who'd try to sneak up on me from behind—like Bain. A shiver danced over me when the brief memory of the last party crowded the edges of my mind.

As Sloane and Mercedes pulled me toward the back of the party, I scanned the open space for him. My feet stalled when I found him standing against a stone pillar with a few unfamiliar guys standing nearby. He was leaning his broad shoulder against the casing, looking just as dangerous as I suspected him to be. Cropped hair close to his skull. A thin scar over his cheekbone. Handsome smile, which was extremely deceiving.

I kept my gaze on his when he found me, as if he knew I was staring at him from afar. His eyes were a deep amber that looked like they'd burn me if I went near. One cheek lifted in a half-smile/half-snarl, and chills raced over my skin. *Shit, maybe Isaiah was right.* I needed to be more alert, especially when sneaking to the art room in the early morning.

"Damn, ladies," a deep voice said from up ahead, stealing my attention away from Bain. I could still feel him staring, though, like his eyes were leaving a trail of warnings over my body. "You three look downright edible."

Warm pools of honey greeted us as we stopped walking. Sloane pushed the guy's shoulder, letting her hand fall from mine. I briefly recognized him, and I was pretty sure he was in my Chem II class. His skin was dark and rich with a smile so bright I felt like I'd been touched by the sun. "How would you know? I wasn't aware you knew what a lady tasted like, Mica."

He tsked a couple of times before grinning at Sloane. "Sure, I do. How would I know that I didn't particularly enjoy the taste?"

I kept my face steady as I tried to comprehend what they were talking about. I had a very strong feeling they were using code. Sexual innuendos were not my thing.

"How could you not like the taste of pussy, though?" This came from behind Mica, and I swiveled around to see the Rebels coming to the group. My heart locked in my chest as I caught the eye of Isaiah who had already spotted me.

Heat kissed my cheeks, and the room seemed to shrink around us. He wore dark jeans and his usual Vans, but he looked more casual tonight. Instead of wearing a shirt like he'd worn last week, showing off his toned arms, this week he wore a zipped-up jacket and had the hood pulled over his head just far enough that it made me pause. My fingers nearly twitched with the need to shove it back from his face.

His famous grin made an appearance, and I swore his hand reached right into my chest, and he squeezed the life right out of it. *Shit*. He had an effect on me. A really big one. One that I wasn't very familiar with. It was like standing on shaky legs or like being pushed underneath icy water and not knowing how to swim.

"Enjoying your night off from tutoring?"

I shrugged just enough that my sweater fell off my shoulder, allowing musty air to dance over the bareness of it. Isaiah's eyes immediately shot down to it, and I watched as a swallow worked itself down his throat. "I guess." My voice was a tiny squeak, and I internally cringed.

Isaiah's head slanted. "You guess?" His eyes were filled with something that caused me to taste that tiniest bit of anticipation on my tongue, and for the life of me, I couldn't figure out what it was. Or what it meant. It was like the last few nights of us "tutoring" in the library with nothing but the sound of his tapping pencil against the thick wood and my racing pulse had led me to this moment right here, where one heated look from him had the small bundle of nerves in my belly exploding to full capacity. "We can always leave now and get back to..."—he took a step closer to me—"tutoring...if you want."

My eyes narrowed as Isaiah's grin grew wider. *Was he toying with me?* Was he making it seem like we weren't tutoring when we said we were? What was he playing at?

Mica, who had moved out of the way some, whistled loud enough that it cut through the music and my racing thoughts. "And suddenly, I wish I *was* into girls. I think I just got a boner watching you two talk."

Sloane threw her head back and laughed as Shiner blew out a breath. "Fuck, I think I got a boner too."

I knew my face was beet red, and I wasn't sure if I was more angry or embarrassed. Once again, I was in the dark with whatever the hell Isaiah was doing at the moment. It was like the lacrosse game all over again, when Isaiah leaned in to kiss my cheek and put on a show for people. Was that what he was doing? Putting on a show again? For Bain? Making people think that he and I were up to something so they'd watch us closely and keep Bain from interjecting himself? I knew the blog had been mentioning Isaiah's and my tutoring sessions, as if there was something else going on.

Isaiah shot Shiner a quick glare. "Shiner."

Shiner winked at me secretly, and I held back a smile. I actually liked the rest of the Rebels, even if they did walk the halls like they had crowns upon their heads. I mean, I did see Shiner throw a serious punch earlier today at the lacrosse game, so I guess I could see why some people stayed out of their way, but over the last few days, the Rebels had been exceptionally nice to me. Cade even introduced to me a game on my phone during lunch this week, and we'd been playing back and forth for the last two nights. I was beating him, and it felt really good to beat someone that seemed to be perfect.

Isaiah sighed agitatedly once more in Shiner's direction before he took another step toward me. The group had parted some, and his walk was more of a prowl than anything else. I swallowed back the need to glance away, knowing that it would only show how confused I truly felt in the moment. But as soon as Isaiah was close enough that his chest brushed against mine, everything else seemed to fade away. There was definitely a shift in the air. I could feel it. Eyes were on us. All of them. They tried to prick my skin, but as Isaiah's hands fell to my hips, a shield that was impenetrable locked down around us.

"What are you doing, Isaiah?" I whisper-seethed, realizing the music had grown softer at some point within the last ten seconds. "Is this another repeat of the lacrosse game? Everyone is going to start labeling me as—"

"Mine." The black hood on top of his head had fallen back, showing off those black-framed blue eyes that sent an icy burn whipping through my body. His fingers around my waist were splayed out, and I was almost certain he could pick me up in one single whoosh, and it would be nothing to him. His hands were large, and my waist was a perfect fit.

My breath caught as his head dipped to my ear, a dark lock of his hair brushing over a sensitive spot. I was suddenly in a frenzy, wanting to pull him in farther, but I was too rational to do so. I wasn't sure what was happening, but my body was feeling all sorts of things, and I was toeing the line of staying in the present and jumping back to the past. *You will remain untouched.*

Richard's voice was like whiplash, but I was quick to dodge the blow.

Stay present, Gemma. Just stay present.

This time, I didn't really care what Isaiah was playing at. I was going to let my instincts lead and push away the uncertainty of right or wrong. This one was all me. I wasn't listening to anyone but myself right here and right now. Not Richard. Not even Tobias, as his last words filtered through. *Survive, Gemma. Just survive.*

"I'm going to kiss you, Good Girl." My mouth opened,

and a rush of heavy-laden breath surrounded us. "Because right now, I need people to know you're mine. I found something today and..." My back curved as his soft lips swiped at my skin. "Just trust me, okay? I'm going to kiss you, and I'm going to act like I'm claiming you." His lips were moving over my ear like some type of synchronized song, and I was falling for it. Every last word. "There is no way I'm letting you out of my grip with Bain in the room." He paused, and I was pretty certain the entire room swayed. "Are you okay with that?"

My hands clamped down onto his wrists, my chest brushing over his. I leaned up on my tiptoes the second he pulled back and placed that dangerous gaze on me. My lips moved over his ear slowly. "I don't know how to do this," I whispered, briefly catching the eyes of our friends at his back. "But I am okay with it." *Was I okay with this?*

Slowly, I placed my boots back onto the ground and peered up at him with a realness that I hadn't shown a single person in this school. I was being completely and utterly transparent with him, even if it did make me feel inexperienced and frazzled. My blood hummed, my heart beating so hard I felt it in every crevice of my body.

He caught the eye of something or someone behind me, but it was fleeting. "You don't know how to do what?" There was the tiniest pinch in between his eyebrows, a small show of confusion on his features.

Another bout of warmth washed over my body as the room grew tighter. Was the music off now? I was pretty sure the music was off. "Kiss," I finally said, glancing to his lips as my chest caved in. "I don't know how to kiss."

His mouth opened almost instantly, those picture-perfect lips parting. His hands around my waist tightened, and his jaw locked. Then, his lips tipped, and his eyes grew hungry. "I thought so. I remember the look on your face when I asked the other night. But don't worry," he said as his hand came up and wrapped around the back of my head. "I'll teach you."

And then... And then he kissed me...and I was floating. I was floating just as high as the butterflies in my stomach, and I didn't care if my feet never touched the ground again.

Isaiah kissed me gently at first, his lips firm but soft at the same time. His hand gripped my hair, and a strange noise left my mouth, and that was when my feet seemed to touch back to the ground, but only for a quick second, because as soon as I caught up to what my heart was doing in my chest, his tongue jolted out, and he licked the seam of my lips, and mine opened without even realizing it. And then...I began kissing him back.

It was a bittersweet feeling. I knew it was fake and that Isaiah was just kissing me like he'd kissed other girls, but it replaced every other time my lips had been touched.

This wasn't my first kiss, but it was the first kiss I'd ever *wanted*. And that meant something to me.

Isaiah's growl vibrated my cheeks as his tongue swept against mine. His grip was death-like around my hip, and something new and hot pulled at my core. Before I could stop myself, my teeth nipped at his bottom lip, and if it weren't for the lights suddenly going dark, I would have pulled back and apologized.

A voice that I'd heard before—Brantley?—flew through the room over the speakers. "I guess we can let that moment right there declare the time for claiming. I think we're all ready now. Lights go back on in one hour. Remember the rules. Don't touch people who don't want claimed. And pick wisely."

"Fuck, Gemma," Isaiah murmured against my lips. "*Fuck.*" Then, his hand clasped with mine, our fingers intertwining instantly, and I was being pulled so fast I could hardly keep up. My eyes hadn't adjusted to the room. Everything was dark, especially with it being underground, but panic didn't creep in like usual.

In fact, the only thing I was thinking about was how my lips were tingling and how every inch of my body was on fire.

I wanted more. Something as forbidden as letting someone like Isaiah touch me and kiss me should have left me feeling tainted and fearful. After all, that was what had been pounded into my skull from a very, very young age. *You are to remain untouched and pristine. Otherwise, you'll end up just like your mother, with a corrupted mind and a twisted heart.*

But after one brush of Isaiah's lips over mine, he could have been the devil asking me to give up my soul, and I would have.

Isaiah just started something that I would make damn sure to finish. His lips made me feel unstoppable.

Richard said good girls didn't break rules, but he could watch me break each and every one.

CHAPTER THIRTY-FIVE

ISAIAH

THE LOCK on the door clicked, and everything intensified. The room was just as dark as the basement had been, but I knew my way around. My hands pushed Gemma's tiny frame up against the back of the cool, concrete wall, and my knee pushed in between her bare legs.

The skirt. The fucking leather skirt. My fingers twitched to unzip it from behind, but I knew I was getting ahead of myself. In fact, this was going against the entire fucking plan.

Kiss her, claim her, bring her in a side room, and ride out the rest of the party letting everyone think you fucked her. That was the plan. Make everyone talk and draw their attention to her, because the more eyes on Gemma meant that Bain would be forced to take a step back. The students at this school were far more loyal to me than they were to him. If he even dared to step too close to her after everyone thought she was mine, they'd rat him out within seconds. Some would even interfere. He'd have more eyes on him than ever. I wasn't confident that the plan would work to its fullest potential, but I had to do something. I had to deter him somehow, especially after finding the photos. This was a plan that was orchestrated by me and the rest of the Rebels. It was all we had at the moment because, unfortunately, Bain was untouchable, per my father's recent orders.

A soft whimper echoed against the stone walls, and I was suddenly brought back to the present. Gemma and I were both still heaving at a complete standstill with our sudden lack of oxygen. My hands touched her soft, warm skin, and my dick was as hard as a rock as it pushed up against her belly. So badly did I want to hitch her legs around my hips and grind myself onto her warmth.

I wondered if she was wet. I wondered what she'd do if I crept my hands up her thighs and pushed a finger into her tight pussy. Would she let me?

Just as I had the thought come through, Gemma jumped up, and her legs were around my waist as if she had read my mind. My head spun, and blood rushed. *Jesus.* Gemma said she didn't know how to kiss, but her tongue was back to being tied with mine, and sexy-ass noises were coming out of her mouth, and it was making me lose control.

I never lost control.

But fuck me, Good Girl was wrapping her tiny little hands around my body—and *Christ,* maybe even my soul—and making them her own.

The strangest pull in my stomach had me faltering for a second.

Fuck. I'd never felt like this. I didn't know what to do with it.

I pulled my mouth from hers, sucking in a chestful of air.

"What the fuck," I said through choppy breaths. Gemma's small frame wiggled in my arms, her warmth radiating to my jeans, and I threw my head back, letting out a ragged breath.

"What?" she asked, her voice heavy with about as much lust as I felt.

My fingers dug into the bare flesh on her legs, and she sucked in air.

Put her the fuck down.

"You!" I growled, fingers still biting her skin.

Lights. Where the fuck were the lights?

I moved us quickly, feeling for the door and then the light switch. A soft glow basked the room from the light above our heads, and I felt the dilation of my pupils as I stared down at her lustful green eyes and swollen lips. The apples of her cheeks were flushed, and when I trailed my eyes down to her split legs around my waist, her skirt was pushed up just far enough that I could see the color of her panties. I almost fell. My knees shook. The entire fucking school shook.

"I'm putting you down."

Hurt flashed behind the lush green, but just as quickly as she looked hurt, she looked...disappointed? Her plump bottom lip jutted out, and it was a swift punch to my dick.

She was pouting, and a twisted part of me wanted to bite that pouting lip. *Fuck yes.*

Was this the Gemma that she liked to hide? The one I caught a glimpse of every once in a while? The one that sat so quietly behind the good-girl act?

Physical pain soared through me as I put distance between us. Her fingers fumbled with the bottom of her skirt as she pulled it down, hiding the marks my fingers had put on her. "Why did you put me down?"

"Why did I put you down?" I asked, almost roaring. My back flung toward her as my hands gripped the back of my neck tightly. Then, I spun around and gave her a look that had her mouth shutting. "You said you didn't know how to kiss."

She nibbled at her lip as she pulled her chestnut-colored hair to the side. "I know."

"You lied!" I snapped. I didn't like to be lied to.

Her gaze flew to mine as she bit back a response. "I did not!"

"You honestly cannot stand there and tell me that I was your first kiss. If so, then you were a fucking stripper in your past life." *So hot. It was so fucking hot.*

Gemma's shoulders stiffened, and a flicker of something went across her face. "I never said that you were my first kiss."

A burning, fire-flaming zip of jealousy slashed up my spine. It was irrational and without logical reason, but that didn't make me any less aware that I wanted to rip any person before me who'd had the opportunity to kiss a girl like her to fucking shreds.

Her shaky voice seemed to ground me. "I said I didn't know how to kiss. Not that I hadn't been kissed."

I thought over her words carefully, repeating them in my head as my hands fell to my sides. "So, then you have been kissed. I wasn't your first?"

Conflict was evident on her face. Her beautiful, angelic traits, even with the rare bout of makeup on her features, pulled together with confusion. "No. But...yes?"

I pulled back, my hands shooting back up to my neck. I felt as tight as a string on a fucking crossbow. "That makes absolutely no sense."

"I know!" she snapped, obviously trying to work through something as she began pacing the small room. There was nothing in her way except for a dingy, tattered couch that had enough cum on it that I could smell the dried sperm before even stepping foot in here.

"I'm confused," I finally said after following her every move. Was that what I was feeling? Confusion? I was defi-

nitely feeling something, but it was so new I couldn't decipher it.

She stopped and spun on her black boots. I caught the
smoothness of her leg and felt the rise of my dick again. *I
wanted her.* I felt wild, staring at her from across the room. My
chest started to heave again as blood pumped harder.

I licked my lips, and she placed her hands on her hips, just
underneath the cream sweater that was now only half tucked
into her skirt. "You're confused?!" she shrieked, and I took a
step toward her. "*I'm* confused!"

My head slanted. "Why are you confused?"

Her eyes shot to every last corner of the room before she
grabbed onto me. I was closer now, and I hadn't even remembered walking the rest of the way over to her. "Because this is
all so new to me! And I like it! I like it a lot, and I'm not
supposed to. It's something that I was taught was *so* bad for
so long."

Bad? My hands reached out for her when she squeezed her
eyes shut, bringing her shaky hand to the bridge of her nose.
Her words were like rapid missiles shooting out of her mouth.
"And it's not even real. You were kissing me because of Bain,
right? I'm just another pawn in a game, and it's whatever... I
know that you're trying to protect me or put more attention
on me so he'll leave me alone or...whatever—"

"Who said it wasn't real?" I interrupted her before she
could get any further.

Two big, beautiful green eyes flew open and snagged me.
My hand came up and rested underneath her chin. My thumb
rubbed her swollen bottom lip, and every nerve ending in my
body stood erect. "This situation is...unorthodox. I know. I
asked you to tutor me and to cover for me when I needed to
leave the grounds so I could have a way to dodge being
caught and expelled by the SMC and still do what I needed to
do..." I glanced away, knowing very well I shouldn't have been

bringing her further into this shit, but she deserved to know the truth—something that I had been contemplating since Tuesday. "I'm here at St. Mary's because of Bain." I couldn't even look her in the eye as disgust and anger filled me. "My father sent me here to report all there is to know about Bain and his father. You want to talk about a pawn? That's exactly what I am. Bain leaves the school, and I follow him. That's why I need you to cover for me and to have a reason to be in the halls after curfew. It's why I leave the school. My father and Bain's father are *bad fucking men*."

Gemma jumped as my words grew angrier, but I continued to hold her chin in place.

My gaze left the couch, and I found hers again when her soft voice echoed in the room. "I know all about bad men, Isaiah. You don't have to explain anything else to me."

My jaw clenched as I fought to keep myself from kissing her again. Gemma was not a pawn. I wouldn't let her be. That was exactly what Bain was trying to do. He wanted to use her against me just like I suspected he was trying to use Journey against Cade, for whatever fucking reason that was still unknown to me.

"I kissed you in front of everyone to put on a show; that part is true. But kissing you wasn't fake. What just happened was anything but fake." I swallowed, licking my lips. Even with the impossibility of her and me ever being anything at the forefront of my head, I couldn't help myself. My body was aching to have her. My heart was beating fast with an intensity that made my blood sing. It was much more than attraction. I wasn't dense. There were things I was feeling that were buried deep below the surface, and that in itself should have pulled me away from her. But instead, I got closer.

I bent my head to hers, shoving any last thought of Bain, my father, the future that awaited me, and the secrets she was keeping away. It was just her and me, locked away in a room underneath the unmoving halls of St. Mary's Boarding School. Something shifted inside my chest, and I craved to know if she felt this way too. She was my little mystery girl. I was bending in half without knowing the things that went on behind those green eyes. Things were moving so quickly. The ability to deny the hole she was carving with just a single glance from across the dining hall was long gone. *Fuck, I needed to touch her.*

Gemma's back curved as she pressed herself to me, and her doe-like eyes nearly stole my breath away. My tongue darted out as I licked my lips again, my chest growing tight as it begged me to shut the fuck up. "We probably shouldn't go here, Gemma." Our eyes caught, and the room was caving in. "It won't last. It can't go anywhere." My mother's face was crowding the outskirts of my memory, and again, that right there should have been the push that I needed to step away, but I didn't.

"I know," she whispered, darting her eyes from my mouth and then back to my face. "I'm leaving this life behind one way or another."

I nodded sternly. "And I can't leave mine."

A short breath came from her sweet mouth, and my eyes shut as I inhaled. "That's the whole point, right? Keeping you here at St. Mary's. Keeping you from being expelled?"

I didn't answer her because I couldn't get my thoughts to stay in that straight, controlled line that they never veered from.

"Isaiah?" My eyes opened in an instant as I locked onto hers. The green pulled me in quickly. "Will you kiss me again?"

My hands around her waist grew firmer until it felt like she was the only thing I'd ever need to ground me. *Shit. This was so bad. So fucking bad.* "My uncle told me not to corrupt you, Good Girl." I knew, staring down at her soft expression and perfect parted lips that she was about as innocent as they came. She may have kissed me like she was made for me, but she had exuded innocence from the first moment I laid eyes on her. And I wasn't going to lie...it was fucking tempting. I wanted to grasp her purity in my devilish fingers and dirty her in every way. I wanted to make her body respond to mine and no one else's.

"And you're going to listen to your uncle?" The sincerity in her question made a deep, throaty chuckle float out of my mouth.

"I never listen to what my uncle says. I will kiss you over and over again until you tell me to stop." *And maybe not even then*.

The smallest lift of her lips made the room tilt. "Good."

CHAPTER THIRTY-SIX

GEMMA

ISAIAH'S EYES shut as I sucked in a shaky breath. His hand splayed out over my torso, resting along the bare skin of my stomach. The feel of his palms on my body was all-consuming. I was suddenly aware of everything he was doing and nothing else. The hardness of him that should have scared me but instead excited me. The way his breath was like a feather brushing against the crook of my neck. The feeling of his chest moving against mine. And at some point, his head had dropped, his hair tickling the side of my cheek as his warm breath coated my flesh, making goosebumps rise on the ends of my arms.

Before I could panic and rethink the last few moments, Isaiah's teeth scraped over my collarbone, and a jolt of something hot rushed through me, canceling out the hidden threats of Richard that laid ever so quietly in the back of my head. Isaiah's presence gave me a fraction of safety...of normalcy, and I was running with it.

"So, you've been kissed," he asked as his lips pressed

against the side of my throat, right over my pulse point. Everything inside of me came to life, and a need so hot was causing my back to bow and my breath to quicken.

What the hell was he doing to me? I'd always thought I'd be afraid or too nervous to actually enjoy myself if I ever got the chance to feel another's touch. But I wasn't afraid. Not at all. I was exhilarated. I wanted more.

"Ye-yes," I answered, tilting my head to the side to give him more access.

"But have you been touched?"

Such a difficult question, and one that I would rather not explain.

Isaiah pulled back just a fraction. The hard planes of his chest still moved against mine. He waited with patient eyes as his grip tightened. The cut arches of his cheekbones were flushed, and his eyes were nearly feral. He was dangerously attractive, standing in front of me like that. Like...like he wanted to consume me.

I swallowed as I let the bitter question leave my mouth. "Touched how?" I knew I was avoiding some of the truth, and he probably knew that too.

Isaiah's eyes had darkened, like a hooded veil covering the depths of his blue hues. "If you have to ask, then the answer is no." He paused, taking his palms from my waist and cupping my hands in just one of his. He pushed them up above my head, and I fought the urge to glance at them to make sure my sleeves were still covering my wrists. "Or..." He was looking at my lips now instead of my face. "Whoever touched you before...didn't know what they were doing. They didn't know just how unworthy they were to have you in their grasp."

His lips were a breath away from mine, and I tipped my head. "But...you do?"

"I know how to do a lot of things, Gemma, which probably makes me that much more unworthy of this moment right here."

He wasn't unworthy. He had no idea what unworthy was. He had no idea the vile things that had been whispered into my ear as my knees hit the cold, damp floor of a dirty basement tucked ever so nicely underneath a pristine house with my wrists in heavy chains. If I thought hard enough, I could still feel Richard's length pressed against my back as I cried from hunger. The desperation in my shaky voice as I apologized for something so completely innocent, like holding my brother's hand. I could sense the way he got off on punishing me. The man I'd never thought of as a fatherly figure *loved* to watch me beg for his help. He loved having me at his mercy, and when I turned eighteen and was back in his grasp, I was sickened with the thought that I'd be at his mercy, and he'd get on with his sick dreams of having me the way he had my mother.

Fury, fear, and rebellion wrapped around my body like a vise grip as Isaiah's lips hovered over mine. "Teach me," I pleaded. The words were jutted out like a sword thrusting forward into its opponent. My mouth brushed against his, and he let out a noise that made my stomach dip. "Teach me what feels good, Isaiah."

"We're going down a rocky path," he answered, pulling back just a second before his lips touched mine again. Sparks flew, and I felt my hips jerk toward him all on their own.

He pulled back and shot me a dark look. "Do that again and I'll end up destroying you." His free hand landed on my hips as some sort of warning. His fingers dug into my skin, branding me as excitement flared within. "I'll make you feel good, Gemma. But trust me when I say you are not ready for what your little hips are trying to do."

He was likely right, but he had no idea how desperate I was to rebel. My body and mind were in sync for what seemed like the first time in my life, and I was rioting on the inside. I wanted to live and breathe in the freedom that I had in this very second. I didn't want to think about the future, or the looming threats, or even finding Tobias. I just wanted to...feel. I wanted to feel like I did when Isaiah kissed me. I wanted that high. I was hungry for it. Things were coiled tightly in my lower stomach, and I wanted them to unravel. I wanted Isaiah to pull the string that was keeping me bundled so tightly.

Before I could plead with him, his palms went underneath my skirt, and he touched the curve of my butt just below the lining of my panties. His fingers gripped the soft skin as he hauled me up against the wall and kissed me feverishly. His wet tongue ravished mine, and I was pushing up against him, and he was pushing right back against me. There were no second thoughts between us. When one of us moved, the other did the same. We were like magnets, unable to pull apart, completely captured by one another like we were ensnared in a trap of hungry kisses and hot touches.

"Do you feel that?" he asked as he hauled himself back for a fleeting moment. My pulse had quickened, and my legs prickled. "Do you feel that burning need inside of you, Gemma?"

My answer came out as a rushed breath. "*Yes.*"

His chest rose as his fingers dug into my skin once more. His jaw ticked, and his voice was as raw as I felt on the inside. "That's how you should feel every time someone kisses you. If you don't feel this way down the road, when you grace some guy with what you're giving to me... You fucking leave and go find someone who elicits this feeling inside of you."

Wow.

At some point during our kiss, Isaiah had let my wrists fall free, and my fingers found their way to the back of his head and intertwined with his thick hair. "Is this how you're supposed to feel?" I asked, fighting the urge to look away as my inexperience and vulnerability came crashing down. "Is this how you feel when you kiss other girls?"

Did it always feel like this? If so, I now understood why everyone got so excited about Claiming Night.

Isaiah's wet lips glistened under the dim light. "No."

The answer shocked me. "No?"

He shook his head slowly as his sharp gaze landed on my lips. A swallow worked itself down his throat, and his next words were nothing more than a whisper. "And you've ruined all future girls for me now." He paused as we locked eyes. "*Shit.*" Then, his mouth was on mine again, and the room was spinning, and all my thoughts vanished. Everything was gone except for Isaiah and the feeling of something so enticing licking over my core.

A soft noise came out of my mouth as Isaiah continued kissing me, moving away from my mouth so we could catch our breath every so often and nipping my ear and my neck, and it was honestly too much to handle, until there was a sharp knock on the door. Both of our heads snapped to attention, and panic cut through me so deep I half expected to be bleeding.

"Isaiah," came a bark through the thick slab of wood. I was pretty sure it was Cade, but I couldn't be certain. My thoughts were so fuzzy that if Isaiah didn't also look at the door, I wouldn't have even trusted that the knock had happened. For all I knew, it could have been my heart thudding to the ground. "Did I finally get your fucking attention?"

Isaiah's tone was as sharp as a whip. "Cade. What do you want?"

Isaiah glanced back down to me, staring directly at my lips like he wanted to kiss me more. "We have a slight problem. He's on the move."

A curse left Isaiah, and his face looked pained as he

glanced at my mouth once more. Hope crashed and burned around me, and I felt the disappointment come between us. The second Isaiah let my legs down, cool air brushed over me, and I felt...damp.

"Fucking hell." A groan left Isaiah as he righted my skirt on my hips and then ran a hand through his hair rather aggressively. "You're..."

My attention flew to him. "I'm what?"

I stood on shaky legs and felt...different. Branded? Less pure? Tainted?

No. I wasn't tainted. I wasn't. Even if Isaiah and I had done more than kiss, I wasn't tainted.

Richard would definitely think that if he ever found out. His words were an echo in my head that seemed to climb out of the darkest areas of my mind. *You are to remain untouched. You belong to me. You are mine.*

But I wasn't his. I wouldn't be. Determination ran through my blood like I was born with the primal notion. The submissive little angel Richard had created was slowly self-destructing, and it gave me the tiniest bit of leverage.

There was a time in my life where I had believed everything that came out of his mouth. I obeyed his rules and thought true to his threats. He told me that if I didn't allow him to punish me, to take care of me, that I'd end up just like my mother. *Dead.*

But it wasn't true.

It was all a fucking lie.

Just like it was probably a lie that my mother had been mentally ill. An omission of the truth. Over the years, I thought long and hard about my mother and her behavior. I was so young when she left that it was hard to grasp onto what was real and what had been fed to me from such an early age, but if my mother had gone through what Richard had put me through (was *currently* putting me through) maybe he was the reason for her illness—if there ever was one to begin with. Maybe he broke her so deeply that she couldn't remember how to put herself back together.

Trepidation started to creep over my shoulder as the thoughts began pulling me under. My mind was trying to remember her laugh or the song she used to sing to me and Tobias, but I was quickly ripped away from the memory when a hand landed on my arm.

"You okay?" Isaiah's other hand found my chin, and I blinked rapidly, focusing on his thick eyelashes and stern gaze. "Where did you just go?"

"Um..." A shaky breath left my lips. "Nowhere. I'm here."

He shook his head once, and a dark tendril of hair fell over his forehead. His brows knitted. "I thought you said you trusted me." I said nothing, and I was pretty sure he was waiting for me to say something. Anything. But I didn't. I couldn't. "I know you're running from him, Gem. But why?"

Another rap on the door sounded, and I jumped. "Isaiah." Cade's voice was less playful and more urgent. "If you want to follow him, you better go now."

"Bain?" I asked as Isaiah's hand fell to mine, and he began pulling me beside him.

Just before he opened the door, he shot me a wicked grin. "Wanna go on a field trip?"

"As in leave the school grounds?"

"Mmhm." He swung the door open, and Cade locked eyes with him before he glanced over at me.

"And what if we get caught? Who's going to be your alibi when your alibi is right there beside you?"

He shrugged once, looking his usual cool, calm, and collected self before that dimple appeared on his cheek. "We better not get caught then, huh?"

CHAPTER THIRTY-SEVEN

ISAIAH

Silence stretched all around us as Gemma placed her shaky hand in mine. My fingers collided with hers as she walked beside Cade and me through the darkness of the party.

I whispered into her ear, "Stay quiet. I don't want people to know we're dipping out early."

"Early from the party?" Her voice was hardly audible.

I straightened my back as Cade answered, "The Claiming."

Sounds of kissing and soft moans came into contact with the three of us as we swiftly made a beeline for the exit. I knew my way around this basement even with the blanket of darkness that surrounded us. My hand reached out as I touched one pillar, then another one, and then one more before I knew we were exactly three yards from the door.

Skin slapping against skin and a flirty giggle came from the left, and Gemma's light gasp filtered out into the heated air. It smelled of sex and alcohol, just like any other claiming, but it was new to her.

Everything was.

A throb settled deep inside my tight core as I let myself picture what was underneath her skirt. She was wet. I could feel her pressed up against me. I had the sudden urge to pull her back into that room and shut Cade out to spread her legs and taste her perfect little pussy.

What an obsessive, wildly hot thought.

Fuck, what was it with her? Gemma had awoken something inside of me, like an unbinding of my most secret desires. A sense of protectiveness and possession came over me the second my hands touched her, and it was a dangerous thing.

It was risky bringing her with me right now.

I knew that.

Cade knew that.

Mixing business with pleasure was likely going to fuck me over in the end, but here I was, shoving her through the door and pulling her along the musty, damp underground hallway made of wet stone and cobwebs.

"You're bringing her with you?" Cade asked, hinting at disappointment.

"She'll be fine," I answered, my hand clenching down on hers. "Who's trailing him?"

"Brantley," Cade answered as we walked briskly through the dark. "As soon as you and Gemma began that very, *very* convincing kiss, he snuck away."

"Goddamnit," I mumbled. "He does know I'm onto him."

I still hadn't informed my father that Bain was suspecting something, mainly because I didn't want to deal with the weight of his words right away. But I knew I had to let him know. I just wanted to be one hundred percent certain Bain knew I was watching him—or at least, that was what I was telling myself. Maybe I hadn't told him because I liked feeling as if I had some type of control, which I didn't. Not really, anyway.

Nonetheless, Bain waiting until I was preoccupied before dipping out was smart and calculating. I had a big feeling he would do it, though. Half the time when I'd follow him, he wouldn't do anything other than drive around in circles before parking his car down the street near the abandoned warehouse and walk back to St. Mary's. The students weren't allowed to have vehicles here, but Bain always had a backup parked down the street. Every once in a while, the type of car would be changed out and the tracker we'd place on it would go rogue, but we still managed to trail him. He was paranoid. Or maybe it was his father's paranoia. Either way, he was a deceitful little fuck.

"Have you told your father yet?"

"No." My answer was as short as it was abrupt, and a second later, I heard Cade sigh. Then, a second after that, we pushed through the doors, and the cool air of the hallway clung to my hot skin.

Gemma stood between Cade and me, staying as silent as a mouse. Her brown hair framed her stoic face, her eyes showing nothing at all.

I pulled my hoodie back onto my head and jerked a nod to Cade. "Let Gem wear your jacket."

I needed her to be in something dark. Her black skirt worked, but her light-colored sweater would catch an eye if we had to hide.

Cade sighed disapprovingly as he unzipped his dark-gray jacket and shrugged it off his shoulders. "You're seriously bringing her with you?"

Gemma shifted nervously and glanced to the floor.

Cade held out his jacket to her and ignored me while saying, "It's nothing against you, Gemma. It's just that Isaiah is being fucking *reckless*." He shot me a glare. "And you could end up as collateral damage."

A throaty laugh erupted from my chest as I tried to remind myself that I wasn't my father, and I'd never act like my father. Sure, I was the Huntsman's son, and I was viewed as the next boss, meaning not only would my two best friends work for me, but so would their fathers—if they managed to stay alive that long—but I didn't want to power trip them. I never would. "You know I wouldn't let that happen, Cade. You more than anyone should know that."

A tick of pain hit me with the quick reminder of my mother and what had happened when she was caught in the crossfire. Cade knew all about it. He and his father had shown up later that night.

Cade's jaw tightened as he helped Gemma zip up the jacket. She stayed silent, and it irritated me not knowing what she was thinking.

"You don't always have that choice, Isaiah." He ran a hand through his hair. "And she's right. What if you two do get caught?"

"We won't get caught. I was careless before. You know this."

Why was I even explaining this to him? Why was I justifying myself to him? I glanced away, knowing why he was so concerned. And I should listen. I really should.

"We need to go. You know what to do if anything arises while we're gone."

Cade shook his head at me before winking at Gemma, and then he slipped through the door to head back to the party.

I grabbed onto Gemma's hand once more, and we began the long walk down the empty hallway toward my uncle's stone cottage.

It was right behind St. Mary's, just through the far left

entrance of the school. Our feet shuffled over the cobblestone walkway as the night air cooled our skin. Leaves rustled
with rising tension as if they knew Gemma and I were
sneaking away from the school in the middle of the night. Or
maybe it was a warning to me that I should send her back
with Cade. But fuck me, I liked having her near.

Stopping just behind the large trunk of a tree that smelled
of pine, I peered at my uncle's far left window where I knew
his bedroom was. This house was an old servant's house.
Small and subtle, nothing more than a bed and a small bathroom inside. But his car was parked just a few yards away in
the makeshift driveway. Gemma and I headed toward it.

My phone dinged, and with my free hand, I pulled it out
and read Brantley's text.

**BRANT: He's on foot. I see a new car up ahead. It's a
Bentley. I think it's his. He must have found the
tracker. Sending a pin.**

I SIGHED and shoved my phone back into my hoodie and
pulled my uncle's spare key from my jeans. Gemma stopped
dead in her tracks, the loose pebbles shifting underneath her
boots. "Isaiah. Are we really leaving?"

Placing a finger to my lips, I nodded once and then
opened the door to my uncle's newly restored '75 Mustang.
Gemma hesitated at first, and I felt the strangest little tug in
my chest at the thought of her backing out, of having to
follow Bain on my own—as usual—without her near. It was
fucked up. Cade was right. I was being risky and reckless. A
taunting voice in the back of my head whispered, "*Selfish.*"

A heavy breath left me as I came face to face with the
realization that I *was* being selfish and impulsive, knowing

very well that whatever it was I was feeling for her was never going to last. I wouldn't let it get that far. Nothing would change for me. I was still taking on the responsibility of my father's fucked-up empire, and I would never put someone like her in a position where she could end up as a suffering victim from the life I led.

I would never let it get to that, even if I could feel the pricking of deeper feelings underneath my skin. Gemma meant something to me—and in such a short time, too. It was fucking terrifying, and I didn't admit my fears easily.

The car came to life a second after I climbed behind the wheel. The engine was loud, but I wasn't worried about my uncle waking up and finding me. He knew I'd taken his car before and why. He likely wouldn't approve of Gemma being with me, but what he didn't know wouldn't hurt him.

"We could get into some serious trouble if someone catches us leaving the school," Gemma whispered, sitting stark still in the passenger seat. "Wouldn't that ruin everything?"

"Put your seatbelt on." I pushed the car into reverse and slowly began creeping away from St. Mary's. I flicked the lights on just as we made it through the entrance, the car dropping down as we rolled over the dip in the driveway.

Gemma's soft tone filled the dark interior after her seatbelt clicked. "Whose car is this? I didn't think students could have cars."

I chuckled, making a right turn to follow the pin that Brantley had sent me. "That's correct." I paused, scanning the street for any other moving vehicles. "It's my uncle's."

Her gasp made me smile.

"What?!"

I rested my hand on her bare knee for a quick second before putting it back on the wheel. *Bad idea.* "Will you relax? I thought you said you trusted me."

Her arms whipped across her chest. "You're totally taking that out of context."

"Ah," I murmured, still scanning the empty street. We were parked across from the address I had on my phone, wedged between a few other cars. "So you only trust me with my hands underneath your skirt. I see."

She gasped again, this time whizzing her entire body toward me. My lip jutted upward, and if it weren't so dark in here, I knew her face would be a *lovely* shade of red. "I...I..."

A laugh started to creep up my throat, and as soon as it was out in the open, bellowing from my mouth, she sighed. I was pretty sure she was trying to act annoyed with me, but instead, her cheek twitched, followed by her smashing her lips together.

My laughing eventually stopped when I watched a midnight-colored Bentley prowl through the entrance of a dilapidated warehouse and whip out onto the road, taking a right up at the stop sign. I crept my foot along the gas before speeding up just far enough that I could keep eyes on which direction he'd gone but not close enough that he'd see me.

Or maybe he had seen me.

Unlikely. But it was possible.

My phone dinged in the cup holder, and I caught Gemma's eye. "Read that to me, will you?"

She looked shocked for a split second before she uncrossed her arms and pulled the phone to her face. "It says it's from Brantley. He says he remained unseen."

I nodded once, and she placed the phone back down and re-crossed her arms. After a few more seconds of tense silence, her voice cut through the stuffy air. "Why am I with you right now?"

My eyebrow hitched as I kept my eyes on Bain. "Do you not want to be with me right now?"

"I didn't say that." She waited for a moment and then

shifted in her seat. "But what if you get caught? You're on probation. Isn't that the whole reason why you have me? To cover for you when you...follow Bain?"

I put my blinker on and turned left, slowing down a little as Bain's speed had decreased.

Gemma didn't give me a chance to answer her as another question popped out. "Do you make it a habit to sneak out of St. Mary's to follow Bain? Is this where you go when you leave tutoring early?"

"So many questions," I deadpanned.

"Isaiah!" she shouted, and I couldn't help but smile. *God, she was cute when she was feisty.* "If I'm going to get in trouble, I better know why!"

"You won't get in trouble, Gemma. I wouldn't let that happen."

She threw her hands out and pushed her lithe frame into the leather seat. "If we get caught, we will get in trouble!"

"We can just say we're studying the stars if they catch us walking back into the school later. Astronomy." I fought the smile wanting to crawl onto my face.

From the corner of my eye, I could see her shoulders slump. "So that's why you brought me? You're still using me as your cover?" She paused. "Do you even take astronomy?" I didn't, but that was besides the fact.

I caught her staring at me intently, and instead of answering her, I threw a question at her. "Aren't you using me too, though? You need fast cash and an ID, right?"

She quickly glanced away, unable to come up with anything to say because I was right, even though we both knew that it was total bullshit, especially now after crashing our lips together for the world's hottest fucking kiss to ever exist.

Bain made another left turn, and I was beginning to think we were going in circles again until he made another turn, and we started on a winding road. There were three cars in between us, making it difficult to keep my eyes on his blacked-out Bentley, so when I spoke next, I kept my attention on the road. "I'm not using you."

Her voice was soft, and I could hardly hear her over the sounds of the car. "You're not?"

"It's a shame that you even have to ask that question after what just happened. And I wouldn't have brought you if I thought we'd get caught." I swallowed back the regret I knew my next words would bring. "I brought you because I like having you near."

"Oh," she whispered, glancing down at her intertwined fingers. It took a moment for her to speak again, but when she did, there was a swift change in the air. "Why do you have to follow Bain for your father?"

Gemma's hands unclasped, and her arm brushed against mine as she placed it on the center console. Even through our clothed arms, I felt the heat. "That's a question I can't answer."

"Can't or won't?"

My response was quick. "Won't. Just like you won't answer any of the questions I want to ask you."

A moment passed before she nodded. "Fair enough." And then an easy silence came over us. It was as if she knew that we were crossing over into those dangerous depths of questions and answers that neither of us wanted to get into. It was so fucked of me to bring her tonight, and even more so if I were to start filling her in on everything that my life entailed. It was better if she were left in the dark on this one.

"So..." I glanced at her, and she caught my eye. Need pulled deep in my stomach as my arm brushed hers again. "Are you liking St. Mary's?"

An abrupt, choppy, squeal-like laugh left her lips, and I snapped my attention over toward her for a second before putting it back on Bain's Bentley. "What?" I asked. "Why are you laughing?" And why did I feel my lips turning upward at the sound?

Her light laugh filled the car again, and it was like an awakening. Why haven't I heard her laugh before? My chest was twisting, and I suddenly wanted to make her laugh again.

"Because..." She dropped her head so low that her hair fell forward, but I could still hear the amusement. "We go from talking about sneaking out of school to follow Bain on some secret mission, and now you're asking if I like St. Mary's?"

My fingers flexed on the wheel. "Don't forget the whole kissing and touching thing before all of this."

Out of the corner of my eye, I noticed how she brushed her hair away from her face, and without even looking, I knew her face was flushed. "Right. How could I forget that?" Then, she began again. "Let's see... My first few days here, I've been shoved inside a closet with the school's most popular bad boy, had a rumor started that I was the new slut of St. Mary's, then I was dragged underneath the school to my first-ever party, and someone attempted to *claim* me before I even knew what that meant, and I ended up with a concussion later that night. Oh, and then I was shoved in another closet after curfew. *And* I somehow started tutoring said bad boy from that first day of school...which really isn't tutoring at all, so..."

I finished for her. "So basically, you fucking love it."

Her laugh was loud, and I grinned. "Actually..." She leaned her head back onto the head rest. "I do."

"Let me guess." I sat up a little taller, squinting through the mist that fell onto the windshield to see where Bain had pulled into. My stomach knotted, but I didn't let Gemma see my concern. "Your favorite part was being shoved into a closet with me on the first day. Am I right?"

Her smile lit up the whole goddamn interior. There was a

glossy gleam to her eye, and at some point, she'd raised the hood of Cade's jacket, making her look adorably mischievous. Most of the time, she looked so focused and stoic, almost sad at times. But tonight? There was a glow around her. A carefree spirit that was just begging for a taste of life. Maybe it had something to do with what had happened earlier.

I wanted to kiss her again.

In fact, I wanted to do a lot of things to her.

Putting the car in park, Gemma glanced out the window. "Where are we?"

My fingers flexed around the wheel. I glanced through the windshield once more and held back a growl. "Somewhere I hope you never learn about."

The Covens.

Why the fuck was Bain at the Covens? Was his father supplying guns here now? This was my father's domain. The Huntsman's. This entire city was my father's, and when he learned that Bain had been over here, he would go on a rampage to find out why. This was grounds for a fucking war.

Gemma's voice brought me back down to the ground as my thoughts began jumping. "*The Covenant Psychiatric Hospital.*" Her head turned away from the window as the sign for the hospital glowed brightly against the wet glass. "Why is that so familiar to me?"

Ice coated my veins. A hand squeezed around the muscle inside my chest. *No.* "Maybe you've driven past it?" A million and one questions rushed to the tip of my tongue as I began fishing for information. It wasn't common for someone to know of this place. It was a psychiatric hospital, yes, and in the front, it looked like any normal facility for the ill. But on the backside? Underneath the floors of those who truly were sick, it was hell. Pure fucking hell. If Gemma knew what the Covens was, then there was a lot more to her than I thought.

"It's unlikely that I've ever driven past." Gemma seemed

to think this over before giving me a quick, fleeting glance. "Before St. Mary's, I didn't really get out much."

I wanted to continue digging and asking questions, but time was getting away from me, and I had a job to do. It was the whole reason I was at St. Mary's and the whole reason why Gemma and I were thrust together in the first place: to keep me here, to feed information to my father, and to keep Jack safe.

I left the car running as I pulled my hood up further onto my head and opened the door. A gust of wet rain rushed in, and I turned toward Gemma. "Climb over here, and keep the car running."

"Wait, what?" she asked, eyes wide and completely shocked.

"I'll be right back." I tapped the top of the car. "Honk if something goes wrong."

Then, I climbed the rest of the way out and watched as she began climbing into my seat. The door slammed as she started to protest, but I knew time was a fleeting thing, so I jogged through the slashing rain droplets and ducked behind a bush, just far enough that I could see through its wet branches.

The hairs on my arms stood erect as I stared at the side entrance of the hospital—the same one my father took me to when I was Jack's age. I knew the inside had lights so bright they could burn your irises if you stared too long and that the hallway reeked of body sweat, blood, and tears that was hardly covered up by antiseptic. My nostrils flared as my mind tried taking me down memory lane, the pinch of my neck still twinging like my father's hand was still there, gripping it, making me watch, breaking that last tiny bit of innocence that I still had in my youth.

Jack entered my head as I stared ahead through the drooping branches of the bush, rain drops clinging to the leaves for dear life. I watched as someone came out of the entrance of the hospital, letting the metal door shut loudly behind him. He was a stocky man, wearing a nicely pressed suit, so I knew right then that he wasn't one of the employees. He didn't have that distinct color of scrubs on: blue for the psychiatric part of the hospital and black for the Covens. I pulled my phone out and zoomed in on Bain backing his Bentley up to the door underneath the awning. There was a bright light that flickered above the man's head, allowing anyone to see clearly.

I snapped several photos of Bain climbing out of the driver's seat and rounding the Bentley with his trunk popped, then a few more as Bain pulled out a bag and rested it on top of the car. Then, out came a sleek, black pistol, and my stomach plummeted as a twist of anger clung to my bones. *Now he's doing his father's dirty work?* It wasn't hard for me to grasp the idea of Bain working alongside his father, because I knew just how dark and deceitful this life could be. And if Bain were anything like me, he'd feel as if he had no choice. But that was the thing with Bain. Even if given a choice, he'd still take his father's side. Bain loved power. The potency of it was clear on his face as he and the man talked back and forth, turning the gun in their hands like it was a gift straight from God.

They were corrupted men.

Both of them.

I wasn't a saint, and I'd witnessed things that I wished I'd never seen and regretted not stopping, but I, at least, had the humanity to feel guilt and torment. I, at least, had the ability to recognize humanity for what it was.

But men like Bain, my father, his father, even Brantley's and Cade's fathers...they looked down upon others and didn't care who got hurt.

A human life wasn't much to them. If it were, then the Covens would be burnt to the fucking ground.

They wouldn't allow torture and the breaking of a person's mind to fester like it had.

They all got off on it.

It made me want to walk over and snap their necks in half.

Maybe that made me as bad as them, but punishments were vital to the world when someone deserved them. And they all did.

After I clicked another photo of Bain handing off several guns to the mystery man, I pushed my phone into my pocket and began to stand up. The ground was slick against my shoes, mud sloshing as I turned my back to get back to Gemma.

That was my first mistake. *You never turn your back on someone with a gun, son.*

The sound whirled past my ear, and for a moment, I paused. *Was tha—?*

The next thing I knew, I was taken to the ground by my own subconscious ability to save myself from getting shot, and then I was ducking and rolling and climbing to my feet before running like hell to get back to Gemma.

That was my second mistake: bringing her here.

What the fuck was I thinking!

I wasn't sure if Bain had spotted me or if it was security. The Covens was highly protected on the inside, and it wouldn't surprise me if it were protected on the outside, especially with a goddamn gun exchange.

My heart lurched as I heard another pop of the gun, and it killed me to have to run right toward Gemma, but I had no other choice.

Cade's voice rung out in my head. *"You're being reckless."*

Reckless should have been my middle fucking name.

My breath was ragged, and my shoes were hardly keeping traction as I skidded to a stop right beside the car. I flung the passenger door open and flew inside.

Gemma was sitting in the driver's seat, and as soon as she saw me, I shouted, "DRIVE!"

CHAPTER THIRTY-EIGHT

GEMMA

I FROZE. My lungs had stolen my ability to breathe.

"Gemma!" Isaiah was completely wet from head to toe. His black hair was even darker than usual as it stuck to his forehead. Tiny raindrops clung to his lashes, and they stayed even as he opened his mouth and yelled, "Gemma, drive!"

A loud noise rang out through the air. *What the heck was that?*

"I can't drive!" I panicked, looking down at the wheel as if the leather would burn my hands. There was panic in his voice, and it only took one look from him to know we were in trouble.

"What the hell do you mean you can't drive?" Then, his hand gripped the shifter in between us. "Gas is on the right, brake is on the left!"

Blood rushed through my body so viciously I itched.

"It's life or death, Gemma! Go! Now!" Then, he popped the car into drive, and my foot moved off the brake, and I slammed onto the gas. The tires spun under wet asphalt, and then we whooshed forward, rushing down the street.

Something from behind sounded again, and Isaiah cursed. "Let off the gas for a second."

I did as he said, my foot completely coming off the pedal, and then he reached over and jerked the wheel to the left, and we went flying onto another street.

He wasn't paying much attention to the front of us but more so behind us. He kept his tight grip on the wheel from the passenger seat, but I was able to straighten it for us before pressing back down on the pedal.

"That's it, Gem. You're doing great. Keep your foot on the gas."

Isaiah was looking out of the side mirror, his jaw set into a tight, firm line. I didn't look for long, though, because the reality of the situation was weighing down on my shoulders, and I needed to keep us on the road.

I'd run before, on foot, but I knew what it felt like to be in a life-or-death situation, and there was no time for worry or second-guessing. What I was feeling was parallel to what I'd felt before, and I knew I'd do what was needed to get us far away from whatever it was he was running from. *Bain?*

"More gas," he urged, his large hand still on the wheel. He glanced out the front for a second before he went back to the mirror. Both of our bodies flew back onto the leather seats as I pushed us forward, trying my hardest to keep us straight on the road. The rearview mirror was too far up for me to see, and I was lucky I'd messed around with the seat while Isaiah was looking for Bain, otherwise my feet wouldn't have hit the pedals.

"Fuck," he muttered under his breath. It was so angry sounding that it sent a wave of caution to my ears. "I need to get you out of here."

"Us," I corrected, pushing even harder on the gas as my

gaze stayed steady on the road. There weren't any other cars in front of us, but up ahead, I saw the white lines curving, and my stomach revolted. *Gas? Or brake?*

"Isaiah, what do I do?"

He snagged a quick look to the road before he answered, "Let up on the gas. I'll turn for you."

My breaths were coming in hot, but I tried my hardest to focus on the task at hand, even with the nagging feeling of being chased scratching at my back. Although I'd been in a similar situation, where I'd been chased before, it didn't make matters better even in the slightest. My body was still just as panicky as it was then, and for a moment, I swore I could still feel the twigs slashing across my arms and legs, my skin burning with the cuts.

"Gemma," Isaiah's voice cut through my foggy brain, and I shook my head. "Breathe. I can feel your slip on the wheel."

I stuttered, shaking my head. "I'm—I'm sorry," I urged through clanking teeth. *Shit, I'm doing it again!* "I do this sometimes."

My fight-or-flight instincts were coming in like stinging slaps against my skin as I decided to fight. I'd fight against the panic. The fear was an exact mold of what I'd felt before. The dread of being caught and the pain that would come with it. It was maddening.

Isaiah turned the wheel for me as I focused on even breaths and letting up on the gas. My foot hovered over the brake and accelerator before he straightened the wheel. "Gas!"

My foot slammed down as my hands gripped the leather.

"You do what sometimes?" He turned the car for me again, although I was pretty sure I was getting the hang of it. Though, I had yet to come to a complete stop, so I knew I probably still needed his guidance.

"I sometimes space out. Black out. Remember with Bain

at the last party? When there is panic rising and it's too familiar to what I've felt before, I…"

He jutted through my confession. "You've run for your life before, Gemma?"

My answer came out before I could stop it. "Yes." Then, my hands squeezed again, righting the wheel so I was in between the lines of the road. "Is that what we're doing? Running for our lives?"

Isaiah's hand dropped from the wheel, and instead, he rested it on my knee. My leg jumped, and little sparks flew to the very tips of my toes. He didn't look at me, still leaving his stern gaze on the side mirror. "I shouldn't have brought you. I'm sorry."

It seemed the panic in his voice had lessened some. He was still glancing out the side mirror, but his jaw was no longer hard like stone. I focused back on the road, the dotted white line growing more blurred as my speed increased. "It's okay."

"It's not okay." I could feel his gaze on me like a million little spotlights. "And how the hell have you never driven before?"

I laughed—actually laughed. "Well…" I began to turn the wheel a little as the road had a slight curve. Isaiah's hand left my knee, and he helped guide me. "No one has taken the time to teach me." That wasn't the whole truth. Richard didn't want me to know how to drive. Just another way I needed to rely on him and ask for his help.

"There is no way I'm letting you leave St. Mary's without having the skill to drive. I'll teach you."

Something bloomed in my chest, and although I could feel the remnants of anxiety still brewing under the surface, a smile graced my lips. "There's no way you're *letting* me leave? I wasn't aware that I needed your permission."

He shrugged. "You don't need my permission, but you do need money and a new ID, so..."

I didn't respond because *yeah, he got me there.*

"We're almost back at St. Mary's," Isaiah said. "Keep up on the gas, though. We're not being followed anymore, but I don't want a run-in with anyone."

I nodded as my foot continued pressing onto the gas. So badly did I want to ask what exactly he was running from and why he was in a life-or-death situation from following Bain to a psychiatric hospital of all places, but I didn't. I knew how it felt to have secrets you couldn't reveal. Not to mention, I had my own answers that I needed to figure out. Like why that psychiatric hospital had felt so familiar to me.

"Make a left then roll into the school slowly. Switch the lights off."

I paused, letting up on the gas and slowly turning my wheel.

"Nice work, Good Girl. You're a fast learner." Just as the compliment came out, he chuckled because we both lurched forward from my foot landing heavily on the brake.

"Sorry," I said as I lifted my foot back off the pedal and inched it onto the accelerator again.

I saw the lazy half-grin appear out of the corner of my eye. "You have nothing to apologize for. In fact, I think you're pretty fucking amazing."

It felt like I'd swallowed my heart. Then, I stopped breathing as Isaiah reached over my body, his damp hoodie brushing over my cheek as he flipped a switch to turn the lights off. Once he was back in his seat, I managed to breathe again. "Amazing at driving? I think you're lying to make me feel better."

His large, warm hand rested back on my bare knee again, and he tapped the inside of it, making me see spots. "I'm not referring to your driving skills."

My mouth opened as a rush of something hot flung to my cheeks. I caught his eye as I glanced over at him, trying to read what exactly he'd meant by that, but then his eyes widened, and he shouted, "Brake!"

Brake?

Isaiah's hand left my leg, and he slammed it onto the middle shifter just as my foot slammed onto the pedal. We both jerked forward, but he was quick to push his arm out to my chest to keep me from colliding with the wheel.

My fingers covered my mouth. "Oh my God! Did I just wreck the headmaster's car?!"

It only took one second for Isaiah's loud laughter to fill the interior. His head was thrown back, his strong jaw catching devious shadows from the lack of light.

Oh my God. "Isaiah! This is all your fault!"

He laughed harder. His shoulders shook as he put his fist up to his mouth to stop himself. I stared out to the stone wall I had run into before slamming on the brake. I felt a shower of embarrassment and fear come down on me like a thousand bricks.

"You are truly fucking amazing," he said through more broken laughter.

"Amazing?!" I shouted. "Isaiah! Never mind the fact that we just snuck out of St. Mary's, but we also just wrecked the headmaster's car! And..." I took a shuddering breath in between my rant. "I don't even have a license! I've broken every rule possible tonight!"

Never in a million years did I think coming to St. Mary's would end up in me wrecking the headmaster's car, in the middle of the night, with someone like Isaiah beside me. Never in a million years did I think I'd be so...careless. Not to mention the fact that I was so blindly ignoring the conse-quences that could follow. But even with all of that, I could feel the amusement bubbling on the inside. It was totally the wrong time to be smiling or laughing, but my cheeks ached to do it.

"Relax." Isaiah was still chuckling with a smile on his face so large it could compel me to do anything if I looked too long. "It's only rule-breaking if we get caught, which we won't."

Then, he opened the door and climbed out effortlessly, taking my panic with him. Sloane had said that the Rebels were dangerous, and Isaiah was just that. He was so incredibly dangerous because he muddled my brain anytime we were alone. Rational thoughts evaporated, fear slowly dissolved, and dread no longer existed. The only thing that did exist was him and my wildly chaotic heart that seemed to soar higher than ever when he was beside me.

As soon as I climbed out of the headmaster's car, feeling the mist of cool rain dampening my hair, Isaiah's hand clasped mine, and we jogged through the wooded area until we got back to the school.

"You are insane, Isaiah," I whispered as he pulled me closer to his body, continuing our conversation. "It's still rule-breaking, even if you don't get caught."

"Says who?" he asked, glancing behind us at the tall trees. "And don't tell me you didn't enjoy breaking the rules."

I didn't answer him as he pulled me the rest of the way through St. Mary's door. He was right. I did enjoy it. I enjoyed it too much.

"You think I enjoyed being chased and then wrecking a car in the process?"

"I sure do," he whispered along my ear, making me jump a little. The farther we walked into St. Mary's, the louder the silence became. Our wet shoes squeaked as we walked along the shiny floors, but that didn't deter Isaiah from keeping silent. His hand still stayed in mine as he leaned in even closer to me, making me freeze. "Just like I think you enjoy it when I whisper in your ear."

He wasn't wrong. I did. My body flamed and ached in such a tortuous way that I was left speechless. It was so incredibly messy inside my head. Feelings and hormones were rioting so much that I stopped right there in the middle of the hallway.

I tipped my head up to his, both of us standing there with nothing but the flicker of sconces along the wall as our witnesses. Isaiah stared down at me, a devilish grin gracing his undaunting facial expression. Things were shifting. I could feel it.

"We shouldn't have kissed like we did earlier."

His sentence threw me off, and I felt my emotions slipping. His eyes didn't change, though. The swirls of blue still held a wealth of wickedness in them.

"Why?" I turned toward him even further.

His chest brushed against mine as he took a step closer, erasing any empty space that was hanging in limbo. His hand gripped my chin hard enough to gain my full attention but not hard enough to hurt. "Because now that I've had a taste of the good girl, all I want to do is corrupt her."

My stomach bottomed out, and my next words surprised me. "Then what are you waiting for?"

Isaiah's face darkened, his dark brows a cloak over his eyes, and then...and then I was spinning.

CHAPTER THIRTY-NINE

ISAIAH

I WON'T CORRUPT the good girl. I won't corrupt the good girl. I won't corrupt the good girl.

No matter how many times I said it, it wasn't getting through. My lips were on hers, and everything else was long gone. Her mouth was sweet and inviting and surprisingly needy. A growl tore up my throat as I pulled her small frame into my chest, and when she shuddered against my hard abdomen, I almost ripped her clothes to shreds.

Need like I'd never felt before drove through my body, mangling every part of me to distortion. I didn't care if she was fragile like my uncle had said. I didn't care if she was inexperienced or that she and I could never be anything more than what we were now. I didn't care that I was feeling something much stronger than desire whip through my blood.

Her kiss sucked me in. *She* sucked me in. A connection. We had something brewing. Something so big that it made everything else just...stop. Her tongue dragged over mine, and I pulled back to catch myself before I began inching underneath her shirt, as if we weren't in the middle of the fucking hallway, and that was when a thundering wave of awareness dragged over my shoulder. *Wait*. Faint footsteps pulled my attention, and I gripped her. We couldn't get caught. Not now. Not after realizing just how hungry I was for her. And possessive. And protective. And fuck, what was I saying?

"Let's go," I whispered, hurriedly pulling us through the nearby door. The second we were inside, I shut it quietly and spun around to check our surroundings. The dining hall was closed as it was the middle of the night, so the expansive area was quiet. The gleam of silvery moonlight shone through the arched windows, allowing me to see just enough to know that we were alone. I turned back to see Gemma nibbling on her lip, looking half scared and half excited. My mouth twisted a fraction, but it quickly disappeared as I saw a light shine underneath the door. *Shit*. Thinking fast, I snatched Gemma's hand, and a sweet puff of air left her mouth as I rushed us three tables down. My back was on the floor within a flash, and I pulled Gemma on top of me in a less-than-graceful way. She toppled and let out a little squeal, and before I knew what I was doing, I was silencing it with my mouth.

As my lips moved over hers, I was somehow able to pull myself from the impulsive behavior and began wiggling us both underneath the long bench and dining table. It was the same damn one I sat in all week, stealing glances at her as she sat with Sloane and Mercedes, looking damn near perfect while eating her oatmeal in the morning.

Gemma dragged her mouth from mine, and I placed my finger over her lips. "What the hell, Isaiah," she hissed over my fingers, her warm breath falling on my face. I inhaled and had to turn my head to stop myself from plunging my tongue down her throat again. "How did one kiss from you end up with me being under a table?"

"Because you're just as hungry as I am. You feel exactly

what I feel when we touch." My tone was hushed, but the validity to my sentence was in full force. Her body tensed on mine but quickly eased as I removed my fingers from her lips and pressed a quick kiss to the tip of her nose. "I like kissing you, and you like it too. There is no shame in that."

My heart strained, and I cursed the fact that her kiss was like a fucking truth serum. There *was* shame in that. I knew deep down that my words were truthful, but I also knew that we were destined to end in tragedy. It felt wrong to be feeding her my emotions, even if they were true, because she and I would never have something real. Even if she were a different girl who wasn't planning on dipping out of St. Mary's with a new identity and handful of money, I wouldn't go down this path with someone.

I needed to push back on the feelings that were there. I needed to stop kissing her, and touching her, and looking for her the second she stepped into the room. I needed to get off probation so I could stop using her as my way off the SMC's radar.

But need and want were two very different things.

Gemma opened her mouth to say something, probably to deny that she liked kissing me back, because I had a feeling she was going through the same emotions in her head, but the door to the dining hall creaked open, and she gasped. "Shh," I hushed over her lips that were still hovering over mine. "We're fine. Stay quiet."

Fuck, I wanted to kiss her again. And touch her.

A few moments passed before Gemma's mouth moved over my ear. "Why..." She spoke so low I could hardly hear her. "Why do I feel like laughing?"

My lips twitched as my hand slowly cupped the back of her head to keep her still. "Because deep down you like breaking rules with me. It's fun."

The softest, throaty noise left her, and she let out a soft

giggle. *Oh, shit.* "Gemma," I warned, also feeling a laugh bubble up in my chest. I saw the sway of light from a flashlight as the dining hall door shut loudly. Whoever was patrolling the halls tonight was suspicious, and I had a big feeling it was someone on the SMC, because why wouldn't it be with us shoved underneath a table in the middle of the night? Part of me wondered if I should have just let us get caught and tell the duty teacher that Gemma and I were walking back from tutoring, but it was late, we were far from the library, and I wasn't done with her yet. I didn't want the night to end.

Gemma's body started to shake on mine as she buried her head into my chest, holding back a laugh. I cursed the fact that we had to be quiet, because I wanted to hear her laugh again. It erased some of the darkness that rested inside me. Like a soothing balm. And I liked the fact that she wasn't panicking like earlier. Did she finally trust me and believe that I wouldn't let her get into trouble?

The light grew closer, and although Gemma's giggles were as quiet as a mouse, a small fraction of reality set in. We couldn't get caught. Even with my grades improving, mainly because I actually turned in my assignments now, I still needed to keep my nose clean. My grades would simply pacify the SMC, maybe sharpen their trust a little, but if I got caught sneaking out again, or alone with a girl shoved underneath a table in the dining hall at midnight—if I got caught breaking any rules, really—I would find my ticket out of here.

Gemma was still shaking on me, and her grip on my hoodie had tightened. *Fucking shit, Gemma.* I wanted to laugh just at the mere fact that she was laughing, but instead, I pushed my hips up and gained her attention. Then, I peeled her head from my chest and smacked my lips onto hers so hard it silenced every bit of laughter that was hanging on her tongue. It only took her a second to move past the shock and begin kissing me back, and although I kept my eyes open, watching the beam of light sway from one end of the dining hall to the next, the heat and intensity that her mouth caused on mine was electric. My hips moved, and Gemma's legs fell to the side slowly, letting my hardness touch her warm core, and *Christ,* I could feel the hot heat sourcing from the only piece of fabric that covered her. My hands gripped her hips to keep her steady so she wouldn't move over my jeans. The scratching noise would only bring more attention to us, and that was the last thing we needed.

Our lips moved in sync with each other, and Gemma must have caught the hint that we needed to be quiet, because there wasn't a single sound of smacked lips. Our kiss wasn't sloppy. Or rushed. It was slow, intense, and hot as hell.

As soon as the door slammed shut again and the beam of light was gone, Gemma pulled herself from my mouth. My hand left her waist, and I brought it up to my lips, telling her to be quiet. She nodded, and a piece of her hair fell forward, landing on my shoulder. The muscles in my neck stretched as I inclined my head and searched through the darkened floor to see if anyone was still standing there. I felt Gemma suck in more air. My hips had pressed up in the action, and she and I were like one. We were so close I could feel the burning throb all the way to my soul.

My eyes clung to hers, and for a second, we just stared at each other, eyes locked, bodies joined. Her chest had risen and stayed, her grip on my shirt never lessening. I gulped down a hot swallow, and then at the exact same time, our lips crashed together again, and our slow and steady kiss from earlier turned vicious and unforgiving. I didn't hold back this time. My hands were on her bare ass, the fabric of her panties bunching as I squeezed. Her hips moved over mine as if she knew exactly what she was doing. I suppressed a grunt and felt the need to growl as I nipped her lip with my teeth. We were moving so fucking fast I didn't have time to even ask if this was what she wanted. If we were going to go down this path, the one where we shared nothing but intense kisses and lustful touches, we were both going to go down afterwards. There was likely to be guilt, maybe even regret.

No. I would never regret kissing her. It was too hot and too pleasing.

I broke our kiss as I pushed us back out from under the dining table, allowing the open air to cool our heated bodies. As soon as we were on our feet, I picked her up underneath her skirt and placed her firm ass down on the slab of wood where we placed our trays for every meal, and then I shoved her legs apart.

"I told myself I wouldn't cross this line with you," I muttered through clenched teeth as her hands laid on my shoulders. "But then we kissed."

"And things changed," she finished, wiggling herself up to be closer to me. Our gazes met, and the air shifted. The truth was evident in her eyes. The same truth that I had. We both knew that this was something much more than a simple touch, and that it was something that would likely punish us in the end, but it didn't matter—at least not to me.

I wanted nothing more than her at that moment.

"Do you want to cross that line?" I asked, tipping her head back with the pad of my finger. Her long hair fell behind her shoulders, showcasing her rising chest.

She glanced at my lips. "I don't know what the line is...but I think I want to cross it with you." She swallowed quietly. "I told you earlier that I wanted you to teach me how to feel good, and that hasn't changed."

My one hand stayed on her delicate chin as she looked up at me with curious eyes. Her body language spoke volumes. The arousal radiated off her so strongly I could hardly focus on anything other than my own racing pulse. The innocent part of her was evident within her gaze, and I wanted nothing more than to take that innocent piece of her and distort it until she was fully fucked and unrecognizable. She was going to know what it felt like to be pleasured and treated like nothing less than a goddamn queen.

"The lesson is long," I started, gripping her knee that had somehow clenched around my hip. "But we'll start at the beginning." A rush of breath left her as my hand trailed up her leg and past the hem of her skirt. I watched as she squirmed under my touch and how her eyes darted away.

"Look at me," I pleaded, gripping her chin again. Once our gazes were joined again, my hand crept up a little higher. "It's okay to feel good, Gemma. If it doesn't feel good, then you deserve better."

A ragged, nervous breath left her mouth. "I was told that this was wrong...what you're doing to me...what I'm feeling."

My fingers stilled for a single second as I filed that little piece away for later. "They lied."

My other hand, the one on her chin, brushed over her slick, bottom lip, and I fought myself when I pictured devouring her mouth again. If I were kissing her, then I wouldn't see the wild hunger on her face as I dipped a finger into her. I wanted to watch her come undone. I wanted to be responsible for the flush on her cheeks.

Her eyes dipped as my hand reached the side of her panties. Her chest heaved. Her back bowed. Her hair flung out of her face, and the subtle moonlight shined directly onto her high cheekbones. Goddamn, she was fucking beautiful. Achingly so. It almost hurt to look at her.

As soon as I hooked a finger inside her panties, she shuddered. *So responsive.* "Isaiah," she whispered, peering up at me with wide eyes. She was already so fucking wet. My finger ran down her slick seam, and she whimpered. I couldn't believe no one had touched her before. Had they touched her before?

A raging dose of jealousy clawed at my back. I couldn't fathom anyone else watching this. I wanted her to be mine. The nerves were intensified in my stomach, and the overpowering protectiveness over her was coming alive in my very being as I stared down at her. "You're fucking beautiful, Gemma." I circled her clit gently, hardly keeping a hold on my steady pace. Rushing this wouldn't be smart. I wanted her to trust me with her body.

"It feels..." Ragged breaths left her as her cheeks darkened.

"*Good,*" I whispered along her lips before I kissed her breathless. Her tongue caressed mine like it was pleading for something, and that was when I pushed the very tip of my finger into her tight, wet folds.

She moaned against my mouth, the echo of it sending a shock of pleasure down my spine. Her hips jutted forward, and it surprised her just as much as it surprised me. My finger inched in even farther, and her hands gripped down onto my shoulders, her tiny fingers digging so hard I could feel them through my hoodie. Our kiss broke, and she threw her head back, gasping as I began to move my finger slowly in her tight embrace. "Do what feels good, Gemma," I whispered along the exposed skin of her neck. I knew what would make her come undone, but she needed to explore this feeling of euphoria. I wanted her to be comfortable, and *Christ* if it wasn't the hottest thing I'd ever seen with her moving her hips to meet my knuckle. *God damn.*

My lips kissed her soft skin again, and I had the sudden urge to suck on her neck, but I knew that would leave a mark, and although I wanted nothing more than the whole fucking world to know that I had left my mark on her, I knew it wasn't in our best interest—at least, not with the SMC. I didn't want them to know I was corrupting the good girl of St. Mary's. My tutor. But that was exactly what I was fucking doing. I was corrupting her, and it was so selfish of me, yet I couldn't stop myself. It felt too good.

"Oh, my God."

My hand moved underneath her shirt, and I felt the tight bud of her nipple against my hand, even through the thin cotton of her bra. Her sweet little pussy began constricting, and that was when I lost my hold on everything. I pushed my finger in farther and curved it toward the spot I knew she was itching for, and my palm brushed over her swollen clit. My mouth was on hers as her legs widened, my hand squeezed her perky breast, and I mumbled, "Unworthy. I'm so unworthy of this." I pulled back just in time to watch her mouth open and her eyes fly shut. I felt her come undone on my finger, and I knew right then I was fucked.

I was royally fucked.

Gemma Richardson had my soul.

CHAPTER FORTY

GEMMA

As soon as I came down from my high and Isaiah pulled his hand out from under my skirt, I flushed so hard I began to sweat. Or maybe I was already sweating before. I wasn't sure. I was incapable of coherent thoughts or sentences, which was exactly why I peered up at him and said, "Th—thank you."

His face split into the biggest smile I'd ever seen, and I wanted to die right then. Actually, no. I didn't. Because if I were dead, then I'd never get to feel what I just felt from his hand again. It was... I was speechless.

Isaiah stood back, peering down at me as I slowly brought my legs together. I was wet and sticky and nearly blinded by another round of embarrassment.

"What are you thinking?" he asked as he pulled his hood back up onto his head. I couldn't see the exact shade of his blue eyes in the darkened room, but I had a feeling they were dancing with amusement.

I sighed, adjusting my skirt as I still sat on the dining

table. *Oh my God.* What if the table was wet from me? "I—I don't know what I'm thinking."

His cheeky grin caught my eye. "That's a lie. Tell me."

"What are you thinking?" I countered, feeling bold.

He chuckled. "You are not ready to hear what I'm thinking."

He was wrong. I was more than ready.

Isaiah had come closer to me, causing my pulse to race so fast I had a hard time focusing. "Tell me what you were thinking," he urged, and there was something in his voice that tricked me into spouting off from the mouth like I had no control over it.

"I'm thinking that I want to do that again...with you." I slapped my hand over my mouth. *Did I just say that out loud?*

Isaiah's eyes clenched for a single second before his hands gripped my thighs, and he pulled me to the very edge of the dining table. My hands fell to my lap. "We will. I promise." He ping-ponged his attention to my eyes and mouth before sighing. "But it's late. We need to get back before the kitchen staff starts prepping for breakfast." He paused, staring at my lips. "And it's almost time for you to sneak out of your room and go to the art room."

My eyes flicked to his, and I paused. "How did you know that?"

A slight dimple appeared. "How do I know you sneak out of bed every morning before school to work in private?"

I nodded.

"You think I'm going to let you sneak through these halls alone after finding out that Bain has some sort of infatuation with you?"

My brows puckered. "He has an infatuation with me? I thought you said he just wanted to use me against you."

He shrugged. "Those two things go hand and hand, which is all the more reason why you shouldn't be sneaking through the halls in the middle of the night." Isaiah's hands gripped my waist, and he plopped me down onto the floor. "But since I know you won't listen, just know you're covered." He winked at me, and I quickly looked away before my pink cheeks gave me away as I pulled my skirt down. I glanced at the table where I was sitting, and when I looked back up to Isaiah, he was smirking.

Why wasn't I more embarrassed? Why wasn't I more embarrassed that Isaiah's finger, the same one that was currently touching mine, was just inside of me moments ago? Why was the thought of him going back to his room without me so disappointing? Why wasn't I looking forward to the moment I was free from my obligation of tutoring him? Because after that, came freedom. That should have been the only thing on my mind. Not Isaiah and what he just did to my body.

"Stop overthinking," he said before slightly opening the door to the hallway. He looked both ways and then pulled me through.

I stayed quiet as we walked through the halls, hand and hand. I was going to break free from his grasp once we reached the girls' hall, but instead, he walked me all the way to my door, glancing back behind us several times.

Once we were in front of my door, I slowly turned to face him with my heart trying to race right out of my chest. Nerves sprouted from the very bottom of my belly as I thought about kissing him again. "Thank you for walking me to my room."

I was sure he had walked me so we didn't get caught by whatever teacher had night duty this evening, probably the same one that almost caught us in the dining hall moments ago, but a small part of me wanted to think it was because he wanted to spend as much time with me as I did him.

"I'm sorry I took you with me tonight. It was reckless of

me." He dropped my hand and took a step away from me. "It won't happen again."

We stared at each other for a scarily long time, and each time I tried to sort my emotions and figure out what exactly I was feeling, I came up short. Because the truth was, I'd never felt like this in my entire life.

I felt different. Isaiah made me feel something big, and even though I understood why he was apologizing to me and why he was telling me that it wouldn't happen again, I still felt the sting of disappointment. It was like he was closing off a part of himself to me, and that was silly because had he even really opened up in the first place?

He had. He told me why he was at St. Mary's. He told me a little bit about himself, and I was certain it wasn't without caution.

He opened his mouth to say something, but I interrupted him. "Remember earlier when you said your father was a bad man? That Bain's father was? That Bain was?"

Isaiah's brows lowered, and he dipped his head in a nod. I gulped back the fear that was crowding my throat and took a step toward him, placing my hand on his hard jaw, splaying my fingers out over his warm skin. "And how I told you that I knew all about bad men?" Isaiah's gaze darted to mine as I whispered something so raw and unforgiving. "My uncle is a bad man too, Isaiah. And you were right. I am running from him."

His hands were around my face so quickly I stumbled backward. Our lips joined together as he cupped my cheeks hard, crashing my body into his with a speed that made my pulse pause. His tongue dipped in my mouth, and that same coiled feeling of sparks that I seemed to feel every time he touched me erupted in flames. Was it the weight of my words that made this kiss even deeper than before? Or was it all in my head?

Isaiah pulled away quickly as he backed me all the way up to the door, pushing my back against it. "Why did you just tell me that? Where did that come from?"

I gulped a lungful of air before saying the same exact thing to him. "You told me some of your truth, and you deserve the same from me."

We stayed quiet for a few moments before Isaiah ran a hand down his face. "We're going to go up in flames, you and I. You know that, right? This..."—he pointed at me and then to him—"is...different."

"Different?" I asked before shaking my head to bypass my question because it didn't matter. "I don't care if I go up in flames." At least here, at St. Mary's, I had the choice.

A quick breath-stealing kiss landed on my lips before he let go of me, and I was met with a shadow of something dark on his features. Torment? Pain? Regret? It was like a knife being lodged into my chest with either option.

"It would be a shame for someone as innocent as you to go up in flames, Gemma."

Then, he turned around and walked down the hall as stealthily as he had crept into my life.

———

SLOANE WAS SLEEPING when I snuck into our room, and I was grateful. I smiled at the sticky note taped to my pillow in her handwriting that read, *Details.* I knew she'd want me to spill everything that had happened with Isaiah, and I didn't want to lie to her. In fact, I wasn't sure what to say at all. Did I tell her about what he did to me? The kissing and the...other stuff? Did I tell her that we'd snuck out of St. Mary's and that I'd wrecked the headmaster's car?

No.

I would take that to my grave. I couldn't believe what the

night had held, and I especially couldn't believe that I didn't regret a single thing. Not even driving illegally with my heart lodged in my throat as someone chased us from behind. I was certain the adrenaline was still flowing throughout and that was why I was so calm at the moment. Tobias would be so proud of me if he knew of all the things I was doing. He'd always been the more daring twin. He used to tell me that I needed to live more and bend the rules. Figure out who I was. Which was probably why Richard hated him as much as he did.

As soon as I stripped out of my clothes and quietly washed up in the bathroom, paying extra attention to how swollen my lips were and how my cheeks held the faintest tint of red on them, I slipped into bed beneath my fluffy covers and replayed the night over and over again as I tried to fall asleep.

I should have been tired, and I was. It was almost three in the morning by the time I'd laid down, but there had been one thing nagging at me from the second I let myself breathe again: the conversation with Isaiah when we'd pulled up to the place that Bain had gone to. I knew there was more to that story than Isaiah had told me, but I wouldn't dig any further than I had. If Isaiah wanted me to know more, he'd tell me. He didn't expect me to tell him my life story, and I didn't expect him to either.

But what confused me the most about the entire situation was that the psychiatric hospital was vaguely familiar to me—like a photo in my head that was clear but tattered around the edges, leaving out the important stuff. And then there was the moment when I'd asked Isaiah where we were, and he said, *"Somewhere I hope you never learn about."*

But I had learned about it.

Or seen it.

Something.

Something had clicked when we pulled up to the dark, ivy-covered building. It was almost as creepy looking as St. Mary's.

I lay in bed for the next hour and a half, tossing and turning, in and out of sleep, willing the visual of the psychiatric hospital to rid from my brain. I'd even thought about Isaiah and his hungry kisses, but each time I'd let my mind wander, the nagging question popped into my head.

Why was it so familiar?

Then, it hit me.

I lifted the blanket off my body and peeled it away slowly, hoping the rustling wouldn't disturb Sloane. Though, she had hardly moved an inch since I'd gotten back into our room.

I pulled Cade's jacket around my shoulders, pushing my arms into the sleeves, smiling as I remembered how Isaiah had pulled the hood over my head as we dashed through the grounds of St. Mary's just hours prior. I tip-toed to my door in bare feet, slowly opened it, and slipped into the darkened hallway.

It was the same eerily silent corridor that greeted me each morning when I snuck out to head to the art room. Thankfully, I'd never run into anyone, but now that I knew someone was "covering" me, I'd made a quick mental note to make sure my back wasn't to the door when I sketched again. No one needed to see what was on my canvas.

It didn't take me long to roam down the stairs or to make it to the art room. I was usually already dressed for class on the weekdays when I'd come here, so the cool floor was jarring on my bare feet as I stepped through the threshold and headed straight for the supply closet.

The door thudded as I pulled it open, and it creaked so loudly I paused for a moment, looking over my shoulder. I half-expected Isaiah to be standing there, but instead, the only thing that moved in the distance were the dust particles as they danced through the air.

After walking a few steps into the supply closet, letting the smell of musty paintbrushes and mildew curve under my nose, I pulled on the tattered string and let the swinging lightbulb bathe the room in a faint glow.

The shake of my hand didn't stop me from pulling down my sketches from the past week, along with my art journal that I'd sketch in when I had any down time during the day. I now replaced most of my down time with the game that Cade had downloaded onto my phone, but that wasn't the point at the moment. With each piece of thick paper in my fingers, my stomach tightened at the things I found beautiful but also horrific.

The first was the sketch I'd done just two days ago, the charcoal still somewhat fresh on the paper. It was almost a blur if you were to look at it too quickly, but I knew by heart what it was even as I pushed it away. The spine of the girl, who I knew was me, was at the center of the sketch. Each vertebra was like a thick knot going down in a straight line with protruding ribs spreading to black smudges. Her head was bent down low with a messy bun of hair in fine detail on top, and the word *mine* was carved into the back of her neck as a thick hand laid on her bony shoulder.

I shuddered a breath as I pulled the next sketch out, which was the one that I'd drawn the first time I'd stepped foot in this art room as the sun still laid behind a blanket of night. It was half my face and the words *Good Girls Don't Break Rules* over and over again, line by line, floating down the other side of the paper.

I didn't even want to pull the last sketch out, so I didn't. Instead, I grabbed the leather binding of my notebook and flipped through sloppy pencil sketches until my throat tightened so quickly I lost my breath.

I knew it.

There, staring back at me, from just a few weeks ago when I'd first started at St. Mary's, was something I'd created in a lull of past trauma. I didn't remember precisely the moment that I'd drawn it, or why, because that was how it was when I took pencil to paper. My mind went to a dark place, and everything else disappeared except for the shunned-away memories that were hidden behind a thick wall in the present. My finger traced over the curved lines of the building, focusing solely on the smeared lead-written words that read *The Covenant Psychiatric Hospital.*

It seemed I was right to feel the sting of familiarity as Isaiah and I pulled up to the chilling ivy-covered stone building just hours ago...but why?

CHAPTER FORTY-ONE

ISAIAH

"Who is this?" I slammed my phone down onto my uncle's desk early Monday morning before anyone was up—well, anyone but Gemma. I already knew she was in the art room, drawing something with that adorable smudge of charcoal that was probably smeared across her soft skin by now.

My uncle sat at his desk and had no intention of moving as I stormed to the front and tossed my phone down.

"Did you wreck my car?" The crease in his brow was deep, but I knew it would lessen eventually.

"Not technically. Who is this man?" I asked again, nodding my head to the photo from Saturday night of Bain handing off a black duffel of guns at the Covens. "Do you recognize him?"

My uncle made no move to look at the phone. Instead, he continued staring up at me with distaste in his eyes. *Jesus Christ. Fine.* I pulled back, leaving my phone on the desk and sitting in the leather chair in front of him. "I didn't wreck your car. Gemma did."

His eyes grew wide. "What?!"

Shame filled me as I glanced at the books on the shelves, too guilty to even look him in the eye. I wasn't afraid of what he had to say about that. But I did feel shame and guilt rock through my body like an avalanche. Cade's, *"I told you so,"* echoed in the back of my skull like my own personal cadence after I'd filled the rest of the Rebels in on Sunday morning.

I glanced back at my uncle. "She recognized the Covens."

His eyes grew even wider. "Wait, you took her to the Covens?" His face was a shade of red that sent a mild line of concern through me.

"Let me explain before you start throwing shit."

His teeth clanked so hard I heard the clink from across his desk. *Impressive.* "Bain had left during a party. So...we followed him. I took your car." I gave him a pointed look. "And don't act surprised. You know I take it when he leaves randomly through the night. Anyway, we followed him."

My uncle's brows were still crowding his face, his jaw molded of marble as he continued to clench it. "And he went to the Covens?"

I pointed a finger at him. "Bingo. But why does Gemma know of the Covens?" An uncomfortable feeling split my chest open, and it shouldn't have surprised me that I was more concerned with how Gemma knew of the Covens versus Bain selling guns in my father's area, but the shock was still there. "If she knows about the Covens..."

"What did she say about it?" He paused, pulling my phone toward him. *And we were past the wrecked car...just like that.*

"She said that it looked familiar to her. But she didn't know why."

"What happened after that?" His eyes squinted as he zoomed in the photo on my phone.

"I got out to take some photos for Dad and told Gemma to slide into the driver's seat, just as a precaution. You never know what you're going to get with Bain involved. And then..."

"And then what?" he snapped, gripping my phone so hard I almost leaned forward to pry it out of his hand.

"And then someone started to chase me." I paused, not wanting to say the next words. "With a gun. So I made a run for it, and Gemma and I sped off. She wrecked because, apparently, she's never driven before." I held back a tight laugh even though it was more sad than anything. "Something I was not aware of until we were in a very compromising situation."

Silence encased the room as my uncle glared down at the screen. It had long since grown dim and eventually shut off. The second the screen was black, his eyes snapped to mine. "That was an incredibly dangerous and stupid thing you did by taking her with you."

"I know," I bit out, not even attempting to deny it.

His hand slapped down onto the desk, but I didn't flinch. I wasn't afraid of my uncle or his temper tantrums. He wasn't my father, by any means. "No. You don't understand." He pinched the bridge of his nose. "The man in that photo is Judge Stallard."

I stopped breathing. My heart seized for a moment, and then the anger came rushing in. "Wait." *Judge Stallard.* The room suddenly seemed colder.

My uncle's hoarse voice scratched at my confusion. "Tell me he didn't see her with you."

"No. There is no way. He was with Bain when I was spotted by someone. My guess is the Covens' security."

He seemed to relax a little before asking, "Did she see him?"

"No. She saw nothing. She did know we were following Bain, but I haven't given her much more than that. I don't want to drag her into this."

"But you have, Isaiah. By taking her with you. What were you thinking?" His expression showed a small amount of pity, and I looked away. "Have you learned nothing from what happened to your mother?"

Anger began to rise again, and I clenched my hands down onto the arms of the chair. "Of course I fucking have! I was there!"

"Then, why are you being so careless?" His voice boomed throughout the room as he stood up and rounded his desk. I didn't dare move in my seat. I didn't even look up at him. If I did, I was too afraid I'd lose the hold on my emotions and start breaking things like a child. I was feeling more and more lately, and I fucking hated it. The numbness I usually felt was gone. Instead, frustration, anger, and maybe even fear were working inside my stomach, and I fought to keep my breathing controlled.

"I thought you and her were just friends—well, that was until I saw the latest blog post. Something about you two and a party? Sneaking away? Was that when you left and followed Bain?" He shook his head. "Don't tell me..."

That stupid fucking blog. I ignored the alert I got this morning, too eager to get to my uncle's office.

I snapped my attention to him. "Don't tell you what?"

"Is that why she agreed to help you? To be your tutor? Are you making her think she's someone special to you? That you care for her?" He scoffed, pinching the bridge of his nose again. "Let me guess, you're fucking her...*goddamnit*. I told you not to mess with her, Isaiah!"

I inhaled a deep breath and glanced down at my shoes. Even if I wanted to explain things to him, I wouldn't know how. It wasn't why she agreed to help me, and I wouldn't tell him why she had, but there was a blinding light in front of my eyes that almost pushed me to tell him that I did care for her.

After a few more deep breaths from me, I took my eyes

off my shoes and placed my stoic expression back on my uncle, only to pause. "Why the fuck are you looking at me like that?" My brows pinched as he clasped both hands and leaned back onto his desk. "Unless..."

"Unless what?" I snapped, leaning forward.

"You do care for her." He hummed out a sound as my sharp glare caught the framed map behind him. *I do, but fuck, I shouldn't. I couldn't.* The admission was there in my mind, but I wouldn't say it out loud. If I said it out loud, then I couldn't take it back and act as if it never happened when our time came to an end. Because it would.

"Gemma is fragile, and there is a lot to her that we aren't aware of. You shouldn't be messing around with her, whether you care for her or not."

"She is not as fragile as you think, Uncle Tate." She wasn't. There was definitely a lot she was hiding underneath her shyness and rosy cheeks, but being fragile wasn't one of them. And she was smart. And courageous. Little did he know, Gemma had a plan. A plan that was full of strength and bravery. Some could say that running away was cowardly, but that was not what this was. Gemma was running away because she knew that going forward was better than going backward. And it wasn't like it was with Jacobi. He ran away and left me behind, along with Jack. There was nothing holding Gemma back, and I fucking envied that.

I moved past the discussion of Gemma, needing to get back to the real reason I came here versus the therapy session that my uncle thought this was. "What was Judge Stallard doing at the Covens in the first place?" Never mind the fact that Bain was selling him illegal firearms.

"My only guess is that he is connected to the Covens in some way, and that makes a lot of sense with what I've uncovered in the last week."

Now that got my attention. "What do you know?"

"What do I know?" He raised an eyebrow as he walked over to his desk and plopped down in his seat. He pulled out the same file that had Gemma's name stamped on it like before. "That he is a far worse man than I thought."

Something ticked inside of me right along with Gemma's confession Saturday night. The thought of her being with someone that she felt the need to run from set an ice-cold feeling straight through my veins. "You knew him before Gemma came here, correct?"

"Yes."

"How?"

My uncle sighed as he looked back down at the file. His muscles tensed, his eyes staring at something in particular, or maybe it was nothing at all. I couldn't tell. When he opened his mouth again, his tone wasn't as cold as before. It was on the brink of devastation, if I had to guess. "Judge Stallard's mother, Anne, used to run a group home for girls."

Silence stretched around us, and my patience began to run thin as he continued staring down at the file that was half closed. But then he began again. His gaze found mine, and his jaw was set like a thick line of steel. "You know how your father donates and makes his charitable dues as a front for what he truly does? How he sways people and misleads them into thinking he's a charitable man with a good heart?"

I scoffed before nodding.

"Well, your grandfather did the same. You know this, I'm sure." I said nothing, and he continued after leaning back in the chair that creaked against his weight. "One of the places he donated to was Anne's group home. They'd take in juveniles who were to serve time in a detention center for a crime they'd committed, but instead of going to prison, they'd go to the group home as a type of punishment. They'd work for free and ride out their sentences that way. Like therapy for young women going down the wrong path. The court would decide if it was the right place for these girls, or sometimes they'd just end up sending them to prison or jail if their age allowed."

"Okay..." I thought for a moment. "And this has to do with Gemma's uncle, how? How are *you* connected?"

He swallowed so roughly it sounded like the pencils that sat at the end of his desk were being forced down his throat. "I had a friend, a good friend. A young woman. We were your age at the time."

I cocked an eyebrow. "A *friend?*"

He ignored me. "She got into some trouble. Judge Stallard was the judge on her case." He thought for a moment. "It was one of his first cases. He was a young judge. I remember that much. He'd been given the job after his father had passed from a heart attack."

Now we were getting somewhere.

"Long story short, Judge Stallard sent my friend to his mother's group home as a favor to our family. With the ties your grandfather had with them, it wasn't hard to sway his decision. It was a well-known group home until recently, actually. Judge Stallard's mother, Anne, had a stroke, and the group home was shut down."

It didn't take long for things to click in my fucked-up brain. "So that's why he said you owed him. Because they took in your...friend? Saved her from what? A few months in jail?"

He grunted. "Try a few years in prison."

Okay, moving on. "So that's how you and Gemma's uncle are connected. What doesn't make sense to me is why he was at the Covens and why Gemma seemed to know what it was —or at least recognized it."

He licked his lips. "From what I've learned as of late, Judge Stallard is not a good man. He's hiding things about Gemma, has ties with the police force in the city, *and* there

have been many rumors floating around about the group
home that I'm pretty sure Gemma came from." He paused,
opening the file again. "My theory is that Judge Stallard runs
the Covens. He is definitely affiliated in one way or another."
He looked up at me. "I'm thinking he sends criminals there
instead of jail. He deems them insane during the trial, sends
them to the psychiatric unit, and from there..."

"From there what? He's there making these criminals even
more unworthy of living? Molding them into men like the
ones my father has working underneath him? Filling the
world with more murderers? What?"

"Yes, Isaiah. That's exactly what I think." His voice was
too calm for my liking. "People like your father pay good
money for the men created in that sinful place. If Judge Stallard is the one sending men there, he's likely to be a multimil-
lionaire."

My anger was back, and my heart was slamming against
my chest. I knew what went on underneath the floors of that
psychiatric hospital. I knew the horrors and spine-stiffening
pain that could be inflicted within those dark rooms. I knew
how they took men and broke their spirit just enough to
brainwash them into thinking they were part of a brotherhood. A family of sorts.

A family of sick murderers and women beaters.

They were weak men.

Each and every last one of them hanging on the promises
of strength, power, and wealth.

All by the hands of men like my father and Bain's. Judge
Stallard, too.

"And Gemma?" I finally asked as I undug my nails from
the leather seat.

"Now that is a mystery I have yet to unfold. But if she's
been living with a man like Judge Stallard for most of her
life..." He flipped a page forward and scanned something. "At

least from a young age, given what I can find... But if she's been living with a man capable of sending people to the Covens, I can't even imagine the things she has seen or heard." He shut the file. "I think she may have been born there."

My brows were crowded. "Where? The Covens?"

"There or maybe at the group home. I suspect that a girl at the group home got pregnant, or was pregnant, and Anne took care of the baby." He raised a brow. "Well...babies, in this case."

"What?" I asked hesitantly.

"Oh, yes. She didn't tell you? Gemma has a twin brother."

What?

"Where is he?"

My uncle gave me a look. "I don't know. There's no record of him. I looked into it after Gemma let it slip. Everything about her is very hush. I can hardly find anything."

My stomach bottomed out.

I had a feeling I knew exactly where her brother was.

And I was wondering if, deep down, Gemma did too.

CHAPTER FORTY-TWO

ISAIAH

MY BLOOD still rushed as I sat in the dining hall, waiting for Gemma to appear for breakfast. I had texted her ten minutes ago.

Me: *You're losing track of time in the art room. It's time for breakfast.*

She texted back within a minute.

Gemma: Cleaning up now. Thanks.

My fingers flew over the screen as my leg bounced under the table that Gemma and I had been shoved under less than forty-eight hours ago.

Me: *Cade will walk with you.*

Her reply came another minute later.

Gemma: *Did you send Cade to spy on me?*

I laughed under my breath as I slipped my phone back into my pocket after messaging Cade that he needed to walk with her. Gemma called it spying. I called it protection. Same difference.

My eyes glanced down to the rich wood that her bare ass

was on Saturday night with my finger deep inside her. Just thinking about it made the itch of concern and anger lessen in my bloodstream, but each time I looked over at Bain with his cropped-to-the-scalp haircut and hardened features, I grew tense. My father had yet to answer a single question I'd thrown at him after Saturday. In fact, I'd heard nothing from him except for the few curse words on the other end of the phone after I'd told him all about Bain's little adventure. Typically, I wouldn't care. I'd feed him the intel and then push him out of my head until he called me again. But now that Gemma was involved, and I knew that our family was tied to hers in some way, I wanted to know more. I needed to know more. I could blame the need-to-know feeling burning inside of me on the fact that I was soon to take over my father's entire gun-trafficking business, but that wasn't why I cared. Not even in the slightest. I could lie to him, or even the rest of the Rebels, but to myself? There was no chance. Gemma's sweet little confession was burning a hole in my brain. *I'm running from my uncle.* Why? What had he done to her, and how could I make him pay?

The thought was there, the minor dip in my rationality that allowed me to wonder what would happen if I made Judge Stallard disappear. I wasn't my father, but his blood ran through my veins. That evil part lived inside of me underneath years of staying in control of myself. I didn't let it out often, but would I for Gemma? Would she be able to stay at St. Mary's if her uncle vanished? *No.* Even if something unfortunate happened to Judge Stallard, which would be totally fucking risky if my uncle was correct with the assumption that he had a healthy relationship with the police force, Gemma and I *still* couldn't be anything. She wouldn't be brought into this life. Not a chance.

I unglued my tongue from the roof of my mouth as the doors of the dining hall swung open, and Sloane walked in, then Mercedes, and then Gemma beside her. Cade soon followed, keeping enough distance behind her that it didn't raise attention but just close enough that Bain's left eye twitched. My attention pulled from him and then immediately went to Gemma's bare legs and then right back up to her cute little heart-shaped face that I hadn't seen since Saturday night.

I hadn't seen her at all yesterday, and I was almost certain it had to do with what we'd done right here in this very spot.

We'd texted a few times, but she'd said she was getting caught up on homework and then having a movie night with Sloane. Apparently, Sloane had said I was taking too much of her time with *"tutoring."* She starred the word *tutoring* in the text, as if we were doing something other than studying in the deep, dark library...all alone.

When our eyes collided, it felt like the room shrunk. The walls caved in, and it was as if all the air was whooshed from my lungs and plowed straight into hers. The slight curve of her lips caught my eye, and I felt mine doing the same.

Jesus Christ. My uncle was totally fucking right. I did care for her. It took me by surprise because I had never let myself even consider the fact that I could feel anything but attraction for someone—so quickly, too. Gemma had grabbed my walls, and with the snap of her finger, they were down.

"I have never seen you look at someone like that in my entire eighteen years of existence," Shiner bemused. "You're scaring the entire student population."

I slowly shifted my attention to him as he held a piece of bacon in the air.

"How am I scaring the student population?"

Brantley grunted from the other side of me. "Because you look like you're in love."

I whipped my head over to him with a set jaw. I wanted to

snap. Recognizing something like that out loud landed on too many ears. It was a slap to my face, and he knew why.

"Don't say shit like that." I flexed my jaw.

"I said it for a reason, Isaiah." He went back to his breakfast, downplaying the intensity of our conversation. "Wake up. That's what I'm here for. To tell you to wake the fuck up."

Cade slipped into the seat beside me. "Thought that was my job. We all know I'm the favorite."

Brantley flicked his eyes up to him over the brim of his cup. "You can't be trusted with this anymore. You've been on both sides of the coin. After Jou—"

"Do not say her fucking name." The dining hall grew quiet, and I shifted my gaze back and forth between my two best friends. Shiner caught my eye across the table and sent a silent warning, as if I didn't see what was unfolding right in front of me. It wasn't unusual for us to argue from time to time, and even though I was technically Brantley and Cade's leader in and outside of St. Mary's, I usually let them hash it out themselves. Aggression faded when you hit shit. At least for people like us.

An annoyed sigh came from my mouth as I placed my hands on the table, watching Cade and Brantley glare at one another. The rest of the dining hall was pretending not to watch, but their attention eventually flickered over to us, one by one. "Guys..." I warned, seeing that a few SMC members were in the dining hall, grabbing breakfast along with some other teachers who had the pleasure of breakfast duty.

The sway of a chestnut-colored ponytail caught my eye, and three girls who were completely unaware of the fight seconds from happening began to walk past us, and my arm lashed out, and I snagged Gemma by the waist.

Her breath hitched, and she whipped her head down to mine, those bright eyes widening.

"Sit with us," I demanded, my voice a little harsher than

usual. "I have some questions on my homework that I think I need my tutor for."

Gemma's soft voice pulled Brantley and Cade's attention. "Um...there are no seats."

I looked to Cade, and his shoulders lowered with the crack of his neck. *Welcome back, fuckwad.* "You can have my seat." He began to scoot down after nodding to a few lacrosse players. They quickly stood up and moved down the bench too, making room.

Sloane rolled her eyes. "I don't want to sit beside you, Cade." She glanced at Mercedes who was fiddling with a curly piece of hair. "Will you sit beside Cade so I don't accidentally stab him with my fork?"

Shiner threw his head back and laughed, trying to lighten the mood, but we all knew that Sloane's insult was like pouring salt in Cade's wound, especially after the spat with Brantley.

Mercedes gave her a look that could only be described as sad and said, "Sure, Sloane." She slid in first, and then Sloane, although Sloane acted like she would rather lick the floor than sit down beside us, and then Gemma went to move next.

Once they had their trays in front of them, Gemma snuck a tentative peek up at me. "What did you need help with, Isaiah?"

Nothing. Not a single thing. My fingers drummed against the hard slab of wood of the table so loudly that Gemma looked down at them. A devilish smirk curved itself on my lips, and I couldn't stop myself from completely veering from anything homework related. "This is a nice table, isn't it?"

Gemma's brows pinched, and her pouty mouth that I couldn't stop glancing at straightened. "That's what you wanted to talk about? The tab—" Her gaze popped up once more, her ponytail swishing with the motion. Her cheeks blushed deeply, and I winked, which only caused her already red face to deepen.

"Why is the table nice?" Mercedes asked, glancing from Gemma to me and then to the rest of our group.

Brantley sighed disapprovingly as he threw his napkin onto his tray. I hadn't told them about what we did on the table, but Brantley wasn't dense. He knew something had happened by the tone of my voice, no doubt.

"Why *is* that table nice, Isaiah?" My entire spine stiffened as Bain's voice came to a screeching halt at my backside. My head slowly rose from Brantley's wadded up napkin, and I locked eyes with him as he slowly put his glass of orange juice down. "Is this where you and Gemma ran off to the other night after...you know. Did you fuck her here too?"

Was he insinuating that he knew we'd followed him? That didn't sit well with me. Not at all.

My chest began tightening as my fist clenched on top of the table. I couldn't even look Gemma in the face because I honestly didn't want to see the utter embarrassment and shame that would be there. It would only strengthen the immediate rage that was billowing in my body. I also did not want her to see the anger that was surfacing. I knew for a fact that the Rebels could feel it. In fact, given my reputation, the entire school was probably waiting for me to wrap my hand around Bain's neck and slam him to the ground.

Bain and I had never physically fought before, and the only reason for that was because of my father's instructions, but hearing Gemma's name roll off his tongue sent me to a dark place.

It was likely the fact that he'd already threatened her once and had that photo of her in his room, plus everything I'd just found out about her, that was mixing things in my head and twisting them in unfathomable ways, but either way, I was going to throttle him across the fucking room. Consequences no longer lived in my head. I'd quickly snapped my fingers and banished them right the fuck out.

For a split second, my thoughts went to my mother. I thought about how my father let down his guard once and caused a chain reaction of hurt and despair. I thought about how someone as equally as fucked up as my father thought they could harm the woman he claimed to love because of something he'd done. They had misjudged his love for her, but that didn't deter my father from revenge. An act of betrayal against him was forbidden in his world.

But make no mistake. We may have been blood, but I would never stand by as someone disrespected Gemma like that. This had nothing to do with the fact that Bain was disrespecting me in front of all of St. Mary's and everything to do with the fact that he was disrespecting her.

Bain's voice came back into earshot, and I cracked my knuckles with my back still to him. "Wait a second. She still has that virgin vibe to her. All sunshiny and cute as fuck. I mean, if Isaiah won't fuck the virgin out of you, then I will gladly do it for him."

That's it.

Something snapped inside of me, and every last thought fizzled right out of my head and evaporated into thin air.

My hand tapped the table twice before I stood up. It was so quiet in the dining hall you could hear a pin drop. I could feel the eyes on us. Even the SMC's. But my target was Bain and only Bain.

"Isaiah," Brantley's warning came into contact with my ears, as did the screeching of the bench as he pushed away from the table, but I still stalked around and glared at Bain who had his chin raised high like some sort of almighty king.

That title actually suited him.

Kings were often insufferable, weak men with too much confidence.

I thought Bain needed to be taken down a few levels, maybe be reminded that he wasn't a king—not in this school and not in our future line of business.

"You think you can talk to her like that?" Something cold came down over my body as I shut the entire dining hall out. It was just me and Bain, like a cord full of burning, red-hot anger connecting us together. He inched closer to me with a grin so smug on his face I felt myself mirror it. "In front of me?"

Bain's smile widened. A twitch under his eye caught my attention. He was just as riled up as I was. "You act like you're someone of importance, Rebel."

I chuckled, and it was menacing. So menacing that I hardly believed it had come from me. I prowled closer to him, stalking my prey like a lion would its next meal. "I'm certain you know just how important I am, Bain. Don't *fuck* with me."

He knew. He knew who I was. There was no doubt about it, and that meant he knew just how lethal I could be if I let myself. Flashes of gun fire and fists that didn't belong to me crowded my vision, but I pushed the past away, focusing on him.

"Isaiah." I felt a hand clamp down on my shoulder, and I quickly brushed it off.

There were too many emotions coursing through my veins, sparking the need to expose all my pent-up anger and resentment. I hated my life. I hated my father. I hated Jacobi. I hated most things, in all honesty. But then a voice flickered in the back of my head, making me pause for a split second. *Jack. Jack and Gemma. All of your friends,* it whispered. *You don't hate them.*

Bain's lips tightened as he took another step toward me. "You don't scare me, Isaiah. Do you want to know why?"

My fist ached as I planted my feet, and the very second I

wound my arm back, ready to punch the smug, arrogant, disrespectful piece of shit in the face, a faint swish of warm-brown hair caught my eye, and then two soft hands wrapped themselves around my cheeks.

Gemma.

CHAPTER FORTY-THREE

GEMMA

HIS JAW WAS like chiseled stone beneath my palms. The feeling was almost jarring as I stood there on tip-toes in the center of the dining hall with every single person staring at me.

"No," I demanded, bouncing my eyes back and forth between his. They were darker than they normally were. They weren't their typical airy, light-blue color that I was used to. Instead, they were dark and troubled, and it made my heart crazy.

Once his clenched fist dropped, he instantly wrapped his hands around my wrists. It took everything I had inside of me not to pull my fingers off his face and pull the sleeves of my school blazer down, but I fought it. Isaiah's hands were large enough that they could wrap around my dainty joints twice if he wanted. No one would see the pink scars.

His words were muffled with a coarseness that rubbed me raw. "He's disrespecting you. I don't like it."

My head shook very briefly. "Maybe. But he's also baiting you. And I don't like it."

I didn't like it. In fact, it didn't bother me in the slightest that Bain was pointing out that I was a virgin in front of the entire school. That insult, which I was well aware—even with my inexperience—*was* an insult to most, didn't even skim the skin. What bothered me was that Bain was causing a reaction in Isaiah, which gave him pure satisfaction. He wanted Isaiah to snap, and he knew very well that messing with me would cause just that.

Isaiah's spine straightened, and I felt mine do it too. Bain had begun laughing from behind me, and Isaiah's glare turned murderous. His eyes narrowed; his cheekbones sharpened. I squeezed his face with my hands until he dropped his gaze down to mine again. "Remember the plan, Isaiah. You are on probation. He knows that. He's trying to get you expelled. You are smarter than this."

His body seemed to relax just a little. "How do you know how smart I am, Good Girl?"

There it was. My nickname. That hopefully meant I was bringing him back down to the present.

I pushed myself closer to him, not caring who was watching. "Are there members of the SMC in here? Watching what's unfolding?"

His jaw wiggled beneath my hands. "Yes."

A smile graced my mouth as I whispered so close to his, "What a perfect opportunity to show them that the bad boy of St. Mary's is actually taming his wildly hot temper for once. Show them that you deserve to stay here. Prove to them that you've changed."

Isaiah's hands left my wrists, and I made no move to look to see if my blazer had crept below the shiny, jagged skin. Once he grabbed my waist, the tension in his muscles seemed to lessen. "You think my temper is hot?"

I let out a light laugh as he put his forehead on mine. For a second there, it was like he and I were shielded together in a room that had nothing but thick walls of stone surrounding us. It was just us. "I knew that would distract you."

Isaiah chuckled as he showed off his white teeth. "I don't think I give you enough credit. The good-girl act is cute and all, but you are a lot more devious than I thought." His lips brushed over my ear. "You're a damn good partner in crime."

Excitement and pride flared in me for a moment before I placed my feet back onto the solid ground and unwrapped my hands from his face. I pulled away from him just enough so I could grab onto his hand and begin leading him out of the dining hall, leaving just about everyone in there with their jaws slacked. As soon as we were passing by Bain, not close enough to where they could get into another tiff but just enough so Bain could hear my icy words as they protruded through the air, I leaned in. "I wouldn't say I'm devious, Isaiah. But I am smart enough to see through people pretty damn well." I said the last part just as I locked onto Bain. His gaze sharpened, and I knew he was angry that his little plan hadn't worked. He was using me against Isaiah, and to be quite frank, I was done with people acting like I had been put on this earth for their own personal gain.

The longer I was away from Richard and his subjective ways of living, the more I felt myself forming into who I was supposed to be. The shattered, submissive girl I had been molded into was slowly slipping right out of his grip. I wasn't stupid enough to act like that in front of him, or during our Monday night phone calls, but in front of Bain? Not a chance. Bain needed to see that I wasn't a little chess piece in his game.

Just as the dining hall doors swung closed behind us, I felt the rest of Isaiah's tension dissipate. The fury had washed off of him, and in its place was the Isaiah that I'd spent Saturday night with. The one that made me laugh and feel all sorts of things I wasn't used to.

Isaiah brought our clasped hands up to his lips and gave my hand a quick kiss. "Thank you." We stopped walking when we reached the hallway that split into two: one hallway led to the library, and the other led to the classrooms. The door behind us pushed open, and dread filled me at the thought of it being Bain, but when I heard Brantley's voice, I let out a trapped breath.

"Are you fucking out of your mind?" He appeared in front of us just as Shiner and Cade walked through the door too. "Were you really about to lose it on him? Your father would—"

Isaiah unclasped our hands and placed his on his hips angrily. The corded muscles along his forearms flexed, and I wondered where his blazer was. "I honestly don't give a fuck about my father."

"No," Cade said, shooting him a look of pity. "But you do care about Jack. Or did you for—"

"Of course I didn't fucking forget." Isaiah's chest rose and fell in swift movements. His anger was back within a flash. "But fuck, I am so sick of this." His hands had fallen onto the top of his head, and he pulled on the thick strands as I stood back and wondered who Jack was.

Brantley glanced down at me, and his set jaw loosened for a second. "You're lucky Gemma jumped in front of you before you managed to take a swing at him."

Shiner chuckled. "Girl has balls, that's for sure. I tried to tell her to stay back because we've all seen that look in your eye before."

"You were in a different mindset, man."

A different mindset? I knew all about being in a different mindset. Physically in the present but pulled to the past was kind of my specialty.

My voice was more of a whisper as I stood in front of the four very tall, strong, intimidating boys who rightly owned their title of ruling the student body. For goodness' sake, people made room for them in the hallway, and I wasn't even sure that they were aware they did it. My peers were like a school of fish. Each and every last one of them in their maroon uniforms, parting the way as one as the Rebels strode over the glossy floor. All except Bain and a few of his friends. They weren't intimidated in the slightest. "I...I just didn't want him to get in trouble. Isaiah is on probation, and I'm pretty sure fighting on school grounds is enough for expulsion, right?"

"Right." Cade pointed to me before glancing back at Isaiah. "And then Jack would be fucked."

Who was Jack? My face fell as the door swung open again behind us. My spine straightened when I saw Sloane cradling her wrist tightly to her body with Mr. Fishers, the PE teacher, looking grimmer than the Grim Reaper himself as he walked beside her.

"What happened?" I asked, running over to her.

Mr. Fishers answered for Sloane, scowling over at Isaiah and the rest of the Rebels. "Sloane took it upon herself to punch Bain in the face after you all stalked out of the dining hall." My mouth fell open in surprise as I grabbed Sloane's hand, inspecting it. Her delicate knuckles were as bright as her pink cheeks.

She let out a feral sound. "Bain is a jerk. He deserved to be punched! He was making sexual remarks about Gemma and also trying to get Isaiah in trouble by picking a fight with him. Yet, *I'm* the one in trouble?! You're dragging *me* to the headmaster's office?"

"That doesn't seem fair," Cade said, noticeably glowering at Mr. Fishers.

Brantley crossed his arms. "Agreed. Did you even ask

Sloane why she had assaulted Bain? Seems kind of sexist to drag her to the headmaster's office without even asking."

I gently pushed Sloane's hand back up to her chest and let her cradle it again. "It's true," I began. "What Sloane had said, I mean. Bain was insinuating that I was a virgin and saying very disrespectful things to me, all while prodding Isaiah to do something so he'd get expelled from St. Mary's. It's no secret that Isaiah is on probation with the SMC. In fact, I'm tutoring him in the evenings, which I'm sure you and the rest of the faculty are aware of, so he can raise his grades in addition to improving his behavior. Bain was being an instigator for the mere fun of it." I and the rest of the Rebels knew that Bain wasn't doing it for fun, but Mr. Fishers didn't need to know that.

"Well..." Mr. Fishers began to stutter as he took in the information I'd fed him. He glanced over to the Rebels and then back to Sloane. "Maybe...you can just do detention with me this evening instead of going to the headmaster. You cannot go unpunished. I do not take physical altercations lightly." He glanced at Isaiah. "Although, I am glad there wasn't a bigger one that I needed to jump into. Thank you for that, Mr. Underwood. Or should I thank Gemma?"

Isaiah grunted an acknowledgement, but that was all. The bell rung just as soon as Mr. Fishers gave Sloane details on her detention and then directed her to the nurse for ice. She brushed him off with an eye roll as students began piling out of the dining hall. Each and every one of them was searching for us like we held the world's greatest treasure in our hands. Mercedes ran over with her mouth gaping, and just as Sloane was filling her in, Bain stepped through the heavy oak doors with blood smeared along his upper lip. Dots of red were sprinkled over his white collar, and I smiled.

I actually smiled.

"Better luck next time," I quietly said as he walked past.

His smile was cold, and it should have chilled me right to the bone, but it didn't because Isaiah's glare, along with the rest of the Rebels', heated up the entire school. When I caught Isaiah staring at me once Bain was down the hall, a wry grin appeared.

I smashed my lips together so I wouldn't smile back at him and then turned to Sloane and Mercedes as we shuffled to class. "Are you sure you don't want ice, Sloane?"

"I'm okay," she answered, flexing her fingers. "I think."

"I can't believe you punched him," Mercedes laughed as she began to hand Sloane and me our books that we'd left behind. "I almost fell out of my chair when you walked over to him."

Sloane's brows pinched together as I snagged her books and held them with my own. "He needed to shut up. No one talks about my friends like that."

"Maybe we should call you girls the Rebel-ettes. Or Rebel-ritas?" Shiner plopped his arm over Sloane's shoulder with entirely too much amusement. He snagged her hand and inspected it as we all walked down the hall. I snuck a timid glance up to Isaiah, and our eyes caught, right along with my breath. How did he manage to do that? How did he manage to take my breath away so quickly?

Before I was able to look away, he snagged me around the waist and pulled me into his side, whispering into my ear, "I think I'm rubbing off on you."

"How so?" I asked, trying to pull my books back that he'd somehow grabbed with just one of his hands.

"I caught your sly remark to Bain. Both of them." His light chuckle vibrated my ear, and my face flamed, remembering what we'd done two nights ago. My body remembered much quicker than my mind. Things heated, something pulled, a slight jolt raced down my back. "And don't think I didn't notice how you avoided me all day yesterday. What was up with that?"

Heat landed on my head. "What? I wasn't avoiding you."

"Your cheeks tell me a different response." There was a light catch to his tone, and I knew he was entertained.

Our friends were up ahead of us, Shiner's arm still draped over Sloane's as her black hair swayed back and forth. I sighed, thankful no one else was listening to our conversation. "Fine. Maybe I was."

He froze for a second before stepping back in pace with me. "Why?"

The heat started at my scalp again, but this time, it continued down to the rest of my body. Why had I avoided him? It wasn't because I'd spent most of the day trying to dig up information on the psychiatric hospital, or because I had a paper to write. It was because there was the smallest part of me that felt ashamed and guilty—and confused.

I liked Isaiah. No matter how many times I told myself not to like him and not to get attached to him, I felt myself clinging to him like he was a reason to stay at this school. My stomach dipped when he popped into my head, his smile from across the room made my own lips curve, and he had made things go haywire in my body that didn't exactly disappear quickly after we'd parted ways Saturday.

I was confused about how much Isaiah had taken up space in my mind, and I was a little ashamed. I was supposed to be focusing on my plan to leave St. Mary's and finding my brother. My heart shuttered with agony each and every time Tobias crossed my mind, which was practically every time I glanced in the mirror, but with Isaiah near, the pain wasn't as unbearable. The stress wasn't as intense.

Isaiah was making me question things like leaving, and that was something that made vomit hit the back of my throat. It was absurd to think that I could actually stay here and keep away from Richard. My eighteenth birthday was soon approaching, and the social worker who dug up things Richard wanted to hide would no longer have an obligation to me. His sick plans would come to light if I didn't slip away unnoticed.

I was too lost in my thoughts to even realize that Isaiah and I had finished walking down the hall. We were somehow already standing outside of my first class, and he'd given Sloane back her books at some point while still holding mine tightly in his grasp.

His strong brow line deepened as he peered down at me. "Did I cross a line Saturday night?" His eyes shut briefly, then his thick black lashes fluttered back open as he shook his head. "I mean, of course I did. I shouldn't have taken you with me. It was dangerous and—"

I placed my hand on his chest. I could feel his heart racing beneath my fingertips. It was...unusual to see him flustered, but he was. His words were too fast; his eyes were darty. The steel arches of his cheeks were a little flushed too. "Saturday was one of the best nights of my life."

Isaiah's mouth clamped shut as shock rolled over his features. I think it may have rolled over mine too. What was I saying?

This. This was why I avoided him. Things were...too much. I wasn't acting like myself when he was near. I was impulsive and careless. I was caught up in him. His eyes. His breathing. Everything. And I wanted his hands back on me. I did. I really did.

"This is why I avoided you," I mumbled, putting my hands on my books and taking them out of his grip. "When you and I are together, I can't quite see the big picture anymore, and it scares me." I glanced away for a second, locking onto one of the oil paintings hanging on the hallway wall. "You scare me... And it has nothing to do with us running for our lives Saturday."

His head slanted as his features softened. "I scare you?"

I nodded as a tiny cut seemed to slice over my heart. I'd never see Isaiah again after I left. I may never feel *this* again, whatever it was. I was excited every time I walked into the dining hall or into the library for tutoring. I anticipated his text in the morning when I'd spent too long in the art room. Even earlier, as I stared over at Bain as he taunted Isaiah, I felt something that I'd never really felt before—I felt protective. I wanted to smash Bain's face onto the floor for messing with him. And then I felt gratitude and love for Sloane as she stuck up for me, right there along with Isaiah. They cared about me. I had people here that actually cared about me and not in the manipulated and twisted way that Richard did. It had been a long time since I'd felt anything but loss and fear.

Isaiah huffed out a breath, running his hand through his perfectly messy hair. The hallway was beginning to empty, and he'd be late for class if he didn't leave now. "You have no idea, do you?" he asked, peering down at me with an awed look in his eye. His hand clamped on my chin, and his thumb brushed over my lip, making my body tighten in the most delicious of ways. "*You* scare *me,* Gemma Richardson. You scare the shit out of me."

The late bell rang out over our heads, but neither one of us stepped away. I blinked once, ping-ponging my eyes back and forth to his. "How do I scare you?"

He swallowed roughly; his thumb laid still on my lip. "Because I'm afraid I'm going to ask you to stay when you try to leave with that fake ID and money."

My heart thudded to the ground, and my knees buckled. My eyes widened. "Don't." I took a step back and stared at the floor. "My only option is to run." The words felt like acid over my tongue, and my mind began to protest them the second they were out. *Is it my only option?* I knew what he was feeling, though. I felt it too. A tie between us. Some type of pull that was resisting as I said the words.

I didn't want to leave. There, I said it.

St. Mary's was like a safe house for me. I was relaxed here. I was becoming myself. *Living. Feeling.* And I was happy. I was happier here than I'd ever been before. If he asked me to stay, it would make it that much harder to leave.

"Is it, though?" he asked, halting my thoughts right there. "Is it your only option?"

"Yes." It pained me to say it; it truly did.

His hands found their way around my cheeks as he lifted my face up to his. His expression was pained, and a small little crease dug in between his eyebrows. A single wave of his hair graced his forehead. "The way you're looking at me right now almost kills me." His lips formed a straight line. "Your eyes are glossy."

My heart beat like a drum inside my chest. I was looking this way because I was conflicted. I had too many emotions piling in that I'd forced away for so long. The resentment, the fear, the loneliness, the uncontrollable need for love and safety and hunger for someone's help.

"What can I do for you? Let me help you." It was as if he'd read my mind.

I glanced away as footsteps began to come down the hall. I knew I needed to open the door that sat behind my back and go to class, but I couldn't move. I was stuck. My mouth was glued shut even though there were screams for help pounding inside my head.

Eventually, I opened my mouth, knowing very well that we needed to take a step away from one another. I was becoming too attached. Too lenient. "You are helping me, Isaiah. You're giving me a way out."

He shook his head angrily, dropping his hands. "No. I'm

giving you a way to run." His jaw tensed as he sliced his eyes to the teacher that was walking down the hall. "Tell me what he's done, and I'll make him pay."

Fear flashed within as I knew very well who he was referring to. "I don't want you anywhere near my uncle." I hardly recognized my voice. It attributed strength, and my determination to keep him far away from anything even coming close to Richard was unsparing. It surprised me.

"I am not afraid of Judge Stallard," he said point-blank, features unmoving.

"You should be."

A throat was cleared, and Isaiah and I ended our conversation abruptly, which I was more than thankful for. "Gemma, if you'll head into class, I'll be right behind you." Mr. Hobbs raised an eyebrow at Isaiah as he backed away from me.

Isaiah's expression told me that he didn't think the conversation was over between us, but it was.

––––––

LATER THAT DAY, Sloane and I sat on the bleachers with the sun dipping behind the clouds every so often, watching the boys at lacrosse. My sketchbook sat in between my knees, and the phone Isaiah had given me was clenched in my fingers as I revisited the Covenant Psychiatric Hospital's website again.

"You and Isaiah were a hot subject matter on the blog today," she started before tearing into a bag of Twizzlers. We were both still in our school uniforms, but I suddenly wished we would have changed, because now that we were nearing November, the weather was drastically getting colder, day by day.

"We were?" I asked, glancing at the side of her face.

She nodded, eyes still on the field. "No need to pull it up on your phone. The blog is already down." Sloane ripped some of the red rope candy from the pack and handed it to me. I glanced at it with suspicion but ate it anyway, and I almost moaned at how good it tasted.

"The blog is already down?"

"Yep." She laughed. "It seems every time you're featured on it, it gets taken down immediately."

I swallowed the last of my Twizzler, and Sloane put another one in my hand. I smiled. "What did the blog say?"

Someone yelled from below during the boys' practice, and I was pretty certain it was Mica. He was jogging with his stick and laughing at something, his bright-white smile so contrasting to his rich skin. Sloane shifted beside me, but I kept my eyes on the field. "It was just talking about how you were able to save Bain from an epic beating, and...it questioned your *friendship* and tutoring obligations with Isaiah. Oh, and there was some speculation as to why Bain and Isaiah hate each other so much." She paused before asking, "Why *do* they hate each other so much? Do you know?"

I stilled for a split second, not really knowing what to say. "Something that happened in the past, I think."

"Interesting. So you and Isaiah don't talk about that kind of stuff during tutoring? Or when he *claimed* you the other night, which by the way, I'm still not forgetting that you have yet to fill me in on what you did for the rest of the night. You two were long gone by the time the party lights came back on."

I opened my mouth, but she cut me off. "And do not tell me you two were studying. I'm not stupid. Isaiah is probably making you keep secrets..." She let out a sad laugh. "Those Rebels have too many secrets. And they're arrogant about it too."

I eyed her from the corner of my eye. "Why do you hate them so much?"

Sloane's fingers clamped onto the Twizzler bag, and I instantly felt bad for calling her out, but Sloane was sort of a closed book. Anytime Mercedes or I would ask her a question that had some substance, she was quick to change the subject. It wasn't obvious, but I was observant when I needed to be.

"I don't hate *them*. I only hate Cade."

"But why?" I asked, now fully seated toward her. I put my phone down, and she looked up at me briefly. Her eyes were troubled, and without knowledge of even doing so, I found my hand on her knee. "You're right, Sloane," I said, whispering even though no one was even close enough to hear us. "Isaiah does have secrets. But everyone does." I took a deep breath. "You can trust me with yours—if you want to, I mean." The conversation was beginning to make my skin itch. I wasn't sure if I was saying the right things to her or if she knew I was being genuine. And how fair was it for her to tell me her secrets, but for me to keep mine?

Her hand fell on top of mine. "I know that." Her pink lips tugged down. "I just feel..." She looked back out to the lacrosse field, and I followed. I immediately caught Isaiah's stare, and my heart flip-flopped. How does he make me react from so far away?

Sloane cut back in. "I don't want to put anything else on your shoulders. You are already..."

"Already what?"

"Troubled. I can just...tell that you're troubled with something." She looked at my covered wrist, and I shamefully pulled my hand away from her leg, but she was right.

"I am," I agreed, pushing back on my anxiety harder than it pushed on me. My fingers clasped my journal, and I almost wanted to just give it to Sloane to show her just how troubled

I was. But I didn't. Instead, I pulled myself back up and smiled. "If I wasn't messed up, I wouldn't be at St. Mary's, right? Wasn't it you that said we were all a little fucked up?"

Her features relaxed, and she laughed. "I did say that. It should be the school motto."

I laughed too before watching Isaiah run down the field with his stick in hand. "They should put it on the pamphlets."

She laughed, but it faded quickly. Her voice was shaky and not at all like the confident girl I knew as my roommate. "I hate Cade because he's part of the reason why Journey is gone."

"Journey was your last roommate, right?"

She sighed, pulling another Twizzler out. "Yeah, we were close. She and Cade were starting to..." She nibbled on her lip. "Date, I guess? I don't know. It was weird. Super intense. Kind of secretive. Kind of like you and Isaiah."

I said nothing, even though I wanted to deny that some-thing was going on with me and Isaiah. Everyone assumed there was something going on with us after Saturday night, which was his plan all along. Some assumed we'd had sex and that I was just *another notch on his bed post,* whatever that meant. Some whispered that we were dating. No one ever said anything directly to me, though—aside from Sloane and Mercedes, of course. I didn't know what to tell them, and I had been too occupied with fighting with myself for most of the day on Sunday, debating whether it had actually meant something to him or not, to tell them anything. But instead of denying it right now, with Sloane staring out onto the field, looking conflicted, I stayed silent as she continued.

"I don't know the full story. Cade said he doesn't know either. But..." Sloane's head turned toward mine. Her eyes were muddied and wet, and my stomach dropped at the hurt that flashed within them. "Isaiah had found her...Cade came right after. They found her with her wrists split wide open, Gemma. She had tried to kill herself."

I gasped, and my hand latched onto hers. I squeezed tight as a chill wracked through me. I wasn't expecting that to come out of her mouth. Her eyes had dipped to my wrists again, and within the blink of an eye, I made sense of her question the other night.

"That's why you asked if I was hurting myself."

She nodded and worked a small swallow down her throat.

My shoulders fell, and I looked her dead in the face. "You don't have to worry about that with me, Sloane. I'm not suicidal."

"Then why do you cover your wrists?" Her voice was wobbly, and I squeezed her hand again. A part of my wall cracked, and I felt the rip down to my very stomach.

I looked down at Isaiah again for a split second and saw his eyes on me. *Trust*, a voice whispered in the back of my head. Trust. Did I trust these people? Did I trust Isaiah? And Sloane? Mercedes? The headmaster?

On shaky legs, I stood up, still holding Sloane's hand. I was half glad Mercedes had to retake a test today so I didn't have two sets of eyes on me when I gave another piece of myself up to someone I wasn't entirely sure I trusted.

But how could I learn to trust someone if I didn't give them a chance?

"What are we doing?" Sloane asked as I pulled her behind the bleachers. A few groups of students eyed us as we rushed away. I mostly knew all the faces that surrounded me now, especially since a lot of them seemed to track my every move when I was with Isaiah, but other than that, no one really messed with me—well...except for Bain. But that, too, was because of Isaiah.

"Showing you why I cover my wrists."

I spun Sloane around so quickly her plaid skirt fluttered

upward. She said nothing, though. She kept her pink lips crushed, and her face was a blank canvas as she waited for me to spill.

"Can I trust you?" I asked, one hand on my sleeve. "This is not something I have shown anyone. Ever."

She gave me a look. "Like...ever?"

"Never," I confirmed. Her brows puckered, and a slight breeze wafted around us.

I pushed my sleeve up, letting the cool air coat my hidden skin, and waited for her reaction.

Sloane's mouth went slack. "What...what are those?"

"They're scars." One on top of the other. Over and over again.

Sloane didn't even ask before she grabbed a hold of my arm and jerked me closer to her. Her eyes widened as she turned my wrist and saw that the pink shiny skin wrapped all around my tiny joint. "Scars from what, Gemma?"

I jerked my hand back and shoved my sleeve down. Anxiety clawed at my throat, and my stomach revolted. I didn't know how to answer her, so I was as vaguely truthful as I could be without lying.

"The past," I said, grabbing a hold of her hand and bringing us back over to the bleachers. "I broke the rules." A knife twisted in my stomach. "And I was punished."

"Oh my God." The words were no more than a breath of air, but they packed a punch so hard my chest caved.

"I'm not suicidal," I whispered, glancing back at my phone to busy myself. I was hot all of a sudden. Sweat coated my back. Nerves tingled along my skin. I couldn't believe I'd shown someone my scars. The only other person who knew about them was the one person who shared the same defective skin. *Tobias.*

"I hope whoever caused those scars is six feet under ground."

The harshness of her words didn't cause a single flinch in my body, because I'd hoped for that on more than one occasion. And maybe that made me just as messed up as Richard was. Or maybe that thought directly stemmed from the fucked-up girl that I was because of everything I'd been through.

But Richard wasn't dead.

And that was something that did make me flinch.

"Gemma?" I stiffened as the headmaster's voice cut through my thoughts. His face appeared through the foggy mist seconds later. "Your uncle called. He wants to have his chat with you earlier this evening. Which works out perfectly. Now you don't have to miss out on the annual pep rally bonfire to kick-start the rival game in Temple on Thursday."

Sloane mumbled under her breath, annoyed that she had to miss out because of her detention with Mr. Fishers.

I nodded at Headmaster Ellison who stood just below the bleachers with his hands in his pockets. "Oh, um, okay," I said before smiling briefly at Sloane. "I'll see you back in our room later."

She nodded as her eyes snapped down to my covered wrists before I began walking down the bleacher steps. The pounding of my shoes against the metal was just as loud as my heart when the headmaster spoke again. "He's waiting patiently to talk with you, so let's get there quickly. I fear that if you're a second too long, he'll show up."

Confusion and a leeriness filled me. "Why wouldn't you want him to show up?"

The warm air from the school hit my face as the headmaster and I walked through the doors. Students eyed us, as usual, some giving the headmaster a high five as they walked past. It was a weird dynamic he had with the students. He was professional while talking to other teachers, and especially Richard, but he was so friendly when it came to the students. Like he actually cared for them.

Headmaster Ellison hummed, thinking over my question. "Well, I guess because I feel that St. Mary's is good for you, and I think if he sees that you're flourishing here, he'll rip you away."

He'd rip me away right now if given the choice.

We were almost to his office when I let myself ask the question, "And why wouldn't you want him to rip me away? Why does that matter to you?"

He sliced his green eyes to mine, and the intense color of them struck a chord with me. My heart skipped a beat as I stared into them, feeling that same sense of familiarity in their depths that I'd felt the first day here. "Because my students matter to me, and I know more about you than you think, Gemma."

I paused as anxiety bubbled in my stomach.

His hand rested on my arm for the briefest of seconds before he pulled away. "That isn't meant to scare you. There is no hidden threat in my statement." A shaky breath clamored from my mouth as we walked into his office. He ushered for me to sit down near the foot of his desk, as always. "Though, I do know you wrecked my car."

Another shaky breath whooshed out of my mouth as it flung open. *How could I forget that I wrecked his car?* Deep down, I knew it was because I was so blinded by what had happened after I'd hit the stone wall. Truthfully, the only thing on my mind was Isaiah and his talented fingers that I couldn't stop myself from staring at today during art. "I... I..." *Deny it!* One look at the headmaster's glittering expression told me that I didn't need to deny it, that there was no point. If he had only guessed that I had wrecked it and was fishing for information, I just gave him the truth right there by not rejecting the accusation right after it came out of his mouth. "Did Isaiah tell you that?"

Suddenly, my heart began to beat harder. Surely Isaiah didn't tell his uncle I had wrecked the car. But what if he did because the headmaster assumed it was him? Or the SMC? Would he throw me under the bus to save himself? There was a reason Isaiah had to stay here, and I had a big feeling it had to do with someone named Jack. I hadn't asked Isaiah who Cade was referring to earlier today, but I saw how Isaiah's shoulders had tensed.

"Isaiah said he wrecked it. But I know how my nephew drives. He doesn't wreck."

My mouth formed an *O*. I could feel the muscles along my lips pinch. *So he didn't throw me under the bus; he tried to save me from it.* I said nothing to the headmaster as I let that sink in. He was staring at me intently, and I had no idea what to even say. Did I apologize? Did I beg him not to tell Richard? *Oh my God. What if he told Richard?* The floor was like water under my feet, and the chair felt like it was seconds from falling in.

"I did wreck your car." I clasped my hands together and felt my head dropping. "And I'm sorry." *What if he tells Richard? Shit.*

"Gemma," the headmaster said, voice a little softer than usual. "I feel like this is a step in the right direction."

"What?" I slowly brought my head up.

A cheesy smile broke out along his face. It was the kind of smile that I would assume a dad to have after saying a silly joke to his teenage daughter. Not that I would have any idea what that would look like, but it just seemed...genuine. In fact, my own mouth wanted to rise at the sight of it. Part of me wished the headmaster was my father. I didn't think much about my own dad. I never knew him, and my mom had disappeared at such a young age that I never even had a chance to ask about him. Tobias once asked Richard about him, and he was locked up for days in the basement. We never dared ask again.

"You didn't lie to me. You admitted wrecking my car." I shifted uncomfortably as I noticed he was still smiling. How could he be smiling when I wrecked his car? "You trusted me enough to tell me the truth. You didn't ask me not to tell your uncle—which I won't, by the way. But that's a step in the right direction, don't you think?"

Was I beginning to trust him?

I pulled at the hem of my skirt nervously. "I guess you're right." I paused. "I'm sorry about your car. I...don't know how to drive."

He laughed. "I can see that."

I bit my lip before asking the question that was nagging me. "Is Isaiah in trouble? For taking me with him?"

Just as he shook his head and relief pooled in my belly, the phone on his desk rang. I jerked upright as my stomach flipped.

"I'm betting that's Ric—my uncle," I said, correcting myself. I leaned closer to the phone. He nodded as he turned it toward me before standing up and rounding his desk.

"You can stay," I blurted, gripping the arm of the chair. The teeniest, tiniest smile found its way to my mouth. "I know you listen through the door anyway."

The headmaster looked surprised at first, and I let myself laugh softly.

"Well..." he said as the ringing continued. "Okay then."

Then, he plopped himself back down onto the chair just as Richard's voice hit my ear.

"Hello, Gemma. I've missed you."

Wish I could say the same.

CHAPTER FORTY-FOUR

ISAIAH

THE FIRE CRACKLED and popped every few seconds as my teammates surrounded it. The glow flickered across all of our team lacrosse shirts, making the white color appear orange with its burning hue. My eyes fell to every single person that circled the team, locking onto Bain for good measure and then scanning the crowd once more for Gemma. *Where was she?*

"Looking for someone in particular?" Brantley grunted, running a hand over his short hair. "A petite, brown-haired girl who has you wrapped around her dainty little *talented* finger?"

I snapped my gaze to him. "What do you know about her talented fingers?" A burning bolt of jealousy flung to my bones before I dug my shoes into the foliage underneath my soles. *Get a fucking grip, Isaiah.*

He chuckled, looking back out to the fire. "I was referring to her artistic abilities...but it's good to know that our little chat earlier didn't help get your mind out of the fucking gutter."

Cade laughed from behind us. "Been there, done that. It won't help, Brantley. Once you're sucked in, you're fucking done for."

"Will you two shut the fuck up, please?" I popped my neck to the side, irritated that I was at the center of their conversation. I was even more irritated that I knew they were right. Both of them. Brantley had pulled me aside after lunch, gripped me by the neck, and brought his forehead down to mine. If it weren't for our friendship, I probably would have swept him off his feet and choked him out, but his eyes burned with such an intensity that I actually waited to hear his reasoning. He was reminding me of my vow. The one I took when I first stepped foot in this school and had girls clinging to my side every single hour of every single day. I could touch, kiss, fuck, but emotions stayed out of it. Always. I made that clear to everyone when the claiming parties started. The claimings were supposed to be anonymous anyway, but some knew who I was, even in the dark, and they thought they could continue the charade well into the next day. *Not happening.*

Brantley and Cade knew of my reasoning: because of my mother, because of my life, because of my future. They made that same vow.

And it was all fine until I kissed Gemma.

She wasn't the type of girl you kissed and forgot, and she wasn't the type of girl you only touched once.

Cade knew how I was feeling. He had felt it with Journey, and just like Brantley was doing now, we all warned him to knock the shit off. It didn't work. And even though Journey was gone, I knew he still felt her deep inside his bones. He carried around the burden every single fucking day. That was probably why he tossed girls out three seconds after fucking them without an ounce of dignity in his tone.

I knew after today in the dining hall, when Gemma seemed to bring me back down to earth, that I wouldn't let her go easily. When she left St. Mary's with the money and fake ID I promised her, she was going to have to truly disappear, because if not, I might just try and bring her back. And it ate away at me that I didn't know more about why she was running. *What had he fucking done to her?*

"What exactly is your plan, Isaiah?" That came from Cade as he tipped back his Solo cup full of St. Mary's punch. I snatched it from his hand and lifted it to my nose, smelling the Bacardi.

"Did you lace the punch?" I glanced behind me and saw Coach talking with Mrs. Graves a few feet away from the punch table. "You better hope to God Coach doesn't catch you drinking that shit the night before a game."

Cade smirked. "I laced *my* punch. No one else's."

"Rude," Shiner snarled, walking up behind us. "Share, fucker."

Cade tipped his head over his shoulder and turned his back on the chaperones. He pulled out his flask next as I scanned the crowd once more for Gemma. A knot began to settle in between my shoulder blades.

"Bain's right there. You can relax." Brantley's voice was low, but I heard the slight uptick of annoyance in it. "What has your dad said about Saturday? Anything?"

"No," I snapped. "I don't know how he expects me to take over when I'm on a need-to-know basis with him."

Shiner smacked his lips after downing his cup of spiked punch. "Damn, that's good." If I weren't on probation, I'd have some too. The burn would surely soothe the coolness of anger pumping throughout my body this evening. I was still irritated that Bain had almost gotten to me earlier. He knew it, too, by the way he kept grinning at me over the fire like a smug fuck.

Cade threw his cup into the fire, and the flames erupted, causing an outburst from a group of girls nearby. He winked before turning to me. "I didn't know you wanted on better terms with him. You're usually avoiding his calls."

"Yeah, well, that was before I realized Gemma was connected."

The three of them nearly broke their necks looking over at me. Our tight group became a little tighter around bundles of students. "What do you mean? Like more connected than Bain fucking with her to get to you?"

I sighed, still keeping an eye on Bain as he wrapped his large arm around one of the girls who he often fucked. "Remember what I told you on Saturday? About Bain dropping guns at the Covens to some man?" They didn't answer, but they didn't need to. "It was Gemma's uncle."

"What?" Brantley's eyebrows raised to his hairline. "Did she see him? Did she point him out?"

I clenched my jaw. "No. But she did recognize the Covens."

"Are you fucking serious?" Cade dipped his head in low. "What does that mean? For her? Surely she hasn't been there."

I shook my head, glancing back at Bain over the sea of people. To be honest, I never used to mind these bonfires to celebrate our biggest rival games, but now that it was running into my tutoring time with Gemma, I found them to be annoying and fruitless. "There is a lot more to her than you guys know." I met all three of their hard gazes, and Brantley swore under his breath.

"There's more to you and her than we know, is what you mean."

Shiner straightened his back, growing serious. "You've fucked her, haven't you?"

"No." But I wanted to. Virgin or not. *Fuck, she was a virgin...right?*

He laughed loudly as he scanned the crowd for what I assumed to be his next smash. Shiner was notorious for snagging a willing participant during the bonfires and fucking her against a tree deep in the forest. "And you're already *this* into her? Interesting..." He paused before looking dumbfounded and mumbling under his breath, "I don't get it."

Cade sighed. "You're already so into her that you're going back on your own morals. You're dragging her into a life that you swore you wouldn't bring anyone into."

"Like the life you wouldn't bring Journey into?"

The muscles along Cade's temple popped as he kept his profile to me. Silence passed through the four of us as we gathered our thoughts. I was growing even more annoyed that Gemma still hadn't shown up. Maybe she was in the art room? Unease settled in, even as Bain stood across the pep rally, clearly not anywhere near her. I scanned the crowd, gazing over the small embers floating into the darkened sky, and sighed. "I am into her. I feel fucked up in the head. I'm possessive of her, protective, even more so now that I've gotten a small glimpse into her life, which by the way, I'm pretty sure is fucked up."

Cade nodded. "She's guarded. There's a reason for that."

"Gemma isn't staying around for long, so this thing between us, whatever the fuck it is—"

"You mean the whole tutoring shit on the front to save your ass but kissing her so possessively at the claiming that everyone cummed in their pants?" Shiner interrupted.

I ignored him as I continued. "As I was saying... This... thing between us won't last. She knows that. I know that. We're both just..." I wasn't even sure what to say. A female had never messed with my head before. I'd never even let someone get close enough.

"Fucked," Cade answered, still locked onto the roaring fire. "You're both fucked. Take it from me, Isaiah. Even if you deny it, you'll be completely fucking destroyed in the aftermath. I see the way you look at her."

The words went unspoken after that. And he was right. I did want to deny it. We all swore that we'd never fall for someone. The reasons were different for me, Cade, and Brantley than they were for Shiner, who was more guarded than most, but we all took the same damn oath one night after the claimings had started. Our lives weren't normal, and we fucking recognized that. Being tied down to someone only ended in two ways, and neither of them were good. I knew that first hand. *So why the fuck couldn't I get my shit straight?*

"It's..." Fuck.

"I know," Cade answered. "I know."

Right before Shiner stepped away, he patted me on the back. "We've got your back—and hers. Won't let anything happen to her as long as she's here."

"I don't approve of this. At all," Brantley ground out. "But we will not have a fucking repeat of Journey. We were caught off guard last time." He leaned forward and shot a look to Cade, which was warranted because Cade had kept her a secret, and if we'd known they were sneaking around, we'd have been able to have a better grasp on things. "And we will not be caught off guard this time. Especially with Bain fucking around. He's already sketchy with the roundabouts he does late at night. And after today, he's on my fucking shit list."

I barked out a laugh as I slid my attention to Bain. "My father says he's untouchable, but fuck me if I'm losing sight of that."

As if I needed a sign from above, my phone vibrated, and

Jack's name flashed on the screen. *Right.* I had more at stake than I liked to let on. "It's Jack. Keep an eye on Bain, at least until Gemma gets here. He wants me to call him."

"She's right there." Cade pointed his head up just as my uncle was walking her toward us. My finger swiped at Jack's message as Gemma smiled at something he'd said. Her perfect, pretty lips curved slightly as my uncle departed, and a breeze wafted around the fire. My breath caught the second our eyes met from across the grassy area, and Cade was right.

I was fucked.

CHAPTER FORTY-FIVE

GEMMA

THE SECOND THE headmaster left me standing in the middle of a rowdy bonfire, I frantically began searching the crowd for Mercedes, since Sloane was in detention, but then I stopped and froze. Isaiah's piercing stare snagged through the fiery flames. Embers danced throughout the wind, floating up to the sky before fading to black. The leaves crunched underneath my shoes, and it was the only indication that I was moving toward him instead of finding Mercedes.

What was I doing?

His eyes flared brighter as his lips tipped. The smallest dimple appeared on his right cheek, and it wasn't a dimple that I saw often. It really never came out unless we were alone in the library, pretending to be busy as he jabbed me with sly remarks and cocky comebacks to my chiding about doing his homework. He may not need actual tutoring, but he did need a little push to do the assignments.

"Hey," he said as he held his phone in his grip. I didn't

think he'd moved even an inch in the time it took me to walk over to him.

"Hi," I squeaked before clearing my throat.

"What took you so long?" Isaiah glanced behind me, phone still resting in his hand. "I was beginning to get worried."

Something tender poked my heart as Isaiah took another step toward me. "Worried you'll flunk without your tutor?" I grinned.

"That's not at all why I was worried." His gaze jolted down to my mouth, and my light and airy attitude was replaced with something much more intense and jarring.

I glanced out to the fire, briefly looking at some of our classmates, who were all dressed in St. Mary's lacrosse apparel instead of their school uniforms like me, before landing on Bain. His body was angled toward Isaiah and me, but he wasn't looking. A pretty, fair-haired girl was wrapped around his side with her head resting on his shoulder, and I wondered what she saw in such an untrustworthy person.

Isaiah stepped beside me, his phone screen bright as he texted someone. I only glanced at his screen for a moment before looking out at the fire again and explaining where I was. "I was checking in with my uncle. That's why I was late."

Out of the corner of my eye, I watched as Isaiah's shoulders stiffened. He was wearing a white St. Mary's lacrosse shirt that fit snugly around the wide berth of his shoulders, and it really did nothing but accentuate the tense way his muscles locked. I leaned forward some and saw that Brantley was also staring out into the fire, but his jaw was rocking back and forth like a ticking time bomb. That wasn't really unusual. Brantley always seemed a little on edge, but both of them? After I mentioned that I was checking in with my uncle? That was something that caught my attention. They were skilled with keeping a hold on their body language; the shift was barely noticeable. But Sloane's assumptions were correct: the Rebels had secrets. It was all part of their allure.

"That's right," Isaiah said seconds later. "It's Monday."

"Yep," I replied, pushing the thought of Richard and his phone call clear out of my head. It wasn't a lengthy conversation. A few hidden threats thrown in when he'd asked how my classes were. He reminded me that my birthday was soon approaching—as if I could forget—and that was about it. The only decent part of the conversation was that he didn't make me call him *Daddy* this time, which was a relief because, although I knew Headmaster Ellison had heard me say it last time, it would have been extremely awkward to say it in front of him, and I wasn't so sure he'd let it slide. He'd ask questions. Questions I wouldn't have answered.

"And how was that?" Isaiah asked. My skin grew warm, and it had nothing to do with the fact that the fire was growing larger and larger. I took a step back, leaves crunching under my shoe again. Isaiah matched my steps, staying in stride with me.

"It was fine."

He chuckled sarcastically. "Look me in the eye and say that."

Slowly, I turned my head and met his intense stare. His chin was raised, that same chin that looked as if it were made from granite, and his eyes gleamed so intently it was like he was trying to reach inside and pull all my secrets out, one by one. I searched his face long and hard before lying again. "It was fine."

His cheek twitched. "And here I thought good girls didn't lie."

A laugh tumbled out of my mouth as I turned back to the fire. I didn't understand how he could make me smile after having thoughts of Richard in my head, but here we were. If only I could take him with me when I left. Maybe then I'd be able to sleep without shit haunting me.

Isaiah's phone vibrated in his hand again as a small smile played on his lips. There was laughter in the air, mixed with the scent of burnt wood, and I felt as if my chest cracked open with light. Isaiah was glancing down to his phone with a hint of smile still there as I turned my head away from him, realizing right then how lucky I was to be standing there underneath the stars and moon with a ginormous school at my back that held a sense of safety so large I could hardly even fathom it.

I felt safe here.

I hadn't felt safe since Tobias left. I hadn't even really felt safe before then either.

It wouldn't last forever, but each day here felt a little more like home, and that made me feel warm. Even if it was only for a second.

"Jack?" Isaiah's voice cut through the happiness churning through my blood, and just like that, it was gone. When I turned toward him again, I saw the blood drain from his face. The healthy glow of his cheeks that were full of innocent laughter seconds ago was no longer there. Instead, it was an ashen gray with shadows of pure panic etching the curves.

"Isaiah?" I asked, not even realizing I'd reached out and placed my hand on his arm. "Are you—" The words died before I could finish. Terror pinched in between his brows as his eyes dipped to mine. "I need my uncle."

I didn't question him. I quickly swept around and found Headmaster Ellison standing with a few other teachers near a table that held some drinks. He was mid-sentence when I interjected myself, trying to appear calm on the outside, but I was twisted on the inside. I'd seen that look before. That look of dread and unease. I'd seen it in the mirror one too many times. I was right there beside Isaiah, feeling what he was feeling.

Only I had no idea *why* he was feeling it.

"Gemma?"

"Isaiah needs you. Now."

His shoulders straightened as he excused himself from the faculty who eyed me with suspicion. As soon as we were out of earshot, he snapped his attention down to me. "What's wrong?"

"I'm not sure. But I think it has something to do with Jack."

He paused for a moment before cursing under his breath. I wanted to ask who Jack was, but I didn't. Instead, we walked in stride. I had a feeling the headmaster was trying to act like he had everything under control in front of me, but he was actually sweating. The heat radiated from his body, and he frantically searched the bonfire for Isaiah.

"Where is he?"

My head snapped back and forth as I began to panic. "He was righ—" My gaze snagged onto Brantley who very subtly nodded his head toward the forest. I wasn't sure what the secrecy was about, but I was sure there was a reason.

I nodded, tapping the headmaster's arm before taking off down the grassy hill. He followed behind me a few seconds later, after Brantley had shouted something about winning their upcoming game, garnering everyone's attention. I wasn't sure if that diversion was planned, but with what I knew, I only had to assume. The headmaster following a female student down to the dark forest probably didn't look too good on the outside—at least not with the way the rumor mill liked to stir up gossip at St. Mary's. I could already practically see the blog post tomorrow morning.

"Jack? What's going on? I can't hear you."

The crunching and snapping of leaves and twigs pulled me

farther into the forest with the headmaster at my heels. A few branches sliced my bare thighs, and I scolded myself again for not changing after class today. Goosebumps raced along my exposed skin the second I was away from the fire, and when I heard even more panic in Isaiah's tone, I shivered.

Something was wrong. Something way bigger than just Bain sneaking off in the middle of the night.

Headmaster Ellison grabbed a hold of my arm as I tripped over a tree stump. "Let me help you."

His grip wasn't firm, but it did hold me in place as we continued to walk. "Isaiah?" he shouted as we both looked through the foggy mist that crowded the forest. It was hard to get my eyes to adjust, but I saw Isaiah's tall dark form up ahead, and I dashed forward, letting my arm fall and getting there before the headmaster.

"Get into the closet and lock it." Isaiah's eyes found mine, their glossiness hitting me right in the chest. His shoulders relaxed for a moment before he squeezed the bridge of his nose and shut his eyes.

"Isaiah? What's wrong?" The headmaster whooshed up beside me, glancing down and landing on my thigh that had a slight sting to it. Our gazes collided, but I shook my head. I was fine. Isaiah wasn't.

"Put it on speaker."

Isaiah stilled, looking over at me, but soon the phone was face up in his shaky hand as a small voice filtered through the other side. "I was already in the clo-closet! She found me, so I ran, and I can hear her looking for me again."

Headmaster Ellison cursed. "Where the hell is Mary, Isaiah?"

"I don't know! Fuck, I don't know! Cade already called her. She didn't answer. I'm afraid Mom did something to her. Jack said the nurses stepped out, and I'm not sure where anyone is! He's alone."

Isaiah seemed to be straddling the line between being terrified and angry. His shoulders were bunched, and the veins along his arms were bulging as he gripped the phone tightly, but his voice didn't sound like him. He sounded broken, and confused, and maybe even a little vulnerable. I wanted to take a step toward him and let him know that he wasn't alone. But I didn't because the tiny, hiccupping sobs on the other end of the phone *was* alone. And that seemed to cause a whole lot of terror for the headmaster and Isaiah both.

"Okay, calm down, Isaiah." Headmaster Ellison stepped forward and tried to take the phone out of Isaiah's hand, but the murderous glare shot his way had him putting his hands up instead. The headmaster ran a hand through his unkempt hair as he looked down to the phone. "Jack? It's Uncle Tate."

"Un-uncle...Tate? It's...Mom. She thinks—" A loud bang sounded on the other end, and I stepped forward as my hand flew to my mouth.

Isaiah's eyes clenched tighter as choppy words left his lips. "She doesn't know it's him. She's saying shit that he doesn't need to hear about that night. I think she's trying to hurt him."

The headmaster pulled on the ends of his hair and snatched the phone out of Isaiah's hands quickly. Isaiah stepped forward as Headmaster Ellison snapped toward me, "Calm him down." Then, he began talking on the phone. "Jack. Listen to me very closely, okay? We're going to play a game."

Isaiah's eyes gleamed with anger as his fists clenched, and I knew what that look meant. It was the same look he had when he almost hit Bain. It was the same look Richard got when he used to snatch Tobias up and keep him for days.

Before I knew what I was doing, I was leaping forward and putting myself between the headmaster and him. Both of my hands fell to his arms, and I peered up into his face. "Isaiah, stop." His jaw was set as he stared behind me. "If you want to keep Jack safe, you need to let your uncle help."

Isaiah's chest was heaving as I put my hand on his chest. The beating of his heart was thunderous against my palm, and my tight belly clenched. "Take a deep breath. Jack needs you to stay calm. Trust me when I tell you that kids can sense terror from a mile away. You stay calm, he stays calm." His steely gaze shot to mine, and the muscles along his face still held a tightness to them that I wasn't sure would ever soften again. "Just breathe and listen."

A rough swallow worked itself down his throat as his nostrils flared. Hot, seedy breath left his mouth and floated around me as I nodded. *There you go.* The headmaster's voice broke through our heavy embrace as we just stayed put. "That's right, Jack. Good job. Take your hand and run it along the side of the wall. Do you feel the little ledge?"

"Ye..yeah! I do!" Jack's voice was less fearful and more excited now.

Headmaster Ellison's chest caved as he put his fist to it. "Good! Push on it with those strong muscles I know you have. I bet you're stronger than Isaiah."

A few seconds passed as Isaiah's labored breathing lessened. My hand was still pressed to his chest, and although his strong heart was still beating wildly, I knew he wasn't going to jump over me and attack his uncle to get the phone back, so I began lowering it. My breath hitched when Isaiah's palm clamped over my hand, keeping it pressed to his body.

"I did it!" Jack rushed out.

"Climb in there. Quick. It's a cool secret tunnel."

Isaiah's gaze switched over to his uncle as confusion covered his face.

"I'm in here," Jack said, sounding more relieved than ever. "Now what?"

The headmaster slowly swung back around, his eyes landing on us. He stepped over a few broken twigs as he rubbed his hand over his forehead. "I'm coming to get you."

"What?" Isaiah's hand fell from mine as he stepped toward him. "But Dad—"

"I know, but until we get ahold of Mary or your mother's nurses, we have no other option."

Just then, Cade came jogging through the wooded area with his phone pressed to his ear. "Mary is there now. She said your father told her she could have the night off. That he would be there all night."

A sarcastic, crass laugh echoed out of Isaiah's mouth as he gripped the back of his neck. "I'm going to fucking kill him."

The headmaster grabbed the phone from Cade's hand and now held both of them out in front of him on speaker. He began talking to both Jack and the woman, Mary, about the situation and how Mary could find him. "Yeah, you know the secret passages from the library to the kitchen? That's where he is. I would find Beth first. Where are the nurses?"

"She locked them out. I found them out front when I pulled up. They're with me. They'll get Beth. I'll grab Jack."

The headmaster and I latched onto each other for a brief moment, and I wasn't sure how I understood what he was telling me, but I did. I felt a sense of understanding between us. It was a strange mix of bitter familiarity that had Tobias' face flashing through my head. *I missed him.* I swallowed as I pulled myself away and came back into the conversation with Isaiah and Cade, ready to de-escalate his rising anger again.

"What's the fucking point?" Isaiah shouted, crossing his arms angrily. "The entire fucking reason I am here, listening to his bullshit and doing his bidding—and for fuck's sake, taking over the family business—is to keep Jack safe. But fuck. He can't even keep his end of the deal? He can't even be bothered to stay at home for one night with his nine-year-old son to make sure he stays away from..." Pain radiated off Isaiah's face so intensely I felt a slight burn in my chest. "From..."

"I know, Isaiah," Cade said, stepping toward him.

"No!" he shouted, his hands running through his hair as his narrowed gaze locked onto him. "You don't. She's a fucking monster, Cade. That night...ruined her. The blood you saw? It all came from her head. It messed her up. She doesn't even recognize us half the time. Neither one of them can be trusted with their own flesh and blood, and fuck, she was the only person who could! Jesus, I had to basically bribe my own fucking father to keep his nine-year-old son safe!"

I stepped forward. "Flesh and blood have nothing to do with it."

Cade's and Isaiah's gazes both shot over to me so quickly I flinched. We all just stood there staring at each other with nothing but the breeze from the tall pine trees wafting around us. I swallowed back the unease wrapping around my body like a twisted vine and raised my chin. "Some people just aren't good people. They don't understand right from wrong. They're twisted and"—I glanced around the forest, not wanting to see the expressions on their faces as I continued on—"and maybe it stems from a fucked-up child-hood, or maybe they're too power hungry and controlling to see that they're causing pain, or maybe they *like* to cause pain, or..." I wrapped my arms around my body. "Or maybe it's an illness, a disease, or...whatever it is, it has nothing to do with flesh and blood. Some people are just...sick. And trust me when I say there is no point in trying to understand it."

Cade stepped forward, the light of the moon peeking through the limbs of the nearest tree over his face. "Sounds like you speak from experience, Gemma."

I shifted my attention and saw Isaiah standing there with

his arms down by his sides, staring directly at me, looking no less than completely defeated. "That's because I am."

Before anyone could say anything else, footsteps approached, and the headmaster appeared with both phones clasped in his hands. His gaze bounced from me, to Cade, and then to Isaiah. "He's with Mary. He's fine."

Isaiah's eyes were like shards of sparkling glass as they landed on his uncle. "He's not fine. No child should go through that."

The headmaster nodded. "I agree. Just like a child shouldn't have to hear their sibling running for their life on the other end of the phone."

My stomach lurched. Something hit me right then as I stared at Isaiah and all his beautiful brokenness and vulnerability that he tried so desperately to hide behind strength and anger. He was really good at hiding it, too. But now I knew that I wasn't the only one with a hidden past that had so much depth that not even an empty abyss could hold it. I wasn't the only one entering adulthood without being unscathed. I wasn't the only one who didn't have a typical, normal childhood. Sure, our childhoods were different, but that didn't mean they weren't just as messed up.

I had been sheltered from the outside world and its monsters, having my own vile one at home, but Isaiah was the opposite. He wasn't sheltered. In fact, I was pretty sure that he'd lived a thousand lives compared to me, and each one of them had something more dangerous than the last.

His shaky, anger-ridden voice cut through the sleepy forest. "I'm not a child. I'm the furthest fucking thing from a child."

The headmaster placed his hands on his hips and garnered all of our attention as his eyes flung from each of us. "None of you are." He glanced at Isaiah first. "Not you with your childhood surrounded by guns, violence, abandonment, fear..." He trailed off before he moved to Cade. "And the same goes for you. Especially with all that you've lost." Then, he landed on me, and I took a step back, wanting to move farther into the dark, wooded area so no one would see me. "And you... From the very moment you stepped foot in my office, I knew."

My heart raced, my breathing so loud I was certain they could all hear the choppy breaths as they climbed from my lungs. "You knew what?"

"That you've been through hell and that you don't plan to go back."

I gulped back emotion, frustrated that he was reading me so easily. I didn't understand. I didn't understand anything anymore. I didn't understand the headmaster for starters. He was so contradicting at times. And did Isaiah tell him of my plans? Did he tell him about our deal? Did he put it together that I was planning on running? That I would soon disappear from St. Mary's all together? Surely not, because wouldn't that go back on him? For not watching over his students closely enough? Did I even want to put someone through that spectacle? Richard would want someone to blame other than himself, and Headmaster Ellison's head would be on the line.

Up ahead, students roared with cheers as a whistle blew. I could see the very faint glow of the fire from the hillside as Cade started to head toward it. He called over his shoulder, "As much as I'd like to stick around and talk about how fucked up we all are, I'm going to get back to the bonfire before Coach flips his shit that Isaiah and I are missing."

Isaiah made no move to leave. Instead, he was staring at his uncle with so much vile that I shivered in my spot.

"I want to kill him." The hate in Isaiah's words rooted me to the forest floor. The muscles along his temples flickered within their shadows. "Same goes for Cade's father, and Brantley's, and fuck, maybe even Jacobi for leaving me high and dry." The headmaster said nothing, and his face was expressionless. Even with the thick darkness that laid around us, I could see that he was calm and collected. Isaiah's gaze shot to mine for a fleeting second before he was glaring back at his uncle. "I want to kill Judge Stallard, too."

My stomach rolled as the name left his lips. How did Richard even end up in this conversation? How did *I* even end up in this conversation?

The headmaster stepped forward and gripped Isaiah's head within his hands. Isaiah's brow line deepened. "You will kill no one, Isaiah. No matter how badly they fucking deserve it."

My lips parted as Isaiah flung his uncle's hands off his face. "And who's going to stop me?"

The headmaster briefly caught my eye before staring at Isaiah directly in the face. He took his pointer finger and pushed it onto Isaiah's hard chest. "You. You're going to stop you. Because you are not your father." He swallowed roughly. "Remember who you are."

Isaiah's head slanted, peeling his glare away. "And how do you know that, Uncle Tate? Maybe I am just as bad as him, because I feel the darkness. I feel that automatic pull to fucking destroy those who deserve it. Starting with Bain."

A faint, choppy laugh left the headmaster. "I know it because your father would *never* give up his wants for someone else. Not like you are doing for Jack. Not like you will do for those that you love. And he doesn't destroy people who deserve it, Isaiah. He destroys innocent people who stand in his way. You know this."

They stared at each other for so long I began to feel uncomfortable. Uncomfortable because I felt like I was intruding. Uncomfortable because whatever they were talking about went much deeper than what was at the surface, and I wasn't sure Isaiah even wanted me around to hear such things.

To see such things. I knew I wouldn't if I were him. If I were digging up something from my dark and twisted life, I wouldn't want anyone to hear it.

Another whistle blew, and we all heard Isaiah's name come from someone's mouth. He sighed as his head dropped.

The headmaster took a step back. "You two go somewhere for the evening. Go to the library. The art room. Somewhere away from here. I don't want you around Bain tonight."

Isaiah gave him a look, but the headmaster shook his head. "I will handle it. I'll tell Coach that your lovely tutor here"—he gestured to me—"is helping you study for a test tomorrow. He wouldn't want his best player getting expelled by the SMC for not raising those grades now, would he?"

"And what about Bain?" Isaiah asked, clearly annoyed that his uncle was banning him from the bonfire. "I'm sure Cade and Brantley will let you know if something seems off. They've always done so in the past, yes?"

Isaiah went to say something, but I took a step forward, snagging his attention. Something flickered across his face, and his shoulders lowered a fraction. "Okay."

The headmaster started to back away, and his lips lifted just a fraction as he threw Isaiah's phone toward him. "Take the night off from Isaiah Underwood, nephew. You deserve it."

Before the headmaster got too far away, Isaiah shouted, "And Jack is good? You talked to him?"

"I talked to both him and Mary. They're together. She has him. Now go be teenagers." He paused. "But...be good." He flipped back around and called over his shoulder. "And don't take my car."

Isaiah grunted under his breath with his back toward me. My lips begged to twitch into a smile, which was so absurd given all that had just happened a few moments ago. From Isaiah's little brother...to the headmaster calling out me,

Isaiah, and Cade on the fact that we had less-than-stellar upbringings...to the emotional conversation between Isaiah and his uncle. It was all so much, yet here I was, wanting to smile. *Don't take my car.* I think I liked the headmaster.

Isaiah's hands found his waist as his head dropped to the ground. He was still facing away from me, and the ridges of his back were hard and tense. I'd bet if his shirt was off, I'd be able to count each muscle along his shoulders.

Taking one step toward him, I said, "Your uncle is...unusual."

A sharp laugh left Isaiah's mouth as his head popped up. He caught a glimpse of me over his shoulder and then began to turn around. "That's what you have to say after all that you just witnessed? That my uncle is...unusual?"

I shrugged, wrapping my arms around my torso. There was a nip in the air, and while I had been warmed by the fire up on the hill, I was definitely chilly without it. "He's just..." A soft laugh floated out of my mouth. "I can't figure him out."

Isaiah and I were only a few feet apart now, standing in the middle of a circle of pine trees that went so high they looked as if they touched the stars. Silvery moonlight cascaded over our heads, and when our eyes caught, I knew the light moment was fleeting. "What are you thinking right now?" He looked away, showing off that flawless skin of his. "I'm honestly afraid to even know."

I chewed on my lip, my eyes burning a hole through his high cheekbone before taking another step toward him. "I'm thinking I want to know more about Jack."

Isaiah's head whipped toward me so fast I felt the strands of his hair fly past my face. "You want to know more about my brother?"

Lifting a shoulder, I smiled shyly. "He seems important to you."

"He is." Silence stretched around us. The faint sound of the bonfire caught my attention, along with the chanting of the forest, but before long, Isaiah's hands dropped, and he began walking farther into the wooded area with me following after him.

The farther we walked, the further the silence stretched. The trees grew more crowded, and the branches and twigs were messier, and they would have slashed at my bare legs, but Isaiah was always quick to move them out the way so I could move by easily. We were still walking when he finally broke the silence. "I've never told anyone about Jack."

My brows furrowed as I tucked a strand of hair behind my ear so I could see him better out of the corner of my eye. "Why not?"

"Because I keep those that I love close to me, and I love him the most."

Isaiah stopped walking and tilted his head up past the trees. I did the same, and a short gasp left my lips. The tall, looming trees that were crowding us during our short walk were no longer blocking the light of the night sky. A million little stars twinkled and sparkled above our heads as if they were putting a show on for us. "That's...beautiful."

His voice was rough. "Agreed." I turned away from the stars and caught Isaiah staring directly at me. My heart jolted as if it had reached up and touched one of the stars in the sky. Heat warmed my cheeks as I quickly glanced away.

Isaiah moved past me a few yards and rested his back along one of the thick tree stumps, kicking a leg up behind him as he crossed his arms over his chest. I stayed in the same spot, too nervous and consumed by the heat creeping into every little crevice of my body to do much more.

"The only people who know about Jack are the Rebels and, of course, my uncle." I opened my mouth to tell him that he didn't need to tell me anything, but he stopped me. "He's nine. Looks just like me, only with a goofy smile and the world's most hideous fucking glasses. He looks like Harry Potter."

I took a small step toward him. "Who's Harry Potter?"

Dark hair flopped on his head as he jerked. "Tell me you're kidding."

Now it was my turn to cross my arms over my chest as I shot him a disapproving stare. "I already told you I had a sheltered childhood."

He kicked off of the tree. "We must rectify this immediately." He paused before pointing at me. "And if you tell anyone I'm a Harry Potter junkie, I'll tell them just how much you like sitting bareass on the tables in the dining hall."

My mouth flung open. "You wouldn't!"

His brow flicked upward as if challenging me, and I rolled my eyes.

"Whatever. I won't tell anyone." I breezed past him and took his spot on the tree, resting my back against it. "But there's no need to threaten me. You could have just told me not to tell anyone, and I wouldn't have."

A sly smile curved on his face. "I know, but then I wouldn't get to see you blush."

"It's too dark to see me blush."

"Not true." He pointed a finger up to the stars and moon gleaming over us, and I clamped my lips together.

"Back to Jack," I reminded him, still feeling the heat simmer in my cheeks.

"There's not much more to tell that you didn't already hear. Jack is my little brother, and he's really the only thing I've ever loved, besides my older brother who..."

Wait. He had an older brother too?

He sighed, running a hand through his hair again. Talking about his older brother was obviously difficult for him. "I don't talk to my older brother anymore. But Jack...I'm really all he has."

I nodded gently as I empathized with a child who I'd never met and probably never would. My brother was all I had, too, as a child. I bet Jack missed him so much. "He's lucky to have you."

"He was until my father sent me here. Now he's alone."

I shook my head but stopped myself as earlier thoughts washed away my previous question. "Is that why you're so adamant about staying here? At St. Mary's?" I jolted forward as puzzle pieces clicked together. Cade had mentioned Jack earlier when Isaiah and I had stepped out of the dining hall after he'd almost lost it. "You're protecting him." My sentence came out in a whisper as my throat began to close up. "Did... did your father threaten your brother? To keep you here to watch Bain?"

That was absurd. Right? Parents didn't do things like that to their children. Did they? My earlier statement had filtered in. *It had nothing to do with flesh and blood...some people are just bad.* I'd always had the thought that Richard was so mean to Tobias and me because we weren't his real family. That he could punish us in such inconceivable ways because he didn't hold that unconditional amount of love that parents were supposed to have for their children. Richard raised us. He was the only parental figure that we had, but he didn't see us as his children. Or even as his niece and nephew.

I wasn't a mother, so I couldn't understand the concept of unconditional love, and the memories of my own mother were so blurry that I couldn't be sure, but I was pretty certain that parents were supposed to protect and love their children above all else. I'd lived with a real-life example of that. Anne, Richard's mother, had loved him even when he hit her and put her down. She had loved him even knowing his plans for me. She had loved him even through his many, many faults.

That was a prime example of unconditional love, but it was apparent that not all parents were like that. I was right earlier. Flesh and blood had nothing to do with it. *Some people were just bad.*

"Yes. That's why I can't get expelled. He's using my little brother as leverage."

Isaiah's answer startled me. I jumped, scratching the back of my thighs against the tree bark.

Shock rippled through me again, and I wasn't even sure why. I knew bad people existed in the world, just like I knew that not all children had a loving home. All the love I had growing up was a fake rendition of such, and you didn't break the things you loved.

"I'm..." I stepped forward just as Isaiah's eyes swung to mine. His head was low, and his vulnerability pulled at the strings inside my chest. "I'm so sorry."

"You are the last person who should say sorry. You're helping me with my probation. You're helping me keep Jack safe, in a way."

Part of me wanted to tell him to forget about our deal. That he didn't have to give me money or a fake ID. I didn't want anything in return if it meant helping him. It was as if I was seeing Isaiah Underwood, St. Mary's bad boy, for the first time. I saw him in a different way now. I saw his vulnerabilities, and to me, that meant everything. It made him real.

Of course I didn't tell him not to pay me or give me what he promised, because that would be insane given all that I had on the line too, but I wanted to. I wanted him to know that I wasn't only in this because of our deal but that I would help him with anything.

St. Mary's had it all wrong. Isaiah wasn't this almighty, arrogant, ruler-of-the-school bad boy.

No.

Isaiah was *good*. And protective. And loyal.

CHAPTER FORTY-SIX

GEMMA

Isaiah and I had been standing silently in the empty forest for entirely too long. Goosebumps continued to rise over my flesh as I wracked my head for something to say to him. For something other than the annoying and unneeded apology that kept trying to escape my mouth.

I knew I had nothing to say sorry for. That whatever else laid behind those icy depths of his wasn't my fault and likely had nothing to do with me, but I was still sorry. I was sorry that he was in a constant battle between keeping his brother safe and losing sight of himself. That had to have weighed heavily on him. It had to. Just like it weighed on me that I was in a constant battle of getting as far away from Richard as possible or getting close enough to him to find out where Tobias was. One made me feel selfish, but the other was like signing my own death certificate.

"Do you want to go back up to the bonfire?"

Moving my attention from the twigs and leaves underneath my shoes, I found Isaiah standing only a few feet away from me. His brows were raised to his hairline as he waited for my answer, and I found myself shaking my head no.

There was a glint of gloss on Isaiah's bottom lip, like he'd recently licked it, and I felt myself pushing my back further into the tree that I was leaning on.

"Well, then what do you want to do? Go back up to the school? Go to the library to pretend we're studying, even when we both know that's total bullshit? Take my uncle's car for a test drive?" He waggled his eyebrows. "I can teach you how to drive."

An abrupt laugh flew out of my mouth. "Absolutely not."

His lip curved until we both snapped to the left as a branch broke. The rustling of leaves quickly followed, and my heart flew up to my throat. The options were honestly endless as to what could have made such noises in the middle of the night, trapped inside a dark forest.

Isaiah was in front of me so quickly that I didn't even have time to register the fact that he'd moved. His body covered mine as his hand clamped over my mouth. I breathed in and out of my nose, smelling pine and his earthy cologne, as fear crowded my thoughts, and shadows began to dance in the distance. Isaiah's forehead slowly fell to mine as he whispered, "Relax. It's probably nothing."

Relax? It could be a bear! Or...or someone from the SMC wondering what he and I were doing sneaking away from the bonfire! Or...or Bain! Not that I would be too concerned if Bain showed up. I knew that I was safe with Isaiah. He wouldn't let anything happen to me.

Another twig snapped in the other direction, and we both turned our heads to see if anything appeared. I glanced up to the stars and moon again as it acted as a spotlight over our bodies, and Isaiah nodded, catching what I was saying. He dropped his hand from my mouth and intertwined our fingers before pulling me a little farther into the forest. We walked slowly so we didn't make too much noise and then nestled in between two more trees that had better coverage. Our hands stayed joined together as my pulse drummed behind my skin. I tried to shake off the unease slithering over my shoulder as I was quickly reminded of the last time I was running through a wooded area. I could almost feel the sharp stabbings of twigs puncturing my legs as I ran as fast I could from Richard.

"Gemma, relax." Isaiah squeezed my hand a few times as I took a deep breath through my nose. "There's nothing to be afraid of. I won't let anything happen to you."

I squeezed his hand back, feeling a slight flutter in my belly. "I know that. I'm not afraid."

He pulled me in a little closer to him, our bodies colliding. "Are you sure about that? You're breathing like..." A quiet chuckle left his rumbling chest. "Never mind."

I felt myself relax against him until we heard some more rustling. Isaiah's hands cupped my waist as he looked over my head, and I peeked around. My brows crowded as I watched something move, and then came a loud smack and a giggle. *Who was that?*

"*Fucking Shiner,*" Isaiah mumbled, flipping me around so my back was pressed to his front as we faced the noises. Isaiah's warmth grew closer as his breath floated over my ear. "Shiner's known for bringing girls out here during the bonfires. I should've known."

And as if on cue, Shiner said, "You like that, baby? I've always heard you like it a little dirty."

My eyes widened as Isaiah began shaking behind me with laughter. Certainly they couldn't be doing stuff...out here? Right?

"What..." My eyes squinted as I watched through the swaying grass and tree limbs as two dark shadows moved languidly with one another. "What are they...wait. Are they...?"

The taller shadow, who I assumed was Shiner, put his hands on the smaller shadow's shoulders and pushed her down below his waist. My brow furrowed even more as I took in her moving figure and the noises that came with it. It sounded like a hiss of an animal followed by Shiner mumbling, "*Fuck yes.*" His head tipped back, showing off his long neck and the side of his straight nose. When I scanned my eyes down to where the girl was, my breathing quickened even more than before. The movement of her head in between the small openings of the branches had my cheeks flushing so quickly I felt the burn.

Isaiah pulled me back a little bit, whispering into my ear. "Did that answer your question?" There was something flirty in his voice, but I couldn't even process it. I was too focused on what was going on in front of me.

My mouth parted as I kept my eyes glued to the girl whose head was bobbing below Shiner's waist, and all of a sudden, things were twisting and curling inside my stomach. His hand quickly fell to her hair, and I pulled back as he began thrusting his hips toward her.

"Is..." I couldn't stop staring. My eyes were glued to them, in awe. It was a world I wasn't familiar with, like dipping a toe inside an ice-cold pool before quickly darting away again. Did I even want to keep looking? Should we leave? Wasn't this...private?

Isaiah's hand splayed over my stomach as he pulled my hair off my shoulder, letting the thick strands fall behind my back. "There are all kinds of places we hook up around here, Gem. Not just the dining hall." He teased me, and I felt his chest rumble against my back. "So, yes. To answer the question that never left your lips. They are hooking up."

A zip of lightning rushed down my spine and pulled at my insides. A ragged breath left my lips as I whispered, "Oh."

Isaiah paused from behind me as I continued staring at Shiner's quickly moving hips. His tempo was getting faster, and I knew I should have looked away. He had come here with a girl to be alone. Not to be spied on by me with curiosity.

"Do you want to go back up to the bonfire? Is this making you...uncomfortable?"

Isaiah's hand stayed glued to my front as his breath grazed over the sensitive skin that laid on my neck. I found myself moving my head to the side for more. I wasn't even sure why I did it, other than that I enjoyed the feeling of sparks flying over my skin.

"No," I answered quietly.

"No?" I looked down to Isaiah's hand that was still laying over my stomach. He was moving his finger, barely notice-able, but I was too hyper-aware to not notice. Did he even know he'd begun rubbing a circle over the fabric of my skirt? Just below my belly button? Did he know how tightly things were coiled there? *This felt so wrong. But so good.*

I shook my head, my neck still craned to the side as his quick breaths filtered over my flushed skin. "No. I... I'm..." I licked my bottom lip, focusing back on the forbidden sounds I was hearing.

"You're what?"

"Curious," I answered quickly. "I'm curious."

I heard Isaiah swallow from behind me, the roughness of it making my heart skip a beat. His finger was still moving in slow, lazy circles, but at some point, his hand had somehow traveled to the side of my hip.

"You're curious?"

My insides spiked with fire as Shiner pulled the girl up and crashed his mouth to hers. *Whoa.* This was intense, and I

THE SAINT MARY'S DUET BOX SET

was hungry to see what else they'd do. It was such a forbidden, dark thing for me to watch. But I needed to know more. I needed to see just what I'd been missing out on while being locked away in a basement for someone else's sick desires. My head tipped to glance at Isaiah for a quick second. It was dark now that we were tucked away behind two trees, but I still found my way to his eyes. "What was she doing? Just a second ago?"

I turned away as I saw the sly grin slide onto his face. "She was giving him a blow job." My brows furrowed. *A blow job? What exactly was that?* I stayed quiet as I began thinking over the words until Isaiah answered my silent question with a tone that made me clench my legs

"She was sucking him..." Isaiah's hand clamped harder onto my hip. "With her mouth."

The shock flew from the very bottom of my belly. "Oh." My attention went right back to Isaiah's hand that had suddenly begun wandering over my hip gracefully and inching underneath my shirt *just* enough to drive me freaking crazy. The pad of his finger against my skin felt like tiny little fires flying throughout my blood. "And...that feels good? When she does that?"

He huffed, his hot, seedy breath touching me like hot coals. "Yes."

I nodded, taking in the new knowledge. My eyes traveled back through the jagged limbs of the forest as I locked onto Shiner and his partner again. My pulse skyrocketed as he quickly picked the girl up, wrapping her legs around his waist. He moved quickly, thrusting them farther into the wooded area and pushing her back up against a tree. It was too dark to see her face, but I could see the way her long hair flew back into the darkness. I could hear her breathy moans as Shiner did something to her that was likely similar to what Isaiah had done to me the other night.

"Gemma," Isaiah whispered again, pulling me flush with his body. "We should go back up to the bonfire."

Disappointment flooded my chest. "Yeah. You're right."

Neither one of us moved. Instead, Isaiah's finger began working even faster. The long finger that was barely moving against my belly was swiping so low that it dipped beneath the waistband of my skirt and touched my panties. I felt the thundering beat of his heart as my head leaned back onto his hard planes. His earthy cologne sent my senses into overdrive along with the sounds of the couple several yards away from us.

"Didn't—" I gasped as Isaiah's other hand gripped even harder onto my hip, steadying me in place. "Didn't the headmaster tell us to be normal teenagers tonight?"

"*Mmhm.*" His rushed whisper awakened something deep inside of me. It took everything I had to keep my feet planted firmly to the ground instead of swinging around and pushing my lips to his. Because that was what my body was telling me to do. It was telling me to kiss him. To touch him. To let him touch me.

"Is this..." I gasped as his lips touched the side of my neck. "Normal? To sneak away from a school bonfire to—"

"To do dirty, dirty things?"

"Ye...yeah." Isaiah pulled me even harder into him with one hand, steadying me so our bodies were flushed together so tightly not even a breath could float in between us.

"We need to go back up to the school, Gemma." The roughness in his tone and beating of his heart told me that he was lying. That he wanted to stay here just as badly as I did. I also wanted to take his hand and push it farther south where the bundle of nerves was. It was an erratic thought that was driven purely from something that had been brought to life by him on Saturday night.

"Do you want to go back?" I asked, watching with hazy

eyes as Shiner rocked his hips forward into a girl that was all but screaming out his name. *"Oh my God, Shiner. Don't stop."*

"Fuck no," Isaiah answered, gripping me so tightly I was likely to have bruises tomorrow. The hand that was swiping back and forth over the top of my panties stilled.

"Then why did you suggest we go back?"

"Because I can't keep my fucking hands off you." Isaiah's nose grazed the side of my jaw so slowly and tediously that I began to throb in places I didn't know I could. There was a sudden pull in my belly that made my stomach dip with his admission. "You're standing here, panting, with my hands on you, watching something so fucking *dirty* with an innocence that I want to taint so badly." His lips gently touched the side of my mouth, and my hand clamped onto his wrist that was so close to where I wanted it. "I'm not a decent person, Gemma. I've seen bad shit. Bad shit that I didn't put a stop to, but fuck...you're good, and I'm not going to ruin you. I've already crossed the line and—"

"And I want you to touch me, Isaiah. So do it." If I wasn't in overdrive from everything else I was feeling, I would have been in shock at my demand. "If anything, just for tonight."

He growled as his teeth nipped my ear. I gasped aloud, my back curving. I felt a heat cling to my skin so quickly that I wished the trees would waft a breeze over us to cool me down.

"Don't say things like that to me." His heavy breath clamored over my skin as he flung me around to meet his dark stare. "I feel out of control around you. I honestly don't know if I can even go slow with you and treat you the way that you deserve." Isaiah's palms wrapped around my face as his fingers dove into my hair. "And you have to understand something, Gemma." His mouth was so close to touching mine that I could almost taste him on my tongue. I licked my lips, and he

somehow pulled me even closer. "You are leaving. I am staying. This won't last."

"I know that."

He shook his head, pushing our bodies flush. I could feel a
hardness lay between us, and I knew what it was. Only this
time, it didn't scare me. "You don't understand. I'm not going
to want to let you go. Especially if we keep this up. Things
are different with you."

There was a slight knock in my heart that understood his
words. I already felt that way. I already didn't want to leave
St. Mary's, but it was absolutely vital that I did.

My shaky hands dropped to Isaiah's waist as I moved my
head just a fraction closer to his. *Can't we just pretend we're
normal? Just for the night? Like we're two teenagers who don't have
a load of baggage at their feet?*

I didn't say this aloud, but it was *so* easy to forget who I
was with him. To forget that guarded girl who was terrified
for the future if she stayed just a moment too long at this
school. It was so easy to just *lose* myself when, in reality, I
should have been finding myself. But there were no fearful
thoughts, no hold-backs, nothing. I just *felt* when I was with
him. I let my mind, heart, and body all come together as one
for the first time, and maybe that was how it was supposed
to be.

Isaiah didn't say anything as he peered down at me. I was
pretty sure that Shiner and the girl had left, because I didn't
hear a single thing except for my own heartbeat and Isaiah's
labored breathing.

"Once I acknowledge that I'm willingly crossing this line,
again, it's going to be hard for me to go back, Gemma. I
fucking can't. I feel wildly possessive over you, and that
should scare the fuck out of you."

"So possessive that when it's time to let me go, you
won't?" My heart raced up my throat, holding me hostage to

the answer that I needed him to give me. *Please just give me this. Just for the night.*

His answer was sharp. "No. Because although I am possessive, I am also protective, and getting away from me is in your best interest. And that has nothing to do with the real reason you're leaving."

I stayed quiet for a few moments. My fingers rested along the hem of his t-shirt as his hands dropped from the sides of my face and ran down the length of my arms so slowly I shivered.

His gulp drew my attention to his mouth as the question floated out. "So what will it be? Do we go back up to the bonfire and stop this before it becomes something more? Or do you want to stay here?"

"Here," I said, gripping his shirt within my hands. "I want to stay right here. With you. We don't even have to discuss it tomorrow. It can just be for tonight."

Isaiah didn't respond. Instead, his hands moved quickly, and his fingers dug into my thighs, hoisting me up to meet his middle. His mouth descended onto mine, and the kiss rocked me. It was rough, our teeth clanking, his tongue diving forward and licking up my innocence like he'd starve without it. My head was dizzy, and I wasn't sure if it was because he had swung us around and stomped through the forest, or if it was a reaction to what his mouth was doing. Either way, I loved it. I loved every single bit of it.

He pulled away when we reached a different area in the forest. I glanced up and saw the opening of the stars and moon again, and I knew we were back to where we started.

"The things I could do to you are endless, Good Girl."

Excitement flooded me as my teeth sunk down into my lip. Anticipation rushed in as Isaiah's eyes traveled down to my middle that was pushed up against him with my legs wrapped around his back. Our gazes collided for only a second before his mouth was back on mine, licking and exploring so tediously that I couldn't think of anything *but* him. I felt him everywhere. His hands roamed, running the length of my body as I pushed myself further onto his hardness. *It felt so good.* He grunted as his hands slapped over my waist, hoisting me away from him as he lowered my shaky legs to the forest floor. Sticks crunched underneath his weight as he erased all the space between us, tipping my head back so it rested along the rough bark of the tree. With the stars and moon above our heads, I could see the look in his eye. That icy blue burned brighter as his thumb rubbed over my bottom lip. "I'm starving." *What? Right now?*

My breaths were rushed, and they grew even choppier as Isaiah held me around my ribcage, right underneath my bra. His hands traveled slowly over my curves as he began to lower to one knee. I peered down at him, slack-jawed, completely and utterly confused. "What.. What..." I gulped as one of his warm palms gripped the inside of my thigh.

His breath coated my skin as he ran a finger up and down my thigh. "When I first saw you walk into the bonfire, I wondered why you hadn't changed out of your uniform before coming." He chuckled before landing the softest, sweetest kiss on the skin right above my knee. Everything grew hot, and I was pretty certain the ground moved. "But I'm really fucking glad you didn't."

I swallowed again, glancing up at the stars before bringing my attention to him hovering right in front of the part of my body that held so much tension I thought I might combust. "Why?"

"Because it's easier for me to do this." The finger that had been running up and down my thigh started at the base of my knee as he slowly trailed it up farther and farther, disappearing underneath my skirt. Our eyes caught, and my stomach tightened. "Do you trust me, Gemma?"

I nodded quickly, clenching my teeth as I forced myself to stay still. He watched me with lazy eyes as I responded to his finger lightly touching me over my underwear. My lips parted as he pressed his thumb slightly into my most tingly part. "I want to taste you."

I pushed myself back into the rough bark. *Wait, what?* Isaiah's arm wrapped around the crook of my back for a second, pulling me closer to his mouth. "No, that's not true." Then both of his hands gripped me again as he made a noise that sent me into complete overdrive. "I fucking *need* to taste you."

"I...I've never done that."

Isaiah shut his eyes and whispered, "Good," before his head disappeared, and my mouth flung open. I didn't know what to expect, but I didn't have time to consider it because the warm heat from his mouth closed in on me, and my hips bucked toward him all on their own. Isaiah's hands traveled up higher, and I felt the rough way he hooked his fingers into the thin cotton, pulling them down to my ankles and flinging them somewhere into the forest. I couldn't even care that my underwear was long gone, because all of a sudden, I was in a frenzy. His mouth was hot as he kissed my center again, licking and sucking as his fingers dug into my soft skin.

I couldn't speak. I couldn't move. I was completely and utterly focused on the way that my body was bundling and curling and throbbing.

My attention was pulled away for a brief second as Isaiah's fingers let up from one of my legs only to prop my calf up onto his shoulder. He popped out of my skirt for a second and peered up at me with a wild and untamed look on his face. "I will never fucking be satisfied again after this. I hope you know that."

He mumbled something that sounded like, "*Only tonight*," but I couldn't ask him to clarify because he'd dipped under-

neath my skirt again and sucked me into his mouth so possessively I cried out. My head tipped backward, and my hands
wrapped around the rough bark of the tree stump behind me.
Isaiah pushed my legs apart even farther, and I was blinded.
My eyes shut; my body sagged. The way his warm mouth felt
as he kissed me all around was too much. It was as if he was
marking me, and I liked it. I felt the shift of his finger as he
ran it over my slick seam. The feeling left me breathless, and
I burned for more. I needed more. I said that, too.

"Isaiah, more." My hips rocked, and he growled, his finger
finding my center as I cried out.

"Anything for you," he whispered before sucking me and
licking up everything I had to offer. The feeling started to
make things tingle, my toes curled against the bottom of my
shoes, and my fingers dug into the bark of the tree so fiercely
I thought they might be cut. "*Fuck*," he said between licks.

I couldn't stop spinning. The trees swayed, the breeze
blew over us, and the second Isaiah curled his finger and
pushed farther into me, I felt the rush. The mind-blowing,
soul-shattering, so-bright-the-stars-didn't-even-match rush. I
cried out, not even realizing until later that the sound had
come from me. Isaiah sucked and licked as I rode out the
most amazing feeling I had ever felt until I was left breathless
and sated. At some point, my leg had been lowered to the
ground, and a jolt went through me, making Isaiah's eyes
grow dark. He crowded my space as soon as he was off his
knees, wrapping his arm around my waist and pulling me into
his body. I felt his hardness in between us, and my head began
to dip down to look at it pressed against my belly, but he
caught my chin and shook his head.

"I don't trust myself."

My brows crowded, still unable to even form words. My
insides felt like jelly, and my heart was hardly back to normal.
I still felt the desire flooding through my veins, though. That

momentary silence that Isaiah had just given to me was enough to wash every last worrisome thought from my head. He had no idea what he'd just given me.

I went to look down again, eager to give him something back, even if I had no idea what to give, but his grip on my chin grew tighter. "If you so much as look down there, I will rip the rest of your clothes off and fuck you right here, Gemma, and that's...too much, too fast. That'll definitely be crossing the line."

My face flamed, almost embarrassed that I found his words so...*inviting.* Did I want that? The answer was simple. *Yes.* I did. And surprisingly enough, it didn't even scare me. It should have, but it didn't. Just like it should have scared me when Isaiah said he felt possessive over me, but I kind of felt that way about him too. I had a sudden rush of anger earlier that St. Mary's had labeled him as such an arrogant, heartless person. That the SMC was giving him so much trouble when they really had no idea what he was up against. What he had been tasked to do. I felt...protective. I'd never felt protective over someone. Not even Tobias. Tobias was always protecting me, not the other way around.

Isaiah gave me a piece of himself earlier. He was completely and utterly bare as his hurt and anger came out in full waves over his little brother. He trusted me enough to talk freely in front of me with his uncle over something so personal.

And there was a hidden part of me that wanted to give him something back.

Especially now.

CHAPTER FORTY-SEVEN

ISAIAH

THE LAST COUPLE of days had been nothing less than torture.

After the bonfire on Monday, and what followed after, all I thought about was putting my mouth on Gemma. Every inch of her skin. I wanted to corrupt her even further. I wanted to get down on my knees, rest them on the dirt-covered floor of the forest, and tongue-fuck her over and over again.

But instead, after I'd handed her back her underwear that I'd found laying several feet from us, I took her right up to her room because she kept giving me those fuck-me eyes that I knew she wasn't even fully aware of, and if we had stayed put, all alone in that wooded area, I would've fucked her. I knew what would have eventually happened, and it just...couldn't. Not yet. Probably not ever.

When I went back to my room after pulling myself from the girls' hall, I lay on my bed, waiting for Cade to let me know if Bain had been up to anything during the bonfire, and thought over her words very carefully: *Just for tonight.*

Deep down, I knew there would be more nights. *There had to be, right?*

It was inevitable because we both seemed to lose sight of the future when we were together. Fears and worries became distorted.

In fact, my future looked a lot like her, and just before I shut my eyes after still tasting her on my tongue, I told myself *no*. I told myself that little word over and over again, and it was fine until I saw her the next day.

She didn't shy away from looking at me like I had suspected she would.

She didn't avoid me.

In fact, during art, when she'd shifted to stand, pulling her journal tightly to her chest, she peeked over her shoulder at me, showcasing her innocent yet *very* inviting smile, and my dick hardened.

If Bain hadn't *wandered* off last night—just to go in fucking circles again—then during our up-close-and-personal tutoring session, where Gemma's leg kept brushing along mine after she scolded me for pushing aside my English 4 paper, I would have kissed her. I would have done a lot more than kiss her.

And when I told her I had to go, because of Bain, I saw a flash of something cross her features.

She was disappointed. It was subtle, but I saw it.

She didn't want our tutoring session to end.

She didn't want the lingering touches to fade.

She didn't want to keep beating around the bush about what had happened Monday, even if there was a shyness to her too.

I was doing my part in crossing back over the line, because her words sat very quietly in the back of my head. *Just for tonight.* They sat along with the Rebels' warnings and my dreadful future, but looking at her all day and remembering what I had felt when I touched her *really* fucking weighed on me.

Just like it was weighing on me that she kept lifting her head to peek at me over her laptop.

I wouldn't get to tutor with her tomorrow night.

It was the big rival away game.

I usually enjoyed away games because I didn't have to worry too much about Bain. I always had it covered. But being in Temple tomorrow meant that I wouldn't get to see warmth rise to Gemma's cheeks when our eyes would catch. I wouldn't get to watch her nibble on her lip as her gaze lingered on my mouth from across this fucking table. I wouldn't get to argue with myself about whether I should cross the line again or sit here and try to decipher if she wanted to cross it too.

She continued to glance up at me every few minutes, and each time I'd catch her, my core grew hot. Her typing was more furious, but instead of listening to the chanting of regret going on in the back of my head, I stared at her. I was minutes, maybe even seconds from flipping the table over and saying to hell with it all when her fingers finally stopped typing, and she slammed the laptop closed.

"I want to show you something."

The next thing I knew, she was standing up, still sporting that goddamn schoolgirl uniform, and placing her hand in mine. The softness of her palm felt sacred in mine. Like I didn't even deserve to be touching her. It felt as if it were grounding me to something that didn't even come close to reality as we left the library and headed toward the hallway.

I suddenly had a feeling of unworthiness go through me over the fact that, on Monday, after I'd completely lost my cool in front of her and threatened to kill my father, she didn't look at me differently. In fact, she looked at me more intently now. Like she understood.

THE SAINT MARY'S DUET BOX SET

And I had tried to give her an out before dipping my head between her legs. I tried to push her into going back to the school and to the bonfire, but she fought hard to stay with me, to show me that she wasn't judging and that she wasn't afraid. That spoke volumes about her. It truly did. And maybe that was why I'd been able to keep myself on a leash the last two days. Maybe I knew, deep down, it was going to be extremely difficult to let her go, because in the end, I would have to let her go. No matter what.

"Where are we going?" I asked, catching up with her just enough that she could still pull me in the direction that she wanted to go. The library doors were shut, and the hallway was dark since it was after curfew.

Her flushed cheeks made an appearance again as a soft smile covered her mouth. "You'll see."

I didn't show my skepticism as I continued to walk with her. I pulled my phone out once to see if I had any missed texts, but there was nothing there, which meant Bain wasn't being sly tonight. I didn't even have a text from Jack. We'd briefly texted yesterday when I checked in to make sure he was okay after the whole *running-from-our-mother* thing, but I hadn't heard from him since. I made a mental note to call my father tomorrow on my way to the game and demand to know where the fuck he was. I would have called him Monday night after I left Gemma, but I knew I needed to wait until the anger subsided all the way before I did that. What I really wanted to do was throat-punch him for leaving Jack alone without Mary as our mother had an episode.

"Isaiah?" Gemma's sweet voice tore my attention away. "Are you okay?" Her doe-like eyes punched me in the core as she looked down at our hands. I quickly let her hand go, pulling my throbbing one closer to my body.

"Fuck, I'm sorry." Anger simmered beneath the surface, right below guilt. "Did I hurt your hand?"

She surprised me again when she reached out and rested her palm against mine, intertwining our fingers. "Are *you* okay? What were you thinking about?"

I let a heavy breath leave my chest as we stayed in the same spot, right in front of the art room. "Nothing. And I'm more okay right now than I ever have been." And that was true.

Gemma seemed to think over my answer for a minute before nodding, her shiny hair swaying off her shoulders. "Me too." Then, she turned on her heel, opened the art room door, glanced down to both ends of the hallway, and slipped us inside.

The smell of paint and clay filled my senses, and it honestly pissed me off a little because, up until now, all I could smell was her. I glanced down to her legs, remembering how she tasted the other night. The thought was never really far from my mind. The second I would taste anything sweet from the dining hall, I thought of her. If anyone else got a taste of her like I did, they'd never ever be the same.

Gemma's hand left mine as the door latched behind us. She made no move to turn the light on. Instead, she walked over to the supply closet, the same one I had pulled her into on her first day of school, and glanced over her shoulder. "I'll be right back."

I nodded and watched her disappear before sitting on the end of Mrs. Fitz's desk, who would likely scold me if she saw me sitting here, but most of the teachers were gone for the night, unless they had duty.

After a few long seconds, Gemma came back out of the supply closet, holding something in her hand.

"What's this?"

Her soft expression caught mine, and there was a quick jab to my chest. "I want to show you something."

Her guard was up. I could tell that much. Her chestnut

hair swayed in front of her face, catching the slight silvery gleam of the moon through the window. Her small hands trembled as she fiddled with the piece of paper.

"Gem?" I asked, taking a step toward her. "Whatever you're about to show me, you don't have to."

Her green eyes struck another chord with me. "I *want* to show you." Her fingers swiped back and forth as she gulped. Gemma and I were close enough now that I could smell her shampoo again, and the strangest feeling flew through me as I stared at her. My stomach knotted, and my chest felt warm. Before I had a chance to say anything, Gemma flipped the paper around and angled it toward me. Her lower lip trembled as I tore my eyes away from her face and glanced down to what she felt so strongly about that it caused her to nearly cry.

Without even knowing I had done it, I grabbed onto her hands that were clenched onto the pale paper. A spark flew from our fingers, and I knew she felt it too. My finger slowly rubbed over hers as my eyes finally adjusted to take in the piece of art that I assumed she'd drawn.

It was fucking amazing. The detail was astounding. So astounding that I couldn't tear my attention away. My head dipped further, a piece of dark hair falling into my eyes as I flicked my head to make it disappear. The boy that stared back at me looked to be a little younger than us. Closer to Jack's age. He had a strong jaw and eyes that were too familiar. There was a faint line of freckles over the straight nose, and the shadows under his eyes were so haunting I was forced to swallow before talking.

"Who is this?" I asked, finally getting a grip and looking back at Gemma. Her bottom lip, the same one that I desperately wanted to suck on, was pulled into her mouth. When our eyes collided, I knew right then who it was. It was her brother. Her twin.

Her tone was shaky as she pulled the paper back to her chest. "I have a brother too."

Of course, I knew this information from my uncle, but I didn't want Gemma to know that. She was being honest with me and giving up one of her secrets, and I'd fucking treasure it.

"A twin."

"A twin?" I asked, sitting back on the desk and giving her the space she was seeking.

She flipped her small frame around, plopping the paper down onto the opposite desk from me. "Yes. His name is Tobias."

The question clawed at me, as did the answer that I was certain she wasn't even aware of. At least not at the surface. "And where is he? Why isn't he here too?"

Gemma slowly spun back around, the green in her eyes glittering with unshed tears, and I almost flew off the desk to wrap my arms around her out of an instinct I wasn't even aware I had. "I don't know. I haven't seen him in four years." Four years? If he was at the Covens for that long...*fuck.* My hand clenched in my lap, and I hoped that Gemma couldn't sense the dread in my posture. Before I could say anything, she spoke again. "I know he's okay, though. I know he's still alive."

That caught my attention. I stayed locked on her, watching the way she fiddled with the hem of her skirt. "How do you know that? Have you talked to him?"

"No." The tremble in her tone cut me. "I think..." She shrugged. "I don't know how to explain it. I just know he's alive. Call it a twin thing, I guess." A small smile appeared, but it left just as quickly.

I thought for a moment, continuing to stare at her as her eyes bounced all over the room. Things were starting to make sense. Now I understood why she was so desperate to leave

St. Mary's, if not for the fact that her uncle was a piece of shit. "Is that why you're leaving? To find him?"

I truly hoped not. Because if she had a hunch that he was at the Covens, and she walked in there without hesitation? They wouldn't give her back.

A shaky breath floated around me as her eyes grew glossier. A mix of anger and fear and—shit—I think hurt etched all over her delicate features, and it felt like my flesh was being pulled from my bones. If she cried, I would rip apart every building, every person, every last living thing on this earth until I could make her tears disappear. I'd tear down the Covens, brick by brick, person by person, to find her brother if that made her happy. If that meant she could stay.

She can't stay, Isaiah.

I pushed the voice out of my head and stood up on two confident feet. I strode over to her quickly, grabbing onto her warm cheeks that I hoped would stay free of tears. I was ready to tell her every last thought I'd just had. That I'd do anything to make her smile, to make the light come back in her eyes that completely messed with my head, but she clenched her eyes shut as she grabbed onto my wrists. "I don't want to talk about him anymore." Her head shook, and my stomach thudded to the ground. It was strange. I'd never felt like this in my entire fucking eighteen years of existence, but I felt the connection. Her feelings were palpable—the pain, the fear. I felt it inside, and it was tearing me apart. I didn't like it. I didn't like that she had this effect on me. And I especially didn't like that I couldn't seem to make her problems disappear. Her voice hitched, and I was suddenly snared within her. "I just wanted to give you a small piece of myself like you did to me. I wanted you to know that you aren't alone in what you feel. Life doesn't seem to be easy for us."

"No, it doesn't," I confirmed, my fingers weaving into her

soft hair. My blood was beginning to run hot again, and I couldn't stop staring at her lips. Passion was licking over every last nerve, and all I wanted to do was consume her. All of her. Her mind, body, soul, and even her heart. Gemma-fucking-Richardson just became the center of my world. And she had no idea. Our lips drew closer, and she peered up at me. "I want to take your problems and make them mine, Gemma." *I shouldn't have said that. What was I doing?*

Her fingers dug into my skin, and if only she knew that that made me want to lay her flat on the desk she was currently leaning against to claim her. "No," she snapped. "I didn't tell you this to make my problems yours. I just..."

"Wanted to give me a piece of yourself."

She nodded, pushing her body closer to mine and resting her forehead on my chest. I was certain she could hear the racing of my heart, the way the muscle ricocheted off the hard planes of my ribs, trying to climb its way out of my body and into hers. "You could, you know. Give me all your troubles," I said, dropping my hands from her hair and wrapping them around her to clutch her close. *To hell with the fucking future.* "If you want me to solve your problems, I fucking will, Gemma. Don't tempt me."

A small, light laugh floated from her mouth. "Some problems only have one solution, and you're already on your way to helping me with that."

That wasn't true. I knew what the problem was. Or part of it. And I was ready to snap Judge Stallard in half and throw his body into the Pacific Ocean.

Gemma and I stood together in the dark art room, intertwined in each other for so long my arms grew numb. I had no intention of moving, but my phone vibrated in my pocket, and reality came crashing back in like a tornado. Gemma pulled apart from me as I wiggled my phone out and read the screen.

"Is everything okay?" she asked, glancing down to the brightness.

I sighed. "Yeah. It was just Cade, letting me know that Bain had left his room, but apparently, he is in Bethany's."

"The blonde who can't seem to keep her hands off him?" She looked disgusted, and I laughed out loud.

"Keeping tabs on Bain now, are we?"

Another glimpse of a smile peeked on her flushed face, and I couldn't even help the rise of my lips. "Just trying to help out when I can. He likes to stare at me, so I stare right back."

I recognized the annoyance poking at my brain as I released a growl. I didn't want to talk about Bain. In fact, I didn't want to talk about anything dealing with the reality of either of our lives, because I knew it would make me want to step away.

"I have an idea," I said, dropping her arms and slowly striding over to the supply closet before giving her a coy smirk over my shoulder.

She crossed her arms slowly after tucking a strand of hair behind her ear. "An idea?"

I nodded before disappearing behind the door and then coming back out again with a box of charcoal and a thick piece of paper tucked under my arm. Her eyes narrowed as her thick eyelashes brushed against her cheek. "What are you doing?"

"Tutoring?"

This time, Gemma was the one to hop up onto Mrs. Fitz's desk, letting her legs dangle below her. *She was perfect.* "And that requires art supplies? Am I suddenly tutoring you in art now?"

I paused, holding the paper out before walking over to an easel and dragging it across the floor to set it up in front of me. "If that'll make you feel better, then yeah. This can be an art lesson."

Gemma fought a smile, sucking her lips into her mouth for a second. "Okay."

Warmth washed over me, just like it always did when I was with her, and up until she had walked into St. Mary's, I hadn't even realized I was so cold on the inside. So...disconnected from life. She was doing something to me. "Okay," I repeated, surprised she went along with it. I walked over to her, standing just a few inches away before quickly grabbing her by the hips. A soft breath flew from her as her eyes widened. "First," I started, pulling her ass toward me so her middle would connect with mine for a brief, antagonizing second. "Don't look at me like that."

"Lik-like what?" She peered up at me all innocent-like, but I saw the fire brewing as I flicked the desk light on. The same damn fire I'd been fanning over the last two days.

"Like you want me to dip my head between your thighs again." *Because I would. I fucking would.*

She blinked a few times, the skin of her legs burning a hole through the sides of my jeans. "And second," I whispered, pushing her hair behind her shoulder. "I need to pose you so I can draw you."

A huge smile broke out on her face, and it was like a swift punch to my core. "You're going to pose me? Can you even draw, Isaiah?"

I cocked a brow as I ran my hands down her thighs slowly, enjoying the way her smooth legs felt against my palms. "What a discouraging thing to hear coming from my very educated tutor."

A loud laugh left her, and it tilted the room on its side.

"You don't do that enough."

"Do what?" she asked.

"Laugh." I licked my lip, gripping her behind her waist

now and slowly lowering her to her back on top of the desk. "And I've gotta say, it might be the best sound I've ever fucking heard." *Next to her little moans of pleasure, of course.*

Gemma glanced away as her cheeks raised. "Who knew Isaiah Underwood was such a sweet talker?"

I hummed, gently gripping her chin and tilting it toward my easel. "If only you could hear the thoughts in my head."

The roll of her eyes made me grin as I made my way back over to the paper and charcoal. Gemma lay flat on the teacher's desk with the soft glow of the lamp caressing her body as she sighed. "Really? You want me to lie like this? Flat on my back...staring at you?"

If only she knew how mind-fuckingly hot she looked *just* like that. I roamed my eyes over her amused face. The small smile playing at her lips was so damn innocent it *almost* made me feel guilty for the sexual thoughts in my head. She sat up a little, placing her elbow on the desk with her head in her palm. "This is silly."

"I don't think it is when you're smiling at me like that." I winked, and she sighed softly.

"Okay, fine. But as someone who draws often, how about I lie like this? I am your tutor, after all." Gemma adjusted herself on the desk after taking off her school blazer to leave only her white blouse. She was half lying on her side and half lying on her back. Then, she slowly rested the back of her head down and tilted her delicate chin toward me, her brown locks swaying out from behind her shoulders, circling her heart-shaped face so perfectly all I could do was stare. Her eyes. The bright green of them somehow vibrant in a hazy room. The perfect tip of her nose and sculpted lips that didn't need even a fraction of color on them to stand out. My eyes slid past her chin and over the hollow part of her neck, the dip nearly begging me to graze my teeth over it.

My dick was growing harder as I continued to gaze over

her curves and the two perfect-sized mounds that I lingered on for far too long before Gemma shifted nervously. I darted my eyes away, knowing very well she had caught me staring.

"Okay, let's get started, shall we?" Gemma giggled at me, and I peeked up over the canvas. "No laughing, or it'll mess me up."

She laughed again. "I can't wait to see what this looks like when you're done. I hope my tutoring skills are up to par."

"Shh," I hushed through a smile. "I'm...creating."

Her lips rolled together, holding back a laugh, as she softened her posture some.

Several minutes passed by as I sketched her on the thick paper with entirely too much charcoal smeared over it. I had no idea what I was doing, and it had nothing to do with the fact that I was totally distracted by Gemma and the smallest of dips over her body. Halfway through staring at her, I decided to just draw a stick figure to make her laugh again, but when I looked up at her once more, her eyes were closed, and all the breath was sucked from my lungs. *Beautiful.*

Her tiny chest was rising and falling slowly, her leg that was twisted to the side had fallen more relaxed, and her hand that was sitting nicely over her hip was sprawled out as her eyes remained closed. Gemma was so damn beautiful that it stole my breath. I couldn't stop looking at her. And I meant, *really* look at her. Not a fleeting glance, not a quick look down at her lips before I had to take a step back so I didn't accidentally kiss her in front of the faculty. No. I mean truly stare at her without any holdbacks. It was world-stopping. She wasn't just hot or someone I'd like to fuck because I was attracted to her...she was more. She radiated beauty, and it honestly made me feel a little uneasy.

Was this what Cade felt when he saw Journey? If so, I regretted every single thing I'd ever said to him about the situation. Everything.

Placing the charcoal down on the easel, I wiped my hands on my pants and started toward her. It was nearing midnight, everyone likely tucked away in their beds since curfew had started hours ago. Cade had texted once more that Bain had gone back to his room and that his roommate had confirmed that he was asleep in his bed—not that I cared at the moment. I was having an even harder time staying on task than usual. Some of that had to do with the brown-haired girl lying in front of me, and some of that had to do with the anger still simmering over my father leaving Jack. What was the point in it all if my father wasn't staying true to his word? If he wasn't watching over Jack like we'd bargained for? I was still so angry about Monday.

Looking down at Gemma once more, feeling the anger drain, I silently cursed because I knew the night needed to come to an end. We both needed to get back to our rooms before the duty teacher became suspicious over our tutoring session lasting this late if we had a little run-in walking back to our rooms. But the longer I stared at her, the more blood rushed to my dick. *Don't do it. Don't cross the line again.*

Just as my hand shot out to wake her, listening to the faint sound of rational thinking in the back of my head, she twitched, rooting me in place. Her head flopped to the side, falling slowly before her eyes squinted as if she were flinching. I waited as my hand stayed stretched out. A few pieces of hair stuck to the side of her face, and that was when I realized that her hairline had a bead of sweat covering it.

Her breathing had picked up as I moved closer to her, and she grew tense. The soft way her hand was lying just a few moments ago sprung open fast, and my spine stiffened. She jostled a little bit, and I wasn't sure what was going on, but I reached out to steady her, to wake her up, but then all of a sudden, Gemma started to pull at her wrists. Both of them, back and forth her hands would move. The left would rub the right, and the right would rub the left. She made a little whimper as I took the last step over to her, and then I froze as she pushed her white sleeves up, the button on the side of the uniform top popping from her aggressively pulling and tugging, and that was when I caught sight of something.

What the hell was that?

My eyes stayed glued to the pink, raised skin circling her wrists. I wanted to pin her hands to the desk to inspect them further, wondering what they were, but another noise came from her, and it snapped me out of my confusion. I reached for her. One of my arms went underneath her legs, and the other went underneath the small of her back. One second she was lying on the hard surface, and the next she was crashing onto my chest as I slid down the front of the desk and cradled her in my arms. Her eyes sprung open, her hand ruffling my shirt tightly in a firm grip.

"You're okay," I said, pulling her in tighter. "You fell asleep."

Her head snapped down to her wrists, and I watched as her expression went from confused to mortified. Her eyes grew wide, her cheeks hollowing out. She knew I saw what she had been hiding, and her entire body tensed.

There was a hot burn that whipped through me. I was angry over the fact that I'd just now noticed her wrists. The pieces clicked together, and I was infuriated that I hadn't thought to question the way she pulled her sleeves down when I grew too close or the reason why she was in her school uniform most of the time, and if not, she was wearing long sleeves. I remembered being frustrated over the fact that she was wearing a sweater at the last claiming, because I wanted to see more of her skin like the rest of the girls. *Shit. What were those?*

Gemma moved to get off my lap, and I pulled her in closer. "No." My words were as cold as I felt on the inside.

"Don't you dare climb off me." Her shoulders sagged, her chest heaving with ragged breath that did nothing but spin shit up in me that shouldn't have been spinning.

I felt the shift of Gemma's head over my chest, and I peered down at her, catching the look in her eye. I wasn't sure what she was thinking, but I planned to demolish every last negative thought in her head. "Don't try to hide from me. I saw them, and even though it's ripping me to pieces not knowing what you were dreaming about so intently that you felt the need to scratch at those scars, I won't ask."

Gemma sucked in a shaky breath and swallowed. I leaned in close, my lips touching the softness of her ear. "But if I find out who put those there, I will fucking kill them. I promise."

And for once, I didn't even care that saying those dark words made me sound just like my father. I was beginning to see that there was no limit I wouldn't go to for her, and that in itself was a total game changer.

CHAPTER FORTY-EIGHT

GEMMA

I WANTED TO KISS HIM. I wanted to kiss him and drink in his promise like it was the only thing that would keep me alive, which was fitting because, with Richard still breathing, death wasn't such a distant thought.

Isaiah's hands were planted firmly on my body, and they were doing nothing but enticing me further. It was the way he said it. The way he looked down at me like he wanted to burn the world to ash instead of looking at me with pity or asking questions that I wasn't ready to answer.

My body was humming. I was angry and desperate in my nightmare—the same one that had been reoccurring since Monday after my phone call with Richard, and maybe even because of what Isaiah and I had done during the bonfire. There was the nagging voice in the back of my head that told me it was wrong that I had let Isaiah do things to me that I knew Richard would kill him for. Even kill me for. If he knew that Isaiah had even touched me with the tip of his finger, he would lose it, just like he had lost it on my mother when a man had looked at her for too long.

I remembered that.

It was one of the only memories I had left of her.

Why did the bad memories always stick out more than the good? I never understood that, and to be honest, it really wasn't fair.

My body was wound up. Like I was seconds from exploding. The nightmares always felt so damn real, and I was usually left shaking afterwards, but being in Isaiah's arms was doing something else to me. Something that was so much bigger and scarier.

The room was warm around us, the moon still streaming through the window behind the desk as the warm glow from the lamp fell upon our heads. Isaiah's thick eyelashes were lowered as he took in my face, his grip on me only growing tighter as his words soothed the goosebumps on my skin.

"Did my promise scare you, Gemma?" The roughness of his voice was like a match lighting me on the inside. It didn't scare me at all. In fact, it...it was *hot*. And I didn't care if that was wrong. "Does it scare you when I say things like that? Because if there is anything I'm willing to give up my humanity for, it may be you."

My heart skipped as his admission floated around me. The drop in my stomach turned to intense fluttering, and I couldn't stop myself from falling. I felt it. I felt the fall as if I had been pushed over the ledge of a tall cliff.

Isaiah.

I felt things for him that I'd never be able to put into words. He was putting me together but tearing me apart in the same breath. I knew, deep down, I needed to put space between us, because the more we were together in these intense and personal moments, the closer I grew to him. I was becoming attached. I couldn't stop the push and pull I was feeling. I couldn't stop as I gripped his shirt tighter and flipped around in his arms, pressing my lips so forcefully against his that he stilled.

But then his hands clamped to my torso, just beneath my breasts, and he pulled me so I was straddling his lap. His long legs stretched out in front of him as I wrapped my hands around his face and moved my mouth over his as if I knew what I was doing.

In reality, I had no idea, but my body seemed to know what to do. There was an instinct buried deep within that was finally crawling out of the darkest parts of my body and allowing me to feel the desire and passion that we sparked to life every time we touched. I felt out of control. *Wild.*

"Fuck, Gemma," he mumbled against my mouth as his hands roamed up my back and into my hair. I felt him beneath me, growing harder and harder, and it felt so good to move above him. To rock myself against him. I didn't understand how it could feel so good, but it did. Even with clothes on. "Gem," he rasped, pulling my face from his. "You've gotta stop."

"No." I shoved his hands away from my cheeks and brought our lips together again, pushing against him once more. His hand flew underneath my blouse, the same piece of clothing that had betrayed me moments ago during sleep as it showed Isaiah the one thing I hid from everyone. *I knew I should have kept my blazer on.* "I want you to just..." I pulled back, and his hand stilled just beneath the bottom of my bra. "Take it. Take it all. Just for the night." There they were again —those four little words that I kept throwing around but ignoring seconds later. *Just for the night.* I had to say it to remind myself that Isaiah and I would never be a long-lasting thing.

His tongue jolted out and licked his lip. "Take what, baby? What do you want me to take? 'Cause I'll take it. Fuck,

Gemma." Isaiah's throat bobbed, and his cheeks grew slightly pink. "I think I would do anything for you."

A ghost of a smile washed over my face. "Take *me*." I wanted to give myself to him. I wanted to cross over that line, because if by any chance Richard got me back in his care, at least he wouldn't be the one to do it. I would have the tiniest bit of control left, even if, in reality, it wouldn't stop him from ruining me all together.

Isaiah's nostrils flared as he clenched his eyes. "Gemma, you cannot say things like that to me, because I want nothing more than to drive my cock into your wet little pussy and make you mine. My hold on myself is slipping faster and faster, and you can't possibly want that. I'm...*fuck*." The more he talked, the more frustrated he sounded. "I'm not the one that should do this! It'll mean too much."

My hands fell to Isaiah's shoulders as I scooted forward, causing a breath to rock out of his mouth. His forehead came down and rested on my chest, his fast breathing hot against my blouse. "Please, Isaiah." My voice was strong, and it felt *so* damn good to take control of something and choose what *I* wanted. Because in the end, this was my choice. Even if Richard didn't think it was. Maybe I was moving too fast, but it wasn't like this exact moment, the moment where I lost every ounce of my innocence, hadn't been whispered into my ear while being at someone else's mercy. I knew the time would come that I would lose my virginity, and I wasn't sure I would have a choice in the matter. But I did right now. "If you don't do this...someone else will. And I need it to be you. Let me have the choice."

That was all it took. It was like a rubber band being snapped throughout the empty room. Isaiah climbed to his feet, wrapping my legs around his waist as he pushed the rest of the contents of Mrs. Fitz's desk to the floor. Pencils flew, the lamp shattered on the floor, and papers swayed softly through the air.

My back was flat against the cool wood as Isaiah hovered over me, spreading my legs so slowly they trembled.

"Are you sure?" He peered down at me, looking so dark and dangerous. The promises I could see lurking behind his hooded eyes made my toes curl. "And this will be the last time I ask you, because if I don't touch you in the next few seconds, I will need to remove myself from this fucking room."

My hand stretched between us as I pulled the collar of his shirt toward me. His middle met up with mine, and desire raced to every part of my body.

"I'm sure," I whispered, and his lips were back. He sucked my bottom lip into his mouth, tugging on it, and I arched my back as his hands went up my skirt, gripping me by the hips and pulling me even closer. A soft sound left me as Isaiah peered down with a look so hot I was left panting. His eyes were lustful, his cheeks flushed and his chest heaving. He looked like he wanted me, and I *loved* how that made me feel.

His fingers left my hips, and cool air hit my legs as his hands came out from underneath my skirt. They landed on the front of my shirt, and Isaiah watched me closely as he popped each button through its rightful hole until my shirt was wide open and my bra was exposed.

Normally, anxiety would have been holding me back, and I'd have been terrified that someone was about to see me bare. The only times I'd ever been naked, other than showering, were the few times Richard *really* upped my punishments and left me cold in the basement, without a single layer of clothing, but this was so different. Isaiah's gaze drank over my skin, his eyes scorching my flesh as he pushed my shirt off my shoulders and down my arms. My plain, white bra was all that stood between his eyes and my breasts, and when his finger traced over the thin delicate strap over my shoulder, I shuddered.

"I've never seen something so goddamn perfect in my life." Isaiah's mouth descended over the thin cotton straps, and he pulled them down, one by one, with his teeth. The scrapes against my skin had me withering underneath him, and I had never been more wound up than I was now. I needed him to touch me. I needed him to ease the bundle of nerves that were coiling in my lower stomach that I was beginning to recognize. And I needed to get lost again. I wanted that feeling that he gave me the other day. I wanted that feeling he gave me hours ago in the forest.

"Isaiah," I whimpered.

The sound of him unclasping my bra shot through the room, and I held back a gasp. "Patience, Gemma. We have to go slow, or it'll hurt you."

My brow furrowed as he stared down at me, pulling my bra from my body and dropping it to the floor. His lips parted, and there was a big part of me that wanted to hide, but his expression changed that feeling in me within moments.

"*Shit.*" His head dipped down, and I felt the warm, wet touch of his mouth over my nipple, and at first, it surprised me, but after a second, I was gasping for air and enjoying it. It felt...amazing.

"Isaiah," I said again, this time even more desperate. His licks and kisses branded my body as he worked his way over both my breasts, my nipples tightening just as quickly as my center. I couldn't believe how good it felt. How lost I became in his touch. I couldn't fathom letting Richard do this—and he wanted to. He wanted to touch and lick and keep me all to himself, like my mother.

"Oh my God," I whispered, and he popped his head up just before his kiss touched my hip bone.

His smirk was devilish, but the look in his eye told me that he was just as infatuated as I was. That he was just as lost as me. "We have to go slow. You have to be ready." His head tilted in the most predatory way I'd ever seen. *Whoa.* "Unless..." His lone finger trailed up the side of my leg, and it tingled all the way to my toes. I opened myself to him even with the small amount of nerves that were there in the back of my mind, and he hissed, slipping past my underwear and running the pad of his thumb over my opening. His eyes clenched as he threw his head back. "It was like you were made for me." His head came back down, and my cheeks flushed. "And only me."

I gulped as I watched him rip off his shirt. I awed over each curve of his chest and abdomen. I knew that he was fitter than most due to lacrosse. I'd watched him play several times, and each flick of his stick showed a thick band of muscles that liked to tease me, but seeing him without his shirt was mesmerizing. There were dips and valleys of hard muscle, and without even realizing it, my hand slipped out from the desk, and I slowly ran my finger over each hard ab. Once I got to the bottom, just above the hem of his pants, his hand gripped mine, and he squeezed it. *He was the beautiful one.* My heart crawled up my throat as something intimate was shared between us. Something that couldn't be described in words. Only actions.

Isaiah took a step back from me, and I sat up from the desk slowly. My long hair fell down in waves behind me, caressing the bareness of my back. The beating of my heart grew as I scooted myself to the very edge and reached my shaky fingers out in front of me. We held eyes the entire time. His baby blues collided with mine. The button of his jeans was slowly pushed through the hole, and my fingers trembled as I pulled the zipper down. Isaiah's stare darkened as the pad of my finger touched over his boxers, and once I pushed the rest of his jeans down to the ground, he stepped out of them and hooked his fingers into the waistband.

I knew what awaited me. I'd felt a man before. But never like this. I'd never come face to face. I'd never actually been *intimate* with someone. I'd never wanted to see. But it was all different with Isaiah. I was hungry to make him lose himself in me like I'd done on Monday when he had pushed me up against that tree. I was eager to do this with him. To have this moment with him.

Our gazes collided as Isaiah pushed his boxers down. I heard the soft fabric hit the floor, and slowly, so slowly, it felt like time had actually stopped. I pushed my hand out and dropped my head.

My heart slowed as I waited for fear, or anxiety, or even surprise, but the only thing I felt was heat. He was hard and long, and my escaped breath propelled me to touch him, to feel him in my hands, to make him come undone, and to please him. I wanted him to feel good. I wanted to drive him crazy. I wanted to do what that girl did in the forest. I wanted Isaiah to want me. Hearing his sharp inhale of breath when I finally reached out and ran my finger around his hardness gave me an incredible amount of confidence. I shot a quick peek up to him, and his jaw was set, and his eyes were pinned on mine.

"Am I...doing it right?" I looked away shyly. "I'm not sur—"

Isaiah's hand came down on mine, and he wrapped my fingers around the thick base. He was warm, and I licked my lips. It was a little intimidating but fascinating, too. "You can't really do it wrong." He paused, taking our joined hands and rubbing them over the length of him. "I'm convinced you can't do anything wrong, Gemma."

Isaiah's hand left mine once I got the hang of touching him. My grip grew a little tighter, and I watched as he grew thicker. His head flung backward, and the muscles along his neck were defined through the shadows of the room. After a few more seconds, he grabbed my hand and held it firmly. His breath was coming in short spurts, his large chest expanding quickly. "You have no idea how wild you drive me."

Isaiah's head dropped back down, and he locked onto my lips. He took my hands and placed them directly onto the desk, the cool wood washing away the heat along my palm that I had felt seconds before. Once I was firmly seated, he leaned into my personal space, his legs brushing against the insides of mine, and he grabbed the back of my skirt and lowered the zipper. "Lift up," he said, breathing down into my personal space. I pushed myself up, hovering for just a moment before he rushed my skirt and panties down past my legs and over my ankles before depositing them to the floor with his clothes.

Another bout of cool air covered my skin, but it didn't last long as Isaiah crowded me once more. His fingers splayed over my hips, and my head fell into his chest. It only took one swipe of his finger over my middle for me to buck my hips forward and for him to catch me in the process.

"Lie back, baby," he whispered softly, pushing me gently so I was lying back on the desk again. My hair fanned out around me as he hovered over me, pulling me just a few inches closer to him so my legs were dangling all the way off the desk. He reached down for a split second, and I heard the crinkling of a wrapper before he popped back up and gripped my legs. He drove his gaze into me with a firm jaw. "I should stop this right here and right now, but I fucking can't."

I swallowed the nerves and licked my lips. "Please don't stop. I need this."

He gritted his teeth. "This might hurt for a second." His

mouth was right above mine, and I had to force myself to lie back so I wouldn't kiss him. "But I promise you, I will make you feel good. Just like on Monday. Do you trust me?"

There was absolutely no hesitation on my part. I nodded quickly as he ran a finger over the side of my face. His hand gripped my chin, and his mouth covered mine, taking away any thought I may have had. His tongue swept over every inch of my mouth, making me spin, before I felt him at my center. He pushed in slowly and paused, pushing up on his forearms to glance down at me. "You okay?"

I swallowed and nodded as his finger trailed past my neck and down my chest. Isaiah had one of his hands gripping my hip and the other moved over to my left breast. He shot me a sexy grin before lowering his head and kissing the tight bud, causing a rush to sweep over my body. I inhaled sharply, meeting him with a small thrust. A pinch of pain came from below as he pulled up and shot me a look. "Careful. Trust me when I say we need to go slow. You're tight, and I have every intention of taking care of you"—his stare grew hooded as he pushed in a little further—"and making you come so hard you'll never be the same."

His words were a little dirty, and it did nothing but make me sweat. I nodded sharply as he came down and crushed his lips to mine again, and this time, the sweetness from earlier was a little more bitter. Our kisses turned urgent, and my breasts pushed up and met his naked chest. A grumble of a sound rumbled out of him and echoed over my mouth, and that was when I felt the fullness of him. He'd pushed in even more, and our middles met. I felt him everywhere. In every inch of my body. In every space inside my head. We stayed like that for a few seconds, his forehead pressed to mine, a bead of sweat running over the perfect curve of his cheek. I moved first, curving my hips up to his for a moment to test the waters. I couldn't believe it was happening. I couldn't believe that somehow Isaiah and I had ended up like...*this*. It was nothing I'd ever expected, and it seemed to happen so quickly, but I was ready. I hadn't known I was ready, but I was. Every interaction I'd had with him from the very beginning felt different. Like we were connected somehow. My body seemed to twist in certain ways when he looked at me from across the hall. And maybe, deep down, my soul begged for him to mend mine. Because that was what it felt like. It felt like Isaiah was taking my deepest scars that laid ever so painfully over my soul, and he was healing them. He was replacing the bad with the good. He was giving me the light, showing me that there was so much more out there than what I'd been given.

"Gemma, goddamnit." Isaiah pulled up, and his hands flew to my hips. His fingers dug into the skin, and I loved it. *I loved it so much.* I felt alive. He could rip me apart, and I would still feel myself piecing together. "I have to go slow, or I'll hurt you. You need to adjust to me."

I wiggled myself under him again, feeling something click into place. I was ready to take what he was giving. I was freeing myself, letting loose to enjoy what I was feeling. My hands found his biceps, and I gripped them hard as I pushed closer to him. His eyes grew frantic, and his mouth opened and then closed. "That doesn't hurt?" he asked, moving my hips slowly before he began pushing farther into me.

"No," I rushed out, arching my back. "My body wants this, Isaiah. It wants you." It did. My body knew what was right and what was wrong. And this? This was right. It felt too good to be wrong.

"Fuck." His mouth fell to mine again, our teeth clanking together. His hips started to move as his arm came around my lower back to steady me. My hair was woven between his fingers as he dug his palm through the strands, and we were in a frenzy. My hips fell apart, his body moving over mine in the most scandalous of ways. "I'm already about to come. You're..." He leaned in and pulled my lip with his teeth, and I whimpered as I felt my body tensing beneath his. "You're so wet and hot, and tight, and fuck me if I'll ever be able to live without this." His hand left mine, and he pushed it in between us. I felt the pad of his thumb rub over me, and I wanted to keep watching him. I wanted to watch his eyes roam over my body like I was the most fascinating thing he'd ever seen, but it was too much. His skin against mine. The fulfillment I felt with him inside me. The way my body pulled and pushed and sang. I moved underneath him, finding the best way to ride how he was filling me, and then I felt it. I felt the wind up. I felt my body twist and curve. The heat started at my head, and all it took was one little movement from my hips and his mouth over my breast, and I was falling. I was falling fast. Isaiah mumbled a curse as he lifted from my tightened nipple and his teeth grazed my neck before he sucked on the skin, and I saw stars.

I felt everything break and come back together again. The wave of pleasure and nothing else was like a drug. It felt so good. He felt so good. Even more so when he stilled above me, making a noise that I would take with me when I left and replay on my loneliest nights. And that was how we stayed. We stayed like that for so long the sweat dried on our skin.

I couldn't move. I couldn't even look at him. I just lay there, completely and utterly sated and...content. I'd never felt so worshiped or...loved. That was the only way I could describe it. Loved. I knew nothing about love, but I felt emotion bubbling up. The realness of it. The raw feeling of a mutual connection.

Eventually, Isaiah pulled out of me. I knew it because I felt the sting and soreness come in crashing waves. But I still couldn't form sentences. I was too afraid of what I would say. My eyes opened briefly as I saw Isaiah hovering over me with a wet paper towel that he must have grabbed from the sink in the clean-up corner of the room. "I'm just going to clean you up. Is that okay?"

I smiled softly and nodded. The cool water felt good against my middle as he wiped me gently, and it made me want to reach out to him and hug him. Isaiah was so much more than what was at the surface. I kept my lips sealed, still too afraid I would say something that would be wrong, and my eyes were so incredibly droopy. They closed a few times as I lay on the desk as Isaiah ran the paper towel over me. My clothes came next, the feel of my panties sliding up my legs slowly then my skirt. The straps of my bra went over my shoulders, and Isaiah pulled me up by my hand, clicking it into place.

When I finally snuck a glance at him as he was buttoning some of my buttons, I saw that he was dressed—well, sort of. His pants were still undone at the waist, but he had his shirt on. When I managed to meet his face, he was staring down at me, expressionless. The blues of his eyes were soft, his mouth relaxed. His hands slowly came up, and he cupped the sides of my cheeks, and my heart was suddenly back to life. It raced as we silently said things neither of us wanted to say aloud.

We knew this was bigger than anything we'd ever felt before.

At least I did.

His thumb brushed over the arch of my cheek, and he shook his head slowly. "What am I going to do now, Gemma?"

My voice broke as I tried to speak words, but I ended up coming up empty-handed. Instead, I shrugged, knowing what he was referring to. There was no future for us. At least none that I could see.

I didn't know what this meant. Or if it meant anything at

all. Nothing was changing. Richard was still a threat. Tobias was still missing, and I was determined to find him. It wasn't like Isaiah could come with me, and it wasn't like he didn't have his own problems to deal with. He'd already told me once before that we'd crash and burn, and I was beginning to see that he was right.

CHAPTER FORTY-NINE

ISAIAH

MY BACK ACHED. It hurt so fucking bad it felt like I'd slept at a nintey-degree angle all night. But I was warm. I was warm, and there was something so peaceful about the way I felt. Why did I feel so content? The first thing I'd always felt when I woke up in the morning was irritation and anger because I wasn't in my childhood bedroom but rather in a dorm room at St. Mary's, acting as an errand boy for my father. But this was different. There was a bright light flashing in my eyes, causing my brows to crowd, and then I felt a slap on my head, and my eyes immediately opened. *Who the fuc—*

Cade's big brown eyes drove into mine, and I saw two things I'd only seen a handful of times: panic and anger. "Get the fuck up, now," he seethed out in a whisper.

"Not sure who you think you're talking to," I snapped before feeling a shift in my lap. It took me a moment to figure out my surroundings, but then I glanced down and saw the peaceful side of Gemma's face with a piece of brown hair over her eyes. I almost moved to brush it away before Cade spoke again.

"Isaiah, get the fuck up. Now. Get into the closet. Mrs. Fitz is seconds from walking in, and if she finds..." The words stalled out in the air as I sprung to my feet.

Fuck.

After Gemma and I...I couldn't even put a word on what we'd done last night because it was so much more than a fuck...we didn't talk. Not much, anyway. I got us dressed, and she seemed to be in a daze, and I felt the same. There were things I was feeling that were so unknown to me that I knew I needed to keep my mouth shut. So, instead of saying anything or discussing the fact that I took her virginity, I wrapped her up in my arms and sat on the floor against Mrs. Fitz's desk. I kissed the top of her head as I ran my hand over her arm, and eventually, her breathing evened out, and she fell asleep.

I fell asleep too, but not before I took her arm and pushed her sleeve up, inspecting the marks around her wrist. That was the last thing I remembered before this moment right here as I rushed us to the supply closet with Cade right at my back.

"What's going on?" Gemma's sleepy voice hit me right in the chest, and I hated that I couldn't see her face in the dark.

"You two are playing with fucking fire," Cade whispered, but I heard the bite in his tone. "Mrs. Fitz is on the fucking SMC, Isaiah. What do you think she'd do if she found you two half asleep in here when, number one, it's obvious you've been here all night, fucking on her desk. And two, you're on probation! Don't you remember that all this bullshit with Gemma is to keep you here? The tutoring? Getting your grades up? She's your cover for the nights you're out past curfew! You can say goodbye to that if they know you two are fucking. Of course she'd lie for you and say you two were tutoring when you were actually sneaking out of St. Mary's. They aren't stupid. In fact, I'm surprised they even believe your act in the first place."

"Cade, back the fuck up." My blood was pulsing through my veins as fast as the rapids. Gemma stilled against my chest as Cade's hoarse whisper grew stern, and it was most likely because what he was saying was right. We were stupid to fall asleep in here. But with Gemma, my mind became messy. Things didn't seem so urgent and testy. I forgot that we had a plan. I forgot about everything the second I touched her. "Don't you think I know all of this? My number one priority is to stay at St. Mary's so my father doesn't ship Jack off just to be the biggest fucking dick in the world. I understand why I'm here. I know what my future holds."

"That isn't your only priority anymore, Isaiah. And you fucking know it." He scoffed as I saw the light underneath the door shine through. Gemma sucked in a breath, and I ran my hands down her arms. Cade leaned in close and whispered, "It's a good fucking thing you have me now, isn't it? Or you'd be trying to explain to Mrs. Fitz why you and Gemma are in the art room at six in the morning, half undressed. It's obvious you two were not studying, unless you two take human anatomy very seriously."

I clenched my teeth, angry with myself that I let us get into this situation. Cade was right. My priority wasn't just with Jack anymore but with Gemma, too. I didn't quite know what I was going to do with any of the knowledge I'd learnt of her this far, but protecting her was high up on that list, and us getting caught like *this* would bring shit down on both of our shoulders. I was sure of it.

The three of us stood quietly as we heard Mrs. Fitz shuffle around, getting ready for her day. We were lucky no one had alerted a teacher that we were missing last night. I wondered what Sloane was thinking since Gemma was her roommate, but I had to hope she wasn't stupid enough to go to someone other than my uncle if she were concerned. Sloane was observant, and she knew much more about the Rebels and me than she let on. After all, she was Journey's roommate.

"How the hell did you even know we were here?" I asked in a whisper so low Cade had to lean into Gemma and me to hear.

Cade held up a finger that I was barely able to see in the darkness of the supply closet. He pulled out his phone, the screen giving way to some light before he turned it in our direction.

A cold hand wrapped around my throat and squeezed as I looked at the newest blog post on Mary's Murmurs. "What the fuck," I muttered, snatching the phone out of his grip. Gemma's hand went up to her mouth. There, staring back at us, was a clear-as-fucking-day photo of Gemma curled up in my arms with her shirt half undone and my pants clearly unbuckled. Her hair was a sexy mess, and it was obvious that she'd been thoroughly fucked, not only by our appearance but by the slightly bruised hickey on her neck.

I quickly pulled the phone up, and my cool hand landed on Gemma's warm skin. I pushed her hair off her shoulders as she tilted her head, and sure enough, there was a mark on her neck. I had fucking marked her. Fuck, when did I do that? Was it my subconscious that came out of hiding when I was buried inside of her?

"Jesus Christ," I growled, nearly snapping the phone in half. I shoved it into Cade's hand and seethed under my breath. "That was taken no less than a few hours ago."

He quickly put it back in his pocket and leaned in close. "It popped up twenty minutes ago. After the last blog post, I signed up to get an alert when they went live again so we wouldn't have any more surprises. Once I realized you weren't in bed, I jumped out and banged on Mica's door. He was able to get in there and take the post down, but Bain is missing from his room, so my guess is the photo came from him."

I silently belittled myself for falling asleep with Gemma. If my phone wasn't currently dead in my pocket from my night spent in the art room, I would have seen that photo— or better yet, the photo wouldn't have been taken in the first place.

It didn't surprise me that Bain was missing this morning. He'd been snapping photos of Gemma and shoving them into his little hiding spot in his room, which was why I didn't want her alone. And surprisingly enough, I wasn't nearly as upset that we were on the blog as much as I was over the fact that he'd seen her with her shirt unbuttoned and in my arms. I didn't like that he was spying on us, just like I was spying on him.

That started a whole new chain reaction in my head concerning Bain. Things were beginning to stand out, and I had a feeling that there was a reason behind every one of Bain's moves. Pushing that thought aside for the moment, I brought Gemma's soft palm into mine and rubbed my finger over her delicate skin. *What was she thinking?*

"So what's the plan? How do we get out of here without Mrs. Fitz seeing us? Usually, I wouldn't care but—"

"But you're on probation, and I cannot, under any circum- stances, get in trouble and get sent home," Gemma's voice broke through Cade's and my testosterone-filled circle. We both shifted uncomfortably. "Please tell me you have a plan, Cade."

The whites of his teeth stood out, and I rolled my eyes. "Of course I do, Good Girl. I told you I had your back, didn't I?"

"So?" I whispered just before I heard the classroom door slam open. Shiner's voice came through, and my lips twitched. I was damn lucky to have the Rebels on my side.

Shiner didn't have the same bleak future that Cade, Brantley, and I had, but at least he had our backs nonetheless.

Mrs. Fitz's voice faded as she followed Shiner out of the room, and then we all quickly darted out of the supply closet and rushed through the classroom. Before we stepped into the empty hallway, I ran back to the trash can and grabbed my used condom and shoved it into my pocket. Gemma's journal was half underneath Mrs. Fitz's desk, so I snagged that, too. Cade sighed annoyingly, and when I caught Gemma's eye, her cheeks filled with blood before she snatched her journal and brought it to her chest. I winked at her, even if it was whole-heartedly inappropriate at the time. Her lips curved before she turned around and followed Cade.

"Now what?" Gemma asked as we rounded the bend in the hallway. Her hand found mine again, and a feeling of satisfaction came over me. I really fucking liked that she still wanted to hold my hand. I didn't think she regretted me taking her virginity, but I was afraid she'd pull away like the last time we had pushed the limits.

Brantley came out of nowhere, slipping beside us and striding down the hallway as if he'd been here the entire time. Gemma paused for a second before catching up.

"We need a 24-hour watch on Bain. He cannot be fucking trusted. What a bastard. He's trying so goddamn hard to get you kicked out of here, Isaiah."

That wasn't all he was up to, but I didn't say that in front of Gemma. Instead, I brushed him off and shrugged. "We'll talk later. I still need to talk with my father. I'll keep you two updated."

"Gemma!" A girly voice filled the hallway, and Gemma's shoulders nearly fell to the floor at the sight of Sloane. She rushed over and grabbed Gemma right out of my grasp. I huffed as she began pulling her toward the south wing girls' restroom with a uniform and Gemma's bookbag in hand.

I glanced at Brantley, and he shrugged. "She came to me, looking for Gemma. Figured we could use her help in getting you two out undetected." He shifted to Cade, and then they both turned toward me. "What are you doing, bro? You're being..."

"I know," I snapped, looking at Gemma and Sloane once more. Sloane was giving her a disapproving look as she ran her finger over her neck, right over the spot that I'd sucked on as I came inside her warm walls earlier in the night. Heat went to my groin before I heard an annoyed sigh.

"For fuck's sake." Brantley stalked off, leaving me staring at Gemma like she was the only goddamn thing that I cared about on this earth. I was in over my head.

Before I knew what I was doing, I stalked over to her and pulled her out of Sloane's arms. The hallway was quiet. The only eyes were Cade's and Sloane's, but I didn't care if the entire school was watching. I wanted them to know she was mine. Only this time, it wasn't for show. I might not have even cared if the SMC had formed a circle around us. I would still grab her just as fiercely, and I'd still tip her head up to meet me halfway.

"What are you doing?" she asked, eyes bouncing back and forth.

"I don't have many choices, Gemma." I dipped in close. "But right now, I'm choosing you before I can't any longer." Then, my lips fell to hers, and everything else ceased to exist. She was willing, too. Her mouth parted, and her tongue moved against mine. I pulled her into my body, crushing us together. Kissing her was like a gift. Or maybe it was a punishment.

Either way, I didn't care. I'd kiss her every day until I no longer could. And then, I'd find a way to keep her. I'd find her one way or another and make her mine again.

CHAPTER FIFTY

GEMMA

"Oh my God." That was the seventh time Sloane had said that in the last thirty seconds. I'd started counting after the third time. "I knew there was more going on than that one kiss and some lame tutoring sessions." Sloane handed me a new pair of underwear and a freshly cleaned bra, and I turned around to put them on. She glanced at my wrists once before quickly moving past that and focusing on Isaiah's kiss. "I cannot believe you and..." She swooped up my uniform and threw it into my backpack, handing me a new one. "Did you want to have sex with him? Did you want him to take your virginity? Did he even know he was taking it?!"

Sloane kept asking me questions, but I couldn't answer her. Every time I would open my mouth, she'd ask another question. It wasn't until she took out her makeup and started covering up my hickey that I finally answered her. "Yes," I said, feeling my stomach dip as I thought back to last night. Butterflies filled me up, and I had to fight to keep my feet on the ground. I was so twisted around all things Isaiah that there wasn't much room for anything else in my head. It was...him. And only him. "I did want to have sex with him, and yes, he knew that he was taking my virginity. The entire school knew I was a virgin, because of Bain, remember? I didn't exactly deny it."

Sloane blew minty breath out of her mouth so fast that it tickled the hair on my neck. She dabbed some more makeup on the sponge thing and got back to work. We were both tucked back into a stall in the girls' restroom, and I knew the morning bell would ring soon. "I'm just surprised."

"Surprised?" I asked, buttoning up the rest of my blouse before pulling on my maroon blazer. "That he would have sex with me?"

Her hand stilled, and she looked me dead in the eye. "No. Not at all." She glanced away. "It's no secret that Isaiah isn't a virgin. He's definitely made himself known in that department." My cheeks burned, and I bit my lip. It didn't even cross my mind last night that he was much more experienced than I was, but it was obvious. He knew how to make my body succumb better than I did. "It's just different with you. From the moment you walked into this school, he's been different."

I bit my cheek as she pushed my hair over my shoulders and ran her fingers down the strands. "Or maybe he's just finally showing who he really is."

She hummed under her breath, handing me my now-zipped backpack. "True, and it's no surprise that it took you to get it out of him." Her cheek lifted. "You're pretty great when you let people in. You know that, right?"

A closed-lip smile fell to my face as she opened the stall door just as the morning bell was ringing.

"He seems consumed by you. Like you are the center of every room you're in. His eyes gravitate toward you. It's not evident to most, but I can see it. I see the way he looks at you. It's the same way Cade used to look at Journey. Like he's afraid you're going to slip through his fingers at the last second or something." *That's because I will, and he knows it.*

Sloane paused before placing her hand on the restroom door. She glanced over her shoulder, and her smile turned down into a frown. "And that's why you need to be careful, Gemma. I don't know why you two seem to be keeping so many secrets, but that's exactly what got Journey a one-way ticket out of this school."

I nodded, and she intertwined her arm with mine as we began walking toward our classes. Just before the hall was swarmed with wandering eyes and the clanking of shoes against the tiled floor, she whispered into my ear. "Just know you can always come to me, okay? I'm here for you, no matter what. Secrets or not."

I nodded, shooting her a smile that was actually genuine.

————

Sloane and I both missed breakfast this morning and rushed straight to our first period. It was likely all in my head, but I felt like everyone knew what Isaiah and I had done last night. I felt different, but I knew it was in a good way, because any time I would feel the twinge between my legs, my stomach would flutter, and I'd have to bite my lip to keep myself from smiling.

I wasn't sure what this meant for us. I didn't think either of us knew. The only thing I did know for certain was that I was half-dreading the moment our tutoring ended. Whenever the SMC decided Isaiah's grades were better and his behavior had improved, gaining their trust back, he'd be taken off probation, and he would no longer be dangling over the edge. Which meant that I would no longer need to tutor him, which would also mean I would no longer be a cover for him if he was caught in the hall after hours, coming back from following Bain. I wasn't sure how that would affect him when it was all said and done. What if he got caught sneaking out after I was gone? And what was going to happen when he handed me payment for our deal? Would I leave without telling him goodbye? Would it be easier that way?

My stomach ached at the thought, so I quickly pushed it aside as I sat down at the art table for class. *No. I wouldn't go there right now.* I peeked behind me only to see Cade and Brantley sitting at the table that they shared, but no Isaiah. When Cade caught me staring, he winked at me, and I shot him a tight smile and quickly turned around and opened up a clean page in my journal and began sketching with my pencil.

The room was loud and chaotic, and my head was no better. Everything was jumbled, and I was antsy. Antsy to see Isaiah. Antsy to be alone with him again. Antsy for the future.

Just as Mrs. Fitz walked in and began shuffling things around on her desk—the same one I was on last night—the room grew quiet. I began lowering my pencil when I felt the shift in the air. The corners of my lips curved, and I closed my journal.

Two smoldering blue eyes were staring directly at me, and the way he walked into the room, commanding everyone's attention, had my heart galloping. His long lean legs in his dark pants, the white dress shirt unbuttoned at the top along with his tie hanging loosely around his neck. The tan of his skin caught my attention, and my mouth went dry, remembering just how hot it felt rubbing against mine last night. I couldn't believe the way my body reacted to him. I couldn't believe what he'd done to me and how mind-numbing it was.

He was in front of me within seconds, pulling out the chair as it screeched along the tiled floor. Mrs. Fitz looked up and shot him a look.

"That's not your seat, Mr. Underwood."

Isaiah gave her the warmest smile I'd ever seen. "I know Mrs. Fitz, but during my last tutoring session with Gemma, she was teaching me a little about the components of drawing. Would it be okay if I sat beside her so we could resume our lesson? I'm not sure how many more tutoring sessions we will have since my grades are drastically improving."

What was he doing? I watched Mrs. Fitz's disapproving glare soften. She looked over to me and then back at Isaiah, placing the backs of her hands on her full hips. "I suppose that's fine. Gemma is doing a wonderful job tutoring you. I'm very glad she is helping you. The SMC is impressed with your overall change, Isaiah. We just discussed it Monday night during the bonfire."

I jumped as Isaiah's hand swiftly fell to my bare thigh underneath the table. I swore my leg caught on fire. My shoulders flew back, and I fought to keep my breathing in check. I snuck a peek at him, and he was looking straight ahead, completely unaffected.

"I'm glad to hear that. Tutoring with Gemma has been nothing less than a godsend." There was a slight shift in his tone, and my brow furrowed as he erased some of the space between us, pushing his hand up higher on my leg. Was he serious right now? I almost pushed it away, but I enjoyed it a little too much. "Oh, and Mrs. Fitz? I meant to tell you how nice your desk looks today. Did you reorganize it?"

I snapped my head straight ahead and clamped my legs shut. My hand grabbed onto his, and I squeezed the life out of it, causing his shoulders to shake for a moment. I was pretty sure I heard Cade snicker from behind, and I threw a glare over my shoulder at him too.

Embarrassment flooded me as I remembered everything flying off her desk last night, but then came the laughter. My own lips started to tremble, and I hated myself for finding it so funny. It could have been catastrophic if Mrs. Fitz had found Isaiah and me half-asleep with our clothes undone. He might have gotten expelled, and Richard would have found out. We were being so careless, but part of me loved taking that risk with him. I liked breaking the rules.

Mrs. Fitz scoffed as she looked over at her desk, and I slowly shook my head, knowing that Isaiah could see me. "The strangest thing happened. I walked in here this morning, and all of my things were completely scattered on the floor. Nash had walked in before breakfast and asked if I had seen the raccoon that had somehow gotten loose in the school. Apparently, it came in here and dismantled things!" She gave a little laugh, and a few of our classmates began murmuring.

A raccoon? Really? That was what Shiner had told her? And she believed that? I thought for a moment... Shiner *could* be very persuasive. Or at least that was what he thought, anyway.

"Is that so?" Isaiah's thumb began rubbing circles on the inside of my leg, and even though my hand was still clamped over his, I let him. I felt the rush of warmth. He whispered down into my ear. "Now that would have been a good headline for Mary's Murmurs, yeah?"

I snuck another peek over at him as he peered down at me. His thick lashes were full of life along with the chiseled smile on his face. We both knew what was on Mary's Murmurs this morning, and I was beyond thankful that Cade had gotten it shut down before anyone had seen it—except the one person who had put it on there, which was likely Bain.

But why was Bain sneaking out of bed in the middle of the night and taking pictures of Isaiah and me? That was beyond creepy. Was it just to get Isaiah expelled?

"Stop worrying about it," Isaiah whispered just as Mrs.

Fitz started to gather the rest of the supplies for class. "I'll take care of Bain." I went to nod, but the rest of Isaiah's sentence stunned me. "And I'll take care of you, too."

My chest locked as I turned fully toward him. The amusement that was there seconds ago was replaced with a steep determination, and the tick of his jaw had my heart thumping louder than I wanted. He raised his brows, and I briefly nodded, turning back to focus on the rest of class.

CHAPTER FIFTY-ONE

ISAIAH

THE FINAL BELL had echoed in the hall fifteen minutes ago, and all of our lacrosse gear was already being loaded onto the one bus that St. Mary's owned. My jersey was resting along my tense shoulders as I waited for Gemma to come around the bend in the hallway.

It was torturous not slamming my mouth to hers every chance I saw her today. Every time I turned around, a member from the SMC seemed to be near, and although I had every intention of kissing and touching her every second I could, I had to remember that if I needed an excuse as to why I was out of my room after curfew, I needed to use Gemma as my scapegoat. If they knew things had shifted for us, it was unlikely they'd believe our tutoring gig, and I was so fucking close to being off probation that I couldn't risk it. I'd save the touching for behind closed doors and hidden nooks in the school.

The thought made me feel wrong. A girl like her didn't deserve to be shoved into closets and kissed behind stacks in the library. It probably made her feel like my dirty little secret, and although that was what she had to be—for now— it didn't sit right with me. She was so much better than that, and I wanted everyone in this fucking school, even the teachers, to know she was mine.

After everything she'd learned Monday and seeing me lose myself to anger and resentment, she still stood there, accepting me. She felt for me. I could see it. It was like we had some tangible connection that made me stop in my tracks. I was so fucked up over her that I had myself coming up with crazy reasons to explain why we were so drawn to one another. Had we been soul-mates in another life? Was she a past lover reincarnated to become just that again? Why couldn't I breathe when she was near? Why couldn't I stop searching for her within every room I stepped into? Was I just *that* afraid she'd leave without saying goodbye?

I didn't even want to think of the moment that was soon approaching. I wouldn't stop her from leaving. I knew it was the only logical thing to do, not only because of the shit I had going on but for her too. That was another thing added to my shoulders. *What did he do to her?*

Gemma's need to keep her secrets close was understandable. I understood. How could I not? I was the same way. But that didn't lessen the need to know. That didn't take away the burning stake that was driven into my chest every time I'd come up with a scenario in my head as to why she was running.

I had every intention of finding out what was really going on, whether she was gone or not.

"There she is." Cade nodded down toward the end of the hall and stepped away near the side door of the east wing. Coach would be wondering where we were if we didn't get out there soon, and the last thing I wanted was a fucking search party for his star players, only to find me with Gemma.

Her soft voice floated down the hall with as much sweetness as a mouthful of sugar. "I can definitely study with you in a few. I don't have to tutor tonight because of the big lacrosse game. Isaiah won't be back until late, so I'm free."

Another voice. "Oh, thank God. Do you want me to just meet you in your room? Or mine?"

"Just come to my room. I'll let Sloane know. She won't mind!"

"Awesome! Thanks so much, Gemma."

"You're welcome!" I could hear the smile in Gemma's tone, and it gave me an unwelcome fluttering in my core. My hand shot out at the last second, and I grabbed onto her arm.

A high-pitched squeal echoed in the tiny crook underneath the stairs, and when the swirl of brown hair settled, I locked onto two big green eyes.

"Isaiah!" A gasp came next as I pushed her small frame against the stone wall gently. "You scared me. I thought you were Bain."

My lip lifted. "Disappointed?"

A half-roll of her eyes deepened my smile. "Quite the opposite. What are you doing? I thought you had an away game."

I took a step closer to her, nestling my knee in its rightful spot between her legs. My fingers intertwined with one of hers, and I brought our joined hands up above her head, resting them against the cool wall of our haunted boarding school. "I do," I said, leaning in close. "But honestly the thought of getting on that bus with twenty sweaty guys is already bad enough without going an entire day without touching you." *What was I doing? This was not why I came to see her.*

A rush of pink swept over Gemma's face, and I loved it. I

loved every shade of red on her skin. She blushed so much. "You've gone eighteen years without touching me. What's one more day?"

I shrugged. "After last night, I don't really intend to find out." My lips closed in on hers, and she paused before opening her mouth and letting me kiss her. I deepened the kiss, completely unable to stop myself, and she fucking loved it. Her tongue jolted into my mouth, exploring like she'd done the night before when her walls seemed to shatter. I dropped her hand and gripped her tightly to my body, trying like hell to reel myself in before I was even more late for the bus.

I broke away just as Gemma's hands started to creep up my jersey. "Fuck, this was not what I had intended to do when I pulled you in here."

Her breaths were soft and fast. Her warm hands were still on my tense abs. "Did...did you need something else?"

I shook my head slowly, peering down at our touching chests and her inviting lips. I glanced away before I kissed her again. The girl was a drug. Intoxicating. Every bit of her innocence nearly begged me to destroy it. *You did destroy it, last night, on Mrs. Fitz's desk.* "Not really. I just wanted to remind you that you need to stay in your room tonight. With me and the rest of the Rebels at the game, Bain will be free, and he is unpredictable at this point."

A tiny smile appeared. "You could have just texted me that. Remember? You gave me a phone."

My finger brushed the side of her cheek as I pushed a stray piece of hair behind her ear. Her little hands cupped me around my stomach, and I fought the shiver that worked itself down my back. "I know." There was a small amount of vulnerability seeping in with my next words. "But I wanted to see you. Every time I turned around today, it seemed like someone was watching us."

She nodded in agreement, sucking her bottom lip in

between her white teeth, and I *felt* my pupils dilate. My chest grew tight as I pushed up along her body, and I felt the war brewing inside of me. A strangled growl crawled out of the deepest parts of my soul, and Gemma paused.

"What's wrong?"

What was wrong? I felt crazed. That was what was wrong. The need to touch her and feel her and kiss every inch of her skin was driving me fucking mad. The rational part of me needed to shove her away, close down my emotions, and get back the numb Isaiah. But that part of me lost. That part of me lost the second I looked into her innocent eyes and perfect bow-shaped lips.

My hands found the small of her back, and my lips brushed over hers before I moved to the side of her neck where I'd left my mark. "Everything feels wrong when I'm not touching you," I whispered before kissing her neck gently. "And that's a troubling thought, Gemma." A soft breath left her, and that was all it took for my temptation to take over. I didn't care if I was late to lacrosse. I didn't care about anything except fueling the fire I felt when I was with her. Gemma had changed me, and I couldn't change back. She was the one thing that I'd get on my knees for, and when the time came, I would look for her. I'd look for her, and I'd find her, and I'd bring her back to me because what I was feeling right now eclipsed the dark future that was clawing at my back like a fucking hellhound. I'd find a way to make my life mine with her by my side. I was through giving my father the choice to dictate me.

"It's like that for me too. I *like* your hands on me." Gemma's sultry tone had me rubbing my growing dick over her pussy that was so close to being completely bare in her uniform. My finger skimmed the outside of her panties as I thrusted my hips upward, catching that plump lip in between my teeth as she gripped onto my shoulders. I was so damn hungry for her that I felt like I'd die if I didn't get a taste. Just one. *Go slow.* I was going too fast, too soon. Gemma wasn't like the girls I was used to. She wasn't experienced, but fuck me if she didn't act like she was.

"Do you like when my hands do this?" I asked, dipping my finger inside of her. Her eyes caught mine, and it was pure euphoria. Seeing her pleasured was life changing. *Fuck, she was already wet.*

She nodded vigorously, her hair sticking to her forehead. "It feels..." Her eyes closed as she rested her head back onto the wall, letting me play with her body all tucked away in a dark corner of the school. I lied earlier. I liked having her to myself. She could be my dirty little secret. No one needed to know what she looked like when I touched her or graced her lips with mine. *No. She was mine.* "I like how you make me feel, Isaiah. I can't stop thinking about it. I've been thinking about it since that night you pulled me into the linen closet and rubbed a finger over my hip."

A whimper left her, and I kept my mouth shut because I felt the same, so much so I couldn't put it into words. My finger pumped in a few more times, and I watched her hand come up and touch her breast, and I had to shut my eyes from whipping my dick out and sinking it into her. If it were anyone else, I wouldn't care to go slow, but I had *just* taken her virginity last night. *God damn, don't fuck it up.* Her wetness coated my finger, and I couldn't control myself. Dirty things started to spew from my mouth into her ear as I ran my thumb against her swollen clit.

"You are the dirtiest good girl I've ever met, Gemma." I sucked her earlobe into my mouth, and she cried out. "I can't wait to do things to you that will have you screaming my fucking name."

Her hips moved back and forth, and her words were ragged. "Like—like what?"

A deep chuckle rumbled out, and she started to move faster against my finger as I added in another. She moaned, and my dick was so hard I almost took my other hand to rub one out.

"Dude, hurry the fuck up," Cade called out. "I'm heading to the bus. I'll tell Coach you're right behind me. You've got two minutes."

Two minutes? No problem.

Shock flew from Gemma's mouth in a fast breath, but I placed my lips on hers, drowning out Cade. It took her a second to relax, but when she started to move her hips again, I pulled back and hovered over her ear. "I'll taste you while you taste me." My blood pumped as Gemma's breathing grew faster. "I'll make you come from that, and then I'll make you come again as I finger-fuck you like this."

A soft moan came from her, and she began tightening around my finger. I grabbed her thigh that was clamped down to my hip and pushed it open wide, letting cool air brush over her sensitive skin. *God, this was so fucking hot.*

"And then I'll fuck your face until we're both seconds from coming and flip you around and sink deep inside your tight little pussy so I can feel you clamp down on me and watch your beautiful face fill with pleasure."

"Ahh," Gemma's cry was muffled as I swallowed her moan. Her nails dug into my jersey, and her hips thrust against my finger one more time before she came undone. My mouth kept moving over hers as I relished in her taste long after she was done orgasming. I couldn't stop kissing her.

"Fuck, Gemma," I said, finally pulling back. "That was fucking hot." My finger slowly left her middle, and a wicked part of me wanted to pop it into my mouth and suck on it. I didn't, though, because was she ready for that? Was I ready to show her what I was capable of? I was hardly hanging on by a thread. I was fucking crazed on the inside.

"I didn't know I could feel like this. I..." she whispered, all doe-eyed and dazed. She was beautiful. So beautiful my chest ached. "I didn't know this was what it was like."

I shook my head, pushing her hair away from her flushed face. "It isn't always like this, Gemma." Her eyes flicked to mine. "There's something different with you. With us. When we touch..." I glanced away, wading through the thoughts that were clouding my vision and making me want to keep her tucked away in this school forever for my own personal gain. When I glanced back at her, the guilt came crashing back, and I knew that we were fucking doomed. I'd seen her shield slip down a few times and watched as the innocence she held so delicately in her hands was washed away by me. Was it wrong? Was she letting her guard down only for me to destroy her in the end? Only for *her* to destroy *me* in the end?

I lowered her leg and straightened her skirt, feeling the truth burn the back of my throat. "I feel like every time I touch you I'm stripping you of your innocence. I'm taking away something that you should have with someone else." *I feel like I'm ruining you.*

Her chin tipped upward, and a determined look came over her face. That fiery girl was back, and I'd missed her. Her hands bunched up into my jersey, and she pulled me closer to her, surprising me. "Don't look so guilty. I want you to take all of my innocence, Isaiah. I want *you* to have it. And no one else."

There was a moment right there, as she said those words, that I felt like I was holding the entire world in my hands. And maybe I was. But the moment was fleeting as something bright caught my eye. Our intimate moment was cut in half as I snapped my head over to the left, just past the break in the tiny crook I'd pulled Gemma into. The air turned to ice.

I quickly turned my back to the flash that caught my eye and bent down to kiss the tip of Gemma's nose. "I'll take whatever you want to give me. But for now, go to your room so I'm not tempted to lose my spot on the lacrosse team for staying here with you." Gemma smiled shyly at me, and I winked. "I'll text you when we're back later. Just to let you know."

Just before she started to walk away, I pulled her back by her arm gently. "Stay in your room, and if you go to the dining hall for dinner, take someone with you. Like Sloane. Don't walk the halls alone, got it?"

Her brows dropped for a moment. "But what if Bain sneaks out while you guys are all gone? Who will follow him to tell your dad what he's doing?"

My hand tightened a fraction as her blazer bunched in my fingers. She shouldn't have been worrying about this, and she looked awfully concerned over it. "I have it covered...and don't even think about it."

Her lips pursed. "Think about what?"

I raised an eyebrow as my hand dropped. I knew what she was thinking, and she was absolutely crazy if she thought I'd allow her to follow him for me *or* my father.

Her mouth twitched, and she sighed. "Just trying to help you. If you need me to do anything, just text me."

What I needed was for her to stay in her room all night long. "I'll text you when I'm back." I quickly bent down and kissed her lips again. "Go the long way back to your room, okay?"

I could tell she wanted to ask me why, but instead, she nodded and turned around, heading in that direction.

I waited underneath the stairwell until Gemma had disappeared, and then I whipped around, knowing very well that it had been more than the two minutes that Cade said I had. Lacrosse could wait, and I wouldn't give two fucks if Coach wanted my balls for being late. I'd gladly lose my spot on the team if it meant catching Bain alone without watchful eyes.

I walked over to the side door that Cade had darted out of minutes ago, pushed it open as if I were leaving, and then slammed it shut. Silence filled the long hallway, and I glanced at the tiny crook that Gemma and I were tucked away in and then to every spot that could have had a visual on us. One small area behind the corner of a classroom snagged my attention, and I slowly strode over on light feet and listened again.

My heart had slowed, and my ears were sharp. My fingers hung loose by my side, and the second I felt a shift in the air, I reached my hand out and connected with bare flesh. "Drop the fucking camera, Bain."

His crazed eyes turned to slits as his face began turning red. His free hand came up out of instinctual panic, and he clamped onto my wrist, digging his nails into my skin. I turned my head and let out a laugh. Did he really think a little cut to my skin would lessen my grip on his throat? Did he have any idea who I was or what I'd fucking seen? My father used to wrap both his hands around my neck until I saw stars, and he taught me to do the same.

Bain's face began turning a shade of purple as I pushed him further up against the stone casing. The panic I saw turned to calculation as he figured out how to get out of my grip. His elbow raised above my arm, and just before he could connect, I let go and flicked my own up to knock the camera out of his free hand. Black pieces scattered all around the floor, along with the Polaroid photos of me with my hand up Gemma's skirt. The photos skittered along the black-and-white tile, standing out like knives in the middle of a goddamn gun fight.

Bain was gasping for air as I bent down and snatched them with my hand, feeling my pulse drum so violently that I could feel it behind my eyes. The side door opened, and I knew it was Cade, coming to get me. He was beside me within seconds and had Bain pinned to the wall. Not that Bain was putting up a fight. A coy grin covered his face as he glanced at the photo in my hands.

"She's quite the moaner, isn't she?" Red covered my vision, and the hold on my resolve slipped through my fingers just as fast as the photo fell to the ground.

His blood splattered on the wall as my fist connected with his cheek. One slice of his skin wasn't nearly enough to calm my anger, but when I met Cade's eye, he was giving me that look that made me pause.

Think, Isaiah. Fucking think.

Bain's laughter was sinister, and my head turned away as I reeled in my irrational behavior and tried like hell to think of the bigger plan. I needed to be smarter. I needed to be the man I was meant to be and not the man my father wanted. But fuck, I was tempted lately.

Cade grunted as Bain forcefully bucked his head back and nearly connected with his nose. "I swear to God, I will fuck you up, Bain."

He laughed, the noise echoing throughout the empty hallway. "Neither one of you will fuck me up. There's too much on the line."

Taking a step forward, I leveled him with a glare. "Looks to me like I just stepped over that line."

"Oooh. There he is. The Huntsman's flesh and blood that everyone fears. The prodigal son. The one that is supposedly going to *end* the war of arms trafficking in the west." Bain threw his head back again and laughed harder as I stood with my arms down by my side and zero expression on my face.

"You mean the war that you're setting up? The war that your father plans to win?" I took another step closer and breathed down on him with as much distaste as I could possibly feel in my body. Bain had no fucking idea that I was one step ahead of him. Cade didn't know either. No one did.

This was something I had to handle on my own. Keeping my secrets close—that was what I did.

Or maybe I just held them close because I knew that the future I was currently choosing for myself and my younger brother may have made me just as bad as my father. I knew Cade and Brantley stood behind me, and they backed my decisions, but when it came to their futures too, would they be so willing to stand beside me if it meant that the people they loved could possibly be caught in the web?

Bain struggled against Cade's hold once more, and although Cade was stronger than he appeared, Bain was just as muscular. He was stocky and knew how to use his body weight, just like me. "You think I don't know what you're up to, Bain, but I fucking do." Something dark began to stir in my blood as I glanced down to the photo of me and Gemma again, and before I knew it, I was spitting in his face and getting as close as I could without risking the chance of him headbutting me like he'd tried to do to Cade. "Take another fucking photo of Gemma, and I swear to God, I will rip your fucking eyeballs out of your head."

There was a slight twitch in his eye as his lips forced out another haughty smile. "You won't touch me."

"Fucking try me." All bets were off when he included Gemma in this little game of ours. Of our fathers'. I wanted to believe that Gemma had nothing to do with this war of weaponry that was brewing and setting up the next line of gun traffickers, but after seeing Judge Stallard with Bain at the Covens, it would have been naive of me to think otherwise. I didn't believe in coincidences.

Bain's voice lowered as the side door slammed open. "Jack's life is on the line, Isaiah. You won't do a damn thing because you know he'll be the one to suffer. Your father is even sicker than mine."

My cheek lifted, and I could sense that Cade was

confused by my reaction. Bain wasn't nearly as good at masking his emotions as he thought, because I could see the confusion brewing in him too. "You mistake me for someone who's selfless, Bain." I laughed as I bent down and swooped up the rest of the photos of Gemma and tucked them into my pocket. "Think again, errand boy. You may be on your father's payroll, but I'm sure as fuck not on mine, no matter the threats he sends my way."

"Boys!" Coach's raspy voice echoed throughout the hall as Cade and I began walking toward the door. He stood there with his maroon polo on and tobacco half hanging out of his mouth, even though tobacco wasn't tolerated on school premises. "Get your asses on the bus now. We're 'bout to be late to Temple, and for fuck's sake, Isaiah...wipe the blood off your knuckles. You're on probation, and this team will be damned if you get expelled."

Cade snorted as we briskly walked out the door with Coach following, leaving Bain with his broken camera on the floor of St. Mary's.

As soon as we were seated on the bus with Brantley and Shiner sitting directly across from us, Cade dropped his voice. "What the fuck was that?"

I leaned back onto the sticky vinyl backing of the seat and stretched my legs out as far as I could, glancing out the window at the high, castle-like dome of St. Mary's. "Bain's been playing us this whole time."

"What do you mean?" Brantley demanded, his face a mask of determination.

I craned my neck toward him. "Do you really think a guy like Bain doesn't know we're following him when he leaves? Do you really think he doesn't know about the fucking trackers we put on his cars? He probably already knows there's one on the G-wagon. From the very second he knew who I was, he changed his path. He's starting a war between his father and mine."

"We already knew there was a war brewing," Cade noted.

I shook my head, glancing back out to the school and wondering why Gemma's uncle, Judge Stallard, seemed to be in the middle of all of this. I wasn't positive if his part was large or small, but what I did know was that Gemma needed to leave now more than ever. Especially if her uncle was more than just a vessel in between two opposing sides. "Bain wanted me to see the deal at the Covens. He knew I'd tell my father that his father was moving into our territory."

Brantley slumped back into his seat. "Therefore, you kick-started things by telling him what you'd seen."

I nodded again.

Silence passed as the rest of the team chatted around us. Shiner sighed and pulled his headphones on, drowning out our conversation out of respect or maybe annoyance that he wasn't as big of a part of it as we were.

Cade glanced over at me. "So now what?"

"Now?" I asked, raising my brows. "Now we decide which side of the war we want to be on."

CHAPTER FIFTY-TWO

GEMMA

TRUST WAS SUCH A FICKLE THING. It was delicate too. Easily broken, but not easily mended. I'd trusted before, and it was a fleeting entity. Trust was volatile. Someone could take the trust they gave you and become unpredictable with it. I was jaded with the term, and the flip in my stomach when I thought about trusting someone made me queasy, but I was nearly there with Isaiah.

And I thought he was there with me too. I knew things about him that others didn't. He shared Jack with me, even in such a small way, but he trusted me enough to tell me about his little brother and the threat of his father. I didn't take that information lightly, which was exactly why I was doing this alone.

I just hoped that it didn't ruin the little trust that we had in each other as of late. He trusted me when I'd told him I would stay in my room all night. And when he'd said it, and I agreed, the idea was just barely a seed sprouting in the back of my head.

Now it was full on blooming, and with each step that I took toward the side door of St. Mary's, well past curfew, another seedling sprouted.

The hallway was quiet and motionless. Sloane had fallen asleep early tonight, which was to my benefit, and either she thought the guys were already back and that I was sneaking out to see Isaiah, or she didn't wake up, because I had no missed texts besides the one from Isaiah that said they were on their way back to the school from Temple.

My heart pounded as my foot hit the pebbled stone beneath my shoes, and the cool moisture from the night air hit my warm cheeks. The hood was pulled up over my head, and the feeling of someone lurking behind me made the hairs on the back of my neck stand erect.

Bain wasn't leaving the school tonight. I knew that because of his conversation earlier in the evening. I called it fate. It was like a stronger force had aligned all the stars and put me in the perfect spot to overhear his phone conversation at dinner, bringing me to my current decision. He had been tucked away in the same little corner that Isaiah had pulled me into earlier to do things to me that made me blush at the mere thought, chuckling into the phone.

"The Rebels took my keys for the night. Or sent someone to do their dirty work."

The other person on the phone rumbled out a grumpy laugh, and it echoed along the stone walls. He must have been on speaker. *"Do they not assume you have a spare? They truly do think you're a fucking idiot, don't they?"*

Bain snorted. *"I'm sure they searched high and low for the spare. Little did they know, it's in the fucking electrical box at the warehouse."* He laughed menacingly before sighing. *"It doesn't matter. It's not like I'm leaving tonight anyway. Who's doing the run tonight?"*

I left the conversation shortly after, feeling my heart

thrash inside from the eavesdropping. It was like listening to Richard on the phone inside his office all over again. The fear of being caught made every nerve in my body fizzle out every single time.

After glancing back behind me a thousand times, sweat lining my hairline, I watched as St. Mary's disappeared in the distance, and I retraced the same route that Isaiah and I had taken. It wasn't difficult to find the warehouse, as there wasn't much more around St. Mary's other than long winding roads and a few streetlights here and there for good measure. My breath fanned out in front of my face from the chill in the air, and my pace picked up when I eventually saw the rickety metal shack up above. The closer I got to it, the more my blood raced. Adrenaline filled me up as I breathed heavily. I kept pushing Isaiah out of my head, knowing he would be upset with me if he knew what I was doing, and there was a little bit of shame and guilt that came with that, but my curiosity was coming in like rolling thunder. *The Covenant Psychiatric Hospital.* I had to know. I had to know why it was so familiar. I needed to know why the hospital was so clear inside my memories that I'd managed to draw it before Isaiah even took me there.

There was nothing on the website that made me think twice, but each and every time I saw that drawing, something pulled at my chest. Something urgent. And there was a nagging thought in the back of my head that said, *What if Tobias was there?* What if it was some weird twin telepathy thing going on?

I sighed, pushing my hair away from my face. There was only one way to find out, and I knew that Isaiah wouldn't take me with him again. It was too dangerous last time, and he regretted taking me in the first place. And I wasn't going to bring him with me or ask him to take me back. Not only would that open up a lot of questions that I wasn't ready to answer yet, but Isaiah had more on the line than I thought.

I wouldn't put him in a position that could extradite him to expulsion. If the SMC somehow found out that I'd snuck out, then that was on me. But if Isaiah was with me, and we were caught off school grounds, *not* tutoring like we were supposed to be? He'd be done for. Expelled just like that. And I didn't want him to cover for me, and I had a big feeling that he would try to.

And if I were being honest, being on my own, making choices for myself—even if I was breaking the rules—felt empowering. Like I was climbing the ladder that I'd been forced to hold for someone else all my life, finally reaching that top rung. Good girls who listen to others and follow all the rules never rise to the top, so I was done being good. I was done being forced to the bottom and doing what I was supposed to do for someone else's benefit.

I needed answers, and I was going to find them one way or another.

The second my hand landed on Bain's spare keys shoved inside the electric box off to the side of the warehouse door —just like he'd said—I was filled with intoxicating pride.

I was doing this.

I slid inside Bain's car with my heart pumping blood to every inch of my body so viciously that my skin singed with anticipation. I really hoped that Isaiah's little driving lesson was enough for me to get to the Covenant Psychiatric Hospital and back without wrecking into any stone walls like last time.

The car came to life as I turned the key and pressed my shaky foot on the brake. I took my time figuring out the seat, wiggling my fingers over the steering wheel, and looking in the rearview mirror every three seconds, hoping to God

Bain's beady eyes didn't pop up in full rage that I was taking his car for a spin, but no one appeared.

It was just me and the open road.

After a few seconds of pushing my foot on the accelerator and jerking the brake once or twice, I was on my way.

I followed the directions I'd written down, knowing my phone didn't work without St. Mary's Wi-Fi, and before I knew it, the curvy roads and blurred white lines gave way to the looming building, and I was there. My head jolted forward as I slammed on the brakes, and my parking job was completely off, but I'd made it.

The sign was flickering ominously, the P in Psychiatric brighter than the rest, and every once in a while, the only letters that were lit spelled the word Coven, but I had made it. Chills raced over my arms, goosebumps rising as I stepped one foot out of the car. I jumped at the sound of my door slamming, even though I was the one who'd done it. I was on edge, and that was probably a good thing.

That meant I wasn't stupid enough to walk into a random place and think I would make it back out. If this place meant something to me in my subconscious, it likely wasn't something good.

Damp leaves smooshed beneath my shoes as I traveled through a small wooded area, careful to keep hidden. It was pitch black outside, and the flickering light of the sign grew dimmer as I rounded the building that I could barely see through the limbs. My breathing was labored, and I could hear my heartbeat in my ears. I stood beside a tree, placing my hand on the rough bark and staring at the small opening that showed the building, and waited for something to happen. Would my subconscious take over and take me back to the time that I'd first seen this building? Would I remember something that I'd suppressed long ago? Would the beating of my heart ever calm enough for me to walk to the side door and peer inside? What exactly was on the other side of that door? Tobias?

The pain I'd constantly pushed down was surfacing. The hole in my heart grew deeper, and the sting of my brother being gone for the last four years was cutting away at me the longer I stood beside the tree. If he was in there, I'd figure out a way to get him back. Just because it was a psychiatric hospital didn't mean that my brother was mentally ill. He was as sane as ever the last time I'd seen him. Back then, I thought he might have been sick. Or maybe delusional. With everything he was spouting off to me and how he had gripped me tightly by the shoulders and begged me to survive, telling me not believe anything Richard said, was alarming. He had acted erratically, and it had scared me. But now I knew that Tobias was telling the truth. He was right.

Why weren't any memories coming back to me? I grunted in frustration, anger and annoyance beginning to force my feet forward. I didn't see anything but the door in front of me, and the closer I got, the more frantic I became. It was a black door with a green awning overhead. My eyes ping-ponged between the two, and when I found myself underneath the tattered green fabric, I found my eyes rising and locking onto it.

This. I remembered this. Only, it wasn't tattered the first time I'd seen it. And the green wasn't as faded.

Why have I been here? I clenched my eyes, bringing my hands up and underneath the hood of my black jacket, fisting at my hair. *Remember, Gemma!*

Just as I started to sort through the dark memories, digging my heels into the hard surface below my feet, I jerked, shooting my eyes open. A hand wrapped around my bicep, and I was swung around violently and thrown up against the door. My head banged off the back of it, and I cried out, fear nearly choking me to death.

I gulped back a scream when I peered up into a man's face who was glaring down at me with sick pleasure in his dark eyes. "And what is a good girl like you doing in a place like this?"

His grip grew tighter, his fingers pulling the fabric of my jacket. My heart climbed to my throat, and I felt the blood drain from my face. *What the hell did I get myself into?* The puffs of air were barely making it out of my chest as panic started to surface. The beady look on his face grew with satisfaction as my body began to shake. He smiled, and my stomach fell. "Where is Bain? Huh?" He dipped his face closer to me, and I smelled the cigar scent lingering on his tongue. Just like Richard. "Where is he, you stupid little bitch?" His arm rose quickly, and before I could duck, the back of his hand landed on my cheek, and I cried out in pain. I blinked a few times, trying to steady my vision, but the trees in front of me swayed even more. "Did he send you to make the sales?"

"What?" The word came out slowly, and I tried to snap myself out of the lull I was in. My head pounded. The throbbing was there at my temples, making me wince, but I dug down as deep as I possibly could and stared at one thing in front of me, steadying my gaze. *You've been in worse places, Gemma. You are strong.* I swallowed as his lip snarled. "Bain isn't with me. I came here on my own."

Regret began to poke at the thick wall I shot up from the second I made the decision to come here. I shouldn't have. It was a mistake. It was apparent that I hadn't learned my lesson with Richard. My plan had holes in it, and I convinced myself that fate was leading me here for a reason, but I was wrong. Fate had tricked me. My plan wasn't concise, and I knew better. I knew better than to jump into action and feed the stupid impulses without a solid freaking plan, and here I was. Caught.

I'm going to end up in that fucking basement again.

No. No, I wasn't.

I leveled my chin and tried to yank my arm out from his grip. "I stole his car."

He snorted, clearly not believing me. I watched as his tongue ran over his white teeth. The man was tall, taller than Richard and slimmer too. He wore a nice black suit that screamed prestige, and his black hair was gelled back to perfection. On the outside, he looked like he could have been a nice businessman in a fancy office somewhere in the city, but I knew better than most that looks could be deceiving. It was the handsome ones that were the sickest. They thought they were untouchable, and that made them unpredictably dangerous.

"*You* stole his car?"

I nodded, ignoring the throb behind my eyes.

"So then that means you know him?"

I said nothing, and his eyes flared. He pushed me up against the door again, and I whimpered as my head hit it once more. *Shit.* What did he want from me? It was obvious he thought Bain had been here. Did he see his car? Had he been following me? "So you say Bain isn't here?" He chuckled, and my stomach convulsed. He was amused, and I had no idea why. "So he didn't bring along his little piece of ass with him on a run? To show her how manly he was? How rich he could get off a few gun sales? In my *fucking* territory!" I jumped as his voice bellowed around me. "Tell me..." He creeped in closer, and I felt his hot, angry breath over my face. My entire body began to shake as the familiar feeling of panic crept over my skin like a slithering snake. "Does he fuck you while he holds those precious guns too? To show you how *dangerous* he can be?" He threw his head back and laughed loudly. It was the only noise I could hear. The forest sounds were gone. Even the buzzing of the light above our heads had vanished. "I'll show him how dangerous *I* can be. This is my area. Not theirs."

Suddenly, I was jerked to my knees as his hand pushed on my head, gripping my hair in his tight fist. The concrete scraped my skin even through my jeans, and I bit my lip to keep from crying. *This was not happening. This was not Richard. I didn't have chains around my wrists. I could run.*

"I'm going to fuck your pretty little mouth and film the entire fucking thing. Then, I'll fuck you until you bleed, and you can take it back to Bain and show him what I'm capable of. He touches my things? Well, I touch his."

My eyes grew wide, and just as I was about to scream from the panic clawing right out of my chest, a voice boomed from behind.

"Dad."

I froze. My heart stopped beating.

The grip on my hair tightened, and I pushed my head up to meet his hand to ease the pain. "Isaiah. How nice of you to show up."

Isaiah. Isaiah was here. And the man who had a tight grip on me, threatening to do horrific things to me just like Richard, was his father. *Holy shit.*

A small amount of relief seeped in through the fear and panic. It was fine. Isaiah was here. He'd tell his father that I wasn't Bain's girlfriend or whatever he thought I was to Bain. He'd tell him that Bain would be glad that he was doing this to me. That it wouldn't even affect Bain at all, and then he'd let me go.

When Isaiah's dad flung me up to my feet by pulling my hair, I fought a yelp and locked onto Isaiah. He spared me a fleeting glance and then looked back at his father with nothing but boredom across his features. *Wait.* I sliced my gaze to Cade and Brantley who were a few feet away, and neither one of them would look at me.

What the hell was going on? Why wouldn't they look at me? Surely they weren't *that* upset that I had left the school. It was a mistake, but... *Never trust, Gemma.* Tobias' voice cut through, and it made me angry. It was okay to trust the right people, and I trusted Isaiah. He would get me out of his father's grip, and it would be fine.

I swallowed past the emotional lump that was sitting nice and still in the back of my throat and leveled my chin, even if it did make my scalp hurt.

Isaiah crossed his arms over his chest, still sporting his lacrosse jersey that had grass stains and mud all over it. "What are you doing here? Isn't this my job?"

His father chuckled, but it was full of cynicism. "You can't do your job right. I got the alert from the tracker. I thought you said you had tonight handled."

Isaiah raised his arms. "I'm here, aren't I? And where is Bain?" Isaiah looked around sarcastically, the moonlight hitting right over the arches of his cheek. "Nowhere to be seen, yeah? That's because he's back at the fucking school." He took a step forward, still unable to look me in the eye. "You say I can't do my job right? Let me ask you this? Where's Jack? Hopefully not all alone with your shell of a wife, like Monday."

Isaiah's words struck a nerve with his father. My hair was pulled, and I was standing on my tiptoes now, trying to ease the pain. "Then who is this? She was driving Bain's car. Are you sure he's back at St. Mary's?" his father asked, full of sarcasm. "I bet he's out here right now, watching me touch something that's his."

I paused. My body seemed to stop functioning. Blood didn't rush. My heart didn't pound. I just stood...and waited. I waited for Isaiah to jump in and make his father let me go.

Isaiah moved his dark gaze over to me so slowly that I almost screamed out his name. I waited for that connection, that small dip in his exterior to show me that he had everything handled and that he'd protect me and take care of me like he'd promised, even if I hadn't responded to his admission earlier. But then he moved his attention back to his father and shrugged.

"Just another piece of fresh ass, I suppose."

The pain. The betrayal. The complete and utter shock from what had left his mouth had my feet touching back down to the concrete even with the pulling of my hair. I blinked once. And then twice. I stared at him, begging myself to scream and kick and demand he give me back what I'd given him. But I couldn't. I just stood there in shock.

Another piece of fresh ass?

"Oh yeah?" his father said, looking over at me. I couldn't even meet his sick gaze. Instead, I stared at Isaiah. Dumbfounded. *I trusted him.* Had he been playing me this entire time? Confusion swept me off my feet so quickly I hardly heard his father ask, "And how was she? I'm sure she was yours first. Otherwise, Bain wouldn't have wanted her."

Isaiah smirked, and it drove a knife into my back. "It was like fucking an angel. Nice and pure."

His father laughed, and I felt the first tear roll down my cheek and land on the concrete below. My knees buckled, and I wanted to feel rage and hate and lash out. But I didn't. What I felt was so much worse. It numbed everything but the pain.

But that numbness was gone as soon as I heard the next words come out of Isaiah's mouth. "I say we get back to the lesson that you were talking about. He touches our things... we touch his right back."

Isaiah's father breathed out a sigh of relief. "Finally comin' around to this lifestyle, aren't ya?" My face burned with his heated look on the side of my face. "And all it took was a pretty little thing like this to make you submit. I'll keep that in mind."

And then I was pushed forward into a pack of untrust-worthy fucking wolves.

TO BE
CONTINUED

Isaiah and Gemma

AUTHOR'S NOTE

Bad Boys Never Fall is the second and *final* book in the St. Mary's Duet. The St. Mary's Duet is a **DARK** boarding school romance intended for **MATURE** (18+) readers. This duet is labeled as dark due to the dark themes (strong language, sexual scenes, and situations) throughout. Be aware that it contains **TRIGGERS** that some readers may find bothersome. **Reader Discretion is advised.**

Bad Boys Never Fall is the second and final book in the St. Mary's Duet and it will end with an **HEA**. There will be more books in the St. Mary's Series but they will feature secondary characters.

WELCOME TO

SAINT MARY'S

BOARDING SCHOOL

WHERE

BAD BOYS NEVER FALL

S.J. SYLVIS

CHAPTER FIFTY-THREE

ISAIAH

I'D LEARNED from a very young age that emotions were fleeting. They were transient. Interchangeable within the blink of an eye. And the range of emotions I'd seen on Gemma's face in the last few seconds were just that. I watched as they shifted behind her jade eyes. Fear turned to relief. Confusion turned to hurt. Heartbreak turned to betrayal.

As I glanced down at the watery mixture of anger and shock, both masking the pain I'd just caused, I knew that I had made a grave fucking mistake seeking her out that first day at St. Mary's Boarding School. And this? This look she was giving as she crouched down below my feet with my two best friends beside me, her knees scraping against the damp asphalt, likely cutting into her perfect soft skin? This was my fucking punishment.

I knew I was playing with fire.

I knew I was inevitably going to hurt her in the end.

I knew that she and I would crash and burn.

Good girls like her weren't made for guys like me. And bad boys never fell for girls like her.

"I hate you," she whispered through clenched teeth, wet tears still glistening over the curve of her cheeks.

It was that exact moment that I hated myself the most. For letting her in. For allowing myself to kiss her and touch her. I had been an empty shell before she walked into my world, and the only thing inside that shell was anger. That was how I wanted it to be because I knew anger was the only thing that would keep me breathing with my future on the horizon. But again, emotions were interchangeable. One brush of her lips against mine, and it was like the floodgate had been unlocked. Possessive, protective, crazed, lust-driven, fearful. I felt everything at once.

I became unhinged when I'd learned that she wasn't in her room earlier.

When the bus came to a complete stop in front of St. Mary's after we'd crushed Temple on the lacrosse field, I got an alert on my phone. My gaze sliced to Cade and Brantley, and we all popped up out of our seats with Shiner following closely behind. In fact, I was pretty sure our lacrosse gear was still on the bus, but at that moment, it didn't matter. What mattered was how Bain, the guy who stirred the very pot of my life, had managed to leave St. Mary's without the keys to his G-wagon.

When we'd met Mica, Bain's roommate, in the hall, he confirmed that Bain was asleep in his bed.

Confusion sat on top of my shoulders as I watched the little red dot move across the screen of my phone, showing that Bain's car was moving to a location that I didn't even want to think about. That was when Sloane came flying down the hallway, well after curfew.

Gemma. What the fuck was she thinking?

"So, who's going to go at it first?" my father asked with

the same amount of distaste as excitement evident in his tone. My eyes burned to see red, to let my guard down and kill him right here. I wanted to wrap my hands around his throat and watch as he fought for life like he'd done to so many other men before him. But I couldn't. I needed to be rational. There were too many things at play. Too many things in the way.

I wasn't him.

I wasn't a replica of Carlisle Underwood even if, at this moment, he thought I was. My father was beaming with pride. He thought I was on his side. He thought that I was going to pass Gemma around like a goddamn whore and let him touch her. He was so blinded by his own misogynistic traits and thirst for power that he couldn't see the way my hands shook with blinding anger. I was fucking trembling. My fists clenched by my sides, my nails digging into the flesh along my bloody palms.

He would never fucking touch her again.

And neither would I.

Not now. Not after this. I didn't deserve her, and she didn't deserve this.

"Cade? Brantley? I always went first and gave your old men the next go around," my father laughed. "I mean, sorry to tell you, Cade, but your father isn't as faithful as your mother thinks."

Gravel crunched beneath Cade's shoe, but I didn't look over at him. This was a good test for our friendship. This moment right here would determine if Cade and Brantley, my two best friends, who knew just how fucked our futures were, trusted me as much as they said they did, just like it would determine if I let them stay by my side in the long run.

Cade's wide shoulder brushed mine as he looked down at Gemma. Her chest was rising and falling, but she kept her teeth bared and her eyes full of lethal determination. My lips ticked upward, and it wasn't for the reason my father thought. I was proud. I was so fucking proud—even knowing that she was full of hatred for me right now—that she wasn't cowering away. Gemma was brave. I'd always known she was. Whatever she'd lived through in the past had hardened her, and that was good.

"I've already had her," I said, swooping down and gripping her arms tightly. Her delicate chin jutted upward, and a flash of fear crossed over her features only to be replaced with a burning fire. I shoved her toward Brantley who was standing a few yards away. She stumbled over her shoes, the loose rocks and gravel kicking up in her wake, landing in a nearby puddle. "Maybe Brantley would like a go?"

He pulled her against his chest and wrapped his forearm around her upper body. Her little hands came up as she clawed at his skin, and the pink scars around her wrists peeked out as her jacket sleeves fell back.

"No!" The tiny word echoed around us, as did my father's maniacal laughter.

He cupped his hands around his mouth. "Do you hear that, Bain? We have your little plaything! Come out, come out, wherever you are!"

Cade managed to chuckle, but I couldn't force it out. I was too focused on the fear seeping into Gemma's eyes as her resolve fell. She caught my gaze from across the space, and her brows crowded as her mouth drew a straight line. "*Fuck you.*"

There it was. That burn of rage. I was glad she was angry, because that meant she had adrenaline, and she was going to need that rush in a second.

"You already have, little one." I winked, and Brantley flung her forward again, as if we were playing hot potato with her. She landed in Cade's arms, and I looked to my father who was watching her with bated breath. *If I killed him, I'd be just like him*. I was smarter than he was. And I wasn't a murderer.

Stepping forward, I tipped my chin. "So, what's the plan? We all fuck her, beat her up real good, and send her back to Bain? He'll know it was me who touched his little whore. It might cause some issues for the future. He'll be even more guarded."

My father took his lingering gaze off Gemma and placed it on me. "There's already an issue, son. Bain knows who you are. They're slowly trying to take each and every last one of my clients." He gestured to the building behind him. *The Covens.* "This one is our biggest consumer. I need Bain to run back to his father and let him know that he can't fucking have it. The Covens buys guns from me and no one else. Bain and his fuck-up of a father touch my shit, then I touch his. Bain's mother is next on my list if they keep it up."

Gemma was struggling in Cade's arms, the muscles along his arm twisting back and forth as he kept her still as my father glared. "Did you hear that, you little whore?" Gemma's mouth clamped shut as she stared at him. The ground behind my feet began to shake. *I was going to strangle him.* "When we're done with you..." He crooked a smile. "*If* you survive, you tell Bain *exactly* what I just said. You got it? You can be a warning."

Her lip lifted, and her white teeth bared again as her head came down. Her eyebrows were crowded above her eyes as she seethed, "I am *fucking* done with men like you demanding things." Then, her head flung back with all her might, and she blasted Cade right in the nose before taking off running into the forest, just like I'd hoped.

Before my father had a chance to grab a hold of the situation and start demanding shit, I stepped forward, taking charge and likely filling him with even more pride. "Time for a game, boys. Go fetch."

Brantley spun around quickly with a devilish smirk on his face, jogging down the hill, and once Cade recovered, he descended too.

My father stood back and lazily placed his hands in his pockets, smiling at me.

"Don't worry, Dad. You've taught me well." I began walking toward the hill that Gemma had disappeared over. "But now that you can see I'm doing what you asked and keeping up with the job you've given me...I expect you to do the same. Leave Jack out of this." I gazed out into the tall trees and foggy air, feeling the bitter taste of deceit in my mouth. "It's not like you'll create a better version of you anyway."

He gave me a curt nod with a glimmer of hope in his eye and started to walk off toward the parking lot. Before he made it to his car, he shot over his shoulder, "Make me proud, Isaiah. Get the point across to Bain...and have some fun. She's a beauty."

Yeah. Fuck you, Dad.

CHAPTER FIFTY-FOUR

GEMMA

I'D BEEN PUSHED AROUND ALL my life. I'd been forced to get on my knees and beg. I'd kept my lips sealed and my tongue clipped, letting threats and insults hinder me. I'd been broken, and torn apart, and had somehow morphed into someone who was vulnerable and weak.

But that wasn't me any longer.

It wasn't my brother disappearing and leaving me false hope that made me snap.

It wasn't Richard and his looming threats.

It wasn't the cool floor of that dirty basement or the abuse that followed.

No.

It was him.

Isaiah.

Isaiah was the one to do it.

There was nothing worse than giving someone pieces of yourself and allowing them the power to destroy every last one. I gave Isaiah the few parts of my heart that were the most jagged, the most tarnished, the ones that held both fear and hope, and he broke them in half.

And in turn, it broke me. But it broke me in the best way. Hope had diminished. Guilt was no longer a notion that I felt. Everything that had been holding me back from taking a hold of my life and fighting back was fleeting.

I wasn't going to sit back and let them have me. I wasn't a piece of trash or a little toy for them to touch for their own sick games. I was done being an object. I was done with people using me. *I was fucking done.*

So, when Cade's breath fell over my ear with his grip hard against my body, I was ready for a fight. "Save yourself, Gemma. Fucking run."

And that was exactly what I did.

As soon as my head had collided with Cade's, his arm loosened, and I ran like hell. The moisture in the air coated my sticky skin, the fog hardly giving way to the forest below. My shoes slid on the wet asphalt, and I tripped a time or two, but I just kept running. Sticks snapped, and slippery leaves stuck to the bottoms of my soles. My hair slashed across my face, and my jacket had fallen down over my shoulder, letting the cool night wash over my skin.

I knew they were coming for me.

Just like I had known Richard would the first time I'd run from him, too.

Hurt seeped in as I jumped over a log, falling to my hands for a second. Mud coated my fingers, but I popped back up and kept on running. *How could he do this to me?* Did Cade tell me to run because he wanted me to survive? Or did he tell me to run because they liked the chase? I could hear them behind me. I could hear the rustle of leaves and breakage of branches.

My feet dug into the ground as a familiar tremor ran through my body.

No.

I wouldn't allow the past to revisit me in a time like this— not when I needed to focus and figure out a plan. My legs picked up pace again, the air in my lungs coming out in choppy spurts as blood rushed through my veins. My legs burned from the fast pace, and I felt another slice of pain against my knees. *Just like last time.*

"No!" I whisper-shouted to myself, causing a nearby cricket to stop chirping. Richard wasn't here. He wasn't the one chasing me. My head snapped up as a thought came through. *But...* My gaze roamed all around the forest as I turned in circles. I was surrounded by large tree trunks and thick branches of pine that seemed to never end. If Isaiah had betrayed me once, he'd do it again. He was using me. Was he using me to lure in Bain? My head began to spin as I tried to make sense of it all. It didn't make sense. The way he touched me. *Kissed me. Looked at me.* It didn't make sense!

Nothing made sense!

My feet pulled me backward as my chest constricted.

I couldn't breathe.

I clawed at my jacket and unzipped it, throwing it off to the side. My feet moved backward again, and I fell to my butt, dirt digging underneath my nails, before quickly climbing to stand again.

Was he even planning on giving me the money?

I needed the money. Where would I go without it?

The fake ID?

Richard would find me if I didn't have one. I'd never be able to work. I'd never be able to survive if I couldn't hide behind the identity of someone else. I would have to find a job eventually. Find a place to live. I couldn't do that as Gemma Richardson.

He would find me.

I'd be his.

The chains would go back around my wrists until I submitted.

He'd make me beg for food. He'd make me beg for him.

"Call me daddy, baby girl. I'm all you have now."

His finger would trail down my spine and curve over parts that weren't his to touch. He'd fulfill his threats. He'd spread me wide and make me think twice about running. He wouldn't stop until I told him I liked it. That I loved him. That I was his. That I wouldn't break the rules like my mother did.

"Gemma! Fucking snap out of it."

His hands were running down my arms, and I shook from fear. Not again. No. "Did you break the rules? I thought you were my good girl? Do you want to end up like your mother?"

I gasped and felt for my wrists. I wasn't chained yet. There was still time.

"Gemma. Come on, don't go to that fucking place."

"I'm sorry. Please don't chain me. I won't do it again." His laugh made me double over. The nausea came in crashing waves.

"Cade, she's trembling. She's not with us."

"No. You won't run again. I won't fucking let you." I felt the tears on my face as he shook me. I felt something hard behind me, but it wasn't Richard. It was scratchy and grounding.

"Shaking her isn't working. We need to open her eyes and—"

"Take her mind back...bring her back to the present."

The scratchiness was gone, but the basement was still in sight. There were hands on me. But...goosebumps covered my skin. There were four hands on me. Four. Not two. And they weren't his.

"That's it. Relax."

Where did the scratchiness behind my back go? It was gone. I was no longer being scraped or cut. The sharp pieces weren't rubbing me raw anymore. Instead, it was firm and warm. There were hands on

my hips and soft touches running over my chest, dipping down low
enough to make me tighten.

"Just let it go. Open your eyes," a deep, raspy whisper
wisped around the inside of my ear. Something wet flicked
my skin just below the whisper, and I felt my head sag.

The hands were moving. My hips pushed back as fingers splayed
over the waist of my jeans. There was a hiss behind me, but it wasn't
angry-sounding. It was hot. I liked that sound. I wanted it to happen
again. My eyes were shut, and the basement was gone. There was the
hooting of an owl overhead, and when warm lips touched mine, I
was suddenly hungry. And eager. And angry. I didn't know why, but
I kissed back. My back arched as another set of lips touched my neck,
and the ones on my mouth were suddenly gone and on my belly.

I gasped, my eyes opening as I shot my head down.

Two big brown eyes peered up at me. Cade's hands were
around my hips, wrapping around me like he was steadying
me before my knees buckled. I watched as his tongue slipped
out from behind his lips and wet the soft skin of my belly,
causing things to throb that shouldn't have been throbbing.
My heart thumped viciously as confusion crowded me. Cade
waited. He stared up at me, looking as hungry as I felt on the
inside but wouldn't dare recognize on the outside. There was
heavy breathing along my neck, and I knew it wasn't Isaiah. I
knew what he smelled like. I knew what his breath felt like
on my skin. I slowly moved my head and peeked behind me.
Brantley's eyes were hooded as my back pressed into his firm
front, but the second he blinked, I snapped out of it.

"Get your fucking hands off me. Both of you."

There was the smallest twitch of a smile on his mouth
before his grip loosened. The ground crunched as Cade
slowly stood up, wiping a hand over his mouth, but he still
kept his other hand on my waist. Brantley stayed behind me
too, trapping me between them.

I was still shaken from my lapse in reality, but I remembered exactly why I was in the middle of a dark wooded area, sandwiched between two boys who were sent here to find me. My only question was why? Why were they touching me? Were they fulfilling what Isaiah's father wanted? It didn't make sense. I wasn't Bain's anything. But they made it seem like I was. Was I something more to Bain than he and Isaiah had let on? Regardless of the reasoning, I nearly growled as I locked onto Cade's face, but before I could say anything, something caught our attention from behind.

Cade peered over his shoulder, and it gave me a direct line to Isaiah. I kept my face steady, but hurt flashed within. His words echoed, and it was the only thing I could hear inside my head. *"I've already had her."* As if having sex with me was nothing more than a goal to be met. Another game.

"Why the fuck are your hands on her?" he gritted, creeping in closer and looking more lethal than I'd ever seen him. His brows were hooded over his black-rimmed eyes, and his jaw looked as sharp as a butcher's knife.

It made me irrationally angry to see him, but there was something that sparked to life, too.

My hands pushed at Cade's chest. He hardly moved but ended up stepping aside to let me through. "Don't you dare act like you care now!" Isaiah's resolve fell quickly when he caught my eyes, but I kept going. I kept charging toward him like I was the strong one here. There were too many emotions flinging at me to make me stop, and the only emotion I wanted to grasp onto was anger. I was so angry. The betrayal wiped away any common sense that I had in me to run. "What do you mean why the fuck are his hands on me, Isaiah? You *asked* Brantley if he wanted a go at me!" His mouth opened, but I kept going. "I'm assuming that invitation extended to Cade as well, right? So don't stand there all pissed off because your two best friends wanted to touch me like you did!" The fear and pain were beginning to surface, but I locked it down, steadying my feet, and the next thing I knew, my hand was raising, and I was flinging it toward the side of his face.

I waited for the burn against my palm. I knew he'd feel the sting across his cheek that I'd felt so many times before, but just as I went to make contact, his hand shot up quickly, and he grabbed my wrist, right around my ugly little scars. "Gemma," he snapped. "Stop it."

"Stop it?" I yelled, trying to whip my wrist back. "You... you..." My eyes bounced back and forth between his, trying to keep up with my courage. "You betrayed me! Have you been using me this whole time? You've been warning me that Bain was using me as a toy, but it's you! You acted like I was nothing more than a simple lay. A conquest. You didn't tell your father that I wasn't Bain's girlfriend. I stood there, with your father's hands on me, waiting for you to tell him that I was innocent in all of this. That Bain wouldn't care what happened to me. That I was nothing to him. Yet, you guys stood there and passed me around, threatening to touch me!"

My voice broke, and I felt my wall slowly slipping down. *No. I would not stand here and look weak.* I glowered up at him as his jaw flexed back and forth. He let go of my wrist, and I snatched it away at the same time, crossing my arms over my chest as my body wracked with a chill.

I was done. I was done playing games. I was done with Bain's threats and Isaiah's need to protect me by keeping things from me. *Things like this.* There were obviously much bigger things going on between the Rebels, Bain, and Isaiah's father. And I knew Isaiah's father wasn't a good person, but what I didn't expect was for Isaiah to take my trust and stomp on it. I didn't expect to hear those things come out of his mouth. I didn't expect to feel the heartbreak just yet and for those reasons. *Did he mean what he'd said?*

"I hate you," I whispered, taking a step back. "And I don't

know if you're using me in this sick game with Bain and your father, but I'm done playing." It wasn't fair when you didn't know the rules. Or the objective. I watched as the wall shot up behind Isaiah's eyes. His nostrils flared. His fists clenched. He crowded my space before I even had a chance to step back, and when he glared down at me, he said, "Good."

CHAPTER FIFTY-FIVE

ISAIAH

I SLOWLY TOOK a step away from Gemma, fighting every last feeling that was trying to escape out of my chest. I was empty before she came into my life, and now, I was flooded with shit I didn't want to deal with.

I hate you.

Hearing those words cut me deeper than I thought possible. But they were needed. They were needed in the most tortuous way. I hated that Brantley was right. I was stupid to think that it wouldn't end up this way. That she wouldn't be standing here, confused and hurt, and that I wouldn't be standing here, holding my bloody heart in my hands as she threw it back at me. She didn't even know I'd given her my heart. I didn't even know. I didn't even know I had much of one to begin with, and here I was, bleeding out with her standing just a few feet away.

"Why were your hands on her when I came up?" I asked again, looking directly at my two best friends. Anger simmered as I shoved my hands in my pockets, putting more space between Gemma and me. So fucking badly did I want to pull her in close and kiss her to erase everything that had just happened. But at the same time, I wanted to express how angry I was that she went behind my back and snuck out of St. Mary's. If she would have stayed in her fucking room like I'd told her to, then we wouldn't be in this position. I wouldn't be standing here, glaring at my two best friends like I wanted to rip their fucking heads off for touching her.

When I'd walked up, after jogging through the forest for what seemed like hours, I stopped dead in my tracks. Heat had spread to my groin as I zeroed in on Gemma's face. Her head was tilted to the side as pleasure coated her features, but then that heat turned to an inferno when I'd realized that not only were Brantley's lips on her neck, but Cade's were on her stomach. Deep down, I knew there was an explanation—or I'd at least hoped—but right now, I was in the mood to break shit. And their faces would work.

"Calm the fuck down, Isaiah." Cade rolled his eyes as he crossed his arms over his chest. "You should know better than to think that we were out here seducing Gemma after your father came close to fucking raping her."

I cracked my neck and growled. *Not the thing to say to me at a time like this.* "Care to explain, then?" I barked, walking closer.

Brantley sighed as he stepped beside Cade, appearing bored. "She was losing her shit. Freaking out. Saying shit that didn't make sense, like she was revisiting the past...and we couldn't get her to snap out of it, so..."

I saw Gemma move out of the corner of my eye. "So they started touching me, and guess what, Isaiah?"

All three of us looked over at Gemma with her sly little smirk.

Jesus Christ. What did I do to her? The sweet, good-girl version of Gemma was long fucking gone, and in her place was this confident, fiery, hot-as-sin girl taking control of the situation. If I thought she was hot before, when she'd spout off those snarky remarks, now, I was certain that she was the only girl on earth that would make my dick hard. *Stop thinking about her like that.*

My tongue ran over my lips slowly. "What?"

Her cheek rose. "I *liked* it. I liked having their hands on me, and you know what else?"

My blood ran hot as I trailed a heated look down her body. She was filthy from being shoved to her knees and running through the forest, but still, I wanted to pull her into my arms and show her that she was mine. *Even though she wasn't. Not anymore.* "What else?" I asked, my voice thick.

"It worked like a charm." She strode over to me, and I heard a snicker come from Brantley. I stood eerily still, unable to move away even if I'd wanted to. "Your two best friends snapped me out of the panic that *you*"—her finger poked into my chest, and my dick jumped—"put there."

"I think this is our cue to go," Cade mumbled.

I stayed locked on Gemma as I dug into my pockets and threw the keys at him. I waited until their footsteps disappeared before I gripped Gemma around the waist and quickly flung her up against the same tree that my friends had her pinned to just moments ago. Her chin tipped upward, and I saw the way her fear flared, but she didn't back down. Her eyes didn't dart away. She kept a hold of me just as firmly as I kept a hold of her, and for some reason, I really hoped that meant she still trusted me—if even a fraction.

"Don't you mean the panic that *you* put there," I hissed through my teeth, knowing I needed to take my hands off her body and take a step back...but fuck, I couldn't. I was selfish.

It was the entire reason we were even standing here in the first place. "You were the one that left your warm bed, climbed into Bain's G-wagon, and came here when I specifically told you not to." Her lips clamped as her breathing picked up. I moved my hands up slightly so I could fold them around her rapidly rising ribcage, realizing how easy it would be to pick her up and wrap her legs around my waist. "I said those things about you so that my father didn't fucking know that I cared about you. If he even saw an ounce of concern on my face when he had a hold of you, he'd know."

Her shaky fingers came up, and she grabbed my wrists tightly. "He'd know what?"

"That you meant something to me! And do you think he'd let you go unscathed if he knew that I cared for you? He'd find a way to use you as leverage to make me do what he wants. He's already using Jack. He'd use you too." My father was manipulative. I knew him better than most.

Her gulp sounded out around us as I stared down at the shadows along her face. Her features were tight, and the anger was still there, but her voice was level as her nails dug into my skin. "You could have told him I wasn't Bain's girlfriend. That Bain wouldn't care if something happened to me."

I laughed sarcastically, tipping my head up to the stars. "And you think that would have saved you from the compromising situation I found you in? He'd still try to fuck you, Gemma." My shoulders tightened as her breaths rushed out in hot spurts. I was certain she was remembering just how terrified she was with him standing over her like he owned her. *God, I hated him.* "And how would you explain knowing that Bain had a car? Or where he parked it? Or how you got his keys? Better yet, how the fuck you knew about the Covens?" I barked the last question out, not knowing exactly how much she knew of the psych hospital, but her mouth slammed shut. "It was either make you seem like you were Bain's little slut and play along, or allow him to see that you meant something to me. One is easily reconciled. The other is not."

Silence fell between us, and it was heavy. Both of our chests were heaving. The air that surrounded us was full of anger and confusion. I gripped her tighter, the cotton of her tank top bundling in my fingers, and her hands around my wrists grew firmer. "And do you, Isaiah? Do you care for me? Because the things you said..."

She trailed off, and I felt my stomach pull. *Say no. Make her hate you. Do it.* "Yes." *Fuck.* Gemma's mouth parted with my admission, and those sweet lips called out to me as heat warmed my veins. "But this..." I pushed my knee in between her jean-clad legs, small pieces of dried mud flying off and hitting the ground below us. "...is over."

There it was. That flash of hurt and confusion all over again. But then the little etch in between her eyebrows smoothed out. "Why? Do you suddenly feel bad for making me a player in your game with Bain and your father? Who's actually using me, Isaiah? Is it Bain? Or is it *you?*"

"I wanna know something," I snapped, ignoring her question solely because I didn't want to answer it. There were too many things that went into my answer, and soon she'd be leaving St. Mary's, and it wouldn't matter. "Why didn't you just wait for me? I thought you trusted me, Gemma. If you wanted to come back here, for whatever reason, I would have brought you myself."

I knew the reason. I knew she had recognized this place, and she was curious. But why didn't she just ask me? Why do this on her own? What was she fucking thinking? If she would have just waited, this wouldn't have happened. My father wouldn't have this perfect visual inside his sick head of her pretty little face, and I wouldn't have stood there, feeling complete fucking terror.

A laugh flew from her mouth and hit me square in the face. Her hair fell behind her back as she looked up to the dark sky in frustration. "It's clear you don't know me at all. Why would I risk you getting caught?" She suddenly brought back those glossy eyes to me, and I stilled. "Did you forget that I know what's at stake if you get caught sneaking out? What happens if you and I both get caught off school grounds, Isaiah? Together? I wouldn't be able to cover for you and lie to the SMC and say we were studying all night! We'd be caught red-handed in our little ploy, and you'd be expelled, and then what would happen to Jack?" Another laugh came from her, and it dripped with sarcasm. "And after meeting your father? I can say I made the right choice. A child shouldn't be left alone with a man like that." Her next words were a whisper. "I should know."

My eyes shut as something in my chest pulled and tugged. I repeated her words in my head, replaying them a few times because I was a glutton for torture. I growled, gripping her torso harder. *Of course I hadn't forgotten that she knew.* Aside from the Rebels, Gemma knew more about me than anyone else. And although I *needed* to stay angry with her over the fact that she put herself in that dangerous situation, I suddenly wasn't any longer. I was more angry with myself, and my father, but not her. *She didn't tell me she was coming back here to protect me and my fucking little brother. Jesus.*

I opened my eyes up again. Gemma was staring at me, and a part of me cracked wide open. "You are too good, Gemma. And that's exactly why this is done." I couldn't stand the thought of her being any more mixed into this than she was. I should have kept my distance once I saw she'd caught Bain's interest. I should have just watched her from afar. It would have been harder, but it was doable. I'd already been keeping hefty tabs on Bain. I could have put even more pressure on him. Get more eyes on her without interfering. Without kissing her. Without making everyone think she was mine and that she was untouchable. I had fucked up by giving her extra attention, by asking for her help with tutoring. I had subjected her to *this*.

Gemma kept a hold of my stare, and I kept going, my grip on her getting tighter and tighter, as if my body knew that this was the last time I'd have her in my hands. "We will continue tutoring. You'll keep meeting me in the library after lacrosse and acting as if you're helping me improve my grades. If anyone asks, you'll say I was there with you, even if I leave. Just like we'd talked about in the beginning. And when it's all said and done, when I'm off probation with the SMC, you'll have everything you asked for, and then you'll fucking leave, and you will never come back." *Then she'd be safe.*

My words were harsh. They implied that I didn't want her to come back. That I didn't want to see her again. And the trembling of her lip told me that she was thinking exactly that. "Fine," her voice cracked as her head turned away.

My jaw ticked, my teeth grinding together as I watched the side of her face nearly crumble. "So, you agree? You and I are done."

Her hands slowly dropped from my wrists, and she brought her gaze back to mine. She put up a good front, but I felt the way her chest caved. She sucked in air as she blinked away the tears. "Yes."

Let her go. Let her fucking go.

The air stilled around us. Everything was frozen. The wind didn't rustle the leaves. The stars didn't glimmer above our heads. Gemma and I locked eyes. My fingers ached to dip underneath her tank top. My mouth begged to be on her warm skin. The perfect bow shape that her lips made opened as a soft breath floated around me. My head dipped down, sweat coating my back even though the night was chilly. My veins flooded with need and pumped blood to every secret spot in my body that only she seemed to bring to life. Our breath mingled as she pressed into my chest. But *no*.

She meant too much.

I'd already hurt her.

My father's hands had been on her. He'd pushed her to her knees and gripped her hair like she was nothing more than a little rag-doll.

I let out a sigh and removed my hands. Her tank top went back down and covered her warm, soft skin. I took one step back, then another, and I felt the cold distance shifting into place. The line was drawn once again.

Gemma pushed off the tree angrily and walked over to her bundled up jacket that was thrown off to the side. I blinked, keeping my face unmoving, wondering if my best friends had taken that piece of clothing off her so they could touch her more.

Although I didn't want to admit it, jealousy was eating me alive. I trusted them, and I believed their excuse as to why things were heated when I had walked up. Gemma confirmed as much.

But she wasn't theirs to touch.

She wasn't my father's to touch either.

Or mine.

When Gemma began to push past me, I grabbed onto her arm and stopped her.

Dark strands of her hair whipped around her face as her stare grew fiery. *Good. She was still angry*. I needed her to keep that wall up so neither one of us was tempted to cross the line again, but there was something on the tip of my tongue that I couldn't swallow. "I'm sorry you had to see that side of my father. I'm sorry he pushed you to your knees and threatened you."

That bright, forest-destroying fire grew wilder in her eye. "It's not the first time I've been shoved to my knees, Isaiah." Then, she peeled my fingers off her arm and kept walking toward the Covens as I stood there with my fists clenched by my side, ready to plow down any mother-fucker who even came close to pushing her down again.

CHAPTER FIFTY-SIX

GEMMA

THE WALK back to Bain's car gave me enough time to shove away the hurt and pull in the anger. My limbs were shaky, and I had a hard time calming my racing heart. I wasn't sure if I was in shock or if I was truly just that angry about everything that had happened in the last hour, but whatever it was, I was ready to lash out.

The Covens. Isaiah had said, *The Covens.* He gave this place a name that I'd never heard before. I stood with my back pressed against Bain's G-wagon as Isaiah thrust his hands out for the keys, but instead, I stared at the building behind him. The sign was still flickering, but the building itself looked to be quiet. I wanted to ask questions, but there was too much tension between us, and I didn't trust myself to be back on level ground with him.

He wanted to push me away.

I'd do the same.

I came to St. Mary's with no intention of forming relationships that were built on trust with people, and that was how I was going to leave. Although a bit bruised, at least I'd have my dignity back intact.

I reached into my back pocket and pulled out Bain's spare keys, shoving them into Isaiah's hand—the same hand that had just been on my hips a few minutes ago, causing things to twist inside of me that shouldn't have been twisting.

I was still confused. Confused about a lot of things. Was Isaiah using me to get to Bain? To lure him in? Or was it the other way around? I understood Isaiah's reasoning as to why he'd acted like that in front of his father. But I didn't agree with it, and the sting was still there. It stung even more when he'd completely glossed over my question about who was actually using me in their little game, which probably answered the question in itself.

"So, tell me..." Isaiah turned the key, and the G-wagon came to life. If there weren't so many other things to be concerned about, I'd wonder if Bain knew I'd taken his car. "How did you get the spare set from Bain? We searched his room high and low before leaving for Temple. Where were they?"

I crossed my arms over my chest and glared out the window as the psychiatric hospital grew distant. "You expect me to answer your questions, but you won't answer mine?" Something evil stirred in my blood, and I fought the bratty smile that was sliding onto my face. I suddenly felt like we were back on day one when he'd called me a good girl and I snarked a response back. "Maybe I let him touch me like I did your friends."

The car suddenly increased in speed, and I held back a smile. I knew I was being immature, but if I didn't keep up with this whole facade that I wasn't hurt and feeling the shocks of panic still surface, I was afraid I'd break down, and that was something I'd have to save for when I was alone.

Because I *was* hurt, and with that came shame. I was

ashamed that I had given someone the power to hurt me again.

When Isaiah looked down at me, just moments ago, as he pressed me up against the tree with his darkened blue eyes and furrowed brow, and allowed the words, *"We're done,"* to hit my ears, it felt like a slap across the face. It was stupid because I knew we hadn't even really started, and I knew we could never be anything anyway, but it hurt to hear him say it. Especially on top of everything he'd said to his father about me, true or not.

"And did you like it?" Isaiah glanced at me once, and I could see that he didn't believe that I'd actually let Bain touch me, but I could also see that my words had gotten to him, and for a fleeting second, I was glad that I saw the hurt on his face.

I shrugged. "Why do you care? I'm just another piece of fresh ass, right?"

The prickles of betrayal were still there. The question of whether taking my virginity meant anything to him ate at me. What if he'd been kissing and touching me all just for show? Even the times that were in secret? Was it all just to prove to Bain that he couldn't have me? Was this some sick way of showing how formidable he was? Did he fool me into thinking that I meant something to him? Did he fool others? He'd all but said it the first time he'd kissed me in front of everyone. *"I need people to know you're mine."*

"Knock it off, Gemma." His grip on the steering wheel grew tighter as the lines on the road blurred even more. "I told you why I said that, and of all people, I thought you'd understand."

I knew we were getting closer to St. Mary's and that I'd be able to go into my room to sort everything out soon, but instead of keeping my mouth shut, I kept going. In a way, it put me back in control, and I needed that. "Haven't you heard the saying: '*Every lie has a bit of truth to it*?'" I clicked my tongue. "Just food for thought."

His fingers flexed as we rounded the bend. The dilapidated warehouse in its run-down glory sat in the distance, and I suddenly couldn't wait to be back at the school. I needed my sketchbook, and my pencil, and a quiet room where I could digest everything that had happened.

I waited as Isaiah's mouth opened. "Oh, I've heard that saying. I believe it to be true in most aspects." There was a hiccup in my chest, and I almost put my hand over my heart to ease the sting I'd felt. "I wasn't lying when I said fucking you was like fucking an angel. Or that it was nice and pure."

I bit the inside of my cheek. I sliced my attention back out my window so he couldn't read my facial expression, because I was certain there was something on my face that I didn't want him to see. I started to breathe heavily, and irritation was poking at my skin like a thousand little needles.

The car came to a stop, and I threw the door open, stepping out and turning on my heel to begin my walk back to the school. I didn't even care if he put Bain's keys back where they were supposed to go. I just needed to get away.

I heard his strides coming up behind me, the gravel being crushed by his shoe. His hands went into his pockets as his arm brushed mine, and I suddenly felt flushed. "Every time I fucking touched you, it was like touching an angel, Gemma. Perfect and captivating. I felt unworthy every single time."

My brow creased as I felt my wall sliding down. *No.* I wasn't going to let his words demolish the shield I'd thrown up the second he played into his father's hand. If I did that, then a whole round of emotions would come through. I gulped back anything trying to come out of my throat, picked up my pace, and didn't stop until St. Mary's came into view.

Isaiah and I stopped right outside the gate before he reached out with a steady hand and pulled it open, allowing me to walk through. We kept our thoughts to ourselves as we passed by his uncle's little cottage, and I shoved the memories away of the last time we'd walked past it together. My arms came up and crossed over my chest as I lifted my chin.

The hallway was as quiet as it usually was, the black-and-white floor shiny and sleek. I didn't dare look at the dining hall because it looked different in the night. It brought back a secret that only he and I shared, and it was something that no longer mattered, even if my lips began tingling at the mere thought.

Isaiah looked back behind us before turning to face me. I saw the way he looked at me, and it sent little shivers everywhere. His blue eyes were swimming with things I couldn't decipher. His jaw wiggled back and forth. His hand came up, and he rushed it through the dark ends of his hair, and he brushed past me, knowing I'd follow.

I just needed to get back to my room.

"I can get to my room from here. You don't have to walk me." My voice was wobbly, and I knew that I would break soon. The ache in my head was pounding. The feelings of anger and betrayal were slowly slipping away. The need to lash out was gone because a part of me understood. Deep down, I knew what it was like to play a part. I knew what it was like to be someone you weren't to save yourself and others. But my heart hurt. My chest cracked, knowing that I wouldn't feel Isaiah's lips on mine again. I was cut right down the middle in the realization that I didn't necessarily feel safe with him any longer. My secrets didn't threaten to spill off the end of my lips, and that was because I wasn't sure if I trusted him anymore, and that hurt worse than anything.

"I'm walking you to your room," he said, voice lacking any emotion at all.

"I don't want you to. I'm fine doing it on my own."

"Just like you were fine sneaking out of St. Mary's alone?"

His response was like a bite to my skin, because he was right. I wasn't sure I would have gotten out of the situation I had been in if he, Cade, and Brantley hadn't chased me off into the woods.

Everything was so messed up, and it was all I could think about as we both silently walked down the hall to my room, both on edge, wondering if the duty teacher would be making her rounds anytime soon.

My hand rested on the iron-clad knob, and I felt the heat from Isaiah's body lingering behind mine. I shut my eyes, breathing heavily as everything came to a sudden stop. The hurt. The fear. The betrayal. The confusion. The realization that he was trying to do the right thing. Maybe this was him trying to be selfless. Or maybe he really had been using me this whole time to get to Bain.

I wasn't really sure. I wasn't sure of anything anymore.

"Gemma?" he whispered, voice soft, likely wondering why I hadn't moved. *Was he hurting too?*

I kept my head down, voice hardly audible. "There's another reason why I didn't ask you to go with me tonight. It wasn't only because I was afraid that you'd get caught and it'd be all my fault. It wasn't only because I was worried for your little brother." I swallowed as one single tear fell over the side of my cheek. "I knew that I was stepping into something that I wasn't quite ready to share with you yet. It wasn't that I didn't trust you, Isaiah. I just wasn't ready to give you something else from my past." My lip trembled as I thought back to the green awning over my head, feeling the memory peek over my walls right before his father had grabbed me. "I've been to the place you call The Covens. That's why I went back alone."

I felt him come even closer, and I clenched my lips together. His hand rested beside my head against the door as my palm shook along the doorknob. My heart raced so quickly I could hear it in my ears.

"I know."

He knew?

All of a sudden, his hand wrapped around my waist, and he spun me around, backing me up against the door. His arms caged me in, and his chest was moving so fast I felt a small amount of fear seep in. "Don't you *ever* go back there. Do you hear me?"

I didn't answer. Instead, I just kept a hold of his steely gaze, seeing the shadows flicker against the wall behind him. He looked like a villain at that moment. And maybe he was.

He dropped his gaze down to my lips, and I froze. We were both breathing erratically, but there was a sound down at the end of the hallway, and his head dropped before he shoved off the door and growled like a terrorized wolf.

A voice carried through the empty space. "Who's down there?"

"It's Isaiah," he answered, keeping me pinned to my spot. "I was walking Gemma back to her room after tutoring."

"Tutoring?" The voice grew closer, and it sounded like Mrs. Fitz, but I wasn't positive. My heart was beating too loudly to hear anything else. "Didn't you have an away game? Surely you two weren't studying this late into the night."

"Get in your room, Gemma. You're filthy."

I didn't miss a beat. The door was opened, and the smell of lavender and chocolate filled my senses immediately. And for the first time all night, I finally felt safe.

I gulped in the air, and Sloane popped up from her bed, holding a Cosmic brownie in her hand as her laptop slid to the side. "Finally! I woke up, and you were gone—"

The second I latched onto her, I cracked. A strangled cry left my lips as the fear and anxiety I'd kept pushing away since the moment I'd taken off toward the forest was back and in full action.

Two warm arms came around me as I sank to the ground and placed my forehead on my knees, letting the tears wash down over my dirty face and clothes. "Shh. You're okay. You're okay, Gemma. You're here. You're going to be fine."

Sloane was right. I was going to be fine because I was leaving soon, and the thought of Richard, Bain, Isaiah, his father, and the sickening memory of the Covenant Psychiatric Hospital was going to be in the past.

CHAPTER FIFTY-SEVEN

ISAIAH

"YOU KNOW what you need to do, bro." I sliced my attention to Brantley, who was resting his elbows against the dining table, looking more smug than usual. He picked up his soda and threw it back before wiping his mouth on his hand. "Just make her hate you. It'll be the easiest way to resist her. There'll be no chance to fuck her."

To fuck her. Like that was all I cared about when it came to Gemma.

Cade chuckled from beside him. "Shouldn't be hard."

"Yeah?" I asked, slapping my hand down on the table, gaining a few quick glances from those who weren't aware that I was seconds from flipping it onto its side. "And how'd that work out for you and Journey, Cade?"

I'd been angry and irritated all day. I couldn't stand to look in Bain's direction, knowing he had a part in last night, even if he wasn't actively present. I had put all the energy I had left into saving face with Mrs. Fitz when she caught me dropping Gemma back at her room well after midnight, which meant, at the present moment, I had nothing leftover to give. My calming vibes and rational thinking were hardly in attendance today.

I could tell Mrs. Fitz had been skeptical when we departed, and why wouldn't she have been? But if she had any suspicion that something other than tutoring was going on with Gemma and me, those suspicions were crushed during art today. Gemma wouldn't even look in my direction, and every time I looked in hers, I wanted to hit something. Her eyes were red, and with the way that Sloane was currently glaring at me, it meant that Gemma had likely cracked when she went into her room last night.

She put up a good front until she turned her back to me and let out her little confession that would haunt me for the rest of my life. Noticing the shake in her voice and watching the lone tear fall down her cheek was so much worse than seeing her hatred brew.

The chip in Cade's hand crumbled. "Fuck off, Isaiah."

Brantley sighed. "Let him be. He's just pissed because we were right." He paused before smirking. "And because he saw us touching Gemma."

My glare was murderous, and I could hear the ticking of the massive time bomb seconds from exploding inside my ears. I didn't have time for this. Although Gemma felt like the biggest issue in my life at the moment, I was balancing something else that neither Cade, Brantley, nor Shiner knew about. Not yet, anyway.

"I'm pissed about a lot of things," I said, my voice seemingly calm, although I still had a load of pent-up aggression simmering on the inside—which wasn't necessarily a good thing. When I was angry but appeared calm and in control, that was when I made bad choices. I was tapping into that overbearing feeling of numbness that cooled my veins, and that was when Isaiah Underwood turned ruthless. "And yes"—I cocked my head at my two friends and dropped my voice—"seeing your hands on her body made me want to strangle you almost as much as I wanted to strangle my fucking father last night."

Shiner peeked up when he heard what I'd said. "What the fuck did I miss?"

Brantley rolled his eyes. "Be thankful you weren't there."

I sensed his agitation before he managed to slump in defeat. Shiner wanted in on the shit that Cade, Brantley, and I discussed privately, and although I'd given him *some* insight on our lives and what I was up against outside of this school, he was still out of the game. It wasn't because I didn't trust him. It was more because the less he knew, the better. "Whatever. Callie's pussy was better than whatever you three got into, I'm sure." He shrugged before snagging his attention away. "But...they're right."

I moved my gaze over to Gemma, seeing her nibble on a carrot stick before I looked back at Shiner. "Right about what?"

"If you want to resist her, make her see you in a different light. Make her see the old Isaiah so *she* resists you. Show her who you were before she stepped foot in this school."

I flicked a crumb off my tie, feeling a shift inside my chest. *Who was I before she came here?* I could hardly remember.

Trailing back down the long table to see Gemma, I noticed that she was smiling at something Sloane had said, which caused my stomach to knot. It was the first time I'd seen her smile all day, and it was like we were back to the beginning, when she had first started at St. Mary's. I had been trying to figure her out from the very second I'd laid eyes on her, and I still was. I distinctly remember thinking she seemed so lost, sitting with Sloane on that Tuesday morning just a couple of months ago. But now? She didn't look so lost, even if I knew, deep down, she was still trying to uncover things about her life that had been hidden from her. Maybe she'd discovered something last night before my father appeared.

Gemma had found her footing in the last few weeks.

But I'd lost mine.

In fact, I was pretty certain that I'd lost myself in her, and she'd found herself in me.

My name on Cade's lips snagged my lingering gaze away from Gemma. "Isaiah can't really go back to his usual behavior. He's still on probation, so there are some limitations, but..."

Shiner played his famous grin, tipping his lip just slightly as he nodded along with Cade. "Oh, yes. I see where you're going, and it never fucking fails."

Their secretive conversation was stroking my irritation. "I'm growing impatient," I snapped, pushing my food away. I hadn't been hungry since I'd seen my father standing above Gemma last night.

"Get a new toy."

I shut my eyes briefly, reeling in my temper. "She wasn't a fucking toy."

Shiner snapped his fingers. "But you played with her."

I was seconds from slamming my fist down onto the table, but Brantley cleared his throat and glanced across the table, gazing into the dining hall. Mostly everyone was seated with their lunches by now, but of course, Bain—being the imperious son of a bitch that he was—slowly strolled the empty space with an apple in his hand, staring directly at me.

Red began to dance in front of my vision, but I dug down as deep as I could to stay grounded. *Calculated behavior was better than impulsive behavior.* I breathed in and out of my nose, hearing something crack in my body from the hostility.

Bain's head tilted with a chuckle as he rolled his dark eyes before turning and going to sit with a few of his friends that were blatantly unaware of his life outside of this school. After last night, I knew that there was going to come a time in the near future where I needed Bain on level ground, so now more than ever, I needed to pull myself back in and stay calm. I gained my smarts from my mother, and I was going to make damn good use of them.

Turning back to the rest of the Rebels, I eyed each and every one of them before I spoke smoothly. "If I find someone new, Bain will think Gemma is free game."

Shiner's eyebrow arched. "And if she's smart, she'll turn him down."

This time, Cade's voice shook, and I was pretty sure I knew why. "And you think that'll stop him?"

I swallowed back the distaste hitting the back of my throat. "Me backing off from her might take some of the threat away. But I have a feeling that Bain isn't only watching Gemma because of me." *And that did not sit well with me at all.*

Brantley nodded, lowering his voice even more. "It has something to do with her uncle, yeah? I mean, they obviously know each other if Bain is his newest gunrunner."

I thought back to the photo I'd snapped that first time Gemma and I went to the Covens. She still had no idea that Bain went there to illegally sell guns to *her* uncle—who was apparently my father's biggest client.

"I think so," I answered as the bell echoed through the vast space, signaling that it was time for the second half of the day. I trailed after Gemma with my heart lodged in my throat. Her smooth legs had two scrapes along the knees that I had to pull my gaze from. "I need you guys to hear this, so listen up." Shiner began to stand, but I held up a finger. "You can stay. This doesn't necessarily apply to you, but you can stay."

He slowly dropped back down into his seat as the dining hall started to empty. Once the ears were away and Bain had disappeared through the doors, not even sparing us a glance, I placed my hands onto the cool wood beneath our trays and breathed out an even breath. "There is going to come a time, in the near future, that I will have to work with Bain."

"You mean work *against*." Cade eyed me suspiciously.

"No." Trepidation crept along my shoulders like a whore running her fingers down the base of my neck slowly and seductively, causing my stomach to hollow out.

Each of my friends was quiet. Neither one of them looked away or spoke. "After I get some things settled, you will have a choice to make." I sniffed, pushing away from the table and climbing to my feet. "I just need you to be prepared."

I turned my back and left them alone, hoping like hell that they chose my side and not the one that was the most familiar to them.

After all, familiar meant comfort even if, in this case, it was morally wrong.

———

"Do you have any whiskey?" I asked, plopping myself down in the same seat I often frequented when I came into my uncle's moody and depressing office. I loosened my tie and propped my foot up against the ledge of his desk, leaning back in the chair.

"What happened last night?" My uncle's glare didn't faze me, and if I were in better spirits, I would have joked with him. But I wasn't in the mood for games this evening, and I had a very important tutoring session to get to in just a few minutes.

"I came to my senses, that's what." And as bitter as the words tasted, they were true. The only thing that kept replaying in my head from last night was the way Gemma looked after I had hurt her and how proud my father was. Two things I never wanted to see again.

My uncle bent down and pulled open a drawer in his desk. He disappeared for a brief moment before popping back up with a bottle of whiskey. *Fuck yeah. Now we were talkin'.*

My eyebrow hitched, and I grinned. "You surprise me sometimes, Uncle Tate."

He scoffed. "This is for me. Not you. Now tell me, what happened? Mrs. Fitz mentioned to me that she saw you dropping Gemma off at her room as she made her rounds last night."

I paused, keeping my face steady. "Did she tell the rest of the SMC?"

The fucking SMC. Always breathing down my neck. They were almost worse than my father. *Almost.*

He shook his head, pouring a single shot that sat in between us. I eyed it carefully, wondering if he would let me have one. Tate Ellison was a man of good word, but he still had Underwood blood running through his veins, which meant that he was a bit rebellious, even if he wanted to hide it.

"So?" he prodded, picking the glass up.

I clenched my teeth, watching the flickering fire. It almost felt like the flames were licking up my arms as anger began to simmer again. "Gemma snuck out last night while we were on our way back from Temple." The shot glass slammed back to the desk, but I kept my eyes on the dancing reds and oranges. "She went back to the Covens. Stole Bain's car. And when I found her..."

"Jesus Christ."

I ignored his muttering. "When I found her, Dad had a hold of her hair, threatening her because he thought Bain was watching from afar or some shit. He thought she was his girlfriend or something." Silence jutted through the room like the crashing of a wave in the middle of a hurricane. It was quick and suffocating, and I had to force the next words out. "I had to interfere in the worst way possible to show him that I was his little fucked-up clone and that Gemma meant nothing to me. That I didn't even know her. I said she was nothing more than a piece of ass and that I would use her to send a message to Bain."

When I glanced back at my uncle, feeling the guilt creep in, his eyes were shut as his nostrils flared. I wasn't sure what he was angrier about, but to be honest, I didn't really care much. He wasn't a part of this life anymore, even if he wanted to act like he was. There was nothing he could have done if he were the one to go after Gemma. Underwood business stayed within those of the same surname, and from the moment Uncle Tate stepped out of the family business, he had to legally change his name and never speak of it again. Same with my older brother, Jacobi.

"And are you, Isaiah?" he finally asked, pouring another shot. Two was his limit. I was half-eager to see if he'd pour a third. I was certain this school would drive him to alcoholism eventually—at least with me in attendance. He cared too much for the students here. He would have never survived working alongside my father. Jacobi would have. But my older brother was even more selfish than I was.

"Am I what?" I put both feet back on the ground and rested my elbows against my knees.

He swallowed, twisting the cap back onto the whiskey bottle. *Huh. Two was still the limit.* "Are you a clone of your father? Are you following in his footsteps? Did seeing him with Gemma change something for you?"

The last we'd spoken of this, I told him I was taking over the business when the time came because of my father's threats against Jack, so I waited for the surprised look on his face when I answered, "No."

"No?"

Last night didn't necessarily change me. It just made me realize what was already there. *I was not Carlisle Underwood.* The anxiety that I wouldn't allow to fester was beginning to cage me, so I quickly changed the subject, knowing I needed to get to the library even if, the entire time, I would be feeling nothing but irritation and regret.

Part of me wanted to be done with the whole tutoring thing so my life could be a little bit easier. But Jack wasn't safe yet, and until he was, I had to keep up with saving face. I had to keep up with my grades. I had to keep up with the tutoring sessions with a girl who made me see nothing *but* her. I had to continue following Bain, even if I was now certain he was just setting me up the entire time anyway. My job wasn't done yet.

"I need to use your phone."

"Isaiah," my uncle's voice grew more intense, and I clicked my tongue back and forth, making the world's most annoying noise, pretending as if I didn't hear the skepticism in the way he'd said my name. "What's going on with you? Now all of a sudden you're not taking over the business?"

"I just need to use your phone. Or maybe one of those phones inside your desk." I snapped my fingers. "That's a better idea. Give me one of those so no one can trace it back to me."

The tiny crease in between his brows was back. "Who are you calling? And is Gemma okay? After last night?"

I ran my tongue over my teeth as my shoulders tensed. "She's fine. And I'm calling the Covens."

He nearly choked on his spit. "Why the hell would you need to call the Covens? Isaiah. Do you know what you're doing?" He let out an exasperated sigh before glaring at me. "The SMC is just about ready to take you off probation.

They've set a date to reconvene. That's why I wanted you to come to my office. What are you up to? Talk to me."

That had something snapping in my neck. *Gemma could leave after I was off probation.* Plus, once Jack was safe, it wouldn't matter anyway. I would be done following Bain, and I wouldn't need a cover *or* a tutor. She would no longer be a player in this game.

I made a mental note to check on her ID and the other various documents I knew she'd need to completely fall off the face of the earth as who we knew to be Gemma Richardson, even if the thought made me sick.

"Isaiah!" my uncle barked, and it snapped me to attention.

"I'm calling the fucking Covens to see if Tobias Richardson is there." My teeth gritted, and I wouldn't have been surprised if dust had coated the inside of my mouth. "She can't go back there again, and I am absolutely certain that the entire reason she went there last night was because she thought he was there."

I hardly got the sentence out before he spoke. "He's not there."

My head tilted with surprise. "What?"

"He's not there—at least not under that name. I've already checked." He paused, placing both hands on the desk and standing up to glare down at me. "I have Gemma Richardson handled, Isaiah."

I rolled my eyes, standing up alongside him. "Do ya now?" *And he thought that would stop me?*

"I have secrets, too. Let me handle her. You handle the plan that I know you have brewing in the back of your head on how to get out from the family business, and let me know if I can help."

I walked over to the door, keeping my back to him. He knew he couldn't help me. I knew it too. He also knew it was useless to ask me anything else about my upcoming plans, because I wouldn't tell them. I kept my secrets close, and there was a reason for that.

"You're too good to be the Huntsman, Isaiah. You are not your father. You're making the right choice."

But was I?

CHAPTER FIFTY-EIGHT

GEMMA

Don't even look at him. Don't do it.

My eyes casually grazed the edge of the laptop that the headmaster had given me, and I hated myself for not being able to keep a hold of my emotions. I'd done so well all day long. I didn't look for him in the hallway, even though I knew exactly where he was. I didn't find those piercing icy depths during lunch, even though I could tell he was looking at me, because Sloane would tense each time. When we'd gone to sit outside during the boys' lacrosse practice, I kept my back turned to the field, resting along the fence as I sketched the same thing over and over again in my journal, trying to keep the momentum of anger and betrayal at the forefront of my brain.

Not the betrayal of Isaiah. Even though everything from last night made my throat close up at the mere thought, I knew him—at least, a part of him. I knew, deep down, he wasn't lying when he'd given me an explanation for his vile words and why he didn't jump in to take his father's hands off me. Did it still hurt? Yes. But the betrayal that I felt from Richard was tenfold. His actions were like sharp shards of glass, cutting into me deeper and deeper as the memory of that place continued to resurface. I had a nightmare last night, which I'd already expected. It was the memory that I seemed to unlock by going to the psychiatric hospital—*the Covens*—by myself. It was a memory that I'd buried away for years because reopening that wound hurt more than being shoved to my knees and chained up from innocently asking about my mother. The older I got, the more confused I became over the lies Richard had fed me. But I'd known this entire time. It just took that tattered green awning from last night to open my eyes. I was on the brink of learning more about that night in my deep slumber, but Sloane had woken me up before things progressed.

What I'd managed to gather, though, was that Richard Stallard was the sick one. He should have been shoved into that padded room. Not my mother.

"Stop researching the hospital, Gemma. You won't find anything on the website."

My fingers stilled over the keyboard as I tried leveling my breathing. My heart pounded as I listened to the clicking of the clock overhead. There was a massive wall between Isaiah and I now. It was much bigger than it was when we'd first met. But just because it was bigger, that didn't mean it was sturdy. It felt fragile. Like it was thrown up too quickly, and it would fall down with the slightest crack.

I straightened my shoulders, thinking back to the pep talk that Sloane had given me before I left to come to the library. She wanted me to blow off tutoring. To tell Isaiah to fuck off and that I didn't owe him anything, much less to help him with *raising* his grades. And a part of me wanted to tell him that, but there was an even bigger part of me that broke last night and formed me into this girl that was strong-willed and determined to be independent without two strong hands gripping her waist with whispered promises of safety inside her ear. I wasn't going to hide from Isaiah. I wasn't that girl anymore. I'd been put in shittier situations, and I knew I could handle this. Living with someone like Richard had groomed me to act in ways I didn't want to. I could act like being near Isaiah didn't make my stomach pull. I could pretend that catching his eye didn't make my entire body hot. It wasn't *that* hard to stay leveled. *Right?*

"I'm serious. Leave it be."

My eyes caught his again as I peeked up over the computer. I wasn't going to lie; intimidation looked good crowding his dark features. "Why don't you just sit over there and pretend we're tutoring? Isn't that what you wanted? For things to go back to how you originally planned?" I shut my laptop and crossed my arms over my uniform. I didn't bother changing after school today. I didn't want to feel the denim of jeans rubbing over my scrapes caused by his father shoving me down to my knees. "You wanted me to go back to knowing nothing about your life. Nothing about you or Bain or your daddy issues. I don't ask where you go when you need to leave in the middle of a tutoring session. I cover for you if anyone asks. Yeah, that's about it. Right? I mean, if you're caught out in the hall after curfew, you were just walking me back to my room from tutoring? Yeah? That's the plan? That's your cover?"

He sighed, gripping the pencil in his fist so tightly his knuckles turned white. "Gemma."

My name was more of a warning than anything, and it pissed me off. "Isn't that what you wanted? Correct me if I'm wrong."

I heard the crack of the pencil, but I stayed locked on his face. The intimidation lingered for a split second before something else came over his features. His jaw untightened, and his brows lowered. "I hurt you last night."

I scoffed, pretending I didn't care. "I've been hurt worse, trust me. Don't flatter yourself." *Lies. Lies. Lies.* The hurt I was used to was tangible. Richard didn't slice away at my heart like Isaiah did, so I wasn't used to this silent, underlying pain. And I really couldn't figure out what was better, the physical hurt or the emotional. The only good thing was that I could hide my emotions. I couldn't do that with the scars along my wrists.

Isaiah leaned back onto the chair and continued to stare at me. I wanted to move in the worst way. I wanted to fidget as butterflies coated the inside of my belly, or better yet, I wanted to burn them all together. Too much had happened last night, and I was left feeling desperate and confused. I should have felt anger when I looked into those icy pools, not this annoying trickle of anticipation. There was a wicked part of me that wanted him to say *fuck it* and take me in his arms. I ached to feel his hands around my waist again. I craved to feel that solitude I felt when he kissed me and showed me things that made me feel rebellious and free.

No.

"He's not there, Gemma."

My chest stopped rising as I repeated his words. There was no warm breath leaving my mouth or silent arguments over my body continuing to react to him. The ticking in my ear only stopped long enough for me to confirm who and what he was talking about. "Excuse me?"

Isaiah moved forward, placing his bare forearms on the table. The corded muscles beneath the skin danced out of the corner of my eye.

"Your brother is not at the Covens." He blinked once, and I tried my hardest to unblur my vision as he confirmed what I'd already suspected. "That's why you went, right? To see if your uncle had sent him there four years ago when he left you? You wanted to know why you'd recognized it that first night."

I bit the inside of my cheek so hard it bled. The metallic taste coated my tongue and sent chills flying down my arms. The longer Isaiah stared at me, the more I wanted to break. "That's none of your business now, is it? What happened to our no-questions-asked policy? That stands now that we're back to our original plan, right?"

I swallowed past the rising lump, wanting to shove the laptop off the table as buried feelings started to suffocate me. I knew why the psychiatric hospital was familiar to me now, but there was still a small part of me that hoped Tobias was there. If Richard had sent my mother there, he could have sent him there too.

"I don't believe you," I remarked, gripping the edge of the table. "And how could you possibly know that? Wait. Don't tell me. You're somehow affiliated with that place? You weren't *only* following Bain that night, huh? You know something else." I laughed sarcastically and mumbled under my breath, "Your father probably runs it. That would make sense. He's just as screwed up as Richard."

"Richard?" he asked, treading slowly.

I ignored him. I didn't care if he knew that Richard wasn't my biological uncle. There was a more pressing issue coming to mind. "How do you know?" I asked, putting my watery gaze on his. "How do you know he isn't there? I'm assuming you didn't ask your father such a question, but then again, do I really even know you?" I shrugged, feeling the betrayal of everyone in my life come at me at once. "I mean, sure, I let you take my virginity, but that's beside the point."

"Gemma," he warned again, but I raised my voice.

"How do you know, Isaiah? Wait. Is that even your real name?"

He turned again, rubbing a feeble hand down his face, trying to hide a smirk. "Yes, that's my real name."

Was he laughing?

I quickly stood up, feeling the tears spring back to my eyes but not because I was sad. It was because I was frustrated and angry. Everything was piling up, and if it was his goal to make me hate him, he was achieving it. It was as if he were patronizing me. Like he wanted me to lash out.

"How do you know?" I asked again, placing my hands down on the cool wood beneath my fingers. My legs were shaky, and my knees were seconds from buckling. *Tobias had to be there.* Because if he wasn't, I had no freaking idea where he was.

Isaiah peered up at me behind those black-rimmed eyes. "Because I called the Covens and asked."

Oh no. "You did what?" The question was hardly above a whisper as I sunk back down into the chair. The final string was clipped, and there it was. *Disappointment.* But just as soon as I let the blow hit me, I stood back up, and the anger was rushing. "Are you kidding me?!" My voice was high-pitched, and I placed my hands on my head, gripping my chestnut strands just as tightly as his father had the night before. "You called and asked for Tobias Richardson?!" *Richard would know.* After all, how many people would be inquiring about a *Tobias Richardson*? I was sure when Richard had changed our last names to his mother's maiden name after our mother died, he had done his research.

I gasped, feeling the memory surface again. The one that I'd dug into last night. The one that told me that Richard was a part of The Covenant Psychiatric Hospital— or *The Covens,* as Isaiah called it. I turned my back quickly and darted away from Isaiah and his unmoving features. I ran past aisles and aisles of books until I got to the very end of the library, tucked away in the dark, as my eyes shut and I was taken back to a time when I was the most vulnerable.

"*You will not get away with this, Richard.*" *My mother's voice was hoarse, like she'd been yelling or maybe she had a cold. We didn't get out much to catch the germs, but occasionally, she'd have the sniffles at night. I could hear her. I'd wake up sometimes, looking for Tobias' warm hand. He and I shared a bed, but every once in a while, I would climb out and go into Mama's. I sometimes felt like she needed my hand more than he did.*

"You mistake me for someone who is weak, Emily." Uncle Richard laughed, and I shut my eyes, pretending that I was asleep in the backseat. Tobias wasn't with us. It was just Mama, me, and Uncle Richard. I peeked up when I felt a shift, and I glanced out the window, wondering how I'd gotten into the back of Uncle Richard's car. My blanket was wrapped around me as I pulled it up to cover most of my face, seeing the blurring stars through the glass.

My mom's voice shook, and I heard another sniffle. Maybe she was sick. I smiled a little as I thought that, maybe in the morning, I would get her some warm tea from Auntie. That would make her feel better. Of course, I would have to have Tobias help me. Auntie liked him better than me.

"Richard. You cannot take me from my children and throw me into a dungeon. My sentence is finished in a few weeks. What will the courts say when I'm missing? I appreciate that you kept me from going to prison, but this will not work."

He laughed again, and confusion filled me. What was she talking about? Sentence? Like a sentence with words? "I own the courts, Emily. You know this, and you'd do good to be by my side. You have a face for politics. I don't understand why you'd want any other life than the one I'm giving you." His words cut off, and the car came to a stop. I almost fell forward onto the floor, but I pushed myself back into the leather seat, gripping my blankie as my stomach rolled. "Don't worry, though, Princess. After you're through here, you'll be just the way I want you. Compliant, submissive, and obedient. You'll spread those legs when I want, hang on my arm at cocktail parties, and we will raise our children to be upstanding citizens. They will follow the rules, just as soon as their mother does."

My eyebrows crowded as his door opened, and I quickly shut my eyes, pretending like I was asleep. I didn't like when Uncle Richard used that tone. It scared me. He did it a lot. It made my stomach wiggly, and sometimes I would run away and hide. Tobias never hid with me, though. He stayed with Mama. He was braver than me.

"Richard, I will tell everyone in there what you've done to me over the years. I'm done being your little doll. You can't groom me into what you want!" My mother's voice shook as it grew louder, and a tear fell down my cheek. I clenched my eyes tighter as I heard the door slam, making the entire car move underneath me.

"Mama?" I whispered.

"Baby, stay asleep."

I shut my eyes again, gripping onto my blankie. My fingers hurt from the grip, but it made me feel safe. The car door opened again, and I peeked one eye open as my mother yelped. My lips smooshed together as I saw Uncle Richard grab her by her pretty hair and drag her out of the car. More confusion filled me as I saw through the crack that her hands were in handcuffs. They looked more real than the ones that Tobias and I would use as we played cops and robbers in the backyard.

Uncle Richard shouted as he pulled her, and I wanted to scream. "If I can't groom you, then I'll just groom her." The door was suddenly shut again, and I counted to five before I sat up taller with my heart feeling like I'd just run through the forest, playing hide and seek. There was a door with a green curtain-like thingy over the top, and I knew it was the door that Uncle Richard and Mama had gone through.

Mama told me to stay asleep, but Tobias wasn't here. He couldn't *stay with her when Uncle Richard yelled. He couldn't hold her hand. She needed me to be brave. I was going to be brave.*

My hand shook on the door handle, and the cool air hit my wet face as I crawled out of the car. The pebbles below my feet dug in as I tiptoed over to the door that they had gone into. I looked behind me and saw my blanket half hanging out, so I ran back over, pretending that my feet didn't hurt, and I snatched it, taking it with me. I knew it would make me feel better if I got scared. I couldn't be scared. Mama needed me.

The door creaked open, and I slowly walked inside, thankful for the shiny cold floor beneath my sore toes. My feet fell flat as my eyes adjusted to the bright lights that lined the white hallway. It smelled funny, like it had been cleaned over and over again. I stayed still, trying to listen for Mama, and that was when I heard a scream.

Mama!

I surged forward, leaving dirty footprints behind me as I dragged my blanket down the hall. I ran as fast as I could, pretending that Tobias was chasing me. "Mommy!" I shouted. My face felt really wet. "Uncle Richard!"

"Baby!" I heard Mama's raspy scream, and I came to a sudden halt. My heart was thumping so fast, and I was scared. I was scared, and my blankie wasn't making me feel any better. I turned and stopped right inside a door that was half-cracked. At first, I only saw Uncle Richard. His brow was raised, but the rest of his face remained smooth. "Baby!" My face was suddenly turned as Mama grabbed onto my upper arms. "I love you. Tell Tobias I love him too."

My eyes welled up, and my lip shook. "Mommy?" My head was suddenly crushed into her warm chest, and my arms came up around her waist as she cried. "Mommy, it's okay," I mumbled, giving her my best hug. "Why are you sad?"

Her breath tickled my ear after she kissed the top of my head. "Find your daddy, Gemma. He will save you if I don't come back. His name is—" Suddenly, my mother was ripped from my arms, and I jolted forward in panic.

"Mommy!" I screamed. "Mommy! Wait!" Two men came forward wearing black outfits and pulled her backward. She fought them. Her brown hair swished in front of her face, getting stuck on her cheeks.

"No! Let me go! You cannot do this, Richard!" She looked to the men holding her arms. "He's raped me! Over and over again! He's going to take my kids! I'm not sick! I don't need to be here!"

Uncle Richard's arms circled around my waist as he pulled me away. My arms reached out, dropping my blanket in the process. "Mommy! Come back!"

"No!" Her hands were freed now, and I was glad when she hit one of the men in the face. But then his eyes grew smaller. They looked like little lines below his eyebrows. He was angry. "Let me fucking go! Baby, I love you! Find your daddy!"

I didn't know who my daddy was. I didn't know! Before I could say that, Richard threw me into the hallway, and I hit the hard floor with a big thump. My belly dropped, and my back hurt. I cried out even louder, feeling for the bump that I knew would be there. The door was slammed, and I looked up quickly through blurry eyes.

"Where's Mommy going?" I asked through choppy breaths. Tears fell, and they made me feel cold.

Uncle Richard came and stood above me as I sat on the floor. I wanted Mama. She needed me. But Uncle Richard was looking down at me with the same look he'd always given her before yelling. He bent down in front of me as I cried and cried. I couldn't stop. I wanted Tobias. And I wanted my blankie. I stared at the door behind Uncle Richard, remembering that my blankie fell. But it was okay. Mama could use it. Maybe it would make her feel safe.

"You remember this, okay, little one?" Uncle Richard's finger trailed down the side of my face, and I cried harder. "This is what happens when you don't follow the rules. You were supposed to stay in the car. Maybe I'll have to punish you too."

Fear like no other came at me. I ducked my head into my knees and tried to hide. I couldn't run to the closet. I couldn't look for Tobias *and hold his hand. Mama wasn't here either. I didn't feel safe with Uncle Richard.*

"Judge Stallard?" I heard a deep voice say from somewhere close by, but I kept my face hidden. I didn't want to be here.

Uncle Richard left my side. I could feel him walk away and hear his feet on the hard floor. I shivered as I grew even colder.

"Ahh, yes. Sorry to keep you waiting, Mr. Underwood. It seems the little one left the car when she should have stayed put. I have to keep my eye on this one. She's like a curious little kitten."

A deep laugh sounded, and I finally raised my head a little, just to see who it was. Maybe he could get Mama for me. The man eyed me for a second before turning back to look at Uncle Richard. "It's no problem. I just wanted to shake the hand of the man I am now doing business with."

Richard shook the man's hand as I hiccupped. I wanted Tobias.

"It's a pleasure. I'm glad I have someone I can count on. I'm assuming the shipment went smoothly? I haven't spoken to my men yet."

"Shipment is nice and tidy on the lower deck. Serial numbers have been scratched. Untraceable."

I put my face back down as Uncle Richard spun on his shiny shoes. "That's great. That's exactly what we needed." I heard his footsteps again but didn't dare look up. Tears kept falling, and I was shaking. I wanted it to stop. "When it's time for another batch, I will let you know. We've been getting requests more and more lately. But I have your contact information, Mr. Underwood. I'll call when it's time. I'm going to get the little one home."

The man cleared his throat, and I was pretty sure he was looking at me. I didn't want to look at him, though. "She's a cutie. Even with tears."

Richard laughed. "Crying makes them cuter, don't ya think?"

I hurriedly swiped at my face, clearing off my tears. I didn't want to cry anymore.

"I think we're going to be great business partners, Judge Stallard."

I heard more footsteps, and my heart hurt because it was thumping so hard. My hands shook as I wiped at my face again, and when I saw two new shoes pop into my vision, my eyes grew watery again.

"Say goodbye to Mr. Underwood, Gemma."

My chin was wobbly. I could feel it wiggle. I looked up at two sky-blue eyes, but I didn't say a word. I was too scared to cry again because that seemed to make Uncle Richard happy, and he just made my mama sad.

I didn't like him anymore.

Not at all.

WHEN MY EYES popped back open, I gasped for air and immediately looked for him. *Oh my God.*

"Gem?" Isaiah was crouched down, resting the back of his legs on his ankles. "Talk to me."

Another gasp came from my chest as my mouth gaped open. I sucked in air, coating the inside of my lungs, and locked onto those familiar blue eyes.

It couldn't be.

"H...he..." *No.*

"Gemma!" My name was urgent as his hands came down and cupped my face, locking onto me.

"He...he was there."

"Who was? Where?"

My lip quaked. "Your father. He was there. He was there the last night I saw my mom."

The blood from Isaiah's face drained, and that was when I felt it. That was when I felt the crack right down the middle of my chest.

CHAPTER FIFTY-NINE

ISAIAH

JESUS CHRIST.

Gemma was shaking in my hands. They were still wrapped around her wet cheeks, and I could feel her entire body tremble as the pain and recollection flowed through her. *Fuck. Fuck. Fuck.* I was right. Gemma was more involved in this than I ever knew. A scary thought flowed through me. *Did my father send her here? Did he know something I didn't?* Every muscle in my body locked up, and I felt an ache settle in my bones. I wanted to punch something, throw every last book off the shelves in this godforsaken library. My fingers begged to squeeze my father's neck because he was part of the reason *she* was fucking terrified at the moment.

I didn't like seeing her like this. My heart screamed, and I needed it to stop. I needed her little snarky remarks to come back. I begged for her rightful anger to rear its head again so she could stop bleeding out in front of me.

"Gemma, baby. I want you to breathe." My forehead came down and rested along hers. It was sweaty, and I shut my eyes, wanting to take everything away from her. I didn't know what I was taking, but I would take it. I would take her hurt and make it my own. I shouldn't have been doing this. I needed to leave her be and get through this last stint of tutoring so she could just...leave. But she was determined to uncover things that needed to stay fucking covered. For her own safety.

"I can't." Her breaths were ragged, and I wanted to breathe for her. I wanted to give her every ounce of oxygen in my lungs.

"You can." I gripped her face harder and pulled back, looking down into her eyes. "Breathe for me."

Her head shook back and forth. "Did you know? Did you know that he was there that night? Did you know that your father knows Richard?"

"No," I answered truthfully, and that was when she took a big gulp of air. The small area we were tucked back in smelled of nothing but dust and old, tattered books. It was dimly lit, and I liked it. It felt like we were shut off from the world, even if just for a second. I wasn't thinking about how I needed to take a step back from her. Or how I shouldn't have been the person that was keeping her steady and calming her down. Or how, just moments ago, before she took off running with fear blanketing her features, I told myself to leave her be. I wasn't even thinking about how my father had her pinned yesterday, ready to hurt her and destroy me in the process. All I was thinking about was *her*.

Gemma continued to shake, tears still wetting her cheeks. Her hands came up and gripped my arms as she tried like hell to pull herself out of the assaulting memory she'd just had. I wanted to know in the worst way. I wanted to dig into her mind and learn every last secret that laid behind those secretive green eyes. "How do I know I can believe you?"

"I didn't know," I said, glancing away. "I suspected, though." I was teetering over the edge of right and wrong.

Pulled in two opposite directions. Gemma deserved to know the truth, but she also deserved to stay safe and untouched by this part of the world that I was all too familiar with.

Her head flicked up, that dainty little chin tipping in my direction. I glanced down to her lips as she said, "Tell me."

My chest screamed with the pounding of my heart. *Shit*. I needed to shove her away. She was better off not being involved in this. But the nagging thought in the back of my head told me that Gemma would probably try to find out more anyway. She had gone to the fucking Covens last night without *me* to uncover things. Maybe if I'd given her some insight, it would've pacified her long enough to get her out. To get her out of this fucking school and the spiderweb of lies, danger, and illicit business that she had no business being a part of.

I slowly pulled my hands from her cheeks, and I saw her hope and fear flicker. Her brown hair came over her face as she glanced to the floor, but she slowly looked over at me as I sat beside her, resting my back against the same bookshelf. "That night I took you to the psych hospital, when we followed Bain... I found out something that I haven't told you about." I kept my attention forward, glancing down the long aisle of endless bookshelves. "Bain met someone at the door —the one I found you shoved against last night with my father hovering over you." I heard her swallow but kept going. "Bain was delivering guns to someone there. Illegally. You've heard me talk about the family business..." I was thankful she never dug too much into it, because I never really wanted her to know in the first place, but now, I was wondering if she already knew.

"Yes," she croaked, hardly above a whisper.

"My father and Bain's are both in the illicit trade of small arms. They're gun traffickers. He's one of the biggest gun runners there is. The whole *family business* that I'm set to take over is illegal gun trade, Gem. That's why my father was so angry when he realized the tracker on Bain's car was going to the Covens last night." I looked over at her and hopefully displayed the disappointment I felt over her taking his car and going alone. "That psych hospital isn't *just* a psych hospital. He went there to catch Bain in his territory, selling guns to..." I paused, bringing my knees up to rest my forearms along them. "Judge Stallard."

I felt the icy whip of her shock even without touching her. Long minutes passed, and I kept my ears perked, listening to hear if anyone decided to pop into the library to check on our studies tonight, and that was when I heard the tremor in her tone.

"That's what they were talking about that night, when my mom was taken from me."

I couldn't even look over at her because I was too afraid to see her expression. *I needed to stop this.* She was confiding in me, and I didn't deserve it, but there wasn't much that would take me away from this very spot, even with my father's face lingering in the outskirts of my brain.

"They talked about a shipment. Scratching serial numbers. Something untraceable. Your father looked me dead in the eye that night and watched as Richard took me away from my mom as she screamed in a padded room that she didn't deserve to be in."

Richard fucking Stallard.

I felt unsettled, and I wanted to ask her more. I wanted to know every last fucking thing about her life, and Richard Stallard, and if she knew what his position was there. But I felt her numbness. The sound of her monotonous voice hit my ears and made them ring. I needed to heed the warning that I sensed. *She wasn't ready.*

Her head turned to me quickly, and I caught the wet stripes across her cheeks. "Make it stop."

I'd do anything she told me to do at this moment. My head was telling me one thing, but my heart was telling me another. My stomach dipped, and my muscles locked. Our eyes collided, and I burned. "Make what stop?"

"Everything. My mom begged..." She sniffled, and I broke. "I don't... I can't..." Her eyes shut, more tears coming out of the corners. "I don't want to feel anything right now."

Leave her be.

Walk away.

Disengage in any interest.

Keep her safe.

Remember what you felt last night.

Make her stay away from you.

"Fuck," I growled, grabbing her by the arm and pulling her into my lap. Her legs wrapped around my waist, her hot warmth heating me from the inside out. Her hair came down and covered us like a shield, as if we were in any need of a disguise. I would regret this later, but if she wanted the world to stop spinning for a little while, then that was what I'd give her.

Our lips touched, and I drank her in like I'd never survive without her taste. My mouth coated hers. It moved languidly, sucking and tasting, coaxing her back to life. Her tongue landed on mine, her shaky hands coming up and grabbing my face. Our breathing was in sync, our bodies pressed together, and just like that, the world stopped. Everything stopped. Everything but her and I.

There was no talk of the past.

No intertwining secrets and lies making either of us tremble.

My father wasn't a thought, and neither was Richard, or the Covens, or gun sales, or Bain. Nothing.

This. This was it.

Fuck regret.

Fuck tomorrow.

This was exactly where I wanted to be. I just needed one last little taste.

My hands moved slowly up her back, untucking her white school blouse from her plaid skirt. Her hot flesh touched the pads of my fingers, and her kiss deepened. Her hands moved to my hair, and she pulled, and I followed. I skimmed up her spine, and goosebumps clung to her skin. Heat shot to my groin as she pressed down, taking her mouth from mine and tipping her chin. My other hand came up, intertwining in her hair as I pushed her back down, taking her mouth. *Mine.*

"You're mine," I whispered against her sweet taste. "Give me everything you have. I'll take it."

I pushed my hips up to her warm center, and it was sinful. She gasped, pushing her chest into my face, and my hands quickly left the skin of her back, and I ripped the front of her shirt open and inhaled. *Jesus.* I wanted her forever. I saw nothing but her. I felt nothing but her. She was my goddamn kryptonite, which was exactly why I needed to let her go.

One last time.

Our eyes caught again, and without even speaking, I knew she was in a different place. A different mindset. The past wasn't creeping up behind her anymore. She was here, with me, in this place, and I'd make her forget everything.

"This feeling won't last," I whispered along her ear, gripping the side of her bare thigh. Her skin was like butter against my palm. "But I'll give it to you, anyway."

My mouth landed on her chest, the fabric of her bra inches from my teeth. I wanted to bite her, suck on her nipple, but I was too concerned with her sweet spot. The part of her that I wanted to devour. I gripped the side of her panties, just underneath her hip bone. My finger crooked into its side, and I rubbed at the skin. She withered above me, breathing hard.

"Isaiah." My name mingled with her breathy moan, and my pupils dilated.

I shoved her legs wider as she hovered over me, my dick so hard it pulsed. I wanted to take her and fuck away all our problems. I wanted to erase the feeling I'd had when I saw my father standing over her. I wanted to erase the surge of jealousy that I'd felt when my friends had their hands on her. *She was fucking mine.* I knew her better than anyone else in this place.

The very second I grazed her groin and pulled her panties to the side, I knew I had to listen to my friends when this moment was over. *Make her hate you. Make her resist you. Make her say no to you.* They were right. I wouldn't be able to deny her a single thing. It was going to have to be up to her.

"Jesus," I groaned before sucking her lip into mine. She whimpered as I sunk a finger into her. Wetness coated me, and I wanted to watch her come undone. I was drunk on her. A high I'd always be chasing.

"*Ah,*" she hummed, throwing her head back, still hovering as I pumped in and out. Her little hips moved to their own rhythm, and I sat back and watched with hooded eyes and a parted mouth. Her neck was there for the taking, and my lips begged to suck on the delicate skin. The hickey I'd left a few days ago was hardly there anymore, and I wanted to mark her again.

"Hello?"

Her head snapped down to me as I lurched my head past her. *Fucking shit.*

I squeezed my eyes shut and wanted to ram my fist into the bookshelf. *Fuck.* I felt the moment break in half. I felt Gemma clam up before she quickly stood, shoving her untidy shirt back into her skirt. Her cheeks were flushed, her hair a mess. I zeroed in on her puffy lips and regretful eyes. Gemma didn't want to cave into me, and I could sense that she felt ashamed. She was so determined earlier. So determined to stay angry with me and push me away. And when she broke, she wanted to pick up the pieces herself, yet she let me do it for her. I gave her the fucking permission. *I just fucked everything up again.*

"We're back here," I shot down the aisle, righting my dick in my pants and glancing away from Gemma's blank face. "Gemma was helping me find a book I needed for my report in World History."

Gemma slowly walked toward me, her light footsteps making no sound at all. My forehead furrowed as my chest seized. *What was she doing?* Her arm shot up, just past my head, as she pulled a book down from the shelf. She shoved the dusty thing into my hand and turned around.

I didn't waste any time following after her to see who'd come to check on things. I knew I'd tipped off Mrs. Fitz last night. I wasn't as elusive as I should have been. Gemma and I were both on a slippery fucking slope that just kept getting slicker.

"Mr. Cunningham. What can we do for you?" My voice was level as I plopped the book down onto our study table, right on top of all our scattered papers and books. I eyed Gemma's open laptop, and an inkling of suspicion came through.

I darted my eyes down both sides of the library, glancing at the darkened sky through the far window, seeing the flags on top of the roof of St. Mary's flicker in the wind in the most ominous of ways.

Mr. Cunningham cleared his throat, looking back and forth between Gemma and me. We couldn't have looked any guiltier than we already did. Her shirt was half-unbuttoned, although tucked back in, and her cheeks were flushed with heat. If Mr. Cunningham did indeed have a dick tucked away in those khaki pants he wore, he would know without a doubt that I'd just had my finger inside her wet, little pussy.

My teeth clamped and ground as I stood and waited for his reply. Gemma was eerily still, face emotionless. I placed my hands on my hips, glancing to the left and right again, looking for a faceless shadow. I hadn't heard Mr. Cunningham as he came through the door. I'd heard the creak of the floor, and then his voice soon followed. Gemma's laptop was shut when she'd taken off down the aisle a little while ago. *Someone else was here.* Someone was always fucking watching. It was Bain, or someone he'd sent, but someone had been here, and that was the nice little reminder I needed to push her away.

Gemma broke through my panicky thoughts, my teeth unclenching at the sound of her sweet voice. "Mr. Cunningham? Did you need something?" Her pink and swollen lips tilted upward, and Mr. Cunningham's mouth flattened. He sighed, looking back and forth between us once more before landing on her yet again.

"No, dear. I just came to check on you two, to make sure Isaiah was still staying on the straight and narrow."

I almost choked. I couldn't have been further away from straight and narrow than this very second. I was still up to my usual bullshit. I was just better at hiding it. Add fucking around with the girl I swore I wouldn't touch again, and yeah, I was just as bad as before.

"All is well." Gemma smiled again, but it fell as soon as Mr. Cunningham looked away. The punch to my chest hurt. Before he left through the library door, he turned and glared at me.

"I think it's time you wrap this up, don't you think? It's getting late." *He knew.* I kept a hold of his stare, hoping he'd keep his mouth shut. Not that he could really prove anything. Gemma and I were right where we needed to be, and I was damn thankful that I hadn't gotten an alert that Bain's car was on the move.

I pulled out my phone when the door slammed, immediately texting Mica and asking if Bain was still in their room. He texted back within seconds, and I was thankful for the distraction. I swore I could feel Gemma's emotions all the way across the table.

MICA: He's here. You know I always send a text when he dips out. He's asleep.

ME: Are you sure?

GEMMA WAS PACKING up her things, pushing papers into a binder and forcefully shoving her journal down into her bag as I stood there, completely stationary. Who the fuck was in here messing with her computer? Better yet, are they still here? *Probably one of Bain's friends, just to fuck with me.*

As soon as Gemma snatched her laptop, I was thankful she didn't seem to notice. When she'd slammed it shut earlier, she was moving in a blur of anger. I wasn't sure she even remembered doing so. But I remembered. I remembered because when she closed it, and my eyes landed on her face, the breath was taken right out of my lungs.

MICA: I'm four feet away from his obnoxious fucking snoring. I'm sure.

. . .

"I NEED you to walk back to your room without me." I couldn't even look her in the eye. "I'll have Cade meet you in a second." The sound of papers rustling stopped. Her quick hands froze along the zipper of her bag. "I need to check on something."

The zipper was quick, and the sound jutted out into the air like a fucking sword. "No, thanks. I'll walk by myself."

My head fell, and a heavy breath climbed out of my mouth. I knew what I needed to do. I let things get out of hand a few minutes ago. I didn't regret it, but it was wrong. This entire situation was wrong. "Gemma, just wait for Cade."

Her tongue clicked as she whipped her backpack off the table, likely not even sparing me a glance. I wouldn't know, though. I still couldn't look at her. If I looked at her, I'd see the regret and confusion on her face again. Or worse, the hurt. "I'm tired of doing things for other people. I will make my own decisions from now on, Isaiah."

I growled, feeling frustrated by everything that was weighing down on me. "You can't really be trusted to make your own decisions, now, can you? You went straight into danger last night! You're being irrational and reckless! Just wait for Cade."

Gemma stormed past me, and I grabbed a hold of her arm. Her hot glare was filled with moisture, and I immediately wanted to retreat. I wanted to apologize, and that was not something I did often. This wasn't fair to her, and I was pretty sure nothing had ever been fair or easy in her life. "Please, just wait."

Gemma whipped her arm out of my grasp, and a part of me wanted to smile at her bravery. She was valiant when she wanted to be. She just needed to dig down to that feeling like I needed to dig down into mine. *Make her hate you.* "I don't owe you anything, Isaiah." Her eyes clenched tightly, and her mouth pursed. "And you know what sucks?" She didn't let me answer as she walked over to the doors that Mr. Cunningham had just gone through. "A big part of me wants to wait here, just because you said so." She scoffed. "I guess old habits die hard. Always trying to follow the fucking rules." Her brown hair swayed as she tipped her chin over her shoulder. "But I'm done doing what everyone else wants. No one tells me the whole truth anyway."

"Gemma!" I yelled, ready to stalk after her, feeling torn between wanting two things. I didn't like the idea of her walking down the dark hallway alone, but I also wanted to stay here and sneak through every last aisle to find out which one of Bain's friends had been in here, messing with Gemma's computer. My head told me to stay, and everything else told me to go after her. My bones were breaking with each stride she took.

I slammed my fist down on the wooden table, the book she'd grabbed from the shelf seconds ago flipping off and falling to the floor beneath a cloud of dust, and I followed after her.

Fucking hell.

CHAPTER SIXTY

GEMMA

"Don't even spare him a single glance, and you know what...forget tutoring tonight. Text him that you're busy with someone else."

Mercedes pulled out the chair beside Sloane. "Yeah, like with another guy. Serves him right."

I tucked a piece of fallen hair behind my ear, almost wishing that I'd worn it down today so I could hide. I had no intention of stooping to Isaiah's level and playing yet another game. It felt like we had been playing a game for weeks. So, to be honest, I didn't have the energy.

I hadn't slept much since Friday, after I completely crumbled in front of him only to flee with anger seconds later as my heart continued to thump from our *moment*. I'd holed up in my room all weekend, thinking about what I'd learned, and each tutoring session that came after felt like an elephant crushing my chest. The only time I left my bed, other than for school and *tutoring,* was in the very early morning to slap my frustrations onto a canvas before breakfast. I was disappointed and confused about what had happened between us in the library, but I also didn't regret it. When he touched me, everything stopped, but I thought it was what I had truly needed at the moment, even as shameful as it made me feel. I was beginning to learn that Isaiah was a sort of isolation for me. Not even sketching was taking away the gnawing thoughts and memories that were distorted and broken. In the past, sketching brought them out, but I'd always been in a trance, unable to sort through them or feel them in the moment. That wasn't how it was anymore. Sketching was replaced with two blue eyes that could see right through me. Everything was just...*gone* with Isaiah. And it was so dangerous. That was why I couldn't even look at him as of late. Not even as we sat a few feet away from one another with a study table in between us. He stayed in the library until eleven each night, never once leaving. He didn't go follow Bain or cut our tutoring time short. I had no idea why, other than maybe he was on edge about Mr. Cunningham checking on us Friday. I couldn't ask, and he didn't give up his reasoning. There wasn't a single word spoken from either of us. Things were left unsaid and lingering.

I shoved my food away, starting to feel weighed down from the week. I'd been feeling the remnants of anger but also anguish from the second I let that memory slip in on Friday. I was sad. I was so incredibly sad for my mom who'd been through something much worse than I thought. I was sad for the five-year-old girl who festered inside me as she watched her mother claw for freedom. I was sad for Tobias because, wherever he was, it probably wasn't a good place. I left both phones in my room this morning, too untrusting of myself if Isaiah decided to text me on the phone he had given me, and too irrational to care if Richard called me on the other.

Something inside me burned to listen to Sloane and

Mercedes and knock Isaiah down a few notches. Everything was so messy between us, and confusion filled every gap that had formed since he found me kneeling below his father at the psych hospital—*The Covens*. I was angry and felt betrayed in a way, but there was the teeniest, tiniest slip in my chest at the mere thought of him that told me just how fleeting those emotions were.

My gaze followed Bain through the dining hall as a whisper of uncertainty graced my ears. According to Isaiah, Bain had met Richard that night at the psych hospital when we'd followed him, and that did *nothing* but stir up anxiety. And although I sensed extreme danger regarding Bain, I also wanted to corner him and demand answers. *Bain knew Richard.* That was something to hold on to.

"Everything is so fucked up," I muttered under my breath, annoyance flashing through because I swore I could feel Isaiah's eyes on me from across the long table. *Was he looking at me?*

Sloane coughed and choked on something, and I whipped my head over to her. "Are you okay?"

Her face was red as she clutched onto her white blouse. She quickly untied the maroon bow around her neck as Mercedes patted her back. Claire, from a few seats down, raised her eyebrows at us and then rolled her eyes, going back to her friends. I didn't pay any mind to her, though. She didn't seem to like much of anyone at St. Mary's unless they had a penis. I couldn't even count how many times I'd seen her sneaking around with a guy following after her. Although, could I really talk much? Isaiah and I had done things on this very table.

My face flamed at the thought, but I wouldn't dare look at him.

"I'm fine." Sloane sipped on her water before putting it

down and looking over at me. "Gemma. I don't think I've ever heard you say fuck."

My lips pursed. "When did I say that?"

Mercedes laughed. "Like, five seconds ago. You said that everything was fucked up."

"Oh." A breathy laugh came from me. "I didn't mean to say that out loud."

Sloane plopped a grape in her mouth before grinning over at me. "You know what you need?"

I half-rolled my eyes, knowing what she was going to say. "To blow off tutoring tonight? I can't." I wanted to. I'd wanted to all week because I wasn't sure how much more I could take, sitting in that quiet library with nothing but the sound of Isaiah's breathing and my rapid heartbeat in my ears. *I couldn't, though.* We had a deal.

"No." She paused. "I mean, yes. But no. You need to let loose this weekend."

"This weekend?" I asked.

"Tomorrow night. Claiming party after the lacrosse game." We met eyes, and she smirked. "You're going to let loose, Gemma Richardson. I demand it. Let's have some fun without the Rebels breathing down your neck like a pack of savages. Fuck Isaiah and the bullshit."

Sloane knew the most about me and Isaiah, although not all of it. She didn't ask what had happened when I came back to our room last week all muddy and in tears. I was certain it was because she knew I wouldn't tell. I wasn't that type of girl. Not to mention, Isaiah and I were like a double-edged sword. Danger on both sides.

Mercedes clapped. "Hell yes! We should pull out all the stops, Sloane. Like..." Mercedes' voice was on the brink of regret. She retreated her next words, but Sloane nodded in agreement.

"Like we used to do with Journey."

Mercedes' lip was held between her teeth as she glanced down the table toward where Isaiah and his friends were sitting. I didn't follow her gaze, though. Instead, I was thinking about tomorrow night and how much the thought of being *normal* seemed so inviting. I needed it. I needed to find another way to deal with everything happening lately, and Isaiah was off-limits. I had to find a way to balance it all until I got out of here, and I had too much dignity to act on impulse with him again. I couldn't rely on his touch. I couldn't rely on Isaiah to silence my confusion and unanswered questions as the blind future dangled right in front of me.

"Oh shit." Mercedes quickly snapped her big brown eyes back to me, and I stilled.

My heart began beating quicker, and my stomach fell to the floor. I was too afraid to look. There were too many possibilities that could have caused her to look panicked. "What? What's wrong?"

"*That mother fucker.* I swear to God, these damn Rebels! They care about no one but themselves!"

Sloane's voice was rising, so I placed my hand on her leg to calm her down. I didn't need any unnecessary looks my way. I hadn't been on the stupid, gossiping St. Mary's blog in at least a week, according to Sloane. I suspected that Isaiah was taking care of it anytime he and I were featured.

"Don't even look down there." Mercedes was trying to appear calm, whereas Sloane was fuming. Her skin was burning hot against my hand.

Slowly, I swung my attention past Mercedes and her wild, curly hair. I saw Claire look down at me with pity before shaking her head at whatever was unfolding. *Why was I nervous?* As long as it wasn't Richard, it was fine. My heart thumped harder. *Wait, what if it was Richard?!* My chest heaved, but instead of looking for Isaiah in the sea of students, I looked for Bain. If Richard were here, coming to get me, it would be his fault. I was certain of it. But Bain's face remained smooth. There wasn't a flicker of accomplishment or even fulfillment there. Instead, he was steady. He watched me, his eyebrows dipping slightly as he tilted his head toward the one place I didn't want to look.

My blood rushed with embarrassment because it seemed like almost every single person was looking at me, which only confirmed that it had to do with Isaiah. Our peers didn't know *everything* that had gone on with us, but Isaiah had made it a point to show them that I was *his*. The kiss at the last claiming was enough to raise questions, even if it had started off as another game in his mind.

Their pitiful stares were the final shove I needed to raise my chin and find those cool blue eyes that I'd grown to love and hate. As soon as I allowed myself to look, it was like ice falling down on my shoulders in the middle of an avalanche.

There he was, sitting with his three best friends, with his white dress shirt undone at the top and his maroon-and-gold tie hanging loosely beneath his neck. His dark hair was standing up like it was Friday evening after I'd run my hands through it in that moment of weakness. I didn't recognize the girl that was on his lap. I was too focused on the way his large hand splayed against her ribcage like he was seconds from gripping her and plopping her down on the dining table like he'd done to me the first night he touched me.

I trembled, feeling sick to my stomach. It was like he had cut me. The feeling was brutal even if I had braced myself. I was back to feeling that overbearing emotional pain I wasn't used to, and instead of letting it envelope me and allowing it to take me down in front of the entire student body, I pushed myself harder onto the seat that was holding me up and looked right back over at Bain. His jaw was set, and his arms were crossed against his chest. He looked angry, and I was too. The rules had changed, and suddenly, I wanted back in the game.

Bain had answers, and I was going to get them, and Isaiah wasn't going to stop me. I wouldn't heed his warnings any longer. Not now.

"Letting loose tomorrow sounds like a great idea," I said, smiling at Sloane and Mercedes.

Sloane's eyebrow raised, and there was a glimmer in her eye. "Heartbreak is code for rebellion. We're gonna have some fun."

"Definitely," I confirmed. But first, I needed to talk to Bain.

———

I wrapped the flannel that Sloane had lent me around my body as the cool wind whipped around us. The boys were down below, dressed in athletic pants and long sleeve shirts, doing their drills for lacrosse. My back was turned toward the field again, and the only reason I'd come to practice today was because I had other things on my agenda. Things that couldn't be stopped because my heart had a little tear in it from Isaiah and his show during lunch.

The girl, who I learned was named Breanna, stayed on Isaiah's lap the entire time. Her long blonde locks fell to her butt when she would throw her head back and laugh at something the Rebels said, and I wanted to throw my salad in their faces. All of them. I was more confused than anything, but the silent touches of shame and betrayal were back, and I was wearing them like a second skin.

No more than a week ago, Isaiah had his arms around me, picking up my broken pieces as they scattered on the ground like the crisp leaves that currently sat beneath me. I shouldn't have confided in him again. He told me on Thursday, after shoving me up against that tree just below the Covenant Psychiatric Hospital, that he and I were over. He was only staying true to what he'd demanded that night, although in a crappy way. He and I were no longer anything. In fact, we hadn't spoken in days, but it didn't matter the reason. Isaiah and I were impulsive with one another; it had shown in the library, just one day later. It was obvious we were both running from a past that neither of us could hide from and racing toward a future that we couldn't have. We were intertwined. Our families were somehow twisted in one way or another, and if he knew more about that than what he'd already said, it didn't show.

But regardless, I should have listened to him when he pushed me away. If I had, maybe I wouldn't have been sitting here with raging jealousy brewing low in my belly as I stared at Breanna up in the bleachers with my back turned to him.

"Are you sure you want to do this? I'm all for pissing off the Rebel who hurt you, but...this? Bain isn't someone you should be alone with, Gemma."

"Bain won't hurt me, Sloane." I wasn't fully certain of that, given the first night he had made himself known to me, but after what Isaiah had reluctantly told me last week—that Bain knew Richard—I was certain that if he wanted me gone or if he wanted to hurt me in some way, he would have done so by now. Richard wasn't here to drag me back home, despite the social worker's threats toward him, which meant that Bain hadn't told him a single thing about me.

When I'd first started at St. Mary's, Bain had said he recognized me; he just didn't know where from yet. At the time, I had no idea just how truthful that was. Bain was definitely hiding something, and I wasn't waiting around for Isaiah to tell me what it was.

"And how do you know that?"

I sighed softly, realizing that Sloane was worried about

me. "I have been in more threatening situations, Sloane. I know what I'm doing. I promise. He won't hurt me."

She rolled her eyes as she looked up into the misty sky. "Gemma..."

"Sloane." I grabbed onto her hand. "You're one of the only people I trust in this school. I may hold back some information from time to time, but I will not lie to you." I thought back to when I'd shown Sloane the scars around my wrists. She had been the only person so far that I'd confided in who hadn't betrayed my trust. Well, Headmaster Tate hadn't either, but it wasn't like I'd told him much to begin with. I was still leery of him at times, even if I did feel safe near him.

Sloane's warm breath made a cloud in the chilly air. "Fine. I'm giving you ten minutes, and then I'm coming after you. Got it?"

I nodded quickly, squeezing her hand. I could have waited and talked with Bain at the claiming party—as long as he stayed there the whole time, unlike the last one—just to drive Isaiah crazy. But I wasn't even sure he'd feel that same burn of jealousy that I felt, and I wasn't going to play that game. I had another game in mind—one I wouldn't let him interfere with.

"Okay, go. Now. Their backs are turned."

I quickly jumped to my feet, locking eyes with Bain who sat at the top of the bleachers, as usual, with his pack of friends. When he caught my attention, snagging those dark, beady eyes with mine, I flicked my chin once and quickly walked down the sidewalk and behind the bleachers.

Resting my back against one of the cold metal pillars, I tilted my head, feeling the chill race down my spine. I wasn't sure if it was from the autumn temperature or fear. I stared up at the gray clouds, taking even breaths, grabbing a hold of this messed-up little game in my two shaky hands. I was done waiting on the sidelines. I was still running when this was all said and done, because I knew with complete certainty that the documents I'd found months ago were, in fact, real. It was confirmed in my shunned-away memory. It just took me a while to dig into the past and find the heavy threat that had been there since I was a small child. Richard would do to me what he did to my mother. He thought because he had taken everything away from me that I'd fall into his lap, allowing him to turn me into someone I wasn't. He thought that all the punishments he'd given me, the threats, the fear, the longing touches against my skin that he tried to manipulate into love, would kill the girl I truly was deep down. He thought that sending me to a place like St. Mary's was a punishment. Just another way to get me to oblige to his rules and demands. He honestly thought that sending me away from *him* would make me realize how worthy I was to be his. Did he expect me to beg to come home? Or to be truthful about it? Richard couldn't see the truth because he was so twisted in the head, and I knew that because I knew *him*. I was thriving here, broken heart or not. I had plans that he didn't foresee coming, and Bain wasn't going to get in the way of those. I wouldn't let it happen.

"Did you enjoy your midnight drive in my car the other night?"

My head came back down to level ground, and I ripped my gaze over to the dangerous boy slowly striding toward me. His hair was cut close to his scalp, a diamond stud glittering through the light fog. His footsteps were easy, and the closer he got, the harder my heart beat. Not from fear, though. I was too eager and wild with power to feel the tingles of fear now.

I turned slowly and propped my shoulder against the side of the metal pole bracing the bleachers. His friends were up too high to hear us, especially with the wind cutting through the air. My lips tipped into a small grin. "It's no surprise that you knew. I think you know a lot more than you let on."

Bain moved closer to me. He reached into his coat pocket, and my heart came to a halt for a quick second before I saw that he was pulling out a pack of cigarettes. The lighter flame was bright before he lit the end of one, and he puffed on it for a few seconds before blowing out the smoke and edging even closer to me.

We stood there in silence, and when I realized that he had nothing more to say, I leveled my voice and said, "My first week at St. Mary's, you pulled me aside and said you recognized me." Bain kept quiet as he sucked on the cigarette again. "But you know exactly who I am now, right? And you know Richard too."

His brow quipped quickly, and I hated the sound of this deep voice. "Richard who?"

He was playing with me.

"Oh, you know, the man you sell guns to at the Covens." I saw the flicker of shock ripple across Bain's features. It was hardly noticeable, but I saw as it tore through him. I laughed sarcastically, unable to stop myself. "I have to admit, you've upset some people. I mean, someone else has been supplying those guns to Richard since I was five years old."

After Friday, I had put more and more information together, like pieces from a puzzle. From the fragments of my memory and from what Isaiah had admitted, I knew much more than anyone thought.

Bain stayed silent, and it gave me the push to straighten my shoulders and raise my chin. Fear was a distant thought in the back of my head. I wanted him to know that I knew things about him. I wanted to prove to him, and Isaiah too, that I was taking things in my own hands. I was tired of the lies and half-truths. I was tired of being dismissed. "Want to know how I know that?"

Bain stepped closer to me, puffing out his smoke, causing my nostrils to flare and my lungs to burn. "I'm sure you know a lot more than I'd like. Tell me." Bain's other hand ran down the side of my cheek, and goosebumps clung to my skin. I still pushed back on the fear, though. I would not be intimidated by him. "Did Isaiah tell you all this? Or are you just as curious as your uncle says? He said you were smart, so did you figure this all out on your own? Unable to stay in your fucking lane?"

There it was. The confirmation I needed that there was more to their relationship than the gun trafficking. Bain knew that Richard was presumed to be my uncle. I still couldn't figure out why there was a need for unmarked guns at a psychiatric hospital or why Isaiah called it the Covens, but none of that mattered right now.

"The better question is..." I pushed his hand away from my face. "Why haven't you told him what I've been up to? He wants you to spy on me, right? Or is that just for your own sick pleasure?"

We both heard the crunching of gravel, and I assumed it was Sloane coming to check on me like she'd promised, but Bain's sick smile appeared, and I faltered. "*Maybeee.* But, sweetheart? You are right where I want you to be. You aren't my enemy."

What the hell did that mean? And that "*maybe*" sounded an awful lot like a confirmation.

"Incoming!" Sloane's shout came out of nowhere. I looked to my left and right, but I didn't see her. Bain slowly pointed upward with the cigarette in his hand, and I saw Sloane's panicked face looming over me from the top of the bleachers.

And that was when I heard the chuckle from Bain and the angry shout from Isaiah. My throat closed, and my breathing stuttered. My entire body felt as if it were plunged into lava as I stared wide-eyed at Isaiah with his hand around Bain's throat as he pushed him up against the same metal pole I had been resting on a few minutes ago. "What did I fucking say would happen the next time you looked at her?" Isaiah cracked his neck, and I saw the veins bulging with his angry, hot blood.

Bain laughed, although it was hard to hear because Isaiah's fingers were plunged deep into his neck. He let up for a second only for Bain to say, "Hey, man...take it up with her. She asked to talk to me."

Shit.

Isaiah's hand still stayed against Bain's throat as he whipped his head to me and glared with those ice-blue eyes. Bain made no move to get out of his grasp. If anything, he looked like he enjoyed it. "You *asked* to talk to him?"

"Let him go, Isaiah." My heart was flying through my chest as I tried to sort through what Bain had said to me. *You're right where I need you to be.* That sent panic right into my bloodstream. Adrenaline pumped, and I suddenly felt lightheaded. "Let him go! You're on probation! Do you really want to get caught in the middle of a fight *during* lacrosse practice?!" With Bain's half-threat in my head, I knew now, more than ever, that I needed to get the hell away from this school and anything relating to Richard. My eyes locked onto Isaiah, and I hoped he knew me well enough to know that there was something else going on here.

"Better listen to her. Wouldn't want to get expelled now, would you?"

Isaiah kept his stare on me, and even from several feet away, I could see the blue in his eyes turn dark. He was angry, but I wasn't sure what he expected from me. He couldn't push me away and then pull me in again. I wasn't a tug-of-war rope. He didn't know me at all if he thought I was going to stay in line and keep silent after knowing what I did now. I would *not* be the girl Richard tried to mold me into. Isaiah might not have realized it, but he was asking the same of me.

"Let him go," I said through gritted teeth, and Isaiah reluctantly dropped his hand.

Bain winked at me, and I turned away briefly, still repeating his venomous words in my head.

"I swear to God, Bain," Isaiah seethed under his breath as he placed his fisted hands on his hips. "I hope you know that the only reason I'm sparing you is because I need you."

Bain's head tilted in a cynical way, but he said nothing as he flicked his cigarette underneath the bleachers and turned around. Before he got too far, he called over his shoulder, "Don't fucking take my car again, Gemma."

Isaiah didn't look surprised at all by the words that came from Bain's mouth. Instead, he looked at me with blinding disappointment. I felt myself retreat for a moment. *But no.* I wasn't going to apologize for anything. Isaiah had no right. He had no right to interject himself in this any longer. I didn't owe him anything.

"What the fuck was that about?" He stalked over to me quickly, but I didn't take a step back. I wasn't afraid of Isaiah. Was I conflicted with him? Yes. Did I think he was keeping things from me? Yes. But I wasn't afraid of him. "I told you that you shouldn't be anywhere near this, Gemma. That's why I'm fucking staying away from you! To keep you out of this entire thing! You don't know what you're messing with."

I scoffed, crossing my arms over my chest in a bratty way, ignoring how my heart buzzed with him only feet away. "But I am in this, Isaiah! I've been in the middle of this the entire time! Which I'm sure you knew well before you dipped your cock inside me!"

I paused. *Did I really just say that out loud?!* Glancing around, I felt my cheeks warm, hoping that no one heard what I'd just said.

"Oh, for fuck's sake." Isaiah turned away, his rising chest climbing in speed. "You should know me better than that."

"But I don't!" I shouted, taking a step closer to him. He sliced his glare over to me, but I didn't hold back. "I thought I did, but I don't. You only show me what you want. You hide things. I get it." My voice was a little softer, but I was still feeling the rage climb. "I hide things too. It just is what it is."

Isaiah's hands came up, and he ran them through his sweaty hair, and I could sense the frustration, but I was frustrated too.

"I told you that I was done acting the way people expected of me. I had a moment of weakness Friday in the library, which is now evident after your show in the dining hall today. You made me feel weak and ashamed, and I will be damned if I am portrayed as weak again. I've been weak for almost eighteen years now, and I'm done. I don't owe you anything, and I surely don't owe you an explanation." I took a hefty step back from him because I could feel his warmth, and I didn't want to crave it. I didn't want to glance at his lips and feel the indignity that would come with it. I didn't need Isaiah Underwood to pick up my pieces and sort through my life—even if our paths were intertwined at some point or another.

Isaiah stood there, taking in my words one by one, with his features even and unreadable. *Typical.* I had no idea what was going through his mind, but I wasn't sticking around to figure it out.

"I will see you in the library for tutoring—unless you would like to change tutors and have Breanna tutor you now? Just let me know. As long as you get me what I asked for, I don't really care what you do."

The lie tasted like the past, and I hated that I was being that version of myself again. I'd always been myself around him. I couldn't not be myself around him, which was probably why I craved him so much. My walls fell when we were alone, and the truth always seemed to spew from my mouth one way or another. But those walls were up right now, and I was lying through my teeth. His little brother came to mind, and the truth was, I did care what Isaiah did. I didn't want him to change tutors, because there was so much more than tutoring going on, and would anyone else understand or even agree to do what he had asked of me? Despite everything, I would still cover for him. I would lie without any hesitation or thought to repercussions, and that drove me *mad* because it wasn't for my sake—it was for his. A part of my heart was latched onto his whether I liked it or not.

Isaiah let out a guttural sound and clenched his eyes shut. He quickly turned around, gripping the back of his neck, and stomped away, leaving me there feeling anything but satisfied.

CHAPTER SIXTY-ONE

ISAIAH

THE PARTY WAS in full swing, but I was ready to snap something in half. The beat of the song overhead was like a blow-horn inside my ears, and not even the shots I'd taken could take me down a notch. I was on edge. My leg bounced up and down aggressively as I leaned back onto the far wall. The plastic shot glass in my hand crumpled up like a wad of paper as Cade and Brantley tried to talk me down from the ledge.

"Isaiah, this was what you wanted."

I growled through my teeth, eyeing the strobe lights, which gave me an instant headache. It was either the lights causing the throb or the stress weighing down on me. I had too much going on, and despite the plan working overtime in the back of my head and the enlightening phone call I'd had earlier, I was still just as concerned with Gemma as I had been from the start. In fact, it was much heavier now.

"This wasn't what I fucking wanted. I didn't want any of this."

Cade's hands clamped onto my shoulders tightly as his

face blocked the multicolored lights. "I got through Journey, and you can get through this. Keep up with the show, make her hate you, and she'll be better off."

I growled, throwing the neon cup to the dirty floor of the school basement where we held all our parties in secret. "No offense," I started, not really meaning it, "but you didn't have to deal with seeing Journey every fucking minute of every day. Imagine it for a minute." I knocked his hands off me. "Imagine seeing Journey every single day and not being able to touch her. Imagine having to pull other girls into your lap to make it clear that you didn't feel anything for her." Having Breanna on my lap yesterday, rubbing her silk panties on my thigh as she straddled my knee, felt like my organs were slowly failing inside my body. I felt hollow. I just sat there, itching for the bell to ring so I could fling her off instead of digging myself into an even deeper grave.

I was one step closer to ending my father but a million steps away from starting with Gemma.

"Yeah, I'm sure it was hard having a hot chick in your lap," Brantley grunted, and I ignored him, knowing he wouldn't understand anyway. He was the one I worried about the most when it came time to choose sides. He was harder to get through to. His walls were thick.

Shiner popped his hand in between us, holding four shots in the middle of his palm. "Let's just get shitty. Bain is right there with a girl pressed up against his dick, chugging even more booze than we are. He isn't going anywhere tonight."

Yeah, but was Gemma?

Cade snatched a green shot glass, tipping it back and swallowing it whole. "You deserve it, Isaiah. Take some heat off your back. Let's go back to how it used to be. Even if it's just for tonight." He slapped my face with excitement clear in his brown eyes as I grabbed onto another shot. *Just for tonight.* I'd heard that before.

Brantley nodded. "We won our game. Let's celebrate that, if nothing else."

I didn't give two fucks about the lacrosse game today, and I wasn't celebrating anything, but I still threw the shot back in hopes that it would help soothe the ache in my chest. I desperately needed something to ground me so I could get through tonight.

Our tutoring session had been intense last night. More intense than the last few. Instead of Gemma and I being indifferent with one another, now we were both angry. She still wouldn't look at me from across the table, which was exactly what I needed, but *fuck* if it didn't sting. I almost pretended that the little alert went off on my phone, telling me that Bain's car was moving, just so I could get away from the suffocating air, but that was too risky with the SMC becoming more watchful since our little run-in with Mrs. Fitz last week. I was lucky that Bain had been staying put lately, but I was sure there was a reason for that. Just like I was sure that Gemma was about to show up tonight with her two best friends by her side to cut me the same way I cut her.

Gemma wasn't going to hold back. That sweet, goody-two-shoes girl she was at the first claiming party had been morphed into someone else over the last few weeks, and it was mostly by my doing. She was no longer hesitant around other people. She seemed so sure of herself, even while talking with Bain yesterday, which sent me straight to the red.

I felt completely out of control, and I wanted to blame it all on everything that was going on with my father, but the truth was, I felt out of touch with Gemma, and that was what made me antsy. The protectiveness I felt for her had intensified since last week, but she didn't want to be protected by me any longer—and for good reason.

I snatched another shot, although I knew I was at my limit. I was seconds from shooting it down my throat with

Shiner's eager nod in my peripheral when the basement door opened, and three sets of bare legs popped through the threshold.

Every single person looked in that direction. I could feel the shift in the room. I wasn't looking at anyone else, though. My attention was solely on the girl in the middle.

Gemma.

My eyes burned with a hot intensity, and I could no longer breathe. My heart halted, and my stomach tightened. She stood there looking *so* unlike herself that I felt the brunt of shame. It wasn't that she didn't look good, because she did. She looked really fucking good. Hot as hell. Her tight black dress hardly reached mid-thigh, and blood shot straight to my groin as I scanned her tanned, toned legs. Her hair was pulled back in a sleek ponytail, showing off every perfect curve of her face, and her red lipstick was like a punch to the gut. But...it wasn't her. It wasn't the Gemma that I knew. This was a girl who was lashing out because she had been hurt—*by me.*

"Hey, Isaiah." Breanna's voice was like a knife being dragged down my back. "Are we still on for tonight?"

Cade pulled me away, and I knew it was because he could sense my hesitation. "Isaiah. Think about how your father treated her the other night." I couldn't seem to snag my attention away from Gemma, even with Cade's face moving in front of mine. *I wanted her.* No one else. I didn't want Breanna. I didn't want any other girl in this school. I wanted her.

"I'll kill my father," I muttered, watching as Sloane and Mercedes dragged Gemma over to the table lined with shots. She inched her head back, and I swore I could feel the burn of Fireball hit the back of my throat too.

"Isaiah, fucking snap out of it. Have you ever thought that maybe Bain was taking those photos of you and Gemma because he's going to give them to your father or, I don't know... maybe use it as blackmail?" *Obviously.* "If you feel for her what I felt for Journey, you will stay away from her."

I finally pulled myself from Gemma and stared at Cade. I needed to stay on track. I needed to keep myself in line, but I wasn't sure I could. This was the hardest thing I'd ever done, and that was concerning, given my upbringing.

Cade tapped my shoulder once and flicked his chin behind me. "Go over there, put your fucking hands on Breanna's hips, and show Gemma and Bain and everyone in this school that she means nothing to you. Because I'm telling you right now, Gemma Richardson will be the death of you, Isaiah. If she gets hurt because of you, you will never fucking forgive yourself."

Cade was speaking from experience, so I took a deep breath, swiveling on my shoe and stomping back over to Breanna. I was sure it was obvious to her that I didn't really want her, but I was hoping that it wasn't obvious to anyone else. There was nothing between Breanna and me. No lust or passion. I wasn't even sure I would be able to get a hard-on unless it was with Gemma.

A future full of celibacy was what I had to look forward to. Great.

When my palms landed on Breanna's waist, I felt like I was fumbling with a grenade. Her head pulled back, and I knew that there was likely something unfolding behind me. My heart was stretching for another girl in this room, and I wanted to pound my fist into the ground to make the music and low chatter stop for just a second so I could breathe. Breanna's hands came up and touched the sides of my face as she whispered, "It's okay, Isaiah. You can pretend I'm her if you want." *Fucking hell.*

I shut my eyes and sucked in even breaths. "Not sure who you're referring to."

It was pretty evident there was something to Gemma and

me, even if some of our classmates assumed it was only a simple fuck during the claiming party. The faculty, however, was clueless because I'd kept the touching to a minimum and didn't spare her many glances when the SMC was around. Mainly because if they knew I was fooling around with my tutor, they'd never believe our story or accept any excuses if we were found wandering the halls after curfew.

In the beginning, before everything had shifted, I didn't hide my interest in her because I needed our classmates to watch her, to envy her, and to speculate on our relationship so Bain would be forced to back away. But that was a mistake.

Seeking her out in the very beginning was a total miscalculation on my part, and deep down, I'd always known it. I'd always known that there was a reason for my need to hover over her and to watch her every move. Gemma dug herself right under my skin, and I couldn't seem to dig her out, not even for a little while.

"We can play that game too." Breanna's hand crept up my neck and into my hair. "We're all trying to just put a pause on things for a while, right? Isn't that the whole reason for the claimings? To shut things out until the morning?"

I swallowed, looking down at her lips. They were nothing like Gemma's, and I hated it. What was Gemma doing right now? Was she watching this? Was she brewing in hatred for me? Would she push me away the next time I came close to her, because I would come close to her again. I would breathe her air again and put my hands on her body. I just hoped she was stronger than I was and would dismiss me like I deserved.

The music grew louder, and Breanna bit her lip with eager excitement. Shiner handed me another shot, and I took it, relishing in the way it burned through my veins. I skimmed my attention to Bain who was opposite of me, making sure I kept my back to Gemma, and I found him watching me suspiciously. We stayed locked on one another, refusing to look away. Bain and I were cut from the same cloth. Dominance was our first language, and neither one of us would submit to the other, which was exactly why we would be forced to work together in the end.

"Fuck yeah," Brantley said, nodding his head at me. "That's the Rebel I know." I gave him a quick look, and I knew he sensed the question on the tip of my tongue. He scanned the crowd at my back before coming back to me. "*She's fine,*" he mouthed, and my throat constricted. Breanna flipped around with my hands still on her hips and began rubbing her ass on my jeans. I hardly noticed, though, because I was too concerned with what was behind my back. Seeing Bain standing off to the side with someone else did nothing to ease my frustrations and concerns. I needed to see her for myself.

I needed to make eye contact with her.

Just once.

But when I tipped my head over, catching a glimpse of her black dress, my stomach plummeted to the floor. I zeroed in on the fucking idiot daring to touch her ass, and the hold on my rational thinking immediately loosened.

Breanna was shoved away, and I was seconds from plowing down any person that stood in my direct path, but just as soon as I turned around, the lights shut off.

I recognized a voice over the speaker that shouldn't have been.

"*It's claiming time.*"

CHAPTER SIXTY-TWO

GEMMA

FIREBALL WAS GROSS.

It tasted like actual fire going down my throat, and it took everything I had not to cough like an idiot after Sloane had handed me the tiny plastic cup. At first, I'd tried sipping on it, but Mercedes and Sloane laughed before demonstrating how to drink it. I was used to Richard drinking his amber-colored liquid in a glass cup, clinking the ice around like a warning before being scolded. But I took the drink anyway, chucking it back and downing it within seconds. I knew why I'd been so bold. I felt Isaiah staring at me, and I wanted to show him that I was fine, that last night's tutoring session didn't bother me in the slightest. Sure, my heart felt a little banged up, and it took every ounce of strength I had to keep my mouth shut as I refused to tell him what Bain had said to me, but *I was fine.*

Except, now that I was being pulled into a dark room with hands that were unfamiliar resting over parts that only *he* had touched, I felt smothered. The fear of being in a damp, cold room without even a sliver of light had my heart flying throughout my chest. I felt almost as scared as the first claiming party, when Bain had whispered things into my ear that made my skin crawl and caused me to panic. Now that I was a little surer of myself, I wasn't *that* scared, but the fear still laid quietly in the back of my head. The past still brimmed the surface, and I had to remember that I saw the face of the guy who came over to me. I didn't know his name, but I'd seen him around the school at times. I'd passed by him in the hallway and maybe even in the dining hall. He wasn't going to hurt me. His genuine gaze drove into mine before the lights shut off, silently asking me if I was up for this, and I nodded in approval.

I wanted to get Sloane's and Mercedes' go-ahead, but if I looked over at them, then I'd see Isaiah and Breanna again, and I couldn't stomach it. I was on my own right now, and I needed to trust myself.

The door latched, and the room was pitch black. My pulse was strumming, and I took a deep breath as the guy slowly backed me up against the wall.

"Wasn't sure you'd agree to this," he whispered along my neck. His breath smelled of the same alcohol that I'd consumed, and I swallowed back the cinnamon taste that still rested on my tongue. "Someone told me that you were no longer Isaiah's. Is that true? Or should I be prepared for him to knock down that door?"

I breathed out a light laugh, trying to force away the excitement that came with that thought. *What was wrong with me?! Isaiah was currently touching someone else!* "Didn't you see that Isaiah found a replacement? He's not coming in here to stop this." I swallowed, tipping my head to the side to allow him access. "He doesn't care."

The truth I felt behind those words made me clam up, but I tried to relax as rough hands skimmed down the sides of my black dress and underneath my butt. "You sure about that?"

"Yeah, I'm sure."

I wasn't sure. I wasn't sure about anything anymore. I wasn't even sure if this was what I wanted, but I was doing it anyway. I slowly turned back to the warm breath I felt against my neck and placed my lips on his. They didn't feel like Isaiah's. They didn't make my knees wobbly or cause a bundle of heat to burrow in my core, but in a sense, it still felt good. When his hands started to move slowly over my hips and up my chest, my breathing picked up a little.

I wasn't panicking, though, and I wasn't trying to push away memories of Richard from my head. I didn't feel that prickle of danger that I'd felt when Bain had shoved me into one of these rooms during the first party. I didn't feel unsafe.

My tongue moved inside his mouth, and I started to feel a little bit hotter. His hands grew more intense, and I began to lose myself in the moment until I realized that the entire reason why I wasn't panicking or forcing thoughts of my past away was because instead of focusing on the way this guy was touching me, I was thinking of Isaiah. I thought about the time his hands had cupped my ass as he placed me on top of the dining hall table. I thought about the way he made my body hum in the library last week. I thought about how good the high felt when he took me in his mouth against a tree. *How enthralling was that?* It was so wrong to do something like that out in the open, but my body responded, just like it was responding now at the thought of it.

I wasn't kissing some random guy in the middle of a claiming party. In my head, I was kissing Isaiah. My nipples hardened, and I whimpered, feeling out of control. *What the hell was wrong with me?! Stop thinking of Isaiah!* I was driving myself mad, and I felt myself getting antsy. I spread my legs, eager for this guy to make me feel him instead of the one who kept reaching inside my chest and twisting my heart.

"No," I said, taking his hands from my pebbled nipples and placing them on my thighs. "I want you here."

"*Fuck*," he muttered over my lips in a breathy way. "Whatever you want."

My head fell back again as I pushed Isaiah out of my head. *It's not Isaiah.*

But...it was. The door flung open, and a tall shadow appeared in the doorway. The guy's hands stopped moving just on the brink of where my panties touched the inside of my leg, and I froze. The lone light bulb was suddenly clicked on, and the air thickened immediately. Isaiah stood there, staring directly at me with a fire brewing in his eyes, and that only made me burn hotter. His cheeks were flushed, and his knuckles were bleeding. My first reaction was to race over to him to see what had happened, but I stopped myself before I could.

"What are you doing here?" I asked, keeping my hands on a set of broad shoulders. *Shouldn't he be with Breanna?*

The guy clicked his tongue. "Told you."

I saw his amusement and paused. "Did you bring me in here to make him mad?"

He glanced away, slowly taking his hands out from underneath my dress. I sucked in a breath as I looked to Isaiah, who had murder written all over his face. *Why did I feel guilty?*

"Bain asked him to. And it's not the first time he has done something that Bain wanted. Jeremy over here apparently likes getting his teeth knocked in. Otherwise, he wouldn't have agreed." Isaiah took a step closer to us, but I ignored him and glared at the guy who was just kissing me.

"Is that true?" *I couldn't trust a single fucking soul in this school! Games, games, games!*

His lip hitched. "It's not the only reason. I heard your moans the other night in the library with Isaiah." His gaze traveled down my body as he licked his lips. "You're fucking hot, babe. Who would say no to you?" I felt so dense, and I was instantly angry.

My leg swiftly came up, and I kneed him right in the balls, relishing as he dropped to the floor. "You're a bad kisser anyway."

I stood over him as he cupped himself, and I felt the urge to spit, but instead, I straightened my shoulders and pulled down the hem of my dress. I was ready to get out of this basement. Actually, I was ready to get out of this school. I left Jeremy on the ground, begging myself to keep my eyes away from Isaiah, and walked over to the door with my dignity only half intact.

I would slosh through cool water in the dark underground hallway and go back to my room all on my own. I didn't need Sloane or Mercedes to hold my hand as the familiar feeling of panic came at me from the small area. I was fine.

"Yeah *fucking* right," Isaiah muttered, grabbing onto my arm. He pulled me right back into that stuffy room and pushed me up against the wall.

Jeremy slowly got to his feet, still wheezing, and he half-laughed while shutting the door behind him.

The intensity of the air grew even thicker. So thick I could hardly breathe. Isaiah's blue eyes drove into mine, and I gulped, pressing farther away from him. I feigned anger, but deep down, I was faltering. I couldn't pinpoint my emotions, but the longer Isaiah glared at me, the more I teetered over the edge.

"Why are you here right now?" I bit out. "What are you doing?"

Isaiah's hands clamped down on my wrists as he flung my arms up above my head. My heart galloped, and the hotness I was feeling moments ago while thinking about his mouth on mine instead of Bain's accomplice only burned me more. *Ugh.*

"What am I doing, Gemma?" He laughed in my face, and I could see the irritation on his features. The vein in his neck pulsed as fast as my chest rose. "What are *you* doing?" Isaiah's face grew closer to mine, and my throat closed up. My body was still reacting, and it felt so right to be this close to him.

"What do you mean what am I doing?" I asked, tipping my chin up and leveling him with a glare just as potent as his. "You interrupted what I was doing!"

He rolled his eyes, and his hands tightened on my wrists. He was the only one I would let touch my wrists without feeling the need to pull away. He knew what laid beneath this black fabric. "This isn't you," he whispered, scanning over every inch of my face before dropping his gaze down my body. Butterflies rushed to my stomach, and when I tried to turn my head away, one of his hands left my wrists, and he grabbed my chin. His thumb came up and swiped over my swollen lips, surely smearing the red lipstick that Sloane told me to wear. "This lipstick isn't you." My brows crowded, and my mouth set into a firm line. Isaiah let go of my chin and touched my ponytail that cleared my face of any stray hairs. "This hair isn't you." I gasped as his finger hooked underneath the tiny elastic holding my hair in place, snapping it in half. My brown locks fell in one single whoosh around my face. He swallowed, his throat bobbing with a force that I felt in between my legs. His one hand still gripped my wrists tightly, but the other crept down the side of my cheek and over the dip of my neck so slowly I began panting. The pad of his finger skimmed over my cleavage, and my back bowed, and I couldn't even become angry at the betrayal of my body. It acted on its own. It wanted Isaiah despite everything. It wanted his touch. His kiss. His soft whispers. My body knew I needed that solitude again. *Reckless. Irrational.* That was what I was when it came to him, and it was rebellion in the form of a single touch.

His hoarse voice snagged my attention, and I stared directly at his inviting mouth. "And this dress." His tongue darted out, and he grazed his bottom lip, and I clenched my teeth so I wouldn't kiss him. "This dress isn't you."

My breath fanned over his face, and we locked eyes. My heart squeezed. "You don't know me as well as you think, Isaiah."

His thumb slowly rubbed over my pinned wrists, grazing my ugly scars beneath the black fabric. "I don't have to know all of your secrets to truly know you, Gemma."

I jerked on my wrists, but he didn't let me go, and I couldn't look away from him. I craved his eyes on me, and there was no way I was willingly leaving this room with him inside it. "I don't even know who I am, Isaiah. So how can you know?"

"That's a lie." His dark chuckle brought me back to life, and suddenly, my mouth was a breath away from his. "You know exactly who you are. You know exactly what you want, and you won't stop until you get it." His knee nestled in between my thighs, and I gladly opened them. His words were intoxicating, and I could no longer feel the alcohol in my blood. Instead, I felt him. "You are determined." He pushed closer, and I nearly whimpered. "You are strong." His hand gripped my thigh, and his fingers dug into my skin. "You are brave." His nose traced the curve of my cheek as he finally let go of my captured wrists. His palm came up, and he rested it along the concrete wall, right beside my head. "Most importantly, you know when to retreat from danger. That's why you're running from Richard."

Richard. Not uncle. He said Richard.

I swallowed, trembling underneath him. I needed it to stop. The push and pull between us. I wanted the room to just stop spinning for a minute so I could get myself together.

His words cut through the room. "Tell me to fucking go, right now."

I glanced around the dusty, dirty room as his teeth scraped over my ear lobe. "Wh-what?"

Isaiah suddenly pulled back, the look of pure agony on his face hardly hidden by the anger brewing. "I'm fucking dangerous for you. Just like Richard. So tell me to go."

My brows came together, but I was too stunned to say anything. He was nothing like Richard.

"Tell me you hate me!" he yelled, letting go of my body and caging my head in between his strong forearms. There was a bead of sweat forming on his hairline, and I knew the reason his hair was messed up was because Breanna had been running her hands through it as she moved over him, but I didn't care. "Tell me you wanted that guy instead of me. Tell me you'd rather fuck anyone in this school besides me! Tell me *no*. Push me away."

That was when it hit me. Isaiah wasn't pulling me in and pushing me away because he wanted to. He was pulling me in because he *couldn't* push me away. He wanted me to be the one to do it. And I should have. I should have placed my hands on his chest and shoved him clear across the room because he was right. He was dangerous. His father was dangerous. Richard was dangerous. Bain was dangerous too. All in their own ways.

But I wavered. My fingers scraped along the stone wall behind me, and I stared. I stared into his eyes, seeing the trouble brewing within the blue specks, and it matched mine. We were both stuck. We were both torn between right and wrong, trying to get each other to understand something we didn't even comprehend.

Isaiah's head dropped, and he reared his hand back and slapped the wall beside me. "Go!" The word was like a mountain falling, but I stayed still. He was hurting. I felt him shake along my chest, and it didn't matter that he'd hurt me the night his father had found me—unknowingly or not. It didn't matter that I was relishing in this newfound independence I'd felt while talking to Bain by myself yesterday. It didn't matter that my stomach bottomed out when I saw him with Breanna. Nothing mattered except him.

Life wasn't easy for him.

And it wasn't easy for me either.

Slowly, my hands fell to his chest. I felt the raging beat of his heart against my palm, and when he opened his mouth, it only grew faster. "Tell me you hate me. Tell me to fucking leave, Gemma. *Please*." His head snapped up quickly, and he pinned me with a look that I felt all the way to my soul. "When tomorrow comes, I'm going to start all over again. I'm going to make you hate me so you'll stay away. I won't fucking stop, so tell me to go."

The anguish twisted inside, jumbling everything up, and it was the only thing I needed to push me over the edge. My shaky hand grabbed his hard jaw, the sharpness cutting into my skin. I pulled him in close and let myself cave. My mouth covered his in hungry strokes, and I pushed everything else away. His hands cupped my waist, and he picked me up, forcing my legs around his back, pressing himself against my middle. I moaned, sucking in the stuffy air trapped inside this room full of too much emotion, and pushed right back.

"I'm not thinking of tomorrow," I whispered before biting onto his lip.

His eyes flared, and it forced a dose of dopamine to surge through. "Fuck tomorrow." Isaiah sat down in the dingy chair that was in the corner, and my legs fell over both sides of him. "You're mine tonight."

I shut my eyes, enjoying the way his hands trailed over my back and up to the zipper near my neck. My hair was brushed over my shoulder, and my skin was so sensitive that I felt the wisps of my strands even through the thick black fabric. The sound of the zipper drew my attention to Isaiah, and his hooded eyes drank in my bare skin as he pushed the dress down over my arms. My breasts were on full display. Sloane told me not to wear a bra, and I was suddenly thankful I listened, because Isaiah's mouth was on me, and my body was receptive. I was wet in between my legs, and I wasn't shy about it.

I wanted this.

It was like all the anger and betrayal I'd felt since the moment his father had found me underneath that green awning was coming in full action, and I needed to release it all.

A breathy moan left me as I moved above him, wanting to feel more than the scratch of his jeans. He pulled my nipple into his mouth, and I cried out, gripping onto his hair. The slight moment of pain was a rush right between my legs. I stopped moving, and Isaiah pulled back, looking at me deviously. My hands left his shoulders, and I moved to his shirt, pulling it up over his head. One of my shoes touched the dust-covered ground, and I scooted myself off his lap, shoving the rest of my dress down past my hips. I stepped out of it slowly, enjoying the way he looked at me. His lingering eyes scorched me from head to toe, and I loved every single second of it.

His abs flexed as I walked over to him, wearing nothing but the strappy heels that Sloane had lent me and my black panties. "I don't deserve you," he whispered, grabbing onto my hips and staring up at me with the same intense look on his face that he'd had when he walked in here earlier.

"Maybe...or maybe not," I whispered, slowly lowering my knees to the ground. My hands found the button of his jeans, and his brow furrowed. "But *we* deserve this moment right here. We deserve to put a pause on reality." I pulled the zipper down and realized I was acting blindly. But I was following the cues of my body, and I was eager to be in this moment with him, past and future be damned.

His head tilted back, and his hands flexed on top of his legs when I freed him from his boxers. I swallowed back my hesitation. There was no room for second thoughts. The throb between my legs grew more urgent as I gripped him and stroked down the base and back up again. I thought back to that time in the forest when Isaiah and I stumbled upon Shiner and a random girl. I wanted to do what she did. I wanted to know what it felt like to have him in my mouth. I wanted to watch him lose control, because more times than not, he *was* in control.

"Gemma." He breathed heavily as his hips moved, and his perfectly sculpted stomach muscles flexed.

My mouth hovered over his hard length, and I licked my lips. I was completely fascinated by the lure of his lust and how it was getting into every crevice of my body, but before I could do anything, his hands clamped down on my arms, and he pulled me up off the floor and plopped me down onto his lap. "Get off your knees."

I sucked in a ragged breath as I felt him rub against my wetness. It was coming through the thin fabric that separated us, and I knew he could feel it. "No fucking way will I let you suck me off in this disgusting, dirty fucking basement with your knees scraped up because of something my father did." He swallowed, lifting up and reaching into his back pocket before shoving his jeans and boxers all the way down. The condom wrapper was in his mouth next, and he ripped the foil, pushing me back just far enough that he could slip it on. My panties came down, and he threw them across the room before gripping me tightly and bringing me closer. "I don't deserve you," he said again, lining himself up with me. I rubbed against him, knowing how good it would feel, and it did. It felt so good I nearly cried.

"*Fuck,*" he said, breathing into the crook of my neck. My hands wrapped around his head as I started moving above him. He was everywhere. His lips touched over every inch of my skin. His tongue coated mine, and his hands seemed to move just as quickly as his thrusts.

"Mmm," I sighed as his hand came in between our bodies, and he rubbed circles over my clit, causing my hips to move differently. I was chasing the high I knew would come soon. The orgasm was building, and things were moving faster. The scrapes against his knuckles rubbed across my belly, and I looked down at the reddened marks.

His thumb never stopped moving, but his lips paused against mine. "I knocked down the locked doors, looking for you when the lights went out." I sucked in a breath, my lungs on fire as I moved. *God, it felt so good.* The twisting and pulling over my lower belly were sparking, and I wanted to feel myself come undone. I wanted that blissful feeling that lied to me and told me that everything was okay and that there was nothing bad that could ever touch me again.

"The thought of someone else's hands on you makes me fucking crazy." He bit onto my lip, and I yelled out, feeling the curl in between my legs tighten. He started to pump into me faster, both of us running in circles, frantic for each other.

"God," I whimpered, moving one more time before coming down in full, thundering waves around his body. His arms clamped around my hips, and suddenly, my back was on the ground as I rode out my orgasm, and it was the most intense, blinding thing that I had ever felt.

Isaiah stilled over me, filling me up to capacity. I hardly registered his words as he came down beside my ear, collapsing. "I think I might fucking love you, Gemma." My heart stopped as my eyes shut, trying to push away the uncertainty of everything to come. "*But I can't.*"

CHAPTER SIXTY-THREE

GEMMA

I KEPT GLANCING at the art room door, wondering when I'd see his face. It had been a few days since everything seemed to come together only to fall apart again in the basement underneath St. Mary's, and things between Isaiah and me were still just as unsteady. He went right back to keeping his distance from me. His eyes stayed to himself; they never wandered in my direction. His hands were almost always clutching a pencil or book during each tutoring session, as if the object itself was grounding him to the chair. He never left to follow Bain or to go back to the psychiatric hospital. Nothing. We just sat there, in that quiet library, festering in our unwanted thoughts, holding back things that neither of us wanted to say.

No one from the SMC had come to check on us again since Mr. Cunningham, and although Bain's stare had locked onto me every time I stepped in the same room as him, he hadn't interfered either. Everything was at a standstill, and it put me on edge because there was always a calm before the storm.

It was often like that with Richard. We'd have weeks of *normalcy* before he would get antsy and say I was disrespectful or he'd make up some scenario in his head that wasn't true, and then he'd punish me.

I was thankful I was able to skip last Monday's phone call with him, though Headmaster Ellison still had me come to his office to chat. My shields were up, preparing to lie through my teeth to Richard as I pushed away the memory of him throwing my mother into that padded room. I needed a level head when it came to him so I could keep things civil. I didn't want to tip him off, especially since my birthday was soon approaching, and things were about to change drastically. I was too stubborn to ask Isaiah when he'd be off probation and when he'd get me the necessary things I needed to run, but I knew it was soon.

If Richard suspected anything before I graduated from St. Mary's, he'd jump the gun and rip me away even with the social worker breathing down his neck, which was what Headmaster Ellison wanted to talk to me about Monday evening. Apparently, Ann, the social worker, had called and wanted to check on me. I had a hunch the headmaster was hiding something, though, because he'd suspiciously brought my birthday up, and I knew that was likely something he and the social worker had discussed. Once I was technically eighteen, I would no longer be an interest to her. Therefore, no one would be watching out for me, or checking on me, or poking holes in Judge Stallard's story full of lies. The social worker would no longer have an obligation, and Richard would make sure she left us alone.

Part of me was half glad that Headmaster Ellison had mentioned that the social worker had called. I was glad to know she was still alive. Though, I was sure there was a reason for that. After learning more about my dearest *uncle*, I had a feeling that I was wrong about a lot of things. I was pretty sure Richard was following her cues and allowing her to insert herself in our life for a reason. Just like there was a reason Bain hadn't told Richard everything I'd done since coming to St. Mary's.

Anxiety was creeping down my arms and into my finger-tips as I swiped the last bit of charcoal on the canvas. I quickly took the thick paper down and rushed over to the supply closet, adding it to my hidden collection of drawings. This was one I didn't want anyone to see—especially Isaiah.

Just as I opened the door to the closet, I saw a shadow outside of the art room. My heart skipped, and a tiny smile crept itself onto my face. Isaiah had mostly been ignoring me, which hurt more than I'd like to admit, especially after our minor lapse in judgment Saturday night, but each morning, I'd see him sit outside the art room door, waiting for me to gather my things and head to breakfast.

He was good at ignoring me and even better at acting like I didn't matter, especially when there were eyes on us, but he still showed up and made sure that I was okay in here. It made me feel protected, even if I told him that his protection was unneeded the first day he'd shown up.

It was our new normal.

He watched from afar, hardly ever looking me in the eye, and I pretended that nothing mattered except my future outside of this school. *Which was exactly how it should have been.*

I straightened my skirt on my hips and grabbed my bag before looking up at the small clock above Mrs. Fitz's desk. I halted with my hand on the strap, realizing that it wasn't time to go to breakfast yet. I turned slowly to the door again, and my heart ricocheted off the walls of my chest. I swallowed the trepidation as I turned the knob.

I had a gut feeling.

Something instinctual, that likely came from all the years of fear and terror that someone was about to catch me doing something I shouldn't have, blossomed in my core, but it suddenly wilted when I saw Cade standing against the far wall with his phone in his hand.

"What are you doing here?" I breathed out in relief, stepping into the open hallway and shutting out the smell of acrylic paints and charcoal dust.

Cade kept his phone in his hand and barely spared me a glance. "Are you planning to go to art college, Gemma? I heard Mrs. Fitz ask you yesterday after class."

The disappointment was there with the fleeting thought of college. But it was the last thing on my mind. "That's not in the cards for me. But you already knew that."

Cade pushed off the wall and slipped his phone in the pocket of his school blazer. His blond hair was pushed away from his face, so I could see the wariness on his handsome features. "How would I know that?"

I rolled my eyes, glancing down the dark hall. "Are you really going to stand there and act like Isaiah hasn't told you that I'm leaving before I even graduate?"

Cade paused in front of me, but I didn't look up at him. I wasn't sure what Cade knew about me. Or the rest of Isaiah's friends. Each Rebel was evasive. They didn't wear their emotions on their sleeves, and they excelled at keeping their faces unreadable, replacing any truth or lie with an even glare, which was why I was having such a hard time knowing what Isaiah was thinking each night in that stuffy library as we pretended to study.

"Why don't you play against me anymore?"

I finally peeked up at Cade's warm, brown eyes. He blinked once, waiting for my answer. "You mean the game you downloaded for me a while back?"

He nodded, looking sincere, but who knew if that was what he was really feeling. I shrugged. "I don't carry the phone around with me anymore." It felt wrong to use a phone that Isaiah had given me. I brought it with me to tutoring, in case Isaiah needed to leave randomly and I needed a way to let him know that someone had come to check on us, but that was it. I didn't want to hold the stupid thing in my hand, waiting for him to text me, only to be disappointed in the end.

Cade sighed agitatedly. "And what if it were Bain in this hallway instead of me? What if he cornered you and threatened you, or hell, what if Isaiah's father showed up randomly and dragged you into some filthy corner inside this school to shove his dick inside you? What would you do, Gemma? Who would come save you?"

Anger rushed to my skin, and I felt the burn on my cheeks. "That seems a little over the top, Cade. Do you really think Isaiah's father is going to come here at six in the morning, pull me out of the art room, and have his way with me?" Never mind about Bain. He wouldn't touch me if he was involved with Richard. He had something else up his sleeve.

He laughed sarcastically. "I'm honestly concerned that you don't seem fearful of that thought at all."

I rocked on my heels. "Cade, you don't know half of the things I've been through. Or what I've witnessed. I know men like Isaiah's father. He wouldn't step foot in this school because there are eyes here. Men like Isaiah's father use other men to do his dirty work." I huffed out a laugh. "Like Isaiah. And you and Brantley."

I nearly choked on the sick feeling I had, remembering how Isaiah's father had shoved me to my knees in front of the Rebels, telling them to have a go at me. He allowed them to chase me through the forest to prove something to Bain, and although that wasn't what happened, or what was planned, he didn't know that.

For all I knew, he thought that Isaiah and his two best friends had raped me and dragged me back to St. Mary's to tell Bain. I wondered if Bain knew what had happened that night. He knew I had taken his car, so did he know what went down after?

Cade ran his tongue over his teeth and shut his eyes briefly before opening them back up and snapping his gaze to mine. He no longer looked like the golden boy that I once thought he was. He looked lethal with his angry scowl and the determined set of his jaw. "Isaiah isn't sleeping."

My head slanted, a piece of my hair tickling my arm. "Okay..." I trailed off because I had no idea what to say or why the sudden change in the conversation. "Did he send you here to tell me that? Is he sleeping in this morning? You know, I didn't ask to have a babysitter. It's fine. You can go."

He dismissed the last part of my sentence. "He's at the pool, doing laps. He does that when he's really worked up about something. He sent me here to make sure you were good. He wants eyes on you at all times, especially now that his father knows your face."

My mouth gaped. "The pool? There's a pool here? It's cold out, though." He had to be freezing.

Cade flicked an eyebrow up as his lips twitched. "It's an indoor pool, Gemma. How did you not know there was a pool here?"

"Is there a swim team?" What else did I not know about St. Mary's?

Cade shook his head. "The pool is off limits. There was a swim team, but..." He shrugged. "Someone drowned or something, so the SMC shut it down. It's supposed to be drained at some point."

My mind got held up on the "*someone drowned or something*"

part, as if that was normal. But Cade continued on past that, once again, dismissing it. "I was hoping you could help."

I took a step back, resting against the door. "Help with what?"

I caught the sharp angle of Cade's jaw as he looked away. "With Isaiah. I've never seen him like this, and..." His Adam's apple bobbed up and down with a harsh swallow. "And I'm worried. I can't get through to him. He has a lot going on, more than you know, and he needs to be sharper. If he's planning on doing what I think, he needs to be focused and tenacious."

A little line of worry etched itself onto Cade's forehead, and it seemed to dig into my belly. I wasn't sure what Isaiah had planned, but for the first time in ever, I could see actual concern on Cade's face. He wasn't hiding how desperate he was, and I ran with it.

"Tell me where the pool is."

———

THE SMELL of chlorine crept under my nose, and a feeling of yearning flew through me. The pool was large, and the dark water looked inviting as it moved effortlessly at the surface. It was so vast and deep that it would be easy to lose yourself in there. To just let the water graciously cover your skin and wash away every last worry.

I heard him before I saw him. His strong arms cut through the deep blue. His dark head of hair would pop up every few seconds, and each time I'd get a glance of his straight nose and jaw, my belly would bottom out. He appeared so strong and capable as he winded back and dove down again. The splashing sprinkled through the air and fell down into the warm liquid, and I felt myself moving closer.

I wanted to learn how to swim.

Maybe I would learn once I grew roots somewhere away from Richard.

"Hey," I shouted, dropping my bag by the door and walking closer to the edge. I was already in my school uniform, except this time, I threw on some thigh-high tights that left a thin sliver of skin showing from below my skirt. My fingers itched to take my shoes off and slide the fabric down my legs so I could at least put my feet in the water.

Isaiah suddenly stopped swimming as his wet face pulled up from the pool. Tiny beads of water ran over the curve of his jaw, and I swallowed. *He was so beautiful.* So dark and dangerous with that constant air of authority surrounding him, but I knew, deep down, he had a strong heart that was desperate for anything good. He tried to hide it, but I could see it. He was right the other night; he didn't need to know all my secrets to know who I really was, and I didn't need to know all of his to know who *he* really was.

"What are you doing here? Is everything okay?" Isaiah waded over to me as I stood above the edge of the darkened abyss. He gripped the side, and I glanced at the popped veins covering his hands and arms from the rush of physical exertion.

"Cade said you're not sleeping."

Isaiah huffed, whipping his head to the left as his temples ticked. A silent moment passed between us before he pushed onto the side of the pool and hauled himself up in one single movement. I quickly took a step back, putting distance between us.

It wasn't that I was afraid to be near him. I'd sat in a quiet library with nothing but the sound of his breathing for the last week. But this felt different. My stomach tensed, and my heart tugged. *Why wasn't he sleeping?*

Isaiah quickly shook out his wet hair, small droplets of water hitting the front of my uniform. He adjusted the low-riding black swim trunks on his hips, and I couldn't help the way my eyes traveled over the hard lines of his abdomen. With every dip and curve, my eyes lingered, remembering how tense he felt beneath me Saturday. A work of art was what he was. I should know, I'd secretly sketched him multiple times this week without even meaning to.

"Cade has a big mouth," Isaiah gritted, standing in the same spot, unmoving as water traveled over his skin and to the floor beneath our feet. "He has no business talking to you about me."

My arms crossed over my uniform as I quickly glanced back at the water, taking my eyes from his body. *God, I couldn't stop staring.* It was one thing being in the library with him, but here? He was hardly wearing anything, and every part of my body reacted. "He said he's worried. That's the only reason he said anything."

His short laugh echoed around us. "And what does he expect you to do about that?"

Hesitantly, I took a step closer to him, ignoring how he was brushing past the matter. "Why aren't you sleeping, Isaiah?"

Isaiah said nothing. Instead, he stared at the wall behind my head, not even looking into my eyes. I craved his gaze so badly it hurt. I wanted to feel that sudden jolt that he gave me when we locked on one another. I hadn't felt it since that night at the claiming. I smashed my lips together, still looking at his perfectly steady face. He had darkened bags underneath the thick mass of damp eyelashes, but he still appeared just as steady as ever. "You know," I started, "I don't sleep much either. Never have, really. Not since Tobias left."

There. Right there. I almost jumped when he flicked his gaze to mine. It was like I could feel the room turn to ice. But it wasn't cold. It was hot. Like the icy burn of stepping into snow barefoot. "I have nightmares," I said, ignoring the way my skin pulled tight at the admission.

"I know," he stated, still staying stark still with the water glistening behind him. I felt the twitch of my brows, feeling the concern whip through me so quickly that I wanted to jump into the pool to wash it away. *How did we get to this?* So much had happened between us in just a couple of months.

Isaiah quickly put his back to me, gripping his neck tightly and showcasing every ripple of muscle along his shoulders and spine. "Do you want to know why I can't sleep? Why I'm here, tiring out my body that's already so fucking tired?"

I stepped closer, and I knew he could feel me. We both studied the pool, nearly standing side by side. He didn't peer down at me, and I didn't peer up at him, too afraid to break the connection. It was heavy and tight. An overpowering tenseness filled the large room, and even the humidity in here couldn't break the cool fluidity of his words.

"I can hear her screams in my sleep sometimes. When things start to get out of control or there's something that I can't fix, it's like my mind instantly goes back to the first time I was ever put into a situation that I couldn't control. My vulnerabilities come out in my sleep."

My hands fell by my side, inches away from his, and I was completely taken aback by what he'd just admitted.

"When my mother was assaulted, I changed. I was barely a pre-teen, but I had seen and knew things that I wished I didn't. So, when the French doors opened, I knew that something bad was about to happen. My father was gone, and so was Jacobi, my older brother. He'd left a while back, leaving me and Jack all on our own." Isaiah sucked in a deep breath, and I knew it was hard for him to talk. I could hear the edge in his voice like a dull razor rubbing over my exposed skin. "It was just me, Jack, and my mom, sitting at the table, eating the dinner the chef had just set down. I saw the panicked look in her eye. The way she looked at me and then to Jack set me into blind action. Once the first man stepped through the door, I dashed forward, grabbed my brother, and I ran. I ran so fucking fast. He was so young that he doesn't remember, but I do. I remember it all. I remember the way his tiny little hands dug into my t-shirt. I remember hearing the blistering screams from my mother as I pushed Jack into the small cubby in the wall between our rooms. I remember every last detail."

Our hands brushed as moisture hit the backs of my eyes. I knew something had happened to his mother, but I never asked.

"By the time I got Jack locked away and ran back to the dining room, it was nearly too late. My mom was lying on the floor in a pool of her own blood. Her face was..." Isaiah paused for a few seconds before finishing. "Her face was unrecognizable."

I wanted to place my hand over my mouth so I wouldn't sob for him. There was a harsh pain nestling in the middle of my chest at the sound of his cracked voice, and although I'd craved to see inside Isaiah's mind since the very beginning, it hurt to do so.

"I don't think about that night often. Everything after was such a blur. Cade and Brantley came with their fathers. They all said I was in shock, but I wasn't." I felt Isaiah move, and I was pretty sure he was looking down at me. "I know how trauma can change people, Gemma. That's why you and I are the way that we are. That's why you and I have something no one else does. That's why we share a connection. We're the same."

My hand shook when his finger hooked with mine. It was a relief to feel him against my skin. Isaiah was comfort and warmth and strength all wrapped up into one person, and with just one single touch, I felt at home. I felt whole. And that wasn't something I thought I could ever feel after Tobias disappeared.

"You asked me why I wasn't sleeping."

My voice croaked as a single tear fell over my cheek and landed on the slippery floor that we both stood on. "Yes."

"I can't sleep because I'm afraid the second I shut my eyes, the same thing will happen to you." I quickly glanced up to him, seeing pure torment and insecurity all over his features. "Whether by my father, an enemy that I haven't even fucking met yet, Richard, or Bain." He swallowed, gripping onto my hand harder and pulling me into his chest. His other hand caressed the side of my face gently, and warmth settled deep within. "You scare the hell out of me because *you* are my weakness, Gemma Richardson, and if the wrong people get a hold of that, like my father or Bain's father, they will show no mercy. You will be used as a bargaining chip, just like my mother."

My bottom lip trembled as I stared up at him. Another stray tear slipped down my cheek, and he quickly swiped it away, the dip in between his brows getting deeper.

"I've been used all my life." It was the only thing I could say. I didn't want to say that I didn't want to be used, because then that meant I didn't choose him, but I wanted to. I wanted to choose him, and I wanted him to come with me and get away from everything that had hurt us or had the potential.

"I know," he whispered, pulling my head into his bare chest. My tears mixed with the water that still blanketed over the curves of his muscles. "Don't worry. I won't let anyone use you anymore."

I quickly pulled back, walls falling and crashing into the pool behind us. Isaiah's face grew serious as I let myself spill. "Bain said something to me."

His jaw wiggled as his hands cupped my face, waiting for

me to tell him, and maybe this was what he had wanted all along—for me to tell him what Bain had said. Either way, I still told him.

"He said, '*You're right where I want you to be, Gemma.*'" I swallowed, letting it all come out in one whoosh. "And his relationship with Richard goes deeper than illicit gun selling. He knows who I am."

The sickening feeling of dread and worry was quickly washed away as Isaiah bent his head down and placed our foreheads together. He nodded against me, our warmth mingling, and then his lips touched mine, and I fell into him. I fell hard and swiftly, and it was irreversible. We gripped one another tightly, and I didn't think either of us wanted to let go.

CHAPTER SIXTY-FOUR

ISAIAH

WHAT HAPPENED when you were in a battle but you were straddling the line between two enemies? Both sides were dangerous and tricky. It was a war where you couldn't walk into it with guns in your hands or without an army to back you up. You had to be precise and gain control, attack them when they least expected it.

And that was the one thing I kept reminding myself as I stood in front of the house that Gemma grew up in, leaning against my uncle's car at one in the morning. No matter what I found inside, I couldn't attack first and ask questions later.

I had two wars brewing: one with my father and the other with Judge Stallard.

"Where are we?" Brantley asked, flicking his cigarette off to the side of the road.

I held back a groan, stealthily walking over to it and crushing it with my black shoe before bending down and swiping it up. Brantley's dark brows lowered as he leaned up against the car, looking as if he wanted to hit me when I shoved my hand onto his chest with the butt crumbling in between my fingers.

Cade chuckled. "Are you suddenly concerned about the planet, Isaiah? Afraid that a lonesome cigarette butt full of nicotine is going to decompose and seep into the ground and hurt the ecosystem?"

Brantley grabbed the butt from in between my fingers, after I told him to shove it in his pocket, and looked over at Cade. "What are you even talking about?"

Cade shrugged nonchalantly. "I learned about it in earth science. Unlike you, I actually pay attention in class."

"That's because you're fucking lame, bro."

I expelled a heavy breath and looked back at the Stallard Manor that stood nearly as tall as the trees out front. There was a chill in the air, and it did nothing but cool me even more to the core. "I told you two a week ago that there was going to come a time when you were going to have to pick a side."

Brantley and Cade both came over and stood beside me, glancing up to the same home that I was staring at, but they stayed silent, likely wondering where we were.

"I asked you to pick up your cigarette because there needs to be absolutely no evidence that we were here. And the person that lives in that house"—I inched my chin to the darkened windows, almost picturing Gemma's face staring out of them as if I were pulled back in time—"thrives on rule-breaking citizens, and he has many ties in this community and can pull strings like you wouldn't fucking believe. A lonesome cigarette butt would only intensify his stance."

Evidence was artillery to men like Richard Stallard.

"Who lives here?" Cade asked, an edge of suspicion to his voice.

I sighed. "Judge Stallard. Gemma's uncle." He wasn't her biological uncle, which Uncle Tate and I had already concluded, but she let it slip one day when she referred to him as Richard instead of Uncle, and it only confirmed what we'd already suspected.

Brantley ran his hands over his head roughly. "Isaiah, what the fuck? I thought you were done messing around with Gemma. Even Bain has taken a step back from her."

I ignored him. "You two have a choice to make. Right here and right now." I quickly looked at both of them before laying it all out in the open. "You're either with me, or you're not." I held my hand up when Cade opened his mouth. "Let me finish."

Both of their faces dropped. I ping-ponged my attention between them both so I could get a feel for how they truly felt when I let it all out. "I am not taking over my father's business." Silence cut through. I was pretty sure that Cade and Brantley had both stopped breathing. "Before I divulge anything else, you need to let me know which side of the war you want to be on. If it's with me, just know that your fathers will likely be going down with mine. Cade," I started, looking over to him, "I want you to remember that you have a mother. It's possible that when it's all said and done, you will no longer have a relationship with her, as little as it is now."

My heart thumped wildly, gaining traction with each word that came from my mouth. I wanted to believe that they wanted out of the fucked-up future our fathers had intended for us and had bred us for since we were young, but I knew that just because I wanted them on my side, it didn't mean that they were. Wants and realities were two very different things.

Surprisingly, Brantley was the first to speak up. "What are you saying, Isaiah? That somehow, you're going to just walk away from everything? That will not fucking fly with the Huntsman. And what about Jack?"

I knew he'd question my father's willingness to let me go,

but I was staying true to my word. I wasn't giving up any more information until I knew for sure they were with me. "You're either with me or you're not. I need to know now."

I counted in my head with each thump of my heart. Blood rushed and flooded my veins with caution. If they weren't with me, that would mean they'd go down too. My muscles were growing tighter with every second that passed.

"I'm with you." Cade stepped forward and stood by my side, causing me to freeze for a second. "I'm a little perturbed that you even had to ask. We've been brothers since we were in diapers." *Loyal. Cade was so fucking loyal.*

"You've been your mother's son for that long, too. You could pack up with her and leave this life if you wanted. Your father won't be able to come after you when it's all said and done." He'd be stupid to.

Cade laughed under his breath. "If you take my father down along with yours, my mother will probably kiss you herself. Last Thanksgiving, she stabbed him at the fucking dinner table. She hates him, but she's too afraid to leave him." I nodded once before we both turned to Brantley.

His jaw wiggled back and forth like a teeter-totter as he pulled his black hood up to his head. His hands went into the pocket on the front of his hoodie. "Are you doing this all for Gemma?"

"No," I answered. "I'm doing it for me and for Jack. But this?" I nodded over to the looming house full of shit I probably didn't want to see. "This is partly for her. Judge Stallard is affiliated with the Covens and has worked with my father in the past and is now working with Bain's, as you both already know. If my assumptions are correct, Bain is planning on using Gemma for something to get closer to him, maybe to secure a deal, I'm not sure. But Gemma is a part of this, and I will not have that. I want to know all there is to know about Judge Stallard and his position in this. Because after I take my father down and hand over the reins, I'm coming for Richard fucking Stallard, and that means I need to know who he is."

What I meant was that I needed to know how much he'd harmed Gemma and what he'd done with Tobias. Because that'd be next on the to-do list: finding Tobias—for her. I couldn't do that if I accidently tripped and happened to choke Richard Stallard in the process.

Brantley observed the house for a few seconds before coming back to me and Cade. "How tight is your plan, Isaiah? Because if your father knows you're planning on taking him down and it doesn't work, he will fuckin' kill us all." He was worried, and that was something I never saw from him. "We've seen him kill men for less."

My plan was mostly solid, as long as Bain agreed to it, which wouldn't be difficult after I revealed my wild card. Jack was already safe as a precaution, because if things went sideways, he'd be the one to suffer the most. And as soon as I got all the necessary documents for Gemma, including the new identity and everything else she'd need to disappear that she didn't even think of, I'd lay it all out in the open for everyone.

"It's tight. But it's a risk. It'll be a war, Brantley. If you want out, then get back in the car. If you want in, just know this is your only warning that things could go wrong."

A swallow worked itself down his throat before a sinister smile broke out over his shadowed face seconds later. "You think I want to be like my father? You think I want to go around taking orders and killing? You think I want to be in an uphill battle against men like Bain for the rest of my life?" He threw his head back and chuckled. "Who the hell do you think I am? Cade is right. We've been brothers since birth. You think we'd actually choose your psycho father, or ours, over *you* and our brotherhood? We may be a little fucked-up, but at least we're loyal to one another." And it was a shame their fathers were loyal to mine.

He walked over and stood beside me, and we all turned toward the house. Relief settled over me, and it was the first time that I hadn't felt weighed down in days—of course, other than when Gemma was in my arms yesterday morning. It was a breaking point I desperately needed, and although I didn't take it any further than a surrendering kiss before the morning bell rang, it was enough to satisfy me until everything else was handled. One taste of her mouth could last me a little longer. The library wasn't as tense last night either, as if we'd come to a mutual understanding. We were walking on broken glass, and one step to either side would cut us in the end.

Brantley grumbled under his breath. "You're a fucking idiot for thinking otherwise."

I pulled my black hood up, and Cade did the same. We slowly began creeping toward Judge Stallard's house. My phone buzzed, and I quickly pulled it out, fearful that either Gemma or Shiner's name would be on the screen, but it was my uncle.

UNCLE TATE: I tell you that the SMC has set a meeting to revoke your probation and you skip off in the middle of the fucking night and test the waters? Did Bain leave this late? Or was it Gemma this time? I swear to God, Isaiah.

ME: Neither. This is purely business. I'll be back soon.

UNCLE TATE: You better not get caught walking the halls this late. They won't believe that you are walking

back from tutoring. Not after Mrs. Fitz caught you at Gemma's door after midnight.

I SHOVED my phone in my pocket and brushed off his warning. I knew what I was doing. In the past, Bain would sneak out during prime time. The time where he knew the duty teacher would be walking. Or better yet, he was probably the one to tip them off. He'd wanted me to follow him from day one. That wasn't his goal anymore. Bain had desperately tried to get me kicked out of St. Mary's for months, but now his plan shifted to Gemma. He had something else brewing, and it no longer included me being expelled.

"So, you mean to tell me that we're about to sneak into a house this big, and we're not going to trip any alarms?"

A deep chuckle rumbled from my throat. "I hate my father, but he taught me well. Alarms and cameras are off. Even the hidden ones."

Richard Stallard was asleep in his bed, unknowing that the three of us were about to uncover every last secret he held between his thick walls.

———

"WHATEVER YOU TWO DO, don't let me fucking kill him." My hand rested on the knob of a door that was on the side of the Stallard Manor. It looked as if it led to a basement as it was below the ground level of the house.

Cade's arm brushed mine as he and Brantley stood close. "What exactly do you think you'll find here?"

Shit that was going to make my blood run cold. I didn't say that, though. Instead, I said, "Hopefully something that will solidify the fact that Judge Stallard runs the Covens and how much he does at that fucked-up place. Uncle Tate and I both think he sends criminals there, deeming them mentally ill, but instead of sending them to the actual psychiatric unit, he's sending them underground."

Brantley gritted his teeth. "He probably sent my father there."

It was possible. Or maybe Richard's father had. I had a hunch that it went back further than we thought.

"What else do you plan to find?" Cade poked, stopping me before I picked the lock. "No more hiding shit, Isaiah. We're on your team. Let us play."

I began picking the lock, my fingers nearly numb from the cool air surrounding us. "I need to know why Gemma is running from him." My teeth snapped as I thought of her terrified face the first time I'd mentioned his name to her. *And the scars.* "He's hurt her, and I want to know to what extent."

"Fucking bastard." That came from Brantley, and I almost smiled. He could put on a good front and act like he was above women, but deep down, he was just as protective as I was. He only pushed girls away after he was through with them because of buried trauma. I had been the same way—until Gemma.

The house was eerily quiet. Not a single sound was heard. No buzzing of the heat as it ran through the walls, no trickling of a leaky drain, not even the soft whirl of the refrigerator, which meant that I was correct. We weren't on the ground level. We were beneath the main floor. I tapped both Brantley and Cade on their left shoulders, and we all turned that way, using a small flashlight to tell us where the steps were. They creaked under my weight, and we all paused, ears on alert. Part of me wished Richard would wake up and come down here. I wanted to look him dead in the eye and ask him some questions. For starters, like why he wanted his *niece* to call him daddy. The thought of overhearing their conversation a while back lurked in the deepest part of my brain.

"Basement." Cade's deep whisper floated around us, and we inched down farther.

The basement wasn't finished. There was no carpet beneath our feet or flat screen TV plastered onto the wall with sports paraphernalia in frames surrounding us. It was dark and bleak, and it sent an icy punch to my chest.

Something splashed beneath our footsteps, and I brought the flashlight up and slowly began scanning the area. My heart was in my gut, and it kept falling as I spun around, pausing on something in the corner.

I walked over to it, the floor damp under my shoes. The smell of mildew and dirt wafted around us, and when I reached the metal chains, I craned my neck, seeing that they were attached to the ceiling. *If he...*

Sickening thoughts were hitting me from every angle, and suddenly, I was alone. Brantley and Cade were no longer there. It was just me, in the dark basement, kneeling in a spot that I had a high suspicion that Gemma had once been. Visuals of her raw wrists, the pink raised skin that she guarded above anything else, made my blood pressure spike. My head fell forward, and my chest heaved.

"Isaiah."

I cautiously raised my head and grabbed onto the hanging chains with small cuffs around the bottom. I pulled myself up, shaking with the overwhelming need to pull them the fuck out of the ceiling. My thoughts were on a rampage, and I couldn't focus. My heartrate was through the roof, thundering behind my ribs.

"What are these?"

More silence passed.

"Isaiah, fucking speak."

I glared over my shoulder at the two shadows behind me, feeling the room shake around us. "They're chains."

"For what?" Cade asked, stepping forward, keeping his voice low. His firm grip peeled my fingers away from the metal digging into my palm, and he hesitantly raised the cuffed bottom closer to his face, inspecting it. His eyes flicked to mine, and Brantley swore under his breath.

"Jesus Christ."

His office.

"We need to go to his office. Somewhere that he would keep his personal documents." I needed to get out of this basement. I was suffocating. *I would kill him.* I glanced back at the chains as they swayed in front of my face, picturing Gemma chained up. For his own pleasure? To harm her? Both?

"Oh, shit. Get over here." My shoe rubbed over gritty dirt as I spun around.

"Wait. Isaiah." Cade's hand clamped onto my shoulder. "Maybe you shouldn't."

I bristled under his grip. "Get the fuck off me. I'm fine."

"Are you?" He met my eye, and I knew I was slipping. Anger was brewing like no other, and it was taking over my conscious ability to control the situation that I would be face to face with in the future.

I nodded once after expelling a deep breath, and we both walked over to where Brantley was standing. His hands were in fists by his sides, rubbing over his black jeans.

Silence followed us like a deadly plague, and I froze, right there in that exact spot, with the chains swaying behind me.

Richard Stallard was a dead man.

My gaze slowly crawled up the wall, and I pointed the flashlight over every last photo of the only girl I'd ever kill for. A hollow numbness flowed through me, and it was a bad fucking thing to feel. Photo after photo of Gemma bound, naked, cold, and starving. His large hands on her body. A finger here or there trailing down her sleeping face while she lay in her bed, surrounded by fluffy blankets, unknowing that he was standing over her.

Scars.

Cuts.

Scrapes.

Bruises.

He had touched her, and she didn't want him to. He hurt what was mine.

Nausea crept up my throat, but I clamped my teeth down. A feeling that I'd never felt so viciously before flew through me, and I was ready to kill. My hands shook as I clutched the flashlight in my hand, and Cade's hand grabbed it out of my grasp before wrapping his palms around my head tightly.

"Calm down, Isaiah."

I couldn't breathe in normal air. I choked on rage and fury. *I was going to rip his hands from his fucking body.*

"Isaiah!" Cade's harsh whisper did nothing to plow through the debris of my humanity falling to the fucking floor like bricks. He slapped my face, and I quickly whipped it back toward the photos. So many. There were so many. He'd touched her while she was naked and chained. His hand on her neck, her back, gripping her hair.

"He needs to get the fuck out of here, now."

"Think of Gemma, Isaiah." Brantley's thick fingers dug into my arms. "You can't be there for her if you're in prison, and if you do anything right now, that's where you'll go."

I had to get out of here.

I was going to blow the house to fucking pieces. I'd pull the pin out of the goddamn grenade without a second thought if given the chance.

"Go to his office. Gather everything about Gemma, the Covens, and someone named Tobias."

Cade nodded. "I'm on it. Go. Now."

Brantley pulled me as Cade stayed behind, and I let him lead me out the side door that we'd come in. I kept my face straight ahead, my body angled away from the house, because if I caught a glimpse of it again, I would turn right back around and kill Richard Stallard with my own two hands.

I said it before, and I'd say it again: Gemma Richardson was the one person I'd give up my humanity for.

CHAPTER SIXTY-FIVE

GEMMA

MY EYES SPRUNG open when the sound of iron against iron rang out. I'd know that sound anywhere, at any time. *Chains.* My throat closed, and my heart skipped a beat. I kept my back turned to Sloane, facing the wall, which meant that I couldn't see who was opening my door. I listened as the chain clamored against the wood, and I held my breath. *Was it Sloane?* The room had a faint glow to it from the fairy lights that Sloane had hung over each of our beds. We usually turned them off when we went to sleep, but after Sloane caught on that I wasn't sleeping, she kept them on, hoping it'd chase away the nightmares.

It didn't. But it was a sweet gesture.

I listened closely to her breathing, realizing that she was, in fact, still in her bed. I felt the cool air of the hallway float into our cozy room, and I shut my eyes. *Shit.* I moved my hand slightly, reaching for the phone under my pillow. It had to have been well into the middle of the night, but hopefully Isaiah had his phone on.

Not that he could do anything for me. By the time he'd answer, it'd be too late.

Whoever was in my room would be done with me by then.

And if it was Richard, we'd be long gone.

I held back a whimper and pushed back on the fear that was too familiar to me. My stomach was tied in knots, and my heart raced. I was hot and tingly from panic, and I didn't know what to do.

It's not Richard. It's not Richard. It's not Richard.

My mouth tasted of blood as I began to feel lightheaded. Terror coursed through me, and when a strong hand landed on my shoulder, I wanted to die right there.

I wouldn't survive if Richard took me.

"Baby."

A shaky gasp left me unable to speak. I quickly turned over and dug my fingers into Isaiah's hand, seeing the worry etched over every perfect curve of his face through the shadows of my room. His dark eyes went directly to my mouth, and his thumb hurriedly brushed over my parted lips.

"Why is your mouth bleeding?"

My eyes shut again as a shudder traveled through my body. I swiped my tongue over my lips, tasting the metallic liquid before swallowing. My whisper was like a broken record playing off in the distance. "You scared me."

Isaiah cursed under his breath, slowly trailing his hand down my arm and clasping our fingers together. I peeked through my heavy lids, willing my heart to calm down as he pulled me up. The covers fell to my lap, and I blinked a few times. "What are you doing here?"

I caught Sloane's staring eyes from across our small room, and she rolled them before turning her back to us. "Fucking knock next time, Isaiah."

He said nothing. He didn't even look in her direction. His

skin felt hot against my palm, and worry nudged me. "Are you okay?"

Again, he said nothing, but his body language said enough. He was tense. All over. He pulled me to my feet, his fingers clenching mine tightly. We padded over the soft rug, and he opened my door, pulling me out into the hallway. "Isaiah, what's going on?"

My mind was reeling. My thoughts were wavering over a fine line of panic and suspicion. I glanced behind me, seeing nothing but the flickering sconces on the wall and the dark-red carpet that lined the hallway. Goosebumps were covering my skin as Isaiah pulled me even faster down the girls' hall and then quickly down the boys' hall until we were outside a door.

"Isa—" I didn't get a chance to finish his name before he opened the door and pushed me inside. It slammed shut, and I realized it was the first time I'd ever been in his room. It was dark, and the bed on the left was messy, whereas the one on the right was made. I wondered where Cade was, since they were roommates, and a part of me wanted to ask, but Isaiah's face was suddenly in front of mine, and he peered down into my eyes with something unreadable passing behind his. He looked unguarded and almost vulnerable.

I raised my hand, my chest rising and falling with concern, as everything else faded away. All of our uncertainties were gone, and I was seconds from feeling his warm cheek pressed to my palm, but he caught my hand in his instead. His stare drove into mine, and with the silvery moonlight streaming through the window behind him, he didn't even look human. He looked too perfect to be real.

My sleeve was slowly pushed up to my elbow with the work of Isaiah's fingers, and I saw that his hands were shaking. *What was wrong with him?* My arm was extended, and I held my breath, briefly glancing down to my scars. He'd seen them already, but he was staring at them with a tight face. I pushed back on the need to secure my wrist to my chest when his lips touched the side of my delicate skin.

"What are you doing?" My voice was breathy as I watched him trail light kisses around the entire diameter of my scarred wrist. Isaiah's mouth stayed on my skin until he slowly dropped that arm and started on the other. The air whooshed over me, and something clicked inside, telling me just how much I enjoyed his lips on my flesh. My wrists didn't get touched often. They didn't even feel the misty air most days. They were sensitive, and Isaiah's mouth overtop of them made heat spread to my stomach.

"Isaiah," I whispered again, my heart bouncing all over the place.

His eyes moved to mine when he dropped my arm. We stayed like that as he fingered the hem of my long sleep shirt and pulled it up over my body. I was too confused and worked up in all the right places to stop him. His touches were soft, but urgent too, like he was cautiously branding every inch of my skin with his.

Isaiah suddenly crowded my space, pushing me up against his door. My back hit the hard wood, and his chest was pushed against my front. I was suddenly frustrated that I'd put on a tight tank top underneath my long sleeve shirt because the fabric felt itchy against my skin. My hands were flat against the solid wood, and my heart climbed with speed as he suddenly gripped my nape and tilted my head up. His mouth grazed the base of my throat, and I was certain he could feel my pulse thumping. The softness of his lips caressed me, and he laid kisses on every part of my neck, dipping just below my collarbone.

"Isaiah, I thought we weren't doing this anymore. After Sat—" To be honest, I wasn't sure what we were doing, but I didn't think it mattered at the moment.

His hands fells to my hips, and he forced me around, covering my back with his heat immediately. My mouth slammed shut, and my eyes widened. My core shrunk as heat pooled in between my legs. The feel of his large hands, so sturdy and protective, gripping my waist had every thought vanishing.

This was just who we were when we were alone.

Too desperate to think of anything but each other.

"I need to touch you," he whispered, his hot breath coating my ear. A shiver raced down my body, and my back bowed, pushing my butt onto his hard front. "Let me touch you, baby. *Please.*"

My cheeks heated, and I smashed my lips together.

His tongue ran a line all the way from my ear to the back of my shoulders, landing over my spine. I wanted to turn around and plant my mouth on his, but something stopped me from doing so. His hands left my hips, and his fingers slipped underneath the thin straps of my tank top. He pulled them down slowly, and a ragged breath left my mouth. The way he was touching me was sensual. He wasn't rushing to strip me naked. He was taking his time. He was slowly running his lips over parts of my body that had only been touched one other time.

My eyes sprung even wider at the thought. *Wait.* My body tensed when his lips touched the skin of my back that I didn't think about often. No one saw my back, not even when he and I had sex. *Could he see it in the dark?*

I stepped one foot back in between his and tried to turn around in a blur of panic, but Isaiah quickly crowded me again so I was unable to move.

"No." His voice was gravelly, and his chest rose quickly against my skin.

"Isaiah," I rasped.

"He doesn't get to touch you anymore." His lips landed on

the faint marks that had since healed and faded. It'd been at least a year or two since Richard had gotten that brutal, probably disgusted with the ugly marks that he had put there. Isaiah pulled the straps the rest of the way down and quickly yanked on my tank top, leaving it to rest along my hips. I was bare in the front, and despite the sudden rush of panic and confusion, my nipples were hard and begged for his touch. His touch did things to me. It quieted me and coaxed me to be in the present.

Isaiah's nose grazed the side of my cheek from behind, his fingers diving low beneath the waistband of my shorts. "Where else has he hurt you, Gemma? I want to remove his fucking touch from your perfect little body."

Tears sprang to my eyes, and my answer was blunt. "Everywhere. He's hurt me everywhere."

Isaiah stiffened from behind me. He wanted to ask me more. I knew he did. But I didn't want to talk anymore. I just wanted this solace I had with him. I wanted to just *be*. With him.

And I think he knew that because he quickly untensed, gripping the waistband of my shorts and pulling them down my legs slowly. My core tightened, and I almost moaned. The fabric ran over my thighs, and it sent tingles up to my middle. My head tipped backward, my hair tickling the bareness of my back.

"He doesn't get to hurt you anymore." His fingers hooked into my panties, and I turned my head, locking onto his eyes. They were wild and untamed, and I wanted to stoke the fire I saw. The passion. There was an unbelievable amount of torture attached to this moment. For us to touch like this, knowing that there wasn't a future. It was almost forbidden from the beginning. With every threat from Richard, Bain, and his father. Yet, here we were, knocking them down one by one for just a little taste.

My mouth was claimed by his, and our kiss was deep. His tongue coaxed mine to life as if he were sucking my soul up my throat and down his. "Put your hands on the door above your head."

Excitement flared, and thoughts of the past were floating away like ashes from a fire. Isaiah's fingers dove further into my panties as he held me in place with his other hand, digging into my hip bone. His finger skimmed over the sensitive bundle of nerves, and my legs grew unsteady. "*Mine,*" he growled, nipping my lips again. "And I will break every one of his fingers for hurting you."

I sucked in air as he circled me, and I felt my wetness coat him. I whimpered, almost begging him to touch me in the way that I wanted, in the way that I deserved. If I could just stay here with Isaiah, in this room, for the rest of forever, I would.

"I'll protect you, Gemma. Even when you're gone."

His finger inched inside of me, and I whimpered, throwing my head back onto his shoulder. Isaiah ground into me, and the tight grip he had on me never wavered, and I loved it. I loved feeling his strong hands. I felt safe with Isaiah, even after I questioned my trust in him.

The dip in my confidence was only a reaction to my past.

I knew all along that Isaiah would never hurt me.

"That's it," Isaiah said, putting another finger inside of me. I moved my hips, basking in the curl deep in my belly. It felt so good. All of it did. His fingers. His lips on my sweaty skin. His hard length rubbing me from behind. "Feel me inside of you. Fuck my fingers and know that you deserve to be worshiped. Do what feels good for you and *only you*."

I moaned, moving quicker. My hands started to slip from the door as I threw my head back. My legs started to get wobbly. Isaiah's grip on my hip left, and he cupped me around the waist, holding me up. "There it is, baby." His mouth was on mine, and his teeth sunk into my bottom lip. "I fucking love feeling you come apart for me. I fucking love feeling you move against me, chasing that high that you deserve over and over again. It's addicting, and I can't stop myself from wanting every single part of you."

Crashing waves hit me from the core and pulled me to the brim of insanity. I yelled out, and Isaiah's mouth came over mine as he quickly removed his fingers and shoved my panties down to the floor. I was still moving my hips, riding out my orgasm, as he spun me around and propped my leg up around his hip. He gripped my bare ass with his hand. "You are fucking beautiful, and you deserve the world," he said, pulling his pants down and pushing himself into my sensitive middle.

Stars coated my vision when he entered me, and it nearly brought me to the edge again.

"Isaiah," I gasped, wrapping my hands around his neck. His muscles were moving fluidly under my touch as he pulled back and entered me again and again. I matched his pace, basking in the way my body was humming. Blood was rushing to every part of my body, and the room was spinning. We met each other's middles, thrusting and gripping one another as if we were about to slip from the other's grasp.

Isaiah pulled away from my mouth, and his eyes bounced back and forth in between mine. "I fucking love you, Gemma. So much that I would burn the world down for you."

My eyes shut as tears pooled. Hearing those words did something to me. It opened up a gate inside my chest that I couldn't seem to close.

"Do you understand me?" he asked, thrusting into me again. I gasped at the rising ecstasy in my blood. "I love you, and I will not stop trying to make the world a better place for someone like you." I could read between the lines. Isaiah knew something about Richard, something that I didn't even want to touch.

I nodded against his chest, placing small kisses over the sweaty skin. I couldn't say anything back to him because I knew if I opened my mouth and said those three little words, I would break in half. So, instead of saying anything, I brought my lips to his, and I kissed him. I kissed him with everything I had, and he kissed me back just as passionately. We met each other with deep thrusts, and I moaned into his mouth, feeling my high come back. His fingers drove into my skin, and I bit down on his lip, feeling myself let loose around him. He pushed in a few more times as I moved my hips, and his hands suddenly left me, bringing my tingling legs back down to the ground before he pressed his hand against the door and shot something warm down the front of my belly.

He hissed in between his teeth as he gripped himself, sweat falling from his forehead and running down the side of his cheek. I watched in awe as he stroked himself as the white liquid left him. *Wow.*

"Fucking hell," he muttered, glancing up at me sharply with hooded eyes and swollen lips. He was still gripping himself, and I bit my swollen lip, not wanting to leave his room to go back into our uncertain realities. I didn't want to think about anything other than this moment right here.

Isaiah shook his head back and forth slowly as he dropped himself and crowded my space yet again. He bent down, grabbed his shirt, and slowly ran it down the front of my belly to clean me. Then, he threw it to the side, gripped my ass again, and picked me up, wrapping my legs around his body.

"Fuck tomorrow," he whispered before depositing us both on the bed until morning.

CHAPTER SIXTY-SIX

ISAIAH

I TRAILED HER EVERY MOVE. From the second we parted ways this morning, it felt like there was a gaping hole in my chest that just kept growing wider the longer we were apart. I wanted to follow her every move, walk her to each class as if danger was lurking behind the paintings on the walls, but the biggest danger of all was the man she had grown up with who hid behind his large, mahogany judge's bench, sending criminals away because they broke the law.

But what about him? No one was above the law, even if men like my father thought so. Judge Stallard was an abomination, and he would never fucking touch Gemma again.

"Hi." Gemma's sweet voice lingered in the empty library, and just like that, I came down off the ledge. The second we locked eyes, her cheeks flushed, and her bottom lip was tucked in between her white teeth in an adorable attempt at hiding a smile.

We hadn't talked much since last night when I stole her from her room and claimed every part of her skin, which was the only thing on my mind today. Even in the dining hall, with the chatter and clanking of the kitchen, the only thing that I could focus on was Gemma sitting at the end of the table with Sloane and Mercedes. We would catch each other's gazes, and something would pull in my chest, and I nearly pushed my chair out and sat with her.

But I didn't.

It wasn't because I didn't want to. It was more because I felt the heavy presence of fear on my shoulders. I didn't feel fear often, but it seemed the more I fell for Gemma, the more it surfaced, and it felt like my profound duty to make everything safe and rid the world of people like Judge fucking Stallard.

Everything felt off since seeing those photos of her and feeling between my fingers the iron links that were held tightly to the ceiling in the basement. Those chains had been cuffed around her delicate wrists at one point or another. *Fucking hell.* It was vital, now more than ever, that Gemma left and stayed away until his actions were brought to light and shoved down his throat.

"Hey," I finally said, smiling down at her. Tonight, we wouldn't be stuck in the library, thinking of all the things we wanted to say or do only to end up keeping silent and sharing stares. Tonight, we were going to forget about it all because I wanted normalcy with her. We didn't have much more time, and it was something I needed in order to keep myself in check. I stared at her a little while longer, the air growing heavy with everything that swam around us, but the longer I gazed, the more her cheeks flushed. "I like seeing you like this," I said, placing my hands down on the table that separated us. Her fingers were fiddling over the woven string of her journal like she was nervous.

"Like what?"

I hummed under my breath. "Flushed." I fought back a

grin when her cheeks grew even more red. "And..." My chest cracked slightly. "And happy. You look happy." Maybe even a little refreshed, too. Like breathing in the air on a spring day. I liked it. I liked her like this.

Gemma's gaze quickly fell to her lap, her fingers stilling on the string of her journal. "About last nig—"

"Nope." I straightened and gripped the edge of the chair I was standing over.

Gemma's head flew up, her bright-green eyes leery. "Isa—"

"No," I said again, this time a little more urgent. "I meant every word I said last night, Gemma." My chin dipped, and my tone grew serious. "You are addicting, and all fucking day, I've had to sit back and watch you from across the room, too afraid to touch you because—" *Shit.*

Gemma's eyes held that same curiosity that I often saw when we were in these heated conversations. "Because what? The SMC? Bain?"

I scoffed. "Fuck the SMC. They're the least of my concerns."

"So you don't care if you get in trouble anymore? You're still on probation, Isaiah. What about Jack? And your father?"

I shook my head, agitated that we were discussing anything regarding them. "The SMC has set a meeting. My uncle tells me they're taking me off probation. Not that it matters. I'm no longer following Bain when he leaves to go on his little business trips. I'm no longer feeding my father viable information." *He just didn't know that yet.*

Gemma's mouth instantly parted. "What? Why?"

"Gemma." My hands left the chair that I was gripping, and I rounded the side of the table. My feet creaked over the old floor, and it echoed throughout the library. "Let's just forget about it all for the night, yeah?"

Her hand landed in mine, and it was warm to the touch.

So warm it melted away the worry that started to creep up at the thought of my father and Bain. Not only was Richard on the forefront of my mind, but so was Bain and our upcoming talk that he had no idea was coming.

"Do you know something?" Gemma's question made me pause for a second. I wanted to squeeze my heart to make it stop beating so fast. "Last night...you—"

I cut her off by pulling her to her feet and grasping her chin tightly with my hand. "You'll be gone soon." My teeth clenched as I felt her body tense in all the wrong places. "I have everything you need. I'm just waiting on one more document."

Her perfectly arched brows crowded, and I zeroed in on her parted lips. "What do you mean? All I asked for was a new ID and some money..." She glanced away, mumbling under her breath. "Part of me doesn't even want it."

"What? Why?" Surely, she wasn't planning on staying. Not after the shit I just saw in that basement.

Her voice broke, and I felt the trembling of her chin. *Fuck.* This was exactly why we were leaving the library. I didn't want this tonight. I didn't want to watch her break and feel the world caving in on us. If anything, we needed to cave in on it. Gemma and I together could put stars in the sky. That was how it felt when we touched. It was...intense and powerful. All-consuming. Like the fucking universe swallowing everything in its path. My ribs felt like they were ready to crack open at any given second with her in my arms.

It was terrifying.

"I... It makes me feel like this thing between us was just part of a shady deal. It all started with you needing someone to cover for you and tutor you, and then I asked for something in return. It feels like I'm being paid to..."

"To what?"

She swallowed and brought her attention back to mine,

bypassing my question. "What other documents are you getting for me?"

I breathed out a loud sigh, conflicted over the fact that she just held something back. I wasn't going to push her, though. She'd been pushed enough, especially last night as I claimed parts of her body that I knew had been touched by Richard. I shifted on my feet when heat shot to my thighs. Last night was more than just hot. The way I brought her body to bliss was fueled by more than attraction and lust. *The things I said to her…*

"Isaiah?"

I cleared my throat, dropping my hand from her chin and pulling her away from the table. "I'm getting you everything you need to disappear, Gem. You'll need more than a fake ID and some money to get away from a man like Richard Stallard." Her fingers clenched down on mine, but I kept moving us toward the door. She stopped for a second and pulled her hand away from mine and went and grabbed her journal from the table. We left everything else, which were just the books that neither one of us planned to open. Once she was by my side again, I intertwined our fingers and walked to shut the lights off. "You'll have a new social security number, a birth certificate, a license—even though you really need some driving lessons…" *Maybe I should teach her how to drive before she leaves.* "A passport…" I trailed off, glancing down the hall before we stepped into it. I didn't want to say any more in case there was someone skulking behind a hidden corner. Bain's plans were still unknown to me, but I knew they had to do with Gemma, and I didn't fucking like that.

Just a few more days.

"Oh." Her whisper was a mix between shock and confusion. "Where did you get all that stuff from?"

Jacobi's face popped into my head at the thought of our phone call. *My older brother.* The person I'd hated for so long yet still held a tiny amount of admiration for. I admired the selfishness he had. If I were as selfish as him, maybe I wouldn't feel the sharp pricks of dread in my back every time I looked at Gemma. "There are people that work for my father who would do anything for money, despite their loyalty to him."

She stayed silent as we continued down the quiet hallway. Most of the faculty members were still awake, but as long as they didn't see Gemma and me actually leaving the school, they would just think we were walking back to our rooms after tutoring. Though, the SMC was hardly a thought in the back of my mind. They could expel me all they wanted. Jack was no longer a loose end for my father to use and taunt me with. In fact, I hadn't heard from my father in days. After the whole thing with Gemma, he'd checked in and wanted to know what Bain's reaction was. After I fed him some bullshit, I told him Bain would likely no longer be messing with the Covens, which was a total fucking lie. He believed it, though, which meant he trusted me, and it was always good to have your enemies' trust in your back pocket. It pushed him to look into his other business relationships that he felt Bain's father was trying to steal. It got him far away from the situation that would soon be in my grasp.

And it was no surprise that he hadn't called to inform me that Jack was no longer at home and in the care of Mary, our nanny. Jack was on vacation as far as anyone knew, and my father didn't even notice.

Fucking piece of shit.

"Not to change the subject," I said, most definitely aware that I *was* changing the subject, "but I have some ground rules for tonight."

Gemma paused, both of us tucked behind the door that led into the side entrance of St. Mary's. "Rules? What exactly are we doing? Isaiah, if the duty teacher sees us..."

I clicked my tongue, stepping back to give her a look. "I thought you liked breaking rules, Good Girl."

She scoffed, rolling her eyes playfully. Even through the shadows, I could see the pink on her cheeks. "Fine. What are we doing, and what are the rules?"

"We're having fun." I winked at her and grabbed her hips, pushing her up against the wall. "Because we deserve it."

————

"FINALLY." Shiner tipped back his flask, swallowing whatever liquor he had in there. "Where have you guys been? You have the only working lighter, and it's fucking cold."

I stepped over the crunchy leaves and pulled Gemma beside me. She was clearly confused as she ran her gaze around the small wooded area, locking onto our friends— Shiner, Brantley, Cade, Sloane, and Mercedes—as they all sat on logs.

"What is this?" she asked, whipping her adorable face over to me. She was excited. Her eyes sparkled underneath the stars, and her mouth split in two. She turned back to everyone else. "Did you all just say screw curfew or...?"

Sloane laughed, popping to her feet and running over to Gemma, taking her from me but not before scowling in my direction. I chuckled, half-annoyed that she didn't like me but half-pleased because I knew the only reason she didn't was because she knew more about me and Gemma than anyone else—or at least I suspected. Sloane was protective over Gemma, and I was okay with that.

"Girl, we used to do this all the time before..."

A twig snapped, and we all glanced at Cade. He was building the fire we were about to light, and his jaw clicked back and forth like a ticking time bomb. "Before I went and fucked everything up," he said dryly before looking over at

Sloane. "Sorry, I just knew that's what you were going to say so I might as well say it myself."

I dug into my pocket and threw the lighter to Cade who caught it with a cat-like reflex and went back to his fire-building. Ready to sit down, I tipped my head to Brantley who remained silent as he watched the girls who sat on the same log together, laughing about something.

"We used to have these small fires on the weekends when there wasn't a claiming party."

Sloane started again, ignoring Cade and his remark. "It used to just be me and Journey and maybe an occasional girl for Shiner over there."

I chuckled when he wiggled his eyebrows.

"Oh." Gemma wrapped her arms around her middle and shivered. I stood up and whipped my black jacket off before handing it to her. She graced me with a thankful smile, and I paused at the sight of it, lingering on her soft beauty.

Sloane was right. These secret bonfires were a norm for us before Journey left. Everything seemed to change after that night, and not just with Cade, but with all of us. It was when reality started to set in, and the Rebels and I saw our futures for what they were.

I knew that things would never go back to normal, and I'd accepted that, but now that I had Gemma, I felt a sense of hope that I didn't know was missing. I was hopeful that things would go my way for once so that we could have more nights like this.

More nights full of normal, harmless shit that teenagers did. Like gathering around a fire with your friends, drinking booze that was stolen from a teacher who was too stupid to lock it up in their desk, eating s'mores, laughing, dancing. All of it. It was all I wanted, and it was all Gemma deserved.

Shiner handed his flask to the girls, and Gemma wrinkled her nose after taking a sip before passing it to Mercedes. The flames came to life a second later. "So, you guys have never been caught doing this? No teachers have ever come out here looking for the fire that was burning?"

Brantley was still staring at Gemma, probably wondering the same thing I was. *How had she survived what she'd gone through at home and still managed to become this decent, kindhearted girl who held respect for people in power?* She was the kindest student we had at this school, even if, deep down, I knew she had a fiery spirit when provoked.

Brantley eventually tore his eyes away before answering her question. "We're facing the opposite end of the teacher's quarters, and we all know Headmaster Ellison doesn't really care as long as we're being safe."

Gemma nodded, looking away from Brantley to land on me. I flicked my chin, and she slowly stood up, staying locked on me as she walked over. I placed my hands on her hips, feeling a fire zip through, and spun her around fast and plopped her down on my lap. A rush of air left her mouth as she wiggled over me, no doubt feeling my growing hardness beneath her. Nuzzling my nose into her long hair, I sighed, letting every worry melt away right along with the fire.

Time passed by quickly. We all laughed and joked around, each of us buzzed on the alcohol that Shiner had brought with him. Gemma had another sip or two, and I felt her body relax along mine and knew that she was forgetting everything that was soon approaching for us. No one other than Cade and Brantley knew that Gemma was leaving. No one knew that, by this time next week, she would be far gone, and people would be looking for her.

"So..." Shiner started, his words elongated due to the excessive drinking he'd been doing. "Mercedes..."

Everyone paused, and I held back a laugh when I saw Mercedes giving Shiner a weird look because he remained silent, appearing deep in thought. I was interested to see what would come out of his mouth.

"This is getting awkward," Sloane whispered, smashing her lips together, looking at Shiner who was apparently thinking of a sleazy line to lay on Mercedes.

He cleared his throat and leaned forward, placing his forearms on his bent knees. "I haven't really met you."

Mercedes tilted her head as Gemma turned on my lap to look at Shiner. I gripped her hips and whispered into her ear, "Are you doing that on purpose?"

"Doing what?" she whispered back, and I chuckled.

Mercedes crossed her arms over her jacket. "You've met me, Shiner. We have world history together. You literally sit right behind me."

Shiner cocked a coy grin and glanced at Cade and Brantley who were also waiting for his ridiculous line. *One-Liner-Shiner. He was famous for his lines.* "Oh, yes. Trust me, I know. You bent over two days ago to grab your pencil."

Mercedes froze, and her eyes widened a fraction, but Shiner kept chugging along. "I meant that I haven't *really* met you."

"What does that even mean?" Mercedes was becoming impatient, and Sloane was shooting him a look like she was about to throw a burning log at his face.

"I mean, like...meet, as in my dick meeting your pussy."

Mercedes' mouth dropped open, and I placed my forehead on Gemma's back and shook with quiet laughter. There it was. The famous One-Liner-Shiner in full drunken action. *I'd missed nights like these.*

"Surely that line isn't part of your famous one-liners." Mercedes rolled her eyes and scoffed. "I don't understand why girls lift their skirts for you when you say things like that! It's so crude."

Shiner threw his hands up in protest. "Okay, fine. So...you don't like dirty talk. Noted."

I couldn't help it. I let out a laugh and felt Gemma laughing too. Sloane was holding back a smile as Mercedes whipped her curly hair away from her face, fully disturbed at what Shiner had said to her. I saw that her cheeks were a little red, though, and I wondered if she secretly liked it.

"You know what I think we should do," Sloane said, swiping the flask back out of Shiner's hands and taking a gulp. "I think we should play a game."

Cade sighed. "We're not playing truth or dare."

For once, Sloane didn't say a rude remark to him. She shook her head, understanding why he'd said that. "No. Let's play hide and seek. Remember when we did that the first time we came out here?"

"Hide and seek?" Gemma sat up a little taller. "I haven't played hide and seek since I was seven." There was a hint of nostalgia lingering within her wistful words. My arms wrapped around her all on their own, and I pulled her back into my chest. Her skin felt so warm as I ran my thumb in small circles underneath her shirt. "I used to play it with my brother."

Sloane and Mercedes both snapped to attention, but my fingers didn't stop moving, even if I was surprised that she had admitted that. Gemma was so guarded and private with everyone. Even with me.

"You have a brother?" Sloane asked, completely baffled. "What?"

Gemma nodded but kept quiet. I took control of the conversation so it didn't bring us back to the heavy moments that I was destined to stay away from tonight. "Hide and seek sounds like a grand idea. Nothing like chasing you girls in the deep, dark woods to keep the night alive."

Shiner clapped his hands and winked at Mercedes, who rolled her eyes in response. "You can run, but you can't hide."

"Girls against boys?" Sloane stood up excitedly, allowing Gemma's admission to pass.

"Always," I answered, tapping Gemma on the leg. She stood up and turned around and mouthed, "*Thank you,*" at me. But she didn't need to thank me for saving her in moments that made her uncomfortable. I was always on her side.

"You up for this?" I asked, pulling her in closer and tipping her chin back. Her emeralds sparkled with excitement beneath the stars, and the shadows of the fire played across her high cheekbones, begging me to take her back to the school to be alone.

"You think you can catch me?" Her white teeth sunk into her lip, and I hurriedly swiped my thumb over it.

I gazed into her eyes, feeling myself snap in two. "I won't stop until I do."

CHAPTER SIXTY-SEVEN

GEMMA

THE FOREST WAS quiet as Sloane, Mercedes, and I descended down the hillside with the fire disappearing behind us. The bushes rustled with the wind, and for the first time, I didn't feel the inkling of panic poking from behind. I was safe. I knew I was safe. I wasn't running for my life from Richard, and I wasn't allowing myself to cave in to the past that I pushed away.

I felt it brimming the surface. I recognized it prickling the sides of my brain, but instead of pushing it away and pretending it didn't exist, I allowed myself to see it, feel it, and dismiss it. All because I knew I was safe. I was with Sloane and Mercedes, two girls that welcomed me into St. Mary's and hadn't judged me once. The two girls that had made me feel better when I was hurt over Isaiah's actions, even if they didn't know all the details. They were my friends, and they cared for me, just like I cared for them.

Isaiah was giving me something tonight, and maybe he

didn't even mean to, but he was gifting me a normalcy I so desperately craved. It was a nice pause on everything else, and I was enjoying it. I was enjoying *him*. *Us*. I was enjoying the laughter and the easy conversation without fear, regret, or dread lingering, and it made me feel strong. It was like he knew I needed this moment to heal what had been broken last week.

"Let's go this way," Sloane whispered, veering us off the worn, dirt path and into an area that was crowded with bushes and trees.

Mercedes and I followed closely behind, and once we were tucked underneath a tall pine tree, we placed our backs against the large stump and watched through the spaced out branches for the guys to finally wander through. *If* they wandered through. How they'd find us in this large forest was beyond me, but I knew eventually they'd show up.

"I cannot believe what Shiner said to me." Mercedes sighed agitatedly and pulled her knees up to her chest. "What a dick."

Sloane laughed. "He just wants in your pants."

"Maybe because there isn't anyone else to feed his ego. He has never even spoken to me in class. It's like I'm invisible to most of the guys in this school."

I peeked forward. "Did you bend down in front of him like he said? To grab your pencil?"

Her lips pursed together as she nodded. "I didn't even think about it."

"Then you're not invisible. He probably hasn't pursued you because he knows you're not like the other girls here."

Her eyes dropped. "What do you mean?"

I smiled. "You're nice, Mercedes. You're kind and pretty." I shrugged, calling it how it was. "He probably feels intimidated by a girl like you. You're not the type to pull your skirt up for a little bit of attention from a guy like him. You have depth. Anyone can see that."

Sloane nodded. "It's true. He knows you're too good for him." She paused before adding, "And you are."

I laughed. "And the same goes to you, Sloane."

She shook her head. "That's not true. I'm not nice. I think most boys are afraid of me because I don't put up with their shit. Not even the Rebels."

We all laughed and discussed how different we all were. It was true. We were all so different, yet we somehow fit together perfectly. They were both really good friends, and I knew my heart would form a tiny gap in it when I left them behind without even a note.

"I'm going to miss you two." I froze the second the words left my mouth. *Wait. Shit.*

"What?" Sloane asked, glancing over at me. Her hair was pushed behind her ear, and she gave me a skeptical look. "You mean, like, when we graduate?"

I nodded quickly, glancing away. *Maybe tonight relaxed me a little too much.* "Yeah, that's what I meant. You and Mercedes are planning on going to an Ivy League, right? Didn't you two already apply?" To be honest, I hadn't really been keeping up with everyone and their college plans. It was never an option for me, so when it was brought up, I usually shut down and detached.

Mercedes blew breath out of her mouth. "Yeah, but that does not mean we will get in."

"Sure you will," I answered. I had faith that they both had exciting new adventures waiting for them after high school. Me on the other hand... I couldn't even see past next week.

"What are your plans?" she asked me as Sloane stayed quiet, seemingly lost in her thoughts. "Art school? Didn't you say that Mrs. Fitz talked to you about putting together a portfolio for one of the schools she was connected with?"

She did, and the entire time we were talking, I felt my heart sinking to the floor.

"Yeah, we're working on it," I lied.

"That would be amazing, Gemma. You'd do so good. It's, like, all she talks about during art class. You're not even in my class, and she pulls out your work as an example nearly every day."

My cheeks heated, and pride went through me. Mrs. Fitz was constantly pushing me to do more and to create things for my portfolio. I was certain she thought that was what I was doing when she'd given me permission to use the art room any time I wanted—within normal curfew times, of course. Except, it wasn't. Not really, anyway. I didn't plan on showing anyone what I'd drawn. Ever.

"Shh," Sloane shushed us, and my thoughts scattered. Excitement bubbled in my belly at the thought of Isaiah's hands wrapping around my waist again. Last night had been on my mind the entire day, and I wanted to ask him more about what went on through his head last night as he ran his mouth and hands over parts of my body that were only ever touched once before, but he had a way of distracting me, and I did exactly as he wanted. I pushed the tough stuff away and focused only on the present moment.

And it felt good to do that. It felt good to be in the moment with him. It always had.

"Listen to them," Sloane whispered above a soft laugh as we listened to the guys arguing about which way to go.

Mercedes bent her head to ours. "We should split up, confuse the hell out of them, and then sneak up when they least expect it."

"Yes! Let's do it. Girl power, baby."

I silently laughed at Sloane, and then the three of us crept out from underneath the tree with the smell of pine flowing through my nose and into my lungs. Sloane went straight,

Mercedes went to the left, and I slowly trotted to the right. I had no idea where I was going, and I really didn't want to venture off too far because, now that I was alone, I was afraid things would start surfacing that I didn't want. Although I felt lighter now than I had in weeks, there was still an edge of caution always present.

I tip-toed toward a large tree in the middle of a large opening and paused, looking up to the sky. A tiny smile stretched on my lips when I realized where I was.

I turned slowly, my hands coming down by my sides that were completely swallowed by Isaiah's large jacket. It smelled like him, and I breathed in the clean scent of his body wash and cologne. It reminded me of safety and something wildly tempting.

I knew exactly where I was in the forest.

I was in the same spot he had brought me to the night of the pep rally bonfire, when he'd told me about his little brother, Jack. It was the first time I saw Isaiah as vulnerable, and it was then that I realized he was just as human as I was.

Closing my eyes, I inhaled his scent, tipping my head up to the stars. Leaving him was going to be hard. Necessary. But hard. *So hard.* I didn't want to leave, and that hurt even worse. It wasn't supposed to be like this. I was supposed to be running from Richard and healing myself in the process from everything that I'd seen and been through, but instead of healing myself, I was leaving with an even bigger broken heart.

"You were supposed to stay with Mercedes and Sloane. It's a good thing I found you."

I shrieked, snapping my head back down as my entire body tensed.

I tipped back, glancing into Isaiah's dark eyes before moving down to his mouth. My heart came to life, and the thoughts of a broken heart left. I knew, without a doubt, that I'd never feel this way again. There was no way something like this ever came twice. The feeling he inflicted in me when our eyes connected wasn't even a word in the dictionary. We were connected, bound by something neither he nor I could ever name. The two of us were thrown together by fate only to be pulled apart in the end by things that were out of our control.

I spun around in Isaiah's grasp and wrapped my hands around his strong neck, pushing my fingers into his hair and bringing our faces closer. He kissed the tip of my nose gently, and I shut my eyes, feeling him everywhere.

"Even when you're far away from here, I'll never stop looking for you." His lips moved over my mouth. "I will find you, Gem."

I didn't wait for him to kiss me. Instead, I kissed him. I kissed him hard, like it was the last time I'd ever kiss him. His grip on my body grew tighter as I slipped my tongue into his mouth, exploring and tasting, trying to memorize everything about this moment. I quickly pulled back and grabbed onto his hand, pulling him farther into the forest with his hooded gaze questioning me from behind.

"What are you doing?

I smirked, feeling bolder than ever. "Do you remember the last time we were in this part of the forest?"

Desire swam inside my veins, and I felt drowned by the need to feel his hands on me. Maybe it was the small amount of vodka that was making me so adventurous, or maybe it was the fact that I knew my time with him was coming to an end. *Don't think, Gemma. Just do.*

Isaiah's tongue darted out as he planted his feet, pulling me into him instead of the other way around. "I remember every moment with you."

A giddiness had me jumping up into his arms, and he quickly caught me, wrapping my legs around his middle. I felt so light in his grip, and with the way his mouth curved into a devious grin, I knew he enjoyed having me there just as much as I did.

He pushed himself into my middle, and my eyes widened. "Tell me what you want, Gemma. What's going on in that pretty little head of yours? I'd love to get in there and see everything you're thinking. You have been a mystery since day one."

His eyes bounced back and forth between mine as he continued moving through the wooded area, surely coming up to the same tree that he had me up against the first time we'd come down here. In fact, I didn't care what tree it was. He could have me anywhere.

"Do you want me to make you come again?" His hoarse whisper was like the tree bark rubbing against my skin. "Is that what you want? To feel what you felt last night?"

I thought for a moment, taking in his blunt question before answering. "Yes," I rushed out, feeling the sturdy tree behind me.

A coy smile worked itself over his face, and I bowed my back, pushing my chest against his. *Why did I get this way with him?* I was an entirely different person when he and I were alone. Like my body did the speaking for me. It craved him. His lips on mine. The way he got lost in me. The way I got lost in him. I loved it. Everything else just disappeared, and that was enticing as hell.

"Say it," he demanded, inches away from my mouth. "Say it so I can hold onto this memory and play it over and over again to get me through everything to come. Let me have this."

I needed it too.

My heart thumped hard as I gazed up at him. Things

suddenly turned dark, and the trees were swaying as my head spun. My lips tipped with a grin, and I'd never felt so bold in my entire life, but seeing Isaiah's reaction to me and knowing that he was seconds from kissing me again, I looked him in the eye and said, "Make me come, Isaiah."

CHAPTER SIXTY-EIGHT

GEMMA

THE DOORS to the library opened, and everything seemed brighter. My eyes found him immediately, and my heart fluttered. I'd waited all day for this. The entire day felt like some wicked form of foreplay for us. The fleeting, heated gazes. The subtle touches as I'd pass by in the hallway that hardly anyone would notice unless they were actively looking—like Bain. Isaiah and I decided to be cautious with each other. Even though we both knew what was coming, Isaiah wasn't all for flaunting me around, and I felt the same. Bain still skulked in the shadows, neither one of us really knowing what his plans entailed, and with his threat about Richard, I was all for being careful. Plus, I liked when Isaiah and I were alone. Our guards were down, as if we were in a safety net.

I knew why he'd used Breanna that one day. I knew why he'd tried to push me away and hurt me. He wanted me to hate him. He wanted everyone to believe that there was nothing between us. I understood, and we'd come to a silent agreement over it. Some things just didn't need to be said or explained because there were just too many uncertainties.

There had always been uncertainties in my life. For the longest time, all I saw when I looked to the future was Richard. I didn't know what the future held, but I always knew Richard would be in it, controlling me, giving me just enough to keep me asking for more. He was a heavy presence in my life from such a young age that, up until recently, I couldn't see past him. Richard Stallard, my presumed uncle, was like a thick wall placed right in front of my eyes, and if he was somehow involved with Isaiah's father and Bain, I wanted absolutely no part of it. I didn't want to tip any scales, even if I did feel that things had changed within me.

I felt more myself now than ever. I was stronger, but that didn't mean I was safe. Isaiah was right. I was smart enough to know when to leave. It didn't make me weak to run; it made me smart. And I'd much rather be smart than stay and risk my life. Because that was what I would be doing if I stayed here, even for Isaiah. I'd be risking my life, because Richard had plans for me, and he knew when to cross his T's and dot his I's.

That wasn't to say I didn't want to stay, though, or that I forgot about the original plan between Isaiah and me from time to time—like when he and I were in our own little world. I couldn't ignore the pang in my chest when I thought of leaving him. Before Isaiah became a constant in my life, I was exhilarated by the idea of a fresh new beginning. But now, I was no longer just leaving Richard when I ran away.

I was leaving Isaiah. Sloane. Mercedes. And I was leaving behind a safety that I'd never felt before and a life that I hadn't seen coming. Like last night, when I was gathered around a bonfire with them. It felt so real and normal. St. Mary's was more a home to me than Richard's house ever had been, and it hurt to think of leaving it behind, especially when I was alone and I thought of Isaiah. He made me feel worthy and like I deserved more than I was given.

"Hey, you." Isaiah sauntered up to the table, and I peeked up at him through my thick eyelashes. The second I caught his gaze, I felt the heat rush to my face, thinking about last night. *And just like that, the dread disappeared.*

"Hi," I quickly said before my smile fell as Isaiah dropped a large piece of paper onto the library table and began unrolling it. I watched as his steady hand smoothed it out and realized right away that it was a map. I was pretty sure it was the same map that was hung in the headmaster's office behind his desk. I would know. Each time I went down there for my weekly phone call with Richard, I would stare at the same place on the map so I wouldn't have to see Headmaster Ellison's wary gaze scrutinizing me.

"What's this?" I asked, pushing my journal into my lap. I'd caught Isaiah glancing at it from time to time as if he were curious of its content, but he never asked to see what was inside. *Thank God.*

"After tomorrow's lacrosse game"—he glanced away from me at the last second, and my core instantly cooled—"I will be obtaining the last document you'll need for your runaway package."

My heart sank to the floor right along with my stomach. I swallowed back the bitter taste of disappointment and nodded my head. Thick tears formed in the backs of my eyes, but I sucked them back down, knowing this was coming. "Oh." I cleared my throat as my fingers gripped onto the leather backing of my journal. "Okay, so..."

"So you'll be leaving the following day."

It only took a second for my eyes to fly to his. I opened my mouth to...protest? I wasn't sure what I was going to say, but I did know that it seemed like my entire body seized up and the room tilted. Sweat started to form on my back.

"Right. Leaving." I nodded, grasping onto the determination in his gaze, hoping it would give me the same strength he seemed to yield.

"You *have* to go the next morning, okay? After the game tomorrow, I'll come get you from your room when the halls are clear. I'll give you what you need and..." His voice trailed off, and he glanced away again. He stared behind me and looked down the aisle with his hands pressed firmly onto the table that separated us. "And then you need to leave."

Something about the way he tensed made me question him. "Why the next morning? What's so significant about the next morning?" I had a weekly phone call with Richard tomorrow night because that was when he returned home from his business trip. The headmaster had already informed me of such. I was to go to his office at 6 o'clock sharp, and I'd call Richard to give him an update on my time at St. Mary's and tell him for the millionth time that I was following the rules and being the good girl that he had *raised* me to be, and then I'd sit with Headmaster Ellison for a little while and chat like we'd started to do over the last couple of weeks. There was another small gap forming in my chest at the thought of Headmaster Ellison. I was beginning to like him. The unexplainable bond I'd felt with him from day one only seemed to grow stronger with my time here at St. Mary's. The familiarity of his presence was no longer a slight acknowledgment to me but more of a constant. He felt safe to me, too.

"Gemma." Isaiah walked over to the side of the table and bent down beside me, resting the back of his legs on his heels. His cool-blue eyes peered up at me beneath his dark lashes, and my heart hurt at the conflict I saw. "Last night, before we went to the bonfire, you asked me if I knew something."

I nodded gingerly as Isaiah's head fell down, showing me his dark head of messy hair.

"I do. And I have something planned. Something big is going to happen, and I can't do it until I know you're gone and you're safe." My throat clogged at the cracking in his voice. I didn't like seeing him like this. I didn't like seeing him worried or conflicted or hurt. I didn't like feeling the insecurity within him. My brows folded, and a tremor of fear coursed through me. Sometimes it surprised me when everything heavy was weighing on us again. It was so easy to lose sight of the mess we were in when he was in front of me. When he and I were alone, touching, looking into each other's eyes, I lost sight of the main goal: leaving for safety. I would be free for the first time in my entire life, and that seemed so scary at times, because although I would never fully feel *alone*, I actually would be. I was a twin. It was like having your soul split in two. I could feel Tobias, not physically but emotionally, and I hoped that someday he would find me. But until then, I would be alone, in a world so much bigger than I ever imagined, without anyone. I'd be navigating the world blindly, running for my life with a new name, and I was pretty sure the only thing that I would be thinking about was everything good that I'd left behind.

I felt incredibly attached to Isaiah, and I knew that all the freedom I'd feel with getting away from Richard wouldn't taste nearly as good because there was now something tying me to this school and this life.

I hated that I felt tethered to someone, and I didn't want to admit it when I was alone, but it didn't matter because my thoughts always came out on paper, and the last few times I'd lost myself to sketching, I'd found myself blending the charcoal until I got the perfect almond-shaped eyes that I was aiming for. The memories that I'd pushed away, the violence in my childhood—all of it—always came to me when I sat, mindlessly sketching. But things had shifted recently. I began drawing other things. Like *Isaiah*. And that was when I realized that I was hiding him, too.

My throat began to throb even thinking about it. So much anger and resentment was buried beneath my thick layers, and a big part of me wanted to tell Isaiah everything. He didn't know all of it. He didn't know the real reason I was running, and lately, there was hardly anything holding me back from telling him.

Except fear.

I was still afraid of Richard, and I was afraid of what he was capable of.

"Isaiah. If you're planning something for Richard...don't. The only thing I need is what you're giving me so I can disappear. It's the only way." My heart galloped in my chest, and I heard the thumping within my eardrums.

"You're still going to disappear," he whispered, reaching up and pushing a stray hair away from my face. "But when things are safe, I will come for you, Gemma. So take this"— Isaiah pulled out a black Sharpie and threw it onto the table —"and mark where you'll be, because I will come for you."

I held my breath as my head spun. "Wh-what do you mean?" I glanced back at the map and then to Isaiah again. "If you're planning on doing something to Richard, please don't." I shook my head as anxiety rattled through me. *He knew something.* "I know that Richard is connected to Bain, and the Covens, your father...whatever...but his plans for me have nothing to do with anyone but himself. Do not do anything to Richard on my behalf, Isaiah. Don't screw up your life for me."

I thought back to last night when he said he wasn't following Bain anymore or giving information to his father, and I began to feel dizzy. Richard's plans for me had nothing to do with anyone else but him. He was selfish and wanted me for himself. I had nothing to do with his business with the psychiatric hospital or the illicit gun selling. I was Richard's little angel that he wanted to keep in a box, up in that big house of his, to do with as he pleased.

"Don't put me in this! Don't do something because of me. What about Jack? What are you planning?" I was frantic and could feel myself spiraling.

"You're already in this, Gemma. I'm just the one pushing you out." Isaiah's words did nothing to soothe me. I wasn't afraid for Richard. I wasn't telling him to leave Richard alone because I wanted to protect the sick bastard. I was afraid for Isaiah. And Jack! Richard was a complex man, and he had more friends than enemies, which was a baffling thought given everything I knew about him.

I glanced at Isaiah's pleading eyes and felt like I could see all the way through him. I knew him, and I knew that he was hiding something. "Do you know why I'm running?"

Isaiah's jaw clenched, and the room grew cold. It felt like hives were eating away at my skin with each passing second, and when he looked down to my wrists, I almost pulled them back.

"I know that he has chained you up." Something dark crowded my vision, and my breathing picked up. "I know he's touched you in places that he shouldn't have." Chills coated my arms. My lip trembled, but I fought back the tears because if I broke, I was afraid of what I'd say. "I know he's cut you and has bruised your beautiful, flawless skin." Isaiah's fingers swiped over my cheek, and I shut my eyes, holding tightly onto the invisible wall to shut out everything Richard has ever done to me. "I know that you told someone that Richard abused you, and they allowed him to twist it all so no one believed you. That's how you ended up here."

"Stop," I whispered with blurred eyes.

Isaiah's hands rested on mine that were clutching my journal. "Please just mark where you're going so I can find you when it's all said and done. It's the only way I'll let you go. I won't look until I know it's safe for us both. I'll keep it safe until I can trust that no one will follow me to find you or hurt you to get to me. I'll keep it safe just like I'll keep you safe."

I shook my head. With the thoughts of Richard crowding my vision, the fear came back, and it slithered into every hopeful part of my body and turned it dark. "I can't risk it." I paused, feeling the cut right to my chest. "That's not why I'm running, Isaiah."

His fingers stilled over mine. "What do you mean?"

I took my hands from his and dug the heels of my palms into my eyes, allowing my shaky whisper to fill the empty library. "From the second I got here, my plan has never veered. *Survive*. I needed to follow the rules, keep my head down, and when I got what I needed..."

"You mean the new identity and money?"

I nodded. "The police know my name and who Richard is. He has friends in law enforcement all across the United States. It wouldn't matter if I went halfway across the country. If my name were to go through their database, it would lead to Richard, and then he'd find me again. It wouldn't matter if I told them everything. He'd just pay them off or lie and tell them that I was mentally ill like my mother—which isn't true. There is no outrunning Richard if I stay Gemma Richardson." I paused, sniffing up the emotions. "So my plan has always been the same. Get a new name and run like hell and never look back." Part of me didn't even care about the past anymore. All I wanted was out.

The library was quiet, and I kept going. I kept going because maybe if Isaiah knew everything, then he'd understand why I couldn't tell him where I was going. He'd have to accept the heartache like I was. We'd have to just deal with our fate. "I'm not running because of the pain he's caused me in the past. I'm not running because he's chained me up and hurt me. I'm running because of what he has planned for the future."

"Look at me."

I began to shake in my seat. I heard the chattering of my teeth but was too blinded by the panic crawling up my back to make it stop.

"Gemma, breathe, baby. It doesn't matter what he has planned, because he doesn't get to hurt you anymore."

My words were choppy and cut short. "It's easy for me to think that when I'm with you. I'm not looking danger in the face when you're in front of me."

"That's because I'm shielding you from it." His hands came around my face, and he pulled me onto the floor and into his lap. "Trust me when I say I'll protect you and keep you safe, Gem. *Please*. What does he have planned for the future? If you're not running from what he's already done, then what are you running from?"

Tell him. I wanted to tell him. The way his strong arms folded around me made me feel like I was in a world where Richard didn't even exist. Nothing existed except for the warm breath of Isaiah moving over the crook of my neck.

"Gemma," Isaiah's voice was distant in my head, and I was afraid that meant I was slipping into the past. "Has he raped you?"

Even my voice sounded far away. "I...I don't know. No. I don't think so. One time, after Tobias was gone...I woke up, and he was there, hovering over me, but..." Isaiah's body tensed, and the memory was surfacing. I quickly shut it down and grabbed onto Isaiah's shirt.

"God, you're shaking like a leaf. It's okay. Don't tell me anything else. It's okay." His graceful touches and warm shushes in my ear didn't stop me from plowing through the walls that were coming up in tens.

"He will," I blurted, feeling goosebumps bubble on my

arms. "He will rape me, and that's why I can't tell you where I'm going. I won't risk it, Isaiah." I pulled up and looked right into his eyes. "And he made Tobias disappear. He'll make you disappear, too, if he thinks you're a threat to me. If he thinks you'll take me from him."

The blue in Isaiah's eyes turned dark and angry. Rage was plastered all over his features when he snarled, "I *will* take you from him."

My hands began to sweat, and everything seemed to crash all at once. Tears spilled over my cheeks, and I shook my head. I saw the way that Isaiah's eyes became worried, and I felt his hand press against my heart.

"Hey, calm down. Your heart is flying through your chest. Gem, fucking look at me."

A sob escaped me, and then everything went dark.

THREE MONTHS PRIOR. September 14th. 3:53 p.m.

MY BACKPACK WAS light on my back as I gripped the straps with my sweaty hands. There wasn't much in there other than a few articles of clothing, my old journal, and the worn photo of me, Tobias, and Mom. Richard's office was unlocked, and I knew it was only because he'd rushed out the door when the school had called him.

I couldn't believe how careless I had been with my drawings, and I wasn't waiting around to see how my uncle would handle the accusations that came with them. I'd heard him telling the principal that I was mentally unstable. That I was making it all up. That everything in that journal was fabricated from my mentally unstable brain.

He was a good liar and an even better manipulator. I knew that now, which was exactly why I was running.

The floorboard beneath my feet creaked as I stepped over the threshold, looking for any indication or clue that caught my eye. I didn't have much time to snoop, but I didn't want to leave until I at least tried to find something that told me where he'd sent Tobias. I knew it had to be on his computer. It was the one thing he guarded above all else, and after the last time he'd caught me in here, it never left his side. He protected it more than anything.

I swallowed past my fear and rising anxiety of the clock ticking quietly in the back of my head. A bead of sweat fell over my temple as I sat on his computer chair and clicked the button, silently thanking anyone who would listen that his computer was unlocked. My heart sped through my chest so hard it was painful as I moved through folders, taking in as much information as I could. There had to be something on here. There had to be.

There were a million folders to sort through, and I wasn't sure I'd be able to get to them all. I knew my time was running out. Each second that I sat here was another second that he could pull his car into the driveway, and I'd be done for. I'd be chained up in the basement for who knew how long. I didn't know where we went from here, and I didn't want to find out. My heart stalled as I clicked through another set of folders. There was one that caught my eye.

The title was a date.

My birthday. Tobias' birthday.

December 6th.

My finger shook over the keyboard as I squeezed my eyes shut, taking a deep breath before clicking on it and reading as quickly as I could.

It could have been another case file of his, but I'd once heard someone say they didn't believe in coincidences, so I didn't either. As soon as the folder popped open, a breath of air got stuck in my throat.

There wasn't a single case file in the folder. Instead, there were tiny thumbnails of pictures.

Hundreds.

And they were all of me.

I blinked a few times as I clicked through them, tasting the bile rise up in the back of my throat.

There were some of me sleeping peacefully in bed, all within the last year or two. It was as if they were in chronological order. My hair got longer, and my breasts got fuller. My cheeks had lost their chubbiness, and the angles grew sharper. I sucked in another breath when I moved from the ones in my bed to the ones in the basement. The rush of cool blood flushed through my veins as I saw my naked form, cowering on the dirty floor with my wrists wrapped in chains. I had no idea when he'd even taken them, but by the look on my face, I wasn't conscious.

A lone tear fell over my cheek and landed on the wooden desk below the laptop, and I had the urge to take the sleek piece of technology and slam it onto the floor. I wanted to stomp on it and destroy every last picture he had of me.

I knew why he had them.

I didn't realize the signs of his obsession until after Auntie left. After Tobias whispered to me in the darkest of nights that what was happening in our home wasn't normal, I started to look at things differently.

Richard didn't care for me like he should.

Our entire upbringing was wrong. So incredibly wrong.

The lies that were fed to me, the punishments, the moral codes and rules that were nothing more than a sheer way to control me. To make me his.

The fear that was buried deep within my chest started to brew, and I was seconds from slamming the laptop shut and leaving, but there was a single file in the bottom left-hand corner of the folder that begged to be opened. The curiosity came from the irrational part of me asking for more fear, and I let it override the rational part, the one that was screaming at me to just leave. To flee.

When the folder popped open, I scanned what appeared to be a spreadsheet of some sort with several dates leading into the new year.

The first date was my and Tobias' birthday with the words: Gemma enters adulthood.

A sickening feeling coiled in my belly as I slowly stood up. The fight-or-flight instinct was going to war inside me as I continued to read the upcoming dates and their purpose.

December 7th: pull from school.

December 9th: meet with Dr. Bink and bring a photo of Emily for reference.

December 15th: first surgery - nose.

My pulse thumped and thumped as I tried to make sense of the spreadsheet. Why would I need surgery on my nose, and why was there was a note to bring a photo of my mother to a surgeon? I didn't understand. But then, small snippets of memories came crashing in, the ones I had pushed away until I no longer could. The things my uncle would whisper to me when I was being punished. The name he would call me as he ran his finger down my bare spine with a thick, raspy voice and a bulge in his pants. "Emily. You'll be my Emily. I won't let you make the decisions your mother made. I won't let you break the rules like she did. You are mine, and you'll do better."

He was turning me into his own messed-up version of my mother. A muffled cry left my lips as I continued to read the rest of his plans. The rest of the surgeries. He had individual notes with each date and appointment. He was even planning to get me colored contacts. Eye doctor: sky-blue contacts. *He wanted to take my vibrant green and change them to the shade my mother and Tobias both had.*

The flight instinct that was fighting to pull me from the computer and force me out the front door won when I'd read the last date on the spreadsheet with the title: Wedding.

That was when I slammed the computer down. That was when it all came back to me. Everything had made sense at that moment.

Richard was planning on keeping me forever.

He was planning on doing more than just touching my spine as he chained me up in the basement.

He wanted me to stop breaking rules and to fear him and his punishments so I would obey him and do what he wanted.

He wanted to turn me into my mother and then marry me.

The videos I'd found a few months ago confirmed that he and my mother were sexual with one another, that they'd had a relationship of some sort, but I remembered when things fell apart. When she wanted to leave with me and Tobias. How she didn't want him to touch her anymore. And then soon after, she was gone.

And he turned into someone else entirely.

I took off through the door and didn't look back. Reading those things was the last thing I needed to take off. Tobias would have to find me, not the other way around. He said he would come back for me, but I couldn't wait any longer.

I just couldn't.

Not if I wanted to survive.

"How long has she been out?" The voice was muffled through my hazy thoughts, and I fought to open my eyes. I wanted to open them so I could stop seeing the dark forest that came after what I'd found on the computer. I could almost feel the sting of the branches whipping at my legs as I ran toward freedom. It was like I was there, but I wasn't at the same time.

Make it stop.

"A few minutes. Off and on. She's been mumbling things. Go get my uncle. See if he can get the nurse."

I could hear footsteps pounding. *Was that real? Was that in my head?*

"Gemma, baby. Open your eyes, please."

I felt the vibration in my throat, and there was a soft touch to my face.

My lashes felt glued together, and although I felt myself coming back, my eyes didn't want to open. The vulnerable, sad, and scared girl that I truly was on the inside didn't want to see the look of pity on the faces that stood above me.

I was afraid.

Embarrassed.

Shameful.

"You're safe with me." Isaiah's whispers soothed the panic that still simmered just beneath the surface. "Tell me what you need."

The tickle on my cheeks told me that my eyes were finally opening and that Isaiah's smooth voice was the one thing that I could hold onto and focus on because I knew I was safe with him. I knew Richard wasn't about to pop out of the corner and beat me for telling someone the things that I knew, and even if he had, Isaiah would take him down. I wasn't in the basement with chains around my wrists. I was in the library with Isaiah's scent wrapped around me like a weighted blanket.

I also knew he wasn't going to tell anyone my secrets if I gave them up. He knew how important secrets were. He had some of his own.

And I trusted him.

I trusted him with my secrets. My body. My mind. Everything.

I trusted Isaiah Underwood, and although my heart felt torn to shreds, I loved him with those tiny, frayed edges.

My eyes chose that moment to spring open. My lip trembled as I locked right onto his face, and all I wanted was for him to make it disappear.

"There you are," he finally said, eyes bouncing back and forth between mine. There was a small divot in between his eyebrows, and his jaw was set to stone. "Don't do that to me, Gemma. I need you to stay with me."

My head was pressed to his chest as soon as he helped me to my feet, and his hand ran down the length of my long hair. His heart was thumping so violently in his chest that I could feel it against my cheek, and I only wrapped my arms around his waist tighter.

"I got a hold of the headmaster. He said he's coming."

Isaiah's grip on me never loosened. "Tell him never mind. I have it handled."

Cade's voice was closer now. "Shiner, you got that?"

"Yeah, I'll let him know."

Silence filled the large library, and although I wanted to know when Cade and Shiner had gotten there, I didn't speak. I didn't want to. All I wanted was to stay in Isaiah's arms and pretend the last ten—or however long it was—minutes never happened. I wanted to go back into my bubble of keeping my secrets silent so I didn't have to face them.

"She shouldn't be alone tonight. I'll stay with Brantley again."

Isaiah's hand ran down my hair once more before his head lifted from the top of mine. He whispered his next set of words, but I heard him clear as day. "I don't want to let her go, Cade. How did you do it with Journey?"

Cade's answer was distant as his footsteps faded. "I had no other choice."

I think Isaiah knew right then that neither did he.

CHAPTER SIXTY-NINE

ISAIAH

GEMMA FELT fragile in my arms, but I knew she was anything but. The images that were forever embedded into my memory of her chained and hurt told me just how strong she actually was. She was braver than most people I knew.

I could see now why she always clammed up when Richard was brought up. The thought of him took her away from me. It took her to a place that her mind couldn't even fathom, so she shut down. That was trauma. I'd seen it before, and I had to say, it cut much deeper when it was happening to someone you cared about.

"Here's some water." Cade walked further into our room, holding a bottle of water he must have snagged from the mini-fridge and handed it to Gemma. Her hand shook when she reached out and grabbed it, opening the top and taking a small sip.

"Thank you."

Cade glanced at me, and I could see the troubled look on his face. He knew what she'd been through. He saw the photos, and although he couldn't get into Richard's office the other night, we'd seen enough to know that he would never get close to her again.

Cade was worried about me, too. I could see it. I was spooked when she'd gone limp. Absolute terror flew through my body when her small frame slipped in my grip. I'd called Cade, and he and Shiner rushed to the library in the dead of night with Brantley not far behind.

Looking over at Cade's bed, I saw that the covers were tossed onto the floor. He must have been sleeping when I'd called, and that was likely because of how hard we'd practiced earlier. We had a big game tomorrow, and Coach made us redo our weakest plays over and over again until we got them right—as if lacrosse was really that big of a fucking deal.

I stared as Cade ran a hand through his messy hair before giving me a subtle nod while pushing his phone back in his pocket. "I'm going to sleep in Brantley's room." There was a quick notch in the way he slanted his head to my phone that sat on the table between our beds.

Gemma finally raised her head. "You don't have to do that, Cade. I don't want to kick you out of your room."

"You're staying in here," I said, swiping my phone off the table as I stood up. I quickly read Cade's text as he assured Gemma that he was fine with sleeping in Brantley's room.

CADE: **Collins texted. The last document is ready. He'll slip it onto the bus during the game. He was inquiring about payment.**

MY STOMACH WAS tense as I put my phone back down onto the table. The question was on the tip of my tongue, and my fingers twitched to let out some pent-up aggression. I knew I had to let her go. I was a strong enough man to push her out the door when I knew danger was soon approaching. But there was something that she was hiding. I was missing a piece of information, and although I wanted nothing more than to just slip under my covers and hold her against me all night long, I couldn't. Not even knowing how desperately she needed my stability instead of the raging monster inside. It was clawing to get out from the dark instinct that was driven into me at such a young age, threatening to make someone bleed—someone being Richard Stallard—but we were running out of time, and I needed to know all there was to know so I could handle it appropriately.

"Isaiah?" Gemma's soft voice brought me back down as I stared at her from across the room. *When did I get over here?*

Cade was almost through the door when he paused and turned back to look at me. Our eyes met, and although his face remained expressionless, I knew he saw the anger stemming from my shaky hands. He knew me better than most, and he would stay if I needed him, but I shook my head, letting him know I was fine. Gemma was my main priority. As soon as the door slammed shut, I glanced over, and she was sitting perfectly still on my bed. Her eyes darted away almost the second I caught her, and a sense of awareness hit me. Her trauma had come back in crashing waves earlier, and those waves were still hitting her.

I knew how that felt.

I slowly crept over to her, and her chin dropped down so low that I couldn't even see her face. I hated that she wouldn't look at me. My knee hit the floor as I bent down in front of her, realizing that I would never bend down for anyone *but* her. My hand came up next and rested on her chin as I felt a single tear drop onto my skin. A stab of pain hit me in the chest, and I didn't even want to speak. I shut my eyes briefly and dropped my hand, resting both of them on the sides of her thighs. My head came down and landed on her knees.

"I know you don't want to tell me," I started, hating how weak and desperate I sounded. Gemma needed me to be strong, but I was slipping, and she was the only one I'd ever slip in front of. She was the only person I'd ever let see through my vulnerabilities, because she recognized my fear. "But I need to know everything." Raising my head, we locked eyes briefly, and I saw the way her mind was moving. "I will tell you what I have planned, if you really want me to, but it won't matter. You will be far away, and I promise you I will not let you come close to this. You don't need anything else fucked-up in that perfect little head of yours."

Her lip trembled as she stared at Cade's bed behind my shoulder. "Perfect little head? It's messed up in my head." A sarcastic laugh huffed from her mouth, and my lip twitched.

"It's messed up in mine, too." I paused. "The only time it's bearable is when I'm with you."

The teeniest, simplest smile formed on her lips, and my entire chest grew warm. *There she was.*

I grabbed onto her chin again, and I swiped my finger over her bottom lip. "Seeing you smile is my favorite thing. You need to do it more often. Promise me you'll smile more when you're gone."

Her head nodded, and the smile vanished along with the warmth I'd felt down to my soul. Silence filled my room, and the only thing I could focus on was the way Gemma's hands were clutching onto my blankets.

"Gem?"

Her glossy, green eyes struck me so quickly it was like a cut to my skin. A faint swallow worked itself down her throat, and my ears began to ring. "He's planning on marrying me."

I blinked once. Then twice. I slowly took my hand from her chin so I didn't accidentally squeeze it tight with the rage engulfing me. *Did I hear her right?* I slowly stood up and placed my hands on my hips, prepared to make her repeat herself, but she pulled her knees up and wrapped her arms around them, continuing.

"He and my mom were in some type of relationship or something. She didn't want him anymore. I remember. She told him no all the time. She cried a lot, and that night..." Gemma glanced up to me as tears brimmed the surface. "That night, when he took her to the psychiatric hospital, the night your dad was there, he acted as if she was mentally ill and unstable, but it was only because she wasn't doing what he wanted of her. She wanted to leave after..." She paused, thinking. "After the court let her go. I'm not sure what that meant. I'm assuming something with the group home Richard's mother ran, but he lied. He lied and said she was sick, but she wasn't, and it was all because she didn't want to be his wife." Gemma sniffled, and my back stiffened at her words. "He plans to make me a replica of her. I saw it all on his computer the first time I ran away. He plans to pull me from school the day after my birthday, and he has surgeries planned." Hands of anger were slowly wrapping around my neck, choking me. "He is going to make me his bride because he thinks, after all the years of abuse and brainwashing, that I'll just comply. That I'll marry him and follow his sick rules and...and..."

"That will not happen." My pulse beat violently against my skin as I pushed Gemma further onto the bed and scooped her up in my arms. She shook as she sobbed, and I felt my heart thud to the fucking ground. It was painful to see her like this, to feel her fear like it was my own. To know all that she'd been hiding and fearing since the moment she set foot in this fucking school. *Jesus Christ.* "Do you trust me, Gem?" Her head nodded quickly as her tiny hands wrapped around my body. I pressed her head hard into my chest, my hand nearly covering her entire face, and whispered, "Trust me when I say he will never *ever* touch you again. I said I would burn the world down for you, and I meant it."

Richard Stallard would be the next to burn, right after Carlisle Underwood.

————

MY PHONE VIBRATED a few times in the early morning hours before the sun had even risen. Cade's bed was empty, his uniform still hanging over the back of his computer chair, so I knew we hadn't overslept.

Gemma's right leg was hooked over mine as her head rested on my chest. The golden-brown strands of her hair covered half her face as I stared down at her partially hidden cheek. Lungfuls of air escaped me as I slowly turned away, grabbing my phone to see who had texted.

UNCLE TATE: **Meeting with SMC is in twenty minutes. Tell me you're awake and you're coming. Let's not give them a reason to not revoke your probation.**

ME: **I'm up.**

UNCLE TATE: **Good. Tell Gemma that I wrote her a note to take classes off today. Is she feeling better? Did she have any more fainting spells?**

ME: **She's okay. She's asleep right now. I'll explain later.**

. . .

I SLOWLY SLID out of bed and couldn't even fathom looking down at her angelic state all tangled up in my covers, but I did anyway. I stared at her the entire time I got dressed. I watched as she mumbled in her sleep, pulling the blankets up to her chin and snuggling into my pillow. I traced the red rings around her wrists and almost bent down to kiss the raised skin, but I kissed her forehead instead.

It was a sweet action. Something I'd never expected of myself, let alone falling in love with someone. But here we were. I was twisted and hooked and willing to change my entire future for her. I was nearly ready to give in to losing a small piece of my humanity.

All for her.

And it was worth it.

"Isaiah?" Gemma's sleepy voice had me pausing at the door with my back to her.

I quietly turned around and began knotting my tie so that the SMC wouldn't roll their eyes when I sat down for the meeting—as if I cared at this point. "Yeah, it's just me. I'm going to my meeting with the SMC."

Her eyes fluttered open, and she pulled down the covers just a little, showing off the tops of her breasts. I tore my eyes away, wanting to savor her body once again. "Oh. I better get up and get ready for classes. I hope Sloane isn't worried about me. I meant to have you text her before we...slept."

I hid a smile at the pink on her cheeks. "Cade let her know that you were staying with me, and my uncle wrote a note for you to skip classes today." I walked over the short distance to her and sat on the edge of my bed, knowing that I was basically eating up borrowed time.

"Oh." Gemma's cheeks burned a bright red as she looked away.

"Stay here for the rest of the day. There's food and water in the mini-fridge. I'll come back before we leave for the game."

Or maybe I'll just come during lunch. A grin started to creep onto my face, but Gemma's question wiped it right off.

"Does he know?"

My head slanted. "Does he know what?"

She gulped, fiddling with the blanket with her dainty fingers. "Does Headmaster Ellison know I'm...leaving?"

"No." I clenched my jaw tightly. I'd fill him in after it was all said and done. He would interfere, and I couldn't have that.

I watched the relief settle onto her face. I smiled at her and ran my thumb down the side of her cheek. She peered up at me shyly, and I couldn't help but bend down to kiss her again.

Our lips connected, and a rushed noise left her as my hands caged her head on my bed. *How will I survive without her?*

I hastily pulled away and stood up. The small indent in between her eyebrows had me considering not even going to the meeting, but instead of staying, I gave her my best smirk and lowered my voice. "I changed my mind. I'll be back during lunch."

"Lunch?" she asked.

"Yeah," I said, walking backward to the door. "I'll come back here to eat."

She smiled innocently, which quickly fell when I said, "*You.* I'll come back here to eat...you." Then, I winked and walked out the door and down the hall with denial stabbing me in the back.

We had only hours left—if that. And denial was the only way I was going to get through it.

CHAPTER SEVENTY

GEMMA

I WAS LEAVING in less than twenty-four hours, yet all I could do was pace my room from the second Isaiah went back to his classes after lunch. I was filled with nerves, and dread, and a whole bunch of other things that I couldn't pinpoint.

Should I pack?

Should I only pack the necessities?

Should I make it seem like I went missing instead of running away?

I made a mental note to go to the art room in a little bit, maybe right before I went down to the headmaster's office for my weekly phone call with Richard, to grab some of the drawings that I'd stuffed in the supply closet. If anyone found those, they'd know for sure that I ran away, and they might not stop looking.

The phone that Isaiah had given me had pinged on my bedside table, and I rushed over to it, seeing that Sloane had texted me.

I asked her to have a full-on girls' night with Mercedes

before Isaiah got back from his away game later, and she gladly accepted, wanting full details on what was *truly* going on with Isaiah and me—especially after I had stayed in his room last night. She, along with Mercedes and the Rebels, knew that Isaiah and I were *more*, but she still wanted the dirty details, and I was fine giving some of those details up.

Sloane: I'm going to the dining hall and bribing the staff to make us something special for girls' night. I passed Isaiah in the hall. He said he was coming to say bye to you in a few when they got the bus all loaded up.

I SMILED, relishing in the tiny moment of happiness before reality came rushing back in.

I was leaving.

I was really leaving. Tomorrow. My throat began to close at the thought, and I realized just how badly I didn't want to go.

"Why couldn't my life be different?" I said aloud, plopping onto my bed. I tried to look into the future, knowing that, no matter what, I would be safe because I would be far away from Richard, but the fear was still there. There were questions without answers being thrown around my head. Like, what if Tobias came back? What if Richard learned of my relationship with Isaiah? What did Bain really have planned? What if Richard hurt Isaiah? Isaiah never did tell me what he had planned, but I knew not to ask again. The only thing it would do was make me stay so I could somehow try to protect him, and I was smarter than that. I had to trust Isaiah, and I did. I really did.

I swiped at my cheeks and nodded sternly to myself. *I trusted him...and I loved him.* Something warm crept down my limbs at the thought of those three little words, and I knew, tonight, I would tell him. I had to tell him because I wasn't sure when I'd get my chance again, and he needed to hear me say it. I'd shown him. I'd given him my everything, so he had to know. But Isaiah Underwood deserved to hear me say it.

I loved him.

And he deserved my love.

Every bit of it.

The knock on my door startled me. My hand flew to my chest, and I glanced in the mirror to make sure my face was clear of tears. We had one day left before things became very, very real, and I was going to make every moment count.

A smile brushed against my lips as my hand landed on the iron knob. The door opened, and I smiled wide only to crash and burn a second later.

Fear sliced at my throat. My tongue was too heavy to move. The blood drained from my entire body and landed right on top of a set of shiny black shoes.

No.

No, no, no.

My lips parted as a strangled gasp left my mouth. Richard stepped into the room as quickly as his strong grip pinched the front of my throat. My natural reaction was to become submissive and cower, but something inside of me had switched the second I came face to face with him. Strength. Determination. Rage.

The sturdy walls of St. Mary's Boarding School that felt so protective were like an invisible shield coming down over my body. I wouldn't submit to him. *Absolutely not.* Submitting to him again was about as dismissive as allowing him to marry me. *Wasn't happening.*

I was angry and so damn close to freedom that I wasn't going to start over now.

This ended here, and it ended now.

"Let me go," I choked through a half-closed throat, trying to jerk out of his grip. Richard pushed me up against my desk, the wood cutting into my back as my journal fell and plopped to the tile floor. The leather binding unraveled just enough to pop open to the last drawing that I'd sketched.

Isaiah.

My breath seized as I tried whirling around in his threatening grip, trying to run as far away as I could because I wouldn't give in this time. I wouldn't go back to that dark basement to play make-believe with him. I knew there would be no more chances for me. He would never let me out of his sight now. I could no longer fool him. He gave me a second chance because he was forced to, and I ran with it.

I turned eighteen in just a few weeks, and I knew that was the end goal.

Legally, I would be an adult, and he would make me his. There was no way around it. He'd already had the marriage certificate drawn up and tucked away so nicely into its own section of the *Gemma* file on his computer. The signatures would be there. Judge Stallard had too many connections with too many important people. No matter what shade of crazy he was.

The deep-brown color of his eyes looked black as he glared down into my face, squeezing my neck so tightly I had no other choice but to claw at his skin.

"I hear you've been a bad, bad girl, Gemma." His hand constricted tighter, and black started to creep into my vision. *No!* I wanted to sob.

How did he get into the school and into the girls' hallway? Did the headmaster lead him to my room? Did I misjudge Headmaster Ellison's good character? How stupid could I have been? To trust him? To trust anyone?

Isaiah. He was coming.

His face flashed before my vision, and a deep instinctual

moment came over me where I thought, for just one fleeting second, that I could get out of Richard's grip by raising my leg and kicking him. But he was too fast. He saw what I was about to do before I even had a chance. His other hand grabbed onto my thigh, and it felt like he'd broken it in half when he slammed my leg back down to the floor. The grip around my neck lessened just a smidge, and I struggled to get away, but instead of letting me get far, he pulled me back and into the bathroom where I fell to the floor, hitting my head off the sink on my way down.

The throbbing came instantly, and something warm ran down the side of my cheek. *Shit.*

"You're just like your fucking whore of a mother," he snarled, pulling me up by the back of my hair. I screamed out in pain, feeling like every last strand had been pulled out. "I thought I could trust you. I thought I had broken you after all these years, molded you into the woman I wanted." His nose ran down the curve of my jaw, and I almost threw up from the recognition of his Old Spice cologne. "At the very least, I thought I could trust Headmaster Ellison, but I was wrong."

I whimpered, wishing like hell that Isaiah would break down the door and find me. Was he coming? If I knew anything about Richard, it was that he could survey an area well, and he never went anywhere without knowing all the ins and outs. He always covered his bases. That was, until his mother had her unexpected stroke, shutting down the group home, but nine times out of ten, he was prepared.

Judge Stallard was fast on his feet, and he didn't make the same mistake twice.

"I thought I told you that you were mine, Gemma."

My vision was growing blurry, but I fought like hell to stay awake and alert. I dug my toes into the bottoms of my shoes as he pulled my head back even further to run his hot breath over the side of my neck. The same side that held a faint bruise from Isaiah's deep sucking from last night. Just as the thought came in, Richard's teeth sunk into that exact spot, and a guttural scream left me, feeling the sharp sting of a bite.

"I told you I would teach you how a man treats a woman. How your body and mind could escape into pleasure by *my* hands. Not some fucked-up little teen boy who has no business putting his dick inside your little cunt." The hand in my hair pulled tightly again, and I cried out. The other hand went in between my legs, and he grabbed me there, stunning me for a quick second before I heard my name being called from my room.

Sloane.

Panic flew through my veins at the thought of him hurting her. Because he would. Richard was in a bad spot. There was blood on both of us. There was even blood on the floor. There would be no talking himself out of this.

Leave, Sloane. Just leave. Please leave. Run.

"Gemmaaaa!" she sang. "Where are you? I got Betty to make us s'mores for tonight! She said we can come get them here in a few. Oh, and I want full details, by the way. Did Isaiah stop by yet?"

My uncle pulled my hair again as he dragged me to the bathroom door, kicking it wide open and startling Sloane. Her eyes flicked from him to me, and then came the horror. Richard gave her no room to speak or even run. He was over to her within seconds, holding me by his side. I was too stunned to do anything. Too confused by the black gun he had whipped out of his pants at some point, directing it right at her face.

"No!" I yelled, pulling away just enough to be pulled back into him again. "Don't! Don't hurt her!"

Sloane's hands went up slowly as she took a small step

back, leaning onto her desk with the twinkle lights hanging just above her head. Her gaze drifted to mine, and something passed between us just before Richard snarled in her direction. "Did you know that she was fucking the Huntsman's son? Did you encourage it?"

Confusion flashed along her features, and I quickly answered, "She didn't know! She warned me against him." *He knows. He knows who Isaiah is and what we've been doing.* I suddenly didn't want Isaiah to come find me. Richard had a gun, and he was crazy enough to shoot Isaiah on the spot.

Richard didn't give Sloane a chance to answer him. Instead, he raised the gun up high and slammed it onto her forehead, making her crumble at our feet.

A muffled cry left me, and I pushed and scratched to get out of his grip, but he was strong. Even with all the fight I had in me, he was too fucking strong.

What was I going to do? *Think, Gemma! Survive.*

"I'll never be yours!" I screamed, throat raspy from the tears and pain. "Never. I will never be yours, just like my mother was never yours."

Richard laughed, letting go of me quickly. I fell to the floor and scooted all the way back to my bed, scrambling to get to my feet. I wasn't going to pretend that I wasn't intimidated. Fear was bubbling up in my core, threatening me as it climbed up my throat, because I was looking into the eyes of a man who'd hurt me. Who had convinced me that he cared for me and that the way he treated me was normal. That my punishments were just what *parents* had to do to make good citizens. But his punishments were set in place to break me. To make me crave his approval. He tried to manipulate me, and when Tobias caught on to his lewd behavior, Richard had gotten rid of him. Just like he'd gotten rid of my mother.

The back of my hand wiped over my face as I smeared away the blood dribbling down my cheek. My uncle squared his shoulders, still holding the gun in his hand, as a pitifully sad smile curved over his lips as he watched me climb to my feet through the swaying of the room. "Oh, baby girl. You have no idea what I have planned for you. You'll be begging for me by the end."

I shook my head, tears and blood streaking over my cheeks and hands as I mentally pushed back on my fear. "I know what you have planned for me, *Uncle*. And you can't make me a replica of her. I will never be her. I will never be what you want. I won't be your good girl, you sick fucking bastard." My attention shot to the door behind me, and deep down, I knew there was no way out. But I was going to try anyway. As soon as he threw his head back and laughed at my insult, I darted forward, but one smack to the head and I was on my back, drifting in and out of consciousness.

Survive, Gemma. Just survive.

CHAPTER SEVENTY-ONE

ISAIAH

MY CHEST FELT TIGHT, like a rubber band was wrapped around my torso, and it just kept getting tighter as the seconds passed. If I didn't have to meet up with Collins in the next town over during my game to get the last document for Gemma, I wouldn't have been going. Lacrosse was only a way to pass the time at this school. A way to blend in and shield myself from prying eyes like Bain. Now, it didn't matter. There were much bigger things going on than beating some lacrosse team full of punks who didn't even know how to hold their own dick.

"Are you good?" Brantley asked, bringing his head down when we both shoved our lacrosse gear into the back of the bus.

My abs flexed with the twisting of my stomach. "Something feels wrong," I admitted, resting my arm along the bus door as other players threw their bags on top of ours.

"That's just tomorrow creeping up on you. Things are about to change. It's heightening your stress."

I shook my head, pushing off from the bus. It wasn't heightening my stress. It was heightening my senses. "I'm going to go say goodbye to Gem. Something feels off. I'll be right ba—"

My words were cut off when I saw Shiner jogging down the sidewalk without his bag. He was lasered onto me, and his face was flush with sweat. Brantley and I both froze, seeing that Shiner's features were pulled a little too tight to be normal.

"What's wrong?" I snapped, meeting him halfway.

He was out of breath but forced the word out anyway. "Bain."

My heart began to slip. "What about him?" I snarled, looking around the school grounds, waiting to see his smug fucking face. All he had to do was wait another day, and he'd have what he wanted.

"I passed him going to my room to get my shit. He was coming out of the girls' hallway. He looked me dead in the eye and said, '*Ask Isaiah where Gemma is.*'"

My feet hit the sidewalk, and I took off running. My heart, lungs, and soul all seemed to stay behind. I felt nothing but panic and rage slithering through my veins as I hopped over the curb and flew to the side entrance. My peers were a blur of maroon as I ran past them, not stopping once until I got to the girls' hall. I paused, silencing the thumping in my ears as I sliced my eyes down the quiet corridor. *Where was everyone?*

It wasn't a good sign. I knew it wasn't. There wasn't a single girl loitering. Their doors weren't opening or closing.

There was no one in sight.

My pulse danced behind my skin in angry booms. I prowled down the hall and stopped outside of the linen closet. The same linen closet that Gemma and I had been in when we first made our deal. I sucked in a heavy breath, swung the door open, walked over to the shelf tucked away in the very back, and reached underneath, unhooking the Glock 19 and pushing it into the back of my lacrosse shorts.

Maybe I was being impulsive, but there was something intuitive about my mechanical thoughts. Too many years of growing up, walking into situations with my father, unprepared. And maybe I knew, deep down, that something was seriously fucking wrong.

I felt it in my bones.

I had felt it in my bones last night when I had Gemma in my arms.

Something didn't feel right.

I felt eerily calm with her tucked away in my bed, and I should have known that something was about to go wrong.

Shit. Shit. Shit.

Leveling my breathing, I exited the supply closet and continued down the hall. I knew my heart was beating a mile a minute, but the only thing I focused on was the single door that was half opened.

"Gemma?" I shouted, pushing my hand on the tall slab of wood. The chain echoed off the side as the door slowly slid open, revealing nothing but her and Sloane's empty room. Gemma's bed was untouched. The phone I'd given her was on her bed. "Gemma!" I shouted again, knowing she wasn't in here. *Fucking shit.*

"Isaiah?" My uncle's voice sounded far away, but within a second, I saw him rushing into Gemma's room with a red face and rising chest. "What's going on? Shiner ran into my office and said something was going on. What the fuck is going on?" He spun around Gemma's room and looked for anything out of the ordinary, just like I was doing. But there was nothing. Everything was in place. The only thing that caught my eye was that Gemma's desk chair was pushed in a little too far at her desk. I bent down and noticed that the two front legs were sticking up from the floor, and that was when I saw her journal.

Sliding it out from underneath, I quickly closed it and held it tightly within my grasp. Cade showed up next as my uncle was walking around the room. The bathroom door was closed, and he was seconds from knocking when Cade said, "She isn't anywhere. I can't find her or Sloane. Mercedes has no idea where she is, and it seems that all the girls had been sent to various places in the school. Mary's Murmurs had some announcement for the girls to meet in the library about some stupid Sadie Hawkins dance that they were planning."

"She was fucking taken!" I yelled, gripping the top of my hair. "Get Bain. Right fucking now."

Cade gripped me by the shoulders, and I was too busy trying to control my breathing to shove him away. "Do you think she might have left early? Maybe Bain tipped her off. Threatened her for some reason? Maybe he forced her to go. Blackmailed her or something."

"What are you two talking about?" My uncle's shout went through one ear and out the other. I shoved Cade's hands off my shoulders and stomped over to the bathroom, knowing that Gemma wasn't in there because she hadn't answered me. I was still going to check, though.

"She didn't fucking leave. I hadn't even given her the documents. She knew that tonight was our last night. She would have told me if Bain had said something."

"What documents?" Uncle Tate threw his hands up. "And leaving? Isaiah, I told you to leave Gemma up to me!"

I got in his face the second I saw red. "Leave her up to you? You don't even know half of it, Uncle!"

Fuck. Was there oxygen in here? Why couldn't I fucking breathe?

"Goddammit! Someone get Bain!"

I shoved the bathroom door open, ready to walk over to

the mirror to slam my fist in it. I didn't even want to see the horror on my face that I knew was there. Reality was sinking in, and everything that I had meticulously planned had just vanished into thin air, like Gemma.

If he had her...

I stopped immediately the second my foot stepped inside the bathroom. My eyes darted to the sink first, and my stomach shrunk. Bright-red blood lined the side of it, and there were drips on the white tiled floor.

"Isaiah." A small voice caught my attention, and my head snapped to the left as my uncle rushed in behind me. He immediately grabbed onto Sloane who was lying in the bathtub half hidden behind the shower curtain.

"Shit!" I yelled, diving down to my knees to look into her eyes. She blinked several times, and I had the urge to shake her tiny shoulders to get her to speak, but fuck, she was bleeding. It was selfish, but a part of me hoped that it was her blood on the sink and not Gemma's. At least Sloane was alive.

Uncle Tate brushed Sloane's matted hair away from her eyes as he bent down and placed her on the floor in between us. "Sloane. Are you okay? What happened?"

Sloane looked from my uncle and then over to me. Her shaky hands gripped onto my forearms, and she cried, "He took her, Isaiah. He...took her."

"Richard? Her uncle?" I asked, placing my hand over hers. Fuck, she was shaking just as badly as Gemma was last night in the library. Shiner's voice carried from the room, and I heard the faint worried tone from Mrs. Fitz, too. None of that mattered, though. It wasn't Gemma's voice that I'd heard, and it was the only one I cared about.

She was gone.

Sloane nodded slowly before wincing. "I think so..."

"What did he look like?" A hopeful part of me hoped it

wasn't Richard that took her, but that would only mean it was one other person. *My father.*

"He was tall..." She winced again. "It was her uncle. I know it. He was saying stuff... I think he's the one that put the marks on her wrists, Isaiah. It had to be. She was so scared."

My chest caved, and my entire being shook. I wouldn't have been surprised if the walls of St. Mary's trembled along with it.

"What marks?"

I met my uncle's eye, and the same determination that I often saw in the mirror was there, and it was prominent.

Sloane pulled us back with her next words. "He asked if I knew she was fucking the Huntsman's son and if I encouraged it. Gemma said that I didn't know. She was trying to pull him away from me." Another tear slid down Sloane's face, and I sat back on my ass, sick to my stomach. "Then he hit me with a gun, and he must have dragged me in here."

"Jesus fucking Christ." Uncle Tate climbed to his feet and began pacing the small bathroom. He opened up the door, and Shiner, Cade, and Mrs. Fitz were all standing there. I could feel their eyes on us, but all I could do was stare at the sink with blood on it. Everything felt out of control.

Everything.

I couldn't get a grasp on it.

"Isaiah," Sloane started, but both of our heads turned at the sound of my uncle's phone ringing. I briefly glanced at Mrs. Fitz. Her plump, rosy cheeks were ghastly white, and I probably looked the same. I slowly stood up and bent over to pick Sloane up. I bypassed everyone, unable to meet anyone's gaze, and sat her down onto her bed.

"Headmaster Ellison, you have to see these. Something is very, very wrong."

As soon as I left Sloane on her bed, Cade walked over and

stood beside her. Our gazes collided, and we both knew that shit was about to turn bad real fucking fast.

"Just a minute, Mrs. Fitz. It's Beth."

"Speaker," I demanded. Beth was my uncle's assistant who knew a lot about the students at this school. She was quiet and often in the shadows, but it was always the quiet ones who knew the most.

"Beth?" my uncle rushed out. I walked closer as he pulled the phone from his ear and put it on speaker. Shiner shut the door because the girls' hall was becoming busier as they came back from their *meeting*. I was certain it was all a big ploy to begin with.

Staring a hole into my uncle's phone, my pulse had begun racing again, and my fingers twitched. *Where the hell was she?* Back in the basement? *Fuck, this was all my fault.* Bain. It had to have been Bain. He must have told Richard. *The fucking photos.* But why?

My uncle's voice came crashing back in. "You didn't see anyone walk in? No other adults other than faculty? Did you see Gemma leave?"

I could tell Beth was leery. "No...nothing suspicious has caught my eye. I didn't even hear the door open. I was calling to let you know the mail came. The results are back."

My uncle's hand tensed on the phone, and my eyes climbed up to his. He was hesitant but must have thought better of putting the phone back to his ear, because he said, "Read them. Right now."

Beth paused. "Are you sure...? I was just going to leave it on your desk. I haven't opened it."

"Opened what?" I asked, noting the way his chest rose a little faster. "Uncle Tate, does this have something to do with Gemma?"

"Open them, Beth. Read them."

The shuffling of a paper came over the speaker, and my

uncle spoke with authority as he looked at each of us. "Not a word to anyone."

Beth's voice had us all looking down to the phone again, and I tensed, fearing nearly anything that could come out of her mouth. *Results?*

Her breath was loud on the other end, and I walked a little closer to my uncle. "Oh, wow. It's...it's confirmed, Tate. Gemma Richardson is your daughter."

CHAPTER SEVENTY-TWO

ISAIAH

MY MOUTH CLAMPED SHUT with horror.

Everything slowed.

The phone fell to the floor, and it felt like hours had passed before I heard the crashing of it hit the ground.

Gemma Richardson is your daughter.

Gemma Richardson is your daughter.

Gemma Richardson is your daughter.

I watched in absolute confusion as my uncle's face morphed from shock into anguish. His clenched fist came up to his mouth.

Gemma Richardson is your daughter.

"No," I said.

Sick. I was going to be sick. I shook my head. "No. No. No. She...she can't be your fucking daughter. The test is wrong." I pointed my finger in his face. "If you suspected she was your daughter..." My hand shook as I felt the blood seep from my fingers. "No. That means..." *Have I been fucking my cousin?* That couldn't be true.

"Isaiah." Uncle Tate's hands came down on my shoulders, and I just stood there in unbelievable shock.

"Have I been fucking my cousin?!" I roared, whipping his hands off my body. *Jesus Christ.* The connection. Was it because we were fucking related? Why was this happening? Why did this feel like the walls were caving in? Why did I feel my heart had stopped beating but I was somehow still alive through it all? "There's no fucking way, Uncle Tate. Are you fucking telling me that I am in love with my cousin?"

"Isaiah." Cade's face came in front of mine as the room flipped on its side. "Calm down right fucking now! Open your ears, and listen to what he's saying!"

I reared back, ready to punch him so I could attack my uncle. How could he have kept this to himself? "My ears are fucking open! She's his daughter, Cade!"

I shook my head, taking a step back until I reached the far wall, and I pushed myself up against it. My uncle rushed over to me and pushed his forearm to my throat so I was forced to look at him. "Goddammnit, get a grip! She isn't your cousin, Isaiah!"

"What?" I yelled, gasping through uneven breaths. His forearm laid tightly on my throat as his green eyes drove into mine. *They even had the same color eyes!* Exact fucking shade of green.

"She isn't your cousin, Isaiah. You are not related."

"What the hell are you talking about? I just heard Beth!" My hand gestured toward the phone that was still laying on the floor. The room was quiet. So quiet you could hear a pin drop.

My uncle's arm slowly fell from my throat, and oxygen swarmed my lungs. He walked away, placing his hands on his hips. "I'm going to make this as short as possible, because she's missing, and every second that we stand here is another second that she is in trouble."

Good. We're on the same fucking page.

"I am not your uncle." My teeth came down on one another as I stood ramrod straight. "And I didn't leave the family business because I wanted to, Isaiah. I was kicked out of it."

I heard his words. I watched as his mouth moved. But I couldn't comprehend it.

"What?"

He nodded. "I am not your father's biological brother. Your grandmother took me in when I was left orphaned because of something your grandfather did to my parents." He swallowed. "Your dad and I didn't know we weren't real brothers until we were around your age. That's when your grandpa kicked me out of the family because I had the wrong blood running through my veins. He had always hated me, and I didn't know why until then." Uncle Tate kept his face even, but I detected the dip in his voice. The low tone of despair and guilt. "Long story short, he and I made a deal, with the convincing of your grandmother and father. He would spare me and do the one thing I asked, and then I would never ever speak of the family business, and I would change my name so I was no longer affiliated." His lips formed a straight line, the light-pale color appearing white as he tensed. "If he helped my friend, *Emily*, get out of some trouble, then I would leave and burn all the incriminating shit I had on him. He wanted to kill me, but believe it or not, your father convinced him not to. Then, of course, once he died, your father and I connected again. Your father didn't trust me. He'd changed over the years, but there was still a slight brotherly bond between us. Bain being here was a coincidence that ended in his favor, thus sending you here to do his dirty work."

"Emily," I whispered. "She was the friend you told me

about. The girl that was sent to the group home by the hands of Judge Stallard instead of going to prison."

He nodded solemnly. "I sent her to the fucking hands of a monster so she wouldn't have to go to prison."

Fuck.

"Emily is Gemma's mother. I didn't know she was pregnant. She didn't tell me, and every time I tried to contact her in the group home, I was shut down. As soon as the five years was up and I contacted Judge Stallard, they had said she finished out her sentence early and had left without even a goodbye. I had private investigators. Everything. She had just disappeared."

My fingers dug into my scalp as I pulled on the ends of my hair, remembering what Gemma had told me that night in the library when another memory stole her from me. "That's because he threw her into the Covens." I shook my head, pacing back and forth inside Gemma's tiny fucking room with too many sets of eyes tracking me. "She watched that sick fuck throw her mother into a padded room all because she didn't want to marry him. He raped her, and he all but told Gemma the same thing would happen to her if she didn't follow his rules." The pictures of her were surfacing in my mind, and I looked at Cade.

"Tell him, Isaiah. Tell him everything."

"He's doing the same to her." I pulled back at the sound of Mrs. Fitz's voice, stunned that she had stolen the words out of my mouth.

"How do you know that?" I asked.

Mrs. Fitz stepped forward with tears gathering. The papers in her hands were thrust outward, and I rushed over and stood beside my uncle...my *not uncle?*...whose entire body tensed like a concrete pillar.

Sketch after sketch of the most horrific drawings shook within Mrs. Fitz's fingers. "These are Gemma's drawings. I saw them while moving some things around in the supply closet. They were hidden, Tate, as if she didn't want anyone to see them."

Cade stepped forward. "That's what she's been drawing in the mornings, Isaiah. I saw her dip into the closet a few days ago when you were in the pool. I assumed she was just putting supplies away."

"What..." Uncle Tate's words slowly evaporated into thin air as his face hardened with each sketch placed in front of him.

These were so much worse than the pictures of her chained in the basement. These were gut-churning, soul-destroying sketches that were drawn so eloquently that only someone who lived them could create. There wasn't a detail out of place. There were scars on one of the figure's bodies— the figure I assumed to be Gemma. The chains hung with her wrists in them. I finally turned my back on the drawing that was half of Gemma's face, as if she had looked into a mirror and traced every last perfect detail of herself, while the other half were the words, *good girls don't break rules,* over and over again.

"Isaiah. Did you know about this?" My uncle sounded just as off as I felt.

I slowly turned back around and faced both him and Mrs. Fitz. "Yes." I found Cade, who was still standing by Sloane on her bed, and at the moment, I felt completely drained. Hopeless. Everything ached. "We snuck into Judge Stallard's house a few nights ago because I knew there was something else going on with Gemma. I also know he is connected to Dad, and the Covens, and Bain. I wanted more info."

"She wanted to run away?"

I nodded and shut my eyes to hold back the emotion. "I was helping her get away from him, and then after I dealt with Dad, I was going to deal with Judge Stallard to somehow fix it all for her. But there's more." *My plans were fucking shredded. What was I going to do?*

"There's more?" Cade questioned, just as confused as my uncle.

"I need to know everything, Isaiah." My uncle and I were feeling the same thing. I could hear it in his voice. Pure fear and desperation were coming down on us. I hardly even registered the words coming out of my mouth.

"Richard was planning on taking her when she turned eighteen. He wants to marry her, and..." I choked the next words out, dropping my head. "Turn her into Emily. Plastic surgery, everything. She found the files on his computer before she ran away the first time." I turned my back, looking directly at her bed. "So, did Richard show up early because of you? Does he know who you are to her? Or did he show up because of me?"

There was a slight shift in air, and the next voice to hit my ears had me stilling.

"He took her because of me."

My hand dug into the back of my shorts, and I spun around quickly, pointing the gun directly at Bain's head.

"Start fucking talking."

CHAPTER SEVENTY-THREE

GEMMA

I WAS SO COLD. My body wouldn't stop shaking. The room was pitch black. My hands were tied behind my back, and although the skin around my wrists was tough from past scarring, I could still feel the slight burn of some type of rope binding me. I wanted to reach up and feel my eyes to see if they were actually closed instead of open. Maybe my body wasn't allowing me to open my eyes because of fear.

The fear settled deep in my belly. My stomach was twisting in unfathomable ways, and my heart had been pounding since I had regained consciousness. I wasn't sure how long I'd been out. My head throbbed with each breath I took, and if I even moved a little bit, the throbbing would be so intense that I would whimper.

He took me.

I sniffed the air softly, trying to calm my senses with the realization that I wasn't in the basement. There was no smell of mildew or dirt. The floor beneath my knees was cushiony instead of lined with the grittiness that laid over the concrete in that godforsaken area underneath Richard's house.

Isaiah.

My heart cracked in between the thundering beats. It had always been the plan to slip right through Isaiah's fingers, but it wasn't the plan to land in Richard's. Isaiah was making sure of that. *He will never touch you again.* But we were too late. We were too careless.

It wasn't Isaiah's fault. I'd waited until the very last second to let my guard down with him, which only made the pain that much worse.

He knew what Richard had done to me. He knew what he had planned. And he would know that Richard was the one to take me. The worry of *his* worries ate away at my stomach like little insects burrowing themselves.

Survive.

I was done fighting for freedom. If Gemma Richardson disappearing was what Richard wanted in the end, then I'd do it for Isaiah, to keep him safe and untouched.

I wouldn't strive for freedom.

I would strive for Isaiah's safety.

I would gladly trade myself for him. I'd do anything Richard wanted if that meant keeping Isaiah safe.

The stronger voice in the back of my head whispered lies and flawed ideas of a future where I could keep Isaiah safe and still escape Richard's plans, and it had me pausing for a moment.

What if? What if I could do what I'd been doing for years? Playing into Richard's hand but still finding a way out? Would I ever really give up? Was it just my fear talking? Shifting plans didn't mean I was giving up. I just had to be smarter.

Fuck him. I wasn't giving up.

The door opened, and I realized right then that my eyes were, in fact, open. The bright glow from the hall was like a punch to the head, and I cried out, dipping my chin to my chest. "There's my good girl with her little sleepyhead eyes on."

It was like nails on a chalkboard.

My chin stayed dipped to my chest as I refused to look at him. I was too afraid of what I'd see if I met his gaze. Would my resolve fall? Would I become submissive and do as he said to survive? Or would I fight back and hope that Isaiah was as strong as he said he was.

Isaiah wouldn't back down from Richard, and Richard wouldn't back down from Isaiah.

My only concern was that Richard had powerful friends that Isaiah didn't.

What was I going to do?

The lights overhead kicked on, and although my eyes were hardly open, the blinding light still hurt like hell. I remembered that he'd hit me really hard before I fell to the ground in my room. *I hoped Sloane was okay.* She would have told Isaiah everything. Panic skated right through me. *What if Richard took her too?*

"Enjoying your new room?" Richard's shoes appeared in my line of vision, and I almost spit on them. "I know your mother sure didn't."

That had my head raising. The second I glowered into Richard's disturbing eyes, his hand grabbed onto my arm, and he pulled me to my feet. The room moved before me, and I fought back nausea with the pain that surfaced.

I scanned the room slowly, wanting nothing more than to whip his disgusting fingers off my arm. I was surrounded by white. The walls looked as if they were made of clouds. Hundreds of them. Puffy, white cushions surrounded every single inch, and my stomach rolled again. I bent forward and bit my tongue so I didn't throw up. *This was the same room.* The memory came at me like sprinkles of broken glass. *My mom gripping me. Richard throwing me out of the room and into the hallway. The two men in black medical attire taking her away.*

"So, you've taken me to the Covens. How sentimental of you."

My face stung the second his hand collided with it, and my vision danced for a moment before I stood up straight and glared. *That hurt.* "I remember, you know," I croaked. "I remember the day you brought her here and locked her away. Tell me..." I sniffed as I felt something running over my lip. Probably blood. "Did she really kill herself, or did you kill her in the end?"

His lip was that of a wolf. A disgusting snarl. "Both. She knew what would happen if she didn't comply."

I kept my face steady. I wouldn't give him the satisfaction of a reaction. I wouldn't give him anything. Richard pushed me with force until my back rested along the cushioned wall. The door was still open behind him, leading out into a hallway, and the second my eyes landed on it, his beefy hand squeezed my chin tightly, forcing me back. I stared at his strong nose and the way his nostrils flared with angry breaths. "I should have never let that fucking social worker live. Nosy little bitch. I should have blinded them all: the ones who didn't want a payoff, the ones who wouldn't take bribes from the officials. I should have done away with them to keep you where you belonged. I never should have trusted you."

A choked laugh came from me. "You think I belong with you?"

His whiskey breath hit the side of my face, and I suddenly wondered how long I'd been out. He hadn't smelled of whiskey when he'd come to my room at St. Mary's. *How much time had passed?* Enough time to be thrown into a room with my hands tied behind my back. "Did he fuck you?"

I stilled, panic rushing. A chill coated me, and Richard snarled, looking down at my chest. "Does the thought of him make your perky little nipples hard?" His hand on my chin grew tighter, and I squeezed my eyes shut at the pain. My chin was likely to have bruises from the pressure. Suddenly, Richard's other hand left my torso, and he gripped the front of my shirt. I heard the tears of cotton as he ripped it from my chest, and I cried out, knowing I was completely bare underneath. His hand cupped me gently at first, and a tear escaped my eye. I knew he would no longer hold back. I knew he would no longer be waiting until I was too unconscious to understand or fight him off. I knew he would no longer wait to creep inside my bed late at night and hover over me with his hard length pressed to my middle only to scramble off in the end when I'd meet his eye.

Richard didn't care anymore.

He was no longer trying to manipulate me and make me love him.

He was going to love me even if I hated him.

Pain bit my skin as his touch turned rough. My eyes flared open, and my fear turned to anger. "Get the fuck off me." I bucked my hips violently, and it surprised us both. Everything else seemed to shut down, and I was in survival mode. Fight or flight. I was doing both. I was fighting so I could take flight. *I needed to get away from him.* "You do not get to touch me anymore! I am not your little doll, Richard!"

His hand came back down on my hip, and his nails dug into my bare skin. He pulled back, and the look in his eye was something I'd seen multiple times, but for some reason, it sent a new batch of dread into me. I was hesitant to do or say anything. "So you do remember," he remarked, brows crowding his dark eyes. His laugh echoed around me as he held me in place. "You're just like her, you know. You and your brother. I thought for a little while that you were more like your father—whoever the fuck he was. You never fought like her. Or Tobias. You were always so compliant."

"That's because you had brainwashed me. Even more so after you sent Tobias away."

His lip curved, and my throat closed. "*Sent* Tobias away?" The tilt of his head was menacing. He found humor in my words, and I didn't like that. I didn't like that at all. "You mean...after I killed Tobias."

My world stopped spinning.

My heart broke off in my chest, cracked my ribs, and fell to the floor.

He's lying. He's lying. He's lying.

"Oh yes, my sweet girl." His hand left my torso. He probably felt the fight leave my body just as I did. "Your mother is dead. Your brother is dead. And if I ever find out who your father is, he'll be dead too. You'll have no one but me."

Tobias was dead? No. No, he wasn't. But I was looking evil right in the eye, and I knew that evil could kill. Evil could destroy and kill, and Richard was the epitome of evil.

"So, let me ask you again." Richard's hand left my chin at some point and now rested over my throat, squeezing it just enough to gain my attention. "Did you fuck that boy? Isaiah? The Huntsman's son?"

I said nothing.

Not even the mention of Isaiah could bring back the fight inside of me.

Fight, Gemma! Survive!

"Oh, boys? Come on in here." The tone Richard carried felt like a storm brewing overhead. Thunder boomed. Lightning struck. I was in the middle of a fucking hailstorm, and I just kept getting pelted. "Go ahead and proceed with the exam. I need to know the truth. I no longer trust her."

"What truth?" I asked as he handed me off to two men wearing black scrubs. Their eyes were as dead and as dark as Richard's. *What the hell was going on?* One of the men, who had a bald head, looked at me like he was hungry. His gaze traveled over my body intimately, pausing at my chest, and I took a step back only to be pushed forward toward the white mattress on the floor. It was the same color and fabric that the walls were. *A padded room and a padded bed.* Both things were made of comfort, but I was as uncomfortable as I was in that basement so long ago.

"If you fucked him, of course. I need to know. The pictures were never as revealing as I would have liked..." Richard walked over to the other man standing above me while the bald one kept his hands on my shoulders. I felt dizzy and faint, and my heart was racing so fast I couldn't breathe.

"Let me go," I gasped, looking up with blurry eyes. "What are you doing?"

"Go ahead with the pelvic exam, and if I find that you are taking pleasure in touching what's mine, I will chop your fucking fingers off. I need to know if she's as tight as she should be. Do an STD test, too."

"What?!" My mouth gaped, and air seemed to be stuck in my lungs. Richard raised an eyebrow at me, as if I should have known this was coming. *No. No. No.* "Let go of me!" My voice was hoarse as I continued screaming. I thrashed as two strong hands landed on my thighs to steady me. Richard bent down and unzipped my jeans all while glaring at me from above.

"What is wrong with you?" I asked through choppy sobs.

I looked back at the two men who had no sign of life in their eyes. This wasn't real. It couldn't have been real.

I fought even harder as they pulled my jeans from my body. My shirt was split open, my breasts half hanging out. My jeans crumpled into a mess at my ankles. "No!" I screamed again, trying to rip my wrists out from the binding. I'd kill every last one of them. "I will never do what you want!

I will never submit. You'll have to cut my tongue out if you think I will *ever* keep my mouth shut."

"Oh, Gemma. You've been such a bad girl. It's almost as if you enjoy the punishments."

Just then, something pricked the side of my neck, and my movements grew slower just as Richard's face started to fade.

"*Good*," I whispered, feeling like I was in a fog. I didn't want to see his face anymore.

Then, suddenly, everything went quiet.

CHAPTER SEVENTY-FOUR

ISAIAH

THE GUN WAS heavy in my hand, and I knew it had nothing to do with the actual piece of metal. My fingers gripped the black handle as my pointer laid over the trigger. "I will blow your fucking head off, Bain. Do not tempt me. Where is she?"

Brantley was holding Bain by the back of his neck, but I knew that Bain could put up a good fight if he really wanted to. He was as large as Brantley and had been raised the same as we had. We all knew how to throw punches.

"I always thought your weakness was your loyalty to your family." Bain's smug grin filled my vision, and I swore to God the room dripped in blood. "I thought for sure that Jack would be your downfall. I mean, your father used him to do his bidding, yeah?" The room grew hot as Brantley pushed him further toward me. I didn't dare look at a single person. I stayed locked on his scheming face, and I felt my muscles tensing like they were preparing for something big. The room was one giant grenade, one exploding after the other. First, Gemma, then my uncle's revelation—or...Tate's, since apparently, we weren't related—and now Bain and his sick fucking game.

"What's the end game, Bain? Why? Why did you fucking have to drag her into this? What is the purpose? How does this benefit you?" I growled, taking a step closer to him. My uncle stepped over closer, too, but didn't get in my line of vision.

"I was wrong," Bain chuckled, glancing around the room at everyone. Even Mrs. Fitz, who I was certain looked as if she had swallowed a bat, stood there with bated breath. "Your weakness was never your family. It was just your inability to shut off those empowering feelings of loyalty and protection." He clicked his tongue. "Look where that got you."

I rushed at him, and his eyes sparked to life like the sick fuck he was. *He was more fucked up than I thought.* The gun was shoved into his chest, and Brantley pulled Bain's arms back with little to no effort.

"Isaiah." My uncle's warning didn't even come close to penetrating my rage.

"You won't shoot me, Rebel." Bain grew more serious. "You aren't like your father. You aren't like me."

"All you had to fucking do was wait one more goddamn day, and you would have had everything without taking down someone innocent like Gemma!" I screamed in his face, ready to blow him to pieces. My humanity was nonexistent when it came to Bain. The only thing that held me in place was the fact that *he* knew where Gemma had been taken. He was the one behind this. He was part of the reason that I suddenly came to the realization that, deep down, I wasn't as damaged as I thought. I used to think I didn't have a working heart, but I did. I did, because it beat for the girl that was taken so suddenly from my hands.

"Where and why?" I asked again, shoving the barrel even farther into his chest. Bain glanced down at it, and I wasn't sure if it was because he saw the coldness in my gaze or watched as my morals shifted, but he began speaking a second later.

"To secure the deal. That's why." Bain licked his lip as my uncle moved in closer. "Your father raised his prices on guns. Did you know that? The greedy fuck just couldn't help himself." Bain shrugged, and Brantley pulled his arms again, stretching the white uniformed shirt over his shoulders. "My dad saw it as a great opportunity and reached out to one of your biggest clients."

I snarled, interrupting him. "Your father is just as greedy as mine. He just can't fucking stand it that he's second best." It sounded as if I was sticking up for my father, but I wasn't. They were both pieces of shit, both too deep in a scheme of a business that did nothing but feed their egos and fulfilled their sick pleasures of becoming powerful and using killing to do so.

Bain nodded but quickly moved past. "Judge Stallard runs the Covens underneath that pesky little psych hospital. Judge Stallard's father was the one that started Operation KFS, did you know that? Never mind. That doesn't matter. Anyway, my father had worked with him in the past, hiring people here and there when need be."

My uncle tensed, and the room was covered in a blanket of ice. Operation KFS, the real story behind the rooms that laid beneath the psychiatric hospital. *The Covens.* Where men were created to kill and hired to do so. *Kill For Sale*—the biggest underground black market for gangsters that were nothing less than murderers and who were praised afterwards.

"So anyway, my father wanted to secure the deal and slowly move in and take all of your father's clients." He tipped his head to me, as if we were fucking friends. "You know all of this. That's why you followed me everywhere like a lost puppy."

"This has nothing to do with Gemma. I don't give a fuck about the business. Or the fucking Covens. Or that Richard runs it!" Gemma quickly moved to the top of the plan. The timeline had shifted dramatically. *At least Jack was safe.*

"Oh." Bain's eyebrows raised, and I wanted to punch him right between the fucking eyes. "But it does. She was my meal ticket. She was what secured the deal, Isaiah. Don't you get that? I knew that Judge Stallard had a niece. I had seen her before. A long, long time ago during a party that my father was invited to. I hardly recognized her, actually. I wouldn't have even known it was her until my father got to talking with Judge Stallard, and he let it slip that his niece was sent to the same boarding school that I was at. Close to the Covens. Not a coincidence there, ya know?"

My heart began thumping faster and faster, and my other hand almost came up to wrap around Bain's neck to drown out his smug tone of voice. *I could fucking kill him.* My bones were nearly shaking to attack.

"He had told my father that if I watched out for Gemma and reported back to him, he may consider switching dealers." Bain's lip twitched, and my stomach fell to the floor. "Imagine his concern when I told him that his precious little niece was *fucking* the Huntsman's son. Say goodbye to your business relationship with him." Bain blew out a heavy breath that hit me square in the jaw. I was too fucking shocked to even blink. *What the fuck.* "Man, he was fucking pissed when I showed him the photos. You better hope he never gets a hold of you."

I crowded Bain, the gun the only thing separating us as I got in his face. "So that's it? You have no humanity left, then? You wanted my father's clients so fucking bad that you gave up an innocent girl that is destined for a life of physical and sexual abuse?"

The pain rocked me so hard that it almost took the anger away. *Almost.*

Bain's brows dropped only a fraction, seeming to halt at the despair in my voice.

"Cade," I barked, knowing that I had to pull the plug now before things moved even further into this. "Go to Bain's room and cover every fucking inch of it. Grab anything that could lead us to Gemma."

The door opened and shut quickly, and I pulled back, lowering the gun from Bain's chest and taking a step back. "It seems my plan is coming a day early, Bain. Sit down and shut the fuck up."

CHAPTER SEVENTY-FIVE

ISAIAH

I PACED the small room a few times as Brantley shoved Bain down into Gemma's desk chair. Mrs. Fitz ran into the bathroom and gathered up some wet towels for Sloane and began cleaning her head up as everyone stayed silent. Part of me wanted to bark at everyone and throw them out so I could be alone with Bain, but I wasn't sure I could trust Mrs. Fitz not to call the authorities. I mean, I did just whip out a Glock with easy movements, and words like rape and abuse were being thrown around like fucking confetti, so it was probably best everyone just stayed where they were.

Except for Cade.

I needed him to leave. It wasn't because I didn't trust him. In fact, I probably trusted him the most. I resonated with him the most. But because I resonated with him and knew the things he felt for Journey, I needed him gone for just a few minutes.

"What plan, Isaiah?" My uncle walked over to me, and we locked gazes. We were both wound tight, but we were way too deep in this to stop and talk about our feelings like a therapist would recommend. The clock was ticking, and my gut churned at the thought of what Richard was doing to Gemma.

Turning my back on Uncle Tate, I walked over to Bain and stood above him. His long legs were straight in front of him, and his hands were tucked behind his head as he relaxed on the chair, looking pompous. He thought he had everything figured out. But he was wrong.

"If you would have waited one more day, you could have had it all without dragging her into this." My lip curved as I bent down to his level, resting the backs of my legs on my heels. "Now, here's the thing. I know you have a heart and some morals, otherwise you wouldn't have done what you did to Journey."

There was the smallest tick on his cheeks as the words flowed effortlessly out of my mouth. His body was unmoving, but the light behind his eyes switched almost immediately. It was the answer to a long-time question of mine. *Did he have something to do with Journey leaving this school?* I was *pretty* certain he was the main proprietor of the entire thing, although he probably thought I actually knew his secret since I called him out on it. Truth was, I didn't know shit.

"You needed her gone from this school. From this life. From Cade. You couldn't stand that she would have been knee deep in this shit. It's bad. You know it. I know it. This life that we both, along with Cade and Brantley"—I didn't even look at Shiner to see the uneasiness on his face from being the odd one out—"are destined to live. It's not safe for girls like her." My teeth ground along one another, and I felt the way my lips pulled back into a snarl. "Or Gemma."

Bain didn't say a word. He sat in the same position, taking in my accusation for what it was. I slowly rose to my feet, putting some space between us so I wouldn't be tempted to take his head and collide it with my knee. I may have appeared calm and in control on the outside, but I was panicky on the inside. I was frantically trying to pull things together with a string that felt knotted on both ends.

"After I got Gemma settled and got her out of this school, *just* like you did for Journey, I was going to make you a deal."

"A deal?"

I nodded solemnly. "You want my father's business so bad? Well, I was going to hand it right over."

Bain's eyes shifted to my uncle and then back to me. "That easy, eh? Just tell your ol' man that you're just going to give us your side of the state? All those clients? The dirty cops? The drug lords? All that money?" He threw his head back, and the room filled with manic laughter. "And you think I would have fallen for that?"

"Of course not." I walked closer to him, causing him to raise his head to look at me. "I was going to tell everyone what you did to Journey that balmy night just before summer hit." I didn't give him a chance to deny it, because I wouldn't have known what to say if he did. I was lying out of my ass, but I was solid with my instincts. I knew he had something to do with her, and if he had, he wouldn't test the waters in fear that I truly did have evidence. "Why do you think I sent Cade away? If he knew what you'd done...he'd break your fucking neck."

"I'm not afraid of Cade."

Brantley hissed out a breath. "You should be."

"So..." Bain crossed his arms over his chest, ignoring Brantley. "Your plan was to blackmail me so I would work with you? How, exactly? Stealing the clients out from your father? That would never work. He hardly trusts you." He laughed, but I sensed his curiosity.

"He trusts me enough. I thought we could work together, take him down, and then you could have it all, Bain. No more bloodshed. No more threats on your family from mine." I glanced up at Brantley, and his jaw was tight, but he shot me a curt nod, telling me that he was still on my side. "I know how to disappear. I'd hand it all over, and I'd be fucking gone. You wouldn't have to worry about the Huntsman any longer."

"And if I would have said no to your grand plan?"

My brow raised. "Would you have really risked it in the end? You have cops on your payroll, and so do we." I threw my hands up cautiously. "The better question is, would you risk Journey in the end? You sent her away; you made it seem like she was unstable." I dipped my head down and lowered my voice. "And I know why."

I didn't.

I had nothing solid that I could have truly shown for proof, but I knew that dangling Journey in front of him was the one thing that caused Bain to flinch and backtrack.

I breathed out an easy breath. "It would be a shame if the truth came out. Your father doesn't know about her, right?" I spun around, putting my back to him for a second. "So, let me ask you again...where the fuck is Gemma, Bain? We are done playing games."

"Isaiah." I felt Uncle Tate take a step forward, but I stayed lasered on Bain, who was undoubtedly thinking and processing everything I'd said. "I need to tell you something, and the only reason I'm willing to do this in front of him"— he nodded over to Bain—"is because we need him to find Gemma. Richard could have taken her anywhere."

The shuffling of papers behind me caught my attention. Over my shoulder, I could see Sloane and Mrs. Fitz both looking through the sketches that Gemma had drawn. I quickly swiped her leather-bound journal off the desk and threw it toward them. "Look in there, too. See if she left anything that could be valuable."

Turning back to Bain, I saw him and my uncle having a

stare off. I moved in a little closer, clenching my fists by my sides, feeling something bubble up in my stomach, threatening to climb out of my throat. "You were right, Bain. I am unable to shut off my loyalty and protection, but do you know what that means?" Hot, seedy breath left me, and my fingers began to tingle. "That means I have no limits when it comes to her. You will tell me, and you will work with me in getting her back." My finger pointed so close to his face that my uncle stepped in and pushed me away. "Or the fact that she's being raped and forced down to her fucking knees with chains around her wrists is on your fucking conscience."

And mine. It was on mine, too. My knees nearly buckled right then, but Uncle Tate's hand dug into the back of my neck, and he looked me dead in the eye. "We will get her back. But you can't kill him."

"I will if anything happens to her." My voice was gritty as I tried to pull back my emotions. I wanted to shut down. I wanted to lock it all down and take my fist and beat Bain until I didn't feel the panic twisting in my body. "She's... You didn't see the fucking photos of her. You didn't see where she was kept in that fucking house!" My voice reached levels that I didn't even know possible. The strain was against my throat, and I knew that if my uncle wasn't holding me upright, I would have fallen. I was terrified. I was fucking terrified and determined to kill every last person on this earth that even dared to touch her. I was spinning out of control and felt untamed, but I didn't even care.

"I'll tell you where she is." The entire room seemed to gravitate toward Bain and his compliance. We locked stares, and his jaw flexed. "If the deal is still on the table, I'll lead you right to her." He sighed. "And we'll take out Richard Stallard in the process."

That was too easy.

"There's a way around this." My uncle took a few steps

back, ripping his tie off with force. "I said I needed to tell you something, and this something can solve our problems right here, and right now."

"What?" I threw my hands out impatiently.

My uncle, the headmaster of this school, placed his hands on his hips and silenced the entire room with five little words. "I'm working with the feds."

Bain's eyes widened. Brantley took a step forward, and I took a step back. *What?*

"I'm working with Jacobi."

My head spun. "What does Jacobi have to do with this?"

"Who is Jacobi?"

We ignored Bain.

"Isaiah." My uncle's eyes softened, and I was stuck on the pleading within them. "Jacobi is in the FBI. He has been since he left." He swallowed, and I stalled. Complete shock and confusion wracked me. Cade chose to walk into the room right then, holding nothing useful, but I was too frozen by the way my uncle was walking toward me and the way his mouth was moving. "We don't have time for an explanation, but your father is about to meet his demise, Isaiah. Jacobi—and I—have been working to take him down for a while. All we needed was to put him somewhere that we could get him. A trap. The feds have so much intel, but...it's all speculation unless we get eyes on him, and someone calls him out on his identity. Your father is very careful. He's extremely smart and elusive. And the feds want more than just him. The feds want his customers too. This isn't just a small sting they're working on."

My uncle looked over at Bain. "You and your father remain unknown to them. They know the idea of you, but not who you are. If you work with us, take us to Gemma, we can make sure it stays that way. They don't want the small fish. They want the shark."

"My father won't step anywhere near this."

"And you?" I asked, once again eating up borrowed time. Jack's face hit the back of my mind, and I had to hope like hell that Jacobi knew what he was doing when he took him in for protection by my request. It was the first time I'd talked to my older brother in years, and he mentioned nothing of this to me. *What the fuck.*

"Is it true?" Bain asked.

"Is what true?"

"What you're saying about Richard and Gemma?"

I stomped over to Mrs. Fitz and Sloane, who were looking through Gemma's journal, and whipped some of the sketches off the bottom of the bed. I shoved them into Bain's lap, annoyed that he was touching something of hers. "What the fuck do you think?" I felt the pain hit the back of my eyes as I looked at her pieces of art. I blinked away the worry and sliced back at the hurt. "Where is she, Bain?"

He blew out a heavy breath. "I'm pretty sure she's at the Covens."

CHAPTER SEVENTY-SIX

GEMMA

I BLINKED SLOWLY, like my eyes were made of lead. The room was so bright that it gave me an instant headache, so I shut my eyes again.

I'll burn the world down for you, Gemma.

I hummed, smiling gently at the thought of Isaiah. It felt weird to smile. My lips cracked with the movement, and I tasted blood on my tongue. I tried to swallow, but my throat felt too dry. Like there was cotton shoved down it. I wanted to go back to sleep.

Just survive, Gemma. I'll come back for you.

"Tobias?" I whispered. My words sounded strange against my ears. Slow and mumbled. I ran my tongue over the roof of my mouth and teeth, searching for rocks. It sounded like rocks were inside my mouth, making my words grumbly.

"No. Not Tobias. I'm just here to give you some more meds. Richard said he wants to keep you sedated until he gets back so you'll stop screaming."

A girly voice hit my ears next. "Whatcha doing?"

My eyes stayed shut as I tried to figure out if I was sleeping or awake. I was too afraid to peek, but I took comfort in knowing that neither of the voices I heard were Richard's.

"What are you doing out of your room?"

The light, feminine voice floated in my ears as she answered whoever was hovering over me. I could feel the person's body heat, and part of me wanted to pull them in close. I was cold. So cold. My blood felt cold. My veins were like icicles. I was pretty sure I was shivering.

"Someone left my door open again, so I wandered."

Warm air wafted over my face as the person above me moved farther away. I slowly pulled one eye open, trying to adjust to the bright lights in the stark-white room. My head rested against the floor, and I remembered sliding off the mattress I was on last time I was awake because of what was done on it. *How long have I been like this?* I was in and out of consciousness and confused. It was like being back at Richard's all over again.

The floor felt so comfy against my skin, but with that comfort came a sickening, nauseated feeling, and I was afraid to dig further into my head to find out what had happened.

"Who'd you spread your legs for this time?"

The girly laugh snagged my attention, and when my eyes finally adjusted to the light, I zeroed in on her. She was pretty, even with the drab clothing she was wearing, and she was definitely my age. She had an innocence to her that felt too familiar to me.

Her blondish-brown hair was parted down the middle and split into easy waves over her shoulders. The slate-colored robe was tied tightly around her tiny middle, and she was barefoot, padding around the white cloud-like floor like she weighed no more than an ounce. The freckles on the bridge of her nose were faded, and her skin was pale, as if she hadn't seen sunlight in a really long time, but the thing that really caught my eye were the long, pink scars running up her forearms. I felt envy for a second because I'd always been so protective of the scars along my wrists, so much so that I wore long sleeves even when the temperature was warm. But this girl? Her cuffed robe sleeves were pushed all the way up to her elbows, and she wore her scars like trophies. The long, skinny, pink, raised marks were shining like diamonds in a desert against her pretty skin.

I wanted to be her.

Not just because she seemed proud of who she was and held an air of confidence to her, but because she was standing in the doorway and could walk the halls without anyone even stopping her.

The man wearing black scrubs crossed his arms over his chest as he gave her a look, waiting for her to answer his question. She shrugged. "Jealous I didn't spread my legs for you, big man?"

I squinted my eyes so it looked as if they were closed as I saw him standing over her. She didn't look fazed in the slightest. Who was she?

He tilted his head, still holding the syringe destined for my neck in his hand. "Maybe. Maybe I'll stick you with this and fuck you while you're unconscious, little one."

I bit my tongue. *Had he done that to me?* No. Richard wouldn't have allowed that. Would he? My heart started to skip in my chest, and I wished I had enough energy to spring to my feet and dart out of the open door, but it felt like my feet were numb. My whole body felt numb and tingly.

"You would never." The girl stood tall and wore an impenetrable expression. "You guys like my banter too much to do such a thing." I caught the flirty tip of her lip, and the man seemed to fall for it.

He rolled his eyes. "Go back to your room so I don't get my ass chewed for letting you roam."

"Who's that?" My eyes quickly shut, and I tried to appear like I was sleeping again, but I was pretty certain the girl had seen me. My movements were too slow. It felt like actual minutes before my eyelashes collided again.

"Newbie. None of your concern. Actually, this bottom floor is none of your concern. How many times have you been caught down here? For fuck's sake, the psych employees are so blinded by your charm."

"And you're not?" I peeled my eyes open once more when I heard the shuffling of fabric. I almost choked when I watched the girl take a step closer, running her hand down the side of his face. The sound of his beard against her skin made a scratchy sound, and her lips were a millisecond from touching his. "Remember the last time we got too close?"

The man's eyes darted down to her mouth, but I quickly moved my gaze to her hand that was moving in between them.

Was she...?

"Mmm, I remember," she whispered. "I wonder what would have happened if we hadn't gotten interrupted?"

I pulled back slowly, wincing at the fogginess in my brain as I watched his hands shoot down to her slender hips. He threw his head back, the veins along his neck prominent as her hand dove down into his pants. "Goddamnit. Stop. You shouldn't be acting like this."

"Maybe you should stop me." Her hand moved inside his pants faster. *What was going on?* I was confused but too stunned to look away or close my eyes. This girl was...different. Bold. Determined. She looked sweet at first. Her calm voice sounded like a child's, with an innocence that I'd held once upon a time. But now she appeared tough and seasoned.

My mouth gaped as the man's hips started thrusting, and the girl's eyes darted away, looking more disturbed than aroused like she'd seemed a few seconds ago. But that was when she caught my eye. She blinked once and froze for a moment before shaking her head, silently shushing me.

Her other hand pulled back slowly, and my eyes widened as I saw her slip something from the man's pocket into her own. He was too blinded by her hand in his pants to realize. His eyes were shut tightly, and his hips were rocking. Loud breaths were coming out of his mouth, and I shut my eyes quickly when his sultry voice rang out.

"You're a little minx."

"What do you expect when I'm stuck inside a prison cell all day being fed little white pills to make me *happy*?" She let out a little moan. "Plus, I like seeing you at your mercy for me. It feels good to be in control once in a while."

"Jesus Christ." His words were a mix of desperation and awe. "You're not in control."

Oh, but she was. She was distracting him so she could take something. *Was this real?*

"Fuck," the word was strained.

"Better hurry, someone's coming."

His breathing picked up, and after one grunt later, every-thing went silent. His breathing resumed to normal, and I heard a faint giggle before he muttered under his breath, "Go back to your room, now."

"I don't get a thank you?" I heard the amusement in her tone. "That was for not telling on me for being out of my room. Bye, big man."

A loud breath clamored through the room right before the door shut, and after a few seconds, I opened my eyes only to pull back with a scream lodged in my throat because the guy was standing over me with a beet-red face.

"Keep your fucking mouth shut." He hovered over me.

"It's the only way you'll survive here." Then, he pricked me again, and for a fleeting second, I was thankful.

———

THE ROOM SPUN AGAIN like I was on a merry-go-round.

He was here.

A tiny voice in the back of my head made the hair on my arms stand erect. There was a shadow in the depths of my mind that was threatening to come to light with the warning. Like some broken part of me that had been shoved down way too far was emerging so I could be prepared. But instead of being prepared, I shoved her down again.

No.

I want to go home.

But where was home? Not with Richard. Home wasn't the place that I had grown up in.

Was it St. Mary's? It was the first place I'd ever felt safe, even if it was proven that I wasn't.

Isaiah.

I felt safe with him. I felt good when I was with him.

A whimper left me, and the warmth of a single tear ran along my cool cheek. "*Isaiah.*"

"Say his name again, and you'll regret it."

I squeezed my eyes shut at the sound of Richard's voice. *Was it real?* It wasn't real. My head shook back and forth as my brain played ping-pong against the walls of my skull.

"How many times did he fuck you? You know better than to lie to me. Think of all the times you'd lied over the years. What happened after I found out the truth?"

The basement was so cold. It always was. I knew Richard was behind me. I felt his heavy presence, and I was pretty sure his hand had trailed down my naked spine. Was that what woke me up? Probably.

"Tell me, Gemma. Did you eat the last cookie? Because Tobias is saying it was him." Richard's laugh cut through my fear like a sharp sword. "A cookie. So insignificant, but I can't have you lying to me. I'm doing this for a reason. You will not break rules while in my home."

"I'm cold, Uncle Richard."

"What did I tell you to call me when you are down here?"

My eyes peeled open, and fear like no other hit me again. I hated it down here. The cookie wasn't worth it. Why did I take it?

"Daddy," I whispered, and then I screamed when something sliced at my back. The sound of leather against skin ricocheted through the dark room.

"I'm sorry!" I yelled out, pulling at the chains imprisoning my wrists.

"You're too old to be doing this, Gemma. Lying to me. You're supposed to be my good girl. I hate punishing you."

"You don't hate punishing me," my voice cracked, and I pulled my eyes open, looking back at Richard's dark eyes that were now aged with fine wrinkles around the edges. I wasn't in the basement. I was in the white room. I was at the Covens.

The sickest smile slithered onto his face. "You're tough this go-around. It was always so easy to break you in the past."

A growl started to curl deep in my throat. Anger lit me up inside, and not even Richard's darkness could put out the flame.

"What?" Richard's head tilted, and I saw that his white button-down shirt was undone at the top, showing off his dark curly chest hair. He looked slimmer, and the dark circles under his eyes did nothing but make him look that much more dangerous. I focused on the bright-pink scratches along his cheek. Where did he get those? "Did having some cock in your pussy give you some sort of confidence? Imagine what mine could do."

I was disgusted, and the remnants of fear surfaced. *No.* He didn't get to have me. "I am not yours, Richard. I won't let you touch me."

He laughed, throwing his head back. I tried raising my hands to lash out, but I couldn't. *What was wrong with my arms?* I looked down, taking my eyes off Richard, which was a mistake. His hand clamped onto my throat, and a scream got lodged. It hurt. It hurt really bad. My neck was sore, and his fingers felt as if they were digging into open wounds. "If you keep screaming and hitting me when I come in here, it'll only be worse for you. No one is coming for you, Gemma. You might as well give up now."

My head thrashed beneath his grip, and I pushed away the pain radiating to my temples. His hand came off my neck, and a look of excitement hit his muddy eyes. He liked when I fought him, and he probably didn't even realize it until now, because in the past, I didn't fight. I had let him have me because I thought it was the only way to survive.

And maybe it was.

"I will never give up."

What if he never let me go? What if I never made it out alive? Panic started to prickle at my vision, and I was seconds from letting it take me under, but I was too afraid of what was going to surface when it did.

A knock sounded, hardly audible through the lush, white, soft walls. I tried to move, wiggling to get away and toward the door. Maybe it was someone sane. Maybe it was someone who could hear me yelling.

Richard's large hand grabbed onto my leg, and that was when I realized I was wearing a gray medical gown, the same color that the pretty girl had been wearing the last time I was conscious. *Was that real? Was she real?*

"No!" I yelled, suddenly snatched from my confusion. "Stop!"

Richard's legs came down as he straddled me, his middle pressing against me so hard that I bit my tongue to direct the pain somewhere else. His hand came over my mouth as he glared like the devil down into my face. "Just be the good fucking girl you're supposed to be, Gemma. I've spent nearly eighteen years taking care of you and waiting for you to grow up. I am no longer going to be patient. You will do as I say. You'll be begging for me after they're through with you. I don't want to let them break you, but I think it's the only way. Why are you women so unaware of what a man like me could give to someone like you?"

My mouth opened wide against his skin, and I clamped down as hard as I could, tasting his blood in my mouth.

"You just have to be fucking difficult!" he yelled, anger taking a hold of his brown depths. His fist came up quickly as his face contorted, and I was suddenly silenced by the pain.

The room was wobbly as my head fell to the side. Dizziness swallowed me, and suddenly, I was back on the merry-go-round. My body was tired, and I was questioning reality again.

"Why is this happening?" I whispered, shutting my eyes because it felt so good to see nothing but the abyss.

Something sounded in my ears, and I opened my eyes again, sour vomit hitting the back of my tongue. The door was open, and I saw Richard standing there with blood dripping from his hand. *Did I do that?* I licked my lips. Yes, I did. I bit him.

"Good." My voice was louder than I thought, and he looked back at me for a brief second before looking at someone else. The room was like a tunnel, and hope sparked in my chest when I caught a blur of a maroon tie.

"Isaiah?" My eyes opened wider, and a ragged breath left

me. *Could I breathe?* I moaned. It felt hard to breathe. My chest hurt from the thumping inside.

Wait. I blinked a few more times, trying to right the room. "Can someone make the room stop moving?" I yelled out, but my voice didn't sound right. It was rough. My throat ached.

"It's none of your business, boy. I switched vendors for a few reasons, one of them being because the Huntsman raised his prices. Don't you think for a second that I owe you now. I don't owe anyone. It's the other way around."

The Huntsman.

"Help!" I yelled, fighting through the fogginess of my head.

"I understand what you're saying, but I have a proposition for you."

I recognized that voice.

Was that...? "*Bain?*"

Richard's glare snapped to me as Bain stepped farther into the room. He was half inside now, and when our eyes connected, his grew wide for a split second before he turned to look back at Richard. "You want Isaiah, right?"

Richard turned his back to me as I squeezed my eyes shut for a second. Everything was fuzzy, like a radio that had too much static. "I can lead him here. He'll want to come after Gemma. He will bring his father, too. He knows I'm the one that gave you the proof of their relationship. Not to mention, the Huntsman is aware that he is no longer in business with you. He knows that you've switched sellers. They'll want blood."

"No." My eyes were open again. *Did I say that?*

Richard and Bain were both looking at me. I could feel their stares without even truly seeing them. "Bain, no," I repeated, trying to focus on him. When we finally seemed to lock gazes, his mouth moved silently. "*It's okay,*" he mouthed. "*Shh.*"

What? It was like seeing that girl again. Was this real?

I closed the room out because I was too confused, and the longer I kept my eyes open, the more nauseated I felt. I didn't want to see him anymore. Or Richard. I didn't want to believe what I was hearing.

Was Bain going to bring Isaiah here?

Richard would kill him. Richard killed my mom...and Tobias.

He would kill Isaiah too.

I cried.

I knew I was crying, because I could hear myself, even if I did feel like I was floating.

Something felt wrong.

It was like I could feel my body, but I couldn't feel my body.

"*Survive, Gemma.*"

"Huh?"

"*It won't be long.*"

I knew I was imagining things. The first voice sounded like Tobias, but the second sounded like Bain.

And neither of them would be telling me anything encouraging. One was dead, and the other had sold me to the devil.

CHAPTER SEVENTY-SEVEN

ISAIAH

"I'M NOT WAITING." The chair I was forced into toppled backward as I jumped to my feet.

My uncle was pacing back and forth in front of me, chewing on his nail. He sliced his attention over to me as he stopped dead in his tracks, and seeing his green eyes made my stomach roll. They were the same fucking shade as Gemma's, and now that I knew she was his daughter, it was hard to look at them.

"You will fucking wait, Isaiah. This is much bigger than your ego, so sit down."

My blood rushed. "This has nothing to do with my ego, *Tate.* He's probably fucking her right now! She's probably screaming for help, and no one is there to scoop her up and take her away from danger!

"You don't think I've thought that already?" The vein on my uncle's forehead was throbbing as we met chest to chest. It was only the two of us in his office. Brantley and Cade were getting things gathered and making sure Sloane and Mrs. Fitz were calm enough to leave alone with the nurse without ruining our plans before we even got a chance to step foot near the Covens. "She's my goddamn daughter, and I'm the whole reason this poor girl is stuck with a man like Richard Stallard!" He turned around and slammed his fists onto his wooden desk, and a few things fell off the side as his head dropped. "This is so fucked up. All of it is. From the moment Emily got caught… I wouldn't be surprised if your grandfather had known she was pregnant with my twins. He probably sent her there on purpose, allowing me to think I was doing a good thing by her, but really, he was sitting back, laughing his ass off over the fact that I was losing everything in my life."

"I don't trust Bain," I said, ignoring my uncle's revelation that my grandfather was a real piece of shit. My father was just like him. Later on, maybe he and I could bond over our paralleled fucked-up childhoods, but right now we needed to go get our girl.

Our girl.

My chest caved in one single swoop. This truly was fucked-up. All of it. Gemma and I were destined to burn from the second we connected. The messy web had grown wider, and it was tangled with a disturbing past and wicked lies. She and I were innocently thrown into a life neither of us wanted or deserved.

And after it was all said and done, I wouldn't be deserving of her at all. I would kill Richard and burn the Covens to the fucking ground and hope my father was inside, too. I didn't care. Bad people deserved bad things. And they were both monstrosities.

My uncle turned back around. "Was it true? What you said about Journey and Bain?"

"Does it matter? The blackmail seemed to work." I paused. "Unless he's playing us. I don't trust him. He could have been lying. We need to go to the Covens."

"We have to wait for Jacobi!"

As soon as my uncle had let the cat out of the bag that my older brother was in the FBI, we immediately went to his office and called him. He was on speaker, and the first thing out of my mouth was, "*Where is Jack?*" Apparently, he was safe, and although I'd hated my brother for years, and the first time I'd spoken to him in a long time was the other day when I told him he *owed* me and I demanded he take in Jack—*his little brother just as much as he was mine*—there was still a part of me that trusted him. I trusted Jack to be in Jacobi's care versus anywhere near my father when he realized that I'd betrayed him.

"No fucking offense, but I don't give a fuck about the FBI's plans to take down my father or Richard. Or the Covens. My only concern is Gemma, and that should be your only concern too!"

We were chest to chest again, and his face was as red as mine. Maddening heat covered every inch of my skin, and every time her name would fly off my tongue, it felt like another part of my soul cracked a little more.

Uncle Tate's hands wrapped around my face, his fingers pushing into my scalp. "Do you really think you'll be able to just walk into the Covens and get her? If she's really there, no one is going to give you the key, Isaiah. You'll probably be shot on the spot, especially if the Covens has switched allegiances. If they are no longer being supplied by your father, they will not think twice about shooting you right between the eyes! You should know this. Why do you think they've been hidden all these years? They're smart and ruthless, and they take any threat they see, whether it's true or not, and demolish it."

"I'll find another way in, then!" My entire body shook with...shock? Fear? Adrenaline? I was ready to break a neck or two if it meant getting his hands off her.

I'm coming, Gem.

"You will not be able to just walk in there, Isaiah! We need to wait for the phone call from Jacobi and figure out the best way to handle this! He's been working with the ATF, and they are constructing a plan right this second. We don't even know if Gemma is actually at the Covens. Can we trust Bain? Probably not. I should have never let him stay at this school. If it had been up to me, he would have been gone. But, Isaiah, you're going to cause more harm to her by harming yourself. Think about her! She will never forgive herself if you die trying to find her! She is just like her mother. She puts everyone before herself."

"Did someone just say Gemma?"

My uncle and I both spun around quickly, and my hands were already in fists. I locked onto two shadowed eyes, one of them black and blue, with dark hair hanging over his sliced eyebrow. He was my height but skinnier than me, standing right there in the threshold of my uncle's office. "Who the fuck are you?"

"He's with me." My stomach was like a catapult to the floor when the person speaking in a shy tone stepped to the left and farther into the room.

My uncle's hands fell to his side as his jaw unhinged. "Journey?"

————

"DID YOU JUST SAY GEMMA?"

My throat constricted as I stared at Journey. It was like seeing a ghost. My eyes immediately flew to her bare arms with the wounds now turned into scars. *What was she wearing?* She had on a...dress? A gray, smock-like dress hid her skinny frame and cut off just above her bony knees. She had on thick gray socks that went up to mid-calf, but they were covered in dirt and mud. The guy she stood next to completely enveloped her short height with his. He took a step forward and placed his body half in front of hers protectively, and my thoughts immediately went to Cade. *He was going to go ballistic.*

"Journey," my uncle whispered, shock rooting him right to the floor.

I quickly moved past the surprise, ignoring the way everything in the room seemed to shrink even further, and saw two blue eyes that looked as cold as mine, staring directly at me. "How do you kno—"

Holy shit.

I was instantly coated in ice. A chill came over me as I took a step forward. "What the fuck," I mumbled, looking at my uncle and then to him. I did that a few more times, and I felt the blood drain from my face. It was obvious. So fucking obvious. "Tobias."

His chin hitched, and the sharp cut of his jaw had fading bruises. "Did you say the name Gemma?"

My uncle instantly crouched to the ground, both fisted hands coming together and up to his mouth. His head shook back and forth as he realized who had just walked in his door. It had to have been like looking into a mirror twenty years ago. The only difference between the two were their eyes. Gemma got her eyes from her father. Tobias must have gotten his from Emily.

"Oh my God," my uncle mumbled, slowly rising to his feet with his eyes shinier than I'd ever seen before. "How did you find me?"

Tobias' cut eyebrow bundled, looking at my uncle in confusion. Journey stepped forward, crossing her arms over her chest. "He didn't find you. I brought us here."

"Where have you been?" I asked. Journey had disappeared after that night, and Cade had let her. He had let her because he knew that if he was aware of where she was, he would have followed her and likely done more harm. We'd assumed that she was sent to a different school after receiving the medical treatment she needed. The farther away from us, the better.

Journey's little jaw wiggled as her eyes darted to my uncle. "Do you know where I was?"

My uncle's head shook as he graced her with a brief glance. "Sister Mary at the orphanage had said you were in the hospital, and afterwards, they would be placing you at a different school and with a foster family, if they could, uh... " My uncle cleared his throat. "Find one that would be willing to address the issues."

A high-pitched sarcastic laugh left Journey, and it was full of sarcasm. I'd know. It sounded a lot like mine most of the time. "That's funny."

"Journey, where were you?" I looked at Tobias as a heavy feeling fell upon my shoulders. "And how did you find him?"

Journey and Tobias turned toward each other before she addressed me. "I've been at the Covenant Psychiatric Hospital since the night I was taken from here."

The room was instantly clouded with something dark and disturbing. The walls changed to black, the lights grew dim, and my heart thundered within my chest. *Fuck.* My nostrils flared, and I hoped like hell that she was a patient on the top floor and had no idea what was on the bottom floor, but with the fact that Tobias was standing by her side, I didn't even want to know. I didn't want to ask.

All I wanted was to move past this, walk out the fucking door, and go get Gemma.

It was like mountain after mountain just kept popping up and getting in my way. The path was winding, and I was sick of not knowing which direction I was being pushed and pulled.

"What?" My uncle's fist was seconds from colliding with the desk again. "This whole goddamn town is corrupted by people like your father and Richard!" He pointed his finger at me, and I didn't disagree.

"Richard? You know Richard?" Tobias crept farther into the office, the door shutting behind him, which was good because we had a whole lot of shit to discuss and not a lot of time.

CHAPTER SEVENTY-EIGHT

ISAIAH

"You mean to tell me that you *think* my sister is at the Covens right now? There's no way. I would have known. The workers talk there. They talk to me."

The tick in Tobias' jaw was moving back and forth, back and forth, much like mine. His voice creaked like a door that was seconds from flying off its hinges, and I was honestly pretty sure he, too, was seconds from flying off the hinges. His face was nearly purple after he got over the hump of shock that my not-so-real uncle, Tate Ellison, was actually his father.

"I need to see a picture of Gemma." Journey finally spoke for the first time since telling us that she had been at the psych hospital.

I stared at her with my leg hopping up and down from across the room. "Why? Did you see her there? She hasn't been there for long." I glanced at the clock and swallowed back panic. *Any amount of time would have been too long.*

"Give me a picture."

"Don't have any."

"She has brown hair. Green eyes. The same color as his." Tobias nodded over to my uncle, *his* father. "I haven't seen her in years, so I can't say much else."

"Scars around her wrists," I said, my voice no more than a whisper. I shut my eyes before opening them again to see Tobias' entire demeanor change.

"From the chains?"

My entire body shook. I gave him a quick nod before taking a deep breath to steady myself.

"Journey, did you see a girl before we left?"

Her hesitant gaze met Tobias' as she crossed her arms over her chest again. Her voice softened when she spoke to him, and my uncle and I shared a fleeting glance.

"Remember when you asked me how I was able to steal the keycard?" Tobias nodded slowly, eyeing her suspiciously. "And I told you to forget about it because we didn't have time for explanations?"

"And I knew you were stalling, and I reminded you that we told each other everything."

Her bottom lip trembled, and it was like going back in the past. Instead of seeing this new, raw version of her, I saw the girl that I'd found with her wrists slit, lying in the middle of the courtyard. So innocent-looking and vulnerable. "Well, I cornered Hank, did something to...distract him, and stole his card. He was the easiest target. So easily swayed. But right before I left the room he was in, I saw a girl. He was about to give her an injection. I'd never seen a girl down there before. I thought it was weird, and I asked who she was, but he blew me off, and my goal was getting us out, and I knew we didn't have much time."

"Journey, what did she look like?"

My uncle asked that question as Tobias and I shared the same blank expression. There was a goddamn war happening in the thick of my brain, and I couldn't form sentences as it fabricated images of Gemma inside that place.

"Not good. She...she looked bad. There were marks around her neck like she'd been choked, some cuts on her face. It looked like her head had bled at some point, too." I climbed to my feet. "I didn't get a good look at her. It was a quick glance, but...her hands were tied behind her back. There was blood on her gown."

"Where at? Where was the blood?"

Journey bit her lip, glancing away from Tobias. "Where do you think?"

"I'm not waiting. I'm going to get her." I stormed to the door with Tobias hot on my heels.

"I can get us in. I'll be enough of a distraction for them. Let's go."

"And what's the plan?" My uncle rushed after us, and I didn't know Tobias at all, but we were instantly on the same side, working together. We were going to get Gemma, and no one was getting in the way.

A blur of dark-blonde hair whizzed in front of us. Journey reached up to her tiptoes and grabbed onto Tobias' shirt. "Do not go back there, Tobias! You promised me that once you were out, you were never going back! No matter what! Not even for revenge!"

His hands landed on her arms gently as he pushed her out of the way. "That was before I knew my sister was there. I've spent four years trying to get back to her. I've spent four fucking years in that place, allowing them to break me over and over again just so I could finally fool them and get the fuck out. Nothing will stop me. Not even you."

"Tobias!" she shouted, tears rolling down her cheeks. "Don't go back in there."

My uncle entered the hallway from his office, his phone pressed to his ear. "I can't stop them." He paused, glancing at the three of us. "Isaiah and...Gemma's brother. He just showed up. He's...he's been at the Covens this whole time."

"Tobias!" Journey stepped in front of him again as he began to shift forward. His jaw flexed, and he heaved a heavy sigh, not even bothering to hide his agitation.

"Journey. I said I would come here with you and make sure you were safe. After that, I was going to find my sister. For once, fate was on my side. I'm being led right to her! Now please get out of my way."

"Remember what they did to you! You can't go back there. They'll kill you if they know you aren't what they thought you were."

He scoffed. "I'm already fucking dead, Journey."

And with that, her hands fell as hurt covered her features. Tobias glanced at me, and I nodded, and we both stepped around her.

"Isaiah." My steps faltered as I heard Cade bellow down the hall. "Is everything set in motion? My dad just called and said your father is on his way to meet with Ric—"

There wasn't a single sound to be heard. I couldn't even hear Jacobi on the other line with Uncle Tate. The doors to St. Mary's were open, and not even the cool night air could lessen the tension inside this entryway.

I glanced over my shoulder and saw Cade standing there, hands down by his sides with his face free of emotion. It was as if he'd seen a ghost, too, and to be honest, Journey was a ghost to us.

"Journ."

Tobias flung his dark hair over his cut eyebrow. He slowly angled his head to Cade, and I saw murder in his eyes.

Cade sliced his attention over to Tobias, and I could feel the tension rise. "Who are you?"

"Are you Cade?"

Journey stayed completely silent as my uncle began talking to Jacobi on the phone again. "We're on our way. Yeah, yeah. Okay. I got it. I'll call you when we're at the spot. Do you have eyes on Carlisle? Cade just said that Carlisle is on his way. I'm assuming to meet Richard regarding his shift in business partners."

Cade stepped closer. "Yeah, I'm Cade. Who are you?"

Right there. That sick grin that covered Tobias' face proved to me at that exact moment that he knew more about Journey than we wanted. His feet took him over gracefully, like he was on the hunt for prey.

"Tobias," Journey warned, taking a step forward. But it was too late. Tobias' arm came back, and he sucker punched Cade without even a flinch of emotion. Blood instantly rushed, and Cade's entire gaze turned dark. He turned toward Journey, but she quickly glanced away, looking afraid instead of ashamed. *Huh.*

I quickly spun all the way around and rushed over to Tobias. "We don't have fucking time for this!" I got in between them. "Let's go. You two can have your WWE match later. It doesn't matter right now."

And with that, we all left St. Mary's behind, knowing we were walking right into a gunfight.

———

THE AIR in my uncle's car was suffocating. The windows felt like the walls inside a prison. No one spoke. Not a single word. Journey stayed behind, and although she had put up a fight, I could see the relief settle when Tobias pulled her aside and spoke quietly into her ear, getting her to agree in the end.

I wasn't sure what would be waiting at the Covens when

we showed up. Jacobi and his team were already there, setting up invisible parameters along with ATF. They'd been working together to take down my father and his crew for quite a while now, which made me wonder if they'd been following me, too, at some point. Although I wasn't the one who carried out the sales, I'd still been involved and had been to the Covens multiple times in the near and distant past. None of that really mattered, though. The only thing on my mind was Gemma. Once I got her out of there and safe, then we could worry about Richard and my father, along with their gun-running business scheme.

That was, if I made it out alive.

If something went sideways and my father slipped out undetected—because he was notorious for being invisible— he would come after me. He would do nothing but hunt me down and kill me. After all, his other persona went by *The Huntsman.*

"So, you know my sister."

I kept my face straight, looking out the windshield. My uncle drove, Cade sat up front for obvious reasons, Brantley sat to my right, and Tobias to my left. We were crammed, and it did nothing but heighten my already rising blood pressure.

"Yeah."

"What is she like now?"

The car turned in jerky movements as my uncle followed the GPS. Jacobi gave him a different location to head to so we were inconspicuous when we arrived, and if we didn't show up at the Covens in the next few minutes, I would open the door and walk there myself. This wasn't the route we usually took.

"At first, she was kind of snappy with me." My lips wanted to curve upward despite the hole in my chest.

Tobias' head whizzed over to me. "She was?"

I nodded solemnly. "Yeah. She seemed annoyed with me, and she was determined to stay on track without anyone poking into her business. She was guarded." My fist clenched over my lacrosse shorts. I still hadn't changed from earlier when we were about to get on the bus for the away game. "For good reason. She was independent. Determined. Strong."

My uncle caught my eye in the rearview mirror, but I looked away.

"But she eventually trusted you? And told you things?"

I tasted blood in my mouth and truly felt sorry for Tobias. He seemed broken, and the curiosity that had piqued in his voice seemed to turn to guilt at the last second—a hopeful guilt, but still guilt.

I nodded. "Yes, she did."

"Does that mean she found out Richard's plans? That he was going to make her his wife? Force her to play make-believe in that fucked-up house he was so proud of. He told me he was going to—"

"Why aren't we there yet?" I interrupted Tobias because everything he was saying was making my anger spike. I was becoming antsier as the road became narrower. I could sense my uncle's anxiety, too, like he was thinking the same thing I was.

Tobias glanced out the window, and Brantley did the same.

"*Tate*." I didn't call him Uncle, and his mouth formed a straight line.

"I don't know, Isaiah." The car suddenly came to a stop, and he pulled his phone closer and started to zoom in on the map.

"He doesn't want me there," I interjected, realizing that we were going in the wrong fucking direction. "Jacobi is controlling and..." I pushed back on the small amount of despair I felt. "Protective. He was always so protective, which was why it was so hard to believe that he'd actually left me. He doesn't want me there. Turn the fucking car around."

My uncle muttered a string of curse words under his breath as he whipped the car around and flew down the same road that we were already on. The center console was opened next as his left hand stayed glue to the wheel. I caught the glint of a small black pistol and nodded in approval.

CHAPTER SEVENTY-NINE

GEMMA

"The Huntsman is on his way, along with his two right-hand men." Richard's laugh made my ears ring. "They'll feel right at home here, yeah?"

I stared at him, feeling so much hate and dread swimming around my head. I was no longer dizzy. The second time I'd woken up, my head wasn't spinning. It hurt, but the room was actually standing upright for the first time since I'd arrived—I thought.

Time was confusing, just like it had been when I was in the basement with Richard all those times.

"Isaiah will be here sooner than him, I bet." Bain's smug smile burned a hole through my stomach. I'd always had a small fraction of hope that he wasn't as terrible as he acted. But I was wrong. I was so wrong about so many things.

"Good. I can't wait to get my hands on him. And you'll take care of his father? Is your father coming, too? I really couldn't care less about The Huntsman and his little minions now that I have a new seller, but a deal is a deal."

Bain nodded. "My father is leaving it up to me."

Richard's eyebrows raised in approval. The conversation suddenly switched from murder and illegal firearm deals to talking about a father being proud of his son. "I have to say, I was nervous about switching vendors, but the local police have been whispering to me that ATF is on The Huntsman's tail." He elbowed Bain, and he smiled, although it didn't reach his eyes. "I have local and county on my payroll, so they give me all the details. Switching to you and your father has been a bit of a blessing."

Richard's stare pinned me to my spot against the wall, and I did everything I could not to flinch under his scrutiny. "I wouldn't have known about Gemma's little escapades, either, if it weren't for you."

There was something stirring inside my belly. Hate was crowding my head, and there wasn't really any point in playing his games any longer. "Oh, you mean spreading my legs for Isaiah Underwood? How do you know I didn't just do it to spite you?" Because at first, a part of me did. A tainted part of me wanted to do everything I could to take back the control that my *uncle* had taken from my grasp. I wanted to prove to myself that he didn't rule me.

"Keep talkin'. It'll make later that much sweeter for me. It's obvious you like it when I punish you, so I won't even feel bad when I bend you over and spank you."

A flush crept up my neck like a fire-burning trail. I tingled all over and *almost* climbed to my feet. For what? I wasn't sure. Richard was bigger than me and stronger, and not to mention, my arms were tied.

My teeth ground along one another, and my mouth was so dry I was surprised I could even form words, but with the adrenaline flowing through my blood, I felt like I could do pretty much anything—like take Richard down and warn Isaiah before he got too close.

I didn't have a plan. I was flying blindly, and I hated that. I'd acted without a plan in the past, and it only ended terribly, but even when I had a plan set in place, it didn't mean that things would go smoothly.

I mean, look at me now. Tied up, beaten, violated, and broken.

That wouldn't stop me, though. Broken pieces were that much sharper.

A head peeked in the white padded room, and Bain and Richard both pushed off from the wall, pausing their totally mundane conversation as if a girl wasn't tied up in the corner.

"Sir, your guests have arrived." My head tilted when I recognized the man. *That was the guy who gave me the injection.* His eyes flew to mine momentarily, and I realized that what I saw earlier was real. There was a girl in here. A girl who stole his keycard. Hope sprung to my very being. *Maybe she would come back for me.* "I would also like to inform you that a patient is missing."

Richard's hands went to his waist. "A patient? From our floor?"

The man's head fell in defeat, and I casually looked over to Bain. My breath halted when I saw him staring directly at me. My brows crowded as something passed behind his eyes. *Was he trying to tell me something?*

"Both, sir. Two patients are missing. One from the psych floor, and one from this one."

"Bain." Bain quickly took his gaze from mine. "Stay in here until I yell for you. I'm going to step out with Hank here and bring The Huntsman in. I guess he arrived before his son. I may be the one to take care of him, depending on how quickly our conversation moves."

"He'll tell me everything you say, so if you want to keep the punishment to a minimum later, I suggest you keep quiet," Richard threatened me.

Then, he walked out into the hall, keeping the door slightly ajar.

Bain's back was to me, and my heart raced. My wrists ached, and my head suddenly pounded as if it were only blocking out the pain while Richard was nearby. My body refused to show any kind of vulnerability while near him.

"How could you do this?" I whispered, shutting my eyes for a moment to ease the throbbing. "Was it all worth it? Did you know who I was from the beginning? Did you plan to use me just to take a customer from Isaiah's father?"

"Gemma, shut up," Bain seethed, still standing near the door. His head turned slightly to meet my stare, and the face he was making didn't match the evil notch in his tone. His amber eyes were pleading. There was a small indent in between his brows, and suddenly, I was back to wondering if this was real. "Shh," he mouthed, and I felt my resolve fall.

Don't trust.

The small voice inside my head was back, and she was pounding against my skull. That leery feeling of trusting someone boomed like thunder, and I listened to it.

"How long have you known who I was? When did it finally click?"

Bain's shoulders tensed. I could see the hardened curves even through his uniform shirt. Did he come here in a hurry? Did he come with Richard after I was taken? I bet Isaiah trashed every last room, trying to find him.

"Did he take Sloane, too? Did you know that you were not only sending Isaiah to his death, but me, too? Do you know what it's like to live with someone like that? Do you know how hard it is to please someone you want dead?"

I swore I saw his head nod, but our attention went back to the door. There were voices outside now. They were muffled, but I could hear the low murmurs. One of them was as familiar to me as Richard's. *Isaiah's father.* His voice had lived inside the deepest parts of my memories. He was the one who had nearly raped me when he caught me just outside the back door to this psychotic place. If Richard knew that Isaiah's father had touched me the way that he did, he would kill him on the spot. Or maybe he wouldn't. Maybe he would play with him like he liked to play with me. Richard liked to taunt and tease. It was always a cat-and-mouse game with him, except he would keep one mouse alive forever.

And that was me.

Their laughter carried into the room through the slight opening of the door. I almost screamed out, but I wasn't sure I could. My voice was hardly above a whisper no matter how hard I tried to speak up. I wasn't even sure how Bain could hear me from across the room. My throat was like sandpaper. Too hoarse to make much of a sound.

I felt a tear escape from the corner of my eye at the thought, and I pursed my lips. *Why was I crying?* Negative thoughts started to peg me, and fear began to dance in the distance. My resolve was falling. The helplessness that surfaced made me double over. *Isaiah.* He was about to get caught in the crossfire, and I would have to live with that guilt for the rest of my life. This was my fault. There wouldn't have been this big of a target on his back if I'd never allowed him to kiss me or touch me...or love me. I should have stayed away like my fear had warned me to do.

Richard's voice grew closer, and my head flew up, my body locking down all emotion I allowed myself to feel. "Yes, I assume you think I called you here to discuss our business arrangement, but that's not exactly the case. We share a mutual problem, Carlisle."

Richard's voice faded, as if he were walking past my room, and I jumped when Bain quickly spun around. He was over to me in seconds, and I pressed my tender back up against the wall when he dipped down in front of me.

"We don't have much time."

"What?" I asked, frustrated that I hardly had a voice. "What are you doing?"

My wrists were jerked, and I let out a whimper. *Oh my God.* They had to have been torn to shreds. The rope felt worse than the chains.

Bain's steely gaze collided with mine, and I hated to admit it, but his voice was soothing. I had no idea why, but he felt safer to me than anyone else so far in this place. "You've always been good at games, Gemma. Play along so we both make it out of here alive. Keep your arms behind your back so he doesn't know I loosened them, and don't run until—"

I squinted with confusion, but Bain quickly stood up when the door swung open. He turned around, and I bit my lip to keep myself from looking startled. My body trembled from the shock and skepticism, but as soon as I saw Richard, I straightened my shoulders and played along like Bain had said.

"What are you doing?" Richard asked as he made his way over to us.

Bain stepped aside. "She was about to scream because she heard people walk past the door. I was telling her to be quiet."

Richard eyed him curiously. He glanced at me, and I glared back when I felt the contact from his hand on my arm. "Well, it's show time. There's movement outside, and I have a good feeling that it's your little boyfriend." He directed the last part of his sentence to me, and not only did dread hit me, but so did hope.

"Where are you taking her?" Bain asked, stepping beside Richard. "Things might get hairy. Isaiah will not come unprepared now that he knows she is here."

Richard threw his head back and laughed. "I'm going to have her watch as I kill him. The ultimate punishment. Maybe now she'll learn that she is mine, and no one else is allowed to touch her." His eyes were like black holes on his face, and I pulled back in horror.

"You want to kill The Huntsman before or after?" he asked Bain, bypassing my horrific expression. *It was now or never.*

I didn't wait for Bain's answer. I saw the open door and the opportunity that I would never be given again. I easily ripped free from Richard's hold because he wasn't expecting it. I fought through the throbs and aches in my body and took off through the opening, dragging my heavy feet with me. *Isaiah.* I had to warn him. I wasn't sure what Bain was up to, but I knew, without a doubt, that Isaiah was about to die by the hands of Richard because of me, and I would fight with everything I had to change his fate.

The hallway was long and bare of anything. The memories of when I was younger tried to break through my resolve, but I was good at throwing walls up, and that was exactly what I did. Each time my hand hit the hard surface as I half-ran/half-stumbled down the hall, another wall would build in my head. I took a left when I got to the end and didn't look back to see if Richard was coming after me, because I knew he would be. In the deepest pits of my brain, I knew my way around this hall, and just as I tried to put walls up to block out the past, there was an instinctual part of me that was trying to tear them down, too.

I'd drawn this before. My memories had been a map of this building—it was the last place that I'd seen my mother—and I was finally going to use it.

"Where is it?" I whispered, heart racing and mind spinning. "Where is the fucking door?"

"Gemma! You cannot escape. You might as well stop

running." Richard's voice was distant, and it gave me the motivation to keep going farther. If he thought I would stop running just by his command, he was even more dense than I thought.

There were loud sounds coming from somewhere close by, grunting and yelling, but it was too muffled to hear with the pounding in my ears. I spun around in a circle, coming to a standstill as Richard popped up at the end of the hall. It was like something out of a horror film. The hallway was bright, and he crept down the length of it like the Grim Reaper. There was an obvious glint in his eye, showing that he enjoyed the chase. *Shit!*

Loud bangs echoed, and I covered my ears to drown out the sound. My back hit the far wall, and there was nowhere to go. I was cornered. *Where was the fucking door? The door was supposed to be here!* In fact, there weren't any doors at all. None. Just one long, skinny hallway with stark-white walls that seemed to go on forever. Did I remember it wrong? Did my five-year-old memory make up a map inside my head to allow me to think there was ever a way out? Did I create some alternate version of this place to drown out the real one? Was I truly trapped? And where was Bain?

"Did you hear that?" Richard shouted as he continued to walk toward me. I almost fell to my knees. "Three gunshots means three men are currently dead. Your boyfriend's father just met his maker." Richard laughed, and it was like being back in his house, sitting across from him at the dinner table as his mother would place hot food in front of us before rushing back to the group home. He was easygoing, like he had the world in his hands. And to him, he probably did. He'd corrupted so many people and had been changing fates by slamming his gavel on the judge's bench for as long as I'd known him. He thought he was the almighty. Untouchable.

"Go to hell!" I roared, which came out like a screeching

whisper. I tasted the salt on my lips from my tears, and I quickly pushed them away, pausing at the sight of my wrists. *Oh my God.* They were torn, and I couldn't tell which was fresh blood and which was dried.

"You think I'm destined for hell? After all that I've given you over the years? Stability, love, steady direction, protection. I've nurtured you, Gemma." My body flattened against the wall as he grew closer, and I didn't know what to do. Fear was wracking my insides, and I knew that if I tried to run around him, he'd catch me. I was looking death right in the eye.

I would die by his hands one day. Maybe not physically, but emotionally, I would be dead.

"Gemma!" My chest rocked as I stifled a sob. That sounded like Isaiah's voice inside my head, urging me to fight a little longer. But this was it. There was no other choice now. The hope I'd felt a little while ago was diminished as I stood alone in the hallway, staring at Richard with a clearer head than before.

"Don't kill him," I whispered, breaking down and meeting my resolve. "I'll do what you want, if you spare him." I swallowed roughly, wincing at the pain it caused. "If you let Isaiah live, I'll do everything you ask. But if you don't, I will scream every second of every day. I'll fight you every step of the way. I will never ever be your wife and play family with you, if you kill him." The thought made me want to vomit. In fact, I felt the burn against my raw throat, but I still kept my chin up and my gaze level.

I knew I was trying to leverage and that it likely wouldn't work.

Richard's hand came up around my throat, and I gasped, beginning to claw at his hands. "You think you can bargain with me? For him?"

I saw the blow before I felt it. My head cocked back and

hit the hard wall behind me, my vision completely vanishing. My legs didn't work, and I couldn't feel the floor beneath me. "You think you have any control here, Emily?"

Emily. He called me Emily. My fingers scratched at his skin, and I felt his flesh beneath my nails. My breath was seizing, and my head was a bomb, exploding with pain. My vision came back in quick jabs, like flashes from a lightning storm. His grip on my neck lessened for a quick second before he squeezed again and shoved me back farther. "Open your fucking eyes when I talk to you. You will watch me kill your little crush, and you'll be sorry you ever let him touch you. I told you the rules, and you broke them. What did I always tell you, Gemma? Good girls don't break rules, and you *are* my good girl."

He shoved me back once more, and I swore every one of my organs jostled on the inside. I wanted to fight back and cry and scream, but my body wasn't acting the way that I needed it to. I could feel the blood dripping over my face and the oxygen leaving my body. *He's going to kill me.*

My heart beat quickly, thumping harder and harder as I tried to stay present. It was the only thing I felt before there was a popping sound, and I suddenly collapsed to the ground.

I fell flat as soon as my knees hit the floor. My head slammed down like a ton of bricks.

My vision was foggy, but I could see Richard lying beside me, writhing around. "You fucking piece of shit! Who are you? You just shot me!"

"If I didn't think sending you to prison was a better idea, that bullet would have gone right in between your eyes. You'll go away for life, Richard. You can't pay off the FBI and ATF."

I groaned, reaching up with a shaky hand and touching my head. It was sticky. *Was my hand sticky? Or my head? Both?* I blinked again, suddenly feeling very cold. Someone in a black

SJ SYLVIS

mask was standing over Richard with a gun pointed at his head. "If I find out that you've touched Journey like you have Gemma, I will fucking kill you with my own bare hands."

Then, his boot raised, and he dropped it down onto Richard's face, silencing every word on the tip of his tongue.

"Bain?" I groaned. *Was that Bain?* It sounded like him.

I felt a light slap to my face, and my eyes opened again. The black mask was moving all over the place, and it was hard to focus. "Keep your eyes open."

Just then, I heard the crash of something, and the person in the mask suddenly stood up. He was there one second, but then he was gone. I turned my head to the left, my head flopped hard, and I cried out. Richard was lying beside me with his eyes shut, and although I felt like I was unable to move, I still tried to get away from him.

"No," I whispered, shoving myself backward, except there was something hard behind me. A wall?

"Gemma!" There was a blur of something dark up ahead. I knew something was coming for me because the dark color stood out in the white hallway.

Wait. Isaiah! I had to make him leave.

"No!" I shouted. "Isaiah...ru...run."

But then, my face hit the floor again, and it was dark.

CHAPTER EIGHTY

ISAIAH

IT WAS CHAOS. A heavy bout of turmoil seemed to blast me from behind, but I kept moving forward. My feet slapped against the glossy tiled floor, and although I'd been in this place before, it all felt so foreign to me because my mind was centered on one thing: the small body lying at the end of the hall that I'd just watched crash to the ground in a heap of blood with my name on the end of her lips.

There was a lot of blood. I zeroed in on it, and the panic hammered through my skin like the bullets I could hear at my back.

I wasn't sure who was shooting: the enemy or the rescuer. I didn't care as long as I got to her. It was selfish, but I was man enough to admit that.

Jesus Christ. My knees hit the ground as I bypassed an unconscious Richard Stallard. If we were in any other situation and Gemma wasn't lying in a pool of red blood, I would have pulled my gun out and killed him right then, but she outweighed any amount of anger that I felt. My heart was in my hands, beating for her and only her, and it canceled out every single thing going on around me.

"Gemma," I gasped. My face was wet, and my hands were shaking. I was always in control until it came to her. Even when I had found Journey bleeding in the courtyard last spring, I'd had my head straight on my shoulders as I picked her up and called an ambulance. I was worried but controlled. With Gemma, I was fucking lost.

Her limp body felt like a feather in my arms as I rushed down the hall, going past the FBI and ATF like they were completely invisible. They ran past me with their guns pointed, and I ran past them with my eyes set on the door.

"Get me a fucking ambulance!" my voice rang through the raging chaos, and Tobias and my uncle, who were two steps behind me when we'd entered the Covens, stopped dead in their tracks at the sound of my demand. Tobias' mouth fell, and the hard shell that he'd formed around himself from the second he stepped in my uncle's office an hour and half ago was shattered like glass.

They rushed over to me as everyone went in the opposite direction. Tobias' hand came up to wipe at his face, but he didn't dare touch her. "*Gemma*, what did he do to you?"

There were marks all over her body. Bruises and blood and her fucking wrists. I *almost* turned on my heel and went back down the hall to grab Richard by his throat, but I didn't. Gemma needed help—right fucking now.

We were back outside a second later, and both Gemma's brother and my uncle were beside me. "Jacobi! Where the fuck is Jacobi? I need an ambulance."

Everything had been a blur from the moment we had gotten here. I went into the side door of the Covens before the FBI and ATF. I didn't know it until I heard my brother's voice from behind, telling me to stand down, but I didn't listen. Neither did my uncle, Tobias, Brantley, or Cade. We stormed the place. Brantley, Cade, and Tobias went in one direction, looking for the guards that should have been there, and then it seemed, seconds later, we had SWAT at our backs.

For all I knew, shit could have still been going down inside the Covens. I wouldn't know, though, because as soon as I grabbed Gemma, I did what I intended to do.

The mist in the air did nothing but add to the sweat glistening on my skin as I ran with Gemma in my arms toward the sight of my older brother wearing his FBI jacket.

"Jacobi, I need a fucking ambulance!" I didn't even recognize the sound of my voice. I felt a heavy hand on my shoulder as Jacobi looked down at Gemma and pushed us toward flashing lights. He pulled his radio up and mumbled something about needing medical attention right away, and then Gemma was ripped from my arms, and Jacobi was in my face, forcing me backward.

"Let them take care of her, brother!" His eyes were the same color as my mom's, and it split me right down the middle. I glanced behind his shoulder and watched as two paramedics started working on Gemma, feeling for a pulse, opening her eyes with a small flashlight and then slamming the doors and turning their sirens on.

"No!" I pushed at Jacobi as his fingers dug into my chest. Tobias and my uncle were holding my arms back as I thrashed. "Let me go with her! I have to go with her. She can't be alone!"

"She is safe, Isaiah. I promise you. She is safe with them." Jacobi's pleads flew into my ears, but it did nothing to settle me. Nothing was getting through the adrenaline and panic.

"How do you know?" That came from Tobias, and I could tell he was just as irritated as I was. "Do you know how many fucking dirty cops there are in the world? Do you know how many men knew about this place and did nothing to stop it?

Do you know how many men were fucking *created* here? How
can we trust anyone?"

Jacobi's hands left my chest, and my fists clenched by my
sides as I stared down the darkened road. The flashing lights
were only at my back now instead of at my front. *I'm going
after her.*

"I would never send her with someone I didn't trust. I will
send some of my trusted men to the hospital. You can go
there now. I don't want you near your father."

Our father. He meant our father. "He's still alive?"

He nodded. "Three shots went off right before you flew
through the side door. My men were already on their way
down the stairs. They went through the psych unit to secure
it first. Your father, along with Cade's and Brantley's all had
flesh wounds. They were trying to flee, along with some
guards, but we got them." Jacobi looked at my uncle. "Take
them and go."

"I want to stay."

That came from Tobias, and my back stiffened. "What?"

There was a cloud behind his blue eyes, something dark
and troubled. "I trust you to keep my sister safe. She'll want
to see you when she wakes."

If. If she wakes.

The thought did not escape me once, and the pain that
came with it radiated all the way down to my heels and back.

"That's good. We need you to stay. We have questions,
and I think you'll be able to answer them."

"I'll answer anything you want as long as you let me see
Richard. Dead or alive."

Murder was in his tone, but nonetheless, Jacobi nodded
and inched his head to everything unfolding behind us.
Tobias turned without saying a word, and I could tell that my
uncle wanted to go after him, but the second he stepped a
foot forward, Tobias glanced back. "She needs to know you

are her father. She needs to know there is one sane person left in our family."

My uncle stopped mid-step as Jacobi interjected. "I'll have an officer escort you to the hospital, along with Cade and Brantley. They're already with Special Agent Gibbons. *A bunch of fucking teenagers swarming the Covens*," he mumbled the last part under his breath and then pulled his radio and began spouting things off as we watched Tobias head toward a group of men and women all wearing the same FBI gear my older brother was wearing.

Jacobi looked at me for a painfully long second, something passing between us that I was unable to sort through with my mind somewhere else. He nodded. I nodded back. And then my uncle and I were both in the back of a squad car, on our way to see Gemma.

To see if she was alive.

———

THE DOCTOR WAS SPEAKING to my uncle about Gemma, although it took a lot of coaxing and explaining.

"Gemma is my student—no, sorry. She is my daughter. But I just found out that she is my daughter."

"The man she lived with abused her."

"He said he was her uncle, but they were not related. He has had her in his custody for her entire life, but it was not formally legal."

"Yes. Judge Stallard."

"He did this to her!"

Finally, Special Agent Gibbons stepped forward and flashed a badge and corroborated on everything, and the doctor finally gave us an update.

"Medically induced coma."

"Possible brain injury."

"Rape kit."

"Severe trauma."

"We need to let her heal and watch her closely. Her body has been through a lot."

I stood there with my arms down by my sides, feeling as if my entire world had been put on hold. The adrenaline was slowly leaving my bloodstream, and the shock was setting in. My legs weren't the least bit steady, and my arms quaked. My face was wet, and my chest felt cracked wide open. If I could take her place, I would. In a heartbeat. She'd been cleaned up for the most part and placed in a clean gown. The blankets were pulled up, so I walked a little closer and began pulling the cotton sheet down so I could hold her hand. I wanted her to know that someone was here. That I was here. She looked so fragile, but I knew she was the furthest thing from it.

"Sir, you can't do that! You really shouldn't even be in here."

Fuck off.

"Let him." I paused at the sound of my older brother's voice and rolled my eyes as he began pulling out his badge, guiding the nurse away for a moment to discuss the situation. It amazed me how pulling a badge out could sway people in different directions. Some people had more power than others, and if that landed in the wrong hands, things like *this* happened—where people got fucking hurt, when they didn't deserve it all, because someone else held the power.

My finger rubbed softly on the white gauze wrapped around Gemma's wrist, and my throat grew tight. I shut my eyes as her beautiful face floated into my head. The sassy look she'd given me on the day I met her. The way her features were pulled in tight as she yelled at me for making the school think something had happened between us in the art supply closet during that first week. How excitement shined bright in her green eyes when we darted through the forest with something much more than attraction pulling us together. It all seemed so trivial now, so innocent and insignificant given everything we'd been through, but there wasn't a moment spent with Gemma that was insignificant. We had no idea the shit we were up against that first time I kissed her. I hadn't known how deep it all truly went.

And I had no idea that she would be able to crawl under my skin and bring to life my deepest, darkest fears. She proved to me that I had true insecurities lying underneath my guarded exterior, and one of the biggest threats was that I would bring harm to someone that I loved because of my choices. I thought I was doing right by her, and in the end, she still ended up here.

There were victories, and there were defeats.

And if she didn't wake up, there would be no victory in this. Nothing would matter anymore. Not my father or his entire empire as it came crashing to the ground. Not Richard or the punishment he would be given and the justice that came with it. Nothing mattered but this moment right here.

Gemma and I were destined to burn from the start, but it felt like I was the only one burning alive.

CHAPTER EIGHTY-ONE

GEMMA

I COULDN'T REMEMBER ANYTHING, and that was so infuriating. Most of my life, I'd been pushing away the dark thoughts and memories that tried to sneak up on me, but now, I was trying like hell to actually remember something, and nothing was coming to mind.

What was the last thing I remembered?

Isaiah? Coming to my room to say goodbye before the game?

I felt my eyes moving behind my closed eyelids as I strained to hear the sounds. Fear was holding me back and blocking things out. I was familiar with the feeling that was nestled deep in my belly. The twisting and bundling of nerves that begged me to keep my eyes closed as I fought to make sense of what was going on.

Richard.

There were beeping sounds that were gaining traction in my ears. They became more persistent as my thoughts jumped in several different directions. *The Covens.* I was at the

Covens. Oh my God. Have they hooked me up to a machine? Was that the beeping? Maybe to keep me sedated and to feed me more drugs?

My eyes flung open. "Isaiah." Did he ever show up? Where did Bain go? Did Richard get to Isaiah?

Things were happening too fast, and I knew I needed to breathe, but I couldn't. I glanced down quickly and saw I was wearing a medical gown. I pulled the covers off my legs next, and I winced at the bruises for a quick second before flipping on my side and clamoring to the floor with a loud thud. Something fell off my finger that held a wire, but the only thing I could focus on was being on the ground.

"Ugh," I groaned, feeling stiff in places that I didn't know existed. My fingers hit the cool tile, and I saw more wires and tubes coming from my arm that trailed to a shiny pole that held something in a clear bag. *Drugs?* I had to get out of here. I pushed myself up on two shaky arms and ignored the bandages around my wrists. I felt weak, too weak to fight Richard if he came here, but maybe, just maybe, I could get to that door and...what? What was I going to do?

My knees wobbled on the hard surface as I began crawling. I heard voices. I pushed past everything that was scheming in the back of my head, telling me to be afraid, but instead, I got to my feet. I hung tightly onto the pole that was following me around like a little shadow.

"Help," I whispered through clenched teeth. My voice was still gritty sounding. My hand landed on the doorknob, and I realized that the room I was in looked nothing like the room from before. I remembered it being white, but this room wasn't white. It was a light blue.

I shook my head, surprised that it didn't hurt that much. The color of the room didn't matter. I needed to get the hell out of here.

The door flung open on its own with my hand on the

knob. I instantly fell forward, crashing to the ground with the metal pole clunking over the tiles. "No!" I jerked back, and my eyes widened at the face standing over me. "Just let me go! Pretend you didn't see me! At least let me warn him!"

"Whoa, whoa." The guy standing over me had beautiful, soft-blue eyes. His face was free of any markings, and he didn't look like any of the men that I'd seen after Richard had taken me. There was something alive in his gaze. Not the dead-to-the-world look that I couldn't forget if I tried. The longer I stared into this person's gaze, the more memories started to surface.

I still wasn't sure where I was, but I didn't think I was at the Covens anymore.

"Is Isaiah okay?" As soon as the words were out, I wanted to suck them back in. What if he wasn't? What if he did show up like Richard had said and...and... My hand flew up to my mouth. "Did he kill him?" And what about Sloane? Then the thought came of my brother and how Richard had told me that he'd killed him long ago.

I shuddered, my shoulders caving. My mind was everywhere. Too many emotions were pulling at me like puppet strings, and I didn't know what to say or do.

The blue-eyed man dropped down to my level. "You're going to be okay, Gemma." He touched my arm, and I pulled back instantly, and then my attention was drawn to the left as I heard something fall to the ground. A Styrofoam cup had crashed, and a black liquid spilled everywhere like tiny droplets from a rain puddle. I traveled up a set of long legs, and it was as if my eyes had truly opened for the first time since waking up.

His gasp landed on my ears as he rushed down the hall, sliding to his knees and picking me up in his arms. I was shaking. My teeth were clattering.

"*You're okay. You're okay. You're okay.*" My head was pressed to Isaiah's chest, and my senses sprung wide open. "It's okay. Just breathe. Take a breath, baby."

His head turned up at the sound of the man who had found me. "I'll get a nurse and her fath—" There was a hesitation. "I'll be back."

The footsteps faded, and I pulled back slightly, taking Isaiah's scent with me. "Isaiah. Where am I?" Our eyes met, and relief fell over me, but I was too afraid to let myself feel it. I shut my eyes and buried my head into his chest again. *Everything was fine. I was fine. I was alive, and he was alive.* "Please tell me that we are far away from that place. *Please.*"

"We're in the hospital, and I promise you that you are safe now. Damn, you're shaking. I need you to calm down, okay? They'll sedate you again, and fuck, just stay with me this time." Isaiah's hands ran down my arms, and I shuddered as things started to come back faster. *Richard had me by the throat.* My fingers uncurled from Isaiah's shirt once again. "Isaiah, where is Richard? He's going to kill you. He knows everything! He told me he had pictures of us...from—" I gasped, feeling panicky. I rubbed at my neck. "From Bain. *Bain!* He was luring you to the Covens! They're going to kill your dad, too! I heard him. Bain was there, and he...untied me?...and then..." I stopped as Isaiah stole my hand from my neck, replacing mine with his. His fingers brushed over the skin as he finished my sentence.

"I know. I know everything." His head dropped as if he were too guilty to look at me. "There are some things you don't know, but all that matters is that you're alive and in my arms for the first time in weeks."

"Weeks?" I swallowed with a dry throat. "I think I need water."

"Come on, I've got you." I peered up at Isaiah, and there were so many things hidden behind his blue eyes. The blue eyes that I pictured when I was taken from St. Mary's and shoved into a white padded room. The blue eyes that I pictured every single time I came to from being hit, or drugged, or worse. His thumb gently swiped at my bottom lip as it trembled, and I smashed them together to keep myself from breaking.

"Don't do that," he whispered. "If you cry, I'll wipe your tears. If you have nightmares, I'll wake you up. If you break down right here in front of me, I will piece you back together. I'm not leaving your side, and you aren't leaving mine, either."

A shaky breath left me as he nodded once, making sure I understood, and then he scooped me up and took me back into the room, scolding a nurse for not coming sooner.

"She finally wakes up, and no one is here to check her vitals. Un-fucking-believable," he grumbled angrily before sitting us both down onto the bed, keeping a hold of me the entire time.

CHAPTER EIGHTY-TWO

ISAIAH

SHE NEVER BROKE her resolve once, even when there were several people in the room, all waiting for her to cry or at least question everything being thrown at her. Anyone else in her situation would have covered their ears and winced at the things coming from Jacobi's mouth, but Gemma was strong.

Stronger than me.

Stronger than anyone I'd ever met before.

The IV was finally taken out of her arm, and there was a slight pinkish hue covering her cheeks that made my stomach dip at the sight. She was beginning to look more like the Gemma I knew, and all I wanted to do was keep her to myself.

She pushed a piece of brown hair behind her ear, showing off how delicate her high cheekbone was. The bruises on her neck were mostly gone now, but they had taken a long time to heal. Every time I caught a glimpse of the fingerprint marks, my vision would turn crimson. I was sure Richard thought he was in a shitty place at the moment and probably couldn't even fathom how a man with his power could end up behind bars, but if he were breathing outside of that metal box, I would take my hands and choke him like he'd choked her.

"So…" Gemma shifted uncomfortably, pushing herself up farther on the bed. It had been quite a few hours since she'd woken, and per the doctor's orders, we were to give her some time before we overwhelmed her with information, but Gemma insisted, and me being me, I advocated for her. She deserved to know everything when she was ready, and if she was ready now, then she was fucking ready.

She had started off at St. Mary's on wobbly feet, but she left on sturdier ones. She didn't shy away from the past any longer. She welcomed it with open arms.

"So…my mom was sent to the group home because she had gotten in trouble with the law? And that was how she met Richard?" Gemma was repeating what Jacobi had told her because it was a clusterfuck.

My uncle—well, not technically my *uncle,* but it was hard not to think of him like that—shifted on the window ledge of the sterile-smelling room, glancing away from Gemma's curious look. "Well, technically, she met Richard when she went for sentencing. He—"

Gemma nodded. "He sent girls to the group home instead of jail. I knew that…I just didn't fully know my mom was one of them. I had suspected a time or two, but from what I remembered when I was little, my mom never really went over to the group home. We lived in the big house. Richard's house."

Uncle Tate's vein was back again, throbbing right there in the middle of his forehead. I knew that, deep down, he felt that it was his fault that Emily had been there. It was a favor from Judge Stallard and the last tie between him and my grandfather. A deal. My grandfather would keep Emily from prison with the help of his ol' pal Judge Stallard, and Uncle

Tate would destroy the incriminating files he had regarding the family business and leave without a word.

It wasn't his fault, though. Although, I knew why he felt that way. It was insignificant at this point. There was so much more that Gemma didn't know.

"Right," Jacobi answered. "From what we've gathered, your mother and Richard had some sort of an affair during her time there, and that would have gone against every ethic and moral that Judge Stallard stood for. So, he kept it a secret, along with you and your brother."

"My mother didn't want to be with him anymore. I remember her telling him no, and he got angry. He said she was mentally unstable and left her at the psych hospital, later saying she had killed herself."

Jacobi nodded again, and I could sense that Gemma was feeling uncomfortable.

I whispered into her ear, "Do you want to take a break?"

Her head shook instantly, so I pulled back and kept a hold of her hand.

"From a psychological viewpoint, Richard seemed to have been obsessed with your mother and with the idea of creating a family with her. When she told him no, his obsession moved to you, and crossing that with an obvious personality disorder along with the different facets of his life..."

"What are you saying?" she asked.

I spoke for my brother. "Richard is fucking crazy."

Gemma laughed. She actually laughed, and her cheeks looked pinker, too. "Um, yeah. I know. But what now?" She looked at Jacobi and suddenly grew serious. "You say you're in the FBI."

He nodded slowly. "We, speaking for the FBI, were working closely with ATF, the Bureau of Alcohol, Tobacco, Firearms, and Explosives, and you seemed to come up on the radar." Jacobi hummed, smiling slightly. "You kind of wrapped everything up for us in a nice and tidy bow, Gemma. We owe you. Not only did we take down one of the biggest illegal gun suppliers in the western hemisphere, we took down their biggest client: Judge Stallard and the Covens, which is wildly popular on the dark web. You were at the center of it all, as complicated as it was."

My brother's half-assed compliment didn't seem to register with Gemma. Her fingers started de-threading the blanket covering our legs, and her nerves were evident. "How many people are on Richard's payroll, though? On the FBI? He has power... I've seen him use it."

I placed my hand on Gemma's, and she stilled, looking up at me, appearing so fucking vulnerable, and I wanted to somehow force it into her head that no one was coming close to her now. "He will not be cut loose, Gemma."

"How do you know that, though? What?" She panicked, looking back at my brother and my uncle—*her father*, which she had no idea about...*yet*. "Is it his word against mine? All the abuse? Who's to say he won't just lie and say I'm crazy like my mother? He's threatened that before! Who's to say I can trust you?"

"Not only do we have him on the abuse, but we have charges relating to the Covens, too. And it isn't just his word against yours..."

Gemma was leery. "What do you mean? Do you have witnesses? Do you have proof of everything he did to me? And I don't even know what *really* went on at the psych hospital...but I can tell you that it wasn't good. The men that came into my room were... What did Richard even have to do with that place? I remember some things that were said and done from when I was younger, but..." She pulled into herself. "The men that I saw in that place were bad people. They..."

My heart thudded to the ground. My uncle visibly tensed, and Jacobi winced. "We know what went on at the psych hospital. Judge Stallard deemed men mentally ill and sent them to the hospital, but instead of treating them for mental illness in the true psych hospital, he..."

Jacobi slowly shifted his attention to me, and I nodded, allowing him to continue. Gemma would tell us when she wanted to stop, but I had a hunch she wouldn't want to.

"He gave those men an option of lessening their sentences for something else in life."

"Like what?"

I answered, staring at the wall. "Gun-runners. Drug-sellers. Hitmen."

Her head snapped to mine. "Hitmen? Like..."

"Professional killers hired on the black market. Yes. That's where Isaiah's father—"

I pointed my finger at Jacobi, correcting him. "Our."

Gemma was already aware that Jacobi was my brother, so she wasn't shocked by this.

"That's where *our* father came into play. He supplied the guns to the Covens for the hitmen. He'd been selling them to Richard for years, thus bringing us all together here today."

"That is not the reason we're here today." Uncle Tate lowered his legs to the ground from the window seat and placed his hands on his knees. I felt the shift in the room and bit my tongue.

"What...what do you mean?" I could hear the exhaustion within Gemma, so I pulled her back, and she rested along my chest, taking a deep breath. *I know, baby. I know.*

My hands rubbed at her bare arms and placed a kiss on her hair.

"You and Isaiah were in the middle of something neither one of you should have had to deal with. You being in Richard's care from birth made you a casualty in a sick game of illegal activities. Not only the abuse that you have suffered but so much more." My uncle turned to me. "And you, being your father's son, had to figure out a way to save the one girl that you loved from not only your future but hers too. You two have been at the center of this the entire time. Like a bridge between two evils."

"I don't know if this..." I started to interject when I felt Gemma shift uncomfortably. She was looking up at me, and I clamped my mouth shut. *She needed to know.*

"I'm not Isaiah's uncle, Gemma."

I grabbed her hand tightly, and she squeezed it right back. "Then who are you?"

His eyes shut briefly. "I'm your father."

CHAPTER EIGHTY-THREE

GEMMA

MY MOUTH OPENED. Then closed. Then opened again. All while the room fell silent. There were four of us in here, but it felt like just me and...Headmaster Ellison...my father.

"Gem." Isaiah's thumb rubbed slow circles over my hand. Headmaster Ellison looked equal parts relieved and horrified.

"I..." My voice was a whisper again, and I cleared my throat, forcing my mouth to move through the emotion straining my vocals. "I don't... I'm confused."

Headmaster Ellison's hands rested over his thighs evenly. His chest rose and stayed for a second before it deflated, and he spilled.

"Your mother and I were a lot like you and Isaiah. We came from completely different backgrounds but were drawn together nonetheless. We were in a sort of secret relationship due to a number of things, but she...helped me through some messed up stuff, and when she got caught in a bad spot—felony theft—I helped her out. Or I thought I was helping. I bargained with my father—or who I *thought* to be my father —Isaiah's grandfather, to help her. Our family had been doing business with the Stallards for a very long time. So, Isaiah's grandfather asked Judge Stallard, *Richard*, for a favor in keeping your mother out of prison, all in exchange for me to leave the family because it turned out I was an orphan, just like your mother was. I'm not an Underwood. I'm not related to Isaiah. And his grandfather knew that from the beginning and wanted me out of the family." Headmaster Ellison's eyes were glossy, and the agony was there, evident on his face, and I felt it just as much. The guilt. He had to have had so much guilt. "I thought I was helping her. I thought I was helping her stay out of prison."

"Did you..." I unclogged my tight throat, looking away. "Did you know she was pregnant with me and Tobias? Did you know who I was the second I showed up at St. Mary's?"

"No!" Headmaster Ellison popped to his feet and walked over to the bed, so I was forced to look up at him. "I tried to talk to your mother after her sentencing, but every time I would try to have contact with her in the group home, I would get shut down. My letters would go unanswered, and eventually, I believed that she just didn't want to talk to me anymore. But I think now I know why. Richard didn't want her to have contact with me or anyone from her past life. He must have seen something in her... Maybe he saw a future with a beautiful young girl who was stuck in a bad spot with two little babies. Maybe he knew I was your father all along. Although, if he had known that, I doubt he would have sent you to me.

"After her sentence ended, I tried to find her again. Ann, Richard's mother, had said that she'd disappeared. I hired private investigators, everything. There was no trail of her. Anywhere."

My head fell in defeat. "That makes sense. There would

be no paper trail when you are no longer alive, and not to mention, Richard is well versed in covering things up. He told Tobias and me that she committed suicide because she was so sick. That's why she left us in the first place. To go to the hospital to get better and...that she killed herself." I slowly raised my head and looked at Jacobi, all while squeezing Isaiah's hand. "That's not true. Richard killed her. Or someone in that place did."

His jaw tensed as he nodded and began scribbling it down in his notebook.

"I'm so sorry, Gemma." I came back and met Headmaster Ellison again. The familiarity of his presence and calmness he always gave me was still there and even more palpable.

"You remind me of Tobias." I bit my lip, squeezing my eyes for a second before opening them back up and taking a deep breath. I pushed up off Isaiah's hard and sturdy chest, suddenly missing the way his heart beat along my back. "From the second I met you, I...you felt so familiar to me. Like I knew you somehow." The realization hit me like a ton of bricks, and I wanted to cry. I really did. There was so much hurt jabbing at me, but one thing was for certain: Headmaster Ellison, my *father*, was not the one at fault. The true evil here was Richard Stallard. All his lies, his cover-ups, his payouts. He was the one who needed to take the blame. All of it.

"It wasn't your fault," I whispered, placing my hand on his. The headmaster's head flew up in surprise. "I know you think you have their blood on your hands, but you don't. It's Richard's fault. Not yours. There were plenty of young girls at the group home that he could have chosen from. Who knows? Maybe this isn't the first time he's become obsessed."

We stayed locked on each other for far too long. My heart hurt, but at the same time, it felt stitched back together. It was banged up, and parts of it would likely never heal. The wounds of losing someone forever would stay, but there were parts of me that were still hanging on. There were parts of me that could care for someone and learn to trust them. I learned that from what I felt for Isaiah.

"Gemma," Jacobi interrupted Headmaster Ellison's and my tense moment. "There is something else that you need to know." He stood up, shifting his attention to Isaiah and then to Headmaster Ellison, which only spiked my blood with more dread.

"Now what?" I asked, feeling as if I were teetering over the edge.

"Like I said, it isn't just your word against his. There are photos that we have collected from the house you grew up in, along with many corroborators who have come forward after the press release on the accusations of Richard, along with those who he tried to bribe and/or pay off. Like a..." Jacobi shuffled through some papers before nodding. "Miss Ann Scova. She was the social worker who had taken on your case after some girls from the group home began speaking up about the *girl in the big house*. That social worker is a tough cookie. Anyway, Richard had tried to pay her to turn a blind eye, but she didn't."

I nodded. "She was the reason I was sent to Wellington Prep. Richard said he had no choice but to send me to an actual school because of a social worker poking around. And then that led to sending me to St. Mary's."

"Yes, and..." Jacobi looked at Isaiah again, and he tensed behind me. I spun around and looked at the wariness pulling along his dark features.

"Gemma, what did Richard say to you about Tobias?" His brows slanted, and his tongue darted out to lick his lips. He pulled himself up higher on my hospital bed and bent a knee, resting his arm on it as I sat in between his legs. "Didn't you tell me that you knew Tobias was still alive? That's why you went to the Covens that one night, yeah?"

My head dropped again, but I thought better of hiding the hurt. Instead, I peeked back up and let Isaiah read my face for what it was. "Richard told me he killed him when I had made a remark. And I know what you're thinking. Why would I believe anything he says? But you didn't see the look in his eye, Isaiah. And it makes sense..." I shrugged, not wanting to believe the truth that had been in the back of my mind for the last several years. "I couldn't find *anything* in that house that was connected to my brother. There were no leads, no clues, nothing. And you even said it yourself: he wasn't at the Covens. Where else would he be?" My heart thrashed, and if the nurse came in here right now and took my blood pressure, I was certain it would be much higher than it was an hour ago. "He killed him."

"Gem," Headmaster Ellison's voice was soft, and like before, I felt calm near him. Almost just as calm as I did with Isaiah. "Your brother is alive."

Chills coated my arms, except this time it wasn't from fear. It was from shock. My heart whacked inside. "He's alive?"

"He's our other witness. There is no way anyone in their right mind could let Richard Stallard walk freely on this earth after the evidence and statements from the pair of you. Even given his judicial stance. There is too much against him now for a cover-up. I won't let it happen."

"Just like you won't let Dad walk either?" That came from Isaiah, but I'd forgotten that his father even had a role in this. Jacobi gave him a look and said something, but I couldn't focus on what he'd said.

Tobias was alive.

My twin brother was alive.

"Do you have him? My brother?" I sat up taller, ignoring

the stiffness in my body. "Is he okay? Where was he? Is he here right now?"

The words were spilling out so fast, and my body was moving quickly as I tried to hop off the bed. Isaiah grabbed onto my waist and pulled me back. "Gemma, take it easy. You're still recovering."

My head turned to him, and I knew that he could see the hope blossoming. "Tobias is alive, Isaiah! My brother is alive."

His lips curved slightly, but there was something sad lingering there too. I knew Isaiah, and I could tell when something wasn't right. "I know, baby. But..."

"But what?"

He sighed, bringing me closer to him as if there wasn't anyone else in the room. I peered up into his blue eyes, and I could see him stalling. "Isaiah, I can handle it. What?"

He chuckled. "Oh, I know you can. I just don't know if I can handle the hurt I'm going to see." My mouth tugged down as he continued. "He's been at the Covens this entire time." He swallowed, licking his lips again. "And...he's working on some things. On himself."

"So..."

"So, he doesn't want to see you...not yet."

My shoulders dropped as hurt crashed and burned around me. *He didn't want to see me?* "Oh."

"Hey, he'll get back on track, okay? He's just..."

"He just wants to be alone right now."

I turned to the headmaster... My father... *Our* father. "Does...he know that you're our father?"

He nodded. "He knows everything."

I nodded in unison with him as I tried to wrap my head around everything. The rollercoaster of emotions and revelations. The ups and down of devastation and hope and then more devastation was making my head hurt again. I didn't know what to say or feel. I should have been grateful that I was alive and sitting beside Isaiah, but now I just felt empty, like my body was locking down emotion because it was just too much.

"Alright. Out." Isaiah pointed to the door as if he read my mind.

I slinked back onto his chest without even realizing I'd done so.

Jacobi stood up, glancing over at me once more. He and Isaiah looked a lot alike, except Isaiah was bad-boy handsome with his coy grin and dark features, and Jacobi was a serene type of handsome. Smooth and put together. Chivalrous. "You are safe now, Gemma. You and Tobias both. Okay? Get some rest." Then, he looked at Isaiah once more and turned around and walked out the door.

Headmaster Ellison patted my leg and slowly began to back away, looking more confused than ever. I felt the same.

"Headma—" I paused. "Ta—" I paused again. *What should I call him?* I shook my head, looking down. "If you talk to my brother, can you just tell him...that..." The vulnerability was so heavy I could hardly speak. "Can you just tell him that I love him? And whatever he's feeling, it's okay?"

His lips gently curved, and the uneasiness that I saw just seconds ago was gone. "I will. Get some rest. I'll be back in a bit."

Once the door shut, Isaiah's hand was on my chin, and he angled my head on his chest to look up at him. His eyes bounced back and forth between mine as his thumb rubbed over my bottom lip again. I was pretty sure it was wobbling. "You are unbelievable. The strongest person I know."

The tears were there, making his face blurry for a second before I blinked them away. I was swimming in everything I'd just been told, and there was shock and fear and a whole bunch of other stuff that was threatening to come out of my mouth, but instead of talking about the fact that my brother was alive, or that I now had a father, I said something that surprised us both. "I love you." Those three little words were the one thing I was sure of in the moment, and it felt good to get them out.

A flicker of shock reached Isaiah, and it was as if everything else just paused for a few seconds. My eyes watered again, and I buried my face back in his chest. "I just wanted you to know that. I didn't say it before, but I felt it. I felt it a long time ago."

"I know. I felt it, too." Then, his arms came around me as his leg popped back down. Mine hooked over his, and we lay like that for so long I thought he might be asleep.

"So now what," I whispered, talking to myself more than anything.

He answered quickly. "Things are going to get messier. We're still stuck in a fucking web. There will be trials. Statements to be made. All of it. My father's entire empire just came crashing down. Some of his people went into hiding, and others are currently being arrested. Richard's name is plastered everywhere, and it's an uproar. The entire state is in shambles."

"What about Jack? And Sloane?"

"They're both okay. I sent Jack to Jacobi before I even knew he was in the FBI, working toward the same goal I was."

I nodded, squeezing him tighter. The future looked even scarier than before, but at least the people I cared about were okay.

"I'll be here no matter what. Okay? We just have to find a new normal."

A small grin covered my face as I tried to lighten the mood. "So, no more hiding underneath the dining hall tables in the middle of the night to reach under my skirt so no one sees us?"

Isaiah's chuckle was abrupt, and my face shook against his chest as he laughed. Somehow, I still managed to let out a light laugh, too.

"Fuck that. I'll have you on top of the table this time. In front of the whole school. Ask me if I care."

I smiled, my cheeks feeling hot, but then a thought occurred to me. "What happened to Bain?" I popped up, and we locked eyes. "He untied me, Isaiah. I think. In that room. He..."

"Don't try to make sense of it."

"Where did he go, though? He was there, and then..."

"He helped us get to you. He had put you there, but he helped get you back after he realized..." He shook his head. "I need you to understand something. Bain won't hurt you. When and if you come back to school, he will be there, but he will not fucking touch you. Okay? Do you trust me? We do not have to worry about Bain."

"Yes, I trust you," I answered swiftly, still stuck on Bain. There was something off about him at the Covens. He wasn't his usual, put-a-knife-in-your-back self. What had happened while I was out the last couple of weeks? *Was Bain the one in the mask after I ran? Did he say those things to Richard? That he would kill him?* What was real and what wasn't?

Isaiah must have sensed that my mind was pulling me again, because the next thing I knew, he was pushing my face closer to his and silencing me with his mouth. His lips covered mine softly, and the things I felt when he kissed me, that had been dormant since I was taken, were suddenly turned back on, canceling out the questions and confusion.

A tiny noise left me as I pushed closer to him. Isaiah's teeth sunk into my bottom lip as he clenched his eyes. He pulled back, and looking into his eyes was like the ocean was pulling me. He drank me in, every inch of my face, especially my lips. "Knock it off, Good Girl."

I smiled.

The twitch of his lips had mine rising higher. He shrugged and said, "Never mind. Don't knock it off." And then he pulled me in again and chased my tongue with his.

CHAPTER EIGHTY-FOUR

ISAIAH

"Go away, Isaiah. She's mine. You've had her to yourself for weeks." Sloane's eyebrow hitched, and there was an evil glint lingering, which was her usual look when it came to me.

My arms were crossed over my uniform as I rested lazily against the far wall of the girls' hallway. It was wild in here at the crack of dawn. Like a fucking zoo. There were girls rushing down the hall with wet hair, and some had green shit on their skin, covering every inch of their face except their eyes. It was frightening, and the excess in estrogen did nothing but make me antsy.

One chick ran past with only a towel on, and when she saw me standing there in a mist of hairspray and perfume, she screamed, and her towel fell. I quickly shut my eyes and pushed forward, running right into Sloane. "She's my girl-friend, Sloane. And yes, I had her for weeks to myself, but she was in a fucking coma. Doesn't really count."

"Does too."

"Oh my goodness, you two! Just let him in, or he'll never

go away. You know how persistent he is." The humor in Gemma's voice made the entire five minutes that I stood in the girls' hallway worth it. In the past, I'd only ever come down here during the late night, even before Gemma. It was a whole new era in the mornings.

"Ugh, fine." Sloane huffed and shut the door behind me, silencing all the catty chatter happening on the outside.

"It's crazy out there," I said, stepping farther into the room. I glanced around their girly dorm and searched for the only person I really wanted to see.

"Says the guy who carried me out of a literal gun fight." Gemma popped out of her bathroom, and it was jarring to see her like this. Her cheeks were painted with a tint of pink, her green eyes brighter than ever. The bags underneath had faded, and it looked as if she had actually gotten some sleep.

I, however, had not. I worried all night long that she would have a nightmare and I wouldn't be there to help her, but she reminded me that she'd been having nightmares and remembering things that she'd forced away for years, and this was no different. Except now, she truly felt safe. Even with Bain here, she said she felt safe. He was still a rat in my eyes, and the Rebels and I would never stop watching him, but he had saved her, and he'd stayed true to his word. So, I would stay true to mine.

Gemma insisted that she get back to classes as soon as the doctor cleared her, despite everything that was unfolding outside of this palatial school. Her name, along with Tobias', had been withheld from the news, and they remained anonymous, so Tate couldn't think of any other reason to keep her from normalcy. If she wanted to come back to school, then she could come back to school.

He'd reminded me that Gemma felt at home here above anywhere else, and it was the perfect place to put her, given that her newfound father also resided here.

Tate—who I now refrained from calling Uncle—had been busy since returning back. There were messes to clean up and explanations to the SMC on his whereabouts—along with mine and Gemma's. And let's not forget the fact that he now had to place two new students at St. Mary's: one being Journey, which was surely going to be the new talk of the gossip blog, Mary's Murmurs, and the other being Tobias—when he was ready.

For now, he stayed away. There was a lot Gemma and I weren't aware of, but I knew that Tate was keeping a watchful eye on him and helping him as much as he could. Tobias was Tate's son, but according to what he'd said to me one night at the hospital when Gemma was still recovering, there may never be a bond between them. There may never be hope for a relationship. Tobias wasn't the same boy he was when Gemma knew him, and Tobias was smart enough to realize that, which was why he was still staying away. I respected that.

And Gemma understood. She knew how damaging trauma could be. But it still hurt her that she hadn't seen him yet. She was quiet about it. Reserved.

But I knew her. I felt her feelings as if they were my own.

Just like I knew that she was nervous for today.

Not because of what had happened over the last few weeks—because, again, no one knew but a few of us. She was nervous because I told her that I was going to pick her up around her waist, place her hot little ass on the dining hall table during breakfast and kiss her senseless in front of everyone because we now had the freedom to do so.

Considering that we were never truly exclusive, I wanted to make a point to show everyone that we were. I explained very calmly that now that she was mine and the dangers that we were faced with no longer hid in the shadows, neither would we.

Gemma was my girlfriend, and the whole fucking lot of St. Mary's would know it. Maybe I was a little possessive, but there was a difference between possessive and controlling. *She was mine for as long as she wanted me.*

"Ready?" I finally asked as Sloane and Gemma packed their bags.

Gemma looked at me out of the corner of her eye, and I winked. "Isaiah, you better not."

"Oh, I am."

She tried to fight a smile, but I saw the cute little way her lips tugged.

"He better not what?" Sloane asked, spraying some perfume on her uniform.

My eyebrows waggled. "I'm markin' my claim."

"You're what?"

Gemma sighed, walking closer to me, but not before shooting me a look. "He said he's going to kiss me in front of everyone to indicate that we are boyfriend and girlfriend."

I shook my finger. "That is not what I said. I said I was going to plop your hot little ass on the dining table and kiss you in front of everyone because I can and I will."

Sloane's lips smashed together as she held back a laugh. "Gemma, your face is so red right now."

"Shut up! Both of you!" She turned back to me. "You know I hate attention."

"But you love me." I winked and grabbed her hand, pulling her toward the chaos. Sloane was right at our backs.

"Everyone knows you two are a thing anyway. It won't be much of a surprise to the students. But maybe to the teachers." Sloane turned to me as we walked down the hall, which was much less wild now. *How did they disappear that fast?* "Are you off probation now? Or was that a lie too?"

I held back an eye roll. Sloane was still a little bitter that we hadn't filled her in on everything when Gemma was taken.

Eventually Cade and Brantley pulled her aside, along with Shiner, while I was at the hospital, and laid it all out for her. Well, Brantley was the one who'd straightened everything out. Cade was still in his feels about Journey showing up out of nowhere. I hadn't talked with him much, but from the times that I did, I could tell he was completely fucked up—especially because she was still at the orphanage until Tate got things settled. It was slowly killing Cade.

"I'm off probation now. That wasn't a lie. The SMC really was going to expel me if I didn't stop fucking around and get my grades up." I pulled Gemma into my chest for a second, pecking her on the nose before we descended the steps toward the dining hall. "Thank God for my tutor."

Gemma laughed, but before we knew it, we were walking into the dining hall. The girl whose towel fell in front of me no more than twenty minutes ago darted past us with her head glued to her chest.

"What was that all about?" Gemma asked, looking back at the girl scurrying away.

I brushed it off, but Sloane answered as we made our way toward Cade, Brantley, Mercedes, and Shiner. "Her towel fell as your boyfriend was waiting in the hall to come into our room. Pretty sure she's horrified."

"Oh my God. That's...embarrassing."

Sloane shrugged. "She could have willingly opened her towel for him, and in that case, we would have had to set her straight. Isaiah Underwood is taken!"

Gemma's face blushed as she elbowed her friend. "Oh my gosh. You're as bad as him!"

Sloane pulled away from Gem and walked over to sit beside Mercedes as if Gemma hadn't just elbowed her.

She and I were left in the middle of the dining hall, and *fuck*, I just got a little nervous. *Did I seriously just get fucking butterflies?*

Gemma's green gaze tilted toward mine, and I dipped down, my tie hanging between us. I whispered into her ear, "I won't do it if you don't want me to."

She paused, looking torn. *Did she want me to?* My lips curled, and she was pinned to them. The thought of her perfect ass on that table did all sorts of things to me. The memory of the last time I'd placed her on the table was not long forgotten. I dipped down to her ear again, seeing a flush creep up her cleavage that had been playing peek-a-boo with me all morning. "But I know damn well, deep down, you want me to. You know you like breaking rules with me, Gem. And I have to say, sitting on the table in the middle of breakfast, tongue-fucking your new boyfriend...is kind of against the rules."

It took half a second for her lips to split in two and one more for my hands to dip underneath her skirt, gripping her firm ass that was hardly covered by her panties and plopping her down in front of everyone.

"You're the baddest good girl I've ever met, Gemma Richardson."

Her brow flicked. "Well, maybe I'm not a good girl, Isaiah Underwood."

And then my mouth was on hers, and the entire dining hall fell silent.

EPILOGUE

GEMMA

THE NEWSPAPER CAUGHT my eye the second I walked toward the dining room with Isaiah at my back. He pulled out my chair for me, and I shot him a playful smile all while Cade, Brantley, and Shiner made no attempt at hiding their snickering. They didn't think their best friend, head Rebel of the school, was a gentleman, but they were wrong. Isaiah was different with me. He was different from what he'd always portrayed himself as on the outside.

I thought, deep down, his best friends knew that too.

They just liked to screw with him.

As soon as I sat down, the guys started talking again about lacrosse and how they wished it weren't an all-year sport for our school. There was a giant elephant in the room, but they pretended there wasn't.

Things were weird.

There...I said it. Sitting here, at my newly found father's home, a very large house behind St. Mary's, having family dinner at his table, was just awkward.

After things had calmed down and I returned to school, Tate had pulled me into his office, looking more disheveled than I'd ever seen him. His tie was loose, his sleeves were pushed up to his elbows, and three half-empty cups of cold coffee sat on the edge of his desk. He very hesitantly told me that he was moving from the servant's cottage just below the school to the actual house that was just a mile or two down the road. He said he'd never wanted to live there because, *"What would a single man like me need a house that big for?"* But now, things were changing. Jacobi, along with Ann Scova, the social worker that had never once forgotten about me *or* Richard, had come together and were allowing Jack, Isaiah's little brother, to move in with Tate. Isaiah's father was behind bars and would be for a very long time given the severity of charges against him, and paired with the fact that their mother was being moved to a medical facility for further care, he had nowhere else to go. Jacobi's job in the FBI wasn't the most accommodating for young children, so this was their best option. Plus, Jack wanted to be with Isaiah, and this was as close as they could get. Jack would attend the primary school down the road and come back home in the evenings. Isaiah would still stay at the boarding school, but he could come and go as he pleased, even if Tate wasn't actually blood related to either of them.

Instead, he was blood related to me.

He offered for me to stay here, too, but I declined politely. It wasn't because I didn't want to have a relationship with him; it was just that things were moving too quickly, and the rest of the school wasn't aware that he was my father.

I was sure it would come out eventually, but for now, no one really knew except our closest friends, and that was how I wanted to keep it.

Now, if my brother came back, then my mind might change.

He was still staying away, and each day that passed that I didn't hear from him made the knife dig in a little further.

But I tried not to focus on it. He was alive and safe, and that was all that mattered.

Grabbing the napkin off the side of the plate, I pulled it to my lap and looked back at the newspaper laying at the end of the table once more.

The headline caused my heart to slip.

"THE GIRL in the Basement Story Unfolds with New Witness Statements"

IT WAS no surprise that the news article was about me, and the future of having to talk with more lawyers and law enforcement did not dampen my foresight at all. Things were going to get harder, but I pushed the anxiety away, reminding myself that I wasn't alone in this.

I had Isaiah, and our friends, and Tate. I also had Tobias, even if he wasn't presently here with me.

As soon as Tate walked into the dining room, holding a box of pizza, Jack—who I'd yet to formally meet—came rushing in behind him with cute little glasses on the edge of his nose, beaming at his older brother and his three friends.

"Isaiahhhhhh!" He ran up to the side of his seat and clenched his arms around Isaiah's middle.

"Hey, little man! Cool bedroom, am I right? I helped paint it."

"No, you didn't. You sat back and watched Gemma. Uncle Tate told me so." Jack released his older brother and turned and looked at me before pushing his glasses up from the edge of his nose. "Are you Gemma?"

I smiled. "I am. Do you like your room?"

He nodded vigorously, his glasses falling down again. "I *love* it. Did you seriously draw Hogwarts on my wall? All by yourself?"

The awe in his blue eyes warmed my heart. I nodded slowly. "I did. Does it look okay? I've never seen *Harry Potter,* so I just looked at a picture on the Internet and tried my best."

His little mouth flew open, and he snapped his head to Isaiah. "She's never seen *Harry Potter*, Isaiah!"

Everyone in the room laughed, even Tate.

"I know, dude. What are we gonna do about that?"

Jack shook his head, taking the seat beside Isaiah. "Well, we have to watch *Harry Potter* after dinner. We have to!" He looked up at Tate, who was still holding the pizza in his hands. "Can we, Uncle Tate? Just the first movie?"

Tate gave him a warm grin. "Sure, if Gemma wants to. They all have to get back to the school here in a bit, though."

"Pizza?" Isaiah asked, leaning back in his seat. His hand made its way to my leg, and small prickles of heat coated my skin. "I thought you said you were cooking."

The pizza was placed down on the table, and his shoulders sagged. "I burned it."

Shiner let out a laugh. "I wasn't gonna say anything, but I could smell that you burned something before I even sat down."

Tate ran a hand through his hair. "I'm... I've never really cooked before. I always ate at the school."

"Aw, look at Tate trying to be a family man." Isaiah's voice was on the brink of laughter, and I knew he was just giving him a hard time, but I thought it was sweet that he was actually trying. He was so unsure when he'd asked me to come to dinner, allowing me to invite Isaiah, too, which then turned into Cade, Brantley, and Shiner inviting themselves along. I was certain once Sloane and Mercedes caught wind that all the guys came, they'd want to come too. Tate was putting in an effort to be there for me, all while not pressuring me to act a certain way or to take control of my life.

"I can cook next week," I said, biting my lip nervously when everyone stared at me. I desperately wanted to pull my hands to my lap to hide my wrists, but I promised myself I wasn't going to hide my scars any longer. It was one more thing I could take back from Richard. He didn't have control over me anymore, nor did I have to hide the scars that he'd put there.

"Oh, good idea. May I put in a request, Queen Rebel?"

I laughed, looking over at Shiner. The nickname started as soon as I had come back to school and everyone realized that Isaiah and I were a thing. It was so stupid, but I secretly loved it, too.

"No, you can't." Brantley sat back in his seat and shook his head. "No one wants to eat fucking liver and onions, Shiner. It's gross, okay?"

"You haven't had it prepared right, then." Shiner clapped his hands as Isaiah sat forward and pulled a slice of pizza from the box. "I have a great idea. We should all take turns. Sunday dinner every week, *but...*" He held up his finger, silencing the room. To be honest, I think we all wanted to know what would come out of his mouth next, because he was so entertaining. "We switch. One week Gemma will cook. Next, I will cook. Then Brantley, Cade, Isaiah, and so on. We should have a competition. Jack can determine who is the best cook, although we all know it's me." He pulled a piece of pizza up to his mouth. "We all know that I'm a winner."

Everyone laughed—even Cade, who had been very withdrawn since everything had happened. I knew it had to do with Journey, who I also hadn't formally met yet. I desperately wanted to meet her, though. I didn't even know her, and

I wanted to wrap my arms around her to thank her for helping my brother get out of the Covens. Maybe it was a mutual thing. Or maybe Tobias helped her. Either way, I felt like she was a piece of Tobias, and I would take what I could get.

After we all got our pizza, I saw Tate casually push the newspaper underneath his plate so no one would see it. We caught eyes, and he paused, knowing that I saw it, but I gave him a little smile and shook my head. Isaiah squeezed my leg, and I began eating until Tate cleared his throat.

"So, about Sunday dinners, then. Is that...a thing?" He was looking directly at me. "Would you like to make this a reoccurring thing?"

There it was again, that small amount of unease that etched over his tired features. He was trying so hard, and it felt so good to have someone not force me into anything. He had no idea how much I respected that.

I nodded. "Sure, I think I would like that." The relief came over him quickly, and his eyes lit up. I turned to Shiner. "But I'm not eating liver and onions."

He threw his hands up as Isaiah laughed from beside me. "Oh, come on! What?"

The table was full of laughter and easy conversation. I couldn't help but feel lighter sitting here, even though this moment and these relationships came from the most messed-up situation ever. It still felt good, though. I felt like I was surrounded by family, and it was then that I realized that feeling at *home* had nothing to do with where you grew up, how you grew up, or who raised you, and it had everything to do with where you felt the safest and the most loved.

And from where I was sitting, I felt loved and safe.

There was still a piece of me missing, but as for the pieces that were there, they were happy. I was happy and at ease. It

THE SAINT MARY'S DUET BOX SET

felt so comforting that I didn't have to watch my back and have fear creeping up behind me.

Shiner was still going on about liver and onions when there was a knock on the door. The table grew silent, and we all turned to Tate. There was a tiny crease present in between his eyebrows as he slowly stood up, placing his slice of pizza back on the table. As soon as he left the room, we all stood up, even Jack, and followed after him.

He turned around right before opening the door and rolled his eyes. "Go back to the dining room."

None of us moved, and he sighed before reaching for the doorknob. The door swung open a second later, and Isaiah, being taller than me, must have seen who it was. His hand grabbed onto mine, and he clenched it.

"What's wrong?" My body instantly went into fear mode. My heart began to thump, and I felt hot.

I slowly peeked around Tate and sucked in every bit of air in the room. A gasp got stuck in my throat, and my legs almost gave out on me.

A voice I recognized, even in this next life, hit my ears. "I think I'm ready to take you up on your offer now. I think I'm ready to see my sister."

Tate took a step back, and there, in the doorway, with the sun setting in the distance, was my twin brother holding a duffel bag over his shoulder.

"Tobias." My whisper was the only thing floating in between us. It seemed everyone was holding their breath.

My eyes watered as Tobias took a step forward, and my heart leapt into the air. He looked different. So different. He was no longer a boy, and he was no longer the light that I grasped onto in some of the darkest times of our lives.

As soon as he was in front of me, he said, "Hey, sis."

My hand slowly fell from Isaiah's, and I shakily reached up and touched the side of Tobias' face. There was a tiny thin scar that cut through his eyebrow that I zeroed in on as my palm collided with his skin. My chest caved, and I wanted to sob. *He was so different.*

"What did he do to you?" I whispered, dropping my hand to wrap my arms around him. At first, he was tense, so tense that I could feel every hardened muscle along his stomach, but eventually, his arms wrapped around me.

His whisper was hardly present. I doubted anyone could hear it but me. "I could ask you the same."

I pulled back slowly, ignoring the tears on my face. Tobias was free of any emotion, but I wasn't expecting much. "We can only go up from here, right?"

He showed me a tired smile. "Yeah."

A few more moments passed before Tate closed the door, grabbing Tobias' bag. "Well...do you want some pizza?"

Tobias let go of me and took a hefty step back. "Sure."

And one by one, we all shuffled back into the dining room. Isaiah's hand was back in mine, and a soft kiss pelted the side of my head. I peered up at him, and he gave me a reassuring smile.

Things were far from being perfect, but that was okay.

Perfect was overrated, and this right here was better than anything I'd ever had before.

The End

AFTERWORD

The **third book** in the **St. Mary's Series** is NOW AVAILABLE. **Dead Girls Never Talk** is Journey and Cade's book and it takes place at St. Mary's Boarding School! **Please be directed to Amazon to purchase!**

Dead Girls Never Talk Blurb:

Cade

Loving her was like breathing air—it was hard to live without.

Journey Smith was quiet and guarded, and above all else... beautiful. When we were alone, I grew to know the girl behind the stormy eyes. Her hesitant touches and hidden smiles were reserved for me, but now they're gone. Stolen moments of happiness were replaced with sharp barbs and fiery glares concealing her fear.

Our past was written in the stone of St. Mary's—a past that I was not willing to repeat. But what I assumed to be the truth was nothing more than a fabrication of such.

Journey was back, but she was no longer mine.

Journey

They say time heals all wounds—unless, of course, your heart was broken by someone like Cade.

Cade Walker was elusive, part of the Rebels who ruled the halls of St. Mary's. However, I got his playboy smile and deep dimples. When we were alone, he said all the right things—until his betrayal.

Now that I was back, we no longer stood on even ground. With every fleeting glance he gave me, my hammering heart tried to obscure my fear. Cornered in the darkened halls of St. Mary's Boarding School, Cade demanded to know the truth.

A truth I wasn't willing to give.

Dead Girls Never Talk is a complete standalone in the St. Mary's Series and ends with an HEA. This book deals with subjects that some may find triggering.

ALSO BY SJ SYLVIS

English Prep Series

All the Little Lies

All the Little Secrets

All the Little Truths

St. Mary's Series

Good Girls Never Rise

Bad Boys Never Fall

Dead Girls Never Talk

Heartless Boys Never Kiss

Standalones

Three Summers

Yours Truly, Cammie

Chasing Ivy

Falling for Fallon

Truth

All of my books are FREE in Kindle Unlimited!

ABOUT THE AUTHOR

S.J. Sylvis is a romance author who is best known for her angsty new adult romances and romantic comedies. She currently resides in Arizona with her husband, two small kiddos, and dog. She is obsessed with coffee, becomes easily attached to fictional characters, and spends most of her evenings buried in a book!

sjsylvis.com

ACKNOWLEDGMENTS

As always, I would like to mention my *amazing* family for making me smile daily and for always supporting me. I love you forever and ever. <3

To my author friends (I can't list you all. I would feel too bad if I accidentally left someone out, so you know who you are!!)--where would I be without you? To our daily voice messages, shares, likes, encouraging words, and writing sprints—I love you all SO much and I am so grateful for your friendship. Here's to many more books!

To my Betas (Andrea, Danah, Emma, & Megan)—Thank you SO much for helping me with plot holes, confusing scenes, and for reminding me that I need to flip imposter syndrome the bird. You four helped me in ways you don't even realize. xo.

To my Editor, Jenn, Thank you for always making my work shine. I would not be where I am without you! xo.

To my Proofer/PA, I honestly have no idea where I would be without you, Mary! Thank you for reminding me to do the things that I forget about, for picking up my slack, and for everything else. xo.

To my Cover Designer/person who keeps me sane—Danah, thank you for everything and for making the St. Mary's covers AMAZING. xo.

Laura, you are so much more than just an author friend. I love you and your friendship! Thank you for helping me with anything I throw your way! xo.

To my readers, bloggers, ARC readers, Tiktokers, anyone who helps spread the word about my books—WOW. You are the reason I can make this writing gig an actual career. Without your support, reviews, & shares, I wouldn't be where I am today. Thank you so incredibly much for everything you do. It does not go unnoticed.

Xo,

SJ

Lightning Source UK Ltd.
Milton Keynes UK
UKHW010639311022
411384UK00004B/340

9 798985 802061

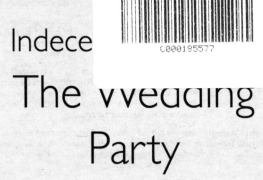

Indece

The Wedding
Party

KATHERINE GARBERA

ANNE OLIVER

STACY CONNELLY

MILLS & BOON

First Published in Great Britain 2022
By Mills & Boon, an imprint of HarperCollins*Publishers,* Ltd
1 London Bridge Street, London, SE1 9GF

www.harpercollins.co.uk

HarperCollins*Publishers*
1st Floor, Watermarque Building,
Ringsend Road, Dublin 4, Ireland

INDECENT PROPOSALS: THE WEDDING PARTY © 2022 Harlequin Enterprises ULC.

Her One Night Proposal © 2020 Katherine Garbera
The Morning After The Wedding Before © 2012 Anne Oliver
The Best Man Takes a Bride © 2018 Stacy Cornell

ISBN 978-0-263-30560-9

MIX
Paper from
responsible sources
FSC® C007454

HER ONE NIGHT PROPOSAL

KATHERINE GARBERA

For Rob, love of my life and my partner in crime.
I'm so glad to be sharing this journey with you.

One

Lunch with her family was always one of the highlights of Iris Collins's week. It was a Wednesday afternoon tradition that had started when she and her twin sister, Thea, were home from boarding school and had followed them into adulthood. They always dined at the club in her father's high-rise office building in the financial district of Boston. Hal Collins was the sole owner and proprietor of Collins Combined, a firm that focused on long-term investments in publicly traded companies.

Iris's phone pinged just as she entered the lobby of the building. She pulled it out of the pocket of her sheath dress and glanced down at the screen to see it was from her so-called boyfriend. She put the phone back in her pocket as her sister came over to hug her.

"I knew you'd be early. I figured I'd get here first so we could chat before Mom and Dad get here," Thea said. "We haven't talked since your trip with Graham. How'd it go?"

"Okay," Iris said.

"Just okay?"

Actually, less than okay if she were honest. During their Bermuda vacation, Graham had pushed her to be more adventurous in bed and that had ended badly. He'd gone down to the bar to drink all night while Iris had sat on the balcony alone listening to the waves. She was trying to keep things going with him until her college roommate's wedding in ten days' time. Graham was her plus one at all the events and she was a bridesmaid so it could get awkward if they broke up. She knew the bride, Adler Osborn, had planned for them to attend as a couple and the last thing that Iris wanted to do was add any extra stress for her friend.

Her phone pinged again, and her smart watch vibrated on her arm. She glanced down to see it was another message from Graham.

"Speak of the devil," she said, pulling her phone out to read the text while Thea looked over her shoulder.

Listen, things aren't working out between us, so I'm done with dating you. I hope you understand.

"Are you kidding me?" Thea said. "He's breaking up with you over a text."

Iris wished she could be surprised but was relieved instead. She quickly typed, Sure, I understand.

Great. Figured you'd get it.

"Get what?"

"Nothing," Iris said to her sister. The last thing she wanted to do was talk about sex in the lobby of their father's building. She was starting to wonder if she was the prude that Graham had labeled her...and did that matter to her?

Thea took her phone from her before she could stop her, typing in a quick message.

That's okay I want more from life than you can offer.

"Thea. Give me back my phone."

She saw the dancing dots that meant Graham was responding and her stomach felt tight. There was no way he was going to take that kind of insult without replying. That was just the kind of person he was.

That's okay I want someone who's not beige, boring and basic. Bye, bitch.

Thea reached for her phone, but Iris just held it away from her and texted back the thumbs-up emoji.

"Why did you do that?" Iris said to her sister. "He was my plus one. I'm going to have to deal with him not being there."

"Who do you have to deal with?" their mother asked as she came up behind them and hugged them both. Always larger than life, Corinne Collins, known as Coco to her close friends and bridge group, was wearing Ralph Lauren.

"Graham. That guy I was dating."

"He just broke up with her over text," Thea added. "How rude."

"Very rude. But not everyone pays attention to etiquette these days."

"They don't," Iris said. "Where's Dad?"

"He's running late," Mom said. "I warned him not to be too late or I'm taking you two on a shopping spree."

They all laughed as it was a family joke between their

parents from back in their early days when her father said
time was money and her mom had said she agreed and liked
to use her time to spend it.

As Iris followed her mom and her sister to the hostess
stand at the entrance to the restaurant on the second floor,
she was seething. How dare he say something so rude to
her? Of course, she knew he thought she was boring…but
basic? She was *so* not basic. She was Iris Collins, television lifestyle guru. Known for her trendsetting style and
Instagram-worthy jet-setting.

She'd known he was douche bag when he'd suggested a
three-way, but this was beyond.

Her mom saw a friend from her bridge club at the bar
and went to chat with her, which meant that Thea and she
were alone again.

"You need to bring someone so hot to the wedding. Show
him who's basic. I can't believe he had the nerve to say
that," Thea said.

"Agree. But who? I don't know anyone. I really don't
have time to cultivate a relationship in only ten days."

"Let me think," Thea said.

"It can't be anyone I know," Iris added. Graham knew
most of the people she worked with.

"True. You should hire someone. Just be straightforward about it. Like a Julia Roberts movie. You can do that."

"No," Iris said.

"Why not?"

"Because it's embarrassing, that's why."

"It's not embarrassing. You could have a hot guy on your
arm, and if you're footing the bill, he has to behave the way
you want him to," Thea said. "I know some hot guys who
might be interested."

"Like who? You work at home with two cats," Iris
pointed out. Her sister ran a very successful blog about

etiquette and deportment. There was a high demand for people who wanted to actually live the life in those swank Instagram photos they saw online, and Thea was in demand when it came to social events.

"I have friends," Thea added.

"Thanks, Thea," she said. "But I'll sort this out. We don't need to waste any more time on Graham."

Their father arrived and they had a nice lunch. Iris had that feeling deep inside as she watched her parents holding hands under the table during coffee and dessert. That longing that she always felt. Was it too much to ask that she could find a partner? She wanted what they had but she seemed to attract men like Graham.

But for now, maybe Thea was right. She could find a hot guy to hire as her date for the wedding. It was only four days and three nights…

Zac Bisset hated being in Boston but there were times when real life intruded on his training schedule and he was forced to leave his yacht and deal with it. It didn't matter that it was a perfectly nice June day. He was wearing a suit and loafers instead of a pair of swim trunks and bare feet. Being born into a family that had wealth, privilege and way too many constrictions had never suited Zac well. He'd found his escape on the sea, sailing. It was a passion he'd pursued through his college years. Then he'd joined an America's Cup team from the UK and done that for the last few years, but he'd recently left the team to start his own bid.

Putting together an America's Cup team was expensive. He could easily ask for and receive the money from his family's company, Bisset Industries. But that money would come with too many strings. His father had been dying to get him to be more active on the board and the last thing Zac wanted was to answer to August Bisset. Or worse, his older brother Logan. He liked having the freedom to do his own thing.

But his options were limited. After the US-sponsored Oracle team won, Zac had craved creating his own team and putting together his own bid to win. He needed a big company to sponsor him or his own inheritance to make a successful run. Time was running out since they needed to already be training.

He left the meeting at the corporate offices of the large telecom company where he'd been discussing a sponsorship. When he got to the bar in the lobby and ordered a club soda, his phone pinged and then started buzzing as a slew of messages came in. The first was from his eldest brother, Darien, who was a politician and not in the family business; he wanted to meet up for drinks before their cousin's wedding festivities kicked off. Then there was a message from the group chat he had with his teammates who were waiting for an update. The last was from his mom, saying she was on Nantucket at Gran's place and urging him to come by early so they could have some mom-and-son time.

He rubbed the back of his neck, not interested in responding to any of them at the moment. Of course, his two favorite people in the family had reached out, which he appreciated. Logan and his dad wanted to boycott Adler's wedding because she was marrying into the Williams family. They were the chief competitors of Bisset Industries; their business had been started by a man his father hated. So there was that.

Zac had no beef with the groom, so he'd volunteered to go to all the events. He liked a wedding party. With booze, pretty girls and lots of dancing, it was his kind of shindig. It was a destination wedding, so everyone was being put up at a luxury resort on Nantucket, the flagship of Williams Inc.'s newest venture. The groom and his family were slowly encroaching on every line of business the Bissets were in. But Zac's youngest sibling and only sister, Mari, had been to a press party there a month ago and couldn't stop singing the resort's praises.

Which had done nothing to make Logan and his father happier about going. Family was trying at times and one of the reasons he preferred to stick to training for the America's Cup.

He texted his teammates first. They had a group chat nicknamed the Windjammers. The team was pretty small at the moment, just Zac, Yancy McNeil and Dev Kellman. The three of them were in New England searching for sponsors and working on a new design for their yacht. The competition was won as much with skill on the seas as it was with the aerodynamic design of the craft.

No-go on the money. Got one more meeting before we are going to have to brainstorm more options.

Yancy was the first to respond.

Damn. I have some feelers out. Heard from a friend that she has someone who is looking for a long-term investment. I'll text you the deets.

Dev quickly chimed in.

I don't have any leads but I do have some margaritas ready to go once you both get back to the Blind Faith.

Zac wrapped up the chat with, Thanks. I'll check out your lead, Yancy.

Yancy texted over the information as Zac signaled the

waiter for a refill of his soda water. He glanced up, his breath catching in his throat as he saw the blond woman walking into the bar. She wore a formfitting dress with tiny sleeves that left her long arms bare. She was tan and fit, and she moved with confidence and purpose. Their eyes met and she stopped, her lips parting in a slight smile. Her eyes were blue like the seas around the southern island of New Zealand. Her mouth was…damn, all he could stare at now. Her upper lip was fuller than her bottom one and it seemed to him that she was very kissable. All he could think about was how her mouth would feel under his.

He stretched his legs under the table and looked away. Yeah, he'd been at sea for too long if his first thought when seeing a woman was kissing her. He needed to get himself under control before he was surrounded by family for a week.

He heard footsteps and looked up, expecting to see the waiter, but it was the woman. She smelled good up close like the summer blossoms in his mother's garden at the house in the Hamptons. She had a direct kind of gaze that he liked. He wasn't a timid man and he didn't always know how to deal with people who were. Up close he could see that her hair wasn't truly blond but darker shades of caramel were shot through it. It curled around her shoulders and he noticed how slim her neck was and the tiny necklace with a flower charm on it.

Iris was still thinking about her sister's outrageous advice as she went to the bar across town after lunch. She glanced around the room; it was midafternoon, and she was meeting her "glam squad" to go over her prep for the wedding in Nantucket. The fact that Adler's wedding was going to be televised and there would be lots of vloggers and online society gossip websites meant that she was going to have to be camera-ready at all times.

She'd built her own platform over the last five years, working her way up from an assistant to Leta Veerland to her having her own style television show. Leta had taken reality television by storm in the late 1990s and early 2000s, starting out by showcasing her sister Jaqs' bridal designs. She had set a standard that many young video channel content creators tried to emulate, with her style and advice on creating the perfect personal habitat. Iris had learned from Leta that she had to always look the part when she walked out her door, even if she was only going to the grocery store. If one of her viewers saw her acting or looking in a way that contradicted her brand image, then she'd lose her believability.

Thea texted to say she'd found a guy who would be her date for the entire weekend for a thousand dollars. She tucked her phone away, not at all interested in some guy her sister found for her.

She glanced around and didn't see her makeup artist, KT, and her stylist and personal assistant, Stephan, so she headed toward one of the tall tables in the back. She almost stumbled when she saw the hunky blond sitting in one of the large leather club chairs near the entrance. He had a clean-shaven, chiseled jaw. His hair was long and brushed the tops of his shoulders, but it was clean and lustrous and reminded her of a Viking…not the pillaging kind but the hot, yummy kind.

Make him an offer he can't refuse.

Thea's voice whispered through her head and she shook it to dispel her sister's ridiculous idea. It absolutely wasn't happening.

But now that Thea had planted the seed, Iris did sort of wonder if she could do it. She ran a multimillion-dollar business. She remembered something her mom had said when she had started to make real money as a social media influencer: *don't be afraid to pay people to do the things you need done.*

Technically there was nothing wrong with showing up at a destination wedding without a date. But the wedding was going to be televised. She was getting ready to launch a domestic goddess–themed range of products and a book. Everyone from her management team to her own staff were looking at the numbers that said she was stagnating while her competition made advances. People like Scarlet O'Malley, the heiress and social media influencer, who was now married and expecting her first child. Iris's peers—her competition—were moving on from single-girl-in-the-city to new-wife-and-mama and she was still stuck in…boring-and-basic land.

Ugh!

If she showed up with someone like the Viking on her arm, it would be a boost to her social image, and it would give her a man to pose with. She could even frame it as a business deal…

He glanced up and caught her staring and she smiled at him. He winked and smiled back. She walked over to him. She wished she'd paid more attention to that movie her mom had made them watch on girls' night… *Indecent Proposal.* She needed to channel her best Robert Redford…or she could *Pretty Woman* him and be Richard Gere.

Confidence was key. She could be confident. Hadn't she convinced her parents to let her start her own YouTube channel when she was fourteen?

"Hello," she said. She'd charm the socks off him, she thought. Glancing down at his feet she saw he hadn't worn socks with his loafers. Fate was giving her a sign that she wouldn't mess this up.

"Hi. Want to join me?" he asked.

She glanced at her watch. She had about fifteen minutes until she'd have to call her team. And Thea's idea was there, nagging at her...though really, if she was going to do this, she had to stop thinking of it as Thea's idea.

"Sure, but only if you'll allow me to buy you a drink," she said.

"I'm never one to turn down a pretty lady," he said, standing and holding out a chair for her to join him.

"You aren't?" she asked.

"Not at all."

"Have you ever regretted that?" she asked. This man seemed daring, just like the Viking she'd compared him too, but she knew that she might be seeing what she wanted to see and not the real man.

"Never. Sometimes it has turned out differently than I anticipated but that's life, isn't it?"

"Your life maybe. I'm pretty much always following a plan," she said. She watched him, carefully trying to gauge his reaction. Was she seriously thinking about Thea's outrageous suggestion?

Yes. She was.

"I've never been one to follow a plan," he said.

"How does that work?"

"I go where the wind takes me," he said.

"The wind?"

"I'm a sailor and compete in yacht races," he said.

Hah, she thought. She'd known he was a Viking and instead of pillaging he was out there conquering the sea.

"Like the America's Cup?" she asked. She really didn't know that much about yachting.

"Exactly like that. I'm currently putting together a team and looking for investors for my bid in four years," he said.

He needed investors...

"Why are you asking?" he asked.

She took a deep breath. If she was going to do this then she wasn't going to find a better man than this guy. He looked good, he needed investors and she liked him. "I need a favor," she said.

"And only a stranger will do?" he asked.

She noticed he had a pile of papers on the table in front of him and as she glanced down, she recognized it as a prospectus—the kind of document someone looking for investors would use to showcase their product. She quickly looked away as he sat back down and straightened the papers, turning them facedown on the table.

"Sorry, didn't mean to read your stuff," she said.

"No problem. But you mentioned you need a favor. I'm already intrigued. Please sit down and then you can tell me all about it," he said.

She sat down, crossing her feet at her ankles and keeping her back straight. Her father had once said that posture was the first step to giving off the air of confidence. She swallowed and then took a deep breath. She had to be careful: sexual harassment went both ways and she didn't want to come across like she was propositioning him.

"I'm going to make you an offer that you can't refuse," she said. Wasn't that what Robert Redford had said? Was that right? Wasn't that the line?

"What are you, the Godfather?"

"No, I'm trying to say I need a man for the weekend, and if that prospectus is any indication you're looking for investors, you need some money, so… I'm making a mess of this."

"Is this an indecent proposal?"

Two

She blushed and blinked at him and then sat up even straighter and tipped her head to the side. "It's more of a business proposal that is personal in nature."

He'd been propositioned before but usually by women who wanted entrée into his jet-set world.

"I'm intrigued," he said. And he wasn't lying. This woman was beautiful. And though the fact that she was offering him money out of the blue was crazy, it was a nice fantasy to think of someone like her sponsoring his America's Cup bid, not a bloodless corporation or his controlling father.

"I'm going to a destination wedding and I need a date. It's four days, three nights, and I'm willing to invest in your project there in return for you accompanying me. It would be strictly for show. I'm not expecting you to do anything indecent."

"Too bad. I sort of liked the idea," he said. Funny, he

was about to attend a wedding that was scheduled to run for the same amount of time. Was she attending Adler's wedding, too?

Her shoulders stiffened and she sat up even straighter if that were possible. He liked her, he realized. She was different from the sporty women he usually hung out with, and though she was polished and clearly moved in the same social circles he'd grown up in, she felt different.

"Well, that's not on the table," she said.

"Why are you hiring a guy?" he asked. Frankly she didn't seem like the type of woman who had to pay someone to be with her, and if she was, what was he missing?

"It's a long story," she said. "And I really don't want to get into all the details. Suffice it to say, I was dating someone, and he broke up with me and I don't want to go stag to this event. It's televised and I'm filming while I'm there so…"

"It's about image?" he asked, a bit disappointed because she'd seemed to be more real than that. But he'd been fooled before so he shouldn't be too surprised.

She shook her head. "Yes, but it's not what you think. It's my business. I'm a lifestyle guru… I have a show and line of products and my mentor's sister designed the wedding dress so I'm doing an entire behind-the-scenes thing. If it was just me and not all the other brand stuff, I wouldn't care."

"Who are you?" he asked. "I hope you don't mind me asking but I've been out of the country and spend most of my time on the water."

"I'm Iris Collins."

He had heard of her, mainly from his sister, Mari, who had mentioned her as someone she wanted to grow her brand to be like. Which Zac had freely admitted he had no clue about. "I'm Zac."

"Am I right in assuming you need investors for your America's Cup bid?"

"Yes, I'm trying to find investors to fund my run. I have some new people and ideas I want to try," Zac explained.

"I think I can help you with that," she said.

"Lifestyle guru-ing pays that well?"

"Very well," she said with a laugh. "Which is another reason why I really need to present the right image. It would mainly involve you dressing up and holding my hand. Maybe there'd be a kiss or two but I just need someone to be my partner at all the events."

He was 100 percent sure that his answer had to be no. He didn't need Carlton Mansford—his father's PR-spin doctor—to explain that hiring himself out as a date for the weekend wasn't going to play well if it ever got out. And he'd been a Bisset long enough to know that this kind of thing wouldn't stay a secret.

He had to come clean with her. Let her know he wasn't desperate for money.

"I…"

He trailed off. He wanted to let her know it was a no-go but didn't want to embarrass her. Under different circumstances he'd have asked her out to dinner, but this wasn't that time. He had a problematic wedding of his own to attend, and he needed to really focus on getting serious investors for his team, not a nice lady who had some money to pay him for a weekend together.

She gave him a wry smile. "Don't say anything else. I knew it was a long shot. My sister said I should be Richard Gere and find myself someone pretty to have on my arm."

"She's right. But I'm not that guy," he said.

She nodded. "Thank you for your time. And the drink is of course on me."

She got up and walked away with way more class and

elegance than he knew he could ever muster. She held her head high and back straight as she went over to the bar area.

Then there was a commotion near the entrance, and he noticed a TV cameraman and several photographers entering as the seating hostess tried to stop them.

They made a beeline for Iris and Zac turned to watch them.

"Ms. Collins, rumor has it that you were dumped by Graham Winstead III?" one of the paparazzi shouted out. "Will this affect the launch of your new Domestic Goddess line? How can you claim to know anything about domestic bliss when you're—"

"Boys, please. Rumors are just that. Rumors. I'm not going to deign to answer them. As my father always says, keeping your ear close to the ground and listening is good business, repeating what you heard is asking for trouble."

Iris Collins smiled winningly at the cameras and then glanced at her watch. "I have to run. I'm meeting someone important."

She turned and started to walk past the paparazzi, but bumped into a table and lost her balance. Zac was on his feet before he had a chance to remind himself he'd already decided this was a bad idea.

But somehow watching her maintain her poise and dignity as she dealt with the gossip had made him forget that. He wanted to know more about this woman. He caught her and pulled her into his arms, looking down into her startled face.

"Angel face, I've got you," he said, making sure he only looked at her.

Angel face?

She clung to his big shoulders and automatically smiled but she was pretty sure she looked like Jared Leto's version of the Joker from *Suicide Squad*. Being ambushed in person wasn't something she'd ever get used to. She preferred to deal with this kind of gossip online when she could rant to her assistant, then just smile and type out a response. Even more embarrassing had been the fact that she knew that Zac had overheard it all.

She'd pretty much used up all of her stores of bravado talking to the paparazzi and the last thing she wanted now was to make things worse. There was a knot in the pit of her stomach, and she was angry. And she couldn't help it; ever since she was a young girl, when she got mad, she cried. She blinked a number of times, refusing to let anyone see tears in her eyes.

Including Zac, but he seemed to get that she needed someone at her side. And here he was, holding her and calling her *angel face*. She had been doing photo-calls for her blog and TV show for the last five years so she was polished and professional or at least she hoped she was on the outside. Inside she wanted to hammer out the details. Did this mean he would come with her to the wedding?

"Thanks," she said, straightening back up. But he continued to hold her close to him.

"Go with it," he said.

"Did you change your mind?" she asked, staring into his blue eyes and hoping that he had. Though a part of her wanted him just for her own, this was easier. No messy feelings, no falling for someone who thought she was basic. Just a simple exchange of favors.

"Yes," he said under his breath.

She wrapped her arms around his neck and planted the biggest, juiciest, showiest kiss on his lips that she could. She knew it had to look good for the paparazzi and she put everything she had into it. She thought he was surprised at first, but then he dipped her low, his tongue sliding over hers, and she forgot about the cameras and the game. Forgot everything but the fact that this man was holding her in his arms, and he made her feel alive.

He straightened them both up and she still felt dazed. She had no problem ignoring the paparazzi, who were calling out questions to them as they walked out of the bar. He just sort of directed her and she followed. As soon as they were on the street, a large Bentley pulled up and a driver got out and opened the door.

"Sir."

"Malcolm," Zac said as he held the door open and she slid in the backseat.

As soon as the door closed behind them and they were on their way, she grabbed her phone and texted someone. Then she turned to him.

"Sorry, I was supposed to meet my hair and makeup people back there. I just texted them to cancel. Now what's going on? Who are you? Did you really agree to be my date for four days? I'm pretty sure you don't need the money... unless you're a professional gigolo—you're not, right?"

He rubbed his finger over his lips and just stared at her as if he couldn't stop thinking about their kiss. If she were 100 percent honest, she couldn't either, but she wanted to pretend nothing had happened. She was beige, right? She didn't kiss a stranger and feel instant passion like this. It was probably a fluke, she thought. Yeah, a total fluke.

"You asked me to help you out in exchange for investing in my project," he said. "I wasn't going to do it, but when I saw what you were up against, I couldn't resist."

"Are you doing this out of pity?" she asked. If so, she was turning into a total loser. She really should never have started this whole indecent-proposal thing.

"No, I'm doing it for money," he said, winking at her. Damn, he was so handsome for a minute she just smiled back at him and then his words sunk in. "But do you need money? You're not a gigolo, are you?"

"I don't know anyone younger than my grandmother who uses that word."

"I don't like the term man-whore," she quipped. "Listen, just answer me. Do you take money from women to hang out with them?"

"Just you," he said.

He was being cute, and she couldn't blame him, but this situation had just gone from a jokey idea to reality and she was committed because those photos of the two of them were going to go viral. Having him by her side would seriously save her bacon, but at the same time it created a bunch of issues she and her team were going to have to deal with.

"Glad to know I'm special. Where are we going?" she asked as she realized the driver seemed to be making a big circle around downtown.

"Wherever you want to discuss this," he said. "Malcolm will keep driving until we give him a location, right?"

"Yes, sir. Ma'am, where should I take you?" the driver asked her, without taking his eyes from the road.

"Take us to Collins Commons," she said, naming her father's compound in the financial district. They could discuss the details in one of the conference rooms there. Her phone started blowing up with texts and she glanced at them. Her team wanting to know where she was and who that hottie was with her.

"What's at Collins Commons?" he asked.

"My father's office. We can discuss your project, my investment in it and what I will need from you this weekend," she said. "I think it's best to get that all in writing so that we don't have any confusion."

"This weekend?"

"Yes. The wedding is the Osborn-Williams one on Nantucket."

Zac stared at her for a long moment and seemed to be pondering something but he finally just took a deep breath and nodded more to himself than to her.

"Your dad does this kind of thing?" Zac asked.

"Investments and contracts, yes. Hiring a man for the weekend, no. I think I'm the first one in our family to do this."

Zac had to give her props for recovering quickly; he realized there was much more to Iris Collins than met the eye. She had handled the online-gossip-site stringers with more aplomb that he ever had. He had seen her mask slip only once and that was when he kissed her.

She was attending his cousin's wedding. He should tell her who he was, but then she might not believe he really wanted outside investors. They were still essentially strangers and telling people he was a Bisset, had complicated his life in the past.

He knew the embrace was meant to be all show for the photographers, but he'd never been good at hiding the truth of who he was. He was ambitious and some would say militant when it came to what he wanted. But then he was a Bisset, and even though he hadn't gone into the family business, he'd brought the cutthroat Bisset drive with him to the world of competitive sailing.

But this was an entirely new situation and he was trying to be chill until he got the lay of the land. The conference room they were led to in the Collins Commons building was well appointed. Not unlike the massively impressive boardroom in the Bisset Industries headquarters in New York.

He knew that at some point he needed to clear up who

he was, but not yet. He was enjoying this. She'd wrested control back from him, and though it was counter to his nature, there was something about her that fascinated him.

Maybe it was that for the first time since he'd left Team GB and came back to New England to start his own team, he wasn't facing a choice that he didn't want to make. He had always been the kind of man who forged his own path. He'd known from watching Larry Ellison's attempts to win the America's Cup with his Oracle backing that it wouldn't be easy. But he hadn't realized how hard it would be to convince investors to take a chance on him without Bisset Industries' money also backing him.

He had always been able to make things happen without his father's assistance. It had been a point of pride for him and now... Well, unless he missed his guess, Iris had the connections to the kind of investors he needed. All he had to do was be her date for a long weekend. Simple enough.

Except his family would be at this wedding and, though he kept his private life private, the kind of splashy relationship she wanted from him...might raise questions. He had to make some decisions quickly.

"Are you freaked out now?" she asked.

"Aren't you?" he countered.

"Yes. I am. Listen, you were so sweet to come to my rescue when I tripped, but I'm not sure you know what you've gotten into," she said.

He leaned back in the large leather chair and steepled his fingers across his chest in a move he'd seen his father make many times when facing an opponent in the boardroom. The fact that the opponent was usually his aunt or his mom had always made Zac smile, but right now he was glad to have that model to draw on.

"Tell me about it," he said.

She nodded and stood up, moving to the other side of the

large boardroom table and pacing in front of the windows that looked down on Collins Commons. The summer sun was filtered through the tinted windows but still provided enough light for him to admire her slim silhouette.

"As I mentioned, I'm a lifestyle television personality. My career started with a blog, and I was a personal assistant to Leta Veerland. I'm not sure if you've heard of her," Iris said.

"I know her," he said.

Leta Veerland was on par with Martha Stewart. She'd built her career in the 1980s and '90s with her lifestyle books, monthly magazine and television show. Yeah, he'd heard of her. His mom had considered her the gold standard for entertaining and had emulated Leta Veerland at all her Hamptons summer parties and events.

"I figured. She's a household name. Anyway, she wanted to cut back on the show and I transitioned into it and brought a younger, fresh perspective—her words—to it. And people seemed to respond. So, I've been doing this for about seven years now. My market has been growing from single-girl-in-the-city to coupledom-and-settling-down—"

"But you're not in a couple?" he asked.

"Well, yes. I mean I was dating someone but that didn't work out. And I'd been teasing that I'd reveal my new guy at this wedding that I'm a bridesmaid in. I'm also promoting a new product launch for brides-to-be and new wives so…"

"It would look really bad if you showed up stag," he said. "Okay, that makes sense. So what exactly do you need from me if I do this?"

She turned around, and he noticed when she talked business there was none of that sweetness to her. She had a very serious go-getter expression that reminded him a lot of his father and his brother Logan when they were going in to close a deal.

"If? The paparazzi just caught us embracing. I'm afraid it's you or no one else," she said. "We just need to work out a price."

He stood up and walked around the long conference table, taking his time. He had somehow gotten the upper hand and while he knew funding and financing an America's Cup bid was way too high a price to ask her to pay for four days as her "boyfriend," they were both in a position where there wasn't an out.

She didn't back up when he moved closer, not stopping until only an inch of space separated them. "I'm afraid what I need is very pricey."

Three

Coming home to Nantucket was always bittersweet for Juliette Bisset. She and her mother, Vivian, had continually had a difficult relationship when they were in the city but on Nantucket they'd always been strangely close. Maybe it was the beach-hair-don't-care attitude that seemed to infuse the island. Juliette had never really thought too much about it, had simply vowed she'd be less harsh if she had a daughter of her own, something she'd failed at.

Her younger sister, Musette, had loved it here as well when she was alive. She'd been gone almost twenty-five years now. Juliette still missed her even though during the last few years of Musette's life, it had been difficult to love her and not live with the constant fear that she was going to kill herself with her reckless lifestyle.

"I figured I'd find you out here."

Juliette turned around to see her niece, Adler, standing there. Musette's daughter. She was the reason the entire family was descending on the island.

Adler's was going to be a no-holds-barred, celebrity-studded, televised ceremony. And as if that wasn't enough to cause stress, she was also marrying into the family of Juliette's husband's business rival. It was completely insane and yet seemed perfectly normal considering she was Musette's daughter. A part of Juliette imagined her sister, who'd never like August Bisset, chuckling in glee at the fact that her daughter was marrying into his rival's family.

"I can't help thinking about your mom this week as we are all here for your wedding."

"Me too. I miss her," Adler said.

Juliette put her arm around Adler and hugged her close. "Me too. I feel like she's here with us."

"I hope so," Adler said. "That's one of the reasons why I picked Nantucket for the wedding. This is where we were always happiest when she was still alive."

"I'm hoping the gardenias bloom in time for my wedding bouquet," Adler said.

Juliette knew that Musette used to leave the blossoms in Adler's nursery when she was a little girl. "I'm sure they will."

Adler turned away to the other headstones in the private family cemetery. This land had been in the Wallis family for six generations and most of their ancestors were buried here.

"Why is this gravestone blank?" Adler asked.

Juliette's stomach felt like lead and her throat tightened. That tiny gravestone held her deepest, darkest secret. "It's for a baby who was stillborn."

"Oh. That's sad. Was it Gran's?" Adler asked.

"No, it wasn't," Juliette said. "Let's get back up to the house before that storm blows in."

Adler slipped her arm through Juliette's as they walked back up the cobblestone path toward the house. Adler was talking about her wedding and the last-minute things she needed to do in the three days before all of her guests arrived. But Juliette's mind was elsewhere—back there with that tiny unmarked gravestone. There were times when she'd wished she'd never hidden that baby.

But there were other actions she'd taken...things that couldn't be undone, so her little stillborn baby boy would always be hidden there.

They went through the house's beachside entrance, switching their sandy shoes for slippers that the butler, Michael, thoughtfully left for them. As soon as they entered the hallway, Dylan, Vivian's corgi, ran toward them. Adler dropped down to her knees, petting Dylan and getting several sloppy kisses.

Juliette petted Dylan, as well.

"Nice walk, Juliette?" her mother asked as she entered the hallway. Vivian was in her seventies but looked younger. She wore a pair of slim-fitting white jeans and a chambray shirt that she had loosely tucked in on one side. While on Nantucket and in beach mode, she let her naturally curly blond hair actually stay curly instead of having it straightened by her lady's maid, Celeste, each morning. She held a martini glass in one hand, and as she came closer to Juliette, she reached over and gave her a loose hug.

Then her mom did the same with Adler but added an air kiss. Juliette had compared herself to others for so many years, and for a moment she started to let the old feelings of jealousy well up before she shoved them aside. She had a daughter of her own that she was finally getting close to. Something she'd never expected to happen at the ripe old age of sixty-one.

"Martini, girls?"

"Yes, ma'am," Adler said.

"Definitely," Juliette said. This weekend was going to be

hard for her in more ways than one, but she was going to do her best to face it with charm and a smile firmly in place.

"When is August coming?" her mom asked when they were all seated in the sunroom.

"I'm not entirely sure. He and Logan have a meeting with a client this week and they will be coming together," Juliette said.

She and her husband were enjoying a new closeness since he'd stepped down and handed the reins of Bisset Industries over to their son, Logan.

"I hope Logan and Uncle August are nice," Adler said. "Zac promised he'd help me ride herd on his older brother, but you know how Logan can be."

"I do. He's so much like your uncle," Juliette said, trying not to let her mind linger too long on that thought.

"How pricey will it be for you to join me?" Iris asked Zac as they continued their negotiation. She was trying to stay focused on business but he smelled good and that kiss earlier… How she'd felt when he'd kissed her kept distracting her. Was it a fluke? That was the one thought that was going through her head.

His mouth continued to be a distraction. It was firm looking, but his lips had been so soft when he kissed her. Had she just imagined it? She wasn't sure that hiring a man to be her date at the wedding was a good idea. She'd barely kissed Zac and she was already losing her focus on the big prize. She had to hustle to stay ahead of the competition. And instead of worrying about that she was wondering about his kiss.

Focus, girl.

"I'm actually putting together my own team for the America's Cup."

She blinked. That wasn't what she'd been expecting to

hear. She knew very little about the America's Cup except that the CEO of Oracle had won for the United States a few years ago and that it had taken him a lot of money and time. "Is that what you do for a living? Sailing? Or is this a new hobby?"

"Yes, it's my job. I have some other interests as well, but the bulk of my time is spent training and participating in yachting competitions around the world. I've been in Australia for the last few years and I had hoped to captain the team I'd been training with, but they went in a different direction and I'm not really that great at taking orders so I'm doing my own thing. I need investors to help sponsor us."

"Okay. I think I can help," she said. "Actually, my dad manages all of my investments and I think this might be something that he would be interested in. He's always trying to diversify but this is niche."

"It is," he said. "You want your dad to know you hired me?"

"No. What I'm now thinking is that you and I would be together the four days at the wedding and then, since this is going to be a big investment, could we possibly extend the arrangement for, say, three months to get through my new product launch? Then you could go off to do your yachting and we could drift apart but it won't look like it was just for the wedding," she said. Now that she knew what he wanted, it was easier to get her head where it needed to be. She turned away from him and moved to the sideboard where she knew pens and paper were kept.

She took two legal pads out and pens and then hit the intercom button on the phone and rang her father's assistant.

"Hello, Bran. It's Iris. Could we send some refreshments into the small conference room and I'll need some time on my dad's schedule in an hour or so," she said.

"Certainly, Iris. I'll get some fresh fruit and those cookies you like sent up. Shall I also bring in cold beverages and some coffee?" he asked.

She looked over at Zac. "Do you want coffee?"

"That'd be great," he said.

"Yes, please. Coffee for two."

"Certainly, Iris," Bran said, hanging up.

She walked back to the table and pushed one of the pads of paper and a pen across to Zac, and then pulled out a chair for herself. He took the paper and pen, then came around and sat down next to her.

Dang, but he was impossible not to watch as he moved. He had a lithe, masculine grace. She was still staring when he sat down next to her.

"What are we doing?"

She shook her head. She had to get over this ridiculous attraction to him. He would be an employee like KT or Stephan. She had to treat him as such.

"I thought we could each write down the things we need. I know you already have a prospectus. Do you have a profit-and-loss sheet?"

"I do," he said.

"Good. How do you feel about the three months?"

"I'm not even sure what it is you want from me," he said.

"I need you to be my boyfriend in public. Take photos with me, of course. You'd have to give me permission to use them on all social platforms. There are four days of events at the wedding, so I'd want you there at all times by my side. Once the wedding is over, I'm thinking we'll need one or two dates a week, as well as some cute social media exchanges and maybe a couple of live videos so I can keep us relevant. My product launch is in six weeks and once it does, I'll be traveling and doing events. We won't be together so maybe we can do some exchanges on social media again and possibly, if it works for your schedule, you could fly out and meet me at one of my appearances. I will give you the full schedule so we can see if that works."

"Uh, I don't know about that. Being your boo for the weekend is one thing, but all that other stuff is a big commitment. I'll have to start hiring my team and get to work on having the yacht I've designed manufactured. My time is going to be pretty well spoken for. I can do the wedding but beyond that you are on your own."

"Forget it then. I need someone... Actually now that you were photographed with me, I need you, Mister... I don't know your last name," she said.

"It's Bisset. My dad is—"

"Mr. Bisset, I don't think we need to go into families right now. All I'm interested in is the details. I'm going to be giving you a large amount of money, you are going to have to work for it."

"You are investing in my racing team, Iris," he countered. "You will see a profit from it when I win. I'm doing this as a favor because I like you, angel face."

He leaned in closer and she felt the brush of his minty breath across her cheek. "I think you like me too or you wouldn't have suggested this in the first place."

Her skin was as soft as it looked and the more time he spent with Iris, the happier he was with his gut decision to help her out. He hadn't liked watching the paparazzi question her, but he knew that was in no small part due to the way that they had treated his own little sister, Mari. Mari had had an affair with a married man when she was younger, and the press had sniffed that story out and made her life a living hell for a while.

As much as he knew that everyone seemed to live for the latest tea, he didn't like it. His sister said that being in the spotlight meant taking the good with the bad, but he wasn't sure about that. And because he wasn't going to lie to himself, that kiss between him and Iris had been hot. Hell, hotter than he'd expected. He didn't want to just walk away. But hanging out with her at the wedding was one thing. Three months of fake dates and appearances would be hard to maintain.

He wasn't at the point in his life where he wanted to focus on anything but winning the America's Cup and that meant his next few years were taken. But she wasn't going to back down; he could easily read the determination in her eyes. And as she'd said, now that they'd been photographed together, it was either him or no one. And he didn't want to leave her in the lurch.

"I do like you," she said, at last, touching her finger to his lip and then drawing her hand back.

A tingle went through him at her touch.

"So then. Let's make this work," he said, shifting back because he couldn't allow this to be anything more than a business deal. He needed investors and unless she was lying—and Iris didn't strike him as a woman who would make things up—she could provide solid backing. This place belonged to her father; she had real money on the table. He would make the three-month arrangement work.

"Yes, let's," she said. "I'm going to make a list of every event I need you at for the next three months. You jot down your schedule, as well."

"Before we do that, shouldn't we make sure that your investors are on board?" he asked. "Or did you anticipate that it would just be yourself?"

"Um, yes, of course," she said. "Let me see what you have. I think an investment group would be better, but I'll ask my dad."

He handed her his prospectus and she started going over

it, making notes off to one side of her notepad. He watched as she flipped through the prospectus and the profit-and-loss sheet. Finally she sat back. "Okay I think you've got a solid plan here. I'm not sure why you weren't able to secure investment on your own."

"Me neither," he said.

"I wanted to sort our part of the arrangement out first, but I think my dad is going to need some time to look into this. So let's get him in here and we can discuss that. Regardless of his opinion, I will be investing in your run."

"Why?"

"Because you are going to help me out," she said. "I like a man who honors his word, and from what I've read in this document, you are qualified and know what you're doing."

"I'm not looking for handouts."

"You're not getting it. I'm not a passive investor. I'll be looking for updates quarterly."

"You will?"

"Yup, but don't worry, you'll be hanging out with me a lot so I can keep up to date," she said, with a wink. She pushed her chair back and stood up, but he stopped her with his hand on her wrist.

That electric tingle went up his arm again and his touch drew her off balance. She started to fall and he caught her and steadied her as he stood up. "I don't want you to think you're the boss."

"Why not? I clearly am. I'm going to work up an employment contract for the next three months for our personal arrangement," she said. "And we will have the investment contract separately, okay? You were right. I don't want my dad to know about this. It would be better for everyone if it seemed like you were into me."

"I am," he said.

"Perfect, keep that up," she said. "I'll go get my dad."

"Not yet," he said.

"What? Why not?"

"Because you're giving me credit for being a much better actor than I really am," he said, putting his hand on her waist and waiting to see if she pulled away.

She didn't. Instead she tipped her head to the side, watching him with those wide brown eyes of hers. She nibbled on her lower lip as she waited, and he was struck again that she was two very different women. Strong and confident in business, a little shy and reserved personally. Which of course made a certain kind of sense when he thought about her asking to hire him for the weekend.

"I'm not sure this is a good idea," she said, putting her hand on his chest. But she didn't push him away.

"Why not?"

"We're *pretending* to be a couple," she said. "I don't want to blur the lines."

"We have to make it look real," he said. "If you push me away when I touch you, no one will buy the act."

She nibbled her lower lip again and he bit back a moan. She turned him on like no one he'd been with in a long time. But he was here for business. Which was part of the point he'd been trying to make to her. They had to appear to be lovers even though they were strangers.

He'd also been determined to make his own path and that had sometimes led him astray, but he had to be honest, this detour was the most interesting one he'd found himself on. Pretend boyfriend/lover to a lifestyle guru...who knew?

Four

"So, my daughter tells me you're putting together a group of investors for an America's Cup bid. I read Ellison's book. That's a risky venture," Hal Collins said. He wasn't a tall man, but he carried himself as if he were. There was a sharp intelligence in his gray-blue eyes and a hint of the warmth that Zac had glimpsed in Iris's. He also recognized where Iris got her confidence and backbone.

"Yes, sir," Zac said. "I've been on two teams since I graduated from college and have a lot of experience and knowledge."

He'd been in the boardroom with Iris for what felt like hours and now her father was here to determine if investing in Zac's America's Cup bid was viable.

"Good to hear," Hal said. "Why are you striking out on your own?"

"The honest answer?"

"Always," Hal said.

"I don't take orders well. I know how to win but when you're cashing a paycheck and not the man footing the bill, not everyone will listen. I'm tired of coming in second," Zac said. Hal reminded him a bit of his brother Logan, who would have asked the same sort of questions. Zac knew he had to prove himself to Hal and he was willing to do that.

"Understandable," Hal said. "I don't take orders well either. So how do you know Iris?"

He glanced over at her where she sat a couple of seats away from him and her father. Her eyes widened. They hadn't finished working out the details of the "favor" she wanted from him. "We're dating, sir. I think you should know that I started dating Iris before I knew she was your daughter, so in no way did that influence me."

Hal glanced at her. "I thought you were seeing someone else."

"I was, Dad, but that ended. Zac and I just met and hit it off," she said. "This isn't about my personal life. It's about a pretty solid investment. You are always urging me to diversify."

Hal looked like he didn't want to let the relationship questions go but he just nodded. "This is a risky investment, but from what I've read, I think you might be worth the risk. I need to do some more research, and I'm not sure when you need an answer?"

"The sooner the better. I have already started the design process and I have two team members, but I'll need to recruit more. To be successful in an America's Cup bid, the longer we have to train and prepare the better we will be."

"Fair enough," Hal said. "I should be able to have an answer for you tomorrow. Iris, will you still need the conference room?"

"If you don't, then yes. We're discussing a few details about our schedules," Iris said.

Hal seemed surprised that she'd choose a business set-ting for a personal matter and Zac knew they were going to end up answering more questions, so he just stood up. "Sorry, that's my fault, sir. I don't live in Boston and didn't want to suggest she go back to my hotel room to talk or to her house. As Iris mentioned, we've just started dating."

"I like that. The other guy was too pushy," Hal said, standing. Iris stood too and smiled at her father as he left the room, carrying all of Zac's financial information with him.

Zac realized he should have mentioned his father and his own fortune and made a quick decision. "I need a pri-vate word, Mr. Collins."

Iris seemed surprised and he wondered if she thought he was going to tell her dad about the offer she'd made him. But he just smiled as reassuringly as he could at Iris.

"I need to return some calls. I'll wait in the reception area, Dad."

Iris left the room as Hal sat back down.

"Are you August Bisset's son?" Hal asked.

"Yes."

"Why haven't you mentioned this to Iris?" Hal asked. "I'm not sure keeping this kind of secret is a good idea."

"It didn't come up, but I'm planning to tell her. As you know my family owns Bisset Industries and I have a large investment portfolio of my own. I'll be putting up some of my own money but I need outside investment."

"Why don't you just go to your brother and ask him to invest?" Hal said.

Zac wasn't surprised that Hal knew his brother, Logan, was the CEO of Bisset Industries. "I don't like the strings that come with that. I need to be free to do this on my own. I'm not saying I won't answer to investors, but when it comes to doing business with family...it's difficult."

"I've heard it can be," Hal said. "Thank you for telling me. I think you'd be safe telling Iris, but my wife has warned me not to interfere in either of my daughters' relationships."

"That's probably good advice. I will tell her but thought you might find it odd when you start doing your research and realize I didn't mention it," he said.

"Makes sense. I have a few investors who like long shots and can take the hit if we lose money. I was thinking of a five to six person investor group. We'd form it as an LLC and you would work for us. I know Iris wants to invest in you and you could put your money in through the LLC too," Hal said.

"That sounds like the right approach. And I've been working on a new cutting-edge design for the fin that I think we might be able to monetize after the race," he said.

"Good to know. I think we can at least get the ball rolling this week once I've done a bit more research," Hal said. This time when he stood, he held his hand out to Zac.

He shook the older man's hand, realizing that Iris had given him exactly what he'd been looking for. So he was going to have to give her what she'd asked for from him.

"I'll let Iris know we're done," Hal said. "I look forward to seeing more of you, Zac."

Hal left the room and Zac walked over to the window, staring out at the city. He felt just as hemmed in as he always did when he was on the land, but this trip had been full of the unexpected. And he definitely couldn't complain.

When Iris left the conference room, she rescheduled KT and Stephan for the next morning at seven o'clock, then went down the hall to the patio area. It was surrounded on three sides by glass walls. She looked out at the city, pretending that this was a normal day. But it wasn't. She had been on a roller coaster since she'd gotten that text from Graham.

Her phone pinged and she saw that it was a text from Adler. Her best friend, the bride-to-be. It was a photo of two martini glasses, captioned, Saving one for you.

She texted back that she needed a drink or two.

Adler's response was immediate. You okay?

Yeah. I'll tell you all about it when I'm on the island. Won't be with Graham at the wedding… I'm too basic for him. Whatever, right?

He's a dick. Are you sure you're okay? Want to chat?

Can't at the moment.

She hesitated.

Believe it or not, I met a guy.

Good. Tell me more.

He's cute, really bright blue eyes, and he has a bit of stubble. You know, normally I'm opposed but it suits him. Also he kissed me, and it was way hotter than anything I've experienced before.

Sounds perfect. Are you bringing him to the wedding?

Yes. Is that okay?

It's fine. Can't wait to meet him. Text me after drinks and let me know how it went.

Will do.

Bran cleared his throat and she looked up.

"Your father said he's done speaking with Mr. Bisset and you can rejoin him," Bran said.

"Thank you. We shouldn't be much longer."

"Your father pays really good overtime so it's not a problem if you are," he joked.

She followed him back into the office area and then went down toward the conference room. On the walls of the hallway were photos from the different companies her father had invested in over the years. Some of them included her father as a younger man and in many of them her mom was by his side.

She felt a pang deep inside of her.

It wasn't that she needed a man to complete her or that she was less than without a guy at her elbow. It was that she wanted a partner. For some of the companies in the photos, she clearly remembered her father struggling to decide to invest in the firm and how her mom had been his sounding board. She knew the stakes because they were in it together.

Iris wanted that. She'd thought that Graham would be that kind of guy. He hadn't shied away from the social media aspect of her career, he liked that she made more money than he did and he'd been nice to have at events and functions. Despite being douchey at times, Graham was very good at a cocktail party. But he hadn't been right for her. She'd sort of sensed it from the first but then she'd put her misgivings aside, preferring to ignore the bad stuff and focus on the good.

But she'd deceived herself.

She wouldn't do that with Zac. He was really going to be just for show, and as much as her heart ached at the thought of that, her mind and her bruised spirit applauded it. How many hits could her soul take before she just turned into... Leta. As much as Iris loved her mentor, she'd had six failed marriages and was very cynical toward the opposite sex.

"Iris?"

She turned toward the conference room where Zac stood in the doorway. She smiled at him. "Just taking a stroll down memory lane. So much of my family is built into Collins Combined that it's hard not to sometimes feel nostalgic."

And envious, she admitted to herself. But then she straightened her shoulders. She wasn't big into feeling sorry for herself. She tucked her phone into the pocket of her dress and turned toward him. "Let's get down to business on this, shall we?"

"There's nothing more to discuss," he said. "I'll do what you've asked. I think it's fair. Your father is offering more than I'd expected from you when you suggested this exchange."

As much as she wanted to hear that news, she had to be sure he understood what she wanted. "Let's go in the conference room and make sure we both have the details the same."

He stopped her as he walked by him. With his hand on her upper arm, she looked up into his eyes and felt that heat running through her at his touch. She had to get this under control. Hadn't she just realized that by lying to herself she'd end up broken? She had to stuff the attraction way down. She'd put her own personal needs and desires aside when she'd started on this path and it needed to stay that way.

She'd built her empire from showing people what they wanted to see and not by being herself. It was too late to change now. She didn't want to lose what she'd built and she had a feeling not keeping strict boundaries with Zac could spell trouble.

"I think we should only be touching when we're in public," she said. "Let's go inside and address this."

"Address what? You want me to be your—"

She put her hand over his mouth to stop him from saying anything else as she noticed her father's assistant coming out of his office.

Zac arched his eyebrows at her as she flushed and drew him into the conference room, closing the door firmly behind them and leaning back against it. She let her tingling hand drop from his mouth. She wasn't normally such a touchy person.

"Well, angel face, that was definitely touching."

Zac could see the conflict in her. There was something about her that was deeply sensual, yet she seemed to prefer to keep it hidden. It was there in her appearance. Her hair was pulled back low on her neck, her clothing was sensibly feminine and conservative, which only made her sensual mouth and her figure stand out more because there was a natural grace and femininity in every move she made.

"What did Dad say?" she asked.

"He's interested in putting together an LLC of five or six investors. You'd be one."

"Good. That works for me. Please, sit down, Mr. Bisset," she said.

"Is this the part where you explain that you're the boss?" he asked as he moved to one of the chairs. He wanted to tease her and see if he could find his way past the bow tied at her neck and maybe loosen up that hairstyle, but he needed to finalize their agreement more. He wanted to know the boundaries and parameters because he was ready to get back to his team and start the wheels in motion. He

had no doubt that once Hal started researching both himself
and his yacht-captaining career, he would get behind him.
And even if he didn't, Zac had decided he'd fund the run
himself. That was what Larry Ellison had done. But part of
the reason Zac had hesitated to do that was ego. He wanted
to know that others believed in him. So that his run was
more about proving something to himself than to the world.

"It is," she said. "So here's the schedule for the wedding.
I think those four days will be the most intense part of this.
Then I just need a few dates after. As I suggested earlier,
at first we'll do a couple a week, and then I have my book
and product launches and you'll be doing your boat stuff,
so we stay long distance—a long-distance couple."

He almost smiled at the way she cut herself off from saying lovers. It amused him that she was...well, the way she
was. He should mention he knew Adler but she was on a roll
with her requirements so he decided to let it ride for now.

"Okay. For the wedding, I'll be your guy at all of the
events. We can hold hands, kiss and do whatever else you
think we should."

"Thank you for that. But maybe we should set a limit
on the kissing—once a day," she said.

"No. We should both be acting the way we would in a
real relationship if we're going to sell it. Your dad is way
too savvy not to notice if we just kiss once a day. We need
to be ourselves."

"Believe it or not, that is me," she said.

"Well it's not me," he countered. "This has to seem like
we're both real people. I can't be someone you made up."

"And yet you are," she said testily.

"Having second thoughts?" he asked her.

"Yes. And third and fourth. And it all comes back to
you."

He scooted around so that his chair faced hers and pulled

her closer to him. "The only way this is going to work is if we are a team. We have to have each other's backs. If we're both playing our own game, it will show to everyone who we meet."

"A team?" she asked.

There was something more going on here than the conversation. He could see it in her eyes. "Yes. We have to be partners. We'll look at the events and make a plan that shows you and me in our best light."

"I… I really like that."

"Good. I know that we have an arrangement, but I think we should try to be friends. That will be fun too. We can learn about each other and that will lend a realness to the relationship."

"It will," she said.

He saw her taking notes and wondered how many relationships she'd been in. Because the way she was acting, it didn't seem like she had a lot of experience. "Isn't that what you normally do when you start dating someone?"

She put her pen down and tucked a tendril of hair that had escaped her updo back behind her ear. "I don't know. Normally I date people I meet at an event. If they are an influencer, then we try to stage photos and go places where our viewers want to see us—"

"That's not what I'm talking about. The last guy you dated—didn't you get to know him?"

"Yes. But he wasn't who I thought he was," she said. "It's so crazy because on the surface we seemed like we were made for each other but behind closed doors… Well, I'm glad that we won't have to worry about any of that."

"What are you talking about?" Zac asked. He wasn't sure what had happened, but it didn't sound like it was pleasant.

"Nothing. I like this," she said, flipping to a blank

sheet of paper on her notepad and writing with clean and neat strokes. When she was done, she turned the pad to him and handed it over. "Read this and let me know your thoughts."

He glanced down at the contract she'd written on the legal pad. It stated a start date for their association, as she'd called it, and it stated an end date of three months from today. She listed out what she wanted from him and then left a blank for the dollar amount of her investment.

"Should we make sure we have chemistry before we try this?" he asked.

She nodded a few times. "Yes, you're right. We need to make sure we're believable as a couple."

He stood up. She did so as well and then held out her hand. He reached out to take it, then tugged her toward him and lowered his head for a kiss.

Five

She clung to his shoulders as every nerve ending in her body went on high alert. His lips were close but he wasn't kissing her but she was so close to those lips of his. And she needed to prove to herself that earlier had been a fluke. That she was the highly business-focused and driven woman with a low sex drive she'd always been.

So she shifted slightly, leaning up until her lips brushed his. That tingle started again in her lips and she saw his eyes widen slightly before he took control of the kiss. Oh, dear Lord, the man tasted so good. Better than anything she'd tasted before. She held on to his shoulders; they were strong and muscly, probably from all that time spent captaining a yacht.

She felt one of his hands on the small of her back and the other at her waist. His fingers moved against her skin, caressing her as someone cleared his throat behind her.

Zac broke the kiss and straightened, turning them both so that the boardroom table was at their backs.

"Dad," Iris said. "Sorry about that. We were just wrapping up in here… I mean it's not what it—"

"Stop explaining, Iris. The last thing either of us wants is to discuss you kissing Zac," her father said.

Iris smiled because her father was right and it seemed like that kiss had lent authenticity to their story that they were dating. "Did you need one of us?"

"Actually, both of you," her father said.

"Both of us?"

"Yes. I spoke with your mom and mentioned I'd met Zac and she wants to meet him too. You know she hates when I know something she doesn't," her father said with a wink.

All the enjoyment Iris had had from the kiss and feeling like she'd fooled her dad went out the window and instead panic started to fill her stomach, making her queasy. Fooling Dad was one thing, but her mom? That was going to be very difficult.

"Oh, I wish we could, Dad, but I promised Adler we'd be on Nantucket in the morning, so Zac and I were going to have a quiet night in."

"That's perfect, sweetie," her father said. "Your mom invited you both to dinner. I think Thea will be there too."

Of course, she would be.

"Zac, will that be okay? I know you said you had a call you needed to make tonight," she said, hoping he'd pick up on her subtle hint and make an excuse so they could skip dinner.

"That's fine. My call can wait," he said, wrapping his arm around her waist and squeezing her close to his side. "I look forward to getting to know your family better."

"Great. That's settled then. I'll text your mom. Be at ours at six-thirty," Iris's father said.

He turned and walked out of the boardroom, closing the door behind him. Iris took a deep breath before turning to face Zac. Before she could say anything, he ripped the page off the legal pad. "We should have two of these so we each have one."

"What?" she asked, not even thinking about the contract. "Yes, of course. Why did you say yes to dinner?"

"If we can't fool your family at dinner, how are we going to make a lot of people buy us as a couple for four days?" he asked. He pulled the legal pad to him and started copying what she'd written word-for-word.

"It will be harder with my mom and Thea. Dad's easy because he only sees what he wants to. But Mom is shrewd, and you should know that Thea suggested I hire a guy for the weekend so she might try to trip you up."

"Thanks for the heads-up. See, this will be a good test run."

"Yeah, probably," Iris said. "I mean, yes."

She felt a little light-headed. Maybe it was that kiss he'd laid on her…or she'd laid on him.

"I'm sorry about that kiss," she said. "I know you meant for it to seem as if we had been kissing if my father came in. It won't happen again."

"I didn't mind at all. I was going to do more than just hold you. I wanted whoever entered to pay attention to us and not this," he said, gesturing to the legal pad. She saw he'd signed his name on both copies. "You sign now and we'll both have a copy."

She went over and signed the second one and then took it and folded it neatly into thirds so it would fit into her purse.

Then it occurred to her that there was no termination clause. "We didn't give ourselves an out."

"You said there was no other option than to see things through for the three months. I'm a man of my word," he said. "And I can tell that you are a smart lady. You won't back out."

She nodded. "Do you have a hotel in town?"

"Yeah, I've got a place," he said. "I have a car there too."

They exchanged phone numbers and she gave him her address. "Do you want to just meet at my parents'?"

"No. I'll pick you up. I think your dad is an old-fashioned kind of guy," Zac said.

"You're not wrong, but he gets that we live in a modern world," she said. "I'll take my car and meet you there."

"You know your family best so that sounds good," he said.

"Okay, so see you tonight," she said, then led the way out of the conference room. As they walked down the hall, she realized she'd said goodbye too soon and now she had to either figure out something to say to him or just walk awkwardly in silence next to him.

In the elevator, he hit the ground-floor button.

"Zac, thank you," she said.

"You're very welcome," he said.

"So how did you get the money for this?" Dev Kellman asked when Zac arrived back at his family's Boston home where he and his friends were staying while they tried to drum up financing. Yancy McNeil was there as well, standing by the bar when he entered.

"Through Iris," Zac said. His friends had never heard him mention a girlfriend, so he figured he'd better start talking about her soon. From watching his sister—whose channel and media following were a lot smaller than Iris's—get dragged when she started dating Inigo, he knew that the attention he and Iris would receive was going to be a lot more intense.

"Who's Iris?" Dev asked as he pulled three longneck

bottles of beer from the fridge behind the mini bar, gave one to Yancy and held one up toward Zac. Zac nodded.

Who was Iris? His objective had been to get financing, and of course he was on the verge of securing it in the most bizarre way possible. Dev and he had been good friends for the last ten years, having met at boarding school. He knew that Iris only wanted the two of them to know about their arrangement and he was going to honor that, but he hadn't really thought through the logistics of being her for-hire man. He was going to have lie to his friends and family or just shut them down with a few terse words. "The lady I'm dating," Zac said.

"Since when?" Dev asked. "We landed two days ago, and you broke up with Zara before we left Sydney so I don't think you had time to get—"

"Since none-of-your-business," he said. He wasn't about to start making up stories about the two of them and Dev and Yancy didn't really need the details.

"Okay, okay, don't get cranky. I was just asking. It's not like you to hook up with a woman this quickly."

"She's different," Zac said at last. "You know I'm not all touchy-feely and *let's talk about our emotions*."

"Me neither. Just when you tie our business to a woman, I want to make sure it's a good decision."

Dev and he both. It was risky. Which was why he'd almost come clean with Hal. He wanted to make sure that the deal with Hal went through regardless of this thing with Iris.

"I'm being careful. The money isn't tied to me dating her."

"Fair enough, but you've got tons of money. Why not just use yours?" Yancy asked.

"I am. Her dad is an investment guy. He puts together groups of investors who go after different ventures. When I mentioned to Iris that I was in Boston trying to raise funds, she mentioned her father might be interested. She said that he was always looking for new things. I don't think this is quite what he had in mind when he said that, but he was game. He's doing some research and is putting together an investment team. I'll be one of the shareholders as will Iris," Zac said.

"Cool. How will it be structured?" Yancy asked.

"I'm not sure yet, but he mentioned an LLC. I want you and me as COOs so that we can be in charge of getting who we need in place. We should know in the next few days about the funding, but I think it's safe to start shopping for a design company that can manufacture our yacht," Zac said. "I mentioned that we are planning to sell our design after the next Cup run."

"The patent is in our names," Dev reminded him.

"They know that. They'd get a share of the profit but no intellectual property claim."

"Great. I'll get the ball rolling. I'm having dinner with some guys who might be interested in joining our team tonight and then we can meet tomorrow to talk more," Dev said.

"Let's meet next week on Nantucket. I've got to be there for Adler's wedding and Iris is a bridesmaid," Zac said. He really needed to tell her about his connection to Adler.

"Ah, so that's how you two met. Cool. Can't wait to meet her. Thanks for putting this together. I was really getting sick of having our ideas overlooked."

"You don't have to thank me. We're a team," Dev said. "I've got to go. Talk tomorrow."

He did the one-armed bro hug with Dev and Yancy that had become their habit, then his friends left and Zac was alone in the town house. He went up to his room and stood in front of his closet. It had been a while since he'd had to socialize with upper-class people so he wanted to look the part.

He had a closet of clothing that the staff kept clean at all times. He didn't know how casual or formal dinner at the Collinses' house would be. He opted for some dark trousers and a button-down shirt and paired it with some dress shoes.

He rubbed his hand over his beard. He kept it neatly trimmed but it was summer and hotter here than it had been in Australia, so should he shave? He'd leave it for tonight.

He showered and dressed, then headed to the address that Iris had given him. When he pulled into the large circle drive, there were two cars already parked there: a green VW Beetle and a sleek beige BMW. He parked behind them, got out of the car and walked up the drive. He had a bouquet of flowers he'd picked up on his way over and a bottle of wine he'd nicked from his parents' wine cellar.

Did he look like he was trying too hard to impress her?

He texted Iris that he was in front of the house, then rang the doorbell. He heard a dog barking, and then the door opened and Iris stood there. She wore a pair of white trousers and a halter-neck top that showed off her shoulders and collarbone. Her hair was down around her shoulders and her brown eyes were warm as she smiled at him.

He wasn't sure why it mattered but he really hoped he impressed her.

"So, when did you meet this guy?" Thea asked as they sat at the counter in her mother's kitchen. She'd arrived twenty minutes earlier and she was just full of questions tonight.

"A few days ago," Iris said, keeping it vague because she'd been so busy making sure they had a legal document that she'd forgotten the details of their cover story. "I didn't want to say anything earlier because I hadn't broken things off with Graham."

"It's kind of quick," her mom said. "But your father was impressed by him."

"He's that kind of guy," Iris said. There was something solid and formidable about Zac. He wasn't like Graham, who, though charming, had at times seemed like he was trying too hard.

"I'm not sure I believe that," Thea said. "Remember what we were talking about at lunch?"

"Thea," Iris said. "I told you that silly plan you had wasn't necessary. You just didn't trust me."

"Sorry, Iris," Thea said, her eyes growing wide. "I was trying to help you. You didn't mention him so I thought that jerk Graham was humiliating you."

"It's okay. I know you were just trying to protect me," Iris said.

"What are you two talking about?" her mom asked, mixing some Aperol spritz drinks for them.

"I suggested Iris hire a guy to act as her date for the wedding weekend. Graham kind of left her high and dry," Thea said. "But you knew that he wasn't right before that text, didn't you?"

"Yes. This weekend he was…well, not what I had hoped he'd be. So I'd already made plans to move on," Iris said.

Oh, God, this had to work, because if it ever came out that she'd hired Zac, she was going to lose a lot of followers. She'd never lied to her audience before. She might stage photos but it was always based in honesty.

Had she made a mistake?

The doorbell rang just as her phone buzzed. She glanced down to see it was a text from Zac. Thea looked at it too. Angel face, I'm here.

"I'll get it."

She left the kitchen and wiped her sweaty hands on her legs as she went down the hall. This would work. She had no choice but to make it work.

She took a deep breath and opened the door. Zac looked good. Damn good. He'd put on a dress shirt and had it neatly tucked into a pair of nice trousers that showed off his slim waist. He had put on dress shoes and socks and his hair was nicely styled. As he took off his aviator-style sunglasses, she realized the navy shirt made his blue eyes more brilliant.

"Hi."

"Hello. I need to talk to you about the wedding."

"Come in," she said. "We can do it later. Not in front of everyone."

Zac stepped into her parents' house as Riley, her mom's thirteen-year-old miniature dachshund, came running down the hall, dancing around Zac's feet and barking.

"Riley, shush," she said, bending to pet the dog.

Zac stooped down next to her and shifted the bouquet of flowers and the bottle of wine he'd brought to the same hand so he could pet the little dog.

"Hello, Riley," he said. Riley loved the attention and started licking Zac's hand. Then after a final pet, Riley trotted back down the hall to the large kitchen where Iris's mom and sister waited.

Iris and Zac stood up. "Thanks for coming tonight. Dad's still at work. Thea and Mom are anxious to meet you. I said we met two days ago."

"Good," he said. "I was in Australia before that."

"Oh, okay. I was on a weekend trip with my ex. They might ask. Maybe we should say we met at the bar today," she said.

"Sounds good."

"Yes."

"Perfect," he said. "You look nice."

"Thanks. So do you. That shirt makes your eyes seem even bluer than before," she said.

He smiled at the compliment. "Should I have shaved? My mom hates stubble, but I figured I didn't want to look like I was trying too hard. Your dad would notice."

"I like the beard," she said, lifting her hand to touch it. It was soft and abraded her fingers slightly.

"Iris, are you going to keep him in the foyer, or can we meet him?" Thea said from the end of the hall.

"We're coming." Iris turned to face her sister and led the way to where Thea was standing. "Zac Bisset, this is my sister, Thea."

"Nice to meet you," he said, holding out his hand.

"Nice to meet you too," Thea said. "Come meet Mom. She's made Aperol spritzes as an aperitif. Do you like those?"

"My brother Darien calls them Kool-Aid for grown-ups."

"He has a point. They are very easy to drink," Thea said.

"Mom, this is Zac. Zac, this is my mom, Corinne," Iris said.

"Nice to meet you, Corinne," Zac said. "These are for you."

He handed her mom the flowers and the wine, then gave her an air kiss on the cheek, which her mom returned. "Thank you, Zac."

"You're welcome. Thank you for inviting me to dinner," he said.

"I'm sure Hal told you that once he met the guy Iris was seeing, I was curious and wanted to meet you too," her mom said.

"He did," Zac admitted.

"No use pretending that we aren't very curious about you," Corinne said.

"I'm an open book," Zac said. "I'm glad to have the chance to meet Iris's family too."

Oh, great. Zac was saying all the right things. And doing everything as if she'd handed him a script. She had to remember it was an act or it would be very easy to fall for him.

Six

Iris walked Zac out after drinks and dessert were over. He had enjoyed meeting her family and it was easy to tell that, despite her online presence and social media persona, Iris lived a very normal life behind-the-scenes.

Thea had done her best to try to trip him up but one thing in their favor was the fact that they'd simply just started dating. There weren't a lot of things a two-day old couple were expected to already know about each other.

"Thea was tough," he said as he leaned back against his car. The sky was clear, and though the stars weren't as visible here as they were in the middle of the ocean, it was still a beautiful night.

"She's a pain in the butt," Iris said. "But I think this was really good practice. So I know I said we wouldn't need to be on Nantucket until Thursday but would you mind going over tomorrow? Adler wants to catch up and of course meet you before everything gets started. She's my bestie so she's curious."

"Not at all. Actually, about that—" he said. He probably should mention that Adler was his cousin at this point.

"Good," Iris interrupted. "I'm going to be bringing some staff with me so we could meet at the hotel in Nantucket or drive down together."

"Staff?" he asked. "Besides me?"

"Yes. I have a glam squad who makes sure I'm camera-ready. Also my production assistant will be there. Aside from my bridal duties, I'm going to be doing a few on-air interviews as part of the recorded show. You'll be free to do your own thing during that time."

"I didn't realize the wedding was going to be televised," Zac said. "I can't drive down with you. I have a meeting with my team tomorrow. I'll meet you at the hotel."

"Yes, it's part of a show that features destination weddings. Adler's wedding will kick it off. Because my reality TV show is pretty much *my life* and the events I attend, I'll be doing some live shoots that will be aired later. I want you in some of them but just to add flavor—that's the part we spoke about earlier."

"Of course," he said, but he really wished he'd paid better attention when they'd negotiated terms because this was sounding more like work than he'd imagined. "Do I need a glam squad?"

She laughed. "No. KT and Stephan will get you camera-ready if need them but I really want to just use shots of the two of us from the weekend in a montage. I don't want you to feel pressured especially since that isn't what you signed up for."

He was beginning to feel like he didn't know what he'd signed up for. Iris wasn't what he'd expected. She intrigued him and he wondered if he'd ever really figure her out. It had been easy to see her as the good daughter tonight but she had demonstrated a wicked sense of humor and her family did a lot of gentle teasing. It was very different from the formal meals he was used to when his father was present. Then everyone was polite and traded thinly veiled barbs. The dinner with the Collins family tonight reminded him more of the meals he had when it was just his mom and his siblings.

Hal Collins was a very different man than August Bisset. Where August was domineering and forceful, Hal was… somehow gentler but in no way less shrewd.

"Great. Will they be staying in the same suite as us?"

"No. Definitely not," she said. "I want us to be able to have some downtime when we can be ourselves."

"Angel face, I'm never not myself," he said.

"Is that true? Even when you told my dad that you were a fan of opera?" she asked.

"Well, I mean, I do like *The Magic Flute*," Zac said. "But you know how it is when you meet the parents. You don't insult things they love."

"Very true," she said. "It's a good thing you'll be in training, otherwise I think he might invite us to join them the next time they go."

"I wouldn't mind at all. My mom loves opera as does my gran. On Sundays before brunch, they both would fill the house with music. Sometimes opera, sometimes jazz, and when we got old enough, rock."

"Sounds like a wonderful tradition," she said. "I would love to meet your family someday."

Uh, yeah. "About that."

"What?"

"I didn't want you to recognize my last name at first, but I'm actually Adler's cousin. My mom is Juliette Bisset, her aunt and godmother. You'll get to meet more of my family than you probably want to," he said.

"What?" she asked. "Why didn't you say anything tonight at dinner?"

"I was trying to let your family get to know me. Plus it's pretentious to introduce myself as August Bisset's son," he said.

"I get that, but you should have said something," she said. "Why do you need my dad to find investors then? Can't you fund the run yourself?"

She looked angry and hurt and he realized he should have handled this better. "I'm sorry, Iris. I never meant to hurt you."

"You didn't. This is a business arrangement. I just like to know all the facts. Does Dad know?"

"Yes, he recognized me and I didn't deny it."

"So why play games with me?" she asked.

He tipped his head back, looking up at the evening sky. "I'm sorry. I didn't mean to hurt you. I could do it with the help of my father and my brother, Logan, the current CEO of the family business, but the truth is they both put too many strings on the money and I don't want to answer to them. I started captaining to find my own thing and if I asked them for money…it wouldn't be mine anymore."

She folded her arms under her breasts and narrowed her eyes as she studied him. "That makes a certain kind of sense. I felt the same way when I started my own brand. I had Leta's backing but I knew I wanted to establish myself before I went to Collins Combine for an investment. It was more fulfilling knowing I'd made it on my own."

"That's what I want," he said. "I'm very successful in my field on someone else's team but I want to be the captain of a winning America's Cup yacht and the only way I can do that is with your help."

"Is there anything else you are hiding?" she asked. "I don't what there to be any more surprises."

"Well, I'm not faking it when I kiss you."

"No. Don't do that. This will only work if we treat it like a temporary thing," she said. "I bought you for three months."

"Angel face, I don't work like that," he said. "I'm not good at faking it and frankly, I'm better at it than you. You were way too tense at the beginning of the meal, waiting for me to—"

"I know," she said. "It's just my business and everything is on the line. I think I made a huge mistake but there's no going back."

Her honesty undid him. He was ready to push her until she admitted that they should sleep together, that the attraction between them was hotter than the sun on a summer's day. But he saw that she was confused by the attraction and this offer she'd made him, which was out of character for her.

He noticed the blinds shifting in the front room of the house and realized that they had been out here too long. "Someone's watching us. Want to go someplace and talk? I have a town house that's not far from here or we could go to a bar."

She sighed. "Okay. Is the town house an Airbnb?"

"No," he said. "It's one my family owns. We have property all over the world and the place in Boston is one my mom uses when she comes up here to visit my gran."

"There is so much I don't know about you," she said.

"That's fine. We've only been dating for two days," he reminded her. "You okay to follow me?"

"Yes. But text me the address in case we get separated."

The blinds at the front of the house were still askew so he leaned in, putting his hand on her waist. Then he kissed her gently on the cheek. "Just to allay any suspicions."

She sighed as her hands curled around his biceps. "I like kissing you too. That's why I don't want to do it too often."

"Let's talk about it at my place," he said. "Want to leave your car here? I can bring you back to get it later."

"No," she said.

He stepped back, putting his hands up. "Okay. Whatever you want."

"Let's go."

He waited for her to get into her beige BMW and then got into his car. He pulled around her in the large circle drive and she followed him the short distance to the town house. There was ample parking for two cars in the driveway and he led her into the house.

She paused in the entrance hall, looking at the picture of the Bissets on the left wall. It included his extended family and had been taken earlier this year when Mari had announced her engagement to Inigo Velasquez.

"I know your sister," Iris said. "Not well, but I do consider her a friend. The ripples from this arrangement we have just keep growing."

Iris shook her head and then walked past him into the house. "Which way to…wherever you want to talk?"

"Second door on the left, wall switch as soon as you enter. I'll be right behind you," he said.

She moved down the hall the way she had moved in the boardroom earlier. She was getting back into businesswoman mode and he was the first to admit he preferred her in relaxed mode. But she was in charge. She had concerns and worries that he knew nothing about and frankly, he didn't need to. They had a deal.

He'd almost forgotten it while they'd been at dinner. Her family had been so warm and welcoming he wanted to be the new boyfriend—for real. He wanted to somehow believe that if he—was what? Someone completely different?

He couldn't fit into that domestic scene in any scenario that wasn't pretend. He spent most of his life on a yacht and he wasn't planning to stop anytime soon. His life was on boats.

She'd taken a seat on the leather sofa in the living room. As much as he wanted to sit next to her, he walked to the large chambray-colored armchair and sat down, putting his feet up on the hassock. "So…"

"Zac, I'm sorry that I've put you in this situation. And I'm not even sure why you agreed. I know you want investors and I sort of understand wanting to do this without your family's interference, but you didn't need to agree to my dating plan in order to make that happen," she said. "I think because we're going to be lying to everyone about our relationship, we need to be honest with each other. We need to be clear so that there are no misunderstandings. Does that sound agreeable to you?"

"Yes, it does," he said. "That's why I told you I'm hot for you."

Her eyes widened for the shortest second and then she nodded. "Me too. But that's a complication I'm not sure I'm ready to handle. To be fair, you should know that I'm not very good at sex."

He was shocked for a second. Then he shook his head. "I highly doubt you're not good. Both players share the responsibility for that."

"Uh, oh…okay," she said. Then she groaned. "Why did I even say that? Even though my reputation is for saying the right thing and hosting fab events, in my personal life… I'm not as together as all that."

"I like it. It's real. I bet your viewers would get it too," he said. "Have you thought about being yourself?"

She shook her head. "No one wants that. Sure, it would be amusing for a short while as a novelty but everyone wants you to stick to the image they have of you. Everyone."

She sounded very sure and he wondered who had been disappointed in the real Iris. But that wasn't a question he needed answered right now.

"What's next?"

Next? She had no idea. She needed to get focused and stop thinking about how strong his arms had felt under her fingers. Or how warm his breath had been on her cheek. Or how she'd wanted one more real kiss instead of that brush of his lips earlier.

"Let's get the wedding details sorted out," she said. "Then I think we can plan to meet on Nantucket tomorrow."

"Sounds good. What are the details?" he asked.

"You might already know them," she said. "Since you're family-of-the-bride. Let me pull up the schedule Adler sent." Iris took out her phone and called up her calendar. "So next Thursday is the welcome lunch at her gran's— your gran's place, then the sailing competition around the harbor. I guess we should do well at that."

"We should since I'm captaining one of the yachts. Are you a good sailor?"

"I'm okayish. I really don't swim well, but I do like being on the water," she said. No use going into details of how she liked to get below deck with a few drinks to calm her nerves.

"Great. That will be fun," he said. "We can do some romantic things on the boat."

She just vaguely nodded. *Like what?* she wanted to know, but kept that question to herself. "Then there's the clambake in the evening. That's a really full day. I think we should just be clear about being a new couple, touchy but not over the top with the PDA. I mean, we want to be cute and romantic, not X-rated."

He crossed his arms over his chest and nodded his head

a few times. "I can do that. Am I staying with you in your suite? Or do I need my own place?"

"I was thinking the suite," she said. "Unless we should just not be lovers…"

"We're not lovers," he reminded her.

"I know that. I mean, will it make me seem too prudish if I don't have you in my suite? It's got two rooms so you can stay with me, and we can let anyone who's inclined to dwell on it, think what they want."

He started laughing.

"What?"

"*Inclined to dwell on it*—are you kidding?"

"No. I mean, it was kind of fussy of me, wasn't it? If people are going to gossip, it's up to them what they think."

"I agree. So, what's on Friday?"

"The golf scramble. Adler is pairing up with her side of the wedding party so we'll be separated for that. Then we have the rehearsal and the rehearsal dinner. Saturday is the big event, so I'll be busy helping Adler get ready and then there's the sunset ceremony followed by dancing all night. Can you dance?"

"I can. Mom insisted I learn. She said women like dancing and a man who says he won't is a turnoff."

"I agree," Iris said. "All that's left is brunch on Sunday and then we head home. Where will you go?"

"I'll stay in Nantucket for a few days unless your father has the investors ready by Monday then I'll come back to Boston with you," he said. "We can see each other frequently until the money is ready and then I'll have to start putting things in motion."

"That's settled then," she said. "I'll forward you the schedule. Remember, I'll be doing some filming as I mentioned. I'll also probably do some photos for my social accounts so I'll need you for those, but I'll use the events we're at for a backdrop."

She put her phone back into her bag and looked around the living room. It was very traditional but with sort of homey touches. There was a large landscape painting of Boston Harbor on one wall and candid family photos on the table by the sofa. She couldn't help smiling at the one of a teenaged Zac standing at the helm of a yacht. "When did you start yachting?"

"When I was nine. It was either that or go with Logan and Darien to the summer internship at Bisset Industries. And…well, Dad and I butt heads a lot so Mom suggested I try sailing lessons, which I loved. She calls me her water baby… I'm a Pisces."

"I'm an Aries but everyone says I'm not typical of the sign," she said.

"Uh, whoever says that doesn't know you at all," he commented.

She stuck her tongue out at him. "I am a tad bossy."

"Yeah, that's one way of putting it," he said.

She liked him. There was a part of her, the one that still secretly longed for a partner, that wished this was real. But she knew she'd never have talked to him if it hadn't been for Thea's suggestion. And he'd never be here if she hadn't made her offer. It was the only kind of relationship she was good at. It was fun and easy because she knew what she was getting and that it would be ending.

Was that really all she was going to have with him?

It was disappointing but she was glad that she had the chance to know him. Because he was so different from the other men in her life. And he made her feel like she was different…well, not different so much as that she could be herself and that was okay.

She realized that she wasn't trying to impress him and she'd have never guessed that would be so freeing.

"I guess I'll be going. Thank you, Zac."

He stood up when she did, and she turned to walk toward the door but he stopped her.

"Angel face?"

"Yes?"

"One more thing," he said, pulling her into his arms and giving her the kiss she'd been craving all night.

Seven

She was so cute, and it had been pretty hard to resist kissing her. He'd been thinking about it all night as he'd watched her and her family interact. He'd grown up in a reasonably supportive household but what he'd seen at the Collins family dinner table was something he'd truly never experienced. There was real love in the family and though he and his siblings had a close bond, their father had always encouraged them to compete against each other. To prove themselves to him that they were the best of the Bisset children.

Darien had reacted by smoking a lot as a teenager and then just skipping the family business, to leave room for Logan who was a lion and had no trouble going in for the kill when he sensed a weakness. That had been the one reason why growing up Zac hadn't wanted to go to the office with his older brothers. As much as he'd wanted August Bisset's approval, he never wanted to have to cut down Darien or Logan to get it.

Kissing Iris made him rethink the entire agreement he'd made with her. He didn't want to be bound by a contract, and for the first time in his life, he felt like he was pretending to be something he wasn't. It didn't sit well with him. He lifted his head to stare down into her face. Her eyes were closed but as soon as he broke the kiss, they flew open.

She put her hand on her lips and then she stepped back. "Did I do something wrong? I'll tell you in all honesty I'm not that great at this. I mean, the posing and looking like I'm enjoying a romantic embrace I can handle but the real—"

He put his finger over her mouth to stem the words that she couldn't seem to control. "Angel face, you're so damned good that you're making me regret I only agreed to be your man temporarily."

She tipped her head to the side and smiled up at him. "Really?"

He nodded.

"You're way sweeter than I bet you let anyone see," she said.

"I'm not sweet," he said. "That's lust talking."

"Lust? Is it because you've been at sea for so long?" she asked.

It was odd to see the woman who had negotiated with him in the boardroom like she was preparing to win *Shark Tank* be so shy when it came to personal relationships. Then again, he knew that everyone dealt with intimacy in his or her own way. Normally he liked to make it a competition because he wasn't comfortable letting his guard down.

But he was quickly coming to realize that he couldn't make this a game. She wasn't the kind of player who would be able to handle this. And that changed everything for him.

She wasn't what he'd expected; even dinner at her family's home hadn't been what he was used to. Maybe he should change his thinking and acknowledge that she wasn't going to fit in any mold he had for her.

She wasn't just the lifestyle guru with the perfect image and confidence to boot. She was real and that enchanted him as nothing else could. Maybe she was his siren, tempting him with something so outside of his normal world that he would unknowingly crash against the rocks to get to her.

But at this moment, he didn't care. His mind might be trying to send out a warning, but his hard-on wasn't having any part of it. He pulled her back into his arms. "This has nothing to do with our deal."

"Why not?"

"Because I want you regardless of that contract," he said. Also, he realized that as a Bisset he wasn't about to let someone else be in charge. He was a bit chagrined to realize he had more traits in common with his father than he wanted to admit.

"I don't... Will you still honor the bargain no matter what the outcome tonight?" she asked.

"Yes, of course," he said. "What kind of men have you—never mind—I really don't want to know. I'm not going to back out now."

"Okay," she said. "I want to say one more time—"

"Don't. Forget about whatever you've experienced in the past, Iris. We've never been together before and I feel like we should both be ready for whatever comes our way."

"Whatever," she said, and he saw a glimpse of the control freak he'd witnessed in the boardroom cross her expression. She closed her eyes and took a deep breath.

He realized thinking wasn't going to help her relax. She wanted him; he'd felt it in her kiss. But she was afraid to move forward.

He pulled her back inside his house and lifted her off her feet, carrying her down the hall to the living room. The room was in shadow when he put her on her feet in front of the French doors that led to the patio.

She tipped her head back as he kept his arms around her waist. "Okay, Google, play 'They Can't Take That Away' by Billie Holiday."

The home assistant acknowledged his request and the music started. He pulled Iris more fully into his arms, dancing with her in front of the doors that led to the backyard. He held her loosely because she wasn't the kind of woman who responded to grasping, greedy passion, at least at this point. There might come a time later in their relationship— he stopped himself from continuing with that thought. Their relationship had an expiration date. It would end. So there was no point in holding anything back.

He could be himself and he could enjoy all of her because there wasn't any expectation that they'd have more than this time together.

He lowered his head and their eyes met. Hers were dreamy, and for the first time since he'd met her, she seemed to be relaxed. Her guard was completely lowered, and he realized that she was probably thinking the same way as he was. That this moment was all they had. There were no consequences.

He put his thumb on her chin and tipped her head back a bit more so he could kiss her again. He swayed to the music and tried to ignore the white-hot passion that was making his blood flow heavier in his veins and hardening his erection. He tried not to focus on the fact that he could tell she wasn't wearing a padded bra because he felt her hard nipples pressed against his chest when she wrapped her arms around his neck and went up on her tiptoes to kiss him.

He tried to pretend that this was like every other first

time he'd been with a woman, but his gut and his heart warned him that it wasn't. His mind wasn't engaged, had been shut down, and consequences and repercussions weren't a consideration. All he wanted was this night with Iris and to squeeze every bit of emotion from it and her that he could.

Iris had to get out of her own way, and once she was in Zac's arms as he danced her around the living room, she sort of did. Part of it was the magic of Billie Holiday—the song was so old-fashioned and such a standard that Iris felt no pressure to be overtly sexy or to bring it. But the other part was just about being with Zac. He sang under his breath as he danced them around the living room; his tone was a bit off-key, but it was endearing. Something less than perfect in the breathtakingly sexy man.

When he kissed her, she forgot everything. She stopped worrying about making sure she kept her stomach sucked in and didn't breathe too heavily. She forgot all the tips she'd read about how to turn a man on and just relaxed. Her skin was wonderfully sensitized and her heart felt like it was beating a bit too fast. When she wrapped her arms around his shoulders, going up on tiptoe to deepen the kiss, she felt the brush of his erection against her stomach. She rubbed against him and would have pulled back, but he made this groan deep in his throat and then reached down to cup her butt, lifting her higher against him so that she felt the tip of his hard-on against her feminine center.

She'd never felt anything like this with a man before. Sure, when she masturbated, she could get there but this was the first time that a kiss and a touch had completely overwhelmed her.

She suspected that Zac was slowly leading her along and she didn't care because it felt so good, so right and exactly like she'd always thought sex should be. It wasn't tongues shoved down her throat or hands that seemed to grasp and pinch her breasts just a little too hard. It was soft caresses and a kiss that she never wanted to end.

He shifted her in his arms as the music changed. It was that song "You Belong To Me." Her heartbeat increased, a warning briefly going off in her mind that he couldn't belong to her, not for long. But she shushed it. The last thing she wanted was to start thinking and lose the feelings that Zac was stirring to life inside of her. When he spun them around and lifted her into his arms again, the world tilted and shifted until she was lying on her back on the couch.

"Still happy to be here with me?" he asked.

She nodded. "Yes."

"Good. If I do anything that makes you uncomfortable, tell me," he said.

"Same."

He laughed in that big kind way of his and she couldn't help smiling back. "Honestly, there isn't anything you could ask me to do that I wouldn't."

"That sounds like a challenge," she said, but she knew she wouldn't dare let herself ask him for anything too risqué.

"I hope you take it up," he said. "But not tonight."

He undid the buttons on his shirt and shrugged out of it, putting it on the coffee table before he sat down on the couch, brushing against her hips. He reached for her sandals and removed first one and then the other.

She reached out to touch his chest. It was covered in a soft mat of blond hair that tickled her fingers when she ran them over his hot skin. His muscles underneath were hard and he bunched them as she touched him. She ran her finger around his nipple and watched it harden under her caress and felt her own nipples do the same.

She drew her finger down the center of his chest and felt the jagged, raised skin that indicated a scar. She leaned closer but in the low lighting there was no way to really see it. She wanted to know more about it, but not now. She let her finger drift lower, following the line of hair that tapered as it approached his belly button. He had the kind of washboard abs that she'd only ever seen in magazines or on TV.

He sat very still and let her explore to her heart's content, but she noticed his erection growing bigger as her touch neared his cock. Her fingers tingled with the need to touch him, but what if she did and he suddenly got impatient, bringing all of this exploring to an end?

She sighed and lowered her hand, tracing the fly of his dress slacks and feeling the hard ridge underneath. He canted his hips forward, thrusting his erection against her fingers, and she curved them around his shaft, stroking him through his pants.

She felt hot and creamy between her legs and she knew she wanted him. She also felt hollow and empty like she wanted him inside of her. It didn't matter that these magical feelings would disappear when that happened. She still craved the feel of him inside her. She shifted around on the couch, reached up under the skirt of her dress and removed her panties.

She tried to straddle him, but he stopped her.

"We aren't in a hurry," he said.

"I am," she admitted. "If we wait too long, this feeling might go away."

She moved awkwardly, because once she started talking, the self-consciousness she thought she'd banished was back. She tried to straddle his lap and lost her balance, falling backward. But he caught her in his arms and lifted her, his biceps flexing under her hands as he settled her on his lap.

"I've got you," he said.

She couldn't say for certain if there was a hint of promise in his words or if she was just imagining it, but she decided to just follow her gut and take it for what she wanted it to be. Take him for what she wanted him to be. The kind of lover she'd always dreamed of finding but never had.

She tunneled her fingers through his thick blond hair and lowered herself, taking his mouth the way she wished he'd take her.

Zac slid his hands up under Iris's skirt and cupped her naked butt as she deepened their kiss. He'd wanted to take this slow, wanted to do this at a pace that worked for her, but at this point he was past thinking about timing. He wanted her and each breath he took sharpened his desire.

He was so hot and hard that he felt like he was going to explode unless he got inside her. He drew her down against his hard-on, thrusting up against her, frustrated by the layers of fabric separating them. He reached between them, pushing her skirt up and out of his way, the backs of his fingers brushing against her warmth. She moaned and lifted her head. He touched her again, holding her with his palm, and she closed her eyes, her head falling back as she gyrated against his hand. When he touched her most intimate flesh, her hands on his shoulders tightened. She made little circular motions with her hips and he adjusted his touch until she was moving more rapidly against him. He shifted his hand lower and entered her with one finger and she threw her head back as he did and moaned much louder this time.

He let her ride his hand until she screamed his name and seemed to come against him. She collapsed against his chest and he held her for a moment before she reached between them and lowered his zipper. He stopped her with his hand on top of hers. If she touched his naked cock, he wasn't going to be able to think of anything but taking her and making her his.

"Are you on the pill?" he asked.

She hesitated and swallowed hard. "Yes. Of course."

"Okay, good. I've got condoms in the other room," he said. "Want me to use one?"

She chewed her lower lip between her teeth.

"I know it's not romantic but a minute of talking now is worth it," he reassured her.

"Yes, I would prefer you use one."

"Wrap your legs around my waist and your arms around my shoulders."

She did it and he stood up, putting his hands on her backside to keep her in place as he walked to the bedroom that was down the hall. He went to the bed and sat down so that she was still on his lap.

"They are in the nightstand."

She reached over and flicked on the lamp first and then opened the drawer. Every time she moved, she rubbed against him and it was all he could do not to twist his hips, find her opening with the tip of his erection and thrust up into her. He was reciting maritime law in his head to keep from doing it and when she finally held up the condom packet, he took it from her with more exuberance than finesse. She slipped back on his lap, closer to his knees, and he reached between them to put the condom on.

Once he had it on, she looked at his erection and then back up at him. He wasn't sure what he read in her expression, but he almost felt like she was unsure again.

Damn.

"Do you still want to do this?" he asked. His voice sounded almost guttural since he was so turned on. Stopping was going to be hard but he'd do it because he never wanted to see fear or disgust on Iris's face.

"Yes," she said, putting her hands on either side of his face and lowering her mouth to kiss him again. She shifted and the skirt of her dress brushed over him. He bunched it in his fist and lifted it all the way up and out of the way. She shifted around, then reached between them to position him between her legs. She opened her eyes and their gazes met as she drove herself down on him.

Damn.

She fit him so tightly, like the best kind of glove, and he wanted more. He had intended to let her set the pace, but he couldn't. He fell back on the bed and rolled over so she was under him. She held on to his shoulders as he brought his lips down hard on hers and thrust his tongue into her mouth. She sucked it hard as he drove up into her, taking her at a pace that was faster and harder than he'd intended. His conscience made him slow down and he started to pull back but she tightened her grip on him and whispered in his ear, "Don't stop."

He didn't stop. He just kept thrusting inside her until he heard those cries he'd heard when she'd orgasmed earlier as she came again he felt her body tightening around his. He drove himself faster and faster into her until he came in one long rush, emptying himself inside of her. He kept thrusting until he was sated and rolled to his side, pulling her into his arms and stroking her back while his heartbeat slowed.

She put her hand on his chest and then rested her head on top of it. She sighed and he lifted his head to look down at her.

"What?"

"Thanks for that. I have to be honest and tell you I wasn't expecting…"

He waited to see what else she'd say. It was clear to him that she hadn't enjoyed sex in the past, but he doubted she wanted to discuss that with him.

"What?" he asked again.

"You."

She rolled to her side and sat up after saying that. Then she got off the bed and went to the bathroom. He watched her go, very aware that she wasn't the only one who'd been caught off guard tonight.

He hadn't been expecting her either.

Eight

Arriving on Nantucket one week later made Iris feel like she was in total vacay mode. It didn't matter that her glam squad had gotten her ready early this morning at her place in Boston to make sure she was casual yet sophisticated or that she had fifteen minutes before she had to meet the photographer on the beach to do a photo shoot for the summer social media shares. As she stood on the balcony of her hotel suite, listening to the crashing of the waves on the beach and smelling the salty air, she felt like she could breathe.

Sleeping with Zac hadn't been her best idea, she knew that, but damn, for the first time in her life she'd felt more than just the urge to get it over with when she'd been having sex. Zac had made her realize that something she'd thought she could live without—an active sex life—wasn't true. She'd had no idea that the men she'd been with hadn't been good lovers. To be fair, it could have been that she wasn't a right fit for those men.

Did that mean she was a right fit for Zac?

Or was it simply because she'd hired him for the weekend that she had relaxed? She wished she could talk to Adler and tell her the truth about what was going on. But she didn't want anyone to know she'd hired herself a man for the weekend.

Her phone pinged and she glanced at it. It was a text from Adler.

Hey, girl! Are you on the island?

Just got in. I have a photo shoot in about ten minutes but want to catch up after?

Yes. Where's the photo shoot? I'll come by and watch.

Private beach two houses down from your gran's place.

See ya there. Is the new guy with you?

He had a few meetings this morning. He'll be here this afternoon.

Perfect. Want to have dinner with Nick and me tonight?

Let me double-check with him.

Iris took a deep breath. This was what she needed to happen. She wanted people in her life to accept Zac as her real boyfriend. And he'd agreed to do whatever she asked for the weekend. She texted to ask if he'd be available around six for dinner. He responded with the thumbs-up. She let Adler know they'd both be there.

Should she mention to Adler that the man she was dating was her cousin? She wanted to tell her in person rather than over the phone. That kind of conversation was going to bring up all kinds of questions about Zac. She tossed her phone on the bed and fell back on the covers, staring at the pristine white ceiling as if she looked hard enough, she'd find some cosmic answer to the question.

There was a knock on her door and she hopped up to go and answer it. It was KT from her glam squad. KT always looked so boho and chic, with her long legs and straight brown hair that she'd styled in a side braid today. She wore a pair of tiny denim shorts with a flouncy top. It was a look that Iris envied but she had never been able to pull off. She was too intense for that kind of outfit. By contrast, she wore a broderie white sundress with wooden buttons and a pair of Hermès sandals.

"Parking is a bear near the beach," KT said. "We should leave now. Stephan is already there and the photographer is setting up."

"I hope the weather holds out," Iris said, grabbing her phone and purse and leading the way out of the room. "There were storms yesterday."

"It's gorg out there today. As soon as your photo shoot is over, I'm going for a run on the beach."

"Sounds like a plan. I shouldn't need you until tomorrow for the clambake. I have the outfit you styled for me and know how to do my paddleboarding makeup… I really hope I don't fall off the board. Did you see that can happen?"

Her assistant put her arm around Iris's shoulders. Everyone in her inner circle knew she struggled with a fear of water. She was slowly getting over it but there were times when it became overwhelming.

"You'll be fine. My sister says the key to paddleboarding is a strong core," KT said.

"A strong core? I'm wearing Spanx 24/7. My core isn't soft at all."

"You'll do fine," KT said. "I've never known you to fail when you put your mind to something. Just remember that your followers are watching and want you to succeed. You're living that hashtag best life."

"I am, aren't I? Also the camera crew will be shooting the paddleboarding so I have that as an added incentive to stay on."

"Perfect. Plus, you'll want to impress your new man," KT said. "You're usually all about keeping up the perfect image so I know you'll do fine."

The perfect image. Was that what she was all about? "Do you think that comes off as me trying too hard?"

"Girl, it's your brand. I think it suits you." KT followed her out of the resort to her car and they both got in.

Iris wanted to be chill about everything that KT had said but it was stirring up the thought that maybe she had been trying too hard for so long that even she didn't know how to relax and just be herself. That brought her back to sex with Zac... Had it been Zac and his fabulously fit body and sensual moves that had been the difference or the fact that she hadn't been trying to be who she thought he wanted her to be?

The answer wasn't going to just show up. Plus, did it matter? He was only with her until Sunday and then for a few more dates and photos before he was out of her life for good. She'd be back to her usual self. Which was exactly what she wanted. Truly.

Now if only she could convince herself of that.

Zac left Boston late, got stuck in traffic, and when he finally arrived on Nantucket, he was ready for a beer or two. He and Dev had spent most of the day on the phone or on Skype calls talking to people that they wanted on their team. Most were excited at the prospect of a new team, but a few were skeptical that they would be able to pull off a winning run with only two years to get the team going.

Zac wasn't interested in naysayers or nonbelievers, so even when Dev had argued to keep a few of the skeptics in the potential pool, Zac had cut them. If he'd learned one lesson from his father, it was to surround himself only with people who had the same goals. His dad had often said if a person was wishy-washy before you shook hands, they weren't going to become more committed after the deal was done.

He rubbed the back of his neck as he followed the map to the hotel where he'd be staying with Iris for the next few days, which he realized was going to be awkward for everyone if he didn't let his mom know. He thought about texting but she would only call him back so he used the hands-free voice command to dial her number.

"Hello, honey. Where are you?" his mom asked when she answered the phone.

"Just got off the ferry," he answered her.

"That's great. Shall we set a place for you at dinner?"

"Not tonight," he said. "I'm not going to stay at Gran's either."

"Why not?" she asked.

All of the sweet chattiness was now gone from her voice. She'd sent all of them an itinerary for Adler's wedding and she'd been very clear that she expected them to show up to all of the events on it.

"I met a woman in Boston, Mom. Turns out she's a friend of Adler's and I'm going to be staying with her."

"Wow, that's quick work," his mom said. "Who is she?"

"Iris Collins."

"Oh, I thought she was dating someone else. She's really nice. How did you meet her?" she asked, chatty again now that she knew he was with Iris.

Zac had never realized what a difference dating a woman who was in his social circle would make. He'd pretty much always picked someone who was in the world of competitive yachting because those were the women he knew the best, so this was a new experience. He wondered if this was how Mari felt when she'd gotten engaged to Inigo Velasquez. The Formula One driver was definitely on Juliette Bisset's approved list.

"We met in a bar," he said.

"Oh," his mom said.

"*Oh?* Don't be judgy, Mom. You and Dad met at a weekend house party," he said. "I'm sure there were drinks served there."

"Did I sound judgy? I didn't mean to be. I was just hoping that you would have a meet-cute story."

"We don't live in a rom-com," he said.

"I know. I just always hope that all of my kids will have a big romance and Iris is definitely a step up—"

"Mom, I'm a second away from driving through a make-believe tunnel and losing my signal with you," he warned her.

"Point taken. Bring her with you to lunch tomorrow. Your father wants us to host the Williamses. Did you see my text?"

"I did and I will. I love you, Mom. I'll talk to you tomorrow," he said.

"Bye, sweetie, love you too."

She disconnected the call and he continued to make his way toward the hotel. His mom was not going to be very happy with him when he and Iris broke up. But that was a problem for Future Zac to deal with. Right now his mom was pleased that he'd landed someone like Iris. He wondered if he could have done it if she hadn't been desperate for a date. He liked to think so, but he wasn't sure.

He didn't know what kind of guy she usually went for but he was pretty sure she didn't often go for athletes or, as his dad like to refer to him, sea bums.

That night together last week, though… If he'd really been dating her that would have changed things for real between them. Instead he had no clue what it had done. He wasn't thinking of when he'd be able to walk away from her. In fact he'd been remembering how she'd felt in his arms all day at odd moments. Dev had accused him of losing focus, but Zac knew that his focus was fine.

It was just on Iris and not on the race or his yacht or the team he was building. Maybe there had been more of a reason to stay away from women in his own social set before this. After all, a sailor would know the score. A fellow sailor would know that he was only interested in having fun until the wind changed, and he was back on the ocean pitting himself against all the other crafts out there. Trying to be number one and conquer the sea.

He followed the signs to the hotel, pulling into line for the valet. As he did, he remembered that little sound that Iris had made when he'd entered her and the surprise on her face when she'd come long and hard. He wanted to see that look on her face again. He couldn't wait to hold her again.

Damn.

He was screwed.

It was a good thing that they had a signed contract. Otherwise he'd be tempted into thinking that Iris was the kind of woman who could make him stay ashore.

He stepped outside into the humid summer afternoon, blaming his agitation on the heat instead of the woman who'd paid him to be her companion.

* * *

Adler Osborn stood on the widow's walk and looked out at the storms brewing on the ocean. Only three more days until she'd be Mrs. Nicholas Williams and she couldn't wait. She'd had a text from her fiancé that he was en route and would meet her at the Crab Shack in town in twenty minutes. She couldn't wait to see Nick.

Growing up, her life had been unconventional to say the least. She'd never known her mother, who'd died when she was twenty-five and her father was a famous rock star who truly lived the sex, drugs and rock 'n' roll lifestyle, but also had oddly been a devoted parent. He wanted her with him on the road but her mother's family had wanted her attending the right schools and getting the proper upbringing.

Her Aunt Juliette and Gran had been fierce negotiators with her father, and they'd worked out a deal where she'd split time between two vastly different worlds. Though she loved both halves of her family very much, she'd always longed to be part of one world. It was hard to go from boarding school and socializing with a lot of rules to life on the road and no rules.

Until college, when she'd met Iris Collins and the two had become best friends, Adler had felt torn in half by her two lives. But Iris had helped her sort herself out. One of the things that Adler had realized was that she wanted all those things she'd never had growing up. A proper home— not a boarding school or tour bus. A home that she came back to every single night. A family that was her own. She wanted a husband, kids and the whole suburban life. But she needed someone who could understand her. Really got her. Not a guy who wanted entrée into her father's debauched world. Or who wanted to attend the jet-set parties her Aunt Juliette threw.

Nick Williams had been perfect. A borderline workaholic who was rich as Jay-Z and didn't give a crap about what anyone thought. He was fun, had the prettiest blue eyes she'd ever seen and the sexiest ass. When she'd first met him, she'd been dazzled. And it was only when things got rough for her, with her father's heart attack, and she found Nick standing by her side, putting work on the back burner to be there for her, that she realized that she'd found the man she wanted for the rest of her life.

She was no longer the illegitimate daughter of a debauched rock star and the runaway heiress who died of a drug overdose, but a respectable member of society. Someone who stayed out of the headlines and lived a normal life.

Gran had said that normal was overrated but then again Gran had been normal her entire life. Adler, not so much. And Iris was another one who lived and breathed for small-town suburbia…the dream, as far as Adler was concerned.

She texted Nick that Iris and her new man were meeting them. He rang back instead of texting.

"Hey, sexy!"

"Hey, gorgeous. Who's the new guy? I thought she was dating Douchey the Third," Nick said.

"I don't have the deets but he arrived about thirty minutes ago and I invited them to join us for dinner. I want to meet him and thought it would be weird if I just showed up in her hotel suite alone."

Nick laughed. "You might seem like a one-woman interrogation squad."

"I know. So, I thought if we met them together, then you could help me make sure he's nothing like Douchey."

"Good plan. Am I picking you up?"

"Nah. Uncle Auggie has just arrived and I think I'll spare us that," she said. Her uncle didn't like her fiancé, which didn't bother Adler because she'd never been a big fan of her uncle. The fact that he'd cheated on her Aunt Juliette hadn't made him Gran's favorite either.

"Thanks for that. You can never doubt that I really love you, gorgeous, because there is no way I'd put up with August Bisset otherwise."

"I know it," she said, feeling her heart fill with joy. "See ya soon."

"See ya," he said, disconnecting the call.

Adler checked her makeup and then grabbed her clutch and headed downstairs. Michael was carrying his silver tray with two martinis and a bourbon neat to the sitting room.

"Will you be joining the others?"

"Nope. Heading out for the evening. I'll probably stay over at Nick's tonight," she said. Since Nick wasn't comfortable staying at her gran's place, he'd purchased a cottage for them that was two streets over. That way she could see the family she loved, and he didn't have to.

"Heading out, dear?" Gran called as Adler walked past the sitting room.

Her Uncle August was sitting in the large leather armchair and had his back to her. His hair was mostly gray now but at one time it had been black. He turned and smiled at her.

"Hello, Adler. Juliette was just telling me that you're all set for the wedding," he said.

"I'm getting there. Still a few last-minute things to take care of," she said, coming over to give him a hug. The thing about Uncle Auggie was that he wasn't a jerk. He was charming and fun. As her Aunt Juliette said, he was hard to stay mad at.

"If there's anything I can do, let me know," he said, then took a deep breath. "I know that there's some tension because of the business dealings Logan and I have had with your fiancé and I want to put that behind us. We'd like to have Nick and his family to dinner tomorrow night. Just so we can all get to know each other. Put everyone's mind's at ease."

Adler was surprised by the offer. "Let me speak to Nick tonight and let him know. That should work with our schedule since most people aren't arriving until Thursday."

"Great," he said, sitting back down. "I'll get Carter to make all the arrangements."

"I'll handle this, Auggie," Aunt Juliette said. "Have fun tonight, Adler. See you tomorrow?"

"Yes," she said, kissing her gran and aunt on the cheek before she turned and left the house.

Her uncle's gesture was surprising and gave her hope that her wedding and marriage could mend the old rivalry between the Bisset and Williams families. Finally she was getting the life she wanted where her name was in the press for a positive reason and not because of scandal.

Nine

Iris wasn't sure how to act when Zac arrived in the suite. She'd been dressed and ready for more than thirty minutes, in fact, since he'd texted her that he was getting close. Now she was hovering in the main living area while he was settling into the smaller room in the suite and getting dressed for dinner.

"I'm ready," he said.

She swallowed hard when she saw him. He wore a pair of shorts, deck shoes and a button-down shirt. His blond hair was tousled as if he'd run his hands through it. Her own fingers tingled as she remembered how soft and thick his hair was and how it had felt to hold his head to her breast while they'd been making love.

She shook her head. *Stop it.* She needed to stay focused. This was the second test of her and Zac as a believable couple.

"Do I look okay?" he asked. "You're kind of staring at me…"

"You look fine. I was just thinking about something else," she said. Yeah, like how good he had looked naked. "So, Adler and Nick are two of my oldest friends. They will be subtle but they're going to dig and try to find out when we started dating and everything."

"So, it's dinner with the family, part two," he said with a chuckle. "Don't worry, angel face, Adler's my family as well so I know how to handle her."

Angel face.

It was a sweet endearment. To be honest, she'd never had one in a relationship before unless *babe* counted. But she'd never felt it had.

"Crapola. I didn't want to tell her in a text and we didn't end up meeting in person this afternoon. She's going to have all kinds of questions. This is a bad idea," she said abruptly. She hadn't really given much thought to the fact that Adler was Zac's cousin. That might make things complicated down the road. As if sleeping with a guy she had hired wasn't already a bad idea. This was what happened when she let Thea get in her head. She started making decisions from a place of panic instead of a place of reason.

Zac came over and put his arms around her, hugging her close and then stepping back. "Relax. Whatever happens, we will roll with it. We're still new to the relationship… By the way, my family is going to be grilling you and probably trying to figure out what you see in me."

"Why would they do that?" she asked.

"I'm pretty much always focused on yacht designs, team dynamics and how to win the America's Cup. I'm told I can be boring AF when I get on a roll about it," he said. "So there is that. I know that we have a contract for me to be here, but I genuinely like you, Iris. I think if we just are honest about our reactions to each other, throw in a few kisses and longing glances, no one will be suspicious."

She stared up into his bright blue eyes and nodded. He made it sound so simple, but she knew that it was way more complex than that. She took his hand in hers. He had some callouses, probably owing to a lifetime spent working on boats, but she liked the way he immediately squeezed her hand.

"I like you too," she admitted.

"I already knew that," he said with a cheeky grin as he led them out of the suite.

He started down the hall, but she stayed to watch the door close and then double-checked the handle. He stopped, arching one eyebrow at her in question.

"Sorry, habit," she said.

"That's a good one," he said.

Graham had hated that she did it and said it made her look like a paranoid weirdo. But then she was coming to realize that a lot of the things Graham had said about her weren't a reflection of her but rather of him. As much as she'd been trying to find the perfect mate, he'd been trying to find a woman who fit what he wanted. A woman Iris realized she hadn't ever been nor truly wanted to be. And that was okay.

Zac came back and double-checked the door as well before taking her hand and walking toward the elevators. He had his faults; she knew he did. No one was perfect—man or woman—but there were a lot of qualities to Zac that she'd never realized mattered to her before. And she knew that it wasn't the qualities per se but Zac himself.

There was an elderly couple on the elevator holding hands when they got on and they smiled at the two of them. For a moment—just the briefest second—Iris saw herself and Zac in them, but she knew that was an illusion and warned herself not to buy into it.

He had said they were friends and could make this work

for the weekend. He hadn't said anything about beyond that. He was here for the time being and she had to remember that he was going to leave once his funding came in and this destination-wedding weekend ended they would start to "drift" apart and their relationship would end in three months' time. So these four days were really all they'd have together.

The lobby was crowded with people as they exited the elevator and walked toward the hotel entrance. There was a pianist playing Gershwin and the buzz of muted conversations filled the room. Iris heard a woman's laugh and turned to see Adler and Nick talking to Nick's mother, Cora. The threesome looked happy as they were talking. Adler glanced up and noticed Iris and waved, then did a double take at Zac.

She shook her head as she started walking over to them.

"Girl, why didn't you tell me your new man was my cousin?" Adler said, hugging her and then reaching over to hug Zac.

"I told her I wanted to surprise you. I wasn't supposed to be here until tomorrow," Zac said effortlessly.

Taking all the pressure off Iris for not saying anything. Adler hugged her close and Iris actually relaxed for a moment.

"He's way better than Graham," Adler whispered in her ear before turning back to Zac. "This is a very good surprise! Come meet Nick and his mom."

"I can't wait," Zac said.

Adler led the way toward them, and Zac kept his hand firmly in hers, bringing her along with him and making it clear they were together.

Adler hadn't seen Zac in person for five years. He had signed a three-year contract with an America's Cup team and had spent the time racing and training. She didn't know the details but her tall blond cousin had fallen out with the captain and hadn't renewed his contract. For as long as she'd known Zac, yachting was his life, so it was interesting to see him holding Iris's hand and laughing at her story of how she'd botched her family's famous lobster roll recipe on the morning show two weeks earlier.

Something seemed...too perfect, too right between Iris and Zac. Adler knew she should just smile and go along with it, but she didn't want to see her friend get hurt.

The thing was, Iris looked vulnerable sitting next to Zac. She smiled when he looked over at her but when he wasn't looking, her friend was staring at him like she was...well, like she really cared for him. Something Adler had never seen Iris do when she'd been with Graham.

Nick pinched her leg under the table and she glared at him. He leaned in to kiss her neck and whispered in her ear, "Stop staring at them. It's clear you're not buying them as a couple."

"What are you two talking about?" Iris asked. "When they kiss like that, they're giving each other the low-down."

Exactly, Adler thought. Iris would know she'd pick up on whatever was going on.

The downside to having been best friends for all of their adult lives was that Adler and Iris knew each other's little social tells.

"Nothing important. I need to powder my nose. Want to join me?" Adler said, jumping up.

"You're not wearing—" Nick said, but stopped when Adler turned to face him, raising both eyebrows. He'd probably been about to point out she wasn't wearing makeup, which her wedding skincare consultant had advised for a few days before the ceremony so she'd be picture-perfect on the big day.

"I'd love to," Iris said with a giggle. "Be right back."

Iris squeezed Zac's shoulder, started to walk away and then turned back to kiss him. It seemed like she was aiming for his cheek, but he turned into the kiss and their lips met. The kiss was the first convincing moment for Adler when she totally bought them as a couple.

Was it just new couple awkwardness?

She glanced at Nick, who smiled and shrugged at her. He seemed to be thinking the same thing. But she'd get to the bottom of it in the bathroom.

Iris's skin was flushed as she brushed past Adler and led the way to the bathroom at the back of the restaurant. Adler followed her friend, knowing that she should have insisted they talk today before the men had arrived. But with her wedding planner, Jaqs Veerland, flying in midday to go over last-minute details, she hadn't had time.

"Okay, spill," Adler said once they were in the ladies' room.

"Spill what?"

"The tea, girl. And don't pretend there isn't any. You and Zac...you almost make sense but something isn't feeling right."

Iris fumbled in her purse for her lip gloss and turned to the mirror. "I'm sure I don't know what you mean."

"I'm sure you do," Adler said, swiping the gloss from Iris and putting on some herself. "That kiss looked real but the rest of it...you were watching him like you weren't sure about him. What's going on?"

Iris shrugged and took the lip gloss back. "I wish I had your skin. You're glowing."

"Thanks. But I'm not going to let you distract me."

"There's nothing to tell. He's hot and we had this zing... I mean, I almost fell and he caught me and kissed me and the paparazzi went crazy snapping photos and it's just sort of gone on from there. We are still in the very beginning of this relationship. Remember when you wouldn't eat in front of Nick?"

Adler did remember. She'd liked him so much she hadn't wanted to do anything to put him off. A previous dude she'd dated had said her chewing was too loud, so she hadn't been able to eat in front of Nick.

"Fair point. I just worry about you, Iris," Adler said.

"I know," Iris responded, wrapping her arms around Adler's shoulders as the two of them stared at their reflection in the mirror. "I love you for that."

Adler reached up and patted Iris's hands. "Nick is never going to let me live this down. He said I was staring at you both like I wanted to do an interrogation."

"You were," Iris admitted. "Which wasn't helping my nerves. Do you like him?"

"Zac?"

"Yes."

"I do. When we were kids, he was always outside on the water. And he could always be counted on to help me disappear when I needed some breathing room by taking me sailing. He's not much of a talker, but that was when we were kids. He pretty much is always away sailing now. How is this going to work?"

"We haven't figured that part out," Iris said. "Right now, we are both here and enjoying each other's company."

"And you'd appreciate it if I let you do that, right?"

"Yes," Iris said. "Also, this is your big week. We should all be thinking about you."

"You should," Adler said with a wink. "I have my final fitting tomorrow after the family luncheon. Will you go with me?"

"Yes. I'm all yours. I'm filming a segment early in the morning. I heard your dad wrote a new song for you."

"Yeah, he did," Adler said. "He's been more…sentimental since the heart attack. He won't let me hear it before my wedding day."

They rejoined the men and Adler was satisfied her friend was going to be okay, which meant she was back to worrying about how her Uncle Auggie was going to be tomorrow when he was in the same room with his most hated rival, Tad Williams—Nick's dad.

"So, you're the America's Cup guy?" Nick asked as the ladies left the table.

Zac reached for his water glass and nodded. "You're the…titan of industry, right?"

Nick gave a shout of laughter. "I'm guessing that's what Adler said. I know for damn sure your father and brother don't call me that."

"No, they usually throw in some derogatory curse words," Zac allowed. Nick was a really nice guy and it was clear to Zac that Nick truly loved Adler. Zac saw real affection between them. Having grown up with parents who had been in and out of love with each other several times, Zac knew how rare that kind of bond was.

"I do the same when referring to them. I'm trying to make peace for Adler's sake," Nick said. "I was surprised by the invitation to your grandmother's for lunch tomorrow."

"Me too," Zac admitted. "I don't think my dad is mellowing, he just knows there will be hell to pay if he upsets Adler. She's my mom's only connection to her sister and she is pulling out all the stops to make the wedding is everything that Adler wants."

"I know. It's so crazy. I like your mom, by the way. She's sweet and funny," he said. "Makes me wonder how she raised a shark like Logan."

"Fair enough, but I think Logan was always Dad's shadow, not Mom's, so that might be one explanation. He's a great guy away from the office," Zac said. He and his siblings were very close, but he was realistic enough to know that they had both good and bad qualities. "We're all very driven."

"I've seen that. What's going on with your America's Cup team? I heard a rumor that you're looking for financing," Nick said.

"I'm not," Zac said. Using the Collins connection to finance his bid was one thing, accepting financing from his families' business rivals would put Zac in direct confrontation with his father and Logan. Something that Zac wasn't interested in doing. He wanted to do this on his own; he had never been looking to piss off his family.

"Okay, but if that changes, I'm interested," Nick said.

"Dude, you know that I can't even contemplate doing business with you," Zac said. "I might spend most of my time on a yacht but if I accepted an investment from you, I'd never be able to come home again. As sweet as my mom has been to you, she'd be royally ticked at the both of us, and let me tell you, that isn't a good thing to be on the receiving end of."

Nick put his hands up. "Gotcha. I'm just always looking for new investments."

"And if it happens to piss off the Bissets, all the better?" Zac asked.

"Sometimes, but honestly that's more my dad's thing than mine. I go after sound investments, not just things I think August Bisset wants," Nick said.

"So you didn't start dating Adler because she's related to my mom?" Zac asked.

"Not at all. She's not a Bisset, which of course is a plus in my opinion, but also I don't spend all of my time trying to undermine your family," he said, leaning back in his chair, glass in hand. "Whatever happened between our fathers happened way before I was born and to be honest it doesn't bother me."

"Glad to hear it. I'm sure Logan wouldn't agree."

"Logan's a douche," Nick said. "He's gone straight after some of my business, but I don't mind a good honest fight."

"Who's fighting?" Adler asked, sitting back down.

"No one tonight," Nick said. "And I promised to be nice tomorrow so we should be good."

Zac hoped they would be. Iris seemed different when she sat back down, not so smiley as she'd been before. Had Adler figured out what they were up to?

But when he glanced at his cousin, she just winked at him so he didn't think she'd found out about their arrangement. He reached for Iris's hand as the check arrived, but she moved away from him, taking the check from the waiter. "This one is on me. Thanks for making time for a quiet meal during your special week."

"Any time, Iris," Adler said.

Zac took the check from her. "Sorry, angel face, but I'll get this."

She glared at him. He guessed that she expected her fake boyfriend to stay quiet and let her pay, but he hadn't been raised that way. And though he knew she made damn good money, there was no way he could tamp down this impulse.

"Angel face?"

"Shut it, Addie. I'm sure Nick has a special name for you," Zac said.

"Does he?" Iris asked as Zac took his American Express from his wallet and handed it to the waiter.

"I do," Nick said. "But I've been warned to keep it behind closed doors."

"Oooh, what is it?" Iris asked. "Now I'm dying to know."

"Stop it," Adler said. "If you were really my friend, you wouldn't want to know."

"Is it embarrassing?" Iris asked. "It can't be. You're too adorable to have a nickname that's not cool."

"It's private," Adler said.

"Fair enough."

Zac smiled at his cousin, who had spent so much of her life in the spotlight. It was nice to know she had someone in her life who would keep her secrets and share things just with her.

Until that moment Zac hadn't realized that there was such a thing. His parents presented a united front for show, but he'd never seen them as a couple in love. And, honestly, that hadn't been something he'd thought he'd wanted in his life until Iris slipped her hand in his and squeezed it.

Ten

A walk on the beach. It was simple. It was romantic. It was expected. Iris told herself that as she slipped her hand into Zac's and followed him down the wooden boardwalk to the shore. In the distance she heard the sound of waves and she stopped for a moment, tipping her head back to look up at the black sky and breathe in the salty air.

Zac just stood next to her, letting her have her moment. She forgot how to breathe sometimes. Not like the normal inhale/exhale thing, but how to take these moments and press them into her mind so she wouldn't forget them.

And she wanted to remember this night with Zac. He'd been funny and charming at dinner—the perfect companion. How had she never noticed that Graham only talked about himself? Zac was the total opposite, asking questions and genuinely listening when everyone spoke.

If she'd had to invent an ideal man for herself, so far he was ticking all of the boxes. The cynical part of her mind warned that he was ticking them because she'd paid him to be by her side. It was a little too convenient.

"You okay?" he asked.

"Yeah," she said, wrapping one arm around her own waist as she dropped his hand. "Why?"

"You looked so relaxed and chill. And then I don't know what happened in that pretty head of yours but you started to look stressed."

She shook her head. "I don't know what happened either. Thea says I overthink everything. She might be right."

Zac reached for her hand and she let him take it. "When I first started sailing, I had a mentor who told me that there were a million things that needed to happen and could go wrong while I was on the water. He said just take each moment as it comes, the strong wind that fills your sails, the spray of water on your face, the storm that blows up out of nowhere. Each moment. That's all you can handle and all you can control."

She knew that. She did. But it was harder to do than Zac made it sound. "I try. Somehow the future always tugs at me, making me anxious to plan for it."

He laughed. "I can see that. I struggle with it as well but then I like finding a solution or a work-around. Want me to help you figure this out?"

She shook her head. "I don't know how to work around you."

"Me?"

"Yes, you. You're not at all what I thought you'd be," she said. "You've been surprising me every step of the way and that keeps making me think things that—"

"Stop," he said, tugging her gently into his arms. "Don't do that. I told you we'd be honest with each other. The way we started out doesn't have to define every moment."

She looked up at him. The lights from the boardwalk

were dim where they stood and his blue eyes were dark. He'd shaved before he'd come to Nantucket. He looked casual, but his jaw was strong, and she couldn't help letting her eyes fall to his lips.

Those lips that she'd kissed last night. Those lips that had charted a path down her body and left her quivering in his arms. She wanted to taste him again. To pretend that they were like Nick and Adler sneaking away to be alone and enjoy the simple romance of an evening at the beach.

She put her hand on the back of his neck as she went up on tiptoe, mesmerized by the thought of that kiss. He tipped his head to the side and she came closer. The warmth of his breath brushed over her mouth as he exhaled. She closed her eyes and his lips touched hers. A shiver went down her spine and she tightened her fingers on the back of his neck.

Swallowing hard as he lifted his head, he stared down into her face. Their eyes met, and she felt like…she wanted to believe that something magical passed between them. Something that would bind them together as a couple. But the truth was she was searching for that connection and she didn't trust her chronic bad taste when it came to men. Didn't trust her gut when it shouted to take him back to the room and make love to him all night.

She wanted to believe she could keep her wits about her, but she knew she couldn't. She was lying to her best friend, lying to her parents and her sister. The one person she couldn't lie to was herself.

She wouldn't be that girl who fell for a pair of blue eyes that promised the moon and woke up in the sand underneath a cloudy sky.

She took a deeper breath as she stepped back. "I think I've had enough of the night air. I'm going to head back to the room."

"Running away from me isn't going to change anything," he said.

She wanted to pretend not to understand what he meant but she wasn't going to play games with him either. "I know that. But I need bright lights and reality instead of this."

"This?"

"This…" She gestured to the sky and the beach and him. "I'm not living a picture-perfect moment that I'm going to share with my followers. This isn't real. Any of it. And I don't want to forget it."

She pivoted on her heel and walked away from him. It was hard, but she knew in the moment that it was what she needed to do. She had to stay focused or she was going to lose control of more than her emotions. She was going to lose control of her life and everything she'd worked for would be gone.

Zac knew he should let her go. She'd been pretty damn plain when she'd said this was an illusion. But he wasn't faking it. He liked her. He wanted her. He followed her, putting his hand on her shoulder to stop her.

"What?" she asked, her tone short and curt.

"You forgot one thing, angel face," he said. "I'm real. You're real. And neither one of us is lying about that."

She chewed her lower lip and he remembered the last time she'd done that: when they'd made love the first time. He was no closer now to figuring out what was going on inside her head than he had been that night. And true, it had only been a week earlier, but it felt like they'd spent a lifetime together since then. He hadn't wanted to believe that he'd ever feel like this about a woman…especially not one that he'd made a deal to date.

He hoped he wasn't. And this wasn't love, was it? Could it be?

It was lust. He was even comfortable labeling it affection and/or infatuation. But beyond that, the answer had to be no. They were in a business arrangement and only a fool would allow it to become too emotional. And despite what his brothers sometimes said Zac wasn't anyone's fool.

"I'm not calling you a liar," she said at last. Her tone was serious and grounded, the kind of tone she'd used when she'd been meeting with her fans earlier in the lobby.

He didn't say anything because he'd noticed that at times she would drop a leading statement and see how he responded. But he wasn't sure what to say to her now.

"I'm talking about myself," she said at last. "We have a contracted agreement and I know what I wanted from it. But here in the moonlight, holding your hand and just standing next to you, I guess I wish we didn't have that. That we were just two people…"

He had thought that, as well. "Would you have spoken to me if you hadn't needed me?"

She shrugged. But they both knew the answer was no. She wasn't at the point in her life where she really wanted a man in it. He was starting to realize that. She liked him and he liked her but it was in spite of their agreement. Neither of them was ready for a serious relationship. He was leaving to train for the America's Cup and she was launching a new line for her brand.

This pact they'd made for Adler's wedding, that was all they had and neither of them should forget it.

"No," she said at last.

"Me neither."

"Why not?"

"You're complicated, angel face," he said.

"So?"

"I like it, you know I do, but the truth is, we're here together because of some very unique circumstances."

"So talking about what-ifs isn't going to work," she said. "I just feel myself wanting to believe this is real in my heart and my mind is warning me that it isn't."

He pulled her into his arms because he hated not touching her when they were this close, and he was tired of denying himself and letting her set the pace. "This is real, Iris. It's just going to end when the weekend is over and we start drifting apart over the next three months. That doesn't mean we won't feel something for each other. I think it would be odd if we didn't. All it really means is that we might look back and wish it had lasted longer…"

He wanted to add that there was no reason it couldn't but that was more complicated than he wanted to be tonight. The wind was blowing off the water and the salt air was making him long to be back out on the deck of his yacht, challenging the elements and competing for his place in history.

But…

He also wanted Iris. He wanted to keep her in his arms and hold on to her until the winds and time forced him to leave her. That was something he knew he couldn't really have.

As much as he wanted to hold her in his moment, when the sea called, he'd answer. Winning the America's Cup with his own team had long been a dream of his. Something he needed to do to prove himself, to show his old man what he was capable of.

She reached up and touched his face. There was a hint of sadness to her smile and he knew she had come to the same realization that he had. No matter how much they both might want to believe that they should have more with each other, the contract they'd signed was all that either of them was willing to give.

He'd thought of her as a siren leading him astray, but he

realized that he didn't want to disappoint Iris. He needed to be his best self and that meant that he couldn't detour from his chosen path because she wouldn't detour from hers.

She needed him to be the man she'd met. The man who was a sailor and a competitor and whose life was on the sea. Not in Boston or wherever her career took her.

He leaned down to kiss her because he knew that these four days were really the most intimate time they would have together, and the pipe dream of more time was hard to let go. But in his heart and soul, he knew that was the only option. He'd taken her up on her indecent proposal never guessing that he would ever feel anything this strong for her or that the thought of leaving her would cut like a knife.

She wrapped her arms around his shoulders, and he knew that no matter what, he wasn't going to be able to stop himself from making love to her over the next four days. They might both know that their relationship would end but he needed to give them enough memories to keep them company over the long dark nights that lay ahead.

She wanted to pretend it was a fluke, that their one night together hadn't changed her forever but she knew it had. Sitting at the table with Adler and Nick tonight had just driven home to her how much she wanted everything about her and Zac to be real. She didn't want it to be just for the weekend and just for show. He'd been funny and charming and just so damn real that it had driven home how wrong her search for a partner had gone up until that point.

He complemented her in a way no one else ever had. A part of her knew it had to be because she wasn't trying to impress him. She knew he wasn't going to leave her alone in a hotel room the way that Graham had. She was paying him to be with her.

God. How humiliating would it be if that ever got out?

But she had no regrets. Being with Zac had shown her a side of herself she hadn't even realized she'd been burying.

It was hard to realize what was missing until she'd found it. She pulled back from the kiss but didn't want to. She liked the way he tasted and it felt as if it had been years instead of a week since they'd kissed.

He kept his hands around her waist. When he turned to shelter her from the wind, she again felt her heart melt just the tiniest bit. He held her as if she were precious to him and she realized that despite the fact that she ran a multi-million-dollar company and she could hold her own with anyone on the planet, it was nice to have someone hold her and shelter her.

She reached up to touch his face, felt the light stubble that was starting to grow on his jaw. In his eyes, she thought she saw the same heaviness that troubled her.

"I know I said no sex, but would you be upset if I changed my mind?" she asked.

He threw his head back and laughed, and she couldn't help smiling. She loved the sound of his laughter. He held nothing back when he did it.

"Uh, no, angel face, I wouldn't mind at all. In fact, I think I'd be downright ticked if you didn't."

"Good. I mean you did say there wasn't anything I could ask you to do that would make you uncomfortable."

"There's something in your tone that's making me think I shouldn't have issued a blanket challenge to you like that," he said.

"You shouldn't have," she quipped but she knew he was safe. She wanted him to herself but would never do anything that would make him feel ill at ease. He had given her a freedom she hadn't realized she'd denied herself. And it was making her regret that she'd waited so long to find it.

She'd never thought sexual confidence was something

she needed in her life. But since being with Zac that one night, she was already a different woman. She wanted to see what happened if they made love twice.

How would that change her?

She was ready for it.

"This is our last night before everyone is here," she said. "Our last night as a quasi-anonymous couple. What should we do?"

"Something daring and not in the rule book?" he asked.

She took a deep breath. She wasn't worried about his suggesting a three-way the way Graham had or that she wear a dildo and take him from behind. That wasn't the kind of man Zac was. In fact, she was excited to hear what he suggested.

"Yes."

"Hmm… Want to take my grandmother's yacht out and make love on the deck with just the sea around us and the moon and stars watching overhead?"

She inhaled sharply, already picturing him nude on the deck of a yacht. She was the tiniest bit afraid of water… But they wouldn't be in the water, and the chance to be the woman with him on the yacht—sharing his world—was too powerful to resist.

"Okay. Let's do it."

He took her hand in his and led the way back up the beach toward the marina. He talked to her as they walked, telling her about his earliest memories of sailing. "It was my gran who first took me out on the ocean and let me get behind the wheel. She taught me about the jib and the wind and how to harness it. She made it seem okay that when my father bellowed and yelled, I ran and hid."

Iris caught her breath as he talked about his childhood. She'd heard from Adler that August Bisset wasn't an easy man to live with. Adler rarely saw her uncle, but Zac had grown up underneath his roof and his upbringing was so different from Iris's. So foreign. Her parents had wanted them to achieve but nothing had been more important to them than making sure that she and her sister were loved.

Something that Iris realized she'd taken for granted.

She stopped Zac when they were on the slip about to board his grandmother's yacht, the Day Dream.

"Changed your mind?" he asked.

"Not at all," she said, hugging him and pulling him closer to her so she could whisper in his ear. "Thank you for being you."

He squeezed her close for a long minute and then let his arms fall to his sides. He didn't respond and she hadn't expected him to. She knew how hard it was to live with someone so demanding, and the fact that Zac had made the relationship with his father work by going his own way was more impressive than he knew. He hadn't chosen the easy path; he'd moved halfway around the world and started over. He thought he was a man who always looked for the horizon because he was running but she knew now that he did that because he was harnessing the bluster he'd inherited from his father and charting his own course.

She wished she could chart a course that would keep her by his side and didn't even care if that made her seem weak. She liked him and she wanted to keep him in her life but she had no idea if that was something that was even possible.

Eleven

Piloting the small yacht out of the marina at night was as familiar to him as the back of his hand. Once he'd gotten them out into Nantucket Sound, Iris stood in his arms at the helm of the boat. He steered them far away from the lights of Nantucket until it felt like they were the only two people left on earth.

And knowing that tomorrow he'd be surrounded by his family and there would be all of the activities of Adler's wedding party, he wanted to make this night last forever. As much as he prided himself on being the anti-Bisset Bisset he knew once he was with his brothers and sister that he'd fall back into the role that he always played with them and, of course, he had the added role of being Iris's boyfriend for the weekend.

But tonight they were Zac and Iris. "I almost wish we were living in a different time. I'd spirit you away on the high seas and we'd stop wherever we hit land, and no one would know who we were."

"You'd run away with me?"

"Hell, yes. Would you?"

She thought about it too long and he knew the answer was no, no matter what she said. Of course, Iris wouldn't run away. She wasn't about running away. She was about making a plan and then following it until its end. No matter what.

"I'm kidding," he said. "The sea just calls to me."

But it was too late to pull back that feeling even though he'd tried to cover it. He'd always know he'd thrown out something that was real and she'd drawn back. He reminded himself that she was a very attractive woman who had decided to hire a man for the weekend instead of finding a real boyfriend.

His thoughts were ruining the night. He needed tonight to be a happy memory for both of them, but maybe it was Nantucket or just thinking about his family that had soured him.

"I'm sorry," she said. "I want to say yes, but I'd be so freaked out about not knowing where we were going and not having a plan that I'd make you miserable. Do I want to be with you…?"

She stopped talking and turned in his arms as he hit the anchor release button and was about to turn away from her. She put her arms around his waist and rested her head on his chest right over his heart.

"More than anything," she said. Her voice was low, but he still heard her.

"Then why do you hesitate?"

"I'm afraid," she said, then let out a deep breath that sounded like a sigh. "I can only let my guard down because I know whatever I do you're not going to leave me. And if we started really dating, I'd let the pressure of that expectation overwhelm me. I know that makes me sound shallow."

"No," he said. "It doesn't. It makes you human, angel face."

She looked up at him then and he didn't care that she knew he wanted to run away with her. He could make whatever excuses he wanted to, he was going to miss the hell out of her when their arrangement was over and he started his training for the America's Cup. He'd go because that was his life, but he'd always look back to this moment and this night with her.

"Want to skinny dip?" he asked, because if he didn't do something, he was going to say all kinds of things that would scare her so much it would send her swimming back to shore.

"I'm afraid of the water."

"I'll protect you," he said. "But no pressure if you don't want to go in."

She chewed her lower lip. "How about if you skinny dip and I stand on the deck and watch?"

"Will you be naked?" he asked.

"I could be," she said. "Seems only fair if one of us is going to strip down, we both should."

"It does," he said, trying not to let himself fall a little bit more for her. There was so much daring inside her but she was afraid to let it out except in little controlled bursts. And he had to admit that made her all the more attractive.

He took her hand and led her to the deck of the yacht, then waggled his eyebrows at her as he took off his shirt and then his pants. He stood in front of her in his boxer briefs and put his hands on his hips. "One of us is a bit ahead of the other one."

"One of us is just wearing a thong under their dress," she said, untying the halter neck and letting the dress fall from her.

His breath caught in his throat as he stared at her beautiful nearly naked body. She stood there in the light of the full moon and the illumination provided by the running lights and reached up to undo the clasp that held her hair back. Her hair spilled down over her shoulders and she lifted her arms as the gentle summer breeze blew around them.

It should have cooled him off but even an Arctic breeze wouldn't have lessened the heat she stirred in him. He was hot and hard and at the same time he wanted to cuddle her in his arms and just keep her safe. He wished the world could see this Iris. The one with her arms in the air, bare breasts uplifted and a huge-ass smile on her face. Gone were her barriers and the proper behavior she used to keep the world at arm's length.

"God, you're gorgeous," he said. His words were low and rumbling but that was all he could manage.

She tipped her head to the side and smiled at him. "I want to point out all the places I'm not, but I can see you think I am, so I'll keep it to myself."

"I'm glad because I wasn't just talking about your body. There's something about you, Iris, that I can't resist."

Zac made her feel different and she wasn't sure she wanted to resist it. She let her arms fall to her sides and stood more fully facing him. He was turned on by her—that was easy to see—but there was a lot more than sexy times between them.

He'd asked her to run away with him and she'd panicked. Not because she didn't want to but because, for a split second, she wished she was the kind of woman who would. But she knew that the contract had freed something inside of her. It was novel and new, and she was enjoying it because it was shocking her to her staid core. But if that was her norm, she didn't think she'd enjoy it as much.

And she knew he would. She didn't want to hurt Zac.

Heck, she'd been hurt too many times by relationships to want to risk another one—hence, the contract.

"Are you still feeling like a swim?" she asked, coming closer to him. She loved his body and honestly it would be perfectly okay with her if he were naked 24/7 when they were alone together. He had been sweet to compliment her but he had the kind of body that would make anyone stop and stare.

"Well, not exactly," he said, reaching out to cup one of her breasts in his hand. He rubbed his thumb over her nipple, and it beaded under his touch.

Remembering the scar she'd felt the first time they'd made love, she reached out and touched it again. She leaned in closer and saw it was jagged and still had some redness around it. "What is this from?"

"Stupidity," he said.

"I've done a lot of stupid things but don't have a scar like this," she said, tracing the edges of it with a gentle finger, wishing she could have soothed the hurt it must have caused him.

"Well, when you combine alcohol with ego and a competitive nature, this is the result. I did a kite-surfing challenge with a teammate, won, celebrated too vigorously and ended up crashing into an outcropping of rocks I hadn't noticed."

"That does sound…"

"Dumb. You can say it. My mom and sister both said it was what I deserved. Apparently, my victory dances are a little OTT."

She had to laugh at the way he said it, but her laughter turned to sensual awareness as his hand moved from her breast to her waist and he drew her closer to him. Her naked breasts were cushioned against his upper body. His chest hair was soft against her skin and his heat was a contrast to the breeze blowing around them. He smelled of his aftershave—a clean, crisp scent—and the sea breeze. She closed her eyes and willed her mind to stop thinking. To just relax and enjoy this. But she wanted to record every second.

Her life had been played out on TV and on social media since she'd entered college. By her own design, of course, but so many of her ups and downs had been recorded and scrutinized on the gossip websites that she almost didn't believe her own reality until she saw it played back. Until she flipped past her profile and saw that smiling face.

She knew she was here with him. She wanted to just enjoy him but—

"Stop thinking," he said. "It's disconcerting to watch you go from enjoying my touch to suddenly seeming to analyze everything."

Busted.

"Damn. I'm sorry. I'm such a freak about things like that. I don't know what my deal—"

He stopped the stream of words with a kiss. She stopped thinking, stopped worrying and calculating her responses. She just clung to his shoulders as his tongue rubbed over hers and his hands splayed warm and wide on her back. She arched into the curve of his body and felt his erection pushing against her. She flexed her fingers against his skin and couldn't help the groan that started deep inside her as her entire body seemed to start pulsing in time with her heartbeat. She wanted this.

She wanted him.

And she wasn't going to allow her own self-consciousness to stop her from enjoying this.

She ran her hand down his arm, felt the flex of his biceps and squeezed them. She loved his strength. Loved how easily he held her and yet how gently he did it. He was aware of his strength and never used it to overwhelm her even though he easily could. He broke their kiss, his mouth moving down the column of her neck, biting gently at the junction where it sloped into her collarbone.

She caressed his chest, flexing her fingers and letting her nails scrape over his skin. He shuddered at her touch and she continued to move her hand down his body. But he stopped her, turning her in his arms and pulling her close against his chest. His erection nestled between her buttocks and he put one hand on her stomach and the other between her legs.

She rocked her hips back against him and he brought his hand up to her chin, tipping her head back and to the side to kiss her again. His mouth was warm and wet, drawing her deeper into the sensual web he was weaving around them. She felt his finger move under the fabric of her underwear to the juncture of her thighs. She reached back between their bodies, fondling him through his boxer briefs, realizing that the only thought she had was how to get him inside of her.

Iris felt so good in his arms that he wanted the moment to never end but he also needed to be inside of her. To take her and pretend that this night could last forever. He pushed her thong down her legs, and she kicked them aside as she turned in his arms and he shoved his underwear off so that her hand was on his naked shaft. He continued kissing her as he walked her backward to the soft cushions on the deck near the railing. He lifted his head for a moment, trying to gauge how quickly he could get to the cushions and get inside of her but she pushed him back on the padded bench and straddled him as she had for a few moments the first time they'd made love.

"I want to be on top the entire time," she said. "I feel

like I let you take control from the very first moment and this time it's all me."

"Yes, ma'am," he said. "I've got a condom in my pants pocket."

"Stay right there," she said.

He did as she ordered, watching her walk across the deck to where he'd dropped his trousers. She bent over and as she did, glanced back at him and realized he was watching her. She stopped just like that, her beautiful backside pointed at him, her hair hanging down as she smiled back at him. She took the condom from his pocket and then slowly stood back up, turning to face him.

He was stroking his cock as he watched her, and this time when she walked toward him, her gait was deliberate and her intent was to turn him on. Her full breasts bounced with her steps and her hips swayed. She was taking control of not just their lovemaking but of the night.

He felt like he was going burst as she stopped in front of him and dropped to her knees. Leaning forward, she stroked her tongue along the side of his shaft before taking him into her mouth. His hips jerked forward and he put his hand on the back of her head, touching her briefly before moving his hand away. She reached between them, stroking his shaft while she continued to suck on the tip. He felt like he was going to come in her mouth and that was the last thing he wanted for this night. He shifted his hips and went down on his knees next to her on the deck, taking the condom from her hand and quickly sheathing himself with it. He turned her around so she was facing the ocean, then took one of her hands and put it on the bench underneath his.

He put his other hand on her stomach, pushed her hips back toward him and entered her from behind. She moaned and turned her hand over underneath his, twining their fingers together, her hips rocking back against him as he entered her deeper. He palmed her breast with his free hand and kissed the side of her neck. She threw her head back as he started to pump his hips and drove himself into her again and again.

She turned her head and he found her mouth with his. He was totally in tune with her as they both ground harder and harder against each other until he felt himself about to come. But he wasn't sure she was with him. He reached between her legs, flicking her clit with his finger, rubbing it the way she'd liked it the other night. She ripped her mouth from his, threw back her head and screamed his name.

He held her hips with both hands, thrusting into her one more time, harder and deeper than before. But it wasn't enough. He drew back and drove himself into her again and again until his release washed over him and he collapsed forward, putting his hand on the bench to make sure he didn't crush her. She wrapped her hand around his wrist, her breath sawing in and out of her body.

He lifted himself from her, pulled her to her feet and then sat down on the bench and cuddled her in his lap. She looked as dazed as he felt. He was totally sated from their lovemaking. She'd done something to him. Snapped that control he'd always relied on to keep his wits about him and make sure he didn't dive in to deep.

But he knew he had. As she curled up on his lap, putting her head on his shoulder and wrapping her arms around him, all he could do was stroke her back and remind himself that he was a man who loved the next horizon more than anything on shore, even though at this moment, with the moon shining down on them, it felt like a lie.

He knew he should say something or get up and start steering them back to Nantucket. But he didn't want this moment to end. She didn't say anything either, just held on to him. He felt like they both knew that something had changed between them.

He thought he might be overthinking it, but he couldn't deny the truth that he felt deep in his soul. Iris Collins was changing him, and he was half addicted to it, half resentful of it. His life had worked for so long because he'd found his place and his way of coping with it. He wasn't sure he was ready to change for her or for anyone else.

And he damned sure knew he didn't want to go into this weekend feeling like this. He needed to be his strongest self, not whatever this was that making love to Iris had made him.

Twelve

Iris had woken up in Zac's arms at 4:00 a.m. in a total panic. She didn't want to dwell on the night before. The moonlight, the ocean, the man.

She was losing control of herself and of the situation with Zac. Last night had changed something inside of her and she didn't like it. She wasn't about to give up on everything she'd worked for because she had a lover who knew how to please her for the first time in her life. And she was ashamed of boiling Zac's good qualities down to the fact that he knew how to make her orgasm, but that was how she was going to cope with him.

She had gotten out of bed at seven o'clock and snuck into the bathroom to change into her exercise clothes. She'd only packed them for lounging in her room, but she needed to get out of the hotel and away from Zac. She needed to think and put everything in perspective.

She had wedding fever, she thought as she started out

on a slow jog down the path toward the beach. But she hated running and as soon as she was out of sight of the hotel, slowed to a walk. She wished her walk would bring her a solution to what she should do. But she'd really made a mess of things this time. It would have been easier if she'd just had Zac show up on the day of the event and look pretty on her arm. But no, she'd found a guy who knew the bride and who was…well, more than Iris had expected him to be.

He was complicating her well-ordered life and she wasn't too sure she liked it.

"Iris?"

She glanced over her shoulder to see Juliette Bisset. "Hi, Mrs. B. What are you doing out here so early?"

"Same as you, I imagine," Juliette said.

God, Iris really hoped not. "I guess hosting your husband's rivals at your mom's house would be a little bit stressful."

Juliette smiled and shook her head. "You have no idea. I've never met Nick's family because…well, Tad and Cora didn't want to meet me. But I'm glad that August is making the effort for Adler. The last thing a new bride needs is tension in her marriage."

It sounded like Mrs. B was speaking from experience. Iris wanted to know more—she couldn't help it—but manners and breeding kept her from asking. "That's true of any relationship."

"I heard you're dating my son," Juliette said.

"I am," Iris said, not sure what Zac had told his mom about them. "It happened kind of quick."

"That's what Zac said," Juliette said. "I'm not going to pry or anything. Just wanted to say I like the idea of you and Zac together."

"I do too," she said. Not just because she thought that's

what she should say but it was the truth. And as Zac had pointed out when they'd signed their pact, if they stuck to the truth as they went along, it would be easier.

"Good," Juliette said. "I should be getting back but I'm not ready for everyone to be here. I hope that Adler is enjoying this quiet before the wedding events take over our lives."

"I'm sure she is. Last night she and Nick seemed to be taking a few moments to themselves. My mom said that she wished she'd done more of that."

"Your mom has always been so wise about relationships," Juliette said.

"You have too. I mean you and Mr. B are a really strong couple," Iris said. She'd heard the gossip about August Bisset's affair that had led to a reconciliation and the subsequent birth of Zac's youngest sibling and only sister, Mari. But since then it seemed that Juliette and August had been solid.

"Thank you for saying that. It hasn't been easy but we are stronger today because of it."

Iris couldn't help but sigh at the way she'd said that. "I want that someday."

"I hope you don't have the rocky road to it that I did," Juliette said.

"If I do, I hope I weather it as gracefully as you did," she said. "I don't feel like exercising. Care to join me for a mimosa before you head back home?"

"I'd love to. I think it's just what I need this morning. I keep thinking about Musette. She'd be completely trying to take over Adler's wedding and I know she'd love every minute of it," Juliette said, referring to Adler's deceased mom.

"It must be hard for you, but I know that Adler thinks of you as her second mom," Iris said.

"And she's my first daughter. I know that sounds bad but I had Adler before Mari and I've always thought of her as mine."

"You two have such a close relationship," Iris said. "I know it means a lot to Adler."

They walked back up toward the resort and went to the restaurant in the lobby for a light breakfast and mimosas. As they were finishing up, Iris's phone pinged. She glanced down to see it was a text from Zac.

Are you okay?

"Excuse me, I have to answer this," Iris said to Juliette.

"Go ahead. I'm going to finish this drink and then head back to the big house. I'm glad we ran into each other this morning."

"Me too." Iris said goodbye, then typed out a response to Zac after Mrs. B left.

I'm in the lobby restaurant with your mom. I'll be back in the room in a few minutes.

My mom?!

Worried? ;)

No... Should I be?

No!

She settled the bill and sat there, taking her time with the final sip of her mimosa. Talking to the older woman this morning had relieved some of the tension she'd been carrying. It was clear that no matter how together a woman appeared on the outside, men and relationships could be a struggle. And in a weird way, that reassured her.

Waking up alone was nothing new to Zac, but when he rolled over and realized that Iris was gone, he wondered if he'd pushed too hard last night. He had a shower, thinking she must have gone for coffee. Then he shaved because he was going to be seeing his father for lunch. And there was no use going into that encounter with one hair out of place.

August Bisset could be charming, and there were a lot of times when Zac actually enjoyed being with his father. But not in social situations where he had to rule the room and the conversation. In such circumstances, his father wasn't afraid to point out the flaws in any of his children. It had been drilled into them to be the best from...well, for as long as Zac could remember.

After he'd shaven and gotten dressed for lunch, he started to worry about Iris. Where was she?

Was she okay?

He fished his cell phone out of his pocket and texted her. He wished he'd thought to tell her to turn on Find My Friends so he'd know exactly where she was, but he hadn't. He was stuck waiting for her to respond.

He saw the dancing dots on his screen and felt a sense of relief until she texted back that she was with his mom.

Dear God. That had *bad idea* written all over it. What were they talking about? He didn't even want to know.

She was cute and funny in her reply, which eased his mind about the night before. He'd be cool today. He was her hired date, and he'd give her what she'd paid for and a little bit more. If he focused on Iris, then he'd be able to deal with his dad without issue.

Or at least that was his hope.

He heard the door open and glanced over to see Iris

entering the living area of their suite. She had on a pair of flower-print leggings and a tank top that hugged her curves. After the night they'd spent together, he shouldn't want her again, but he did. She smiled at him and raised her eyebrows as she took in his navy pants, button-down oxford shirt and loafers.

"You're ready really early," she said.

"Usually we have a family meeting before events like this, so I'm anticipating a text from Carlton," he said.

"Good to know. Who's Carlton? Is that your dad's PR guy?" she asked.

"Yeah, he is. He kind of goes over the family image and the dos and don'ts for the event. Normally I'm not in town so I get to miss them, but I'm pretty sure I can't skip this one."

"Probably not. I'm going to shower and get dressed for the day. Should I plan to meet you later or come with you?"

He rubbed the back of his neck. "I'd like you to come with me. I mean, you don't have to, but if you are there, you're going to up my image rating."

She shook her head. "Your image rating is already pretty high."

"With you maybe," he said. "But I'm not as polished as Dad and Carlton would like. And I seem okay now, but when you see me next to Dare, Logan and Leo, I do seem like the scruffy one."

"Good thing I like scruffy."

"Good thing," he said.

She gave him a little wave as she walked toward the bedroom. "I better get moving."

He leaned back against the sofa and turned on ESPN as he waited for her. She'd been so peppy this morning. He'd thought she'd be dwelling on what had happened last night.

Well, hell.

She was ignoring it, wasn't she?

Was she going to pretend that nothing had happened? Should he?

He knew that he couldn't do that. He wasn't built that way. But she was in full-on wedding-pact mode and that meant they were the picture-perfect couple. He had planned to use their arrangement to sooth his father and keep the criticism at bay, but now that he knew Iris was back to just playing a role, it bothered him. He wanted her to talk about last night or at least be thinking about it so that he'd know she was as affected as he was.

Didn't it mean anything to her?

He got up and went into the bedroom. He stood there, staring at the closed bathroom door until he heard the shower shut off. Then he ran for the bed and lay down on it, trying to look casual as the door opened and a cloud of steam preceded Iris into the room.

"What are you doing in here?"

"Waiting for you? We're lovers now, angel face," he said.

"I know but that was last night. The wedding stuff starts today. This is the contracted thing—"

"I'm not going to embarrass you but I'm also not going to pretend that last night and the other night didn't happen. There is more between us now than a contract."

She put her hand on her chest and toyed with her diamond necklace. "You know it still has to end, right?"

"Yes, of course, I'm not sticking around, hoping you'll put a ring on my finger," he said. "I have other commitments, as well."

"Good. Then I see no reason for you not to be in here."

But she didn't smile or talk to him while she got ready and he knew that something had changed between them again. They weren't closer now; there was a new barrier between them and he had the feeling it came from both of them ignoring the truth of what they felt and wanted to say.

Iris didn't want him as her lover while she was doing the wedding stuff this weekend. And he wanted her to be that. He wanted more from her than he'd contractually asked for and it was too late. He'd signed the agreement and he had to live up to it.

And he would. Come hell or August Bisset.

Iris didn't like the fact that Zac was on the bed, but she wasn't about to let him see he had shaken her. And he did have her in a state. Enough of one that she'd had to leave the room to clear her head and get it on straight. Which was when she'd run into his mom.

Ever since Thea had grabbed her phone and responded to Graham's text, nothing had been in her control. Her sister had goaded her without even realizing what she was doing. It wasn't Thea's fault that Iris always had to appear to be in control. And as much as she hated to admit it, it wasn't Zac's fault she'd blurred the lines between them.

She could admit that the first time she'd fallen into bed with him had been sheer lust. She hadn't had that kind of experience with a guy before. But she'd been hot for him. The second time… Hell, she had no excuse. Last night had been a slip in judgment and from where she stood in the slightly steamy bathroom, pretending she was still putting on her makeup, it seemed downright stupid.

He was hot and sweet and unexpected. And not for her. She wasn't trying to talk herself out of a good thing; she was reminding herself of her reality. She couldn't let the romance of Adler finding a great guy influence her. It didn't matter that she'd wanted a man to grow her brand into "coupledom." Zac wasn't that guy—he was only acting the part.

No amount of sex was going to change that.

But would it hurt her to keep having sex with him?

That was the million-dollar question.

She wanted to be a modern woman and say no. She could have sex with a guy and not fall in love with him. After all, look what had happened with Graham. But that had been bad sex. Not the melt-her-panties-off sex she had with Zac. That kind of sex made a girl dream of something more. Something forbidden and as hard to find as a unicorn in Times Square. And as much as she was all about her preppy, practical lifestyle, she was still a dreamer at heart. Underneath her Lilly Pulitzer navy dress with the white embroidery, she was dreaming of a man who'd stand by her side.

The knock on the door startled her and she put her hand to the diamond charm on the necklace before opening the door.

"You okay?" Zac asked.

He looked so sincere and sexy, dressed up to impress his parents. She wanted to tease him about it but frankly she got it. It didn't matter how grown-up or successful she became, she still wanted her parents' approval and it made her fall a little bit more for him that he wanted his.

"Yeah," she said. Her heart wasn't in putting up her normal shield this morning. Or at least not with him.

"We said no lies between us."

She sighed and brushed past him, trying not to let the scent of his aftershave send sensual tingles of awareness through her body, but she couldn't help remembering how strong that scent had been on his naked chest last night.

"I know," she said, going to the wardrobe where she'd stored her shoes and pulling out a pair of strappy white sandals that would give her a few extra inches of height. "But you're throwing me off my game, Zac."

"What? How am I doing that?" he asked.

She wished she could be Thea and just bluntly tell him that sex was making her addle-brained, but she wasn't her twin. She was Iris, and there was no way she was going to bring up sex now. They were on their way to lunch with his entire family, and she had to keep the new girlfriend act going.

"Nothing. I think I'm just tired this morning and nervous about meeting your family."

He nodded, then walked over to her and put his hand on her shoulder. "They're going to be so impressed that you're with me, you're not going to have to worry about anything. I'm the black sheep of the family."

Only the Bissets would consider an America's Cup team member the black sheep. She smiled and realized he'd done it again: eased her nerves by being himself. She had to find a way to make her feelings more casual. But everything about him made her want to cling.

She wasn't a clinger.

She didn't want to be the woman Graham had accused her of being.

Heck, was she reacting this way because she was trying to prove something to Graham?

She hoped not. She wouldn't be that petty and spiteful. But she always knew a part of her would love to rub in his face that she'd had a fabulous night of orgasms in Zac's arms.

She groaned.

"Iris?"

"Sorry. I just had the worst thought."

"Want to share it?"

"No, you'll think I'm a lunatic."

"Now I have to know what it was," he said, with that crooked smile of his.

"You know that guy who broke up with me, forcing me

to hire you?" she asked. "Well he called me a cold fish because I couldn't climax with him and said lots of other mean things about me in the sack. And I was just thinking I wish I could tell him about last night. I think the issue was him, not me."

Zac smiled at her, pulled her into his arms and kissed her with passion. When he lifted his head, he said, "Angel face, it definitely wasn't you."

She put her arms around his shoulders and kissed him back, pouring all her fears and hopes into the embrace. When she stepped back, she told herself that was the last behind-closed-doors kiss they'd share. From now on, everything between them would be for show.

Really.

Thirteen

Juliette stood in the corner of the large conservatory that her mother always used for welcoming guests when the weather allowed. The July sky was gorgeous. Juliette almost wished she were the kind of woman to allow herself to believe in things like signs from heaven because she could have sworn that it was her sister looking down on them and giving Adler a perfect day.

But she didn't.

Her husband had changed his jacket three times, wanting to appear casual as he welcomed his one-time friend—and now enemy for more than thirty-five years—to lunch. Over the years Juliette had seen newspaper articles and some photos occasionally of Tad and his wife, Cora, but August always left events if they showed up so she'd never met them. Watching him try had always been the one thing that she hadn't been able to resist about him. August was a big man with big appetites, big ambition and a very big temper, but she'd glimpsed the vulnerability in him that he hid from the world.

They'd been married almost forty years so she knew that was to be expected.

"There you are, Jules," her mother said as she entered the room. "I have Michael and his staff ready with the welcoming drinks. I assume most of our guests will drink but he told me you asked him to include a nonalcoholic one, as well."

"I did, Mother. I hope you don't mind," she said. "I'm not sure what to expect from the Williams family, but I wanted to give everyone a choice."

"Good thinking."

Her mom had a way of making her feel like her party-hosting skills had stopped developing when she'd been throwing tea parties for her dolls even though she had a reputation for throwing the best parties in the Hamptons.

"Thanks."

"Do you really think she might make you a grand-mother?" her mom asked.

"I don't know. And we shouldn't be discussing this now. Though I am ready," Juliette admitted.

"I am too. And what's with your boys? I thought they'd be more like Auggie and marry young, but they seem to be waiting," her mother said.

"They are like Auggie but on the business side, not in terms of starting a family," Juliette said. All of her children were determined to make their mark on the world, and she didn't blame them. She'd often wondered if she'd had a career whether her marriage would have been different. Her life certainly would have. She might not even still be married to Auggie.

They heard the door open and Juliette was glad that the

guests had started arriving. She liked socializing because it distracted her from her own thoughts and her own life.

"Gran," Zac said, coming into the conservatory with Iris Collins on his arm.

Iris was too sophisticated for her son, and if Juliette were being honest, she thought the younger woman was a little too prim. Zac liked his women more…well, sporty for one thing. And loose but not in a negative way.

"Zac, so good to see you. Your mother and I are both delighted you're back from Australia," her mom said as she went to hug him.

Juliette hugged Iris and then stepped back to hug Zac. Her boys were all taller than her now and his hug engulfed her. She held him longer than she knew she should, but she'd missed this tall blond boy of hers. He always made sailing seem like it was a gentleman's sport but she knew it was dangerous and she worried about him.

"Mom," he said, kissing her on the forehead.

"Sweetie," she answered. "Tell me why you were in Boston and how you met Iris. I know that's where it happened but the details are murky."

Zac put his arm out, drawing Iris in to the curve of his body. "Nothing murky about it, Mom. I quit my old America's Cup team and was in Boston looking for sponsors for my run in the next one. If I asked Dad, there'd be strings attached. Iris's father runs an investment group and we met when I was waiting to speak to him."

"I stumbled and he caught me," Iris said.

Zac looked down at Iris and winked and suddenly Juliette loved seeing her son with this woman. There was something about them that made her want to smile.

"Your dad won't be happy about the investment but I think everything else will be fine," Juliette said.

"I know but once I caught Iris I told myself not to let her go. It's not every day I meet a woman like Iris."

"So true," Nick Williams said, coming up behind Zac and clapping him on the shoulder.

Juliette smiled at Adler's fiancé. She'd met him a few times before and found him to be a very likeable man. But, of course, he was a thorn in Logan's side, always foiling his business deals and trying to beat him to market. So she understood that not everyone in her family was happy to see him, not to mention that he was marrying Adler.

"Hey, man," Zac said, turning to shake Nick's hand as Adler came in with an older woman.

There was something familiar about the tall brunette, Juliette thought as she came closer. Then their eyes met and both women froze. *Dear God.*

It was the other woman who'd been in labor the night Juliette had given birth to her unnamed stillborn baby. Except she was a brunette now, not a blonde, and she wore the trappings of wealth as easily as if she'd been born to it.

Was this Cora Williams? The girl—Bonnie, she'd said her name was. Bonnie Smith. They'd both been in that post-delivery room crying. Juliette because she'd lost her baby that she'd hoped would save her marriage and Bonnie because she'd been cut off from her family, had no job and no way to support twins.

She remembered that moment when they'd realized there was a solution that would serve them both. If Juliette raised one of the fraternal twins as her own son, it would solve their problems.

Juliette had made a deal that only she, Bonnie and the nurse Jennifer had known about. They'd switched her still-born child for one of the healthy boys. Juliette had given Bonnie a large sum of money from her private trust fund so she could go back to school and raise her son. Jennifer had taken a small sum to falsify the documents.

There wasn't a day that went by that she didn't think about the deal she'd made. How her Logan wasn't really hers. But until this moment she'd expected to keep the secret until her grave.

She'd never met Nick's parents…that meant that Nick was probably the other twin. She saw stars and thought she was going to pass out.

Crap.

This wasn't good.

The woman… Cora. Heck, she remembered everything about that night but at the time she'd called herself Bonnie Smith.

"Auntie Jules, this is Nick's mom, Cora," Adler said, bringing them both face-to-face. Cora seemed as shocked as Juliette felt.

But manners guided her and Juliette put out her hand. "So nice to meet you."

"You, as well," Cora said, but her hands were clammy. "I feel like I know you from all of Adler's stories."

"Me too," Juliette said. She knew they needed to talk but not now. Not today.

"Adler, is this your fiancé? I'm so eager to meet him and get to know his family," Auggie said as he came in.

Cora turned and Juliette saw the look on her husband's face as he saw her. She knew that look. Cora and Auggie had been lovers.

"Cora?"

"August," Cora said, then turned to Juliette. "You never said your husband was August Bisset."

"I didn't know you knew him."

"We need to talk," Cora said.

"I think we do," Juliette said.

* * *

Zac saw the color leave his mother's face and the shock on his dad's when he saw Nick's mom. Nick looked at him and they both seemed to be of the same mindset. Carlton had entered the room and looked at Cora and then blanched.

"Why is Bonnie Smith here?" Carlton asked as he came into the room. The older man had been his father's PR man and spin doctor since the beginning of his career. In fact, Zac had never been at a family meeting that wasn't chaired by Carlton. He was the one who cleaned up messes for the family. There were times when Zac liked the older man; he was nicer than his father. But there were other times when Carlton could be tough as nails. This was one of those times.

"Bonnie? This is my mother. Cora Williams," Nick said, stepping to Cora's side and putting his arm around her shoulders. "Is there a problem?"

"Don't worry about it, Nicky. I need to speak to August and Juliette alone. Will you keep an eye out for your dad?" Cora said.

Nick pulled his mom aside, away from everyone else, and Adler was looking at Zac's mom like she wanted to ask a million questions, but she wasn't saying a word. His father just walked out of the room with Carlton, turning around briefly. "Vivian, may we use your study?"

"Of course, Auggie."

"Ladies, will you please join me in there?" August asked.

Zac watched as his mom nodded but Nick stepped in front of Cora. "I don't think so. She's not going anywhere with you. I want to know what's going on. Why are they calling you Bonnie?"

"I agree with Nick," Adler said, going over to her fiancé and taking his hand. "What's going on?"

Juliette stood up and looked at Iris and Gran, and both

of the women walked out of the room. But Zac stayed. This was his family and he wanted to know what was happening.

The butler closed the door to the conservatory. The groups in the room formed an odd triangle. Zac and his mom were on one side, his father and Carlton on another and Nick, his mom and Adler finished the formation. His father looked like he was going to lose his temper, his mom looked scared and Cora looked defensive.

He glanced over at Adler. She looked pale and afraid.

"Dad, how do you know Nick's mom?" Zac asked.

"I don't think you should be—"

"Just answer him, August. Tell our son how you know Nick's mom," his mom said.

From the tone of his mom's voice, Zac had the sinking feeling that Cora had been one of his father's other women. God, this was a mess. Had his father become her lover to get back at his rival Tad Williams?

"They were friends," Carlton said. "A long time ago. She was an intern who worked at the company just after Darien was born."

"Friends?" Nick asked, looking down at his mom. "With August Bisset?"

"Yes, dear," Cora said. "It was before I knew your father. We were friends."

"How do you know Juliette?" Nick asked. "Were you all friends?"

His mom's shoulders straightened and she shook her head. "No. That's not how we know each other. I met your mom the night I gave birth to Logan."

"We were in the hospital together. Both of us. In that rural hospital in the middle of a storm."

August looked at Cora and then shook his head. "You gave birth the same night as Jules?"

"I did," she said. "Unfortunately, I was a single mom and Juliette was kind to me."

"I know how hard it can be," Zac's mom said.

There was more to it. He could feel it in the room. A single woman giving birth at the same hospital as... Zac looked at his dad as he came to a conclusion that he hoped was wrong. Had his dad been Cora's lover? Was he Nick's father? *Hell.* He hoped not because then this entire wedding weekend was going to be a lot tougher than he'd thought it would be.

"Dad?"

"Zac."

"Is Nick your—"

"Niece's fiancé?" Carlton asked. "Because that's really the only question that makes sense, Zachary."

"Carlton, enough. It's just us. I want the truth," Zac said. "Adler deserves that. Hell, I think we all do."

He turned to look at Nick, who was staring down at his mother, and he saw the truth on the older brunette's face. She started to cry and before anyone could say anything else, the door burst open and Tad Williams walked in. He went straight to his wife's side. "What did that bastard say to you?"

But Cora couldn't answer. She just shook her head and Tad pulled her into his arms. Nick was looking at his mother and then back at August and then he just walked out of the room. Adler ran after him and Zac wondered if he should leave, but when he started to go, his mom held on to his wrist, keeping him by her side. He looked over at her.

"Please."

He nodded and put his arm back around her shoulder. Zac knew he shouldn't be surprised because his father had never been a one-woman man. But in recent years he'd started to mellow and settle down. He'd been a good husband to his mom since Mari's birth. But this was a secret from the past and it was coming back to bite them. The kind of secret that could hurt them all. Not like the secret he and Iris had. That one was just between the two of them.

He'd made damned sure of that. "Dad, is Nick your son?"

"What?" Tad asked. "What is he talking about?"

Juliette had never felt like this before. She knew that Nick was August's child, which meant that Logan, the twin she'd raised, was August's child too. She'd always felt bad about deceiving her husband but now she felt sick. This complicated game that she and August had been playing with each other for forty years was now going to ensnare too many other people. And their sons would be hurt. Mari had been the product of their reconciliation after August's blatant affair in the early '90s but this was from almost a decade earlier. At the time, Juliette had never suspected her husband was having an affair.

She'd had some postpartum depression after Darien's birth and it had taken her a long time to get pregnant with her second child. The pregnancy had made things start to feel better between them. She had the feeling now that she'd been fooling herself. Because Cora had been pregnant at the same time with who she now truly believed were August's twins.

"I asked a question," Tad said.

"Tad, honey, August and I—"

"She worked for me, Tad. After you left the company, we had those interns come in and Bonnie—I mean Cora—was one of them."

Zac knew there was bad blood between Tad Williams and his father but not being a part of the day-to-day operation at Bisset Industries, he didn't know the details.

"Did he work for you?" Zac asked.

"I was an intern at the company for a short while until your father had me fired," Tad explained.

"You weren't performing up to expectations," August said.

"Whatever. How could you have an affair? You had a new wife and baby at home," Tad said.

"You're right, I did," his dad said. "I can make no excuses, only apologies. I wasn't the man I am today. When I saw something I wanted, I went after it. I didn't care who I hurt. And, Jules, my love, you know I regret that. I don't regret it if Nick is my son. Cora was my lover at about that time. But I assumed he was your son."

"No, Cora and I started dating when Nick was three months old," Tad said. "Cora?"

"August is the father. I never told him I was pregnant. I ended things as soon as I realized that he had a wife and baby at home."

Zac wasn't sure what to say. This wasn't at all what he'd been expecting when he'd come to his gran's house for lunch with Adler's fiancé's family.

The conservatory doors opened again, and this time Logan and Leo walked in. Both of his brothers came straight toward him and his mom.

Logan put his hands on his hips, "What's going on? Adler is in tears. I really couldn't understand a word she said but she mentioned Dad…"

"Oh, God," Zac said. "Dude, there's no easy way to say this but it seems like your archenemy in business might be related to us."

"What the f—!" Logan didn't handle the news well. He turned on their father, who held his hands up.

"I just learned about it a second ago," their dad said.

Their mom put her hand to her throat and walked out of the conservatory and August followed.

"No one talks to the press. We need a meeting to figure out how to do this properly," Carlton said. "Mr. and Mrs. Williams, do you have a PR person, or would you like me to run point on this."

"We don't have a PR person," Cora said. "Nothing like this happens to us."

"I'll handle it for you," Carlton said, patting Cora on the arm. "Don't worry. This isn't going to be a big deal."

"I guess when you're used to cleaning up after August Bisset, it seems that way to you," Tad said. "But we are straight shooters. The Williams family doesn't cover up the truth."

Carlton nodded. "I know you and August have had issues in the past, but there is no way that you and your wife look good in this scenario if you go public with just the truth. August has a child he knew nothing about. You can see how that will play in the press."

Cora started crying and Tad put his arm around his wife. Zac walked over to them. He wasn't involved in the Bisset business. He felt that of all his brothers, he was the one who could liaise most easily with the Williams family.

"Carlton will make this right for all of us," Zac said. "He's not going to do anything that will put you in a bad light, Mrs. Williams. Isn't that right?"

"Of course. I'm sorry if it seemed I might," Carlton said. "We just have to cover all of the bases."

"I can't do this right now," Cora said.

"You don't have to," Carlton said. "I'm sorry I came on strong. Would you both come with me and we can figure out how you want to handle this announcement? I can tell you from past experience that we want to be the ones controlling the narrative."

Carlton led the Williamses out of the room and Zac turned back to his brothers. He hadn't seen them in person in over six months. "This isn't how I envisioned our reunion."

"Damn," Leo said, coming over to hug him. "It's good to see you, but what the hell happened?"

"Let's go get some cold ones and I'll tell you," Zac said.

"I can't," Logan said. "Is Nick really related to us? I mean, I hate that guy. I know Adler's marrying him and I was willing to be cordial but he can't be our half brother. I mean, he's the worst."

Zac clapped his older brother on the shoulder and squeezed. "I think he is. We'll figure out how to deal with him. Maybe he's not as bad as you imagine."

"Who's not?" Dare asked, coming into the room. He had his phone in one hand and a whiskey glass in the other. "Carlton told me you'd catch me up."

"We're all going to need something to drink," Leo said, leading them out of the conservatory to the lounge down the hall with the built-in bar. Iris and Gran were already sitting there and the women glanced up as they came in. Zac heard his brothers talking to his grandmother but he ignored them as Iris smiled at him. Who knew their charade would be the least exciting secret this weekend?

Fourteen

Iris didn't know how to help the actual situation they were in, but she did know how to be a good friend. When Adler came to the doorway and Iris saw the tears on her friend's face, she didn't even hesitate. She grabbed her friend's hand and took her upstairs to the bedroom that she knew Adler used when she was at her grandmother's house.

"What's going on?" she asked. "How's Nick?"

"Nick's mad. He's mad at his mom, his dad and August. It's just too much. You know I never thought that he'd have anything like this happen in his life. Oh, my God, this is something I'd expect from my dad. He's going to be completely crazy about this. He told me that I couldn't escape the chaos of life," Adler said.

Her friend was rambling and pacing around the bedroom. Iris saw that her hands were shaking.

"It's okay. Chaos is your friend," Iris said. "Your dad is going to be protective. Is he on Nantucket yet?"

"I don't know. I was supposed to text him when everyone was here. He was planning to come over and diffuse the tension between the Bissets and the Williamses," Adler said. "Given these new developments, I don't think even Dad can do that."

Adler stopped in front of the big bay window looking out at the ocean and Iris went over and hugged her. "What do you want me to do?"

"Make this all go away," Adler said.

"I can do that. We can leave Nantucket and go off grid until this passes."

Adler started crying and Iris hugged her friend harder. She didn't know how to fix this. She didn't know what impact Nick's paternity was going to have on Adler. Clearly she and Nick weren't related, as Nick was Cora and August's son; Adler wasn't a blood relation to August. But still, this was the kind of thing that Adler hated. She didn't like the jet-set party scene, or the bohemian live-for-the-moment mind-set. She wanted normal.

"Nick was supposed to be my Cory."

"I know," Iris said. Adler was referring to Cory from *Boy Meets World*. Growing up, the show had been their favorite to escape into. They'd loved that family dynamic and Adler had craved it for herself.

Adler's phone started ringing but she didn't make a move to see who it was.

"Want me to handle that?"

"Who is it?"

Iris glanced down at the screen. "It's your dad."

"Let me talk to him," Adler said. She took the phone and Iris stepped away to give her some semblance of privacy.

Iris was worried about Nick and Adler. This wasn't the news they needed two days before their wedding. She

pulled out her own phone and texted Nick to ask if he
was okay.

She got back a thumbs-up emoji.

She couldn't leave Adler and she knew that Nick needed
someone. She didn't have any of his siblings' phone numbers and she wasn't sure if it was the right solution or not
but she texted Zac.

Would you go and check on Nick? I think he's alone and
he might need someone to listen.

She got an almost instant response. Where is he?

Iris used the location service on her messaging app.
Nick was at the yacht club. Probably in the bar. At least he
wasn't driving.

She sent the information to Zac.

On my way to see him. I'll tell him you sent me. He might
not want to talk to me.

At least he won't be alone. Thanks.

No problem. This wasn't how I saw the day going.

Me either.

I'm glad you're here with me.

Me too.

She didn't have to think too hard about it. Seeing the
people she loved, a family she thought she knew, thrown
into a maelstrom was hard to witness. Knowing that they
were going to have to put on a good public face when all

of the guests started arriving made her glad she was here. She could help with that. And being with Zac was giving her a safe base to do it from. She wasn't just Adler's friend; she was posing as Zac's girlfriend and this family drama included her.

Adler collapsed back on the bed as she ended her call with her dad. "What am I going to do?"

Iris went over and lay down next to her on the bed. "About what?"

"Nick. The wedding. Everything. This isn't what I signed up for."

"Do you love him?"

"I thought I did."

"Do you still want to marry him?"

Adler leaned up on her elbow. "I don't want the media circus that this could become but I do want to marry him. But Nick isn't the same guy now."

"I wish it were simple. I've never seen two people as in love as you guys were," Iris said. "Are you strong enough to handle this?"

"I don't know," Adler said. "Our love has been easy. We've never been tested like this."

"You've handled way worse," Iris said.

"But that was easy because I was sort of removed when dad was having his issues with the media," Adler said. "It's simpler when I'm not in the direct spotlight."

"I know. But you won't be for long. If I know your dad, he'll do something outrageous to keep the attention off you. He loves you more than any other person on the planet."

Adler nodded. "That wouldn't be good either because he's just started to settle down. He can't go back to being outrageous again and living that rock'n'roll lifestyle. I mean he's barely recovered—"

"He won't," Iris interrupted. It was hard enough for

Adler to worry about Nick, let alone having to worry about her dad.

"Oh, my God. I shouldn't have let Nick leave alone. I freaked out about my perfect wedding," Adler said. "He's just found out a man he hates is his father."

"I know. I sent Zac to find him," Iris said.

"I think I need to go to him. We have to talk about what this means for us."

Iris agreed. Her friend was too emotional to drive so she went with her. They snuck out of the house because Adler didn't want to risk running into any of her cousins or her uncle on the way.

Zac picked up two Maker's Marks, straight, before approaching Nick. The other man looked like Zac had felt when he'd walked away from the UK team he'd been part of and decided to strike out on his own. He'd had no idea if any of his friends would come with him and it had been a lonely, lonely feeling.

"Nick, would you like some company?"

Nick glanced up at him and for the first time since Zac had known him—which, granted, wasn't long—the man didn't look at ease. His eyes were bloodshot and Zac noticed that his knuckles were scraped as if he'd punched a wall.

"I brought a double, figured you could use it," Zac said.

Nick took the drink and pushed the chair opposite him out with his foot. Zac sat down and took a swallow once Nick drank some of his.

"Iris sent me. I would have come on my own but had no way of getting in touch with you."

"Thanks, man. I'm not sure what the hell is going on and I know I'm not the best company right now."

"That's cool. I spend most of my time on the ocean fighting against the wind and waves and trying to prove I'm nothing like the rest of my family," Zac said.

"Your family…"

"It's yours too, right? I mean we don't have to talk about it but I want you to know that we're not as bad as you might think."

Nick downed the rest of his whiskey. "I can't do this right now. I was already a little nervous thinking of marrying Adler and starting my own family and then to learn that everything I knew about myself was a lie…"

"It wasn't a lie," Zac said. "I don't know much about your family but your dad is Tad Williams. No matter what biological matter my dad contributed, Tad raised you and the man I saw today is a good man. He defended your mother and mine."

"He is a good man. I've always wanted to be just like him," Nick said.

Zac realized that Nick might not know it but he had a better relationship with Tad Williams than he ever would have had with August Bisset. August was mellowing but he was still a difficult man to have as a father.

"That's good," Zac said. "Nothing's changed. Did you know he wasn't your biological father?"

"I did."

"Did your mom ever say anything about my dad?" Zac asked.

"She said she'd fallen for a man who was charming and funny, and when she'd realized he belonged to someone else, she left. She said he wasn't in the picture and that Tad was the only father I'd know."

Zac wished that had been the case. "I'm sorry."

"Thanks," Nick said, pushing the glass back and forth between his hands.

"Want another?"

"Yes. But I have to fix things with Adler. She tried to say things would be okay and I yelled at her."

"I think I'd do the same thing in your situation," Zac said. "That kind of news is hard to hear."

"It is, but Adler didn't deserve that. She was freaking out too, I know it, even though she didn't say anything."

"But she loves you," Zac said. "I've never seen her this happy before."

"That's the worst part about finding this out now. It's going to be a cloud over the wedding. Hell, I don't even know if she'll still marry me after I yelled at her the way I did."

The door to the bar opened. Zac caught sight of Iris and Adler. Leave it to Iris to get the couple back together and salvage the weekend. That was one of the things he admired about her. She didn't hesitate to do whatever she needed to in order to make things run smoothly.

Look at how she'd contracted him to be her man when she'd been dumped.

Where had that thought come from?

There was a hint of resentment inside him as he realized he might be just another quick fix that she was so good at administering.

"There's only one way to find out," Zac said to Nick. "Adler just walked in."

Nick pushed his glass to one side and sat up straighter. His shoulders went back and all the doubt and anger that had been dominating his expression and posture were subdued. It was as if he were putting on a show for Adler.

Instead, he was the confident man that Zac had seen the night before at dinner. He ran his hands over his hair and then noticed the scraped knuckles. Zac pulled his pocket square out and handed it to the other man. "Use this."

"Thanks."

Nick cleaned his knuckles, passing the square of fabric back just as the ladies arrived at their table.

Nick and Zac stood and when Nick turned to Adler, Zac looked away. They were hugging each other, and it was so intimate that really no one should be watching them.

He glanced at Iris and saw the longing on her face. She wanted what Adler and Nick had but she'd settled for a contracted boyfriend.

He wondered why. Was it convenience? Or was there something deeper that kept her from really committing to a man?

"Let's give them some privacy," he said.

She nodded and slipped her hand into his as they turned away. He looked down at their joined hands. After the morning they'd had, filled with lies and betrayals and secrets that should have stayed that way, he wondered what he was going to do about his woman he'd agreed to pretend to care for, since he had already realized that he had never been pretending with her.

She had gotten to him from the first moment they'd met and he should have done the smart thing and walked away. But she had him ensnared, and he had to admit he didn't mind it as long as she felt something for him.

Which he couldn't be sure of.

Iris walked with Zac to the other side of the yacht club bar, which wasn't very busy at this hour. She was worried about Zac. She knew he and his father had a contentious relationship and finding out that his dad had cheated on his mom…that had to be a blow.

"Are you okay?"

He held out a chair for her and nodded. "Do you want a drink?"

"I'm okay, but you can get one if you want to."

"I don't like to drink alone," he said.

"I'll have a Perrier with a lime," Iris said, realizing he needed something to do. She would bet that everyone in his family was doing their best to keep busy and not think about what had happened.

He walked to the bar and Iris realized she should probably cancel all of the filming she'd planned to do around the events for the day. She sent a text to her staff, letting them know that the family had decided to have a quiet day together and told them to enjoy the bonus day off. She also texted her friend Quinn, who was producing the televised wedding ceremony, and told her that Adler wasn't going to be available today.

Quinn called back instead of texting. Considering that Iris, Quinn and Adler had been good friends since their freshman year of college when they'd met at the sorority house, she wasn't surprised.

"Is Adler okay?"

"Yes. There was some unexpected drama with the Bissets and the Williamses and I don't know that she's in the right state to film. Just wanted to give you a heads-up."

"Thanks for that. Is she okay? I'm going to text her. Just send her some virtual hugs. I'm on the damn ferry right now. This thing seems to go slower and slower every time I get on it."

Quinn was a big city gal used to moving at a fast pace. Iris had once seen her friend pay for and bag up another woman's groceries because she was moving too slow. "There's nothing you could do if you were here sooner."

"Except see Ad and if needed, kick some Bisset butt. They have to be the trouble, right?"

"It's complicated," Iris said. "Text me when you get here. Do you need a ride?"

"No. The traffic will be heavy when the ferry gets in. I'm going to run to the hotel. I need to burn off some energy."

"Okay, I'll see you later then."

"Bye."

Zac set the glasses on the table before sitting down across from her. He rubbed the back of his neck and turned to look out at the ocean. His clean jaw and sharp blade of a nose gave him a gorgeous profile but then everything about him struck the right note for her.

"Wish you were out there?"

He turned back and took a sip of what looked like whiskey. "Yes and no. I mean, my mom would've been alone when she heard the news about my dad today if I hadn't been there."

"That was a shock," Iris said. "I was glad I got to escape."

"I bet."

He didn't say anything, just swallowed his whiskey in one long sip.

"Do you want to talk about it?"

"Which part?"

"Whichever part you want to," she said.

"I'm not sure. This isn't part of the contract."

"So? You said it yourself. We're friends, aren't we?" she asked. She had stopped thinking about the contract when shit had gotten real in the conservatory. It had made her feel very shallow to realize she'd been worried about showing up stag when something like this was going down.

"Are we?"

She wasn't sure if he was being cagey because of what he'd learned about his dad or if he had some beef with her. She knew if it were her, she'd want to fight with someone… probably Thea because she knew that she could say mean things to her sister and, in the end, Thea would forgive her.

"Yes, we are. Listen, I can't begin to imagine what you're feeling but if you need to talk or yell or go sailing or—"

"Have sex?"

Her eyes widened but she nodded. Whatever he needed. She hated to see the people she loved hurt… Wait, did she love him? She wasn't sure if she did because she'd never been in love before, but this felt…well, not like anything she'd experienced before.

"Yes. Even that. Whatever you need. I'm here," she said.

He reached for her hand and laced their fingers together. "I don't know what I need. I guess I'm in shock. I've always known my dad wasn't faithful to my mom. He had a very public affair before Mari was born. But I thought we knew the worst of him. Catting around on Mom while she was pregnant with Logan…that is something I can't forgive."

"You don't have to," Iris said. "You get to decide what you feel about that and if you can't get past it, then that's fine. He's always going to be your father, but you don't have to let him be a part of your life."

Zac nodded. "I know what you are saying but here's the kicker. I want him in my life. I've always worked so hard to make him proud. To prove that I was better than he was. And now, knowing in my heart how petty I want to be about this, I don't think I am any better."

Iris went around to sit next to him at the table. She put her arm around him and her chin on his shoulder. "No one is. That's something I had to figure out the hard way. But no one is better than anybody else. We are all messed up and trying to figure out how to get through each day. Your dad had a shock, as well. He screwed up and probably thought that he had put all of that in the past. And then today his mistakes were front and center for his entire family to see."

"You're right. I know you are," Zac said. He pulled her around onto his lap and just held her in his arms. She knew she should get up, that people would see them, but she didn't want to. She wanted to give as much comfort to this man she loved as she could. And it didn't matter what kind of image they presented to the world.

Nick took Adler to the new home he'd had built for them on Nantucket. She watched him pacing around the living room, that she'd had designed for their future. But as she looked around she saw it was all the things she wanted them to be and maybe not who they really were.

"What are we going to do?" she asked him.

"Do about what—the wedding?"

"Yes." What did he think she was talking about?

"I really don't know. We have all these people coming to Nantucket. If we cancel—"

"Are you thinking about not marrying me?" For the first time she had to face her fears about Nick. He was questioning everything about himself and his life. Maybe he was questioning a future with her, too?

"I don't know," he said, shoving his hands through his hair. "My gut says this isn't going to blow over easily. I want to manage it."

"I get that. Managing the news about your parentage should be the top priority. But are we going to do it as a team?"

He turned on her and she saw anger in his eyes. "Can we have one minute where it's not all about you, Adler? Is that possible?"

She took a deep breath and nodded. She was about to start crying and blinked rapidly to keep the tears from falling. "Take as much time as you need. I'm going to my gran's."

"Run away. That's what you do when life gets too real, isn't it?"

"It's what I do when I'm confronted with a bully who is lashing out because he doesn't want to admit he's hurting," she said. Her voice was low and rough from trying to choke back tears. "Let's have the clambake tonight and tomorrow we can figure out if we should still get married. We have a lot of people coming. Try to remember it's not all about you, either."

Adler left the room, tears streaming down her face. She wished her mom were here so she could talk with her about this. She had no idea how to handle Nick right now.

Was the man she loved gone? Had Nick disappeared when he learned he was August Bisset's biological son?

Fifteen

Iris and Zac ended up taking a lead role in entertaining the guests who were attending the clambake on Thursday evening. The elder Williams and Bisset couples had spent the day with Carlton coming up with the spin on today's revelations in case the story somehow got out to the press.

Iris just stayed by Adler's side and did whatever her friend asked her to do. It was odd to see Adler so fragile because she'd never been like that before. This thing with Nick had rattled her.

It was safe to say the couple hadn't resolved things. They were still going through with planned events but Iris could tell nothing was right.

Nick was drinking a lot; Iris had known him in his frat boy days so that was saying something. Zac was keeping pace with him and she had to say she was both surprised and happy to see that he was a really funny drunk. His brother Logan, who had the fiercest rivalry with Nick in business, had surrounded himself with a group of women that Iris wasn't sure were part of the wedding party. Leo, Zac's younger brother, was keeping an eye on Zac and Nick and running drinks back and forth to them. Nick's brothers, Asher and Noah, were hanging with Leo and Nick's sister Olivia was at Iris's side, helping Adler out.

The food had been prepared by a catering company Adler had hired, which meant there was little for them to do but keep the conversation going and that horrible truth buried.

Iris saw Toby Osborn before Adler did. He still had a full head of hair despite being sixty. He had a mustache and short beard and carried his legendary guitar, Martha Mae. He had his usual entourage with him, including his live-in girlfriend, whom Iris had met before and liked.

As soon as Adler saw her dad, she ran to him and he pushed his guitar around to his back and caught her. Iris knew that Adler had always wished for a more normal upbringing but there was no denying she had been well loved by her father. She was his world.

"What'd I miss?" Quinn asked, coming up beside her and handing her a gin and tonic.

"Nothing. The elders are back at the house having a meeting, Nick's getting drunk and Zac is helping him, and Toby's just arrived."

"Are you dating Zac?"

"That's what you got out of my rundown?" Iris asked.

"Well, I did see it on my newsfeed. He's not your usual type, is he?"

"Uh, no. Graham kind of put me off my usual type."

"Graham was a douche bag," Quinn said.

"Did everyone hate him?" Iris asked.

"Yes," Quinn said. "I'm glad you aren't with him anymore."

She glanced over at Nick and Zac, who were singing along to Sister Hazel's "All For You." She especially loved when they tried to harmonize and neither of them sang a note that was near the other's. Toby set Adler down and went over to the two would-be singers and joined in.

"Oh, my God, they're hilarious," Iris said, grabbing her phone so she could capture the moment. She knew that Nick would want to see this happy moment later, after a day that had been filled with so many ups and downs.

Zac caught her filming and wriggled his eyebrows at her. The next time the chorus came on, he gestured to her as if to say he only wanted to be with her. She knew he was drunk and kidding around but she wanted this to be true.

Adler came up beside her and looped her arm through hers and Quinn took her other arm. After the crazy day they'd had, she was so grateful to have these two women by her side. She wasn't sure that anything was going to come of her and Zac but she'd have this memory to last forever.

And after the way she'd seen the past come back to haunt August and Cora, she wondered if she shouldn't come clean about hiring Zac to be her man for the weekend. She didn't want that to come out at some odd time when they were both older and more established...maybe with other partners.

The thought hurt and dimmed her joy of the moment, but she had to be honest with herself. She loved Zac but that hadn't made her blind to how impossible it was for the two of them.

He was in the spotlight, dancing and singing and loving the attention, and she would never be comfortable out there. She needed her glam squad and her prepared scripts to be comfortable in front of the camera.

She stopped filming the video as the song ended. Toby started singing some of his hits and Adler drifted over to Nick and they walked down the beach. Quinn's phone went off and she turned away to take the call. Iris was left standing by herself. Zac was surrounded by his brothers. She watched him and realized that he always knew how to handle every situation and she envied that.

It was something she'd never been able to find in herself. She could only function with rules. She took a step backward as she realized that she had let herself love Zac because it was safe. She'd let her guard down, thinking her contract and her end date would keep her from getting hurt. Never realizing that letting her guard down was the thing she should have been avoiding.

It wasn't a certain type of man who could hurt her—it was herself. Her own flaws and fears had been driving her to this moment ever since she'd become an adult.

She looked at Adler, trying so hard to find a man who was nothing like her father and then finding out on the eve of her wedding that he had a scandalous secret, even though it was no fault of his own. Then Iris thought of her own secret with Zac, one she was 100 percent responsible for.

There was no way to protect herself from herself. She wished she'd realized this in Boston before she'd walked into that bar and seen that sexy man for the first time. She wished she'd had the strength to know herself and be real about her fear of being alone then. She wished… Hell, it hurt her to her core but she wished she'd never talked to Zac Bisset.

Without saying a word to anyone, she quietly left the party and went back to the hotel.

She was in her bed for a good four hours before she heard Zac in the other room with some other guys. They were laughing and shushing each other and she lay there alone in her bed, realizing that even paying for a man hadn't changed her.

* * *

Zac woke up with a fuzzy mouth on the couch of the suite he'd been sharing with Iris. He had one shoe on and his belt was removed but otherwise he was fully clothed. He blinked, surprised he didn't have a headache. But he'd been very well hydrated the night before. He blinked again, seeing the light through the window, and then Iris sitting in a chair opposite him. She watched him with that prim expression she had when she was in an awkward situation.

He scrubbed his hand over his face, felt the stubble on his jaw and something that might be a bruise later—did he punch Logan last night? Then he forced himself to sit up and tried to smile but the light was really bright and he had to close his eyes for a second.

"If you can manage it, I've put in an order for a bacon, egg and cheese biscuit for you," Iris said.

"You really are an angel. Coffee too?" he asked.

"Coffee too."

He knew he should go and wash up. He'd been in this situation before. Women didn't always respond positively when he came home drunk and passed out on the couch.

He washed his face, brushed his teeth and debated a quick shower. After a whiff of his clothes as he took them off, he decided that there was no debate and spent three minutes under the hot jets of water.

He felt closer to human as he left the bedroom dressed in a pair of basketball shorts and an old America's Cup team T-shirt. His food was on the table under a cloche, along with a cup of coffee and a plate of fresh fruit.

Iris sat at the table, looking so elegant and put together, like a woman with a mission on her mind.

"I'm sorry about last night. I knew Nick needed to drink because I would in his situation. My brothers were being uptight and his were too, so someone had to be the one to break the ice," Zac said.

"That's okay. Honestly, you were so funny and probably exactly what everyone needed," she said.

He opened the cloche and took a bite of the bacon, egg and cheese biscuit, and closed his eyes. It was perfect. Exactly what he needed.

"What about you? I know I wasn't delivering on my duties last night," Zac said.

"About that," Iris said. "I think we can agree that your behavior last night can't be repeated. Starting today, I need you to be everything I asked for in the contract."

"I'll try," he said, taking another bite of the biscuit. Honestly, at this moment, he was only half listening to her. The food was making him feel a lot better.

"You'll do more than try or you will be in breach of our agreement and I will call my father and tell him that I don't think you're a good investment," she said.

That he heard.

He put his biscuit down and his hands on the table next to his plate. "Are you threatening me?"

"I am. I know your family is going through some messy things, but your first priority is the commitment you made to me."

"Other than last night, have I shirked my duties?"

"Last night was the first time you were supposed to be doing your duties in front of other people."

"I sang to you, Iris. Even Toby said that was romantic," Zac said.

"I came home about four hours before you did," Iris pointed out. "You didn't even notice I was gone... Not very romantic."

"Sorry I wasn't paying one hundred percent attention to you," he said. "I already apologized for last night."

"You did and I appreciate it. I'm just saying don't let it happen again."

She stood up and walked past him to go to the bedroom but he stopped her by catching her wrist lightly in his hand. "Are you okay?"

She nodded, tugged her hand free and kept on going.

But he knew she wasn't. He wanted to blame it on his hangover but he knew he was missing something. He'd done something last night that had changed the way that Iris was looking at him. Damn him if he could remember all of the details clearly enough to figure it out.

He finished his biscuit and coffee. He wanted to make this right. He stood up and went to the bedroom door, knocking on it before entering. She was standing in front of her wardrobe when he entered.

"Hey, I'm sorry about last night. Whatever you need today, I'll be there for you. I think we have the scramble golf tournament and you wanted me to pose for some photos, right?"

"Yes. My glam squad will be bringing some clothes for you and I'll text you when I need you. I kind of like the stubble so if you want to leave it for this morning and then shave before tonight's rehearsal dinner—if it's still even on—that would be fine. Did you see Adler last night?"

"I don't remember," he said. "Angel face, I really am sorry. I never meant to drink like that. It's not every day I find out I have another brother."

She nodded. "I know. I'd be a monster not to understand it, and I definitely am not upset that you drank last night."

"Then what are you mad at me about?" he asked. "Don't deny it, you are upset with me."

She shook her head. "I'm upset with myself because I thought you were something that you aren't."

Something he wasn't. He'd been more himself with her

than he'd ever been with anyone else and she still thought he was phoning it in.

He was tired, he knew that, and a wiser man than he would have kept his mouth shut. But hell, no one had ever labeled him the smart Bisset.

"I'm not what you thought?" he asked, approaching her as she turned away from the wardrobe to face him. "Iris, you hired a guy you met in a bar to be your boyfriend for a four-day wedding. What exactly were you expecting?"

"Don't get defensive, I wasn't attacking you," she said, folding her hands neatly in front of her.

And that right there was enough to push him over the edge. He'd seen glimpses of the real woman beneath all the prim and proper behavior but more times than not, this was what he was faced with. Some cardboard cutout of the real woman. No man wanted that. Actually he felt safe in saying that no one wanted to have a relationship with someone who was always hiding behind the perfect smile, clothing and manners.

"I've gone above and beyond for you. I actually like you as a person most of the time, but I can't with this," he said, gesturing to her holding her coffee cup with one hand while smiling serenely at him. "It's not real. I get that we have a contract, but I've never been anyone other than myself with you. Who does that?"

"I do, according to you."

"You can't fight properly. Tell me what's on your mind. Don't worry about hurting my feelings or how it might make you seem human instead of a social media goddess with the great life. Just be you, Iris. Do you even know who you are?"

"Screw you, Zac. That's not a very nice thing to say. Of course, I know who I am," she said.

"That's it. Get mad, girl. Show me what's really bothering you," he said. He wasn't sure where this was going but after last night, learning that most of his life he'd been lied to by his father, he was tired of half-truths. He was no longer interested in playing a part. Any part. He was going to live life on his terms and he wasn't holding back. Iris should do the same.

"What's bothering me?" she said. "I don't think you really care that much, Zac. We both know you're only here until my dad and Collins Combined come through with your funding. Then you are off to train and race for three years. We both know that you are playing a role even though you want to pretend that you're, what, better than me, more honest than me? You're not. You're here dressing in jackets with pocket squares, shaving and trying to fit into a role as much as I am. You're judging me while excusing yourself."

"I didn't say I was disappointed in you," he pointed out.

"Well you didn't have to. I'm disappointed in myself. You know what's the matter this morning? My dad sent over some paperwork for both of us. He has assembled your investors and you will have the money wired into your account on Monday. And I know you'll be out the door. Sure, you'll be sweet and polite about it, but that's it. You'll move on.

"And while I watched you singing and dancing in front of the fire last night, I realized I didn't want you to leave. I didn't want to see you walk out of my life because I'm an effing idiot and fell in love with you. Sure, I knew I shouldn't. Hell, you're not even the kind of man I usually fall for. But you know that perfect image you're so sure I'm hiding behind—well, I wasn't. I was myself. Sorry I'm not more exciting and can't deliver nonstop fun the way you can, but that was me. Guard down and being totally myself."

He was stunned. He was pretty sure in the middle of her rant she'd said she loved him. Iris Collins, the most sophisticated, sexy, sweet, charming, smart woman he'd ever met, loved him. He'd lashed out because he knew he wasn't worthy. Even now he realized he'd let her down. Again.

He should apologize. He knew that. But his brain was working slowly this morning and Iris just shook her head and blinked a lot before she walked out of the hotel suite.

Why was she leaving?

He hadn't had a chance to tell her any of the things he needed to. He ran out after her, but she'd gotten in the elevator and was gone. His gut told him if he let her go, he'd regret this for the rest of his life.

This wasn't a moment where time was going to make things better. She needed him now.

He went to the balcony. They were only on the third floor and he climbed over and lowered himself onto the balcony below and then one more time until he was on the ground floor.

The gravel path was rough on his bare feet, but he made it around to the front of the building just as Iris exited. She had her large black sunglasses on and a sheath dress. He stood there with dirt and rock embedded in the bottom of his feet, looking like a beach bum instead of a Bisset.

He was never going to be the picture-perfect man on her arm, but he knew that no one would love her better or give her more adventure in her life.

Now to somehow show her that.

Sixteen

Iris walked straight past him and he realized that maybe it was better if he just let her go. She was definitely not thinking straight. He knew women tended to get all those romantic feelings during a wedding weekend and Adler and Iris were best friends.

He stood there next to the valet, barefoot and looking like he'd just come off a night of binge drinking, which he had. Watching the woman he loved more than he'd ever thought he could walk away from him was sobering. This was the reality of life with the two of them. They were both busy people and weekends like this would be the best they could hope for.

She deserved more, and in her own words, wanted more. Shouldn't he just let her have it? He watched her get into her sensible car and drive off and then he slowly made his way back into the hotel.

His brother Logan was slinking in, as well. He had his

eyes shielded behind his Ray-Ban Wayfarers and as he saw Zac, he lifted his hand in a weak wave. His brother looked worse than Zac felt, and he wasn't sure how that was possible given that Zac's world was crumbling. Everything he'd ever believed about himself was shattered. He wasn't the man who was looking for another horizon—he had been looking for Iris. No other woman had ever made him feel like he was okay just as he was.

"Dude, you look rough," Zac said. "Where'd you go last night?"

"Took a trip down memory lane and I'm not sure how but we ended up in bed," Logan said. "I think it's going to end up biting me in the ass."

"Her too," Zac said. Logan hadn't always been the type-A, driven COO he was today. Once upon a time he'd been a very competitive kid with a girlfriend who liked to one-up him. Quinn had gone on to take television by storm. She was one of the top producers today. But Logan had caught up and maybe even moved past her, making a name for himself at Bisset Industries. It was interesting to think of the two of them hooking up. And it was just the distraction he needed after Iris walked away looking broken.

"Yeah, I know," Logan said. "What are you doing in the lobby looking like a hobo? If you have even the slightest chance of keeping a woman like Iris Collins, you have to up your game," Logan said. "Come up to my room and I'll get you some decent clothes."

"Thanks, bro," he said, trying to play it cool but knowing he failed when Logan put his hand on his shoulder. Everyone could see that he and Iris weren't meant to be. He should just take the investor money and start focusing on the one area where he was good. Sailing. Captaining a racing team. He could do that.

"You okay?"

"No. I screwed up, Logan. I have no idea how to fix it or if I should even try. I'm hungover. I might still be a little drunk. I've had the kind of morning that Dad should be having but he probably is too coldhearted to realize that everything is slipping out of his grip."

"Z, Dad's not the heartless monster that the media and Carlton play him up to be, you know that. Despite everything else happening right now. What's wrong that you are lashing out?"

He shook his head. He had no idea where to start. "Never mind."

"I'm on your side. I'm always on your side, no matter what happens. Talk to me. If there's one thing I'm good at, it's solving problems," Logan said.

He was good at it. "All right. I agreed to be Iris's plus one this weekend in exchange for her getting some investors for my America's Cup run. We both said it would be temporary, but it didn't feel that way until this morning. Now I don't want to let her go, but even you pointed out that she's too good for me and you hardly ever notice stuff like that."

Logan put his hand on Zac's arm and urged him to move out of the lobby. For the first time, Zac was aware of their surroundings—the fact that it was a crowded lobby and that people had been staring at the two of them.

Damn.

Hell.

He was the biggest asshole on the planet. He'd had blinders on because he wasn't used to anyone caring what he did when he was on land.

"Do you think they heard?"

"I have no idea, but let's get up to my room and figure out what's next," Logan said.

"She'll be ruined by this, Logan. I can't believe I didn't

think before I spoke. She's all about image. I mean that's why we—"

Logan put his hand over Zac's mouth as they got on the elevator. The door closed and Logan dropped his hand. "Paparazzi are all here trying to get the scoop on the latest Bisset scandal. You have to stop talking."

"I know."

Zac didn't say another word until they were down the hall and in his brother's room. "Why aren't you staying at Gran's?"

"I didn't want to make Adler uncomfortable. I've been a douche about Nick and he's her groom. But I do love our cousin. I figured the least I could do was stay out of her way."

"Yeah, that's a good call. Nick's not a bad guy."

"I know. It's just that for as long as I can remember, I've always been trying to beat him. Sometimes I do and other times I don't. I hate losing and he's a Williams, so it makes it harder to let it go," Logan said, tossing his sunglasses on the bed and then looking over at him. "Now about Iris… We need to get ahead of this before it comes out."

"What am I going to do?" Zac asked his brother. "I love her. I was trying to ask you how to win her back, but it seems impossible now, doesn't it?"

"Nothing is impossible. You told me that when we were teenagers. If you were smart enough to realize that back then, you can fix this," Logan said.

Zac wasn't sure his "wisdom" as a teenager was anything more than bravado, and he didn't know how to fix this. But he regretted that he might hurt her and had to try to make things right.

Iris didn't have a destination in mind as she left the hotel behind. She could think of only one person who actually needed her this morning and that was Alder. Sure Iris wanted to escape. She'd never been in love with anyone before and confessing it to Zac and having him just sort of blink at her wasn't the reaction she'd been hoping for. She'd had two breakups fairly close together and honestly she had to say this one was affecting her way worse than the first.

Not that she and Zac had broken up. She started crying as she realized how messed up this truly was. She pulled her car off the road and just sat there for a few minutes, realizing that the only place she wanted to be was off Nantucket. But she couldn't do that to Adler.

She was trapped by her own bad decisions. She almost texted Thea something mean but it wasn't her sister's fault that she'd decided to choose a man to be her fab, fun plus one and Zac Bisset turned out to be the one. She couldn't have predicted it and she couldn't blame it on Thea.

She drove her car back to a public parking lot and left it there, walking toward the beach because going back to the room she was sharing with Zac was completely out of the question. She took her shoes off as soon as she was on the sand. Tendrils of hair started to escape from the chignon she'd put it up in, when she was still trying to pretend that she had it all together. She reached up and took the pins out, knowing that she was done fooling herself.

Since she'd gotten the internship with Leta Veerland, she'd promised herself she wouldn't waste a moment. That she'd craft a life that was successful and leave no room for failure and she'd done that. On every front except on the personal one. But there was no way she was ever going to be successful in a relationship unless she let herself be. The problem with men, and Zac in particular, was that she didn't want to be vulnerable to him. She didn't want him to see that she wasn't that social media person. The one with the fabulous life who made good choices. But until him, she'd never found a way to be comfortable with herself.

Now she had no choice and she was failing.

Big time.

She took a deep breath and tipped her head back, letting the sea air sooth that troubled part of her soul. She'd taken a risk, a real gamble, when she'd approached Zac. And it had given her so much more than she'd expected. She had to let herself have that.

Her phone vibrated but she ignored it. She wasn't going to respond to anything right now. She needed this walk on the beach to gather her thoughts and regain her equilibrium. She knew she was the maid of honor at the wedding and Adler might need her.

Adler. Something had been up with her and Nick last night. Iris pulled out her phone to text Adler and saw on the Find My Friends app that she was on the beach as well. She walked toward her position and found her friend standing on the shore just staring out at the water.

"Hey, Ad," she said, coming up behind her and hugging her. "Everything okay this morning?"

Adler wiped her eyes and immediately Iris knew it wasn't.

"Nick and I had a big fight last night. I'm just not sure if we should cancel everything. He was too hungover this morning to discuss it and said whatever I decided he'd go along with."

That didn't sound like the Nick she knew. "He didn't mean that."

"I'm not so sure. He's reeling from learning that August is his father."

Iris held Adler's hand. "I know, but he loves you."

"He did."

"Stop that. This is just bridal jitters on steroids. He's

not himself because of the news, but I'm sure how he feels about you hasn't changed. Do you want to cancel the wedding?"

Adler hesitated and Iris's heart, already sore and aching, broke for her friend. Men. Love was kicking her ass and now Adler's ass, too.

"I can't cancel it. Everyone is arriving today."

Iris took a deep breath. She completely understood where her friend was coming from. If she cancelled a televised wedding she was going to bring a lot of unwanted attention down on herself and Nick. "If you're not sure about Nick, then you should postpone things. You're going to spend the rest of your life with him."

She nodded. "I hate this. It's like when dad had that affair with that stupid eighteen-year-old. The media isn't going to be kind."

"Are you cancelling things?"

"I need to talk to Nick," she said.

"Okay. Do you want me to go with you?"

"No. I have to do this on my own," she said.

They both went their separate ways, Adler walking up to the house that Nick and she had purchased on the island and Iris walked back to the hotel. She started up the path toward the hotel, stopping at a bench to wipe her feet off and put her shoes back on. She took her phone out and glanced down to see that she'd missed a call from Quinn and one from Zac.

Good.

She wasn't ready to talk to Zac. She had to figure out how to pull herself back from what she'd admitted. From now on, she wasn't going to let her emotions get the better of her.

She texted Quinn and got back a call.

"Hey."

"Where are you?"

"On the beach, fixing to walk back to the hotel. Why?"

"Stay there," Quinn said. "I'm tracking you with the friend app, hold on."

She did as her friend asked, looking up at the sun. "Still there?"

"Yes, what's up? Did the media already start pinging you about Nick?"

"Yes. But that's not all. Something else has come up and it involves you."

"What?"

"Zac blurted out that you paid him to be with you this weekend in the lobby at the hotel. It was overheard by a bunch of reporters and everyone is running with the story."

"What?" Shock warred with anger and betrayal inside of her.

"Yeah, I know. Listen, it gets worse. Someone videoed him saying it on their phone, so everyone has it. There's no denying it," Quinn said.

"What am I going to do? I'm prelaunch on the new couples line. This affects everyone who works for me. My partnership deals," she said, but she stopped talking. Had Zac done it to prove he didn't love her? Had he thought that he needed to make it clear that things between them would end when the wedding weekend was over?

She was horrified and angry. She felt tears burning in her eyes as she fumbled in her bag for her sunglasses and put them on. She wasn't about to let him know how badly he'd hurt her. She texted her team to get another room at the hotel and meet her there in forty-five minutes. She was going to have to go on the offensive to save her business.

Quinn showed up a minute later and sat down next to her on the bench. She looked at her friend and all the betrayal and pain inside of her welled up. Quinn hugged her close.

"He's an idiot."

"He is," Iris agreed. "But I think I might have been the bigger one. I love him, Quinn."

"I know," her friend said. "I could tell last night."

"I'm going to have to spin this," she said.

"I think he cares for you too," Quinn started.

Iris shook her head. "It doesn't matter. We can't be together after this."

She hoped if she said the words out loud enough, her heart would get the message.

Zac didn't have the chance to talk to Iris before the rehearsal where she pretty much ignored him the entire time. Nick and Adler looked fragile and both went their separate ways after they were done. Zac wasn't sure what was going on between the two of them but he wanted to fix things with Iris.

He didn't blame her for ignoring him. Stephan from her team had come to see him and had advised him that he wasn't needed for any promo or to do anything with Iris for the rest of the weekend.

He'd tried to talk to Stephan, but it was clear the other man wasn't having it. He'd left Zac feeling even worse about what had happened. And when he got to his grandmother's house, his entire family was tense. Even Mari, who usually found a way to lighten the mood, looked somber.

They were all gathered in the formal living room when Mari walked over to him and gave him a hug. "I love you, big bro, even though you are totally clueless sometimes."

"I'm not used to having anyone care what I say."

"But you knew she does," Mari said. "I like Iris a lot. I'm surprised at what you said, but I can see how it would be something she'd agree to. She's really smart about her brand and has been careful about how she manages it."

"Yeah, until I majorly messed it up. That wasn't my intent," Zac said. He'd spent all day thinking about the business side of it but he knew that if he'd handled the declaration of love better, they wouldn't be in this situation and she probably wouldn't care because she'd know he was on her side.

"No one thinks you did it intentionally," Mari said. "How are you going to make it up to her?"

He had a few ideas. So far none of them had been that great. He'd hoped he could talk to her. He knew that he was going to have to show her how much she meant to him. Make the big gesture and prove it to the world. His family was all for him doing something with Iris, anything that would take the spotlight off his father and the illegitimate son that no one had known about until yesterday.

Now that the media were beginning to hint they had the scoop on what had transpired at the Bissets' yesterday, Carlton was releasing a statement that had the backing of both the Williams and Bisset families. But no one believed that the scandal would go away that easily.

"I'm hoping that when the time is right…it will come to me."

Mari punched him in the shoulder. "Don't wing this, Zac. If she's important to you, then show her and make an effort."

"I am," he said. He had spent the entire day thinking of all of the things he'd learned about Iris since they'd met. It might not have been a long time but they'd both been real with each other. He was pretty sure he knew her better than anyone else.

He knew how badly he'd hurt her. He had humiliated her

without meaning to and he knew he was going to have to bare his soul in order to have a chance at winning her back.

The rehearsal dinner was being held in the ballroom at his grandmother's house. It had been set with large round tables that would seat eight and a large dance floor in the middle. There was a live band and later on he knew that Toby Osborn was going to perform.

There was media at the event as Adler and Nick's wedding was being filmed and most of the wedding guests were present. He had an idea and knew that if he was going to pull it off, he needed to get to work.

"Bye, kiddo. Wish me luck."

"Good luck," she said as he turned and walked out of the ballroom to find Toby. If there was a man who knew how to survive scandals, it was Adler's father. He didn't need advice because he knew what he needed to do, but he could use some backup.

He found Toby outside smoking a cigarette.

"Hey, I need your help. I'm not any good at this sort of thing and I screwed up royally with Iris."

"After last night? I thought you were going to propose," Toby said.

Drunk Zac had been prepared for that. Unfortunately that wasn't an option until he fixed things with Iris.

"Yes, I really messed up today. I want to do something that will show her what she means to me. Can you help me with some lyrics?" Zac asked. "I want to use the old song 'They Can't Take That Away From Me.' The song means something to us."

Toby listened to everything that Zac had to say and then nodded. "Okay. If that doesn't work, be prepared to grovel."

"I am," Zac said. And he was. He didn't want to lose Iris over this. Not when he'd finally realized that she was the person he wanted to always come home to. The one woman he needed to be his home port.

He told Toby what he wanted to say and the other man wrote it down, wordsmithing it as he went along. When they were done, he handed the paper to Zac who read over the words and hoped that Iris would understand that she was his world. She was the ocean underneath his yacht and he needed her.

He hurried into the ballroom. The band was almost ready to take a break but he asked them if they would stay and play for him while he sang for Iris.

They agreed and Zac took a deep breath.

"We have had an odd request and I hope you won't mind helping this man out by welcoming Zac Bisset to the stage. He has a special song he'd like to perform for Iris Collins."

Seventeen

The last thing Iris was interested in was seeing Zac dressed in a dinner jacket and tie looking way more handsome than someone who'd broken her heart should. She almost got up but Mari came over and put her hand on her shoulder.

"Give him a chance," she said. "If this doesn't make it right, then I'll be surprised."

She thought Mari was giving her brother too much credit but she sat back down and looked up at the stage.

"Thank you for allowing me to take the stage," Zac said. "Many of you may have heard about a pact that Iris and I made for the weekend and I'm sure you've inferred all sorts of things about it. But whatever you've come up with, it's not the truth. I'm sorry, Iris, for not being more care- ful when I spoke. I'm not used to the spotlight but that's no excuse. You asked me for a favor, which I agreed to and then broke my word. This in no way makes up for it, but I hope it will help you accept my apology. The sentiment is my own, the song is borrowed and the lyrics were tweaked by Toby Osborn."

He turned to the band and they started to play the beginning notes of "They Can't Take That Away From Me." She was flooded with memories of him dancing her around his living room and singing under his breath. That was the moment, she thought, when she'd first let her guard down and started to fall for him.

Zac started to sing in his off-key tone. He was singing the actual words of the song until he got to the chorus. Then she stopped breathing as he sang. Because the chorus was all about her and how he hoped she'd give him another chance.

He ended with, "Please don't take my angel face away."

Her heart was in her throat. Today had been long and she'd been through the wringer. But she'd missed him. Her manager had called and she'd done a live video on her YouTube channel talking honestly to her viewers, and it had resonated. A lot of them had made mistakes and understood how hard it was to find love. It had led to a good discussion, one Iris intended to keep going.

One of the brands she'd partnered with had dropped her but Iris understood they needed someone who was perfect, not human like her.

He stood there on the edge of the risers waiting for her, and she hesitated for a second before she got up and walked over to him. The band started playing one more song as Zac led her to the corner of the ballroom.

"This morning when you said you loved me, it was buried in a bunch of other stuff and my foggy brain was still processing it when you walked out the door. I climbed down to the ground floor to go after you but...there you were, all you, and there I was, sloppy me in bare feet. And we both know you deserve better than that."

"No," she said. She could tell he still had more that he wanted to say but she wasn't going to let him go on believing she wanted more than him. "I think I made you feel like you wouldn't be good enough if you weren't fitting into my image of life, but I like life with you. I like me with you."

"I do too. I honestly am in love with you, but I feel like we could both use some time to believe it," he said. "I'm so sorry I blew our cover. I didn't mean to. For the first time in my life I was on rough seas and had no idea how to navigate myself through it. I realized after I blurted everything out to Logan that you are my keel, angel face. You keep me on course. I didn't know I needed that until we found each other."

"Me too. I love you, Zac. All of you. You embrace life in a way that I have never been comfortable allowing myself to. I guess I thought no one would accept me if I wasn't perfect but you have done that from the beginning."

Everyone applauded as he took her in his arms and kissed her.

A moment later there was a commotion and Iris looked up to see Adler pulling away from Nick and throwing her engagement ring at his feet.

"I can't do this," she said as she ran from the room.

* * * * *

THE MORNING
AFTER THE
WEDDING BEFORE

ANNE OLIVER

To Sue. You're loyal, generous, compassionate and caring, touching people's lives in the best way, and a true friend on life's amazing and unpredictable journey.

Thank you for always being there! Anne

CHAPTER ONE

EMMA Byrne refused to give in to the nerves zapping beneath her ribcage like hysterical wasps. She was a sophisticated city girl, she wasn't afraid of walking into a third-rate strip club. Alone.

But she paused on the footpath in King's Cross, Sydney's famous nightclub district, and racked her brain for an alternative solution as she eyed the bruiser of a bouncer propped against the tacky-looking entrance.

Six p.m. on a balmy autumn Monday evening and the Pink Mango was already open for business. Sleazy business. She gulped down the insane urge to laugh—she'd been naïve enough to think the Pink Mango was an all-night deli.

But she'd promised her sister she'd deliver the best man's suit to Jake Carmody, and she would. She could.

Pushing the big sunglasses she'd found in her glove box farther up her nose, she slung her handbag and the plastic suit bag over one stiff shoulder and marched inside. The sound system's get-your-gear-off bump and grind pounded through hidden speakers. The place smelled like beer and cheap cologne and smut. Her nostrils flared in distaste as she drew in a reluctant breath.

Her steps faltered as a zillion eyes seemed to look her way. *You're imagining it,* she told herself. *Who'd give you a second glance in a dive like this?* Especially given her knee-length buttoned-up red trench coat, knee-high boots and leather gloves, all of which she'd left on the back seat of her car since last winter. Which, when she thought about it, could very well be the reason she was garnering more than a few stares…

Better safe than sorry. Thank heavens for untidy cars and a convenient parking spot.

Ignoring the curious eyes, she turned her attention to the décor instead. The interior was even tackier than the outside. Cheap lolly pink and gold and black. The chairs and couches were covered in a dirty-looking fuchsia animal print. A revolving disco ball spewed gaudy colours over the circulating topless waitresses with smiles as fake as their boobs.

At least they *had* boobs.

Most of the early-evening punters were lounging around a raised oval stage leering over their drinks at a lone female dancer wearing nothing but a fuzzy gold string and making love to a brass pole. A hooded cobra was tattooed on one firm butt cheek.

Far out. Despite herself, Emma couldn't seem to tear her fascinated gaze away. *What men like…* She'd never have that voluptuousness, nor the chutzpah to carry it off.

Maybe that was the reason Wayne had called it quits.

Shaking off the self-doubt, she blew out a deep, slow breath and turned away from the entertainment. Just what she *didn't* need right now. A reminder of her physical inadequacies.

I don't care if you and Ryan are getting married next weekend, little sister, you owe me big-time for doing this.

'I've got an appointment to get my nails done,' Stella had told her with more than a touch of pre-wedding desperation in her voice. 'Ryan's in Melbourne for a conference till tomorrow and you don't have anything special on tonight, do you?'

Stella knew Emma had no social life whatsoever since the break-up with Wayne. Of course she'd be free. Wouldn't have mattered if she wasn't. As the maid of honour, how could she refuse the bride's request? But a strip joint had *not* been part of the deal.

A man in an open shirt with a thick gold chain over an obscene mat of greying chest hair watched her from behind a desk nearby. His flat, penetrating gaze—as if he was imagining her naked and finding her not up to par—made her stomach heave. A bead of sweat trickled down her back—it was stifling inside this coat.

But he seemed to be the obvious person to speak to, so she moved quickly. She straightened her spine and forced herself to look him in the eyes. Not easy when those eyes were staring at her chest.

But before she got a word out he twirled one fat finger and said, 'If you've come about the job, take off that coat and show us what you've got.'

The hairs on the back of her neck prickled and, appalled, she tightened her belt. 'I *beg* your pardon? I'm n—'

'You won't need a costume here, darlin',' he drawled, eyeing the garment bag over her shoulder. 'We're one down tonight so you can start on the tables. Cherry'll show you. Oi, Cherry!' His smoke-scratched voice blasted through the thick air.

Emma cringed as people looked their way, glad of her dark glasses. She summoned her frostiest tone. 'I'm here to speak to Jake Carmody.'

He shook his head. 'Won't make a scrap of difference, y'know. Seen plenty just like you pass through the door hiding behind a disguise, expecting to make a quick buck on the side.'

'*Excuse me?* Just tell me where I can find Mr Carmody so I can finish my business with him and be *out of here.*'

Those pale flat eyes checked her out some more as a woman approached toting a tray of drinks. She was wearing eighties gold hot pants and a transparent black blouse. Beneath her make-up Emma saw that she looked drawn and tired and felt a stirring of sympathy. She knew all about working jobs out of sheer necessity, and was grateful she'd never been quite so desperate.

'Lady here wants to see the boss. Know where he is?'

The boss? 'There must be some mistake…' Emma trailed off. His PA had told her she'd find him at this address, but…he was the *boss* of this dive?

The woman called Cherry gave a weary half shrug. 'In the office, last I saw.'

He jerked a thumb at a narrow staircase on the far side of the room. 'Up the stairs, first door on the right.'

'Thank you.' Lips pressed together, and aware of a few gazes following her, she made her way through the club, keeping as far away from the action as possible.

The *boss?*

Despite the heat, she shivered inside her coat. His lifestyle was none of her business, but she'd never in a million years have expected the guy she remembered to be involved in a lower-than-low strip joint. He already had a career, didn't he? A degree in business law, for goodness' sake. *Please don't let him have chucked in years of study and a respectable livelihood for this…*

Sleaze Central's business obviously paid better. Money over morals.

She knew Jake from high school. He was one of Ryan's mates, and the two guys had often turned up at home to catch up with her more sociable sister and listen to music. Emma had been either working one of her after-school jobs or experimenting with her soap-making, but there'd been a few times when Stella had persuaded her to chill out with them.

Jake the Rake, Emma had privately thought him. A chick magnet. Totally cool, ever so slightly dangerous, and way too experienced for a girl like her. Maybe that was why she'd always tried to avoid him whenever possible.

Hadn't stopped her from being a little in love with him, though. She shook it away. Obviously her young eyes had been clouded by naïveté and love was definitely not in her life plan. Not ever again.

She heard him before she reached the door. That familiar deep, somewhat lazy voice that seemed to roll over the senses like thick caramel sauce. She *was* well and truly over her youthful crush on him, wasn't she? He was on the phone, and as she paused to listen his tone changed from laid-back to harassed.

The door was open a crack and she knocked. She heard a clatter as he slammed the phone down, a short, succinct rude word and then an impatient, 'Come in.'

He didn't look up straight away, which gave her a moment to slide her sunglasses on top of her head and look him over.

Sitting at a shabby desk littered with papers, he was writing something, head bent over a file. He wore a sky-blue shirt, open at the neck, sleeves rolled up over sinewy bronzed forearms. Unlike the rest of this dive, his clothing was top of the line. Her gaze lifted to his face and her heart pattered that tiny bit faster. God's gift with a sinner's lips…

An unnerving little shiver ran through her and she jerked her eyes higher. His rich, dark hair was sticking up in short tufts here and there, as if he'd been ploughing his hands through it. Her fingers itched to smooth it down—

Good grief, she was lusting after a man who owned a seedy striptease venue—a man who not only used women but exploited them. Wanting to touch him made her as low as him and as bad as those pervs downstairs. But, despite her best efforts to ignore them, little quivers continued to reverberate up and down the length of her spine.

'Hello, Jake.' She impressed herself with her aloof greeting and only wished she felt as cool.

He glanced up. His frown was replaced by stunned surprise. As if he'd been caught in a shop window with his made-to-measure pants down. She blinked the disconcerting image away.

'Emma.' Putting his pen down slowly, he closed the file he'd been working on, took his sweet time to stand—all six-foot-plus of gorgeous male—and said, 'Long time no see.'

'Yes,' she agreed, ignoring the tantalising glimpse of masculine hair visible at the neck of his shirt, the way his broad shoulders shifted against the fabric. 'Well…we've all got busy lives.'

'Yeah, it's all go these days isn't it? Unlike high school.' He came round to the side of the desk with a smile that was like a lingering caress and did amazing tingly things to her body.

She took a step back. She needed to get out. Fast. 'I can see you're busy,' she hurried on, keeping her gaze focused on his black coffee eyes. 'I j—'

'Are you here for a job?'

What? She felt her jaw drop, and for a moment she simply stared while her brain played catch-up and heat crawled up her neck. The sod. The dirty rotten *sod.* 'I phoned your office—your *other* office—and your PA told me you were here.'

Her lip curled on the last word and she tossed the garment bag onto the desk, sending papers flying every which way. 'Your suit for the wedding. If it needs altering the tailor says he needs at least three days' notice, which is why I'm dropping it off tonight. Ryan's interstate, and Stella had an appointment, so I—'

'Emma. I was joking.'

Oh. She glimpsed the twinkle in his eye and took another step back. Twinkles were dangerous. And why wouldn't he joke? Because no way did she measure up to those voluptuous creatures downstairs. 'I don't have time to joke today. Or anything else. So...um...you've got the suit. I'll be off, then.'

He watched her a moment longer, as if saying *What's your hurry?* Beneath the harsh single fluorescent light she saw the bruised smudges and feathery lines of stress around his eyes, as if he hadn't slept in weeks.

Well, good, she thought. He deserved to be stressed for making her feel like an inadequate fool. As if her self-esteem wasn't suffering enough after Wayne ending their relationship, and in this place...

'So, it's *Gone with the Wind* for us two, eh? Hope I can do Rhett Butler justice.' He glanced at the bag, then aimed that sexy grin at her. 'And you're to be my Scarlett for the day.'

She stiffened at the darkly delicious—no, *bad* thought. But her blood pulsed a bit more heavily through her body. 'I'm not your anyone. Why they had to choose a famous couples-themed wedding's beyond me.'

He shrugged. 'They wanted something sparkling and original and wildly romantic—and why not? Might as well have some fun on the big day. Everything's downhill from there.' His long, sensuous fingers curled around the edge of the desk and he aimed that killer smile again. 'Thanks for dropping it off. Can I get you a drink before you leave?'

Good heavens. 'No. Thank you.'

Crossing his arms, Jake leaned a hip against the desk, inhaling the fresh, unfamiliar fragrance that had swirled in with her. She was an energising sight for tired eyes. What he could see of her.

Tall and slim as a blue-eyed poppy. Even angry she looked amazing, with that ice-cold sapphire gaze and that way she had of pouting her lips. All glossy and plump and…

He fought a sudden mad impulse to walk over and taste them. Probably shouldn't have made that wisecrack about a job here. But he'd not been able to resist getting a rise out of her. On the few occasions she'd been persuaded to join them she'd always been so damn serious. Obviously that hadn't changed.

The muffled thump from downstairs vibrated through the floor. He rasped his hands over his stubbled jaw. 'If I'd known you were coming I'd've arranged for you to drop the suit at my office. My *other* office.'

She drilled him some more with that icy stare. And he felt oddly bruised, as if she'd punched him in the gut with her…gloved hand.

'I have to go,' she said stiffly.

He pushed off the desk. 'I'll walk you down.'

'No. I'd really rather you didn't.'

The tone. He knew well enough not to mess with it and crossed his arms. 'Okay. Thanks again for dropping the suit by. Appreciate it.'

'Glad to hear that, because it's a one-off.'

'I'll see you tomorrow night at the wedding dinner.'

'Seven-thirty.' She hitched her bag higher. 'Don't be late.'

'Emma…' She glanced back and he thought once again of poppies. About lying in a field of them on a summer's day. With Emma. 'It's good to see you again.'

She didn't reply, but she did hesitate, staring at him with those fabulous eyes and allowing him to indulge in the cheerful poppy fantasy a few seconds longer. And he could have sworn he felt a…*zap*. Then she nodded once and her head snapped back to the doorway.

He watched her leave, admiring the way she moved, all straight and sexy and *classy*. He wondered for a moment why he'd never pursued anything with her back in the day. He'd seen her look his way more than once when she'd thought he wasn't watching.

His lingering smile dropped away. He knew why. Emma Byrne didn't know the meaning of fun, and she certainly didn't know how to chill out. She wore *serious* the way other women wore designer jeans.

Jake, on the other hand, didn't do serious. He didn't do commitment. He enjoyed women—on his terms. Women who knew the score. And when it was over it was over, no misunderstandings. No looking back. But, *hoo-yeah*… He couldn't deny this lovely, more mature, more womanly Emma turned him on. Big time.

The door closed and he listened to her footsteps fade, stretching his arms over his head, imagining her walking downstairs. In that neck-to-ankle armour—which only added to the sexual intrigue. Did she even realise that? He should have escorted her down, he thought again. But the lady, and everything about her body language, had said a very definite no.

Shaking off the lusty thoughts, he rolled down his shirt-sleeves. Damn Earl, the SOB who'd fathered him, for dying and leaving him this mess to sort out. No one knew of Jake's connection to this club, with the exception of Ry and his parents and more recently his PA.

And now Emma Byrne.

'Hell.' He checked the time, then shoved his phone in his pocket. He didn't have time for that particular complication right now—he had an important business meeting to attend. Grabbing his jacket from the back of his chair, he headed downstairs.

CHAPTER TWO

AND she'd told him not to turn up late.

'She'd better have a good excuse,' Jake muttered the following evening as he swung a left in his BMW and headed for Sydney's seaside suburb of Coogee Beach, where Emma lived with her mother and Stella. As Ryan's best man he'd had no choice but to elect himself to conduct the search party.

Or maybe she'd decided she didn't want to run into Jake Carmody again so soon.

She'd always been big on responsibility, he recalled, and tonight was her sister's night, so he figured she wouldn't opt out without a valid reason. But she hadn't answered her mobile and concern gnawed at his impatience. He tapped the steering wheel while he waited at a red light. A trio of teenagers skimpily dressed for a night on the town crossed in front of him, their feminine voices shrill and excited.

Maybe Emma wasn't the same girl these days. Maybe she had decided to swap those self-imposed obligations for some fun at last. After all, apart from those few minutes yesterday, when neither of them had actually been themselves, how long had it been since he'd seen her?

His gut tensed an instant at the memory. He knew exactly when he'd last seen her. Seven months ago at Stella and Ryan's engagement party. He knew exactly what she'd been wearing too—a long, slinky strapless thing the co-lour of moon-drenched sea at midnight.

Or some such garment. He forced his hands to loosen on the wheel. Unclenched his jaw. So what if he'd noticed every detail, down to the last shimmering toenail? A guy could look.

He'd arrived in time to see her leave hand in hand with some muscled blond surfie type. Wayne something or other, Stella had told him. Apparently Emma and Wayne were a hot item.

Maybe Surfer Boy was the reason she'd lost track of time…

Frowning at the thought, he pulled into the Byrnes' driveway overlooking the darkening ocean. The gates were open and he came to a stop beside an old red hatchback parked at the top of a flight of stone steps.

Perched halfway down the sloping family property was the old music studio, where he remembered spending af-ternoons in the latter days of high school. Early-evening shadows shrouded the brick walls but muted amber light shone through the window. Emma lived there now, he'd been informed, and she was obviously still at home. In the absence of any other car on the grounds, it seemed she was also alone.

Swinging his car door open, he pulled out his phone. 'Ry? Looks like she hasn't even left yet.' He strode to the steps, flicking impatient fingers against his thigh. 'We'll be there soon.'

Pocketing the phone, he continued down the stairs. If *he* could make it on time to this wedding dinner after the hellish day he'd had, trying to stay on top of two busi-nesses, so could Emma. She was the bridesmaid, after all.

Some sort of relaxation music drifted from the window, accompanying the muted *shoosh-boom* of the breakers on the beach. He slowed his steps, breathing in the calming fragrant salt air and honeysuckle, and ordered himself to simmer down.

The peal of the door chime accompanied by a sharp rapping on her front door jerked Emma from her work. She refocused, feeling as if she was coming out of a deep-sleep cave. She checked her watch. Blinked. *Oh, no.* She'd assured Stella she'd be right along when the family had left nearly half an hour ago.

Which officially made her the World's Worst Bridesmaid.

She stretched muscles cramped from being in one position too long and assured herself her lapse *wasn't* because her subconscious mind was telling her she didn't want to see Jake. She would *not* let him and that crazy moment yesterday when their eyes had met and the whole world seemed to fade into nothing affect her life. In any way.

Rap, rap, rap.

'Okay, okay,' she murmured. She slipped the order of tiny stacked soap flowers she'd been wrapping back into its container and called, 'Coming!'

Running her hands down the sides of her oversized lab coat, she hurried to the door, swung it open. 'I…'

The man's super-sized silhouette filled the doorway, blocking what was left of the twilight and obscuring his features, but she knew instantly who he was by the way her heart bounded up into her throat.

'Jake.' She felt breathless, as if she'd just scaled the Harbour Bridge. Ridiculous. Scowling, she flicked on the foyer light. She tried not to admire the view, she really did, but her eyes ate up his dark good-looks like a woman too long on a blond boy diet.

Tonight he wore tailored dark trousers and a chocolate-coloured shirt open at the neck. Hair the colour of aged whisky lifted ever so slightly in the salty breeze.

'So here you are.' His tone was brusque, those black-coffee eyes focused sharply on hers.

'Yes, here I am,' she said, trying to ignore the hot flush seeing him had brought on and reminding herself where she'd seen him last. The flashback to the strip club made her feel like a gauche schoolgirl and it should not. But she was the one at fault tonight—and the reason he was standing in her doorway.

She gave him a careless smile, determined not to let yesterday spoil this evening. For Stella's sake. 'And running late,' she rushed on. 'I assume that's why you're here?' *Why else?*

One eyebrow rose and she knew he wasn't impressed. 'You had some people concerned.' He said it as if he didn't count himself amongst those people—where had yesterday's twinkle gone?—while he stepped inside and scanned the dining room table covered in the hand-made goat's milk soaps she'd been working on.

'You weren't answering your phone.' His gaze swung back to hers again. 'Not handy when people are trying to contact you.'

Her smile dropped to her feet. Was that *censure* in his voice? 'This from the guy who was too busy at his *other business* to answer his own mobile yesterday?' she shot back. 'You do realise I had to pry the info as to your whereabouts from your PA?'

He nodded, his eyes not flinching from hers. 'So she told me. I apologise for the inconvenience, and for any embarrassment I caused you.'

Emma drew in a deep breath. 'Okay.' She forced her mature self to put yesterday's incident to the back of her mind for now. 'As for me, I have no legitimate excuse for forgetting the time, so it's my turn to apologise that you had to be the one to come and get me.' She tried a smile.

He nodded, his dark eyes warmed, and his whole demeanour mellowed like a languid Sunday afternoon. 'Apology accepted.' He leaned down and brushed her cheek with firm lips, and she caught a whiff of subtle yet sexy aftershave before he straightened up again.

Whoa. Yesterday's tingle was back with a vengeance, running through her entire system at double the voltage. 'So…um…I'll just go…' Feeling off-centre, she backed away, ostensibly towards the tiny area sectioned off by a curtain which she used as a bedroom, but he didn't take the hint and leave. 'Look, you go on ahead. I'll be ready in a jiff and it's only a ten-minute drive to the restaurant.'

He shrugged, stuck his hands in his trouser pockets. 'I'm here now.'

Slipping off her flats, she glanced about for her heels. But her eyes seemed drawn to him as if they were on strings. He dressed like a million bucks these days. Still, those threadbare jeans he'd worn way back when had fuelled more teenage fantasies than she cared to remember. She watched him wander towards her table of supplies. With his hands in his pockets, drawing his trousers tight across that firm, cute butt…

No. Sleazy club-owner. Dragging her eyes away, she scoured the floor for her shoes. 'There's really no need to wait…'

'I'm waiting. End of story.' She heard the crinkle of cellophane as he examined her orders. 'Your hobby's still making you some pocket money, then?'

Irritation stiffened her shoulders. She glared at him. 'It's *not* just a hobby, and it's never been about the money.' *Unlike others who shall remain Nameless.* Exhaling sharply through her nose, she swiped up a black stiletto and slipped it on. 'I have to wonder why it is that helping people with skin allergies seems to you to be a waste of time.'

'I never sa—'

'Why don't you go while I…?' *Calm down.* 'Find my other shoe.'

'So uptight.' He tsked. 'You really need to get out more, Em. Always was too much work and not enough play with you.' He scooped her shoe from beneath a chair and tossed it to her. 'Maybe the wedding'll help things along.'

She caught it one-handed, dropped it in front of her with a clatter and stepped into it, then bent to do up the straps. She'd had it with people telling her how to live her life. Get out more? She let out a huff. She had familial obligations. Had she told him what she thought of the way he was living *his* life nowadays? No.

She finished fastening her shoes and straightened, pushed at the hair that had fallen over her eyes. Forget his uninformed opinion. Forget him, period. She had her *un*-fabulous job at the insurance call centre—but it paid the bills—and she had just finished her Diploma in Natural Health. And if she chose to fill her leisure hours working on ways to help people use natural products rather than the dangerous chemicals contained in other products these days, it was nobody's business but hers.

'So how's…what was her name…? Sherry?' she asked with enough sweetness to decay several teeth as she slipped open the top button of her lab coat. 'Will she be missing you this evening?'

His brows rose. 'Who?'

'The one…' *draped all over you* '…at Stella's engagement party. Stella mentioned her name,' she hurried on, in case he thought she'd actually asked. Which she had. But he didn't need to know that.

'Ah…You mean Brandy.'

She shrugged. 'Brandy. Sherry. She looked like more of a *Candy* to me.' With her suck-my-face-off lips and over-generous cleavage. And everything else Emma was lacking. 'You didn't say hello and introduce us. Was that because she was one of your *exotic dancers?*'

'You and your date left as we arrived. Was that just a curious coincidence?'

Jake watched her cheeks flush guiltily and felt an instant stab of arousal. Hell. He kept his expression neutral, but something was happening here. And the hot little fantasy he'd had last night about what she'd been wearing beneath that red coat yesterday wasn't helping.

And now she was undoing the second button of that lab coat, revealing a pair of sexy collarbones and putting inappropriate ideas into his head.

He ground his teeth together as images of black lace and feminine flesh flashed through his mind. 'Are you going to get ready or what?' The demand came out lower and rougher than he'd have liked. Then he held his breath as she shrugged out of the coat, tossed it over the couch.

'I'm ready already.' She flashed him a cool look. 'I use the coat to protect my clothes when I'm working.'

His gaze snagged on her outfit—a short black dress shot through with bronze, hugging her slender curves to perfection. He swallowed. The legs. How come he'd never noticed how long her legs were? How toned and tanned? He did *not* imagine how they'd feel locked around his waist.

Cool it. He deliberately relaxed tense muscles. He'd wait outside, get some air.

But before he could move she picked up an embroidered purse from the couch and walked to the front door. 'Shall we go?'

He walked ahead, opened the door. 'We'll take my car.'

'I'm taking my own car, thanks.' She locked the door behind them, then headed towards the hatchback, her heels tapping a fast rhythm on the concrete.

He pressed his remote and the locks clicked open. 'Hard to get a parking space anywhere this time of night,' he advised. 'And we—make that *you*—are running late already. Stella and Ryan are waiting.'

Swinging her door open, she glanced back at him. 'Better get a move on, then.'

He started to go after her, then changed his mind. She was in a dangerous mood, and he was just riled enough to take her on. And it might end… He didn't want to think about how it might end. Because he had a feeling that anything with Emma would need to be very slow and very, *very* thorough. If you could find your way through those thorns, that was. 'I'll see you there.'

She clicked her seat belt on, turned the ignition and revved the engine. 'Ten minutes.'

Emma's stomach jittered. Her pulse raced. Trouble. She'd seen more than enough of it in Jake's hot brown eyes. As if she was performing some sort of striptease. She'd not given it a thought when she'd peeled off her lab coat. But he had. *Sheesh.* She scoffed to herself. As if he'd give her less than average body a second look when he was surrounded by all those Brandies and Candies and brazen beauties at the Pink Mango.

Flicking a glance at her rearview mirror she caught the glare of his headlights. She deliberately slowed her speed, hoping he'd overtake, but he seemed content—or irritated enough—to cruise along behind her. She could feel his eyes boring into the back of her head.

She let out a shaky sigh and drew a deep, slow breath to steady herself. Easier to blame him than to admit to that old attraction—because no way was Jake the Rake the kind of man she wanted to get involved with on an intimate level.

She accelerated recklessly through a yellow light, Jake hot on her heels. She wasn't herself tonight. Wrong. She hadn't been herself since she'd come face to face with Jake in his dingy office yesterday.

Even as a teenager he'd always made her feel…different. Self-conscious. Tingly. Uncomfortably aware of her feminine bits.

Her fingers clenched tighter on the steering wheel. She needed to get herself under control. She didn't figure in his life at all, nor he in hers. And tonight wasn't about her or him or even *them*; it was about Stella and Ryan.

She tensed as the well-lit upscale restaurant came into view, and glanced in the mirror again just in time to see Jake's car glide into a parking space she'd been too distracted to notice right outside the restaurant.

Oh, for heaven's sake, this was ridiculous. The restaurant was on a corner and she stopped at a red light, tapping impatient fingers on the dashboard. Seriously, if it wasn't Stella's night she'd turn around and go home, pull the covers over her head and not surface till Christmas—

The thump on the car's roof nearly had her foot slipping off the brake as Jake climbed in beside her. 'Don't you know better than to leave your passenger door unlocked when you're driving alone at night?'

She hated his smug look and lazy tone and looked away quickly. 'Don't you know better than to scare a person half to death when they're behind the wheel?'

'Light's green.'

She clenched her teeth, pretending that she hadn't noticed his woodsy aftershave wafting towards her, and crossed the intersection. 'What are you doing here? There's no sense in both of us being late.' She saw a car pulling out ahead, remembered at the last second to check her rear vision and slammed on the brakes.

'We'll walk in together, *Scarlett.*'

'Don't remind me,' she muttered. She slid the car into the parking spot, yanked the key from the ignition, jumped out and locked her door before he'd even undone his seat belt.

Jake took his time getting out, watching her walk around the car's bonnet to the footpath. Not looking at him. No trace of the blue-eyed poppy tonight, he thought, locking his own door. She was as prickly as a blackberry bush.

The pedestrian light turned green. She left the kerb and he fell into step beside her. 'If we're going to pull this wedding business off, we need to be seen to be getting along.'

She jerked to a stop outside the restaurant. 'Fine.'

Catching her by her slender shoulders, he turned her to face him, noticed her stiffen at the skin-on-skin contact. 'We'll need to have a conversation about that at some point.'

'There's nothing to talk about.'

Light from the window spilled over her face. Wide eyes stared up at him, violet in the yellow glow. He slid his hands down her bare arms, felt her shiver beneath his palms and raised a brow. 'Nothing?'

'Nothing.' She rubbed her palms together, her gaze flicking away. 'It's chilly. I should've brought a jacket. I left it on the bed…'

No, he thought, she'd been distracted. Grinning, he let her go. 'Lighten up, Em, and give yourself permission to enjoy an evening out for once.'

CHAPTER THREE

WITH a light hand at her back, Jake ushered Emma into the upstairs restaurant. Exotic Eastern tapestries lined the burgundy walls. On the far side, through double glass doors was a narrow balcony crowded with palms. Dreamy Eastern music played softly in the background. The tempting aromas of Indian cuisine greeted them as they made their way towards the round family table already covered in a variety of spicy smelling dishes.

'Apologies, everyone.' Jake nodded to the happy couple. 'Glad to see you've already started.'

Emma murmured her own apologies to Stella while Ryan spooned rice into two empty bowls and passed them across the table. 'We wondered whether you two had decided to play hooky.'

'We thought about it—didn't we, Em?' Jake grinned, enjoying her appalled expression, then turned to Ryan's father.

Gil Clifton, a stocky man with wiry red hair and always a genuine smile, rose and shook hands. 'Good to see you again, Jake.'

'And you. We must get around to that tennis match.'

'Any time. Just give us a call and drop by.'

'I'll do that.'

Gil's smile faded. 'I was sorry to hear about your father. If there's anything I can do…'

The mention of the old man left nothing but a bitter taste in Jake's mouth and an emptiness in his soul that he'd come to terms with years ago. As far as he was concerned Gil and Julie Clifton were the only adult support he'd ever needed. 'Got it covered, thanks, Gil.'

He kissed Julie's cheek. 'How's the mother of the groom holding up?'

'Getting excited. And, to echo Gil's words, if you want to drop by and chat…you're always welcome.'

If Jake was ever to be lost for words now was that time. Ryan's family were the only people who knew about his dysfunctional childhood, and now the whole table knew about Earl. He forced a smile. 'Thanks.'

Emma watched Julie give Jake's arm a sympathetic squeeze. It occurred to her how little she really knew of his background beyond the fact he was Ryan's mate.

'So how's business?' Gil asked as Jake moved to the two empty chairs.

'Busy as usual. Evening, Bernice.'

'Jake.' Emma's mother acknowledged him coolly, then turned the same stony gaze on Emma. 'Thank you for collecting my unpunctual daughter.'

Emma reminded herself she was Teflon coated where her mother's barbs were concerned. The others resumed their conversations while she took the empty seat that Jake pulled out beside her mother and whispered, 'Sorry, Mum.'

'Have to admire our Emma's work ethic, though,' Jake remarked as he sat down beside her. 'It's not easy juggling two jobs.'

'Two jobs?' Bernice bit off the words. 'When one's a waste of time, I—'

'Mum.' Emma counted to ten while she reached for her

table napkin and smoothed it over her lap. 'How are you enjoying the food?'

Bernice stabbed at a cherry tomato on her plate. 'You need two *proper* jobs to be able to afford a dress like that.'

Jake smiled at Bernice on Emma's other side. 'And it's worth every cent. She looks sensational, don't you think? Wine, Em?'

'No, thank you. Driving.' She acknowledged Jake's support with a quick nod and reached for the glass of water in front of her. She took several swallows to compose herself before she said, 'I bought it at Second Hand Rose, Mum. That little recycle boutique on the esplanade.'

When her mother didn't reply, Emma turned to Jake. 'I didn't know about your father,' she murmured as other conversation flowed around the table. 'I'm sorry.'

He didn't look at her. 'Don't be.' He tossed back his drink, set his glass on the table with a firm *thunk* and turned his attention to something Ryan was saying on his other side.

Ouch. Emma reached for the nearest dish, a mixed vegetable curry, and ladled some onto her plate. He didn't want to talk about his father—fine. But there was a mountain of pain and anger there, and... She paused, spoon in mid-air. *And what, Emma?*

He clearly wasn't going to talk about it. He didn't *want* to talk about it—not with her at any rate—and she had no business pursuing it. It wasn't as if they were close or anything.

A moment later Jake turned to her again. 'I was abrupt. I shouldn't have been.'

An apology. Of sorts. 'It must be a tough time, no matter how you and he...' The right words eluded her so she reached for the nearest platter instead. 'Samosa?'

'Thanks.' He took one, put it on the side of his plate.

'I've been thinking about you, Emma.' He leaned ever so slightly her way, with a hint of seduction in the return of that suave tone.

She could feel the heat bleed into her cheeks. 'I don't—'

'Have you considered selling your supplies over the internet?' He broke off a piece of naan bread. 'Could be a profitable business for you. You never know—you might be able to give up your day job eventually.'

'I don't want to give up my day job.' *I'm not a risk-taker. Mum depends on me financially. I can't afford to fail.*

'I could help you with your business plan,' he continued, as if she'd never spoken. He lowered that sexy voice. 'You only have to ask.'

His silky words wrapped around her like a gloved hand and an exquisite shiver scuttled down her spine. She could imagine asking him…lots of things. She wondered if his sudden interest and diversionary tactics had anything to do with taking the focus off his own family problems. 'I don't have time to waste on the computer, and I told you already it's not about the money.' *Business plan? What business plan?*

'Lacking computer confidence isn't something to be embarrassed about.'

'I'm n—' With a roll of her eyes she decided her protest was wasted—men like Jake were always right—and topped up her curry with a broccoli floret. 'I'm flat out supplying the local stores. I don't need to be online.'

'It would make it easier. And if your products are so popular why wouldn't you want to see where they take you?'

She would—oh, she *so* would. Her little cottage business was her passion, but technology was so not her; she wouldn't know where to start with a website, and her meagre income—which went straight into the household budget—didn't allow her to gamble on such a luxury. 'As I said, there's no time.'

'Maybe you need to change your priorities. Or maybe you're afraid to take that chance?' He eyed her astutely as he broke off more bread. 'The offer's always open if you change your mind.'

Was she so easy to read? An hour or so with Jake and he saw it already. Her fear of failure. Of taking that step into the unknown. He was the last person she'd be going to for help; she felt vulnerable enough around him as it was. 'Thank you, I'll keep it in mind.'

Over the next hour the meal was punctuated with great food, toasts to the bride and groom, speeches and recollections of fond memories.

Jake watched on, feeling oddly detached from the whole family and the getting-married scenario. What motivated sane, rational people to chain themselves to another human being for the term of their natural lives? In the end someone always ended up abandoning the other, along with any kids unlucky enough to be caught up in it.

Then Emma excused herself to go to the ladies' room and Julie claimed Bernice's attention with wedding talk. He breathed a sigh of relief that for now he wasn't included in the conversation.

A moment later he saw Emma on her way back and watched, admiring her svelte figure and the way her hips undulated as she walked. Nice. Last night's fantasy flashed back and a punch of lust ricocheted through his body. She'd been fire and ice yesterday at the club, and he couldn't help wondering how it might translate to the bedroom.

He saw her come to an abrupt halt as a newly arrived couple cut across her path. His eyes narrowed. Wasn't that…? Yep. Wayne whoever-he-was. Jake watched on with interest as Wayne's dinner partner hugged his arm a moment then walked to the ladies', leaving Emma and Surfer Boy facing each other.

More like facing off, Jake thought, studying their body language. Even from a distance he could see that Emma's eyes had widened, that her face had gone pale and that Surfer Boy was trying to talk himself out of a sticky situation fast. Emma spoke through tight lips and shook her head. Then, turning abruptly, she headed straight for the balcony.

Uh-oh, he thought, *trouble in paradise?*

Emma's whole body burned with embarrassment as she hurried for the nearest sanctuary. She pushed blindly through the glass doors and took in a deep gulp of the cooler air.

He'd had the nerve to introduce the girl. *His fiancée.* Rani—a dusky beauty, heavy on the gold jewellery—had flashed a brand-new sparkle on the third finger of her left hand and said they'd been seeing each other for *over a year.*

While Emma and Wayne had been seeing each other. *Sleeping* with each other.

The bastard.

He'd broken it off with Emma only a month ago. Said it wasn't working for him. No mention then of a fiancée. Obviously this Rani girl had what it took to keep a man interested.

The worst part was that Emma had let her guard down with him. She'd done what she'd sworn she'd never do— she'd fallen for him big time.

Shielded by palm fronds, she leaned over the railing and stared at the traffic below. But she wasn't seeing it—she was too busy trying to patch up the barely healed scars and a bunch of black emotions, like her own stupid gull-ibility. She'd been used. Deceived. Lied to—

'Emma.'

She jumped at the sound of Jake's voice behind her. Embarrassment fired up again. He must have seen the exchange. No point pretending it hadn't happened. 'Hi.' She ran a palm frond through her stiff fingers. 'I was just talking to an ex.'

'A recent ex, by the look of things.' Warm hands cupped her shoulders and turned her towards him. He lifted her chin with a finger, and his eyes told her he knew a lot more than she wanted him to. 'Should I be sorry?'

She shook her head. 'I'm not very good company right now.' Shrugging off the intimacy of his touch, she looked down at the street again, at the neon signs that lit the res-taurants and cafés.

'You didn't answer the question, Em,' he said softly. 'But, if you ask me, I'd say he's not worth being sorry over.'

'Damn right, he's not. That was his *fiancée*. According to her, they've been together over a year.'

'Hmm. I see.'

'Unfortunately for me, I didn't.' She stared at the street. 'We were both busy with work and after-hours com-mitments, but we always spent Friday nights together.' Frowning, she murmured, 'I wonder how he explained that to her?'

'Friday nights?' There was a beat of silence, then he asked, 'You had, like, a regular slot for him, then?'

She watched a couple strolling arm in arm below them and felt an acute pang of loss. 'We had an understanding.'

'He *understood* that you scheduled him into your work-ing life like some sort of beauty session?'

Her skin prickled. Wayne had actually been the one doing the *scheduling,* and Emma had been so head over heels, so desperate to be with him, she'd gone along with whatever he'd asked. 'He had a busy schedule too.' Obviously. 'But Friday night was ours. And he was cheating all along.'

Why the hell was she telling Jake this? Of all people. She turned to him, dragged up a half-smile from somewhere. 'I'm fine. I was over it weeks ago.'

'That's the way.' He smiled, all easy sympathy, and gave her hand a quick pat. 'The trick is not to take these things too seriously.'

These things? Being in love was just one of *these things?* 'And you'd be the expert at that particular trick, wouldn't you?' She and Wayne had had an understanding. He'd betrayed her and *that was serious.*

To her surprise, he spoke sharply. 'Contrary to what you may think, I don't cheat.'

'Because you're not with a woman long enough.' As if *she* would know his modus operandi these days…she wasn't exactly a social butterfly. She looked up and met Jake's eyes—dark, intense, like Turkish coffee. 'Sorry.' She shrugged. 'It's just that you're here, you're male, and right now I want to punch something. Or someone.' Her gaze flicked down to the street. 'Nothing personal.'

He shoved his hands in his pockets. 'Emma, yesterday—'

'You live your way, I live mine.' She waved him off. 'We're not teenagers any more.'

But was she living her life her way? she wondered as she paced past the balcony's foliage and back. Or was she living for other people?

After her father had died, leaving them virtually penniless, Emma had spent years working menial jobs after school so that they wouldn't have to sell her maternal grandmother's home, and then had supported herself through her studies. Her mother had been diagnosed with clinical depression soon after their father's death, and Stella had taken on the role of main carer, but Emma had been the one with the ultimate financial responsibility.

She didn't mind giving up her time or her money, but her mother was recovered now and Emma's sacrifices went unacknowledged and unappreciated.

And now she'd discovered the man she'd loved had been cheating on her for God knew how long, and in Jake's opinion it was because she was so focused on her work.

But Jake knew nothing about it, and she intended for it to stay that way. It did *not* excuse Wayne. Even the fact that the girl was more exotic than she was, more voluptuous... more everything...was no excuse. She was tempted to run downstairs and tell him what she thought of him, let Rani in on his dirty little secret—except she never wanted to see him again and she'd only make herself look like a fool. 'If nothing else, I expect honesty in a relationship.'

'You call a regular Friday night bonk a *relationship?*' he said.

She met his stare with a defiant stare of her own. 'It suited us.'

'It suited *you.*'

She bit her lip to stop unwanted words from spilling out. 'I thought what we had was what he wanted too.'

'Yeah, I'm sure it was.'

His dry comment riled her further. She rubbed the chill from her arms while inside her the anger and hurt and humiliation burned bright and strong. Better him thinking she was an idiot than knowing the embarrassing truth— that she was a naïve, gullible idiot.

'Sometimes I get so damn tired of doing what everyone else wants. What other people expect...' She trailed off when she saw Wayne and Rani outside an Italian restaurant on the street below. While his *fiancée* studied the menu in the window he glanced up and met Emma's eyes.

Renewed outrage surged through the other emotions in a dark wave. She refused to step back, refused to be the one to break eye contact. How dared he? Their weekly love-in had been a lie. They'd been seeing each other for months and the whole time he'd been deceiving her.

Making a fool of her.

In an uncharacteristic move, she made a rude hand gesture…and it felt good. Especially when Wayne looked away first. She spun away towards Jake, finding an oddly reassuring comfort in his presence. 'And sometimes I just want to live my own life and to hell with everything and everyone.'

'So start now, Em,' he said, his voice gentle yet firm. 'Change your life. Do what you want for a change.'

She stared into those dark eyes holding hers. What *did* she want?

All she saw was Jake.

Every rational thought flew away. Every drop of sense drained out of her as she stepped nearer to him, her eyes only leaving his to drift to his mouth.

What I want…

Before she could warn herself that this was a Really Bad Idea, she launched forward, cupped his jaw between her hands and plastered her lips to his.

Her heart gave a single hard jolt, and a little voice whispered, *This is what I've been waiting for.* The sizzle zapped all the way to her toes and back again before frustration and fury liquefied into heat and hunger. She flung herself into the moment, indulging her senses. The warmth of his mouth against hers was a counterfoil for his cool, refreshing scent—like moss on a pristine forest floor.

Caught off guard, Jake rocked back on his heels before

steadying himself, and her, his hands finding purchase on the smooth slope of her hips as he kissed her back.

Emma. Her taste—new and unforgettably sweet. The fragrance of soap and shampoo and woman all wrapped up in the texture of skin-warmed silk beneath his fingers.

She was a rising tornado of emotion and needs, and it whipped around the edges of his own darker desires. The word *complication* lurked somewhere at the back of his mind. He shrugged it away and instead, sliding his palms around to her back, hauled her closer and settled in to savour more of the exquisite sensations battering him.

'Ohh…' The sound was exhaled on a strangled gasp as firm hands pushed at his chest. She jerked out of his hold, eyes wide. 'I didn't… That was…'

'Nice,' he finished for her. His hormone-ravished body protested the gross understatement even as he knew she was just using him to get back at the drivelling idiot probably still watching the performance from the other side of the street.

As quickly as it had blown in the whirlwind subsided leaving only a tantalising whisper as she stared up at him, rolled her lips between her teeth and said, 'I don't know why I…did that.'

'You were upset. I was here.' Enjoying the way her eyes reflected her conflict, he couldn't help but grin. 'Have to tell you it wins hands down over the punch you threatened to dole out earlier.'

'I…need to see if Mum's ready to go home.'

'Emma.' He lifted a hand, dropped it when she edged farther away. 'Don't beat yourself up. It was just a kiss. And I'm sure Wayne got the message.'

She flinched as if he'd hit her. '*He* wasn't the… He wasn't look— I was… Oh, forget it.'

And in the light filtering through from the restaurant

he glimpsed twin spots of colour flag her cheeks before she whirled around and made a dash to the door.

Shoving his hands into his pockets, he leaned a hip against the railing while he waited for his body's horny reaction to subside. *You kiss me like that, honey, I ain't gonna forget.*

It was too bad she'd come to her senses so quickly. He didn't mind being used when it came in the form of a beautiful woman in distress—particularly when the woman had seemed oblivious that she *had,* in fact, used him. He looked down at the street. No sign of the scumbag.

He could still smell Emma; the fresh, untainted fragrance lingered in the air, on his clothes. The flavour of that one luscious kiss still danced on his tastebuds. The surprise of it—of *her*—like the first green sprout emerging from the carnage of a bushfire, still vibrated along his bones. She'd reacted without thinking for a hot and heavy moment there, and he'd enjoyed every second.

So had she.

And he wasn't going to let her forget either. Her weekly love-in arrangement proved she did casual. And she expected honesty from her lover. They had something in common on both counts.

He watched her walk towards a group who were preparing to leave and smiled to himself. The upcoming wedding weekend was looking better and better.

Emma gulped in a calming breath, drew herself tall, and walked unsteadily towards her table, trying not to remember she'd just kissed Jake Carmody senseless. Correction: *she* was the one who was senseless. The dinner left-overs had been cleared away. Only a rumpled and food stained red tablecloth remained. And a few curious faces were aimed her way.

'Emma…' Stella trailed off, her gaze sliding over Emma's shoulder.

The back of Emma's neck warmed. Her cheeks scorched. 'Um…sorry.' Was it possible to speak more than one word at a time? She waved a hand in front of her face. 'Needed some air.'

'We were starting to wonder whether you two had slipped away without—'

'Jake and I were just catching up.' She collected her purse. 'Mum, are you ready to leave? I've got some work to do before I go to bed.' She didn't wait for an answer, moving around the table saying her goodnights.

'Can I get a lift with you?' Stella reached for her own bag. 'Ryan's taking his parents home, and I want a couple of early nights this week.'

'Sure.' Emma steered clear of Jake, muttering a quick goodnight without looking at him, and from a safe distance on the other side of the table, then headed for the stairs.

'You okay, Em?' Stella asked beside her as they drove home. 'You're awfully quiet.'

'Wayne came into the restaurant while we were there,' she said, her voice tightening. 'With his fiancée.'

'Oh. Oh, Em. I'm sorry. You guys split up—what?—only a month ago?'

'What did you expect?' her mother piped up from the back seat. 'If you mixed with the right people like your sister, instead of hiding away in that studio night after night, y—'

'I'm not hiding.' Emma sighed inwardly. Stella had nursed their mother, then fallen in love with a wealthy man; in Bernice Byrne's eyes her younger daughter could do no wrong. 'I enjoy what I do, Mum.'

'Like you enjoyed cleaning other people's toilets and

stocking supermarket shelves after school too, I remember. Just another excuse not to meet people.'

Emma pressed her lips together to stop the angry words from rushing out. *Yeah, Mum? Where would we be if I hadn't? In a rented bedsit on the wrong side of town. Not in Gran's home, that's for sure.*

'Mum, that's not fair.' Stella spoke sharply.

'It's not, Stella. But then, life's not always fair—right, Mum?' Emma glanced at her mother in the rearview mirror. 'And sometimes it makes us hurt and lash out and say things we shouldn't. So I forgive you. You're not sorry about Wayne, Stella, and neither am I. And I don't want to talk about it. *Him.*'

'No, you'd rather kiss that good-for-nothing Jake Carmody behind the palms like some floozie,' her mother muttered.

Emma jolted, her whole body burning with the memory. And her mother, of all people, had obviously seen the entire catastrophe. Something close to rebellion simmered inside her and made her say, 'Jake's hardly a good-for-nothing, Mum—he has a well-established practice in business law.' She couldn't help feeling a sense of indignation on his behalf.

The strip club aside, she knew enough about Jake to know he'd worked hard all those years ago, taking jobs where he could get them to pay his way through uni.

Whereas Ryan came from old money. He'd graduated in the sciences and held a PhD in Microbiology—all expenses paid by Daddy. Then he'd volunteered his skills in Africa for a couple of years before hooking up again with Stella.

From the corner of her eye she saw Stella shift in her seat and turn to look at her. Suddenly uncomfortable, Emma lifted a shoulder. 'What?'

'Jake *kissed* you?' she said slowly. 'Like a proper kiss?'

'Not exactly.' Emma couldn't resist a quick glance at her mum in the mirror again. 'Mum got it right. It was more like…I kissed him.' As she relived that moment something like exhilaration shot through her bloodstream. 'What about it?'

'Ooh, that's so…hmm… You and Jake?'

Emma heard the smile in her sister's voice, could almost hear her mind ticking over.

'Wouldn't it be cool if—?'

'*Not* me and Jake. You know him. Every red-blooded female in Sydney knows him. Didn't mean anything.'

'But—'

'No buts.'

'Okay. *But*… The wedding will give you two time to catch up. You liked him well enough when we were younger, I remember.'

'Yeah—in a galaxy far, far away.'

'Not that far, Em. He lives in Bondi now. Only an hour's stroll along the coast…if you feel inclined.'

'I don't. I won't.'

But she couldn't blot him from her mind when she crawled into bed that night. She *had* been looking forward to seeing Jake again, even if it was only to assure herself she was well and truly over him.

But she didn't want to catch up with a seedy strip club owner who used women for his own purposes—both for his personal satisfaction and his burgeoning bank account.

But, oh, that moment of insanity…his lips on hers, his hands tugging her against the heat of his hard, muscled body…

And it *was* insanity. She stared up at the music room's low stained ceiling and tried not to hear the thick elevated thud of her heartbeat in her ears. She could have kept it simple. A friendly few days in the company of a good-looking guy. But she'd kissed him like one of his Brandies or Candies…and she'd changed everything.

CHAPTER FOUR

STIFLING a yawn, Emma glanced at her watch and wondered if Stella's hen's party would ever end. Twelve-thirty. The male stripper had done his thing and left to raucous feminine laughter and a wildly improper proposition or two over half an hour ago. The girls were now sitting around Emma's table drinking what remained of a bottle of vodka.

Emma had sat on one glass of wine the entire evening. She needed a clear head. She still had half a dozen orders to fill when the others left.

Emma glanced at the bleary-eyed girls in various stages of intoxication as Joni poured the remains of the vodka into her glass and laid the bottle on its side on the table. 'Don't any of you girls have to work in the morning?' she asked.

'It's Friday tomorrow,' Joni said, spinning the bottle lazily between two fingers. 'Nothing gets done on a Friday anyway.'

'Well, I don't want to be a party pooper but I've got work to finish tonight.'

Karina pointed at her. 'You need to get a life, Emma Dilemma.' She downed her drink, slapped her glass on the table and slurred, 'Seriously. Your hormones must be shrivelling up with neglect. When was the last time you got laid?'

'Kar, give it a rest.' Stella shot Emma a concerned look. 'She broke up with her boyfriend a few weeks ago.'

Karina squinted at Emma through glazed green eyes. 'You had a *boyfriend*?'

Emma could see it in Karina's eyes—*How did you find the time?*—and her whole body tightened. 'He wasn't a boyfriend as such…' She picked up her glass, touched the rim against her lips. 'He was convenient. More like a bed buddy.' Even if Wayne *had* seen their relationship that way, in Emma's book bed buddies didn't cheat. When the gaggle of giggles subsided she angled her glass in Karina's direction. 'You'd be familiar with the concept of bed buddies.'

'Totally.' Karina grinned. 'Way to go, Em,' she enthused, then raised a hand. 'Okay, enough of the true confessions. We're hungry, aren't we, girls? And since you're the only sober one here, Emma Dilemma, how about being a good little bridesmaid and fetching us a burger from that shop down the road?'

'And fries,' Joni added, stuffing another chocolate in her mouth.

'I'll go to the drive-through. It's closer.'

Karina shook her head. 'Nuh-uh. We want real hamburgers with proper meat—not that cardboard stuff.'

'Yeah,' Joni agreed. 'With lashings of bacon.'

Stella leaned to the side and massaged Emma's neck a moment. 'Come on, Em. I *looove* you, sis,' she cajoled in a boozy voice, then pulled her purse from her bag. 'My treat.'

Emma pushed up. Anything for peace. 'Okay. Providing you take your orders and eat them somewhere else. I've got to work.'

'You're a good sport, Em.' Karina stood, slung an arm around Emma's neck. She patted Emma's backside, then grinned hugely. 'Off you go, now.'

* * *

'Told you they'd still be awake,' Ryan said as the limo pulled into the Byrnes' driveway.

They'd dropped off the rest of the guys from the bucks' night, but Ry had got it into his head to kiss Stella goodnight before going home, and Jake—well, he was along for the ride. It was his responsibility to ensure nothing happened to Ryan before the big day. It had nothing to do with Emma living here too.

'Not sure they'll appreciate us gatecrashing their evening.' With a few beers under his belt, Jake stretched his long legs out in front of him. He'd assured Stella he'd look out for Ryan, and he'd done a pretty good job. He glanced at the slightly worse-for-wear groom-to-be. Mostly. Then he looked down to the well-lit studio. 'What do you suppose the girls get up to on a hens' night?'

'We're about to find out.' Ryan was already fumbling with the door.

'Steady, mate. I promised Stella I'd get you home in one piece.'

'Whoa…' Ryan murmured as the limo's lights swept an arc across the driveway, whitewashing the unexpected view of a female figure half-in, half-out of a car. 'Nice arse.'

Jake blinked at the flash of leggings-clad backside poking out of the open door, then took his time to admire the slender thighs and shapely calves rising from a pair of silver stilettos. A spark of interest danced along his veins. 'Careful,' he murmured with a grin. 'You're practically a married man.'

'Doesn't mean I'm dead.'

But Jake's attention had focused on what looked like a neon sticker in the shape of a hand on the girl's backside. 'What *is* that?' He squinted. The words *Pat Me* glittered in gold. 'Don't mind if I do,' he murmured, still grinning. His grin faded. 'Isn't that Emma's car?'

'Reckon you're right.' Both men looked at each other. *'Emma?'*

They turned back to see her unfurling from the car's depths. Dropping a loose soda can into the carton on her hip, she righted herself only to freeze in the headlights like a stunned, lanky-legged gazelle.

Incredulous, Jake felt his whole body tense as he took in the view. *Hot.* Over the leggings she wore a slinky white sleeveless top with a scooped neckline, blanched in the glare and highlighting enough curves to start her own Grand Prix.

'Eyes off, buddy.' He cleared his suddenly dry throat. 'She's about to become your sister-in-law.'

But Jake wasn't honour-bound by any such restriction. Eyes still feasting on the mouthwatering sight, he unfolded himself and climbed out, leaning an elbow on the open door. Cool air hit him. He could smell burgers.

'Emma. Wow.'

He gave himself a mental kick up the backside. *Well said.* Spoken like a freaking teenager. Where the hell were his sophisticated, urbane conversational skills? But his brain didn't seem to be functioning because all his blood had drained below his belt.

She seemed to come out of her daze, eyes widening as they met his. 'You're not supposed to be here,' she said, tight-lipped, as she turned and headed for the door at a rate of knots.

'Careful…' he called. Too late—he was already moving forward as he saw her stiletto bend and her ankle crumple. He heard her swear before she landed on that watch-worthy rear end in front of him, the carton she'd been carrying landing beside her.

Ryan rescued the carton with a muffled, 'I'll get Stella,' and made his escape as Jake squatted beside her. 'Emma?' He reached for her elbows. 'Are you okay?'

Emma groaned, but not nearly as much from the pain shooting up her calf as from her spectacular fall from grace in front of *this* man. She felt Jake's hands on her, his warm breath washing over her face, and closed her eyes. 'Just let me die now.'

She heard that rich caramel chuckle of his. He had both her shoes off before she could stop him. Gentle fingers probed her ankle, and a voice laced with calm concern and a hint of amusement said, 'So this is what you girls get up to on hen nights. Ry and I were wondering.'

She started to shuffle away from him but felt her leggings snag on the rough cement. She heard a strange sound, like Velcro parting, and stopped abruptly. 'I'm okay,' she said, gritting her teeth. Or she would be if she didn't die of embarrassment first. 'Now go away.'

He moved around behind her, slid his hands beneath her arms and hauled her upright so that his body was in intimate contact with her back. His big, hot *masculine* body. Her practically naked back. And nothing but thin torn jersey between her bare bottom and his...pelvis. Liquid heat spurted into her cheeks, along her limbs and everywhere their bodies touched.

'I told you I'm fine.' She tried to shrug away from the intimate contact but he didn't budge.

'Test your weight on it,' he ordered.

Her ankle tweaked when she set it on the ground but she stifled a wince and said, 'See? Fine.'

'Yeah, I can see.'

Ryan and the girls spilled out of the studio just as Jake swept her up into his arms. In an automatic reaction she clutched at his shoulders, and for an instant of lunacy she wallowed in the strength and heat surrounding her.

Being held against Jake's chest and carried inside was like being lifted into the clouds. She gazed up at his square shadow-stubbled chin. And just above that were…those lips.

Instant tension gripped her insides and refused to let go. Had she so quickly forgotten she'd kissed those lips? And *how?* That she'd flung herself at this man in an instant of heightened emotion was going to have to live with the re-minder for the rest of her life? Or until after the wedding at least.

'It's going to be okay, Stella, don't worry,' she told her sister as Jake set her on the saggy old couch. Right now she was more concerned with that ripping sound she'd heard. 'Pass me that sarong on the armchair, will you?'

'Are you chilled?' Stella said, her voice anxious. 'Do you want a blanket or something?'

'No—and stop hovering.'

Stella pulled the sarong off the chair. 'I'm not hover-ing.'

'Are too.' She grabbed the proffered garment. 'Thank you.'

'Um… Before I go, I should tell you that Karina…um…' She exchanged a look with Jake, who shook his head.

Emma darted a glance between the two of them. 'What?'

Stella let out a strangled sound behind her hand. 'Never mind.'

Squatting in front of Emma, Jake prodded her ankle and began issuing orders. 'Get rid of the girls, Stella. And then you might like to kiss your fiancé goodnight and send him on his way.'

Hearing their cue to leave in that no-nonsense masculine tone, the girls scuttled out with muffled giggles.

Panic rose up Emma's throat. 'No, stay, Stell. Let Jake go.' She glared at him, winding the sarong about her torso as high as possible under her arms. 'I bet he has a million things to do.'

He met Emma's eyes full-on for a few seconds, then studied her foot again. 'Some ice would be good here, Stella, before you go.'

Seconds later Stella produced a pack of frozen peas from Emma's fridge, handed it to Jake. 'I feel responsible...'

'Don't,' Emma said, tight-lipped. 'If these guys hadn't turned up everything would've been all right.'

'So this guy'll take care of it.' Easing the improvised cold pack around Emma's ankle, Jake waved her sister off. 'You have guests to see off and a fiancé to farewell. You've called the girls a taxi, right?'

Stella nodded.

'Okay, go to bed.'

'If you're sure...' Stella's eyes flicked between the two of them.

Emma couldn't decide whether there was a glint of something playful in her sister's baby blue eyes, but her voice was concerned enough when she said, 'Phone up to the house if you need anything, Em.'

Then she disappeared outside with the rest of the gang, leaving Emma alone with Jake. The voices faded and the bustling atmosphere disappeared, leaving a tension-fraught anticipation in the gaping stillness. So still that Emma could hear the nearby surf pounding the beach. The sound of her heart beating at a million miles an hour. Jake had to be able to hear it as well. Fantastic. She groaned inwardly. 'But you have to go too,' she told him. 'The limo...'

'I can call him back. He's booked and paid for till 3:00 a.m.' His voice lowered a notch. 'Unless you want me to stay longer?'

His head was bent over her foot so she couldn't see his eyes. Just the top of his glossy dark head and those impressive shoulders making the fabric of his sexy black shirt strain at the seams. Before she could tell him no, not on his life, he straightened.

'It doesn't seem to be swollen. You sure that's the only casualty?'

'Yes.' In his line of work he might see more than his fair quota of bare backsides, but he wasn't going to see hers. She squeezed her still smarting butt and trembling thighs tighter together. 'I can take care of myself.'

'It's not your cute *derrière* I'm interested in right now, Emma,' he said, and she wondered if she'd voiced her thoughts. *And what did he mean 'right now'?*

Her cheeks flamed and she pushed the frozen pack of peas away. 'I can walk.' Holding the edges of the sarong together, she rose, ignoring the glint of pain in her ankle, and took three tentative steps. 'See? Now I want to go to bed. I appreciate your concern, but I'd like it if you'd leave.'

He ignored her. 'You should rest it. You need to be fit for Saturday.' He picked her up again and moved swiftly across the room and past the privacy curtain. He set her on her bed, laid the peas against her ankle again, then placed his hands on either side of her lower legs. Looked into her eyes. 'And, remember, as best man I've got the first dance with you.'

He'd come to her rescue and allowed her to keep her dignity. And now he sounded so genuinely caring that a wry half-smile tugged at her mouth.

'With you to remind me I'm not likely to forget.' She had to admit it felt good to be pampered for once in her life, to have someone care enough to look out for her and not even remotely laugh at her embarrassment. She relaxed a little. 'Thank you. I feel like a kid again. All I need is the warm milk and honey.'

'Warm milk and honey?'

'Mum's panacea for everything. Rather, it used to be.' *Twenty years ago.*

Jake knew Emma had always been a keep-to-yourself kind of girl, whereas outgoing, fun-loving Stella had made friends easily. He knew, too, how Emma had changed when her father had died.

Leaning in, he watched her gorgeous eyes widen, smelled her soft feminine scent. 'No milk and honey, but this—' he touched his lips chastely to her forehead '—might help.'

He heard the barely-there hitch in her breath and drew back. His gaze dropped to her mouth and lingered. Unglossed but luscious. So tempting to lean down and... He felt his blood pressure spike. His good deed damn well wasn't helping *him*.

Don't. Her lips moved but no sound came out.

'Why not?' he murmured. 'You kissed me the other night and I can't return the favour?'

'That was...different.' Her voice was breathless and he got the impression she'd have pressed her rigid spine through the wall if she could.

'Yeah,' he said, recalling the firestorm which had engulfed them both for one unguarded moment. 'It was.'

'It was impulsive and selfish and I used you.'

Straightening up, he looked at her eyes, almost violet in the dim light from the single naked globe above the bed. 'I didn't mind. And, if we're being honest here, you didn't mind either.' He saw colour bleed into her cheeks and patted her leg. 'Take it from me, Surfer Boy wasn't right for you.'

'And you'd know that how…?' She stared at him out of soulful eyes. 'I sure as heck don't know Jake Carmody. You work in the sex industry.' Her voice rose with disapproval. 'You *own* that…that place. So you… It follows naturally that you're not ashamed to use and exploit women—often women with no other choices—to make money. And it's just *wrong*,' she went on. 'Does—?'

'I didn't buy the strip club. I inherited the place when Earl died.'

She frowned. 'Earl? Who's Earl?'

'My father.'

'Oh…' A slow exhalation of breath accompanied the word. She curled her fingers beneath her chin. 'So…your dad owned it.'

'Not "dad." That word implies some sort of familial bond and there wasn't any.' He refused to allow regret to intrude on his life. He didn't need family. He didn't need anyone. 'And before you say I should shut it down and walk away and there'd be one less sleazy club in King's Cross I have the staff to consider. I've found a potential buyer but we're negotiating; I want to ensure a fair deal for everyone.'

'Oh. Yes. Of course. I…' She trailed off, and maybe her eyes softened, but he couldn't be sure because for once in his life he wasn't really seeing the woman in front of him.

He scratched the niggling sensation at the back of his neck that he'd learned long ago to recognise as insecurity. He hadn't felt it in years. He made his own rules, controlled his circumstances, his life. Himself. Always.

Not this time.

He clenched his jaw against the feeling that the rules

had suddenly changed and his life was veering off course. And he might have left then but for Emma's soft voice.

'Your mother…is she…?'

'She lives in South America. She doesn't keep in touch.' After nearly two decades, her abandonment still had the power to slice at his heart. He'd always made a point of not getting personally involved in other people's lives because it would involve opening up his own.

'Do you have any siblings to help? Extended family?'

'No.'

'That must be tough for you, handling everything on your own.'

He shrugged dismissively. 'I'm a tough guy.' It was baggage he'd left behind years ago and he wasn't going there. Not for anyone.

She nodded slowly and smoothed the sarong over her legs. 'Look, I'm sorry if I sounded over the top, it's just that I have very firm thoughts about men who use women for their own purposes.'

He knew she was thinking of Surfer Boy. 'Acknowledged and understood.'

'Still, I am sorry about your dad…I can see it hurt you. If you wa—'

'Okay. Let's leave it at that.'

'So…um… How did it go with the guys' night?' She didn't seem in such a hurry to kick him out now, and he didn't know whether that was a good thing or not.

'Ry may need me to remind him tomorrow that he had a good time.'

'Did it include a visit to King's Cross by any chance?'

'Every bucks' night worth its mettle has to include a stop somewhere in King's Cross.' Unfortunately. He must be the only straight guy in Sydney who didn't find striptease a turn-on.

'Well, we girls enjoyed our own private stripper right here.' With a theatrical flick of her hair she drew her knees up to her chest, tucking the edges of the sarong beneath her feet.

'And how did that go?'

'Man, he was *hot*.' The instant the words were out her hands rushed to her cheeks. 'I've never seen a guy strip… well, not that way.' She sucked in her lips. Her cheeks were pink beneath her hands.

'Am I detecting a double standard here?' He couldn't resist teasing her. 'Okay for the girls to look but not the guys?'

'Oops!' Her pearl-tipped nails moved to her lips. 'Can I say I didn't look?'

'Afraid not.' He leaned closer. 'I have to tell you, you looked hot too, last night, in that sexy little number.'

Her smile, when it appeared, was a delight to behold. 'It *was* fun dressing up and feeling attractive for a change.'

'You should try it more often.'

'Try what?' Her smile disappeared. Her hands fell away from her face. A shadow flickered in her eyes—a blue moon sinking into an inky sea—as she crossed her arms and hugged her shoulders. 'Looking attractive? Gee, thanks heaps.'

'Fun, Emma. Just try having some fun.' He was barely aware that his hands had somehow moved towards her thighs, so close he could feel the heat from her body, and barely caught himself in time.

He jerked back and away. Pushed to his feet. If he stayed he was just un-sober enough to show her something about having fun…and he didn't want to think about the consequences if he did.

Not tonight.

'Since you don't seem to need me for anything, I'm

going to see if I can catch up with Ry after all. I haven't heard the limo leave yet.' He didn't know what demon prompted him to add, 'The night's still young. Might as well enjoy my evening off...'

He winked—he *never* winked—leaving Emma staring wide-eyed at him as he lifted a hand, then turned and walked away. ''Night.'

He let himself out and headed towards the limo at the top of the drive. He needed the brisk evening air to cool his groin. So much for keeping his past where it belonged. He'd moved on, made something of himself. Until Earl had died and all the old bad had rushed back.

He didn't need Emma messing with his head, trying to make everything all right. Maybe he should just keep things as they were. Acquaintances. Casual friends.

He came to an abrupt halt. Except...now he'd tasted her on his lips, enjoyed the slippery slide of her lithe womanly body against his. Seen and felt her respond as a woman did to a man she fancied...

Friends, *hell*. It was too late for that.

CHAPTER FIVE

'DID you ever see such a view?' Emma leaned over the balcony outside the room she was sharing with Stella for the night. 'You sure know how to pick a wedding venue. It's like some god has spread a knobbly green carpet over the Grand Canyon, then sprayed it with a fine indigo mist.'

'It helps that one of Ryan's uncles owns the place,' her sister said cheerily behind her.

Nestled on the edge of the escarpment at Echo Point, in the famous Blue Mountains west of Sydney, the exclusive boutique hotel was pure luxury. The majestic view of Jamieson Valley stretched out below them, equally breathtaking. As evening approached, soft golden light coloured the sky. Inky pools were swallowing up the valley floor, and the sun's last rays hammered the streaks of exposed rock with vermilion, carving deep purple shadows between.

Stella joined Emma at the balcony's wooden rail. 'The guys won't be seeing anything like this where they are.'

'No,' Emma murmured, drawing her tracksuit jacket closer as the air chilled. The guys and Ryan's parents were spending the night at a cosy little bed and breakfast in Katoomba, a two-minute drive away. 'But I'm sure they'll find something to entertain them.' Her tone was more caustic than she'd intended.

She was still brooding over the way Jake had swaggered out of the studio last night. She couldn't stop wondering what he'd got up to afterwards. Her fingers tightened on the cool wood. He'd *winked* at her. She knew exactly what he'd got up to.

And why on earth was she tying herself up in knots over it? It was precisely the kind of behaviour that reminded her that he had been, and obviously still was, a chick magnet. And why he was such a knee-buckling, sigh-worthy *experienced* kisser...

'So, Stella.' Forcing him from her thoughts, she linked arms with her sister and guided her back to the little glass table. 'Ryan can't wait for tomorrow. He's going to make a wonderful husband, and you're going to have lots of babies and live happily ever after, the way you always dreamed.'

She picked up their Cosmopolitan cocktails and offered a toast. 'To your last night as a single woman.'

As she sipped, Emma's gaze drifted inside, through the floor-to ceiling glass doors, to the two four-poster double beds with their embroidered snowy white covers and mountains of soft lace pillows.

Ryan's parents had footed the bill for the entire wedding and the wedding party's accommodation here tomorrow night. Ryan was their only child, and for them this extravagance was a drop in the ocean.

'You're marrying money, Stell. We might have been rich too if Dad hadn't made those bad investments just before he died.'

Stella nodded. 'Yeah, Mum never got over losing her inheritance that way.'

'She never got over *Dad*.' Even now their mother was in her own beautifully appointed room down the hall, alone. 'She let him destroy her,' Emma went on. 'Even beyond the grave she's still letting him colour her life grey.'

Emma reminded herself that she wanted no part of that pain. Wayne had temporarily clouded her vision with his good looks and smooth-talking charm, but now she saw everything through the crystal-clear lens of experience. No man would ever have that power over her again.

Stella set her glass down and touched Emma's hand. 'You've kept us together all these years with a roof over our heads and I want to thank you—'

'It was my responsibility as the elder sister to keep us safely off the streets.' She shook her head. 'You looked out for Mum—I had it easy compared to you. But I wanted a career too. All you ever wanted was to find the right man and get married.'

'Yeah.' Stella sighed. Then she smiled, her face aglow with a bride's radiance. 'But now I'm marrying Ryan I'll be in a position to help out. I've already decided—'

'Stella—'

'He and I have discussed it.'

'For Mum, then. Not for me.'

Stella met her eyes. 'You don't want to give away a bit of that independence and find someone to love and share your life with some day?'

'Love? No.' Because Stella's question had unsettled her, she cupped her suddenly cold hands beneath her armpits. 'I prefer lust. Less complicated.'

'You're hurting after what happened with Wayne,' her sister said gently, 'and that's okay because—'

'I told you last night. It was lust, not love.'

'Bed buddies?' Stella murmured, then shook her head. 'I don't believe you for one minute, Em. And I don't care what you say. You *do* want love somewhere down the track when you're over the love rat. I remember when we were kids and used to talk about the men we were going to marry. Your man had to own a house by the sea, he had to love animals, 'cos Mum refused to let us have pets and he had to own a cupcake shop.'

Emma smiled at her childish fantasies. 'What about your ivory castle?'

'We're staying in one in France.' Stella hugged her drink close to her chest. 'Not ivory, but a real medieval castle with its own resident ghost.'

Emma heard the signal for an incoming text and dug her phone out of her pocket to read the screen.

'How's the view where U R? J'

She frowned as a butterfly did a single loop in her stomach. She texted back: *'Glorious.'*

Setting the phone on the table, she reached for her drink and considered switching the thing off. She needed a clear head for tomorrow, and interacting with Jake beforehand—in any way, shape or form—wouldn't do her any favours.

A moment later another text appeared. *'Did U bring work?'*

She sipped her drink and looked at her phone a moment before answering: *'Yes.'*

Seemed he wasn't put off by her one-word texts, because the next one appeared a moment later.

'Not allowed. This weekend is about having fun.'

Fun and Jake…? A shiver tingled down her spine. He was a man who definitely knew how to have fun. She texted back: *'Is she a blonde?'*

'I have a certain brunette in mind. Meet me downstairs 4 a drink.'

The shiver spread to her limbs. *'Spending evening with sister. Remember her? 2moro's bride.'* She switched her phone off, shoved it back in her pocket.

'Who are you texting?'

'Jake.' She threw Stella an accusatory glance.

'Anything wrong?'

'He asked me to meet him for a drink.' She felt Stella's gaze and looked away, out over the darkening valley and the gold-rimmed purple clouds in the distance.

'Something you're not telling me, here?' Stella asked behind her.

'No.' She had the niggling feeling she was being set up by her sister.

'Jake likes women, but he's a good guy. Nothing like the love rat. He's not into commitment right now and, as you've clearly pointed out, neither are you…so are you going?'

'Of course not.' She turned around and met her sister's scrutiny full-on. Stella had a half-smile on her lips, as if she didn't quite believe her. Emma glared back. 'This is our last night together—you and me.' And she wanted to place some orders and research some alternative suppliers on her laptop at some stage.

'Well, I'm going to have a long soak in that to-die-for spa tub.' Stella rose, collected their glasses and walked towards the door. 'I won't miss you for an hour or so if you want to change your mind.'

'Nope.' Emma followed her in. 'I've got my music to keep me company.' So much for placing orders. Right now she couldn't remember a single item she needed, and music seemed a more soothing option.

The hotel's phone rang as Emma closed the balcony's glass doors and Stella stretched out on her bed to pick up. 'This is the bride's room,' she announced, with a bounce in her voice. 'You're speaking to the bride, who's just about to enjoy her own candlelit spa bath.' She grinned over at Emma, then rolled onto her back, listening to whoever was on the other end of the phone. 'Uh-huh. In the lobby. Ten minutes. Okay.'

Emma's pulse blipped. She sat on her own bed and unravelled her earphones. 'No.'

'But it's Ryan.' She hugged the phone to her chest. 'The guys had Chinese take-out and he has a fortune cookie for me—isn't that sweet of him?'

'It's not sweet, Stell, it's subterfuge.' Emma lay back and closed her eyes. 'Jake put him up to this, and I'll bet you your fortune cookie that it's Jake, not Ryan, down there.'

'Please, Em. You have to go to make sure. I can't see him now before the ceremony. It's bad luck.'

'And Ryan would *know* that.'

'Pleeease?'

'Fine,' she huffed, and sat up, clipping her iPod to her jacket.

'She said fine,' Stella told her caller, and hung up then grinned. 'Thanks, bridesmaid.'

Emma grabbed an elastic band from the nightstand and dragged her hair back into a tight ponytail. 'Only for you, and only because it's your wedding day tomorrow. Then I'm going for a run.'

'Take your time,' she heard Stella call as Emma let herself out of the room and headed for the stairs.

Jake disconnected with a satisfied grin. 'You don't need me for a while, do you, Ry? She said yes.'

Ryan was stretched out on the couch, checking out their honeymoon destination on his tablet PC but he glanced up as Jake pulled on a clean T-shirt. 'You're a sneaky devil.'

'Make that *smart* and sneaky.' He stuffed his wallet in his jeans. 'And your fiancée's as much to blame as me.'

'Then she's a sneaky devil too.' He tapped the screen. 'I don't know why I'm marrying her.'

Jake grinned and waggled his brows. 'Having second thoughts? It's not too late to back out, you know.'

'Ah, but the reception's paid for. Why waste good grog?'

'There's that.' His humour fading, Jake sat down on the end of the couch and studied his best mate. 'Seriously, Ry. Why the big commitment?'

Ry looked up, and Jake saw the furrows of concentration in his mate's brow smooth out and the corners of his mouth tip up. 'When you meet the woman you want to spend the rest of your life with you'll know why.'

'But *married?*' Jake mentally shuddered at the word. 'Why would you want to spend your life with one woman? Man wasn't meant to be monogamous.'

'Says who?'

'I read it in an article. Somewhere. A reputed scientific journal, if I remember right.'

'Okay, well, *this* man's monogamous.' Ry resumed tapping his screen.

'Maybe *now*,' Jake said. 'I remember when you and those twins—'

'Past history. I was at uni and Stell and I weren't seeing each other then.'

'But how do you *know* she's the one?'

Ry's finger paused. 'When I saw my children in her eyes I knew.'

Jake stared at the guy he'd thought he knew. 'Crikey, mate—break out the violins.'

Ry squinted at something on the screen, slid a finger over its surface. 'Just because you're not into the matrimonial thing doesn't mean others aren't.'

'Fair dinkum—*your children in her eyes?*'

Ry looked up, a lopsided grin on his face. 'Yeah. We want kids. A whole bunch of 'em.' His expression sobered. 'I guess the bottom line is I love Stella. For better or worse. I don't want to imagine my life without her.'

Jake didn't want to imagine a life without women either. But *one* woman for ever? Absolutely for worse. But a curious sensation gripped his chest, as if somehow Ryan had betrayed their friendship and left him standing on the outside looking in.

'So, are you going to tell me why you're playing sneaky devil?' Ry asked, his eyes focused on the screen once more.

Jake rose to hunt up the keycard for the room. 'Because the girl needs a kick up that seriously sexy backside—'

'Which I didn't notice, remember?'

'Yeah, I remember.' Something that might feel like possessiveness—if he were the type—clawed at the back of his neck. He didn't care for the sensation and rubbed it away, swiping the keycard from the bottom of his bed. 'She needs to come out of that shell she's been living in for the past however many years. There's more to life than work.'

Ry looked up, expression thoughtful. 'And you're going to be the one to show her? Careful. That's Emma you're talking about—she's not just any woman. And she's my future sister-in-law.'

'I'm aware of that,' he muttered, fighting the scowl that came from out of nowhere to lurk just beneath the surface of his skin. He planted a grin on his face and grabbed his jacket. 'Trust me.'

The moment the door shut behind him his smile dropped away, his own words echoing in his ears. Problem was, could he trust *himself*? But from the moment Emma Byrne had walked into the club in that sexy red coat, those blue eyes smoking and sparking with every challenge known to man, he'd not been able to think past getting her naked. He'd never intended acting on it—he liked his women without prickles, after all—but then there'd been that kiss at the restaurant... Sparks that hot demanded at least some sort of exploration.

He decided to walk the short distance to sample autumn's crisp mountain air. Cold. Bracing. Invigorating. Mind-numbing. Just what he needed. His breath puffed in front of him as he strode along Katoomba Street towards the girls' hotel.

After tomorrow it would never be the same between him and Ry again. He passed a warmly lit café, packed with Friday-evening diners, and hunched deeper into the warmth of his jacket. It reminded him that back in that room with Ry he'd felt…shut out. As if Ry was about to join a club Jake wasn't eligible for. Would never be eligible for.

Clenching his teeth against the chill, he crunched through a pile of autumn leaves, sending them scattering and twirling along the pavement in noisy abandon. He didn't want to join the matrimonial club.

Shut out.

His mother had shut him out of her life too. 'You look just like your father,' she'd accused her five-year-old son. Jake was reminded of that every time he looked in a mirror. She'd left her cheating husband and young look-alike child for a new life and a new marriage. Rejected him— her own flesh and blood.

And, yeah, he might be his father's spitting image— but had he inherited Earl's genes? He'd learned a lot about women in his formative years. After all, how many kids got to grow up in the back room of a strip club? With the smell of cheap perfume and sex in their cramped living arrangements. Falling asleep to carnal sounds through his tiny bedroom's paper-thin walls.

As a teenager blocking out those same sounds while trying to finish homework, because he'd known that to escape the place, to take control of his life and become a better man than his father, he needed to study.

Jake knew how to have a good time. A good time involved no strings, no stress. No emotion. Was he like his father in more ways than looks? He clenched his jaw as he turned a corner and the hotel came into view. *Shoot me now.*

He picked up his pace. Earl had used women, whereas Jake respected his partners. The women he associated with were professional career types more often than not—unlike Earl's. They were confident, intelligent and attractive, and they understood where he was coming from. He made it clear up front that he wasn't into any long-term commitment deals and they didn't expect more than he wanted to give.

It was honest, at least.

Emma was braced to see Jake, not Ryan, waiting in the lobby. So she took the three flights of stairs rather than the elevator. Deliberately slowly. Admiring the delicate crystal lighting along the hallway, the local landscape paintings on the walls as she reached the top of the ground floor. The thick black carpet emblazoned with the hotel's gold crest.

But seeing Jake standing at the base of the sweeping staircase as she descended, one bronzed hand on the newel post, dark hair gleaming beneath the magnificent black chandelier, with his jacket slung over his shoulder like some sort of designer-jeans-clad Rhett Butler...

Her hand was gliding along the silky wooden banister or her legs might have given out. She might even have sighed like Scarlett; she couldn't be sure. She was too busy shoring up her defences against those dark eyes and the heart-winning smile. Because she knew in that instant that this man could be the one with the power to undo her.

Slowing halfway down, she leaned a hip against the staircase, sucked in a badly needed breath. *Stay cool,* she told herself. *Cool and aloof and annoyed.* He thought he'd tricked her into coming but she knew better. Didn't she? She frowned to herself. She was here, after all.

Because Stella had asked her.

Right. Straightening, she resumed her descent, concentrating on not tripping over her feet, her eyes drawn to him no matter how hard she tried to look away. That sinner's smile and those darker-than-sin eyes…

'Are you feeling all right?' he asked when she reached the bottom step.

She looked at him warily. 'Why wouldn't I?'

'You looked as if you were swaying there for a second or two. I thought you were going to swoon, and then I'd have been forced to play the hero again.'

'I did not sway. Or swoon. And you are *not* my hero. I'm guessing there are no fortune cookies either.'

He grinned. 'You're guessing wrong.' He took her elbow, led her across the glittering marbled foyer. At intervals floor-to-ceiling glass columns illuminated from within threw up a clear white light. He stopped by a little coffee table with two cosy leather armchairs. 'Sit.'

She did, gratefully, sinking into the soft black leather.

He pulled two scraps of paper from his jeans pocket, checked them both, then placed one on her lap.

'This isn't a fortune cookie.'

'I have to admit Ry and I ate them. But we saved you girls the messages.'

She unrolled the little square. '"A caress is better than a career."' Where the heck had he found *that* little gem? 'Says who? *And* it would depend on who's doing the caressing.'

But her traitorous thoughts could imagine Jake's warm, wicked hands wandering over her bare skin… Lost in the fantasy for a pulse-pounding moment, she stared unseeingly at the paper in front of her. *For heaven's sake.*

She forced her head up, regarded him with serene indifference. 'This isn't from a fortune cookie. You made these yourselves.'

He spread his hands on his thighs, all innocence. 'Why would I do that?'

'To get me downstairs, perhaps?'

His smile came out like sunshine on a cold day. 'You have to admit it's inventive.'

'Deceptive, more like.'

'Hey, Ry has to take some of the credit.'

She felt the smile twitch at the corner of her mouth. 'What does Stella's say?'

'"Two souls, one heart." Appropriately romantic, Ry thought.'

And Cool Hand Jake didn't, obviously. 'She'll probably sleep with it under her pillow tonight.' Desperate to distance herself from his enticing woodsy scent and the thought of those coolly efficient hands on her heated body, she pulled her earphones out of her tracksuit pocket. 'Okay, now that's out of the way I'm off for a run.'

'Not so fast.' He reached over, circling her forearm in a loose grip. 'You're going to say you've got soap orders to type up or some such rubbish when you get back. Right?'

Right. If she could only remember what... The heat of his hand seemed to be blocking her ability to process simple thought. 'I—'

'To avoid me.'

She swallowed down a gasp. He was flying too close to the truth, and it threw her for a loop. 'Why would you matter th—?'

'You know it. I know it.' Cutting her off, he leaned forward, his hold tightening a fraction, his eyes boring into hers. 'Admit it.'

'Why?' Little spots of heat were breaking out all over her body.

'I matter to you.' He smiled—grinned, actually—teeth gleaming white in the light. 'How much do I matter, Emma?'

She pushed a hand over the crown of her head, her mind a jumble. 'Stop it. You're confusing me. This is the last evening I'll see my sister before she gets married. I...I'm going to spend the evening with her—a maid of honour thing.'

'Of course. And you can. In a little while.' His thumb abraded the inside of her wrist, sending tiny tingles scuttling up her arm. 'She won't mind,' he continued in that same liquid caramel tone. 'In fact I'm betting she's enjoying her soak in the spa right now.'

'It *was* you on the phone.'

'Guilty.' He grinned again, totally unrepentant. As if he pulled that kind of stunt all the time to bend women to his will. 'She's confiscated your laptop, by the way.'

'What?'

'Your sister agrees with me that you need time out from work.'

She gaped at him, incredulous. 'You two discussed my *needs?*' The image popped into her mind before she could call it back, along with the overly explicit, overly stressed word, and the whole calamity hung thick in the air like a sultry evening.

His eyes turned a warmer shade of dark. 'Not all of them. But we'll get to that. Stella wants you to enjoy her wedding, not be distracted by orders and schedules. She's concerned about you. And frankly—'

'What do you mean, "we'll get to that"? Get to what?'

Her voice rose on a crescendo. A couple of heads turned their way.

'This isn't the place,' he murmured, his voice all the quieter for her raised one.

Changing his grip, he pulled her up before she could mutter any sound of protest. He was so close she could feel the heat emanating from his body, could smell expensive leather jacket and freshly showered male skin.

'The place?' she echoed. 'Place for what?'

He entwined his fingers with hers. 'Why don't we take a walk and find out?'

CHAPTER SIX

Emma blinked up at him through her eyelashes. It took her a scattered moment to realise she was still holding her earphones in her free hand and that her other hand was captured by the biggest, warmest hand it had ever come into contact with. She told herself she didn't want to be holding his hand…but who was she kidding but herself?

'*Run*,' she managed, pulling out of his grasp. 'I was going for a *run*.' And if she was sensible she'd keep running all the way back to Sydney.

'I'll join you.'

She glanced at his leather jacket and casual shoes, deliberately bypassing the interesting bits in between. 'You're hardly dressed for it.'

'I'll try to keep up.' *His* gaze cruised down her body like a slow boat on a meandering river, all the way to her well-worn sneakers. 'What about your ankle?'

'It's fine.' He'd be offering to carry her next, so she conceded defeat. 'Okay, we'll walk.' Stuffing her earphones back in her pocket, she accompanied him outside and onto the street.

The air had a cold bite and an invigorating eucalypt scent that called to her senses, and she breathed deep.

'I saw a little café on the way here,' he suggested.

'I didn't come to the mountains to be shut in a stuffy café with a bunch of city slickers up for the weekend.'

'Of which we're two,' he pointed out.

'I want to see the Three Sisters by night and sample some mountain air. Come on, it's a ten-minute walk to Echo Point.'

He took her hand again. 'What are we waiting for?'

They followed the hotel wall that enclosed the beautiful garden where tomorrow's ceremony would take place until it gave way to bushland fenced off from the road. Beyond, the ground fell away more than two hundred metres to the valley floor. Neither talked, but a feeling of camaraderie settled between them. Both were absorbed in the mutual appreciation of their surroundings.

The minute the famous Three Sisters rock formation came into view Emma came to an awed stop. 'Wow.' She hung back from the main vantage point where a few tourists were milling about, unwilling to share the moment with strangers.

Floodlit, the Sisters gleamed a rich gold against the black velvet backdrop, surrounding trees catching the light and providing a lacy emerald frame. The never-ending sky blazed with stars.

She sighed, drinking in the sight. 'Aren't you glad we didn't go for coffee?'

'That first glimpse always packs a punch, that's for sure.'

His voice rumbled through her body and she realised he'd let go of her hand while she'd been taking in the view and was now standing behind her, his chin on top of her head.

'Did you know the Aboriginal Dreaming story tells us there were three brothers who fell in love with three sisters from another tribe and were forbidden to marry?' She hugged her elbows, and it seemed natural to lean back into Jake's warmth.

In response, a pair of rock-solid arms slid around to the front of her waist. 'Go on. I'm sure there's more.'

'A battle ensued, and when the men tried to capture them, a tribal elder turned the maidens into stone to protect them.'

'And right there,' he drawled lazily, 'you're viewing a lesson to be heeded about the dangers of love and marriage.'

She turned within the circle of his arms. 'The sad thing is the sisters had no say in any of it.'

'But you do,' he murmured against her brow. And bent his head.

Warm breath caressed her skin and her heart began to pound in earnest. He was going to kiss her... And she wasn't in a fit state to be running anywhere.

Her legs trembled and her mind turned to mush as anticipation spun through her and she looked up. His face was so close she could feel the warmth of his skin, could see its evening shadow of stubble. He had the longest, darkest eyelashes she'd ever seen on a man. And his eyes... had she ever seen such eyes? As bottomless as the yawning chasm they'd come to view.

Then a half-moon slid from behind a cloud, bathing his perfect features in silver, as if the gods had hammered him so.

'You can tell me no.' He loosened his hold around her waist slightly. 'Right here in front of the Sisters you can exercise your free will as a modern woman. Push me away if you want. Or you can accept what we've been tiptoeing around for the past few days and kiss me.'

'Tiptoeing?' she whispered. 'I haven't—'

'And it's time it stopped.'

'Kiss you...?' Her words floated into the air on a little white puff as she looked up into his eyes. Dark and deep and direct. Had he mentioned free will? Her will had suddenly gone AWOL; she'd felt it drift out of her and hang somewhere over Jamieson Valley with the evening mist.

His gaze dropped to her mouth. Strong fingers curled around her biceps. 'And this time I'm warning you I'm not letting you go until I'm good and ready.'

The way he said it, all male attitude and arrogance, sent a shiver of excitement along her nerve-endings. Emma heard a whisper of sound issue from her throat an instant before his lips touched hers.

Then she was lost. In his taste: rich and velvety, like the world's finest chocolate. His cool mossy scent mingled with leather. The warmth of his body as he shifted her against him for a closer fit.

She should have stopped it right there, told him no—he'd given her the option. But her response was torn from her like autumn's last leaf in a storm-ravaged forest. Irrational. Irresistible. Irrevocable.

Voices ebbed and flowed in the distance but she barely heard them above the pounding of her pulse, her murmur of approval as she melted against him like butter on a barbecue grill. Her arms slid around his waist to burrow under his jacket, where he was warm and solid through the T-shirt's soft jersey.

Jake felt her resistance soften, her luscious lips grow pliant as she opened for him, giving him full access, and he plunged right in. Dark, decadent delight. Moans and murmurs. Her tongue tangled with his, velvet on satin, and her taste was as sweet as spun sugar.

Dragging her against him, he moved closer, his fingertips tracking down her spine, over the flare of her backside, where he pressed her closer so he could feel her heat.

So she could feel his rapidly growing erection butting against her.

He felt the change instantly—subtle, but sure. A tensing of muscles. A change in her stance. She didn't move away and her lips were still locked with his, but...

Breaking the kiss with a good deal of reluctance, he leaned back to look at her. They were the same age—both twenty-seven—but she looked impossibly young with her hair scraped back from her face, her eyes huge dark pools in the moonlight, her mouth plundered.

He stroked a finger over the groove that had formed between her brows. 'You're thinking too hard.'

'One of us should.' She didn't look away. Nor did the frown smooth out.

'Okay. Talk to me.'

She took a step back. 'This...thing between us is getting way too complicated.'

'Seems pretty straightforward to me. So I'm proposing a deal,' he went on before she could argue, resting his hands on her shoulders. 'This weekend neither of us talks about work.' He touched his forehead to hers. 'We don't *think* about work. We're both between partners, so we'll enjoy the wedding and each other's company...and whatever happens *happens*. No complications. One weekend, Emma.'

'One weekend.' She leaned away, her eyes clouded with conflicting emotions. 'And then what?'

'Put next week out of your mind, it's too far away.'

Come Monday they'd go their separate ways. Back to real life and working ridiculous hours. Emma and the Blue Mountains would be nothing but a warm and pretty memory.

'Think about this instead,' he said, sliding his hands down her upper arms. 'Neither of us wants to be tied down, and we both work our backsides off. We deserve some playtime.'

'*Playtime?*' She stared up at him, her eyes the colour of the mist-swirled mountains behind her. 'No deal. Not with you.'

'Why not? Afraid you might enjoy yourself?'

She rolled her lips together, as if to stop whatever she'd been about to say, then said, 'I just don't want to play with you, that's all.' She turned and began walking back the way they'd come.

'Liar.' Grabbing her arm, he walked around her, blocking her path until they stood face to face. 'Tell me you didn't enjoy that kiss just now.'

She studied him a moment. 'I didn't enjoy that kiss just now.'

He laughed. 'You started it. That night at the restaurant. You blew me away with your enthusiasm and got me seriously thinking about you. And me. I haven't stopped thinking about you and me—together—since.'

'I told you, that kiss was an overreaction to a particular circumstance,' she said primly. 'And what are we—kids? *"You started it"*,' she muttered with a roll of her eyes, but he thought he saw a hint of humour there too.

She looked so delightful he couldn't resist—he planted a firm smacking kiss on those pouted lips then grinned. 'I'd better get you back. Stella'll be starting to think I've kidnapped you.'

Grabbing her hand, he tugged her alongside him along the path towards the hotel. The weekend had barely begun, plenty of time to convince her to change her mind.

'So. Seen any good movies lately?'

She kept up a brisk pace beside him. 'No.'

'Me neither. Stella mentioned you swim every morning, come rain or shine. Is that true?'

'Yes.'

'So…if I were to change my early-morning jog—'

'One weekend.' She jerked to a sudden halt and looked up at him. 'And whatever happens happens?'

A strand of hair had come loose and blew across her eyes. He smoothed it back, tucked it behind her ear. 'We'll take things as they come. It'll be good, I promise.'

Oh, yes, she knew. Emma stared into those beguiling eyes. 'I bet you say that to all the girls.' She couldn't believe she was having this conversation with Jake Carmody.

She resumed walking, hoping she was headed in the right direction. Everything seemed surreal. The moonlight distorting their combined shadows on the path in front of them. The sharp eucalpyt fragrance of the bushland. The way her body was responding to his proximity even now.

His seductive charm really knew no bounds. No wonder women swooned and fell at his feet. She firmed her jaw. Not *this* woman. Still, she didn't have to swoon, exactly…

He was suggesting what amounted to nothing more than a weekend of sex and sin. Heat shimmied down her spine. A weekend on Pleasure Island. She had no doubt Jake could deliver, and couldn't deny the idea called to her on more than one level. But was she game enough? Why not? It wasn't a lifetime commitment, for heaven's sake.

Since her father's death eleven years ago she'd worked her butt off to make things better for them all. Jake had made it clear to her that it was past time she took something for herself. One weekend to be free and irresponsible. And this weekend, with Stella leaving home and the love rat a disappearing blot on her horizon, was it perhaps a good time to start?

They reached the hotel and she hesitated on the shallow steps out front. Her cheeks felt hot and super sensitive, as if a feather might flay away the skin.

She turned to say goodnight and met his gaze. The heat from that kiss still shimmered in his eyes, and it took all her will-power to keep from flinging herself at him and kissing him again.

Deliberately she stepped back, aware she hadn't given him an answer and just as aware they both already knew what her answer would be. She turned towards the building.

A liveried porter swept the wide glass door open with a welcoming smile and warm air swirled out. 'Good evening, madam.'

'Good evening.' She smiled back, wondering if her cheeks and lips were as pink and chapped as they felt. From the safety of distance, she turned to Jake once more. 'Till tomorrow, then.'

'Get a good night's sleep.'

His smile was pure sin. *You'll need it*—no mistaking that message in those hot dark eyes, and her heart turned a high somersault. It continued its gymnastics all the way up the three flights of stairs.

Stella was bundled in a fluffy white hotel robe on the couch, watching a TV cook-off, when she entered.

'Traitor.' But there was no sting in the word as Emma pulled out the fortune cookie note and dropped it on Stella's lap. 'For you.' Because her legs were still wobbly, she flopped down on the couch beside her.

'"Two hearts, one soul." Ooh, I've gone all gooey inside.' Smiling broadly, Stella tucked her legs up beneath her. 'What does yours say?'

She shook her head, that overly warm sensation prickling her skin. 'Never mind.'

Stella stuck out her hand, palm up. 'Come on—give.'

'Oh, for heaven's sake.' Emma dug into her pocket again, then glued her attention to the TV screen, but she wasn't seeing it. 'It's not romantic, like yours. And that's okay because I'm not a romantic like you.' She pressed a fist to her lips to stem the flow.

'"A caress is better than a career." Of course it's romantic, silly. It's telling you to take time out and enjoy… To… *Em.*'

'Where's my computer, by the way? Jake said…never mind.' Emma could feel Stella's gaze on her and jerked herself off the couch without waiting for an answer. 'I'm going to take a bath.'

'Oh. My. Lord.'

'What?' She was in the process of ripping off her tracksuit jacket but stopped at her sister's tone. 'What's wrong?'

Stella was staring at her. And pointing. 'What have you done with my sister?'

'What are you talking about?' She shrugged her shoulders. Ran a hand around her neck. 'What's he done?'

'Ha!' Stella jabbed her finger in the air again. 'I should be asking what *Jake's* done with my sister.'

'No. It's nothing. Don't you say one word to Jake or I'll—'

'*Not* nothing.' Stella craned forward, studying Emma as if she was counting her eyelashes. 'My big sister with fresh whisker burn around her mouth. And stars in her eyes. She's never had stars in her eyes. *Never.*'

'Don't be ridiculous.' Panicked, Emma swiped at her mouth, then sucked in her lips and backed away. Tugged her T-shirt over her head and threw it on her bed. 'Do you know how cold it is outside? The air… A hot bath…'

'Emma Dilemma.' Stella grinned. 'You've just had it on with best man Jake.'

'*No.* It's such a cliché to get it on with the best man. I kissed him, that's all. No. He kissed me. We kissed each other. He started it. No biggie, okay?'

Stella shook her head. 'My sister never gets flustered when she talks about a guy. *Never.*'

Emma fumbled through her suitcase. 'He's not a guy, he's Jake. And I'm not flustered. It's nothing.'

'It's something.'

She yanked her pyjamas from her overnighter and blew out a breath then turned to Stella who was watching her with her chin on the back of the sofa. 'Okay, it's something. But it's just a weekend something. Or not. I haven't decided yet.'

Stella smiled. 'You know you'll have this room all to yourself tomorrow night…?'

'Not another word.' Emma flung up a hand. 'You breathe so much as a syllable of this conversation to Jake or anyone else and I'll sabotage your wedding night.'

And, swiping up her cosmetics bag, she fled to the bathroom.

CHAPTER SEVEN

THE wedding day dawned bright and clear. And cold. Clad in her complimentary terrycloth robe, Emma took her early-morning coffee onto the balcony to admire the cotton balls of cloud that hid the valley floor. From her vantage point she could see the garden below, where even now staff were setting out chairs, toting flower arrangements, twining white ribbon and fairy lights through the trees.

A few moments later Stella stumbled out, hair wild, eyes sparkling. 'Good morning.' She leaned a shoulder against Emma's. 'It's just perfect. Isn't it perfect? Not a cloud in the sky. By afternoon it'll be warm and still sunny. Hopefully... Can you believe I'm getting married in a few hours' time?'

Emma dropped a kiss on her sister's cheek on her way back inside. 'And there's a lot to get through before that happens.' She checked her watch. 'Breakfast is due up in ten minutes. The hairdresser will be here in half an hour.'

With less than an hour to go, the bride's dressing room on the first floor was pandemonium. Underwear, costumes, flowers. A blur of fragrance and colour. Sunshine streamed through the window. Champagne and orange juice in tall flutes sat untouched on a sideboard, along with a plate of finger food.

Stella was with Beth, the wedding planner, and her two assistants—one aiming a video camera and catching the memories. The excitement, the laughter, the nerves.

In one of the full-length mirrors Emma caught a glimpse of her reflection in a strapless bustier. Crimson, with black ribbon laces at the front, it looked like something Scarlett O'Hara would have approved of. She yanked the ribbon tight between her breasts and tied it in a double knot, staring closer.

Wow. She actually had breasts today. Enhanced by the bustier's support, they spilled over the top like something out of a men's magazine. The garment pulled in her waist and flared over her hips, leaving a strip of bare belly and the tiny triangle of matching panties tantalisingly visible. A pair of sheer black stockings came to mid thigh, held up by long black suspenders.

For an instant she almost saw Jake's reflection standing behind her, his eyes smouldering as he leaned over her to dip a finger between—

The tap on her shoulder had her spinning in a panicked one-eighty. 'What?' Her breath whooshed out and her heart skipped a beat. 'Stella. Sorry. I was—'

'A million miles away.'

Not as far as that. 'I'm here. Right here.' She gave a bright smile, then forgot about her erotic meanderings as she gazed at the bride. 'Oh, my! Gorgeous.'

Stella's figure-hugging floor-length Guinevere gown was bottle-green crushed velvet. A dull gold panel insert in the bodice gleamed with tiny emerald beads, replicated on the wide belt cinching in her waist. Full-length sleeves flared wide at the wrist and fell in long soft folds. Her coronet of fresh freesias, tiny roses and featherlike greenery complemented her rich auburn hair.

'You look stunning, Stell. Radiant and stunning. I can't wait to see Lancelot's face when he gets a load of you.'

'Neither can I.' She looked down at Emma, waved a hand. 'Um…are you planning on wearing something over that? I'm sure the guys won't mind, but this is my day and I know it's selfish but I want all the attention.'

'Getting there…' With the help of Annie, one of the assistants, Emma stepped into a voluminous skirt and shimmied into the bodice. 'I told you, Stella. You should have been Scarlett, not me.'

'And I told you already, Scarlett's the brunette. She's playful and coquettish and I really, really wanted you to be that woman today. Whereas Guinevere was pale and intense and totally and unconditionally in love with Lancelot.'

'Well, you'll have that attention,' Emma said, admiring her sister. 'Ryan, not to mention the rest of the male population, won't be able to take his eyes off you.'

Annie slipped buttons into the tiny loops at the back of Emma's dress, then handed her black lace gloves and a parasol.

'Don't forget the bridal bouquet.' Emma passed Stella a simple posy of flowers to match those in her hair. She paused with her sister at the top of the wide sweeping staircase. 'We're a clash of eras, aren't we?'

'We are. But it's going to be fun. For both of us.' Stella squeezed Emma's hand. 'Thank you for helping to make it a perfect day.'

'It's not over, it's just beginning.'

The harp's crystal clear rendition of 'Greensleeves' floated on the air as they arrived at the garden's designated bride spot. At a signal from Beth, the music segued beautifully into Bach's 'Jesu, Joy of Man's Desiring.'

'You're up,' Beth murmured to Emma. 'And don't forget to *smile*.'

She'd taken but a few steps along the petal-strewn manicured lawn when she saw Jake and Ryan up ahead. She forgot about smiling. The garden might look like a fairytale. The costumed guests might look magnificent or they might be naked for all Emma knew, because her peripheral vision had disappeared.

Rhett Butler had never looked so devastating. Black suit, dove-grey waistcoat and dark mottled cravat beneath a snowy starched shirt. His eyes met hers and he smiled. A slow, sexy, come-away-with-me smile.

'*Hi*,' he mouthed.

'*Hi*,' she mouthed back, and, *Oh, help*. Her knees went weak but she seemed to be moving forward. What was wrong with her? No man had ever captivated her this way.

Deliberately freeing her gaze, she aimed her smile at Ryan instead, looking regal in a black tunic and cowled top over silver-grey leggings and black knee-high boots. The Clifton family crest was emblazoned on his tunic— she could make out a lion and a medieval helmet in the black-and-gold embroidery.

Not that he was looking at her; his eyes were for his bride, a few steps behind. As they should be. Emma wondered for a quickened heartbeat how it would feel to have someone look at her that way, with shiny unconditional love. She rejected the thought even as it formed and concentrated on keeping her smile in place, her steps smooth and measured.

Jake's eyes feasted on Emma. The deep colour complemented her lightly tanned complexion. A wide-brimmed hat shaded her face, and he couldn't quite read her eyes, so he contented himself with admiring the seductive cleavage and the way the crimson fabric hugged every delectable curve as she moved closer.

His fingers flexed in anticipation of becoming more intimately acquainted with those curves. How long would it take him to get her out of that dress? To lay her down on the grass right here in the sunshine and plunge into her while the birds sang and the cool wind blew up from the valley....

Then she moved out of his line of sight to take her place beside the bride. Probably just as well, because any longer and it might become obvious to all where his thoughts were.

He turned his attention to Ry and Stella, and watched the couple blindly promise to handcuff themselves to each other till death did them part. A life sentence, no parole. His collar itched on Ry's behalf, and he shifted his shoulders against the tight sensation inside his shirt.

They looked happy enough. But it never lasted. There were exceptions, of course. Ry's parents—Henry VIII with a fake red beard and Anne Boleyn—were holding hands, eyes moist.

He glanced at the girls' mother in her white Grecian goddess robe, looking, as always, eternally constipated. Her marriage disaster had turned her into a bitter and twisted woman. Nevertheless, she was still beautiful. He imagined Emma would look as beautiful in thirty years' time.

But he didn't want to contemplate Emma's lovely face marred with that same perpetually pinched expression, those sparkling sapphire eyes clouded with sadness.

Who in their right mind would take the marriage risk? Only those temporarily blinded by that eternal mystery they called love. Not him, thank God.

Formal photographs followed in the gardens, then on

to the decking overlooking the mountains as the sun lowered, turning the sky golden and the valley purple.

Emma couldn't fault Jake's behaviour. He was the perfect gentleman. The perfect Rhett. He only touched her when the photographer required him to do so. During the five-course meal he was seated next to Ryan at the top table, so conversation between them was limited, but there was a heated glance or two when the bridal couple's heads didn't block the view.

After the speeches guests chatted over music provided by a three-piece orchestra as the desserts began coming out of the kitchen. Anne Boleyn, aka the mother of the groom, made her way to the top table.

'Beautiful ceremony, my darlings. It must be your turn next, Emma.'

'Oh, I don't think so.' Emma smiled back, then lifted her champagne glass and swallowed more than she should considering her duties. 'It's not for me.'

'Ah, you just have to find the right man.'

Smile still in place, Emma set her empty glass on the table with a thunk. 'And isn't that the killer?'

'And Jake?' Ryan's mother smiled in his direction. 'When's some clever woman going to snap you up and make an honest man out of you?'

'Alas for me, fair lady.' He put his hand on his heart. 'You're already taken.'

Laughter from the bridal couple. 'You never know, Em,' Stella murmured into her ear as her new mother-in-law walked back to her chair. 'He could be closer than you think.'

'What I'm thinking is it's about time you two cut that white skyscraper.'

The guests applauded as Stella and Ryan laughed into each other's eyes and fed each other cake. Weddings,

Emma thought. They always whipped up those romantic, dreamy, nostalgic emotions. It was hard not to be caught up in the euphoria.

She deliberately veered from those too-pretty thoughts and watched Karina knock back one glass of champagne after another. Emma pursed her lips, remembering the *Pat Me* sticker she'd discovered stuck to her backside after the hens' night. She narrowed her gaze as Karina plastered herself all over one of Ryan's cousins up against a wall. Weddings also came with too much booze and indiscriminate physical contact.

But when Ryan and Stella took to the floor for the bridal waltz to the seductive beat of 'Dance Me to the End of Love', she knew her own moment of up close was imminent and her legs started to tremble.

Jake rose and held out his hand, his eyes as beguiling as the song. 'I think it's our turn.' Emma caught the undertone in his voice and her whole body thrummed with its underlying message that went way beyond the dance floor and upstairs to that big soft bed.

When he grasped her fingers to lead her into the dance space there was something…different about the contact. And in the centre of the room, when he slid his hand to her back, firm and warm and possessive, she felt as if the floor tilted beneath her feet.

They'd never danced together, and his proximity released a stream of endorphins, stimulating her senses. The throb of the music echoed through her body. His cool green aftershave filled her nostrils. The sensuous brush of his thighs against hers beneath the heavy swish of her full skirt had her breath catching in her throat.

'Sorry,' she muttered, missing a step and trying to create some space between them—she needed it to breathe, and to say, 'I'm not a very good dancer.'

'Lucky for you I am.'

She flicked him a look. 'Lucky for you I'm feeling congenial enough to let you get away with that.'

Was there *anything* in the seductive sciences he wasn't accomplished at? She sincerely doubted it as his palm rubbed a lazy circle over her back, creating a deliciously warm friction and at the same time drawing her closer and causing her to misstep—again.

'Is it the dance, or is something else distracting you, Em?'

How typically arrogant male. But she smiled into his laughing eyes. 'Do men always have sex on their minds?'

His answering grin was unrepentant. 'Pretty much.' He dipped close and lowered his voice. 'It's on your mind too.'

She dragged in a breath that smelled of fine fresh cotton and hot man and tried not to notice. 'I'm finding it hard to concentrate on the steps, that's all.'

As Ryan swept his bride past them Emma saw Stella's eyes twinkling at her and looked away quickly. Apart from the bride and groom and Ryan's parents they were the only couple on the floor. 'People are watching us.'

'And why wouldn't they? You look amazing.' The hand holding hers tightened, and his thumb whisked over hers as he leaned in so that his cheek touched her hair. So that his chest shifted against her breasts. 'You feel amazing,' he murmured into her ear. 'Forget the audience. Listen to the music.'

Forget the music. Listen to the Voice. Her head drifted towards his shoulder, the better to hear it. When other couples joined them on the dance floor he swept her towards the window with its panoramic views. Not that she was interested in any view right now except the one in front of her.

He crooned the song's lyrics about wanting to see her beauty when everyone had gone close against her ear. She nearly melted on the spot. 'You think I've changed my mind?'

'Honey, I don't even need to ask.' His hand tightened around hers and then she realised that couples were swirling around them and they were standing still. And close. That the fingers of her free hand had somehow ended up clinging to the back of his neck. That the song had changed to something more upbeat.

How long had they been standing there? How long had she been showing him exactly how she felt? That those options she'd thought she had were down to one? Somehow she managed to yank herself into the present and remember her bridesmaid duties.

She let her hand slide down the smooth fabric of his jacket, slipped the other one from his grasp. 'I need to go.'

'Are you sure?' He lifted the heavy mass of hair from her shoulder with the back of his fingers and stroked the side of her neck, then linked his arms loosely around her waist, trapping her against him. 'Because I'm kind of enjoying where we are right now.'

She felt a series of little taps track up her spine.

'How many buttons would you say this dress has?' He slipped the top one from its tiny loop. Then another.

Her breath caught and her blood fizzed through her veins like hot champagne. 'What do you think you're doing?'

He swirled a finger beneath the fabric. 'Your skin feels like warm satin. How many buttons?' he asked again.

'Twenty two.'

He muttered a soft short word under his breath.

'Is that a problem?'

His eyes burned into hers. 'I've never encountered a

problem with female clothing I couldn't solve one way or another.' And with a slow sexy grin he released her. 'Okay, you're free. For now.'

For now? But she couldn't deny the thrill of knowing he wanted her. That he was already figuring a way to get her out of her dress. That the women casting admiring glances his way were not even on his radar tonight—Emma Byrne was.

His proprietorial hand at her back manoeuvred her through the dancers as she made her way towards the bridal table. A middle aged Fred and Wilma Flintstone twirled by, a gay couple dressed as King Arthur and Merlin, a Beauty and a Beast.

'Who's the Roman warrior chatting up Bernice?'

Emma followed Jake's gaze to a nearby table and snorted a half laugh. 'He won't get far with Mum.' But to her surprise her mother smiled at something the middle-aged guy said. Then laughed. 'Amazing.' Emma smiled too. 'Maybe I should invite him around some time as a distraction when I'm fed up with her.'

'Hang on—that's Ryan's Uncle Stan from Melbourne. Divorced last year and looking good. Go, Stan.'

Emma took that moment to break away. 'I have something I need to take care of.'

Leaving the sounds of laughter and music behind, she made her way to the honeymoon suite in another wing of the hotel with a basket of rose petals. A glance at her watch told her she had half an hour before the happy couple were due to leave the party and celebrate the end of their special day.

More than enough time to catch her breath and take a moment. Letting herself in with the keycard she'd been given at Reception, Emma flicked on the light. A soft glow filled the room, glinting on the massive brass bed and lending a rich luxury to the sumptuous gold and burgundy furnishings. She leaned a shoulder against the door, drawing in air. She really needed to increase her daily workout.

Rubbish. Emma knew her lack of fitness wasn't the reason her lungs felt as if they'd shrunk two sizes. She could try telling herself her underwear was laced too tightly. The ballroom had been badly ventilated. She'd had too much of the fizzy stuff.

But there was only one reason, and thank God he was downstairs—

'Need a hand?'

That familiar seductive drawl coated the back of her neck like hot honey, causing her to jolt and drop her little basket. She drew in a ragged breath. His question, which wasn't a question at all, could only mean one thing, and it wasn't an offer to help sprinkle her rose petals over the quilt.

'Jake…' The word turned into a moan as a warm mouth bit lightly into the sensitive spot where shoulder met neck. She simply didn't have the strength or the will to pull away. 'What are you doing here?'

He soothed the tender spot with his tongue and her toes curled up. 'What do you think I'm doing here?' In one fluid move he spun her around. The door swung shut behind them and he rolled her against the wall, his hands hard and hot and heavy on her shoulders.

He didn't give her time to answer or to think. One instant she was staring into a pair of heavy-lidded dark eyes, the next her mouth was being plundered by the wickedest pair of lips this side of the Yellow Brick Road.

He lifted his mouth a fraction and his breath whispered against her lips. 'Is that clear enough?'

Perfectly. And just clear enough to have her remember where they were and what she'd come here to do. 'Are you out of your mind?' She pushed at his chest. Uselessly. 'Housekeeping could show up here any minute.'

'Then we've got a minute.' He grinned, dark eyes glinting. 'Better make the most of it.'

Excitement whipped through her as his hands rushed down, his thumbs whisking over taut nipples, the heat of his palms searing her skin through the satin as he moulded them around her waist and over her belly with murmurs of appreciation.

There was nothing of the suave, sophisticated gentleman from this afternoon except perhaps the scent of his aftershave. This man was the wickedly handsome rogue bent on seduction that she'd always known him to be. Nothing for her to do but to look into those eyes and oh-so-willingly acquiesce.

He gathered handfuls of her voluminous skirt in his fists at either side of her, creating a cool draught around her knees as he ruched the fabric higher. 'Do you want to tell me to stop?' he murmured, leaning down to sip at her collarbone.

Only to stop wasting time. A moan escaped as the tips of his fingers grazed the tops of her stockings, then came into smooth contact with naked flesh. He slid one sensuous finger beneath a suspender and up, to track along the edge of her panties.

He grinned again as he tossed her skirt up over her breasts. 'How many layers have you got on under here?'

'I don't remember...' Moisture pooled between her legs, dampening her silk knickers, and she didn't know how much longer she could remain upright.

He watched her eyes while his finger cruised closer, curling inward, between her thighs, along the lacy edge of her knickers, almost but never quite touching where she wanted him to touch her most. And the spark she saw in his gaze ignited a burn that wasn't about to be extinguished any time soon.

'Jake...Housekeeping—'

'Tell me what you like. What you want.'

The husky demand turned her mind to mush, and she arched wantonly against his hand. Forget Housekeeping. 'Anything. Everything.' Clutching her skirt, she let her spinning head fall back against the door. 'And quickly.'

He stepped between her legs, the sides of his shoes pushing her feet wider. One sharp tug. Two. The sound of fabric ripping. And she felt her knickers being whisked away from her body by impatient hands.

She trembled. She sighed. She hissed out a breath between her teeth. 'Hurry.'

'No.' His thumb found her throbbing centre. 'A job worth doing...'

'Ah, *yesss...*' A slow, sensuous glide over her swollen flesh—one touch—and the burn became a raging inferno. *So* worth doing...

How could one finger cause such utter devastation? Her eyes slid closed. Golden orbs pulsed across her vision. She felt as if she was standing on the rim of a volcano, yet she was the one about to erupt.

He touched her a second time, and she flew over the edge and into the hot and airless vortex, her inner muscles clamping around him.

She flattened her palms against the wall for balance, her breathing fast and harsh. She felt him step away on a draught of air, and opened her eyes in time to see him grin with promises yet to be fulfilled as he slipped out through the door.

CHAPTER EIGHT

Oh...My. God. Emma sucked in a much needed calming breath. If she'd had the luxury of time she'd have slid down the wall and possibly passed out for the rest of the night.

He'd touched her twice. *Twice.* That was all it had taken to bring her to the most intense orgasm of her life. And then he'd nicked off like some pirate in the night, stealing her breath and her composure and leaving her with the possibility of facing Housekeeping alone.

Out. She realised she was still clutching her skirt up to her chest and pushed it down quickly, her cheeks flaming, at the same time thanking her lucky stars that no one had turned up yet.

A hank of hair fell over one side of her face. She pushed it behind her ear. Panicked all over again, she scanned the floor for her knickers. No sign of them. Picking up her forgotten basket, she stumbled to the bed and dumped the petals in the centre, arranging them in a hasty circle. She placed the two heart-shaped soaps she'd made with Ryan's and Stella's names in gold leaf in the centre, then made her way quickly downstairs, where the couple were preparing to farewell the guests.

She didn't see Jake amongst the crowd until he appeared in the doorway ten minutes later. Their gazes clashed hotly across the room. He was the only one who knew she was naked beneath her gown and her cheeks flamed anew. She prayed he'd stay away from her for the next little while, because they both had their respective duties before the social part of the evening was over.

Neatly sidestepping as Stella threw her bouquet in Emma's direction—she wasn't falling for that old trick—she saw Jake follow the bridal couple out.

She moved among the guests, catching up with friends and relatives. She was on tenterhooks, expecting Jake to tap her on the shoulder at any moment, and she didn't know how she was going to hide the guilty pleasure from her expression.

The band was still playing and guests lingered, enjoying the music. Some danced; others gravitated towards the bar next to the lobby. A while later, when Jake still hadn't shown his face, the glow cooled, to be replaced by an anxious fluttering in the pit of her stomach. Was he coming back? Was he expecting *her* to look for *him* after his impromptu seduction?

She didn't know what game they were playing—had no idea of the rules. *Damn him.* Collecting her hat and parasol from behind the concierge's desk, she made her way towards the bar.

Jake waved Ry and Stella off and headed straight for Reception. Business taken care of there, he stopped to collect a couple of sightseeing brochures on his way to the lobby bar.

He found a comfortable armchair in the corner, from where he could see the ballroom, and signalled the waiter. He knew Emma was still in there. He'd give her some space but if she didn't materialise in ten minutes he was damn well going in there and hauling her out.

Folding the brochures, he slid them into his jacket

pocket. His fingers collided with silk. Emma's panties. He remembered her surprise, the passion in those deep blue eyes, when he'd stripped them off. The way her lips had parted on a moan of pleasure when he'd first touched that intimate flesh.

His body tightened all over again. The next time Emma writhed and moaned against him... He smiled to himself in anticipation. He had definite plans for the way their evening was going to go.

Han Solo and Princess Leia exited, with a lone cowboy in tow. No sign of Emma. He exhaled sharply through his nostrils and rechecked his watch. Was she saying a personal goodnight to everyone in the bloody ballroom?

His order arrived with a paper napkin and a bowl of peanuts. He set the unopened bottle of champagne and two glasses on the floor beside his chair and reached for his beer.

'Good evening, Rhett.'

Jake took a second or two to catch on that the sultry come-hither voice was directed at him. He glanced up to see a well-endowed woman in her mid-thirties or thereabouts, in an embroidered medieval get-up, holding a cocktail glass brimming with blue liquid and a cherry on a stick.

He lifted his glass and drained half of it down then set it back on the table. 'Hi.'

She took his half-smile as an invitation and spread herself out on the chair opposite him, placing her glass up close to his. She lifted the little stick to her mouth.

'So.' He kept his eyes off the cleavage obviously on offer and leaned back, crossed his legs. 'Who are you tonight?'

Slipping the cherry between her glossed lips, she tossed her mane of auburn hair over her shoulder and aimed a killer smile at him. 'The Lady of Shalott.'

He took his time to say, 'No Mr Shalott?'

She giggled. The sound grated the way feet scrabbling down a rubbled cliff face to certain death grated. Clearly she thought he was interested in her as the night's entertainment. And at some other time he might have been interested. Or not.

'There *was* no Mr Shalott. It's a poem,' she informed him, in case he didn't know.

'Yes, Tennyson. Tragic circumstances. The girl loved Lancelot but he really wasn't that into her, was he?'

She leaned forward on the edge of her chair. 'But he didn't *know* her. If he'd taken the time, things might've turned out different.'

'But not necessarily for the better. Lancelot had his eye on someone else. The lady would've been disappointed.' A thought occurred to him and he tried to recall if he knew her. 'You and Ry weren't…?' He jiggled a hand in front of them.

She grinned. 'No. I had no idea the groom was going to be Lancelot. I'm Ryan's cousin. Kylie. From Adelaide.'

'Ah…yes. Cousin Kylie from Adelaide.'

He'd heard about Wily Kylie—two husbands down, on the prowl for her third. He suddenly needed a drink, and lifted his beer.

Following suit, Kylie raised her glass and tapped it to his. Her eyes drifted to his mouth. 'To a good night.'

Not if I hang around here it won't be. Like an addict, he suddenly craved the woman he'd partnered all day, not this silicone bimbo looking for rich husband number three. *Emma.* A woman with a real body and a smile that could quite possibly melt his heart if he wasn't careful.

'And a good night to you too.' He drained the glass and set it down on the napkin, then picked up his bottle and glasses, rose and executed a bow. 'Welcome to Sydney, Lady Kylie, enjoy your stay.'

He didn't wait for a reply, simply turned on his heel and headed towards the ballroom to find Emma.

Emma's hands shook so much she could barely swipe the keycard through its slot. On the third try she managed to let herself in and lean back against the door. She felt physically ill—as if the five-tiered wedding cake had lodged in her stomach.

One hand clenched on her parasol, she rubbed her free hand over her heart and up her throat. Jake hadn't come near her since their upstairs 'encounter'. For want of a better word. Never mind that she'd stupidly tried to avoid him; that was totally beside the point.

Flinging her hat into the air, she watched it sail across the room. She'd been hanging around in the ballroom, expecting him to come and find her. But he hadn't. When it came to guys like him she really was *so* naïve.

Then *she'd* found *him.* In the lobby bar…with a woman who *looked* like a woman, not some under-developed teenager.

The soft knock at the door behind her had her whirling around. Heart pounding in her throat, she yanked the door open.

Jake leaned on the doorjamb, his jacket slung over one shoulder, shirtsleeves rolled back. His hair was a little mussed, his cravat was gone, and the top button of his shirt was undone, leaving his throat tantalisingly exposed. He dangled a bottle of champagne and two glasses in his free hand.

His eyes met hers. They burned with such hot, unsatisfied hunger her throat closed over and she couldn't raise so much as a whisper. All she could think was he'd come for her. *Her*.

He lifted the bottle. 'You going to let me in? Or do you want the entire floor to know the best man's planning a hot night with the bridesmaid?' He grinned as he slid sideways and passed her, brushing his liquor-tinged lips over hers on his way. 'I hope you hadn't planned on starting without me.'

She took a moment to catch his meaning, then a wild fire swept up her neck and into her cheeks. All she managed was a gurgling sound at the back of her throat.

She closed the door and leaned back against it, heart pounding as she watched him toss his jacket over the couch, watched the way his muscles bunched beneath his shirt. His hair held the gleam of burnished gold threads amongst the brown.

He glanced back at her as he walked to a little round table topped with a crystal vase of fresh blooms. 'You weren't running out on me, were you?'

'You…you were otherwise occupied.' She found her voice.

He frowned. 'I was *waiting* for you.'

'I didn't know.' The door felt hard, the row of buttons digging into her spine.

He set the bottle and glasses down, brows raised, eyes dark as midnight. 'You *didn't know?* Jeez, woman.'

'I thought maybe you'd…' *found someone more desirable, more attractive* '…changed your mind.'

'What? This weekend's about you and me, remember?'

Her chin lifted. 'I never agreed.' Exactly.

'You…' He shook his head, eyes changing, finally comprehending. 'Come on, Emma, do you really think I'd go for that type downstairs?'

'I…hoped not.' She swallowed, relief softening her

limbs, and allowed herself a smile. 'Because then I'd have to hit you with my parasol.'

He grinned back at her, eyes wicked. 'Maybe I'll let you. Later.'

'Um…' Was she really up for an experienced man like Jake?

He popped the cork off the champagne bottle. 'Tonight's been a foregone conclusion all along, and we both know it.'

Yes. And for this moment, for what was left of the weekend, or for however long this spark burned, she knew without a doubt she wanted to make love with Jake more than her next breath.

He set the bottle down. 'Come here and kiss me.'

She needed no second bidding. Crossing the few steps between them, she flattened herself against his chest, her arms circling his neck, fingers diving into his hair as she fused her mouth to his.

Heat met heat. Not sweet and tender—not even close. Not with Jake. Nor did she want it so. This melding of selves and mashing of lips was a dark, dangerous mix of pent-up passion and long-held desires. Exactly what she wanted.

Hard hands dragged her closer, then zigged down her spine to press her bottom against him so that she could feel the steel ridge of his erection. Persuasive pressure. Promised delights.

He lifted his lips to murmur, 'Emma, Emma, you've been driving me crazy all evening. All week.'

His admission thrilled her to her toes. 'Same goes…' Dazed and dizzy, she arched her hips against his hardness and clung to him, welcoming the scrape of evening beard as he worked his lips and teeth up her throat, down the side of her neck, over her décolletage.

Impatient hands skimmed over her breasts, kneading and squeezing, deft fingers finding her aching nipples through the satin and rolling them into hardened peaks.

The delicate fragrance of the valley's sweet-scented wattle and eucalypt from the arrangement on the table mingled with the hot scent of aroused man as he laved the swell of her breasts above the neckline of her dress, then bent his head lower to nip and suck at her nipples through the fabric.

He made a sound of frustration, lifted his head and leaned back slightly to look at her. Light from the chandelier wall bracket glinted in his eyes, but the heat, the purpose she saw there, burned with its own fire.

'How many buttons did you say?'

Oh. 'Buttons…' She raised her arms to help but he didn't give her time. In a frenzy of movement, he fisted his hands in the fabric at her shoulders and yanked. She felt the satin give way down her back as buttons popped and pinged. 'Uh…'

'I know a dressmaker…'

Of course he did.

Dropping to his knees, he pushed the ruined garment and accompanying petticoats to her feet. She stepped out of the mound of puddled satin, kicked it away, leaving her wearing nothing but her laced bustier and stockings.

'You're gorgeous,' he murmured, voice husky. A corner of his mouth kicked up in a wry smile. 'And armour-plated yet again.'

Goosebumps of heat followed his gaze as it swept up her corset-trapped body to meet her eyes. 'Not quite. You do have my panties…don't you?' she finished on a slightly panicked note.

'They're mine now.' He looked down at the feminine

secrets exposed below the suspenders, then back, his eyes burning. 'I want to see all of you.'

He knelt in front of her, took off her shoes then un-hitched her stockings, warm hands gliding them down her legs, breath hot on her naked skin. She lifted each foot so he could slide them off and toss them away.

Hands shaking, she started to fumble for the laces. Her breasts weren't… 'I'm not—'

Laying a finger on her lips, he shook his head.

Taking her hands in his, he spread them wide so that their bodies bumped in all the right places, then, fingers entwined, brought them in close and began to waltz. Tiny steps, his thighs pressing against hers. He swayed her to-wards the massive four-poster bed. She could almost hear the dusky beat of Stella's chosen song that they'd danced to earlier.

She felt the corner of the bed against her thighs as he backed her up against the bedpost. Watching her, he turned her hands palm up, kissed the inside of each wrist, where her pulse beat a rock concert's applause, then curled each finger around the smooth wooden bedpost above her head.

'And don't let go,' he ordered, squeezing them for good measure, fingers trailing down her raised arms, leaving little shivers sparkling in their wake.

The erotic pose triggered within her an avalanche of wild needs and urgent demands. Her breasts thrust up-wards, straining at the bustier's confines, nipples tight to the point of pain and on fire for his touch.

'Jake…' She sighed. Wanting it all. Wanting it now.

His eyes swept over her and his smooth seduction van-ished in the blink of an eye.

His fingers scrambled for the laces. When she loosened her hold on the post in a frantic effort to hasten the process he grabbed her wrists, pinning her in place, a firestorm in his dark gaze. *'Stay.'*

A thrill spiralled through her body, clenching low in her belly as he renewed his task. His hands weren't steady, she noticed, and his breathing was ragged. He swore, then a hand dived into his trouser pocket and reappeared with a miniature Swiss Army knife. A handful of condoms spilled onto the floor.

She glanced down at them, then met his eyes. 'Boy Scout?'

'Just prepared,' he muttered thickly.

His eyes darkened. She knew his intent, and her pulse kicked into a wild erratic rhythm. No trace of the suave urban sophisticate—just prime, primitive male. She loved that he'd lost control with *her*—plain and ordinary Emma Byrne.

He flicked the tiny blade open and nicked the first ribbon. The second. Her breath sucked in. So did her stomach. His knuckles grazed a nipple as he worked his way down. The erotic response echoed in her womb, drawing it tight at the same time softening and moistening the internal muscles, slackening her inner thighs.

'Jake…'

Snick, snick, snick. 'I'll buy you another one.'

'Doesn't…matter…it's…only ribbon.'

The undergarment fell apart and slid to the floor and her breasts spilled free. And suddenly it didn't matter that she didn't have the breasts she'd like to have, because he was looking at them with awe and appreciation.

'Gorgeous,' he whispered. 'Absolutely perfect.'

Dropping the knife, he filled his hands with her, thumbs whisking over the tight buds, rolling and pinching them between his fingers until she thought she'd pass out with the pleasure. Wayne had never, *never* worshipped her body the way Jake was doing.

She writhed against the post, tilting her hips and arching her back. Closer…she had to get closer… She needed more. Him inside her. *Now.*

A groan rumbled up his throat and she heard the sharp rasp of his zipper. Without taking his eyes off hers, he somehow produced a condom that hadn't fallen from his pocket and ripped the foil packet open with his teeth.

Her breath stalled in her throat as he quickly sheathed himself. 'Hurry.' Anticipation and that aching, devastating need had reached flashpoint.

Hard wide palms clamped onto her hips, a sensuous vice, holding her in place. With unerring precision he plunged deep and hard and true. A torpedo finding its target. Invading her, stretching her, filling her.

Where he belonged.

Somewhere in a dark corner of her pleasure-fogged mind she fought that concept even as she embraced it. Then all thought melted into oblivion as she gave herself wholly over to layer after layer of sensation.

His hard thighs abraded hers through the rough weave of his trousers while he hammered into her. The sound of his laboured breaths, shockingly harsh in the room's stillness, and her own rapid sighs of response.

The golden light pulsing behind her eyes as she felt her climax building, building… Her legs threatening to give way, she clung tighter to the satin-smooth pole behind her, then Jake's hands were covering hers, holding her upright. From heads to toes their bodies collided, naked skin to fully clothed.

She was slick, hot and unbearably erotic, and Jake couldn't remember the last time he'd been so turned on. She bucked against him, all wild, wanton woman, meeting his thrusts with an eagerness and energy that rivalled his own.

He hadn't expected Emma to be so utterly responsive, and the pleasure of it, of *her,* slapped through him, sharp and viciously arousing. Clenching her hands between his own he drove into her, the urge to plunder and possess riding roughshod over anything sane and rational.

He'd not known it could be like this. That need for a woman—for one woman—could be so desperate, so powerful, so consuming. Some kind of madness had seized him.

She came in a rush, all but sobbing his name, her internal muscles clamping around him, silky walls of heat that triggered his own climax.

Their joined hands slid down the sweat-slicked post and he released her, and they flopped onto the bottom of the bed together in a tangle of sated limbs, their ragged breaths filling the air.

'Come here,' he murmured when he felt able enough to move again, shifting up the bed and dragging her with him. He hauled her on top and she lay spread-eagled over his body like one of those ragdoll cats. Against his thundering heart, he felt hers pounding in unison.

'Do you realise this is the first time we've actually been horizontal together?' she said drowsily.

'Mmm,' he answered, almost as lazily. Her body fitted seamlessly against his, curves to angles, womanly soft where he was hard, as if she'd been made exclusively for him. She made him feel like the king of the universe. Already he was becoming aroused again, his body stirring as she arched a bare foot over his calf.

'Hey, you gonna get naked with me or what?' Her voice was slurred with fatigue.

He tilted her face so he could look at her, skin peach-perfect and sheened with a translucent film of moisture, eyes still glazed with residual passion.

Emma.

An unfamiliar feeling stole through him. One he wasn't sure how to deal with. He eased her off to one side. Her hair was in disarray; he smoothed it away from her face and kissed her damp brow. 'Give me a minute.'

In the bathroom he dealt with the condom, then splashed cold water on his face. He'd just had wild sex with Emma. *Emma.* Looking away from the frown he glimpsed in his reflection, he swiped a towel and dried his face.

When he came back she'd burrowed beneath the quilt and was fast asleep, dead centre in the middle of the bed, one arm flung across a pillow, long dark lashes resting on cheeks the colour of dawn.

She looked tiny, all alone in that master bed. As if the snowy mountain of quilt might swallow her up.

Vulnerable.

That odd feeling intensified. He watched the slow rise and fall of the quilt as she breathed. He'd not anticipated this…this surge of emotion. What had he done?

He should go back to his own room, he thought, even as he stripped off his shirt, tossed it over the chair. Collect a few essentials. She might need some space. Hell, *he* needed some space.

But he toed his shoes off, shoved down his trousers and jocks and stepped out of them. Retrieved the condoms from the floor, dropped them on the nightstand, then slipped into bed beside her.

She snuggled against him with a sleep murmur. Her warmth seeped into his bones, her exotic fragrance…fresh and floral and exclusively hers, surrounded him. He'd never forget that exotic fragrance. And when this attraction had run its course...

He closed his eyes.

Tomorrow. He'd think about that tomorrow.

CHAPTER NINE

THE sound of a man's steady breathing woke Emma. A hard-muscled, hairy thigh was draped over one leg, its weight effectively pinning the lower half of her body in place. A warm hand curved around her left breast.

Jake.

Her heart leapt and her body burned as images of last night with the man of her dreams flooded back. She knew it was morning because a dull apricot light shimmered behind her eyelids, but she didn't open her eyes. She lay still, not wanting him to wake yet, because she wanted to replay every glorious, mind-blowing minute. Her skin felt as if it had been rubbed all over with a stiff towel.

He'd made love to her again while the soft darkness cocooned them in its blanket of intimacy. Horizontally this time. And slowly, skilfully. Sinfully. The way only a man with Jake's experience could.

And again and again. Always different, always amazing.

Her eyes blinked open and she turned her head on the pillow to study him. As innocent as a baby but she knew better. Those perfectly sculpted lips, so relaxed in sleep, could wreak absolute havoc. Everywhere. A quicksilver shiver ran through her.

His hair was sticking up and it was an odd feeling knowing she'd had something to do with it. She smiled to herself. She itched to run her fingers through its silky softness again. Couldn't wait to feel the weight of his body on hers, to feel him come inside her again. Now. Tonight. Next week.

But reality intruded like a thief, stealing away the lovely feeling and her smile faded. This weekend was all he'd offered. All they'd agreed on. Just for fun.

And that was all she wanted too, right?

So make the most of it, she told herself, determined to ignore the feeling tugging at her and pleading for more. *Live in the moment.* They still had a late checkout and the rest of the day to spend together however they chose. A lot of fun could be packed into those few hours.

Easing her leg from beneath his, she slid a hand down between smooth sheets and hard-muscled belly… She found him semi-erect and wrapped her fingers around him. His eyes snapped open and that innocence disappeared in an instant, replaced with hot, not-quite-sleepy desire as he hardened beneath her palm.

'Good morning,' she murmured, and slid her hand down his satin-steel length and up again. 'Sorry to wake you… Actually, I'm not sorry.' She squeezed gently. 'I've got big plans for the day.'

He stuck one hand behind his head and watched her. A smile teased the corners of his mouth. 'Have you, now?'

'Mmm.' Positioning her top half over his chest, she rubbed against him once, twice, enjoying the rasp of masculine hair against her nipples, before reaching down to cup the heavy masculinity between his thighs. *Very big plans.* Resting her chin on his breastbone, she looked into his eyes. 'What about you? Any ideas?'

'I'm up for anything.' His smile was wicked and wide awake, like the rest of him.

She pushed the quilt down and took her time to admire the magnificent view of tanned skin over hard-packed muscle…and the proud, arrogant jut of his masculinity. 'I noticed.' Before he could flip her on her back and have her at his mercy again, she took charge and straddled him, reaching for a condom. 'Let's start the day on a high.'

A short while later, snuggled against him, she stretched lazily. Sunday mornings didn't get any better than this.

'Speaking of high,' Jake said, running his fingertips up and down her arm. 'What else are you up for today, Emma?'

A sneaky premonition snaked down her spine. 'Depends.'

'I'm thinking there's a playground of world-famous tourist attractions within walking distance that we should make the most of.'

She knew, and her stomach was already doing somersaults. Did she want to be suspended two hundred and seventy metres above the forest floor on a wire cable? Or be slung down the side of a cliff on the steepest funicular railway in the world?

Her whole body recoiled. She wasn't a fan of heights and she didn't care who knew it. 'Or we could explore the local galleries, or take a drive to Leura and have lunch in one of the cafés before we head home,' she suggested hopefully.

He grinned and shook his head. 'Come on, Em, where's your sense of adventure?'

'I lost it somewhere. Really,' she insisted, when his grin remained. If anything it broadened. 'I think maybe I used it all up in this room,' she finished. She stared at him, her whole body blushing at everything they'd gotten up to last night. Suddenly feeling way too naked, she sat up, pulling the sheet over her breasts. 'Is this…*us*…weird?'

His grin faded, and for a long moment he didn't answer while they watched each other. In the stretched silence she heard a service trolley lumber past the room, the clatter of dishes. Had she ever seen his eyes so dark? Something behind that gaze had her heart stumbling around inside her chest... It was supposed to be just physical. *A weekend on Pleasure Island, remember?*

'You're thinking too hard again.' Jake reached out, smoothed her hair behind her ear. 'I rebooked my room. I want another night with you. What do you say?'

Yes, please?

One more night. Her pulse was on a fast track up the side of that mountain. Free and irresponsible was calling her, and she wasn't ready to go back to her boring job and busy *unsociable* life just yet.

'It'll mean a very early start tomorrow if we're going to make it to the city in time.'

'I've decided to take tomorrow off. You?'

'Monday's busy. I've got—'

'Stay with me. Call in sick.'

'I can't just take a day off.'

His brows rose. 'Why the hell not? Your sister just got married. Your boss'll understand.' His voice turned low and smooth and seductive. 'If you want, I can convince him you need the day to recover.'

She frowned. How she chose to use her recreational time was one thing, her job was quite another. An income was a necessity. A one-night stand, even a two-night stand, was a luxury.

And didn't every woman deserve a little luxury now and again?

Still... 'I haven't interfered in your working life, Jake. Please respect mine. And, just so you know, my boss is a woman, and it happens she's a real soft touch when it comes to love and romance.' She leant over and soothed his lips with hers. 'I'll organise it myself.' And deal with the repercussions later.

'Good decision.' She felt his fingers on the back of her head, holding her still while he turned her smooch into a meltingly irresistible kiss.

'Are *you?*' he murmured against her lips a moment later.

'Am I what?'

'A soft touch when it comes to love and romance. You feel soft enough...' He drifted a finger over her cheek, a bare shoulder.

She drew back, shrugged off the words and the associated emotions she didn't want or need. Jake and love and romance were mutually exclusive. In that they were equally matched. But she couldn't quite look him in the eye, and drew circles on the crisp pillow-case with a fingertip. 'I don't want the complication of either in my life.'

'You're a career girl.'

'At least you can count on your career.' Unlike counting on a man.

'Okay, career girl. We'll both play hooky tomorrow and then take a leisurely drive back to town.' He sat up, swung his legs over the side of the bed and reached for his trousers on the floor. 'I need to go back to my room, take a shower and change. Meet me downstairs for breakfast in half an hour and we'll discuss our plans.'

'Okay.' She watched him pull last night's clothes over his magnificent taut backside. The way the muscles in his shoulders bunched as he shrugged into his shirt. Biting back a sigh, she rose and picked up the terrycloth robe she'd worn the night before, which still lay on a nearby chair. She tied the sash and followed him to the door.

'See you in a little while,' he said, bending to kiss her

before opening the door. Then Emma saw his shoulders tense as he came to an abrupt halt.

'Jake.'

She heard her mother's chipped ice voice and Emma's skin flushed to the roots of her tousled bedroom hair. Shrinking into her robe, she hugged the lapels up to her chin with both hands.

'Good morning, Bernice.' Jake's back was towards Emma, and if he was surprised or embarrassed his voice gave no sign. 'Em's about to take a shower,' she heard him say as he sauntered out, his jacket and waistcoat slung over a shoulder. 'You just caught her in time.'

Emma sucked in a fortifying breath. 'Mum.' She moved forward and pulled the door wider while she imagined slamming it shut. 'Jake was…just leaving.' Obviously. And he seemed to have taken her thought-processing skills with him.

Her mother stalked in, missing none of last night's carnage strewn across the floor. 'I came to tell you I'm driving back with Ryan's Uncle Stan.'

Was that a flicker of *excitement* in her mother's eyes? But when Emma blinked it had vanished. 'That's…great, Mum…' She trailed off. What to say?

'I wanted to make sure you'd arranged a lift, but I assume now that you're driving back with Jake.'

Emma heard the underlying criticism loud and clear. 'Thanks, but actually I'm staying on another night.' Defiance streamed through her veins. 'Make that *we're* staying another night.'

Her mother had been staring at the rumpled bed but she swung to face her. 'What about work tomorrow morning?'

'I'm taking the day off.'

'Have you no sense of responsibility, girl? And with

a man like Jake.' She exhaled her disapproval audibly through pinched nostrils.

'I never take time off. As for Jake, I like him, Mum. And so does Stella.' She hugged her arms to ward off the chill in her mother's eyes. 'He's an interesting, honest, hard-working man. I make my own decisions about the men I choose to see. And my own mistakes.'

'So you already think he's a mistake, then?'

Maybe it *was* a mistake, but she'd never know if she didn't take the risk. Jake had liberated something inside her last night and she wanted explore it, even if it was only for what was left of the weekend. 'I want a chance to find out.'

'Very well, then,' her mother replied, tight-lipped. The stony expression remained as she moved to the door. 'I'll see you at home.'

'Right. Drive safely.' Emma maintained an outward calm until the door closed with chilling formality, then swung around to lean back against it and slap her palms on the smooth wood. And a big goodbye to allowing her mother to put a blot on the morning.

It was only a little risk, she told herself, gathering her discarded garments and all the loose buttons she could locate. She tossed them into her suitcase, took out her casual clothes. A relaxing day playing tourist in the Blue Mountains was just what she needed.

And tonight… Her newly energised body tightened at the thought. It was going to be fun. Just fun.

CHAPTER TEN

AFTER waving the newly married couple off on their honeymoon, Jake convinced Emma to walk to Echo Point again later that morning. The air was cold but the sun was out for now, turning the Three Sisters a stark orange against the blue-tinged foliage. A bank of clouds was building; it would rain before nightfall.

'So Stan's driving your mum home,' Jake said as they gazed over the valley. Bernice finding him in Emma's room had been an unexpected and awkward moment. 'Did she give you a hard time?' Neither of them had spoken of the episode over breakfast, but it needed to be said.

'No more than usual.' Emma spoke casually, but he saw her posture dip as she leaned on the railing as if it might prop her up. 'I hope Stan can put her in a better mood.'

'If anyone can cheer Bernice up, Stan's your man.'

Hanging on to the rail with both hands, she leaned back at a crazy angle and looked at the sky. 'You know what? I don't want to think about her *or* work today.'

'Good girl.' He covered her hands with his. 'Today's for us.'

'Sounds perfect.' Turning to him, she tipped her face up to his, last night's sparkle still dancing in her eyes. She wore a faded tracksuit, scuffed sneakers and her hair was tied back into a loose coil which hung between her shoulderblades. Without make-up, her face glowed with good health except for some luscious-looking peach-coloured lipgloss.

She looked...radiant. Last night's gymnastics had done her a world of good. 'Let's go.' Keeping her hand clasped firmly in his, he headed towards a walking trail which pointed to Katoomba Falls.

Seeing the spectacular World Heritage sights with Emma, he discovered their mutual enjoyment of exploring nature on foot. She shared his interest in the environment and the native flora and fauna they came across. Ancient ferns, rainbow lorikeets. They even glimpsed an echidna fossicking in the bushland nearby.

He persuaded her to cross the valley on the Skyway with the promise of lunch at the revolving restaurant at the other end. She buried her face against his chest as they swung out into space so high that the shadow of their cabin was the size of a newborn's thumbnail on the Jurassic forest below.

Jake couldn't remember a day he'd enjoyed more in a long time. Simple things like sharing a can of soda while they sat on a rock with the breeze at their backs and listened to the crystal sounds of the nearby Katoomba waterfall.

He was as interested in Emma's mind and her opinions as he was in her body. Connecting with her, seeing that rare smile and finding out what they had in common, was as much a part of the day as the hot, lingering looks they exchanged, knowing the evening ahead promised to be as special as the last.

By mid-afternoon it was becoming increasingly difficult to keep his hands off her, so they cut the sightseeing short and made a fast trip back to the hotel and his suite.

Later, surrounded by white candles in the gleaming

black spa of the stunning black bathroom, with its wide uninterrupted view, they sipped bubbly and watched the constantly changing panorama. A curtain of rain filled the valley floor, a blur of dull gold with the setting sun behind as the shower moved through in brilliant contrast to the encroaching stormy black sky.

But the best view was right in front of him.

Emma's hair was catching the sun's last feeble rays, and the soft glow of candlelight shone on her cheeks as daylight faded.

She was facing him across a mountain of bubbles, and in those sapphire eyes, with their stars and luminosity, he could see a load had been lifted. She'd let herself go for once in her life and had a good time.

How long would it take for the pressures of real life to tarnish that glow and eclipse the sparkle? After tomorrow's short return journey to the urban rat race it was back to business for them both.

Which made it all the more important not to waste a single second of what was left of tonight.

He took her glass, set both flutes on the side of the spa, then slid forward, knees bent, so that his legs came around hers and her belly came into contact with his. Put his hands on her shoulders so he could look right into those eyes. 'You're a pleasure to be with, Emma Byrne.'

Emma stared into his warm brown eyes. She was going to pay for that pleasure sooner or later. This weekend had been one amazing adventure after another, one she'd remember for ever.

'Hey, that's supposed to make you smile, not frown.'

'I'm not fr—'

'You are. You get that little line between your eyebrows...' He smoothed it away with a fingertip. 'Okay, I've got something guaranteed to make you smile.' His deep voice rumbled between them and he pressed closer, his burgeoning hardness hot and impatient against her belly.

'Mmm…'

'See? Smiling already.' He nipped his way up the side of her neck to the sensitive spot beneath her ear. 'How am I doing?' Tugged her earlobe between his lips, making her tingle.

'Pretty well.' His hands were a slippery delight on her shoulders.

'Only pretty well?'

She closed her eyes the better to savour it. Him. 'You can do better.'

A slow hand cruised down to her left breast to toy with her nipple. 'How about this?' He moved his mouth over hers and murmured, 'Is this good?'

'Mmm. Good.' *Very good.* She sighed and her lips opened under his probing tongue. It wasn't only his fabulously sexy body and his skill as a lover, it was their easy rapport, their shared interests.

Or was it something deeper?

Before she could ponder or react to that significant and scary thought he surged forward, his hands on either side of her face, his dark eyes holding hers. Slowly, slowly, he pushed that glorious hardness inside her. Slow and slippery and…oh, he was persuasive. Addictive.

'Tell me it's the best you ever had,' he demanded against her lips, withdrawing inch by excruciatingly exquisite inch, leaving her breathless and arching her hips in anticipation.

'Ha!' she managed. 'Isn't that what you guys all want to know?'

'Tell me you want more.' He leaned back just enough for her to see the wicked glint in his eyes and withdrew.

'Yes,' she moaned. 'More.' And moaned again as he pushed inside her, faster now, on a wild ride to paradise.

'Come with me.' His words sounded harsh and ragged against her ear as he came deep inside her.

'Coming,' she gasped as she rode over the edge of the velvet chasm with him.

Jake had chosen the room for its awesome view and the gas fire. The flames that licked over attractive smooth river stones provided warmth and intimacy. They sat in matching hotel robes on the rug in the flickering glow and shared the cold lobster and mango salad Room Service had delivered earlier.

He watched Emma slip a slice of mango between her lips. Tousled damp hair framed her face. Her eyes reflected the fire's orange glow, turning them violet and mysterious.

He wanted to know more of her secrets. More about the product line she'd developed and why she was so passionate about it that she'd spend so much of her free time immersed in it and yet not pursue its potential further.

Was it a front to hide behind? Was she lonely or a natural loner? Was she a risk-taker or not?

She was different to the women he usually got involved with. *So* different from the synthetic types to be found in King's Cross. Emma was sparkly and refreshing, a glint of dew on spring grass on a sunny morning. Her body was slender, firm, natural. Curves in all the right places and they were all real.

'Taste.' She swirled a sliver of lobster into the buttery sauce and held it to his lips. 'It's divine.'

He opened his mouth and let her feed him. Chewed a moment, savouring the flavour, the slight pressure of her finger against his lips.

The room's muted glow cast intimate shadows. 'Nothing beats romance, huh?'

She wiped her fingers on her napkin, her movements a

little jerky. Her eyes were still on his but rather than the dreamy violet from moments ago they were quicksilver-black. 'I don't do romance.'

The flat comment surprised him. 'No?' He waved an all-encompassing hand around the room—the flickering firelight on the walls, its warmth against his skin. 'What do you call this? The candlelit spa we just enjoyed?'

'Ambience.'

'So define romance.'

'Hearts and flowers and pretty words.' Silver sliced through her gaze, a knife's glint against ebony. 'I don't need them and I don't want them.'

'Why not?' He saw the pain in her eyes before she looked away. 'Surfer Boy wasn't the romantic type?'

She shrugged. 'That's just it. He was. Something special every Friday night and a dozen red roses every Wednesday, with a pretty note to say he was thinking of me...'

Her story didn't make sense to Jake. 'You weren't being totally honest with me about him the night of the dinner, were you?'

'Just because I don't want rom—'

'It's in your eyes. That's why you're not looking at me.'

'I'm...' Her shoulders drooped. 'Okay. I didn't slot him into my schedule. He slotted me into his. And I let him. Because, you see, I was stupidly in love with him.'

Jake reached out, trailed a finger down her cheek. 'He's even more of an idiot than I thought,' he murmured.

She shook her head. 'Romance is a lie to cover a lie.'

'It doesn't have to be, Emma.'

'No romance, okay? No lies.'

'Okay...' He pressed her down and rolled her onto her back on the rug, unknotting her belt and spreading her robe wide. 'Does that mean I can't tell you you're the sexiest woman I've ever made love to by firelight?'

She reached for his robe, pushing it away, fingers stretching and flexing over his shoulders, her eyes duelling with his, a smile on her lips and that little dimple in her cheek winking as he lowered himself on top of her. 'I'm okay with that.'

They had a late checkout on Monday morning so they spent it in bed and then enjoyed a quick lunch in a charming little rustic café before returning to Sydney. Emma had phoned in sick to work—something she'd never done before.

On the trip back she was almost tempted to open her laptop which Jake had returned to her, and catch up on the orders she'd neglected. But she knew she'd not be able to concentrate. Her mind was chock-full of distracting thoughts. So she watched the scenery flash by, and with it the slow return from fairytales and magical rides—of any kind—to civilisation and real life.

Real life. Depressing thought. Closing her eyes, she feigned sleep as they reached outer suburbia and let her mind drift back over the past two days.

She heard Jake speak on his mobile with his PA about some problem with a client that couldn't wait, enjoying the deep, authoritative timbre in his voice, remembering how it sounded when he came deep inside her.

Emma's phone signalled an incoming text. She considered ignoring it, but her responsible self wouldn't allow her to. She opened it and stared at the message. 'I don't believe it,' she murmured.

Jake glanced her way. 'Something wrong?'

'Mum's gone to Melbourne. With Stan.'

'Good for her.' Jake's voice was laced with a smile.

Emma texted back a reply before slipping her phone back into her bag. 'She's never done anything so impulsive in her life.'

'Then it's time she did.' With his eyes on the road, Jake put a hand on her thigh. 'Stan's a good guy. She'll be fine.'

'Of course she will.' She hoped. Because she wasn't looking forward to the fall-out if things went wrong.

'Your mum's a hard woman, Em,' he said, moments later. 'I know she was ill for a long time…'

'Clinical depression.' Emma hugged her arms, remembering the stress she and Stella had endured as a result. 'She's recovered now, but the after-effects linger on.' *And on*.

'Your dad's death caused it?'

She shook her head. 'She was depressed long before that. Dad didn't love her and there were other women.'

'Why didn't she just kick him out or walk away?'

'Because he had absolute control of her money. Remember, her generation isn't ours. And maybe she *wanted* to play the martyr.' The angst spilled out and it felt good. Really good. As if she was sweeping it out of her life. 'Just before Dad died he invested what was left of her inheritance and lost the lot.'

She heard Jake exhale loudly. 'That's tough, Emma. That's why you were always working?'

'I couldn't let the house be sold. It would've finished Mum off. Stella, being the nurturing soul she is, took on the role of carer.'

'So, forgive me if this offends you, why the hell does Bernice treat you the way she does? And why do you let her?'

A question Emma had asked herself often enough. 'Mum never appreciated the financial side of what I was doing—she just didn't see it. And Stella's been there for her in a more physical and emotional way.'

'So you erected a barrier to protect yourself from the rejection.'

'I guess I did. She doesn't get to me any more.'

He glanced at her. 'I disagree, Emma. It's still there.'

She shrugged—maybe he was right—and watched the glimpses of the ocean through the windscreen as they neared Coogee. 'She allowed my father to ruin her life. It spilled over to her daughters.'

And it reminded Emma why she wouldn't allow herself to think of what she and Jake had as anything more than a sexy encounter. She'd enjoyed it for what it was. But never again would she rely on anyone for her own happiness.

It felt odd, pulling up in her driveway in the middle of a work-day afternoon. She felt as if she'd lived a lifetime since she'd been home.

Jake switched off the engine, and the sudden silence in the car's confines seemed to shout. She busied herself searching her bag for her keys then realised she was already holding them.

She felt his gaze as he said, 'I guess you'll want to jump straight on your laptop and check out those orders that have piled up in your absence.'

His tone suggested that even if *she* wasn't down from the clouds and quite ready to settle to work just yet he was. He was probably used to switching from pleasure to business without a blink.

She fought down an absurd disappointment and turned with a smile fixed on her face. 'It doesn't go away, does it? Even when we do.'

He smiled back. 'Okay, then.' He pushed open the door and walked around to the boot to take out her belongings.

She took a careful, calming breath before climbing out and following him to the front door. She unlocked it and he ushered her past him and inside.

'Where do you want your gear?' he said behind her.

'Here's fine.' She gestured beside her and turned to him,

suddenly feeling like a stranger in her own surroundings. Everything felt different and she didn't know what to say. How ridiculous. She was experiencing morning-after awkwardness *now?*

He set the suitcase down and placed the garment bag on top, then straightened.

'Thanks.'

'No worries.'

She didn't know what to do with her hands and clasped them in front of her. How did you say goodbye to a man you'd just spent the past couple of nights having the best sex of your life with?

You said it casually, as if it happens all the time. 'Thanks for a great weekend.'

'My pleasure.' A flicker of heat darkened his gaze.

Mine too.

'I'll let you get to it, then.'

No *We'll have to do it again sometime.* 'Yes. Better get started. So...I'll see you...around.' God, did she sound needy? Clingy? Desperate?

He nodded, those dark eyes fixed on hers but giving nothing away. 'I'll give you a call some time.'

'Right.' Tomorrow? Next week? Next year?

He bent to kiss her. Just a brief brush of those expert lips over hers. Then he must have changed his mind because his arms slid around her waist and pulled her close. Her mouth opened beneath his and she let him in, tasting him as his tongue slid over hers. Her heart thudded against her chest and she clung to his shirt a moment before he lifted his head.

His eyes had changed, she noticed, like hot treacle. But she instinctively knew he wasn't going to act on it, so stepped back first. *At least maintain a little dignity.* 'Bye, then.'

'Catch you later.'

As he turned to leave his mobile buzzed and he yanked it out of his jacket pocket. 'Carmody.' He paused on Emma's doorstep, not looking at her while he listened to the caller. He didn't look back, walking into the sunshine, his attention already focused elsewhere.

Emma closed the door and listened to the purr of his car's engine as he drove off. She rubbed a hand over the familiar ache in her chest. It couldn't be love. Not again. She wouldn't let it be.

CHAPTER ELEVEN

EMMA found it tough going over the next couple of days at work—unable to concentrate, thinking of Jake, remembering their time together, wishing she could see him again even if it was just to remind herself that he was a one-weekend wonder. But she didn't hear from him.

Get over it. They'd had a fling. One wild, sexy weekend of pleasure. He'd never promised more. He'd been totally upfront with her. At least he'd been honest, and after Wayne that counted for a lot.

She felt different, though. Being with Jake had given her a new-found confidence in herself. As a woman, as a lover, as a person. She wanted to take on the world. She wanted to get serious about her business.

She wanted to see him so she could tell him that.

Meanwhile she filled her orders and surfed the internet for new soap-making recipes and considered how she might extend her client base.

On Thursday evening, humming along with her favourite jazz CD, she collected the ingredients together for honey soap. She melted glycerin bars and honey, poured it into a shallow pan, then melted the goat's milk, adding it to the mix. She'd just set it aside to cool when she heard the doorbell chime and went to answer it.

Jake.

He was leaning on her doorframe, reminding her of the last time she'd seen him standing there, and her heart tripped and she was breathless all over again. A burst of happiness sang through her veins as she met his warm brown eyes. Tonight he wore a luxurious-looking cream jumper over black trousers.

Her smile was spontaneous. 'Hi.'

'I was on my way out and passing this way…' The timbre of his deep, familiar voice turned her insides as hot and syrupy as the mix on her kitchen bench. 'Have I caught you at a bad time?'

'No…no.' She forced the surprise and excitement from her voice. *Act natural. He's on his way out, after all.* 'Come on in. I'm just finishing some soaps.' She turned, casting a deliberately casual glance over her shoulder as she moved to the kitchen. 'What brings you by?' When he didn't answer, she stopped at the kitchen table and turned. He almost crashed into her.

'You,' he said, his eyes melting into hers.

The heat from his body seemed to shimmer right through her. He smelled of warm wool and apple and cinnamon pie.

'More specifically, your soaps.' He rubbed his knuckles together audibly. 'It's my PA's birthday next week. I'd like to buy some for her.'

'Uh-huh. Well…' She swished her own hands down her coat. Her palms were sweating. 'I've got some pretty flower-shaped ones with a "Happy Birthday" imprint somewhere. I'll—'

'No birthday imprint.' He caught her arm as she started to move away.

'Oh. Okay…' She blinked once.

'She doesn't want anyone to know.' He lifted a shoulder. 'She's shy about birthdays.' Jake lowered his voice, curling his fingers around the lab coat's thick fabric. He felt Emma's gentle warmth beneath, the smooth muscle over bone against his palm, before letting his arm drop to his side. 'I thought I'd take some extras into the office at the same time. Let some of the staff try them out.'

'Really?' Surprise and humour glinted in her eyes and her lips curved and he knew she was wise to his game.

'Really.' He smiled back. 'What can you recommend?'

She moved to the plastic containers stacked along the wall. 'They're all made with goat's milk for sensitive skin, but I have a range of fragrances. How about amber, which has a sweet woody note suitable for both sexes? Or vanilla? Or, for something extra special…' She pulled out a container, carried it to the table. 'I've got some gorgeous little cupcake shapes in different fragrances—vanilla, blueberry, cinnamon, coconut. They're my favourite stock and very popular. I can pack them in a little basket for you if you want.'

He grinned. 'Do you wash with them or eat them?'

She opened the box, closed her eyes briefly and inhaled the fragrance, her ecstatic expression reminding him of when she'd come apart in his arms. She lifted out a pretty pink sample that matched the colour in her cheeks. 'I love cupcakes to death, but I wouldn't recommend eating these.'

Amazing, this transformation from the solemn girl who'd greeted him at her door only last week. The obvious joy she got from her creative work. The sparkle it put in her eyes and the glow it brought to her cheeks. And she was right; this was no mere hobby. Little wonder she'd been insulted he'd called it such. She had something unique here, a marketable product.

He leaned a hip against the table. 'Have you given any more thought to expanding this business online? Because

I see a different woman standing here tonight. One who might be willing to take that chance now.'

'Maybe I *am* a different woman.' He noticed her eyes had turned a darker hue as she looked at him. 'You've had something to do with that. And I *am* thinking about it.' She picked up a green cake, held it to his nose. 'What do you smell?'

'Fresh mown grass?'

'It gives a bathroom a pleasant scent.' She set it down. 'So many fragrances. I love them all.'

'Which one do you use?' He leaned in to catch more of that scent he'd missed over the past few days, heard her tiny intake of breath.

'Tahitian Fantasy.' Her breath hitched again. 'Why are you really here, Jake?'

Her husky voice vibrated against his lips as he set them on her smooth neck. 'Nothing like a little Tahitian Fantasy. Because I wanted to see you again. Are you okay with that?' His hands drifted to her waist, lips tracing a line over the fragrant flesh beneath her ear.

'Ah…yes…'

'Good, because I can't seem to stay away.' He nipped at her earlobe. 'What's in it?'

'The tiare flower. Tahitian gardenia.' She arched her neck. 'It has healing properties.'

'I've got this itch…'

'Where?' she murmured.

'Everywhere,' he murmured back, moving nearer, pressing open-mouthed kisses up her neck, over her jaw. 'I itch every damn where.'

'That sounds serious.' She stepped back to see his eyes, her own dancing as she slid his sleeve up to his elbow, fingers lightly massaging his forearm. 'Do you exfoliate?'

He had to lean forward so he could drop a lingering kiss on her lips. 'Only when I'm with you.'

Her blue eyes twinkled up at him. 'Ha-ha.' She picked up a dark-coloured soap that looked like congealed breakfast cereal. 'Honey and oatmeal,' she said, and gave his chest a light prod with one finger. 'Sit down…if you've got a moment?'

'For you, yes.' He yanked out a chair and watched her fill a shallow bowl with warm water.

The last time he'd been in her place she'd been uptight and defensive and prickly. Tonight she was the relaxed woman he'd enjoyed the weekend with.

Was it only four nights ago? It felt like four weeks. He'd spent those nights in a kind of limbo, caught between wanting to call and ask if he could come over and reminding himself they'd agreed on a weekend and the weekend was finished.

Had she spent the last few nights thinking of how good they'd been together? In bed and out of it? She was fresh, honest and fun to be with. He regretted putting a time limit on their affair.

'It's almost as good as sex.' Her words had him sitting up straighter as she carried the bowl to the table, set it in front of him along with a handtowel.

'What is?'

'Push up your sleeves and put your hands in the bowl.' She moistened the soap in the water and worked it between her palms till it glistened, then slid it over and around his hand in a slow, slippery massage. 'Good?'

He watched, fascinated, her small fingers with their short neat nails gliding over his, between his. He looked up, met her eyes. 'Very good. Exceptionally good. But… Do I need to work on my bedroom technique?'

The twinkle in her eyes sharpened. Her lips stretched

into a full-on smile. 'Okay, that was my selling point before the weekend. Damn—now I'll have to think of something else.'

'We could always test the theory again, just to be sure…'

'There's nothing wrong with your technique, Jake.' She twined her fingers against his. Silky heat on silky heat.

'Nor yours.' He reciprocated, pressing his thumb into her palm and drawing lazy circles, watching her cheeks pinken, her eyes turn to liquid pools of blue desire.

His own vision was growing hazy as they continued to watch each other while they made out with their joined hands. 'Do you give all your clients the personal treatment?'

She leaned in so that her lips were a whisper away from his. 'Only the ones who knock on my door.'

'I've been thinking,' he murmured back, 'there's no reason why we can't continue seeing each other, is there?'

Her whole body stilled. 'What are you saying?'

He soothed his lips over hers just once. 'I like being with you. Don't look too far ahead. Let's just enjoy the ride. What do you say?'

'Uh-huh…'

He lifted her damp fingers to his mouth, kissed them and released her. 'In the meantime, I've got an appointment in King's Cross. If tonight goes as planned, tomorrow the Pink Mango could be looking at a new owner.'

She continued to stare at him, unblinking, gaze unfocused. 'Uh-huh.'

But she didn't seem to hear him. 'Don't congratulate me yet,' he said anyway. He wiped his hands on her little towel, then pushed up. 'Talk to you tomorrow evening.'

'Uh-huh.'

He folded the towel, set it on the table. 'I'll let myself out.'

He smiled to himself when he heard her call, 'Yes!' as clear as crystal as he walked to the door.

For Emma, the following work day dragged. Unlike what was happening with Jake, which seemed to be taking off at warp speed. She couldn't focus on anything except their unexpected sexy interlude last night.

He liked being with her. He wanted to be with her some more. It brought a smile to her lips every time she remembered. So often that her co-workers cast more than a few Emma-had-got-lucky glances her way over the course of the day.

She left the call centre five minutes before closing time; something she'd never done before. She tapped along with the beat of the latest pop song on the radio as she drove home, looking forward to Jake's call.

It was nearly six o'clock when he rang. Emma picked the phone up on its first ring.

'It's done,' he said without preamble. 'The Pink Mango's history.'

She almost heard the drum-roll of satisfaction in his voice and smiled. 'Hooray for you.'

'Can you clear your evening schedule and come out to celebrate with me?'

Her smile broadened. 'Consider it cleared.'

'I'll pick you up in thirty minutes?'

'*Thirty* minutes?'

'You'll look gorgeous whatever you're wearing,' he said, obviously familiar with the female ritual, 'and I've got somewhere casual in mind.'

Thirty-five minutes later, after three changes of clothes, she'd decided on her best jeans and an ivory jumper with a bright turquoise-and-orange scarf when he arrived.

Seeing him was like cresting the top of a rollercoaster

wave, all excitement and anticipation. He wore black jeans and a black T-shirt beneath an often washed black, white and navy flannel shirt, open down the front. Definitely casual.

'Hi.' She sounded as breathless as she felt.

'Hi.' With one arm still propped against the doorframe he tugged on her scarf, pulled her towards him and kissed her.

He tasted *sooo* good, and she felt herself rushing down the other side of that slippery breaker. Then he straightened, and with a wickedly hot twinkle in his eyes, said, 'If we don't get moving we might never get there.'

'Wait up. You forgot something last night.' She picked up a little cellophane-wrapped basket from the shelf by the door and held it out with a grin. 'Tell your PA happy birthday from me.'

He nodded, eyes twinkling. 'How much do I owe you?'

'Nothing. Free sample.'

'Are you sure?'

'Positive. Promotion's good for business.'

'Okay, but don't forget to write it off as an expense.'

Moments later they were cruising along a well-lit Bondi street bustling with Friday-night shoppers. But Jake bypassed the usual restaurants and turned into a suburban street.

She looked out at the luxury homes, roofs glinting in the streetlights. 'Where are we going?'

He pulled up in front of a buttercream wall. Beyond, Emma could see an expansive red-tiled roof. 'Welcome to Jake's Place. Home of great food and magnificent views.' He pressed a remote and the gates swung open revealing a large two-storey house.

'Wow.' She took in the view as the car came to a stop under an open carport. A long curve of beach, dark now but for a couple of lights blinking near the horizon. 'It's magnificent, Jake. You've achieved so much in such a short time.' The location alone had to be worth a fortune.

He swiped the keys from the ignition, his gaze on the black waves laced with a fine line of white in the distance. 'The bank still has a share, but we're getting there.'

Reaching across the console between them, he cupped the back of her neck with one hand, unclipped her seat belt with the other, his gaze hot with smouldering promise. And before she could blink he meshed his lips with hers.

He'd had no intention of jumping her until he'd fed her, but when Jake looked into those sapphire eyes which had kept him from the precious little sleep he'd managed over the past few nights, every thought flew out of his mind bar one. Having Emma.

'Have you missed me?' he murmured against her lips. When had he ever asked that question? he wondered vaguely, and was stupidly happy when he felt her lips curve against his mouth.

'Yes.' She sucked in a breath.

His impatient fingers found the hem of her jumper and rushed beneath to feel the firm, warm flesh of her torso, the ridges along her ribcage, and higher to the curve under her breasts. Her nipples tightened as he swirled his fingers over the crests. Beneath his hands he felt the same urgency that whipped through his own body as she strained against his palm.

'Emma…' The breathless sound registered somewhere as his own voice. 'Missed you too.' Flicking the clasp, he loosened her bra, shoved it up and out of the way so he could feast on the sweet taste of an engorged nipple. He slid his palm between her thighs, cupped her hard through the hot denim, felt her shudder and arch in response, heard her muffled sigh as she forked her fingers through his hair and pulled it tight against his scalp.

He heard a rushing noise in his ears; it might have been the sea, or her ragged breath, or the fizz of his own blood. All he knew was if he didn't get out now he'd have her here, in the car, before sanity could prevail.

Swearing and fumbling with the latch, he pushed the passenger door open. Somehow they were both out of the car and stumbling together towards the house.

His keys... In the car—somewhere. The hell with them. He had her up against the wall, mouths fused, teeth clashing, his raging erection pressing into the soft give of her belly before either of them knew what had happened.

Did she have any idea how much power she wielded over him? He never lost it like this. Her pupils were dark and dilated when he lifted his head to watch her while he snapped open the top button of her jeans.

She returned the favour, hard little knuckles against his belly as she loosened the stud.

There was a harsh zipping sound as they freed each other. And then he was lifting her against the wall and pushing into her familiar sultry heat, his tongue mimicking the action as it dived inside her mouth to drown in her taste.

Fast, furious, frantic. No time to think. Just blind, burning lust, passion and pleasure. She seemed to struggle for air, and he lifted his lips, as breathless as she, and watched her, head thrown back, neck pale and slender in the cool wash of light angling in from the street.

Then his mouth was there, on that galloping pulse, her smooth fragrant skin. Exquisite taste. Pure sensuality.

But the need she conjured in him as he rode the wave to completion, this desperation, as if she was tearing something from deep within him, was beyond his experience.

Moments later, his body still humming, he lowered her to her feet, rested his brow against hers. 'What is it with you? I can't seem to get enough—'

Protection. He froze. He'd not given it a thought. Not given Emma's welfare or safety a thought. What kind of man did that make him? He lifted her chin with a finger and stared into her eyes. 'We just had unprotected sex, Emma.'

'We didn't use a condom, no.' She didn't look fazed or alarmed. Her eyes were clear and calm, like the sea on a summer day.

'I…if anything happens…'

'It won't. I'm still on the pill.'

He relaxed a little. 'You didn't tell me.'

'You didn't ask.' She lifted a shoulder, then wiggled back into her jeans. 'And I wasn't as sure about you then…'

He caught her drift. 'I'm healthy, Emma.'

If they'd been in full light he'd have sworn her eyes darkened, and she rolled her lips together in that way she had before saying, 'I wanted *you* inside me, not a piece of rubber.'

Her words hit hard, right where his heart suddenly pounded like a hammer on steel. His fingers tightened as he adjusted his own clothing. 'I should've been more careful. I always use condoms.' Just not this time.

'I take care of my own protection,' she said.

Emma didn't want to talk about it. Not another word. *Oh, no.* Her heart suddenly cramped, twisted as she realised the full import of what she'd just admitted. She'd wanted that closer connection with him. Craved it like an addict. *Dangerous.* Had she made the right decision to continue seeing Jake after all?

She rubbed a hand over her chest. 'It's cold out here,' she said, hugging her arms. 'Can we go inside?'

He mumbled something about keys and walked to the car, fishing around in the luxury interior a moment before coming back, keys in hand. 'Come on—you can take a look around while I cook.'

She used the time alone to refocus her thoughts while she explored Jake's domain. The décor was essentially masculine but comfortable. Lots of glass, dark furniture with splashes of colour—maroon, grey, red. The wood-panelled kitchen was surprisingly clean and tidy, putting hers to shame. But then, he had enough cupboard space and mod cons for the both of them. An office with two computers and three monitors, and a fortune in the latest technology in the living room.

The upstairs bedrooms were mostly empty except for Jake's. A massive king-size bed dominated the room with its tan and navy quilt and minimal furniture. She backed away from the reminder that other women had no doubt enjoyed themselves there and hurried downstairs.

He'd slapped a couple of thick steaks on the grill and was slicing an avocado when she returned to the kitchen, but he waved away her offer of help so she wandered to the living room. Windchimes filled the balcony beyond the floor-to-ceiling windows, the sound tinkling and clacking in the gentle breeze. Solar-powered balls of crackled glass slowly spun multi-coloured lights over the deck.

He appeared moments later with the aromatic steaks, a bowl of healthy-looking salad and a loaf of crusty bread.

They ate while a blues CD poured music out of the speakers with only the solar-powered balls for lighting—'ambience', he was quick to point out—and washed it down with a nice cabernet sauvignon while they watched a passenger ship track north, myriad tiny lights blazing.

He topped up her glass. 'What's the latest on your mum?'

'She's still in Melbourne. Staying in Stan's house, of all places. *And* she's still deciding when she'll come home.'

'Having a new man in her life's obviously done her good.' He grinned. 'Maybe she'll be a little more mellow on her return.'

'Maybe.' It helped that Jake understood, and Emma was glad she'd opened up on that topic; it felt good to share.

He rose, collected their plates. 'Why don't you go make yourself comfortable on the couch and I'll make coffee? What's your preference?'

'Cappuccino, please. With extra chocolate?'

While he attended to the coffee machine she walked out onto the deck to feel the salt breeze and hear the sound of the sea. She told herself that she was right where she wanted to be. With a guy whose company she enjoyed. She refused to let herself think beyond the ride he'd promised.

When she walked inside he'd brought the coffee and a bowl of dark chocolates and she snuggled against him on the couch. She listened to his heart beating strong and solid against her ear, the fresh fragrance of sun-dried clothes and his clean scent in her nostrils. He turned on the TV. Some old adventure movie was playing. She tuned out, closed her eyes, and moments later felt herself drifting...

'You're tired,' he murmured. 'Stay the night.'

The spell she was falling under shattered like glass. She kept her eyes closed but her mind was instantly alert. Unlike their fantasy weekend in paradise, this was the real world. And in the real world she was...falling in love with this man.

Even as the words formed in her mind she was shoving them away, squeezing them out of her heart. She refused, *refused* to fall in love again. She'd been there, done that, and had the scars to prove it. Her mother had fallen for a man who'd not loved her and it had brought nothing but pain and misery to herself, her husband and her daughters—even long after he'd died.

'You're thinking too hard again.' He curled a hand around her head and stroked her hair. 'You won't need pyjamas, and I've got a spare toothbrush.'

Oh, yes, she'd bet he did.

'So…spend the night with me?'

She opened her eyes, looked into his and felt her heart tumble further. 'I can't,' she all but whispered.

A puzzled crease formed between his brows. 'I'll drive you back in plenty of time in the morning. I can even wait while you get your swimsuit and drop you off at the beach if you want.'

'We'll see each other, Jake, but I won't be staying nights.'

A beat of silence. 'I'm not Wayne, Emma,' he said quietly.

'I know. I just need my space for a bit. This is all happening too fast.' She couldn't help it. She reached up, touched his clean-shaven jaw. 'Okay?'

'Okay. I won't pressure you. It's too soon. I get that. But if you change your mind…'

She nodded, feeling the strength drain out of her. 'Thanks. But you're right. I'm tired and, if it's okay with you, I'd like to go home now.'

He exhaled a slow, deep breath, then pushed off the couch. 'I'll get my keys.'

When a woman didn't want to spend the night with him, he… He what? Jake frowned at his darkened ceiling later that night. He couldn't remember the last time.

He swung out of bed, dragged on old shorts, T-shirt and sneakers, then headed downstairs and out into the salty night air. The chill spattered his skin with goosebumps as he made his way along a couple of streets to the beach. Black waves surged and thumped on the sand as he jogged off the road and onto the esplanade.

She had good reasons, he reminded himself, and it wasn't personal—the scumbag surfer had done a real number on her.

He'd respect her space, give her time. That fragile heart of hers was still healing, and no way was he going to be responsible for further damage. Meanwhile they could continue to enjoy what they *did* have, keeping it casual.

A car skidded to a stop a short distance away, drawing his attention. The back door swung open, something flopped onto the road and the vehicle sped off. What the...? Switching direction to the way he'd come, he increased his pace.

The small bundle of dirty fur moved, and two frightened eyes looked up at his. Jake's heart melted. 'Hey, fella. Steady.' He looked the dog over, murmuring soothing noises. No ID. Beneath the matted white fur he was skin and bone, and alive with fleas. Abandoned in the middle of the night. Poor little scrap.

'Come on, Scratch. We'll find you some place safe.' Sliding a finger beneath the grimy collar, he picked the little guy up and set off for home. In a different life he'd have kept him, but he had no choice but to hand him to the nearest animal shelter first thing.

With Scratch contained in the laundry, with a bowl of water, a left-over sausage and an old cushion to sleep on, Jake's thoughts turned to Emma again as he climbed the stairs to snatch a couple of hours of sleep.

She was sexy, had a sense of humour, and was good company in and out of bed. If she wouldn't stay the night he'd accept that. Because she was Emma. She wasn't only a lover, she was a friend. There was something so easy about being with her, and she brought more to his life on so many levels than any woman ever had.

Careful, mate. He was starting to sound like Ry. *Hell.* He flopped backwards onto his bed. That was one very dangerous thought.

CHAPTER TWELVE

THE sea was as calm as glass on Sunday morning, but the air chilled Emma's body as she waded in for her morning workout. The sun had lifted out of the ocean, spreading crimson and gold across the sky.

Sliding beneath the surface, she kept close to the shoreline between the red and yellow safety flags, swimming hard until her limbs warmed and softened. She trod water, watching the sun glimmer on the surface, and waved to a regular fellow swimmer before heading back the other way.

Jake had come by yesterday evening, late and tired. Working his day job and dealing with the sale of the club would take a toll on anyone. She'd made popcorn on one occasion and they'd made love—on every occasion. On the couch. In her tiny shower stall. In her too-small bed. But he hadn't stayed. She'd been unable to sleep for the rest of the night, knowing there was a big warm man in a big warm bed a few kilometres away who'd have been happy to share.

She headed for her towel farther up the beach. Sunday mornings brought out tourists and locals alike. Walking up the shallow steps towards the lawns bordering the esplanade, she watched a group of families set up for a picnic breakfast.

Only now, with Jake in her life, was she realising how isolated she'd let herself become over the years. She needed to make an effort to go out and socialise more.

She wrung out her hair, tied it into a high ponytail, then changed into her track suit in the change rooms, dumping her swimsuit and towel into her hold-all.

On such a beautiful day she didn't want to go home and deal with business, shut away from people and life. She'd splash out on a take-away hot chocolate on the way home. She might even add a cake to her order and sit at an outdoor table on Coogee Beach Road and people-watch awhile.

A big guy with a black-and-white dog on a leash was approaching when she reached the traffic lights. He waved and she pushed up her sunglasses. Jake? With a dog?

She waved back, and suddenly that sunshine seemed a whole lot warmer. The whole world seemed that much brighter. He was looking at her as if he wanted to eat her while he waited for the lights to change.

He crossed the road and kissed her right there on the footpath. 'Hello, gorgeous girl,' he said when he let her up for air. 'Mmm—salt.'

She licked his familiar taste from her lips. 'I wonder why.' He was a beautiful sight, even in a ratty T-shirt smudged with what looked suspiciously like doggy paw prints. She bent to pat the gorgeous black-and-white pooch of indeterminate pedigree at his feet. 'I didn't know you had a dog.'

'He's not mine, unfortunately. I walk him for an elderly neighbour who can't get out much these days. Say hello to Seeker.' He patted the dog's head. 'Shake hands, boy.'

At Jake's command, Seeker sat down and lifted a paw, big puppy eyes looking up at her and a doggy smile as wide as the beach. 'Oh, aren't you *gorgeous?*' She squatted down to ruffle his well maintained fur and was rewarded with a sloppy kiss. 'I always, always wanted a dog, but Mum said no.' *And hadn't she decided her perfect man in her perfect world would love animals?*

'I still do, but these days with my lifestyle it wouldn't be fair, so I get my animal fix with Seeker, here. Some people don't deserve pets.' He frowned. 'I had to turn an abandoned dog in to a shelter yesterday.'

'That's so sad—not to mention criminal. If you can't give a pet the time and love it deserves, don't have one. I'm going for hot chocolate. Would you like to join me? We can get take-away and walk if you like.'

His grin was one-hundred-percent contagious. 'I would. I didn't stop for breakfast. Had to give Seeker his doggy bath.'

'You groom him too?'

'It's part of the fun. He's all mine every Sunday morning unless I'm out of town. There's a dog-friendly park a ten-minute walk away. I can let Seeker off the leash. I've got his *B-A*-double-*L*.'

She laughed. 'He's gorgeous *and* smart.'

Like you, Jake thought, watching her bury her face in fur.

'So how come I've never seen you down here before?' she said, straightening.

'I don't usually come this far. I was on my way to see you, as a matter of fact. Good timing—I was hoping to catch you on your way home from the beach. If not I was going to hunt you down at your place and interrupt you.'

'Oh? Why?'

Because I can't get you out of my mind. I want to be with you all the damn time. 'Can't a guy see his favourite girl?'

She blushed, and her smile was the best thing he'd seen

all morning. 'I thought you said you were going in to the club today.'

'I am. Later.' He'd delayed his meeting with the buyer by a couple of hours—something he'd never have done for any other woman. He slung an arm around her shoulders with an unnerving feeling that with Emma he was swimming in uncharted waters. 'But here you are, so let's get that breakfast you promised and take it to the park.'

'*I* promised?' She smiled up at him, the light in her eyes reflecting the sun's sparkle off the sea. 'I never promised breakfast.'

'Okay, you buy the hot chocolate; I'll spring for the rest.'

They took their purchases to the park: two hot chocolates and a couple of cupcakes drizzled with icing. They shared half a soggy bacon and egg burger with wilting lettuce and mayonnaise, and let Seeker snaffle the other half.

After a vigorous game of chase-the-ball, which Emma threw herself into with enthusiasm, Jake suggested they walk back to his place, return Seeker on the way, and he'd drive her home on his way to the club.

They headed towards Bondi. Emma jogged a few steps ahead with Seeker, chasing a white butterfly, her slim figure as watch-worthy as any catwalk model, her ponytail bouncing and swinging in time with her steps.

They'd been lovers just over a week. With a little of the edge gone after those first frenzied encounters he'd expected the attraction to fade somewhat, as it invariably did. It hadn't. They'd had fun this morning. She'd not fussed over her sea-damp hair and lack of make-up like other women he dated would. Her tracksuit was smeared with paw-prints and covered in fur.

He'd never in a million years considered asking a

woman to come out and play ball with a dog in a park on a Sunday morning. With Emma it came naturally.

'Hope you weren't worried,' he said when they reached Mrs G's front door.

'Of course not, Jake.' The white-haired lady turned her smile on Emma. 'And you found your friend.'

'Mrs G, I'd like you to meet Emma. Emma, this is Grace Goodman—everyone calls her Mrs G.'

'Pleased to meet you, Emma. Jake was hoping to run into you.'

Emma smiled up at him, then at Grace. 'Nice to meet you too. We've had a lovely morning.'

'I don't how I'd manage without this young man here,' Mrs G told Emma. 'He's taken good care of both of us since my Bernie died. I broke my hip last year, and I can't get out like I used to.'

'Afraid I can't stay,' he said, with an apology in his grin and handing the leash to Mrs G. 'Got work.'

Grace shook her head. 'You work too hard. You and this lovely girl here should be out enjoying yourselves.'

Emma smiled at him. 'Work comes first.'

He knew Emma understood. She believed it as much as he—something some of his other lovers hadn't. But he was also working on the playtime her life had been lacking. The idea of convincing Emma to let him take the rest of the day off with her was tempting, but he had to meet the new club owner and go over the books.

They farewelled Mrs G, then picked up his car. He dropped Emma home first. But he lingered over a long hot kiss before letting her go. 'See you tonight.'

On Tuesday Emma had a rostered day off—and her first luncheon date with Jake.

Since Jake had clients all morning, she was meeting

him at his office. His *real* office, which he shared with two other professionals. In a respectable building in the commercial heart of the city.

She rode the elevator to the fourteenth floor, smoothed the lapel on her black jacket as she stepped into a bright reception area with wide windows and glimpses of the Harbour Bridge between the skyscrapers. A dark-haired woman with exotic eyes that hinted at her Asian heritage greeted her with a professional smile at the desk. So different from the first time she'd met him at his place of work—and in so many ways.

Emma smiled back. 'I'm Emma Byrne and I'm here to see Jake Carmody.'

'Oh. Emma, hello.' Her professional smile widened to friendly interest. 'I'm Jasmine. Jake told me to expect you. He's with someone at the moment. Can I get you a coffee or something while you wait?'

'Thanks, I'm fine.'

'And thank you for sending in the soaps. They're a real hit. I'm making a list of people wanting to buy more.'

'That's very kind of you.'

'Are you sure I can't get you a coffee?'

She shook her head, smiling back. 'I'll just admire the view.'

'It's not nearly as spectacular as where you're going for lunch. I booked the table.' She lowered her voice to a conspiratorial whisper. 'Oh, and I probably wasn't supposed to tell you that.'

Emma had expected to grab something in the little café downstairs, and was pleasantly surprised. 'I didn't hear a thing.'

'Don't plan on getting any work done for the rest of the afternoon. I— Excuse me a moment,' she said when the phone rang. 'Carmody and Associates.'

Ten minutes later Jasmine was still handling what seemed to be a complex call. Emma glanced at her watch and flicked through another magazine. Maybe they should postpone their lunch for another time. He was obviously busy.

Even as she considered it, she heard a door open and Jake's voice in the corridor. '...Any time—and don't worry. It's all going to be fine.'

'Thank you, Jake,' a woman's voice said. 'For everything.' Her voice trembled. 'You've given me a chance to start over and I'll never forget it.'

'Just put it all out of your mind for now, and concentrate on spending some quality time with Kevin while I get things rolling.'

The woman appeared first, in jeans a size too big on her too-thin frame and a faded black top slipping off one shoulder. Her hair was scooped into a knot on top of her head and she carried a thumb-sucking toddler on her hip.

Familiar...Emma racked her brain, trying to place her as Jake followed close behind. He walked the woman to the elevators on the other side of Reception, squeezed the woman's bony shoulders as she entered the lift.

Then Emma remembered where she'd seen her. The waitress from the Pink Mango. Cherry.

Obviously a woman like her couldn't afford to be paying Jake for his professional services, yet he was treating her with the care and respect he'd offer any fee-paying client.

Then he turned and saw her, and his frown cleared and his face lit up. 'Emma. Sorry to keep you waiting. Unexpected delay. Hang on a sec, I have something for you.' He disappeared again into his office.

Jasmine, still on the phone, smiled at Emma and rolled her eyes as she spoke to the caller.

Then Jake returned with a fluffy black-and-white stuffed dog. 'According to the tag, his name's Fergus.'

'Oh…' A warm squishy feeling spread through her body. 'You got me a dog.'

'I hope you like stuffed animals.'

'I did, I do. I guess I never grew up.' She'd mentioned never having pets and he'd bought her the next best thing. 'Thank you.'

He jerked a thumb at the busy Jasmine to indicate they were off, then walked Emma to the elevator. It was crowded with office workers headed out for lunch. He flagged down a cab, then they took a short ride to the Centre Point Tower.

She stared up at the famous landmark, as high as the Eiffel Tower. 'We're going up there?'

'I know you hate heights, but I'm sure you'll enjoy the food,' he said as they shuffled towards one of the elevators that shot sightseers to the observation deck, the Skywalk and other adventures Emma had never felt the urge to discover. 'Don't look till we're there.'

She slipped her hand in his and looked up at him. 'Maybe it's time I did.' Steeling her stomach muscles for the inevitable drop, she let out a nervous laugh. 'I might even surprise myself and enjoy it.'

And she didn't shut her eyes once all the way to the top—which seemed to take for ever. The three-hundred-and-sixty-degree revolving restaurant afforded magnificent views of Botany Bay and as far away as the Blue Mountains. She was so proud of herself she even ventured to the slanted window for a quick dizzying glimpse to the street way below.

Jake's hand on her shoulder and his 'Congratulations' made it even more special. She might never have had the nerve to try if he hadn't been there to encourage her. But her legs were still shaky as she set Fergus on the edge of the table.

Jake ordered white wine and a shared seafood platter for starters. He'd made the right decision about the venue— seeing the almost shy pleasure in Emma's eyes when she'd faced her natural fear was worth it.

'Any other plans for your day off?' he asked, setting the menu aside.

'I have an appointment with a potential client at two-thirty.'

'New client?' He leaned forward, interested. 'That's great, Em. Where?'

'It's a new natural products shop in the mall where I work.'

'So we've plenty of time.' He raised his glass. 'Cheers.'

'Cheers.' She tapped her glass to his.

'Emma, I've been thinking about you getting your products out there. Letting people sample them. Why don't you ask one of the shops you supply if you can set up a display one Saturday morning or during late-night shopping hours? I'll give you a hand. You might sound out this place this afternoon, since they're new, and see if they're interested.'

The seafood platter arrived and she selected a prawn. 'That's an idea.'

'We'll need to set up a website first, in case customers ask, and get some business cards printed so they can contact you.'

'You really think my products are good enough for all that hoopla?'

'Hoopla?' Had no one ever encouraged her to aim for the stars? 'Are you kidding? After that sensual demonstration the other night?' He pointed the crab claw he was holding her way. 'You'll never know if you don't give it a go. Honey, have a little faith. In yourself *and* your products.'

'I'm trying to. I *do*,' she corrected, and gave a half-laugh. 'Force of habit. I'm not used to others sharing my enthusiasm, and I'm still getting accustomed to the different mind-set.' Setting her palms on the table, she leaned forward with a grin. 'Of *course* you have confidence in my products; why wouldn't you? They're the best you ever tried, right?'

'Right.' He grinned back. 'We'll make a start tonight,' he decided. 'I'll come over when you get home and we'll make plans.'

Emma took another sip of cool fruity wine while she thought about his ideas. She didn't want to let him—or herself—down, especially when he was so busy. Surely she could try it on her own? Even if she just let him help her with the IT side of things? 'You're very generous with your time, Jake. As if you haven't got enough to do with your practice and winding up the club. Are you sure?'

'Of course I'm sure. I want to help you any way I can.'

'Cherry obviously thinks you're pretty wonderful too.'

He looked slightly stunned. 'You know Cherry?'

'I recognised her from the club. I didn't know she had a child, though. I guess you don't think of people in that industry as being mums and having otherwise ordinary lives. She looked pretty down...' She waved a hand. 'Sorry, it's none of my business.'

'Cherry and her kid were evicted from their accommodation a couple of weeks ago. She came to me for help.'

Emma understood that feeling, that desperation, all too well. She'd had to work after school to help pay the bills when her mum had been too depressed to get out of bed for weeks on end. 'That's a horrible, gut-wrenching feeling, and even worse with the added responsibility of a child. What about women's shelters?'

'Do you have any idea how many homeless people there are in Sydney?' His expression changed, and his eyes met hers with an understanding she'd not expected. 'Maybe you do.'

Emma nodded. 'It wasn't that desperate with us, but it so easily could have been. So Cherry came to you?' She remembered the woman's tremulous and relieved voice outside Jake's office. Cherry saw the kind of man Emma saw. An approachable man, an honest man, someone she could trust to help her and her child in a time of desperate need. A man who was generous with his time and expertise. 'It shows how highly she thinks of you.'

But he shook his head as if it was nothing. 'She needed a place for the night, for herself and Kevin. I told her there was a room at the back of the club she could use until we sorted something out. She's staying there for the time being.'

'If anyone can help it'll be Jake Carmody.'

They didn't talk for a moment while they sampled more of the delicious food. 'So...who looks after Kevin when Cherry's working?' Emma asked between mouthfuls.

Jake chose a prawn, peeling it carefully while he answered. 'The girls take shifts. They're a tight bunch. Protective. Mostly they're just people trying to make a living the best and sometimes the only way they know how.'

Emma didn't miss the slightly defensive tone. As if he had a personal interest or understanding. She speared a piece of pickled octopus. 'So what happens next? Obviously that can't work for ever.'

'I've bought a place. It needs some work, but I'm using the sale of the club to finance it. Temporary accommodation for people like Cherry to stay until they get themselves on their feet. I've asked Cherry if she'll run it. It'll get her out of the club scene.'

She took a moment to consider his words before she answered. He seemed so sure—as if he'd thought this through over a long period of time. 'This is very important to you.'

Jake nodded, selecting another crab claw, snapping it open. Damn right it was. It was the only good thing to come out of his inheritance: an ability to make a change for the better. If he only helped one person it would be worth it.

'I've been around that strip club for a big chunk of my life, Emma. Seeing women and their kids come and go. Seeing their lack of power over their own circumstances, the hopelessness in their eyes. Wanting to do something to break the cycle. That's why I went into law. I may not have had the world's best upbringing, but I've turned it around, I think.'

He saw her shift closer, elbows on the white tablecloth, her fresh, clean fragrance wafting towards him. 'I reckon you have,' she said softly. 'You should be careful, Jake, a girl could fall hard for a guy like you.'

His head shot up. Her eyes… Maybe, just *maybe,* there was a hint of those for ever stars in that blue sparkle? He shredded another prawn while his heart tumbled strangely. 'Not a girl like you, Emma. You're too smart.'

The little crease dug between her brows as she popped an olive in her mouth. 'Why not a girl like me?'

Careful. The last thing Emma needed right now was another crack in that heart. 'We're both career types, you and me,' he said, avoiding her gaze. 'Work hard, play hard.'

But were good times all he really had in common with

Emma? He'd never discussed the club or his upbringing or his reasons for his choice of career with anyone. Not even Ryan. Though his mate knew of his father's business they'd never talked about it. Yet he'd talked about it with Emma. But she didn't need to know his whole life history.

Shaking the thoughts away, he lifted his glass, drained his wine, then said, 'Tell me more about this shop you've discovered that's going to help send your new career soaring...'

Emma drove home, her mind abuzz. The new shop was happy for her to promote her products with a display—this coming Friday evening, no less, to coincide with their first week of trading.

Jake was the only one who'd ever shown an interest and inspired her to take the plunge. Jake's encouragement and support had lifted her spirits and caught her enthusiasm. With his help she might just be able to make it work. Correction: she *would* make it work.

With his help so many people were better off, she thought. She thought too, how he'd chosen a career so he could help people like Cherry—the girls and their plights had made a lasting impression on him.

Because he'd grown up around the strip club. For how long? she wondered. Had his mother been a stripper? How long had it been since he'd seen her? She remembered the fleeting expression in his eyes when he'd spoken of her, just once, on the night of the hens' party—at odds with the casual indifference in his voice.

She hadn't let herself become interested in his past because what they had was based around the present. But now she simply couldn't ignore it. His past had shaped him into the man he was. He might be fun-loving, casual and outgoing but there were shadows there too.

She switched direction and headed for his place. There was so much more she wanted to know.

CHAPTER THIRTEEN

EMMA pressed the intercom on the wall outside Jake's home. 'It's me,' she said, when he answered. 'Let me in.'

The gate slid open and by the time she'd reached the door Jake was waiting for her, naked but for a towel low around his hips. 'I thought we arranged to meet at your place, but if you've come to share my shower…' His sexy grin faded when he realised she wasn't smiling back. 'Something wrong? Didn't it work out with the new clients?'

'No, no, nothing like that. It went well, really well, and I'll tell you about it later. But…' She waved a hand. 'Can we talk?'

He gestured her inside. 'Let's go to the living room.'

She followed him, then went to the window and looked out at the sea while she took a calming breath. She didn't know how it was going to go. Whether he'd resent her for what he might see as an intrusion on his privacy. But this was too important to ignore.

'I've been thinking about what you said this afternoon,' she said slowly. 'About Cherry and the place you've bought. How important it is to you.'

'It is, yes. Is that a problem for you?'

'Of course not.' She turned to face him. 'But why buy

a place? Why be personally involved? Why not give to a homeless charity instead? *Why* is it so important?'

Jake listened to her rapid-fire questions while he dragged in a slow, slow breath. Having Emma come into his life was one of the most life-changing events he'd ever experienced. To his surprise, he discovered he wanted to answer them, to have her listen and understand. His only concern was if once he started he might not be able to stop.

He crossed the room, gripped her shoulders loosely and steered her towards the couch. 'Sit down.' He sat down beside her, fisted his hands on his thighs. Took another breath. 'I lived there, Emma. The back of that strip club was home sweet home. So I know first-hand what it's like to be powerless.'

'Oh…Jake.' She lifted a hand, thought better of it and drew it back. 'How long?'

He shifted a shoulder, always uncomfortable with sympathy. But that wasn't what she was offering. Just support and a willingness to listen with an open mind. He'd never realised he'd needed it until now.

He gazed through the windows into the deepening twilight. 'I was five when Mum left in the middle of the night. I hadn't started school yet. I had no friends. Can't blame her, Earl cheated on her as regular as clockwork. She worked late-night shifts cleaning offices, so I saw all sorts come and go at our apartment. One night she just didn't come home. It was like losing an arm.' Or a heart.

Emma didn't speak, but he felt her reaching out to him with streamers of warmth that touched the dark, secret places inside him.

'It was lonely and isolating—after all, I could hardly ask schoolmates to come over and play. As I grew up I understood what had happened, and I swore I'd never be like *him*.' His fists tightened against his thighs. 'But the

one person I'd counted on, the one person I'd loved and
trusted, left me there. She didn't take me with her and it
hurt like hell.'

He felt her hands cover his fists and looked into her
moisture-sheened eyes.

'Your mum stayed in a loveless marriage, Emma, but
she stayed. Even a mum who gives you grief is better than
no mum at all—at least yours had some compassion, some
sense of loyalty. But then, that's my opinion. We're always
going to see it from our own perspective.'

'How do you know she went to South America?' she
said softly. 'Did she come back for you?'

'She sent a postcard once, when I was ten. New conti-
nent, new husband, new life. Anyway, after she'd left Earl
didn't see the point in paying rent on two places and we
moved in to the back of the club. At least I had a roof over
my head and food in my belly.'

'A child living in the back of a strip club?' Her eyes
changed—ice over fire—and she exhaled sharply. 'The
authorities? Didn't they ever catch up with Earl?'

He shrugged, remembering times when he'd been fer-
ried to some stranger's home in the middle of the night.
'Earl was clever. Always one step ahead. It wasn't so bad,'
he went on. 'The girls used to make me breakfast sometimes before they went home. They helped me with my
homework. Substitute mums of sorts.'

'Your young life must have been very confusing. How
did you cope with it all?'

He wrapped a hand around the back of his neck. 'Kept
to myself. Studied. Swore one day I'd get out. I was seventeen when I left and found a part-time job and a room
to rent.'

'I'll never understand a mother leaving her own flesh
and blood.'

He remembered the despair and heartbreak he'd seen too often in his mother's eyes. The guilt that had tormented his youth. The pain of that rejection and abandonment he'd never really got past. 'Because when she looked at me she saw him.'

'Ah...' She shifted closer, the fresh, untainted scent of her skin filling his nostrils. 'But you're *not* him. And she's missed out on knowing someone amazing.' She combed her fingers over the back of his hair. 'You're kind and generous and thoughtful. You're also a man of integrity, and don't let anyone tell you different or make you feel less or they'll have me to deal with.'

A band tightened around his heart. Even knowing his past, she didn't judge. 'Using my inheritance to pay for a safe house is one way of addressing the injustice. My mother didn't benefit, but others will.'

'You're one special guy, you know that?' Her compassionate blue gaze cleared and brightened, and she touched the side of his face with gentle fingers.

He hauled her against him so he could feel her generous warmth against the cold. 'I need that shower.' He needed the water's cleansing spray and her caring hands to rid himself of unwanted memories. Memories that no longer had a place in his life. He closed his eyes. 'You want to wash my back?'

'Does that mean I have to get naked too?'

He drew in a breath and opened his eyes. She was smiling. He touched her hair. 'Unless you want to drive home dripping wet or wearing my bathrobe.'

'Yeah, there's that. Whatever would I do if the car broke down on the way?'

Or you could stay here...

Only he didn't say it. She might be ready to hear it now,

but he didn't want rejection of any kind tonight. He undid the top button of her blouse. 'You *want* to get naked too?'

'Try stopping me. You know what?' She pressed her lips to his chest. 'I even have some spare soap left over in my bag from this afternoon's meeting.' She opened her mouth and flicked out her tongue, leaving a damp trail as she worked her way up to his Adam's apple then his chin. 'There's a new fragrance I'm trialling...' She let her hands wander over his hips, drawing tight little circles through the terry towel with her fingers. 'Eygptian nights. Musk and sandalwood.'

'First Tahiti. Now the East. A round-the-world tour, huh?'

She grazed her fingers over his hardening erection. 'More like a journey of discovery,' she whispered, drawing the towel away. 'Just the two of us.' She reached behind her neck, unfastening her zip and sliding it down so that her dress slipped to the floor. Stepped out of her panties and unsnapped her bra, tossed it away. 'One back scrub coming up.'

At Emma's place later that evening, Jake worked with her on a website design for Naturally Emma. They drank instant coffee and ordered business cards and composed her website pages. It helped take their minds off the earlier conversation. There was a new understanding, a comfortable silence between them as they worked.

Emma took shots of her products for Jake to upload to her computer. She was literally bouncing off the walls with enthusiasm. And nerves. 'Where will I put the extra stock?'

'You'll find a place. I have an empty room under the house if you need it.'

'What if this thing explodes? How will I keep up?'

'Now, *that's* the confidence I like to hear.' He smiled at her, the computer screen's glow reflecting the encouragement etched on his expression. 'You'll give up your day job and employ someone to help you.' He stretched his arms over his head, then reached out to take her hand. 'You'll be fine. If you need help I'm here.'

She breathed deep. 'You don't know how much it means to have you in on this with me, if only to get me started.'

As usual, he shrugged off the praise. 'No worries. I'll have the website ready for you to look at tomorrow night.'

When Jake left, she worked on into the wee hours. She made a start on some mini soap samples and selected a collection for display.

The following day Emma took off in her lunchbreak to slip further down the mall and make arrangements with the shop, collected her business cards from the printer, then caught up with Jake in the evening and approved the website.

Naturally Emma. She stared at the screen, biting her lips, hardly able to believe it was really happening. The lavender background with elegant flowing script and artistic design. The photos. The little piece about her background and qualifications that she'd composed.

'Only two nights to go,' she said, hugging her arms.

'I'll be here to pick you up,' he said, rising. 'But I need to get going. I've got some of my own work to catch up on.'

'I'm sorry. I've monopolised your time.'

'Not at all. Glad I could help.' He pulled her up for a quick kiss. 'Get some sleep.'

The mall was bustling with late-night shoppers when Emma and Jake carried her boxes in at five-thirty on Friday evening. Lights gleamed on the shiny store windows, the smell of roasting nuts and popcorn mingled with perfumes and hair treatments. Elevator music tinkled in the background, along with the ever-present underlying tide of urban chatter.

Kelsey, the shop's proprietor, had set up a table for the products just inside the entrance, and was serving a customer as they arrived. She smiled and waved when she saw them.

'I've got a severe case of killer butterflies,' Emma told Jake as she pulled stock from her box and began arranging it on the table. Her hands weren't steady, her pulse was galloping, and she really, really wanted something to moisten her dust-dry throat. 'What if no one stops by?'

'Looking at you, why wouldn't they?'

She glanced at Jake over her box. He was smiling at her, his eyes full of encouragement. He believed in her, she couldn't let him down. She couldn't let herself down. 'I'd rather they look at the products, but thanks.' She swallowed. 'Would you mind getting me a bottle of water? I forgot mine.'

'Sure.' He put down the box he'd been emptying. 'Back in a moment.'

Kelsey, with curly red hair and moss-green eyes behind her rimless glasses, stepped up as Jake walked away. 'Your guy's a superstar.'

Her guy. Emma started to deny it then stopped. Her heart took a flying leap. Yes, she realised. He was. 'None of it would've happened without his support.' She drew out a cellophane-wrapped basket full of soaps and held it out. 'This is for you. You can take them home, give them to friends. Whatever. I hope your new venture's a success.'

'Oh, Emma, thank you. It's beautiful.' Kelsey admired the basket with a smile, turned it in her hands. 'I think we'll both do well. People look for natural products these days. I'll leave it here for now, so customers can see it. Thanks so much. Oh, I've got a customer...'

Jake slowed as he arrived back, then stopped, watching Emma talk to a couple of elderly ladies. The shop's down-lights glinted on her glossy dark hair. She wore the same white top she'd worn for the hens' night, with a slim white knee-length skirt. Tasteful, professional. A chunky gold bracelet jangled on one wrist as she gesticulated.

She'd ditched the nerves, obviously, and was deep in animated conversation, smiling, eyes alive with friendly interest. Calm, in control, and the sexiest girl in the mall. In all of Australia. How different was this Emma from the Emma he'd seen wearing that top only two weeks ago?

He felt a twinge around his heart—he seemed to be getting a lot of those lately—and his fingers tightened on the red foil balloon with its twirling ribbons he'd purchased on impulse after remembering her edict about no flowers.

He shook his head. No matter what she said, Emma was a woman made for hearts and flowers and pretty words, and he was discovering, to his surprise, that he wanted very badly to give them to her. Because, unlike with his previous lovers, with Emma they would mean something more than traditional and often empty gestures.

He watched her pack soaps into a bag, pass it to one of the women with a smile as they handed over their cash. They continued down the mall. Then a guy in a snazzy business suit stopped at her table.

Jake watched Emma smile some more. Watched her flick back her hair as she talked. Pretty boy leaned closer, head tilted to one side, listening. Nodding. He picked up a soap flower and held it to his nose.

Jake scowled and wasted no time making his way to her table. 'Sorry I took so long, honey.' Slight emphasis on the endearment as he handed her the balloon and her water, then nodded at Mr Businessman. 'How's it going, mate?' He stuck out his hand. 'Jake Carmody. Emma's accountant.'

The man shook his hand. 'Daniel McDougal.'

Beside Jake, Emma made a noise at the back of her throat, setting water and balloon aside. 'Thanks.' Then she darted him a disconcerted glance. 'Jake, Daniel is from Brisbane. He owns a large health food chain and is interested in trialling my products up there.'

'That sounds great.' Jake nodded again. 'I'll let you two get on with it, then.' He dropped a firm hand on Emma's shoulder, let it linger a few seconds longer than necessary. 'If you need me, my phone's on. I'll be back to help you pack up.'

'My accountant?' Emma said on the way home.

'Yeah.' Why the hell had he got so proprietorial back there? He didn't *do* proprietorial. He dismissed the unsettling notion from his mind and concentrated on the traffic. 'Because I'm coming over on Monday night to look over your financial records,' he said. If this was going to take off, Emma needed someone she trusted from the get-go to help her manage the financial side.

'Oh. Okay. Thanks.' She bopped her little balloon against his arm. 'And thank you for tonight.'

'Pleasure.'

He glanced her way. She had a dreamy expression on her face. He looked away quickly. *Accountant? Sure.* She knew exactly what had gone through his mind.

On Saturday Emma caught up with all the things she hadn't been doing, such as grocery shopping, washing and cleaning. In the evening Jake took her to a little out-of-the-way café where the pasta was hot and the jazz was cool.

She was thrilled when Jake asked her to share dog-walking duties the following morning. They took Seeker for his walk before Jake went in to the office to catch up on his own neglected work.

Emma spent the afternoon looking forward to seeing him again at dinner while she put together a gourmet beef casserole and whipped up a batch of Jake's favourite lemon poppyseed cakes.

But how long would this thing with Jake last? How long before he tired of her? The way her father had tired of her mother and taken a mistress. The way Wayne had tired of her and found Rani. A guy like Jake with good-looks and all the charisma in the world could have any woman he wanted.

He'd never mentioned anything lasting. *Don't look too far ahead,* he'd told her. *Enjoy the ride.*

And it was one amazing ride.

She could handle it if—when—it came time to let go. Whatever happened, she'd be fine. Because he'd changed her, made her a confident woman who could meet life head-on. She loved him. But a wise woman knew if her love wasn't returned there was nowhere for it to go. She hoped she was strong enough now to let him move on. At some point.

She needed to stand on her own two feet with this business. And she could. He'd given her the belief in herself to give it a really good go. After he'd shown her what to do with the accounting side of things she was going to say thank you very much and be her own businesswoman.

When Jake arrived after work on Monday night, Emma was looking more than a little harassed.

At the front door they spent a moment with their lips locked before she broke away with a sigh. 'This is impossible,' she said, walking to her work spot at the dining room table. She flicked at an untidy pile of papers, sending a couple sailing to the floor. 'I can't do figures. It's a mess.'

'First off—calm down.' He took her hands in his. 'I'm in business law. That makes me a figures guy. Brew us a coffee while I look over your books.'

She stared up at him, eyes panicked. 'Books? I don't have books. I have paper. Piles and piles of paper.'

'Okay. Why don't *I* make us coffee while you gather them together? Then I can take a look. And don't worry. That's what I'm here for.'

'But it's *not* your worry. I have to be able to do it on my own…'

She trailed off, but not before he heard the hiccup in her voice. A sombre mood fell over him, a dark cloud on a still darker night. He squeezed her hands that little bit firmer. 'I'll be available for however long you need my help.'

She looked away at the clutter on the table. 'I'm not a complete moron. I should be able to handle it myself.'

'You're not and you will,' he reassured her. 'I'll sort it, show you how it all works, then you can take over.'

A few hours later he'd organised her paper filing system into some sort of order. He'd set up an accounting program on her laptop and entered her details. All he had left then was to show her how to manage it.

He'd hardly been aware, but at some point she'd finished packing and stacking and made another coffee. He sipped his, found it stone cold. Stretching out the kinks in his spine and neck, he turned to see her zonked out on the couch, fast asleep, a book on the Pitfalls and Perils of Small Business still open on her stomach.

He didn't get nearly enough time to watch her in that state, so he took the opportunity while it presented itself. Turning his chair around, he straddled it, resting his forearms along the back.

Her waterfall of glossy dark hair tumbled over the side of the couch. Her long, dark eyelashes rested on pale cheeks. Her mouth…a thing of beauty, full and plump and turned up ever so slightly at the corners, as if waiting for one chaste kiss to awaken her…

Her eyes would open and that glorious sapphire gaze would fix on his and he'd kiss her again…not so chaste this time…

His lips tingled with sweet promise. His heart beat faster, re-energising his bloodstream, reawakening sluggish muscles. Desire unfurled deep in his belly. Amazing— this feeling, this need for her, never waned. In fact, it was stronger than ever.

But he touched only her silky hair. She needed her sleep. She looked pale, worn out. He should leave, let her rest. They'd catch up tomorrow. But he couldn't leave her to finish the night on that spring-worn couch.

Gathering her in his arms, he carried her to bed, laid her down, and for his own peace of mind pulled the quilt right up to her chin.

She stirred and looked up at him through sleepy eyes…

And it was as if he saw all the days and nights in a fantasy-filled future when he'd wake and lose his heart over and over every time he gazed into those captivating blue depths—

When I saw my children in her eyes…

A bowling ball rolled through his chest. His throat tightened as if the air was slowly being squeezed out of him by an iron fist, and for a few crazy seconds he thought he might black out.

But his moment of panic slid away like an outgoing tide over hard-packed sand, replaced by a shiny and unfamiliar warmth which seeped deep into his heart.

Love.

It had to be love. What else could it be? He'd not recognised it before because he'd never experienced it. Never believed in it. Not for him. Love had always been an unknown. His childhood had been one of rejection and indifference. His entire adult existence had revolved around relationships that never lasted. The women in his life had been about fun and good times. He'd never really taken the time to get to know them on a deeper level. Hadn't wanted to. Maybe he'd been afraid to.

But he knew Emma. And she'd opened his eyes and his heart to a different world. A world where life held more meaning than he'd ever imagined.

'Jake... Wha...?' Her drowsy murmur drifted away.

'Sleep, sweetheart,' he murmured against her temple, and she snuggled into her pillow, eyes already closed again.

He woke before dawn, still fully dressed on top of her quilt, his eyes snapping open to the fading sound of a car's tyres screeching in the distance. Emma was spooned against him as warm and soft as a kitten. He shifted carefully off her bed and let himself out into the pearl-grey of early morning.

He hurried to his car. He had plans to make before his working day started.

CHAPTER FOURTEEN

JAKE was wearing a groove in the floorboards in Emma's studio. He'd left the office at lunchtime, dropped by Emma's workplace and asked her for a key so he could work on her computer. She'd told him she'd be home by six.

It was now twenty minutes past.

The mustard chicken and orzo casserole he'd ordered from his favourite gourmet kitchen was in the oven. A bottle of her favourite bubbly was chilling in the fridge, along with a couple of his favourite gourmet cupcakes.

He'd cleared the work from her table and covered its scarred surface with a cream lace cloth he'd found in her kitchen drawer, placed on it a bunch of red poppies he'd bought.

Should he have taken her to some fancy restaurant instead? No. He didn't want a bunch of strangers intruding. He wanted to share the moment with her. Only her.

A beam of light arced through the window and the familiar engine's sound had him reaching for gas lighter and candles.

Grabbing the plastic carry bag of fried chicken and a bottle of fizzy stuff from the passenger seat, Emma swung her bag over her shoulder and almost danced down the steps.

She couldn't wait to tell him her news. She hadn't phoned. She needed to say it in person.

'Honey, I'm home,' she sing-songed as she pushed the door open.

She was met by some herby, aromatic fragrance. On the table, tall red poppies speared out of a jar alongside two squat red candles already lit.

Jake was pouring fine pink champagne into two glasses that were far too elegant to have come from her cupboard. *He* looked too elegant, in slim-fitting black trousers and a snowy-white shirt that looked as if it had just come out of a box.

'Seems you beat me to it.' She set down her own cheap bottle of fizz on the sideboard and admired the candlelight reflecting on crystal and silver. 'This looks wickedly romantic.'

'I thought it was time I took a chance on the romance bit. You don't mind, do you?' Hands occupied with wine and glasses, he grinned and leaned forward so that she could plant an enthusiastic kiss on his lips. He smelled of some exotic new fragrance.

'I don't mind. Taking chances is what it's all about, right?' Overflowing with excitement, she sashayed over to the oven, peeked at the delicious-looking meal inside. 'And I bought take-away. You should've let me know you were planning a seduction.'

'I wanted to surprise you.'

'You did. And I've got—'

'Everything's ready. Sit.'

He didn't appear to hear her. Okay, this wasn't the moment, she decided. He'd obviously gone to a lot of trouble. 'It smells yummy.'

'It tastes even better.' Pulling out her chair, he waited till she was seated, then walked to the oven. He removed the casserole, set it on the table, then sat down opposite her.

'You okay?' She studied him. 'You seem a little...' she circled a finger in the air '...preoccupied.'

His mouth kicked up at one corner as his gaze drifted over the front of her shirt. 'If I am, it's your fault for looking so sexy after a day at work.'

'And don't you know just the right things to say?' While he spooned the meal into shallow bowls, she fingered a poppy. 'I didn't know poppies had blue centres.'

'These do.'

'Made-to-order poppies? Hmm. You *have* put thought into this.'

'They remind me of you in that sexy red coat of yours. Tall, slim. Blue-eyed. Gorgeous.' He raised their glasses, handed her one. 'To happiness.' Did his eyes look different tonight? Deep and dark... Maybe she was imagining it.

Because everything looked different tonight. From the sunset to the sea, even her old studio apartment. Everything *felt* different tonight. Her life was about to change.

'To happiness.' She took a sip, then set her glass down. She was bursting to talk but she squashed it. She didn't want to spoil his evening's plans. She wanted him to see her make time and enjoy the meal he'd obviously taken so much thought with first. The crystal flutes were sparkly new and very expensive. He'd used her best silver cutlery and china and her grandmother's tablecloth.

She spread a matching cloth napkin over her knee. 'Did you cook this yourself?'

'It's from a gourmet shop in Bondi. I shop there so often the owner's thinking of making me a partner.' He passed her a bowl. 'I'd have cooked, but today's been a bit of a rush.'

So while they ate she asked him about his day. One of his colleagues in the office was taking on a high-profile case. He'd almost finished entering her data on the computer.

How was it going with Cherry and Kevin? He'd driven Cherry to the safe house and they'd chosen paint for the walls. Cherry and a couple of the other girls were starting that job next week in their spare time.

When they'd polished off the last cake crumb from their plates and were enjoying their filtered coffee, Jake decided the moment was right now. He took a gulp of coffee to moisten his throat and steady his nerves. His fingers tightened on the little box in his trouser pocket.

'Emma, I—'

'I have some news—'

Both spoke at the same time.

She was clutching her hands together beneath her chin. Her sapphire eyes shone like stars, reflecting the candle-light.

A premonition snaked down Jake's spine and his breath snagged in his chest. Why did he suddenly feel as if the floor was about to give way? He nodded once. 'You first.'

Her shoulders lifted and she leaned forward. Her familiar fragrance curled around his nostrils.

'You talked about taking a chance earlier—on romance. And it's been lovely. Everything. Thank you for making the evening so special.'

He acknowledged that, but didn't speak.

'I've taken a chance too. I've been offered work in Queensland. *Real* work. Work I love, work I've wanted all my life but never had the opportunity to do.'

Jake was having trouble processing the words. *Queensland.* He was grateful he was sitting down because his legs suddenly felt like lead stumps. 'Queensland?'

'I know. Isn't it exciting? I can't believe it.'

Neither could Jake. 'Where? Who? You've made plans?' *Without discussing it with me?*

'You remember Daniel McDougal? From the mall last week? Well, he was so impressed with my products he had them analysed and everything, consulted with his partners, and rang me this afternoon. He wants to invest in my product line *and* take me on as a consultant to liaise with his client base all around the state.'

Daniel McDougal. Mr Pretty Boy. 'But what do you know about him? Aren't you jumping in without the facts? God, Emma, you can't just—'

'Turns out he's Kelsey's cousin. You know—the owner of the shop? I talked to her, and checked him out on the internet to make sure. Danny's a real success story up there.'

So it was *Danny* now? Jake clenched his jaw. 'You don't have to make a decision right away, Emma.' But she didn't seem to be listening.

'He's got stores around Australia. He's booked me an airline ticket for tomorrow morning to meet the staff and look over the factory before I commit to anything. He emailed me the information. I have a copy right here. Since you're the expert, I'd be grateful if you'd check it out?' She reached into her bag, pulled some papers out, set them on the table.

Damn right he'd check it out. He picked them up with a restraint he was far from feeling. 'This isn't something you simply say yes to, Emma.' He flicked through the first couple of pages. 'There are other considerations to take into account.' *Us, for starters.*

'Of course, and I know that. Jake, put those pages down and look at me.'

He did. He'd never seen her so happy. That sparkle in her eyes, excitement glowing in her cheeks.

'We've got something special,' she said. 'But it was only ever temporary, I'm realistic enough to know that. I'm a career girl, you said so yourself. This chance to do something meaningful with my life is what I've been waiting for. And if it wasn't for you I'd never have had the courage to go for it. I have to try or it'll all have been for nothing. Do you understand?'

His fingers clenched beneath the table. 'Yes.' She was thinking with her head, not her heart—she was doing the right thing. He knew she had to give it a shot. Because if he told her he loved her and asked her to stay and she missed out on her big opportunity he'd never forgive himself. He forced himself to smile. 'I'm proud of you, Emma. You've come so far.'

Her answering smile and the dancing sapphires in her eyes faded a little. 'It's such a big decision, and I have to make it on my own, but... Oh, Jake, I...' She bit down on her lip. 'I...I almost wish I could ask you to make the decision for me. *With* me.'

Damn. Her heart was bleeding into the mix, threatening to sabotage everything. He needed to leave soon, because he didn't trust himself not to try and change her mind—and that would be the worst thing he could ever do for her.

'That's the old Emma talking. Don't listen to her. You know what you want, so go for it.'

A memory of his mother flashed through his mind. She'd left him too. The circumstances were at opposite ends of the spectrum but the hurt was the same. All these years he'd never allowed a woman into his heart, and in a couple of weeks Emma had managed to do what no other woman had.

'Emma. You're a very special woman and I've enjoyed being with you. But circumstances seem to have made the decision for us. And I want you to go. I want you to have that opportunity to shine because I know you will.'

Rising, he swiped his jacket that hung over a chair, shrugged it on—he'd never felt so cold. He picked up her papers. 'I'll look this over and get back to you.'

'Jake, wait.' She pushed up, eyes wide. 'Why are you leaving so soon? Didn't you have something you wanted to tell me just now? You let me have my say—it's your turn.'

He shook his head. 'I was going to tell you I'm flying out too—tomorrow morning. A client's set up a new business in Melbourne and wants my advice.' He waved a hand over the table. 'The meal was to...sweeten things.' He smiled again but it felt as if his lips had turned to stone. 'Turns out it was a celebration after all. And if I know anything about women, you'll need the rest of the night to sort what you're taking and pack.'

He took her in his arms, kissed her beautiful lips just once. Inhaled the scent of her shampoo, drifted his fingers over her silky cheeks as he stepped back and looked into her eyes one last time.

'Go, Emma, and make me proud.'

CHAPTER FIFTEEN

EMMA yawned as the taxi pulled into her driveway at ten p.m. on Thursday evening. She paid the cabbie, jumped out to key in the gate's security code, then collected her cabin bag from the footpath.

As she rolled it across the pavers she saw her mother exit the back door, the old cardigan she'd wrapped around her shoulders flapping in the breeze as she came to meet her.

Just what she didn't need right now, but Emma pasted on a smile. 'Hi, Mum. You're back.'

'Yesterday. I got your text. How was Brisbane?'

'Warm and sticky.' And lonely.

'Jake dropped by this afternoon to drop this off for you.' She held out a large envelope. 'Said he'd rather leave it with me than in the letterbox.'

'Thanks.' She frowned. 'I thought he was going to Melbourne.' It must have only been an overnight stay. Emma knew she should wait until she was alone, but she needed to see what Jake thought of the offer of employment. She so needed to see his handwriting. Anything. Something of him.

She slid the documents out. A green sticky note was attached to the top page.

Hi Em. Looks OK.
Remember, go with your gut—if you think it's right,
do it. And good luck.
J.

'My offer of employment.'

Emma blinked back tears as she slid the contents back into the envelope. Forty-eight hours ago she'd thought it was worth more than gold. Now she knew it wasn't. A successful career was an empty one if she couldn't share it with the man she loved.

Rubbing the chill air from her arms, she reached for the handle of her case. 'I hope you were pleasant to Jake?'

Her mother pursed her lips, but then seemed to relax a little, and something like a smile twitched at her lips. 'Bit of a charmer, that one. Done all right for himself, hasn't he?'

'Yes. He has.'

'Come inside for a few moments.' She turned and began walking the way she'd come.

The kitchen, when Emma entered, was warm and smelled of fresh-baked cinnamon cake. She hadn't smelled that comfortable homey aroma in this kitchen in years.

Her mother pulled a carton of milk from the fridge. 'Would you like a hot chocolate? I could do with one myself.'

'Thanks.' Emma sat down at the kitchen table. 'You've been baking.'

'Stan's coming up to Sydney tomorrow.' She put milk in the microwave, then set slices of fresh buttered cake on the table. 'Try this and tell me if I got it right. I tried a new recipe.'

Emma took a slice and broke a piece off, bit into it.

'Mmm—yum.' She dusted off her fingers. 'So how long will Stan be staying?'

'Not sure yet.'

'He's staying here?'

'Yes.' Her mother stirred chocolate powder into the hot milk and poured it into two mugs, then carried them to the table and sat down.

Emma cupped her hands around the mug and blew on the steaming surface. 'This smells good.' Almost as good as the old milk and honey fix. 'So…things are going well for you two?'

'We have a lot in common.'

'That's great, Mum. What are you planning while he's here?'

'We'll take it as it comes. What about you and Jake?'

Emma could feel her mother's eyes on her and stared into her mug. 'He… We…' She swallowed the lump that rose up her throat.

'He was the mistake you thought he might be?'

Still staring at her mug, she said, 'It was one of those get-it-out-of-your-system things…' Only she hadn't.

'So you're going to Brisbane to work?'

'I thought I was. But I've changed my mind.'

She flashed Emma a look. 'Why?'

'Mum, why did you stay with Dad when you had so many reasons not to?'

'I had two children.'

Emma's jaw tightened. 'And you made us pay for your unhappiness. Every day of our lives.'

She saw her mother flinch, then she put her mug down and folded her arms on the edge of the table. 'Yes. I did. I'm sorry for it. I was wrong.'

Emma studied her, thoughtful. Jake's mother had abandoned her child and he'd suffered the consequences his whole life. Emma's had stayed, even if it would have been better for all if she hadn't. But maybe her mother had been too afraid to leave—afraid of the changes it would bring. The way Emma had been afraid.

Basically her mother had made what she'd thought was the right decision, and it wasn't Emma's place to judge.

'Sorry, I shouldn't have said that,' Emma murmured.

'It needed to be said. I needed to hear it. But a good man, a man who takes the time to look beneath the hard shell and find the woman inside screaming to be let out…' Her mother's voice softened. It was a tone Emma hadn't thought her capable of, and an unexpected smile brightened her whole demeanour. 'Well, he can change your life.'

Emma nodded. 'Yes. He can.' Stan had instigated the change in her mum without Bernice even being aware of it. And wasn't that what Jake had done for Emma?

Friday

'Good afternoon, Carmody and Associates.'

'Hi, Jasmine, it's Emma Byrne.'

'Emma, hi.' There was a smile in Jake's PA's voice that wasn't only professional courtesy. 'What can I do for you?'

Emma's fingers tightened on the phone and she rolled her lips together before saying, 'I was wondering…is Jake there?

'Yes. He's free at the moment. Do you want me to put you thr—?'

'No.' She swallowed. 'Thanks. I wanted to know… I want…' She sucked in a deep breath. 'Actually, I was hoping you could help me…'

Jake checked his watch, then pressed the intercom. 'Jasmine? Looks like your friend's a no-show. Why don't you give him a call, tell him to reschedule? I'm knocking off early—'

'She'll be here,' she assured him. 'Do me a favour and wait a few more moments.'

Jake was already shutting down his computer with his free hand. Jasmine hadn't mentioned her friend was a woman. The only woman he wanted to see walking through that door was a million miles away.

'I gave her my word you'd see her tonight,' Jasmine continued. 'Hang on…' He heard a muffled sound then, 'I can see her from the window. She's walking into the building now.'

Emma refused to let the nerves zapping beneath her ribcage win. She was a woman on a mission and nothing was going to stand in her way. So she wasn't afraid of walking into an office high-rise to face the most important meeting of her life.

Six p.m. on a chilly autumn evening in Sydney's CBD and the business day was over. Workers were trickling out of the building on their way home.

Her work was just beginning. The most important work she'd ever done. The most important work she'd ever do. She'd promised herself she'd talk to Jake Carmody, and she would. She could.

Shrugging her bag higher, she marched inside. A couple of men in snazzy business suits exited the lift. She clutched the miniature hat box at her waist as she passed them. Did they know her life was on a cliff's edge? Could they hear how hard her heart was pounding? She hit the button for the fourteenth floor and watched the numbers light up while her stomach stayed on the ground floor.

The doors slid open smoothly and she stepped out. Jasmine looked up and smiled, collecting her bag from her desk on her way out. 'Go straight in. He's getting a little impatient.'

'Thanks.'

Emma heard him on the phone before she reached the open door. That deep, lazy voice that rolled over her senses like caramel sauce. Only three days, but she'd missed hearing that voice. She loved that voice. She loved the man it belonged to. It was time she took the big, scary leap and let him in on that fact.

She took a fortifying breath, then knocked and entered.

He was sitting behind his desk and looked up sharply, eyes widening when she closed the door behind her.

'Something's come up. I'll speak to you tomorrow,' he said into his mobile without taking his eyes off her. He disconnected and set the phone on the desk. 'Emma.'

'Hello, Jake.'

'I'm expecting a client…' He studied her face. 'I'm guessing it's you.'

'Jasmine told me you'd be here. She asked you to wait, so thank you.'

His eyes raked over her coat and she felt a flush rise up her neck. Heat, desire, longing. Her body reacted to his gaze as if it had been programmed for his exclusive use, and her nipples hardened beneath her finely woven cashmere jumper. She wished she knew what he was thinking, how he felt about her turning up without calling first.

He checked his watch. 'I was about to leave. I need to get home.'

Her heart clenched so tight she wondered that her blood still pumped around her body. Her fingers tightened so hard on the little box she wondered it didn't implode. 'A… date?' She had to force the words out.

He stared at her with those beautiful, dark, unreadable eyes. 'What do you think, Emma?'

'I think...if it was...I'd try to talk you into cancelling because I need to talk to you first.'

'No need—there is no date.' He was turning his mobile over and over in his hands. Watching her. 'How was Brisbane? Is the new job everything you wanted?'

'Yes. And no.' She focused on those eyes. 'It's everything I wanted in a career. Double the income I'm making at the call centre. A spacious office with my name on the door. The chance to build my own business on the side. A chance to travel.' She sucked in her lips. 'But it's not enough.'

'Not enough.' Rising, he came around to her side of the desk, leaned his backside against the edge. 'Why isn't it enough, Em?'

He enjoyed being with her, she knew that. He made love to her as if she were a goddess. He believed in her. But did he love her? How would he respond if she asked him? There were no guarantees in life and love, but wasn't taking that leap of faith what it was all about?

She tightened her fingers on the little box and sucked in a lungful of air. 'It's not enough because I want more. I want it all. What's the point in being successful if you're lonely?' She pushed her gift into his hands. 'I love you, Jake. I need you in my life. No matter what else I do or don't have, I need you.'

He shook his head slightly, as if he couldn't believe what he was hearing, then looked down at the box. Back to her.

'Open it.'

She forgot to breathe as he lifted the lid. He met her eyes. A slow smile curved his lips and her breath whooshed out. He lifted out the cupcake with its red heart piped on top.

'It's not soap. It's chocolate—you can eat this one.'

'I'm not so sure I want to. It's too special.'

She twisted her trembling fingers together in front of her. 'Jake...do you love me back? I really, really need to know if I'm making an idiot of myself here...'

'Emma.' He set the cake and its box beside him on the desk, then covered her hands with his. 'I know that when I'm with you, when I look at you, I have this feeling inside me that makes Everest seem like an ant hill. It makes me want to go out and climb its highest peak with my bare hands. It gives me a reason to get up and watch the sun rise and thank the universe for bringing you into my life. I'd say that's love, wouldn't you?'

'Yes. Because that's how you make me feel too.' She was beyond terrified that she might have let this chance slip through her hands. It gave her strength to continue. 'I came here to say...to ask...Jake, will you marry me?' The last words rushed out on a trembling breath.

His eyes darkened, warmed. And his slow smile was the most wonderful, heartbreakingly beautiful sight she'd ever seen. 'That's going to be one hell of a story to tell our children some day.'

Our children. Her heart blossomed with all the possibilities of a future together opening up inside her. 'So...is that a yes?'

He brushed the back of his hand over her cheek, the side of her neck, leaving a shimmer of heat, the scent of his skin. 'I'm not planning on having our kids out of wedlock, sweetheart.'

He bent his head towards her and she rose on tiptoe, slid her arms around his neck and pressed her lips to his with all the pent-up emotion and love she had inside her. He kissed her back without hesitation, without reservation, dragging her close so that she could feel the fast, hard beat of his heart against hers.

Finally she drew back so she could see him, cupped

his treasured face in her hands. 'I was afraid to love you. Afraid of its power. It can lift you up, but it can bury you so deep you can't see a way out. I saw what it did to my mother. I saw how she let it destroy her.

'But when I went to Brisbane I realised I wasn't like her. You showed me that, by pushing me out of my comfort zone and allowing me to see another side of myself. And I want to thank you for the rest of our lives.'

He smiled down at her. 'And I want to let you.' Then his expression sobered. 'I was afraid too, but wouldn't admit it—even to myself. I've never let anyone close. It was easier to play the field and move on. But with you I couldn't seem to let you go. Until you told me about the new job. I wanted you to have that career you worked so hard for. That success. I had to let you go and find it for yourself, even though I knew I loved you.'

'It's not enough. Not without you.' She tugged his hand. 'Can we get out of here?'

'Sure thing.' Tightening their clasped fingers, he headed for the door. 'I've got a surprise for you.'

Jake handed his address and a healthy wad of notes to the parking attendant on their way to pick up Emma's car. 'Find someone to take care of it and there's enough cash for a cab back,' he told him, then, slinging his arm around Emma's shoulders, he hustled her along the street. He wondered that his feet touched the ground. Half an hour ago he'd been at the lowest point in his life and now he was flying.

A short time later he kissed her on the front door step. 'Welcome home. I love you, Emma, and I'm never going to tire of hearing myself say it.'

'I'm never going to tire of h—' A long, low whine interrupted, vibrating through the door, followed by a whimper and a series of sharp barks. '*What* is that?'

He unlocked the door and a flurry of paws and joyous barks greeted them. 'Meet Scratch.'

'You bought a dog? So *that's* why you had to get home.'

'He's the abandoned dog I told you about.'

'And you rescued him.'

'I just couldn't bring myself to leave him at the shelter, so I picked him up yesterday.' He bent to scratch behind his silky ears. 'I think we rescued each other—didn't we, boy?'

'We were all in need of rescue,' Emma murmured. 'Hey, there, you little cutie, you.'

Jake watched her wasting no time getting acquainted, crouching down so Scratch could sniff her and approve. With a joyous yelp he rolled onto his back, his tongue lolling out, adoration in his eyes.

Jake squatted beside Emma to scratch the dog's tummy. 'So what do you think—you and me and a crazy pooch? You didn't know he was part of the deal—you sure you still want to marry me?'

'Are you kidding? He seals the deal absolutely.'

He looked at Emma, his heart overflowing with that mysterious thing called love. It had eluded him all his life but now… Now he had it all.

A few moments later, with Scratch tucking into his dinner, Jake put the little velvet box into Emma's hands. 'To make it official.'

Her eyes widened. 'What's this? How…?'

'I was going to propose to you the other night. Until you told me your news.'

Realisation dawned in her bright blue eyes. 'So *that's* why you went to so much effort. Oh, Jake. I was so focused on myself I didn't—'

He placed a finger on her lips. 'Just open it.'

'Oh, my…' she breathed. 'It's beautiful.'

Three diamonds on a platinum band winked in the light. 'One for you, one for me, one for the kids we're going to make,' he told her, sliding it onto her finger.

He lifted her off the floor, twirled her around and around until they were both dizzy, then waltzed her to his bedroom the way he'd waltzed her to bed that first time they'd made love.

He tugged on her belt. 'I'll have you know the first time I saw you in that coat I wondered what you were hiding beneath it. Now…take it off and let me see.'

Later, Emma cuddled against him in his king-size bed. Scratch snored doggy snores in his basket nearby. 'I think I'd like to stay right here for the rest of the weekend.' She stretched, feeling satisfied, in love, and entirely too lazy.

'Sounds like a plan. But I doubt Scratch will agree.'

'Our house by the sea and a dog,' she murmured. 'This really is home. What a wonderful life…'

'And what do you want to do with that life…' he nuzzled the sweet taste of her breast '…besides making love endlessly till dawn?'

'I want to concentrate on Naturally Emma. Danny's still going to market my products in Queensland, and I might go up once a month to see how it's going.'

'Maybe I can accompany you sometimes. As your accountant.'

'Nuh-uh. If you accompany me it'll be as my husband.'

'Even better.' His hand created a warm friction over her belly. 'I'm shifting some of my office work home. When I decided to take on a dog I made the commitment to be home more.'

'We'll neither of us ever get any work done.' She drew a line up his shin with her toes and draped her top half over him like a scarf.

His laugh was more of a choke as his arms went around her to pull her all the way on top. 'Reckon you're right.'

She buried her face in the musky warmth of his neck and breathed in his scent. 'I'm always right. I asked you to marry me, didn't I?'

'So…how does a wedding as soon as Ry and Stella come back from their honeymoon sound?'

She lifted her head so she could look into those warm coffee eyes and see his love for her shining through. 'Perfect.'

* * * * *

THE BEST MAN
TAKES A BRIDE

STACY CONNELLY

To all my fellow romance readers out there and the ongoing search for happily-ever-after...in (and out) of the pages of a romance novel!

Chapter One

This was going to be a disaster.

Jamison Porter eyed the dress shop with a sense of dread. Early-morning sunshine warmed the back of his neck and glinted off the gilded lettering on the plate glass window. Frilly dresses decorated with layer after layer of lace and ribbons and bows draped the mannequins on display, a small sample of the froth and satin inside. All of it girlie, delicate and scary as hell.

The forecast promised a high in the low seventies, but Jamison could already feel himself breaking into a sweat.

He swallowed hard against the sense of impending doom and fought the urge to jump in his SUV and floor it back to San Francisco. Back to his office and his black walnut barricade of a desk, matching bookshelves lined with heavy law books, and rich leather chairs. All of it masculine, substantial—the one place where Jamison never questioned his decisions, never doubted his every move—

He felt a tug at his hand and looked down at his four-year-old daughter's upturned face. Big brown eyes stared back at him. "I wanna go home now."

Never felt so useless as he did when he was with Hannah.

His daughter's barely brushed blond curls tilted to one side in a crooked ponytail. Her mismatched green T-shirt and pink shorts, both nearing a size too small, were testimony to the crying fit that ended their last attempt at clothes shopping. Jamison at least took some small comfort that Hannah had been the one to leave the store in tears, and not him. Because there were times...

Like now, when he didn't even know which home Hannah was referring to. Back to Hillcrest House, the hotel where they'd be staying for the next couple of weeks? Back to his town house in San Francisco? To her grandparents' place? To the house where she'd been living with her mother...

"I know, Hannah Banana," he said, fighting another shaft of disappointment when the once-loved nickname failed to bring a smile to her face. "But we can't go home yet," he added as he set aside the question of where his daughter called home for another time. "We're here to meet Lindsay, remember? She's the lady who's getting married to my friend Ryder, and she wants you to be her flower girl."

Hannah scraped the toe of a glittery tennis shoe along a crack in the sidewalk. "I don't want to."

Her lack of interest in playing a role in Lindsay Brookes's wedding to Ryder Kincaid didn't bother Jamison as much as her patented response did. Not because of all the things Hannah didn't want, but because of the one thing she did.

The bell above the shop's frosted-glass door rang as the

bride stepped outside. Dressed in gray slacks and a sleeveless peach top with her dark blond hair caught back in a loose bun, a smile lit Lindsay's pretty face. "Hey, you made it! Not that I thought you wouldn't." She waved a hand, the solitaire in her engagement ring flashing in the sunlight. "I mean, it isn't like any place around here is hard to find!"

Ryder had told Jamison his hometown near the Northern California coastline was small, and he hadn't exaggerated. Victorian buildings lined either side of Main Street and made up the heart of downtown. Green-and-white awnings snapped in the late-summer breeze, adding to the welcome of nodding yellow snapdragons, purple pansies and white petunias in the brick planters outside the shops. Couples strolled arm in arm, their laughing kids racing ahead to dart into the diner down the street or into the sweet-smelling café across the way.

It was all quaint and old-fashioned, postcard perfect and roughly that same size. Jamison figured it had taken less than five minutes to see all Clearville had to offer even while obeying the slower-than-slow posted speed limit. "No trouble. Didn't even need to use the GPS."

Finding the shop had been easy. Making himself step one foot inside, that was a different story.

"Good thing," Lindsay said with a laugh, "since cell coverage can be pretty spotty around here."

Jamison fought back a groan. In a true effort to focus on Hannah and leave work behind, he hadn't brought along his laptop. But he'd been counting on being able to use his phone to read emails and download any documents too urgent to wait for his return. "How does anyone get things done around here?" he grumbled under his breath.

She lifted a narrow shoulder in a shrug. "Disconnecting is tough at first, but before long, you find you don't miss it at all."

"Can't say I plan to be in town long enough to get used to anything," he replied as the driver of an SUV crawling down Main Street called out to Lindsay and the two women exchanged a quick wave.

And despite his own words, Jamison couldn't help thinking that, back in San Francisco, had a driver shouted and stuck an arm out the window, the gesture wouldn't have been so friendly.

"That's too bad. Clearville's a great town. A wonderful place to raise a family," she added with a warm glance at Hannah, who dropped her gaze and retreated even farther behind his back.

So different from the adventurous toddler he remembered…

He sucked in a deep breath as he tried to focus on whatever Lindsay was saying.

"But why don't we get started? I'm here for my final fitting, and I've picked out some of the cutest flower girl dresses. Our colors are burgundy and gold, but I think that would be too strong a palette for Hannah since she's so fair. Instead I've been leaning toward a cream taffeta with a sash at the waist—"

Catching herself, Lindsay offered a sheepish smile. "Sorry, Ryder's already warned me I tend to go into wedding overload on even the most unsuspecting victim. The other day, I talked a poor waitress's ear off and all she asked was if I wanted dessert. If there's something else you need to do, you don't have to stay—"

"No! Daddy, don't go!" Hannah's hands tightened in a death grip around his as she pressed closer to his side.

Lindsay's expression morphed into one of sympathy that Jamison had seen too many times and had grown to despise over the past two months.

But not as much as he hated the tears in his daughter's

eyes. "I'm not going anywhere," he vowed, disappointed but not surprised when his promise didn't erase the worry wrinkling her pale eyebrows.

"Pinkie promise?" she finally asked, holding out the tiny, delicate digit.

Jamison didn't hesitate as Hannah wrapped him around her finger. Love welled up inside him along with the painful awareness of how many times he'd let her down in her short life. His voice was gruff as he replied, "Pinkie promise."

"Your daddy can stay with you the whole time," Lindsay reassured Hannah gently. "I bet he can't wait to see you try on some pretty dresses."

Jamison had thought Hannah might enjoy being a flower girl, but the truth was, he didn't have a clue what would make his little girl happy anymore. Sweat started to gather at his temples along with the pressure of an oncoming headache. "Look, Lindsay, I appreciate you thinking of Hannah and wanting her to be part of the ceremony, but I don't—"

"Sorry I'm late!" The cheery voice interrupted Jamison's escape, and every muscle in his body tensed. That need to run raced through him once more, but his feet felt frozen in place. Still, he couldn't help turning to glance over his shoulder, bracing himself for the woman he could feel drawing closer.

The wedding coordinator.

Ryder and Lindsay had introduced them not long after he'd checked into the sprawling Victorian hotel. He'd been exhausted from fourteen-hour workdays, worn out from the long drive from San Francisco and far more overwhelmed by the idea of taking care of Hannah on his own than he dared admit even to himself.

That was the only logical explanation he'd been able

to come up with for why that first meeting with Rory McClaren had sent a lightning bolt straight through his chest. Her smile had stopped him dead in his tracks and her touch—nothing more than a simple handshake—had shot a rush of adrenaline through his system, jump-starting his heartbeat and sending it racing for the first time in... ever, it seemed.

But logical explanations failed him now. One look at Rory, and Jamison was blown away all over again.

Big blue eyes sparkled in a heart-shaped face framed by dark, shoulder-length hair. A fringe of bangs, thick lashes and arched eyebrows drew him even deeper into that gaze. A sprinkling of freckles across her nose kept her fair skin from being too perfect, and cherry-red lipstick highlighted a bright smile and a sexy mouth Jamison had no business thinking about again and again.

A white sundress stitched with red roses revealed more freckles scattered like gold dust across her delicate collarbones. The fitted bodice hugged the curves of her breasts and small waist before flaring to swish around her slender legs as she walked.

She looked as fresh and sunny as a summer's day, and Jamison almost had to squint when he looked at her, like he needed sunglasses to shield him from her stunning beauty.

He sure as hell needed some form of protection, some barrier to establish a safe distance from this woman and the unexpected, unwanted way she made him feel. If his disastrous marriage had taught him one lesson, it was that he far preferred being numb.

"Mr. Porter, nice to see you again."

Her smile was genuine, but Jamison couldn't imagine her words were true. He'd been abrupt the day before, unnerved by his reaction and bordering on rude. "Ms. McClaren. I didn't know you'd be joining us this morning."

"All part of Hillcrest House's service as an all-inclusive wedding venue," she said with a smile to Lindsay before turning that full wattage on Jamison. "But we are a hotel first and foremost, so I hope you enjoyed your first night under our roof."

He'd heard his share of come-ons in his lifetime. There was nothing the least bit seductive in her smile or her voice. But his imagination, as suddenly uncontrollable as his hormones, had him picturing an intimacy beyond sleeping under her roof and instead sleeping in her bed…

Jamison didn't know if his thoughts were written on his face, but whatever Rory saw had enough color blooming in her cheeks to rival the roses on her dress. Her lips parted on an inhaled breath, and Jamison felt drawn closer, captured by the moment as the awareness stretched between them until she dropped her gaze.

"And Hannah!"

That quickly, the enticing image was banished, but not the pained embarrassment lingering in its wake. He wasn't some gawky teenager lusting after the high school cheerleader. He was a grown man, a father…a father with a daughter he was terrified of failing—just like he had her mother.

"How are you this morning?" Undeterred by the lack of response, Rory's lyrical voice rose and fell, and Jamison didn't want to think about the slight tremor under the words. Didn't want to think she might be as affected as he was by the chemistry between them. "Do you like your room at the hotel? You know, the Bluebell has always been my favorite."

The Bluebell…

What kind of hotel designated their rooms by a type of flower?

"It's all part of Hillcrest's romantic charm," Rory had explained.

He had no need for romance or charm or bright-eyed brunettes. He wanted logic, order. He wanted the normalcy of sequential room numbers, for God's sake!

But the Bluebell was one of the hotel's few two-room suites and, while small, it offered a living space and tiny kitchenette. The comfortable room was subtly decorated in shades of blue and white.

If only it wasn't for the name…and the reminder of flowers that had him thinking far too often of Rory's dark-lashed, vibrant blue eyes.

"I like purple," Hannah answered, surprising him too much with her willingness to talk to a virtual stranger for him to point out bluebell wasn't a color.

"Me, too," Rory agreed as she caught on to his daughter's twist in the topic.

Hannah's forehead wrinkled. "You said you like blue."

"Actually, Hannah, rainbow is my favorite color…" The wedding coordinator bent at the waist so she and Hannah were almost eye to eye as she shared that piece of nonsense with the little girl. "That way I never have to pick just one."

A lock of her hair slid forward like a silken ribbon and curved around her breast. The dark strands were a stark contrast against the white fabric, but it was the similarities that had Jamison sucking in a deep breath. Soft cotton, soft hair, soft skin…

Realizing he was staring, he jerked his gaze away. Falling back on good manners now that good sense seemed to have deserted him, he ground out, "Hannah, you remember Ms. McClaren?"

His daughter nodded, her eyes too serious for her still-baby face as she peered up at the wedding coordinator. She wrapped her index finger in the hem of her shirt, holding on the same way she had to the pink-and-white blanket Jamison remembered her carrying with her everywhere when she was a toddler. "She's Miss Lindsay's fairy godmother."

Jamison blinked at Hannah's unexpected announcement. "She's… Oh, right." That was how Lindsay had introduced the woman. The bride had sung Rory McClaren's praises, complimenting her on finding the perfect music, the perfect flowers, the perfect menu—as if any of that attention to detail would lead to the perfect marriage.

Jamison knew better. He was cynical enough to wonder if Rory knew the same, but not cynical enough to believe it. Everything about her was too genuine, too hopeful for him to convince himself it was all for show. But even if the wedding coordinator believed what she was selling, that didn't mean Jamison was buying.

"She's not really a fairy godmother," he told his daughter firmly.

"Of course not," the dark-haired pixie said with a conspiring wink at the little girl, who gazed back with shy curiosity. "And you can call me Rory."

Jamison's jaw tightened. No doubt Rory thought the shared moment with Hannah was harmless, but the last thing he needed was for his daughter to put faith in fairy tales. Especially when the one thing Hannah wanted was the one thing no one—not even a fairy godmother, if such a thing existed—could give her.

Rory's smile faltered when she glanced up into his face. Straightening, she rallied by getting down to business and glancing between Lindsay and Hannah. "So, are we ready to start trying on some gorgeous dresses?"

"I can't wait!" Lindsay announced, clapping her hands in front of her as if trying to hold on to her excitement.

"I've picked out some of the cutest dresses, and you have got to help me decide which one to choose."

"That is what I'm here for. Anything you need, all you have to do is ask!"

And with statements like that, Jamison thought, was it any wonder Hannah thought the woman was some kind of fairy godmother? Even he half expected a magic wand to appear in the delicate hand she waved through the air.

Better to leave now before he—before *Hannah*— could get sucked any further into a belief in fairy tales and happily-ever-afters.

"About that. I think Hannah might be a little too young for all of this."

Lindsay sank back onto her heels, her earlier excitement leaking out of her. He wasn't a man to go back on his word, but he never should have agreed to have Hannah in the wedding in the first place. With his in-laws pointing out the need for a female influence in Hannah's life, he'd thought—hell, Jamison didn't know what he'd thought. But the whole idea was a mistake. "Trying on clothes isn't her idea of fun."

This time, though, the wedding coordinator's smile didn't dim in the least. If anything, an added spark came to her eyes. "The shopping gene hasn't kicked in yet?"

"I'm hoping it skips a generation."

Rory laughed as though he'd been joking, brightening her expression even more, like a spotlight showcasing a work of art. "You and all fathers everywhere."

It was a small thing—Rory categorizing him as a typical dad—but some of the pressure eased in his chest. Maybe it wasn't so obvious from the outside that he was at such a loss when it came to his own daughter. Best to quit while he was, if not ahead, then at least breaking even.

But before he could once again make his excuses, Rory

turned to Hannah. "Well, maybe Miss Lindsay can go first. What do you think, Hannah? Are you ready to help?"

"Ms. McClaren—"

"Why does she need help?" It was Hannah who interrupted this time, coming out from behind him far enough to look from Rory to Lindsay. "She's a grown-up, and big girls should be old enough to get dressed by themselves."

Jamison closed his eyes and wished for a sinkhole to open up in the sidewalk and swallow him whole at his words coming out of Hannah's mouth. *Crap.* Was that really how he sounded? So...condescending and demeaning?

"Hannah..." He'd only pulled out the big-girl card because Hannah was so filled with ideas of what she would do when she was older. Or at least she had been.

But if Rory was ready to take that "typical dad" title away from him and flag him with "worst father ever," she didn't let it show as she knelt down in front of his little girl. Close enough this time that he could have stroked her hair, as dark as Hannah's was light, and he shoved his free hand into his pocket before insanity had him reaching out...

"You know, Hannah," Rory was saying, her voice filled with that same touch of sharing a secret she'd conveyed earlier with that wink, "funny thing about being a big girl...sometimes we still need help."

As she spoke, she reached up and slipped the bright pink band from Hannah's hair. With a few quick swipes of her hands and without a comb or brush in sight, she had the little girl's curls contained in a smooth, well-centered ponytail. "Not a lot of help. Just a little, just enough to make things right."

To make things right... Jamison didn't have a clue how to go about making things right in his daughter's world. Especially not when he saw the open longing and amazement in Hannah's face as she reached up to touch her now-perfect ponytail.

"So what do you think?" Rory asked as she straightened, her full skirt swirling around her legs. The roses on her dress might have been embroidered, but somehow Jamison still caught a sweet, fresh scent, as if she'd risen from a bed of wildflowers. "Do you want to help Lindsay with her dress for the wedding?"

Hannah hesitated, and Jamison braced himself for the "I don't want to" response. Instead, she surprised him, nodding once and sliding a little farther out from behind him.

"And maybe, after Lindsay's done, we could find a dress for you. Just to try on—you know, like playing dress-up. And then you can put your everyday clothes back on, because who wants to wear dresses all the time?"

Hannah reached out and brushed her tiny hand over Rory's skirt. "You do."

Rory tilted her head to the side as she laughed. "You caught me. I do like wearing dresses. But not *all* the time."

Jamison might have only met the woman, but he already sensed how Rory's clothes—elegant and old-fashioned—suited her. He had a hard time picturing her in anything else.

Now, if he could only stop himself from picturing her wearing nothing at all...

Chapter Two

When Rory McClaren was five years old, she went through a princess phase. Her cousin Evie would likely say she never fully recovered from her belief in true love and happy endings and fascination with gorgeous ball gowns. Or the hidden longing to wear a tiara. On a Tuesday. Just for fun.

And while Rory had denied those longings throughout her adult life, her new position as wedding coordinator for Hillcrest House brought out every once-upon-a-time memory. She might have laughed it off when Lindsay Brookes had introduced her as a fairy godmother, but it was secretly how she viewed her job.

Of course, Rory also knew what Evie would say about that.

Coordinating weddings is a serious business, not a game of pretend. And Hillcrest House isn't a fairy-tale castle, no matter what you thought as a kid.

Neither she nor Evie had planned on this recent stay in Clearville, but the two of them were in this together—doing all they could to keep Hillcrest House running while their aunt was going through cancer treatments. Evie, a CPA, was handling the books and the staff while Rory was taking on a guest relations role as well as event planning for the venue.

So far, Lindsay Brookes had been a dream to work with, but her wedding to Ryder Kincaid came with some extra pressure. Not only did Rory consider Lindsay a friend, the pretty businesswoman also worked for Clearville's chamber of commerce. She was constantly promoting the small Northern California town and its businesses.

Rory wanted to prove all the brochures and promotions touting Hillcrest House as *the* all-inclusive wedding destination were as good as gold. The weight of responsibility pressed hard on her shoulders, but she was determined not to crumble.

She could certainly withstand a reticent best man and his shy flower girl daughter. Despite Jamison's claims that she didn't enjoy shopping, Hannah was gazing at the elegantly posed mannequins and racks of lacy dresses lining the walls of the small shop while her sharp-eyed father watched from close by.

With her tiny hands clasped behind her back, the little girl was clearly familiar with the phrase *look but don't touch*. Under her breath, she named off the color of each dress she came across in a singsong voice, and Rory didn't think it would take much to rid Hannah of her uncertainty in her role as a flower girl.

Her smile faded, though, when she caught sight of the storm clouds gathering in Jamison's eyes. Something told her erasing *his* concerns wouldn't be so easy.

Rory had hoped her initial impression of Ryder Kincaid's best friend had been a rush to judgment. She'd told herself that with a good night's sleep and a chance to relax and unwind, Jamison Porter would be a different man. A man she could handle with professional competence as she guided him through the duties of the best man from suggestions for a fun yet tasteful bachelor party to tips on a heartfelt toast.

But Jamison Porter was still every bit as intense and edgy as he had been the day before—and not a man easily handled.

It wasn't the first time Rory had been to this shop with a reluctant man in tow. Not every couple held to the superstition that the groom shouldn't see the bride in her gown. But none of the men had seemed so out of place as Jamison did. At over six feet, with rich chestnut hair and cool gray eyes, all rugged angles and sharp planes, he wore the tall, dark and handsome label to perfection. The airy dresses around him seemed as insubstantial in comparison as dandelion fluff, ready to disintegrate with a single puff of breath from his lips.

Not that Jamison Porter's lips were anything Rory should be thinking about...

"So, you're the best man," she said, cringing at the exuberant sound of her own voice.

"That's what Ryder tells me."

The hint of self-deprecating humor loosened a strand in the single father's too tightly laced personality. One that made him even more attractive than his classically handsome good looks.

But that was the last thing Rory needed. Their first meeting, as abrupt and tension filled as those moments had been, had sparked an awareness that had her thinking of the handsome single father far too often.

And just now while standing outside the bridal shop,

when she asked what she'd thought to be an innocent question about his first night at Hillcrest...

The intensity in his expression served notice there was nothing innocent about Jamison Porter. Everything about the man had Rory on high alert, raw nerve endings leaving her jumpy and out of sorts. Off her game at a time when she needed to be at her best.

Evie had taken a leave of absence from her job at the accounting firm to help out their aunt, confident they would hold her position for her, and had sublet her fabulous condo in Portland.

Whereas Rory—

Rory had nothing left. She couldn't afford *not* to come to Clearville. Back in LA, she had no boyfriend, no apartment, no job and a reputation left in tatters all thanks to her professional—and personal—failure.

Pushing thoughts of her short-lived interior design career aside, she focused on the most important aspects of the wedding.

"Ryder and Lindsay make such a wonderful couple. It's amazing the way they've reunited after so many years, and seeing them together... Well, they're crazy about each other."

Jamison gave a sound that wasn't quite a laugh. "*Crazy* is one word for it."

"And what word would you use?"

He paused for a moment, and Rory had a feeling he was searching for the least offensive description. "*Sudden,*" he said finally. "They just got engaged."

"True, but they've known each other since high school." Lindsay had filled Rory in on the couple's history, how she had been a shy bookworm with a huge crush on the popular quarterback. "They went their separate ways after graduation, but from what Lindsay says, she never stopped loving Ryder."

And while Ryder had gone on to marry another woman, Rory had no doubt he was in love with his future bride.

"She's a wonderful person. A great mother..."

The dark clouds in Jamison's eyes started flashing lightning and Rory's voice trailed away as she realized that was one box she shouldn't have opened. Unable to leave well enough alone, she couldn't help asking, "Have you met Robbie?"

He gave a quick nod. "I have."

"He's a great kid."

"One Ryder didn't even know about until a few months ago."

Rory sucked in a startled breath. Okay, so Jamison was breaking out the big guns to take on the elephant in the room. Fortunately, the curtain to the dressing room opened and Lindsay stepped out before he had time to reload.

Hannah's breathless voice broke the silence that followed. "You look beautiful."

This was the first time Rory had seen Lindsay in her wedding dress, and she couldn't hold back a whisper of her own. "Oh, Lindsay. Hannah is right. That dress is perfect."

Having worked on the flowers, the music and the table settings for the reception, Rory knew Lindsay had an elegant, timeless vision for the wedding, so it was no surprise her dress reflected that same taste.

The sheath-style gown was gorgeous in its simplicity; lace sleeves capped a straight column of white satin, and a hint of beadwork decorated the bodice and the lace insert that veed out into a modest train.

Lindsay gave a self-conscious laugh as she glanced at the silent member of the group. "It's not bad luck for the best man to see the bride in her gown, is it?"

To his credit, Jamison tipped his head at Lindsay. "You make a beautiful bride."

Lindsay blushed at the compliment, but while the words were right, Rory knew in her heart Jamison thought Ryder and Lindsay getting married was wrong.

A gentle tug on her skirt distracted Rory from the troubling thought. "Miss Rory, is it my turn to dress like a princess?"

She smiled down at Hannah. She was an adorable little girl with a riot of blond curls, big brown eyes and a shyness that tugged at Rory's heart.

But it was the expression on Jamison's face that had grabbed hold and wouldn't let go. A mix of love and uncertainty that held him frozen in place, as if he, too, were bound by the *look, don't touch* mantra.

"It sure is, sweetie," Rory said, injecting a positive note into her voice though she didn't know which of the Porters needed her encouragement more. "Miss Lindsay has a whole bunch of dresses for you to try on." Tilting her head in the direction of the changing room, Rory asked Jamison, "Do you want…"

Looking torn between Daddy duty and a man's typical reaction of running as far as he could from anything girlie, he said, "I, um, think I'll wait out here."

"What do you think, Hannah?" Rory asked when the little girl hesitated. "See, your daddy wants the princess dresses to be a surprise, so he'll wait in that chair over there."

Like father, like daughter. Hannah looked indecisively from her father to the curtained dressing room and back again. Finally her blond head bounced in a nod. "You wait there, Daddy, and no peeking."

Rory wouldn't have thought Jamison Porter could look any more uncomfortable than he had two seconds ago, but his daughter's instructions for him not to go peeking into the women's dressing room had a slight flush darkening his cheeks.

Rory fought to hide a smile, but judging by the narrowing of Jamison's eyes, she didn't succeed.

Biting the inside of her lip, she shot a stern look in his direction. "You heard the girl, Mr. Porter. No peeking."

For a split second, their eyes met, and Rory's smile faded as something electric and powerful passed between them. Heat flared in Jamison's eyes, a warning beacon, and she swallowed hard. He might not have looked behind the curtain, but when it came to her attraction to him, Rory feared he saw way too much.

The jingle of metal rings cut through Jamison's relentless pacing, and he glanced over in time to see Rory slip through the curtain.

The one his little girl had warned him not to peek behind. His faced started to heat again at the thought. Not because his own kid made him out to sound like some kind of Peeping Tom—she was only four, after all. But because of the moment that had followed.

The moment when Rory had echoed his daughter's words and his gaze had locked on hers and there'd been nothing—nothing—in his power that could keep him from mentally pulling back that curtain and picturing Rory McClaren wearing something far less than the old-fashioned dresses she favored.

Judging by the way her eyes had widened, she'd known it.

Clearing his throat, he asked, "Is Hannah—"

"She's fine. The seamstress is taking some measurements, and Hannah wanted me to make sure you're still waiting for her. She was a little nervous at first, but I think she's getting into the spirit of things. So, please..." She nodded her head at the waiting chair. "Sit down and relax."

He all but glared at the floral-print cushions that might as well have been covered with sharp thorns. Without some outlet for his excess energy, he'd likely explode. "Relaxing doesn't come easy to me."

"Really?" Rory drawled.

"That obvious, is it?" He supposed he shouldn't have been surprised. Maintaining a single-minded focus and blocking out the world around him had been a reflex since he was a kid.

His parents' divorce—hell, their entire marriage—had been a battlefield, his childhood collateral damage. The fights, the cold silences, the endless digs when the other wasn't around—Jamison had hated it all.

That volatile home life had made Jamison even more determined to keep the peace in his own marriage. He'd worked hard to give Monica everything she could need, everything she could want, everything she'd asked for and more.

And none of it had been enough to make her—or their marriage—happy.

Monica had always complained about the long hours he put in. Of course, Monica had complained about so many things that work became even more of a refuge.

A sweet giggle came from behind the curtain, and Rory murmured, "She's a beautiful little girl."

The innocent comment slammed through him. He needed to spend this time away from work with his daughter. He needed to find a way to reconnect, but he was at a loss to know how. And it galled him, he had to admit, how easily, how naturally Rory related to Hannah when for him it was all such a struggle.

"Thank you," he said stiffly, wishing he could take more

credit for the amazing little person Hannah was. But she even looked like Monica, a tiny carbon copy of his blond-haired, doe-eyed wife.

"She'll make an adorable flower girl," Rory said.

"I'm sure she will," Jamison said. "I'm just not sure about this whole wedding thing."

Rory cocked a questioning eyebrow. "The *whole* wedding?" she asked.

"Hannah's role in it," he amended, knowing he'd already said too much.

"I can see how she'd be nervous, walking down the aisle in front of all those people. But you'll be standing at Ryder's side, so all she has to do is keep her eyes on you, knowing you'll be watching her the whole way, and she'll do fine."

"You make it sound so easy."

"I have faith," she said lightly.

Of course she did. The Hillcrest wedding coordinator had faith, hope and light shining out of her. "Still, it's a lot of pressure to put on a little kid."

"Oh, I wasn't talking about Hannah. My faith is in you."

"In me?" Jamison echoed. "Why would you—" why would *anyone* "—put your faith in me?"

"Because I see the trust Hannah has in you. All you have to do is show her you'll be there for her, and she'll find the courage and confidence to move forward all on her own."

All you have to do is be there for her. Little did Rory know how seldom he'd been there for Hannah during her short life. First because of how hard he'd been working, and then because of Monica… But now he, as Hannah's only parent, was responsible for her health and happiness.

The weight of that responsibility pressed on Jamison's chest until he struggled to breathe. And he couldn't help wondering if his in-laws were right and if they weren't so much better equipped to raise Hannah...

"Ever think maybe you put too much faith in people?" he asked Rory, his voice rougher than necessary and so out of place in this shop filled with feminine softness.

"Sometimes," she admitted, surprising him with the candid answer. "And sometimes they let me down."

"Rory—" A hint of sadness clouded her beautiful features. And that restless energy inside him changed into an urge to close the distance between them, to pull her into his arms and wipe the lingering shadows from her blue eyes...

"Daddy, look!" His daughter's excited voice broke the moment, saving him from making a huge mistake, as she popped out from the dressing room. "It's a real princess dress! Just for me."

She giggled as she spun in a circle, the cream-colored lacy skirt flaring out around her tiny legs and glittery sneakers. The happy sound only magnified the ache, the guilt, pressing down on his chest. When was the last time he'd heard Hannah laugh?

"Just for you, Hannah," he vowed.

From now on, everything was just for his daughter.

Because if there was one thing he'd already done far too many times, it was let the females in his life down.

So despite the attraction, despite the knowing, tender look in the wedding coordinator's gaze, Jamison was going to keep his distance.

Chapter Three

"Oh, my gosh! Didn't Hannah look so cute?"

Seated at a wrought iron bistro table outside the café, Rory smiled as she listened to Lindsay describe every detail on the flower girl's dress. Not that she minded. The time with the sweet little girl was still playing through Rory's thoughts, as well.

Which was much better than thinking of the girl's not-so-sweet but undeniably hot father...

The bride-to-be's recitation stopped on a sigh as she paused to take a bite of a double-chocolate muffin. "Why did you bring me here?" she demanded. "That was supposed to be my final fitting, and after eating this dessert, I'm going to need to go back and have the seams let out at least two inches."

Eyeing Lindsay's slender frame, Rory laughed. "I think you're safe, and besides, we're splitting, remember?" she asked before breaking off a piece of the moist top rising above the sparkling pink wrapper. She gave a sigh of her own as rich chocolate melted in her mouth.

"Perfect, so the seams will only need to be let out one inch." Despite the complaint, Lindsay went in for another bite.

"You have nothing to worry about. Ryder is going to take one look at you walking down the aisle and be blown away."

The other woman smiled, but as she wiped her fingers on a napkin, Rory could see her heart wasn't in it. "Hey, everything okay? I know how busy you've been between the wedding and the benefit next week."

As part of her job promoting Clearville and its businesses, Lindsay was helping Jarrett Deeks with a rodeo at the local fairgrounds. The benefit was aimed at raising funds and awareness for the former rodeo star's horse rescue.

"Everything's on track. Jarrett lined up enough cowboys to compete, and local vendors have been amazing about donating their time and part of the proceeds from their booths." Despite the positive words, worry knit her dark blond brows, and she crumpled the napkin in her fist.

"So then what's wrong...and what can I do to help?" Lindsay was a Hillcrest bride, but she was also a friend. "Whatever you need, I'm here for you."

"You might wish you hadn't made that promise."

"I never make promises I don't keep," Rory vowed, her thoughts drifting back to her ex, Peter, and his many, many broken promises, but she shoved the memories away.

"Okay then," Lindsay exhaled a deep breath. "Here goes... It's Jamison. He and Ryder have known each other for years, and I can tell by how Ryder talks how close they are. He's already told me there's nothing he wouldn't do for Jamison, and I'm sure Jamison feels the same."

The last part was said with enough worry for unease to worm its way into Rory's stomach. "And what do you think Jamison's going to do?"

"I'm probably being paranoid. But my relationship with Ryder… Well, let's just say we didn't get off to the best start." The bride gave a shaky laugh at the understatement behind those words.

Rory might have moved to Clearville recently, but her frequent visits as a teenager had given her a taste of small-town life. Everyone knew everyone's business. Which was why it was still something of a shock among the local gossips that Lindsay Brookes had managed to keep her son's— Ryder's son's—paternity a secret for so long.

"But the two of you are together now," Rory reassured her friend, "and that's all that matters."

She might not know the whole story of how Lindsay and Ryder had worked out a decade of differences, but she'd seen for herself how in love the couple was. The way Ryder looked at Lindsay—

Rory pushed aside the pinpricks of envy jabbing at her heart to embrace the positive. If Ryder and Lindsay could overcome such odds and find their way back to each other, then surely there was hope for her. True love was out there somewhere, but right now her focus was Hillcrest House and helping her aunt. Her own happily-ever-after would wait.

"I know. Things are going so well, but I can't shake this feeling that something's going to go wrong. Like I'm waiting for the other shoe to drop."

"And you think that shoe's a size-eleven Italian loafer?"

Lindsay laughed. "You noticed that, huh?"

"I think it's safe to say Jamison's strung a bit tight for a guy who's supposed to be on vacation."

And was it any wonder she was determined to ignore

the instant, unwanted attraction? If Rory had a type, she certainly didn't want it to be Jamison Porter. He was a corporate attorney, for heaven's sake! A shark in a suit when she was looking for more of a—a puppy.

Someone sweet, lovable…loyal. Someone willing to defend her and stay by her side.

"From what I've heard from Ryder, Jamison doesn't do vacations. Ryder really had to push him to take this time off. I guess Jamison has some big deal in the works, but I think if he would take a day or two to relax, it might give him a different perspective on the whole wedding and, well, on me."

"Lindsay, Ryder loves you. And as for Jamison, I think he and Ryder need to go out for a couple of beers and a game of pool over at the Clearville Bar and Grille. They can do the whole high-fiving, name-calling, competitive guy thing, and all will be well."

Even as she said the words, Rory had a hard time picturing Jamison Porter at the local sports bar. He seemed like her ex, Peter, who was more interested in being seen by the right people in the right places. But then again, so much about Peter had all been for show…

"And Ryder's asked, but Jamison won't go. He doesn't want to leave Hannah."

And *that* did not sound like Peter at all. Maybe Rory had been too quick in making her comparisons.

"She's had a hard time since the accident."

"Accident?"

Lindsay nodded, sympathy softening her pretty features. "A car accident a few months ago. Hannah sustained a mild concussion and a broken arm, but she was the lucky one. Her mother was killed instantly."

"Oh, no." That lost look she'd picked up on in Hannah… and in Jamison. Rory had assumed it was nothing more than a single dad on his own with his daughter, far away from the comforts of home. She should have realized it was something deeper… "Poor Hannah. And Jamison, to lose his wife."

"They were separated, and from what Ryder's said, things hadn't been right between them for a long time. But still…"

"I guess you can't blame him if he has his doubts about love and marriage."

"That's what Ryder keeps telling me. Not everything going on in the world revolves around our wedding."

"You're the bride, Lindsay. Everything *does* revolve around the wedding."

Lindsay dropped what was left of the mangled napkin on the table and leaned forward with a relieved smile. "I knew you'd understand, Rory! You're the best wedding co-ordinator ever, and I knew I could count on you to help."

Rory's eyes narrowed. "What exactly am I helping with?"

"Well, with Jamison, of course. I thought if you could show him around town, spend some time with him—"

"Wait! What?" she asked in alarm. "Why me?"

"You have such a way with people. Of keeping calm and helping them relax. Not to mention how taken Hannah is with you. You saw that, and I know Jamison did, too."

Yes, Rory had noticed Hannah's shy fascination. Knowing the little girl had lost her mother added a sense of heartbreak to the tiny fingers that had wrapped around her hand. But it wasn't enough to erase the memory of the dark, disapproving clouds brewing in Jamison's gray gaze.

She'd dealt with enough parental disapproval in her relationship with Peter to last a lifetime.

"I don't think that's such a good idea, Lindsay. With everything Hannah and Jamison must be going through—"

"That's why this is so perfect!" her friend insisted. "Back home they're surrounded by memories, but Clearville—and you—are a clean slate. I know this isn't some miracle fix for what they've lost. No one expects that. All I'm asking is for you to show them around town. Give them a tour of Hillcrest House. You're always saying how magical the place is."

"So no miracles required, just performing a little magic," Rory said wryly as she sank back in her chair. But she was already caving despite Jamison's disapproval, despite her own reluctance to spend time with a man who made her heart skip a beat even when he was frowning at her.

Because once upon a time, Rory had found magic at Hillcrest House, and while her belief might have wavered a time or two over the years, it had never left her.

And when she thought about Hannah and the seriousness in her big brown eyes, Rory couldn't help thinking that belief in happily-ever-after was what the little girl needed.

As for Jamison... Well, there was some magic Rory wasn't sure even a fairy godmother could perform.

As a corporate lawyer at Spears, Moreland and Howe, one of the most prestigious firms in San Francisco, Jamison Porter was at the top of his game. He was vying for a promotion that would make him the youngest junior partner in the firm's history. He had a track record of success and negotiated million-dollar deals for breakfast.

So why was it he couldn't win an argument with his daughter when it came to *eating* breakfast?

"I want pancakes."

Still in her ladybug pajamas, her hair a tangled mess of curls—proof of another battle he'd already lost this morning—Hannah slouched in the dining room chair in a classic pout.

"Hannah…"

The key to winning any negotiation was coming to the table from a place of power, and in this, Jamison had none. Zip. Zilch. Nada. Not after he'd given in to her request for pancakes the day before.

But how was he supposed to say strong when his daughter's willful tantrum broke down and she'd whispered, "Mommy let me have pancakes," with tears filling her eyes?

And so he'd given in and learned the hard way a sugar rush was not a myth. Hyped up on the sweet stuff, Hannah had talked almost nonstop after leaving the bridal shop—mostly about the very woman Jamison was trying so hard not to think about.

"Rory says I can wear ribbons in my hair.

"Rory says I'll get to carry a basket filled with roses and can throw them like it's raining flowers.

"Rory says…"

But no matter how much his daughter talked, it was Rory's voice Jamison heard. Her smile that flashed through his mind time and again. Her challenge to him to reassure Hannah that everything would be okay and her misplaced confidence that he would succeed.

His daughter didn't need him to encourage her to walk down the aisle and be the best flower girl she could be. Rory had done all that on her own. Jamison doubted there was much the woman couldn't talk a person into if she tried.

Sometimes people let me down.

Whoever the man was—and Jamison would bet the partnership up for grabs that it was a man—he had to be the biggest kind of fool to put that shadow of disappointment in Rory's eyes.

And Jamison was no fool. He learned from his mistakes and the biggest one he'd made was in believing he could make a woman happy. So he'd be smart and keep his distance from the pretty wedding coordinator before she could learn the hard way he could only be another man who would let her down.

Jamison scraped a hand over his face, feeling the stubble he had yet to shave away. He'd grabbed a quick shower that morning, but Hannah had been up by the time he'd gotten dressed. He had hoped she might sleep in, but she awoke first thing...looking as bright eyed and well rested as if she hadn't taken ten years off his life when she woke up screaming in the middle of the night.

His mother-in-law, Louisa, had warned him about deviating from Hannah's schedule. *She's been through so much. She takes comfort in a stable routine.*

In that, they were alike, but lately he'd noticed his daughter's routine—or more specifically, Louisa's routine for his daughter—left very little time for him to spend with Hannah.

After the accident, he'd welcomed his mother-in-law's help. Though not life threatening, Hannah's injuries had left her bruised and broken, and Jamison had almost been afraid to touch her. Louisa, a former nurse, had the knowledge and experience Jamison lacked. But now that Hannah had healed, it was time for Louisa to take a step back—whether she wanted to or not.

Which was one of the reasons he'd insisted on this extended trip with Hannah. He'd thought his mother-in-law had exaggerated the problems he might cause, but now he had to wonder.

The first night at the hotel, bedtime had been accompanied by multiple requests for night-night stories, drinks of water and trips to the bathroom. Had those delay tactics been something more than a child's typical resistance to bedtime in a strange location? Were the nightmares that haunted Hannah enough to make her afraid to close her eyes?

Jamison hated the helplessness that gripped him and how the sound of her cries took him back to that horrible day.

On the phone fighting with Monica, Hannah crying in the background...his wife's shrill scream, the sickening crash of metal and after that...nothing. Just a dead phone clutched in his hand.

Eventually Hannah had drifted off to sleep, her breathing still shaky from lingering tears. But Jamison hadn't slept a wink. Blinking through blurry eyes, he figured he looked every bit as rough as that sleepless night had felt.

He was relieved Hannah didn't seem to be suffering any ill effects, but the sense of anxiety that had kept his eyes wide-open still lingered. The monster under the bed ready to jump out at any minute, even during the day with the sun shining.

"I've already ordered breakfast," he reminded her now as he sank into a chair and was met with her pouty face.

Stick with the routine, he reminded himself.

When he first read through Louisa's list of approved foods, dominated by fruits and vegetables, he'd wondered if his mother-in-law wasn't setting him up for a fall. Really, what kid wanted oatmeal for breakfast? But the pancake incident and last night's nightmare made him realize he didn't need to blame Louisa for his failures.

He could fail spectacularly all on his own.

"But I want—"

A quick knock on the door interrupted the brewing

tantrum, and Jamison wasn't sure when he'd felt more relieved. "See, there's room service now with breakfast."

"Pancakes!" Hannah finished in a voice loud enough to have him cringing as he opened the door. And then cringing again at who was on the other side.

"Morning!" Looking bright, chipper and far too tempting for so early in the morning, Rory McClaren met his frown with a beaming smile.

Her dark hair was pulled back in a high ponytail that made her look even younger than he guessed she was and brought to mind old sitcoms set back in the '60s. So did the halter-style dress with its soft floral print and full skirt. His mind still foggy from a sleepless night and too many hours spent thinking of her, Jamison could only stare.

After Hannah's nightmare, Rory looked like something out of a dream. As the rich, strong scent of caffeine hit him, he belatedly noticed the silver serving cart in front of her.

"What are you doing here?" Still on some kind of sleep-deprived delay, the question didn't form until Rory had already wheeled the cart between the floral-print couch and coffee table in the living area and into the dining room.

She shot a questioning glance over her bare shoulder. "You did order room service, didn't you?"

Her blue gaze was filled with wide-eyed innocence, but Jamison wasn't buying it. Realizing he was still holding the door open, he let go and followed her inside. "Yes, but I didn't expect the wedding coordinator to deliver it."

She waved a dismissive hand. "Small hotel. Everyone pitches in." Smiling at his daughter, she asked, "Are you ready for breakfast this morning, Miss Hannah?"

Despite her earlier fascination with the woman, Hannah retreated back into shyness. She drew her bare feet up onto the seat and wrapped her arms around her ladybug-covered legs, looking impossibly tiny in the adult-size chair. "I want pancakes," she repeated, her voice more of a whisper this time.

Instead of a wave of embarrassment crashing over him, Jamison couldn't help feeling a little smug as Rory's cheery expression faltered a bit.

"Um—" she glanced at the ticket tucked beneath one of the covered trays "—it looks like the chef made you oatmeal this morning." She lifted her gaze to Jamison for confirmation.

He nodded. "Oatmeal's good for you. Healthy."

At least that was what his in-laws thought. It wasn't something his mother would have fixed when he was a kid. Not that his mother fixed much of anything in the way of meals—breakfast or otherwise. Jamison had mostly been on his own and, in all honesty, more than content with sugary cereal eaten straight from the box, parked in front of morning cartoons.

"Good for you. Right..." Rory drew out the word as she pulled the cover off the bowl of plain, beige cereal. No fun shapes, bright colors or magically delicious marshmallows there. "What do you say we make this oatmeal even yummier, Hannah?"

Somehow, Jamison should have known a bowl of mush wouldn't be enough to throw her off her game.

"How?" A wealth of doubt filled that one word, and just like that Jamison's amusement vanished.

Yesterday, Hannah had been ready to believe Rory was a fairy godmother who walked on flower petals. And okay, so he didn't buy into Rory McClaren's brand of happily-ever-after, but his daughter was still a little girl. Did he want her doubting something as simple as breakfast couldn't somehow get better?

"I'm guessing Rory has an idea about that," he murmured.

He caught her look of surprise before pleasure brought a pink glow to her cheeks. "That's right. Thanks to your daddy, who also ordered some fruit, we are going to turn this into happy oatmeal."

"Happy?"

"Yep. This oatmeal's a little sad and plain right now," she said as reached for the platter of fruit beautifully arranged in the middle of the tray. "But with a little bit of color..." Her hands, as delicate and graceful as the rest of her, sliced up the fruit as she spoke. A moment later, she'd outlined a blueberry smiley face in the bowl of oatmeal, complete with banana-slice eyes, a strawberry nose and an orange-wedge smile.

Scrambling up onto her knees, Hannah peered into the bowl Rory set in front of her and let out a soft giggle. "Look, Daddy, the oatmeal's smiling at me."

And his daughter was smiling at him. Jamison would have liked the credit, but Rory McClaren had the magic touch. A woman who thought rainbow was a color and turned plain beige oatmeal into a bright, happy-faced breakfast.

"I like smiley-face yummy oatmeal." Grabbing the spoon, Hannah leaned over the bowl, ready to dig in, her blond hair falling into her face.

"Oops, hold on a second, Hannah."

Skirting around the whitewashed oak table, Rory reached up and pulled the peach-colored band from her ponytail. Jamison's mouth went dry as she gave her head a quick shake and sent her dark hair tumbling over her bare shoulders.

His tongue practically stuck to the roof of his mouth; he fought to swallow, assailed by the image of that silken hair spread out against a pillow or tumbling over *his* shoulders as Rory leaned down to kiss him...

"Thank you, Miss Rory." Her riot of curls contained, Hannah beamed up at the beautiful brunette.

Cupping her chin in one hand, Rory bent down until they were eye to eye. "You are welcome, Miss Hannah."

Hannah giggled at the formality before digging into her breakfast. She bounced up and down in the chair in time with chowing down on a bite of banana, drawing an indulgent smile from Rory.

"And what about you, Mr. Porter?" she asked as she walked back over to the serving tray and waved a hand. "I don't see another bowl of oatmeal for you."

"Coffee," he said abruptly, still trying to get the erotic images out of his mind.

Mistaking the reason for his short response, her earnest gaze met his. "I'm sorry if I overstepped with the ponytail. My only excuse is to say it's an occupational hazard."

"So, wedding coordinator, room service attendant and hairstylist?"

"Oh, I'm not a professional stylist by any means. But in my short time as wedding coordinator, I've learned to be a jack-of-all-trades when it comes to last-minute emergencies. Whether it's figuring out how to turn three bridesmaids' bouquets into four because the bride made up with her best friend at the last second or pulling out a hot-glue gun for a quick repair to a torn hemline, I feel like I've already been there, done that. And now it's like I can't help fixing things… Not that Hannah's broken or you need help and—I have got to learn to keep my mouth shut and my hands to myself!"

Rory wasn't the only one with that second problem, but it wasn't his daughter's hair Jamison longed to get his hands on. "It's all right," he said gruffly, even though it wasn't. Her actions were innocent. His intentions…not so much. "About the ponytail thing, I mean. Anyone can see I can't get it right. And I do mean anyone, since even Hannah tells me her hair looks funny when I'm done with it."

"I'm sure you're doing fine."

"Are you?" The sympathy in her eyes told him he and Hannah had been a topic of conversation once they left the bridal shop. "Because I'm not sure of a damn thing."

He half expected some meaningless platitude, but instead she reached for the carafe on the serving tray and poured a cup of steaming coffee. "Rough night?" she asked as she handed him the mug.

His fingers overlapped hers, the warmth seeping through coming more from her soft skin than from the hard ceramic. For a brief second, they both froze, connected by the fragrant cup of coffee. And he found himself desperate for someone to confide in.

"Nightmare," he admitted as Rory released the mug and took a quick step back. She set about tidying the serving tray, her lashes lowered as she avoided his gaze.

"You or Hannah?"

Jamison gave a quick laugh. "Hannah," he said as if he hadn't had more than his share of bad dreams over the past months. Not about Monica, like the dreams that had Hannah crying out for a mother who would never again kiss away her tears, but ones about the accident.

He'd seen pictures of what remained of the run-down sedan Monica had been driving—a mangled wreck of metal Hannah had somehow survived. As if those images weren't bad enough, his subconscious tormented him even further. In his nightmares, the car burst into flames, plunged into a river or fell from a cliff while he could do nothing but watch.

In reality, Jamison hadn't seen the accident, but he'd heard it.

Worse, he'd caused it.

Chapter Four

"Oh, Ms. McClaren, I have to tell you we just got back from the wedding-cake tasting, and every one of them was to die for. I think all those tiny little bites added up to an entire cake by the time we made up our minds."

Rory smiled as the beaming, sugar-filled bride-to-be rushed to her side in the middle of Hillcrest House's elegant, dark-walnut-paneled lobby. She had offered to take Jamison and Hannah on a tour of the grounds, but so far they hadn't made it out of the hotel. She'd been stopped a handful of times either by guests or employees with questions about upcoming events.

Susannah Erickson was the latest interruption. "I'm glad you enjoyed the tasting. I learned within my first few days here not to accompany brides to the bakery. Too much temptation."

And why, oh, why did she have to say *temptation*? Just speaking the word out loud had her thinking about that morning, and not about food. The image of Jamison opening the door, dressed but fresh from the shower, was seared in Rory's mind. The scent of soap and shampoo had clung to his skin, and his damp hair had been rumpled from a quick toweling. Add to that the dark stubble he'd yet to shave away, and all she'd been able to think about was the seductive rasp of that rough skin against her own…

Almost against her will, Rory sought Jamison out. He stood off to the right with Hannah at his side, but Rory had already known that. She'd felt hyperaware of his proximity since he'd opened the door. Telling herself in the intimate setting of the Bluebell suite, of course she would notice the overwhelming presence of a masculine, six-foot-something man.

But even now, surrounded by guests and employees in the spacious lobby, she was still conscious of him. Of the way his gray gaze focused on her. Of the way the air crackled with electricity when their eyes met. Of the restless energy that seemed to pulse inside every inch of his broad-shouldered frame.

As Rory spoke with the bride-to-be about menu options and table settings, her words trembled and tripped on her tongue as though she were the one experiencing a high-octane sugar rush. Fortunately, her client didn't seem to pick up on her nerves and promised to call back and book Hillcrest for her wedding as soon as she had a chance to talk with her fiancé.

After saying her farewells to Susannah, Rory braced herself to face Jamison again. He had taken the opportunity to shave and comb his hair during the time it took for her to return the breakfast dishes and serving cart to the kitchen. Too bad she didn't find that strong, smooth jawline and the hint of an expensive, spicy aftershave any less attractive.

But the clean-cut version was a good reminder of who the man was. In the suite this morning, he'd been a harried father who'd needed her. A man dealing with the heartache of raising a child on his own. A man her heart urged her to help...

This, though, was Jamison Porter, Esquire. A businessman in control of himself and immune to his surroundings as his thumbs flew over his phone. Including, she feared, the daughter twisting restlessly at his side.

Rory knew what it was like to be pushed aside, forgotten, ignored...

She'd been a few years older than Hannah when tragedy struck her family. As an adult, she understood that her parents loved her every bit as much as they loved her brother, Chance, but in the weeks following his accident she'd felt like a ghost wandering the hospital halls—unseen, unheard.

Shaking off the memories, she scolded herself for projecting her own past onto the father and daughter in front of her. *Focus, Rory. Jamison Porter is part of a wedding party and dealing with him part of your job.*

Pasting a professional smile onto her face, she apologized as she joined them. "Sorry about all the interruptions."

"If there's one thing I understand, it's work." He thrust the phone into the pocket of his slacks, but Rory couldn't tell if he was reluctant or relieved to break the connection. "I'm good at what I do."

Rory frowned. The words didn't sound like bragging as much as they sounded like...an apology? She wasn't sure she had that right until his gaze dropped to the top of his daughter's head and his throat worked in a rough swallow.

Suddenly the puzzle pieces fell into place. Successful businessman, not-so-successful family man. His fingers tapped on the outside of his muscular thigh, and Rory could sense his need to reach for his phone again—tangible proof of the predictable, logical world he'd left behind.

"Jamison—"

"I want cake for breakfast," Hannah cut in, her tone grumpy enough for Rory to know the little girl hadn't totally gotten over having to eat oatmeal that morning.

"Only brides get cake for breakfast," her father answered quickly.

"I wanna be a bride."

His daughter's comeback was even faster than his and left Jamison groaning in response. Rory couldn't help but laugh. "Relax, Dad, that's one worry you can put off for a few years." Gazing down at Hannah, she asked, "Do you want to go see where Miss Lindsay is going to get married? You can practice being her flower girl."

Hannah was quiet for a second before her eyes lit up. "Do flower girls get cake?"

"They do—but not for breakfast."

After heaving a sigh at the unfairness of that, Hannah nodded. "Okay."

"All right then. Let's go!"

"Wait, Miss Rory," the girl demanded. "You hafta hold my hand."

Hannah held out her left hand, her right already wrapped around her father's. Rory hesitated even though she knew she was being ridiculous. In her short time at Hillcrest, she'd held more than her share of little and big girls' hands leading up to a wedding. This was nothing different. But with Jamison on the other side, his daughter joining the two of them together, Rory felt a connection that went far beyond a professional capacity.

Something about the corporate lawyer, something in the shadows lingering in his silver eyes, grabbed hold of her. She'd been telling the truth when she said she'd become a jack-of-all-trades with a quick fix for prewedding emergencies. But she had to be careful. She'd be foolish to think she could step in and fix Jamison and his adorable daughter. Foolish to invest too much of herself when their time in Clearville was temporary. Foolish to think he'd want her to.

Though Rory didn't want to be so in tune with the man just a child's length away, she sensed the deep breath he exhaled as they stepped out into the cool morning air. Hannah bounced between them down the wraparound porch's front steps, but it was Jamison who seemed to have released a negative energy bottled up far too long.

As they walked down the gravel path leading from the house, Rory couldn't help glancing back over her shoulder. Even though she'd been back for almost three months, the sight of the Victorian mansion never failed to steal her breath.

She loved the history and old-fashioned elegance of the place. The way it brought to mind a simpler time. With its high peaks, glorious turrets and carved columns and balustrades, an air of romance surrounded the house and property.

Not that romance was anything Rory should be thinking of—at least not as her gaze met Jamison's.

"Um, did you know Hillcrest House was built in the late 1800s? The original owner made his fortune decades earlier down in San Francisco during the gold rush. Not that he ever found gold, but he was one of the enterprising men who figured out the more practical side of gold fever. The thousands of men dreaming of striking it rich were going to need tools and equipment, and he was one of the first on the scene to set up shop."

"Let me guess...at ridiculously inflated rates?" Jamison

asked, the corner of his mouth lifted in a cynical smile that still managed to trip up Rory's heartbeat.

"Oh, but he wasn't just selling metal pans and shovels and pails... He was selling the miners the tools they needed to follow their dreams." Catching the look of utter disbelief on Jamison's face, Rory let out the laughter she'd been holding back. "Yeah, okay, even I can't pull that one off. He robbed the poor suckers blind, selling on credit and then cashing in on their claims when they couldn't pay him back."

"So much for the romance of a time gone by."

Rory started, feeling as if Jamison had read her thoughts moments earlier. "Well, uh, if it's any consolation, karma did bite back, and he ended up losing his fortune—and Hillcrest House—when the stock market crashed."

"Hmm, sounds like cosmic justice but, again, not very romantic."

"Ah, but that's when the house's luck changed. After it stood empty for years, a wealthy industrialist from back east came to California and fell in love with a young woman. He bought Hillcrest as a wedding present for his bride. The story goes that their plan was to have a dozen or so kids—"

"A dozen?"

"At least," Rory emphasized, smiling at the overwhelmed expression on his face as he glanced down at his lone child. "Sadly, they were unable to have children, but as time went on and more and more people were traveling to California and taking vacations along the coast, they decided to turn Hillcrest into a hotel so its rooms could still be filled with families and children and laughter—even if those families only stayed for a short time."

The reminder was one Rory needed to focus on. Jamison and Hannah were only staying for a few weeks.

She couldn't allow herself to be drawn in on a personal level, to let herself start to care too much, too quickly. But with the little girl's hand tucked so trustingly in hers as she sang under her breath, Rory couldn't help wondering if it was already too late.

Hannah's shy sweetness reminded Rory of a kitten she'd once rescued. The frightened Siamese had been all eyes in a skinny body covered with matted fur. It had taken time to build up enough trust for the kitten to allow her to pet it and even more time for the tiny bundle of fur to completely come out of its shell. To learn to run and play and chase. But Rory hadn't given up, because even at the beginning, underneath all the wariness, she had sensed the playful kitten longing to come out.

And as much as the kitten had needed to be rescued, Rory had needed something to save. She couldn't compare her experience as a child to what Hannah was facing in losing her mother so young, but Rory understood a little of what the girl was going through.

That beneath the sadness and loss, a silly, playful girl was struggling to break free.

"And what's your family's connection to the hotel?"

The summer breeze blew a lock of chestnut hair across Jamison's forehead and let loose a flurry of butterflies in her stomach. He was so good-looking, she forgot the question, forgot everything as she met his gaze over his daughter's head.

"Rory."

Heat flooded her cheeks as she tore her attention from the heat shimmering between them and back on what should have been her focus all along. "Right...my family's connection to the hotel. Um, the couple owned the hotel for decades, but with no children to leave it to, they put it up for sale. My grandparents met at Hillcrest—"

"Another romantic story?"

"Exactly," she answered, pleased with his guess despite the cynical tone of the question. "My grandmother was working the front desk and my grandfather was a guest here. Years later, when they heard the hotel was available, they bought it as an investment. They visited all the time but never lived here.

"My father and my uncle both worked here when they were younger, but the hotel and the hospitality industry were never their calling. Not like it was for my aunt Evelyn. Everyone knew she would run Hillcrest one day. She's smart and strong and independent."

Rory's worry over her aunt's health stung her eyes, but she blinked, banishing the tears before they could form. Her aunt wouldn't appreciate Rory getting teary in front of a guest. Not even if that guest was ridiculously handsome with the kind of broad shoulders and strong arms where a woman would be tempted to find comfort.

"And you and your cousin are here helping out?"

That was the explanation she and Evie had been giving people. Their aunt kept a strict line drawn between her personal and professional life, and she didn't want anyone outside of family to know of her health problems.

"Hillcrest House has always been a popular location for weddings with the locals in Clearville and Redfield," Rory said, naming another nearby town, "but last year my aunt decided to expand Hillcrest as a wedding destination. The couples now have the choice of an all-inclusive ceremony, with the hotel handling everything from the cake to the music to the photographer."

"And that's where you come in."

"I work with the couple to get a feel of the type of wedding they're looking for and design all the elements to match that theme."

Jamison shook his head at the notion of a wedding theme, which had Rory wondering what his wedding to Hannah's mother had been like. Not that she was about to ask.

"You're good at this."

Feeling her cheeks heat at the surprising compliment, Rory shook her head. "I've had Hillcrest House facts drilled into my head since I was a little girl. I could recite this information in my sleep. A couple of times, in the midst of wedding madness, I think maybe I have!"

"Not just the tour. I mean the way you dealt with the guests and the staff earlier. You're friendly and encouraging but firm enough to get your point across."

"I—thank you," Rory said, far more pleased by the compliment than she should have been. She didn't like thinking of herself as hungry for approval, but after her failure at the interior design firm in LA, finding success—especially at Hillcrest House—was so important to her. "I didn't expect…"

"Expect what?"

She gave a small laugh. "You and my cousin Evie have quite a bit in common when it comes to the whole wedding thing."

Jamison and her by-the-book cousin likely had more in common than their negative views on weddings and marriage. A CPA, Evie was smart, well educated, as razor sharp as the blunt cut of her dark, chin-length hair. She was practical, pragmatic and more than a little cynical—the kind of woman Rory figured would impress a successful businessman like Jamison.

Ignoring the stab of jealousy at the thought of Jamison and her cousin forming their own mutual-admiration society, Rory said, "Evie's a genius when it comes to handling the books and the last person to believe in fairy tales, but sometimes she acts like I pull off these weddings with nothing more than a wave of a magic wand. She doesn't seem to notice the hard work that goes into them."

"Look, Daddy!" Hannah's impatient tug on their hands brought the conversation to a halt as they reached a curve in the pathway. An intricate lattice-arched entry led to the rose garden—a favorite spot for many brides and grooms to say their vows. Pink, red and white blooms unfurled amid the dark green bushes and the thick, rich lawn.

Turning to Rory, Hannah asked, "Is that where you grow the flowers for the flower girls?"

Not about to ruin the moment for the child, especially when she saw some of that curiosity shining through in her big brown eyes, Rory said, "It sure is. Why don't you go look for the perfect flower? But don't touch, okay? Some of the roses have sharp thorns."

Hannah's pale brows furrowed as she glanced between the rose garden and back again. "Will you stay right here, Daddy?"

"I'm not going anywhere, Hannah Banana."

A small smile tugged at the little girl's lips, and Rory swore the sweet expression was somehow tied to the strings around her heart. She couldn't help smiling as Hannah tucked her hands behind her back before racing— somewhat awkwardly—over to the garden.

But it was Jamison and the unabashed tenderness in his eyes as he gazed at his daughter that had Rory's emotions all tangled up in knots.

He was a guest. And like any other guest who passed through Hillcrest House, Rory would quickly forget all about him. She'd forget all about this day, about walking with Jamison and Hannah beneath a cloudless sky. About the warmth of his skin as his arm brushed against hers. About the rich, masculine scent that tempted her to move closer and breathe deeper. About the longing to reach out and take his hand, knowing how something as simple as entwining her fingers with his would form a bond she would feel right down to her bones…

Yes, indeed, she would forget all about that. Might just spend the rest of her life forgetting all about that.

The strict talking-to had Rory straightening her shoulders and adopting a polite smile, neither of which were any protection against the power behind Jamison's gaze.

"I'll say it again, Rory. You're good at what you do," he repeated, the intensity behind his words preempting any denial she might have made. "Anyone who doesn't appreciate you is a fool."

"Like this, Miss Rory?" Hannah asked over her shoulder as she placed a single rose petal on the verdant green grass.

"Just like that!"

Jamison shook his head at the beautiful brunette's unrelenting encouragement. "You do realize, at that rate, it'll take her an hour and a half to walk down the aisle?"

"She is the flower girl, and they are her flowers. She has every reason to enjoy her moment."

How was it that Rory McClaren seemed to enjoy every moment? A hint of pink touched her cheeks, and he couldn't help wondering if it was from the midmorning sun—or in response to the words he shouldn't have spoken.

Mouth shut and hands to yourself, Porter, he repeated, glad he'd at least stuck to the second part of the mantra despite the serious temptation she posed at every turn. His finger itched to discover the softness of the dark hair that trailed down her back, to trace the splash of freckles across the elegant line of her collarbones, to strip away the strap of her dress marring the perfection of her shoulder…

He hadn't touched, but he couldn't seem to stop himself from speaking. He'd seen the self-consciousness she tried to hide as she talked about her aunt and cousin—smart, successful women—as if she were something less. And everything in him had rebelled at hearing it.

Yes, Rory was beautiful, but desire was something he could control. Listening to her put herself down, even if the words had been unspoken, that was something he couldn't let go. Not after all she'd done for Hannah in as little as two days.

And yeah, it scared the hell out of him, when at times his daughter still felt like a stranger to him. When he felt at such a loss for what to do or what to say. When he felt himself start to shut down like he had when he was a kid and his parents' fighting was enough to send him underneath the covers—or sometimes even underneath the bed—where he'd cover his ears and close his eyes and wish himself away.

But right now, in this moment with Hannah jumping from one spot to the next, playing some kind of flower-petal hopscotch, he wouldn't have wished himself anywhere else in the world.

"Thank you."

Rory blinked in surprise. "For what?"

"For Hannah. I haven't seen her this happy in—I'm not sure I remember when."

She shook her head. "It's not me. It's Hillcrest. This place is magical that way."

When Jamison offered a disbelieving snort in response, she held up a silencing hand. "Hear me out." And when that hand came down and she entwined her fingers with his, he couldn't have said a word anyway.

Holding hands hadn't made it into his fantasy, but it might have if he'd known how something so simple would make his pulse skyrocket, his heart race, his stomach muscles tighten in response. The softness of her skin seemed to telegraph through his entire body until he swore he could feel her caress…everywhere.

He wasn't sure how he got his feet to move as she led him over toward a white wrought iron bench. Tucked off to the side of the garden, the shaded spot offered a perfect view of Hannah playing a few yards away.

"Rory—" His voice was a strangled croak, and even when she let go, the feel of her hand gliding away branded him. It was all he could do not to scrub his palm against his pressed khakis.

She patted the spot beside her. "Have a seat. Please," she added when he stood ramrod straight at her side.

Somehow, he made his muscles move and forced himself to sit on a bench too small for the arm's-length distance he needed between them. So small the cool breeze carried the sunshine-and-wildflower scent of her skin closer and a strand of her hair danced over his biceps like a caress.

It took everything in his power to focus on the words she was saying rather than following the tantalizing movement of her lips, but the seriousness in her blue eyes soon caught his complete attention. "I have an older brother, Chance, who I adore. He's four years older than I am, and growing up he was always my hero. The big brother who looked out for me. When I was a few years older than Hannah, he was in an accident."

Even though years had passed, Rory sucked in a deep breath before telling the next part. "He was showing off for his friends, fell off his skateboard doing some crazy jump and hit his head. He ended up in a coma. The doctors did everything they could, but for a long time, they didn't know if he would wake up or what kind of shape he would be in if he did."

"I can imagine how hard that must have been on you and your parents." Hannah's injuries hadn't been that severe, but it was the months leading up to the accident when he hadn't known if he would ever see his daughter again and the agonizing hours after that final fight with Monica when he hadn't even known if Hannah was still *alive* that gave him an idea of what the McClarens had gone through.

"It was. Our family had always been so together, so strong, but Chance's accident proved how everything could change. Like that," she said with a snap of her fingers. "As the weeks went by, and his condition didn't change, eventually my dad went back to work. Not because his job was more important than Chance, but because—I just don't think he could sit there, feeling so hopeless, anymore.

"My mom refused to leave my brother's side—eating, sleeping, living at the hospital. She never came out and said so, at least not when I was around, but I think she resented my dad for not doing the same."

"And what did you do," Jamison asked, "during all that time?"

Rory met his gaze before ducking her head, looking almost embarrassed that he'd asked about her. He could imagine she must have felt like the forgotten child, the healthy, happy one no one had the time or energy to pay much attention to.

"I split my days between school and the hospital. I mostly tried to be quiet and stay out of the way, but as the weeks went on… I don't know, maybe I got to be more like my dad, where I couldn't sit there and watch anymore. And then one day, after my mom had run down to the cafeteria for coffee, she came back and I was kneeling on the bed, shaking Chance and shouting at him to stop messing around and to wake up."

"Rory."

Shaking off his sympathy, she talked faster, as if eager to get through the worst of it. "After that…incident, my aunt and uncle, Evie's parents, brought the two of us here for an extended vacation. We ran and laughed and played and explored every inch of this place.

"Not that I forgot about Chance. Every game of pretend Evie and I played over the summer had something to do with breaking a curse or casting a spell or rescuing him from a dragon. I knew if I believed strongly enough, one day Chance would open his eyes and wake up… And one day, he did."

"I'm glad your brother got better, and I can see why, as a little girl, this place would seem so magical, but Rory—" Jamison stopped short and heaved out a heavy sigh. "Hannah's mother isn't going to open her eyes and wake up. Not for all the faith or magic or fairy tales in the world."

"No, she isn't. And Hannah's been through a horrible tragedy, but she's still a little girl who wants to run and laugh and play again, and she needs to know it's okay for her to do those things."

"Of course it's okay."

"And she knows this…how? By watching you? When was the last time you ran or laughed or just enjoyed life a little?"

"Give me a break, Rory. I'm a grown man, not a kid."

"Right. But you're a grown man *with* a kid. A child who's lost her mother. She's looking to you to see how she's supposed to react to a loss she isn't old enough to understand."

Jamison jerked away from Rory's imploring gaze to focus on Hannah. She was no longer dropping petals but was instead gathering them up, one by one. Picking up the pieces…

He didn't want to admit Rory was right, but the truth

was he'd spent his entire life burying his feelings. Was it any wonder he'd done the same when Monica died?

But he hadn't thought about how his emotions—or his lack of emotion—were affecting Hannah. He'd seen how she had retreated into herself after the accident, so different from the smiling, laughing girl he remembered.

How had he not seen his own reflection staring back at him when he looked at his daughter?

"Even before...Monica," he confessed, "I wasn't the running and laughing kind of guy."

A small smile played around Rory's lips, telling him she wasn't shocked by his confession. "And that's why I wanted you to come along today. So you could see that here, at Hillcrest House, you can be."

"Wait a minute." Jamison reared back against the wrought iron bench and waved a hand in the direction of the path they'd taken. "You're telling me this whole tour was for my sake and not for Hannah's?" It was by far the most ridiculous—and quite possibly the sweetest—thing anyone had ever done for him.

"Hillcrest House is special that way," she told him. "Its magic seems to touch whoever needs it the most."

Somehow his scoffing laugh stuck in his throat. There was no magic, and hadn't he already decided there couldn't be any touching? He wasn't the kind of romantic fool who would buy into such whimsical nonsense.

But in the peaceful setting with the dappled sunlight streaming through the trees and the gentle understanding reflected in Rory's midnight blue eyes, Jamison almost wished that he was.

Chapter Five

Jamison Porter had to think she was the world's biggest fool. Had she really spent the past five minutes trying to convince a corporate lawyer, a man who lived his life based on rules and regulations, to believe in magic?

No wonder he was staring at her. The poor man was probably trying to figure out a way to grab his child and run before the crazy lady totally fell off her rocker. She would have been more embarrassed—probably *should* have been more embarrassed—except she believed every word she said. Hillcrest *was* magical, the kind of place to bring people together, and if he gave it half a chance, Jamison might feel that, too.

A tug on her skirt broke the moment, freeing her from that intense silver stare, as she turned to Hannah.

"Miss Rory?" The little girl ducked her head shyly as she pointed to a glimpse of white showing between the trees in the distance. "What's that?"

"That, Miss Hannah, is my favorite spot in the world."

"Your favorite spot in the whole, whole world?"

After pressing her knuckles to her chin and pretending to think for a moment, Rory nodded. "The whole, whole world."

Hannah offered a lightning-quick smile, one Rory couldn't help returning. Playing to the child's curiosity, she stood and held out her hand. "Do you want to go see?"

After hesitating for a moment, Hannah asked, "Can Daddy come, too?"

Without looking his way, she offered, "I bet your daddy would love to come with us."

Jamison made a sound Rory decided to take as an agreement as she led the way down the flagstone path. "What about you, Hannah?" she asked the little girl. "Do you have a favorite place?"

The little girl gave a soft giggle. "The hidey-hole in Daddy's office."

Rory laughed. "A hidey-hole, Jamison? I mean, I've been known to duck behind an ice sculpture to avoid a bridezilla or two, but I've never had to install a hidey-hole."

"It's not a hole, it's—" He shook his head. "Your favorite spot, Hannah? Really?" he asked, surprise softening his expression.

His daughter nodded as she swung the two adults' arms back and forth in time with her steps. "Yep. It's just my size an' when I'm real quiet, nobody knows I'm there. Like the time I hid from Nana."

"Yes, well, your grandmother isn't as good at hide-and-seek as you are," Jamison said, his wry tone telling Rory the older woman hadn't been as amused with her granddaughter's game as Hannah was, either. With a glance at Rory, he said, "And it's not a hole. The furniture set in my home office came with a liquor cabinet. I'm more a beer-on-the-weekend than a three-martini-lunch kind of guy, so I never bothered to stock the cabinet. Probably a good thing, since someone—" he gently shook Hannah's arm "—thinks it's a fun place to hide."

Jamison thought he was struggling as a father, but he must be doing something right. Didn't he realize Hannah's favorite place was one she associated with him?

As they rounded a bend along the flagstone pathway, Rory announced, "And here it is. My favorite place in the whole, whole world."

Rory was accustomed to breathless reactions at this point, and Hannah did not disappoint. "Daddy, look! It's a playhouse."

"I see it, Hannah," Jamison answered, and Rory couldn't help wondering *what* he saw.

With its crisscross latticework, carved pillars and wide steps leading toward the circular platform, the gazebo was breathtaking. The gleaming white woodwork could be transformed by wrapping the columns with gorgeous flowered garlands, adding colorful organza swags to the decorative eaves or bunting to the airy facade.

It was one of the most romantic spots Rory could imagine, and she'd shown it to dozens of couples in her short time as Hillcrest's wedding coordinator. But showing it to Jamison felt...different.

She felt oddly vulnerable, as if she were revealing a part of herself to the enigmatic, troubling man at her side.

Needing to create some distance, she let go of Hannah's hand and tried to pretend this was no different from any other tour. "It does look like a playhouse, but it's a gazebo, and this is where Lindsay is getting married." Pointing to the wide steps, she added, "Ryder and your daddy will be standing right up there, waiting. Because you're the flower girl, you'll go first—"

"An' get to throw my flowers."

"You'll throw your flowers and Robbie will carry the rings. Lindsay's bridesmaids will walk down the aisle and finally Lindsay."

"'Cause she's the bride and gets to eat cake for breakfast," the little girl piped with a definitive nod.

"That's right, and she'll walk right up here and—" Rory had barely set foot on the first step when she heard a creak and a crack. Neither sound registered until the board splintered beneath her sandal and pain shot up her leg. Her abbreviated cry got stuck in her throat as she lost her balance and fell—

Not to the solid ground but against Jamison's solid chest as he caught her in his arms. For a stunned moment, neither of them moved.

"You okay?" His low murmur stirred the hair at her temples and the vibration set off tiny shock waves in her belly.

Staring breathlessly up into his silver eyes, Rory could do little more than nod. Her heart pounded, and she wished she could blame the reaction on her near fall. Instead, she was pretty sure it had everything to do with the man who'd caught her. She braced a hand against his chest, knowing she should move, but her body refused to listen to her brain. The soft cotton was warmed by the morning sun and held the scent of soap combined with 100 percent pure male.

His face was inches from hers, so close she could feel the kiss of his breath against her lips, a prelude to the touch of his mouth against her own…

"Miss Rory!" Hannah's startled cry broke the moment so quickly Rory wasn't sure she hadn't imagined it.

"Stay back, Hannah. It's not safe," Jamison instructed. Bending down, he carefully maneuvered Rory's foot from between the jagged, cracked boards. She winced at the raw scrape on the outside of her ankle.

"She's all bleedy."

The wobble of tears shook Hannah's voice, and Rory focused on the little girl instead of the throbbing pain. "Hey, Hannah, do you—do you know what would make me feel better? If you'd sing a song. Can you do that for me?"

Nodding her head with a big sniff, she started singing a song Rory had heard her humming under her breath on their walk. She wasn't sure which was the bigger distraction—Hannah's sweet voice or the feel of Jamison's hands against her bare skin. She swallowed hard at the sight of the gorgeous man kneeling at her feet and swayed slightly.

Jamison caught her around the waist and lowered her to the first step. "Here, have a seat while I take a look at your ankle."

"Thank you. I—I don't know what happened."

"I can tell you that. The wood's nearly rotted through."

She shook her head. "No, that can't be. Earl, our handyman, just finished remodeling the gazebo last week." She had noticed some wear and tear and had put the gazebo on the handyman's to-do list.

"I'd say all your handyman did was slap on a coat of white paint. Judging by the way that step cracked beneath your feet, that new layer of latex is about all that's holding this thing together."

Dismayed, Rory struggled to push to her feet, but Jamison held her in place. "But this is where Ryder and Lindsay are getting married. It's where I—"

Where *Rory* wanted to get married. Okay, she wasn't even dating anyone and her last relationship had ended in disaster, but none of that meant she'd given up hope of finding true love. She wanted love, marriage, a family... and it all started here. She'd imagined dozens of scenarios for her perfect dream wedding, and while the dress, the flowers, even the guy had changed numerous times, the one constant had been speaking her vows beneath the lacy, romantic gazebo.

"Hey, it's going to be okay." Jamison's voice cut into her thoughts, and only as she met his silver gaze did Rory realize how close he was sitting.

He'd taken the step below her and slipped the sandal from her foot. He cradled her instep in one large hand while he brushed sharp slivers of wood from her abraded skin. The warmth of his body seeped into hers, radiating out from his palm, and Rory shivered in response. She caught the scent of his aftershave again, mixing with the pine-scented breeze surrounding them.

She drew a quick breath in through her mouth, trying to somehow stop inhaling the heady combination, but that only made matters worse as Jamison focused on her parted lips. Her pulse pounded and it was all Rory could do not to lean closer, to close the narrow gap between them, to press her mouth against the temptation of his.

The wind shifted again, rustling through the trees and carrying the sound of Hannah's sweet voice as she started singing a new song…

Jamison reared back, a look akin to horror flashing across his features so quickly, Rory wasn't sure what she had seen. But just like that, it was as though the tender moment never happened.

"You're lucky it wasn't a guest nearly breaking an ankle on that step," he was saying. "This whole thing is a lawsuit waiting to happen. You need signs and a barricade cordoning off the area until someone can tear—"

"Tear it down?" She stared at him as she jerked her foot away. Instantly, the warmth of his touch disappeared, and the throbbing in her ankle multiplied. Was this the same man who'd come to her rescue, catching her when she would have fallen? The same man who'd cradled her foot in those big, warm hands? The same man she'd thought was going to kiss her?

With his arms crossed over his broad chest, *he* might as well have had signs and barricades warning her off.

"I am not letting anyone tear down the gazebo!" She'd as soon rip her own heart out and douse all her dreams of finding true love. Without the gazebo—

He reached out and gave the wobbly railing a good shake. "You won't have to let anyone tear it down. A stiff breeze, and the whole thing will fall over."

Still feeling foolish over the almost kiss she was starting to think had only happened in her own head, she glared at him. "You'd like that, wouldn't you? After all, you've made it clear how you feel about this *whole wedding thing*. You'd probably just as soon tear it down yourself."

"You're being ridiculous," Jamison muttered, but the baleful look he cast at the gazebo told Rory he was considering doing some damage to the structure—with his bare hands.

Pain shot up her leg the instant she pushed to her feet, and Jamison shot her a frustrated look. "Would you sit back down? You're lucky you didn't break your neck, thanks to your beloved gazebo, and you should go to the hospital—"

"No, Daddy!"

Jamison started at his daughter's shout. "Hannah, what?"

The little girl rushed over, but instead of latching onto her father, she threw her arms around Rory's legs, almost knocking her off balance.

Jamison frowned as Rory flinched. "Hannah."

"Don't make Rory go to the hospital! Don't make her go! Mommy went to the hospital and she never, never came back!"

* * *

Jamison froze at his daughter's cry, the sound piercing straight through his heart. In those first dark days after the accident, he'd tried to be there for Hannah, to be the one to care for her, to hold her when she cried. But her tears had been for her mother, and Jamison's fumbling, painful attempts to explain that Monica was now in heaven didn't seem to penetrate Hannah's sorrow.

"No! I want Mommy!" Accusation had filled her dark eyes, as if Jamison was the one keeping Monica away, the one responsible...and in so many ways, he was.

He'd seen the sympathy of the doctors and nurses at the hospital. *Give her time*, they'd advised. *She'll come around.* Before long, he'd learned to step back, to let someone better prepared handle Hannah when she was upset. One step, and then another and another, and before long, he'd stood on the fringes of his daughter's life. Present but accounting for nothing.

"Hannah." He could barely get the word out, barely make himself move to brush a hand against her curls. Half afraid to touch her and 100 percent certain she'd pull away.

Rory had no such fear. "Oh, Hannah, sweetie." Despite her injured ankle, she dropped down to his daughter's level to give her a hug. "I'm fine! All I need is a Band-Aid or two."

She brushed away Hannah's tears, reassuring the little girl who managed a watery smile in response, her ease with his daughter making Jamison feel like even more of a failure as a father.

"See, Daddy? Miss Rory doesn't need to go to the hospital." Hannah stared up at him, her chin set at a stubborn angle.

Jamison fought back a sigh. How did he end up the bad guy in all of this when he was only trying to help? "Hannah..."

"Your daddy was worried about me. And even if I did have to go to the hospital, I promise you I would come back."

He caught sight of the wince she tried to hide as she pushed to her feet and warned, "You need to get some ice on that ankle to keep the swelling down."

"I'll be fine," she repeated with a big smile, and Jamison couldn't figure out if it was for his benefit, his daughter's or her own.

At her first awkward step, he sighed again, wrapped an arm around her waist and under her knees and lifted her against her chest. Her startled gasp brought them face-to-face. Close enough for him to count the freckles dusting her cheeks. Close enough to feel her breath against his skin. And Jamison wondered how long he could have resisted before pulling Rory into his arms—banged-up ankle or no banged-up ankle.

"I'm not letting you hobble all the way back to the hotel."

"Well, you can't carry me back!"

He gave her a light toss, fighting a grin at the way her arms tightened around his neck. "I'm pretty sure I can."

"Not into the hotel. I can't—please, Jamison."

His smile faded. Rory was more than simply flustered by the idea. Pained embarrassment etched her pretty features. He didn't know the reason for the lack of confidence he'd sensed earlier, but he could understand why she wouldn't want her coworkers to see a guest carrying her through the hotel—regardless of the situation. Still, he couldn't let her limp back on her own. "Rory…"

"You, um… My place isn't far from here."

"Your place? You don't have a room at the hotel?"

She shook her head. "Evie does. She's staying in my aunt's room while she's…away. But I wanted a place of my own. I thought it would be easier."

"Easier?" he asked.

He did his damnedest to ignore the dizzying thought of taking Rory back to her place, but that was as impossible as ignoring the feel of her in his arms as she gave him directions to something called the caretaker's cottage.

She's injured, you idiot, he warned himself. *And your daughter is right beside you.*

Hannah skipped along the path, carrying the shoe he'd slipped from Rory's foot and still humming the song she'd switched to earlier. A song Monica used to sing to her.

It might not have been his dead wife's voice calling out from the grave, but it had still chilled him to the bone.

"I thought it would be easier keeping my professional and personal lives separate," Rory was saying, "if I wasn't staying at the hotel." She didn't meet his gaze, but judging by the color in her cheeks, she was well aware whatever was happening between them was a serious mixing of the two.

She wasn't simply the wedding coordinator any more than he was just the best man.

The best man… He wasn't anywhere near the best man for a woman like Rory. He needed to keep his distance, so how the hell had he ended up with her in his arms, about to carry her into her home?

"Yeah, how's that working out for you?"

She lifted her chin, but the stubborn angle only emphasized the pulse pounding at the base of her neck. "Just fine," she insisted, but as he rounded a curve on the path and the small cottage came into view, he thought he heard her whisper under her breath. "Until now."

Rory had always loved the caretaker's cottage, as the place was still known even though many years had passed since Hillcrest had live-in staff. From what her aunt had told her, the tiny wood-and-stone structure had nearly fallen into disrepair, but decades ago, Evelyn had saved it from the brink of destruction and had kept it up over the years.

Still, it had needed some sprucing up and some serious elbow grease to turn it into a place Rory called home, but now it was her sanctuary. A place she could retreat to where she didn't have to deal with demanding brides, cold-footed grooms or the mess she'd left behind in LA.

As Jamison set her down on the tiny porch, she insisted, "I'll be fine from here."

He'd said little on the walk from the gazebo, but Rory had felt the rock-hard tension gripping his muscles—a tightness she doubted had anything to do with carrying her weight.

She'd practically thrown herself at him thanks to the broken step, and he probably had whiplash from pulling away from her so fast.

"There are still splinters stuck in your ankle. If you won't let me take you—you know where—you're going to need some help."

She felt the weight of his frown as she hop-stepped over to the door and slipped the key out from beneath a brightly colored mosaic pot of pansies. She held her palm out in the universal stop sign as he moved closer. "I'm good. I've got it."

The very, very last thing she needed was Jamison Porter carrying her over the threshold!

"I like your house, Miss Rory," Hannah announced before bending down to take an exaggerated sniff of the pansies.

"Thank you, Miss Hannah."

"She probably thinks seven dwarves live here," Jamison muttered under his breath as Rory pushed the door open. She shot him a look over her shoulder, though she had to admit the tiny cottage in the woods did have a fairy-tale feel. The front door opened into the living room, a comfortable space Rory had filled with secondhand finds from the Hope Chest, an eclectic consignment store in town. Two floral-print sofas faced a steamer-trunk coffee table, all in pastel shades with white accents. Hannah was drawn to the patchwork bear sitting in a miniature white wicker rocking chair in the corner, both mementos from Rory's childhood.

"I have a first-aid kit in the bathroom." Rory waved a hand toward the partially open door down the narrow hallway.

"I'll get it. You sit."

Rory flopped onto the sofa with a huff. Sit? What was she, a dog? But as she reached down to massage the bruise already forming on her ankle, she had to admit it felt good to take her weight off. A clatter sounded in the bathroom—something falling into the porcelain sink—followed by Jamison's curse.

"Everything okay in there?"

"Fine. I dropped the—never mind."

Groaning, Rory dropped her head back on the back of the couch as she tried to remember what else she kept in the medicine cabinet along with the Band-Aids and iodine. Just what she wanted—a superhot guy getting a peek at her anti-aging wrinkle cream, Midol and other assorted feminine products.

He returned a moment later, first-aid kit in hand, and while Rory couldn't be sure, she thought his face was a shade or two more red than when he'd entered.

Great.

"Find everything?"

"Uh, yeah. I think so."

And then Rory wasn't so worried about Jamison's embarrassment or even her own as he knelt down in front of her and placed her foot on his khaki-covered thigh. She could feel the muscles and heat beneath her foot and it was all she could do not to flex her toes like some kind of attention-seeking kitten. And while Jamison might have made reference to Snow White, Rory couldn't help feeling a little like Cinderella as he cradled her foot in his large hands.

"How's that?" he asked.

A perfect fit...

Rory snapped herself back to reality as she realized he'd already removed the last of the splinters with a pair of tweezers, dabbed some antibiotic ointment on the scrape and was getting ready to smooth a Band-Aid over the area.

"Good. Fine. Thank you."

His nod sent a lock of hair falling over his forehead, and she gripped the cushions at her side to keep from reaching out. Jamison glanced up and their gazes locked, and Rory knew.

"I'm not imagining things."

His forehead wrinkled in a frown. "I wouldn't think so. I've never heard of a twisted ankle causing hallucinations."

"You were thinking of kissing me earlier."

This time it was Jamison's turn to look like he'd taken a blow to the head. He sucked in a breath that fanned the flames burning in his quicksilver eyes. "Rory. That's not—" His gaze shot to Hannah, who was sitting in the rocking chair, her attention still captured by her newfound stuffed friend. "We can't."

Maybe Rory should have been more disappointed as he turned his attention to cleaning up the cotton balls and wrapping from the first aid, but instead a tiny kernel of hope bloomed in her chest.

Because *can't* was a different story than *didn't want to.*

Chapter Six

"What do you mean, you fired Earl?" Her head pounding almost as loudly as her ankle, Rory stared in disbelief across the wide expanse of her cousin's cherrywood desk. She'd spent a painful half an hour searching for the handyman before stopping by her cousin's office, where Evie had stunned her with the news that she'd let the man go.

"Is that—" Evie frowned as Rory hobbled over to a chair and reached down to rub her ankle. "Why on earth is there toilet paper wrapped around your foot? And why are you limping?"

Rory straightened, heat rising to her cheeks. "Never mind."

Before Jamison and Hannah left the cottage, the little girl had ducked into the bathroom and returned with a long length of the paper trailing behind her. Her blond brows had pulled together in concentration as she'd tried to wrap the "bandage" around Rory's ankle before her father stepped in.

The last thing she'd expected was for Jamison to indulge his daughter's attempts to play doctor, but he'd showed the same seriousness using the toilet paper as when he'd applied the antibacterial ointment and Band-Aids.

Yes, she should have ripped the silly "bandage" off already, but she'd been touched by Hannah's sweetness. Not to mention Jamison's...

"How could you fire Earl without telling me?"

"We agreed when we both started working here that staffing decisions fall under my purview." Evie gazed back at her, slender hands folded in front of her. Sometimes her cousin's crystal-cool demeanor was enough to make Rory want to scream. It made her want *Evie* to scream, to show some emotion, to go back to being the warm, funny girl Rory remembered instead of the calculating woman she'd become.

"Earl wasn't a handyman you can replace with a snap of your fingers." The potbellied, fiftysomething man had worked for the hotel almost as long as Rory could remember. "He was—"

"He was stealing from the hotel," her cousin cut in.

Rory's jaw dropped. "Stealing?" she choked, the word lodging against the lump in her throat.

Pamela Worthington's voice whipped through her mind so clearly, she half expected her former employer to be looming behind her, anger and disappointment written across her aristocratic features. *I trusted you, Aurora. I gave you a chance despite your limited experience, and this is how you repay me? By stealing from our clients?*

"Are you—" Rory cleared her throat before her words could break into ragged shards. "Are you sure? Maybe there was some kind of mistake—"

But Evie was already shaking her head. "He turned in an invoice from Hendrix Hardware a few weeks ago." She tucked a strand of perfectly straight dark hair behind her ear. "Not long after that, I ran into Howard Hendrix, who told me he was sorry the parts Earl special ordered for the new irrigation system didn't work out and if we needed him to order more, to let him know."

"Maybe the parts didn't work. Maybe he bought them somewhere else."

"Where? And why wouldn't Earl have a copy of that receipt? You know Hendrix gives us a better deal than the big-box store over in Redfield. No, Earl returned those parts and pocketed the money."

"But I saw him working on the irrigation."

"And for all we know, he patched everything together with duct tape and used chewing gum. I already have a call in to a landscaping company. Which means spending even more money."

Focusing on the money side of her job was not Rory's strong suit, but Evie had been clear on how tightly the two were tied together.

I know you like picturing yourself as some kind of fairy godmother, but you can't solve things with a wave of a wand. Aunt Evelyn wants to expand the wedding destination aspect of the hotel, but doing so only make sense if it makes money.

Her cousin had also told her about an offer on the hotel. Their aunt Evelyn had fielded offers from large hotel chains before, but with her recent health issues, Rory feared she might be considering it. Selling Hillcrest...

Rory couldn't even imagine not having the hotel in her family.

"I spoke with Susannah Erickson this morning. She's almost committed to having the ceremony here," Rory told her cousin. "I'll give her a call this afternoon. If I can get them to sign off on the paperwork, I can request a deposit—"

"Rory," Evie said slowly.

Just the sound of her cousin's voice had her stomach sinking. "What is it? What's wrong?"

"As Earl was leaving, he said something under his breath."

Rory frown in confusion. "You just fired him, Evie." She held up a hand as her cousin opened her mouth to protest. "Rightfully so, but I'm sure he had a whole bunch of things to say."

"It wasn't about his being fired, at least not exactly."

"What did he say?"

Evie dropped her gaze to her hands, her inability to make eye contact making that sick feeling in the pit of Rory's stomach even worse. "He said that if his last name was McClaren, he wouldn't be getting fired. He'd be getting promoted to wedding coordinator."

Rory sucked in a quick breath that fanned the flames of humiliation rising in her cheeks. "How—how could he know? How could anyone here know?"

Silence had been a stipulation in keeping the Worthingtons from going to the police. The last thing they wanted was for their clients to know one of their employees had stolen from the multimillion-dollar homes they were hired to stage.

Somehow, though, word had gotten out. And the Worthingtons quickly pointed the finger at Rory—the designer they had fired after finding pictures of the stolen items posted to online auctions from her computer.

She'd not only lost her job, but her career, her friends, her boyfriend, as Peter had taken his mother's side. Only later, once the hurt and humiliation started to wane, had Rory realized why he'd turned on her so easily...

"I don't know, Rory," Evie said, pulling her from the dark memories and how badly things had ended in LA. "I certainly haven't said anything."

A touch of self-righteousness underlined her cousin's words. Of course, Evie wouldn't say anything. Evie would never do anything wrong. Evie would never cross a line and date someone she worked with. Evie would never find herself framed for a crime she didn't commit.

Rory blinked back the tears burning her eyes. She'd thought she'd left it all behind her—the accusations, the whispers, the "thanks but no, thanks" responses to every job she applied for.

But it was her family's reaction that hurt the worst. Not that they didn't believe she was innocent. But she couldn't shake the feeling they thought she'd somehow brought this on herself. By being too naive, too trusting, too *something*.

"Regardless of what Earl does or doesn't know... I think it would be best if I'm the one who deals with collecting the deposits from now on."

"Evie..." Rory gaped at her cousin, as stunned now as she'd been when Pamela Worthington had confronted her with the "proof" that Rory had been behind the rash of thefts.

"It's not that I don't trust you. You know that."

"Do I?" She couldn't help asking.

Evie lifted her gaze and straightened her shoulders. "You should. But these couples are spending a great deal of money, and it's their trust we can't afford to lose. Besides, collecting deposits falls more into my job description."

That's not the point! The words were on the tip of her tongue, but Evie had already turned back to her computer screen. *I didn't do anything wrong. I didn't deserve to be fired, to be blacklisted from every design firm in Southern California!*

But deserved or not, those things had still happened. Yes, she'd been glad to come to Clearville to help her aunt Evelyn, but the truth was, she'd slunk out of LA with her tail between her legs. And now the fallout had followed her, and Rory felt she had no choice but to duck and run once more.

She was halfway to the door when Evie asked, "Why were you looking for Earl, anyway?"

"I'd asked him to fix up the gazebo last week."

"The gazebo?"

For a split second, Evie's gaze lost focus, a sadness shadowing her expression, and Rory couldn't help wondering if her cousin was thinking about her own plans for her wedding and the ceremony that was to have taken place there years ago. And how, back then, it had been her relationship—and not the gazebo—that had ended up in shambles.

"It was looking a little worn around the edges, and with Ryder and Lindsay's wedding coming up..." She shook her head. "Anyway, it turns out it's in worse shape than I first thought."

Rory didn't know if Evie picked up on the sympathy in her voice, but if she did, her cousin knew all too well how to make people stop feeling sorry for her. "If the gazebo is in bad shape, that makes it a liability. A—"

"A lawsuit waiting to happen," Rory filled in, recalling Jamison's words earlier.

Her throbbing ankle echoed its agreement. Not only did they have to protect their guests, they also had to protect themselves. If Aunt Evelyn were still in charge, she would feel the same way Evie did. The two strong businesswomen didn't have any trouble following their heads. And maybe they had it right. After all, where had following her heart gotten Rory except into a boatload of trouble?

"Lindsay and Ryder's wedding can still take place as planned," Evie said pragmatically. "They can always use the rose garden."

The garden was lovely. A place where numerous weddings had taken place. But it wasn't the gazebo. It wasn't where Lindsay and Ryder wanted to say their vows. It wasn't where Rory dreamed of having her own ceremony.

Rory wasn't giving up. Not on her dreams of the future and not on the wedding Lindsay and Ryder wanted. "There's still time."

Evie raised a disbelieving eyebrow. "Less than two weeks."

"Like I said," Rory responded with a confidence she didn't entirely feel, "plenty of time."

Her cousin shook her head. "I know you want to believe everything ends in happily-ever-after, but you need to be practical about this. Talk to Ryder and Lindsay about moving the ceremony now. Don't put it off with the hope that a bunch of talking rodents are magically going to fix the place."

Rory offered a quick curtsy. "As you command, my evil queen."

Her cousin rolled her eyes and turned her attention back to her spreadsheet. Evie might not believe in fairy tales, but Rory still did. She wasn't about to lose faith in giving Ryder and Lindsay the wedding of their dreams.

"Ready, Robbie?" Ryder Kincaid called out to his son. "Okay, go long!"

Cocking back the golden arm that had carried him all the way from small-town Clearville to a college football scholarship, Ryder threw a perfect spiral to his son. The ball arced through the late-afternoon summer sky, hitting the boy right in the hands...and then bounding off to land in the sand a few feet away.

Smiling sheepishly behind too-long bangs and pair of wire-rimmed glasses, Robbie scrambled after the pigskin. "Almost had it!"

"So close, bud!" Ryder called back, his smile as wide as if his son had caught the winning touchdown in the Super Bowl. "Kid's smart as a whip. Can't catch to save his life."

Jamison couldn't help thinking the boy's skills would have benefited from playing catch with his dad from the time that he was Hannah's age, instead of just over the past few months. "Maybe if he—"

"Maybe what?" Ryder asked as Robbie chucked the ball back in an end-over-end toss.

"Maybe Robbie takes after Lindsay."

"You got that right." Ryder's grin was just as big as he thought of his fiancée, and Jamison knew he'd made the right decision in not speaking his mind.

Ryder was crazy about Lindsay. That much Jamison could see, but he couldn't understand it.

In the months after he and Monica separated, she'd done everything she could to keep Jamison from seeing Hannah. Canceling visits, conveniently forgetting when he was scheduled to come by the house, insisting Hannah was sick, asleep or any other excuse she could come up with to keep him from seeing his daughter.

He hadn't wanted to fight with Monica. After his parents' endless battles, he'd learned to bury all emotion, knowing even as a kid that anything he said or did would only throw fuel on an already out-of-control fire. He'd retreated into himself, playing the childish game of closing his eyes in the hope no one could see him.

He'd never intended to fall back into that same pattern

with Monica. He'd done his best to ignore her constant complaining, her out-of-control shopping sprees, the way she'd started spending more time out with friends than at home with Hannah. He'd buried himself in his work, not wanting to admit his own marriage was headed down the same rocky path as his parents'. By the time he'd finally opened his eyes, his daughter had grown from a toddler to a little girl he hardly recognized.

He glanced over to where Hannah was playing off away from Robbie and his cousins, building a Leaning Tower of Pisa sandcastle on her own. Was that missing time the reason why he struggled so much to connect with her now? Or was it something more, something lacking in him, that all his relationships seemed destined to fail?

All Jamison knew for sure was that he'd never forgive Monica for keeping Hannah from him for all those months. And if he'd been Ryder, and Lindsay had kept Robbie away from him for years... There was no way.

"I'm sorry we haven't had more time to hang out since you've been here," Ryder said as his older nephew took over and the three boys started a game that looked far more like dodgeball than football. "But we'll have time with Cowboy Days coming up."

Jamison had seen the signs advertising the event during his trips into town. Normally attending a benefit rodeo—any kind of rodeo—would be last on his to-do list. Here in Clearville, it was evidently a can't-miss event, but his response was noncommittal. "We'll see," he told Ryder. "Hannah isn't comfortable in big crowds. And I know you're trying to get as much as you can done before the wedding and honeymoon."

"Yeah, I can't believe the wedding's coming up so soon. But when Rory told us about a cancellation, we couldn't pass up the chance to have the wedding at Hillcrest House even if it did mean putting a rush on things."

"It did happen fast, didn't it?" Jamison couldn't help murmuring. And why was he somehow not surprised Rory had a hand in the abbreviated engagement?

"Depends on how you count. As far as Lindsay, Robbie and I are concerned, we've already waited almost ten years to be a family."

Jamison's gaze cut to Ryder as his friend spoke those words, but no buried anger, no lasting bitterness over the past lingered in his expression. Nothing but excitement and anticipation for the future.

"We're lucky Rory was willing to work with us, and she's done an amazing job with the wedding preparations."

"What's her story, anyway?"

Ryder's eyebrows shot upward. "Seriously? You're interested in Rory McClaren?"

"I didn't say I was interested. I'm…curious. Hannah thinks she's some kind of fairy-tale princess and fairy godmother all rolled into one, and I want to know more about her."

"Well, from what Lindsay says, the woman can perform miracles when it comes to weddings." Ryder shot him a sidelong glance. "It's a pretty sure bet Rory's got plans for her own dream wedding someday."

Jamison felt his face heat. He needed to put on some more damn sunscreen. "Not interested," he repeated, "just curious."

And maybe if he kept telling himself that, he'd start to believe it.

You were thinking of kissing me.

Thinking about it? Jamison still didn't know how he'd escaped her house without pulling her into his arms and tasting those lips that had tempted him from the start.

"Right… About Rory. Her family's owned Hillcrest for years. Her aunt's been running it the past three decades or so, but she recently brought Rory and her cousin Evie in to help out with the wedding destination packages they're promoting. From what I've heard, Rory had been living in LA. She worked for some hotshot interior design firm— the kind that decorates houses for Hollywood stars and stages million-dollar mansions for putting them up to sell."

Jamison could picture Rory in the role—dream weddings, dream houses, all part of her belief in happily-ever-after. "Sounds like a job she'd be good at."

"Yeah, well…"

"What?" Jamison asked when his friend's voice trailed off.

Ryder shook his head. "Small-town gossip about the reason why Rory was let go from the job. Like you said, not a whole lot else to do around here."

"Hey, Uncle Ryder, catch!" One of the boys tossed the ball back, an end-over-end lame duck Ryder still managed to deflect up into the air at the last minute and catch one-handed—much to his nephew's delight.

Ryder grinned as he spun the ball between his hands, cocked back his arm and returned the ball in a perfect spiral.

"Show-off," Jamison muttered under his breath, more annoyed by his burning curiosity about the gossip about Rory than he was by his friend reliving his golden years.

It was hard to imagine any scandal connected to Rory McClaren. She had such a sweetness, such an air of innocence surrounding her. But he'd seen a hint of the shadows hiding behind her wide blue eyes.

If his marriage to Monica had taught him anything, it was that everyone had secrets. Had he paid more attention in the final months of his marriage, maybe he would have seen what was coming. Maybe he could have stopped her, and if he had—

Jamison looked over at his daughter, carefully crafting her sandcastle, the expression on her sweet face so serious, even as the boys yelled and laughed and raced around her.

Maybe if he had, Hannah's mother would still be alive.

"What can I say?" Ryder raised a shoulder in a negligent shrug. "Some of us have still got it. Hey, man, you okay?"

Jamison pulled in a deep breath. He couldn't close his eyes and pretend everything was going to be okay. If Rory was going to be in his—in *Hannah's* life—even for a short time, then he needed to learn everything he could about her. For his daughter's sake.

"You were telling me about Rory and her life in LA."

"Oh, yeah. Look, I'm sure it was nothing, but the story goes that she got involved with the boss's son and it didn't end well." Ryder shook his head. "As someone who once worked for his in-laws, I can sympathize. I guess things got pretty ugly at the end, with lots of accusations being thrown around about Rory stealing some stuff…not that I believe it for a second."

The whole thing sounded rather petty and ridiculous. What had Rory done—refused to return the gifts her ex had given her? Kept some of the things he'd left at her place? Ryder was right. The rumors were likely nothing more than a bad breakup blown out of proportion thanks to the Clearville grapevine.

"Has Rory talked to you about the gazebo?"

"She said it's in bad shape and even asked if she could hire me to do the work, but with trying to get our scheduled jobs finished—" Ryder shook his head "—I don't see how I can squeeze another project in. Lindsay's disappointed, but she understands. Plus, Rory's done such a fabulous job on short notice that she doesn't want to make her feel bad."

The image of blue eyes flashing wide with hurt and disappointment jabbed at Jamison's conscience. *He* had made Rory feel bad, snapping at her the way he had when she'd been nothing short of amazing with Hannah.

And before Jamison realized what he was saying, he told his friend, "I could do it."

"Do what?"

"Fix up the gazebo."

"Seriously? You haven't done any remodeling work in years. I bet a judge's gavel is the closest thing to a hammer you've been around since we were in college."

Although it was quite possibly the worst idea he'd ever had, Jamison insisted. "It'll all come back to me the minute I put on a tool belt."

The two of them had met while working construction part-time. Despite the differences in their backgrounds and the fact that Jamison was a few years older than Ryder, they had struck up an instant friendship.

And it was that friendship that had him saying, "Consider the gazebo your wedding present."

That was the reason he'd made the offer. It had to be. No way should he be doing this as a way for Rory to see him as some kind of hero when nothing could be further from the truth. He was simply helping out a friend.

Nothing more.

Right. Helping out Ryder by fixing up Rory's favorite place in the whole, whole world.

A wide grin split his friend's face. "Hot da—dog!" he exclaimed with a glance at the kids. "You have made my day. No, my wedding! Lindsay is going to be thrilled, and this is much better than some high-tech coffee maker ordered off the bridal registry!"

His face heated at how closely his friend had him pegged. A perfectly wrapped present had been delivered to the hotel the other day, compliments of his assistant's efficiency. He had no idea what the box contained or even what the card said. "I would never buy something so lame."

"Are you sure about this, though? Isn't the point of this vacation for you to spend time with Hannah?"

Jamison rubbed at the back of his neck. "I'm going a little stir-crazy here, Ry. I'm used to nonstop meetings and calls and conferences. This is all getting to me."

Restlessness and frustration stacked one on top of the other inside him, like the brightly colored blocks Hannah used to play with. Higher and higher until a crash was inevitable. He had too much time on his hands. Too much time to worry about Hannah. Too much time to—

You were thinking of kissing me.

"Right..." his friend drawled. "I can see how tough this is, you know, when life is literally a walk on the beach. Tell the truth—you've been dying to check your phone the whole time we've been out here."

"There's no reception," Jamison grumbled as Ryder laughed. "Doesn't it drive you crazy? This small-town living?"

"This small-town living has given me the chance to know my son."

"You could have done that in San Francisco," he argued even as Ryder pinned him with another knowing look.

"I'm not that far removed from the corporate world, Jamie," he said, breaking out the childhood nickname only Jamison's father still used and only to remind him of who he used to be. "You can't tell me you'd be doing this in San Francisco." His friend tipped his head toward the kids running along the windblown beach.

"I have a job," Jamison argued. "A career—"

A child. One he'd already let down so many times in her short life.

With his gaze locked on Hannah and her precarious sandcastle, Jamison admitted, "I don't know if I can do this, Ry."

His friend was silent for a moment before he advised, "Do your best, Jamison. That's all any of us can do as parents."

Jamison nodded as his friend clapped him on the shoulder before jogging over to join the boys in their game. *Do your best...* Good advice, but other than in his professional life, doing his best had never been enough. Not for his mother, who tried to fill the emptiness in their lives with one failed marriage after another. Not for Monica, who'd taken to wild spending sprees and late-night partying with friends during the final months of *their* failed marriage. And not for Hannah, who would grow up without a mother thanks to the choices he had made.

You're her father. Rory's gentle yet insistent voice seemed to echo in the ocean breeze at his back, a warm, buffeting push in his daughter's direction. *She's still a little girl who wants to run and laugh and play again...*

"Hey, Hannah Banana," he said as she upended another bucket of wet dark sand to start another tower of her leaning castle. "Can I give you a hand?"

She squinted up at him in the sunshine, her sweet face adorably wrinkled, and Jamison stepped to the side so his shadow blocked the glare. "I dunno. Do you know how to play?"

His own father had taught him how to fix, repair, build any number of projects. How to start with the best materials and use the right tool to guarantee what he crafted was solid, sturdy, dependable. Built to last...

But when it came to forming lasting relationships—with his father, his mother, Monica...Hannah—Jamison felt as though every foundation rested on shifting, unstable sand, always ready to give way at any moment.

I have faith in you.

Rory's words rang in his ears. He didn't have that kind of faith in himself. But maybe he didn't need to. Maybe for now, for as long as he was in Clearville, Rory's faith in him would be enough...

Sinking down onto his knees in the cold, damp sand by his daughter's side, he brushed some dried grains from her pink cheek. "I was thinking maybe you could teach me."

Chapter Seven

"As you can see, the rose garden is a beautiful spot for a wedding. In fact, we have a ceremony scheduled here in a few days." Rory forced a smile as she turned her gaze to the young couple who'd come to tour Hillcrest.

The rose garden was beautiful, and if they had to move Lindsay and Ryder's wedding to this location, the ceremony would still be as touching and emotional as it would be taking place in the gazebo. But it wouldn't be the wedding Lindsay and Ryder had imagined, and that was the problem. Rory wanted to give every couple the wedding of their dreams, not some kind of runner-up.

The couple exchanged a glance. "On the website, we saw pictures of a gazebo. It looked like the perfect backdrop. We'd love to see it in person."

Her heart sinking, Rory admitted, "I'm sorry. The gazebo isn't available at the moment. We have some renovations in the works. I'm sure it won't be long before the work is completed, and there's still plenty of time before the two of you plan to get married. For now, why don't we take a look inside at the ballroom?"

Twenty minutes later, the young couple left…without signing a contract. It was a big decision, and Hillcrest House wasn't the only option for couples looking to get married, but Rory couldn't help feeling like she'd failed. Again.

She'd hated having to call Ryder to tell him about the sorry shape the gazebo was in, but in the back of her mind, she'd hoped he might have a crew she could hire. Evie would blow a gasket if she learned Rory had tried to solicit a Hillcrest groom to do manual labor at the hotel, but construction work *was* Ryder's job. But he was also in high demand, booked solid and rushing to get several jobs completed before he left on his honeymoon.

He had told her he would see what he could do, but Rory hadn't heard back, and her other efforts to find someone on such short notice had turned up empty. She didn't want to admit defeat, but maybe Evie was right. Maybe she needed to be practical—and not just about the gazebo.

She hadn't seen Jamison and Hannah in the past two days, and she hated how much she missed them. More than once, she'd done a double take when she spotted a dark-haired man out of the corner of her eye or stopped midsentence at the sound of a child's voice only to be disappointed that it wasn't the man or the child she was instinctively looking for.

She was getting too close, too fast. She'd made the same mistake with Peter, certain she could overcome the obstacles between them and trying to make molehills out of mountains. She'd fallen hard—and landed even harder. If she wasn't careful, when Jamison and Hannah returned home after the wedding, she'd be left behind nursing something far more painful than a bruised ankle.

If only Evie's "be practical" advice didn't feel so much like quitting without trying her best. How could she give up on having the gazebo ready for Ryder and Lindsay's wedding before she'd exhausted every possibility of getting it fixed?

And how was saving herself from heartache later more practical if it meant being miserable now?

Rory was still waging that internal battle as she headed for Evie's office, tucked back behind the registration desk. A group of hotel employees had gathered over to the side near an empty luggage rack, and Rory recognized the tall redhead in the middle.

Trisha Katzman had worked at the hotel for years. The thirtysomething woman had made it clear she, and not Rory, should have been the one to take on the expanded wedding coordinator role. Rory had done her best to smooth things over, to reassure Trisha she wasn't taking over her job and the increase in weddings would create more than enough work—and reward for a job well done—for everyone.

Her efforts had met with little success. The redhead was coldly polite face-to-face, but Rory could feel the daggers the other woman shot her way the second her back was turned.

And something had changed lately. The subtle disgruntled looks were no longer so subtle, and Trisha's smug expression reminded Rory of her last miserable months in LA.

The other women in Trisha's clique returned Rory's greeting before picking up their conversation. "I still can't believe that store's computer got hacked and some loser stole my credit card number," one of them was complaining as she walked by.

The other two made sympathetic sounds, but Trisha pointedly looked over her shoulder, tracking Rory's movements as she said, "Hard to know who to trust these days, isn't it?"

Rory froze.

She knew.

The patterned carpet shifted beneath her feet as her stomach listed and sank. Rory didn't know how the other woman had found out about what happened in LA, but she had no doubt Trisha was responsible for the rumors swirling around the hotel.

Once Rory would have walked over and confronted the group. She'd learned back in junior high that showing fear in front of a group of mean girls was the worst thing she could do. But after everything that happened in LA, when nothing she said made any difference and keeping silent had ended up her only defense, the words stuck in her throat.

Ducking her head, Rory headed away from the group and down the narrow hallway to Evie's office. Her cousin glanced up at her quick knock. "Oh, good. I was about to come looking for you—what's wrong?"

"It's—nothing." Rory didn't need to see the "I told you so" look in her cousin's eyes. She'd been fooling herself thinking she could have a fresh start in a place she'd always loved.

Evie's gaze narrowed, but she didn't press. "Good, because right now we have enough trouble. Mrs. Broderick called. She swears she and her daughter requested veal *piccata* and not chicken as part of the reception menu."

"They went back and forth before deciding on chicken." Rory specifically remembered. The conversation had gone on so long, by the time the two women made up their minds, she thought she might scream if she heard the words *veal*, *chicken* or *piccata* ever again.

Evie lifted an eyebrow. "That's not what she says."

"I'll talk to the chef. Hopefully it won't be too late to cancel the order."

"And if it is? They signed the contract, which states chicken," her cousin pointed out. "If you talk to them…"

"What difference would that make?" If Mrs. Broderick didn't believe what was in front of her in black and white, what was the likelihood the woman would believe anything Rory had to say?

"Then I'll talk to them," Evie decided.

"No, Evie, this is my job. I'll handle it."

Rory held her breath, waiting for her cousin to take yet another responsibility away from her because she couldn't be trusted—

Finally, her cousin gave a short nod. "All right."

Half an hour later, after dealing with their disgruntled chef and butcher, Rory stepped outside. She inhaled a deep breath, taking in the scents of forest pine and salty ocean and hoping the combination would clear her head.

She had a dozen phone calls and emails to return on everything from placing orders with the florist to confirming the chairs and bunting with the rental company to sending a new song list to the band for a wedding. But nothing needed to be done right that second. And with Trisha and her clique still inside the lobby, Rory wanted a few minutes to herself.

But as she followed the meandering walkways leading from the hotel, she didn't take the curve that would lead toward her cottage. Instead, she found herself walking down the tree-lined path toward the gazebo.

Her steps slowed on the flagstone steps, not wanting to

see the caution tape she'd asked one of the groundskeepers to put up, cordoning off the damaged and dangerous steps.

It was a simple wooden structure. Her hopes and dreams for a future and a family with a man she loved were not tied into its decorative pillars or carved eaves. Even if it might feel that way...

"Miss Rory!"

Her mood lifted, concerns about Trisha and the gazebo melting away when she saw Hannah tugging on Jamison's hand as the father-daughter duo headed her way. Maybe she should have been worried how happy the simple sight of them made her, but Rory had never been one to question a good thing. She'd always been more inclined to embrace it—easy enough to do when Hannah broke free the last few steps and threw her arms around her legs.

Bending down to return her hug, Rory breathed in the scent of little girl, baby shampoo and sunshine. Words spilled out of Hannah as she filled Rory in on the past two days—time spent going into town, including an all-important trip to the café for a cookie, and a day at the beach.

"Me and Daddy builded a sandcastle this big!" Hannah threw her arms out wide, and Rory met Jamison's gaze for the first time.

"You did?"

"We *built* a sandcastle," he automatically corrected.

"Daddy," Hannah sighed, "I just tol' her that. And it was this big!"

"Well, I am very proud of you," Rory said, her words not for Hannah alone, something Jamison picked up on based by the eye roll he gave her.

She had a hard time imagining Jamison on the beach, let alone playing with his daughter in the sand. And yet she could see a hint of sun in his cheeks and on the forearms left bare by the shirtsleeves he'd pushed up to his elbows. She wouldn't go so far as to say he looked relaxed—his silver eyes were too intense, too watchful to fit that description—but he did seem more at ease than when he'd arrived at the hotel.

He was even dressed more casually in a faded gray Henley and jeans. The comfortable clothes molded to his broad shoulders and muscular legs and had Rory wishing he would sweep her up into his arms again…and not because she'd injured her ankle.

As if reading her mind, he asked, "How's the ankle?"

Rory lifted her leg. "Almost as good as new. The scratches are healing and the bruises are already starting to fade…" It hadn't been her intention to draw Jamison's gaze to her legs or the strappy white sandals she was wearing despite the still-tender ankle, but she couldn't argue the results or the masculine appreciation in his expression.

"Toilet paper must have done the trick."

The wry humor in his voice did as much to set the butterflies in her stomach fluttering as the heat in his gaze. "I couldn't agree more."

"I'm glad you're all better, Miss Rory, 'cause me and Daddy have a surprise!"

"Hannah, you're not supposed to tell her. That's what makes it a surprise."

Her big brown eyes wide with innocence, Hannah protested, "But I didn't tell her, Daddy! I didn't tell her about fixing—oops!" The little girl clapped her dimpled hands over her mouth to keep the words from spilling out.

Rory laughed. "Okay, well, someone needs to tell me! What are the two of you up to?"

With a nod at his daughter, Jamison said, "Go ahead."

Throwing her hands out wide, she exclaimed, "Daddy's gonna fix the playhouse!"

Rory looked from the exuberance written across Hannah's face to her father's much harder to read expression. "Fix... You mean the gazebo?" she asked, her voice filled with disbelief. And then even more disbelief as she asked, "You?"

But if she'd offended Jamison, he didn't let it show as he stepped closer and bent his head toward hers. "What's the matter? You don't think I'm up for the job?"

A day or two ago, she might have said no, but in the T-shirt and jeans, he looked the part of a calendar-worthy handyman. This ruggedly physical side of him was something Rory would never have imagined. So different from the cool, composed lawyer. Add a tool belt and a hammer swung over one broad shoulder and—

She had to stop herself right there. No need for a hammer when her heart was doing all the pounding.

"I'm sure you're—" Rory snapped her mouth shut, his turn of phrase getting stuck in her throat. Feeling a rush of heat rise in her cheeks, she finished, "Perfectly capable."

Desperate to ignore the glint in his eyes that said he knew what she was thinking even if it wasn't what she was saying, she said, "But I don't understand—"

"I was talking with Ryder, and I offered to fix the gazebo. You know, for their wedding."

"Oh, Jamison..."

As if hearing the wobble of tears in her voice, he quickly went on. "Ryder's going to provide any of the materials or tools I need so long as I swear not to cut my fool hand, foot or head off."

Rory laughed in return even if she was still blinking back tears. "You're not, um, likely to actually do any of those things, are you?"

"It hasn't been that long since I had my hands on a power tool."

There was nothing overtly sexual about that statement,

but Rory had to pull her gaze away from the muscular arms and chest his T-shirt put on display. Definitely some powerful tools there, but it was his offer—his thoughtfulness—that had her throwing her arms around his neck.

"I can't believe you'd do this. It is so sweet of you."

He started, caught off guard by her impetuous hug before wrapping his arms around her waist. "It's hard, sweaty, manly work. Nothing sweet about it."

"You're helping give your friends the wedding of their dreams."

"Don't you dare call me Ryder's fairy godfather. I'd never live it down." His wry smile faded as he pulled back far enough to meet her gaze. "Besides, I'm not just doing this for him."

"No?"

Rory counted out the time it took for him to respond by the rapid beating of her heart. "No." He frowned as if annoyed by his own admission. "I'm doing this for you."

She sucked in a quick breath. "For me?"

"You know," he clarified, "for all the help you've given me with Hannah."

"Oh. You don't owe me for that, Jamison." She took a step back, brushing at the material of her full skirt where it clung to his denim-covered thigh. She could have used the reminder that he was a guest—a member of the wedding party—before she'd thrown herself into his arms.

She turned her focus to Hannah, who'd wandered a few feet down the path toward the rose garden. "I've enjoyed spending time with her, and since she's one of my flower girls, it's part of the job."

"Is it?" he challenged. "Because if that's the truth, then maybe I'm the one imagining things."

"Imagining things…"

His hand closed around her wrist, trapping her palm

against the muscular strength of his thigh. "Yeah, like that you're thinking of kissing me right now."

Her breath caught in her throat, and her fingers instinctively flexed, her nails digging into warm denim. Jamison's eyes darkened from silver to steel and suddenly she was imagining so much more than kissing—

"But we still can't," she echoed his words from the other day.

Can't, not *didn't want to*, because, oh, how she wanted to.

Without taking his eye off her, Jamison called out to his daughter. "Hey, Hannah, how'd you like to play a game of hide-and-seek? Close your eyes and count to one hundred."

"One hundred?" she asked as Hannah's singsong voice filled the air.

"She only knows up to twenty."

Turning her wrist until her hand clasped his, Rory tugged Jamison toward the closest tree. "Then we better make this fast."

She was already breathless with anticipation by the time they circled around the large pine, and he hadn't even touched her. By the time he pulled her into his arms, Rory thought her heart might explode. Yet despite her instructions to hurry, Jamison didn't kiss like a man in a rush.

He kissed like a man who'd traveled far and had finally, at long last, come home. Like a man who'd thought of nothing else, who had dreamed only of this moment. He caught her bottom lip, tugging in a gentle tease, before delving farther. His tongue swept inside, and her senses reeled, spinning off into a world she'd never known existed.

A world of pleasure. A world of sensation. So bright and startling all else seemed dull and gray.

And Rory had to have more.

Digging her hands into his dark hair, she pulled him closer. Arousal poured through her veins, centering low in her belly and striking sparks wherever their bodies touched. But the contact, her mouth eagerly seeking his, her breasts straining against his chest, wasn't enough. She had to have more and almost cried out in protest when Jamison broke the kiss.

"Rory," he ground out, words barely registering beyond the pulse pounding in her ears, "we better stop…"

Though the haze of desire, Rory heard Hannah's voice. On a breathless whisper, she said, "We still have ten seconds left."

"Nine," Jamison corrected, his breath warm against her skin as he trailed kisses down the length of her throat.

Her head fell back in pure pleasure. She thought she just might melt into the rough bark of the tree at her back, but Jamison pulled her tight and she melted into him instead. "Nine?" she asked weakly.

"Hannah always skips fifteen."

Sure enough, the little girl missed the number, and Rory started her own countdown. "Four, three…"

Recognizing the challenge, Jamison covered her mouth with his in the hottest, fastest kiss of Rory's life. One that left her gasping for air even as Hannah yelled out, "Twenty!" and started to search for them.

Ready or not.

Rory stepped back and sucked in a single lungful of air that wasn't superheated by the attraction burning between them before Hannah rushed around the tree and stopped short at the sight of them.

"Daddy, you're s'posed to hide." Shaking her head in disappointment, she said, "You and Miss Rory aren't very good at this game."

Jamison met Rory's gaze, and beneath the shared amusement was enough heat to set another round of fireworks shooting off in her stomach. Rory didn't want to argue with a four-year-old, but this game was one Jamison was very good at.

As it turned out, Jamison was quite as bad at hide-and-seek as his daughter feared. That wasn't as much of a surprise as the enjoyment he found in the game. Of course, part of that was the grown-up version he and Rory were playing—stealing kisses while Hannah's eyes were closed, finding a hiding spot of their own before tracking the little girl down in the rose garden.

But they'd both been careful to keep those stolen moments lighter, more playful. Not that the spark had dimmed. If anything, it built with every touch, every glance.

A controlled burn instead of an out-and-out wildfire like their first kiss.

"You know, I was so excited earlier—" Catching sight of his raised eyebrows, Rory rolled her eyes, but not before her cheeks turned a flattering shade of pink. "About the *gazebo*," she stressed, "that I didn't ask what you plan to do about Hannah while you're working."

Hannah had skipped ahead on the flagstone path only to get distracted by a colorful butterfly flitting by. The joy and awe on her sweet face brought a lump of emotion to the back of his throat. He'd seen his daughter break free and spread her wings over the past few days, and he was terrified of doing anything that would send her back into the cocoon of sadness and loss.

"I talked to Ryder about hiring a teenage girl they've used before."

Seeming to remember how reluctant his daughter sometimes was to leave his side, Rory asked, "Do you think Hannah will be okay with someone new watching her?"

"I hope so. If not—" Then he might soon have bigger problems than finding time to fix the gazebo.

"Does she have a babysitter back home she's comfortable with?"

"I haven't used any sitters back home…not since before the accident. Hannah's been staying with her grandparents. With everything that was going on, it seemed better that way."

"She's here with you now. That's what matters."

"Yeah." He sighed. "She's with me for now."

"For now," Rory echoed, "but not for long? Is that what you're saying? What happens when you go back to San Francisco, Jamison?"

Even though she'd asked the question, the disappointment in her expression said she knew the answer as well as he did. "Monica's parents want Hannah to live with them."

And they didn't even know about the promotion, one that would mean long days and even longer nights. Times when he would be leaving for work while Hannah was still asleep in the morning and wouldn't be home until after she was in bed in the evening.

"Hannah's grandmother is a retired nurse. She can be with her all day, every day. And Hannah loves her grandparents. After Monica and I separated, Hannah spent as much time with them as she did with Monica. And far more time than she spent with me."

Something Louisa was quick to point out. He carried around plenty of guilt on his own and didn't need his in-laws piling on, but Louisa knew what button to push—reminding him what a detached and absent father he'd been even before he and Monica separated. And now that Hannah needed him to be both mother and father…

"I'm sure they do love her, but Jamison, you're her father and your daughter needs you. I'm not trying to compare what I went through to Hannah losing her mother, but after Chance's accident, I needed my parents, too. As an adult, I get it. They could only handle so much, and almost all of their time and energy was focused on Chance getting better. But for me, as a kid, I felt like they were as lost to me as Chance was in that coma."

Even after so many years, Jamison picked up on the tremor in Rory's voice, the whisper of a little girl who'd gone unnoticed, unheard. He hated thinking of her feeling that way. Hated thinking of *Hannah* feeling that way.

"Rory—" He swallowed against a lump in his throat. "I—I just want what's best for her."

"I know. I see that, Jamison. I do." The certainty in her gaze turned sorrowful as she added, "What I don't understand is why you don't think that would be you."

Rory knew she shouldn't have been surprised when Jamison didn't answer her question. Just because he'd kissed her senseless didn't mean he was going to spill his guts. And just because she'd poured out the old ache in her heart when she spoke of the horrible days following Chance's accident didn't mean Jamison would pour out his.

Instead, his expression closed off, reminding her of the man she'd first met and not of the man she'd just kissed. Avoiding the emotional discussion, he'd gotten down to the business of inspecting the gazebo. Or at least trying to with Hannah hanging by his side, wanting to "help."

"Got it, Hannah?" he asked, as he ran a measuring tape along the length of the gazebo railing. "Are you holding on tight?"

"Got it, Daddy!" Stretched up on her tippy toes, Hannah held on to one end of the tape.

Jamison jotted down some figures in the small notebook he'd pulled from his pocket. "Okay, kiddo. You can let it go."

Hannah released the small tab and the yellow metal tape zipped back into the casing, bringing a giggle from the little girl and drawing a smile from Jamison, but the shadows lingering in his expression made Rory's heart hurt.

Did he think Hannah would break if he were to unbend enough to hug her—or was he afraid that he would? His love for the little girl was obvious, but so was the fear.

He needed more time. Time with Hannah, not time spent fixing the gazebo. As touched as she was by his offer to help his friend, to help *her*, his daughter needed him far more than Ryder and Lindsay needed the perfect setting for their wedding.

Swallowing against the lump of disappointment in her throat, she opened her mouth, but Hannah beat her to the punch.

"Did ya see, Miss Rory?" The little girl bounced on her toes. "I'm being a big helper!"

Rory met Hannah's wide smile with one of her own as the perfect solution bloomed. "I did see, Hannah. You are such a good helper, and I just had the best idea ever!"

Chapter Eight

Maybe it was something in the water.

Something that made him say yes to harebrained schemes and even come up with a few of his own. Bad enough he'd offered to fix up the gazebo, but what the hell was he thinking yesterday when he agreed to let Rory and Hannah help?

I just had the best idea ever!

Rory's eyes had glimmered with such hope that Jamison had found himself holding his breath in a combination of dread and anticipation. Even before she started talking, he'd had a feeling that whatever the crazy idea swirling in her pretty little head was, he was going to hate it. And an even worse feeling that whatever it was, he was going to be fool enough to agree to it. Just to keep that light in her eyes and the smile on her face…

Jamison fought back a groan as he and Hannah made their way down the flagstone path. He adjusted the tool belt at his waist even as he gave serious thought to smacking himself upside the head with a hammer. How was he supposed to work and keep an eye on his daughter…when he couldn't keep his eyes off Rory?

He'd reached for his phone a dozen times already, prepared to call Rory and then Ryder and tell them both the whole thing was off. He could tell his friend the work was too much and the ceremony could take place in the rose garden with Lindsay and the guests none the wiser.

There was only one problem.

"I'm going to be a big help, right, Daddy?"

Even if Ryder was smart enough to keep his mouth shut with the woman in his life, Jamison had already blown it by telling the pint-size girl in his.

Excitement radiated from her tiny body as she bounced by his side, jumping from one flagstone to the next, one hand holding the oversize yellow hard hat on her head.

"I get to help Miss Rory fix the playhouse."

"It's a gazebo," he corrected. "And I'll be the one fixing it," he added before realizing he sounded like a total jerk.

In the months since Monica's death, Jamison couldn't think of a single suggestion he'd come up with that Hannah hadn't met with *I don't want to.* Even her favorite activities back home—going to the park or the zoo—had all been shot down.

But not this chance to work on the gazebo.

Did it matter that Rory was the bigger draw when it came to Hannah wanting to lend a hand? Wasn't his daughter's happiness, no matter the reason, most important?

And what happens when you go back home? When there is no Rory around to add a hint of sweetness to everything she touches and to make more than smiley-face oatmeal happy?

Construction wasn't easy work, and Jamison had had

his share of injuries—the worst of them a pair of broken ribs and a punctured lung thanks to a fall through some rotten floorboards. But the sharp pain and struggle to breathe were nothing compared to what he felt when he thought of trying to care for Hannah on his own.

"But we get to help, right, Daddy?"

"Sure thing, Hannah Banana. I need all the help I can get," he sighed, wishing the words weren't so blatantly true.

And that was why he found himself trailing after his daughter as she raced ahead toward the gazebo.

"Hi, Miss Rory!" Hannah cried out as she rounded the curve in the path.

Jamison should have been prepared, thanks to his daughter's early-warning signal, yet somehow he was still caught off guard. Because standing in front of the gazebo, gazing up at the aging structure as if the rotting wood and cracked paint had already been stripped away and restored to its once-gleaming glory, Rory turned to greet them with a brilliant smile.

"Look, Miss Rory! We both have hard hats!" Hannah clamped both hands on top of hers as if expecting her sheer excitement to blow the thing right off her head at any second.

And Jamison couldn't help feeling like he should hold on to his own, considering how the sight of Rory in a pair of faded skintight jeans and a pink—hot-pink—hard hat was threatening to blow his mind.

"I see!" And then meeting his gaze over his daughter's hard hat, Rory shot him a wink. "Safety first, right, Jamison? After all, it has been a while…"

She had no idea. If she had, she would have brought a fire extinguisher instead. Something in the intensity of his gaze must have given him away because her smile faded.

His heartbeat quickened as the awareness between them grew. Try as he might, he couldn't keep his eyes from drifting down her body.

He'd never seen her dressed so casually—couldn't have imagined her wearing denim, a fitted white T-shirt, that outlined her breasts far too clearly for his comfort, and honest-to-God work boots. And yet there she was, like some kind of construction worker Barbie.

"This is never going to work," he mumbled under his breath.

Despite the rush of color blooming in her cheeks, Rory pretended she hadn't heard him. She waved a hand at a shaded area several yards away from the gazebo where a picnic basket and blanket waited. "Are you ready to get started, Miss Hannah?" At his daughter's nod, she said, "We have a big bucket of screws and nails we need to separate so all the same sizes are in their own little cups. And then we'll use scissors to cut sandpaper to the right size to fit your daddy's super noisy sander.

"When we're done with that, we have paper and pencils and paint so we can draw pictures of the gazebo and practice on them until your daddy is ready for us to help him paint the real thing. And then we can make sandwiches with the stuff I brought in that basket over there, because all that hard, hard work is going to make us all hungry. What do you think?"

Jamison shook his head. He thought she was amazing. All those little projects would keep Hannah engaged and entertained. And he never would have thought of any of them. Somehow, though, instead of his inadequacies as a father casting a dark pall over his mood, gratitude rushed through him.

He caught Rory's hand as she walked by and gazed down at her in that ridiculous hat. Her blue eyes sparkled and her pale pink lips curved in a smile that had him thinking about their kiss…

She might not have been dressed like one, but he couldn't help asking, "Are you sure you aren't some kind of magical fairy-tale princess?"

"Why, Jamison, I didn't think you believed in fairy tales."

"I don't," he insisted. "But I believe in you. You have this way of making things—even the most everyday, average things—special."

And if that wasn't magic, then he didn't know what was.

Despite Jamison's initial concerns over the shape of the gazebo, a more thorough inspection revealed the overall structure—the support beams, most of the main floor and the roof—was sound. The steps, the lattice facade and the railing needed the most work, but he'd assured her the repairs were all doable and could be fixed before the wedding.

With Hannah occupied on the blanket with some of the little games she'd come up with, Rory had worked at Jamison's side, hoping effort made up for what she lacked in experience.

"Admit it…you're impressed." Rory pointed a plastic water bottle Jamison's way as they took a short break.

He gave his typical snort of disbelief as he raised his own bottle. But before he took a long swallow, he murmured, "Only every time we're together."

She took a quick sip of the cool liquid, thinking it might do her more good to dump the whole thing over her head. Her heated thoughts at watching Jamison do something as simple as drink from a bottle didn't bode well for completing the gazebo without her jumping his bones.

I believe in you.

How long had it been since someone had that kind of faith in her? Months? Years?

Evie had always been the practical one, Chance the adventurous one and Rory the dreamer. The girl with her head in the clouds, whose ideas were always too impractical, too over-the-top, too silly to be taken seriously.

But Jamison believed in her.

With Hannah close by, they had no chance to repeat the kiss from the day before. But the little girl's presence wasn't enough to keep Rory's thoughts from straying in that direction or to keep her from imagining Jamison felt the same way.

More than once, their gazes had locked over some small task—their fingers brushing as he handed her the hammer, his chest pressing against her shoulder as he reached around her to help with a particular stubborn nail, his breath against her neck raising gooseflesh on her skin as he offered some words of instruction.

"You told me you're a jill-of-all-trades, but this seems a bit much for a wedding coordinator."

"Well, I wasn't always a wedding coordinator," she told him, only to instantly regret it. She didn't want to talk about LA. Didn't want to think about Pamela or Peter or the thefts she'd been accused of.

"So what did you do before this?" Jamison asked.

"I worked for an interior design firm." She forced a smile. "Way too girlie for you to find interesting."

"Still not sure how carpentry falls under interior designer... And for the record, I happen to find girlie very interesting."

His appreciative glance coaxed a genuine smile out of her, and she sighed. "I started at the bottom with big dreams of working my way up. As low designer on the totem pole, I was stuck with all the jobs no one wanted—

including getting my hands dirty to get a remodel done on time. If that meant ripping out carpet because the sub-contractor no-showed or repainting an entire kitchen because the client changed her mind at the last minute and the painter had already walked off the job, then I was their girl."

"So what happened?"

Rory started. "What makes you think something happened?"

Jamison shrugged casually. "You're here, aren't you? Something must have happened."

"I had the chance to work at Hillcrest with my family. This place means so much to me, I wouldn't have missed that for the world." Even if she hadn't been without a job and weeks from running out of rent money for the ridiculously expensive studio she'd called home.

"So…no heartbroken guy left behind?"

"Heartbroken? Definitely not."

"But there *was* a guy."

Rory squeezed the water bottle, the thin plastic crackling in her hands. "His name was Peter, and he's the boss's son. I should have known better than to get involved with someone at work." But some lessons were hard to learn. By no means could she classify her relationship with Jamison as strictly professional.

"Pamela, his mother, had far greater aspirations for him than dating a lowly assistant in her company. I tried not to let it bother me, and Peter assured me his mother would come around. All I had to do was to give her some time."

"But that didn't work?"

"The longer we dated, the more uncomfortable things became at work. I don't think it was coincidence that I was always assigned to the most difficult clients. My friends all thought I should quit, but—I don't know. I guess I was too stubborn and the job wasn't the problem. Quitting wouldn't make my relationship with Pamela any easier. If anything, it would have proved to her that I could be run off."

"And you weren't willing to give up on Peter."

"I thought he was the one. So I put up with so much crap from his mother. She'd turned a job I loved into one I hated. I dreaded waking up in the morning, knowing I'd have to do battle with that dragon, but I did it. I did it for months, because I told myself it was worth it. I was willing to fight for our relationship, but Peter..."

The worst of her ex's betrayal caught in her throat, as did the humiliating circumstances that had led to her leaving LA. She should tell Jamison the entire story, she knew she should, but—

I believe in you.

She didn't want to lose the faith he had in her, not when it meant so much, not when there was a chance he *wouldn't* believe in her once she told him the whole truth.

"Looks like someone's ready for a nap."

Lying back on the picnic blanket, his eyes closed to the bright, cloudless sky overhead, Jamison said, "You have no idea."

Muscles he hadn't used in years groaned in protest at the slightest movement, thanks to the hard work he'd put in over the past three days, but Jamison was determined to have the gazebo ready by Ryder's wedding. If he had to throw in the towel, his friend would never let him hear the end of it.

Rory's low chuckle brushed over his skin on the warm summer breeze. "Like father, like daughter."

He cracked an eye open to see Hannah slumped to one side, half-eaten peanut butter and jelly sandwich in hand.

She looked angelic, peaceful. Pushing up onto his elbows, he said, "It's hard work being a number one helper."

The title was one his daughter wore with pride, overcoming her shyness with strangers to tell anyone who would listen—the big, burly guy at the lumberyard, the skinny teen in the paint department, the gum-popping cashier at the hardware store—that she was the best helper ever.

He'd had his doubts about taking Hannah along on those trips, certain he could get in and out much faster and more efficiently on his own, but Rory had insisted. And since he seemed incapable of saying no to either of them, the two ladies had accompanied him. And yeah, maybe it had taken more time, but it was time spent with Hannah…and with Rory. She'd pushed Hannah around in a basket, managing to turn even the countless trips up and down the aisles in the huge home improvement store while he looked for the right L-bracket into some kind of adventure.

"When will we be ready for the big reveal?"

"I'm sure we'll be done at least an hour before the rehearsal dinner next Friday."

Rory tossed a crumpled napkin at him. "Very funny."

He grinned as the wadded-up ball sailed past without hitting its mark. Despite having to work around Hannah's nap time and Rory's scheduled fittings, tasting and meetings with clients and potential clients, they'd made real progress.

They'd torn out the splintering lattice fasciae and trim, and pried up the rotted steps and any warped boards on the circular platform. He'd cut the replacement boards and had spent the morning sanding them smooth, filling the air with the slight scent of burning wood. A fine layer of sawdust covered just about everything. Including Rory's toned arms, left bare by the pink-and-white-striped tank top she wore.

Suddenly not feeling so tired, he could think of better things to do while Hannah slept than to take a nap of his own...

"So tell me the story," Rory said, catching Jamison off guard.

Talking wasn't where his mind had gone.

"You sound like Hannah," he said with a laugh, "but if she were awake, she'd tell you I suck when it comes to fairy tales. I can't tell her a bedtime story without the CliffsNotes in front of me."

Rory laughed. "Don't worry. You already know this one. It's the origin story of a successful lawyer with a hidden background as a blue-collar construction worker."

"Not hidden," Jamison argued, feeling his face heat at the lie.

"So this is something you do a lot?" she pressed. "Help friends with projects or volunteer with Habitat for Humanity?"

The simplest thing would have been to agree and hope Rory would leave it at that. But from the moment they met, she'd challenged him not to take the easy way out. Not when it came to Hannah and not when it came to telling the truth about himself. "I haven't picked up a hammer in almost a decade," he confessed.

"But once upon a time..."

A gruff laugh escaped him at the teasing look in her eyes. "Once upon a time," he began, "I worked construction while I was in college. That's how Ryder and I met."

"So you weren't—" Rory cut herself off, but Jamison had a feeling where her thoughts had gone.

"Born with a silver spoon in my mouth?" He shook his head, hardly offended by the assumption when he spent most of his life trying to give that very impression. "Not even close. My parents had me when they were barely out of their teens. Neither one of them took more than a few college courses. My mom worked as a receptionist off and on, and my dad was a handyman, taking on whatever jobs he could find."

"And he's the one who taught you how to do this," Rory said, waving a hand at the gazebo with an expression of pride that sent guilt stabbing through Jamison's heart.

"Yeah, my dad taught me a lot of things." And Jamison had repaid him by being ashamed and spending most of the past fifteen years pretending the man didn't exist.

"But the things my dad could do… It was never enough for my mother. They fought all the time. Over everything, it seemed, but mostly over money. My mom was the one who always encouraged me to do more, to be better, to—"

Do whatever you have to do so you don't end up spending your life cleaning toilets like your father.

Jamison shook his head, trying to dislodge his mother's bitter words from his memory. "Anyway, when I was ten or so, she got it in her head that public school wasn't good enough and that I needed to go to prep school."

"Prep school? As in matching uniforms with jackets and ties and argyle socks?"

He gave a mock shudder. "It was that bad and worse."

"Hard to imagine worse."

"Worse was knowing I didn't belong in that uniform. That I was the charity case—the kid who could only afford to go to Winston Prep because my dad took a job there as a janitor and my tuition was waived.

"My mother was the one who was so determined I go to that school, and my dad made it happen the only way he could. But that wasn't good enough for her, either. She hated that he worked there, was always putting him down, and after a while, I started to feel the same way. I didn't want the other kids knowing he was my dad."

"It's hard to think of anyone other than yourself when you're a kid."

"When they divorced my freshman year, I thought the constant fighting would be over. But in some ways it got worse. Like they no longer had to even pretend that they cared about each other. I got caught in the middle and felt like I had to make a choice, and I chose to stay with my mom.

"After so many years of hearing how we deserved better and how I had it in me to 'be something' so long as I didn't let my dad bring me down... I don't know. I guess I started to buy into it. I wanted the expensive shoes and the latest electronics and the fancy cars like everyone else at Winston had, and when my mom remarried that first time, to a rich guy she met thanks to her making friends with the parents of kids who went to Winston, I got all that stuff."

"The first time your mother remarried?"

"First, but not last. She's on her fourth marriage. Fifth, I guess, if you count that she married number three twice."

"Ouch."

"It's made Father's Day interesting."

"I'm sorry, Jamison."

"Don't be. I made my choice. I could have gone to live with my dad, but I liked have all those shoes and toys and cars." Jamison shook his head. "You know, even after my mom remarried, and my stepdad was footing all the bills and could afford to pay my tuition a thousand times over, my dad kept working at that school. A thankless, low-paying job he must have hated...just so he could still see me."

"I'm guessing that made it all worth it for him."

"I wish I'd appreciated all he was willing to do for me and that I hadn't cut him out of my life the way I did."

"But that was then. What about now?"

"It's been better...especially over the past few years.

Mostly thanks to Hannah." A smile touched his face as he said his daughter's name. "I reached out to him after she was born, and he's made a real effort to get to know her, to be there for birthdays and holidays. He enjoys being a grandfather."

"I'm glad…for Hannah, but also for you and your father."

"Yeah, me, too," Jamison agreed, but he couldn't help thinking of the years he'd lost—both with his father and with Hannah.

Two of the most important people in his life, and he'd failed them both. First as a son and then as a father.

As much as he'd enjoyed the past few days and as familiar as a hammer felt in his hand, Jamison couldn't see giving up everything he'd worked for—the struggle to put himself through college, the countless hours of studying to get through law school, the prestige of working at Spears, Moreland and Howe, and the promise of the partnership— even if it would be best for Hannah.

His dad had made that kind of sacrifice, but Jamison couldn't help feeling he was very much his mother's son. He loved his daughter, he did, but Jamison couldn't help feeling something lacking inside him kept him from loving her *enough*.

Chapter Nine

The first annual Clearville Cowboy Days was in full swing by the time the sun started sinking behind the horizon, painting the sky with a pinkish-orange hue. Warm summer air carried the sound of laughter and, as long as the wind wasn't coming from the arena, the mouthwatering scent of smoky barbecue. Along with the draw of the rodeo, walkways led toward a fenced-off petting zoo and a carnival-style midway lined with cheesy stuffed-animal prizes. Bells and whistles rang out mixed with groans and cheers from the spectators gathered around the games.

"I still can't believe this turnout."

"Yeah, it's impressive," Jamison responded, trying to match his friend's enthusiasm as he, Ryder and Lindsay dodged the boisterous crowds checking out the Rockin' R benefit rodeo.

"The chamber of commerce has worked with Jarrett Deeks and his wife, Theresa, on the event," Lindsay chimed in. "The hope is to raise money and awareness for their horse rescue, but it's also a chance for Clearville to shine."

"A chance for you to shine," Ryder told his fiancée with a proud smile that had Lindsay shaking her head.

"Theresa and Jarrett already had much of this in place before I moved back and came on board. They're the ones who deserve credit."

"Says the woman who's been working tirelessly on promotion and sponsorship and vendors—"

"All right, all right! I'll take some credit if it'll make you hush up!"

"I bet you can think of better ways to shut me up," Ryder challenged with a suggestive lift to his eyebrows.

"You do realize other people can hear you, right?" Jamison's pointed comment had his friend grinning even more unrepentantly while Lindsay gave his shoulder a quick shove.

"You're crazy, you know that?"

"Only about you."

At that, Lindsay showed she did indeed know how to shut Ryder up as she rose onto her tiptoes to keep his mouth occupied with a kiss.

Jamison jerked his gaze away to focus on a trio of dusty cowboys, complete with hats, chaps and bandannas, laughing with a group of wide-eyed, flirty girls, none of whom looked old enough for all the makeup they were wearing, let alone the beers they were drinking.

All in all, Jamison felt as out of place as…well, a corporate lawyer at a rodeo.

But it wasn't the retro Wild West setting that had him feeling so uncomfortable. It was playing third wheel to Ryder and Lindsay, an unnecessary cog to the obvious affection and attraction between them.

"Are you sure the kids are okay going off by themselves?"

"They're fine, Dad," Ryder teased.

Lindsay's response was more sympathetic. "I know Robbie, Tyler and Brayden are still young," she said, referring to her son and his two cousins, "but they're good boys. They'll keep an eye on Hannah, and the carnival games are all being run by locals who'll watch out for them, too."

"Yeah, I'm sure you're right."

He'd worried about Hannah's reaction to the loud noises, huge animals and large crowd, but his concerns had been misplaced. After little more than a brief hesitation, Hannah had taken off with the boys, leaving Jamison feeling... bereft. Suddenly, he was the one feeling out of place and overwhelmed.

They'd spent so much time together the past few days, he missed having his daughter at his side...as much as he found himself missing Rory.

He still didn't know why he'd agreed to go to the rodeo—other than the thought that Rory might be there. And if that wasn't the stupidest move ever, he didn't know what was. Going to the rodeo on the off chance of catching a glimpse of the beautiful brunette when he could have gone *with* her.

She'd issued the invitation as she'd packed up their picnic lunch the day before. "From what Lindsay says, they'll have all kinds of music, food and even games planned for the kids. Anyway, I was wondering if you and Hannah would like to go. You know—" she rolled her eyes, a hint of color brightening her cheeks "—with me?"

Jamison had swallowed the instant agreement that came to mind. "Rory... I'm leaving in just over a week."

"I know," she'd shot back quickly, her eyes and smile still bright. "But fortunately for us, the rodeo is tomorrow. You're still here tomorrow."

He should have expected she wouldn't give up easily,

not a woman who'd been willing to fight for a man she thought was *the one*. But like the ex who had let her down, Jamison knew he'd done the same.

The disappointment in her gaze should have been enough to make him keep his distance. Rory wasn't the type of woman to have a summer fling, and he couldn't offer her anything more. He'd be going back to a life that already felt overbooked with the pressure of the upcoming promotion and the responsibility of raising Hannah on his own.

"Lookie, Daddy, Tyler won me a fuzzy unicorn!" Hannah's voice broke into his thoughts as she raced toward him, and Jamison wondered what it said about him that he was as eager to see his daughter as she was to see him.

"He did, huh?" Jamison bent down to examine the purple-and-white stuffed animal she proudly held out.

"Uh-huh! For me!" His daughter nodded, her ponytail bobbing exuberantly. She didn't seem to care that the poor thing was slightly cross-eyed, its golden horn already bent, as she gazed at the older boy with a look of pure hero worship.

The brown-haired boy trailing behind her with his younger brother and Robbie scuffed his oversize tennis shoe against the loose gravel. "No big deal. It was one of those dart games where you have to pop the balloons. The prizes were all lame—uh, kinda girlie."

Ryder smiled at his nephew's deflection of Hannah's praise. "Way to go making a little girl's night, dude."

Tyler ducked his head, but he still held up his hand for his uncle's high five.

"I think someone might have a little crush," Lindsay teased, and Jamison didn't know which of them was more horrified—ten-year-old Tyler or his thirty-one-year-old self.

Just the thought of makeup, short skirts and puberty

had panic racing through him, and he longed to hold on
to the unicorn and hope for a miracle that would keep his
daughter a little girl forever.

"Hey, Dad, can we have some money to go get something to eat?"

As Ryder handed the boys some cash, Lindsay warned,
"Not too much junk food."

"Yeah, right," Ryder snorted as the boys took off, jos-
tling each other as they went. "I'm sure they're heading
straight for the booth selling the organic quinoa."

A few yards away, Robbie turned back. "Hannah, you
wanna come?"

"Can I, Daddy?" She looked up at him, her eyes filled
with happiness and hope, and something caught inside
his chest.

"Yeah," he said, his voice husky. "Go have fun."

She turned to race after the boys before circling back.
"Here." She thrust the unicorn into his arms. "You can
hold Uni. He'll keep you comp'ny."

Bending down to her level, he tapped the mythical crea-
ture's bent horn against her forehead. "Thanks, Hannah
Banana."

She giggled at the nickname and threw her arms around
him in a quick hug that had Jamison swallowing against
the sudden lump in his throat.

Rory might not have been by his side, but she was there.
He could feel her presence in Hannah's smile. She'd given
his little girl back her laughter, her sense of adventure, her
willingness to try…and he wondered at what might be possible if only he was half as brave as his daughter.

"Come on!"

Rory stumbled, trying to keep up with Debbie Pirelli as
her friend dragged her through the Clearville fairgrounds

toward the sound of country-western music. Boots might have been the right fashion choice, but they weren't the most comfortable. She slipped more than once on the fairground's loose gravel before they reached the stage. A local band had taken their place in the spotlight, and a dozen or so wannabe cowboys were boot scooting their ladies across a makeshift dance floor.

"I'm not sure this is a good idea," Rory protested.

"Trust me! This will be fun!"

Following at a slower pace a yard or so behind, Drew Pirelli laughed. "I can't tell you how many things she's talked me into with those same words!"

The vivacious blonde sent her husband a grin over her shoulder. "Like you're complaining!"

"Um, he might not be," Rory said after Drew offered to stand in line for drinks at the nearby booth, "but did I mention I'm not a fan of country music?"

Her friend laughed again. "You do know this is a rodeo, right? I don't think they'll be playing too much classical music around here tonight!"

Debbie was Hillcrest's exclusive wedding cake designer, and Rory had gotten to know the talented baker and café owner over the past few months. She'd been surprised and pleased when Debbie had called to see if she wanted to go to the rodeo. The last thing she wanted was for her new friend to think she wasn't enjoying her company. "Thanks again for inviting me. I'd been looking forward to this night, but I wouldn't have come by myself."

"Ah, now I get it," Debbie said as she bounced on her toes in time with the music.

"Get what?"

"You wanted to come with someone else."

"No, I—not really," she mumbled. She'd hoped to go with Jamison and Hannah. Rory loved seeing the little girl come out of her shell, how her first few steps in trying something new were always a little hesitant, but once she found her footing, she was ready to hit the ground running.

And Jamison...he was running, too. Only he was running away.

"I can't figure him out," she muttered, not realizing she'd spoken the words out loud until Debbie jumped on them.

"Who?"

"What?"

"Who is this mystery man we're talking about? The one you can't figure out but would like to be two-stepping across the dance floor with right now."

That was enough to startle a snort right out her. "Two-stepping is the last thing I can picture Jamison..."

Rory swallowed a curse as Debbie crowed with laughter. "I knew it! I knew there was some guy you'd rather be with right now." Her eyes widened further. "Wait... Jamison. Isn't that the single dad who's been bringing his adorable daughter into the café for cookies this week? No wonder you're not into cowboys if a guy like that is your type."

"That's part of the problem. Jamison is the exact opposite of my type."

Debbie raised a knowing eyebrow. "Funny. That's what I said about Drew. Once upon a time."

Ignoring her friend's words, Rory said, "He can be so serious, so logical, so lawyery..." And he probably would have been the first to call her on making up words, had he been there.

"Not to mention seriously sexy, practically gorgeous—"

"Okay, stop. I don't need to hear all of that. Especially not after making a fool out of myself over him yesterday."

"Ooh, that sounds promising." Debbie's blue eyes lit up with curiosity. "Give me the gory details."

Rory might have made it seem like Debbie was pulling the information out of her, but deep down, she needed someone to talk to. No way could she go to Evie when her cousin's line between business and pleasure was more like the Great Wall. And Rory didn't feel comfortable talking to Lindsay about her fiancé's best friend.

She was careful, though, not to reveal too much of Jamison's past. He'd opened up to her in a way she doubted he did with too many people, and she would hold fast to what he'd told her in confidence.

"I know this attraction between us isn't meant to last, that he'll be going back to San Francisco after the wedding." And if she wasn't careful, she'd be heartbroken when he left her behind. "Maybe he's right. Why bother to start something that's destined to come to an end?"

Debbie glanced past Rory and her grin widened even further. "We need to find you a dance partner."

Thrown by the abrupt change in topic, Rory said, "I'm not sure how that's going to help."

"Oh, believe me, it will. Jamison thinks he's being all noble by keeping his distance, but that's sure to fade fast when he sees you in the arms of another guy."

"Sees me?" Rory's heart skipped a beat even before she glanced over her shoulder to what had captured Debbie's attention a few seconds earlier. Or more specifically who...

Jamison stood outside the crowd gathered near the beer garden. His chestnut hair gleamed even in the artificial light. He wore a black T-shirt and jeans, perhaps in an effort to fit in, but for Rory, he still stood out. He was more masculine, more striking than the men around him, and that was even with the stuffed unicorn he held in one long-fingered hand.

She jerked her attention back up to find her gaze snagged on his lips and the memory of his kiss. Thirty feet and two dozen or so people separated them, but the distance, the crowd, the music, all of it faded away until only the two of them existed. Right up until the moment he turned away…

"Dance," Debbie commanded and just like that, the rest of the world rushed back in. Only it was too close, too crowded, too noisy.

"I don't feel like dancing," she protested weakly as she lost sight of Jamison in the line of people milling around the drink booths.

Debbie shook her head. "This isn't about how you feel. This is about making Jamison face how *he* feels."

"I don't even see him anymore. He's probably not even paying attention."

"Oh, trust me, he's still watching." Her friend grinned "And it's up to you to make sure there's something to see."

He couldn't stop watching. Try as he might to pull his gaze from the crowded dance floor, to stop staring at Rory like some kind of stalker, his attention returned to her time and again. In the brief seconds when he would lose sight of her during the turns and twists of complicated line dances he couldn't begin to follow, his heart would stop…only to start racing double time when he once again caught a flash of her ruffled denim skirt or the red bandanna material of her sleeveless top.

She was far from the best dancer on the floor. She'd stumbled once or twice, turned the wrong way and even bumped into a dancer next to her. But through it all, she kept smiling, laughing despite her embarrassment, her blue eyes sparkling and her dark ponytail swaying in time with the music.

"Here you go," Ryder said as he handed Jamison the chilled bottle of beer that had brought them over to the area by the dance floor in the first place. "Sorry it took so long. Man, those lines are crazy."

The brew was cold and crisp but did little to douse the fire in his gut as the music changed, switching from a boot-scooting beat to the slow, mellow strains of a waltz. Like some kind of switch had been flipped, the crowd of people who'd been standing side by side started pairing off, leaving Rory alone. But only for a moment...

A split second in time when her gaze met his, the pull strong enough he caught his body swaying in her direction.

I'm leaving soon.

His reasoning for keeping his distance hadn't changed, but neither did Rory's response. He didn't need to hear the words to read what was written in her expression.

You're here now.

A blond cowboy stepped between them, blocking Rory from his sight. The other guy was tall and wide enough that Jamison couldn't see Rory's answer to the question the cowboy asked, but a second later, her slender hand curved over the guy's broad shoulder as he took her into his arms.

Dragging his gaze away with a curse, Jamison sucked in a lungful of air, suddenly realizing he'd forgotten how to breathe in the last few moments. He needed to get out of there before he made the best worst mistake of his life. "I need to check on Hannah," he said, but Ryder was shaking his head.

"Lindsay's already talked to Robbie. They're having a great time. They've left the food court and are heading over to the kiddie rides."

"Maybe I should go—"

"She's fine, man. She doesn't need you to hold her hand...but maybe you need her to hold yours?"

"What the hell is that supposed to mean?"

"Just that strangling that unicorn isn't helping your mood any. Maybe you think having Hannah around will keep your mind off a certain wedding coordinator strutting her stuff out on the dance floor."

"I'm not—she's—" Cutting himself off, Jamison set the stuffed animal he'd forgotten he was still holding on a nearby table and took another long pull of the beer he no longer wanted. "Rory's free to dance with whomever she wants."

"Yeah, right," Ryder gave a doubting scoff, and Jamison couldn't blame his friend. Even the cross-eyed unicorn seemed to be gazing at him disbelief, but it was the truth...

"Go ask her. Unless you're afraid she'll say no."

He was afraid she'd say yes. Rory might have been in the arms of another man, but it didn't matter whom she danced with or how many times.

That could have been me.

It *should* have been him.

"Hannah! Oh, sweetie, what happened?"

Lindsay's cry jerked his attention from the dance floor in time to see three guilty-looking boys leading a sniffling Hannah their way. Tyler and Robbie exchanged a quick glance before Tyler said, "She, um, kinda got sick after we went on the merry-go-round."

"Yeah," the youngest boy chimed in, "it was super gross and—"

"Brayden, dude."

"Oh, right." The boy ducked his head at his uncle's reproach and mumbled, "We're real sorry she got sick."

"Daddy, I don't feel so good." A flood of tears balanced on Hannah's lower lids, and Jamison froze.

The sight of his daughter's tears instantly sent him back to those first horrible days after the accident when all

Hannah could do was cry for her mother and there'd been nothing—*nothing*—Jamison could do to soothe her fears.

Lindsay reached out to smooth Hannah's hair back from her sweaty forehead in the way all mothers seemed to know how to do. "Poor thing. They have a first-aid station set up near the front entrance—"

Alarmed, Jamison broke out of his paralysis. "You think she's that sick?" Knowing Hannah's fear of hospitals—the place where her mother had died—he didn't want traumatize her further unless a trip to the doctor was absolutely necessary.

"No, not at all. I think she had too much junk food combined with too much excitement, but they can help clean her up and maybe give her something to settle her stomach."

Bending down, he tried to keep his own stomach from roiling as he took in the bluish-purple mess staining the front of his daughter's T-shirt. What on earth had she eaten that would be that color coming back up? "What do you think, Hannah? Do you want to go get cleaned up and see what we can do to make you feel better?"

But Hannah shook her head, her lower lip protruding in a trembling pout. "No." She wobbled. "I want—I want m—"

Jamison braced himself only to be blown away by a request he never saw coming. "I want Miss Rory."

Chapter Ten

Her heart still in her throat, Rory ducked into the first-aid tent. She barely took in the small space with its two empty cots and a rolling cart stacked with bandages, gauze and bottles of peroxide and iodine before her gaze locked on the third occupied bed.

"Miss Rory…" Hannah's brown eyes filled and her lower lip trembled as she spotted her. "I got sick."

"I know, sweetie. I heard, and I'm so sorry you don't feel good." Hazarding a glance at Jamison, standing like a sentinel near the foot of his daughter's bed, Rory added, "Your daddy called me and said you wanted me to come see you."

She'd heard the reluctance in his voice as he explained how the little girl had gotten sick and that he'd taken her to the first-aid area. How he hadn't wanted to bother her…

But Rory had the feeling Jamison was the one who was bothered—by Hannah needing her. And maybe, just maybe, by how he needed her, too…

The little girl nodded, giving a watery sniff and wiping at a tear with the back of her hand. She was wearing one of the Rockin' R souvenir T-shirts. The oversize sleeves hung down to her elbows, making her look even smaller and more vulnerable.

As soon as Rory sat down on the cot, Hannah climbed onto her lap...and right into her heart. Closing her eyes against the undeniable realization, she breathed in the sweet scent of baby shampoo combined with mint toothpaste. Little more than a week, and Rory had fallen hard, and she didn't dare think about her feelings for the sad-eyed girl's father...

"I'm feeling better now," she mumbled into Rory's shoulder.

"Don't count on it."

At Jamison's dry comment, Rory couldn't help but glance up at him. He too looked a little pale and green around the gills, and she finally noticed Hannah wasn't the only one wearing a brand-new souvenir T-shirt.

She pressed her lips together to keep from laughing, but judging by the way he shook his head, she didn't succeed in hiding her amusement. "So glad you—and everyone— find this so funny."

"I don't think it's funny, Daddy." Hannah wrinkled her nose in an exaggerated expression of disgust. "I think it was yucky."

"And that," a female voice chimed in, "is what we in the nursing field would call a spot-on diagnosis."

Rory looked up as Theresa Deeks handed Jamison a plastic bag containing Hannah and Jamison's damp shirt. She hadn't realized the pretty nurse would be overseeing the first-aid station, though Theresa was certain to be on hand after all the work she and her husband, Jarrett, had put into making the rodeo such a success.

"I rinsed them out, but they'll still need a good washing."

"That wasn't necessary."

The dark-haired woman laughed. "It was if either of you hoped to wear them again."

"That's my favorite shirt," Hannah chimed in, her voice forlorn.

Jamison looked slightly exasperated by his daughter's "woe is me" sigh but merely said, "Then I thank you for saving my daughter's favorite shirt."

"You're welcome, and as long as Hannah is feeling up to it, you can take her home."

"Come on, kiddo." Jamison reached out, but the little girl burrowed deeper into Rory's arms.

"I want Miss Rory."

"Hannah—"

"It's okay, Jamison. I'll ride back to the hotel with the two of you."

"Are you sure?"

At her nod, he leaned down to reach for Hannah. The move brought Rory and Jamison face-to-face, and even with his daughter between them, her breath caught at his nearness. Nerves danced in her stomach as if she'd been the one to have way too much junk food.

Jamison stood, lifting his daughter from her lap, and Rory was surprised at how empty her arms felt. Picking up the unicorn that had been tucked against Hannah's side, she was glad to have something to hold on to. Something to occupy her hands and to stop her from reaching out to smooth the oversize shirt over Hannah's back...or to try to ease the frown from Jamison's forehead.

"This is my fault. I should have been paying closer attention to Hannah and not—"

Watching you.

He didn't say the words, but Rory still heard them, and

even though he was blaming himself, she couldn't help feeling like he felt she, too, was somehow at fault. She'd taken more than her fair share of blame when she'd done nothing wrong, and this was one time where she wasn't going to keep quiet.

"Mrs. Deeks…"

"You can call me Theresa," the dark-haired woman offered over her shoulder as she wheeled the cart out of the way.

"Theresa, is Hannah the only child to come in with a bellyache tonight?"

"Are you kidding? We've had half a dozen or so little kids come through already. And don't even get me started on the big kids," she added as she crossed her arms over her chest. Offering a sympathetic smile, she told Jamison, "Your daughter's going to be fine. In a little while, you can try to get her to drink some flat soda to keep hydrated and crackers or dry toast if she's hungry. By morning, I'm betting she'll be back to her old self."

Jamison didn't say much once they left the first-aid tent and headed for his SUV. He strapped Hannah into her car seat, tucking her stuffed unicorn in next to her, and had pulled out of the parking lot before he glanced Rory's way.

The fairgrounds were located outside town, connected by a two-lane highway lined with towering pines but not the typical streetlights. Without the passing glow, the interior of the car was too dark for Rory to read his expression.

Hannah drifted off to sleep, and Rory might have found the soft sound of her breathing soothing if not for the tension she sensed coming off Jamison in waves.

Was he still blaming himself for Hannah getting sick? For not paying more attention to how much junk food one little girl could eat in a very short time span? They were almost back at the hotel when he spoke.

"I'm sorry. I'm sure this isn't what you had in mind for how tonight would end."

"And what do you think I had in mind?"

"I saw you earlier. Dancing. Having fun."

She must have been a better actress than she gave herself credit for if Jamison had thought she was enjoying herself. She'd tried. She had, appreciating the effort Drew and Debbie had put into including her.

But that hadn't stopped her from wishing Jamison had been on the dance floor beside her, that he had been the man to pull her into his arms and hold her body close as they swayed in time with the music.

And when her phone rang and his name lit up the screen—

"Actually, this is exactly how I hoped tonight would end."

She didn't need passing streetlights to recognize the incredulous look he shot her. "Leaving early with a sick kid?"

"With the three of us spending time together."

"Rory." Jamison made a sound that was half laugh, half groan. "I'm trying to do the right thing here."

"And if we disagree on what the right thing is? Then what?"

"We're leaving in just over a week. If we start something—if we—then what?"

She knew the answer as well as he did and couldn't deny the ache in her heart at the thought of saying goodbye. But worrying about the future wouldn't stop it from coming. All they could do was make the most of the time they did have. As far as she was concerned, that was the only right thing to do.

"If you left tomorrow, I wouldn't miss you any less."

Rory heard his quick intake of breath, but he didn't reply as he pulled into the Hillcrest House parking lot and cut the engine. The golden glow from the safety lights bathed the SUV's interior, and she could see what she'd missed before. The muscle working in his jaw, the tendons standing out in stark relief along his forearms, his hands tight on the steering wheel as if they were flying down the freeway. Holding himself back when every fiber in her being ached for him to hold her...

Deciding to put her cards on the table, Rory shifted on the passenger seat to face him. "I adore your little girl, Jamison, and I—I like you."

His hands clenched around the wheel tight enough that the leather squeaked beneath his grip.

"I know that makes me sound like a twelve-year-old with a foolish crush—"

Now he responded, quickly cutting off her words. "I think you're smart and brave and amazing. Which is why I can't do this."

"Do what?"

"Pretend to be the kind of man you deserve. A good father...a good husband...a good son... Name any kind of relationship, and it's one I've already failed. I don't know what this is between us, but I don't want it to be—I don't want *you* to be one more person I fail."

Debbie was right, Rory realized. He really did think he was being noble by keeping his distance. She might have admired his effort if she wasn't so tempted to smack him upside the head.

"You only fail when you stop trying. You haven't stopped trying with your father and you won't stop trying with Hannah. Not because that's the kind of man I deserve, but because that's the kind of man you are. And as for the two of us..." She sucked in a deep breath of her own. "I know how this ends, Jamison. With you and Hannah saying goodbye. Whether we spend those days together or not, that doesn't change. Whether you kiss me right now or not, that doesn't change. So the only question is…why not kiss me?"

Why not kiss me?

The words, the temptation, pounded through Jamison's veins in time with the blood beating from his heart. At the moment, he wasn't sure which was more vital. His heart had maintained the steady rhythm for the past thirty-one years, but he'd never felt this…aware. This alive.

Fortunately—or unfortunately, damned if he knew which—he hadn't had a chance to answer Rory's question. With the motion of the vehicle no longer lulling her into sleep, Hannah woke up and he'd lifted his sleepy, grumpy daughter against his chest. She held on tight to her new toy and the stuffed unicorn rode along his shoulder as she wrapped her arms around his neck.

The warm weight of her in his arms, combined with the trust and faith she placed in him, brought an ache to his throat. He pressed a kiss to her tangled curls as he breathed in her baby shampoo scent. Rory was right. He wasn't quitting on his little girl. He didn't know how he'd manage being a full-time single dad and a full-time lawyer, but he'd find a way.

Even though it wasn't very late, the hotel lobby was quiet—most of the guests were either at the rodeo or out enjoying dinner. Even so, Jamison was conspicuously aware of Rory walking by his side toward the Bluebell suite.

They needed to talk, to finish the conversation they'd started in the car but—

Why not kiss me?

Jamison sucked in a breath as they turned down the narrow hallway. He was going to have one hell of a time focusing on talking when he had Rory alone in a hotel room.

He carried Hannah straight into the suite's connecting bathroom and, within minutes, had her surrounded by a tub full of bubbles. Rory joined them a few seconds later, making the small space positively claustrophobic as she placed a hand on his shoulder and set a pair of pajamas on the toilet seat.

"Can you, um, hand me that washcloth?" The folded cloth at the edge of the tub wasn't so far that he couldn't have reached it, but Jamison found himself wanting Rory to stay. As she knelt by his side, helping Hannah hold the washcloth against her face as he rinsed the warm, sudsy water from her hair, it hit him this was the first time he'd ever shared Hannah's bath-time duties.

Before their separation, Monica—or, he later suspected, the nanny the Stiltons hired to "help out" their daughter—had been responsible. Now the nighttime duty was his alone.

I won't miss you any less if you left tomorrow.

God, wasn't that the truth, he thought as Rory wrapped his daughter in an oversize towel, drawing out a sleepy smile. Within minutes, she had Hannah dressed and still giggling from her first attempt to put the little girl's pajama top on inside out and backward.

But once Jamison tucked his daughter into bed and Rory kissed her good-night, Hannah hugged her unicorn to her chest, huge tears filling her brown eyes.

"Oh, Hannah, do you still feel yucky?"

Nodding her head vehemently, Hannah gave a watery sniff. Then, with a single blink, the dam burst. Silent tears coursed down her chubby cheeks.

"Sweetie…"

As Rory sank down on the bed beside her, the little girl threw her arms around her neck. "Can you sleep in my bed tonight?"

"Hannah," Jamison started but he could already see

Rory melting like Hannah's cotton candy at the first splash
of water. He didn't doubt his daughter wasn't feeling well.
He had a souvenir T-shirt and a possible lifelong aversion
to brightly colored spun sugar to prove it.

But that didn't mean Hannah wasn't playing on the
grown-ups' sympathy and using tears to get her way. After
all his years with Monica, he'd built up a slight tolerance.
Rory had no such immunity.

"Of course, Hannah." Curling up on her side next to
the little girl, she promised, "I'll stay right here until you
fall asleep."

Having done their trick, Hannah's tears performed a magical disappearing act as she snuggled beneath the covers.

"Daddy, too."

Hannah patted the empty spot on the other side of the
bed, and Rory's eyes flew wide. The startled look and
instant color heating her cheeks were reminders that she
wasn't as bold as her words.

He knew he should play this smart and keep his distance. Starting something determined to end in such a
short time made no sense in his logical, well-ordered
world. But then again, he'd never met anyone like Rory
McClaren in his logical, well-ordered world.

A little over a week ago, he wouldn't have believed such
a charming, magical woman existed. And the chance to
spend eight days—hell, even another eight minutes—with
her would make spending the rest of his life missing her
a price he was willing to pay.

The last thing Rory expected when she closed her eyes
and pretended to sleep was to drift off. But as she lay on
the bed with Hannah curled up against her side, keeping
her breathing slow and steady—thinking that might encourage her rapidly beating heart to do the same—trying

to lull the little girl into a peaceful slumber, she somehow followed right along.

She woke slowly, taking in the unfamiliar warmth pressed against her side and something soft and furry brushing her face. She blinked as she waited for her eyes to adjust to the dim light shining in from the doorway. Brushing the unicorn's fluffy tail aside, Rory smiled at the sight of Hannah's angelic features, sweet and soft in sleep. She looked over the little girl's blond head to Jamison's handsome face. Not sweet, not soft.

Not asleep.

Her mouth went dry as she met his glittering gaze. "Um, what time is it?" The question wasn't the one she wanted to give voice to, but she couldn't quite bring herself to ask how long he'd been watching her sleep.

She was tempted to pull the blanket over her head as the humiliation of another question she shouldn't have asked throbbed in the stillness of the night. She might as well have begged him to kiss her, and that was after he'd already turned her down once!

"Late…or early, depending on how you look at it."

"I should go." Sliding out of the bed, she placed the stuffed animal under Hannah's arm and smoothed out the blankets, wishing she could smooth her rattled nerves as easily.

Focused on getting Hannah ready for bed, Rory had pushed the final minutes of their conversation out of her mind. But now the words pinballed through her skull, pained embarrassment flashing all around. She'd thought the way Jamison had kissed her, the way they'd opened up to each other, sharing hurts and fears from their pasts, had meant something.

But she'd been wrong before.

Ducking out of the bedroom, Rory hurried down the

shadowed hallway as fast as her boots could carry her. She'd keep her attention where it should have been all along, on Ryder and Lindsay's wedding, on getting through the next week, and then she could forget all about Jamison, all about Hannah, all about how her heart was breaking inside her chest…

She'd barely made it to the living room when Jamison caught her by the shoulders, stopping her short and drawing her back against him. His warm breath stirred her hair and sent shivers running down her spine as he murmured in her ear. "If you leave now, I won't miss you any less."

For a split second, she allowed herself lean into the warmth and strength of his body before growing a backbone and pulling away. He let her go, and Rory spun to face him, ready to remind him he didn't want this, didn't want *her*, but the sheer longing in his expression sucked the words right from her chest.

"Jamison—" The whispered sound of his name hovered in the charged air between them. A connection drawing them closer as he reached up to cup her face in his hands.

His thumbs caressed her cheeks, her lips, charting a sensual path that held her captivated. Her heart pounded, running a hundred beats a minute, but she couldn't even move. "Jamison—"

Light as a feather, his lips moved against hers as he spoke. Her stunned senses barely recognized the words. "So why not kiss me?"

Rory didn't know what it was about this man that was magic, but one kiss and she'd swear she could fly. She fisted her hands in the crisp cotton of the Rockin' R T-shirt as if he might somehow keep her grounded, but how could he when it was his touch, his kiss that had her body, her heart, her soul soaring? And then her feet really did leave the earth as she sank onto the couch cushions, Jamison following her down, his body strong, warm, *perfect* above hers.

He deepened the kiss as her mouth opened to his—touching, tasting, teasing. His hand found the narrow gap between the bandanna-print shirt tied at her waist and the top of her skirt. Her skin sizzled at the contact, and it was all she could do not to arch her body into his, wanting, demanding, needing more—

But she could feel him holding back. Like a kite with a string still tethered to the ground, Rory could feel the tug of resistance, the slow, unrelenting pull reeling them back to earth as he broke the kiss.

This time she didn't let old insecurities get in the way, didn't doubt his desire for her. "Jamison," she whispered softly once she'd found the breath and ability to speak.

He dropped his forehead against her shoulder, his body rock hard as he fought for control. "We can't," he started as he lifted his head.

"I know," she smiled, his willingness to put his daughter first one of the reasons why she loved hm.

Loved him?

No! She couldn't—she didn't—she—

Loved him.

Rory slammed her eyes shut, too afraid of the emotions Jamison might see. "I should go."

The cushions shifted beneath her as he pushed into a sitting position and lifted her up beside him. She felt as well as heard the words he spoke against her ear. "Rory... I wish—I want—"

"I know." Her heart was suddenly filled with wishes and wants, but closing her eyes wasn't going to be enough to make them come true. Lifting her lashes, she repeated, "I should go."

"As long as you know how much I want you to stay.

You were right before. I want us to spend the time we have left together."

Rory didn't know if she wanted to laugh or cry. She'd convinced Jamison—straitlaced, logical Jamison—to take a leap, and now she was the one who wanted to play things safe. To protect her heart, to take a step back from the edge rather than risk a nasty fall.

"Tell me you still want that, too, Rory," he urged, his hands bracketing her shoulders. "I'm here now, and I don't want to start missing you until I have to."

If you leave tomorrow...this won't hurt any less.

"I want that, too," she promised.

"Good." Pulling her back into his arms, he pressed a kiss to her temple. "Good."

Rory wasn't sure how long she stayed in his arms, her head resting on his chest as she counted out the beats of his heart. If only it didn't seem like the steady rhythm was going backward, counting down the time they had left...

It was still dark and Jamison was still sleeping when Rory eased out of his embrace and slipped out the door. The old-fashioned hallway sconces had been dimmed for the night, casting a soft golden glow on the familiar dark walnut wainscot and richly patterned carpet.

So overwhelmed by the emotions still careening through her, Rory barely noticed the two women she passed in the hallway until their sharp laughter stabbed her in the back.

"Guess those stories Trisha heard were right. She really can't keep her hands off the merchandise."

Chapter Eleven

Jamison jerked awake, startled by the unfamiliar ring of a telephone. Pain shot down his spine as he lifted his head, blinked a few times and realized he'd fallen asleep on the couch.

Rubbing the kink at the back of his neck, he pushed into a sitting position on the too-soft blue floral cushions. He hadn't planned to spend the night on the couch, but then again, much of what happened last night had been completely unexpected…

He took a quick look around to confirm what he already knew. Rory was gone. He didn't blame her for leaving. The last thing she would want was for someone to see her slipping out of a guest's room in the middle of the night.

That didn't mean he didn't wish she'd stayed. Call him selfish, but he'd had the pleasure of falling asleep with her in his arms. He wanted to know what it was like to wake up the same way.

Still, maybe she was calling to check on Hannah and see if she felt up to another batch of smiley-face oatmeal. Anticipation wiped away the last traces of sleep as grabbed the hotel phone off the end table.

"Jamison, my boy! How are you doing up there in Smallville?"

He cringed at the sound of his former father-in-law's voice. Gregory Stilton was as big and imposing in person as his booming voice was over the phone. When Jamison first met Monica's father, he couldn't help being impressed by the businessman's wealth, status and importance. At the time, those things had still mattered to Jamison. Having just passed the bar and eager to make his mark, Jamison had seen Gregory Stilton as having it all.

"It's Clearville, Greg," he told the older man, "and everything's fine."

"Good, good. Glad to hear it. And how's our grand-daughter?"

His hand tightened around the phone. "She's doing fine."

His gaze locked on a piece of paper on the coffee table, a project Hannah had worked on the day before. It took some imagination, but even he recognized the lime-green grass, turquoise sky and silver gazebo. Three stick figures held hands in front of the structure. He might have wondered at his daughter's Picasso-like image of him if not for the big red smile filling up half his face.

"Better than fine," he added, hearing the pride in his voice. "She's doing great. She's looking forward to her role as a flower girl in Ryder's wedding."

"Well, that's great."

Over the years, Jamison had learned to distrust Greg's over-the-top friendliness. More often than not, he was hiding his own agenda behind his smile. He'd come to appreciate Louisa's open disdain. At least with his mother-in-law, he never had to guess where things stood.

Proving his suspicions correct, Greg casually commented, "Of course, this vacation of yours couldn't come at a worse time—what with the junior partnership up for grabs."

"How do you know about the partnership?"

Gregory's laughter ratcheted up Jamison's suspicion even more. "You're nearing the big time now, Jamison. The law firm of Spears, Moreland and Howe taking on a new partner is news. People have been taking about it at the club."

The firm's partners ran in a tight-knit circle of powerful men and women in San Francisco. It was possible Greg had heard the rumors. But it was also possible that, as a powerful man himself, Gregory Stilton would use his considerable influence to weigh in on which direction he wanted the firm to go.

"Greg…"

If the older man heard the warning in Jamison's tone, he ignored it. "You know if you get the promotion, you'll be spending even more time at the office—long hours, weekends. Have you thought about what you'll do with Hannah?"

"We've talked about this. She'll be starting preschool once I get back."

"Half days in the mornings," Greg pointed out dismissively. "And that's if you can get her to stay. You know how leery she is around strangers."

"Hannah's getting better about that."

Silence filled the other end of the line, and Jamison realized what he should have known all along when his mother-in-law's voice came across the speaker. "Getting better? What strangers have you been leaving her with up there?"

"Not strangers. What I meant is she's getting better about meeting new people." Knowing his in-laws would dig the information out of Hannah given the chance, he added, "Rory McClaren is the hotel's wedding coordinator, and Hannah's taken a shine to her. She's made the whole idea of being a flower girl fun for Hannah. That's a good thing, Louisa."

"Is it? I thought this trip was about you spending time with your daughter, not about finding someone else to watch her while you go off and—do whatever."

"I'm the best man. The only *whatever* I've been doing is lending a hand with the wedding, and I wasn't always able to do that without someone to help with Hannah."

Jamison heard Louisa mutter the words *party planner* and *responsible sitter* under her breath before Greg came back on the line. "We're glad our little girl's looking forward to the wedding. How about you put her on so we can both say hello?"

A loud yawn sounded from the bedroom doorway as Hannah shuffled out, rubbing one eye before she pushed some serious bed-head curls out of her face. "She's right here, but don't expect too much. She just woke up and might be a little cranky."

He held the phone away from his ear rather than listening to what Louisa thought of him letting his daughter sleep in late and past her scheduled breakfast time. "Hey, Hannah Banana, want to talk to Nana and Papa?"

Giving a sleepy nod, Hannah took the phone and scrambled onto the couch next to him. Some of the tension caused by speaking with his in-laws faded as she snuggled by his side. "Hi, Nana. Hi, Papa."

Jamison might have questioned if he'd done the right thing in bringing Rory up in a conversation with his in-laws, but his daughter proved he'd little choice as she launched into a recitation of everything she'd done over the past few days—with almost every sentence filled with "Rory this" or "Rory that."

And after his daughter capped off her story with a detailed account of throwing up the brightly colored cotton candy, Jamison figured Louisa was about ready to faint.

"I didn't feel good, so I wanted Miss Rory to spend the night. Daddy, where is Miss Rory?" Hannah frowned before thrusting the phone back at him. "Nana wants to talk to you."

I bet she does, Jamison thought grimly.

"What kind of example are you setting, having some strange woman spend the night—"

"She didn't spend the night, Louisa. She stayed until Hannah fell asleep."

No need for the woman to know what happened after Hannah fell asleep. Covering the mouthpiece, he told Hannah, "Rory had to go back to her house, but we'll see her in a little bit if you're feeling okay."

"I feel good, Daddy. But I don't think I should have cotton candy for breakfast."

"Wise decision, kiddo."

He'd barely paid attention to the final minutes of Louisa's tirade. He was sure he'd heard the lecture about strict schedules and maintaining routines a dozen times before. "It was one night of too much sugar and too much excitement," he finally interrupted. "She's fine now, Louisa. In fact, I'd say Hannah's happier than she's been in a long time."

I'm happier. And he refused to feel guilty about that even as a cold silence filled the other end of the line.

"And I suppose you think this Rory person has something to do with that."

"It's not about what *I* think, and if you were listening to anything your granddaughter had to say, you'd know that."

"My granddaughter is four, a child who can be easily manipulated and fooled. As her father, it's up to you to know better."

Jamison rolled his eyes. "No one's manipulating or fooling anyone."

"I guess we'll see about that."

"What does that mean?"

"It means I hope you know what you're doing," she told him before ending the call, the warning in her voice making it clear she didn't think he had a clue.

Jamison hopped down from the stepladder after putting the final touches of paint on the trim along the gazebo's roof and tossed the paintbrush into an empty bucket. "What do you think?"

"It's be-yoo-tiful, Daddy!"

Rory couldn't agree more. The gazebo gleamed against the bright blue midday sky as it never had before, shining like new and yet still maintaining all the old-world charm and romance that made it a perfect part of Hillcrest. She loved the elegant scrollwork along the eaves, a more delicate pattern than what had been there before. Jamison had found matching spindles to replace the loose railing, making the stairs as good as new.

But it was the special touch he'd added, one no one else could see, that meant the most. Beneath the top step, on the underside of the tread, Jamison had carved all their initials.

He hadn't inscribed them within a heart, but he didn't need to. He and Hannah had already etched a permanent spot within her own.

He smiled when he got a good look at his daughter's

face. "Hannah Banana, I think you have more paint on you than on the gazebo."

Their roles as helpers had involved touch-up work, painting over screw and nail heads with Hannah doing her best and Rory following behind to fix any missed areas and clean up any drips.

"Uh-uh!" the little girl argued before wrinkling her paint-splattered nose and turning to Rory. "Do I, Miss Rory?"

"Well, maybe not that much." Dipping the tip of her finger in an open paint can, Rory said, "But you do have some here...and here...and here."

Hannah giggled as Rory tapped her nose, cheeks and chin. "Now look, Daddy!"

Shaking his head with the slightest bit of exasperation, Jamison said, "Nice polka dots, kiddo."

"I like poky dots."

"Well, you can't have poky dots if we're going to go into town for something to eat, so we better get cleaned up."

"Yeah, pizza!"

"With lots of anchovies, right?" Rory teased as she grabbed a semiclean cloth and a bottle of water off the top of a cooler.

The little girl made a face. "Anchovies, yuck!"

"Hannah, you don't even know what anchovies are," Jamison pointed out.

"Are they good?" his daughter demanded, her doubt obvious.

"Well, no," he admitted, clearly failing to prove his point.

Hannah turned back to Rory in triumph. "No anchovies!"

"All right. How about—" Rory paused for a moment to think "—pepperoni?"

"Okay!" With the promise of pizza in the air, Hannah

bounced on her toes, making Rory's efforts to clean off her face like a new version of pin the tail on the donkey. "No anchovies, just pepperoni."

Once Rory had Hannah's face as clean as she could get it without a tub full of bubbles, she cupped her cute cheeks in her hands. "There you go. All clean."

Hannah responded with a definitive nod. "Daddy's turn."

Jamison had dropped down to sit on one of the step-ladder's lower rungs, and when he brushed a hand across his damp forehead, he left behind a streak of white.

"Hannah is right." Lips quirked in a smile, she told him, "You're wearing almost as much paint as she was."

He took in his white-flecked shirt with a careless shrug as he cracked open the water bottle she handed him. "What can I say? Construction work is an ugly process."

Ugly was not the word that came to Rory's mind as she grabbed the damp towel and walked to his side. "Come here."

He leaned forward, and she lifted a hand to brush his dark hair back from his forehead. His gaze caught hers, and she paused, almost forgetting why she'd embarked on this task.

She dabbed at the paint just as she had with Hannah. The actions might have been the same, but Rory's response was completely different. Her hand trembled as she traced a path across Jamison's forehead, his temple and along one cheekbone. She lowered the towel but didn't back away, staying whisper close, as his gaze searched hers.

"Better?" he murmured.

"Not quite so ugly anymore." She'd meant the words as a tease, but the huskiness in her voice gave her away.

Hannah had grabbed the empty water bottle, seeming to enjoy making the thin plastic crackle and pop in her small hands. Crouched along the edge of the pathway, her interest soon turned to scooping loose dirt into the narrow container.

Rory had learned the little girl's attention didn't stay captured for long, but for now...

She brushed her lips against Jamison's, their equal height giving the illusion of equal footing until Jamison caught her face in his hands, took control and shattered any pretense of staying grounded.

It was a quick kiss. A prelude for what was to come. A promise of more...but enough to send her head spinning into the clouds, leaving her breathless and dizzy with desire. She didn't know if her feet would have actually left the earth, but Jamison held her fast. He caught her hips and pulled her into the cradle of his thighs.

The gazebo had always been her favorite place, and that was before. Now every time she closed her eyes, Rory would see Jamison leaning against the carved post, paint streaked across his forehead and a gleam in his eyes. His low voice would echo through the whisper of wind in the trees and Hannah's lilting laughter would ring out with the trilling call of the birds. Pizza would never taste the same again, and paint fumes would always bring her back to this moment and this man.

Her favorite place and her favorite people in the whole, whole world...

"Ryder's bachelor party is tomorrow night."

"I know, so is Lindsay's bachelorette party."

"Do I even want to know what goes on at a bachelorette party?"

"Probably not." Rory was touched Lindsay had invited her and had been looking forward to hanging out with a group of women who weren't pointing and whispering behind her back.

Ever since the night of the rodeo, she'd lost count of the conversations that had stopped the moment she stepped into a room or neared a group of Hillcrest employees. As usual Trisha Katzman was right in the middle, surrounded by her flock. Whenever the redhead spoke, the other women leaned in like hungry birds, eyes wide and mouths open, pecking over a tasty morsel of gossip as they whispered back and forth.

Thrusting the thought aside, she asked, "What do you have planned for Ryder's last night as a free man?"

"You know me, something wild and crazy."

Rory couldn't help but laugh at his deadpan delivery. "It's always the quiet ones you have to watch out for."

Jamison smirked a little. "Per the groom's specific instructions, we're having a guys' night out at the Clearville Bar and Grille for a debauched evening of pool, darts and beer."

"Hmm, if not for the beer, you could invite Ryder's son and a few of his school friends along."

"Oh, you are funny."

She was glad he thought so. The bachelor and bachelorette parties were among the last events leading up to the wedding. The rehearsal dinner was scheduled at Hillcrest House the evening before the wedding, and after that— After that, it would all be over.

Lindsay and Ryder's life as a married couple would just be starting, but her relationship with Jamison would come to an end.

A smarter woman might have tried to keep her distance, to guard her heart, but Rory didn't have that kind of strength. She did know she was right about one thing, though. Ending their relationship now wouldn't make her miss him any less, so she was determined to enjoy what time they had together now.

She was afraid she'd have plenty of time to be miserable later.

Jamison cleared his throat and glanced over to where Hannah was now sprinkling the collected dirt along the walkway. "I, um, talked to Ryder. His parents are watching Robbie and his cousins tomorrow night. He said they'd be happy to add a girl to the mix."

"Do you think Hannah will be okay staying with them?"

Jamison huffed out a sigh. "Ever since the night of the unicorn, Hannah's been asking when she can play with Robbie and his cousins again."

Rory laughed. "But that's a good thing, isn't it?"

"A good thing for Hannah…and I'm hoping a very good thing for us."

Their time alone since the night of the rodeo had been limited to stolen kisses when Hannah was preoccupied with some game of make-believe or in the evening after the little girl had gone to bed. But Jamison was careful not to go too far, pushing them both to the brink before pulling back from the edge.

If Rory didn't know better, she might have thought he was trying to drive her out of her mind.

But if Hannah was happy staying with a sitter for a night…

"Don't tell me," Rory said, keeping a light note in her voice despite the bass drum beating inside her chest, "you have something wild and crazy planned?"

"Oh, sweetheart, you have no idea."

Chapter Twelve

"Am I the only one who thinks this is a bad idea?" Rory's words fell on deaf ears as she and the rest of Lindsay's bridal party scrambled out of the SUV amid constant chattering and bursts of laughter.

"I'm afraid so," Sophia Pirelli Cameron said. The petite brunette met Rory's exasperated glance with a sympathetic look. "You've been out-Pirellied."

"I had no idea that was even a thing."

Sophia laughed. "When you have as much family in town as I do, you learn to go with the flow."

At the moment, the five women, including Sophia's sister-in-law, Debbie, were flowing toward the Clearville Bar and Grille, a local watering hole offering beer, chips, an assortment of burgers and every sport imaginable on large-screen TVs. The place was popular with locals and tourists alike, and for tonight, it was the hot spot for bachelor parties. As in Ryder's bachelor party.

The girls were supposed to be out for their own night on the town, but halfway to Redfield, Debbie had had the great idea of crashing the guys' night out. The exuberant blonde's enthusiasm was contagious, and it hadn't taken much convincing for Lindsay's future sister-in-law, Nina, to turn the car around and head back to Clearville, where all of their guys waited.

Well, not her guy.

Jamison would be there, of course, but the other women were all married or about to be married to the men inside. While she and Jamison...

"That's a pretty heavy sigh for a Saturday night," Sophia commented as the two of them fell into step a few paces behind Lindsay, Debbie and Nina, who were already racing toward the bar. "I don't suppose it has anything to do with a certain best man, does it?"

"Jamison is part of the wedding party and a guest at our hotel—"

"Not to mention single...and hot...at least according to Debbie and my cousin Theresa."

Rory groaned. "You're right. Your family really has taken over the town, haven't they?"

"Pretty much," Sophia said. "But what can I say? Clearville's home, and I'm glad to be back. I'm only sorry I stayed away so long."

Music and light spilled out from the open double doors leading into the bar. Their steps slowed as they neared the entrance. "Considering how much family you have here, why did you stay away?"

The brunette lifted a shoulder in an easy shrug. "Small towns have long memories. When I was in high school, I screwed up. I trusted the wrong person and did something I shouldn't, and when we got caught, I took the blame. I'm not proud of what happened, but the thing I regret the most is the guilt that drove a wedge between me and my family. I never should have let that happen, especially not when they forgave me long before I got around to forgiving myself."

I trusted the wrong person.

Boy, did Rory know how that felt! And maybe she had carried her guilt around for too long—when that was the only thing she'd done wrong.

"Thank you, Sophia."

The brunette shot her a curious glance. "For what?"

"For helping put the past into perspective."

"You're welcome, and while I'm doling out pearls of wisdom, let me tell you that trips to the past are best served with fruity cocktails."

Rory's laughter faded away as they stepped inside the bar and she spotted the combined bachelor and bachelorette parties gathered near the pool tables. Music blared from the jukebox in the corner, making it impossible to hear what they were saying. But even in the dim lighting and neon glow cast from the beer signs hanging on the walls, what she saw made her heart sink.

Ryder was furious. Lindsay stood in front of her fiancé, her pretty face distraught, as the rest of the bridal party milled awkwardly around the couple.

He couldn't be so upset because Lindsay had crashed his stag party! In all the time Rory had worked with the groom-to-be, he'd been nothing but laid-back and relaxed, happy with whatever made Lindsay happy. Watching them together, Rory had thought they were the perfect couple...

In an instant, she switched from member of the bach-elorette party to wedding coordinator. There had to be something she could do to fix this!

Cutting through the crowd gathered in front of the bar, Rory reached Bryce Kincaid's side. "Bryce, what is going on?"

"One minute everything was fine, and then in the next—" Ryder's brother shook his head. "All I know is that I heard Ryder tell Jamison he's not sure if he even wants Jamison to be at the wedding, forget having him *in* the wedding."

Jamison? This was about *Jamison*?

A tearful Lindsay caught sight of Rory and hurried to her side. "This is awful! Jamison is the best man. Ryder's best friend! I know how much he wants Jamison standing beside him." She brushed the backs of her fingers beneath her eyes. "I'm not going to be so dramatic as to say Jamison's absence will ruin the wedding, but I know how much it will hurt Ryder if he's not there. Something like this could ruin their friendship."

"Do you know what the fight was about?"

"Other than me?" Lindsay asked with a sad little laugh. "No clue."

"Okay. You keep working on Ryder and see if he'll open up. I'll find Jamison. Between the two of us, they don't stand a chance."

"Thank you, Rory."

"Wedding coordinator to the rescue," she promised, glad to hear a genuine laugh from her friend as she gave her a quick hug.

Oh, Jamison, what did you do?

Turning to Bryce, she asked, "Do you know where Jamison is now?"

"He drove separately from the rest of us in case he had to leave early to pick up Hannah." At her questioning glance, he added, "I've already called my folks. They haven't heard from him, and Hannah's asleep on the couch after somehow talking my boys into watching a princess movie with her."

"I rode over with the rest of the bachelorette party—"

"I can give you a ride if you know where he might have gone."

"Let's start at the hotel."

Once Rory spotted Jamison's SUV in the parking lot, she convinced Bryce she could handle things from there. Faint moonlight lit the way to the lobby, but a gut feeling had her veering away from the elegant building and following a familiar path instead.

She ducked under the yellow caution tape barring the way to the gazebo. The elegant structure was draped in shadows, still and silent, and a dark figure sat hunched on the top step. Her heart ached at the loneliness, the isolation he seemed to have wrapped around him like a moth-eaten-yet-familiar blanket.

Oh, Jamison, she thought again. *What did you do?*

She set foot on the first step, noticing the six-pack of beer, and sank down beside him. Smoothing her skirt over her knees, she kept her gaze focused straight ahead as she asked, "Come here often?"

Jamison tipped his head back to take a swallow from the beer in his hand before stating, "I'm not even going to ask how you found me here."

"I think the better question would be *why* are you here?"

"I'm getting drunk," he said, the clarity of his words and the barely touched bottle belying his words. "Isn't that what tonight is all about?"

"Actually, tonight is about spending time with your best friend and celebrating his upcoming marriage."

"I don't think Ryder would call me his best friend anymore. Even though all I was trying to do was to look out for him."

A bad feeling sinking into the pit of her stomach, Rory asked, "Look out for him how?"

"I told him it wasn't too late—"

"To call off the wedding?" She reared back in shock and might have tumbled from the step if he hadn't steadied her with his free hand.

"No, no, not to call it off. Just to have one of the lawyers at the firm draft a prenup."

"Oh, Jamison."

"I didn't think he'd—I'm trying to protect him, you know? Isn't that what a best man—a best *friend*—does?"

"I think a best man should be happy his friend has found the love of his life."

Wincing, he ran a hand through his hair. "I tried to have a good time. I did, but all I could think about was that I'd been there, done that, and look how it ended."

"Been there?"

"I was best man at Ryder's last wedding, too."

"Oh."

"Yeah. And that time, I did keep my mouth shut, even though I sensed Ryder was feeling pressured into the marriage. I told myself it was cold feet and everything would work out."

"And everything did work out."

He shot her an incredulous look. "They were miserable together. They ended up getting divorced."

"Yes, so Ryder and Lindsay can get married now."

"You are incredible."

"Thank you."

"Not a compliment. You can't be that naive."

Rory sucked in a lungful of cool night air and tried not to let that arrow strike her heart. He thought she was naive for believing Ryder and Lindsay's love was meant to last. How foolish would he think she was for falling for him when she'd known all along their relationship was destined to end?

Keeping her voice steady despite the trembling inside, she said, "Believing in love isn't being naive any more than being cynical makes you smart. All it does is blind you to the good things in life. I don't know anything about Ryder's first marriage, but I do know he's crazy about Lindsay."

"Lindsay kept his son from him for nine *years*! Ryder didn't even know Robbie existed. At least Monica only—" Cutting himself off, Jamison shook his head and took another drink.

"What did Monica do?" Rory asked, her words blending in with the rustle of wind through the trees, the distant rush of waves against the shore.

For a long moment, she didn't think he would answer, that he would keep his words—like his heart—locked up in the past. But finally, he started to speak. "We'd been fighting a lot, so much that I was afraid it would start to affect Hannah."

"And you didn't want that…not after the way you'd grown up."

"It's the last thing I wanted for Hannah. I did my best to ignore the worst of Monica's habits—the extreme shopping, the time she'd spend out with friends instead of at home with Hannah, her complaints that I was the one who spent too much time at work to be a good husband and father. Although she was right about that…"

Jamison still didn't know if his marriage had failed because of all the time he put in at work or if he put in all that time at work because his marriage was failing. But he did know Hannah had paid the price.

"Jamison—"

Ignoring her softly voiced protest, he continued, "Before long, Monica and I couldn't seem to be in the same room together without arguing, and I felt like I had no choice. I moved out. We called it a separation, but I think we both knew we wouldn't be getting back together. I don't know why I didn't ask for a divorce right then."

"Maybe because you still were holding out hope you would work things out."

Jamison gave a rough laugh, his hand tightening on the beer bottle. "Well, if that is the reason, it was a foolish hope. We might not have fought as often, but when we did, it was as bad, if not worse. That's when she started keeping me from seeing Hannah. It was small things at first. Dropping her off a few minutes late, picking her up early. But before long, she was canceling visits altogether. Hannah was sleeping or not feeling well or had a playdate with friends. One excuse after another until I was lucky to see Hannah once a month instead of every weekend."

It was his father who had warned him not to make the same mistakes he had. "I let your mother convince me you were better off without me," he'd told Jamison. "I was never going to be rich or successful. I was never going to be the kind of man she would be proud of. But the one regret I have is that I didn't fight as hard as I could for you, Jamie. You are rich and successful, but I can promise you, none of that will mean a thing if you don't have that little girl in your life."

Rory shifted closer to him, slipping the cold, hard bottle from his hand and replacing it with the warm, soft reassurance of her own. "And that was wrong of Monica, but—"

"That's not all she did, Rory." Jamison had to take a deep breath to get out the words, buried deep in his memory where he tried his damnedest not to think about them. "I couldn't let things continue the way they were going. So I told Monica I was filing for divorce. I was prepared for her to go ballistic, but she barely reacted. I left that day feeling this huge sense of relief and went on an out-of-town business trip, thinking everything would work out. I should have known better."

The wind picked up, drawing a curtain of clouds over the full moon. Dark memories crouched in the shadows, trying to drag him back into the past, but Jamison held on tight to Rory's hand, her touch, her presence keeping him present.

He thought of the first time he saw her, how her smile, her beauty had warmed him like a summer day... She was his sunshine, his ray of light.

"I tried calling while I was gone, and when she didn't call me back, I started to get this bad feeling. She'd been so calm when I left, acting so out of character... I tried her parents to see if they could get ahold of her, but they couldn't reach her, either. Finally, I left in the middle of a meeting and took the first flight I could get home. I didn't know what I would find."

"Oh, Jamison."

Even though he had moved out, he'd convinced Monica to allow him to keep a key in case of emergencies. "When I got there, everything was the same as when I left, and I felt foolish for overreacting. It's not like it was the first time Monica had avoided my calls. But then I found her phone on the counter. She never went anywhere without that phone."

He'd torn through the house after that, the missing items as telling as the phone she'd left behind. Suitcases, clothes, Hannah's favorite toys... "Monica was gone, and she'd taken Hannah with her."

"Jamison... I am so sorry. How awful for you to have to go through that!"

There was more. There was what happened the day of the accident, but Jamison couldn't bring himself to tell Rory about that. Couldn't watch the sympathy and understanding in her beautiful face fade into the condemnation he saw whenever he looked in the mirror.

"How long were they gone?"

"Almost four months. One hundred and seventeen days."

Gazing at his granite profile, Rory could still see the toll that time had taken on Jamison written in his tense jaw, the brackets around his mouth and the hand fisted at his side. Her heart ached for all he—and Hannah—had been through, emotion building inside her as she wished for something to say to wipe those bad memories away. Instead, she scooted closer to him on the step and rested her head on his shoulder.

"I know it doesn't sound like a long time—" he started.

"It sounds like an eternity," she protested and felt a small sense of victory when Jamison sighed and some of that tension eased out of him. And when he leaned his head against hers, Rory wished this was a moment she could make last.

"Between the separation and the time she was gone, I only saw Hannah a handful of times in almost eight months. She'd grown so much, when I first saw her in— when I first saw her again, I hardly recognized her."

"But all of that happened to you and Monica. It didn't happen to—"

Us.

Monica had let him down, betraying him in the worst way possible, but Rory wanted him to know he could count on her. That he could trust her with his heart, and even more important, he could trust her with his daughter. She would never let either of them down.

"To Lindsay and Ryder."

"I don't know how he can forgive her."

But it wasn't Lindsay Jamison needed to forgive. He needed to find a way to forgive himself.

"It's not your fault."

But instead of soothing his pain, her words caused Jamison to jerk away. He vaulted off the steps only to turn back and point an accusing finger at her—as if condemning her for trusting him, for loving him. "You don't know, Rory—"

"I know you." She stood slowly before she deliberately made her way down the steps. "I might not know the man you were, but I know the man you are. A good father, a good friend, a man who—"

"A man who killed his wife!"

"What?" Rory stumbled on the final step, but this time Jamison wasn't there to catch her. She regained her balance at the last second, her legs, her entire body trembling at the force of his words. Words that couldn't be true. "I don't understand. Monica died in a car accident. Were you—were you the one driving?"

His arm fell to his side, and his chin dropped to his chest. "I was a thousand miles away."

"Then how—"

"Monica called me. When she figured out I had a detective looking for her, she called me. We were yelling at each other, ugly, hateful things—and then I heard her scream."

"Oh, my God. You heard the accident?"

"Heard it? I *caused* it."

"Oh, Jamison, you can't believe that! You know it isn't true. Monica called *you*. You didn't know she was behind the wheel."

"I should have. I should have realized she'd take Hannah and run again—"

"Maybe, maybe you could have guessed she'd do that. But you couldn't know that she would crash."

He closed his eyes as if that could block a truth guilt wouldn't allow him to believe. He might not listen and he didn't want to see, but Rory could still make him *feel*. She lifted her hands to his face, and the scrape of his late-night stubble sent chills up her arms. The sensation was as powerful as if he'd run his jaw over her sensitive skin from her wrist all the way to her shoulder.

And she knew in the split second before she raised her mouth to his, that this kiss wouldn't be the caring, consoling kiss she intended. But then their lips met, and she stopped worrying about what the kiss was supposed to be and focused on what it *was*.

Raw. Intense. So close to perfection, she could have been dreaming. But the tension in Jamison's body, the lingering anguish, was all too real. The need to take that pain away had Rory parting her lips beneath his, as if she could somehow draw out the darkness trapped inside him.

Touching and tasting, the kiss grew more and more heated, and the air seemed to sizzle around them. It burned in her lungs until she had to break the kiss and gasp for breath.

"Rory." He groaned her name in what might have been a protest, but the plea in his rough voice and a tiny thread of hope let her know how much he wanted to believe.

"There are a million things you could have done differently then, but there's not a single one you can do now to change what happened."

"So I'm just supposed to forget?"

"No, you're supposed to remember. To remember how lucky you are that Hannah survived and that she's okay."

"I am. You have no idea how damn grateful I am that she wasn't badly hurt."

"I know. I know." Rory swallowed hard, knowing the words she needed to speak and knowing how hard they would be for Jamison to hear. "And you have Monica to thank…because no matter how angry she was, how determined to run, she still took the time to buckle Hannah into her car seat. To make sure your daughter was as safe as possible in case of an accident no one could see coming."

His fingers flexed at her hips, and Rory tensed, waiting for him to push her away. To reject her and the forgiveness she wanted for him. Instead, he pulled her body to his. Close, then closer until she could hear his ragged breathing and feel his heart thundering. Until she resented every article of clothing, every millimeter of distance separating them.

"I can't. I know you want me to forgive Monica, but I can't."

"It isn't about what I want, Jamison. It's about what you need."

"I need you, Rory. All I need is you."

He swept her up in his arms, but instead of carrying her away from the gazebo, he climbed the stairs to the shadowed platform. It was dark, and the secluded gazebo seemed a million miles away from the hotel and its slumbering guests. As he sank down onto the top step—the one with their hidden initials carved in the wood—and drew her into his lap, no one else existed outside the world they created for each other.

He murmured her name against her mouth, her cheek, her throat. Each husky whisper sent shivers running up and down her spine. The seductive, potent promises set off tiny explosions along her nerve endings—fizzy and sparkling and all building to a grand finale. She tugged his shirt from his jeans and shoved her hands beneath the soft material. The tight muscles and smooth skin of his back made her greedy for more.

His eyes blazed at the proof of her impatience, and he

reached behind his back with one hand to pull the shirt over his head. She smothered her startled laughter at the unexpected move against his neck, breathing in the scent of his skin and the anticipation of what was to come.

With his shirt gone, she had the freedom to explore his broad shoulders, muscled chest and stomach, first with her eyes and then with her hands. His hair-roughened skin tickled her palms, but it was Jamison who flinched as she worked the button on his jeans.

"Rory." He caught her hand, his grip a little rough as he held her fingers against his rock-hard abdomen. He didn't ask the question, but the words were written in his glittering gaze.

I'm leaving...

Leaning forward, she gave her answer as her lips found his. *You're still here...*

Their affair might not last, but Jamison seemed determined to make it one she would never forget as his hands slid beneath her skirt and he set out to brand every inch of her body. He stripped away her panties and found her wet and waiting for him. Heat flooded her bloodstream, a tidal wave of desire that washed away the worries of what tomorrow might bring and left her bathed in his kiss, his touch...

Until the tide turned, and Rory was the one painting kisses over his chest, shoulders and stomach. She'd studied dozens of swatches over the years—paints, fabrics, ribbons—but she'd never before realized that kisses came in colors. The innocence of pink, the glorious revelry of gold, the rich decadence of red...

She'd nearly completed a rainbow when Jamison stopped her. She muttered a protest that was silenced when he reached for protection and then lifted her above him. Her body sank onto his, and Rory welcomed him just as she'd welcomed his kiss, his touch, his heartache. Her arms and legs wrapped tight, never wanting to let him go...

With his hands at her hips, he slowly began to move, increasing a pace destined to drive her wild. Her body rose and fell with every thrust, and a kaleidoscope of colors burst behind her eyelids as the pleasure broke, showering down over them in a burst of fireworks.

His breathing was still rough in her ear, his heart pounding against hers, when Rory pressed her lips to his shoulder, fighting a smile he evidently felt against his skin. "What's so funny?"

"I was thinking we should do something to celebrate the gazebo's reopening, but this is so much better than anything I had in mind!"

Chapter Thirteen

Jamison woke slowly, blinking against the early-morning light. The sun streamed through the curtains, and he suffered a moment's disorientation. He never slept this late. Hannah never let him sleep this late. At the thought of his daughter, his eyes flew open and took in the unfamiliar, feminine surroundings. Lace curtains. White wicker furniture. Pale pink walls and sheets embellished with tiny pink roses. At the sound of a soft sigh, the memories from the night before came rushing back.

Rory. In his arms at the gazebo last night. Rory. In bed with him this morning.

Wide-awake now, he rolled his head on the pillow. They'd made their way back to her cottage after leaving the gazebo, stumbling through the darkened rooms before falling into her bed and making love a second time. She slept on her side facing him, one hand cradled against her cheek. Her dark hair spilled in disarray across the pillowcase, her eyelashes forming soft shadows against her cheeks. Sheer amazement filled him. He'd never seen a lovelier or more amazing sight.

He felt the ridiculous urge to wake her, as if that might somehow prove last night hadn't been a dream.

As if she could read his thoughts, her eyelids fluttered, then drifted open. Unlike his momentary confusion, her eyes were clear. "Morning," she whispered.

"Hi," he murmured, almost afraid to break the silence.

"What time is it?"

"Early," he insisted, ignoring his previous admission.

She smiled at his white lie. "Not that early. When are you supposed to pick up Hannah?"

"We didn't have a set time, since no one knew how late we'd stay out."

Reaching out, she cupped his face in her hand. "You know you have to make things right with Ryder."

Jamison didn't want to lose his oldest and best friend, but Ryder wasn't first on his mind as he pressed a kiss into Rory's palm. "I didn't plan for this, you know."

"Uh-oh." Her smile trembled a little as she tucked the sheet beneath her arms. "Do I hear another 'do the right thing' speech coming?"

"Too late for that," he sighed.

"But not too late for this." Leaning forward, her dark hair framing her face, she brushed her lips against his. The gentle, giving kiss still had the power to kick his pulse into overdrive and send desire crashing through his veins.

"Rory…"

"I know you're leaving, Jamison." Was it his imagination or was the shine in her blue eyes the glitter of tears? Before he could know for sure, she ducked her head again, punctuating her words with kisses on his face, his throat, his chest. "But not today…and not tomorrow…"

And before long, leaving Clearville—leaving Rory—was the last thing on his mind.

An hour later, Jamison pulled up in front of the Kincaid residence. Ryder's parents lived outside town in a ranch-style house with a wraparound porch and lush green front yard. The sounds of laughter and a dog barking filled the air as he headed for the front door.

"Kids are all out back." Ryder stepped through a side gate, coffee mug in hand, and let the door slam shut behind him. "Hannah has the boys playing some kind of game where she's a princess and they're trying to rescue her from a dragon. Who in this case is my brother's Border collie."

"Sounds like they're being pretty good sports about the whole thing."

Ryder shrugged as he climbed the steps to the porch. "Robbie's been begging for a dog, so any game that includes Cowboy is one he's up for."

Jamison opened his mouth, the apology stalling in his throat. "Seems like you survived last night."

"Yeah, it was a real blast." Ryder's poker face folded slightly as a wry smile kicked up one corner of his mouth. "Especially once the bridal party showed up."

"So that's what happened." He'd been too caught up in the moment last night to wonder how Rory had found out about the argument at the bachelor party.

"Huh?"

"It's—nothing. I was an ass last night."

Ryder took his time, lifting the mug, blowing on the steaming dark roast, taking a swallow before saying, "Got that right."

Jamison sighed. He was going to make him say the words. "I'm sorry. I know you love Lindsay and she loves you, and I...hope everything works out."

His friend tipped his mug in Jamison's direction. "But you don't think it will."

"Dammit, Ryder, I'm trying really hard not to get into another fight with you."

"Good thing, since I'd kick your ass."

"And I'd sue yours until you didn't have a penny to your name."

Ryder smirked, and Jamison figured they could call their insult battle a draw. His friend lifted the mug for another drink, and Jamison noticed the gold trophy and the words *World's Greatest Father* on the side.

"You want to know how I can forgive Lindsay? The truth is, that's the only way I could expect her to forgive me. The only way I could forgive myself."

It's not your fault. Rory's words whispered through his mind. *And you have Monica to thank...*

He couldn't. Maybe if he had Rory's capacity for love, for hope, for forgiveness, he could forgive Monica. But he was a man who lived the law—right and wrong, black or white.

Jamison shook his head. "You didn't do anything wrong! You didn't know Lindsay was pregnant."

"I didn't want to know," Ryder stressed. "I slept with her. I knew the baby could be mine—forget what the Clearville grapevine had to say. But I had plans, big plans, and you better believe being a teenage dad wasn't part of them." He rubbed his thumb over the trophy emblem on the mug. "That's not an easy thing to admit, even now, but it was something I had to face when Lindsay told me about Robbie. Something we both had to get over in order to move on."

And he was moving on. To a life with the woman he loved with a confidence and faith Jamison...envied. "I really was trying to look out for you."

"I get it. I do. Your head was in the right place."

"Isn't the expression your *heart* was in the right place?"

"Oh, hell, no. Your heart's all messed up, dude."

"What is that supposed to mean?"

"Just that half the stuff you were saying was way more about what's going on with you than anything to do with me."

Bits and pieces of his argument echoed across the lush green lawn.

You have to protect yourself.

You made a mistake before.

Don't leave yourself open to getting hurt again.

Jamison swore under his breath. "When did you end up being the smart one in this friendship?"

"I was always the smart one. Playing the dumb jock was how I got all the girls."

"You are so full of it."

Jogging down the porch steps, Ryder spoke over his shoulder. "Yep. But I'm right."

He'd always had a bit of showman in him back in his college football days, and Jamison couldn't help thinking his friend hadn't lost his touch as he followed him around to the side of the house. Ryder pushed the gate open wide, and Jamison saw what was behind door number one.

In the middle of a green tree-lined lawn, Hannah held a beat-up red Frisbee over her head, running and laughing as the black-and-white dog and three boys chased after her.

Her pure joy grabbed hold of Jamison, and he didn't want to let go. Didn't want to step back from the emotion pouring through him. He wanted to embrace it for all it was worth, and he only wished he had Rory at his side to share in this miracle.

Hillcrest's magic touches whoever needs it most.

She was magic. She was his princess and fairy godmother

rolled into one, and Jamison didn't know what he would do without her in his life.

As if reading his thoughts, Ryder said, "You have a good thing going with Rory, Jamison." At Jamison's questioning glance, his friend added, "Your daughter isn't exactly a vault when it comes to Miss Rory and how much time you are all spending together."

"Rory's…amazing. She's been so good for Hannah."

"She's been good for *you*. That's what's made the biggest change with Hannah. Kids are smarter than most adults give them credit for. She's taking her cues from you. If you're happy…"

"She's happy," Jamison finished, but he still wasn't sure he believed it. Or maybe he was too afraid to believe it. Too afraid he couldn't be this happy in San Francisco. That he wouldn't be this happy anywhere that Rory wasn't. "When we get back home…"

"What happens when you get back?"

"I don't know." Hannah had come so far, and maybe Ryder was right. Maybe he too had taken some serious strides when it came to being the kind of dad Hannah deserved, but without Rory…he didn't know if he could keep going in the right direction.

And yet… "Rory and I both agreed. After the wedding, we go our separate ways. No hard feelings." And no broken hearts.

It didn't take a genius to figure out a woman like Rory wanted more than a short-term fling. The woman lived and breathed weddings and had made her belief in romance and a love of a lifetime clear.

All of which asked the question of what the hell she was doing with him.

He was jaded, cynical, so wary of love he'd almost blown a longtime friendship because he wasn't ready to believe Ryder had found a love that would last beyond the honeymoon stage.

"So that's it?" Ryder twirled the now-empty mug around by the handle, and Jamison had the feeling his friend was thinking of chucking it at his head. "You meet this amazing woman and you're going to kiss her goodbye?"

Thoughts of kisses and goodbyes took him right back to Rory's bed that morning. Their relationship was temporary. It had to be. They'd agreed. And nothing this good could last.

He might not know much about fairy tales, but he knew what happened when the clock struck midnight. Their magical night would be over.

"What else am I supposed to do, Ryder? My life is back in San Francisco."

"Your *job* is back in San Francisco. Don't fool yourself by calling that a life. And if you're going to walk away from the best thing that ever happened to you, at least be honest about the reasons why."

"I wanna see Miss Rory!"

Jamison sucked in a breath, struggling for patience—with his daughter and with himself. *He* wanted to see Rory. He wanted to talk to her about his conversation with Ryder, to let her know he was back on track as Ryder's best man and as his best friend. He wanted to thank her for that... and for a whole lot more.

A handful of hours had passed since he'd left her bed that morning, and his eagerness to see her again surprised him. Worried him.

I won't miss you any less if you leave tomorrow.

He wasn't leaving tomorrow. The wedding was Saturday and his reservation lasted through the weekend, but he couldn't deny their time together was coming to an end.

He wasn't worried so much about missing Rory as he was about finding the strength to leave.

"Daddy!"

"Hannah—" Catching himself before he could snap at his daughter, he reminded her, "We can't see Rory right now. She's working."

She'd told him about the small afternoon wedding taking place in the rose garden. She'd spent most of the day yesterday preparing for the event in the hours leading up to the bachelorette party.

"But I wanna tell her about the sleepover! We played games and watched princess movies and Mrs. Kincaid doesn't know how to make smiley-face oatmeal, but she made smiley-face pancakes instead!"

Pancakes... Jamison closed his eyes with a sigh. That explained the sugar rush that had the little girl bouncing around their suite like the Energizer Bunny. "Why don't we go outside for a walk?"

"To the gazebo?" Hannah asked, her brown eyes wide.

What kind of father was he that he wanted to keep the memory of his night with Rory and the gazebo to himself? That he wasn't ready to see the magical spot in the full light of day?

"How about down to the beach instead?"

"Can we hop like bunnies?"

"If we do will it make you super sleepy so you take a big nap this afternoon?"

Hannah wrinkled her forehead. "I don't think bunnies take naps, Daddy."

"Of course they don't," he muttered as they headed out of the suite and into the hallway. All the time wondering at the odds of convincing his hopping daughter to be a giant sloth instead.

With Hannah tugging at his hand, Jamison stepped out of the lobby and into the sunny, cloudless day. A slight breeze blew off the ocean, cooling the sun's rays and adding a hint of sea salt to the air. He couldn't help giving a slight chuckle at the first thought that came to mind.

It really was the perfect day for a wedding.

As they headed down the path leading to the rocky shoreline, a familiar sound rang out in an unfamiliar setting. Reaching into his pocket, he pulled out his cell phone. He still kept the thing charged, carried it with him everywhere, even though away from the hotel, he rarely had reception.

In San Francisco he could count on one hand the number of times he didn't respond to a call within half an hour. Here, he'd gotten used to missed calls, lengthy messages and unreturned emails. Most of the time, he waited until the evening when Hannah was asleep to respond.

But not last night.

Last night, San Francisco and the law firm had been the last things on his mind.

But when he saw the name on the screen, he swiped his thumb to answer the call.

"Jeez, Porter, where the hell are you, the dark side of the moon?" his friend and fellow lawyer Donnie Lipinski demanded. "I've been trying to get ahold of you for days!"

"Sorry, cell coverage is pretty spotty around here."

His friend swore so loudly Jamison automatically looked to Hannah who was tugging on his arm. "Give me a second, will you, Hannah Banana?"

"I wanna see Rory!"

"In a minute."

Hannah dropped to her butt in a pout, arms crossed

over her chest and bottom lip stuck out as far as it would go. "Count to one hundred and I'll be ready to go," he promised.

Lifting the phone back to his ear, Jamison caught Donnie midstream. "...middle-of-nowhere vacation?"

"One! Two! Three!"

Hannah's counting reached an almost-obnoxious volume, and Jamison covered his ear with his free hand. "I'm here for a friend's wedding," he reminded Donnie.

"A wedding lasts what, a day? Maybe two if you get suckered into going to the rehearsal dinner. You've been there almost two weeks." Lowering his voice, he added, "Do you know how many clients Martinez and Harris have met with in two weeks? And word has it Martinez grabbed the Langstone account."

Jamison took his turn swearing, though he was careful to do it under his breath. The firm encouraged competition between its employees, with a "may the best man win" mentality. Langstone Communications was a coveted account, one he'd thought he had a good shot of landing... two weeks ago.

"They're pushing hard toward the finish line, and you're still stuck in the blocks, man."

Hannah finally reached twenty, and Jamison dropped his free hand. "I needed to come here, Don. It was important."

"More important than your career?" Incredulity filled his friend's voice, as if he couldn't image what could top that. The thrill of the chase, the euphoria of landing the biggest, brightest account had been a rush beyond anything Jamison could imagine.

But he never could have imagined a woman like Rory. Making love to her, kissing her, hell, even making her smile made him happier than any client, any account ever had.

But he'd been a lawyer for years, and everything he felt for Rory was so new, so fragile. And hadn't the personal relationships in his life taught him that nothing lasted? His feelings for Rory would fade, and he would need the comfort, the security of his career to fall back on. "I'll be back on Monday," he told Donnie.

His friend snorted. "Who knows how many accounts your competition will have brought in by then? Forget the promotion—you'll be lucky to still have a job."

Jamison opened his mouth to retort, but Donnie had hung up. As much as he loved modern technology, what he wouldn't give for an old-fashioned phone he could slam back into its cradle right now. Instead, he dropped the cell into his pocket.

He wasn't in danger of losing his job. Donnie was busting his balls with that comment. But the promotion... Yeah, he had a feeling he could kiss that goodbye.

You're destined for bigger things, Jamison. Never forget that. Never settle for less when you can take more.

His mother's words echoed through his thoughts as he ran a hand through his hair. He didn't want to end up like her—grasping and grappling to hold on to something fleeting that had already passed him by. He'd worked hard for that partnership, dammit! He'd put in the long hours, the nights, the weekends. He'd given his all! He'd sacrificed—

He'd sacrificed his marriage just to be considered.

What would he be expected to sacrifice to win it all?

Reaching into his pocket, he powered down his phone.

"Hey, Hannah—" His shoes crunched on the loose gravel as he turned. "Are you ready—"

His words—his heart—stopped at the sight of the empty path behind him.

Chapter Fourteen

"Hannah!" He called her name, but this was no game of hide-and-seek with his daughter giggling, hardly out of sight, a few feet away. She was gone. "Hannah!"

He froze, unsure where to go, what to do…but then he knew.

Hannah had gone to find Rory.

He had to believe that, just like he had to believe he'd find the two of them together. He couldn't bear to think anything else. The rose garden wasn't far from the front entrance of the hotel, and he ran the distance in record time. His heart pounded in his ears so loudly he could barely hear the strains of a harp floating on the air. But that sound and the activity around the wedding had to have drawn Hannah to the one spot where Rory was sure to be.

She *had* to be there.

He stopped short as he rounded a curve, his shoes skidding beneath him. Two dozen people filled the white chairs lining the lawn, all focused on the couple standing beneath the delicate arched trellis. He scanned the crowd but didn't see Rory. Didn't see Hannah.

The bride's tremulous voice barely carried to the back row. It was all Jamison could do to not hold his peace and to start calling out for his daughter…

"Psst, Daddy."

At first, he thought he'd imaged the faint whisper blending in with the breeze rustling through the trees. That the sound had come from one of the guests, murmuring under their breath about the bride or her dress or the ceremony. But then he heard it again.

"*Psst*, Daddy! Over here!"

The call was louder this time, enough for a few heads in the back row to turn his way. Jamison paid them no attention as he scanned the garden off to his right, where he finally spotted golden curls amid the verdant green bushes and red roses.

"Hannah."

Too relieved to have found her, Jamison didn't care about making a scene as he wound his way through the fragrant bushes until he could crouch down at his daughter's side and yank her into his arms. "Hannah, what are you doing? You know better than to go off without me!"

Her lower lip sticking out in a pout, she said, "I wanted to see Miss Rory's wedding."

"Hannah, this isn't Rory's wedding."

"Uh-huh," his daughter insisted. "See? She's right over there."

Jamison followed his daughter's outstretched hand and spotted Rory standing off to the side. His breath caught at the sight of her—her hands clasped in front of her chest and a beaming smile on her face. No one was supposed to be more beautiful than a bride on her wedding day, but as far as Jamison was concerned, no woman was more beautiful than Rory—ever.

Her outfit—a pale yellow sweater and narrow cream-colored skirt—was a little more sedate and businesslike than the flowery dresses she usually wore, and her hair was caught back in a professional-looking bun. But nothing she wore could ever downplay how stunning she was, and that was only on the outside.

Her inner beauty—her kindness, her compassion, her caring—that would shine through even in the darkest moments. Wasn't that why his first instinct when Hannah was missing was to run to Rory? Yes, he'd figured that Hannah had gone to find her, but even more than that, *he* had wanted to find Rory. To have her tell him that everything would be all right. To make it all better, the way she'd made everything in his life better.

And he couldn't help wondering if he was only fooling himself. If his feelings for Rory were destined to fade, then why did they grow stronger every time they were together?

"You know, we've never had a Hillcrest House wedding crashed before." Up until a minute ago, Rory wasn't sure how she'd feel the next time she saw Jamison. She hadn't imagined she'd be fighting laughter, but she found herself doing just that as she confronted the guilty-looking duo crouched at the back of the rose garden.

"Look, Daddy! It's Miss Rory!"

"So I see." His silver gaze swept over Rory with an intimacy and something...*more* that left her trembling in her sensible shoes. The wedding guests were focused on the bride and groom, but it still wouldn't do for her to launch herself into Jamison's arms in the middle of the ceremony. Even if she wanted to...

The soloist had started singing about the power of love,

providing enough ambient noise for Rory to feel comfortable murmuring, "You're not planning to rush the aisle when the pastor asks if anyone objects to this wedding, are you?"

"I wouldn't be anywhere near this ceremony if a certain someone—" he landed a pointed gaze on his oblivious daughter "—hadn't decided she wanted to come to your wedding."

"*My* wedding?"

"That's what she said."

"So this is my fault?"

"Clearly. My daughter is obsessed."

"With weddings?"

"I wish it were that simple."

As much as Rory wanted to deny she was a complication in Jamison's life, it was hard to do when his daughter scrambled over to take her hand. "Did you see the flower girl, Miss Rory?" Hannah asked. "She had a blue basket for her flowers and ribbons in her hair and she went like this!" Throwing out an arm, she exuberantly mimicked the other girl's flower-tossing technique.

Raising an eyebrow, Jamison murmured, "Was she throwing rose petals or a ninety-five-mile-an-hour fastball?"

"You hush," Rory scolded under her breath but with a smile. "I did see her, Hannah. But you don't have to lurk in the bushes."

"Are you sure?" Jamison asked. "As you pointed out, we aren't guests."

"You're my guests. Wedding coordinator's prerogative. Besides, it's not like the bride and groom will notice."

The young couple only had eyes for each other, and Rory led Jamison and Hannah closer in time for her favorite part.

"As long as we both shall live."

The tall, thin pastor beamed as he announced, "I now pronounce you husband and wife. You may kiss your bride."

The guests burst into applause as the groom cupped his bride's face and pressed his lips to hers in a kiss that was as much of a vow as the words he'd spoken.

It was a moment that would never get old, no matter how many weddings she witnessed, and one that never failed to bring tears to her eyes. The love, the hope, the promise of a future where two lives joined together as one… Her heart was filled with so much emotion, she couldn't stop some of it from overflowing.

She was struggling somewhat blindly with the clasp on the tiny clutch hanging from her wrist when Jamison's hand flashed in front of her face. Rory blinked, dislodging a tear or two, when she saw what he was holding out to her.

Snatching the tissue, she touched it to the corners of her eyes, trying not to do too much damage to her makeup. "Don't make fun. I always cry at weddings."

"Tears of joy that all the hard work is over?"

"No!" Her protest faded into laughter as she admitted, "Well, maybe. A little."

"I've also started carrying wet wipes if you really feel the need to break down."

"Hmm, those would have come in handy at the rodeo. Goes to show you're learning."

A muscle twitched in his jaw as he glanced down at his daughter. "She got away from me, Rory. I was on the phone. I swear I only turned away for a second, and when I looked back…"

She could only imagine the panic that must have raced like wildfire through Jamison's veins. Hannah's disappearance, even for a few minutes, must have taken him back to those long, agonizing months when his daughter had been gone and he'd had no idea when or if he'd see her again.

"Look at her now, Jamison." The little girl was focused on the ceremony taking place, throwing her arm out and tossing imaginary flower petals. "She's fine."

"No thanks to me."

"Jamison…"

"I don't know if I can do this, Rory. To be the kind of father Hannah deserves. I've already made so many mistakes. I wasn't there when she needed me most—"

"You're here now."

"But when I get back home…"

Jamison raked a hand through his hair. How was he supposed to juggle being a full-time father and full-time lawyer when he couldn't keep an eye on his daughter during a five-minute phone call?

"You can do this." Rory caught his hand in hers, her blue eyes shining with the faith that had been there from the start. A faith that made him believe he could do anything…as long as she was by his side.

"I can't—I can't do this without you. I don't want to do this without you," he blurted out. "I don't want to say goodbye."

"What?"

Pulling Rory into his arms, he pressed his forehead against hers. "After Ryder and Lindsay's wedding, I don't want that to be the end."

"Jamison, what—what are you saying?"

"Rory, I—we can make this work, right? Somehow?" He heard the desperation in his own voice but couldn't make the words stop spilling over one another. "We can call and text and maybe I can make it up here for Labor Day weekend…"

"Labor Day," she echoed weakly.

"We're good together, Rory. I want to give our relation-ship a chance."

Reaching up, she traced her fingers along his jaw, her touch tender, but her smile as sad as he'd ever seen. "Labor Day is a holiday, Jamison. Not a relationship."

"Rory—"

"We agreed, remember? When this is over, we say goodbye."

He stepped back, his hands dropping to his sides. She was turning him down? Sticking to the rules as if this was some kind of game they were playing?

"You can't mean that."

"I know you're scared, Jamison."

"Scared?"

"Of taking care of Hannah on your own."

Scared? Hell, he was terrified! But that wasn't why he wanted Rory in his life…was it? Okay, maybe his words had come across like a knee-jerk reaction to the panic rush-ing through him, but he'd still meant them.

"Miss Rory," Hannah piped in, breaking the moment. "Are you crying?"

Lifting her chin and turning her face away from him, she murmured, "Just a little." More now than when the couple had spoken their vows a few minutes earlier.

Vows joining two lives as one, to have and to hold, from this day forward… Vows of forever.

Not for a weekend. Not for a holiday.

Was he really surprised Rory had turned him down when he'd offered so much less than she deserved?

Gazing up at the two adults, the little girl said, "You hafta kiss her, Daddy. Like when my tummy didn't feel good. You kissed me and the next day—" Hannah threw her arms out wide "—I was all better."

"Listen to your daughter, Jamison." Rory offered him

another sad yet tender smile. "You can do this. You already know how to make it all better."

If this was better, Jamison thought as he followed his daughter's instructions and gave Rory a heartbreaking kiss that already felt too much like goodbye, he'd sure as hell hate to see what he could do to make things worse.

Hannah twirled back and forth in the middle of the bridal shop, the full skirt swishing around her knees. The cream-colored taffeta with its burgundy velvet sash and hint of matching lace at the hem fit perfectly. "Do I look like a real princess?"

"The prettiest princess ever." Rory and Hannah had met up with Lindsay at the shop to double-check the alterations and pick up the dress. The little girl beamed back, and her joy was enough to bring the sting of tears to Rory's eyes.

The days leading up to Ryder and Lindsay's wedding were the best and worst of Rory's life. She lived each day they were together—whether it was window-shopping in town, having a picnic at the gazebo, buying clothes for Hannah. But a part of her mourned the moment she closed her eyes, knowing each morning meant one day closer to Jamison and Hannah leaving.

But, oh, those nights…when Jamison pulled her into his arms, determined to remind her just how *good* they were together…

Making love with him was so magical, so amazing, Rory almost gave in. Almost agreed to what he offered. To late-night phone calls, video chats between meetings, the occasional stolen weekend. And she would have—if he'd told her he loved her.

"I think I'm the one who's supposed to tear up at this part," Lindsay said gently as she handed Rory a tissue once Hannah went to change back into her regular clothes.

"Although I can't blame you. If I didn't know better, I wouldn't even think that was the same girl from just a few weeks ago."

Rory dabbed at her eyes. "Time here in Clearville has done wonders for her."

"*You* have done wonders for her. For her and for Jamison."

She crumpled the tissue in her hand. Oh, how she wanted to believe Jamison had changed but, forcing a laugh, she said, "The same Jamison who wanted Ryder to get a prenup?"

Lindsay gave her a chiding look along with another tissue. "The same Jamison who apologized to Ryder and to me. He was looking out for Ryder—I can't really blame him for that."

He was a good friend, a good father, a good man... Was it any wonder she'd fallen so in love with him?

"We agreed. When our time together is over, we say goodbye."

"Well, it's not like it was written in stone. You can change your mind. Something tells me you *have* changed your mind."

"It doesn't matter if I've changed my mind. Not if Jamison hasn't changed his."

"And you're so sure he hasn't?"

I can't do this without you.

She'd heard it before from grateful brides and grooms. How Rory was the glue bringing together all the thousands of tiny details that made up a wedding. How they never could have managed it all on their own. But then the big day was over, and the newly married couples went on with their lives.

It would be the same for Jamison and Hannah. They would go back to San Francisco, back to their lives.

Without her.

"You're sure he hasn't changed his mind?" Lindsay pressed.

"He—he said he doesn't want our relationship to end after the wedding."

Lindsay's brows shot to her hairline. "But that's huge!"

"It's not—he said we're good together…" Aware of Hannah on the other side of the curtain, she mouthed, "As in—in bed."

An impish smile played around her friend's lips. "And are you?"

"Not helping!"

"Look, Rory." Turning serious, Lindsay said, "I can only imagine how Jamison had to bury all his feelings, all his emotions simply to get through a single day when Hannah was missing. And considering how long she was gone, that's digging pretty deep."

Rory's heart hurt for all he had gone through. "I know."

"So how close do you think you have to get for a man whose feelings are buried that far down to admit he needs you—even a little?"

Chapter Fifteen

"Last chance, man," Ryder warned. "Speak now or forever hold your peace."

The groomsmen had gathered in a small room at the back of the hotel to get ready for the ceremony. Standing in front of the full-length mirror, Ryder was straightening his bow tie for the tenth time. Jamison might have thought his friend was nervous if not for the huge grin on the other man's face. "Still don't know why we couldn't have gone with clip-ons."

"Leave the stupid thing alone, will you? It's fine. And the only speaking I'll be doing is when I give the best man's toast."

"I'm not talking about that. I'm talking about…her." Ryder tipped his head to the right, and Jamison felt his heart jump to his throat, pressing against his own too-tight tie.

Rory had slipped in the back. Like at the previous wedding, her dress was simple, understated, a sleeveless beige-colored sheath she probably thought would help her fade into the background. As if that could ever be possible.

She smiled at Robbie, giving the boy a high five when he showed her the rings carefully tied to the pillow he would carry. She adjusted Drew's bow tie, helped Bryce with a cuff link and made Lindsay's and Ryder's fathers laugh at something she said.

It was ridiculous to feel jealous, but he was. Of all of them. Of the ease and laughter they were sharing with Rory. An ease that had gone out of their relationship as the tension of a ticking clock marked each moment they were together.

"No hard feelings, right?" Ryder mocked after taking one look at whatever was written on his face.

"I told her I'd changed my mind." But he knew now what he'd only started to figure out then. It wasn't his mind Rory needed him to change.

Seeming to come to the same conclusion, Ryder reached over and gave the back of his head a light tap. "Did you tell her you love her?"

From the very beginning, from the first moment they met, Rory had told him she was a woman who lived and breathed love, romance and happily-ever-after. Little wonder she'd turned his half-baked, half-assed offer down.

Never settle for less.

Maybe his mother had had one thing right after all. And maybe it wasn't too late to grab hold of more.

"One final touch!" Rory announced as she faced the groomsmen. They all looked so handsome, from Robbie to his grandfathers, but Jamison... She didn't know if her heart could take seeing him so suave, so stunning, so *San Francisco*.

If Hannah had changed into a girl Rory hardly recognized, well this—this was a man she didn't know. The other groomsmen looked somewhat uncomfortable in the formal wear, clothes that didn't quite fit despite quality tailoring. But Jamison... The tuxedo suited him, and why not? This was who he was. Jamison Porter, hotshot corporate lawyer.

Her hands trembled as she reached for the white florist's box. The pair who had brought the flowers were putting the final touches on the centerpieces in the ballroom and had asked if she might deliver the boutonnieres. She handed out a single burgundy rosebud to each of them, leaving Jamison for last.

He caught her wrist as she reached out to hand him the flower. "I think I could use some help."

Ryder muttered, "You got that right," as the groom turned toward the mirror, but the words hardly registered. Her pulse pounded in her ears as Jamison's fingers stroked the underside of her arm.

You can do this, Rory. It's part of the job.

The pep talk didn't steady her nerves, but it was enough to jolt her into action. She slid her fingers beneath the lapel, doing her best to ignore the strength of his chest against her knuckles, the body heat transferred to the smooth fabric.

"We need to talk."

She shook her head. "Not a good idea when I'm pointing a sharp instrument at your heart."

His chuckle vibrated against her fingers as she finally, finally slid the pearl-tipped pin into place. "After," he qualified. "Tonight."

It would have to be tonight. Because there wouldn't be any *after* tomorrow.

Rory didn't know how she made it through the wedding. Hannah was the perfect little flower girl, practically skipping down the lace runner toward the gazebo, tossing the petals up in the air and then giggling as they rained down over her. The guests laughed along with her only to fall reverently silent as Lindsay stepped into view.

She was a beautiful bride, but it was the love shining on her face that was truly breathtaking. And Ryder—the groom had laughed and joked his way through the rehearsal dinner the night before, but this time he was the one Jamison had to hand a handkerchief to as Lindsay walked down the aisle.

Rory couldn't meet Jamison's gaze, not if she had any hope of smiling her way through the ceremony. She'd told the truth when she said she always cried at weddings, and if the tears streaming down her face when the couple spoke the words *to have and to hold from this day forward* weren't tears of joy, well, no one else had to know.

"Did you see me, Miss Rory? Did you see me throw the flowers?"

Rory managed a genuine smile as Hannah raced into the ballroom, darting between the white-covered tables and fancifully dressed wedding guests. She'd been double-checking with the band, the servers and the bartender while the bridal party finished with the pictures. Everything was running smoothly, something Rory normally appreciated, but tonight, she could have used a minor emergency. Something to get her mind off the best man.

She wanted to believe Lindsay could be right, that Jamison cared for her more than he was able to admit. But she was afraid of fooling herself again, of building another relationship on a lie—this time one of her own making.

Bending down, she scooped Hannah into a hug and spun her around. "You were the best flower girl ever! I am so proud of you."

As Rory set her back on the ground, the little girl

reached up to touch the crown of flowers circling her blond curls. Her eyes were wide as she said, "There were *lots* of people!"

They'd talked about that at the rehearsal dinner. How the empty chairs would be filled with wedding guests watching her walk down the aisle. "Was that scary?"

"Kinda scary. But then I saw my daddy waiting for me, and I wasn't scareded anymore."

Rory wasn't sure what made her turn at that moment, but as she did, Jamison walked through the ballroom's carved double doors. His chestnut hair gleamed in the wall sconces' warm lighting, and she knew the instant he spotted them. The joy, the anticipation...

How many times had she seen it before—on the face of a groom waiting for his bride? Nerves trembled in her stomach, and Rory wrapped her arms around her waist. Not trying to still the overwhelming, frightening emotions swelling up inside her, but embracing them instead.

Jamison was waiting for her...and maybe she didn't have to be afraid anymore.

Hillcrest House's dark-paneled ballroom was decked out in all its finery for the reception. White tablecloths covered a dozen or so round tables. Each chair had a large bow tied at the back. Burgundy and cream roses sparkled in cut-glass vases beneath the crystal chandelier, and a matching garland draped the front of the band's raised platform stage, the cash bar and the tables offering a mix of appetizers and crudités.

But for all the romantic touches and tasteful decorations, he could see only Rory. She might as well have been the only woman in the room. The only woman in the world. The only woman for him...

Their gazes locked, and even from across the room he

could see a slight shudder shook her slender body at the powerful impact.

That's it. You can do it. One foot in front of the other.

But this time it wasn't Hannah who needed the silent encouragement. He wove his way through the round tables and milled with wedding guests, his heart thundering in his chest. Past a growing collection of brightly wrapped wedding gifts, past the towering three-tiered wedding cake, past the photographer setting up to capture the moment when Lindsay and Ryder walked into the room as husband and wife…

So focused on the beautiful wedding coordinator, he barely heard his name over the romantic ballad being played by the band.

"Jamison!"

But when a hand clamped down on his shoulder, he turned and did a quick double take, hardly believing what he was seeing. "Louisa? Greg?" He stared at his in-laws. "What the—what are you doing here?"

His beefy, sterling-haired father-in-law blustered about missing Hannah and wanting to see their little flower girl. Jamison raised a brow at his mother-in-law, wanting to know the real story.

Blonde and trim with classic features she had passed down to her daughter and granddaughter, Louisa lifted her chin. "We want to make sure Hannah is being properly cared for while she's here."

"Properly—is this because she got sick at the rodeo? Good Lord, Louisa! Hannah is fine! See for yourself."

Waving a hand toward his daughter, he expected Louisa's rigid stance to loosen once she spotted her granddaughter. Instead, the woman froze, her expression icing over until Jamison half expected her to shatter. He followed her chilly gaze, his own reaction completely different as he saw Hannah and Rory together.

Standing on the edge of the parquet dance floor, Rory held Hannah's hand overhead as the little girl spun around, making her full skirts flare out from her skinny legs. Their combined laughter rippled through the elegant ballroom, washing over him like a warm wave.

"I take it that's your wedding coordinator."

"That's Rory McClaren, yes." Jamison sighed, trying to hold on to his patience.

She's lost her daughter. It can't be easy for her to see Hannah so happy with a woman who isn't her mother, who isn't Monica.

Rubbing his forehead, he said, "I still can't believe you came all this way when we'll be home on Monday."

"That isn't what Hannah said."

"What?"

"She said you didn't want to say goodbye."

Jamison swallowed a curse. Clearly he needed to pay more attention to the conversations his daughter was having with her grandparents. Maybe he shouldn't have been surprised by his mother-in-law's overreaction, but he wouldn't have expected Greg to go along with it. "And you came all this way because of that?"

"So are you saying it's not true? That you're not planning to come back?"

"My plans are none of your business."

"You're a fool, Jamison Porter."

"Excuse me?"

"You've been here just over two weeks, and you've already let that woman get her hooks into you. Worse, you let her get to you through your daughter."

"Now, Louisa—"

"Don't!" She raised a silencing hand, and her husband

took a step back as if to avoid the blow. "This has to be said."

"No, it doesn't." Steel undercut Jamison's words as he stepped closer and lowered his voice. "If you're here for Hannah, that's fine. But my relationship with Rory is my business. You don't know her—"

"Oh, and you do? Did you know the hotel is losing money and that one of those massive hotel chains has made an offer to buy it?"

Jamison glanced at his father-in-law, who merely shrugged. "Word gets around."

"Right. Probably something you heard at the club," he added sarcastically. "Even if that is true, it doesn't have anything to do with me and Rory."

"Oh, really. So you don't think she'd be interested in a wealthy lawyer who could save her family business?"

"She isn't like that."

"This isn't even the first time she's latched onto a rich man. Did you know that? She went after her boss's son at her last job."

Jamison swore under his breath. "Yes, she told me, Louisa, but who the hell told you? You have no right—"

"I have every right where my granddaughter is concerned!"

"Nana! Papa!" Hannah's happy voice bubbled over the harsh whispers, and Jamison forced himself to take a deep breath and a step back as she rushed over. "Look, Miss Rory, it's my nana and papa!"

Rory laughed as Hannah tugged her over toward the older couple. She looked so happy, so beautiful. He wished for a way to warn her Louisa was on the warpath.

Louisa was wrong about Rory. He was sure of it. He trusted Rory. He trusted her with his daughter. He trusted

her with his heart. He couldn't be so wrong about her...
couldn't be so wrong a second time.

"Welcome to Hillcrest House," Rory said as Greg lifted
his granddaughter for a kiss. "Hannah has told me a lot
about you."

Louisa's greeting was less exuberant, patting Hannah on
the back as the little girl leaned over for a hug. "Yes, well,
our granddaughter has had quite a bit to say about you, too."

Picking up on the tension, Rory crossed an arm over her
chest as she fingered the pendant she was wearing. "All
good, I hope," she said with a tentative smile.

"Hannah, my girl, why don't we go take a look at that
big ol' wedding cake?" Greg suggested, leaving a heavy
silence behind as he and Hannah walked away.

"It's funny how small the world can be sometimes,"
Louisa stated, but Jamison knew he wouldn't find any-
thing amusing in what she had to say. "I used to live in
LA, and it turns out we have a mutual acquaintance—the
Van Meters. You know them, don't you, Ms. McClaren?"

Rory went pale, the color leaching from her face, as she
took a stumbling step backward.

"In fact," Louisa continued, "the Van Meters hired the
company you used to work for to stage their house. Jo-
hanna Van Meter has wonderful taste. She was devastated
to realize some of her priceless antiques had been stolen."

Ignoring the uneasy feeling worming its way through
his stomach, Jamison demanded, "Louisa, what are you
talking about?"

"Ms. McClaren knows. Would you like to tell him...
or should I?"

This was a nightmare. It had to be. Standing in front
of Jamison as his mother-in-law blamed her for stealing
from the Van Meters.

This couldn't be happening and yet—

Rory had to swallow a burst of hysterical laughter. God, Louisa Stilton even bore a slight resemblance to Pamela Worthington. And the look of disdain—well, that was identical.

"Rory." Jamison grabbed her arm, shaking her from the dreamlike paralysis that, no matter how far or how fast she ran, she could never escape. "Tell me this isn't true."

He loomed over her, a commanding presence in the dark tuxedo he wore so well, and she was struck again that this was the real Jamison Porter. Not the hard-body handyman with paint splattered on his jeans and T-shirt. Not the tortured soul who'd made love to her by the gazebo. Not the laughing father who'd played hide-and-seek with his daughter. This was Jamison Porter, Esquire—a man of wealth and power and status.

One who suddenly reminded Rory how it felt to be powerless.

"Tell me!"

Shock had wiped all reaction from his expression as Louisa spit out her accusations, but now Rory could see the emotion creeping back in. She could see the questions; she could see the doubt.

Trust me, she silently pleaded. *Believe me... Love me.*

But he'd never said the words. She wanted forever, and he wanted a weekend. A holiday. A fairy tale...

But this was one without a happy ending. "What do you want me to say, Jamison? That it's all true? That thousands of dollars' worth of belongings disappeared from a house I staged? That I was fired when pictures, receipts, transactions from online auctions were found on my computer at work?"

Tears clogged her throat and burned her eyes. "Fine, I'll tell you. It's true. It's all true."

* * *

"Go ahead and say it," Rory told her cousin the next morning as she sank into one of the chairs in her office. "I know you want to, and I deserve it."

Evie had pulled Rory out of the lobby on the verge of a breakdown. She'd overheard one of the porters speaking with a new hotel guest as he wheeled a loaded luggage cart past her. "You're lucky we had a family check out early. The Bluebell suite is one of our best…"

The Bluebell…

Gone. Jamison was gone. He'd already left. Without giving her a chance to explain. Without giving her a chance to say she loved him before saying goodbye…

Maybe it wouldn't have mattered. Maybe their relationship was destined to end from the start.

Evie handed her a box of tissues before circling behind the refuge of her desk. "You're right. You deserve to hear this…so here goes." She took a deep breath. "I'm proud of you."

"Yeah, right." Rory pulled out one tissue and then another. "Real proud."

How many times had Evie warned her not to mix business and pleasure? She still hadn't learned the lesson and totally deserved an *I told you so* from her know-better cousin.

"I am. It wasn't that long ago that you and Peter broke up."

"And here I am—" she waved a tissue in surrender "—four months later, stupidly falling in love again."

"Bravely falling in love again." Evie glanced away, swallowed hard and glanced back again. Her professional demeanor dropped away, leaving her looking vulnerable, raw, real… "It's been two years since my engagement, and I haven't had the courage to let a man close since."

"I didn't think you wanted a relationship," Rory

murmured, embarrassed she'd been so caught up in her own troubles that she hadn't seen the loneliness her cousin tried so hard to hide.

Evie gave a short laugh. "It's a lot easier to tell yourself you don't want what you can't have."

"But you could… You're smart, beautiful, sophisticated. Any man would be lucky to have you in his life."

But Evie was already shaking her head. "It doesn't matter whether some guy would or wouldn't get lucky with me. I can't bring myself to put any kind of faith into a relationship, and what guy is going to put up with a woman who doesn't trust him?"

"Maybe one who understands what you've gone through? One who's willing to earn your trust?"

"No one wants to work that hard."

"Someone will. The one man who's worth it will."

Evie shook her head again. "Never mind all that. This isn't about me, anyway. It's about you and the way you never let life get you down. That even after everything that's happened, you still believe in love and romance and happily-ever-after."

This time, it was Rory who shook her head as she wiped the tears from her eyes. "I don't know about that…"

"I do. I know you, and I know you won't let some corporate lawyer jerk change who you are."

"He's not a jerk," Rory murmured. He was the man she loved. The handyman, the lover, the father, even the lawyer—all were different sides of the man she'd fallen in love with.

And maybe Lindsay had been right. Maybe Rory had touched something inside Jamison, but she hadn't reached deep enough. She hadn't been able to grab hold of the trust he'd buried so deeply, and without that…

"See?" Evie announced triumphantly. "You still have

faith in people. That's what makes you so good at your job. I know we don't always see eye to eye, and that sometimes it seems like we're too different to agree on much of anything. But the truth is, your strengths are my weaknesses, and vice versa. And that means if we work together, we're pretty damn unstoppable."

"I had no idea you felt so strongly about the hotel after… everything."

"The truth is, I haven't let myself feel much of anything in a long, long time. But this is where I belong. Where we belong."

Where we belong… "Now if we could get Chance to come back."

"That would be the icing on the wedding cake. But for now, it's just the two of us, and heaven help any guy who gets in our way."

Chapter Sixteen

"Hannah, you need to sit still." Jamison struggled to cling to his patience as he tried to figure out how to keep hold of the brush with one hand, the neon-green rubber band with the other and his squirming daughter with his third, nonexistent hand.

"That's too hard!" The little girl cringed away from the soft-bristled brush as though he held a branding iron to her head. "It hurts!"

"I'm trying not to pull your hair, but you have all these tangles." How was it that every strand of his daughter's blond hair seemed to be tied in knots? How was it that his whole freaking life seemed to be tied into one giant knot since he'd left Clearville?

As if reading his thoughts, Hannah argued, "Rory did it better."

Jamison wished he could convince himself his daughter was simply talking about the uneven, frizzy ponytail springing from the top of her head, but he couldn't. Rory had made everything better.

"We've talked about this, Hannah." And they had. Incessantly in the week since they'd been home.

Hannah's frown and saucer-size pout told him what she thought about that, but like it or not, Jamison gave a final tug to tighten the haphazard ponytail before grabbing his briefcase and Hannah's backpack and ushering her out the door.

"I don't wanna go to school."

"You like school," he reminded her—or maybe he was trying to convince himself—as he belted his daughter into the booster seat in the back of his SUV. "And after school, your grandmother is going to take you for a girls' day out."

Jamison didn't know what that entailed and didn't want to know. He was grateful to his in-laws, he really was. But by giving in and having them watch Hannah in the afternoons, he was playing into Louisa's hands. He might have viewed it as a short-term solution, but he didn't fool himself that she had given up on her long-term plan.

She needs you to fight for her.

Rory's voice rang in his memory along with the stricken look on her face at the wedding. She had needed him to fight for her…and he'd failed miserably. She hadn't stolen those items, no matter what the evidence might have said.

And if she'd told him what had happened, if she'd trusted him with what had happened, he would have been prepared for his in-laws' accusations. Instead he'd been blindsided by the secret Rory had kept. And for a moment, when faced with the realization that maybe he didn't know her as well as he thought, that maybe—like with Monica—he didn't know what she was capable of, he'd shut down.

He'd retreated back into the shell that had surrounded him in the final months of his marriage and during the desperate, agonizing weeks when Monica and Hannah were missing.

Somehow, he'd found his way back home, where the familiarity of work waited. Where Hannah had started preschool and where, for a while, Jamison had thought he was going to have to enroll himself after spending the first few sessions seated in a humiliatingly tiny chair beside his daughter, who refused to let him leave.

He'd interviewed almost a dozen nannies, but none of them had been right. None of them had been... Rory. He couldn't see any of them knowing how to turn a boring breakfast into smiley-face oatmeal. He couldn't imagine any of them showing the patience Rory had when Hannah asked her to watch her practice walking down the aisle for the twentieth time. He couldn't picture any of them healing old hurts, breaking through a protective shell, making him feel again...

And that was the real problem. Not that those women couldn't be the nanny Hannah needed, but because they couldn't be the woman *Jamison* needed. The woman he loved.

"I don't want a girls' day with Nana! I want Rory!" Hannah's petulant demand so closely echoed the one in his heart that it was all Jamison could do not to snap at his daughter.

Instead, he finished buckling her in and climbed into the driver's seat. "We can't always have what we want," he muttered under his breath as he jammed the key into the ignition.

Traffic into the city was a tangled mess, with cars locked bumper to bumper on the freeway. Not that that stopped other vehicles from trying to weave through the lanes, cutting off drivers and jamming on their brakes. When a red sports car nearly took off his front bumper while slicing toward one of the exits, Jamison swore and slammed on the horn.

Hannah's scream nearly sent his heart through his throat. "Hannah, what—"

"Don't go, Daddy! Don't go!"

Glancing into the rearview mirror, he saw the tears streaming down Hannah's chubby cheeks. The hysteria in her voice told Jamison this was more than worry about him dropping her off at school.

Taking the same exit as the sports car, he pulled off into the first parking lot he came to. Hannah was still crying when he climbed into the back. Strapped in her booster seat, she reached out, clinging to him as tightly as she could.

"Hannah, honey…" Jamison undid the buckles at her chest and pulled her into his lap. "I'm right here, and I'm not going anywhere."

Another horn blasted from the nearby freeway, and Hannah cringed again. Swearing under his breath, Jamison asked, "Did I scare you when I honked the horn? I'm so sorry, sweetheart."

Her chin tucked against her chest, Jamison could barely make out the words his daughter was saying. "What did you say, Hannah? What was that about Mommy?"

"Mommy was mad on the phone. She said we weren't coming home. Never, ever, ever again."

His fight with Monica… The accident… Jamison had heard the whole thing. How stupid of him not to realize that, sitting in the back seat, *Hannah* had also heard her parents' final, fateful fight. "Oh, Hannah…"

"I tol' her I wanted to go home. I wanted to see you and Nana and Papa. Mommy said I had to stay with her." Tears streamed down her face. "But I told her I didn't want to, so she went to heaven without me."

"Hannah, sweetie. Mommy—Mommy didn't want to leave you." His heart broke at the thought of his little girl thinking her mother had left because of something she'd said, something she'd done. "It was an accident."

The words lifted a weight from his chest, and he sucked in a deep breath. The first he'd taken without the crushing guilt pressing on him since the day he walked into an empty house and realized Hannah and Monica were gone. They'd both made mistakes, but he was lucky. He had the chance to make up for them, while Monica—

"She loved you." The words Rory had spoken that night in the gazebo, words he hadn't been willing to embrace, came back to him. "She loved you so much, and she wanted you to be safe so that you could come back to me and Nana and Papa. Because we missed you."

"Like I miss Mommy?"

"Yeah, like that."

"I don't want you to miss me anymore."

"Neither do I, Hannah."

Not when he'd already missed so much. "What do you say we play hooky today?"

"I don't know that game."

Jamison laughed. "It's a fun game. One where you skip school and I skip work and we have a daddy-daughter day."

"Really? Then what do we do?" Hannah's eyes lit up with hope, and for a moment, Jamison panicked. He didn't know any more about a father-daughter day than he did about a girls' day out.

All you have to do is be there for her.

"We can go to the park and have a picnic. We can color in your coloring books and then watch one of your videos."

"An' have ice cream and popcorn?"

"Maybe ice cream *or* popcorn," he offered, not wanting a repeat of the night at the rodeo. "Does that sound like fun?"

"That sounds like the best! I love you, Daddy."

Breathing the words against his daughter's blond curls, he murmured, "I love you, too, Hannah Banana."

It wouldn't always be so simple. But maybe it wasn't always as hard as he made it out to be. Maybe he did have a chance of making things right…and not just with Hannah.

He'd finished belting Hannah into the booster seat when the sound of his phone ringing jarred him from his hopeful thoughts. His boss's name flashed across the screen, but Jamison didn't immediately reach into the front seat for the device.

"Are you okay now, Hannah?"

His daughter nodded, but even he could see she wasn't as excited as she'd been seconds before. "I bet Miss Rory would like to go on our picnic."

"I bet she would, too."

Slipping back into the driver's seat, Jamison reached for his phone. "Mr. Spears."

"Jamison, good of you to pick up."

He heard the dry reproach in his boss's voice but refused to make excuses. "I'm glad you called. I was about to phone in to let you know I won't be coming in today."

"Jamison—"

"I'm spending the day with my daughter." Catching Hannah's gaze in the rearview mirror, he shot her a wink.

"We're gonna watch a princess movie!" she shouted, and he grinned, not knowing—or caring—if his boss could hear her.

Silence filled the line before the older man commented, "You do realize the partners are going to make a decision about the promotion soon."

"I do."

"You've worked hard for this, Jamison. I'd hate for you

to lose out now when you're so close. I probably shouldn't be telling you this, but you're first in the running."

"Why?"

"Well, we want to let all the candidates know at the same time—"

"No, I mean why am I first? Harris has seniority, and Martinez landed the Langstone account. So why me, Charles?"

"I don't understand what you're asking," Spears said stiffly, but Jamison had a good idea the other man knew exactly why he was asking, just like Jamison knew exactly why the older man wasn't answering.

"You can tell my father-in-law I said thanks but no, thanks."

Jamison didn't wait for his boss's response before ending the call. He didn't know for sure that his father-in-law had influenced his boss's decision and would probably never know, but if he took the promotion, he would always wonder. But it was more than stubborn pride keeping him from accepting, more than a need to know that he'd earned the partnership on his own merit.

Taking the job would be taking a step backward—back to the man he'd been before he and Monica separated, back to the man he'd been before the accident, back to the man he'd been before Rory.

He didn't want to go back. He wanted to go forward, to step toward a future that a few weeks ago, he wouldn't have dreamed was possible.

Jamison paced his office impatiently, his hand tightly gripping the phone as he counted out the rings. "Come on, pick up."

The masculine space with its solid furniture and shelves

lined with law books used to be his sanctuary. But now he saw it for what it was. *His* hidey-hole.

He'd had to wait until Hannah went down for a nap after their impromptu daddy-daughter day to make this call, and he didn't want to wait anymore. Just like he didn't want to hide from his emotions anymore.

"Hi! Hello," he almost shouted out a greeting when he heard the voice on the other end of the line. "It's Jamison Porter, and I need your help."

Silence answered his desperate plea before Evie Mc-Claren asked, "Why exactly would I want to help you, Mr. Porter? You broke my cousin's heart."

His own heart gave a painful jerk at the thought of hurting Rory. "I know. I made a mistake. When my mother-in-law told me what happened—"

"You thought Rory was guilty."

"No! Not really. Not once I had a chance to think about it. But Louisa sprang the information on me, and I was—I was blindsided by it."

The same way he'd been blindsided by Monica. By coming home to find the house empty. To find Monica had left without a word and taken Hannah with her.

"It totally caught me off guard, Evie, and I didn't handle it well. I know I was no better than her ass of an ex, who didn't stand by her—"

"Stand by?" Sharp laughter pierced Jamison's eardrum. "Is that what you think happened? You think Peter didn't come to Rory's defense when she needed him?"

Jamison swallowed, suddenly fearing whatever happened might have been so much worse. "Isn't it?"

"Peter didn't let Rory down. He set her up."

"You mean he—you mean the boss's *son* is the one who stole from their clients? And he framed Rory for it?"

"I don't know if he was framing her or simply covering

his tracks. But all of the proof—the online auctions, the storage shed, the emails—all of it traced back to Rory's computer."

Jamison swore under his breath. "How could he do that to her? When she trusted him—"

Like she trusted you? Like she counted on you to be there for her, to believe in her the way she believed in you from the very beginning?

Sick to his stomach, Jamison sank back into his chair.

"Guys are jerks," Evie said succinctly. "Unfortunately, Rory was so shocked by the accusations, by the evidence planted against her, she didn't realize until later Peter was the only one with that kind of access. And by then, it was too late. Anything she said would have seemed like she was simply trying to throw blame on someone else.

"Rory came here for a fresh start. Instead the stupid rumors followed her, and if that wasn't bad enough, your mother-in-law had to show up—"

Jamison closed his eyes. "I have even more to make up for. So I'll ask again, Evie. Will you help me?"

"What do you need me to do?" she asked, suspicion still underlining her words.

Even so, he felt the first kernel of hope start to sprout. "I'm looking for my very own fairy godmother."

Evie let out a short scoff. "And you called me? Mr. Porter, you must be even more desperate than I thought."

"You have no idea."

"Oh, there you are, Rory." Evie breathed out as she reached Rory's side in the middle of the lobby. "I've been looking everywhere for you."

"Why? What's going on?" Rory had tried to take her cousin's words to heart, to believe her unshakable faith in people and her belief in happily-ever-after were her greatest strengths. But some days she felt like the only news was bad news.

It wasn't easy dealing with so-in-love couples, with helping them make their wedding dreams come true, when her own heart was broken. She knew it wasn't their fault. That they hadn't somehow stolen her happiness and taken it for themselves. But she couldn't help wondering how their relationships seemed to be smooth sailing when falling in love had left her beaten and broken, stranded on the ragged shoals.

Evie rolled her eyes but wouldn't meet her gaze, her attention focused across the lobby. "Oh, you know. The usual. We've got some crazy-in-love guy who wants to plan an over-the-top, surprise proposal for his girlfriend. He's waiting to meet with you at the gazebo to go over all the details."

"A surprise engagement. Well, that could end badly..."

That statement caught Evie's attention, and her cousin turned to meet her gaze. "Stop being so cynical. That's my job. And something tells me this guy has nothing to worry about. So go!"

Great. Just what she didn't want to deal with. A crazy-in-love fiancé-to-be gushing over the woman he loved.

Don't make comparisons, she sternly warned herself. *What you and Jamison had wasn't love. Not really. Not on his part. Which is why you're going to get over him... someday.*

Catching sight of Trisha and her friends huddled near the concierge desk, Rory straightened her shoulders. First things first.

Surprise lit the other woman's eyes when Rory walked toward the clique instead of hurrying by with her head ducked down as if she were invisible. No, worse...as if she were guilty.

Tell me it isn't true, Rory. Tell me!

She'd been so sure he wouldn't believe her. So afraid Jamison saw what they had as some kind of escape from the real world. That his feelings for her weren't strong enough to survive the challenges of everyday life. But the truth was, it wasn't Jamison she hadn't trusted.

"Trisha, I'd like a word with you."

The redhead raised her sculpted eyebrows before glancing at her friends with a smug smile. "I'm kind of on break here."

Rory met their laughter with a smile of her own. "Break's over."

The three other women exchanged startled glances before murmuring their goodbyes and heading off in opposite directions—hopefully to get back to doing their jobs.

Trisha huffed out a breath before demanding, "So what do you want?"

"There have been some rumors going around, rumors that might have been intended to hurt me, but that could end up hurting Hillcrest."

Trisha blanched slightly, as if she hadn't considered the more far-reaching consequences.

"This hotel has been in my family for decades, and I'm not going to let anyone damage its reputation. So if you—" The threat stalled in Rory's throat as Evie's words played through her memory. Her cousin was right. She did still have faith in people. "If you hear anyone spreading those rumors, I'm counting on you to help put a stop to them. You've worked here for years, and the staff looks up to you. I'm sure we won't have any of these problems going forward, will we?"

Trisha blinked. "I, uh—no, no trouble," she agreed, clearly startled by the turn of the conversation. "I'll make sure none of those rumors get spread around."

"Good." Rory sighed with relief. "I'm glad to hear that."

As Trisha hurried away, Rory straightened her shoulders and turned toward the lobby doors. One confrontation over, one more to go.

She'd avoided the gazebo in the week since Jamison left, but she couldn't stay away any longer. Lindsay and Ryder's wedding had brought even more attention to Hillcrest House, and Rory was fielding call after call from couples looking to plan their ceremonies there. More brides would say their vows framed by the elegantly scrolled woodwork.

But not Rory. Not when she couldn't look at the graceful structure without thinking of Jamison... Picturing his sexy smile as he teased her about his abilities. Remembering the thoughtful way he'd included Hannah in the work... Torturing herself with the memory of making love in the moonlight...

Evie was right. Rory wasn't going to give up. She still had faith that she would fall in love again, have a family of her own. But while her cousin admired her ability to get over Peter as quickly as she had, Rory didn't think getting over Jamison would be nearly as easy.

The sun was sinking behind the horizon, painting the sky with a gorgeous pink-and-purple haze and casting a golden glow over the gazebo. The groom-to-be stood with his back to her, one foot on the first step and a hand braced on the railing. His tailored dark suit was a stark, masculine contrast to the delicately carved white spindles.

Rory's heart seized at the sight. How long would it be before she stopped imagining Jamison in every tall, broad-shouldered man she saw?

"Good evening, I'm—" The introduction stuck in her throat as the man turned and the faint rays highlighted his face. "Not imagining things..."

"Hello, Rory."

"What—what are you doing here?" she asked, still unable to believe he was real.

"Didn't Evie tell you?" he asked.

"Yes! I'm meeting a man who's planning to propose to his girlfriend at the gazebo. Which is why I can't do this with you right now. He'll probably be here any minute and—"

A small smile played around Jamison's lips. "What?" Rory demanded.

"He's here."

Throwing her arms up in the air in frustration, she demanded, "Who's here?"

"I'm here, Rory," he told her.

"You—you're—"

"I'm the guy who was an idiot not to trust you, not to fight for you. I'm the guy who couldn't let go of the darkness of the past long enough to see the bright future right in front of him. I'm the guy who never should have left and the guy who will do anything it takes to convince you to forgive him."

Tears flooded her eyes, but Rory quickly brushed them aside. After seven days, she was too starved for the sight of him to let anything get in the way. "Oh," she said softly. "That guy."

"That guy," Jamison agreed. "The one who loves you. I love you, Rory. I love your openness, your faith in people, your willingness to see the best in them. In me, even when I probably didn't deserve it."

Rory blinked again, but nothing could keep the tears from spilling down her cheeks.

"I said it all wrong before, and you were right to turn me down. I don't want a holiday or a weekend. I don't want to reach for a phone when I want to talk to you at night. I want to reach for *you*.

"Evie told me what happened at your last job, but I didn't need her to tell me the whole story. I know you wouldn't have stolen from a client. I know *you*." He shook his head. "I've been miserable since I left, Rory. Even after the partners at the firm offered me the promotion, I wasn't happy."

"You turned the partnership down?"

"Turned the partnership down and turned my resignation in."

Rory's jaw dropped in shock. "You...resigned?"

"The job wasn't right for me, not anymore, and it was never what was best for Hannah."

If Rory had ever had any doubt Jamison deserved all the faith and belief she'd had in him, his words brushed them away as easily—as tenderly—as he brushed away her tears.

"I can't believe you quit."

"Well, fortunately I won't be unemployed for long. Turns out a lawyer over in Redfield is getting ready to retire and is looking to take on a partner."

Rory wasn't sure how much more her heart could take. "You mean you'd move here? To Clearville?"

Jamison shrugged a shoulder as if giving up his life in San Francisco to live in the small town was no big deal. "I'd move wherever you are. I missed you, Rory. Hannah missed you, too." He smiled, but a hint of vulnerability reflected in his sterling gaze. "I realize I've sprung all this on you suddenly, but I'm hoping at least some of it has come as a good surprise."

Realizing she'd been too shocked to do much more than echo what he'd told her, Rory reached up to cup his face in her hands. "Well, there is one problem."

"Yeah, what's that?"

"I came out here because Evie told me a man was look-ing to propose to the woman he loves…"

Turning his head, Jamison pressed a kiss to her palm before lowering to one knee. Despite what her cousin had told her, Rory still gasped when he pulled a small blue box from his suit pocket. "Rory McClaren, you might not be a princess, and I know you're not a fairy godmother, but Hannah and I think you would make a wonderful step-mother.

"I love you, Rory. In such a short time, you've brought light and laughter back to both of our lives, and if I can spend the rest of my life making you as happy as you've made me over the past few weeks, I'll be the luckiest man alive."

Her heart ready to burst from her chest, Rory sank down in front of him and threw her arms around his neck. "I love you, Jamison Porter, and I can't think of anything that would make me happier than to be your wife and Hannah's stepmother. I've spent my whole life imagining the perfect wedding, but you're the one who's made my dreams come true. You're the best man, the *only* man, for me."

Epilogue

One year later

"That's the fifth time you've looked at your watch in the last ten minutes," Ryder murmured as he adjusted the cuff link on his tuxedo. "Is this my turn to remind you that it's not too late?"

Jamison met his friend's cocky grin with a wry look. "Very funny." And no less than he deserved now that their roles had been reversed. Now that Ryder was the best man and Jamison—

He sucked in a deep breath and ran a finger beneath the starched collar and bow tie. He was the groom.

"So no cold feet?"

No cold anything.

The summer day was perfect for a wedding. The sun shone down on the gleaming white gazebo with only a hint of clouds above, and the scent of roses carried from the garden on the warm breeze. Dozens of chairs lined either side of a lace runner as their friends and family had gathered to celebrate his marriage to Hillcrest House's very own wedding coordinator.

Rory's parents sat in the front row. So, too, somewhat surprisingly, did his parents. And Monica's.

A lot could change in a year.

"I'm not nervous," he insisted. Despite the way the second hand on his watch seemed to move in slow motion and the bow tie threatened to cut off all the air to his lungs, the words were true.

He'd been waiting for this moment—for this woman, for Rory—his entire life. He didn't want to wait anymore.

His heart jumped in his chest as the familiar music began to play, and his wait was over. Oohs and aahs rose from their guests as they caught sight of Hannah, looking like an angel in her lacy white dress, and a huge grin split Jamison's face at the overwhelming rush of emotion he felt for his daughter.

She met his grin with a dimpled smile of her own. A flowered crown perched on her riot of curls was already slightly askew, and a white wicker basket swung from side to side as she skipped down the aisle, remembering to drop a rose petal or two on the way.

The music swelled, and Jamison's breath caught as the guests all rose to their feet. But then at his very first glimpse of Rory in wedding white, the rest of the world fell away.

He'd told her once that he didn't believe in fairy tales, and in a way, that was still true. Because this was no fantasy, no game of pretend, no story that would come to an end on the final page. The emotions pouring through him as Rory climbed the gazebo steps and placed her hand in his were as solid and as real and as lasting as anything he could ever hope to build.

Even if she did *look* like a fairy-tale princess...

Sunlight glittered on the lace and beads, the shimmering white satin hugging her curves. Her skin was as luminous as the pearls around her slender neck, and her dark hair was held back from her beautiful face by a rose-adorned headband.

"Did you see Hannah?" she whispered, her sapphire eyes sparkling, as the minister began his greeting. "She was perfect."

"I knew she would be."

Hannah had been as eager—almost as eager—for this day to arrive as Jamison.

"You did?"

He nodded. "I had faith."

Those were the same words Rory had spoken a year ago, but so much had changed since then. For him and for Hannah. Gone was the shy, fearful girl he'd first brought to Clearville. She'd blossomed beneath Rory's care, growing happy and confident, blooming into, well, the perfect flower girl.

And why not? He and Rory weren't the only couple to be touched by Hillcrest's magic. His daughter had had plenty of practice in the past few months.

So, yes, Jamison had faith. He had hope...

And when he vowed to take this woman to be his bride, when he sealed that promise with a kiss, and when Hannah turned back to the happy crowd, tossed the rest of her bright red rose petals straight up into the air and shouted, "Now we get cake!" Jamison couldn't help but throw his head back and laugh.

He had love.

* * * * *

LET'S TALK
Romance

For exclusive extracts, competitions
and special offers, find us online:

- **f** facebook.com/millsandboon
- 🐦 @MillsandBoon
- 📷 @MillsandBoonUK

Get in touch on 01413 063232

For all the latest titles coming soon, visit
millsandboon.co.uk/nextmonth

MILLS & BOON
A ROMANCE FOR EVERY READER

- **FREE** delivery direct to your door
- **EXCLUSIVE** offers every month
- **SAVE** up to 25% on pre-paid subscriptions

SUBSCRIBE AND SAVE

millsandboon.co.uk/Subscribe

JOIN THE MILLS & BOON BOOKCLUB

* **FREE** delivery direct to your door

* **EXCLUSIVE** offers every month

* **EXCITING** rewards programme

50% OFF
YOUR FIRST
PARCEL

Join today at
Millsandboon.co.uk/Bookclub

MILLS & BOON

THE HEART OF ROMANCE

A ROMANCE FOR EVERY READER

MODERN

Prepare to be swept off your feet by sophisticated, sexy and seductive heroes, in some of the world's most glamourous and romantic locations, where power and passion collide.

HISTORICAL

Escape with historical heroes from time gone by. Whether your passion is for wicked Regency Rakes, muscled Vikings or rugged Highlanders, awaken the romance of the past.

MEDICAL

Set your pulse racing with dedicated, delectable doctors in the high-pressure world of medicine, where emotions run high and passion, comfort and love are the best medicine.

 *True Love*

Celebrate true love with tender stories of heartfelt romance, from the rush of falling in love to the joy a new baby can bring, and a focus on the emotional heart of a relationship.

 Desire

Indulge in secrets and scandal, intense drama and plenty of sizzling hot action with powerful and passionate heroes who have it all: wealth, status, good looks…everything but the right woman.

HEROES

Experience all the excitement of a gripping thriller, with an intense romance at its heart. Resourceful, true-to-life women and strong, fearless men face danger and desire - a killer combination!

To see which titles are coming soon, please visit

millsandboon.co.uk/nextmonth

JOIN US ON SOCIAL MEDIA!

Stay up to date with our latest releases, author news and gossip, special offers and discounts, and all the behind-the-scenes action from Mills & Boon...

 @millsandboon

 @millsandboonuk

 facebook.com/millsandboon

 @millsandboonuk

It might just be true love...

GET YOUR ROMANCE FIX!

Get the latest romance news, exclusive author interviews, story extracts and much more!

MILLS & BOON
MODERN

Power and Passion

Prepare to be swept off your feet by sophisticated, sexy and seductive heroes, in some of the world's most glamourous and romantic locations, where power and passion collide.

MILLS & BOON
True Love
Romance from the Heart

Celebrate true love with tender stories of heartfelt romance, from the rush of falling in love to the joy a new baby can bring, and a focus on the emotional heart of a relationship.

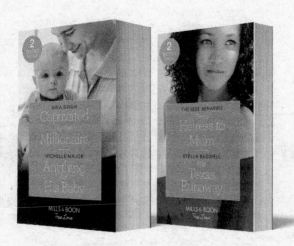

MILLS & BOON
Desire

Indulge in secrets and scandal, intense drama and plenty of sizzling hot action with powerful and passionate heroes who have it all: wealth, status, good looks…everything but the right woman.

Four Desire stories published every month, find them all at:

millsandboon.co.uk

Indecent Proposals

About the Authors

USA Today bestselling author **Katherine Garbera** is a two-time Maggie winner who has written 108 books. A Florida native who grew up to travel the globe, Katherine now makes her home in the Midlands with her husband, two children and a very spoiled miniature dachshund. Visit her on the web at katherinegarbera.com, connect with her on Facebook and follow her on Twitter @katheringarbera

Anne Oliver lives in Adelaide, South Australia. She is an avid romance reader, and after eight years of writing her own stories, Mills & Boon offered her publication in their Modern Heat series in 2005. Her first two published novels won the Romance Writers of Australia's Romantic Book of the Year Award in 2007 and 2008. She was a finalist again in 2012 and 2013. Visit her website anne-oliver.com

Stacy Connelly dreamed of publishing books since she was a kid writing about a girl and her horse. Eventually, boys made it onto the page as she discovered a love of romance and the promise of happily-ever-after. In 2008, that dream came true when she sold *All She Wants for Christmas* to Special Edition. When she's not lost in the land of make-believe, Stacy lives in Arizona with her two spoiled dogs.